THE MAGDALEN

a novel

or, rather,

a probability

D1127686

BONNIE JONES REYNOLDS

iUniverse, Inc.
New York   Bloomington

The Magdalen
A Novel

iUniverse books may be ordered through booksellers or by contacting:

iUniverse
1663 Liberty Drive
Bloomington, IN 47403
www.iuniverse.com
1-800-Authors (1-800-288-4677)

ISBN: 978-1-4401-7207-6 (sc)
ISBN: 978-1-4401-7206-9 (ebk)

Printed in the United States of America

iUniverse rev. date: 02/17/2010

With forever thanks to

Jane Roberts
and
Robert F. Butts

and to the
Energy Essence Personality

Seth

for the many volumes of wisdom
which they bequeathed to this probability.

Also by Bonnie Jones Reynolds

FICTION

The Truth About Unicorns
The Confetti Man

NONFICTION

Bikram's Beginning Yoga Class – co-author
If Only They Could Talk, The Miracles of Spring Farm – co-author

He that hath ears to hear, let him hear.

Mark 4:9

PREFACE

I began *The Magdalen* in 1982 and finished it in 1984. It has had a remarkable odyssey in the intervening twenty-five years.

In a way, that odyssey encapsulates the amazing changes of the last twenty-five years—in technology, the publishing world . . . and in the collective mind of Humanity.

Upon completion of *The Magdalen*, I sent it to my, then, agent, Roberta Pryor. Roberta submitted it only once. The editor to whom she submitted it was scandalized by its content. Roberta returned it, saying that she felt that it was "too controversial to sell."

I then sent it to Renni Browne, who had been the editor on my first two novels. Renni said that at least fifty percent of the content had to go. And, of course the ending had to be changed.

Yes, cutting fifty percent would have produced a tight, fast, commercial read. I had become a pretty fair editor, myself, during the merciless cutting that Renni had demanded on my first two novels. And, yes, I also knew that the ending would raise more than eyebrows.

But *The Magdalen* had not come into being in order to be a tight, fast, commercial read. And the ending had not been written in order to shock or to raise controversy, but because, in the probability described in this book, that is the way that things happened. *The Magdalen* was not written because I just woke up one day and decided to write it. I can see now that it was an organic process. During the preceding years, my every experience had been preparing me for the task. When I was ready, *The Magdalen* was ready. It insisted upon being written, and it virtually wrote itself. It intended that every word should be put out there for the world to read. It was/is my task to facilitate the "putting out there." I am a foot soldier, one of the many keepers of the message, given my marching orders, I firmly believe, two thousand years ago, alive again at this time, in this probability, to carry out those orders, and publish this teaching document. Those with the ears to hear will hear, and those with the eyes to see, will see. There will be many more of those now than there were two thousand years ago. Because the Magdalen's time has come.

Oh yes, I did physically write *The Magdalen*. I remember sitting at the keyboard doing so. I remember the hundreds of hours of technical research, so time-consuming way back then—crawling through libraries and searching through books, painstakingly gathering information that now pops up on your screen after a few key words tapped into Google.

But, for the most part, what was said and done in the book just came streaming into my mind. The actions, the people, the teachings of "Josh"—were just there, waiting, as soon as my fingers reached the part where they should be written down.

Many authors feel that they "get help" from other realms when writing. I have no doubt that the people in this work, themselves, coached me in the recording of their stories. Whenever I re-read any part of it, I am as a first time reader. "Can I have written this?" "I don't remember writing that." "Where in the world did those words, that wisdom, come from?" "How the heck was I able to write this in just two years?"

Additionally, I am unable to separate my own heart from theirs. No matter how many times I read what was written, it moves me to the core of my being, and re-*minds* me of what I know so very well, but keep on forgetting.

So, of course, cutting the book and changing the action was out of the question. Unfortunately, my determination in this regard meant that, in the publishing world of 1984, *The Magdalen* was not publishable. I did think of self-publishing. But, in those days, self, or "vanity," publishing, was looked upon with scorn, as a joke.

The Magdalen was no joke. And it was certainly meant for a wider audience than just family and friends. So it would have to wait. Wait for its time to come.

I did give the manuscript to some friends and family to read: my mother, Willa Dean Jones, who was horrified as to what her Bible study class would think; my sister Peggy Miller, who didn't say much of anything until just recently, when she wondered if publishing the book would put me in any danger; my late cousin, Gail Andrews, who gave me a 1984 version of a high five and a "Yeah! You go, Girl!" while asking if she could keep the manuscript long enough to read it again; and my friend, Dennis Hayman, a man totally on *The Magdalen*'s wavelength.

I also sent a copy of the manuscript to my friend, Andy Magyar, who lived in Australia. In order to make the shipping less cumbersome and expensive, using the technology available in those days of yore, I took the manuscript to a copying place and had the thing reduced so that two pages fitted onto a standard 8x10 sheet of paper. (Nowadays, of course, I would simply have e-mailed it to him!)

Only one other person read it—my friend and business partner, Dawn Hayman, who, upon finishing the manuscript, had a t-shirt made. On the t-shirt were the words, "There is no such thing as a dead fig tree." (That will make sense when you get to Chapter Nine.)

After those initial readings, I put *The Magdalen* into a trunk, saying, "Someday its time will come."

It was still there in its trunk on the night of October 31, 1993, when my home was destroyed by fire.

Gone. *The Magdalen* was gone, along with another, nearly finished, novel. There were no other copies.

Or so I thought. Two years later, in 1995, it occurred to Andy Magyar—who had moved to the U.S. and was living with us in the upstairs of my family's little, red farmhouse—to ask if I would like to have that copy of *The Magdalen* that I had sent to him

E-gad! I had forgotten all about that copy! It was a miracle!

Lowering myself back down from off of the ceiling, I began to wonder. Was this it? Had *The Magdalen*'s time finally come? Should I try again to submit it for publication?

If so, there was a major problem. That reduced-in-size copy that I had sent to Andy was not appropriate for submission to a publisher. Trying to enlarge it would also not work. I would have to type it all over again. I am a miserable typist.

Someone then told me that I could have Andy's copy scanned and put onto what they called "floppy discs." The material could then be uploaded to my computer.

There was technology that would do that? Wow. Would wonders never cease?

I found someone to do that job, and eagerly loaded the floppies when they were delivered to me.

It is hard for people living in the year 2009 to remember back to the dark ages of computer and communications technology. Suffice it to say that the technology for the scanning of documents in 1995 left something to be desired. What came up on my screen was fifty percent gibberish interspersed with the fifty percent that was legible.

I was going to have to type the whole thing over after all. I would also have to recreate much of it as I went.

At least I now, sort of, had it on computer, with floppies safely stored elsewhere.

The re-typing process took three years of spare-time work. It was not just the typing that took that long. As any writer knows, the urge to edit and re-write oneself is so powerful that some writers never even get around to submitting a manuscript. They just keep editing and re-writing.

But, once I again had a perfect manuscript—now saved on the computer and with computer backups plus multiple hard copies stored elsewhere . . . . . . what had I? *The Magdalen*'s time still had not come. Roberta Pryor had retired, I had no agent, no way to even begin to go about getting a publisher.

Back into the trunk it went. I was not concerned. I was beginning to realize that *The Magdalen*, the document, had a mind of its own. *The Magdalen*, itself, would tell me when its time had come.

In 2004, miracle of miracles, I was contacted by Fran Collin, a literary agent who was interested in having me and my partner, Dawn Hayman, write what was eventually published as *If Only They Could Talk, The Miracles of Spring Farm*—Spring Farm being the animal sanctuary that we had co-founded, and that had largely occupied my time since about 1986.

When that book was finished, I submitted *The Magdalen* to Fran.

It wasn't her cup of tea.

Back to the trunk with you, Magdalen.

It was a morning in January of 2009 when I woke up and knew that the time had finally come. No trumpets or fanfare. It was just suddenly apparent.

The Magdalen had waited for the world to catch up with it.

It had been written before its time. Minds had not been ready for it. The means of publishing had not been ready for it.

But, in the twenty-five years since its writing, other books had been published, and films had been made—some quite wonderful—which had touched on various elements contained in *The Magdalen*, and which had enjoyed wide public interest and acceptance.

At the same time, the publishing industry—along with almost everything else—was falling apart, being forced to reinvent itself. It was turning to electronics—as in, for instance, the case of Kindle— and was now also using the services of self-publishing firms in order to print books on demand, rather than in the huge, risky "printings" of old. Gone was the label of "vanity," as more and more authors bypassed traditional publishers and did their own thing through self-publishing houses—which now provided links to major sales outlets.

The chaos repeatedly predicted by "Josh" was upon our civilization. The fabric of our society was unraveling, everything coming apart at the seams.

While the magic, mysterious, Maya date of 2012 was just around the corner.

The world was now ready—desperate—to receive the message of *The Magdalen*.

I selected a self-publishing house and plunged into the daunting task of editing for grammar, etcetera, and copy reading, aided by another cousin, Whyla Beman.

My thanks to all who read the manuscript, including more recent readers, my third business partner, Margot Unkel, and friend, Janine Schlaudraff.

Beloved Renni, editor *extraordinaire*, you didn't get a shot at cutting, but I hope you appreciate the paragraphing.

As to Andy Magyar . . . Andy departed this Earth some ten years ago.

How wonderfully droll that it was Andy who saved *The Magdalen*—dragging it all the way back from Australia with him—so that it can finally be published—in its entirety as it was meant to be published, unafraid, and unmutilated.

For Andy was a dyed-in-the-wool atheist, who did not mince words as to his utter disgust for any and all religious notions, and who did not attempt to hide his disdain for any "idiot" who believed that there was anything other than annihilation come death.

Andy, Old Friend, I know that you now know how very wrong you were. I know that it all seemed so "stupid and unbelievable" to you because, as it has been presented to most of us for two thousand years, it *is* stupid and unbelievable. I know that you now know that "God" is All That Is, and is so much grander, more beautiful, more exciting, and wonderful than anything that our little minds will ever be able to completely wrap themselves around.

Because of you, those with the ears to hear, and those with the eyes to see, in this desperately searching world, will be helped to that same understanding.

Andrew Magyar, I send you my thanks for being the savior of *The Magdalen*. And I send my love. Now will you *please* stop haunting the upstairs of the red house?

Bonnie Jones Reynolds
Spring Farm – July, 2009

Chapter 1

Bethabarah

A crescent of strong young men, knee-deep in water, separated Johannan from the crowd that lined the banks of the Jordan. That crowd pressed inexorably forward, each unit of the beast intent upon experiencing immersion.

Johannan knew that the crowd was not actually a sprawling, mindless beast. Yet, after a morning of teaching, and an afternoon of steady dunking, he could not help but think of it as such.

He released his grasp from the neck of the old man whom he had pushed briefly beneath the silky, green waters and set him upright, his big hands steadying the man. He summoned The Energy from within, and beamed his conviction into the bleary eyes.

"You are clean now, Old Father. This sacred river has entered your every part, washed every bit of you, floated away the old. You are new, with opportunities as though just born. Return to your home. Remember my words. Weigh again your previous conceptions, re-think those things that you have understood to be the truth until now, and know that the good news I have given you is the truth. The Kingdom of God is within you. Laugh and be joyous in that knowledge for the rest of your days."

"But what of my sins?" said the old man. "Have they, too, been washed away?"

"There is no 'sin,' Man. Only spiritual ignorance—misunderstanding of the true nature of our reality."

"But am I now forgiven?"

Johannan sighed. The man had heard his words, but he had not listened. So few of them did. He embraced the man.

"There is nothing to forgive, Old Father. You are beautiful by the mere fact of being. Go now, and try to remember my words."

He pushed him gently toward the living wall that separated him from the crowd. The concave center opened to allow the man exit, and to allow the next candidate ingress. A tall, slim boy formed the left side of that portal. The boy glanced at Johannan.

"Are you all right, Jo? Would you like to rest? Or perhaps some bread, or water?"

Johannan grinned.

"Just like your kind."

"Yes," growled the young man on the right. "And hold your tongue, Merovee, your tones betray you."

The delinquent cast the speaker a scathing glance and repeated pointedly . . .

"Do you require refreshment, Jo?"

"One smile is all," said Johannan.

The smile came readily, and, behind it, laughter unlaughed. That smile did, indeed, refresh the man who would be known to later generations as John the Baptist. He passed it on to the quaking young girl who waded toward him, speaking words of encouragement to her. No women had come to the river for immersion at first. It was unheard of among the children of Israel that a man should in any way touch a stranger who was female—even more strange that a prophet should consider women on an even basis

1

with men, a part of, or in need of, the same spiritual ceremonies. But word had got around, and now some brave women did come, or, as in the case of this girl, were brought by brave fathers.

The immersion of a female always brought murmurs of disapproval from the Pharisees in the crowd. The Sadducees, however, remained silent. Unlike Pharisees, their only intent was the literal application of The Law as set down in the Five Books of Moses. Nowhere in those five books did it actually state that men and women should not touch. The Sadducces did not like what they saw, but no Law was being broken. Let the Pharisees with their endless interpretations of The Law mutter all they wished. The Sadducees were content to bide their time. This "Elijah returned" would make a slip someday. When he did, they would have him.

Ignoring the angry stares even from two of his own men, Johannan put his hands upon the shoulders of the girl and once more tapped into The Energy within.

"Daughter. You have heard my words. The Tabernacle of God dwells within you. Within you is the Power and the Glory of what you call God. Whether or not you believe, you daily create your own personal world with this Power. Are you courageous enough to understand and believe that I speak truth, Little One? Courageous enough to believe in me? In what I say? If you will, if you will forevermore know of this Power, and recognize what you daily do, I promise that the Kingdom will come. It will come and reign upon this Earth just for *you*, as it does for all who understand in a like way. Believe in my words and you will be saved from all the misunderstanding which has afflicted Humankind until now, saved from fear, misery, unhappiness, want. Yes, even from death, for you will understand the true nature of the change that you call death.

"I will now cause you to sink beneath the water. As I do so, I want you to imagine that that water flows, not just over your body, but, into it, through the skin, and through your innards, cooling, soothing, cleansing, floating every old idea and impurity away from you. As the old is washed out, allow yourself to fill with the glad tidings and joy of what I tell you."

The small, pliable body sank beneath the pressure of his palms. Johannan sighed. He had come to know about people from their muscle tone. This was a harmless little person. She had made hardly a ripple as the water closed over her. Her life would be the same. She had come, she would exist, and then go, and there would be hardly a splash to testify that she had been. Like the old man, the girl had heard without listening. She would never understand that The Power was her birthright, hers for the using at any moment.

But no! He must not think that way! Why go on if that was the way it was? What was the purpose if it was all for naught?

At least the girl was young. Young in age and young in Spirit. And had she not come to him this day? So what if it had been only at the bidding of a parent? Someday, years—maybe lifetimes—from now, the person she had then become would wrinkle the brow, and, as with a forgotten and then dimly remembered dream, think one of the thoughts he had given her this day. From that moment, her path through eternity would be holy. She would be on her way to knowing her Self, and so to knowing the true god.

After knowing would come the even greater task. To remember what one knew. Steadily. To keep the trust, the belief, constant, a bastion against doubt.

How difficult was that task, Johannan well knew. How difficult sometimes even to remember that the reality of his mission exceeded one time, one place . . . that he was not just some crazy old man standing waist-deep in water beneath a blazing sun, giving other poor idiots a bath.

. . . not just some poor fool, crying in The Wilderness.

* * *

He came for his immersion at the end of the day, as the sun was setting and the crowd all but dispersed. It was that tall, young person called Merovee who spotted him first. Johannan had come to depend upon Merovee for much, and with good reason. Merovee seemed to have the invisible feelers of an insect, whiskers of a cat, the darting tongue of a viper. Merovee could raise the nostrils and sniff the wind as did a wolf, and know who was coming, how many, where they had been, whether they were friendly. Merovee sometimes seemed to remember the future equally as well as the past. There were those who would have said that the sensitivity of Merovee was bestowed by some Prince of Darkness. Johannan knew differently.

"Hsst! Jo!"

Johannan looked up from the body that he was holding beneath the waves. He caught the shiver of Merovee, and let it run through him.

The object of Merovee's attention was lounging against the trunk of a palm at the top of the bank, obviously hanging back, wanting to be the last. He was tall, and as graceful as a lion, but, though his posture spoke of negligence, his eyes upon the scene were avid. He wore a robe of soft, eggshell linen. His hair, beneath the small, linen cap, was shorter than was the style of either Judeah or Galilee, more like that worn by the Greeks of Athens, itself. The hair was dark, but its topmost layer had been bleached as fair by the sun as his face had turned golden-brown from the same. Again contrary to local custom—indeed, in what most would have called flagrant disregard of The Law—he was shaved clean and wore no earlocks. He had angular, but regular, features, and lines at the corner of the mouth which suggested a propensity to laugh. His eyes were the color of honey, with startling flecks of blue.

Johannan felt a mighty heaving beneath his hands. Remembering, he raised his nearly drowned initiate, helped him retch out the water, then delivered a long benediction, explaining to the man that, being extra clean now, he was doubly blessed. A light came into the eyes of the initiate at those words. He seemed truly impressed. So much so that, as he departed, Johannan wondered if he had stumbled onto a new and better technique.

It was another half hour, with the sunset and darkness spreading over the river, before all had gone . . . save the man in the linen robe, who now came to the edge of the water. He stood for a moment looking across the distance of a dozen feet at the impressive bulk of Johannan, the wild man from The Wilderness of Judeah, whose hair and beard radiated in a great silver profusion, who dressed himself in cloth woven of camel hair, who girded his great trunk with leather—the Prophet, whom some claimed was Elijah, himself, returned at the end of days, to usher in the Kingdom of God.

Returning that direct regard, Johannan at first felt nothing—that initial shiver had been an excitement caught from Merovee.

But then he saw, deep in the eyes of the stranger, a knowing as profound as his own. Suddenly he did feel something. Gratitude. Relaxation. *The* one had finally come.

"Do you have strength for one more?" said the man.

His voice was as sure as his eyes. Johannan smiled, and spoke words which he now knew would be understood.

"I am human, so The Energy is boundless."

"Is it permitted to partake without my robe?"

Johannan hesitated.

Merovee turned.

"Johannan, as we are no longer needed to hold back the press, will you excuse us to lay the evening meal? This man can then have the privacy he needs."

As always, the mind of Merovee was quickest.

In silence, Johannan and the man waited as the bodyguards splashed up onto the bank. The newcomer smiled at Merovee as the boy passed him, watching after him until he and the others disappeared, glad of the release, eager for food and drink, south along the bank to the palm grove where Johannan had his camp.

In near darkness, then, the man shed his robe, and, in violation of The Law, his under-linen as well. Naked, he waded into the water. Shivering with the sudden chill, but relaxed no less, he approached the Prophet. The two stood eye to eye, each searching for something.

"I am Joshuah," said the stranger, as though he hoped it would explain.

"Where are you from?"

Joshuah did not conceal his disappointment.

"Bethlehem. You had no sign, then. No pre-knowledge of my coming?"

"Not I," said Johannan. "It was Merovee who recognized you as special."

"Merovee?"

"The one who suggested that they depart to prepare a meal. Merovee supplies much that I, myself, lack. For some days now, Merovee has been expecting the Messiah to arrive and request the cleansing."

"You, then, do not consider yourself to be the Messiah?"

Johannan smiled.

"If the prophets speak true, how could I be? I am of the lineage of Aaron, not the lineage of David."

"Ah yes. The prophets. How men do search, and stretch, and twist the innocent words of yesteryear to find evidence of what they wish to prove today. Have not the Essenes of Qumran even decided that Scripture predicts *two* Messiahs, one from the priestly House of Aaron, the other from the royal House of David?"

Johannan nodded ruefully.

"As you say, each man finds in Scripture what each man wishes to find. I care not for any of their interpretations. I do not consider myself any form of messiah. I consider myself a harbinger, a bird with a song to sing. What of you?"

"Cleanse me and fill me. Perhaps then I can be certain myself."

"You are, then, I take it, of the House of David."

"You know it if you would but remember, my Samaritan cousin. We met many times as boys, when your parents brought you up to Jerusalem for the Passover. On the last occasion, we escaped our parents and ran to the Temple to tease the Pharisees."

4

Johannan's mouth dropped.

"Josh!"

They wrung hands gladly, and kissed upon the lips, as was the custom among male friends and family.

"How you have grown," said Johannan foolishly.

"And you," replied Joshuah just as foolishly.

"Do your parents still prosper?"

"They do."

"Miriam and Joseph, are they not? He of the Triple Ramah, the Prince of the House of David, and she a cousin to my mother."

"Yes. And your parents?"

"Both passed."

"I am sorry."

"Their years were already advanced when they conceived of me. But I left even before they had died. Left not by design. In an excess of zeal, soon after my ceremony of manhood, I rose in our synagogue and expounded at length upon the complete misunderstanding of the children of Israel as to the intentions of God, and on the manifold stupidities of my elders." He smiled in response to Joshuah's chuckle. "It did not go down very well."

"Elders do tend to be unreasonable."

"On my dear mother's advice, I was gone before the next sunrise. I traveled to the north and came across a community of Essenes where I dwelt for many years. But I could never bring myself to take any beyond the vows of lay servitude. Even among the Essenes, you see, my ideas were continually out of countenance. When finally I left . . . it was once more under duress."

Joshuah laughed outright.

"I then went down to Petra to dwell with Zoroastrians. Again I found myself out of step. I came back into Judeah, to Jerusalem, and tried for a time to be a Pharisee."

"Do please tell me that you went to Hillel and not to Shammai."

"Of course to Hillel," grinned Johannan. "How can you offer such insulting mistrust on such short re-acquaintance? When I was asked to leave the House of Hillel, I tried my hand at becoming a proper Sadducee, and even presented myself at the Temple to learn to fulfill my priestly duties according to the Judean tradition. In due course, I again found it necessary to be on my way in the dead of night."

"It is the best way to avoid the heat."

"I went down to Egypt, and dwelt once more with Essenes, this time with a group who admitted women with men on an equal basis, and who understood the importance of individual revelation. These were perhaps the best of the lot, the closest to the mark. But not quite.

"In the end, I simply wandered about in The Wilderness of Sinai, trying to develop clearly what I, myself, believed—for, obviously, it was at variance with anything that any others believed. Once I understood the differences with surety, I had to decide whether these different beliefs of mine would be of benefit to my fellows, whether I had a calling to teach them . . . whether to speak up or to keep my mouth shut. Once I realized that I had been born—destined—to speak these strange, glad tidings, I had to decide how to go about it."

He shook his head.

"It has been a long road, Cousin. And a lonely one. Just once in a great while did I have a sense of . . . someone, walking along purposefully, somewhere behind me."

Joshuah's eyes sparked.

"I am glad," he said. "Glad that your way was made more companionable by a sense of me. For certainly my way was eased by knowledge of you. I actually saw you. Quite often. In the dream state. I did not know who you were, but I knew your face.

"I, too, set out upon that lonely road just after coming of age. I, too, left many a place in the dead of night, and under duress as you would say—one jump ahead of the local priests most usually, for I specialized in speaking out against their kind. My path led me first to India. I studied the teachings of the Djainists, and of Lord Krishna. Then I traveled to the mountains which they call Hima-ahlaya, to understand what the Great Buddha had had to say."

"You did not, in the end, neglect to visit Greece to study the thoughts of their ancients, that is obvious from the nakedness of your countenance," said Johannan with a twinkle. "Are you not afraid that you will take a chill with no whiskers? And is it the Greek manner that prompts you to come naked to the immersion?"

Joshuah laughed and shook his head.

"I simply want to be closer to what I seek."

Johannan sighed. He, himself, was beginning to tremble in the gathering evening chill and after so many hours in the water—while a breeze was whipping up.

"I hope that you do not want the full sermon, Josh. My belly is rumbling in anticipation of Merovee's stew pot."

"I have known the sermon in my heart for as long as I can remember, as have you, my counter part. Only put your hands on me, Johannan, and cleanse me of all but The Essence, so that I may experience it anew."

Johannan obliged, there in the darkness, in the cold of the Jordan. He did not have to hold Joshuah down. The man stayed long, in no distress, but prolonging the cleansing. He rose with teeth chattering, hugging himself.

"Come to the bank, get your robe," said Johannan.

Joshuah did not seem to hear. He stood as though rooted, locked in the embrace of himself, and Johannan then understood the chattering teeth to be caused by something other than the cold.

The man was in ecstasy . . . a state that Johannan knew well. Joshuah hugged himself and rocked, smiling, laughing, and talking to himself.

"It *is* so," he crooned. "All is reaffirmed. It feels like a dove. A white one, all soft, and warm, settling down, nesting upon every part of me with its downy belly and pulsing heart. I am its son. its dear, speckled egg."

Johannan listened patiently. The words reminded him of ways in which he, himself, had felt, and he did not need to ask how Joshuah knew that "it" was so. Better than any man, with the possible exception of the one who stood before him, Johannan understood what the Greeks termed Gnostic experience . . . that personal inner knowing, that comes seldom, and to few. He understood that, after gnosis, one *knew*, with a certainty that made a mockery of physical evidence, but in a way that was impossible to explain to those who had not, themselves, undergone gnosis.

So he waited, allowing the man his experience. As he did so, a sadness stole over him.

6

At last, Joshuah dropped his hands to his side, sighed and opened his eyes. In the darkness, his teeth showed white against the sun-darkened skin.

"Thank you," he said simply.

He took Johannan's shoulders and kissed him lightly upon the mouth.

"You are trembling, Johannan. And you must be weary. Come. I should not have kept you in the cold so long."

They waded to the bank, where Joshuah donned his garments.

"That robe is Egyptian linen unless I miss my guess," said Johannan.

"You have a good eye."

"So you also went among the Egyptians. Did you learn the ways of the priests of Isis?"

"I did." Josh got his bed roll and they started down along the bank toward the welcoming campfire, it being understood without speech that Joshuah would share the meal.

"Such wide travels," mused Johannan. "I wish I had had the chance."

"You had the same chances as I. You made different choices."

"I stand reminded." Johannan shivered again. "I wish you had come in the heat of the day. I would like to have taken more enjoyment from our time together. Instead, I can only think of a warm fire and food for my belly. I must be nearing the end of my days."

* * *

The stew was of goat's milk, bought from the Ford Master, who kept a small herd. Mushrooms which Merovee had gathered in the morning mist had been simmered with artichoke hearts and grains. A flat bread with nuts, of which Johannan was especially fond, was cooking on the coals, and there was warmed wine.

Johannan took his place cross-legged before the fire, on sheepskins which comprised the place of honor. He motioned Joshuah to the place beside him, offering one of his skins. Joshuah made himself comfortable on it, leaning against his bed roll Roman style. Johannan, along with two of his men, did not drink of the vine, but Joshuah accepted his own measure with alacrity. All ate heartily, silent until they had finished their portions.

Then Joshuah stretched, sat up himself, and grinned at Johannan.

"Men speak true when they say that you do not drink of the vine. I can now, though, testify that they err when they say you eat only of locusts and wild honey."

"They certainly err, praise be."

"I have eaten many unspeakable things when driven by need, but never locusts. Are they tasty?"

"About as tasty as the bark on the trees, and you have to catch a hundred of them to make a decent meal. Do you know how long it takes to catch a hundred locusts? A man has better ways to spend his days I have decided. Since Merovee arrived, my meals have appeared before me as magically as manna from Heaven."

Johannan grinned at the boy, reached over and gave him a manful slap on the back. The one who had admonished Merovee for his speech at the river, whom Johannan had introduced as Chandreah, laughed at the gesture, seeming to find it a great joke.

The other men did not laugh, or even smile.

There were six of them. Mathiah, Ezekiel, Salmon and Eli, then the two who had refrained from wine . . . a young man named Judah, whom the men called Sicarius, and his eldest brother, called by two names, Simon Yeshuah.

It was the face of this Simon Yeshuah that Joshuah fastened upon across the flames. It was not simply that Simon Yeshuah regarded Merovee with hostility, which he did. The thing upon his face went beyond even hatred. It was one of the most disturbing expressions that Joshuah had ever encountered.

But he *had* encountered it before. Where?

This Simon Yeshuah, like his young brother Judah, was of a build and of coloring to match that of Joshuah. But his hair was worn in the long, uncombed, never cleaned or shorn fashion that signaled a man under the ancient vows of the Nazorite, while his features could hardly be seen, hidden as they were beneath equally profuse and untidy facial hair.

Nothing, however, could hide his burning eyes.

The man was a fanatic. Joshuah knew the type only too well. And there was something about this particular man that went even beyond fanaticism. There was a purpose within him that reached across the fire and laid itself upon the heart of Joshuah like a rod of iron.

Joshuah returned his eyes to the one called Merovee, Without knowing it, he smiled.

That young person was but a few inches shorter than Joshuah, and Joshuah was accounted a tall man. Merovee's body was broad-shouldered, slender, and angular. Yet there was a markedly female quality to it. The black hair was worn long, un-oiled, braided at the back, clean and combed to the tastes of the Pharisees and Essenes. The earlocks were prominent, but, as with many young boys, there was not even the hint of a fuzz upon the square, handsome face. There was a slight pout to the lips that formed the broad mouth, and the large, dark eyes were the most beautiful that Joshuah had ever seen.

Again he smiled.

"It gladdens my heart, Cousin, to see that you suffer a woman amongst your followers."

A hush fell upon the group. It was Simon Yeshuah who broke the silence with an angry snort.

"Surely you jest, Stranger. This creature is an abomination before her own sisters and before the Lord."

"Simon Yeshuah." The voice of Johannan was deadly quiet.

"She should be stoned, even as the adulteress in the street. Yes! For her crime is even greater than the adulteress. She dresses as a man! She seeks to take to herself the privileges and prerogatives of her betters, to act in ways that are forbidden to her sex by the commandments of God, himself!"

"Simon Yeshuah, I have told you before. I will now tell you again, and for the last time. Miriam is welcome here. I have much work to do, and but a short while in which to do it. She dresses as a man, not by choice, but, because of just such foolishness as you are spouting. She came to me with a pure heart and a desire to serve me, and she has served me as well or better than any of you men. As far as I am concerned, God, whose mind you presume to know so well, has changed that mind. As far as I am concerned, he sent this woman to me to ease my burdens in the last days of my ministry."

"You are beguiled!" It was Judah the Sicarius who cried out.

He was a man of not much more than twenty, in height, coloring, and features a younger version of Simon Yeshuah, though his hair and beard were neat, so he was not a Nazorite. Between the two brothers Joshuah guessed there to be an age difference of nearly a generation.

8

"You are beguiled just as Adamah was beguiled by Chavvah and her serpent. What of this woman's unclean periods?"

"I keep aside from all of you at those times," said Miriam sharply. "We have been over this repeatedly, Judah."

"That is what you say. How do we know it is true? Look at us, made even to eat alongside of you! My own mother waits respectfully until we men are sated, and then eats apart, knowing her sinful place, respecting The Law, and never presuming. How do we know when you are clean and when you are not? How do we know that you have not defiled us, again and again?"

"And even if she has not," said Simon Yeshuah, "her presence here with you, Rabban, is in violation of every Law of God *and* Man. Think you your Essenic brothers would support the scandalous manner in which you encourage women to all manner of sinful practices?"

"To which Essenes do you refer, Simon Yeshuah? There are Essenic groups which recognize women as human beings, you know."

"Aha, perhaps! But do even those foolish ones allow the daughters of Chavvah to break bread with the Sons of Man?"

"To the everlasting shame of the Sons of Man, no. Simon Yeshuah, explain to me, please, how a woman can contaminate you by sitting beside you at table, when the fact that she has made the meal, touching it repeatedly with her hands, does not? I would that we Sons of Man would begin to use the powers of reasoning of which we are so boastful. The first thing that might then occur to us is that we are more primarily the Sons of Woman."

"And thus arises our error!"

"*Our* error? Was it not God who created it thus? Do you proclaim God to be in error?"

"It was done to try us and to teach us."

"Camel dung! Simon Yeshuah, it is you who try *me*. And you teach me once again that Humankind is in need of my message. The thing I am unable to understand, Simon Yeshuah, is, what are you doing here with me? Why do you persist in calling me Rabban—a title reserved for only the highest of masters and teachers, and for married teachers at that—when you agree with nothing I say or do except the eschewing of wine? I invite you now, as I have invited you before. All of you. Any of you. If you object to Miriam's presence, then leave. Right now."

There was a moment's silence.

Miriam broke it.

"Nay, Jo. Better I should leave than any of these strong arms. We have heard the growling in regard to Herod Antipas. If the tongues speak true, and he sends his minions to take you, you will need men, not a girl, to stave them off."

"What thinks this cousin of yours?" said Simon Yeshuah. "Surely you did jest when you congratulated our master for countenancing this woman? Is it not clearly written that a woman cannot enter the Kingdom of Heaven?"

"No. Not at all. Those such as yourself have merely found it to their liking to make such an interpretation of Scripture. As much as I deplore animal sacrifice, I would personally sacrifice a prize ox upon the altar of the Temple every day for the rest of my life to assure that you are wrong. For if 'Heaven' is without women, I would not care to go there."

He leaned forward, elbows on knees, chin on hands.

"Your attitude has served our people for thousands of years, Simon Yeshuah. As it was meant to. For reasons which would clearly be beyond you at the moment, the female principle was forced into subservience. Yet I tell you that Johannan, and I, are bearers of a *new* covenant. A new understanding of the 'word' of 'God.'"

One eyebrow lifted sardonically. The ghost of a smile touched his lips.

"Or do you not grant to your god what you would grant to mere men? The right to change 'his' mind, amend 'his' contracts, develop and grow along with the times? Or the right simply to withhold information from growing children to reveal when the time is ripe? I do grant 'God' those privileges, Simon Yeshuah. And, as Chapter One in 'his' new covenant, as the first writing in this new book, I tell you that a woman can enter the Kingdom of Heaven . . . if she becomes as a man."

The smile could no longer be concealed.

"She has but to come courageously forth from the bondage that the old covenant imposed upon her, exercise her mind, develop her talents and forgotten abilities, like some creature stretching, emerging from a magically inspired sleep . . . and the Kingdom will belong to her as readily as to any man.

"For the Kingdom of Heaven is within, Simon Yeshuah . . . within each man, woman, child, rock, snake, drop of water, or star in the sky. It always has been and always will be, it has never been withheld, not from anyone or anything. We men conveniently forgot that fact somewhere along the way, and decreed that women must forget it, too. The Kingdom of Heaven is right at hand. Any may grasp it at any instant. The trick is simply to know, to trust, to understand that this is true.

"Which is more easily said than done. It takes a courage that few can muster. But that courage does not know sex, Simon Yeshuah. Neither, I assure you, does The Creator.

"This woman *has* become as a man. And not simply by dressing in a way that enables her to enjoy the freedom of action that our garments allow to us men. She has become as a Man in the true sense of what the word means. More of a Man than most men. For she has found the courage to think for herself, to act upon her own convictions, her own inner faith, with no fear of the condemnation of others. So she has at last set her foot upon the path that will eventually lead her inward, to her own personal Kingdom of God, and to an understanding of her own divinity."

"You are a fool and a blasphemer," said Simon Yeshuah, rising.

"Call no one 'fool,' Simon Yeshuah. Too often it is yourself who most closely resembles the slander. And I tell you that it is you who blasphemes, you who insults your god. I say to you, Simon Yeshuah, that you have lived many lives. And not all of them as a man."

"What is this you say?"

"Our finest hopes are in those born female, Simon Yeshuah. They are the repositories of all we need to remember about ourselves. But the old covenant has also given them the hardest path, the longest way to travel, into the sunlight so freely accorded to us men."

For a moment, Simon Yeshuah simply stared, speechless. Then he strode over to where his bed roll hung on a bough and snatched it down.

"I came to the Jordan to be immersed by this man Johannan. I stayed to serve him because I hoped to find one wiser and greater than myself. I am grieved to say that I found no such thing. As a matter of fact, I now understand that what I did find is the den of the Evil One. My way is now clear. I see the path I must take in order to save my brethren."

The burning eyes turned to Judah.

10

"Do you follow me, Brother, or do you remain in this nest of evil?"

Judah hesitated. Then he got to his feet, got his own bed roll, and hurried after Simon Yeshuah. The two of them disappeared into the darkness.

For a while the only sound was the snapping of the fire. Then Johannan sighed.

"Is it really so difficult, what we try to tell them, Joshuah? It seems to me to be so very simple, so obvious, such joyous . . . good news! Yet either they refuse to listen or they accuse us of evil intent."

"The simpler the truth, the more reluctant the acceptance," said Joshuah. "They have been so comfortable, believing themselves the chosen of The Chosen, believing that 'God' begins and ends within the pages of their Scripture, or in the interpretations of the Pharisees. How easy it has been to have it all mapped out in The Law, 'Heaven' secured without thought, by mindless obedience alone. They will never thank us for disturbing their complacency with the news that each of us is responsible for drawing his own map to the Kingdom. Of course they will revile us as evil. And they will kill us rather than accept the responsibility of their own Souls."

Johannan roused himself and looked around.

"Are there any others who wish to leave with those two?"

There was a hasty disclaimer from Chandreah and the other four men.

"Then it is time to rest," said Johannan.

"Shall I rub you, Jo?"

"I shall be grateful, Miriam."

The girl ran for his bed roll, stretched it out, and, as he settled his tired bones onto it, she fetched a pot of sweet-smelling ointment, the precious balm from Gilead. She moistened her fingers with the little that was left and began to massage him—first his face, then his neck and the muscles of his shoulders. Joshuah opened his own roll and laid down, watching. Her movements were strong and sure, filled with solid love and tenderness. She rubbed his arms, and then the hands, cracking the joints and eliciting grunts of pleasure. Then she moved downward and worked the ointment into his feet and calves.

At the moment that Joshuah was sure his cousin slept, Johannan turned his head and smiled a drowsy smile.

"I have told these young people from the beginning that I but prepared the way for one greater than myself. Yet I did not recognize you when you came. Is that not strange? It was Miriam who knew."

The girl glanced up. Her great, dark eyes met those of Joshuah for a moment, then returned to the work at hand.

Johannan smiled a smile of great contentment.

"And so now I have naught to fear. My mission is ended."

"Jo!"

"Nay, Miriam, do not start so. I am a tired old man."

"You are not old," she protested.

"Age has nothing to do with old, Dear Girl. I hope you never have to know what it is to pursue a mission, year after year after endless year. Knowing, knowing what you must do, but with only yourself to sustain and confirm the true god that you know to be within yourself. A person grows weary."

He reached across and grasped the hand of Joshuah.

"Now he has come, he whose shoe latches I am not worthy to unloose. I see that I did read my task rightly, and it is now done, to my satisfaction. And, I do not mind saying—to my relief. And my burden?"

He rolled his head to the side, grinning hugely at Joshuah.

"That burden now passes to the new Lamb of God. Sorry, Lambkin. But I know you will not shirk."

Shortly thereafter, Johannan slept deeply. Miriam remained at his side for quite some time, arms wrapped around her knees, her chin between them, watching his face and the rise and fall of his breast.

The stranger soon slept as well. Openly then, she could study his features.

She knew who he was. There was a place in her mind where she knew things so certainly. Yet, tonight, she could hate him. She wished he had never come.

Her gaze returned to the face of Johannan. The image blurred through silent tears.

Inwardly, she began to pray.

* * *

Joshuah stayed on for two more days, filling the gap created by the departure of Simon Yeshuah and Judah. Merovee had never seen Johannan happier. He delighted in the blue of the skies, thought the clouds the most beautiful he had ever seen. He swore he could hear the grasses growing, and wished to match the green of the Jordan in a gown, to show the world what a beautiful creature was his favorite bodyguard.

And he drank of the vine.

"Yes, I said I would never again drink," he admitted to the stunned Merovee. "Not until the Kingdom of God had fully come. But for me now, it has. So stop scowling. Let an old man enjoy himself."

Even his sermons were soft. His love flowed palpably as he gazed upon the initiates—and spies from the Temple of Jerusalem—thronging the bank.

"Oh, you generation of vipers," became a caress.

"Crawling on your bellies, refusing to stand. Refusing even to believe that you are able. Earless like the viper, refusing to hear, deaf, no matter how many times we come among you to tell you the glad tidings."

His eyes swept the faces compassionately.

"Yet it will not always be so. There are vipers who have grown feet. There are vipers who swim. There are vipers who rear up. There are vipers who reach for the stars, if only by climbing the trees. I am told that there are even vipers which fly. And if it takes a thousand, no, two thousand years, I have trust that you will even grow ears, and a few of you will learn how to listen.

"When you do, you will, of yourself, weigh again, re-think, the things you have believed, and you will understand at last what I now tell you. This new thinking will bring forth sweet fruit, such as you cannot now imagine. As it must if you are to find the Kingdom. For I say to you that the fruits you put forward into the world, to be savored by others, will save you, while those which you keep hidden inside yourself will rot and destroy you. Think not that you can sit content, smug that all is well simply because you are children of Ibrahim. What you think of as 'God' can make children of Ibrahim out of rock! So be ware."

His voice had hardened with emotion. It softened once again.

"Yet think not that my words offer an ax to the roots of your tree. I tell you that the gardener of the garden in which you grow is ridiculously patient, offering nourishment and encouragement even to trees which do not put forth. But no gardener can waste his time forever. One season, two, three, even four. Then the gardener will turn his back, and minister to the more worthy plants.

"That, my friends is the only damnation possible—the turned back of the gardener. Show but one sickly bud, and the gardener will cry out in pleasure and come rushing back with water and eager words, smiling, loving, hoping that his silly tree has finally decided to fulfill its own Self."

Those last two days were warm without being hot, bright without a glare, the breeze soothed but did not chill. Even the crowds were gentle, they were quiet, and did not push. So that, on what was to be the final day, when his group had drawn a little apart for the noonday meal, Johannan suddenly suggested that they share their food with the entire crowd.

"But Jo," laughed Merovee, convinced that the wine had gone to his head, "I did not make enough bread to feed all these people."

"How much bread do we have?" said Joshuah.

His tone was light. Yet, when she looked at him, she found that he and Johannan were staring at one another.

"Five small loaves," she said softly.

The two men continued to regard one another. Mischief crept into their eyes, and smiles lifted their lips.

"Shall we try?" said Johannan.

"I have never done it," said Joshuah.

"Neither have I," said Johannan. "But between the two of us . . . "

"There are three smoked fishes as well," ventured Chandreah.

Johannan slapped his leg.

"That settles it. Bring them to us."

The loaves and the fishes were brought.

Like plotting boys, the two men bent over the two baskets.

"Which do you feel best able to influence?" said Joshuah.

"I think . . . the bread."

"Excellent. I lean toward the fish."

They then sat down, Johannan with the basket containing the bread on his lap, Joshuah with the basket of fish on his. Johannan placed his fingers lightly upon the rim of the basket and commenced to stare at the contents. Joshuah refrained from touching his basket. Instead, he fixed his eyes on the fish and began to breath in a deep and unusual fashion.

They remained that way for some minutes.

Then, in a voice that seemed to come from a long distance, Johannan said . . .

"Lay out a coat, Merovee, to receive the bread."

"Likewise the fish," said Joshuah.

Quickly, not knowing what to expect, Merovee spread her coat at the feet of her teacher. Chandreah spread his before Joshuah.

Each man reached into his basket and began to break off pieces of food, tossing them onto the coats.

The other disciples drew close. They watched with no sound. The pile of bread and fish upon the coats grew until there was no more room.

"Carry that to the people," said Johannan.

In shock, the disciples lifted the coats, and carried them to where the people waited. Those gathered were surprised and grateful for the offering, for not all had brought a noonday meal. The coats emptied quickly, and the disciples returned.

"How much more is needed?" said Joshuah.

"At least twice again as much," said Mathiah.

Once more the two men began to tear off pieces from the contents of their baskets and toss them onto the coats.

Three times more, in like manner, the cloaks were filled, and the people fed.

Then Johannan and Joshuah divided the five loaves and three fishes among their group and they, themselves, ate.

The food was consumed in silence. Both men seemed elated, but exhausted, and in need of private thought. Indeed what was there to say? Since, when the food was being multiplied, Johannan's group had been drawn aside, the multitude was not aware of the manner in which the meal had been produced. But even the disciples, who were aware, could hardly admit to it. With their own eyes they had witnessed it, yes. But it could not be.

At last, Johannan, who had been lying back with eyes closed, sat up.

Merovee touched his hand.

"How did you do it, Jo?"

"In exactly the same manner in which you daily materialize your own body and the world in which you exist, my dear. With The Energy. With the mind. It is that simple and that complicated. Through experience and lifetimes far in excess of your own, my cousin and I have obviously learned the focus needed to speed the process and materialize objects almost instantaneously, instead of over the lengthy physical periods called 'time,' which our race assumes are needed."

He smiled at Joshuah.

"We proved that even to ourselves this day, did we not, Cousin. We gave each other courage and daring, our energies fed each the other, and we did what we each had singly but wondered at and been too cowardly to attempt. We have done each other a great service this day. We have banished the only remaining doubt as to our true natures.

"You will need that validation in the years to come, Joshuah. Even such as you. You will have to think back to this feat again and again, to remember. To renew your courage."

"Was the food which we served the people then real, or of the mind?" said Merovee.

"They are one and the same," said Johannan. "All—everything—is an illusion, a mass dream if you will, created by thought."

"I saw you sneak a morsel of that 'imaginary' fish," said Joshuah, grinning at Merovee. "Did it taste real?"

For a long moment, she studied him. Then she tilted her head.

"Frankly, it could have used some salt."

Joshuah threw back his head. He and Johannan laughed until they cried.

The mirth was ended by Mathiah, who fell to his knees before Johannan.

"Master, you mentioned your true natures. Are you and your cousin . . ."

He hesitated, reddening. What he was about to ask was blasphemy to a Hebrew mind.

"Are the teachings of the priests in error? Are there many gods and not just one? Are you and your cousin gods come to walk amongst us?"

It was Joshuah who answered, by raising Mathiah precipitously to his feet.

"Would you kneel to yourself, Mathiah? I tell you that you have as much, and as little, cause to kneel to yourself as to this man, or to me, or to any god. The true god is All That Is. Therefore, the priests are correct. There is only one god.

"But, since the true god is All That Is, 'God' is also each one of us, and every lily and every camel—and every thing that creeps, crawls, walks, sits, swims, or blows. The true god is the earth you are standing on and the air that you are breathing, the sky, the stars, the waters, the fires . . . All That Is. Therefore, the priests are wrong, and the number of gods is beyond our ability to count.

"This is the Divine Dichotomy. Only when you realize that the full Power of the true god dwells within you and in every atom of your company on this Earth—even more than the full Power of wheat is contained in any little grain—will you find the Kingdom for which you quest . . ." he tweaked Mathiah's nose, "and realize that it was right under this handsome appendage of yours all along.

"What Johannan and I did just now is nothing more than any one of you can do if you will understand and know as we do. We demonstrated The Power that is your birthright, but which you stubbornly refuse to recognize and so utilize. Only in that are Johannan and I your 'masters.' You have but to open your minds, remember what you already know deep in your hearts, and understand what you remember. In the moment that you do, you will become our equals. You will become us, and we will become you, so that identical twins would be no more alike than we.

"So do not hide from the knowledge of 'God' in your own self, Mathiah. Such denial will only prolong your own misery and that of your fellows."

He crossed his arms, regarding the young man.

"Do you now understand?"

"I think so."

"Where, then, is the Kingdom of Heaven?"

" . . . In the sky?"

Joshuah threw up his hands.

Johannan sighed.

"In that case, Mathiah, the birds will be there before you."

He rose and went to the river to continue the immersions.

* * *

"I have immersed you in water," he told the crowds on that last afternoon. "That water has cleansed and prepared you. Yet I say to you that there is one who comes after me, who is even now amongst you, who will immerse you in fire. The fire of the Spirit, which is the motivating Essence of all things living, and even of those things which you think have no life—Spirit, which, of all things, deserves to be called 'Holy.' For that Spirit is The Energy, the vehicle, the manifestation of the true god in this world. It is a fire that burns but does not consume.

burning bush

"To Moses, it made itself <u>symbolically visible</u>, appearing as apart from his own self, as in a burning bush. The one who comes after me, who is far greater than I, shall give you knowledge of this Spirit, and bathe each of you who have ears to hear in its Holy Fire. It will burn into each heart ready to receive it, and dwell forever, never consuming, rather, instead, providing The Energy for greater heights of accomplishment.

"Where it dwells, there will be true understanding of the nature of the true god. The bodies of this elect shall be temples of the Kingdom, their hearts shall be its tabernacles. This is a new covenant, tidings of great joy which are for all the people, if only they will listen.

"And I tell you that, once you have understood the Kingdom of Spirit that is naturally within you, climbed in your understanding onto a higher mountain, there will never again, for you personally, be any war, or famine, or sorrow, or sickness, or even death as you now understand it. These will be the former things, the ignorance and misunderstanding of your spiritual childhood which shall have passed away, even as the swaddling in which your mothers bound you."

He sent each initiate forth from the waters with . . .

"Go now in sure and certain knowledge that the grace of the true god is within you. Love your Self. Not in the false way of one who secretly feels himself to be worthless, helpless, and who, to hide his own lacks, struts and postures and grabs and bullies. But love yourself out of true understanding that your own Self is a part of the true god. The god that loves you and that waits patiently for its love to be returned.

"<u>When you</u> have learned to love, and to respect your own Self for the god that dwells within, then love for your <u>fellows—those other</u> portions of the true god—will flow sweetly from you. Until then, all your protestations of love will be as the clicking of desert sands.

"So you now know how to love 'God,' the true god, with all your heart, and soul, and strength."

After the worst of the day's heat had passed, Johannan took Joshuah aside.

"I had a dream last night. My time is exceedly short. I want you to take Miriam away from here now . . . to your home. It is near Bethlehem, you said. So if you leave now, you can easily reach it this night."

"Yes."

"I do not need to tell you that if the soldiers of Antipas were to discover Miriam to be a woman when they come for me, and posing as a man, she would be handled without mercy. I spoke with Chandreah at the noon hour. He agrees to go with you. We settled on a story. In my newfound freedom, I have developed an insatiable thirst for some of the good wine which you have told me you have in your cellar. Additionally, I want some good fruit, and nuts from my own Samaria, which can be got in the bazaar of Bethlehem. Naturally, Miriam would not trust a man to make these selections, or even trust Chandreah not to lose himself in your cellar and forget to return.

"Chandreah will have spoken to her by now. It will be no surprise when you suggest setting off immediately, so that the provisions may be gotten in the morning and the return journey made after the midday heat tomorrow. Once you have her away, it will be up to the two of you to find convincing reasons to delay that return. Keep her until word comes that I have been taken. It might even be tonight."

"You have thought of everything. Except her habit of knowing the thoughts of others and peering into the future."

"I have not forgotten. Lock her up if necessary. Do what you will. But keep her safe."

He spoke these last words with difficulty, and turned his face away.

"I will try to do as you say," said Joshuah gently.

Johannan took his hand.

"She is the best of them, Josh. My most beloved disciple. And . . . my beloved. Though she knows it not. Cherish her. She is our sister in Spirit, and will learn quickly. I send her with you not only for her safety, but because you will have need of her. When her wrath against you dies, she will love you and succor you and fill the lonely places you will find along the way. In a manner that is hers alone."

"I will cherish her as yourself."

"My eternal thanks. Beyond that, between us two, I think there is nothing more that must be said."

"Not if you are decided to yield to Antipas."

"For me, all is accomplished, and I am very tired. May all your futures be joyful, my dear friend."

"May you return as a great tree, just for a rest."

Johannan laughed. Then his face straightened.

"There is one question. Have your ever thought . . . that there is yet another one?"

"A third major part of us? Yes. I have entered his thoughts in the dream state. I am not sure I like him. He does not yield. Like the toughest of bread, he will need to be well-chewed before being swallowed by even the most hungry."

"It is a man, then. I sensed the third, but could not get an image. I had often wondered if the third might even be Miriam, herself."

"In another era. If the present parameters of belief among us Jews will hardly countenance a female as follower, how then could she be accepted by our people as a teacher?"

"You are right, of course. You have climbed onto a higher peak than my own, and so see farther into the distances."

Johannan rose.

"Come, then, my other part. I have tried to make the way straight for you. Let me now see your foot set upon that path."

* * *

Merovee had no objections to the journey. Indeed, stores were getting low. She needed provisions for the making of bread, and it was the season for melons—orange, green, and luscious pink. And peaches, oozing with juice. Oranges, and pomegranates. Not grapes. Too early for the good ones. But she would get cheeses. And raisins . . . fresh figs, and grains for soups . . . she was glad that Chandreah was coming, they would probably need a pack ass to carry it all back, maybe two. She had dug up her money belt from under its rock, and, as they left, she was already envisioning Johannan's delight with what she would bring him. He had no idea about her money. The wine would, of course, be a gift from Joshuah, but the few coins which Johannan had given her would hardly, she knew, buy the nuts which he desired. Poor Johannan had been living in one wilderness or another for so long that he did not realize how prices had risen.

So Merovee took her leave from Johannan with an abstracted little smile and hardly a backward glance. She gave the two men no cause for complaint, girding her loins—tucking the flowing folds of her garment up into her gird to allow free movement of the legs—and striding purposefully along the narrow and dusty shepherds' paths which led to Bethlehem. She even set the pace, for the paths climbed steadily into the mountains. The welcome cool of darkness would be on them soon enough, but she had no mind to be traveling all night long. Tonight would be the full moon, which would make the going easier . . . and she was almost out of her balm. Would they have it in the bazaar at Bethlehem?

Yet, there were hours to be passed, and one might as well use them.

"Master . . ."

"Only Joshuah, please, Merovee. Or Jesus as I am called in the Greek."

"Then I shall call you Josh, for that is how Jo addressed you. Josh, when you multiplied your fishes . . . where did you go in your head?"

Joshuah smiled. Johannan was right. She understood and aimed for the core, unawed, as it should be.

"I sent The Energy directly, from a place in the forehead between the two eyes. There are many different techniques, both for receiving and sending. I do not know where Johannan went in his head, but he obviously channeled it out his fingertips. The teachers to whom I responded the best, however, were those in the north of India, the followers of the Great Buddha. They understand there to be a third, invisible eye in the spot just above and between the eyes. Most frequently, that is the place that they use for sending."

"What is best then, if one wants to learn?"

"There is no best. There is only what is right for you. Listen often inside your own mind. Become acquainted with the secret little things which are continually going on beneath your notice. Sounds, scenes, voices, emotions, fantasies . . . you spend so much time looking outward, you see. Much too much. You need the balance of inward vision. Learn to listen to what you think are the silences. In those silences hides The Power of the Universe and of your greater Self."

"That does not tell me how to multiply fishes."

He laughed.

"It does. Better than you know. I will make you a promise. Allot just half of one hour each day for a month to quiet listening inside your self. Then we will talk of this again. If you have done this with diligence, you will already have a feeling about your own best channel, and I can then aid you in strengthening it."

"But what is this?" said Chandreah. "Do you seek this man's powers, Merovee?"

"No. I seek my own."

"But power like that is not for such as you."

"I do hope," she said archly, "that you really meant to say such as *us*, Chandreah. Or do you mean that, because I am a woman, I must not presume?"

Chandreah shook his head and gave no answer.

"Perhaps," said Joshuah, "Chandreah is not sure what he means."

Chandreah nodded.

"You have put it the best."

"Let me tell you a story as we go," said Joshuah. "Once, a very long time ago, a king and a queen ruled over a beautiful land. They ruled equally and with justice, and the people were very happy. But the queen was exceedingly lovely, which made the people adore her, and she was exceedingly wise, so that they sought her counsel as much as that of the king.

"And the king had a brother who had nothing to rule for himself, and, since he had never bothered to learn a trade, he sat around the palace examining his thumbs and thinking of mischief which would keep him from remembering what an empty fellow he was. This brother grew jealous of the queen, and begin to whisper in the ear of the king that the people loved the queen better than the king, and that she grew too much in power by virtue of her goodness, and that soon she would take all the power and lord it over the king, and that the justice and equality for which they were famed would no longer be the mark of their reign.

"Though he should have known better, the king soon began to believe this spiteful brother, and to be jealous of his queen. The more beautiful she became, the more he resented it. The wiser she grew, the more threatened he felt. The happier were the people, the more he saw it as a sign that soon the queen would take everything for herself.

"The idle brother then proposed that, instead of the queen, he, himself, should rule with the king. Indeed, he said, in order to preserve the justice and equality for which the kingdom was famed, women should never ever be allowed to rule again.

"And the king agreed that this was a wonderful plan.

"The brother then proposed that they simply kill the queen. Here, the king refused. He was fond of his queen, and, since she was beautiful, he liked to look at her. So it was agreed that she would simply be put into eternal sleep.

"A magician was looked for, one who could brew a proper potion. But all the magicians were out performing tricks for the people that day. So an old sorceress was found, and brought to the palace. The king explained what he wanted . . . a potion to put his queen into peaceful sleep forever. And the sorceress complied.

"Except that, being a woman, she did it her own way. Unbeknownst to the king, she administered a potion that would keep the queen in sleep only until a man as wise as herself kissed her and bade her wake.

"Well, years passed. The foolish king and the spiteful brother ruled, and beauty was gone from the land, and wisdom and goodness. And the people began to be unhappy, and to quarrel amongst themselves, and the men of the kingdom, seeing that all this unhappiness had come about because the queen had gone to sleep and refused to wake, blamed her, and all women, for their woes. So they made their wives into slaves, and bade them not to speak unless spoken to, and to walk behind, and to sit in the corners in the temples, as unfit to worship their god—who also had his goddess taken from him.

"And things went from bad to worse, and there was a blight on the land, and famine, and wars without end. And the cry of the people went up. 'Our God! Why have you forsaken us?' But no answer came.

"In the palace, the king grew old, and the brother died, of a malignancy he had brewed from his own spite. With the whispers of his brother gone from his ears, the king began to remember, and to re-weigh his beliefs.

"And he realized how foolish he had been. How very happy he and the people had been before his queen was sentenced to her eternal sleep. And he went to the room where she lay, and knelt beside her and wet her face with his tears.

"'Oh Woman, how I wish that you would wake and take your place beside me once more. For I understand now that there are things our people need which a man alone can never supply.'

"And he kissed her."

They walked on in silence for a moment.

"Well?" said Chandreah. "Did she then wake?"

"I know not," shrugged Joshuah. "That is the end of the tale."

"It cannot be the end," said Chandreah.

"Why not?" said Joshuah.

"It has no resolution."

"Make your own."

"What a miserable storyteller you are!"

"That is because my mother was put to sleep by a sorceress when I was only a boy."

Merovee began to laugh. In mock anger, Chandreah scooped up a handful of dirt and flung it at Joshuah.

"Anyone know a good walking song?" said Joshuah, "How about this one?"

And he began to sing. An impious ditty about a very fat priest, riding a very small ass, jogging toward Jerusalem.

* * *

They attained the farm of Joseph of Ramah in the hills between Bethlehem and Jerusalem an hour after full darkness. Their merry songs could be heard from afar off, and they were met by two, laughing, young girls, and a boy. The girls flung themselves onto Joshuah, hugging and kissing him until he begged for mercy. The boy, who was almost thirteen and so nearly a grown man, hung back in a more dignified fashion.

"Did you find him?" demanded the oldest girl.

"Did he dunk you?" said the youngest.

"Is it true that he dresses like a camel?" said the boy.

"Yes, yes, and yes," laughed Joshuah. "Chandreah, Merovee, these discourteous persons are my sisters, Annah and Rachel, and the youngest of our family, Joses. Now do not disgrace me, you three, for I will have you know that these two young gentlemen are disciples of the Prophet, himself."

"How lovely to make your acquaintance," said Rachel. "Did you bring us some presents, Josh?"

"Now what could I bring you from The Wilderness, a scorpion or two?"

"Is the Prophet as great as they say he is?" said Joses.

"That and more," said Joshuah. "Among any man ever born to woman, he is the greatest."

"He cannot be greater than you," said Annah quite seriously.

"We are as twins," said Joshuah.

The three young people nodded as though they understood perfectly. Joses took Chandreah's hand companionably, while the two girls took Merovee's.

"But what is this?" said Annah after hardly a heartbeat.

She raised that hand of Merovee's that she held in her own and studied it in the moonlight. Then she peered at the face of Merovee.

"If you are to pass as a man, you had better toughen your hands, Maiden."

Joshuah let out a hoot.

"What a marvel you are, Annah. It took even me longer to divine the secret. Do not fear, Miriam. My family is as my own bosom. Your secret is safe with them."

20

"I am not so sure that Mother will approve," said Annah darkly.

"Josh, she is in a dreadful rage," said Rachel.

"Father has not come back from Jerusalem," said Joses. "He sent word that the Sanhedrin extended its session, and, this morning, with the largest field of grain to be got in, our overseer quit us."

Joshuah muttered something beneath his breath.

"How did Mother provoke him?"

"The usual way," shrugged Joses. "She knew better than he on all matters, till the poor man knew not which way to turn. He finally threw up his hands and left. I did the best I could to take his place, Josh, but . . . "

Joshuah put an arm around the boy and sighed.

Then he grew thoughtful and cast a glance at Merovee.

"Well, no matter, Joses. I am back. Chandreah, Miriam, I do apologize, but, as you see, we will have to delay our return to the Jordan, for I shall have to oversee the harvest on the morrow, awaiting my father's return. I assure you that our hospitality will make your stay a pleasant one. You will have more time in the bazaar, and then we will take asses from the stable of my father for a swift return."

For the first time, a worry creased Merovee's brow. She was not allowed the privacy of that worry. Rachel still had hold of her hand.

"So, you are Miriam, too, like our mother. I certainly hope you have a better temper."

Chapter 2
Into The Wilderness

"Where in the name of all that is holy have you been!"

Miriam, wife of Joseph of Ramah, shrieked the words as her eldest son and his entourage appeared in the cool, tiled, tree-sheltered courtyard where she had been sitting at her prized, Egyptian-style table with chairs, munching on bread and cheese and drinking watered wine. In the corner, a young slave boy took fright and stopped his strumming of the lyre.

"Do not stop, you fool! What else have I to calm my aching nerves? Joshuah, you have no idea what a day I have had."

Joshuah patted the young musician on the head.

"I do know, Mother. Joses described the problem."

"Joses? What does he know? He is a boy now, but soon he will be a man, Heaven forgive him. Why is it, just tell me why it is that every year at the time of the grain harvest the Sanhedrin calls an emergency meeting?"

"Mother, these are my friends, Chandreah and Merovee."

"Hello. Welcome. Sit, sit. Unless you have objections to sitting with a woman, in which case you can go to the kitchen, for I am not moving. Oh, look at those feet of yours. Naomi, bring basins with water and linens so that our guests might wash the dust from their feet. And more wine. Are you hungry? And bread and cheese! Every year, Joshuah. And they do not think we women notice. What sort of fools do they take us for?

"Or, more to the point, what sort of fools are they? They will prolong their meeting, and their holy moaning and marching, then come rolling home, well done for wine, I can assure you, after we women have done all the work. If the harvest is good, with never a word of thanks to us, they will go galloping back to the Temple to thank God for his goodness, and then stay to dispute some earth-shaking theological point such as, were the sandals of Moses made of calfskin or goat.

"But if the harvest is bad, you can be sure they will not leave until they have first blamed us wives. Then they will go galloping back to the Temple to moan and wail and beat their breasts and wonder why God has visited this travail on such as they. Then someone will suggest that the sandals were made of camel."

"Is there fruit as well, Mother?"

"Naomi! What is the matter with you, do you not see that the young master is here with guests? Bring that melon, and the dates.

"What is a woman to do? A husband who can not tear himself away from the Temple, an eldest son who disappears for years at a time and can hardly wait to run off again the moment he comes home, a second eldest who disappears into the desert to live with those ridiculous Essenes . . . you should see my Jacob," she said angrily to Chandreah. "Those people starve him! He looks like a hundred-year-old vulture waiting for his own self to die so that he can have something to eat. I hope you are not an Essene."

"No, Mistress."

"Very sensible. And I have not the slightest idea where Jude has gone to, he is probably with those awful Zealots, sticking knives into pro-Roman ribs in Caesarea."

"Oh, Joshuah, I thought it would be so different now. You said that you were home for good."

"I am, Mother."

"Strange way you have of showing it, hardly here a month, when off you go again. Did you find that young fool of Elisheba's?"

"Yes, Mother. Mother, what . . . "

"What was his name again?"

"Johannan."

"Oh yes. He ruins everything. If it were not for him, I could claim that all this bad blood came from your father's side."

"Mother, what did the overseer do that necessitated your interference?"

"What did he do? I will tell you what he did. Due to the lack of rain this year, he ordered that water for the workers be cut to one third of normal."

"Ah!"

"Yes! When they are already laboring for half the normal price due to the upset after the uprisings over the aqueduct that Pilatus tried to build with the Corban funds. One third ration, for even the children, Joshuah."

"You did not tell me," said Joshuah to his sisters and brother, "that the trouble was of this nature."

"And you have not heard the half of it," continued Miriam. "He forbade the gleaners."

"Impossible!"

The right of the poor to glean was inalienable, one of the best-kept injunctions of Mosaic Law.

"Yet it is so. I first heard of it yesterday morning. Naomi came to me, all shy, did you not, Naomi."

"Yes, Dear Mistress."

Joshuah grew thoughtful.

"What in the world possessed the man?"

"He said that, due to the poor rainfall, we would need the gleanings ourselves, and he sent word through the countryside."

"Father will die of shame when he hears."

"Quick!" cried Miriam. "Spit over your left shoulder! What can you be thinking of, Joshuah, to tempt the jinns in that manner?"

"Now Mother, how many times have I told you . . . "

"Too many times."

She leaned forward and grasped his hands.

"I did do well to oppose that terrible man, did I not, Joshuah?"

He smiled and touched her cheek.

"Yes, Rosula. I am proud of you."

"Good. Ohhhhh! The day I have had! It was so hot in that field, Joshuah. How do the poor people stand it?"

For the first time, she looked full at the newcomers. The scowl lines smoothed and she was suddenly quite handsome—in the same way, thought Merovee, that a raucous scrub bird was handsome. Her personality was as imposing as though she were large. Yet she was a small woman, coming barely to Merovee's shoulder. Her eyes were quite green, her hair, though streaked with gray, was red, while her freckles proclaimed that the red was not gotten from the henna so currently popular among the aristocratic Sadducean matrons of Jerusalem.

"So who are your young friends?"

"This is Merovee, and this is Chandreah."

"You already told me their names. Who are they?"

It was obvious, from Joshuah's grin, that he took secret delight in his mother. He turned with a mock whisper to Merovee.

"Though her given name is Miriam, we call her 'Rosula.' It is much more fitting, do you not think?"

"I cannot be sure, for I do not know the word. It sounds Latin."

"Humph!" said Rosula. The slanted green eyes examined Merovee then turned upon Chandreah. "You. You are Galilean."

For, though Galileans spoke Kione, the same Aramaic dialect as did Judeans—heavily influenced by the recently ended Greek occupation—the Galilean accent was, to the Judean ear, foolish and rude, the butt of cruel jokes.

"But you." She swung back to Merovee. "You puzzle me. Your accent, and that strange name of yours. Is it not Canaanite, the name?"

"Yes, Mistress. It has been in use in my mother's family as long as anyone can remember. Her grandfather was Merovee, and his grandfather before him. Nobody really knows why."

"But you are Hebrew . . . "

"Yes."

"And what is your accent?"

Merovee shrugged, wishing Rosula would turn her attention to another topic.

"It is a mixture of many things. My mother was born in the Greek Peloponnesus. Yet, when she was still a girl, her family removed to Galilee."

"The Peloponnesus?" said Joshuah. "Then you must be Benjaminite."

"Yes."

"That explains the use of a Canaanite name in your family," he said. His voice was smooth, but his eyes twinkled. He was enjoying her discomfiture at the prolonged analysis of her name. "When the Benjaminites left Judeah, most of them moved north, at least passing through Canaan and Phoenicia, if not actually settling there for a time."

"On the other hand," said Merovee, pushing on, "the people of my father are of Bethany near to Jerusalem. Hence, Mistress, I have spent equal time in both Galilee and Judeah. But then I also speak Greek fluently, for, aside from the fact that it was the language of my mother and my grandfather, I spent time in my childhood in Athens and the Peloponnesus, and again in Alexandria. My grandfather traveled a great deal on business, you see. He loved me dearly and often took me with him on these travels. Sometimes, Mistress, I am not really sure just how I should speak."

"To speak fine Judean is infinitely the best," said Rosula, emphasizing the gutturals in the proper fashion, and she nodded as though the matter were settled. "But you had best begin to learn some

Latin. Greeks are of our past, young man, while Rome will be with us Jews until all of us here are in our winding sheets.

"So I will teach you your first Roman word. Rosula. It means Little Rose."

She leaned forward on one elbow, grinning evilly.

"It was bestowed upon me by our praefectus, Pontius Pilatus, himself. Do you not find it apt? Do you not find me to be as a small, delicate rose?"

Merovee hesitated, then returned Rosula's grin.

"Most certainly. For seldom can one pluck even the most delicate rose without losing some blood to the thorns."

The mother of Joshuah let out a shriek of merriment, sounding for all the world like the women who hawked their fish in the towns along the Sea of Galilee.

"You will do well, my fine young fellow. And what a pretty boy you are. Now, what is the name of this Galilean grandfather of yours who had need of so much travel?"

"His name was Nathan. He was a potter."

"A potter with business in places like Athens?"

"And Rome," said Merovee with a mischievous smile. For she had not said that she did not know Latin, only that she did not know the word 'Rosula.' And when it came to her grandfather, Nathan, she could not squelch her pride. "He founded a factory near to Migdal—or Magdala as you probably think of it. Among other things, the factory produces the postal cylinders."

"Your grandfather was Nathan of the Magdalia?"

The wife of Joseph nearly dropped her wine.

The bulk of magdalia—as the Romans termed the sealed postal cylinders used throughout the civilized world—were made by the House of Nathan.

Rosula's green eyes narrowed, appraising the boy Merovee with embarrassing frankness.

"Naomi. Bring more wine. A jug from the bottom cellar. And that new goat cheese. Fix a lettuce with oil and vinegar and herbs, and put some of those nice olives into it, my son and his friends are ravenous from their journey.

"Annah, dear, come sit next to Merovee. There is my good girl. Do you not think that Annah is comely, Merovee? She is the eldest daughter. Naturally, she will have an excellent inheritance."

Annah flushed and began to giggle. Merovee squirmed and looked at Joshuah. Chandreah laughed outright. And Joshuah found his voice.

"Mother, there is something you ought to know."

Miriam looked from one to the other.

Then a look of hurt flooded the green eyes, and they hardened.

"Oh. Is *that* it? Yes. Forgive a stupid mother out of step with these cosmopolitan times. Yes. I should have known. You return after half a lifetime away from us with your hair cut off as though for mourning, not a whisker on your face—so that we hardly know how to explain you to our friends—with those soft robes and sophisticated Greek ways, preferring even to be called Jesus in the Greek manner. And now I am to understand that you have entirely adopted Greek habit. After the wonderful things I expected of you!"

"Mother, that is not it."

"Do not bother, 'Jesus.' I can be modern, though you had best not let your father know of this.

"And it is a pity to rob from your lovely little sister, what with such a dearth of eligible young men in this God-ridden land. It seems that they are all either out with the Zealots killing Romans, or becoming Essenes and doing little but to worry over whether there are any specks of dirt on their pure white robes, or else rushing to be Pharisees, muttering prayers morning, noon and night and seeing who can wear the largest tefillin—with their duty to marry the farthest thing from their minds, all of them ignoring sweet young things like my Annah, here."

Joshuah had been doing his best not to laugh.

"Mother, I assure you," he said with lowered voice, "if what you think about Merovee and me were so, I would announce it to you proudly, for no real love between human beings is reprehensible. But you have rushed ahead of the tidings. The others smile only because they already know what I was just about to tell you. Merovee is, in truth, Miriam, like you. She has served our cousin Johannan in the guise of a boy, and continues to travel in that guise for safety."

Rosula's eyes widened and fastened on Merovee.

"You ought to be whipped!" she hissed. "Does your father know where you are at?"

"My father is dead. But, though my mother has no way of knowing where I am at this exact moment, Rosula, she knows how and why I went to Johannan, and she approves."

"What sort of mother is she? Allowing you to travel—live—with men, and not even a chaperone? What can she be thinking to let you do this?"

"She thinks, I am sure," said Merovee stiffly, "that I know what I am about, that I am honorable, that the men I chose to deal with are also honorable, with greater things to think of than mere animal rutting. And that I have the right—nay, the duty—to govern my own life."

Naomi arrived at that moment with the oiled lettuce and the good wine. The slave boy continued to plunk diligently upon the lyre. The night was gentle and the moon bright overhead. The wife of Joseph poured wine for her family and guests and gave herself a measure full to the brim, with no room for water. She took a deep draught and examined, anew, the young person who sat at her table. Then she turned to Chandreah.

"And what do you do?"

"I fish."

"How nice. I wish you had brought some of your product with you, it would go nicely with our meal."

"Ask your son," said Chandreah. "If you insist, he will make you a basket full."

Rosula turned away. The younger generation had gone mad. She would love to have blamed it on left-over influence from the pleasure-loving Greeks, but the Romans were really just as bad, what with their idols, and their opulence, and their precious empire. Their mere presence and example was dividing the people into seemingly endless camps, sects, parties, and cults, each one becoming more fanatical by the day, each propounding a different belief and calling it the only way, so that it grew tedious trying to remember who stood for what and why.

And, all the while, the struggle between the Sadducean old guard and those upstart Pharisees for control of the Temple grew more intense, and religious demands proliferated until it was next to impossible to get through a day without seriously violating what one or the other of those groups considered to be The Law.

And how quick the Temple authorities had become to punish those infractions, rather than sensibly waiting for God to do it. Why, the action that the overseer had taken this morning could still have repercussions.

Perhaps he had been an agent of the High Priest, sent to create an embarrassing incident that could be held over the head of her husband.

Or perhaps he was a Zealot, plotting their destruction because of their friendship with Pontius Pilatus.

Or he might simply be someone with a grudge against them because of the activities of one of her sons.

Who knew? Life of late had become as a journey through a field of quicksand. Each step had to be considered in advance, and, even then, seemingly solid earth could give way and swallow a person. How, she had secretly to admit, could the young people help but develop strange ideas in the midst of such insecurity?

She sighed. Life had used to be so blessedly simple.

Her gaze settled upon Merovee once more. Imposing, if one considered her as a female. No beauty in the strict sense of the word, and impertinent in the extreme. Yet the inheritance of Nathan of the Magdalia was not to be sniffed at. Were there brothers? Was she at least the eldest daughter?

Miriam, wife of Joseph of Ramah, smiled. All was not yet lost.

"I trust you have noticed what a fine sort of a man this 'Jesus' of mine is, 'Merovee.' Can you imagine? Closer to forty than to thirty, the first heir of his father, yet he has so far escaped the right of his father to have him wed."

* * *

A mother exercised her own rights shortly. She ordered her youngest children to retire, and, with them, smoothly, their female guest.

"We need not involve any of the servants in your retiring, my daughters. Act as the hostesses of the house in my place. It will be good training for you. Give our guest the best guest chamber, my favorite, fancy quilt, and see that all the amenities for a bath are laid out."

"But, for Heavens sake," she whispered, "do not linger. Remember, she entered this house as a man. Servants have keen eyes, large ears, and even larger mouths."

"Good night to you, 'Merovee.' Since Joshuah is here to see to the fields, I shall accompany you to the markets in the morning. I have some buying of my own to do."

"I shall be honored of your company, Rosula. Thank you. Good night."

Rosula waited until the young people had disappeared into a corridor which led to yet another courtyard, around which the sleeping chambers were ranged. Then she turned on her son, voice again lowered.

"Heavens above us, Joshuah, of what can you be thinking? If the Sadducees get wind of what this girl is up to with her male attire, I shudder to think what they will do to her. Or to us!"

"I fear more the Pharisees," interjected Chandreah.

"What matters it?" said Rosula. "If a man can be stoned to death simply for disobedience to his father, would they do less to a woman who so flouts every convention? There were two stonings to the death at the pit in Jerusalem just last week, Joshuah. There is insanity in the air. One cannot be too careful."

"I am not really sure that they would do anything to her," said Joshuah thoughtfully. "True it is that Scripture says that a woman should not wear the clothes of a man, but it does not mention any specific punishment, or even say that the violation must be punished."

"That is why I fear the Pharisees," urged Chandreah. "Daily, they add to The Law to suit themselves. They will invent the demand for punishment. Joshuah. Miriam makes a mockery of every custom concerning women, they could not afford to let her get away with it, for then other women might begin to act in the same way. Since she first came to Johannan, I have been telling her, and him, too, of the danger in which she puts herself *and* us men. Oh I do beg your pardon, Rosula, if my accent makes it difficult for you to understand."

Rosula blushed and poured more wine. Joshuah laughed outright.

"Do not worry about my mother. She understands Galilean only too well."

Chandreah did not press. Instead he said earnestly . . .

"From the very beginning, the spies of the High Priest and Sadducees have been among those who come to hear Johannan, and there have been so many Pharisees that the rattling of their tefillin sometimes drowns out his voice.

"And they do not come to learn anything, Joshuah, no, none of them. They come to catch him in some infraction of The Law, or in some phrase that they can construe as an infraction.

"Oh, how they watch, with their sweet-as-honey eyes, their ostentatious modesty. Rapacious as vultures! Sadducee or Pharisee, one is as bad as the other. One group seeking to create Law, to extend the ways in which one must bow and scrape to God, the ways in which one can offend God, and to force all the rest of us to their view. The other group seeking to apply the existing Law so rigidly that our people will soon die from lack of the ability to breathe. Both factions seek to lay their clutches on every corner of your life and my life, extend their insidious authority, and make us slaves to their insanity!

"Just look how we whisper here, afraid to be overheard, afraid to offend, lest we be reported to these fanatics who have gained all the power in Jerusalem, and who have the ability to visit calumny on any one of us or on our families.

"And, as far as I am concerned, it is not out of any real piety that they do this, but for their own political ends and comfort!"

Chandreah's voice had risen. Smoothly, Rosula turned to the young musician.

"You may retire now, Coel, Dear. Thank you for playing so sweetly. And, please, forgive that I was short with you earlier. My day was hard."

"I understand, Dear Mistress, As I sleep, I will try to dream of a new song to play for you."

"Give me a kiss."

The boy complied, adding a hug with the kiss.

"My apologies," said Chandreah when the boy had gone.

Rosula smiled, and, aloud, said graciously . . .

"The child is devoted to me. His mother died when he was but a toddler. I have raised him. Still, one can never be too careful."

To herself, she thought . . .

'Galileans. Hotheads, every one of them.'

"No, you cannot be too careful! Exactly a case in point!" Chandreah continued angrily. "Do you wonder that we flock to Johannan? Those such as myself, and even a female such as our Merovee. Bless her, I say. I can name you a thousand men who have not her courage, not even if you join them all together.

"You speak against her mother. I honor her mother, for she is ten times more courageous than even Merovee, knowing what could befall her and her entire family as a result of this girl's doings. Yet she sends her forth with blessings.

"Do you not see, Rosula? It is *freedom* that is at stake here!"

"Freedom? Are you a Zealot? Do you wish to oust the Romans?"

"No! What bother are the Romans? Until recently, they did not even tax us. They have left us free to govern ourselves and live as we please. It is our own people who are the oppressors! The Sadducees and priests, the scribes, and Levites, the Pharisees, the Zealots. *They* are what send men like me to men like Johannan. And to your son.

"You see how much I trust in your son? I did not even ask, 'What sort of household is this?' Though you are obviously rich, and you speak of a husband off to attend the Great Sanhedrin of Jerusalem, so that you are probably Sadducees. Yet I know, from the things your son has done and said, that I am not in a den of the oppressors."

"Oh my goodness," said Rosula. "I certainly hope not. Joseph is . . . conservative. I suppose one *could* call him a Sadducee."

"Heaven preserve me."

"But he is very fair. And everyone nowadays belongs to some sort of faction," said Rosula testily. "One has to have *some* sort of stance, especially in my husband's position. He is the ranking prince of the House of David, of triply high lineage—Mount Ephraim, Bethlehem, and Hebron. He is of great importance. What would you have him do? He has to fit himself *somewhere*. We all do. Even you. What *are* you? If not a Zealot, what then do you call yourself?"

"I call myself Chandreah," said Chandreah proudly. "I belong to no sect. I know myself to *be* without having to belong to a group! I want only to be allowed to live in the dignity of my own knowledge. I deny the right of any other person to tell me how to live my life, or how to worship my god."

"But this is laid down!" said Rosula desperately. "You are Hebrew, for all you are from Galilee— what is your tribe?"

"Naphtali."

"Well, so you are not of Judah and so not a Jew, but you are Hebrew. You are a son of Ibrahim, of Jacob. And The Law is simply *there*. You must live it. You are one of a chosen group. You are designated by God, himself, to live by that Law. You cannot refuse."

"Mistress, I beg to differ. I can refuse and I do refuse. I insist on my own right to interpret God in my own way. If it were only between him and me, I could probably live in reasonable harmony with his Law all my days.

"But, can you not see? That is not what pertains anymore. God is no longer present in all this niggling and naggling. I can now turn neither right nor left without some pious fool popping up to tell me how I have offended against his interpretation of The Law.

"And not only can this pious fool berate me, but he can imprison me, try me, flog me until I cry out that I agree with him, or stone me until I am dead, or else claim that I have committed some treason against Emperor Tiberius and turn me over to Rome for crucifixion.

"*And* bring my loved ones to ruin in the bargain!

"I do not have to belong to any sect to say that I will not tolerate that. Daily, there are more like myself. And, for such as us, leaders like Johannan, like your son, will come forward. They will lead us as Moses once led us, out of bondage, out of this excessive interference in living, back to . . . "

"To what?" said Rosula scornfully. "You are so young. Too young to remember anything else. Even I can hardly remember a time . . . "

She sighed.

"Oh, I suppose when Herod still lived . . . for all his horrendous abuses, it was a lighter life. He was so loved by Caesar Augustus that, even though a tax was threatened, and we were, in fact, counted for the purpose of being taxed, no tax was actually imposed.

"Oh, it is this tax! This damnable taxation which Rome *has* imposed in these last few years which has so inflamed our people and driven us into all this madness."

She shook her head.

"Is it not strange? I never really thought about it till now. Herod murdered his father-in-law, his brother-in-law, his mother-in-law, his beloved wife, his two young sons, and countless more innocents besides. And to those moral outrages we Jews hardly murmured a protest. But just let Rome impose a tax. On *us*? We are the *Chosen* people, no one has a right to tax *us*!

"And so we protest. And how do we protest? By tearing each other asunder over our own internal religious matters. Now what sense does that make, I ask you?"

She halted. For Joshuah was laughing.

"Oh, Josh," she said. Tears came to her eyes. "I can not laugh with you, my son. Neither with your brave young friend here, nor yet with that demented young female whom I have just sent off to bed. I can understand in some small way what you all protest about, and what you seek. But I think you seek it in the wrong places. You fight against your own people, your own Law, which has nourished and sustained us for over a thousand years. You but compound the error of the sects which visit this oppression upon you. If you came to me and told me that you were Zealots, going out to fight the Romans and free us from their yoke, I would be more content. For I think this foreign domination is really the root of the problem."

Joshuah took her hands.

"Do you know that I love you, Mother?"

Miriam's eyes grew dimmer with tears.

"Yes. I know."

"Hear me then. The Law as we know it has served its purpose to our people and to Humanity. The time of its rule is about to end. The foreign yoke is only the catalyst.

"The answer is not out there, Mother. It is not the foreigners. It never is. Not in any instance. Always, the answer lies within . . . within each society, and, inevitably, within each person. Each idea outlives its usefulness and eventually becomes a millstone upon our understanding of ourselves. Ideas are meant to be—not replaced—but built upon, so that, continually, we climb higher. The greater the idea, the greater the build, the higher the step that appears, the more confusion amongst the masses, the more fear and resistance from those who have grown fat and comfortable and do not wish to make the climb.

"So it is with our Law. Our Law is one of the greatest Ideas of this current experiment to date. But, of its own greatness, it has bred many sons. I am one of those sons. And, Mother, I am about to find my voice."

There were tears even in Joshuah's eyes.

"I do not make mockery of our Law. I revere it as I would a dying parent. And the fact that most of us Jews turn upon our own selves in our frenzy, and not upon the Romans, is tribute to our instinctive understanding of the Idea that we have guarded in the guise *of* The Law! All of us really, in our hidden hearts, understand that that Idea is no longer an egg, and is in the throes of becoming a caterpillar."

Miriam tilted her head poignantly.

"Not a butterfly?"

"Someday, Rosula. But not quite yet."

"And you think," she said, "that you are come to be midwife to this . . . caterpillar."

She drew a weary breath.

"Are we to be green or brown? I have seen both kinds."

* * *

Chandreah and Joshuah sat late over the wine after Rosula retired.

"I wish to stay with you, Master," said Chandreah.

"If Johannan had not wished you to stay, he would not have sent you with me. You are welcome. But call me not master. Not even Joshuah. In my many years in India, they called me 'Isa.' It was their translation of the Greek translation of Joshuah, which is Jesus. During my last years in Greece and Alexandria, I answered to Jesus. As my mother so tartly stated, I have come to think of myself in terms of those sounds."

"Then Jesus it shall be. What did Johannan tell you? How long before he is taken?"

"He was expecting the minions of Herod Antipas hourly."

"It is only a blind you know, this fanciful story that Johannan has spoken against the incestuous marriage of Antipas to Herodias, and so incurred their wrath. Johannan has offered no such personal affront. But the chief priests and Pharisees, whose directives even Antipas is afraid to ignore, have caused this legend to be spoken abroad as an excuse for Antipas to seize Johannan."

"Ah, Jesus, it has been with fainting heart that I have watched the snakes from the Temple hissing in the multitude these last weeks. Not a day passed without them. And Johannan would not yield to counsel. He insisted upon speaking his heart, knowing that each utterance shook their citadel the more, and so brought his ruination closer. His teachings after your arrival were certainly the last straw."

"I know. I saw men of my father's acquaintance among the faces."

"Do you think they recognized you?"

"How could they help it?" smiled Jesus. "My dress and manner are unmistakable, and they all know of the wanderings and recent return of Joseph's eldest prodigal."

"Then you, too, have put yourself into danger."

"We are each in danger from the moment we decide, yet again, to take root in a womb, and to make that awful, suffocating trip forth into this world. The time of such a one as I is seldom long, Chandreah. What those who dispose of us refuse to note is that the Ideas we bestow upon humanity do not die along with our bodies."

"Nonetheless, you will need stout men to defend you."

"Johannan has stout men. Think you they will be of any use at the end? No. They will fade away, disappearing behind trees, lifting no hand in defense. The only followers who would have stayed, defending to the death with their own bodies, are here in this house with me. That is why you were both sent hither."

"Be that as it may, you have need of strong men. I have an older brother in Galilee, a fisherman as myself. Simon. He is not too bright, but he is a big man, strong and true to what he believes. And I am sure I can find others. Probably fishermen as ourselves. Come down into Galilee. Teach there, with us to guard you. People there are more free, not the bigots which you grow here in the south. We are accustomed to different ideas in Galilee. Is Galilee not scorned by the Temple snakes as the seat of every vile heresy and foreign corruption? Your ideas can take root in our fertile, Galilean soil. They can then spread out in all directions, along the caravan tracks of which we are the center, instead of shriveling in the seed as they would surely do here in barren Judeah."

"How could such eloquence be refused?" said Jesus smoothly. "Come I shall."

Chandreah stared.

"Just like that?"

"Why not?"

"It is much too easy." He tilted his head. "Have I but given voice to your own thoughts and plans? I have, your eyes are twinkling. If I had not asked you, you would have told *me*."

Jesus only smiled.

"To add to your arguments, my activities here in Judeah would be severely curtailed on account of my father and his position in the Sanhedrin."

"Is he against you, then?"

"Neither for nor against. Since he has not had me stoned to death as a disobedient son, one could say that he is moderate. But I do not care to put his back to the wall, neither do I care to endanger him nor my family.

"Additionally, the rock on which I will build my new edifice *is* The Law. I need, then, to begin with those who know that Law, while those same people must be open enough to listen and to understand the greater heights—and depths—to which I shall lead them.

"And who knows both heights and depths better than fishermen, who must watch the sky for the weather as well as the sea for the fish.

"So, yes, Chandreah. Go ahead of me into Galilee. Find me some stout friends, and I will teach all of you to fish for your fellow men."

* * *

On the following morning, however, the household of Joseph of Ramah woke to confusion.

Merovee was gone. Her bed had not even been slept in, the treasured, fancy quilt lay as Annah and Rachel had left it.

Tearfully, Rachel supplied the men with what they needed to know.

"Yes, now that you mention it, we did speak of Herod Antipas. She asked if we had heard aught of his movements, and I told her yes. A Roman post rider stopped yesterday, craving water for his horse. As his horse drank, he mentioned to me some of the gossip from Jerusalem, and he said that Antipas was stirring himself. Rumor said that the guard from the Herodian Palace was preparing to march toward the ford of the Jordan at Bethabarah."

"Why did you not tell me of this!" cried Jesus.

"I did not know that it was important!" wailed Rachel.

Leaving a disgusted Rosula to see to the harvest yet again, Jesus and Chandreah set off upon stallion, riding asses from the stable of Joseph. They reached the ford at Bethabarah at mid-morning.

Where multitudes usually gathered around Johannan, there was now only trampled grass.

Likewise, the camp of Johannan was empty. The Ford Master was not in his hut, only his goats grazed placidly nearby. Not a person was to be found. And there were no signs of any struggle.

The two men sat down on their haunches and thought upon what to do next.

* * *

Merovee had waited only until her young hostesses had entered their own sleeping chamber on the opposite side of the courtyard. She then filled her water skin from the pitcher beside the sleeping couch, filled the folds of the girdling belt at her waist with the contents of a dish of nuts and dried fruit so thoughtfully provided, and, carrying her sandals, stepped out onto the tiled walkway.

The center of the court was planted with fruit trees and the bushes of Rosula's pet name. Though the moon was still bright, those trees concealed her movements should Annah or Rachel glance through the vents of their windows. Shadow-silent, Merovee glided to the farthest corner of the courtyard, into a corridor that, as she had rightly guessed, led to the stable court.

For a brief, yearning moment she considered borrowing an ass. But the danger of discovery was too great. From experience, she knew that those opinionated beasts would bray at the slightest provocation. Being awakened from slumber and prodded out into the night was more than slight. She continued to the gate, stealthily lifted the bar, and slipped out.

Her first impulse was to run. Better sense conquered that impulse. Bright as the terrain was beneath the moon, the shepherds' paths over the Judean hills from Bethlehem to Bethabarah were not like the main trail from Jerusalem to that same place. They were rough and often treacherous, especially traveling downhill. She could not risk a turned ankle, or torn sandals, or bruised or bloodied feet. Not at the first. Neither could she exhaust her strength. So she strapped on her sandals, girded her loins, and started off at a smart, but sane, stride.

She understood all of it now. How could she have been so dense? She, the seer, the one who could sniff the wind and tell the future. What had happened to her famous senses, that Jo had known, ahead of herself, that he was soon to be taken? The sudden drinking of wine these last days had been part of his calculated ruse. And nuts from Samaria, indeed. What was wrong with the nuts that grew on the banks of the Jordan, which she gathered for him daily?

How could she have allowed herself to be so gulled?

Angrily, she stopped the tears. They but blurred her vision and increased the chances of misstep.

Of course she knew why Johannan had done it. She could reconstruct his instructions to Chandreah and Jesus regarding her safety, and the promises he must have extracted from them.

Yet she could still hate those two men for implementing his instructions.

Her strides ached to lengthen, to carry her faster. Were the soldiers of Antipas already arrived? Was it already too late?

Her inner sense said no, she was in time. But she did not trust that inner sense any longer, not after it had abandoned her so shamefully this last day.

When the soldiers came, would Mathiah and the others make a stand? Or would they run, leaving Johannan alone, defenseless except for his innate greatness.

Thanks be to the gods for the moon.

There was a goddess of the Moon. To the Greeks, she was Artemis, to the Romans, Diana, to Canaanites and Phoenicians, Astarte. She had been the goddess of the Canaanites. And, yes, the Benjaminite ancestors of Merovee *had* passed through Canaanite lands when forced to flee Judeah all those centuries before. And, yes, they had sojourned there for many generations. Joshuah had been chillingly close to the bone with that hypothesis.

Merovee knew all about Artemis-Astarte. In all her manifestations. For, truth to tell, the ways of the Canaanites were far from forgotten by the people of her mother.

And Merovee knew very well why the name "Merovee" still occurred in the family, swimming up from its Phoenician-Canaanite depths.

Anxiously, she glanced at the sky. Clouds were gathering. If they covered the moon, the way would become so hard, so slow.

"Mother," she breathed. She drew an amulet from the folds of her gird, kissed it, and spoke to the moon, to blessed Artemis hunting her stags somewhere overhead. So what if the Jews did consider it a sin to pray to any god but theirs? Right now she needed all the help she could get, and she had no trust whatsoever, and no love, for the thoroughly unlovable god worshiped in the Temple of Jerusalem.

"Continue to light my way. Let me speed across these hills as swiftly and safely as they say that you do, Mother. Lend me your fleetness for just this night . . . my beloved Jo is in mortal danger."

Yes. He was her beloved. She had finally to admit it to herself.

And would he ever know? Should he ever know?

Of course not. How ridiculous. A man such as Johannan was beyond such considerations.

* * *

The moon remained her constant protectress. She arrived back at the ford in much better time than had been made earlier in the day with the two men. Some distance from the river she slowed, and took to the scrub and rocks, watching and listening.

Naught seemed amiss.

She made her way down to the shore, to the camp in the palm grove. At the edge. she squatted, silent, waiting for her eyes to adjust to the gloom.

As she saw, her heart fell.

No. Crashed.

The bed rolls of the followers were gone. Only her own bed roll, and Johannan's, and Johannan's sheepskins, remained. There was not even a glow in the ashes of the campfire.

She was too late. The disciples had fled. The minions of Antipas had been here. They had taken him.

She sank down onto her knees, then threw herself flat out upon the earth. Her wail went up, uncaring now for listening ears.

"Johannannnnn!"

Tears gushed out, and her sobs filled the night.

Then, as in a dream, she heard his voice.

She lifted her head, looked around.

He stood on the top of a nearby hillock, seeming to be the ultimate destination of a moonbeam. Was it an illusion?

She rose, ran toward him, stumbling up the slope . . . straight into his solid, outstretched arms.

"Merovee. You fool. Why did you come back?"

"You tricked me, damn you!"

"I had to. Go, Merovee. Now. Please. You must."

"I will not."

"I order you."

"To Gehennah with your orders! Where are the others?"

"They left. I sent them."

"And the cowards did leave?"

"They are not cowards. They but obeyed me."

"Cowards! Cowards!" she shrieked.

She pulled him to her, so closely that she thought his body would have to blend straight into hers. She held him in a grasp that dared the world to take him from her.

"Oh, Jo. My darling. My love. Do not make me leave you. Do not make me go. If you must die, let me die with you."

Johannan stood for a moment, his arms gone stiff, held outward now, suddenly not daring to hold her.

Then, with a great exhaled breath, he relaxed toward her and around her, returning her love.

"All right," he whispered. "I tried. All of Creation knows that I tried. Yet it defied me, and sent you back to me. The reason is clear."

He pulled her down, into the hollow of the hillock where he had been lying, thinking, awaiting the arrival of his enemies.

He did not waste time. There might be none to spare. How he wished it were otherwise, as his lips sought hers and he felt the shocked, glad flood of emotion that she gave back to him. He allowed his own tears to flow.

"Oh Miriam. If things had been otherwise . . . I would have served you all my days."

"If you were the mere sort of man to have had all that time to serve me, perhaps I would never have loved you. So think not of that. Only love me now, this once, with all your heart and strength."

For one fleeting moment, he wondered if he remembered how.

Then he forgot to wonder if he remembered.

* * *

They lay together beneath the moon.

"I prayed to her again, Jo," whispered Merovee. "To keep the clouds away and speed me to you. Did I sin in your eyes?"

"You prayed to Artemis, you mean?" He smiled. "No, my darling. I have told you. Artemis . . . any god, any goddess . . . they are all our friends. Like you and like I, deities are but attributes, beloved children, of the Great God Which Is Everything."

He hugged her closer.

"Anything that Humankind can imagine, is a part of 'God,' my darling. So never fear to take your comfort and your help from where you may, and as it is presented to you. I promise you. There is no path in this world upon which you can place a sandal that is even so much as a sneeze away from The Power that sustains us."

Merovee smiled. Then laughed. She reached into the squashed, disarrayed folds of her gird and withdrew an offering.

"I almost forgot. I completed at least part of my assigned task. Nuts and fruit from Bethlehem, Master."

He laughed and took the food gratefully.

"I did go without my supper this night."

"You see the trouble you get into by sending me away?"

She emptied the belt, searching out each morsel.

"Just like your kind," he smiled.

"Ah, Jo."

She lay back against the hillock, the better to see him in perspective. She was aware of the coarse, but giving, grass and dirt, and of the unyielding rocks beneath her body, as she was acutely and blissfully aware of every sight, sound, and smell of the night.

"You seem so young now. How old are you really, Old Man?"

"In my heart right now I am newly born. In years? As I said before, I am only a few years older than my cousin Joshuah."

"Joshuah has become Greek," she said tartly. "We are all to call him Jesus."

"So be it then. How come you to scorn things Greek, my love? You above all?"

"You reprimand me."

"Never. Not you. I seek only to give you what wisdom I may in the little time that is left to us. Your wrath is not at things Greek, or at the name by which Joshuah chooses to be called. Your wrath is at the man, himself.

"Please. For my sake—and yours—love him."

She nodded, and sighed almost indifferently.

"All right. They will be here soon, Jo. Our enemies. A sister of Josh had word yesterday that the soldiers of Antipas were preparing to march. I feel them gathering toward us."

It was as if she gave the signal. Far in the distance, the first faint clink of metal was heard.

"Oh!"

She dove back toward him, clasping him desperately.

"Hold me. Kiss me just once more."

He obeyed. With all his heart.

"Do you think they will kill us immediately? Or will they take us to a prison?"

He smiled . . . and almost wanted to laugh for gladness at a Soul such as hers. There was, in her voice, no care for herself, but only for him. She was already scheming at how to feed him, minister to him, arrange for his comfort should they not be killed outright, but cast into some foul dungeon. He savored, for one last moment, the scent of her hair. Then he put her out to arms' length.

"Whatever they do, Miriam, it will be done to me, alone. You are to remain here."

His hand shot out, silencing her retort. Over his hand, her eyes were wide and frenzied.

"No. Listen to me. I said that you were sent back to me for a reason. I yielded to that. If you truly love me, you will yield as well.

"I poured my seed into you this night, Miriam. Seldom has seed been given and received so gladly, and with such love. If only for that reason, it is blessed."

He held even more firmly against her struggling.

"But there is more. Your body has become a chalice, and that chalice is sacred. I have not spoken to you before this moment of my own greater reality. But I have known it. And so have you. Yes, I am a man. But I am more besides.

"And so now, as to our coupling, I have not the slightest doubt. You would not have come back here tonight except that you knew, at a deeper level of yourself, that you are the Chosen One. Of all women on earth, you are my match, Miriam. My brave Merovee. It is you who were born, made, to bear this seed and see it raised to a tall, full plant."

She went slack, just staring. He released her from the iron grip.

"Do you understand what I am saying, Merovee?"

"Yes."

"The Law of our people states that it is a despair and dishonor to any person to leave this Earth knowing that he or she leaves no body child behind. I do not agree with this at all, and, myself, was leaving behind so many mind children to benefit my fellows that I barely gave thought to physical progeny. Until this night. Now I see the beauty and rightness of this additional gift that your love has enabled me to leave for Humankind. I have taken you for my dear wife, Miriam. Merovee. Have you taken me as your dear husband?"

"With all my heart."

He unloosed his great gird of leather, and put it about her waist. It went twice around.

"Since I have no other token, this will have to do. To those who know me, it will serve even better than any document, for it will be recognized, and they will believe what you tell them, that it is a token of our marriage, valid under customs of our people."

He smiled a rueful smile.

"They will then respect the child as both lawfully and naturally born, rather than having to make stories about angels or swans or lights from Heaven to explain the child's presence in the world, as I hear some have already began to tell of my own birth.

"Guard this child of ours, Wife. Teach it all the things that you know I would have taught it. For you, above all, have listened and understood, and I trust you to say it rightly. The seed has a certain undying memory all its own. But give to my child, and to the children of my child, and all who come after us, a mindful knowledge of me, of what I taught, and of their special importance in the world because of their descent from me. And from us. Will you do that, Merovee?"

"Yes, Jo."

Another clink of metal, much closer this time.

"Lastly, I enjoin you, as under the Law of Leverite marriage, to take yourself to my closest, unmarried, male relative, who is Jesus, and, once you know yourself to be a widow, give yourself to him in marriage."

"No."

"Yes. Do not trouble me now, Merovee."

"That Law is seldom observed nowadays except in the case of brothers."

"Jesus and I are more than brothers. He, before any man alive, will understand and protect you and the child."

"I will not promise to marry him. I will protect the child with my own life and wits which you admit to be both great and planned. But I will not promise to give my body to another man."

They stared at one another in the moonlight. Tears rolled down her cheeks.

"I am sorry, Jo. You will have to trust me to make the right choices as they need to be made."

"Josh is as myself."

"Not to me."

He sighed.

"So be it. Will you at least say that you will go to him and show him my gird and enlist his protection as a friend to my wife?"

"My wits, which you value, would have made me do that without being told."

The proximity of the sounds made it clear that there could be no further conversation.

"Lie down flat," he whispered. "Neither stir nor make a sound until they have taken me well away."

His hand rested upon her head for another brief moment as she complied.

"I know that I am giving you the hardest of our two tasks. Pray that I will be worthy of your courage. Goodbye, Beloved Disciple."

Then he was on his feet. To be sure that he was noticed as he strolled down the hillock, he began to hum a song to himself. It was the same one that Joshuah had sung. The fat priest, on a very small ass, jogging toward Jerusalem.

Merovee wrapped her arms around her head and buried her mouth against a shoulder to keep that mouth shut. Her fingers moved convulsively against the earth, found some pebbles, and clutched them for support.

"Hey! Hello. Who is there? What? Yes, I am the Prophet. Have you come for immersion? Who? Hold there, Fellow, there is no call for roughness. I am alone and unarmed. If Antipas yearns for my company, I shall be happy to satisfy his need."

Merovee lay flat until there was sufficient distance between her and all sounds. Then she sat up.

They were taking him up the bank to the hut of the Ford Master. She watched as they awakened that man, as they loaded men, beasts and equipment onto the ferry barge and set out for the Peraean side . . .

. . . and as they then killed the Ford Master, pushing his body out into the current of the river. Vultures would soon rid the world of that carrion.

Poor man. He could have testified to the fact that they had seized Johannan upon Judean soil. Now there were no witnesses. It would be said that Johannan had been taken on the Peraean side, within the jurisdiction of Herod Antipas.

She watched them head south, along the track that edged the eastern shore of the Salt Sea. Toward Machaerus.

Unconsciously, then, her hands lowered to her abdomen. She sat for a minute, rocking, cradling the child. She had no doubts as to its reality. The moment that Johannan had mentioned it, she had felt it quicken within her. As though his pronouncement, itself, had sparked the conception.

Finally she rose. She went to the palm grove, where she gathered up the few items of clothing, and her cup and bowl, that were there in her bed roll, rolled them together with Johannan's sheepskins, and tenderly bound the sheepskins into a parcel to be easily carried. Someday, she would give those skins to his child. For now, they would be her own bed.

She then went to the hut of the Ford Master, where she loosed that poor man's goats, lest they be overlooked and starve. He had loved them like children.

Then she girded her robe up into her leather wedding band and set off across the river, using the hidden footings that she knew so well . . . set off after her husband.

Yes, she had said that she would go to Jesus. But she had not said when.

* * *

And so, in that late morning, Chandreah and Jesus sat in consultation, laying their plans. Chandreah was sure that Johannan would have been taken to Jerusalem. Jesus thought not.

"Too dangerous. Antipas has no real charge against him. If the priests had taken him, it would be because they had found a legitimate violation of The Law. In which case they would stone him to death today. If the Romans had taken him, it would be for valid treason against Caesar. In which case he would be crucified, also today.

"But those at the Temple who have plotted his capture could find no valid charges. So they persuaded Antipas to make the arrest on personal grounds, which are not capital.

"Now Antipas in the midst of a problem. With no grounds to execute Johannan, he must simply keep him in prison. And Johannan is too popular with the people. To imprison him in Jerusalem—which is in the jurisdiction of Pilatus, and where Antipas is little more than a private citizen—to imprison him there for long would certainly invite insurrection from the people and interference from Pilatus.

"No. Antipas must take Johannan to some out-of-the-way stronghold within his own territories and keep him there, until the furor has died and the populace has all but forgotten him. Then, on some pretext, they will dispose of him."

He looked across the Jordan.

"Over there somewhere. In Peraea. Galilee is too populous, too filled with those who would support Johannan. It is into Peraea that they have taken him. And that is where she has followed. If she was not even taken prisoner along with him."

Still, it was possible that Jesus was wrong.

So it was agreed that Jesus would head for Peraea, while Chandreah went, first, back to Bethlehem to return his steed, then, to Jerusalem.

"And if," said Jesus, "on arriving in Jerusalem, you find that Johannan has not been taken there, go ahead of me, down to Galilee. I will be at Kapher Nahum by the next full moon."

"With or without her?"

"With or without her. At least I will have learned her fate."

Chandreah tilted his head.

"Why do you bother?"

Jesus smiled.

"I could tell you that it is because I promised Johannan that I would look after her. That would be the truth. But there is truth even beyond that."

He rose and mounted his stallion.

"Fare you well, Chandreah. Get me those stout fellows you promised in Galilee."

He set off toward the ford. But then he reined in.

"Oh. Be sure to tell my mother that I will not be home for the evening meal. Or for the harvest, poor lady."

He laughed, slapped the rump of his steed, and was off across the Jordan, into The Wilderness of Peraea.

Chapter 3

Machaerus

The territory known as Peraea was the second inheritance of Herod Antipas after Galilee, east of the Jordan and of the Salt Sea, and encompassing the city of the balm, Gilead. To the south was the citadel of Machaerus. It was to that fortress that they took Johannan. It was situated on a mountaintop between the track that followed the shore of the Salt Sea, and the grander King's Highway to the west—available to travelers or caravans using either of those routes should they care to turn aside a few miles from either one. The settlements near to the citadel were of little account. Two miles to the east was a small town with a dusty caravansari, a slightly better inn, a third-rate bazaar, and a small camel market. Just outside the walls at the northernmost tower, and entrance, to the citadel, was a collection of mud-baked hovels and a small market serving the garrison. The outer appearance of the fortress was grim, making no pretense at being anything but what it was, a prison of no return. It had been built by Alexander Janneaus and rebuilt by Herod the Great, and filled with more blood and treachery in the lifetime of the latter than could have been accumulated in the lifetimes of a hundred others.

Incongruously now, Antipas had caused a most pleasant palace to be built within the walls and adjacent to the northernmost tower. It commanded a spectacular view of the Salt Sea and of the surrounding hills, and had become a favored retreat for Antipas, away from the cosmopolitan hubbub of the Herodian Palace in Jerusalem, or the constant clang of construction in his new city of Tiberias in Galilee.

Merovee wandered around the little settlement beside that northern tower for half a day, examining all, listening to gossip, ascertaining that Johannan was, indeed, in that tower. Then she left.

Days later, an itinerant trader riding a small ass wandered back into town. The trader was but a lad. It was obvious that he had been on his own for much of his young life. He was filthy and trail worn, surly, suspicious, and secretive. A few, second-hand pots and tatty items of trade clanged and rattled. Mostly, however, the boy had a store of the prized balm of Gilead. He slipped a piece of silver to the head guard at the gate of the citadel, took possession of a stall near to that gate, and commenced to hawk his wares.

Did Johannan, there in the tower above, hear the high, sing-song voice? Did he recognize it as hers?

"Gilead, Mistress. Gilead, Master. Mine is the balm to soothe you. You will find no better price. Let me lighten your load. Do your muscles need refreshment? I come to help you, to give you release. In the balm is the answer to release. It was used by Elijah, himself. Buy, Master, buy the balm."

She sang out unceasingly, in her best Aramaic, believing that he heard, filling her jargon with messages for his understanding alone, hoping that, just knowing that she was near, and safe, and caring, would give him comfort. Otherwise, she kept to herself, short and silent with customers—though with ears tuned to each bit of gossip—preparing her meals on her own little brazier, eyes as darting and warning against overtures as a dog with a bone.

A week after her arrival, the head of the palace guard sent one of his soldiers to purchase some balm.

"So," she muttered in her brassy boy's voice. The tone was difficult for her, causing her voice to break often, adding to the impression of a lad whose voice was just changing. "Your superior has a sore back perhaps?"

"Oh, the balm is not for him," said the soldier. "The Princess Salome has heard your cry and wishes a jar for her bath."

"Salome, the daughter of Herodias? I thought she had been married to her Uncle Phillipus and sent off to rule with him at Caesar Phillipi."

"Where have you been hiding yourself, Lad? Tetrarch Phillipus died last December—died as the girl was on her way north to join him. He never even got to bed her. I know, for I was part of the guard that was taking her north—though she was his wife by any law, you may be sure, there was a proxy ceremony before she set out."

"I am sorry to hear of the death of Phillipus. They say he was a good and a just ruler."

"The best of the sons of old Herod for my money. But, if he had to up and die, it was good he did it before he bedded her. Antipas can get a fine second marriage for her, her still being virgin."

"Who of the royal family is here besides Salome?"

"Only Herodias, though Antipas will arrive any day. There are going to be big doings. Antipas is going to war against King Aretas. He will be gathering an army here in Machaerus."

"So it has come to war, has it?"

Aretas was the outraged father of the wife who, three years earlier, Antipas had divorced in order to marry Herodias. Since that time, Aretas had kept the border between Peraea and his own land of Nabataea bloody with skirmishes and raids of retribution. Merovee, however, cared nothing for talk of war. The soldier had given her the opening that she sought.

"So, Herodias is up there in the palace. What does she think of your prisoner? They say he is not entirely to her liking."

"The Prophet? Psaww! Why should she care about him one way or another?"

"The talk is that he has spoken against her, and that that is why he was taken prisoner. They say that she demanded it."

"Do not believe all that you hear, Lad. The man has offended the priests of the Temple, pure and simple."

"How so?"

"That which he teaches would put them out of business if people would but understand it."

"You have heard him teach?"

"No. But we talk. I am often set to guard him."

Her heart gave such a thud that she wondered he had not seen it.

"How fortunate for you. I would give anything to hear him. I was on my way north to Bethabarah to be immersed when I heard that he had been arrested. Were . . . you one of those who captured him?"

"To my shame, yes. I wish that I had broken my own leg and stayed in Jerusalem. I will never be rid of the guilt . . . to have helped to bring such as he into prison."

"Think you that he is the Prophet Elijah returned, as they say?"

"More than that," said the soldier.

"The Messiah?"

The man shook his head.

"Greater than even that."

Merovee frowned and studied the face of the man as she finished filling a jar with the balm. He was mature, full-bearded, and of kindly mien. It was a comfort to know that Johannan was guarded by one such as he.

Even more striking was the fact that he seemed to be one who understood the words of Johannan. Really understood. For only one whose understanding went beyond the ordinary could say that Johannan was "even greater than" the promised Messiah.

She handed him the jar. Taking the coins which he offered, she made change slowly.

"Has he immersed you?" she said.

"Nay. Where would he get the pool? There is not even a place for him to bathe himself. Anyway, my captain would not allow such a ceremony."

She turned, filled a second jar, and corked it.

"Here. If the poor man has no means to bathe, the fragrance of my balm will soothe him. You would make me happy if you would give him this gift. It is fitting if he is, indeed, Elijah returned, for Gilead was the birthplace of Elijah. Tell him that a poor trader lad sends him the gift and begs his blessing."

The soldier hesitated, glancing around.

"I am not sure I can do that, Son."

"Perhaps he might even give you the rite with the drops of oil which gather on the top of the balm. I have heard it said that such as he has no need of a whole pool, that he can do the rite with only one drop of any liquid."

What insanity. Where were such words even coming from?

"Tell him that. Ask him to do it for you. Then I will have the pleasure of knowing that I gave both of you a great gift."

The idea seemed attractive to the soldier. He took the second jar and thanked her.

"Do not forget!" Merovee cried after him. "Beg his blessings for me as well."

"I will do it, Lad."

"Come this way again. Please. Come and tell me what he says."

Bright-eyed, she watched him disappear through the gates of the citadel. Would he do it? Or would he keep the balm for himself. More probably he would give it to a woman for a favor. If even he used a bit of it, though, and Johannan smelled it, Johannan would know. And if he told Johannan that crazy thing about the oil and the rite, Johannan would know immediately from whose mind it came. What a laugh it would give him, and hours of smiles. She hugged herself, chuckling, as she imagined the things he would think—of that additional gift of laughter that she sent him along with the vial.

"Oh, Soldier. Please do not fail us."

* * *

He did not fail. He returned the next afternoon, and hung about until she was without customers.

"Hello," she said, trying to be so casual that her voice squeaked more convincingly than usual. "Did the Princess Salome like the quality of my balm?"

"Oh, her. I could not tell you, for the uppity, young thing does not allow me into her bath."

Merovee made a sound that was meant to be a knowing, male chuckle.

"And the Prophet?" she said.

The man's face broke into beaming.

"That is what I came to tell you. I can never thank you enough. He did give me the rite with the oil."

"He *did*?"

"He said you are a very clever young man to know it can be done that way. Indeed, it is a great secret among the masters. He says that the use of oil from the balm of Gilead is probably the single most potent way to do the rite. He says that a clever lad such as yourself ought to immediately seek out someone called Jesus, and follow him."

"Oh." She turned away. "That will not be necessary. The mountain is on its way to Moses."

"What?"

"Nothing. What else did the Prophet say?"

"That he had heard your voice outside the wall, and was longing for your balm, but had no money to send for any. So the gift was wonderfully welcome. He sent to you his blessing, as you asked. And he said, in place of the rite for yourself, each time he uses the balm upon himself, he will remember you with great love. It will be as though you, yourself, soothed him with it. Is that not a beautiful thing?"

Merovee sank onto the ground and lowered her face into her hands.

"Most beautiful. Thank you, Friend."

"It is certainly no more than you did for me."

The man sank down also, took a piece of bread from his gird, broke it, and offered her the half.

"My name is Nathaniel," he said companionably. "I am from Kapher Kana of Galilee. Where are you from?"

Kapher Kana!

Merovee shot him a sideward glance. His face called forth no memories. He had probably left to go soldiering before her own birth. Surely he would never recognize, in this dirty urchin, the beloved granddaughter of the man who provided employment for most of the citizenry of his village. Yet she must drop him no clues.

"I am from wherever I last plied my trade."

Nathaniel found nothing suspect in that answer. The caravan routes saw many lads such as this, most of whom probably did not even know their parents, much less their places of birth.

"The Prophet has made me a chief disciple," he confided happily. "He said you could be one, too, if you like."

Merovee studied his face more openly now. Her inner sense said he was a good man, lacking in artifice—a rock to which one could cling. And Merovee knew only too well about clinging to rocks.

"Tell him I accept to be a disciple. Nathaniel, you said he does not have any money. Do you mean that, if he did have money, he could buy some things for his comfort? It would be allowed?"

"Of course. That is always the way of it. That is how captains of the guard grow rich and retire to olive farms on Mount Ephraim."

Merovee reached into the folds of the girding leather that was her secret wedding band, withdrew a purse of silver, and gave it to Nathaniel.

"See that he gets this, then. Should he need more, he can depend on me."

"I will tell him," said Nathaniel, pocketing the purse. "But I have also been thinking, now we are his chief disciples, is it not up to us to find a way for him to escape?"

A shadow darkened their conversation. Merovee looked up.

The man who stood over them wore a burnoose and the simple, nondescript coat of a traveler. He was leading what Merovee knew to be a highly bred Syrian riding ass. Yet his dust-caked face and dirty feet testified to the fact that he had been dragging the stubborn creature along for quite some time, rather than riding in style, as was the point of having such an elite beast.

Beneath all that dust, and a ragged two weeks' growth of beard, the face was barely visible . . . only the bloodshot eyes, blazing with anger.

Merovee's lips curled upward in disgust.

"So. You finally got here. What took you so long? I have smelled you on the wind for days now."

Jesus would gladly have yanked her to her feet and slapped that insolence off of her face.

Instead, he closed his eyes for a moment, breathing in Pranayama. His heartbeat and pulses slowed in immediate response. When he opened his eyes, he was able to summon a smile. He felt it crack the dust upon his face, saw the girl laugh as the dust showered downward, stifled the impulse to kick her, and said as kindly as possible . . .

"So, my dearest son. You thought to run away from your father, did you? Do you not realize that your poor mother has been worrying herself nigh unto death? While I have been up one side of Peraea and down the other in search of you. I should stake you out for the carrion birds, or else have the priests stone you for such a lack of respect. But my love for you is great, and I will give you another chance. Pack up your things and we will begin our return journey immediately."

"No," said Merovee quite simply.

Jesus blinked. He crossed his arms and scowled, considering what to say next.

Merovee saved him the bother. She rose, fetched her water jug and her basin and returned.

"Sit you here upon my stool, Father Dear. I shall wash the travel from your feet and rub you with my balm and then you will feel less like a bear." She poured water onto a piece of linen and handed it to him. "Your face could use a wash as well."

As Jesus sponged off his face, Merovee sank to her knees and commenced to wash his feet. Not, however, before she was sure that he had noticed the leather girdling her waist.

She did not look up, but worked diligently at the cleansing.

"This is my new friend Nathaniel, Father. Nathaniel, this is my father, Joshuah. And I can not return home with you, Father, because Nathaniel and I have been given an honor. The Prophet Johannan is imprisoned in yonder tower. Nathaniel is one of his guards, and the Prophet has bestowed a great honor upon the two of us. He has made us his chief disciples."

She raised her eyes at last.

"I know how much you, yourself, esteem this Johannan, Father. Nathaniel was just saying that, as chief disciples, we two ought to devise a means for the escape of the Prophet. Now that you are here, perhaps you would like to join our endeavor."

For a moment, Jesus lost himself in wondering just exactly how to describe the color of her eyes.

Then he roused himself and looked up at the grim mass of the tower.

"Nathaniel," he said, studying the fortifications, "has the Prophet told you that he wants to be rescued?"

"Well, no. He has not said so, but certainly he would want it."

"Not necessarily."

Jesus returned his gaze to Merovee.

"You take much for granted, my son. Do not force your own wishes upon the Prophet."

She rose onto her knees.

"You have not gotten all of the dust from the lines of your face, Father. Here. Allow me."

She wetted the linen once more, and applied a few drops of the balm. Gently, she cleansed the resilient dust from the furrows of his brow, and the laugh creases about his eyes and lips.

"You really must take some pumice to those feet of yours, Father, or you will have more scales than a fish. This is quite a nice beard you have started."

Her nearness sent his pulses racing. With them, his anger.

"Did you hear what I said, Merovee?"

"Yes, I did. But I must do what I must do."

Nathaniel rose.

"I have got to be getting back, and I can see that you and your father have things to discuss. If I do not see you again, Merovee . . . "

"You will see me. I am not going anywhere."

"Nathaniel," said Jesus abruptly, "please be good enough to carry a message to the Prophet. Tell him that Joshuah, the father of this young man, has come to take him home. Ask him what he recommends."

"It will not matter," said Merovee.

"Ask him, Nathaniel."

"Well, he already did say," said Nathaniel helpfully, "that he thought your son ought to go and find someone named Jesus and follow after him."

Jesus rose, his eyes holding those of Merovee, still there upon her knees.

"I tell you I am staying," she repeated.

"Ask him also, Nathaniel, whether he wants to escape. Tell him I await his answers."

"I am not set to guard him again till the morning. I could not get back here without arousing suspicion until the afternoon."

"We will be waiting. Thank you," said Jesus.

Nathaniel hesitated, looking from one to the other, troubled without knowing why.

Then Jesus reached out and took his big, calloused hand.

"That is a nasty cut. Beginning to fester. How did you get it?"

"Just a sharp edge on the windlass at the well last evening."

"Was there rust on the edge that cut you?"

"I suppose."

Jesus passed his palm over the wound, then smiled and released the hand.

"It will be improved by the morning, I am sure. If not, ask the Prophet to heal it for you. We will see you tomorrow afternoon, my friend."

Nathaniel nodded and lumbered away, staring down at his hand, which he held out quite stiffly before him.

Jesus turned back to Merovee.

"Come with me. To a place where we can talk."

"I can not leave my stall. I will be robbed."

Jesus walked briskly to the next stall, and smiled at the middle-aged proprietress hunkered down before a potting wheel.

"Good woman. I am the father of yonder boy, come to fetch him home. Will you watch his stall while we stroll away to discuss the matter?" He held forth a silver coin.

The woman looked at the coin, seemed about to reach for it, then she smiled and shook her head.

"Go talk some sense into the lad. I will see that no one pilfers while you are gone."

"My thanks and my blessing," said Jesus.

He returned to Merovee.

"Can you think of any more excuses?"

She shrugged, and followed after him. They passed down through the market, Jesus walking so rapidly that she had often to skip to keep up with him. He maintained that pace, silent and unsmiling, for more than a mile along the narrow trail that led down toward the Salt Sea. Then he turned off from the road, keeping on until they reached a secluded spot overlooking that sea, still several miles away.

For some time then, as Merovee fanned the perspiration from her face, he stood staring out at the milky expanse. Then he picked up a stone and flung it as though trying to skip it over the surface of the sea.

"Isn't it amazing," he said at last. "You can hardly sink in that water. You would have to struggle all day, with great perseverance, to drown yourself. It is the salt which makes it so. I do not really understand why."

He turned.

"There is a salt in the earth, as well. Some of it is people. Like the woman guarding your stall. They are particles of the invisible salt which keeps all that is good in Humankind afloat, and will never allow it to sink, no matter how we insist that it must.

"Merovee. Please come back with me. Johannan, himself, has already requested it. And you know the message he will send back with Nathaniel on the morrow."

"Of course I know." She sat down. "But I can not and I will not, Joshuah."

"Girl! You know who and what he is. You have some idea of who and what I am. Have you no respect for our advice, knowing what you know?"

"Not in the least. No matter who you are. So do not try to intimidate me with that argument, 'Jesus,' for I have heard Jo teach, and he has told me privily much of the underlying truths which the masses are not yet able to understand. I have listened to your own words, and I have understood what you are saying. You seek to convey the same truths as does Jo."

Her eyes flashed.

"But do you practice what you teach or do you not? Perhaps even you have to make up your mind once and for all. Do you have one line of thought for your pretty speeches, but yet another when you wish to get your own way? What sort of a disciple would I be to either of you if I followed your wishes blindly, having none of my own? I must do what *I* must do. I am *my* creature, this is *my* life, *my* living experiment. How well I perform will be on *my* head, *my* Soul, forevermore. I, not you, must answer for my results, and you know that better than any man on the face of this Earth.

"Shame on you, 'Jesus'! You would tell the multitude as much, yet expect me to have no Self or guts of my own, and come trotting after you like a dog."

Her eyes narrowed.

"Yes, even like a bitch in heat if I read some of your glances correctly."

His face had crimsoned with rage as she spoke. At this last, he wheeled and walked away from her. He stood for some time kicking at stones. Then he bent and seized one and again hurled it toward the sea . . . picked up another and hurled one that as well.

His anger seemed to melt then. His muscles relaxed. When he turned, his face was composed, and a smile tugged at his lips.

"Thank you, Merovee."

He seemed suddenly so beautiful that she was shamed. It was her turn to redden. She ducked her head and sat down.

"You are welcome, I am sure."

He came back, sat down beside her, reached over and took her hand.

"Lift your head, Girl. You hit your mark squarely."

He squeezed the hand, released it, and leaned easily back onto one elbow.

"Do you know that that is the true meaning of 'sin'?"

She cast him a quick, sideward glance.

"I do not understand."

"The words originally used were words which applied to archery. Those words meant 'to miss the mark.'

"What a lovely example of the way in which translations and usage change meanings—allow our languages to begin to lie to us. You must always think twice, and then yet again, about the words that you use, Merovee.

"'Sin' has come to mean codified, eternally unchanging transgression, from which there is almost no recovery, save by the most abject groveling and beating of the breast and sacrifice . . . some dreadful act that one does, or thought that one thinks, for which one must beg forgiveness from an unreasonable and completely arbitrary god."

He put out a finger to an ant. It climbed onto the offering and scurried upward to explore. Idly, he watched as it charted the jungle of golden hairs upon his forearm.

"Those of us who first used the allusion in our teachings never dreamed the turn it would take in the minds of people. Does one who misses the mark with his arrow transgress against the target? Of course not, what stupidity. He has failed only himself. And, perhaps, his teacher. If he is an experienced archer, and it is himself he has disappointed, he will try again, and again. He will vary his posture, his aim, his grip, fuss with his arrows, perhaps get another bow, change the string, study the wind . . . he will keep at it until his accuracy improves, until, with some degree of confidence, he can shoot and hit, or come respectably close to, the mark. And if the archer is new, with a teacher standing alongside, will that teacher rise in anger at a miss, and cast the pupil into a bottomless pit of fire to roast for all eternity? Save me from archery lessons if that is so. No. With patience or impatience—depending on how often the teacher has delivered the proper instructions, or how dense or frivolous the student—the teacher will explain it once again, then stand back and watch the next try, hoping fervently for improvement. Only the most stubborn or stupid of students will ever be abandoned . . . cast, not into any fire, but, out into the desert of themselves, until, of themselves, they begin to hunger and thirst for perfect aim, and find their own ways back, and seek out those able to teach, and apply themselves with new insight. That, then, is what was originally meant by what is now called a 'sin against God.' One aims for 'God.' 'God' is the target. One tries to understand how to hit that invisible target. One fails, again and again. But one keeps trying again and again. Until one gets it right. Until one's understanding is a part of Self, not just some words prated by others. Until one, too, is qualified to patiently teach."

"And the trick," said Merovee quietly, "is that 'God' is the target, the teacher, the bow, the arrow, the wind, and the student all at once."

Jesus smiled.

"An apt student sets a teacher's heart to singing. I missed my mark when I sought to demand your obedience, Merovee. I 'sinned.' But you stayed true to your own aim—which you are learning very well—and so reminded me of my own. Call no person master ever again, Merovee. Not Johannan, not even I."

Once more, he took her hand.

"He told me I would have need of you in the days to come. And I will. I will need you to be you, to help me remember to be myself."

A fluttering warmth filled her as a current of energy flowed from his hand to hers. She tried to pull away, but could not. She tried to think of something to say. No words came.

"What is the significance of his gird about your waist?" he said gently.

"He had no other token. It signifies our marriage."

"In every sense of the word?"

"Yes."

He was silent for long moments, still holding her hand. A sea gull, ventured inland in hopes of good hunting, and puzzled by the fishless sea, flapped down from the sky. It stood regarding Jesus with round, red eyes, then settled companionably beside him.

"Two weeks ago that you lay in your bridal bed," he said at last. "Where were you in the space between your woman's times? . . . Do not turn away like a simpering child. Has your next time come upon you as yet?"

"No. I do not expect it."

He did not seem surprised.

"Of course. I see the rightness of it."

"That is what Jo said."

"All the more reason why you should come back with me. You have become a chalice, Dear Friend. A sacred chalice."

She could not help laughing.

"You two really are as one."

"There is no way that the entity of which we two are a part could have contained itself in one body," he said in all seriousness. "There is yet a third major part of us. Then there are many junior fragments." His eyes met hers. "Such as yourself."

He could not help smiling at how her lovely eyes widened. He decided that they were, indeed, a deep violet.

"Miriam, Johannan wants to 'die.' His Energy has completed its task within this current body. It must move on to its next challenge. If you love him—and I understand how very much you do—you will let him go in peace. He will have no peace if he must worry night and day for your welfare."

"You are trying to intimidate me again."

"Not at all. I am talking common sense. I admire your bravery, but I am entitled to my opinion that you are being foolhardy, chancing, as I now understand, not only your own life, but that of his child." Anger stole back into his tones. "You think your disguise as a boy protects you? Granted, you are somewhat convincing, for you are as flat and shapeless as any boy."

"Well, thank you very much."

"Should I say less than the truth? On the other hand, you have a way that is enticing beyond words." His voice had softened again. "Your tattered clothes and well-applied grime cannot hide you, Merovee. You stand out in any crowd. Did you not see the hungry eyes that followed you as we walked through the market and along the road?" He threw up his hands at her look of puzzlement. "No, of course you did not."

"What are you saying? No one in this place has the slightest idea that I am anything but a boy."

"Which desert rock have you been hiding beneath? Even my mother knows of these things. Do you not remember the conclusion she leaped to regarding us two? Those eyes follow you not because the beholders think you are female, but because they do believe you to be male!"

She stared. She had heard of such things, of course, but it had never occurred to her that . . .

"Do you not realize how they would use you, what they would do to you, if the truth were discovered either way?"

She averted her face.

"I will be very careful in my movements. I will entice no one."

Abruptly, he began to laugh. It was her turn to get angry. She rounded on him, wanting to put a doubled fist through that grinning white crescent of teeth.

"Damn you! You worry only for yourself. Your feelings, your concerns, Jo's feelings, Jo's concerns. What of mine?" Tears rushed to her eyes. "I can not leave, can you not understand? I love him. You say you have lived lives as a woman. But this time you are a man, and you have forgotten how a woman loves, how a woman feels. Flat and shapeless or not, I . . . "

"Miriam." He reached out in sudden contrition.

She recoiled from his touch, forming herself into a protective ball hugging its own knees.

"You and he teach of trust," she said through clenched teeth. "In your teachings, you applaud those who trust the underlying goodness of all, the salt, as in that sea, and in the woman guarding my stall. You encourage us to walk through fires, and into the dens of lions, knowing that our own understandings and expectations create whatever befalls us, trusting that we understand and believe firmly enough to create safety and goodness for ourselves. Well I do understand and believe, 'Jesus.' I trust myself. I told that to Jo and I will say no less to you. I trust myself to stay here and see to him in any way that I am able, and still, if it must needs be that I am widowed, return to you unscathed, the seed inside of me all safe and secure. If you do not believe that . . . "

She turned and looked him squarely in the eye.

"If you do not believe as I do, then you do not deserve to have me return to you. When my task here is complete, I will take my bow and my arrows and go in search of a better teacher."

He stared at her speechlessly for a moment. Then he shook his head and expelled a long breath.

"I will be broken in heart if you do not come to me, Merovee. Please say that you will. You will always be free to leave if you find me unworthy."

She lowered her eyes.

"Of course I will come. I told Jo that I would."

"I do not want you to come because of any promise to Johannan."

She lifted her eyes to the brackish sea. Suddenly she could not stop the tears.

"It will not be for that. You must know better. Oh, Josh!" She buried her face into her knees and hugged herself for dear life. "If they kill him—will they at least let Nathaniel and me have the body?"

"Even Antipas would not dare to refuse the corpse a ritually proper burial," he said quietly. "Yes. We must take Nathaniel into full confidence before I leave. I sense fine depths to the man, simple though he seems, do you not think so?"

"I stopped trusting my intuitions in these matters after I let you and Jo and Chandreah trick me as you did."

"The things we assent to consciously, and the things we assent to below the level of usual consciousness, are, more often than not, different matters, my little friend. By claiming no conscious forewarning of things that transpire, one can then claim innocence of what occurs, shrug one's own responsibility off onto some nebulous 'fate,' or the perversity of 'God.' The task of such as we is to become aware of our unconscious informations and motives, and to take full responsibility for our own selves, our actions, and fates in this world." He grinned. "Though I hardly need to tell you that, for it is another version of the lesson you have been teaching to me in these last minutes."

"I suppose it is." She sighed and shook her head, her voice still breaking with tears. "How easy it is to forget in one instance what one knows so well in another."

"None of us are above that forgetting, Merovee. Not a single human being born of woman will ever be above reminding."

She flushed.

"I am sorry I presumed so."

"I told you not to be. Never hesitate, Merovee. I mean that. Look at me."

"I can not."

"Look at me."

"No. Please, Josh, I am feeling too much right now. There is so much, and it is all so confusing. I am not sure I can handle it."

"Please."

She remained for a moment with her face buried against her knees. Then, with a sigh, she raised her head and turned her tear-filled eyes to him.

He smiled gently.

"Your eyes are redder than that sea gull's."

She laughed.

"That is better. Keep your laughter in all things, Merovee. Laughter is God's favorite sound. It is a contagious sound, that makes God laugh, too. And when God—the true god All That Is—when that god laughs, rain falls out of blue skies filled with rainbows, and every sort of seed giggles and gurgles as it grows, and nothing that is negative can flourish. I will not ask you for any promises. But I want to tell you some things that I hope you will keep in mind. Firstly, take no chances. Guard yourself, not only for your own sake, but for Johannan, and me, and for generations which are not yet born. And know that your importance to those generations is not confined to the seed that you carry. Secondly, do not interfere with the course that Johannan has set for himself. Succor him where you can, yes, but do not try to interfere. You just told me, in no uncertain terms, to respect your course, your choices, and the answer you will have to give on your own account when you finish this particular life. Accord to Johannan what you demand for yourself. Next . . . ”

His own eyes dropped, then returned, and he smiled.

“I understand much of the confusion within you. For I have it within myself. Do not fear it. Do not take it for a shame. People with only a little love to give love little and few. Those with much love to give love much and many. At the moment, Humanity sees the range of Love as it sees one of those rainbows I just spoke of. Humanity does not understand that its limited understanding of Love allows it to see only a handful of colors in that rainbow. A rainbow’s colors are without limit, Merovee. Rainbows go on forever, with colors of which Humanity has not even dared to dream. As does Love. And so what you feel for me . . . ”

She dropped her face back onto her knees.

“ . . . and what I feel for you, is no cause for shame. Johannan would tell you that. Never hide your face when you feel a truly loving impulse, Merovee. Raise your face and smile for joy. For Love is synonymous with joy. Love is the Prime Power of this world. And only by loving can you gain the sight to see the next color in the rainbow of Love, and then the next, and the next. Give me your hand again.”

She stuck the hand out, but did not raise her face.

He laughed as he took it.

"Annah would approve. You have managed a few calluses. The last thing I will ask you to keep in mind and to consider is what, without being told, I know Johannan asked of you. If you are widowed, come to me, and be my wife.”

He held tightly to her hand as she tried to pull back.

“Only consider it. First of all, Rosula and my father, who have despaired that I would ever fulfill my obligations as a proper Jewish male, would be delirious with joy. Secondly, you have done me more service here today than you can know, Sweet Girl. I, too, must answer for my performance in this world. Not to any punishing god, but to myself . . . to my own expectations of what I wanted to do while here. I can see that you would be an excellent galley master, to keep me rowing with all my strength, straight and true, and with a full stroke every time. Just consider it. Please.”

She jerked the hand back.

"I do not need to consider it. I do not fancy the life of a galley master.”

“Wait!”

For she was on her feet.

“A fine one you are! Prating of Love! I shall not govern myself to please either your mother or your father, and, if you want a galley master, go hire one.”

She spun on her heel and was off.

Jesus stared after her, his face a study in puzzlement. In the back of his mind, he made a note to tell her not to allow her hips to swing in just the way that they did. Then he looked for the ant, to off-load it, could not find it, and stood up, hoping he was not crushing it somewhere beneath his robe. The sea gull made a clucking sound.

"What did I say wrong?" he asked of it.

'A fine one you are, prating of Love.'

Love.

The light dawned. With it, a grin.

Chuckling, he stood for some moments, hands on hips, looking out at the sea. Then he grabbed up another stone and, with a yell, sent it sailing out toward those unyielding depths.

He chuckled all the way back to Machaerus.

* * *

Nathaniel did not return till near sundown of the next day. There was a difference as he approached. He walked slowly, seemed taller, larger . . . yet the bumbling quality was gone. His largeness had become quiet, and quite fine.

Jesus sat mending the bridle of Merovee's little Gilead, chatting with Susannah, the woman from the next stall. He missed nothing of Nathaniel's approach, and smiled as the man halted in front of him.

"Friend Nathaniel. How is the hand?"

Nathaniel extended it. There was no sign that it had ever been wounded.

"It was like this before I reached the citadel yesterday afternoon," he said flatly.

His eyes flicked over Susannah.

"I have need to speak with you privately."

"Sit you down right here," said Jesus. "Susannah, this is Nathaniel, Nathaniel, Susannah. Speak freely before her, Nathaniel, we have had long discourse, and she has enlisted gladly in our cause."

Nathaniel hesitated, glancing into the recesses of the stall, to where Merovee sat in sullen withdrawal upon Johannan's skins. Then he sank down cross-legged.

"I may say all?"

"All," said Jesus.

Once more, Nathaniel glanced toward Merovee.

"The Prophet told me who that really is."

"He revealed to you that Miriam, known to you as the boy Merovee, is his wife," said Jesus quietly.

"When I showed him my hand and told him what you had done, he knew it for a sign and message from you, and told me all. Including . . . who you are."

"Fine," smiled Jesus. "That saves my own breath. Do you still wish to help us, Nathaniel?"

Tears came into the big man's eyes.

"More than ever, Jesus."

Jesus reached out, grasped his shoulder, then inclined his head in Merovee's direction.

"Come here, Dear Son. Our friend has things to tell you."

Merovee rose and came forward, moving with the tight-hipped slouch that Jesus had taken pains to recommend.

"I doubt he brings any surprises for me," she said caustically, and sank down cross-legged into the circle.

"He begs you most humbly to depart with Jesus," said Nathaniel.

"I will not."

"He expected as much," continued Nathaniel. "He wants you to know, however, that he does not wish to be rescued and would not cooperate in any attempt."

Merovee nodded dully, her eyes fixed upon the ground.

"So be it. I already saw a vision of his death. His head . . . "

She broke off, covering her face.

"Severed from his body," she whispered.

Nathaniel drew in his breath and glanced at Jesus. From the gravity upon that face, he understood that Jesus took the girl's vision for fact, not fancy.

"When will this be?" said Jesus gently.

"That was not given. I heard music. Entertainment. A banquet. That is all."

Jesus sighed, collected his thoughts and spoke briskly.

"I shall leave you coins with which to purchase burial spices."

"I have enough," said Merovee.

"One always needs more than one expects." He took a purse from his gird, extracted a variety of coins, and passed them to Susannah. "Tell the Prophet of Susannah, Nathaniel. It will comfort him to know that there is a good woman here with his wife, and it will comfort you to know that Merovee is looked after when you cannot be here. Susannah and Merovee are to combine their stalls for greater security. Merovee has promised to exercise all caution and to at least consider your counsel and that of Susannah."

Nathaniel studied Susannah more closely. She had been handsome in her day. Even now, everything about her seemed fashioned as from stone, with no extra lines or superfluity. She might not even be so very old—perhaps it was just that the sun had chiseled her skin.

"Have you a husband, Woman?"

"As far as I am concerned, no," said Susannah. "He was a camel driver. Twelve years ago, he left with a great caravan, headed for the silk lands beyond India. I never received a word. If he still lives, he obviously chooses to do it without me, and I certainly prefer to do it without him. The girl will be safe with me. Men have given me a wide road all to myself for a long time now."

"You do not look as bad as all that to me," said Nathaniel.

"Watch how you speak," said Susannah shortly. "If the head of the guard were to find out that you are blind, you would lose your job."

Jesus laughed and got to his feet.

"I will be on my way then."

All three looked up in shock.

"Now?" blurted Merovee. "But—there will be no moon, it is not a fit night to travel."

"Pharisee is an extremely sure-footed beast," said Jesus, nodding toward the tethered ass.

"Why do you call him Pharisee?" said Nathaniel."

"Because he halts often, cares not how he holds up traffic, and can, in no wise, be persuaded to continue until he has finished braying to the Great Ass in the sky."

Susannah let out a shriek of merriment. Nathaniel covered his face.

"Oh Jesus," said Susannah, "I do like you."

"The feeling is mutual, Susannah. Goodbye for now then, Disciples. I am leaving the two of you with great responsibility. Merovee is the beloved disciple of Johannan and of myself. I will never stop thanking you two when you have delivered her safely to me in Kapher Nahum after your task here is complete. Places of honor will be yours always. Now and forever. Merovee? Will you accompany me down the road for a bit?"

Merovee hesitated, then got to her feet. She went into the stall, got a jar of the balm, came back and handed it to him.

"It is most soothing at the end of a long day."

"Thank you, my dear."

They started slowly down the street, Jesus leading Pharisee.

"You are managing the hips much better now," he said. "Put a touch more movement into the shoulders. Clench the fists just slightly . . . too much . . . better. Imagine that, at any moment, you will have to use those fists in a fight. Lightly swim those shoulders toward the imaginary attacker . . . too much . . . perfect. Let the fists move ahead of the shoulders. Yes! Very convincing. A man would think twice before accosting another male walking with just that hint of menace, and it certainly conveys no welcome. You must be a fine dancer, you coordinate so well. Do you like dancing?"

"Very much."

"There are few things I would rather do."

He gave a little hop just thinking about it, so that Merovee had to laugh.

"To the Universe belongs the dancer," he half chanted, moving rhythmically. "Those who will not dance will never know what happens. Follow my dance. See yourself in me who speaks." He resumed a normal gait. "We will dance together, Merovee. Someday."

"Together?" she said, puzzled.

"Do you not know that, in some times and places, men and women dance with one another?"

She hesitated at the curious way that he put it.

"I cannot imagine such a thing."

"Then begin to try. When we meet again, I will show you."

They continued in silence for a moment.

"Was Johannan Elijah, Josh?"

"No. Could you seriously imagine Johannan giving voice to the vicious and hate-filled utterances of Elijah? Elijah was of a great, but still growing, entity. One that is still struggling toward an understanding of Love. Or wisdom."

Suddenly he halted.

"Of course!" he cried. "I wondered where I had seen those burning eyes before. That Simon Yeshuah! The one who walked away from Johannan's campfire that night. How could I have been so dense? He is of the Elijah Entity. Oh, there is trouble going forth to happen. We have not seen the last of that man."

He resumed walking, muttering, shaking his head as though trying to drive away some stinging insect.

"Of course. Of course that entity would respond to the call as well."

"What call?"

He stopped again, stared at her, and came back to the place where they were.

"The call of the dreaming mind of the species. In dreams, Merovee, all parts of All That Is can be—are—in contact with one another. In the dream state, information is exchanged, desires are expressed, conversations are held, decisions are made, teachers are summoned. We come among you so often, Merovee, sometimes in memorable ways, but, more often, in very unassuming ways. Seldom are we recognized for what we are. But we are here among you more often than we are not. Humankind is never left without our help, if only it seeks it." He shook his head again. "Our help or, in the case of such as our friend, Simon Yeshuah . . . hindrance."

Merovee walked on for a moment, feeling oddly detached.

"So, from what you said yesterday, there are many teaching entities—obviously of differing stages of development—but each able to send many Souls, or fragments, forth into a time period. And I am included in the 'we' you just spoke of, in regard to Johannan and yourself."

"You are." He smiled. "Would you care to know some of the people you have been?"

"Not just yet if you do not mind."

"Actually I am not at all sure who you might have been. Or will be. But I could make a few educated guesses. Then, of course, there are the probable Merovees or Miriams, who split off onto their own courses at each point of decision." He glanced over and saw her wrinkling brow. "I am sorry if I go fast. But time is short. Think about what I am saying, and you will figure the thing out for yourself. Just remember that, as I have told you, time is simultaneous. Past, present, and future, in all possible versions, are as much in existence at this moment as is this moment." He smiled again at the expression on her face. "And suffice it to say that you have been 'being brought along' by our entity, Miriam/Merovee. An apprentice if you will. One whom, I think, is due for graduation from apprentice to master in this lifetime."

"There are things I would rather hear. What you are talking about is all so frightening."

"None of us ever stops being frightened, Merovee."

"One such as yourself is frightened?"

There was no levity in his expression.

"Such as I, and such as Johannan above all others. But it is a different kind of fright, that you could not imagine at this point. A tortoise fears but little. In truth, it has little to fear. Most men pass their lives like tortoises, sticking their necks out but seldom, retreating into their shells at the first hint of danger. Those such as myself are as tortoises who have willingly shed their shells, made ourselves naked, totally vulnerable. We have separated ourselves from any chance of retreat, crushed our shells behind us. We march forward into the world with no armor except our superior knowledge, understanding, and trust—gained, earned, bled-for over many lifetimes. Because we understand so much more, because we understand the true nature of things, our powers are greater, so that we are capable of things which others would call magic. Which makes us all the more obvious—and threatening—to our fellows. And increases even more our chances of being . . . disposed of."

"By the tortoises?"

It got a smile out of him.

"You never thought of tortoises as such vicious creatures, did you. Try to deprive one of its shell, and you will find out quickly enough. But the fears of such as Johannan and I are not fears for physical safety. We have long ago made ourselves masters of the physical. We dwell in the endless universes of

56

the mind—in realities, and on levels, which cannot be described, only experienced. I can only say that there is always a higher daring. With each level of daring comes a more exquisite version of fear."

"I can hardly wait."

He threw back his head and roared with laughter.

"As Susannah said to me, I do like you, Merovee."

"I hated you at first."

"That does not still pertain?"

"I . . . am not sure."

"Oh? Well then, you must be careful. For I will tell you one of the unalterable rules of the Universe. What you hate, you draw to you."

She gave him a quick, sidewise glance. His eyes sparkled with mischief. At the same time, he was serious.

"Equally," he went on, "if you fear something with enough insistence, you will inevitably bring upon yourself that which you fear. Now why do you think that might be?"

"Well . . . I suppose because you could never learn to stop hating it, or fearing it, without experiencing it, learning to understand it. Without making it your own, so to speak."

His eyes widened and he shook his head in respect.

"That is not what I had in mind, but it is certainly one aspect of it. A rather advanced aspect. I could not have said it better. I wonder that Johannan can bear to leave you. Do you understand the courage, the daring that takes, Merovee? Loving you as he does? Having found a partner such as yourself? Oh, what a seldom thing that is! What a temptation to stay and enjoy it. And here is one of those exotic fears which perhaps you can understand. He goes on about his task, trusting that he is not really leaving you, that he can always communicate with you on levels of which he believes himself to be a master, that there will be other times, others lives, that his beloved friend is his forever." His eyes clouded. "But then the fear. What if he is wrong? What if he is a deluded fool? What if there is nothing . . . nothing on the other side of death?"

"Surely you and he could never even consider such possibilities."

"My dear girl, the true god, itself—All That Is—gets frightened sometimes, and questions its own reality. Without such questions, and the resulting quest for affirmation, there would be nothingness for even All That Is. The answer is always contained in the question, and the desire to Know will, of itself, always generate Being."

"You called God 'it.'"

"I will do that often with those who can understand. Only the tortoises are unable to conceive of that which is really god as having attributes which have nothing to do with the rules of this world."

"There are other worlds then?"

"Beyond number. Each more unlike this one than the next."

"Have you visited them all?"

"Only All That Is, being all, could possibly know them all. Though even All That Is has a hard time keeping up with new developments. Each world generates endless versions of itself in simultaneous time, and each version generated then generates endless versions of its own self, and on and on. And now tell me, does everything that I have been saying make you feel small and inconsequential?"

Merovee considered the question for a moment.

"No. Quite the opposite. As I understand it . . . I am learning to become like you. What you have just told me promises to me an infinity of discovery and experience, what with all these endless versions of myself, and endless worlds, to explore and learn to understand. But what I feel most strongly right now is . . . love. Love for what I have right here. Everything suddenly seems more dear. As you spoke, I thought that the dust beneath my feet became warmer, silkier. I smelled Pharisee, and the scent was precious. I noticed those lovely colors in the sky, and heard the birds for the first time today. If this Earth is the only place where they have these special, wonderful things, how very much more worthwhile it all is. I think . . . knowing what you have just told me, I can begin to truly love the world for the first time. I want to know everything there is to know about it, and experience all that it has to offer. I want to cherish it, so that I can never forget it."

She turned and looked up at him, and was surprised to see tears in his eyes.

"At any time in the future, when you wonder if the true god All That Is loves this world, or has forsaken it—could ever forsake it—remember this moment, Merovee. For what you felt just now was All That Is seeing through your eyes, and All That Is expressing its own Love with your lips. And if you wonder why such as Johannan and I return to teach, again and again, even though we now have much greater realities in other worlds, remember this new understanding, and know that we share it. It is Love that draws us back each time. And that is the other part of the rule I just gave you. Even as you draw what you hate and fear to yourself by concentrating upon it, by concentration you also draw to yourself that which you have learned to truly Love."

She could not keep looking at him. He seemed suddenly brighter than the sun. She looked down at the silky dust, and allowed her toes to drag against its warmth.

"The tortoises, Josh—are they what Jo calls the generation of vipers?"

"They are. But I think the tortoise image is much more apt, ummm?"

She smiled.

"Do not ask me to chose between orators." They had long ago left the village, and were nearing the place where the trail from Machaerus joined the trail along the sea. "Do you have enough food and drink with you?"

"Now that I do not have to wander the dusty length and breadth of this Wilderness of Peraea in search of you, my trip will be swift. I shall be back at Bethabarah by midnight. In another two to three days' time, I shall be in Kapher Nahum."

"Following along the river you can catch fish in the shallow pools if you are lucky. And the mushrooms are wonderful now. Do you understand how to select the ones without poison?"

"I do."

"The cypress has a seed that is quite good . . . "

She stopped, for he was laughing.

"Just like your kind," he said.

She felt a rush of resentment, that he would use Jo's own teasing words.

"Yes, you are right to laugh," she said tartly. "Who am I to tell you how to get food? If you get hungry you can make food out of thin air."

"That I could. I was tempted to it these last days in The Wilderness. I also considered flying over to Jerusalem, landing on the topmost eminence or the Temple, and using the Pharisees for spitting targets. I thought of flying up onto the top of the highest mountain in the world, and subjugating all the lands to my sway. All these things were temptations. But I did none of them. For such things should not be done merely to satisfy my own wants, or merely to amuse myself. For one thing, such tricks take tremendous Energy. I save my Energy for constructive purposes. In the second place . . . it is hard to explain. By taking this body in this time and place, I accepted certain rules, limitations. It somehow seems unfair to take shortcuts to gain one's own ends, not to adhere to rules which others think they have to follow."

"You could really fly?"

The eyes he turned to her were merry. Such nice eyes. The flecks of blue in the honey were especially brilliant today.

"We will never know, will we," he said.

They had reached the place where he would leave her and head toward the north. Merovee felt a sudden surge of panic. All at once she wanted to beg him to stay.

"Is a father permitted to embrace his son?"

He turned, took her shoulders, pulled her lightly to him, and kissed her upon both cheeks.

"Master!" she breathed, her fear finding words. "Give me your blessing."

"I told you never to call me master. And of course you have my blessing. But, as you already know, the only really important blessing is that which you give to your own self."

He mounted Pharisee.

"Goodbye, Beloved Disciple. Remember to walk toughly."

And he rode away.

She stood watching after him, breaking into laughter sometimes as Pharisee stopped in his tracks and brayed his prayers before continuing. At long last, they disappeared from sight. Merovee turned and headed back to Machaerus, practicing her new walk, gaining confidence with each stride, thinking that, on a religious ass such as Pharisee, it would be more like a week to Kapher Nahum.

* * *

A week after the departure of Jesus, Machaerus and its surroundings were hardly to be recognized. Gone, the relative quiet of the sleepy little market, and the hours of ease with nothing to do but listen to the quiet places as Jesus had suggested, or to investigate in more detail the life story of Susannah. The projected war of Antipas against the Nabataean king seemed to be fast approaching. There were more soldiers with each passing day, mercenaries from throughout the Mediterranean world, and camels, asses by the tens of hundreds, even horses, wagon after wagon of provender, siege equipment—and, of course, camp followers. A stream of couriers hurried backward and forward, hither and yon. Splendidly caparisoned foreign contingents arrived—generals, rulers, come to talk of the terms of allying themselves with Antipas in the forthcoming fray. The population of the little village by the gate doubled, tripled in size. The roadsides, the ridges, came ablaze with campfires by night. The shouts, laughter, and carousing of the soldiers seldom stilled. Traffic before the stall of Susannah and Merovee was constant from dawn until darkness.

Each night, music could be heard floating down from the terrace of the palace, as Antipas entertained his generals and potential allies.

Music. Banquets. The time was fast approaching. There was a cold place in Merovee's heart where she knew it so well.

Nathaniel continued to come each day, pretending, without much pretense, to be smitten with Susannah as an excuse should his superiors grow curious. The two women had considered moving to a stall on the outskirts, to be not so much in evidence. This, Nathaniel vetoed. They were actually safer right here by the gate, where any alarm would bring guards running from the citadel. He was also of the opinion that often the way to invisibility is through total visibility.

And so it seemed. They were taken as part of the furnishings, assumed to be a woman with her young son, patronized profusely for the precious oil and for Susannah's items of pottery, and left respectfully alone. Indeed, if money had meant anything to Merovee, she would have been happy. She ran out of jars, and had to have Susannah create a multitude of tiny, clay vessels. To stretch her store of balm, she cut further and further back on the amounts she gave, but found that the soldiers, with nothing much to spend their wages on, paid any price she cared to name for that precious little. She took their money without blinking, and packed it all away, nursing a forlorn hope that Johannan would change his mind, and that the money could be used to bribe his way out of his prison.

Indeed, the news that Nathaniel brought to them several weeks following the departure of Jesus sent her hopes soaring into the sky.

"The Prophet was sent for by Herodias and the Princess Salome! We got him a bath, and he spent the morning in their reception chamber, answering their questions and teaching to them. He is to return on the morrow. The young Salome has asked for the immersion!"

"Will it be allowed?" said Merovee, clutching her racing heart.

"He is not sure. But he says their interest is genuine, their questions intelligent, and that they are decent women. They were distressed that he has been kept in such mean circumstances. Herodias had the straw of his bed changed, and Salome sent him a good quilt, and some fine wine as well."

"Wine?" trilled Merovee in pure delight.

Susannah poked her.

"You are supposed to be a boy."

"Yes, he did drink it," grinned Nathaniel. "With great relish. He said I was to be sure and tell you, and that you should tell Jesus when next you see him, for he knows how you two will enjoy the joke."

The reference to her next meeting with Jesus took the edge off of the pleasure, implying as it did a time when Johannan would no longer be living. Still, the turn of events was more wonderful than anything she had dared to hope. She sank down cross-legged.

"Go on, Nathaniel. Tell me everything that he said."

Nathaniel discoursed for onto an hour, covering all the points that had been discussed with the royal women, passing on any gossip that he had gleaned.

"And that slander," said Merovee, "that Johannan had spoken against Herodias. Was it mentioned between them?"

"He said not. He gathered that she knew that he knew that she knew that it was merely a face-saving falsehood, and so was not worth discussion. He was most impressed with Salome. He says she is superior. Oh, and yes! She noticed the scent of the balm upon him, and he on her, and she asked about it. He told her he got it from the boy who hawked without the gates, and she seemed to feel a comradeship, because of the balm and because they had got it from the same boy."

All the next morning, and into the afternoon, Merovee waited for Nathaniel's next visit, hoping for news that Salome had been immersed. A move like that would be of immense political importance.

Antipas could not, would not, kill the man who had performed such a sacred rite on his young step-daughter.

Would he?

She was deep in thought when she heard the light voice behind her. She turned and stared dumbly at the girl who stood there. She was richly dressed, in a silken toga of canary yellow, edged with a Greek key design and embroidered with blue and red. Her face was pale, unpainted, and freckled. Her eyes were translucent blue, and her hair, falling in maidenly abundance beneath a sheer, blue veil, was gently red. She was small, slender, and fragile beyond words, hardly out of childhood. Behind her stood two serving women.

"Yes?" said Merovee. She knew of no fine families in these parts. This must be one of the guests stopping at the inn of the nearby town "How may I serve you, Maiden?"

"I wish some of your ointment as a gift for a friend," was the shy response.

Merovee turned and began to measure a sparse portion.

"My friend the Prophet," the voice continued, eagerness pushing the shyness aside. "He immersed me today. I am as though newly born."

Merovee turned back, staring.

"Can you see anything different about me?" said the girl hopefully.

"Indeed . . . I could not say, Maiden, for I have never seen you before today."

"But of course!" The smile was enchanting. "I had forgotten. He and I both got our balm from you before, you see, so I thought of you as sort of a friend. My name is Salome. What is your name?"

Merovee fought the lump in her throat. The girl was, indeed, impressive. Innocence flowed from her being like a humbling river.

"Merovee. And I shall be happy to stand your friend, my princess."

She turned back, filled her largest container to its maximum, corked it and held it out.

Salome emptied a handful of coins from out of a silken purse and stared at them, in the manner of one unaccustomed to dealing with such matters.

"My gift to him is in thanks for my immersion, so I wanted to purchase it all by myself." She thrust the entire fistful at Merovee, coins ranging from copper to silver to gold pieces of enormous value. "Which of these do you need?"

Smiling, Merovee selected coins amounting to the pre-army price. She felt one of the serving women move forward.

"Are you sure that is enough?" said Salome as Merovee returned the rest.

"Yes, my princess."

Salome glanced dubiously at the serving woman. The woman nodded.

"It could have been more, but it is fair enough."

"Oh. Well . . . thank you then." Salome backed away, all the more enchanting for her awkwardness in taking leave of a mere merchant lad. "I go now to present my token to the Prophet."

"Tell him that the hawker lad at the gate sends greetings."

"Oh yes?" Salome seemed genuinely delighted. "I will do that. Every little bit counts, you know, to lighten his lot in that wretched cell. Goodbye then."

The girl moved away. Merovee sank to the earth.

Susannah, who had been motionless at her potter's wheel, found her voice.

"I would never have imagined she was like that. Like an angel down from Heaven."

For the next week, Johannan continued to be taken each morning to the women's reception chamber, to there teach to the mother and daughter, and even to their women, Nathaniel reported.

It was at dawn on the morning of the eighth day, as Merovee squatted before the stall, cooking breakfast for Susannah and herself, that the travelers from Jerusalem came halting up the street. They moved haltingly because those bringing up the rear of the procession stopped every few hundred feet to mutter prayers, causing those ahead to stop and wait as well. Exaggerated tefillin dangled from the foreheads, and encircled the arms of these pious men. Their faces were lost in bushes of sacred hair. Their sanctity filled the air like a miasma.

"Pharisees," said Susannah, coming to Merovee's side. "Traveling with Sadducees and priests and scribes. What a strange bunch of birds to be flocking together. And some of those Levites are police from the Temple. It must be a delegation from the High Priest. What do you suppose they want here?"

Merovee could not answer. The hopes of the last week had congealed in a heart turned cold again.

* * *

Nathaniel's report that afternoon was indeed grave. The palace was in an uproar. Herodias and Salome had been confined to the women's quarters. Johannan had been moved to the deep dungeon below the tower, his prior guards, including Nathaniel, dismissed, replaced by the dreaded Temple Police.

"Ah, had I but known!" cried Nathaniel, striking his breast in anguish. "I would have warned him. Only now do I realize that those foolish women did it all without the knowledge of Antipas. Word of Salome's immersion was carried back to the High Priest in Jerusalem before ever Antipas even knew that the Prophet had visited their quarters! Antipas is wroth beyond words, made to look a fool who cannot so much as govern his women-folk. And those treacherous saints from the Temple have him white as a wraith, with their insinuations that he is aiding and abetting insurrection, that he might even be guilty of treason against Rome. What have we come to? What sort of god is this God of the Jews, that he will make us slaves to such as they? We did not escape bondage when we left Egypt, we plunged deeper into it!"

"For the love of God, lower your voice," said Susannah.

"Love God? How can I love a god who makes me a slave, who gives others the right to silence, intimidate, imprison, murder any who do not agree with them?"

"They are guardians of The Law," said Susannah nervously.

"Then it is time for the rule of The Law to end," gritted Nathaniel. "Does not Torah enjoin us to listen to God in our hearts above the voices of men? By what right do the Pharisees presume to dictate all that we must believe and do, making it up as they go along to suit themselves? By what means have the Sadducees found the way to destroy someone like the Prophet simply to keep themselves on their cozy and cushioned terms with Rome? By what right do the priests send out this execution squad to destroy a man who offends against no one and nothing but their own power? How has it arrived so that such as they seek to set themselves above God in my heart? Never has my Soul sung so sweetly as in the hours that it has been my privilege to listen to the Prophet. Never have I heard God so clearly within myself. And they would kill that blessed man, all in the name of The Law. They make me hate them *and* their Law. By my sword, I hate them with a passion so deep . . . "

"No!" cried Merovee suddenly. "Hate them not, Nathaniel!"

"What would you?" he said in amazement. "That I should love them?"

"Yes . . . No . . . That would be as foolish as asking you to love the god you just described. I am not sure of the answer, Nathaniel. Help me to it." She repeated what Jesus had told her just before they parted. "So if what he says is true—and I believe with all my heart that it is—by hating these men you will only draw them closer to you. They will hound you all your days, become more entwined in your life the more you hate them, until you destroy your own self in the cauldron of your own hatred."

"What then is the answer?" said Nathaniel. "I cannot just suddenly stop hating them."

She shook her head, at a loss. There was an answer, there had to be.

"The answer is always contained in the question, that is what he told me. Could it be . . . Concentration!

"Yes, there it is! He said you draw to yourself what you concentrate on. So the answer is not to concentrate upon these men. No, not on them, or on the fact that Johannan might die. We must all . . . release those things. Leave them to the true god. For that god, All That Is, is made sad by what these men do, I promise you, Nathaniel. They will have to answer to All That Is. And so they should be pitied. Those poor men. They harm only themselves. They cannot really harm us, they cannot really harm Johannan."

Her voice swelled, and tears rolled down her cheeks. But they were tears of gladness. She saw Johannan's face, felt, almost, that he spoke through her lips.

"For they cannot kill him. They will only think that they do. In the belief that they *can* kill, will be the 'sin' for which they will have to account."

Suddenly she seized Nathaniel's hand. Without explanation, saying only, "Come, come," she led him down the street and out of the town, along the trail toward the sea, then off the road and to the place where she and Jesus had talked together. Hardly pausing to catch her breath, she picked up a stone.

"I am going to stone the bastards!" she cried.

With all her might, she hurled the stone toward the sea.

"I got a Pharisee right on the nose!"

She picked up another stone.

"Yahhhhh! Did you see, Nathaniel? I split that priest's skull clean open!"

Nathaniel let out a whoop. He scooped up a stone and let it fly.

"There is one Sadducee who has fathered his last child!"

"See how they beg for mercy?"

"Do not give them a drop!"

"Not one whit!"

"Die, you demon!"

"This one is for Johannan!"

"This one is for Herodias!"

"This one is for Salome!"

"This one is for Jesus!"

"This one is for me!"

They stoned those luckless priests and scribes and Levites, those Sadducees and Pharisees, until they could think of no more parts to hit and no one else to hurl a stone at or for. Until their strength was exhausted and they collapsed, laughing, onto the dirt.

They laughed until they cried. And they cried until they became silent, staring up at the sky.

Merovee reached over and took Nathaniel's hand.

"And now that we have released our hate, we can release Johannan's oppressors, my friend. See how blue the sky is. Feel the warmth of the dirt. How wonderfully the whole Earth supports us. She holds us as in a cupped palm. The breeze is cool. The vegetation is dry, even dead, yet how sweet is the scent. Concentrate on the honor it has been to know Johannan, to have heard his words, to have served him. Think of how you and I will be able to help our fellows, those who will listen to us and understand. Think of the great good we can do, all the rest of our days, as a result of Johannan's gift to us. Think of the step upward we take on the ladder of our own understanding. These are the real things. Death, unfairness, Sadducees, hatred . . . are but passing illusions. Do you love life right now, Nathaniel?"

"It feels very good."

"Do you love all these things around us?"

"At the moment, I do. Look at that pretty little bird."

"Always remember this moment, Nathaniel, when you are tempted to believe that 'God' has forsaken us. Because the love that you feel right now is the true god, All That Is, seeing and feeling through you. And that which you are loving as you look and feel is also the true god, All That Is. Even those misguided men from the Temple, prating of their vindictive god, are parts of All That Is. In a way, those men are angels, sent to help us realize, remember, recognize the real god All That Is, that is with us always, that supports our every step. And so you *can* love God, can you not?"

"Yes. I can."

She sat up.

"We will both concentrate upon these things, Nathaniel. Each time that hatred for Johannan's oppressors creeps in to distress our Souls, we will release the hate in some way, as we did just now, and then concentrate on the positive things around us. It will not be easy. Not for either of us. Susannah never met him. It will not weigh as heavily on her. For me, of the three of us, it will be the worst. Help me, Nathaniel. Help me to keep strong in a way I suddenly see we must all keep strong. I know so deeply at this moment that we must keep this hate away from our hearts. For, eventually, we go to Jesus. If we have drawn the Temple snakes to ourselves with our hatred . . . we will lead them straight to him."

She stopped in dismay. Nathaniel had taken her hand and was kissing it.

"Beloved Disciple," he murmured. His eyes lifted to hers, and they were filled with wonder. "You are blessed as well."

Her first impulse was to yank her hand away, to protest. Surely, she had presumed too much, to have spoken and acted with such authority in the last minutes. She, a mere woman. Much less could she allow this man to call her 'blessed.'

Then she remembered the words of Jesus, and she smiled.

"We are all blessed, Nathaniel. Each of us is God Incarnate, experiencing itself in every possible way. The meanest beggar on the Temple steps is God among us. Our task in life is to learn just that."

They walked slowly back to the town and to the stall. Though off duty, Nathaniel returned to the citadel to hear what he could hear. Merovee lay down on Johannan's sheepskins and covered her head with a quilt.

Where had all those words come from? Some had paraphrased Johannan's teachings, others she had heard from Jesus. But she had not "thought" a one of them. They had simply and suddenly been there. And she had *understood* what was simply and suddenly there, understood it with dazzling clarity, while new ideas had seemed to come from nowhere. The idea to "stone the bastards." That had just suddenly "been."

She tried to figure it out. But figuring was too tiring. So she tried to worry about Johannan. Her brain could not seem to concentrate on worry. She concentrated instead upon the mindless, musical babble of human voices in the street, and on the softness of the sheepskins, and the comfort of the quilt hiding her head. She peeked out from beneath that shelter, swiped some balm from a jug, and smoothed it over her face. She pretended to be back beside the campfire at the Jordan, supper finished, conversation low and relaxed. She asked Johannan if he would like a rub. He smiled. Yes, of course. The sheepskins remembered, the balm smelled sweetly, and his muscles were firm beneath her fingers. He moaned with pleasure. Smiling, she drifted into sleep.

* * *

The Temple delegation began its return journey to Jerusalem that same night, for it was a Wednesday, and there could be no thought of being on the road when the Sabbath arrived. Even more, men such as these would not think of being separated from Jerusalem and its Temple on the Sabbath. For the delegation which had come to Machaerus represented a particular sub-species among the children of Ibraham. These men made the Temple and the observance of The Law their reason for living—and considered that what they were doing should be every Hebrew's reason for being. The only reason. In Palestine, on that day in what later ages would consider to have been August in the thirty-fifth year of a new era, there were priests . . . and then, again, Priests. There were levites and there were Levites, scribes and Scribes, sadducees and Sadducees, pharisees and Pharisees. Throughout the country, in cities, towns, villages, there were humble and simple men who called themselves by one or the other of those names. On the other hand, there were those, called by the same names, who felt that those names were titles, ordained by heaven, entitling the bearer to special privilege and rule over their fellows. Those titled ones flocked to Jerusalem, and could hardly thereafter be driven from their chosen perches. The quiet, simple men of the provinces were in the majority, yet, as is often the way, the vocal, aggressive minority of self-styled 'holy men' in Jerusalem ruled the country and held their fellows in almost hypnotized thrall.

Among the priests of the delegation, there were none whose turn it was to perform Temple duties directly related to the coming Sabbath. Indeed, the descendants of Aaron, the physically perfect males of whom, by the mere fact of birth, secured the inalienable right to sacred dominion over their fellows and to monetary support and homage from the same, had already been so numerous even a thousand years before, in the days of King David, that special thought had had to be given as to what to do with them all. A system of rotating service, which divided the Aaronites into twenty-four groups called "courses," had been proclaimed by David and further expanded by his son, Solomon. So that, for several weeks each year, every priest in the land got a chance to actually participate in services at the Temple of Jerusalem. The rest of the time, they were thrown back onto their own devices. Most, without worldly ambitions, returned quietly to their homes once their course had finished its service, there to rule over local synagogues and teach the men and boys of their villages. But others became scribes, dedicating themselves solely to the study and interpretation of Scripture and of The Law, setting up schools in Jerusalem, the most renowned of them teaching in the Temple, itself. Others just hung around the Temple in perpetuity. The most talented or fortunate among those hangers-on curried enough favor with the family of the High Priest to win appointments as assistants, secretaries, treasurers, ambassadors, elders of the courses, or even members of the Great Sanhedrin. But there were still a lot who just hung around.

Of course no priest had actually to earn a living . . . his living was provided, according to Mosaic Law, by the people. Yet it did not look good to have so many idle priests, and a man did like to feel useful. So, over the centuries, the occasions when each citizen had to make sacrifice at the Temple steadily increased in number, while the sins and offenses which could only be expiated with sacrifice doubled and tripled. Now a priest so inclined could always find a way to look busy at the Temple, assisting in the endless daily burning of little carcasses. The nose of each sacredly entitled priest marching out of Machaerus that day could almost be seen to twitch, in anticipation of the sacred smoke to which it would soon once more be treated.

The number of Levites, those supporters, protectors, and servants of the unimpeachable Aaronites, had increased as embarrassingly as had the number of Aaronites—but, then, so had their duties. Aside from acting as police and hatchet-men for the High Priest and rulers of the Temple, theirs was the honor of slaughtering the animals for the priests to burn. Even after this short absence from Temple duty, many there were amongst them who ached for the solid beauty of the sacrificial knife within the hand, for the short, despairing cry of a dove or kid or lamb or calf as its throat was slit, for the sweet, sticky gushing of blood. Those among them who served primarily as musicians missed the solidity of the stairs outside the Inner Sanctuary where, during daylight hours, their Levite chorus indulged in endless Psalms-singing. As long as the sun could be seen, that song must be kept sailing heavenward, lest their god, who lived within the Temple in the Ark of the Covenant in the Holy of Holies—but, also, confusingly, somewhere in the sky above—be made irritable and restless with a moment's silence, and wreak some dreadful punishment upon his beloved children.

To have been denied so many days at the Temple was, to both the sacredly endowed priests and the Levites leaving Machaerus that evening, equivalent to having been expelled from the womb, into a sinful and ugly place. They hastened back toward the Temple, where all was good and right and ordained, and one's salvation was guaranteed with one's performance of rites. Toward the Temple, where the comforting scent of the burning animals was ever-engulfing, the sacrificial smoke ascending along with the Psalms, in appeasement of both the bloodlust and the ego of the god in whom they believed. To the Temple, where the ecstatic cries and adulation of worshipers daily underscored their own power and prestige.

As for the Pharisees in the procession leaving Machaerus that night, they were of the harsh and unforgiving House of Shammai, rather than of some gentler school such as the House of Hillel. Their leader was a man named Zakiah, secretary to the Rabban of Shammai. Their presence was only to be expected. The House of Shammai, more often than not, joined with the Sadducees. Together, their supposedly opposed philosophies worked to perpetuate their own existences and power. Whatever the school, however, to a Pharisee, the Sabbath was the single most important observance in life.

Many considered the Sabbath to be the Queen of Earthly Existence, with Jerusalem her throne. In the hair-splitting that occurred in the synagogues and schools, some claimed that Jerusalem, itself, was the queen, spread in stately splendor, awaiting the coming of her master, the King of Heaven, and that the Sabbath was her gift to this heavenly consort. Others insisted that it was the Temple that was the queen, sitting on the throne of Jerusalem. One thing was universally agreed upon among Pharisees. The Temple was the most sacred place on Earth, the only spot where one could truly contact God. Without the Temple, there would be no Law . . . and thus no Chosen People. Some had even wondered if, without the Temple, there would be a God. The excessive sacrifices of animals were, to the Pharisees, repugnant. But they were tolerated. Because the sacrifices were the lifeblood—physically and financially—of the Temple, and the Temple was the heart of Jerusalem and the giver of their own power.

Jerusalem, Jerusalem. Toward Jerusalem and all her sacred parts, the Pharisees hastened. To walk her hallowed streets, to pray each day in her Temple, to converse in her synagogues, learn from mighty rabbis or, themselves, teach their students, to sit in endless study of Torah, endless argument of Oral Law, and celebrate the Sabbath within the sacred womb of this Queen of Heaven was, to them, the highest honor that life could bestow upon a man. The journey had sullied them, they had must needs come in contact with multitudinous persons, places, and objects that offended their obsessive rules of personal purity. They must have a full day after the return during which to cleanse themselves of bodily and spiritual impurities that might have been encountered on the journey, to make themselves ready for the Day of the Lord.

And so, whatever the persuasion or philosophy of each individual in the delegation, each man hastened toward Jerusalem, and to the Temple whose existence gave privileged reason to his own.

A small detachment of Temple police issued first from the gates of the citadel, marching abreast, carrying lanterns, their imperious eyes warning pedestrians, who willingly made way. Headed by the notorious Alexander, these Levites brooked no insult. Their power to take prisoners and to punish was great. No man cared to cross an eye in their direction.

Behind these came the priests and scribes, on fine riding asses. The foremost was Mattias, a nephew of the High Priest Annas, riding a splendid stallion ass of near-white color, that moved with stately grace, lifting its manicured hooves as daintily as any fine Arabian horse. At his side rode a man named Noah, the personal secretary of Annas.

Behind the priests and scribes rode Sadducean elders, most mounted on asses, some few walking. Then came more Levites, on foot. Behind them, at a discrete distance, came an ass carrying a man ringing a bell. The questionably clean populace must make even wider way. Pharisees approached. Those holy men must not be defiled by so much as a breath.

Merovee stood in the foremost rank, forcing herself to watch it all, talking back to the rage within her breast. She must not hate them. Especially the priests. To hate these priests was to hate a part of her own self. And a part of her Aaronite love, Johannan. And were not the songs of the Levites within the Temple courts as angel song to the ear? Did not the scribes support the children of Israel in their learning and progress? Were there not, among the Pharisees, rabbis such as Rabban Gamahiel of the House of Hillel, whose wisdom and fairness was a byword in the streets of Jerusalem? Was not each of these men honestly trying, in his own way—right or wrong as it might seem to her—to praise and to serve that which he believed to be God?

See the pure white garments of the Pharisees, edged with broad bands of blue in accordance with Scripture. See their phylacteries, the tefillin—not so clearly commanded by Scripture, but convenient for advertising one's holiness to the world—lashed with black leather to the arm nearest the heart and to the forehead between the eyes. These Shammites seemed to vie with one another over who should wear the largest, the most obvious of these black cubes enclosing fragments of Scripture, which fragments repeated the name of the Lord twenty-three times! More holy even than the plaque worn on the forehead of the High Priest, for that proclaimed the name of the Lord only once.

Oh, there was much to love and respect here!

Hysterical laughter pushed into her throat. She forced it back, gritting her teeth.

The earth supported her. God's hand would not suddenly withdraw, allowing her to plummet into an abyss. The sun that had just set would rise again, and shed its warmth upon her and upon all growing things. Her heart was still beating. And the Spirit did not die. There were so many good things to dwell upon. One simply had to make the effort!

The ass bearing the hindmost Pharisee stopped dead in its tracks and commenced to bray at the sky.

Merovee lost control. Her laughter bubbled out. She felt those near her drawing away, not wanting it to be thought that they condoned such impious behavior. She felt Susannah plucking at her arm.

"Get hold of yourself."

Control returned. She passed her hands over her eyes and then raised those eyes to the Pharisee upon the ass. He was smiling.

"Augustus is a great trial to me," he said. "Like Caesar, he regards himself as a law unto himself. I am fond of him no less. Peace be with you, my son."

"And with you, Pharisee."

The efforts of the Pharisee's slave boy to urge the animal onward with a brush whip bore fruit. The Pharisee trotted after his comrades.

"He did not seem at all bad," whispered Susannah.

"No. I must remember his face. I want to remember it always when I search for something to love among Pharisees."

She turned and gazed at the citadel. No longer could she look to the heights for Johannan. He was down in the depths, in the filthiest of holes, guarded by those whom the priests of the Temple set over all men. In the back of her stall, the burial preparations waited. Myrrh. aloe, oil of peppermint, fine Egyptian linen. She had purchased these after waking from her sleep, for her dreams had told her that they would be needed this very night.

She walked back into the stall and sank to her knees upon the sheepskins.

"I shall lift my eyes to the Lord," she prayed, "from whence comes my help. And yes, though I walk through the valley of the shadow of death, I shall know that death is just that. A shadow. I shall fear no evil, for you are with me. I am within you, and you are within me, and so wherefore can there be any evil? It is only my imperfect understanding that makes it appear so. Your rod and your staff, they comfort me. You have put them into my own hands. I have but to take hold of them. You prepare a table before me in the presence of my enemies. You would break bread even with me, a lowly woman, whom Pharisees and their ilk would consider impure. But you would sit with me, even serve me. You anoint my head with oil. You consider nothing too good for me. I am your beloved child. My cup runs over. And I must not waste a drop. I must take my cup, this chalice of myself, and share it with all, let them drink of my bounty, from the spring of yourself that is within myself, an eternal spring, that can never go dry. Surely goodness and mercy shall follow me all the days of my life . . . humbly, waiting for me to turn, look back, and notice that they are there. And I will dwell in the House of the Lord forever. How could I not? For you are All."

She remained on her knees deep into the night, praying thus. Susannah sat beside her, eyes shining with pity. From the great terrace of the palace came the sounds of music. Laughter. Yet another banquet for the allies of Antipas.

It was near midnight when the news came, sweeping down from the gate of the citadel like a fire in a field of dried grass.

"They have killed the Prophet!"

Merovee sucked in her breath, eyes wide and staring. Then she gave a despairing cry. Her hands flew upward and disheveled her hair. Her fingers curled into talons and poised to rake her own cheeks.

Her hands were seized by Susannah.

"No! You must not mourn as a woman or they will know." For, though it was forbidden for women to disfigure themselves in grief, that injunction was often ignored.

"I do not care if they know!"

"You must care! He still lives. In your womb."

Merovee fell onto her face and gave way to sobs. Susannah threw quilts over her head to muffle the sound, and ran out to gather information. Some minutes later she returned, sank down onto a stool, and commenced staring at the glowing coals of the brazier. Merovee had crawled into a corner of the stall. She sat, back to the wall, staring listlessly. At last she spoke.

"What are the particulars, Susannah?"

"My heart faints to tell it."

"Speak on."

"They say that . . . Antipas commanded his daughter Salome to dance for his guests. Her dancing pleased them mightily. Antipas was so moved that he vowed she should have anything in the world that she desired. They then say that Salome went to Herodias, for advice on what she should request. Herodias . . . bade her request that the head of the Prophet should be brought to her on a salver."

"Herod Antipas! You filthy worm! You disgrace to Humanity!"

"It was not his fault. He was broken-hearted they say."

"A bowl of jelly has no heart to break."

"But he had made a vow. He was honor-bound to satisfy the demands of his women."

"Just as Adamah's arm was twisted by Chavvah, I suppose, so that he was *forced* to eat the forbidden fruit. Oh, Antipas. You pile lie onto lie, treachery onto cowardice. You will be one million lifetimes righting this wrong."

"The guards went straight to the cell of the Prophet and . . . did as they were instructed."

"And his beautiful head, so lately filled with love and wisdom . . . do not tell me. See if I can guess the mind of Antipas. Jo's head was taken to Herodias and Salome in their chamber, and they gloated over it. Salome danced around the chamber in triumph."

"Why yes. Exactly. I would never have believed it. Salome looked like such an angel."

"And so she is, Susannah. To the Universe belongs that little dancer. You, of all people, should suspect the words of lily-livered men."

Nathaniel's bulk hove into view. Upon his back was a pack, containing his worldly goods.

"You have heard?" he said tersely.

"Yes."

"I am doing my best to keep the hatred away."

Merovee rose. She took a series of deep breaths, as she had seen Jesus do. She had to stay strong, to live up to all her fine words, to be worthy of what she knew in her heart.

"I, too, am trying, Dear Friend. Our task now is to see to his body. Go for me, please, and say to the powers-that-be that a disciple of the Prophet is without the gate, desiring his body to give it proper burial."

"I have already done that. We have permission to go immediately to prepare him and bear him away."

The words struck Merovee like a rock-quarry hammer. To say the words was one thing. To go now and see him, touch him . . . mutilated, covered with filth and gore . . .

Without knowing, she had stumbled backward. Nathaniel took her arms.

"If you cannot stomach it . . . "

She recovered herself.

"I can. I have the spices and the linen right here. Bring those jugs. They hold fresh water with which to wash him."

"I am coming with you," said Susannah.

"Susannah, it is not required."

The horror of corpses which The Law engendered was extreme. The dead were unclean. Those who touched so much as a bleached bone remained ritually impure for seven days, enjoined to keep their distance from their fellows and contaminate no one else. Hence, the haste for burial, to, as soon as possible, remove carrion from the proximity of the living.

So it was, Merovee suddenly realized, that the insult of sending that dead head to Herodias and Salome in their quarters was more subtle than met the eye. The mere presence of that dead member "contaminated" them, but it also implied that they were touching it, Salome even dancing with it. Ah, the beauty of it. By Law—to which, though Idumeans, the entire Herodian family was nominally converted—the two women should now stay closeted for seven days. By the time they emerged, and had opportunity to deny the version of Johannan's death invented by Antipas, it would be too late. Machaerus already buzzed with the slander. Tomorrow, all of Judeah would know it, and believe it.

"I want to come with you," Susannah persisted.

Merovee started to say yea. Then she grew thoughtful.

"No, my friend. You can serve us and the Prophet better. I think that, when we go out to bury the body, we should not return here. It will be safer for us all. So stay you here. Pack that which you value onto your little Solomon . . . not your wheel or tools. In Galilee I have access to any potter's material that you will need. Then pack Gilead and prepare her to carry Johannan's body. Use his sheepskins. Have all in readiness. This will give us the advantage of one face in our party that is unknown to the fortress guards, while, not having touched carrion, you will be able to transact any needed business on our way down to Galilee. In good conscience, we should not cause others to be unwittingly defiled."

Nathaniel grunted affirmation. Susannah could not but agree. They left her there, already packing, and, weighted down with the burial materials, they entered the fortress of Machaerus.

* * *

A guard with a sputtering torch led them down a spiral staircase, into a circular horror dug through the earth beneath the tower proper. He was a regular citadel guard, known to Nathaniel. For, now that the deed was done, the Levite police had melted away as though they had never been there in the first place. The air grew closer, more deadeningly still, the lower they went, so that one found oneself gasping for breath along with the torch, and thinking that, with the next gasp, there would be no more air to be had, but only that odor, the filth and agony of over a century of prisoners. Cells descended along with the spiral, each cell meaner, more cramped, more uncongenial to its contents. None seemed empty. Merovee could feel the eyes. Then they rounded a final turn in the downward spiral. Without ceremony or preparation, she saw him.

Her world spun. She clutched at the wall, slipped on the dry scum, and sat down hard on the stairs.

"I agree. It is not a pretty sight," said the torchbearer.

The body lay just as it had fallen. Johannan's last prison had been little better than a hole beneath a grate, a torturous place constructed so that a man could neither stand nor sit upright nor yet lie down. He had been yanked up out of this place, made to kneel on the rough stone floor, drop his head forward and expose his neck.

"Pretty clean, though," observed the guard. "The man who did it was a master. One blow, and whop! The old man hardly knew what hit him."

Merovee forced herself to stand and to look squarely at the corpse. There was surprisingly little blood, that was a blessing. Her voice was hard to find.

"Where is the head? Why has it not been returned?"

"Oh, I do not suppose you will get that back. The ladies are dancing with it, I hear. They will probably sleep with it. I would not mind being a mouse to see what goes on in their beds this night."

Merovee swallowed the rising bile.

"Be good enough to leave us while we prepare him," she said curtly.

The guard was more than happy to comply. He, no more than the other guards, wanted to touch that body, or to be with it any longer than was necessary. He planted the torch in a holder on the wall and removed himself to a level above.

With halting steps, Merovee went to the corpse, reached out and laid a hand upon one massive shoulder. She swallowed a sob. The body was still slightly warm.

"So near and yet so far."

"Shall I see to him?" said Nathaniel.

"No. It is for me. Only help me lie him down."

They laid the body gently onto its back, and removed the tattered, camel-hair clothing. Nathaniel gave her a jug of clean water. She tore fresh linen and washed him, while Nathaniel laid out the linen in which to wrap him. She did not think about what she did. She could not allow herself to remember that this lifeless, faceless thing was Jo.

At last he was washed, to her satisfaction and as thoroughly as the jugs of water would allow. They lifted him, then, onto the linen, and she rubbed him first with her own balm, then with the oil of

71

peppermint, that was said to dry and shrivel the flesh. She then applied the aloe. Then the myrrh. In the fetid, airless vault, the scents were nearly overpowering. Awash with perspiration, they covered him with the linen then wrapped that linen round and round with narrow linen strips.

"I hope we have done it properly," she gasped as they finished.

"Knowing him," said Nathaniel. "I am sure he would congratulate us, thank us most sincerely, then ask us please to get him out of here so that he can breathe."

Merovee looked up in shock. There was a smile upon the broad, kind lips. His eyes coaxed and nudged . . . and did finally win her smile in return.

"Thank you, Nathaniel."

Had not Jo loved her smile? And had not Jesus, himself, urged her never to put her laughter away?

"And after all," she said, addressing the corpse with what passed for light spirits, "it is not as though we do this each day, Jo, or that you have been what could be called an ordinary corpse, losing your head and all that. You will just have to be satisfied with our work or hire someone else."

Tears pressed too closely on the heels of the manufactured levity. She stifled a shiver, clenched her teeth, and glanced at the stairway.

"I think you had better take his shoulders, Nathaniel, that is where most of the weight is . . . but you go first, then some of the weight will come downward to the feet. I can manage."

"Are you sure?"

"Yes."

The spirals that had seemed to go on for a lifetime coming down were forever going up. The guard carried the torch, but in no wise would he touch the body, neither was he asked.

There were those who did ask, however. The eyes that had only been felt on the way down, as their owners huddled in the darknesses of the cells, now approached the bars. Blazing eyes, behind unkempt Nazorite and Zealot beards, for such were the sort who gave trouble to governmental authorities nowadays.

"The Prophet?" asked a soft voice.

"Yes," said Nathaniel. There was little breath to spare.

"Are you his followers?"

Nathaniel glanced at Merovee. For all her unwomanly strength, it was all she could do, in this fetid atmosphere, to manage her end of a dead-weight load.

"Yes," he said, relieving her of any need to speak.

"But are you not one of the guards?" said another voice.

"No more," said Nathaniel. He hesitated, then summoned the breath. "The Prophet made the way straight for a man called Jesus. We go now to Galilee, to find him. If you get loose from this place, come along, too."

A hand reached out.

"Let me touch him."

"He is carrion," Nathaniel warned gruffly.

"He is the Prophet."

Another hand, then another. The way became slow and ever more torturous. Cries and whispers filled the tower. What cared these men for seven days of ritual isolation. What cared they for the irritation of the guard who bore the torch. A Prophet of Israel was passing by.

"Some say he was the Messiah."

" . . . the way straight."

" . . . a man called Jesus."

"'Perhaps this Jesus is the Messiah."

"Galilee!"

"Can you go on, Merovee?"

"Yes.

"We could lay him down and rest for a moment."

"No!" cried the torchbearer. "You are not to let that body touch a floor I have to walk on! Come on!"

"I can make it, Nathaniel."

They arrived at ground level slippery with sweat, staggering, and desperate for clear, fresh air.

"Keep going! Right out the gate, get him out of here."

They staggered onward, the fresh air helping to some extent. As they approached the gate, a murmuring arose. A surprising number of people waited without. Two figures detached themselves from the crowd and rushed forward. Without a word, they took the body from Merovee and Nathaniel and lifted it up onto their own shoulders. Confused, Merovee cried out.

"Hush," said one of the men. "Direct us, Merovee. Where shall we take him?"

The face of the speaker swam in darkness and in the stinging salt of her sweat.

"Judah Sicarius!"

He who had followed his brother away from the campfire on the night that Jesus was immersed.

"And Mathiah," offered the other young man. "Where to?"

"Oh thank you. Thank you for coming. Just down here . . . the potter's stall . . . on the left. We have an ass to carry him."

Susannah was waiting, all in readiness, her prized red silk shawl laid over the sheepskins on Gilead's back, bells and desert flowers affixed to the small beast's bridle. Judah and Mathiah lowered the linen-wrapped form onto that strangely gay bier and began to tie it into place.

"May we accompany you to the burial?" asked Judah as they worked.

"Johannan's heart would be glad, both for your return and for the honor you show him. Susannah, Nathaniel, these are our fellow disciples, Judah, who we call Sicarius, and Mathiah bar Boaz. We three do not plan to return here to Machaerus after the burial though, Judah. We continue north, down to Galilee."

The two young men exchanged glances.

"We, too," said Judah, "were preparing for a journey down to Galilee when finally we received news of where they had imprisoned Johannan."

"We came in all haste," said Mathiah sadly.

"There is nothing you could have done," said Merovee, forcing from her mind memory of the fact that Mathiah had been one of the men who had run off, leaving Johannan to face his captors alone.

The body was securely tied. Judah straightened.

"Is it to join the one they say is the Messiah that you, too, travel to Galilee, Merovee?"

"Yes, it is to Jesus that we go."

"Jesus?" said Judah. "Who is Jesus?"

Merovee's mind was tired. His question seemed foolish.

"Why, the Messiah, of course."

But then she remembered.

"Forgive me. You and Mathiah will remember him as Joshuah. He is the one with whom your brother quarreled the night that you left Johannan's fire."

Judah frowned.

"There must be some mistake."

"The Joshuah of whom you speak is a Judean, a prince of the House of David," said Mathiah. "Certainly he is a magician of sorts, for, with my own eyes, I saw him multiply fishes, but . . . "

"The Messiah who is teaching in Galilee is of the House of David but of humble origin," said Judah flatly. "He is described as a Nazorite, the son of a Nazorite carpenter. He is called Yeshuah. From the description, I have no doubt that he is my own brother."

"But whoever he is," said Mathiah staunchly, "we are convinced that he is the Messiah, and so we go to him."

"Well for Heaven's sake then let us get started!" said Susannah impatiently. "Or do you propose to stand here disputing until Antipas thinks up a reason to throw all of us into that tower as well?"

Merovee's mind was in such a muddle that she welcomed the opportunity to just walk, and not dispute. Walk, and never again have to think.

They set off down the street past silent stalls, the bells upon Gilead's bridle announcing, "Carrion! Stand away!" A respectful crowd followed to the edge of the town. There they dispersed, melting solemnly off into the night, leaving the disciples to travel on alone, down the trail that would join the road to Bethabarah and the Jordan.

The lights of Machaerus were gone from sight, and only the moon lighted their way, when some sixth sense told Merovee that not every member of that crowd had stopped at the edge of town. They were being followed. She turned.

On the rise just behind them stood a small, pathetic figure, clutching a package to its breast. Hesitantly, the person came forward. The hair was disheveled, the clothing rent. The face was a ghostly white.

Merovee cried out and rushed to meet her. She stopped a few feet short, staring at the girl, and at the linen-wrapped package clasped to her breast.

Salome's eyes were wide enough to contain the world.

"I swear I did not do what they say," she whispered.

"I know that."

And then they were in each other's arms, sobbing, cradling between their two grieving breasts the head of the man who had said . . .

"I come to make the way straight for one far greater than myself."

Chapter 4

Down to Galilee

The site of Johannan's grave had finally to be decided by the drawing of lots. Everyone wished to do proper honor to the Prophet, but each had a different idea of just how.

Salome, who refused to return to Machaerus until she had seen the Prophet interred, wished to take him to an ancient Hasmonaean tomb in the hills north of Machaerus, and bestow upon him the honor of burial with Palestinian royalty.

Judah was for carrying him all the way to Samaria, for burial upon the mountain near to where Johannan had been born, and where Elijah had confounded the priests of Baal.

Mathiah opted for Gilead, birthplace of Elijah.

While Merovee, knowing that the association with Elijah was spurious, wished for a simple spot on a Judean hillside looking down upon the ford of Bethabarah.

A bit of papyrus was torn into bits, each piece marked with one of the choices. Susannah was then asked to draw one from a cup, the disciples agreeing to abide by whichever piece she drew.

So, at sunrise, they arrived once more at Bethabarah, and made their way on foot through a river lower than ever in the hot summer.

No Ford Master was in evidence at the hut upstream. No doubt the murdered man would not be replaced until winter rains again turned the waters deep and treacherous. Merovee saw Nathaniel look toward that hut, and toward the place where they had taken Johannan.

"Bethabarah does not hold good memories for you," she said.

He shook his head.

"Was it you who dispatched the Ford Master?" she asked gently.

"The head of my squad did it. The blood is on my head no less. As is the blood of the Prophet."

"No, Nathaniel. When the Prophet gave you the rite with the balm, he washed it all away."

Nathaniel shook his head.

"With due respect to the rite . . . the blood will never come off."

A splendid tomb site was found on a hillside overlooking the ford—a shallow cave in the rocks, with even a shelf of stone on which to lay the body as in a proper tomb. There was no particular ceremony. They stretched him out reverently, putting the bundle containing the head in place at the neck. No one looked again upon his face, for Salome and Herodias, themselves, had carefully washed the head, combed the hair and beard, anointing it with their own tears, with the last of the balm of Gilead, with spices, and then they had wrapped it round and round with clean linen. Anything further would not be seemly.

They worked for an hour then, moving heavy stones into place at the mouth of the little cave, then bringing smaller stones, till they had sealed the entrance tight, to keep the body safe from wolves and bears and lions, while also, with the arrangement, signaling to any shepherd who might chance upon it that a body lay within, and that he should keep his distance to avoid defilement.

Merovee was well satisfied. The tomb was as she had envisioned it, with the cool, green Jordan flowing in eternal baptism at its base. One could see the spot where Jo had immersed Jesus, the palm grove where his camp had been, the hillock where they had lain together that last night and conceived their child.

"Come," she said when they had finished. "We are hot and tired and dirty. Let us go down to the ford and cleanse ourselves and renew our immersions in honor of him." She looked at Nathaniel, but spoke to Susannah. "Susannah, you have not even had your first immersion as yet."

"But who can give it now that Johannan is gone?" said Mathiah.

"Any of us" shrugged Merovee. "Do not the Essenes immerse themselves almost daily? What a useless rite it would be to posterity if only Johannan could bestow it."

"How come you to utter such blasphemy!" cried Judah. "Who are we? Who are you? Did he ordain you?"

"I can answer for that," said Nathaniel quietly. "Yes. He did ordain her. He spoke of her repeatedly in the days that I guarded him. He called her his Beloved Disciple, and he said that, above all others, he trusted her to carry on in his own true spirit after his death. He enjoined me, for love of him, to follow her and guard her with my life for all my days, for in her, he said, he, himself, would dwell." He smiled at Merovee. "And so I shall be honored to have her hold me beneath the waves and re-cleanse my soul. I have much need of cleansing. I will understand there to be two pairs of hands upon my neck, those of the Prophet, and those of his wife."

The two young disciples started back as one. For the first time, they seemed to see, and to grasp the import of, the leather gird about her waist.

Merovee smiled into their astonishment.

"He took me to wife just before he was captured."

"You lie!" cried Judah. "He could not have—he would not have—defiled himself with a woman!"

"Since when does a Hebrew consider it anything but an honor and duty to God to take a wife?" said Susannah.

"And," said Merovee quietly, "why refuse him his humanity because he also happened to be great?"

"Again, I can testify to the truth of the marriage," said Nathaniel. "With my own ears I repeatedly heard him call her his wife."

Little Salome had plunked down onto a rock, her fragile body exhausted from unaccustomed toil.

"So can I testify." She stared up at Merovee, comprehension piercing her innocence and grief. "He spoke to my mother and me of his friend Nathaniel and told us that he had taken a wife just before his capture. No wonder he was so pleased on that last afternoon, when I took him my gift of balm and told him I had made friends with the trader lad at the gate. I gave him two gifts without knowing it. You make a fine boy, Merovee. I would never, ever, have guessed."

Merovee could not help but laugh.

"My sweet little princess."

Sweet and plucky. What courage it had taken, to defy all convention surrounding defilement, then to escape the palace to bring that bundle for proper burial. With those thoughts, Merovee allowed herself to consider the problem that Salome now presented.

"We have got to find a way to get you quickly back to Machaerus."

"I am strong! I can keep up with you."

"That is not the problem," said Mathiah kindly, for it was difficult to be anything but kind to Salome. "Surely you would be punished or disgraced if it were found . . . "

"My mother and her women helped me go. There are seven days of confinement due to the defilement. Even after that, Mother and our women will make excuses for me. Please let me go with you to Galilee."

"Salome," said Merovee, "I might be able to trot about the countryside without arousing attention, but you, never."

"And think of *us*," said Susannah. "Your presence is liable to land us all in prison. I wonder that your father's soldiers have not already come looking for you and arrested us for stealing the daughter of the tetrarch."

"Herod Antipas is not my father," said Salome testily. "He is but the husband of my mother. And he cares not one whit for me now that he has used me and shamed me and blackened my name before the world."

"You are still a princess," said Merovee. "You are a commodity. Men like Antipas keep track of their commodities."

"No suitable second husband has yet been found for me, neither will Antipas even begin to consider the matter until after his silly war. That matter will consume many months. I assure you that Antipas will not so much as think of me until its conclusion."

Even Judah had to smile.

"Let us go to the river," he suggested. "After we have bathed, perhaps we will all see things more clearly."

So they went down to the river, to the shallows where they had stood day after day with Johannan.

"How quickly the grass forgets," mused Merovee, gazing at the fresh green growth which all but obscured signs of those who had thronged this bank not two moons ago.

"We might never even have been here," agreed Judah.

"And yet," said Merovee, cocking her head, "something here remembers. Do you not feel it?"

Judah looked about, listening carefully.

"I cannot be sure what is me remembering and what is *it* remembering." He shook his head. "Perhaps it *is* all for naught."

"If you think it is," said Merovee, "then, for you, it will be. Come, Susannah. I will immerse you."

She took her friend by the hand and they waded to the spot where Johannan had used to stand. The touch would technically defile Susannah, but, since Susannah had been careful to at no time touch Johannan's corpse, the defilement would be of a secondary degree, lasting only until sundown.

And might not the rite of immersion, itself, be enough to end any defilement?

The water was delicious upon their hot bodies.

"Feel it. How it wants to cleanse you. When I put you under, use your mind. Imagine that the water flows into every part of you, washing away all the impurities, all the old ideas, all the mistakes, all the hates, the fears, the aches, the pains, the transgressions. Feel yourself becoming as a new-born babe, ready to learn, to receive the truth . . . the joyous tidings of Johannan and of Jesus. Let that joy flood through you. Within that joy, you will find All That Is."

Gently, she pushed her friend under. Susannah stayed and stayed, playing with the water, moving against it. She came up smiling.

"Are we allowed to do this every day?"

Merovee laughed and gave her a playful shove.

"Nathaniel. Come let me dip you. You have had nothing but a drop of balm."

"No!" said Judah. "It might be well enough for you to immerse a woman, but it is not to be countenanced that you should perform the rite on a man. I doubt most severely that any of us is justified in performing it, but, if it must be, then Mathiah or I will do it."

Merovee shrugged.

"It is up to Nathaniel."

"I believe in the Prophet's *new* covenant," said Nathaniel. "Which does not teach any sort of inferiority or uncleanness in women, or a need to avoid their touch or to segregate ourselves from them. Johannan's own attitude, and that of Jesus, makes this abundantly clear. How could she be unworthy if the Prophet expected to be present in her after his death? Would the Spirit of such as he take up residence in a body that would defile or in any way degrade it? No, Judah. With no disrespect to you or to Mathiah, I wish to receive the honor from the widow."

Judah stood back, his face a study in conflicting emotion. Silent, he watched Nathaniel wade out to Merovee.

Then he jumped, for a small hand tugged at his sleeve.

"I will let you do *me,* Judah. Will that make you feel better?"

"No!"

He backed away from the forbidden touch.

"You have missed the point of the whole thing, Salome. You are female. I cannot."

"The Prophet did."

"The Prophet was misguided."

"How can you think that, yet honor him as you do?"

"'I do not know. But I do."

"I know what it is. You are afraid I will defile you. It is not that time, I promise most faithfully."

"No! Stop pestering me! . . . . Oh. Now please, Salome. I had no wish to make you cry. Please."

"What good is being a princess? It does not count for anything if you consider me too slimy to touch! The only thing that being a princess does is get me into trouble anyway."

"Salome. I did not say that you are slimy, you are anything but. You are lovely."

"Then why will you not immerse me?" she wailed.

"Perhaps, Salome," said Mathiah, "Judah considers you *too* lovely, and does not trust himself to touch you. That is another part of the reasoning in the Law against touching women you know."

Salome stopped crying. She stared at Mathiah.

The blue eyes, so full of love and innocence as a rule, snapped in anger.

"You say there is a Law? Whose? Certainly I have had an upbringing unlike yours, and have been treated differently than most young girls, but my family has adhered to your faith for several generations and we dwell amongst you Hebrews, and I know of no such Law. I am sure that my step-father has not enacted any such statute, and certainly the Romans have not . . . "

78

"This is part of the Law of God," said Mathiah.

"Who said so? Is it in Torah?"

"No. But the rabbis say . . . "

"Rabbis? Aha! So this is no Law of God, but a law of men. What am I to think, that Judah is some mindless animal to go mad and ravage me after one touch? Would he fight off all these others in his sudden, insane lust? Is that as little or as much as a woman means to Hebrew men? A brood mare good only for mounting? What possible excuse can you give me? If a woman is in her time, she keeps herself apart, so that if she is amongst you she is obviously not in her time, and so why should she not be touched? What foolishness is this Law of the rabbis that does not give human beings credit for any sort of fineness, or civility, or honesty, or truthfulness. Has it been around for long? Well thanks be to Heaven that the Prophet came to set things straight, and this Jesus, too. I can hardly wait to meet him. Perhaps I will wait and give *him* the honor of renewing my immersion."

"Ohhhh . . . all right! Come on."

Like a diver who has found the courage to throw himself off the precipice, Judah reached out and took her hand. He pulled her into the river and, with no ceremony, pushed her under. After an instant so short that she hardly had time to get wet, he set her back upright.

"Now are you happy?"

Salome's smile was radiant.

"Yes, Judah. Thank you. I will never forget. I will endeavor to always be your friend and to return the favor one day."

Judah stood frowning down at her, his sun-streaked fairness managing to seem dark in his consternation. Then he threw himself backwards and swam away.

They stayed thus for well onto an hour, enjoying the water, washing themselves and scrubbing the grime from out of their garments. Then they went up and sat down on the bank, to dry themselves in the sun and to eat a meal of bread and cheese.

And wine. To Merovee's surprise, Judah accepted a measure. Away from his hot-eyed brother, it seemed he could be quite human.

"I have been thinking," said Nathaniel, watching up the road. "Travelers who set out from Jerusalem with the dawn will soon be reaching the ford." He squinted up at the sun. "We have all spent the night without sleep, so I propose that we get some. The day promises to be scorching. Most of the travelers will halt beneath the trees here at the ford till the worst of the heat is done. Surely, somewhere amongst them, there will be a good, trustworthy family including their womenfolk, heading down Machaerus way. To them we will consign Salome, so that she will be returned home this very day, properly chaperoned and in all safety."

"Consign?" said Salome haughtily. "You sound as if I were a piece of papyrus, to be shoved into one of those magdalia and handed to a messenger."

"Salome," said Susannah, "it happens to be a good plan. You know that you have to go back."

"I know nothing of the sort. I am determined to go with you down to Galilee and meet this Messiah, this Jesus."

"What is this foolishness about a Messiah named Jesus?" said Judah sharply.

"Besides," said Salome craftily, "you could not consign me to *any* travelers. I have touched carrion and am unclean for seven days, though I think God is very silly to say that, when I have just had such a thorough bath, and how could such as the Prophet contaminate us in the first place? Be that as it may, I am sure that Judah's rabbis would agree. You could not consign me to travelers without telling them of my defilement, for you would then cast them into unwitting sin. And if you told them of that defilement they would refuse to take me. No. I will go with you. I suggest we start immediately."

Merovee and Susannah exchanged glances. Innocent the girl might be, pure and loving. She was also a wily little baggage with a head on her shoulders, a mind of her own, and a knack of getting her own way.

"Salome," said Merovee patiently, "if you were anyone but who you are, I would not hesitate to take you. But you cannot come. For all your assurance that Antipas will not miss you, he will. When he does, he will leave no stone unturned until he finds you, neither will he leave any whom he finds in your company unpunished."

"Merovee, please believe me." Salome's eyes were wide and earnest. "I would die before I would endanger any of you. Truly. You do not understand how things are, living with Antipas. Firstly, as far as he knows, my mother and I will be closeted for seven more days. When the seven days are up, he will move with unseemly haste to the apartment of my mother, for he is besotted with her . . . and my mother . . . poor woman . . . despite all his failings—and his strange attachment to a man named Manaen, who claims to be his foster-brother—and now despite even this last horror—she loves him so. It would be difficult to tell you of the torments she has suffered with the man. But she will not betray my absence, neither will our women. They have been with my mother since she was a child, and they love us both dearly. They all know where I have gone and why. The Prophet had told us of his disciples, Nathaniel and Susannah, and the trader lad at the gate. It was one of our women who sneaked out of the womens' quarters and learned that you were leaving Machaerus with Johannan's body. It was my mother who immediately gave permission when I begged to follow. She knew that I would be safe with disciples of the Prophet. She also knew, as do I, that Antipas will not know that I am gone. He and I despised each another on sight. He cares more for the welfare of his dogs than for mine. And I care more for their welfare than for his. He has never been known to ask after me. In the three years since my mother married him, I have seen him but a handful of times, when I was paraded at state functions, or for my late husband, my Uncle Phillipus. Now that Antipas is playing soldier with his generals, and will soon be off to fight Nabataea, we may be perfectly certain that I am the furthest thing from his mind. Even if the unexpected did happen, my mother and our women are experts with excuses. In addition to which . . . well, suffice it to say that my mother has a way to make Antipas believe that I am still at Machaerus. So what I propose is this. I will go north with you and I will meet Jesus. Then I will be content. I will leave you in peace and go to my step-father's new palace at Tiberias on the Sea of Galilee."

"How will you explain arriving there all by yourself?" said Mathiah.

"And will Antipas not be wroth at your mother should he discover her complicity?" said Nathaniel.

"I told you he is besotted with Mother. He is incapable of sustaining an anger against her. As for my story, I will make it a good one. Should the affair come to the attention of Antipas, he will allow it. As a matter of fact, if my story is not good enough, he will think up a better one, himself—you were witnesses last night to his talent at making up stories. No hint of scandal, or of my 'running away,' can be allowed, do you not see? Antipas needs me. I am one of his most important, political gaming pieces, the 'Virgin Princess,' whose properly arranged remarriage can forge an important alliance. In the game that Antipas plays, a blemished bride of questionable virginity is unthinkable. He would be the very last person on Earth to sully my chaste reputation, or to let it be known that I have been out traveling the roads like a camel driver, doing Heaven knows what with whom."

Throughout the speech, Salome's face and smile had remained that of an angel. The others sat silent for a moment, all thinking much the same thing. A girl so innocent in so many ways, yet so knowing, so calculating, in others. How sad that the facts of her existence had forced her into such cynical maturity. Yet how wonderful that, in spite of that maturity, she remained a creature of light.

"Well," sighed Merovee at last, "since it is possible that your reading of the situation might be wrong, and that the rest of us would then be in danger, would you abide by a majority vote, Salome?"

Salome hesitated. Then, reluctantly, she nodded.

"I suppose it is only fair."

"Do all the rest of you agree to abide by the will of the majority?"

There was muttered assent.

"Should the ballot be secret?" said Merovee.

"Not as far as I am concerned," said Nathaniel.

"Or I," snapped Judah.

"Does anyone wish it to be secret? . . . No? In that case . . . Nathaniel, what say you?"

"I say to take her. I would not have it on my Soul to have stopped her from meeting Jesus."

"Susannah?"

"I must ask a question of her. Do you have any idea at all as to the mate Antipas might have in mind for you?"

"One of my young cousins has been discussed . . . he will be inheriting his own tetrarchy some day."

"Have you ever met this cousin?"

"Once. He is nice. I like him. But he has pimples."

"Most young boys do," said Susannah. She shook her head. "I am afraid I must vote against your accompanying us. If you had said that Antipas was considering some diseased old man, or some cruel tyrant, it would have been different. But you could well end up with a sound, young fellow with whom you could have a wonderful life. My darling, take it from one who knows. Few women are fortunate enough to be given to good men, for the simple reason that there are not many good men to be had. Not for a moment would I be the cause of jeopardizing your possible marriage with one of those rare beasts."

Merovee hesitated.

"I will go next. I vote to take her along. Like Nathaniel, it would be heavy on my Soul to keep one so determined from meeting Jesus. Mathiah? What say you?"

"I am sunk in confusion. If Johannan was right, then we have not sinned by associating with you all these months, Merovee, or now with these other two women. If Johannan was right, it is not an abomination that you dress and act as a man. If he was right, then we have no call to worry over defilement even from eating beside you. But if he was wrong . . . then Judah and I are sunk so deeply into sin against the Law of God that I fear we may never find enough sheep to sacrifice to him to atone for our errors. I can not . . . " His eyes met Salome's. "I can not further compound a situation that has me so confused. I am sorry, Salome, but I vote against taking you."

Salome's face fell. Tears flooded her eyes.

"Well," said Merovee, "I guess that is it then."

"No!" cried Salome. "Judah has not voted!"

"Judah?" Merovee had purposely left him till last, considering his vote a foregone conclusion.

So it was with amazement that she heard him say . . .

"I vote yes. We take her."

There was a moment's stunned silence. The most stunned amongst them was Judah, himself, who looked around as if wondering who had uttered such traitorous words.

Salome let out a shout and flung herself forward, seizing him in an ecstatic embrace.

"Oh thank you. Thank you, Judah. My brother. I shall call you my brother, for I always did want one. That is two great deeds you have done me today. My debt to you grows, and how happy I shall be when I find a way to repay you."

"You may begin by unhanding me," he muttered.

"Oh. I do beg your pardon. I forgot about that silly worry of yours." She jumped to her feet. "Let us start. Right now. Surely none of you want to sleep. Look what a beautiful day it is."

Nathaniel chuckled.

"One can see that you have always been carried about in a covered litter with a slave to fan you. Beautiful it may be, but the hottest hours of the day are just beginning. One hour's march in that sun and you would be wilted, my little lily. And so, yes, I do want to sleep, and so should you."

Merovee would have wished it otherwise. She had been dreading the moment. But the shadiest, most private, and safest spot was the palm grove of Johannan.

She was not the only one who halted at its edge, remembering. Mathiah and Judah stood for some moments, staring. The bedrolls were gone, but the circle of stone still held the ashes of the last fire. Mathiah had walked away from that last fire, leaving the Prophet to his doom. While Judah had strode away from a deeper layer of ashes, following his wild-eyed brother after Merovee had been called an abomination who should be stoned. Now Judah returned, with that surprising vote in favor of a woman such a short time ago escaped from his lips.

She glanced toward him. His handsome face was screwed up by the conflict that always seemed to bubble just below his surface. Beneath his robe was the outline of the sicarius, that wicked, double-edged dagger from which his surname was derived, a weapon so much in use among Zealots in the dispatching of Romans and Roman sympathizers that 'Sicarii' had become another name for the Zealots.

Judah the Sicarius had twenty-five little nicks on the hilt of his weapon. Why then had he always seemed, to Merovee, to be so . . . vulnerable? And why, of all people, had the 'little lily' picked Judah the Sicarius to love?

* * *

She could not sleep. She was exhausted, yes. But it was a clean and good exhaustion. She had done well by Jo, she could feel his approval in her mind, and body, and in the air around her. And a strange exhilaration filled her.

She had been feeling differently in her woman's parts these last few days. At no moment now was she without an underlying awareness of what was growing there. She hoped it would be a boy, so that he could move freely in the world, and not have to fight every step of the way.

She thought then of Jesus, and pushed the thought away. It was not mete to think of him. Not yet.

Why could she not sleep? None of the others had had any difficulty, even Salome, who had gone dead to the world the moment her head touched the coat that Nathaniel laid out for her.

An image of a man riding an ass flitted across her mind. She had seen it several times now. This time she could see that it was a priest, for the image had grown closer with each viewing, as though the priest was traveling . . .

She sat up, stood up, and walked quietly out of the grove. The sun was blinding after the gloom. She shielded her eyes, waiting for them to adjust, focusing on the Jerusalem road.

He had just come over the crest of the hill, about a quarter of a mile away. She drew a deep breath, walked up to the road and sat down to wait.

He jogged along at a brisk, comfortable rate, confident that his mount would not suddenly stall and pitch him over its head. It was a superior sort of ass, a Syrian riding mare, who took her role in the world quite seriously.

About a hundred yards from Merovee, the beast began to bray. It increased its speed, eager for a drink of river water, one would have thought. Merovee smiled and got to her feet. The ass bore down, heading, not for the river water, but, straight for Merovee, almost at a gallop now. As it reached her, it stopped dead.

"Hello, Ruthie, my sweet heart." She hugged the steaming head and laughed as the ass pumped that head up and down and brayed its glad hello. "Hush, my love, you are disturbing the sleep of my friends." For Gilead and Solomon, back in the grove, were answering her brays. "Bring her down for a drink, Lazarus, that will quiet her." She backed away as the priest slid down. "But do not touch me, Darling, for we have buried the Prophet and I am defiled."

The priest hesitated. Then he smiled, showing strong white teeth in an angular, handsome face. So much did he resemble Merovee that they might have been twins.

"So be it. I, too, will be defiled."

Still smiling, he came forward and enfolded her.

"How could I not hug my best girl when it has been so long? And who would miss me anyway, if I drew apart into defilement for the rest of my life."

She ignored the bitterness of this last.

"I would. Oh, Lazarus!" Her strength cracked at the seams. Tears oozed from her eyes. She wanted to give herself up to his arms and never think about anything again. "I am so glad you are here."

"Merovee?" came a voice.

Nathaniel stood at the edge of the palms. In the shadows behind him, she could make out Judah, weapon drawn.

"All is well, Nathaniel. This is my brother. My twin. I am sorry that Ruthie's braying woke you. She is my pet, happy to see me again. Go back to sleep. I will wake you when it is time to leave."

Nathaniel hesitated, noting the emblems of attire which marked this unexpected twin as a priest. Then he waved and went back to his sleeping spot.

Judah hesitated longer. To a Zealot, a priest from the Temple, as this one obviously was, was a Sadducee, a boot-licker of the Romans. There was a reluctance to his figure as it faded back into the gloom.

"Come, Ruthie." Merovee turned and slid the bridle from off of the ass. "Come on, Baby, let us race." She took off, running for the water's edge. The ass kicked up her heels and gamboled along beside her. Laughing, the priest slowly followed. One might have thought that he forbore to join the race out of dignity. A second look revealed his limp.

"You have kept her well," said Merovee as he reached her side. She stroked the drinking mare, pridefully examining the luster and cleanliness of Ruthie's coat, the aristocratic delicacy of her limbs.

"She deserves all the care I give her. Many who see her riding gait and manners are jealous, I can tell you."

"Have you found a good Syrian stallion for her yet? The world needs get from such as our Ruth."

"What stallion could be worthy? Besides," he grinned an engaging grin, "I am not her master. You nursed the orphan, fed her, trained her. It is to you who she brays, 'Where you go, I shall go. Where you lodge, I shall lodge. Your people shall be my people . . .'"

His smile faded. He turned away.

"It is for you to decide upon the stallion for Ruth. Please come home and see to it. Please, Miri. You are sorely missed."

Merovee sighed, undid the belly strap that held Ruthie's cushioned riding pad, and laid the pad beside the bridle. She nudged the mare away from the water.

"Enough, my sweet. Too much when you are hot is not good for you." She took a handful of reeds and began to scrub the perspiration from the pearly gray coat.

"How *is* Martha?" she said, addressing the source of her brother's depression.

"The same."

"And Mother?"

"Escaped from our sister's carping tongue in the usual way. Some problem came up at the factory, so she hastened off to Magdala to see to it."

Merovee looked up sharply.

"Mother is in Galilee at this very moment? How soon does she return?"

"Never, if she can help it. You know that. When there are no more problems to be seen to, she will invent some."

Ruthie moved off to graze. Merovee and Lazarus sank down onto the grass.

"And how do you happen here, Brother? How did you know where to find me?"

He grinned.

"How did you happen to be sitting by the roadside, little witch? Know you not that I am forbidden to associate with wizards and diviners and necromancers? You have even been carting a corpse about the countryside, which underscores your necromancy." He saw the change in her face, and his own face straightened. "I apologize. I should not make light."

"Go ahead. Make light. Laughter is God's favorite sound, or so a trusted friend has told me."

"I came down here to the ford one day . . . the day before they took him. I stayed at the back of the crowd."

"You were here that day? When we shared the bread and fish with the people? But why did I not see you? You should have made yourself known. How I would love for Johannan to have met you."

"I hid from you at the lunch hour. I did not wish to make things awkward. I only wanted to hear the man, to know what it was that you found so remarkable."

"Did you find out?"

Lazarus frowned.

"I am not sure. The things he said were . . . quite wonderful. If one could only believe them. Anyway, this morning, when I heard of his horrible death at the instigation of the daughter of Herodias, I knew that you must be there as well. So I set out for Machaerus, hoping to find you."

Merovee sat staring for a moment.

"At what hour did you hear of Johannan's death?"

"Oh, it was before sunrise. In the Temple. I went to assist the Levites in preparation for the morning sacrifices. It was all the talk."

"Interesting. Johannan was killed at just about midnight."

Lazarus frowned, figuring the hours which it took for even the fastest of couriers to travel from Machaerus to Jerusalem.

"Word was abroad in the Temple before it should have been," he murmured. "Even if it had been done by beacon fire or pigeon, that would mean that the rulers were waiting for the news."

Merovee rose. Thoughtfully, she went to the grazing mare and stroked Ruthie's back.

"Lazarus, I, along with my party, am on my way down to Galilee."

"No! Oh, please do not tell me that you, too, are off in search of this insane 'Messiah' we have been hearing about."

"Just what have you heard about him?"

"That he is a builder, or some say a stone mason, under the vows of a Nazorite as are most craftsmen . . . a Galilean who claims to be the foremost prince of the House of David. Can you imagine? A penniless Galilean builder, the scion of the House of David? Why, we all know that Joseph of Ramah is the foremost heir."

"What is the name of this Messiah?"

"Oh . . . Yeshuah, Joshuah. Sometimes you hear it in the Hebrew, sometimes in the northern Aramaic . . . "

"Have you heard the Greek? Jesus?"

"Yes, that, too. What does it matter? It is all the same name no matter which language you speak it in."

Merovee glanced toward the palm grove.

"It is all the same provided that all these linguistic versions apply to one and the same man."

"Heaven help us. You think there are two Messiahs, as the Essenes have predicted?"

"No. There is only one."

She was thoughtful for a moment. Then she turned, smiling.

"Lazarus, I have decided on the stallion for Ruthie."

"Excellent."

"And how fortuitous that Mother is in Galilee."

"You mean the stallion . . . No! Miri, I am not going with you to Galilee! Neither is Ruthie."

"Calm yourself, Lazarus. I have many things to tell you. First of all, the stallion's name is Pharisee."

* * *

They set out at the tenth hour after sunrise, up a trail along the eastern bank of the Jordan. It was not an actual road, such as the one to the west, that passed through Jericho, and was the main north-south route between Jerusalem and Galilee. Neither was it a major route, like the King's Highway, a few miles farther to the east, that, for over a thousand years, had connected the lands of Arabia, Moab, and Edom with Damascus, Babylon, and destinations beyond. The trail was actually little more than a rough path, sometimes not wide enough for two people to walk abreast, used essentially by shepherds, and by locals traveling from one small village to another. It was, however, quite straight, ignoring the winding of the river as it did . . . while travelers upon that trail might almost have been in another time and place, private and relatively safe from curious eyes. Or from pursuit.

They would have company soon enough, when they reached the point where most of those traveling between Jerusalem and Galilee crossed the Jordan, avoiding Samaria. That province bounded the western bank of the Jordan for many miles between Judeah and Galilee, and Samaritans were often less than cordial to those who paid homage at the Temple of Jerusalem.

The problem was not that Samaritans were not Israelites. Indeed, they considered themselves to be the only true Israelites. Samaria comprised the area of Palestine that, in the days of the Judges and Kings, had been known as Israel. In name and fact, that Israel had become extinct when its people were removed to Babylon. But the spirit of that Israel had never died, not in the hearts of those who populated Samaria. To their minds, they were the custodians of the only true Word and Law of God. To most Samaritans, Jews, those of the tribe of Judah, were the enemy, and Jerusalem in Judeah was one vast blasphemy, while the Samaritan capital of Sechem was the true throne of God upon Earth. Some Samaritans still came up to Jerusalem to worship, and a few of their priests—such as Johannan's father, Zachariah—still joined in the courses at the Temple. But they did so in secret from their countrymen, for the rivalry between the powerful, ostentatious priesthood of Jerusalem and the painfully austere priests of Sechem had become so intense that religious Samaritans had taken up the cudgels, persecuting neighbors who looked toward Jerusalem, and laying into any whom they suspected to be coming from, or going to, the Temple of Jerusalem. Unless traveling in the company of Romans or caravans then, Judeans or Galileans who were not looking for a fight took the path of least resistance.

They traveled as briskly as possible, pushing themselves even—Salome, by mutual insistence, mounted on the dependable Ruthie, the others taking turns on Gilead and Solomon. They could afford to tire themselves at the first. At the following sunset, the Sabbath would begin. At that point, by Law, they would be forced to stop and rest until the next sundown.

All save Susannah were familiar with the province of Galilee. Mathiah was of Beth Sham, on the border of Galilee and Samaria. Judah called no particular town home. He was of Galilean parentage, son of a Nazorite craftsman named Jethro, and Nazorites were itinerants, finding work as they might. His mother's people were of a small village in the Galilean hills southwest of Nathaniel's village of Kapher Kana. Merovee and Lazarus were best acquainted with the area from Kapher Kana to Magdala and Kapher Nahum. While Salome knew only the cloistered luxury of her step-father's new palace in Tiberias.

They traveled in silence at the first, saving their strength against the last of the sun's heat. At least that is the excuse that any of them would have given.

In reality, the silence was on account of the presence of Lazarus. Priests cast a pall over any gathering. Additionally, there was, to a greater or lesser degree in the minds of all of them, the feeling that Merovee had betrayed them in not revealing that she was of a priestly family. An Aaronite.

So it was that, once the sun had dropped below the horizon and the coolness was upon them, Merovee called out to her brother.

"Lazarus! Do you know any good walking songs? How about this one?"

She launched into the one about the very fat priest jogging toward Jerusalem. Lazarus laughed and joined in. Susannah shrugged and took up the song, then Salome, and, finally, Nathaniel.

"Do you think that ever such an ill-assorted group has kept company down to Galilee?" laughed Merovee when they had finished.

Even taciturn Judah smiled. The atmosphere eased.

"What my sister is trying to tell you," said Lazarus, "is that there is no need to be overly impressed with me." He kept his humor, but Merovee understood the bitterness beneath his words. "You see before you a blemished lamb, my friends, unfit for sacrifice to the Lord. Have you not noticed this limp of mine? You thought perhaps I had only stubbed my toe. Would that it were so. Instead, I was born with a deformed left foot."

All knew his meaning. By the Law of Moses, only perfect, unblemished animals could be sacrificed to the god of the Jews, and only perfect priests, with no physical imperfections, could make those sacrifices . . . could perform any ceremony in the Temple.

Lazarus had thus been relegated to a half-life. He had a position while having no position. He had duties while being forbidden to perform them. His place in the Temple was little better than that of a Levite. He could but hang about at the edges and assist, wondering often why he had been born at all, and what sort of god it was to have visited this living death upon him.

The one brightness in his life was his twin. Strangely, he had never envied her own perfection. How could he, when she gave him so such love, and when, in her own way, she was as handicapped as he, having been born female into a society where only men had rights or status . . . and when her courage and persistence in fighting that handicap gave him courage to bear his own.

By midnight then, barriers were down. All walked near to Lazarus, pumping him for news from Jerusalem. What had Pontius Pilatus done to anger the rulers of the Temple this week? What was the latest bone of contention between Sadducees and Pharisees? What did the House of Shammai have to say about Johannan, and now about this new Messiah? What was the pronouncement of the House of Hillel? Had Lazarus visited any of the synagogues to listen to the disputations of the people, themselves? What had been their tone? Had the Zealots been active? Who had they most recently assassinated? Were there any new edicts from Rome? Or from the Temple? How many were languishing in the prison of the Temple? How had they offended? Had there been any stonings? Had the harvest been bad throughout all the land or only in Judeah? Was wheat being rationed? Water?

They stopped at one in the morning, close to the ford of the Jabbok River. They ate, then slept for several hours before continuing—no longer alone now on their journey. For they had passed the crossing-over place between the east and west banks. The path had become a road, and traffic was heavy, with most of it headed down to Galilee. Notable were the number of family groups, many of them carrying old or invalid members on litters.

They kept on then until an hour before the noon, at which point they sought the shade of a palm grove, finding space with difficulty among all those resting there. They touched no one else, aware of their uncleanness, and they talked with no others, uneager to draw attention to themselves. Salome wore one of Susannah's garments, her own having been rent in her grief for Johannan—an obvious sign of personal defilement to any who chanced to notice. She wore, as well, one of Susannah's headdresses, the veil drawn about her face as though to protect her fairness from the sun. They ate, ears tuned to the conversations around them, and slept again until the worst of the heat had passed. Then they rose and pushed on, eager to cover as much ground as possible before the enforced Sabbath halt.

By sundown, they reckoned themselves to be almost halfway to Tarichaea, which was at the southern tip of the Sea of Galilee, some thirteen walking miles from Kapher Nahum.

Kapher Nahum, in whose precincts all of Jerusalem's gossips, and those in the palm groves along the road, agreed, the man who might be the Messiah was teaching.

* * *

In the first hour of Tuesday morning, they spread their bedrolls and took some sleep just past the ford at the confluence of the Yarmuk with the Jordan, and within sound of the barking dogs of Tarichaea.

Still in darkness then, they rose and continued, crossing the bridge over the Jordan into that city with the sun.

Tarichaea, like all Galilean cities, was a place of means. In the dozen cities and large towns on the shores of, or near to, the "Sea" of Galilee, whether in Galilee on the west of that lake or in the Decapolis to the east, there were no squalid tenements, no sprawling suburbs of the poor, no beggars, as in Jerusalem. All was tended, prosperous, often even opulent. No dweller upon the shores of the lake that its own people called Gennesareth lacked for bread.

For Lake Gennesareth, with Tarichaea at its southern tip and Kapher Nahum at the north, was a hub of commerce, and a caravan staging area between Judeah, Samaria, the ten Greco-Syrian city states to the east, Phoenicia and other Mediterranean ports. Citizens of Galilee were not only Hebrew, but Greek, Roman, Syrian, Phoenician, and of a dozen more exotic extractions as well—so that most of the two hundred villages and cities of Galilee were, in one way or another, in vital daily contact with Rome, Athens, Alexandria, Carthage, Massilia, Damascus, Ephesus, Babylon, even with the Isle of the Britons, and with India and the mysterious silk lands beyond India. The merchants of Tarichaea were thus traders, agents, and suppliers, while many of its forty thousand inhabitants worked in the shipbuilding yards, or as fishermen, or in the factories where the fish which were a delicacy even on Roman tables were pickled and packed for export. The bazaar of Tarichaea was extensive, there were luxurious public baths, a theater, a stadium, and a substantial camel and livestock market not fit for fastidious noses.

"If a man seeks wealth, let him go to the north. If he seeks knowledge, let him come to the south of Palestine," the priests of the Temple were fond of saying when attempting to demean their prosperous and cosmopolitan northern neighbors, and to excuse the ghettos of Jerusalem.

Yet now it seemed that the world knew something that the priests of the Temple did not know. All the world seemed to be traveling into Galilee in search of knowledge.

Since joining the main roads from both Samaria and Bethania, and from the Decapolis the night before, Merovee and her party had found themselves in an intensified flow of humanity. Small, motley family units packed the route, some camping, some trudging doggedly along. While the lakeshore of Tarichaea was a sight to behold.

The boats of the Galilean fishermen were seemingly without number. On a normal summer morning in Tarichaea there would have been a couple of hundred bobbing gently at their moorings, or hauled up for repair, with many a fisherman willing, in the hot, stagnant, low-tide off-season, to earn extra coins by ferrying travelers up to Kapher Nahum. Today, despite the early hour, the shore was devoid of boats. But not of people.

Far more than a thousand were encamped there. Some were stirring, preparing a morning meal. Most still lay on their pallets. Indeed, it became apparent that those on their pallets would not rise at all. They were aged, infirm, crippled, sick.

The disciples paused at a stall where a fishwife was doing a brisk business in fishcakes—sweet, white meat, fresh from the waters of the lake. At the instigation of Merovee, they goaded and teased until Lazarus agreed to buy one of the treats for each of them.

"Where are the boats, Old Mother?" said Lazarus as he made the purchase. "And forwhy all these invalids?'

"Well now that is a foolish question," said the woman, her eyes snapping with typical Galilean disrespect, pleased to make a fool of a priest. "Why are *you* here?"

"We travel to Kapher Nahum to find the one they say is the Messiah."

"So do these. They go to be cured. The boats have been back and forth for weeks now, carrying those who cannot walk. Do you have any cripples in your party?"

"Not a one."

"Then keep walking, Priest. There are too few boats and room only for those who really need the ride."

"*Is* the Messiah in Kapher Nahum?" said Judah.

The old woman cackled.

"Some people to the west of here, who tossed a preacher fellow down a hillside after he stood up in their synagogue and tried to tell them how to live . . . those people might say no, there is no Messiah up in Kapher Nahum. But you will have no difficulty finding those in Kapher Nahum who will point you in the direction of the Messiah. Just pay no mind to those walking in the opposite direction who think that they are going to see the Messiah as well." She cackled again. "More power to them. My son and I are growing rich on the flapping of their tongues."

Merovee and Judah exchanged glances and they pressed onward, hoping to be as near to Kapher Nahum as possible before the full heat of the day.

But the route along the edge of the lake—always slow as one traveled through bustling town after bustling town, and what seemed endless suburbs between—on that day was made excruciating by the number of pilgrims.

"I doubt that we will get farther than Magdala before the heat of the day," said Lazarus after two hours. At that point, the party had progressed not much beyond Sennabray, and only halfway to Tiberias.

Merovee nodded. Shrugged. Sighed.

Lazarus laughed.

"You are thinking she will make you dress in women's clothes before continuing."

"Probably."

"Well, perhaps it is best. After all," he cast her a mischievous glance, "you do go to present yourself to your new bridegroom." He shouted and leapt aside as she swung.

"Well do you not?"

"No!"

She subsided into moody silence. She had not planned to halt in Magdala and announce her presence to her mother just yet. Fate and timing seemed to have planned otherwise. After all, it was silly to just pass by, sweltering, when, up there on the hill, the cool, thick-walled rooms of her grandfather's townhouse waited, with sparkling fountains, smooth, tiled floors . . . even a bath. A bath *would* be nice before continuing on to Kapher Nahum. And grain and a rubdown for Ruthie and plucky Gilead and Solomon—old Jesse was wonderful with animals. Salome and Susannah would appreciate baths as well.

Poor Salome. Merovee glanced up at her. She had been strong as promised. She had never complained. But Merovee knew that, beneath the veil, her face was made tight by the aches accumulated from all the unaccustomed hours on Ruthie's back, and great, dark circles had formed beneath her eyes. Tiberias could now be seen, several miles ahead, its white marble shimmering as though it were a mirage at the water's edge. Salome was trying not to look at it.

Merovee reached up and touched her arm.

"You can go in when we get there."

Salome shook her head.

"I must meet Jesus."

Merovee sighed and made her decision.

"In Magdala is my grandfather's town house. We will rest there before going on. And we can bathe."

"Oh!" A sound of pure delight.

Merovee smiled.

"My mother will even have some fresh, clean robes for us."

Yes. It was for the best. She allowed her heart to quicken at the thought of her dear mother's arms and cool, fair thoughts. So what if Deborah did make her don female attire again. She, Merovee, was rather handsome when dressed as the maiden Miriam.

What would be the expression on the face of Jesus when first he saw Miriam, rather than Merovee?

She laughed out loud just thinking about it.

* * *

The commerce of the town known to some as Magdala, and to others as Migdal—"tower" in Latin and Aramaic respectively—was doves, dyes, and pottery. From Magdala came the best white doves sold for sacrifice in the Temple courts. And from Magdala came brilliant dyes used throughout the Mediterranean world, and exquisite pottery—these last two the products of the House of Nathan, founded by Nathan of the Magdalia.

Merovee supposed he had not been all that big and grand. Yet she could see him now only through a haze of years, and with the eyes of an adoring little girl. He had seemed as large and enduring as the great lighthouse tower of Magdala, clean-shaven, with his hair close-cropped in the Greek fashion, and his eyes forever crinkled in laughter. How he had loved her. And she him. Poor Lazarus. Despite his deformity, he still had had to spend all of his time at his lessons and in the Temple schools. While Martha had always been so good that she had never been any fun. So that it had been she, lucky Miri, who got whisked up from time to time and carried off to wonderlands across the sea. To Alexandria, to Athens, to Cyrene, Cyprus, Carthage, Ephesus, Corinth, and Rome.

"There is no reason at all why Hebrews should not enter into artistic commerce with the world!" he would thunder, berating her as though it were all her fault. " . . . no reason why we should not be originators, creators, exporters, rather than passive middlemen. Look at us, still importing most of our fine pottery from Greece. Why? Why, I ask you? What is there about Grecian pottery that is finer than anything we Hebrews could do? The answer, Young Lady, is . . . nothing. Nothing! It is only that we have been kept back. It is our Law that has done this. Artistically, commercially, in every way, our Law discourages normal intercourse with other peoples. When it comes to art, we may not make images of anything on Earth, or in the oceans, or in the skies, or in the heavens above. Which does not leave much to play with. So for centuries we did nothing. Tell me about Hebrew art. Go on. Define it. You cannot. There is none. What we must do in the face of our Laws is to use our imaginations! We must create! Create that which is not on Earth, or in the oceans, or the skies, or heavens above, but only in the hearts and minds of our people. Designs which represent none of the prohibited images but which are an art unto themselves. Oh yes! I know that, in our land, you have seen a few lions and eagles and flowers and angels carved in stone . . . even in our synagogues. I have nothing against those who went against the commandment and carved those things. In fact, I applaud them. But the House of Nathan will follow The Law!" The crinkling eyes, a mischievous wink. "That way, we cannot possibly get into trouble, can we."

Long before Merovee's birth, after the death of his wife, Nathan had set off in quest of his goal. He had selected that area of Palestine which he considered to be the most free, the most innovative, the most cosmopolitan, the most commercially receptive, and also the richest in good potters' clays—Galilee—and moved there from the Greek Peloponnesus with his daughter and his younger brother, returning his family line to Palestine after an absence of only one thousand years.

For the family of Nathan had left in that initial expulsion chronicled by the Book of Judges. The argument had not, however, been over any slain concubine, as the Book of Judges so simplistically stated. It had been a schism of religious ideology, a struggle for religious freedom . . . in which the Jews of the tribe of Judah, and the priesthood of those Jews, had been victorious. Rather than submit to the rule of the Jews, and renounce their beloved Astarte and her consort Baal, whom they had worshiped in easy comradeship with the god of the Jews, the greater part of the Benjaminites had done what many brave peoples had done before them, and which many would do after them. They turned their backs on the homeland that persecuted them on account of their beliefs and set off into the unknown, migrating northward.

They passed through Phoenicia, where many were still to be found. But most sojourned there for only a century or two or three, then continued northward, settling, finally, in the Peloponnesus. The family of Nathan had been "Greek" for over seven hundred years—indeed, Nathan's wife had been a daughter of the Arcadian royal house.

Yet their Palestinian roots were never forgotten. The memory of their Hebrew heritage, of their persecution at the hands of the priests of "Jew-dah," and of their sojourning, had been passed from father to son, mother to daughter, and was as fresh and real in the mind of each Greek Benjaminite as the events of the prior week. And, from childhood, Nathan had been obsessed by a dream . . . to return to Palestine . . . to give to the Hebrews some of the artistic sophistication of Greece, along with the business acumen he had gained through his family's many ventures—to help the Hebrews to develop an art form of their own.

He began by encouraging the potters of Gennesareth. Their pottery was already fine, and known throughout Galilee, for Galilean soil contained a particular quartz which, when ground to just the right consistency, made the pottery shinier, harder, far more durable than the average. But now Nathan encouraged them to experiment with form, and to create new designs, to use some of the rich regional dyes, and find brilliant new glazes. He subsidized the most promising artists, awarded prizes, hired them at superlative wages, then, with samples in hand, he went traveling, hawking their designs, winning export contracts.

Despite all this, the pottery, while remaining a lifelong passion, was not the cause of his immense wealth and renown. That had been an accident, the result of a stray observation.

In ancient days, most postal communications had been impressed upon clay tablets—the message imprinted while the clay was wet, then the clay baked. Some die-hards still used that method, but modern men inscribed their messages upon parchment, or upon the sheets obtained from papyrus, such as grew in Egypt and in dense marshes just above Lake Gennesareth at Lake Huleh. Parchment and papyrus, while handier and more versatile than clay, were not as durable. Both had to be protected from weather and rough usage in transit.

To protect them, then, messages were put into cylindrical clay tubes shaped like tiny towers— dubbed "Magdalia"—and baked closed. Barring breakage of the cylinder while in transit, those contents arrived at their destinations in perfect condition.

Nathan abhorred waste. It occurred to him one day, after seeing a number of smashed cylinders in the office of a client, that there was a better way to do it. The clay of his area was almost proof against breakage, and what if a more permanent tube were to be manufactured, with a reusable top? One could seal the top into place, which would guard against tampering while in transit, but the recipient could then slit the top off with a knife and reseal the cylinder with his own waxen seal to send his reply, or even save the tube for a new communication to another party.

There were even more possibilities. What if an important merchant had his own distinctive cylinder manufactured, decorated in a way, with information, that was his and no other's? Suppose he sent out a great many of these, and that clients then reused them in their own businesses and sent them on to yet others? Well then, the name and prestige of the original merchant was being sent abroad. As many times as the cylinder was reused, that merchant and his wares were being brought to the attention of the entire commercial world.

Nathan introduced his idea to prestigious merchants ringing the Mediterranean and his fortune was made. Not that he kept a corner on the market. While purists, and those concerned with quality, continued to give their contracts to Nathan, copyists moved in. The fame, the credit, though, remained

Nathan's. And ancient Migdal, which had taken its name from the stone tower erected upon its shore to measure the rise and fall of Lake Gennesareth, and to light a sailor's way in the fog, found yet a second reason to call itself by a word meaning 'tower'—expressed this time in the language of the Romans, Magdala.

One night when Merovee was eleven, Nathan of the Magdalia died in a storm off Delos. All had been calm when he tucked her into her bunk for the last time. Then she was being awakened, snatched up into his arms, carried onto deck . . . into a screaming hell of black wind and water. The mast and sail had snapped and was dragging alongside. The captain and crew of the ship, the *Magdalia*, struggled grimly with the tiller and oars. It was no use. Inexorably, they were being carried toward the rocks.

Nathan saw what must come. He took from its hiding place in his gird an ancient amulet of the Phoenician Astarte—one that had left Phoenicia with his family seven hundred years earlier—and slipped its golden chain about the neck of his granddaughter. About her waist he tied two of the circlets of milkweed floss bound in clay-surfaced linen, which circlets floated on the water, and to which one could cling and not drown. Putting one about his own waist, he pulled her to himself, holding her, telling her that soon they might have to go overboard into the water, assuring her that, if they did, he would keep hold of her hand, but telling her also what she must do just in case he did let go of her hand for a minute.

"My little Miriam. Would for your own sake that you had been a boy. For you are the finest of the lot. Make your grandfather proud, Miriam. Keep your head above water. Fight for air with everything you have in you. Dig. Kick. Never give up. Not ever, in any matter. And always remember what your grandfather has taught you. Never accept as inevitable what others tell you. Never let others box you in. Escape their boxes. Find ways out, through, over, around. Never stop finding new ways to express the you that is you. I do not care what your father's family might tell you. Remember what I, your mother's father, tell you—what I believe with all my heart. It is escapees who please the gods, not prisoners."

When they hit the rocks, the world became one vast, screaming voice. The *Magdalia* screamed, the rocks screamed, the sea, the wind, the sailors, and her grandfather screamed.

She had never been sure whether she screamed as well. She must have. For suddenly the ship stopped still and she was flying through the air towards the water. Her grandfather flew with her. She could feel him, clutching, grabbing at her. Then something went wrong. They hit the water with an awful shock—a roaring pain filled her ears, and she began to swallow water. There was no way to breathe! She began to kick, and to dig, just as her grandfather had told her. Why was he not holding her hand anymore?

She surfaced some yards from him just as he also came up. He saw her, shouted, and started to swim toward her. He did not see the wave behind him, or the jagged piece of mast that that wave wielded. She saw it strike him in the back of the head as the wave curled over. She never saw him again.

The day seemed strangely cool, as, in her mind, she fought the waves of the Aegean all over again. The only warmth was in her eyes, in the slow tears that always filled them whenever she approached that house in Magdala.

It was on an elevation well back from the shore, catching the breezes which swept both off of the lake from the east and down onto the lake from the west. It was not a palatial home, not even as large as the home of Jesus in Bethlehem. But Nathan had designed it himself, and he had created a jewel.

He had placed it in one of the few remaining groves of the fir trees which had once blanketed this region, but which had long ago been harvested off. The trees lent cool permanence. As did the soft cooing of white doves in their cotes . . . doves never sold to the Temple of Jerusalem—for doves, to the House of Nathan, represented the goddess Artemis, and were to be cozened and admired, not slaughtered and burnt. The house was of typical Galilean style—white stucco, square angles, roof gardens, high walls, no hint from the outside of what the interior might be. But that interior incorporated the best of what Nathan had found in his travels. The floors were of bright, glazed tiles—in sophisticated, non-representational designs which could not offend against The Law. The walls, when not tiled, were frescoed, using, again, color and design, rather than images. The rooms ranged around two garden courts, in the center of which were burbling artesian springs. From these springs, an elaborate system of pipes carried the water to many of the rooms, providing, in some, little waterfalls, pools, or fountains, while the baths of the sleeping chambers were supplied with water from one of the hot springs for which the area was famous.

The House of Nathan was a delightful place in which to be. Merovee well understood why her mother found every excuse to leave the house in Bethany near to Jerusalem—where one either froze or melted—visit the Galilean properties to which she was sole heir, and prolong her stay.

Old Jesse, who was watering the flowers without the wall, was the first to note their approach. He stared for a minute, then shook his head, grinned, and came forward.

"Reb Lazarus! Good to see you. And you can see how old and fuzzy I am getting, for I could have sworn that your twin was a girl."

Merovee laughed and reached out to hug him.

Then she stopped.

"Oh. We are defiled by carrion for two more days, Jesse."

"Well, soon I shall be dead and defiled myself, so give me my pleasure while I still have the chance."

She laughed and went into his arms, clinging an extra few moments. It had been Jesse bar Eli, once a boat builder of Lake Gennesareth, then captain of the *Magdalia*, who had pulled the half-drowned granddaughter of Nathan up onto a rock that night, then clung there for two days, comforting the delirious child, until they were spotted by a fishing boat.

"We have brought you our Ruthie, dear Jess."

"Ruth! Mistress Deborah has told me what a fine young lady you have made of her, Miriam. Hello, Ruthie. Oh! Look how quick she is with her kisses. And who are her highness' little friends?"

"Mine is Solomon," said Susannah.

"And mine is Gilead," said Merovee.

"Well now, as much as I admire these flowers that I have been watering, I am better with animals. Would you that I see to their comforts?"

"We would be forever grateful, Old Love."

Jesse moved to Ruthie's midsection. With surprising strength for a graybeard—and in accustomed disregard of any "Laws"—he lifted Salome from the mare's back and set her onto her feet. Knowingly, he steadied her as she got her land legs back.

94

"Be strong yet a while, Girl. The mother of these two reprobates is within, and she will see that you are properly rested." Grinning, basking in heartfelt joy at the arrival of the twins, he took up the reins of the animals and led them toward the stable.

For just a few steps. Then he turned.

"You are staying for a bit are you not?"

"We intend to leave toward sundown, Jesse. But . . ." Merovee reddened and gritted her teeth at a snicker from Lazarus. "We go only to Kapher Nahum. I think, then, we will be staying hereabouts for quite some time."

* * *

They did not leave that night. Deborah bat Nathan might be the daughter of her late father, but she was also the wife of her late husband, a priest of one of the most powerful Aaronite families in the land. Appearances must be maintained. The House of Nathan must watch its step. For more reasons than one.

"Miriam. Lazarus."

Deborah had seated herself upon a finely carved Egyptian chair in the reception salon. There had always been, in Deborah's smallest gesture, in each detail of her dress, of her speech, and in her calm, lovely visage, a natural regality. Her two youngest children hung their heads. Never had the queen of their lives been unfair to them, and never was she arbitrary. If she was angry, it was with good cause.

Nathaniel, too, hung his head. Only upon arriving at the House of Nathan had he understood who Merovee—Miriam—was. Why, he had known Miriam and Lazarus when he was a young man, before he went off soldiering, when they were but babes, playing about their grandfather's farm at Kapher Kana, trying to help the workers from the village with the grape harvest and managing only to be in the way. Nathan and his family were held in such respect by the people of Kapher Kana as to be nearly deified. So when the daughter of the revered Nathan—in whose honor Nathaniel had, himself, been named—spoke sharply, Nathaniel bar Ezra bar Kapher Kana hung his head.

"You especially, Lazarus," Deborah chided. "A priest should know better. Where is your sense of fair play at least? It is forgivable for you to bring your defilement here, where each of us can individually know of it and acquiesce. But do you not understand the chaos of Gennesareth at this moment, the number of people camping around Kapher Nahum? Would you go amongst the unsuspecting and possibly pass on your defilement? Even your grandfather, Miriam, would rebuke you. The cornerstone of his philosophy was free choice. Perhaps you do not truly believe that a body becomes instantly unclean at death, but you must have respect for those who do believe in immediate uncleanness, and not defile them unbeknownst to themselves. Think of the anguish they would suffer if they should find out—the endless chain of guilt they would imagine themselves to have begun. Always, before yourselves, my children, you must take care in regard to what others believe will cast them into sin."

Fresh tears filled Merovee's eyes. She went to her mother, sank down onto the cool tiles, and buried her face into the sweetly scented lap.

"You will not try to continue tonight, will you Miriam."

"No, Mother."

"That is my good girl. Or boy." Deborah's sudden laughter trilled with the splashing of the fountains. "Look at you, Sweetling. Just look at Mother's Demure Little Girl."

Deborah's face lifted to the others, dark eyes dancing. The others found themselves laughing as well.

Deborah held out her hand.

"Come here, Salome."

The girl flew to the comfort of Deborah's lap as a baby bird to food.

"So this is the 'fatal temptress,'" Deborah crooned, petting the pale red hair. "The 'wicked dancing girl' of whom all Galilee buzzes. No. There now, do not cry, Child. Do you know . . . " She lifted the wan, wet face. "My father was a very wise man. He would have told you that there is only one opinion of yourself in this world that is worth your slightest attention. That is your own opinion of yourself. It is hard sometimes to hold your head up when others whisper and do not understand. But if you can learn to do it, you will be the person that your god hopes you will become." She tweaked the freckled nose. "Look at you, a princess, and my children have dragged you about the country and gotten you all sweaty and dirty. We must get you a warm bath and a soft bed. Later we will find you a lovely, clean robe in which to meet your Jesus." She sighed, stroking the two heads, one dark, one light.

Then she frowned.

"You have been so unthinking as to defilement, Miriam . . . "

She glanced at the men, and at Susannah.

"I am no longer troubled by those times," said Susannah.

"I am not in my time," said Salome.

Deborah's eyes settled on her daughter.

"Miriam?"

The great, violet eyes lifted.

"Mother, there is no worry of that with me. I became the wife of Johannan. I am with child by him."

Deborah understood, from the gasp of all but Nathaniel and Susannah, that she was not the only one to be shocked by the news.

"Forgive me," said Merovee to Lazarus. He looked so wounded. They had always shared their secrets. "Had I revealed my condition it would have slowed our journey. You would have worried constantly that I was overdoing, and insisted upon more frequent rests. Well would you not?"

"I suppose so."

Precipitously, Deborah rose to her feet, clapping her hands. Serving girls appeared.

"My women will see to your comfort, my friends. Do not hesitate to ask for anything that you need. Sweet dreams. As for you, Daughter, come with me. It is obvious that we two have much to discuss."

* * *

The quarters of Deborah were luxurious—to a pagan degree some would have said. The sleeping chamber was large, with an expansive, raised sleeping couch, a sitting area that contained both pillowed platforms and chairs, and a writing table at which Deborah did the accounts and correspondence of her personal and business life. The bathing room was large, totally tiled in abstract blues and greens, yellows and golds, but so cunningly executed as to suggest to the bather that he or she was a fish, lazing about in the depths on a sunny, Aegean day. In the center of the room was a sunken place, a small pool rather than a tub, where one could sit, or float, or splash, and bathe in the warm water circulating there.

Gratefully, Merovee shed her trail-worn garments, gently folding the great leathern girdle of Johannan. As she slipped down into the pool, Deborah seated herself on a stool, appraising her daughter's figure.

"How far along are you?"

"The child was conceived at the full of the moon of Tammuz."

"The exact full?"

"Yes."

Deborah was silent for a moment.

"An auspicious child," she said at last. "But there is still time if you wish, Miriam. We can lose it for you safely."

It was only a gesture. Deborah would be boiled in oil before she would aid in the aborting of a child conceived at the full of the moon—for that was the time of Artemis.

Merovee smiled.

"I, too, would sooner die."

"Good. You truly exchanged words of marriage with your prophet?"

"Yes. His leathern gird was his token."

"You must have loved him greatly."

"I do."

Deborah nodded.

"I am glad, then, that you brought some of your defilement here and touched me with it. Perhaps some of his wisdom rubbed off onto me with that touch."

She rose and went to a small cabinet, selected a key from the ring in her gird, and opened the case. Inside, in a tiled niche, stood a statue of gold. The case had been opened at least once before during the day, for fresh flowers lay at the feet of the idol. Deborah bowed, touched a kiss to the head of the statue, and returned to her stool.

"We will let The Mother hear our speech so that her wisdom may fill us as well."

Merovee smiled. For as long as she could remember, this representation of the Arcadian Artemis had presided over serious discussions with her mother. Each time that that cabinet was unlocked, Deborah took her life—and the life of anyone with her—into her hands. Of all Mosaic Law, the injunction against idolatry was the most fearsome. A follower of the god of the Jews who was found to be also worshiping idols could be dragged by anyone, with no recourse to even the most summary of trials, into the street and forthwith stoned to death.

How droll was life, Deborah had often thought, how mischievous the fates, that the only love of her life should have been a Jewish priest. But there had been no escaping it—neither for him nor for her—from the moment they had lain eyes upon one another. She had just turned eighteen. Nathan had brought her up to Jerusalem for the Passover, staying an extra week for Nathan to see to some business. And, one day, exploring the bazaar with her women, she chanced to stumble on an uneven place in the walk. A strong hand saved her from falling.

How crimson-faced he had been to have lost his head, thoughtlessly reached out and touched a strange female. Perhaps that is exactly why she fell in love with him then and there. As for him, when their eyes met he had ceased to worry about convention. He did not care who might have seen, or what they might think. How beautiful he had been, her Jeremiah.

Neither family had been pleased with the match. Nathan spoke to her of the spiritual prison to which she was condemning herself, while his people objected to the fact that she was Benjaminite rather than Aaronite, as was fitting for a promising young priest of prime lineage and brilliant intellect. But the love of Deborah and Jeremiah had been no less blind or stubborn than that of other young lovers. Both families had finally, regretfully, consented to a marriage. Deborah's position as sole heir to Nathan's vast fortune had, in the eyes of Jeremiah's parents, sweetened the tribal difference somewhat—though, at Jeremiah's request, it was not mentioned to them until after the marriage that Deborah's mother had been, not Benjaminite, but, Arcadian Greek. Since "Jewishness"—not according to Torah, but according to oral tradition—was traced matrilineally, through fully Hebrew mothers, rather than through fathers, this technically rendered Deborah a Gentile. That despite the copious Benjaminite blood which had mixed with that of the Arcadian royal house over the many centuries during which Benjaminites had dwelt in Arcadia. The truth about Deborah—and thus the embarrassing fact that her children, like Deborah, were not technically Jewish, was kept a closely guarded secret by the parents of Jeremiah once they learned of it. Deborah had often thought that the stress of keeping that secret had shortened the lives of both of those dear people.

All the more reason why Deborah had endeavored to be the best among Aaronite wives. During the short years which she had with her beloved in the house at Bethany, in deference to his position and to the sensibilities of his parents—not to mention her own family's safety—Deborah had eschewed Artemis completely. No Sadducean matron was more conscientious of her duties, religious or social. No up-and-coming young priest of the Temple could have wished for a better wife and hostess.

He never saw his twins. As Deborah was brought to bed in one chamber, Jeremiah lay dying of a sudden fever in the next. The physicians never could say what had caused it. Deborah had always blamed herself. It was the judgment of the Fates upon her. She had not been true to herself. She had lived a lie, pretending to worship a god she could not love, denying The Mother whom she did love. For, unlike Nathan, who, like many Benjaminites of the Arcadian Peloponnesus, revered the god of the Jews equally with Artemis, Deborah had never been able to warm to that restricting and unforgiving god of her forefathers. If only she had not turned her back on The Mother, if she had but kept her there in the house at Bethany, just hidden, instead of left behind, locked away in a chest in Galilee . . . then Artemis would have been there to help Jeremiah when she, herself, could not.

Perhaps the harsh punishment had even been served up by the goddess, herself. Artemis was not above occasional fits of jealous rage.

Foolish? Perhaps. Yet Deborah had not taken the same chances with her children. Artemis had been sent for. From that moment on, Deborah had led her dangerous double life—Sadducean widow, mother to a young priest of Aaron in view of the world—devotee of Artemis in the privacy of her own chamber. Each of her children had been offered the freedom of choice that she now demanded for herself.

"All the gods are capricious," she told them, "more selfish and jealous than the most spoiled of children on occasion. But we have to put up with them. Since we must, it is important that each of us chooses the ones *we* want. To my mind, the god of the Jews is so . . . male. But male as only the most hateful of men ever are. He insists that we love him, while he has no real love for us. No, not even so much as the poorest sort of parent has for the most troublesome of children. What the Jewish god needs is to have his woman returned to him. Asherah. The priests of Judah did away with her many hundreds of years ago. Shame on them. Maybe that is the very reason why their god is so angry. Asherah would soften him back up quickly enough, you would see . . . if ever she could find him, that is. That is another big problem with this god of the Jews—this 'invisible' business. How can a woman find her man if he keeps himself invisible?"

Of the three children, Martha had rejected Artemis totally. She still showed tight-lipped anger over the matter, which was one reason why, with the three of them grown and able to see to themselves, Deborah spent so much time in the tolerant and cosmopolitan atmosphere of Galilee. As for Lazarus, he did not care one way or the other, neither for Artemis nor for the Jewish god who so cruelly shunned him. Ironic that Lazarus had found no comfort in any god, thought Deborah . . . for Lazarus was the one who most needed some rock to cling to, a god to say, "Rise, Lazarus. Walk. And proudly. You are beautiful by the mere fact of being, and I love you."

It was Merovee who had taken to the goddess as a baby duck to water.

Now Merovee sighed, leaned back and let her arms float limply to the top of the water. How she had loved the Artemis stories that Deborah, and Nathan upon their travels, had used to tell her—some merry, some bloody, some warm, some sad. But always they were great adventures, with a person there, a beautiful woman, bold and free, striding through forests and across the heavens, conquering all with her mighty bow. Free. Free. No one could tell Artemis what to do, especially men. Why, Artemis could wind even the mighty Zeus around her little finger. Most of all, Merovee admired her energy and strength of purpose. Only minutes after her birth in Arcadia, so they said, Artemis had helped her mother across the ocean to Delos, saving her from drowning on the way, and then acted as midwife at the birth of her twin brother, Apollo.

As always, at the thought of Delos, Merovee's eyes clouded.

"I wish she had been there to save Grandfather."

Deborah knew of what she spoke. They had discussed it often.

"She *was* there, Sweetling. She saved *you.*" She bent and retrieved the Astarte amulet from the folds of the great leathern gird, stroking the gird respectfully as she did so. "The more I think of it, the more I am convinced that Father knew what he was doing when he gave you this amulet. He set such store by it, it had protected seven hundred years of forefathers, and had been passed on scrupulously from generation to generation. When he relinquished it to you that night . . . he knowingly made a trade with Artemis. His life for yours. He had had a wonderful life, Miriam, while yours was only beginning. I think it was a sacrifice that he was happy to make."

Merovee sighed and sat up.

"Perhaps . . . but Mother, I . . . I do not feel the same about Artemis anymore."

There was silence for a moment. Deborah had instructed Merovee to the Fifth Mystery of Artemis, and had hoped to see her journey to Greece to complete the Sixth and Seven Mysteries with the teacher of Deborah's own girlhood.

"Is it the teachings of Johannan which have changed you?"

"I . . . was beginning to change even before. Artemis and her stories were lovely when I was a child, Mother, but they never did really answer my questions about anything, any more than did the god of the Temple. That is why I went in search of Johannan, to find out what he had to say, to see if his teachings matched the whispers that I heard within myself. And, yes, his words were the means by which I was finally able to understand, and to sort out the confusion of my own mind."

Deborah could not keep the sadness from her voice.

"Will you, then, go back to the worship of this harsh creature insisted upon by the Jews?"

For the first time that day, in her disappointment, Deborah gave the word "Jews" a special emphasis, filled with disdain for that one particular Hebrew group, the tribe of Judah, who now, in popular usage, gave their name to the whole people. A thousand years it might have been since the tribe of Judah had ousted the tribe of Benjamin from their Mosaic inheritance of Jerusalem and environs, and then forced them to flee their homeland in order to preserve their religious freedom. But, among a people so intent on recording traditions and maintaining genealogies, a thousand years was as yesterday. Old grudges did not die. They but found new ways of expressing themselves. A Benjaminite would be the Hebrew most apt to explain to a foreigner that he was not a Jew. Should that foreigner persist in calling that Benjaminite a Jew, it was the Benjaminite who would be most apt to punch the foreigner in the nose. And, since it had been the tribe of Judah, under the leadership of David and in league with the Aaronites, that had forced its own conception of its own god onto the rest of the Hebrews, that god would forever remain, to such as Deborah, a symbol of oppression.

Merovee smiled a gentle smile.

"Mother, you have no idea how far removed Johannan's teachings were from the teachings of the Jews. As far away as . . . from here to the Isle of the Britons. Oh Mother, you must come and hear him talk. I will still love the goddess, and so will you, how could we ever forget her? And we should not. But what he has to say is so exciting that it takes the breath away. Nothing like it has ever been heard in our lifetime."

"I do not understand. Who is 'he'?"

"Why, Jesus, of course."

"What is 'of course' about it? I thought you were traveling to see him out of curiosity. Do you mean to tell me that you know this magician fellow?"

"He is not a magician, Mother."

"He most certainly is," said Deborah indignantly. "They say that he makes the blind to see, the lame to walk, that he cures lepers . . . and, most certainly, he flies."

"Flies?" Merovee frowned. "I do not understand why. He told me he would not do that."

"Ah! Then you do know that he flies."

"Well, he could if he wanted to, but . . . where has he flown to?"

"Everywhere. He must. One day he is reported in Caesar Phillipi, the next day in the Decapolis, then Chorazin, then here in Magdala, then in the hills to the west, or even in cities of the Mediterranean coast. Yet, every night, he seems still to be back in Kapher Nahum. You cannot be everywhere at once unless you can fly."

Merovee drew a long breath.

"So it would seem," she murmured.

"What have you to do with this man?"

"He is Johannan's eldest unmarried kin. I . . . will probably marry him."

Deborah jumped up, paced over to the goddess, then back.

"I must be getting old, you go too fast. I thought you said you would not adhere to The Law of the Jews. You know that I never pressured you to marry anyone in the first place—indeed I have been delighted that you preferred to go out searching into the world. But, now that you are a widow, you want to follow Jewish Law and marry your dead husband's cousin? Why? Certainly not on my account. I will require remarriage of you no more than my father required it of me. My darling, you have access to all the money you could ever want, why put yourself into bondage again? Miriam, besides being a public magician, which is sure to get him into trouble with the Temple, this Jesus puts it about that he is a prince of the House of David. His tribe is thus Judah. He is a *Jew*! Miriam, *Darling*! You are so special. Do not throw yourself away on this charlatan. We will return to Greece, you and I, and the other two if they choose. I do not know why I have not proposed a return before this. Martha probably will not come, she fancies that Boaz of hers and thinks only of becoming his wife. But it would be the exact thing for Lazarus. In Greece, he would not be excluded from the religious life. And there you, too, would have more latitude. Women are allowed to study with physicians and become expert in women's ailments. Or you could become a priestess. Priestesses are accorded great honor in Greece. Or we could go to Alexandria. Women enjoy even more freedoms in Egypt. Anywhere, Miriam! But for the love of any god that you choose, do not give yourself to a man whom you do not love!"

Merovee dabbled at the water, watching the droplets.

"I do love Jesus."

"A scion of the House of David? He must be a Sadducee!"

Merovee laughed.

"No. He is Jesus."

"Miriam. Think what you do. Even if he gives up his rabble-rousing and does not get himself stoned to death, to marry a Jew of his class and position is to put yourself into prison."

Even as she spoke, Deborah realized that her words were the same as had been spoken to her by her own father, twenty-three years before. She saw the placid dreaminess in her daughter's eyes. Had she, Deborah, had that same look in her eyes back then?

Still she kept on.

"Take it from me. You know how I loved your father. From first sight. My father tried to warn me, as I am warning you now. I would not listen. But he was right. Miriam, I have never before voiced this. But had your father lived . . . had I been forced to go on in that artificial existence, robbed of all that my Spirit held dear, I do not know what would have become of me. Eventually, your father's love would not have been enough. I would have had either to escape . . . or to go mad."

"Mother, Jesus does not hold with The Law in regard to women any more than did Johannan. As a matter of fact, he hardly holds with The Law at all. And he will not give up his rabble-rousing. He cannot. I believe him to be the Messiah, Mother."

Deborah sat down, thought a moment, and tried a new tack.

"I had no idea that I had raised such a fickle little beast. Your affections certainly blow with the wind, my girl. I thought you said you loved your late husband."

"I did and do. He and Jesus are as one."

Merovee lifted her eyes to Deborah's troubled face.

"Do you want me to try to explain why they are as one or do you wish to sit there eating my dust as I disappear down the road?"

Deborah stared for a moment. Then, with a sound that was half snorting disgust and half laughter, she bent, scooped the water and dashed it squarely into Merovee's face.

"So the kitten thinks it can teach the cat?" She laughed outright at the spluttering. "All right. I am not so old that I cannot learn. Say on, oh Wise One."

They talked through the afternoon. Deborah, the daughter of a free-thinking iconoclast—a daughter who had continued to think freely, and who had passed the family propensity on to at least one-and-a-half of her children—who had watched her youngest daughter stride off in man's clothes to find some wild-eyed prophet, but who had rested content for close to a year, knowing that Miriam could take care of herself come what may—a woman of courage, strong enough to believe that individuals should be free to make their own choices, and to act upon their own beliefs. There was much that Deborah could understand. But some of the things, some of the private teachings that Johannan and Jesus had given her daughter . . .

"They are as strange as the things I was taught in the last mystery of Artemis. The Seventh Veil of Mystery. Yet . . . those things I was taught *were* as veils. Misty, floating, faraway. One memorized the words, the texts, the chants, the dances, the motions. One learned them without really thinking about them, or really, I can see now, *believing* them. Now you tell me that this Jesus says that much of what I memorized, and took for pretty symbolization, is so . . . that the mysteries approach the truth as to what we are, and as to the true nature of the world around us. But this Jesus goes even beyond what I was taught, into truths which make me faint even to contemplate. What childs' play it makes of all the rest of it if it is so. And perhaps it is. For, if the rumors speak truly, your Jesus seems to be able to physically demonstrate what he claims."

They sat at table now, with fruit and wine.

"Did your Johannan know of your love for the goddess, Miriam?"

"I told him. I showed him the amulet."

"And he approved?"

"He said that Artemis is a beloved aspect of the Great God Which Is All."

"Does your Jesus know?"

"Not yet. He will understand."

Deborah sighed.

"An unusual man, indeed. And an unusual *Jew*. I think I will go with you and meet my future son, the Great Magician. Oh! Does *he* know that you are going to marry him?"

"I am sure," said Merovee, "that he has known for a million years."

* * *

Merovee should have slept as if dead that night, but her mind would not lie still. She seemed to hear a roaring, as of some great wave traveling towards her, gathering, gathering toward that last moment when it would curl and come crashing down over her.

She had no fear of drowning in it. Her excitement built with the roar. A whole new part of her life was about to begin. Of her own free choice, she was here, swimming *toward* the wave even.

Yet she could remove herself from out of its path at any moment if she so chose. She had thought a great deal about the things that Jesus had touched upon that last morning at Machaerus. She had begun to understand. She understood that there were many Merovees and Miriams of Migdal-Magdala-Bethany—living out the lives that each of them had chosen at each juncture of existence.

Or not particularly "living" them out. There was a little Miriam who had died at the age of eleven, drowned in the Aegean. Jesus had told her that that Miriam had already been born again. The strangest

102

part of what he had said was that that Miriam had been born into a life a thousand years into the future, that she was a queen, and lived in the north of the cold, dread Isle of the Britons.

Time is simultaneous, he had told her. All that had ever been, that was right now at this moment, and that would or could ever be . . . it existed all at once, in a shining Eternal Moment. It was hard to understand how such a thing could be. Almost harder than understanding the probable Miriams and Merovees who had split off at moments of decision. All of them must now be living in their separate realities somewhere in simultaneous time. So there must be a Miriam much like her sister Martha, who had never gone in search of Johannan in the first place, never taken the name of Merovee. There would also be a Merovee who had not returned to Bethabarah that last night, and one who had returned, but had not run into Johannan's arms and become his wife. There would be a Merovee who had not followed Johannan to Machaerus, and one who had not come down to Galilee. There was a Merovee who had listened to her mother this afternoon, and who was even now deciding not to continue into Kapher Nahum, but, instead, to go to Greece and become a priestess, or study the curing of women's ills with some physician. According to what Jesus had said, all those Merovees and Miriams were real, each as valid as the other. In a way that she did not understand, but knew to be the case because Jesus had said it was so, at moments of decision, one's energy split, multiplied, as Johannan and Jesus had multiplied the fishes—each split as real as any of those fragments of food—and the splits, themselves, kept multiplying, until there were enough Merovee-Miriams to act out all the possibilities of any given juncture, present, future, or *past*.

All those other Miriam-Merovees, she wondered—by means of some gigantic communications network between minds, such as Jesus said existed in the dream state—were each of them thinking of *her* at this moment because she was thinking of them? Were each of them sensing, or in any way understanding, *her* existence? If they were, each of them was thinking that she, herself, was the *real* one, and that she, Merovee, was the ghost. How droll. When she, Merovee, was the one who was going to continue on, link her destiny with a man such as Jesus, and follow his road wherever it led.

What an incredible sense of power it gave, to know, not only, that she could live out whichever possibility she chose, but that all the others were there, living out every possibility that she had ever entertained but rejected. How wonderful to think that, in her dreams, she could be in contact with all of them, and share, to some extent, in their experiences.

How vast she was!

She had the sudden sensation of being the hub of an eternal spider's web of Energy—and of people and of consciousnesses that, in a way, were, all of them, Her.

Things seemed gray at the edges for a moment, and she could sense the one who had decided to go to Greece. She lay upon the same bed, staring at the ceiling. Tears rolled down her face. She did not look quite as Merovee imagined herself. She was softer, weaker. She was not as committed, nowhere near as sure of herself. She was not sure she had made the right decision. But, still, she was going to go to Greece.

Merovee smiled. The poor thing. It was a wonder she had been brave enough to come even this far. Mentally, she called to the girl, trying to reach her mind.

'Have no regrets. I am brave enough to do what you can not do. I will go to him. For us. You go on to Greece. Take the knowledge he has given you and put it to use there. Be happy. Live that road fully and hone a different sort of bravery. We will each benefit from the experience of the other as we dream . . .'

The vision faded. But not the excitement.

At last, unable to lie still, she rose, went out into the garden court of the sleeping wing and up the stairway onto the roof.

The night was balmy and still, the doves asleep, no breeze to move the firs. One could see through those trees from up here, down onto the lake. That grove of fir trees was no accident. Nathan had chosen the site of this house carefully. Fir trees and high places, like doves, were sacred to Artemis . . . whose moon was nearly full again tonight, shining across the water. Considering the season, there were a surprising number of boats out trawling. Many other boats, brightly lighted, moved purposefully, still ferrying invalids to Kapher Nahum—from Tarichaea, but also from the cities of the Decapolis, which glowed like diamonds there across the lake—Hippos, Gergesa, Bethsaida . . .

What must it be like in Kapher Nahum? Its lights could be clearly seen, just six miles further on up the coast—so many lights, so late at night. Kapher Nahum seemed, from this distance, to have grown as large as Jerusalem. The place must be a beehive of activity. Where were they putting all the people? How were they feeding them? She smiled, remembering the fishwife in Tarichaea . . . getting rich on the flapping of tongues. The merchants and farmers of the area would love Jesus as long as their saleable goods lasted.

A sound made her spin about.

"Judah! I did not see you."

He had been so silent there in the shadow of a fir. He came forward.

"You could not sleep either." He looked up toward Kapher Nahum. "Soon we will know, will we not."

It had been unspoken between them throughout the journey.

"It is my brother they are speaking of, Merovee. Simon Yeshuah bar Galilee. You will see. He is the Messiah."

"I am sure that, in a way, you will be found to be right, Judah."

"In a way? You speak only in riddles of late! How can there be any doubt? My brother is the Great One of whom the prophets foretold. I have known it since I was a boy, and so has he, but he would not give a name to it as did I. No one, not any Sadducee or Pharisee, is more learned in The Law than my brother. His love of his people has no end, His only thought in life is to redeem the children of Israel from sin. And he has powers that can only come from God."

He hesitated, then went on.

"This has never been known by any except my mother. But I think you should know. You need to see the truth. When I was a boy—Simon Yeshuah struck down one of my playmates in anger. A Greek lad it was, son of a trader of Kapher Nahum—an idolater, of course. Simon Yeshuah came to fetch me from my play. When he saw me with the Greek, and knowing of his idolatry, he became wroth. Ah, the rage of Simon Yeshuah is a frightening thing to see, Merovee. But the foolish boy persisted in defending his sinful ways when Simon Yeshuah would have shown him his error. So my brother struck him with a rock. The boy's head split wide open. I was paralyzed by terror, not on account of the idolater, who surely deserved to die, but out of fear for my brother. What would the elders do to him for this act? Might they even kill him? My brother realized the danger as well. He knew that, for the sake of his people, he must save himself. You know Simon Yeshuah's eyes, Merovee. He can move mountains with those eyes of his. And now he fastened them upon the boy and laid his hands upon the broken head. I tell you, I saw it. The sinner became whole once more. He got up and walked home with us, seeming not even to remember that Simon Yeshuah had hit him. The next morning, he did not rise from his mat. He had well and truly died during the night—yet no one suspected that he had died by my brother's hand. Thanks be to our Lord. All this I saw with my own eyes. Can power such as I have just described signal anything but the Messiah?"

Merovee was silent, stunned by the story. She did not for a moment think that Judah was lying. His sincerity was apparent. And, yes, she did know the eyes of Simon Yeshuah. Could the man possess such power? To heal? To raise from the dead? Was it possible for two men to have such extraordinary abilities? Everything within her said that Jesus, not Simon Yeshuah, was the looked-for Messiah. She had felt his coming for days before he had arrived at Bethabarah, like a drumbeat in her mind, growing louder and louder. Then there he had stood, at the top of the bank, shining as Apollo, himself, must shine. The drumbeat had stopped. There had been blessed silence, like water after a thirst.

"The only value of your Jesus, Merovee, is that his blasphemies at Johannan's campfire that night so enraged my brother that he was at last able to admit to himself who he is. Until that moment, he had still wondered if Johannan, and not he, himself, was the Messiah. But, as we walked away that night he said, 'You have spoken well all these years, Little Brother, when you have said that I must be the Messiah. I know it now. I am the Anointed One.'"

Doubt, cold and painful, crawled into Merovee's mind. She had felt the coming of the Messiah like a drumbeat . . . had thought it heralded Jesus. Was it possible that it had signified only the coming of the catalyst who would cause the true Messiah to declare himself?

"Why did you part company from him then Judah? How came you to be with Mathiah?"

"My brother, the Messiah, wished to go into The Wilderness of Judeah to fast and to meditate upon his new knowledge. He told me to bide a while and I would hear of his doings, and that, when I did, I should come to him. So I went to Jerusalem to spend my time in devotion at the Temple, and to dispatch a few Romans in the dark of the nights. It was in Jerusalem, in the Temple court, that Mathiah found me after he, too, left Johannan. We two decided then to go to Qumran and bide for a while with Essenes. Hence, we were late in hearing of the place where Johannan had been imprisoned. We heard it almost simultaneously with news of my brother's works here in Galilee. We were torn as to where our duty lay, but we finally determined to go first to Machaerus and see if there was aught that could be done for the Prophet, and then go to Galilee. You know the rest."

Merovee sank down onto the parapet and stared out at the lake. Confused she was. Yet . . . not confused. There was something so completely right to her mind about all that Jesus said, and about all that he was. And there was something so very wrong about Simon Yeshuah—a true part of the Elijah entity according to Jesus.

"You say that Simon Yeshuah made that Greek boy whole and raised him from the dead only to save himself, not out of any love for the boy, or regret of the murder."

"How should the Messiah love a blaspheming idolater or regret the killing of him? Is it not plainly written by Moses that we shall slay idolaters wherever we find them?"

Merovee smiled gently.

"Yes. It is plainly written."

She did not mention that, conversely, God had also said to Moses, "You shall not kill." She could sense that that contradiction had occurred to Judah even as he spoke.

She realized suddenly what was "wrong" about Simon Yeshuah. Deborah had only today complained that the god of the Jews was invisible. But he was not. The god of the Jews had taken earthly form. In Simon Yeshuah.

. . . a man in whom there was no love, for all that he thought, and claimed, that he loved his people. A man in whom there was only childish, arbitrary, contradictory, unreasoning, righteous wrath.

Simon Yeshuah was, indeed, made in the image of his god.

A god whom Merovee had always disliked. A god upon whom, even as a child, she had had the sense to turn her back.

She understood now why she loved Johannan. Why she loved Jesus.

'You shall love the Lord, your God, with all your heart, and soul, and strength,' said another commandment of Moses.

Johannan and Jesus had introduced her to a god that she could—and did—love in just that way.

All That Is. The god of Johannan and of . . . a man who was beyond even the Messiah.

A god of whom Jesus and Johannan were the thoroughly lovable images.

"I think there *can* be more than one Messiah," she murmured.

"Do not be ridiculous."

"Do the sages, themselves, not bicker over who he will be, when he will come, what he will do? The House of Hillel says he will be one thing, Shammai says that he will be another. The priests have yet a third idea. Then there is the Sadducean version. Then the Samaritan version. To one he will be a priest, to others a teacher, to others a king, to others a conqueror. And what say the Essenes?"

" . . . they . . . are misguided."

"That does not answer my question."

"They expect two Messiahs," he admitted. "A priestly Messiah and a kingly Messiah."

"While you Zealots expect just one Messiah . . . a wild-eyed killer who will rid the Earth of Romans and lead the Jews to world domination. Do you not see, Judah? Everyone has a different definition of 'the Messiah.' Each man interprets what he reads differently. Who is right?"

"We Zealots, of course."

"If so, then Simon Yeshuah is the Messiah. *Your* Messiah. Not mine. My Messiah comes with a new message, he does not come merely to underscore the old. My Messiah comes to me with tidings of love, of joy, and freedom, and creativity beyond my wildest imaginings. Your Messiah would bury you ever more deeply into angers and hatreds, rules, regulations, fears, sin, and guilt."

"There cannot be two Messiahs!"

"I suddenly think that that is exactly the key. As a matter of fact, I think that there can be as many Messiahs as there are interpretations of that concept. Each of us will receive in accordance with our idea. We will each find the Messiah that we believe we will find."

"I must not listen. It is evil what you say."

Merovee smiled. What would he say if he learned of golden Artemis in the casket in her mother's bath. She, Merovee, would probably never know what he would say. For he would hurl the stone before he spoke. He would kill her along with gracious, beautiful Deborah.

Judah and his Messiah brother would also have considered her grandfather, with the thrusting ideas and forever-smiling eyes, as unworthy of life.

"I take it, Judah, that your family is of the House of David."

That was one element upon which all agreed. The Messiah would be born out of David. With genealogical charts the cornerstone without which the Laws of Moses could not be implemented, each family—especially of the tribe of Judah—knew its lineage from at least the departure from Egypt to the present. Vast chambers had been built beneath the Temple of Jerusalem to store the genealogical records of all the people.

"We descend through Nathan."

One of David's numerous younger sons, an inferior descent. But the prophecy stipulated only "from the loins of David." Simon Yeshuah was thus qualified to be thought the Messiah.

What a dangerous Messiah he could be, she realized. Politically a Zealot, religiously a Nazorite fanatic, dedicated to the expulsion of Roman authority from Palestine, and to the supremacy of the god of the Jews upon Earth . . . with the power to work miracles, and the charisma to inspire those who thought like himself, to then declare himself King of the Jews, and to lead a revolution. It would be madness. Rome would crush such a revolution as one squashes a bug.

It was so peaceful there on the roof, in the warm darkness of the Galilean night. Merovee wondered suddenly if it would be the last night of true peace she would ever find . . . if, in years to come, she would envy that timid Merovee who was preparing to run away, turn her back on messiahs of every sort.

It was not yet too late. Even now, she could go down to her bed, fall asleep, and wake in the morning as that other girl.

But then, what would Ruthie do for a proper mate?

Chapter 5

Gennesareth

After the hottest hours of Thursday had passed, with their seventh day of ritual uncleanness to end with the setting sun, freshly clothed, with Merovee dressed as Miriam and accompanied by Deborah, they left the House of Nathan and walked the six miles to Kapher Nahum.

The last two miles of the trip after Heptapegon, the place of the seven springs, were one continuous camp, the road lined with the booths of fishermen, farmers, and merchants of all sorts. More than once, Salome dropped behind, exhilarated by freedom in such a setting, unable to resist this purchase or that, or wanting only to watch some show. For, those with neither goods nor food to sell provided entertainment and services. An enterprising Syrian had roped off a ring and, for a copper coin, was giving children twice around the perimeter on the back of a crabby, old she-camel. Greek and Cyrenean physicians ministered to the ill for a price. A Sidonite had himself a dancing bear, and there was a jet-black man from the land below Egypt who had a monkey, which funny little creature many of the pilgrims had never seen. He was making a great deal of silver, many people being as eager to watch a jet-black man as to watch his comical pet. There were a plenty of Roman soldiers, ostensibly on guard lest there be a breach of the peace, but enjoying the fair-like atmosphere and the change from their normal routine. There were hairdressers, tailors, cobblers, tinkers, fortune-tellers, astrologers, and professional storytellers.

These last passed among the sick and crippled, telling, for a price, where the rabbi had gone that day, what he had done, dramatizing all that he had said.

Merovee and her group stopped aside one such man and Lazarus inquired as to the whereabouts of the rabbi. The fellow was not put off by the priestly garments. He stuck out his hand. Lazarus shrugged and gave him a coin.

"He lodges near Chorazin this night."

Nearly another three miles beyond Kapher Nahum.

"Are you sure?"

"Of course I am sure, I have just come from there."

"Brother," murmured Merovee, acting the respectful female, "ask him what this rabbi looks like."

"For another shekel I will not only tell you what he looks like, Maiden, but I will tell you what he said, in the very voice and tones that he said it."

"No thank you," said Lazarus.

Merovee poked him.

"Please, Brother, I should love to hear it."

Reluctantly, Lazarus fumbled in his gird for another coin.

"Let me," said Salome, and, as was her wont, she produced a piece of silver large enough for all the stories in the storyteller's head.

Hastily, he took it and gathered himself for a fine rendition.

"The rabbi said . . . "

"No," interrupted Merovee. "Tell us first what he looks like."

"Oh. Well, he is taller then most, well built . . . "

"Does he have the hair and beard of a Nazorite?"

"No. His beard is quite short, and his hair as well. He must have been recently in mourning." Which was the only reason why a devout Hebrew male would drastically shorten his hair or his beard.

Merovee frowned. The gestures of the story teller had indicated hair a bit too long for Jesus even if he had been letting it grow along with his beard. She glanced at Judah.

He was as puzzled as she, and suddenly worried.

"Perhaps," he whispered, "there has been a death in my family, though I cannot imagine Simon Yeshuah cutting his hair . . . "

"Go on," said Merovee to the storyteller. "Tell us the words he spoke."

Again the story-teller gathered himself to perform.

"He said, 'Be ware! Mend your ways!'"

He spoke in low tones so that others could not hear without paying, but with drama worthy of his craft and of the subject.

"'The Kingdom of God is at hand! Only those who follow me will be saved from the wrath to come!'"

"Thank you, that is quite enough." Merovee smiled at Judah. "So now we know that it is your brother who is in Chorazin."

"How do you know it is not Jesus?" said Lazarus.

"Jesus would not be caught dead spouting such rubbish," muttered Nathaniel.

"Jesus, is it?" said the storyteller. "The Jewish prince with the Greek habits and the fine, soft robes? That one is no rabbi, my friend, he is not even qualified for the title, he has never taken a wife. He is one of the false prophets against whom Scripture warns us. It is the Galilean you want to follow, take my word. There are those who say that the Galilean is surely the Messiah, though you must know that already. This Jew from Bethlehem is sent by the Prince of Darkness, intended to confuse us."

"Still," said Lazarus, "it is he who we have come to see. Where will we find him?"

Again the eyes of the storyteller studied the priestly garb, and now also the rich robes which Deborah had provided for the women.

"He took sail over to Bethsaida this morning, but by darkness he will be back in Kapher Nahum, never you fear, getting drunk at the inn of Obed with his friends. With the rich and with *tax collectors*, those Roman lackeys. With any manner of vile sinner, the more offensive the better. That is the scum that flocks to your Jesus, your Joshuah *ben* Joseph *ben* Bethlehem."

His Judean emphasis was derisive, and his eyes, blazing with indignation, fastened on Judah.

"You. Did I hear this woman say that Yeshuah of Galilee is your brother? Why, then, are you traveling with friends of that charlatan from Judeah? Go to your brother. He needs stout followers. He is doing the work of the Lord, casting out demons, redeeming the children of Israel, Get you to him, Lad!"

Judah colored . . . seemed about to reply. Then he walked on ahead.

It was Salome who answered the storyteller. Whipping aside the veil from her face, she rounded on him.

"Hypocrite! If you feel so strongly about this Yeshuah, why are you standing here making money for yourself off of his words? Get you, yourself, to him, and become his follower!"

She rushed after Judah.

Merovee had already caught up to him.

"I am sorry," she said.

"Not at all," said Judah. "The man is right to berate me."

"Judah, Brother!" It was Salome, innocently taking his arm. "He was not right. He was rude, that is what."

"Will you part from us now then, Judah?" said Merovee.

"Oh! No! Please do not!" said Salome.

Her lack of guile could not tease from Judah the usual, grudging smile.

"Actually I will not leave you yet. I intend to stop with you in Kapher Nahum, for I have family there and must discover if we have been visited by a death. Besides, I want to take a better look at this wine-house rat of yours. I am curious to see what magic he works, that makes you all so sure that he, and not my brother, is the Messiah. When I have understood that, I can make a report to my brother so that he will better know how to combat your false prophet. Salome. What are you doing? Stop that!"

Salome had stepped quickly behind him and was trying to match her steps to his, while also desperately trying to refasten the veil over her face.

"Hide me, Judah, hide me!"

It was no use. The woman had seen. She came straight to Judah and peered around him.

"Your Highness," she hissed. "For I know it is not Scota. *She* would know better. What in the name of God are you doing here?"

"I could ask the same of you, Johannah." Salome adopted her most imperious expression. "Why are you not occupying yourself with your duties at the palace?"

"When the lion leaves, the lambs do gambol. I am up to visit cousins near to Heptapegon for the month. You are not putting me off, you little scamp. What are you up to this time?"

"I am on my way to an audience with the Messiah," said Salome grandly, not for a moment dropping her tone of command. "Miriam, I should like you to meet Johannah, wife to Chuzah, my step-father's steward in Tiberias. And this is Judah, and . . . "

She introduced all in the party. At the name of Deborah, daughter of Nathan of the Magdalia, Johannah reacted and visibly relaxed. Her young mistress was at least traveling in suitable company.

"We were going to come back down to the palace after we had conferred with the Messiah, who is a personal friend to this company," continued Salome, desperate lest Johannah take her by the ear and drag her away. "Would you care to come along?"

Johannah tilted her head.

"You have not answered me. What are you doing here alone?" She glanced at Deborah. "Without your women or your step-father's guard, I mean. Feelings are high over the death of the Prophet. If this crowd were to realize who you are . . . "

Salome lifted her chin.

"I shall explain all that on the way. You will come, will you not?" Better to keep her with them than to have her send word to the palace and raise an alarm.

Johannah, for her part, was young, and not above a bit of adventure to break the monotony. For all her assumed sternness, she had assisted Salome in many a girlish escapade before this day. Besides, who could resist such an invitation?

"Of course I will come. Is it not my duty now to watch after you? But with which of the two Messiahs do we have an audience, Your Highness?"

* * *

Kapher Nahum was a place of industry and a caravan center like unto Tarichaea, but even larger, sitting, as it did, on the Imperial Roman Road from the Mediterranean to Damascus and beyond. It was also headquarters to the Roman troops garrisoned in the province of Galilee. Partly because of that Roman presence, the atmosphere inside the town was in marked contrast to the carnival atmosphere of its approaches. The streets were thronged with people, yes, but they moved, sat, stood, conversed with decorum. Despite the background of sound from the activity on the outskirts, the usual hubbub of the market place and caravan-staging areas, and the murmuring of the crowd that jammed the Thursday gathering at the synagogue, it could almost have been said that there was a hush in the air—a hush of expectancy. One did not have to ask to know that Jesus had not yet returned from Bethsaida. The crowd grew denser the closer one got to the little harbor, and the eyes of all those who waited in the streets—a great many of them on litters and crutches—were turned as one great pair toward that place, watching out to sea. It would be at least an hour, they were told by one of the watchers, before Jesus returned. He had put out the word when he had set sail that morning that he would return with the darkness, and, after taking some refreshment and rest, would open the door of the inn where he lodged and treat as many of the ill and infirm as possible.

Judah and Mathiah detached themselves from the group, heading for the home of Judah's mother's brother, Judah anxious for word of his family. The others presented themselves at the house of Deborah's uncle, Alphaeus, younger brother of Nathan.

The old man was a widower, blinded with cataracts, living alone except for servants. His son Jacob, and Jacob's son Lebbaeus, lived in Magdala, managing, for Deborah, the House of Nathan's pottery and dye works.

But Alphaeus was far from infirm in body. He moved about with sprightly step, confident in his own surroundings, greeting Deborah and the long-absent twins with pleasure, hustling his servants to bring basins for their washing, wine for their refreshment.

There was no question but that the guest chambers would be prepared for them.

"For you will find no room at any of the inns, I can tell you that. All are filled, even the roofs are rented, while this Jesus has hired the entire inn of Obed for himself and for his people. There are hardly places in which to stretch out in the street. Not since the uprising of Judah of Galilee has this town seen so many people."

And, when he learned their errand, his ears seemed to prick. Almost, a light appeared in the cloudy eyes. There was nothing for it but that he would accompany them to meet this Jesus.

"I will be the envy of all my friends, I can tell you that. Some have tried for weeks, but have never been able to get near to him, what with the pushing and shoving of all of these outsiders. We must go now, this very moment, so as to get a place near the door of the inn. For, once the crowd sights his boat, if you are not near, you will never be able to call out to him and let him know that you are there, that is how great the roar and the press become."

So they went to the shore and patiently, unobtrusively, gently elbowing, moving into spaces as they opened, got themselves into position near to the door of Obed's inn, which door Obed kept locked during the absences of Jesus. Seeing their chance, Merovee and Salome even managed to get up onto the mounting block by that door. From that height, they had a view over the heads of all.

It was Salome who spotted Judah and Mathiah some distance away.

"Judah! Brother! Here!"

The two men patiently jostled their way over.

"Was it bad news?" said Salome, squatting down to the height of Judah's eyes.

"My uncle, brother to my mother, died during the month of Tammuz."

"I am so sorry," said Salome.

"Thank you." He glanced at Merovee. "My aunt tells me that Simon Yeshuah did, indeed, clip his hair and beard in token of mourning. She was much impressed. He would not clip his hair when even our own father died. But he was always mightily fond of our uncle . . . and both of us of Aunt Sarai."

"I hope you will not cut *your* pretty hair," said Salome.

Judah reddened.

"I shall have to confer with Simon Yeshuah," he muttered, and turned away.

The sun had already set when a small fleet of sails was sighted in the twilight. A sigh went up, and rippled backward through the town. He was coming, in the lead boat, followed by those who had been rich or fortunate enough to procure a craft and follow him over to Bethsaida for the day. The crowd pressed forward, the sigh building, heading toward that roar that Alphaeus had predicted. Merovee's party stayed put, Merovee and Salome still up on the block, the rest of them managing to get right up to the door.

Merovee counted six men in the lead boat, but she could not tell one from the other in the gathering dusk. Finally, sail lowering, the boat coasted toward its mooring spot.

As it did, the mouth of the crowd opened, into a full-throated cry. Merovee swayed, unprepared for the desperate energy that swept over them all like a flash fire. She fought the fear, the sudden horror in the pit of her stomach. She had never really gotten used to the crowds which she, herself, had helped to hold away from Johannan. As frightening as those crowds had been, they were as pups beside this full-grown wolf.

Two figures slipped over into the knee-deep water and tied the boat to its post . . . two pimply-faced boys, unknown to her.

A third man slid over the side. Chandreah!

Then a fourth—tall, thin, and dour.

A fifth—a big man, not tall, but as broad as a bear.

Then she drew in her breath. Josh.

Unafraid, smiling even, Chandreah and the four strangers splashed toward the shore with Josh following.

As they emerged from the water, the phalanx closed, forming a ring around him. Slowly, in that manner, they eased through the screaming crowd. Like the calm in the midst of a storm, thought Merovee. For Josh and his men proceeded with smiles, friendship, and many pauses. Only the tall, dour man found no hands outstretched to him, seemed to find no acquaintances to salute, talk, or laugh with.

Especially long halts were called before those in the press who were crippled or in some way ill. To each of these Josh spoke earnestly, touching each of their heads and smiling before passing on.

Some distance from the door of the inn, his eyes lifted, scanned the crowd, and met Merovee's.

A look of such gladness came onto his face that her heart gave a thud.

She saw his eyes sweep the crowd before him, felt him consider the possibility of simply pushing through to her side. Then he looked back up at her, gave a comical shrug, and continued his slow, caring progress.

"Merovee!" Chandreah was first to the door. Unthinking, he swung her down and embraced her, laughing above the din. "Thanks be that you are safe. He has watched for you hourly, ever since we had the news of Johannan. Mathiah. Judah! *Good men!* We should have known that some of you would be there at the last."

A hand reached through the crowd and took Merovee's. Holding soundly, Josh continued his discourse with the last few people.

"Enough now, friends," shouted the bear of a man. He brought up the rear, holding back those who would still press forward. "Let Jesus rest himself for an hour. Obed will then open the door just as Jesus promised, and those of you who have ailments can come in and get his help. Let him be. Come on, let him rest. He is only human, you know."

As if by signal, the door to the inn opened. Merovee found herself moving inward, drawn by a sort of suction and propelled by Josh's hands on her shoulders.

"Josh!" she cried, panicking and gesturing. "All these others! Do not leave them, they are with me!"

"All? You have found yourself more followers than even I."

"And the veiled lady on the mounting stone!"

Laughing, Jesus reached up, swung Salome down and through the door.

"All these people are to come in, Petros. Hello, Friend Nathaniel. Help Petros sort out your party, would you, please? Obed!" he called to the innkeeper. "Wine! Quickly and for the love of Heaven. Make it your best, for Miriam has arrived."

Behind them, Petros managed to close the door. Jesus embraced Merovee, then Susannah and Nathaniel.

"I am wet, dirty, and exhausted beyond telling. But my joy at seeing you people safely arrived is also beyond telling. Mathiah!" He hugged the boy.

Then his eyes fell on Judah. His face straightened.

"Judah called Sicarius, is it not?"

"Yes."

"You were in Machaerus at the end?"

"Only just. Mathiah and I arrived in time to help them bury him."

"On behalf of my cousin Johannan, I thank you and Mathiah for even that. And, on both of our behalves, I thank you for accompanying his widow to this place."

Judah exchanged a look with Mathiah. There could be no doubt if even Jesus acknowledged the marriage.

"It was no trouble, Jesus."

"Oh. Of course. You must wish to join your brother. He is . . . where did we hear that he is preaching today, Jacob?"

"In Chorazin, they say." Jacob was evidently one of the two young boys.

"We heard that as well," said Judah. "Thank you for your trouble. If you do not mind, though, I will stay here with you this night."

"Stay as long as you like. I have need of good men."

With no further attention to Judah, Jesus returned his gaze to Merovee.

"And of good women."

He smiled, acknowledging her female attire.

"I would be hard put," he said softly, "to decide which way I prefer you, my friend. You are like unto that desert creature that so admirably changes its color to suit its needs. Now tell me, who are the rest of your friends?"

"My mother, Deborah . . . "

"Oh!" He laughed outright. "That may prove convenient. Hello, Mother of Merovee."

"Hello, Jesus. So far you seem worth the trip."

"Good. How long was it?"

"Six miles."

"I will endeavor to be worthy of much longer journeys."

"And my Uncle Alphaeus," said Merovee.

"Alphaeus?" Jesus studied the old man thoughtfully. "An auspicious name. In Arcadia, that is."

For the river Alphaeus rose suddenly in the Arcadian highlands of the Greek Peloponnesus and, just as suddenly, disappeared back into the ground. Some claimed that the river arrived in Arcadia by an underground tunnel from Ephesus, home of the Ephesian Astarte, and that, after it disappeared once more, it resurfaced at the southern tip of Italy.

Whatever the case, the river Alphaeus was sacred to Artemis, integral to her worship in Arcadia.

"You are, then, a Benjaminite, uncle to Deborah, here."

Alphaeus hesitated, wishing he were not blind . . . wishing he could see the face of a man who knew so much—who knew perhaps too much.

For Alphaeus, like Deborah, also had an Artemis hidden in his closet.

Jesus forestalled his fear by embracing him.

"Welcome to you and yours, Alphaeus. I am your friend."

He reached up and put the palm of one hand over the old man's eyes.

"You will soon be able to see that for yourself."

"And this is my twin brother Lazarus," said Merovee.

Once again, Jesus grew serious, studying the young priest.

"You certainly did neglect to mention some pertinent and fascinating facts about your family, Miriam."

"Consider not my 'priesthood,'" said Lazarus lightly. "Our father is dead, while I am deformed and cannot serve God."

"Cannot serve God?"

Slowly, Jesus reached out and took both of the boy's hands.

"I cannot imagine why not. I find you quite beautiful."

"You do?"

"I do. Will you remain with me, Lazarus, and help me in my teaching, so that injustices such as you have suffered may be erased, and each member of Humankind be finally treasured for his or her unique worth to the great god whose true name is All That Is?"

The breath seemed to leave Lazarus, along with the color from his face.

"Yes," he whispered. "*Yes.*"

"Good." Jesus smiled. "I think I shall call you 'Didymus.'"

"Twin?" said Lazarus.

Deborah clapped her hands.

"You know Greek! Jesus, I am liking you better by the moment."

Smiling, Jesus turned to the last two women.

"Josh," said Merovee, "this is Johannah, wife to Chuzah, the steward of Herod Antipas at Tiberias."

"Surely you are jesting."

"And the young lady whom you rescued from the mounting block is one about whom you have heard much bad report. All false. Our good friend, and true disciple of Johannan, the Princess Salome."

"Well I will be damned," said Jesus softly.

* * *

Obed, the proprietor of the inn, was brother to Zilpah, who was in turn wife to a man named Zebediah. "The Zebedee," as the Greeks called him, was the most prosperous fisherman on the lake, with a fleet of eighty-four boats and a factory where fish were pickled for export. He had his own camels and drivers and carried freight, as well as his own fish, to Jerusalem, Hebron, Jaffa, Akko, Caesarea, Tyre, Sidon, Damascus, even Babylon, and ports between. All in all, he employed or worked on a cooperative basis with over seven hundred men of the area, and was a power to be dealt with. Two of the new followers of Jesus, Jacob and Johannan, the pimply-faced youths, were the sons of the Zebedee.

The tall, dour man was Levi. He was the publican of the town. That is, he was the collector of Roman taxes. Small wonder that no one had had a smile for him. Yet, now, out of public view, his face was relaxed, his smile gentle, and his eyes held a comfortable glow.

The broad bear of a man was Simon, older brother to Chandreah. He was in his thirties, with a balding head and a square, curly beard. He held the important position of foreman to the Zebedee's fleet, and lived with his mother and wife in Bethsaida, on the opposite side of the lake. Jesus called him by yet another Greek pet name. "Petros"—a moveable rock or stone—as opposed to Petra, which was Greek for bedrock.

"For he is a rock," said Jesus as he introduced the man.

They sat now "at table," cross-legged on the floor around a large reed mat in the common-room of the inn. In another part of the inn, in the upper room, were more luxurious accommodations, with silken couches Roman-style. But nothing fancy was needed this night . . . it was only a break between work and work.

"Look at that frame," said Jesus, continuing his admiration of Petros. "A rock indeed. A boulder. Whenever crowds must be held back, my rock becomes a wall that even Joshuah and all his trumpets could not breach."

The two young Zebedees, he called "Boanerges."

"Sons of Thunder," smiled Deborah, translating the Greek. "Are you that stormy, Jacob?"

The "Sons of Thunder" were near to eighteen, just emerging from gangliness, tall and skinny, with large hands and feet, and that acne beneath their scraggly beards.

"We do have tempers," said Jacob, but in such a mild-mannered fashion that all at table laughed.

"It is not for our tempers that Jesus named us, though," whispered Johannan.

"Forwhy then?" said Nathaniel.

The boys' Uncle Obed entered with a second jug of wine. Jacob poked his brother.

"Leave off. Let them figure it out for themselves."

Simon Petros gave a guffaw. Jesus grinned.

"Obed," he said, "this is indeed fine wine. You must have dug deep."

"As you said, it is an occasion."

Obed glanced reverentially in Merovee's direction. All among the initiates of Jesus had been prepared for her arrival. They knew of whom she was widowed, and they knew that she carried the Prophet's child. It was even more impressive to Obed that she should turn out to be the granddaughter of Nathan of the Magdalia. The House of Nathan was even more of a force in the region than the Zebedee.

"The wine *should* be good," he said, bowing to Deborah. "It is from your father's vineyards at Kapher Kana."

"Indeed!" smiled Deborah. The soil of that plantation was the best in Galilee. "Of which vintage year?"

"Alas, Lady. It is from the year of your father's death."

Deborah's eyes flickered, but she kept her smile.

"That was our very best vintage. And completely apt. As you must know, Miriam nearly died in that storm along with my father. But through the mercy of . . . God, and a man named Jesse, she was saved. Mayhap for some higher purpose." Her eyes met those of Jesus, "Which truly begins this day."

Jesus raised his cup to Deborah.

Then his face grew somber.

"Petros, Obed . . . I will want to admit as many of the sick and crippled as possible this night, help as many as I can,. Because tomorrow I will leave Kapher Nahum. I have waited here and returned here each night only because I had told Miriam that this was where she would find me. Now I can move on. And none too soon. The crowds are too large. and their confusion is growing. While the merchants make a mockery of my purpose. It is best that I remove myself from the proximity of Simon Yeshuah."

"But Master . . . " said Jacob. He colored at his "master's" quick, reproving glance. "I mean Jesus. If you leave this place, you leave all these people a prey to the wrongful things which Simon Yeshuah preaches. Ought you not to stay and countermand his effect?"

The eyes of Jesus met those of Judah.

"No teaching is 'wrong,' Jacob. It is simply that any teaching is right only to certain ears. Further still, any teaching is right only to certain ears at certain stages of their development. No one can truly teach anything to any other human being. Teachers can only open doors inherent in the spiritual structure of the student, re-awaken memories long dormant. A true teacher knows this. A true teacher simply re-*minds* a student, helps that student to remember. To re-*member*. To join, once again, a body of information that has been forgotten—but which was *fore gotten*. Hence," his eyes once more met Judah's, "some teach, while others preach. A teacher knows that we are all masters, needing only to be re-minded of what we already know. A preacher thinks that only he knows, and that others are dunces who do not know, so that they must be verbally beaten into submission, and forced to believe as he believes."

His eyes swept all of them.

"Those with the ears to hear—whose mental doors are ready to open—those people, and only those people, will hear, truly hear, what I teach. Some, like yourselves, will understand it more profoundly than others. While, to those of my inner circle, I will often speak even more profoundly—as I have already begun to speak to Miriam, my Beloved Disciple."

He smiled at young Jacob.

"So do not fear. Those who are ready for my message, who can understand—if only to the level of a seed cast abroad, laying on the earth, yearning within itself to burrow deeper, to take root and to grow—those ready ones will follow after me, seek me out, somehow manage to find me. They will hear, and be richer for the hearing. That is all that I ask. This particular lifetime is only one stanza in their eternal song. In the next lifetime, or a dozen lifetimes from now, that seed that I will have planted will finally take root. In another dozen lifetimes, or even a hundred lifetimes, it will finally bear fruit. I say to you that none of my seed is lost. Not forever. None."

"You are telling us, then," said Judah slowly, "that those who go to my brother, listen and believe what be says . . . would not come to you—or, if they did come, they would not understand your words?"

"Not at this time. It would be as though I shouted down to them from a high mountain, and through a raging wind."

"Why?" said Judah intently. "How does this happen?"

Jesus seemed to sink deeper into himself. His eyes unfocused, his voice grew small and dry, and seemed to journey back to them from a far place.

"There are concepts for which you Hebrews as yet have no words. Among those civilizations of your living area, only the Greeks have as yet attempted such definition. These concepts have to do with the composition of your Universe. That composition is particulate, as some Greeks have divined, but to a greater degree than even they can imagine. Whether or not you can discern it with the eye, or yet believe it with the heart, the totality of these particles—which is the true god—work in magnificent order upon unfailing principles.

"The first great principle is Emotion. E-*motion* is the motive force of the Universe. The most powerful e-motion is Love.

"Added to the principle of E-motion is At-traction—that which gathers, grips, and holds. Your life will form itself around, adhere to, gain a footing to achieve motion from, your dominant Beliefs, the Ideas which you hold to be true about your world.

"If your dominant Ideas engender the E-motion of Hatred within you, if you concentrate on those things which you hate above all other things, you will draw to you hateful thing after hateful thing.

"If your dominant Idea and Belief is Sickness, you will draw to yourself one illness after another.

"If your Idea and Belief is that the world is an untrustworthy place, and if you propel yourself on the E-motion of Fear, all that you fear will eventually find you.

"By the same token, if the Ideas and Beliefs which fill your mind engender the E-motions of Joy and Love, then those things will bubble from you as from a spring. Your cup will run over, your days will overflow with goodness, and nothing will ever have the power to prevail against you.

"For, all seeming evidence to the contrary, Love is not only the most powerful E-motion, but the most powerful physical energy unit of the Universe.

"Know that, even though you cannot see them—can only see their results—your Ideas and E-motions are *real things*, composed of the physical particles of which I speak.

"Examine your Ideas, then. Determine which E-motions you are using as At-tractions, and so allowing to shape your experience and move you along . . . for the events you construct out of them will faithfully reflect their basic qualities.

"In the same way, you will be drawn to those Ideas which suit your most closely held Beliefs, and to teachers who will appear as and when you are ready to open whatever doors you have already decided to open for yourself."

There was silence.

Jesus seemed to come back into himself. His voice returned to normal.

"Did you understand those words, Sicarius?"

Judah nodded.

"Tell me what was said so that I can be sure."

Judah drew a breath. A sheen of perspiration appeared on his brow.

"I was told that my way will not be easy. I will be torn, as if between two horses racing in opposite directions."

Jesus was silent for a moment. Then he nodded.

"You understood."

His eyes returned to Petros.

"So we will work late tonight, my friend, and help many before I move on."

"Before you move on." The face of Simon the Petros worked painfully. "You said that before, Jesus. What about me? And Chandreah and the others? Are we not welcome to go with you?"

"I was hoping you would ask," smiled Jesus. "Of course you are welcome. I need you. All of you. But I will not tell any of you to leave your homes and livelihoods and families. Those decisions—choices—must be your own."

"Master!" said Johannan, youngest of the Boanerges, ignoring the prohibition against that word. "Our parents expect us to go with you. Our mother would never cease berating us if we do not."

"And I had prepared my wife and my mother for my departure," growled Petros.

"Then come you shall," said Jesus. "Any of you who wish. And I will make of you the arrows by which Ideas composed of Love are sent flying to the farthest corners of this Earth—in any past, present, or future."

A scraping was heard. Petros glowered upward

"They crowd so closely that now they are even up on the roof. Can they give you no rest?"

Jesus shrugged.

"Perhaps you could lie down for a while," said Merovee.

"My mind is too active."

"Then have yourself a wash," she said. "Why has Obed brought you no basin and pitcher as yet?"

Provisions for the washing of feet and hands were the first order of business among Hebrews. Indeed, it offended against The Law to drink or eat without having first washed . . . though in the press of daily life this was often ignored.

Jesus smiled tolerantly.

"If you will recall, my first demand was for wine. Then more wine. We have kept the poor man running."

"Jacob," said Merovee. "Please fetch a basin and water. And bring a chair."

"And you will wash me?" said Jesus, his smile broadening.

Merovee had no chance to answer. Salome thrust forward.

"Let me! Please. Look what I have brought you, Jesus. I got it today, from one of the merchants along the route. Especially for you. It is nard! All the way from India. Smell." She unbunged the jar. "Is it not wonderful? They say that those of India anoint their kings with nard, and so it is apt that you should be anointed with it. It is good for aches and pains as well."

The smile had departed the face of Jesus as Salome spoke. Not that he was angry. Indeed, his eyes upon her were gentle. But suddenly far away.

"I know spikenard well. I studied in India for many, long years, did Merovee not tell you? How strange that, of all things, you should have chosen spikenard."

"You studied in India? No. Merovee had not told me. Are the streets paved with gold as they say?"

His focus returned. He leaned forward, his head tilted, studying Salome.

"Hardly, Little One. The streets are paved with dirt and dust which all but boils in the sun."

For a moment, he stared even harder.

Then he leaned back, smiling again.

"I will appreciate your balm, Salome. First Merovee shall wash me, then you shall anoint me, all right?"

"How much did that stuff cost?" It was Judah, suddenly indignant. "You throw your silver about as if it grew wild in the fields, Salome! A hundred poor people could have been fed this night for the cost of that wretched jar of goo. Why did you not give alms along the route, rather than buying this wasteful stuff? Is that not the truth, Jesus?"

"Yes and no, Judah."

The footsteps and scraping upon the roof intensified.

"The first barrier you must overcome in your search for 'Truth' is the mistaken Idea that, in any instance, there is only *one* truth."

"What E-motion would that Idea be based on," interrupted Merovee.

Jesus nodded.

"You never fail me. It would be based on Fear."

"Fear? How?"

"Insistence on just one truth is a *narrowness* of thought. People who think narrowly are afraid to stray from the well-trodden, well-marked paths that they have chosen for themselves—or rather, most usually, that others have chosen for them. Such people are afraid to explore for themselves, lest they lose themselves. Thus, they lay great emphasis on keeping things well-marked and labeled, so that they can always feel safe. To protect their positions, they are forced to insist that only those paths which they follow are the 'true' paths, and that the only 'true' signs are the signs upon those 'true' paths. To venture onto unmarked and unexplored paths would terrify such people. Many of them would even deny that such paths exist. Many doors must be opened in the mind before one realizes that the unknown, unmarked paths are as 'true' as those that have already been explored and marked."

He observed Judah kindly.

"For any 'truth' that you can find me, Sicarius, I will find you an exact opposite, equally true. And then I will find you a hundred million true truths in between those two opposites. This is as it should be. Such is the nature of reality. Truth is individual, Judah.

"Now, certainly it is true that the cost of this spikenard would feed a hundred 'poor' people tonight. It is also true that I am greatly pleased with Salome's gift, and that I shall be eased in mind and body and Spirit to have it rubbed onto me. And I *will* have it. And the honor accorded to her who applies it will echo through the ages.

"Because the relaxation of my mind and body and Spirit is of more importance to your 'poor' people than all the meals they will ever eat, Judah. That relaxation will allow me to work with greater strength and clarity this night, and for longer hours. The effects of that work will ripple out into the days to come. What I will do tonight, and in the coming days, will benefit the 'poor' far into the future.

"For it is not by bread that Humankind obtains life. One more meal would benefit the present bodies of your 'poor' people for one more day. And do not mistake me. The body is worthy of its due. The body is to be honored and cared for. But bodies are only the temporary vehicles in which eternal Spirits transport themselves in this reality. While the sustenance that I offer the 'poor' will nourish their Spirits, and hence all other bodies which they will ever create for themselves, in either past, future, or present probabilities."

"What insane prattle is this?" cried Judah. "It is nothing but a justification of decadence, that is what it is."

"Judah. The poor will always be with us. In any time, in any place, in any group in the reality here on this Earth, there will be those who, for their own reasons—reasons which perhaps only their own Souls can understand—remain at the lowest levels in comparison to others, defying every effort of society to help or lift them. But such as *I* you will not always find, Judah. The 'I's' who are 'we'—we come to you much less frequently than the poor. Our price is far beyond spikenard."

"You certainly do think a lot of yourself."

"Indeed I do. Hopefully, Judah, I will be able to lead you to the threshold of a like regard for your own self, with a full understanding of *why* you should have that high regard. For, only when you truly understand your own value—your divinity—can you be of value to others, and give them back to themselves—help to open their hearts to the Joy that is All That Is."

Jesus smiled.

"As a start, should you chose to follow me, I would make you my bag-man. You seem to have an eye for finances, and would tend the purse-strings admirably."

A large, bony woman with big hands and big feet slipped, panting, through the front door.

"Idiots! Fools!" she expounded, glaring back at the door.

Then she turned.

"Hello, everyone. That crowd is larger than ever. I had to stave in some ribs to get here. And look what I have brought you!"

She held up a huge fish.

"A prize comb! Have you ever seen one this big? Not an hour out of the water. I swear the seeds of its mating are still in its mouth. Obed! Come get this comb!"

Obed appeared in the kitchen door.

"Slice it thin as papyrus, then drench it in your most fresh olive oil and add salt. Let it sit for five minutes, then smother it in . . . "

"I know how to do it, Zilpah."

"You ruined it the last time. Smother it in garlic and oregano. *Fresh* garlic and oregano," she called after him. Then she turned.

"Hello, my darlings!" She hugged Jacob and kissed Johannan. "Did you do wonderful things today? Who are all these people? Oh my, what a wonderful aroma! Is that nard?"

Merovee was kneeling, washing the feet and forelegs of Jesus in preparation for Salome's nard, deftly massaging the muscles as she worked.

"Ah, Widow," he smiled with half-closed eyes. "That is good."

"The widow, is it?" boomed the bony woman. "Well at last! Welcome! Oh. And, of course, my condolences, my dear."

"Jacob," murmured Jesus, "will you introduce your mother to all of our friends?"

Jacob did the honors. If Zilpah was impressed by Deborah bat Nathan, she was struck nearly dumb by Salome. But "nearly" was the closest that Zilpah would ever get to silence.

"What in the world are they doing up there on the roof?"

It sounded now as though someone was digging through the stucco.

"Could it be a rat?" said Susannah.

"Oh much bigger than that," said Jesus absently. "I think a bear might be digging itself a den."

"Well, we cannot allow that!" said Zilpah. "Jacob, why do you not do something? Besides the cost of repair to your uncle, the beast might attack someone. Do you not understand that there are hundreds of people out there in the street?"

"Which is probably why the poor creature is trying to hide itself," murmured Jesus.

Stifling her laughter, Merovee rose.

"He is ready for the spikenard now, Salome."

She backed off, grinning. With each moment, the sounds from the roof became more alarming. Jesus merely gazed at the ceiling.

"What is the matter with you people?" cried Zilpah.

She ran to the door of the kitchen.

"Obed! Get out here! No, forget the fish. There is a bear on your roof!"

Salome was kneeling before Jesus now, working the ointment into his feet.

"May I put some on his forehead and temples?" said Deborah.

"Here, hold out your fingers."

Obed emerged from the kitchen and stared up at the roof.

"That is no bear. Too many people have climbed up there, they are weakening the structure and will crash right through."

"Jacob!" said Zilpah. "Go up there this minute. Tell them to get off."

Stucco dust began sifting down onto the table. Jesus opened his eyes a slit.

"Move the wine please, Petros, it is too good to waste."

"Susannah. Now you," said Deborah. "Put some onto Susannah's fingers, Salome. Do his right hand, Susannah."

A clump of stucco dropped onto the table.

"How can you people just sit there?" cried Zilpah. "Johannan! Go up there and help your brother!"

"Now you, Johannah," directed Deborah. "Do his left hand."

Stucco and straw began descending in a shower.

"Move back, move back!" cried Zilpah.

Chunks of stucco came down with a crash. A hole two feet in diameter appeared in the ceiling. Down through the hole came the shouts of Jacob and Johannan, and up through the hole went the curses of Zilpah.

"Fools! Sons of dogs! My sons will take your names! You will pay the damages! Get off, get off, lest the whole roof go!"

"Now you, Miriam," said Deborah.

Merovee bent down beside Salome and took a bit of the spikenard onto her fingers.

"This is much more fun than Tiberias," said Salome. "I think I will not go there after all."

"Anoint the top of his head," murmured Deborah.

With strong, sure movements, Merovee worked the balm into his scalp.

Legs appeared at the edge of the hole in the ceiling. Midst more plaster and dust, a whole man appeared, seated in a sling of rope.

"Swine! Cloven-hoofed beast!" screamed Zilpah, beating at him with her fists as he was lowered into the room.

"Sons of Thunder," whispered Merovee to Jesus. "I thought the title was taken from mythology, but even now I hear the Thunder."

Jesus burst into laughter.

"Is it tickling?" said Salome.

"Master! Mercy!" cried the man in the sling. "Stop hitting me, Woman. Master, help me!"

Jesus stood up, murmuring thanks, ending the women's ministrations.

"Zilpah, cease. Let him descend."

Petros came to his side.

"I know this man. A Gentile. A Greek of my own town, Demetrius of Bethsaida."

"And so," said Jesus to the dangling man. "What ails you, Demetrius?"

The sling was twirling. Demetrius craned his neck this way then that, trying to keep track of Jesus.

"It is the pain in my joints so that I cannot walk or stand, Master. My sons tried to carry me to you this afternoon in Bethsaida, but the press was too great. So they brought me over here. We saw only more crowds. I despaired of reaching you and we thought that, as we are Gentiles, you might refuse us as that other one, Yeshuah, did. Then my eldest son had this idea. Oh, mercy! Heal me. The pain has been on me most all of my life. If I could have just one year free of it, I could die in happiness."

"And you believe that I can heal you, Demetrius?"

"Yes! Yes! We have heard. We have talked to many whom you have cured."

"But do you agree to give up the Idea of pain and infirmity?

"Why . . . I suppose so."

"Do you believe that you deserve to be healed?"

"Yes, Master. I have paid then paid again for any sins I might have had. And I believe in your Hebrew god, Jesus. I am not circumcised, but I had my sons circumcised, and I revere only him. Please ask him to forgive me at last. I want to walk upright before him just once more before I die."

"I can grant you that temporary respite. But is there not anything else that you would like to do before you die?"

Demetrius blanched.

"Master, please do not say that I should be circumcised."

"Calm yourself, Demetrius." The eyes of Jesus twinkled. "I am sure that 'God' would agree that you have suffered enough already. But think. If you had more than just one year . . . what would you do with that time?"

Demetrius thrust out his lower lip, considering the matter. Finally he looked up at the ring of earnest faces—now including those of Jacob and Johannan—that were thrust through the breach in the ceiling.

"I have not been pleasant to my wife these many years," he said at last. "Or to my sons, or to their wives. They are all good people who have tried hard to help me. They have not deserved the meanness that, in my self-concern over my pain, I have shown to them. I would make up for that if I could. I would take them in say arms and tell each of them of my love and gratitude. I would try to return the kindnesses that they have shown to me."

Jesus nodded.

"If that is so, then you shall live many more years in perfect health, my friend."

He reached out, put his hands onto the man's head, and said two words.

"Release. Allow."

With no more ado, he took hold of the man's arm.

"Take his other arm, Petros. Do not be afraid, Demetrius. You can stand now. Trust me yet a bit further, Friend. Understand what I say. It is not enough that someone else has forgiven the sins that you think you have, even if that someone else is I. It is not even enough that you believe that the 'Lord' has forgiven those sins. My power to heal can grant you perhaps the year that you craved—a short time in which to make amends to your family. But then, unless you forgive yourself for what you believe to be your sins, your joint pains—or some other symptoms—will return. The only true cure—the only cure that can last—must come from within the one who suffers, and not from any outside source. Forgive yourself, Demetrius. Forgive yourself out of an understanding that 'God' did not create your infirmity. 'God' did not, and never does, punish us. All that befalls us—everything—we create ourselves. We do it all to ourselves. Come now and stand, and then turn your cure to good use. Come! Stand! As Petros and I release your arms—let go now, Petros—release, Demetrius. Empty yourself of guilt. Allow Love to flow into its place."

Demetrius stood, swaying, completely on his own.

"How does it feel?" said Jesus.

"Wonderful," breathed Demetrius at last.

He looked up at the faces ringing the hole in the roof.

"Phillipus. I stand."

"I see, Father. You will walk as well."

"Thank you, Beloved Son."

"Phillipus, is it?" said Jesus, smiling up at that handsome, clean-shaven face. A fine mist of dust still drifted downward. "You and your family will be needed here on the morrow to repair friend Obed's roof."

"We will be here."

"In the meantime, come down to me. I have need of clever men."

"Me?"

"Are you not the one who engineered this feat?"

"Yes."

"Then get down here. Bring your family."

Phillipus disappeared.

Jesus sighed.

"Is my hour of rest gone yet, Petros?'

"More than half, I would say."

"Obed. How fares Zilpah's fish?"

"Immediately, Jesus. And more of the good vintage as well. And bread, fresh baked, and cheese and a green-leafed vegetable."

The company ate in silence—not for lack of matters to discuss, but out of hunger and for lack of time. Any morsel that Obed would produce was consumed.

Then Jesus ordered the door to be opened.

Petros, Nathaniel, and the Sons of Thunder made a fence, allowing in only about a dozen people at a time. Chandreah, Levi, Mathiah, and Judah kept order amongst them once they were in, while Demetrius and his sons were allowed to sit with Merovee and her company, quietly watching. There were other watchers as well—a circle of faces at the hole in the ceiling.

The sick and crippled came hour after hour. Jesus did not heal them all. After long and earnest conversation he sent some away, saying sadly . . .

"You do not believe that your malady *can* be healed. For, at base, you do not *want* to release the malady. It suits your purposes. Without it, you would have to face a whole new way of functioning in this world, and you are not yet brave enough to do that. So do not waste my time. Do not ask me to drain myself trying to combat your own set purpose. Only remember . . . if ever you change your mind and want to be whole . . . the power to heal yourself lies completely within yourself. There is no other rule."

At an hour past the midnight, he quite suddenly put his hands to his face.

"I can do no more," he said softly. "My Power is exhausted. I must sleep. I must give my Soul its freedom to fly home for a bit and re-energize itself."

Never had the watchers seen a human being so drained. He did not even look like Josh anymore.

Petros went to him, put a protective arm about his shoulders. Merovee and the women rose. It had been decided that they would sleep at the house of Alphaeus, leaving the men to bunk about the inn as best they were able. They moved quietly toward the door, thinking to tiptoe out without bothering Jesus. But he stayed them.

"Petros, do the women have their instructions for the morning?"

"They do."

"Alphaeus."

The old man smiled.

"Yes, Jesus."

"Did you enjoy the evening's spectacle?"

"It has been many years since my eyes have had such a treat, Young Man."

"Do you need a lamp to lead your flock to your home?"

"My sight is suddenly so sharp that I am sure I can see in the dark."

Jesus rose, came to them, and drew Merovee aside. His eyes, in the tired face, were intent.

"You see now what life by my side will be like. It will get worse, not better, for we have not yet run afoul of the authorities. I will understand if you turn away from it, Merovee."

"Egotistical as always. Thinking only of yourself. *You* will understand. What of *me*? Is it not I who must understand my own actions?"

He smiled a wan smile.

"You have not changed."

"Would you have me change?"

"Never."

She wanted to take him in her arms. Instead, she stretched up and kissed him on the cheek.

"Good night, Jesus. Sleep well."

* * *

There were but a few hours of sleep that night. Well before dawn, the women re-traced their steps back to the harbor. The night was still deeply dark, a darkness made strange, thick, and dreamlike by their own exhaustion and by a fog laying upon the town, so that Alphaeus, himself, insisted upon leading them.

He had said little about the clearing of the mists from his own eyes. So striking had been some of the healings which he had seen the night before, that the disappearance of his cataracts seemed hardly worth mentioning. Only to Deborah did he murmur . . .

"I did not sleep this night. I lay pondering on why I had given myself those clouds in my eyes. It is so clear, when once you decide to be honest with your own self. I needed another challenge. While I managed the factory for Nathan and then for you, I had challenges a-plenty. But then the time came when convention said that I must retire and give the management over to my son. And, suddenly, I had nothing to overcome on a daily basis. And so I made myself blind and gave myself the challenge of merely walking from one room to another without bumping and falling. How *proud* I have been of the way in which I moved about. I felt an inner glow after each successful trip. Nothing could keep Alphaeus down, I would tell myself.

"But, of late, I have become bored again. Do you know, Deborah, that I even found myself thinking last week that, if I did fall, and break a limb, I would surprise you all once again. I would still manage to get around, even if I had to crawl. And I thought for a long while about the various injuries I could receive, and I planned the ways in which I would overcome them. If Jesus had not come along, I can see now that, very soon, I would have decided on which sort of tumble to take, and I would have taken it . . . and set happily off about my new challenge."

125

"Since you released the blindness and have decided not to take your fall," smiled Deborah, "you must have an even greater challenge in mind. What is it?"

"Ah." Alphaeus grinned. "It is to follow the thinking of this Jesus, of course. To learn as much as I am able in the years which are left to me. Send me word of all his doings, Niece, while I wind up my affairs in this place."

"Wind them up?"

"I have decided to sell my house and property so that I can follow after him," said Alphaeus blithely. "I want no encumbrances cluttering my mind."

The progress through the darkness to the shore was slow, for there were people sleeping even in the streets, and the point of this early departure was to get away without being seen. Muffled sounds led them at the last, and they came upon the men. A second boat had been pulled up onto the shore beside that of Petros.

"Where is Jesus?" whispered Merovee.

"We will not wake him till the last," said Petros.

He and the other men helped Merovee, Deborah, and Salome into one boat. Susannah and Johannah were helped into the second. All were in evidence except Judah and Mathiah.

"He and Mathiah were gone when we woke," said Lazarus.

Phillipus was there, however.

"Are you not staying behind to mend the roof?" smiled Merovee.

Phillipus grinned.

"That is what a man has younger brothers for."

They continued to move quietly back and forth from inn to boats, loading sparse but essential gear. At last they were ready. Petros went for Jesus.

He came as if sleepwalking. Only at the last did he lift his head, survey the occupants of the boats, and then climb in and sit down into the bottom beside Merovee and Deborah. As Petros and the Zebedees shoved off their respective crafts, he dropped his head onto his chest and appeared to doze.

All was dead calm, with no breeze to fill the sails. It was deep, quiet, oar strokes which carried them out onto the lake, into an even denser mist, so that old Alphaeus, back on the shore, was quickly obscured. Indeed, one could hardly see the occupants of his own boat, while only the occasional splash of an oar told the occupants of one craft that the other one was still there.

"I wonder where Judah went," came the plaintive voice of Salome.

"Hush!" whispered Petros. "Sound carries far over water. Do not speak till I tell you that it is safe."

They glided on, straight out onto the lake.

"We are far enough," Petros said finally. "Speak if you wish, but softly."

Jesus stirred.

"Like thieves in the night."

Petros grunted.

"You deserve a respite. They have been at your heels more thickly than fleas, day and night, on land or on water, for more than a month now. So what if we did give them the slip and they must search for you for a day or so. They will find you soon enough again."

Jesus inclined his head toward Merovee and, beyond her, Deborah.

"I am sorry to be such dull company. I am still very tired, besides which, when I sleep, I go to a far place. It is often difficult to return."

"No apologies are necessary," said Deborah. "Go ahead and sleep."

"We shall have to wait here till this fog lifts anyway," said Petros. "Even if there were a breeze, I would not know which way to go. I have never seen it this bad. I cannot tell which way is which. When it does lift, to where shall we go, Jesus?"

"I am hoping for an invitation to the House of Nathan in Magdala."

"But of course," said Deborah. "My home is yours for as long as you wish."

"You can accommodate this many?"

"And more. When we run out of room in the house, we can bed them in the stable."

"Thank you, Deborah. With the Sabbath upon us at sundown, I would not be able to accomplish much of anything today. And my Energy is lower than I have ever felt it. To take an extra day of rest would be a good thing for me now. For all of us, I am sure. For, the mission that we here are embarked upon drains both emotionally and physically, in ways which one does not even suspect—until, suddenly, the legs collapse and one finds oneself sitting ignominiously in the dust—or else shouting irritably at others for no reason at all. In addition to which . . . " A spark of mischief lightened the tired voice. "I have some contractual matters to discuss with you and Didymus, Deborah."

"I have not said yes as yet!" said Merovee sharply.

"Oh, do not be such a simp," said Deborah. "You told me only the day before yesterday that you plan to marry him, so do not trouble the man, let him sleep."

Jesus put his head back against the boat and shook with silent, helpless laughter.

"I could not have said it better had I thought for a thousand years. Be ware, Merovee. I am falling fast into love with your mother and may ask for her hand instead."

"Ah well," said Merovee, "then you would have to take us both, for, if you do not marry me, I will sue before the Temple authorities upon your breach of promise."

He turned his head in the darkness.

"You will be my wife, then?"

"In a way, I already am."

"Give me a kiss to seal it."

She leaned toward him.

"Master," came the gruff voice of Petros. "It will be to Migdal, then?"

As it was surely intended, the forbidden title got the attention of Jesus.

"Call me not master! Yes. Migdal."

"As I say, we will have to wait here until this fog lifts."

"Fine."

"Would you that we drop lines for some fish while we wait? With this many people, even the House of Nathan might welcome them."

"Fish, Petros."

"Later I must go over to Bethsaida and tell my wife and mother that I will be absent for a while."

"Petros, why are you trying to stop this woman from kissing me?"

" . . . I had not noticed."

"Camel feathers," growled Jesus. Then he shrugged. "It is probably best kept for later anyway."

"Jesus," came the voice of Salome from out of the darkness beside Deborah, "do you have a stallion riding ass?"

One could hear his perplexity.

"Yes."

"Where is he?" said Salome.

"Developing new quirks at his leisure in the stable of the Zebedee. Why?"

"You will want to send for him, that is all." Salome poked at Merovee and the two of them burst into laughter.

"Hush!" said Petros.

"Forbid them not their laughter, Petros. Never forbid people their laughter."

He shifted his position, trying to get comfortable.

"Take my lap," said Merovee.

Gratefully, he eased himself downward and laid his head onto her lap. There he heaved one large sigh and was fast asleep.

Merovee gazed down at the dark bulk of him for a moment.

"I wish I could fall asleep like that," she said at last.

"If you gave as much of your self as does he, and took yourself over the edge of exhaustion each day, you would develop the ability as well."

Merovee glanced up. She could not see the face of Petros in the darkness. But she could not have mistaken the hostility in his voice. Her first thought was to meet that hostility head on, to nip it in the bud. But she was only half awake, herself. She laid her head back against the boat. Deborah moved toward her. Feeling the movement, Merovee let her head fall sideways, onto the welcoming shoulder. Deborah rested her own head against Merovee's. Salome crawled over and nestled down into Deborah's lap. Within moments, all three had followed Jesus into sleep.

* * *

Merovee was not sure when she woke that she *was* awake. She seemed to be in a nightmare.

The fog had become a swirling, wind-driven white. Waves were crashing over the sides of the boat. It had been one such, slapping her in the face, that had wakened her . . . that and the cries of the others.

Petros was wrestling the tiller, shouting instructions to Chandreah and Levi, who struggled with the sail. Deborah and Lazarus had found pots and were bailing. Salome clung to the side. From the other boat, somewhere off to the right, came more shouts. They were in the midst of one of the sudden and vicious storms for which the Lake of Gennesareth was notorious. Merovee could think of nothing but that night off Delos. For a moment, she was weak with terror.

Then she realized that Jesus was still asleep in her lap. His face was wet, his clothing drenched from the wave that had awakened her . . . yet still he slept, gone to that faraway place of which he had spoken.

A calm came over Merovee as she studied his face. He was having a bad dream. His features worked. He muttered, and threw his head from side to side.

Another wave washed over them. It did nothing to wake him. Instead, it seemed to increase his frenzy. His fists clenched. He ground his teeth.

"Saul, you *traitor*! You have destroyed it all!"

A horrific burst of wind seized the sails, laying both boats over onto their sides. Shouts became screams of despair.

"We perish!" cried Petros.

"Jesus!"

Merovee seized his shoulders and shook him. He fought back, mistaking her for his adversary.

"Josh! Wake up! You will drown us all!"

She slapped his face. Hard. Harder.

His eyes opened and he saw Merovee. But he was not seeing Merovee. He was still seeing a dream enemy. His eyes blazed with fury. For a moment, she was sure he would kill her.

"Lord! Lord!"

It was Petros, lurching the length of the boat to kneel beside him. "We are going to die, Lord. How shall we pray?"

"Die?"

Jesus pushed himself up onto one arm and gazed at the world which raged about them.

"Oh. No. Not yet, Petros."

He took hold of the side and got to his feet. Impatiently, he gestured at the waves.

"Cease. Desist."

He began, then, to breath deeply, eyes closed, face ever more serene.

As he did so, they sailed into another world.

The storm that had been there was suddenly not. The fog ended as though at an invisible wall. The sky beyond was streaked with the delicate tones of sunrise. All that could be remembered of the storm was a brisker than normal chop, that flattened as they increased their distance from the cloud bank.

Then, even the cloud bank dissolved into the brightness of the new day.

Petros remained on his knees. A row of heads lined the side of the second boat. Every eye was fixed on Jesus.

His own eyes swept them. He shrugged.

"I had heard of the capriciousness of the storms on this lake," he said easily. "I swear, they are as nowhere else on the face of the Earth."

He turned, stretching, and squinted toward the distant shore.

"Where are we, Friend Petros? I am beginning to yearn for the delicious fare with which my mother-to-be will help us break our fast."

Petros roused himself and hunted for landmarks.

"Why . . . that is Migdal right there," he said, pointing to a tower that could be seen almost directly in front of them. "How could the storm have blown us so far?"

"I am no expert on storms," said Jesus. "Only food and drink. Pray move me toward it with all dispatch."

He sank down onto a bench, rubbed his jaw, and cocked a brow at Merovee.

"You hit as well as any man."

"Better that than that we all lie at the bottom of this lake."

How could it be?

"Was the lake responding to your emotions, or . . . was the whole episode a sort of dream?"

"Both. All of life is a dream, Merovee. Quite literally. It is the phantasy life of that far place to which I told you that I go, and which is the true reality."

Deborah and Salome drew close, listening.

"Is this world of no importance then?" said Salome.

"Never think that. By its dreaming, here and in those many other worlds which I told you about, that far place learns to know itself better and better, and so improves itself with each moment, learning and experiencing right along with you."

"How far away is this place?" said Deborah.

"To understand that, you would have to forget your usual concept of distance. *In* your terms of distance, it is no farther away from you than one blink of your eyelashes. But, to *consciously* travel there, one has got to know how to travel through *intensities* of *e-motion*. And that, presently, is beyond the conscious ability of most of Humankind."

"Josh," said Merovee. "Who is Saul?"

His head snapped around.

"I said that name?"

"You called him 'traitor' . . . said he had destroyed it all."

"So. *Saul* is it? I have seen him again and again in dreams, but never got a name. And I said he *had* destroyed it all? Past tense? Then I was in a future place when I spoke, glimpsing a probability that . . . Ah, no!" He pounded the boat. "It shall not happen. It *must* not happen."

Merovee realized suddenly.

"Saul is the third. The other part of you and of Johannan."

"He had put it all into a box," mused Jesus. "A huge box, with a door upon it. There was a large place in front of the box. I think the box must have been a building, and it might have been in Egypt, for there was an obelisque there in that space in front of it. He had taken all that I had said and done and put it into that box, but in a way so that it could not be recognized. He kept cutting pieces of flesh off of me, and breaking up my words, distributing the pieces here and there throughout the box, so that nothing of me could be understood . . . putting my pieces into locked cupboards in vast rooms, and into niches, oh, so many niches. I was running from niche to niche, and cupboard to cupboard, trying to find all of my words, and all my bits of flesh, to put everything back together again. But every time I found a bit of flesh he laughed and grabbed it away from me. And ate it! And washed it down with wine. And my words he snatched away and tossed into the air, and blew on them. His breath was like a great wind. The words flew down corridors, into rooms, under doors, here, there, everywhere, all fragmented, all in pieces. Like my bones, and those of others, stuffed into niches and cupboards. He even had yours, Merovee. But he called you by another name. I was made wild with horror, and I ran like a mad person, trying to find all of me, and all of you, and to put one word back with another again. And, while I was running, he went and told the people what I had said, and it was not what I had said at all, and he raised a statue of me in the center of this box, grotesque and tortured and covered with blood. It was *not* I! Yet he insisted that it was, and the people came and groveled before this horror, and cried to it that they were as worms, and begged it to forgive them for being alive . . . begged that disgusting, dead statue for forgiveness that they were alive."

His brow creased further. He turned and stared at Petros, back at the tiller now.

"He was there, too. Petros. He helped Saul do these terrible things."

An arm slipped softly around his shoulders. Deborah.

"It was only a dream. You are badly in need of rest. I have good wine from the farm at Kana, and there will be berries from the garden. Fresh goat cheese . . . "

"Merovee, the bread you cooked upon the coals at Johannan's campfire . . . "

"It takes only a few minutes."

"I would like that. With honey, perhaps?"

"Our bees are the best."

"And then more sleep," said Jesus. "I grow so defeated at times. Forgive me, You think I should always be strong, but I am not. Sometimes I wish to lie down and go to sleep and never wake up."

"What endearing and encouraging words to murmur to your intended," smiled Merovee.

He turned. His eyes cleared.

"Yes. Of course. You will make a difference. A great difference. Give me my kiss now. Quickly, before Petros thinks of something else to say."

Laughing, she kissed him.

His arms felt like Johannan's . . . completely comforting, composed of Love.

She did not mind thinking of Johannan.

She would have minded if she had not.

* * *

When Jesus and his party had pushed off that morning, Judah and Mathiah had been but yards away, lying upon their bed rolls beneath an overturned boat. Neither of them spoke . . . only watched and listened till the gentle splash of oars was heard no more, and Alphaeus had disappeared back into the fog. Then they climbed out, rolled up their quilts, and left Kapher Nahum, taking the road to Chorazin.

They left the fog behind as they climbed upward from the level of the lake, and made good time, the road lit by a nearly full moon. Both were silent, sunk so deeply into thought that they were hardly aware of each other.

The dawn was only hinting at itself when they arrived at Chorazin. The last half mile resembled those last two miles of the road into Kapher Nahum. Those encamped were just beginning to stir. The two men asked directions of one of the early-risers, went on through that town of black basalt buildings, and left the road at one of the rolling wheat fields beyond. Skirting its perimeter for half a mile, they came at last to the base of some hills, and to a group of caves there in the rocks.

A burley sentry hailed their approach.

"Hold. Who are you? What do you want of the Master?"

"What do I want? Why, to slit his throat of course, for I am Judah called Sicarius, bar Tolmei."

"Ho! He has looked for you! Welcome, Judah. But he is at his devotions, so you must wait a bit. Eleazar! Wake up, Boy. It is your young uncle."

A boy, not yet thirteen, lifted his sleepy head from out of his roll.

"May the blessing of our Lord be on you, Uncle Judah."

Judah smiled, went to him and hugged him.

"How you are growing, Eleazar."

"I shall be a man before the next Passover."

"How did your father wean you away from your grandmother?"

Eleazar wrinkled his nose and whispered . . .

"He did not. She insisted upon coming. She is there, in yonder cave."

"Oh, I ache!" Judah blurted.

Eleazar giggled.

"She will be *very* happy to see you, Uncle Judah."

"Are your other uncles here?"

"Joseph, Baruch, Isaac, and Jacob. And their families. And some of the Prophet's followers. A Salmon, one called Eli, and Ezekiel. Grandmother is wroth that you, alone, have delayed in joining us, Uncle Judah."

Judah shrugged.

"Then I have done her a service. If she had nothing to be wroth about, she would pine away and die."

He motioned to Mathiah. The two sat down before bar Tolmei's fire and ate of the bread that he offered. Each had wine in his bed roll, but neither produced it—they were on their best behavior again—wine would not be countenanced in this camp.

Simon Yeshuah, himself, emerged from one of the caves some minutes later. How strange he looked. Judah had never seen his brother except with such a bush of hair on head and face that one could hardly tell what he looked like. He was really quite handsome, Judah decided now. And he could suddenly see why people were confusing Simon Yeshuah with Jesus. The resemblance was superficial to one who knew them both, but it was strong enough to confuse any who did not know both of them well.

Simon Yeshuah saw Judah, strode to his side, kissed him upon the lips and grasped his shoulders.

"I was beginning to despair of you, Son."

Simon Yeshuah was the eldest of the children of Jethro the Nazorite and his wife Meraiah, while Judah was the youngest. Twenty years lay between the two men. Often, since the death of Jethro, Simon Yeshuah had adopted the role of father to Judah. In moments of affection, especially, he was prone to referring to Judah as his son.

Judah deepened the embrace, putting his arms about his brother and hugging him.

"I have not been idle. You will not mind my tardiness. When you left for The Wilderness, I went to the Temple." He grinned and patted his sicarius. "I managed to track two Romans who profaned the Temple courts with their presence and send them to the nether regions."

"God will bless you and increase your seed upon the Earth."

"Then Mathiah came along."

"God be with you, Mathiah."

"And with you, Simon Yeshuah."

"We went and sojourned with the Essenes of Qumran. Greetings to you from Reuben ben Hezekiah, by the way. Word finally came of you. At the same time, we learned the place where they had imprisoned the Prophet."

Simon Yeshuah nodded.

"I understand and am well pleased. Did you help to bury him?"

"Yes."

"You are cleansed of the defilement, are you not?"

"We have not yet made sacrifice for cleansing, but the days of defilement are ended. I would not dream of coming to you in an unclean state, Brother."

Simon Yeshuah closed his eyes.

"I would have it that all proper homage be paid to the Prophet. I would have it that we be known as the true followers of the Prophet. For he came as a voice from out of The Wilderness, and prepared the way for me and for my mission, just as Scripture foretold. He and I spoke as with one tongue, our insights agreed in all ways. It was the day I first went to him, as I arose from my immersion, that I understood my calling. I heard a voice from out of Heaven say, 'This is my only begotten son, in whom I am well pleased.' You were there, Judah. You heard it, too."

Judah's mouth had fallen slightly open. Inadvertently, he glanced at Mathiah, and saw that the consternation was not his alone.

"Uh . . . " Judah searched for words. "Well I did hear something. But I did not realize that it was the voice of God."

"Of course you did not." Simon Yeshuah regarded him kindly. "To such as yourself, it would only have sounded like wind in the palms, or as the fluttering of the wings of birds."

"Yes. That is the way it sounded."

"It was the Word of God . . . the very Spirit of God, himself, descending into me."

"I had not realized. I am sorry."

"I did not tell you. I was afraid you would be over-awed."

"I probably would have been."

"But now my predecessor, the Prophet, is called by my heavenly father, to sit with the angels. And the truth of my mission must be trumpeted from the tops of the highest hills."

Simon Yeshuah grasped a shoulder of each of the young men.

"All is pre-planned . . . which plans are known only to me. Yet I can tell you, my sons, that I will be King of Israel. But king in a way—the glory of which—neither of you might ever be able to perceive. Only *I* have the vision to lift myself to the pinnacle of glory that my father, who is in heaven, prepares for me."

"Simon Yeshuah . . . " Mathiah struggled to find words. "I am sure that I am not understanding you correctly. You seem to be saying that you are a god. That you are the *son* of Yahweh."

"I am the Messiah," said Simon Yeshuah quietly.

"Fine. Perhaps," said Mathiah. "David was a messiah. Solomon was a messiah. The High Priest of the Temple is the Priest Messiah. Messiahs are our anointed leaders, our rightful kings and priests. But not gods."

"I told you," said Simon Yeshuah, "that I am *the* Messiah."

"There is no prophecy that says that *the* Messiah is to be divine. The Messiah will be a man. Such as I. Such as . . . "

"Do not include me in your tabulation," said Simon Yeshuah.

Mathiah was not deterred.

"This smacks of paganism! You cry out against the Roman emperors who declare themselves to be gods, yet now you do the same thing!"

Simon Yeshuah was struggling to be kind to Mathiah.

"My son, do not even the demons cry out at my approach, and flee in terror from those whom they have possessed? I make the lame to walk, the blind to see, and I proclaim to the children of Israel the means by which they may redeem and save themselves from the wrath to come. *God* has sent me into this world! I am his *only begotten son*! How can you doubt? How can you?"

Mathiah took a deep breath.

"Forgive me, Simon Yeshuah. But, last night in Kapher Nahum, we saw the one called Jesus also make the lame to walk and the blind to see."

"Fool! Spawn of this generation of vipers! Do you not understand that his powers come from the Prince of Darkness? Did he cast out the demons? Did he?"

"Well, none with demons came seeking aid."

"None with demons came? How many came?"

"Oh . . . at least . . . "

"I counted one hundred and six," murmured Judah.

"One hundred and six afflicted? Plus family members bearing them?"

"Yes."

"So at least three hundred people came before this Jesus last night."

"At least."

"And you seriously imagine, in this sinful age, in a world that God is ready to destroy yet again for its transgressions, that there were no demons hiding in any of those three hundred?"

"Now that you mention it," said Mathiah, " . . . there must have been."

"Of course there were!" cried Simon Yeshuah. "Yet they did not cry out, neither did they flee before the face of your Jesus. And do you know why? Because they were right at home. They were part of the plan of the Prince of Darkness to deceive the people with this false messiah and lead them ever more deeply toward the pit of fire from which there will be no return."

"Mathiah," said Judah. "Do you suppose that that is why Jesus refused to heal some of the people?"

"He refused?" said Simon Yeshuah.

"He said that they were not ready to give up their afflictions. He said that the power to effect any lasting cure rested entirely within themselves, and that his power could give them only temporary relief at best."

"Ha!"

Simon Yeshuah rose to his feet, towering above the other two, eyes shining.

"And you two are too lame of wits to understand. Does or does not all power, *all* power, come from God?"

"Of course it does," said Mathiah.

"Through God and now through his son. Do you think that any affliction could stand before the power of God or his son? Of course not! Ah, what darkness this Jesus leads them into. Shall worms have the power to heal themselves? Do you not see that, if each man begins to think that he is a little god, and that his own welfare abides within himself, the world will descend into utter darkness, and there will be redemption for none? Those that this Jesus would or could not heal were the ones with the demons! He and they laughed and giggled to one another as he spoke! Those bodies which he would not heal were bodies which already belong to his master, the Prince of Darkness. And now all those whom he did cure are sent forth thinking that the power reserved to God abides in them alone, and demons are finding their ways into those misguided Souls. *Oh*!" Simon Yeshuah cried out as though in pain, and collapsed onto his knees. "I must save them. I must. With my own sacred body, I must redeem the lost sheep of Israel."

"Simon." In tears, Judah knelt and embraced his brother.

"Swear, Judah. Swear now, by all that is in Heaven and all that is in Earth. I know that such an oath is forbidden to mere mortals, but to swear to such as myself is mete and proper. Swear that you will uphold me in all that I do and say, and that you will obey me without questioning whenever I call upon you. Swear. Quickly!"

"What is happening? Yeshuah, my son, are you hurt?"

Meraiah, mother of Simon Yeshuah and Judah, stood in the mouth of one of the caves. She was a woman so small that a child was of greater girth and height. Yet she filled every space that she entered with herself even if that space was all of the outdoors.

The largest thing about her was her eyes. They burned more fiercely than those of Simon Yeshuah. Like her eldest son, Meraiah had a mind composed of sure and certain thoughts. Doubts had no place therein—for such as Meraiah and her eldest could never possibly be wrong about anything.

"Oh. So. Judah. It is you. No wonder Simon Yeshuah cries out. You have wounded us deeply with your absence."

"No, Mother," said Simon Yeshuah. "The boy has been about good works. He has brought me tidings that I needed to know."

"And I killed some Romans," said Judah hopefully.

"Ah. Well, that is commendable, but you need not have bothered. My first-born will soon rid our land of Romans forever, and, after that, the world. Come and give your mother a kiss. What is this? Do I smell wine on your breath?"

"Wine?"

She had the nose of a wolf! He had taken but one swallow just after waking.

"Let me see your bed roll."

"Mother . . . "

"Let me see it. Your friend's roll as well."

With a sigh, he brought her the rolls. She dug out the jugs and smashed them upon the rocks.

"Not again in this camp," she warned them both. "We who walk with Simon Yeshuah are consecrated to the Lord and may not indulge in worldly pleasures."

Simon Yeshuah still knelt upon the ground.

"How do you come by this wine, Judah? What evil companions have you fallen in with?"

Judah swallowed,

"That was the next thing I meant to tell you, Brother. Mathia and I were not the only followers of the Prophet's at Machaerus. Merovee was there."

Simon Yeshuah's eyes went cold in a way that never failed to turn Judah's spine to ice.

"That abomination among women. She has seven demons within her. I was shown it in a dream."

"Simon Yeshuah." It was Mathia who found the courage to speak. "The Prophet did her great honor. He made her his wife. She is with child by the Prophet."

"Blasphemy! Would you damn yourself?"

"It is the truth!" cried Judah.

Slowly, Simon Yeshuah got to his feet.

"Did either of you witness the marriage? Did the Prophet tell you with his own lips?"

"No, but . . ."

"Then she lies! The seed within her is that of her whoring!"

"The Prophet told other witnesses of the marriage," said Mathiah.

"And he gave her his great leather gird in token," said Judah.

"His gird? His gird? Since when has a gird signified marriage? Who are these witnesses?"

"Nathaniel of Kapher Kana, who guarded the Prophet in Machaerus. And Jesus, himself."

"Jesus?" Simon Yeshuah was honestly perplexed. "How could this Jesus-person be a witness to anything to do with the Prophet and the woman? Had he ever met either of them?"

Judah stared.

"But I thought . . . Simon Yeshuah, Jesus is the one called Joshuah, who so offended you that last night beside the Prophet's campfire."

Simon Yeshuah took a step backward. For once in his life, he was speechless.

"It was he to whom Merovee wished to go after we buried the Prophet," said Judah lamely. "Johannan had asked it of her. And so—since we were traveling in the same direction—we accompanied her and her party northward. When we reached Kapher Nahum, we stayed the night with this Jesus, so that I could observe him and report upon him to you."

Simon Yeshuah turned and walked apart. For some minutes, he stood motionless, staring off across the wheat fields, down toward Kapher Nahum. Then he returned to his brother's side.

"You did well, Judah. My opponent now has a face, and I can study upon how to defeat him. Sit you down while I break my fast and tell me all that you know of this man and of his followers . . . including the whore, may her womb wither and be consumed by worms."

"Think you that she is Jezebel returned?" whispered Mother Meraiah. "Returned once more to lead the children of Israel astray?"

Simon Yeshuah considered the question. A glint crept into his eyes.

"Jezebel. Yes. That is exactly who she is. Why did I not recognize her before? She who worshiped the idols Baal and Astarte. She who forced our good King Ahab to raise altars to those false gods. She who brought down onto Israel the wrath of God."

"How did she do that, Father?"

It was Eleazar who spoke. Simon Yeshuah stared at his son.

"What?"

"*How* did Jezebel force King Ahab to raise altars to false gods? Was she bigger and stronger than he was?"

"You would not understand, Eleazar. Women are the emissaries of the Prince of Darkness. Only a handful of women on the face of the Earth, such as your grandmother and your late mother, have ever risen above the swine-swill that is their birthright. The blandishments of these temptresses are more powerful than any might of arms or strength could ever be—for the Prince of Darkness gives these creatures sway over any man ever born to women."

"But how?" said Eleazar. "When Jezebel asked him—could King Ahab not have just said no?"

136

"Eleazar," smiled Simon Yeshuah. "You betray your lack of scholarship and understanding. Go in and re-read, if you please, the account of the perfidy of the first woman in the garden of our God. Later, we two will discuss it."

Eleazar took a few steps. Then he turned.

"Father, if you are the son of God . . . . . . what am I?"

"Go!"

Reluctantly, the boy went.

"Mother."

The woman jumped to her feet, anxious to please her eldest.

"Go and counsel him. Such as yourself can teach him of women far better than can I."

He waited until she was gone. Then, breathing a long sigh, he washed his hands and took the bread that bar Tolmei offered and blessed it, saying . . .

"Lord God of Israel. Help me to combat Jezabel anew. Keep me perfect as you are perfect. Keep me safe from the ways of the unrighteous, and give me the wisdom always to lead the wicked back to the path. Nourish my unworthy body with your manna, and guide me purely through another day. In belief and certainty."

He put the bread into his mouth and munched thoughtfully.

"She was there, then, last night—Jezebel, with the seven demons. Yet not one of those demons cried out. Do you still doubt what I tell you about this Jesus?"

"I suppose not," muttered Mathiah.

"No, Brother," said Judah.

"Then swear, as I asked you before. Swear by everything that is in Heaven and everything that is in Earth. Swear that you believe that I am who I say I am. Swear to uphold me in all, and to obey any order that I give you without question."

Mathiah lowered his head and looked at his hands.

"I swear," he said.

"Judah?"

"Simon Yeshuah . . . "

"Swear!"

"I swear."

"Good. Now tell me the whole story again from the beginning. Omit nothing, no matter how inconsequential it may seem."

* * *

An hour later, Simon Yeshuah called in a loud voice to all of his followers. His brothers and their families came forth from out of nearby caves, yawning and scratching themselves. They were pleasant enough fellows, his brothers, but lacking in any attributes which Judah had ever found remarkable. Then there were Salmon, Ezekiel, and Eli, who, along with Mathiah, had abandoned the Prophet on that last night. Then Samuel, Ephraim, and David. Along with bar Tolmei and Judah, these men had traveled with Simon Yeshuah for years. Simon Yeshuah's band was the most respected and feared of all the Zealot terrorists in the land—these men did not even bother to hide their sicarii, but wore them proudly exposed, protruding up from out of their girds.

"Get your rolls," Simon Yeshuah told them. "The false messiah has abandoned Kapher Nahum. I must go to that place and gather my strayed sheep."

In the town of Chorazin, shopkeepers were opening their shops and the day's traffic was beginning. Some cast curious glances at the rumored Messiah and his followers as they passed through. Beyond that, Chorazin gave little attention, and certainly no homage, to the man who called himself the only begotten son of God. Was he not merely the eldest son of Jethro the Nazorite and of Meraiah, whose own mother had been born and raised in Chorazin? How could the grandson of one of their own be the Messiah?

Fury at the lack of perception among the townspeople built in the eyes of Simon Yeshuah. He had been treated even more shabbily in a place to the southwest, where his mother had been raised. In that place, the elders had dragged him out of their pathetic excuse for a synagogue and thrown him down a cliffside! The people of Chorazin must know of that shameful happening. All of Galilee probably knew. They must be sniggering behind those bland glances.

He would tell them! He would show them!

So it was that, as they passed Chorazin's synagogue, and he saw an aged Pharisee approaching from the opposite direction, Simon Yeshuah stopped square in the Pharisee's path.

"Seldom are the great recognized in their own countries," he growled to the surprised man. Then he threw back his head and wailed at the sky. "Woe to you, oh Chorazin! The son of the All High has been amongst you, and you knew him not. I say to you that, in the wrath to come, in that day when my father and his angels shall come from the heavens in chariots of fire to separate the wheat from the chaff, Sodom and Gomorra shall have been luckier than you, Chorazin. There shall be weeping and wailing and gnashing of teeth. But naught shall avail you. I turn my back upon you and cast you into the pit, Chorazin!"

He marched on, leaving the Pharisee gaping.

Only outside the town did he attract the attention he craved. Those who had traveled from afar to see him set up a cheer. Hastily, they packed and ran, hobbled, dragged themselves in his wake. Those with afflictions hailed him from every side.

"Rabbi! I am halt. Heal me."

"Rabbi! My sight fails. Cure me."

Simon Yeshuah but smiled and passed on.

"Hahhhh! What do you here? I know you, you Son of Man. Go away! Leave me to my work!"

The words came from a woman who had thrown herself into his path. She writhed in the dust. Spittle dripped from her mouth. She clawed at the dirt and glared up at Simon Yeshuah with eyes which reminded Judah of Simon Yeshuah's own. About her was a reek that spoke of incontinence.

Simon Yeshuah stopped.

"You demon of Beelzebub," he said. "So you know me, do you?"

"Be gone! What think you to avail against my master?"

"I command you to go out of this woman."

"I will not."

"Do you not understand that my master is the master of the one that you call Master?"

"You lie! Spawn! Scum! Ooze of a putrefying wound!"

"You think I lie? *Go!*"

"No! Do not say it! Where will I go?"

"Fly to the Decapolis and find yourself a pig. That is all that you are fit for."

"Ohhhhhh!"

It was a terrible wail. The woman rose upward. Then she fell back down into a senseless heap.

Simon Yeshuah raised his arms to the crowd.

"By my works you shall know me!"

He looked back down at the woman. His lips twitched in disgust.

"Someone wash her," he said, and strode on.

Judah followed quietly along at the rear. Mathiah dropped back to walk beside him.

"You saw that," he said.

"I saw it," said Judah.

"Then we *have* to believe . . . . . . well do we not?"

"We have taken oaths," said Judah.

Mathiah hesitated.

"I did not want to, Judah. I wanted time, to think the matter over carefully. But your brother is so . . . absolute. Who could tell him no?"

Judah smiled.

"You know, it is funny. I have been thinking . . . what he said about Jezebel and the power given her by the Prince of Darkness to convince any man born of woman. I thought that my young nephew asked a very intelligent question. Why did King Ahab not simply say no? Or even Adamah to Chavvah for that matter? Were these not grown men? Men who pretended to be wise, to be the leaders of their people? Yet someone with Simon Yeshuah's power came along—and they could not say no."

"Well of course," said Mathiah, "it is as your brother explained. The power of the Prince of Darkness cannot be overcome."

Judah's eyes swung slowly toward Mathiah. A terrible smile twisted his lips.

"Do you understand what you just said, Mathiah?"

"I . . . "

"Do not trouble yourself. For, among other considerations, even my brother has told us this day that *all* power comes from God. And so how could the Prince of Darkness have any power? How, indeed, could there even *be* a Prince of Darkness unless he is simply another attribute of God? But let us deal with the more mundane. You say that this certain power cannot be overcome. Can it not?"

Judah's face was pale. He walked as in a dream.

"I could have said no to my brother this morning, Mathiah. I could have said, 'Brother, I would like to convenience you, but, until I have decided within my own self what is right, I will not make this terrible swearing that you demand of me.' If *I* could have done that, Mathiah, what of you?"

"I . . . but he is so frightening, Judah."

"So we both took the easy way. And we swore an oath forbidden by Torah—swore by all that is in Heaven or in Earth—to believe in him and defend him and obey him without questioning."

"The oath need not be kept, Judah."

"Need it not? You have learned differently in regard to oaths than have I."

"But he put us under duress to obtain it!"

"What duress? Did he snatch a coal from out of the fire and threaten to blind you? Did he so much as twist my arm?"

"No," muttered Mathiah.

"On your life, no. He simply spoke some words and looked harshly at us. And, as easily as Esau, we gave him our birthrights. And the question that keeps coming to my mind, Mathiah, is . . . Who was the real sinner? The woman named Jezebel, who insisted to a man that he do a certain thing . . . or the fool named Ahab who went out and did it? And if the wrath of God then descended onto Israel . . . at which of those two, Jezebel or Ahab, was God truly wroth?"

Chapter 6
The Builders

For the next two days, the House of Nathan was a place of peace and of silence, of light steps and hushed voices. For, after his meal, Jesus went into Deborah's chamber—that she insisted he take for his greatest comfort—and did not come out again. In the late evening of the first day, Merovee tiptoed in with fruit and wine. He did not stir. She left the food at his bedside and went out.

The next morning she went in again with more wine, and with bread, freshly cooked for him despite the Sabbath . . . and she drew a sharp breath as she saw him there on the bed.

He had not moved from the night before. The quilt lay upon him in exactly the same manner. Nothing from the previous night's tray had been touched.

Fearfully, she went to him, looked closely at his face—found it a deathly white—watched his chest for the rise and fall that would signal life.

There was none.

With pounding heart, she felt his forehead. Cold.

She lifted one of his hands. Pliable, but, again, cold.

She ran to find Petros. He sat in the stable, swapping sailing yarns with Jesse.

"Does Jesus ever sleep so soundly that he seems to be dead?"

"Cold and with seemingly no breath? I have seen it once before. It will do you no good to try to rouse him. You may shout and pound upon him for hours, but he will not wake until he is ready."

Reassured, Merovee went back to his chamber, finding Deborah on the way. "Come with me, Mother. Tell me if you have ever seen a man sleep this way."

Deborah felt of his forehead as had Merovee. Then she lifted his hand and put her thumb to his wrist below the mound of his own thumb. For some time, she stood, her head cocked as though listening. Then she smiled.

"Here. Let me show you how to find the life."

She positioned Merovee's own thumb upon her own wrist.

"Do you feel that steady pulsing?"

"Yes."

"The physicians of Greece and Cyrenea make much of it. What you feel now is normal. It increases if you work hard or run, and decreases with relaxation. Only with death does it cease entirely. Now take his wrist in the same way."

". . . . . . I do not feel anything."

"Wait."

Merovee waited. Many seconds later, she felt one strong, sure beat.

"Keep hold," said Deborah.

Many more seconds elapsed before Merovee felt the next beat.

"So slow! How can that be?"

"I do not know. And I do not know how to achieve this slowed pulsing for myself. But we were told of it in the Seventh Mystery of Artemis. The priests of Isis know the secret, but they will share it with

141

no one. To learn it, then, one must travel to India. That is where masters called 'yogis' are to be found, and they gladly teach all seekers."

"Jesus spent many years in India."

"And became a yogi himself, that is obvious. If he wanted, he could will the pulsing to cease completely, and he would die."

Merovee shivered and laid his hand gently back onto his breast.

"What is the point of this strange sleep?"

"I believe it begins as an exercise in mental control. The student begins to understand how completely his body obeys the will of his mind. I am told that, once each year, the High Priest of Isis takes this 'death sleep.' He sleeps for three days and three nights to signify the death and resurrection of Osiris. I suppose, in this case, Jesus has done it to afford his body total rest. He might also be traveling."

"Traveling?"

"We touched upon it lightly in the Fifth Mystery, Daughter. Do not tell me you have forgotten so soon. Each of us has at least two bodies. Some say three. They are imprinted one upon the other, all taking up exactly the same space. But only the first one, the physical body, can normally be seen in physical life. In sleep, in dreams, and especially in a state such as we see here, the mind, which is in reality one of those invisible bodies, separates from the physical body and goes upon adventures of its own."

"I wonder if he will be able to tell us his adventures when he wakes," mused Merovee.

"Such as he could certainly tell us. If he wanted to. This is a strange man that you have gotten for yourself, Miriam. Strange and quite wonderful."

"He told me . . . Mother, he says that I am special. He says that I am a part of his own entity, but of a lesser degree of development than he, himself."

"I can believe it. I suggest then that you study him well. Do not leave his side, never stop questioning, learn all that you can during the little time that he will be with you."

"Do not say 'little' time!"

Deborah smiled gently

"Surely he, himself, has warned you that your time together will be short. And you, my little seeress. Do your powers stop at what is unhappy to you personally?"

Merovee lowered her eyes.

"No. I have seen . . . "

She shook her head.

"Jerusalem. Something dreadful."

"What?"

"I can never see it clearly. People come to take him away. And then there is a vast confusion. I wake knowing only that I must lose him."

"Then you must live for each moment, Miriam. Fill each one of those moments with all the awareness and love and joy that you can find."

"Do you think . . . would it be wrong for me to stay here with him now? To sit beside him until he returns to the body and wakes himself?"

"Would you consider it wrong?"

"No. After all . . . he already regards me as his wife."

"Then why ask my opinion?" Deborah pinched her cheek, kissed her, and quietly left.

Merovee sat beside him then for the rest of the day. She memorized each hair on his head, each line on his face, counted the gray hairs that showed themselves in his growing beard.

And, often, as she sat, it seemed that what she saw blurred, began to shimmer, and then to glow. At those moments, the walls of the room seemed to fall away. At one point she saw mountains—low, but dense and impenetrable, composed of massive, swirling rocks, and sculptured, blunted pinnacles— mountains such as she had never really seen. And she heard sounds, people speaking, in a language that she did not know.

At another time, she reached for her wine and drew swiftly back, convinced that the cup contained poison.

She shook her head, lifting the cup, staring into it.

Where had she been? What had she been thinking to imagine such a thing?

She glanced down at Jesus and smiled. Silly of her. Even if there were poison in the cup, with him there beside her, she could drink it and come to no harm.

At sundown—the end of that Sabbath—as though by pre-decision, Jesus made a slight sound. Then, slowly, he reactivated his limbs. Merovee watched in fascination as fingers, then hands, arms, shoulders moved, shrugged, stretched—while, beneath the quilt, his toes, feet, and legs did the same. His torso arched and moved from side to side. A flush of pink crept back into his face.

At long last, he opened his eyes and looked up at her. His lips lifted in a slight smile. He said nothing, but eased himself up onto the side of the sleeping couch and rose.

Merovee turned away, for he was naked. She heard him pad phlegmatically around the room, yawning and scratching himself. He stopped at the table beside the bed, broke off a chunk of the morning's bread and chewed upon it absently. At last, he seemed to realize that he was naked. As she heard his linen under-trousers being drawn on, she turned back to him.

He smiled.

"Excuse my ill manners. You have had a long vigil."

"I hope you do not mind that I sat with you."

"I knew that you were here. I returned to the room often to check upon the state of the body. I would have come fully back into the body to greet you, but then putting oneself back out again is a long and involved process. And when one *is* out, it is much too pleasant. There is little desire to return. Goals not yet realized . . . and Love, are the only things that bring such as myself back to the body. I will teach you how to do it if you wish."

"I wish to learn everything that you care to teach me."

"Your mother is a wise woman."

Merovee looked up sharply.

"You were spying on us!"

An eyebrow cocked.

"Merely minding my own business in my own appointed chamber, Widow. Can I help it if curious women insist upon crowding around? So." He forestalled her retort. "Your mother has the Seventh Mystery of Artemis, and you the Fifth."

She flushed.

"We were going to tell you. We were not going to withhold it. Do you still wish to marry me?"

He sat back down onto the bed and propped himself against the wall.

"More than ever. It is partly because of your exposure to that ancient wisdom that you and your family are prepared to understand the things I say. Ishtar, Isis, Asherah, Artemis, Astarte, Ashtoreth, Selene, Kali, Diana . . . and Ninkhursag, the original of the great mother goddesses, also very interestingly known as Mama—whatever you wish to call her—she encompasses symbols which are in fact *knowledge*, that reaches backward to the dawn—literally to the birth—of Humanity as we now know it. For that very reason, she is the stone that the Builders rejected."

"That is in one of the Psalms. 'The stone that the builders refused is become the head stone of the corner.'"

"A female scholar." He tilted his head. "My cup runs over."

"Do not tease me."

"I am perfectly serious. Women are forbidden to study Scripture. How do you come to know yours so well?"

"Lazarus and I were very close as children, Josh . . . I hope you do not mind that I persist in calling you Josh."

"Now that we have things straightened out between the two of us, Merovee, you could do little that would annoy me."

"Is that because very little annoys you or because . . . "

"There is much that annoys me. You have become a constant pleasure."

She flushed again, and lowered her eyes.

"Even your girlish blush pleases me. You, who I so carefully taught to walk as a man."

She laughed outright.

"I got very good at it you know."

"I have endless confidence in your ability to be good at anything you decide to be good at. Now tell me how a female managed to insinuate herself into the exclusive male realm of Scriptural study."

She shrugged.

"By having a twin with whom I was so close that his scratches hurt me and mine hurt him. We tried to do everything together when we were children. So, when he had to study, I studied, too."

"And, since you had a wise mother, it was allowed. She is a jewel, our Deborah. She caught my meaning exactly last night when I said that to her who rubbed me with the balm will go everlasting credit. She saw to it that every woman in the room had a hand in the rubbing, and thus gained a piece of that credit."

"Every woman but Zilpah," laughed Merovee.

"Ah, Zilpah. A raw soul made vicious and rude by its own insecurity and terror. 'Zilpah' has many more frustrating lives to live before she becomes even moderately likable. One day, however, she will shine as the sun."

"Please go on, Josh. That passage about 'the stone that the builders rejected' has always mystified me. Who are the builders?"

He filled a cup with wine from the decanter and picked up a peach.

"Noah, Enoch, Peleg, Ibraham, Isaac, Jacob . . . "

"What?"

"Joseph, Daniel . . . at least those are some of the names by which we recognize them. Other cultures call them by different names. They were, quite literally, Builders."

"Do you mean they built buildings?"

"Houses, palaces, temples, dams, roads, bridges, pyramids, tombs . . . you give a name to it, they built it."

"As slaves you mean. As in Egypt and Babylon."

"Occasionally they were held against their wills, or invited rather roughly to attend the festivities. But they were, for the most part, the leading craftsmen of the world, made wealthy and privileged through their knowledge. They and their people formed an independent, floating nation of Master Builders, a nation of many parts, states, and provinces, for whose services the kings of the Earth eagerly vied."

"How can this be? Why does Scripture not speak of it?"

"It does. When you know what to look for."

"But . . . Ibraham, for instance. He was a shepherd."

"A rather strange shepherd, would you not say? With three hundred and eighteen servants born and trained in his own house? Three hundred and eighteen fully grown men, trained for warfare, whom he could arm on a moment's notice, lead off to battle, and with whom he could defeat the kings of Elam and Babylon. Not only that, but he trotted those three hundred and eighteen men two hundred miles to catch up to those kings. Three hundred and eighteen men *born* in his own house. Think what that means. Those men were either his own sons, born of concubines, or born of his sons, or of his slaves, servants, or entourage of whatever description. Now, coincidentally . . . "

His look prompted her.

"There is no such thing as coincidence," she said.

"Good. The numerical equivalent of three hundred and eighteen expressed in Old Hebrew adds up to the name Elizar, who, we are told, was a steward—a steward to a shepherd, mind you. We are also told that, for want of legitimate sons, Ibraham feared that he would have to leave his entire inheritance to this Elizar. Whether or not Elizar was one man who, himself, had three hundred and eighteen sons, male relatives, and servants, or whether 'Elizar' was a term that applied to a sum total of slaves and servants and children by concubines, hardly matters. Keep in mind that these three hundred and eighteen were only the men grown, trained, and prepared to do battle. What of the mothers of these men? What of their wives? Their children? What of young women? What of the old? What of those whose duties were other than that of guard or soldier? How large *was* the retinue of Ibraham? Did it include, as a sub-section, the retinue of Lot, the man whom Ibraham was marching his men to rescue? Why was Lot, this underling of Ibraham's, so important that he and his people had been 'taken prisoner' by the greatest kings of Mesopotamia? What would you say of a man such as Ibraham, with such mysterious wealth and power, with a steward, and with such valuable friends?"

"If I did not know it was Ibraham we were talking of . . . I would assume that you had just described some kind of a king."

"And you would be correct."

"But we know he had flocks . . . "

"Of course he had flocks. 'Ibraham,' my dear, was a traveling nation of a hundred parts. Every time a contingent was called somewhere to build a city, or a new temple, or to complete some road or irrigation system for a *stationary* king, it had to feed its people on the way to the work site and also while working, did it not? Have you never wondered at the restlessness of Ibraham? He could not seem to stay put, not even so much as a normal shepherd who must move occasionally to graze his flocks.

"It is recorded that his ancestors came from Elam—from where the Aryans and Iranians lived, and where their descendants, the Persians now rule. We are told specifically that those ancestors came to Ninevah and Ur and to Shinar, which is now Babylon, *as they were being built.*

"We are further specifically told that those ancestors built the Tower of Babel!

"Then we are told that 'Ibraham' came many more hundreds of miles west, with his 'father' 'Terah,' to Harran in the land of the Hurrians—who are 'coincidentally' the ancient Elamites—into the north of Syria. Again, coincidentally, Terah and Ibraham decided to make this move just as Harran was being built.

"After Harran was built, 'Ibraham' went on his travels yet again. He came hundreds of miles south, to Sechem. And what did he do there? Built an altar.

"Then he went to Bethel. What did he do? Built an altar.

"Then he went many more hundreds of miles to Egypt, had business with the pharaoh, and left Egypt a wealthy man.

"He then went to Hebron . . . again, coincidentally, as it was in process of being built.

"Then he went back north again, to Kadesh—two hundred and fifty miles. There he again had business with a king.

"He then journeyed back down to Beersheba.

"Then he went to Jerusalem to see yet another king about yet another altar.

"Then back he went to Hebron.

"What sore feet his poor sheep must have had."

"But," said Merovee, "if Ibraham was as you say, why does Scripture not state that fact?"

"It does! Were we not just able, on the basis of what Scripture says, to figure it out between the two of us?"

"Now just a minute. No. I do not know from where you get your information, and I do see your point—it all seems quite strange when one pulls the story apart. But I can not agree that what you say is all there in Scripture."

"To what did 'God' change Sarai's name?"

"To Sarah."

"What does Sarah mean in Old Hebrew?"

"Princess. But it was only a title of respect!"

"What did the people of Heth say to Ibraham when he asked to buy a burial lot amongst them?"

"Oh. Well, they . . . told him to take any sepulcher that he wanted."

"Come now, you have not finished. Why?"

"Ohhhh . . . all right. They called him 'Lord' and a 'Great Prince.' But a prince of *God*. One naturally assumes they were only respecting his holiness."

"What holiness? In the days in which Ibraham lived that word had not even been invented! It is amazing how easily and how much we assume . . . how easily we take so much literally that we should *not* take literally, while glossing over the very things that *should* be taken literally. Because we are not thinking for ourselves. Instead we are letting our priests do our thinking for us, and acting like blind people, who cannot see what is right in front of their eyes. Never take anyone else's word for anything, Merovee. Not even mine. Always think for yourself. All ways.

"If," he went on, "'God' changed Sarai—which means contentious—to Princess, and the sons of Heth respected Ibraham as a Prince of God, you may be sure that 'God' meant something totally different to the sons of Heth than it does to us today. The God of Ibraham was not a deity. The God of Ibraham was more than one thing. It was the secret knowledge guarded by the nation of Builders that came to be known by Ibraham's name, *and* it was the ruling elite, the organizational structure of that nation—the bosses, the keepers, the givers and dispensers of that secret knowledge.

"Have you never wondered why, every place that Ibraham went, he dwelt with kings, did business with kings, was forever being loaded down with presents from kings—sheep, camels, slaves, cattle, gold, silver—why he did battle with kings, had relatives kidnapped by kings, had his wife taken away from him by a pharaoh?

"And we are to complacently believe that these were the adventures of a common sheep herder?

"Have you never wondered why Ibraham married his own sister, why Ibraham's brother married his own niece, why Ibraham's son married his own first cousin, and his nephew, Lot, married his own two daughters?"

"Of course I have wondered," said Merovee. "But that all took place before God prohibited incestuous marriages. It was not wrong when Ibraham did it."

"No, not wrong, but ill-advised, for reasons of the strength of the species. This, the species has always unconsciously known. The only group that persistently, as policy, for dynastic reasons, marries incestuously is the ruling class. Royalty. In particular, the royalty of Elam, from whence Ibraham's forebearers came, and of Egypt to whence he traveled, and where his sister, who was his wife, was also the wife of a pharaoh—which pharaoh could not seem to leave off showering Ibraham with sheep and camels and wealth when finally he departed—those two royal groups in particular—of Elam and Egypt—were notorious for incestuous marriage.

"Ah, Merovee. The story of 'Ibraham' is a much broader history than the exploits of one man, and *much* more exciting! It is a symbolic statement of the history of our present world. It is the story of the family of consciousness that symbolically and physically *built* that world. And it is all right there in Scripture for those with eyes to see. When the ancients told or wrote their stories, they could not anticipate our own ignorance of the world in which they lived, or the errors that would be made in translation. Neither could they anticipate what their 'God' would become—how that concept would be so badly twisted and misunderstood, nor could they foresee a power-mad priesthood that would order scribes to edit, rewrite, and even forge those stories to suit their own greedy interests.

"But we can still find the truth if we stop hanging on the words that are there, and listen to the spaces *between* the words . . . to the silences on which those words ride. It is exactly in the places where the scribes could not quite make things fit—when we find our senses jarred, our intelligence insulted—that we must stop, cock our heads, and listen. Sometimes all that is needed is a little common sense."

Merovee shook her head.

"Why did *I* never understand these things? As many times as I read the story of Ibraham, I made excuses for exactly the items that you have mentioned. I never, ever, questioned them."

He nodded ruefully.

"Even you, who, more than others, insists upon thinking for herself. And there are areas which you still do not recognize, where you still, without question, accept the pronouncements of others."

He poured the last of the wine into his cup and shook his head.

"Ah. What am I doing here? You are hard enough to get along with as it is. When I finish having taught you, you will be insufferable."

He ducked at a thrown pillow.

"Be that as it may," he went on. "Rule Number One. Accept at face value *nothing*—no written word, no law, no spoken word, no idea or pronouncement—which assumes to regulate your actions, your health, your mind, or your Soul. Just as the poor will always be with us, so those who seek, for whatever their own purposes, to Control us and our thinking will be ever with us.

"Rule Number Two. *No* attempt to Control, no matter how seemingly well or piously intentioned, is Good. There will come a time—millennia from now—when laws, when rules, and rulers, will be things of the past . . . when, in place of Control, we will have Release and Allow, and Humanity will soar to the heights of both individual and collective Creativity of which it is inherently capable. When Humanity reaches that point of understanding, I will be in the midst of it again— teaching and leading—and a more 'God'*like* Kingdom will come into being here on Earth. Until then, I will teach you how to find the *real* Kingdom, which is the divinity, the true deity, within your own Self."

He took another peach.

"Now, as to the history of the Builders, do not take any of the names which I listed—Noah, Ibraham, any of the others—do not take them literally. In the first place, because of changing languages and translations, while names offer clues, they can also be misleading. Also, as I indicated, the names do not necessarily apply to individual men.

"Not that men with those names did not actually live. As in the case of Enoch. I was, and in simultaneous time am still, that man. He definitely lived. But, more often than not in Scripture, the names have been applied to whole family dynasties, or to places—sometime even to *concepts*, or organizational structures, and/or the ruling elite of those structures, as with the original 'God.'

"And while, of old, the human life span was much longer than it currently is, often the number of years that the patriarchs and their sons are said to have lived are the lengths of time that those dynasties, places, or concepts held away. Many of the dynasties were even concurrent. Others occurred in epics other than those to which they are ascribed.

"Now, for ease of reference, and unless I say otherwise, when I refer to a patriarch, I will be referring to a dynasty rather than to one man. And the dynasties which thrived after the cataclysm are what I will call the Builders. Noah is the earliest. These are excellent peaches."

"There *was* a flood then?"

"There was a cataclysm of unprecedented proportions. The Earth changed the tilt of its axis, causing devastating tidal waves and extremely nasty weather conditions that took quite some time to settle down. This did not occur because any god was unhappy with 'sinful man,' but because Humanity, itself, decided—on a mass, subconscious, cooperative basis—to use its consciousness in a totally different way. The change in the Earth's attitude was a *symbolic statement* of this new beginning.

"Pay attention to that. Begin to put *symbols* at the top of your awareness. Symbols are, literally, the bricks with which Humanity builds the events which it experiences.

"Now, in actuality, Noah, the man, with his ark and his animals, was largely a *mass dream event*, shared in basic detail by all the consciousness then on the Earth."

"You mean there was no Noah? And no ark?"

"I did not say that. I said only that Noah and his ark occurred on a dream level. Your mistake is to suppose that dreams have less reality than do those things which are actualized on a physical level. In truth, dreams are much more real, much more powerful than is physical reality. Physical reality is the *product* of dreams, not the other way around. And if a dreamer decides that he will find the ark near the summit of Ararat, he will. I, myself, have seen it. Others go to the mountain and do not see it. That is the true nature of 'reality.'

"So. Between the actual physical upheaval and the dream of mass destruction and redemption, the species imagined that it had been destroyed and reborn. Noah is called by other names in other areas of the Earth. I will remind you again to set very little store by names. But, by whatever name, in whatever place, Noah was an *advanced family of consciousness with a particular focus*. It was the lineal mental descendant of Adamah, which had been a rogue consciousness of the previous experiment. This consciousness chose, generally, to incarnate into particular families or tribal groups, so that the seed of Adamah, and then Noah, came to be composed almost entirely *of* this consciousness *wherever it was found in the world.*

"This is often the way, that consciousness of a particular inclination will repeatedly incarnate in and around a genetic group whose energy and thrust it admires. You have brothers and sisters on the other side of the world, Merovee. And in other 'times.' They are not brothers and sisters of the body, but of the mind, which is the most important family relationship.

"So. Noah took the fore in the structure of the new experiment. As symbol of this—again, that all-important symbol—Noah became the *Builder* . . . first of an ark, that supposedly saved all living species and is the symbolic equivalent of the Ark of the Covenant—and then of the cities and great works which appeared after the cataclysm."

"But *why* was only Noah the Builder?"

"The Noachites were the most advanced consciousness *in the areas needed to structure the new experiment.* The antediluvian world had been structured upon much different lines. In all places, but very specifically in our area, the Adamah consciousness had been the rebel, always at odds with the mass intent, striking off on its own to develop in its own ways."

"The expulsion from Eden."

"You have it. Adamah offended the mass intent, the psychological power structure—that had created and structured that previous phase, the previous experiment."

He smiled.

"But note that it was not Adamah who got blamed for acquiring new knowledge and so causing the expulsion from 'Eden.' Pay close attention to the cleverness of the Adamites, and the later Noachites, in this power transition.

"Supposedly, Adamah, through Chavvah, offended 'God.' And the symbolic representation of that god, my dear, the prime god of that antediluvian phase, was god*dess*."

"Artemis!"

"The female principle. The Great Mother, with her varied consorts. The god, the power structure that Adamah offended, and by which Adamah was expelled, was matriarchal. Rather than being expelled, however, the Adamites, and the later Noachites, were really involved in a massive power grab—a transfer of power, and of spiritual understanding, from the unconditional love of the Great Mother, to a ruthless, aggressive, arbitrary—and seemingly sole and celibate—Father. This changeover took millennia to achieve. It was a psychological takeover that eventually, with the Noachites, became physical.

"But, of course, the men involved in this power grab could not admit to what they were doing. Hence, the story of Creation as written and edited by our priests in our Genesis is a conscious effort to degrade the female principle—and so disenfranchise and enslave women—through the character of Chavvah—or Ava as she is called in the Greek. It goes without saying that the prime drive of 'Noah's' descendents has been to wipe Artemis and her adherents from the face of the Earth."

"Oh! Please! Can Mother and Lazarus hear this?"

"I want them to. Go and call them. But only them. Say to the others that we must discuss our contract. That will be no lie. And, while you are gone . . . " He smiled. "Despite the sweetness of your peaches, I have the most dreadful taste in my mouth. I should like to do something about my teeth. On top of which, after two days, there are certain bodily functions which . . . "

"Oh!"

She rose so rapidly that the chair in which she had been sitting toppled over backwards.

"How thoughtless of me! Yes, by all means. I am sure that you will find all that is needed in the bathing room, and certainly you will wish to bathe."

"It would be pleasant."

Disconcerted, she moved toward the door.

"I will send Lazarus with clean linen immediately. Then Mother and I will come with a supper for us all. Will half of an hour be enough time?"

Jesus smiled.

"Just do not forget the wine."

* * *

Merovee found her mother and brother on the roof, enjoying the evening air with their guests. She felt a twinge of guilt, but Jesus had been specific.

"Mother. Lazarus. Jesus has awakened. We must discuss our contractual and other private matters."

Once away, she whispered the rest of the story.

"And he wants *me* to come and hear?" said Lazarus in disbelief.

"And me?" said Deborah.

"Do we have a Genesis scroll in the house?"

"In one of the chests in the storeroom," said Deborah.

"Find it, Lazarus. And extra papyrus, we might want to take notes. But, first, take him a fresh robe and linen. Come, Mother, we will get a supper and I will tell you what he has said as best I can."

Half an hour later, Merovee and Deborah entered the bedchamber.

Freshly robed, Jesus lounged on the bed. At his feet sat Lazarus, listening, rapt, to his words. Jesus broke off.

"Behold, the Beloveds, bearing wine. What is this? Deborah! You blush as nicely as does your daughter."

"I am honored to be included in the category of Beloved . . . Jesus."

He nodded.

"You were going to say 'Master.'"

"No. I was going to say 'Lord.'"

"That would have been even worse."

"I did not do it."

"You pay attention. You understand what you see and hear and do not have to be told a thing twice. That is why you are here. All three of you. You are all of a consciousness that I know I can work with."

"Could we . . ." Deborah hesitated. "It is only a matter of habit. But could we include the goddess? May she listen?"

That eyebrow cocked once more. Seeing it, Merovee felt a tug inside her breast.

"I had wondered," he said, "what was locked in that case in your bath. By all means, bring her out. I would like to meet her."

Deborah disappeared into the bathing room and reappeared with the statue cradled in her arms.

"Beautiful," said Jesus. He reached out.

With tears of gladness, Deborah relinquished her treasure.

"Just look at that workmanship," said Jesus. "And this detail etched into the robe. It is so good." He leaned closer, studying the motif. Doves, endlessly entwined. "Do you know why one of her symbols is the dove?"

"I have heard many reasons," said Deborah.

"But not the basic one. It is an example of the way in which Humanity's unconscious mind retains what the conscious mind has forgotten, and how it stores that knowledge in the symbols which the conscious mind then believes itself to have chosen at random. What happened the last time that Noah sent the dove forth from the ark?"

"It did not return," said Lazarus.

"Neither, as far as the Noachites were concerned," said Jesus, "did the goddess. Instead, she presented the masculine principle of Noah with an olive branch as a sign of her submission, and left forever." He stroked golden Artemis. "At least so they hoped. This piece is ancient."

"So my father always believed," said Deborah. "He thought that she dates from shortly after the expulsion of the Ionians from the Peloponnesus."

"I think he was correct." He set the goddess on the bedside table and gave her a nod. "I am honored of your company in this discussion, Your Highness. I have never been one to deny an ally. I take my comfort and help as it is presented."

Merovee drew a sharp breath.

"Is it the baby?" said Deborah in alarm.

"Jo." Merovee bowed her head, ashamed of the tears which gushed in a sudden, warm river. "What Josh just said . . . Johannan spoke the same words about Artemis on that last night . . . when I became his wife."

Jesus took her hand.

"There are all kinds of twins, are there not."

"So it would seem," she whispered.

He kept hold of the hand.

"While we are on the subject, Deborah, Lazarus. I wish to take my cousin's widow to wife. What bride price do you ask for her?"

Deborah glanced at Lazarus.

"My sister will be freely given."

"Ah," said Jesus. "A bride freely given, the most treasured among women. I accept the honor you accord to her and thus to me. But I suggest that we invite our guests and have our wedding at the earliest possible moment. I do not have much time to spare."

Deborah cleared her throat. Lazarus turned away.

Merovee squared her shoulders.

"I took the liberty of dispatching a messenger south yesterday morning. He is to bring your family down for the festivities."

She, too, then turned away . . . though the grin of Jesus was beautiful to see.

"What a shameless baggage you have raised, Deborah."

"It is enough to make a mother cry."

Merovee shrugged.

"Like others of my acquaintance, I have no time to waste. I chose a Greek messenger who is without duties toward the Sabbath, and I put him on Ruthie, our best riding ass—who, unlike your Pharisee, has even fewer religious duties than the Greek. They should be almost to Jericho by now."

"I thought," said Deborah, "that we might celebrate the marriage at our farm near Kapher Kana. It is pleasant there in this hot season, and remote . . . it would afford the two of you some quiet time together. You may not have many more quiet times in the days to come."

"My wise new mother. It shall be as you say.

"And now, Mother, Brother . . . Wife . . . " for, with the matter settled between all parties, the marriage was actually valid, with any subsequent ceremonies being a mere social nicety, "I shall continue with my story. I shall state things plainly, for I believe that you are ready to hear them. Some fresh wine with which to inspire myself, Merovee? And so where were we?"

"You were talking about the Adamah consciousness," said Merovee, "and how it offended against the old goddess—against the prevailing consciousness."

"Yes. The Adamah phase was not, by the way, Humanity's first episode on this planet Earth. Consciousness has been experimenting here for hundreds of millions of what we call years. Be that as it may, the Adamites were 'cast out' of the 'garden' by the mass consciousness in that experiment. On their own, alienated from the rest of their fellows, they developed, over millennia again, the seed that grew into an Idea that was gradually accepted, under the Noachites, as the basis of the new experiment. The Noachite Idea became the mass intent. Four thousand years ago, that intent solidified and became the new creator of mass events."

"And so the new 'God'?" said Merovee.

"Any family of consciousness knows its role on a sub-conscious level, knows its history, its purpose. And so, yes. Sub-consciously, the Noachites knew themselves to be the creative force, and understood the narrowness of focus that they had to maintain to be successful in their particular brand of creativity. Consciously then, they developed an arrogant, jealous, completely male god, narrow, intolerant, unforgiving, ready to cast any who did not obey him into everlasting torment. That god was, of course, a very gradual development. He reaches his pinnacle of intolerance and oppression just now—at a millennium. It is, in fact, a milestone of two-thousand years, which is the more important cycle.

"I hope this begins to answer your initial question, Merovee. You wondered why it was that the Noachites took the fore. The other types of consciousness left upon Earth after the cataclysm were in no way inferior to Noah, merely different from Noah. But, for the duration of the new experiment, they retired to the background.

"Now, even before the cataclysm, the Adamites were in possession of fairly sophisticated sciences necessary for building. These sciences had been given to them, as is often stated in myth."

"By whom?" asked Lazarus.

Jesus hesitated.

"The answer to that is extremely complex. What I tell you here is complex enough without getting into that just at this point. However, I, myself, was one of those who gave knowledge of the sciences and of building, in the guise of the man that Genesis calls Enoch.

"Over the centuries, Noah perfected those sciences and those skills. They did not invent the refinements, they merely re-membered them . . . for the sciences have been used again and again in one Idea-form or another during the millions of years of experimentation which I told you about. No Idea belongs, or is original, to any one person or to any one group. Ideas belong to the species and ultimately to all consciousness. Any place that a person has an Idea, a million other people, not only in the same time band, but in all other times, experience a version of that same Idea.

"Now . . . one of Humanity's most amusing mistakes, and one from which it never seems to learn, is to constantly imagine that it can keep Ideas a secret. The Noachites were no exception. They made, of writing, mathematics, geometry, a knowledge of chemicals, and the true nature of matter—skills which were as indispensable to building as is a knowledge of the proper way in which to put materials together—a system of esoteric, ritual teaching requiring secret indoctrination, and open to only a few. In this way, they thought to control the rank and file of craftsmen amongst their number."

"Where did the Noachites of our area build their first cities?" said Lazarus.

"Just as their trade was symbolically important, so were the areas in which the Noachites first plied that trade. They chose areas in which there was annual flooding. That annual event served both as a repetitive subconscious reminder of their origins, and, consciously,, as a problem that had to be overcome and even subdued."

"Egypt?"

"That and Mesopotamia in the main. The connection between the two places is as close as twins joined at the head. Noachites were the guiding geniuses of both areas. And, wherever they went, they were protected by their own version of god, the 'God of the Fathers'—that is, a god exclusively male. They were his Chosen. They had a mandate, they believed, to structure the world as they saw fit."

"In their own image," said Deborah quietly.

"They called themselves by the name of Man. Tents were their home, for, though they built things of physical permanence for others, they had no physical permanence of their own. Indeed, they wanted none. Their permanence rested on mental, not physical, concepts—which is an irony in that their mission was to foist a *physical focus* onto the rest of Humanity. But they required none of that for themselves. They had been wanderers since the 'expulsion from Eden,' the wilderness was their home, their friend, their refuge, and, in its harshness, so like their god who was themselves.

"So the wandering in the wilderness, that Scripture condenses to forty years, has been, in this experiment, of a duration more closely resembling forty centuries. The 'Moses' phenomenon—the definition and transformation of 'Israel's' very special 'God,' the creation of the Law, and the organization of the people—was also a gradual process that took fully as long."

"Was there, then, no Moses?" said Merovee.

"There was an Egyptian. A . . . . . . well I will just describe him as an Egyptian prince. A brilliant man. An opportunist, as are most brilliant men. And a Noachite himself. For remember, Noachite consciousness is not confined to Hebrews, even though its largest concentration is there. This prince became the leader of the Joseph Noachites, who had been doing the building for Egyptian pharaohs for several centuries. It was his vision that finally saw certain Noachites seemingly settled into a stationary nation, that we now know as Palestine.

"Though Noachites will never create nations of any great duration. Their consciousness is much too restless. It must travel, it must contribute its 'structure' to others. A homeland, a permanent place, especially Jerusalem, will remain a goal, a dream to be consciously striven for. But, for us, the dream of permanence will remain just that. The Noachite, himself, will ensure that never does he remain in one place too long. His own actions and attitudes will repeatedly ensure his expulsion from whatever Eden he finds.

"Look, at this very moment, how we Hebrews are spread, how we persist in moving around the face of the Earth. No other people can match our geographical distribution, save only the Romans. We have persuasive enclaves in Greece proper and Asian Greece, in Anatolia, Egypt, Phoenicia, Syria, Cyrenia, Rome, Carthage, Gaul, Iberia, Sicily, in Frankland, on all the shores of the Caspian, in Babylon and every part of Mesopotamia, in India, in the Silk Lands beyond, and even in the Isle of the Britons. We will not stay at home!

"And it is no accident, you see, that we are constantly overrun by other civilizations and even transported away from our lands. The leading Noachite consciousness chose the natural world crossroads of Palestine as a 'homeland' for that very reason! Our 'Promised Land' was never meant to be a land of peace and contentment. No. It was meant to keep us always in contact with the most important cultures of the moment, for, to those cultures, we are subconsciously impelled to make our contribution. Yes, even to change those cultures, to mold them into something much closer to our own image—even, if need be, by the inter-marriage with, or proselytizing of, those of Noachite consciousness encountered amongst them. Why do you suppose we are so widely spread throughout this world? For trade? As a group, we are not inclined to mercantile things. Our only real product is our 'God.' The Romans would conquer the world by force. Our subconscious goal is to conquer it with an Idea. And so we go traveling. Specifically, we "Jews" of Jerusalem and environs are preparing now for another great dispersion—those who manage to escape the slaughter or slavery will disperse, that is."

"What are you saying?" cried Merovee. "Josh, does this have anything to do with you and me?"

"No. All here have time. I am not sure just how much time. But the probabilities are so intense as to be certain that, within your lifetimes, Jerusalem will be laid waste, the Temple will be gone, with not one stone left upon another, the priesthood will be destroyed, and our self-rule ended."

There was stunned silence.

"Is it Zealots who will bring this about?" asked Deborah at last.

"Quite so. In their determination to save our nation, such extremists will, instead, bring Jerusalem down in flames. Though they will only really be doing the will of our mass, Noachite mind.

"You understood, Deborah, that I was traveling while I slept. I was working with probabilities, looking into the various futures which will play out from this point in time. I check these futures frequently, in order to keep my own work on track, as probabilities change with each moment. There are, though, overall patterns. Mass consciousness works cyclically, with a rhythm that can be depended upon. Mass consciousness subconsciously picks up this pulse from the Universe, itself. And the Universe pulses in intervals and multiples of ten. Now, there are certain junctures, intersections, moments in the course of events and multiples of ten, that . . . how to say it? That bulge. The probabilities become too many, too large, the intersection too *filled*, for things to be contained in a normal way. And so that intersection—time itself—actually bulges.

"Think of a stalk of the tall, coarse grass which grows on the hillsides. The stalk is tubular but, ever so often, there is a nodule, a place that bulges. It is in that bulge that vital inner workings of the plant take place, and, out of it, comes the next section of growth.

"Events—the *course* of events—have these occasional bulges as well, where large probabilities governing the future of the species meet, exchange, and generate the next events. At times of the greatest exchanges—those which change the destiny of the species—this bulge elongates. Many great probabilities run along parallel with each other for what can amount to centuries. Until the most turbulent are played out.

"Then synthesis takes place and the overabundance dwindles to the more usual number. Like the one, slim, healthy stalk of the plant, events then flow smoothly onward until the next nodule begins.

"In terms of time, these intersections are roughly what we think of as millennia, and, generally, a nodule would be the century preceding, and then the century following, a millennium. Not, however, the change of millennia as currently reckoned and absolutely marked to occur on certain days by any calendars now in use, but the change of millennia as felt by the pulse of the Universe, itself.

"Now, major mass *experiments* in consciousness tend to occupy a period of about six-thousand years before transitioning to a different experiment. Again, this happens in relation to a universal pulse. At a double millennium within any six-thousand-year experiment, the nodule can be even longer than just one century before and after the millennium change. In our terms, we are in a nodule that would include the last two centuries, the one in which we are currently living, and will probably include much of the century to follow. What I was examining in my sleep in these last hours was the overall structure of this nodule and the complexity of the intersection. And I can tell you that all and any of the probabilities which will play out from the given circumstances, being variations upon one major theme, will not be termed good by people who have no overall perspective . . . certainly not good for the future of this nation."

He took Merovee's hand again.

"That is why a mass dreaming consciousness—not the Noachite consciousness, but a gathering amalgamation of *several* consciousnesses—summoned my Spirit to again take human form. In this time and in this place, we set the stage for the final two millennia of the experiment of the Noachite Builders. The experiment that is to follow at the end of those two thousand years *can* be one in which Humanity begins finally to attain the heights of love and wisdom and creativity of which it is capable. On the other hand, that coming experiment can be one of such rampant idiocy that Humanity, as we know it, will be erased from the face of the Earth. I am here to try to set Humanity on a course that will insure the former, and not the latter. That is why much of what I will do, as far as teaching, takes place here in Galilee, the true current crossroads of the world. Here in Galilee, one has a finger on the pulse . . . "

He smiled at Deborah.

" . . . an example of which your mother has showed you, Merovee . . . a finger on the pulse of the planet Earth. Galilee is as the center of the planet right now. One would think that Rome was the center, but it is not. Here in Galilee, I have immediate mental access to Grecian, Roman, Egyptian, and Hebrew cultures, while the caravans make this a nexus of more farflung cultures as well—those of Africa, Anatolia, Mesopotamia, India, the Silk Lands, Gaul, the Isle of the Britons . . . even, though you know it not, to a land far across the Great Sea to the west of the Pillars of Hercules, a land known at this point in time only to Egypt and certain of the sea-faring peoples.

"And, of course, through Rome, one's access to far-flung cultures is intensified.

"So this 'time,' this nodule, is the culmination of a two-thousand-year cycle. In preparation for the next two-thousand years, in your lifetimes, you will see the beginning of the 'deaths' of two important cultures. Not total death, but change so vast that many will consider it death. I have already spoken of the change in store for our current Jewish culture. The next cultural death, the throes of which will take several centuries, will be that of the Romans."

"Roman!"

The exclamation came from all three of them.

"How can *Rome* die?" said Merovee.

"Rome is so mighty!" said Lazarus.

Jesus smiled.

"It is ironic that Jews hate the Romans so much, for both the Roman and Jewish cultures are Noachite. Supremely Noachite. And it is the Noachite consciousness that the new amalgamation, which I will call the Aquarian Consciousness, called Johannan and me to help begin to supplant.

"And who will destroy these two great Noachites? They will destroy—forever change—one another. First, Rome will destroy Jerusalem. Most Hebrews, those outside of Jerusalem, will remain in Palestine, living quietly, farming the land. Over the centuries, freed from the Temple, they will turn to new religions and lose their identity as Hebrews. Others will go wandering with the four winds. Some will spread a modified version of the religion of the Jews through the world. Others will take with them the new Idea, the new understanding that Johannan and I came to impart to them. It is this new Idea, carried to the Gentiles, that will eventually destroy the Roman Empire."

"I find it impossible to imagine a world such as you describe," said Deborah.

"Which is why our prophets spoke of an *end* to the world at this time. There will never be an end to the world. Only continual change. But seers, looking into the future, catching glimpses of vast changes at the turn of each millennium, and especially at the turn of double millenia, usually interpret what they see as an end to the world."

He reached out and touched Merovee's cheek.

"Perhaps, Dear Wife, this will help you to understand why I am here, what I must do, and why our time this 'time' will be short. This is the *prime moment* during this current experiment for new ideas to be inserted into the world mind. At no time before this nodule have the conduits of communication, that we know as the Roman Empire and as the worldwide Jewish culture, been as vast, as powerful, and as ready for change. From this point on, those conduits will steadily weaken. Not for another two thousand years will the world be again in possession of such incredible communication conduits between peoples and cultures. Not again until those two thousand years have passed will the Aquarian Consciousness be ready to be birthed as the mass consciousness. Until then, that consciousness will but swim in the womb of the world mind, growing and preparing itself for that birth."

"Will we be together again to witness that birth?" asked Merovee softly.

"I promise you faithfully, my beloved. We will, all of us, be there together. All of my inner circle will be midwives to the birth. If I, if all of us, do our jobs well now, the child will not be stillborn, or even sickly. It will be straight, strong, and healthy.

"In the meantime, on a mundane level, Deborah, I suggest that you and yours begin to sell all of your holdings in Judeah or Galilee while there is still a market. I will suggest the same to members of my own family. My father has much not only in Judeah, but in Samaria. I promise you that proceeds from these sales will be needed. And for important work. Soon. When possible, sell to Gentiles—to Roman citizens of whatever nationality. Such as they will not be harmed in the changeover when Rome devastates Jerusalem, their claims will be respected. Be sure to give all buyers solid descriptions and written proof of their purchases to decrease any chances of future confusion. Transfer as many funds as possible out of the country.

"And, if I might make another suggestion, you should send those funds to some trustworthy banking establishment in Massilia of Gaul."

"Gaul!"

Again, all three of them said the word at once.

"That is so far away!" said Deborah.

"I went to Massilia once with Grandfather. It is not so bad," said Merovee.

"But the country, itself, must be awful," said Lazarus. "Gaul is a place of exile, to where Rome sends those whom it wishes to sentence to living death."

Jesus shrugged.

"Actually, Gaul is a place of beauty. But you are not required to act on any advice that I give.

"In any case, you took me afield with your question about Moses. It carried me into the future, when I have still not finished telling you about the past."

He moved to the writing table and took up papyrus and stylus.

"We were wandering with the tent people who called themselves Man. That is what Adam, or Adamah, or the more ancient Chadam or Chadamah, means. Man," he said, writing out the differences.

"In many cultures, Man was the highest class. In old Assyria, there was a class called Avelum or Awelum or Chavelum—from which we derived our Chavvah or Chawwah—literally, Mother Of Man. You can begin to see the similarities. The Avelum were the most privileged class in old Assyria, above and *distinct* from Assyrian citizens. Avelum. Literally, Son or Sons of Man."

"Son of Man," said Lazarus. "Is that what the Essenes are talking about when they say that the Messiah will be called the Son of Man?"

"I will tell you a secret," smiled Jesus. "The Essenes do not know *what* they are talking about. They read ancient manuscripts, find kingly status applied to the Son of Man, and seize upon it as a prophecy of their Messiah . . . when, in reality, it is nothing but a social description from a civilization four thousand years dead."

He returned to the bed and made himself comfortable, sitting propped against the wall, cutting himself some cheese.

"Again and again I will caution you—implore you. Be ware of language. Of words. Of titles. Know that you can *never* read the word of any god. Only of men. See how even that one simple word—Man—has changed in our minds from what was originally meant? The first people with the name of Man considered themselves the only worthwhile people to have survived the cataclysm. Hence, when they spoke or wrote their histories and legends, they did not even bother to mention the fact that there were others beside themselves on the face of the Earth. This is excellent cheese, Deborah. Goat?"

"No, it is of cattle."

"I hope you have a lot of it. Pass the bread again, would you please, Didymus?"

"I always did wonder," mused Merovee, "where the grandchildren of Noah found wives and husbands."

"One could only think the most forbidden thoughts," said Lazarus. "I assumed that they married incestuously for many generations until they had re-populated the Earth."

"Had they done that," said Jesus, "Humanity would be even more imbecilic than it often seems. The arrogance of the storytellers left us with the same problems as to the children of Adamah. When Cain slays Hebel and is reprimanded by his god, Cain is afraid of all those people out there who might now slay him for slaying Hebel . . . that despite the fact that we have been specifically led to believe that he and his parents must now be the only three people left on Earth. His god tells him, however, that he shares his concern, and that he will put a mark on him so that all those mysterious people will not kill him. Cain then goes into a land called Nod—which is obviously peopled by people, where he readily finds a wife who is also obviously not his sister—and, in passing, note what Cain did next. He 'built him a city.' The Adamah consciousness, that would culminate in Noah, was already at work.

"Lately, the embarrassing problem of Lilith has surfaced in the writings of groups such as the Essenes. She is said to have been Adamah's first wife. '*First* wife?' say the Sadducees. 'How could there have been a first wife? God made only Adamah and Chavvah."

" . . . which are both linguistic variations of the same original concept!" interjected Lazarus.

"Exactly. But our Sadducees do not know this. They assume that their god made a person named Adamah and then a person named Chavvah during the first week of the existence of the Earth. Hence, there could have been no women before Chavvah.

"Which points up another mistake which Humankind, in the form of rulers and priests, makes when it decides to lie about the past, and to subvert the truth for its own special interests. The mistake is to imagine that knowledge of What Is True can be kept from the people, that it can be lost to them, taken from their memory. The people might go along for centuries *acting* as though they are ignorant of the truth, but the knowledge of it is always within them. That knowledge will, finally, if only during the nodule at the turn of a millennium, boil to the surface and change the existing order, sweeping lies—and governments—aside."

"You sound dangerously like a Zealot," said Deborah.

"You and my mother will get along beautifully. No, I am not a Zealot. I have no need to foment revolution when I know how nicely the nature of consciousness takes care of revolution for me.

"The point is that Scripture is replete with evidence of what I will tell you. Try as they would, the priests and scribes could not piece together, from what had come down to them, a history that made sense, in the way that they *wanted* history to be understood. And they had too much awe and superstitious reverence for the documents with which they were working to change them completely. While, also, if they had more than one version of the same story, not knowing which one to be right, they included them both. Sometimes they stuck one version onto the end of the first. At other times, they changed the various versions just a bit and stuck them in as fresh incidents in other chapters. When they found scraps which mystified them completely, they just stuck them in any which way, thinking it would do no harm, and it might just possibly be something that should be saved.

"What we are left with is uneven at best. But, midst the welter, the truth can easily be found. One has only to study the inconsistencies themselves, and the story that the priests rejected, the cornerstone that the authorities would deny, will take form between the lines."

"Look here," said Lazarus, studying the Genesis scroll. "These are things I always wondered about. To my mind, Genesis has three separate versions of the Creation. I have heard people say two, but I read three. The third is very short. It says nothing of sons named Cain or Hebel, but speaks only of a son called Seth. On top of which, it makes Cain's sons, Enoch, Methusael, and Lamech, into grandsons of Seth, and might even make *Cain* a grandson of Seth. And here, in that third version, it says, ' . . . male and female created he them, and blessed them, and called *their* name Adamah.' That bears out what you say. That it was a *group* that was called Adamah, not one man. And look here in the first version . . . when God gets ready to make Man, he says, 'Let *us* make man in *our* image.' And, in the second version, he says, 'Behold, the man is become as *one of us*.'

"When I questioned the priests as to who God was talking to—who 'us' was—they said that God was talking to his angels. I had to accept that. They told me that the 'sons of God' who took the 'daughters of men' to wife were angels as well, and that the 'giants in the Earth' were the children of angels and women. I had to accept that as well.

"But it did not make sense. Who were these angels in the first place? If God was omnipotent, why did he need these angels? If the angels were 'as him,' were they not gods, too? If they were the sons of God, why did we never hear of their mother? And why, then, until the Essenes began to talk of them of late, did we hardly ever hear of angels again? Why were they only male? Why did God have nothing but sons? And, if God was above such matters as mating with women, why would his sons—who were 'as him'—do so? And how could men have been sinful if they were the children of God's own angels?

"I had so many questions, and the priests never answered them, neither did the scribes, nor the rabbis. I see now that, first of all, the terms 'God' and 'Man' *then* meant something much different than we now suppose. And that, also, these strange references are clues as to the experiment even *before* Adamah! As for instance, when God says he has made Man in the image of 'us,' might that not be a hidden reference to both male and female? A deity both female and male at one and the same time? Or else a male deity and his consort goddess. Am I right?"

"You are. Some scribe, five hundred years ago, not knowing what to make of these references, simply recorded them as he found them. Were he here, I would pat him on the back, give him my undying thanks, and a cup of wine.

"Only in one thing are you wrong, Lazarus. Twice you told us that you *had* to accept the explanations of others. You did accept them, and were outwardly content—even when, in your core, a voice kept saying, 'That is not the answer. Something here simply does not make sense!' It is my hope, dear Didymus, that, from this day on, you will listen first to that still, small voice within yourself, and never again be content with any explanation of anything if it does not satisfy that voice."

"I will try, Jesus. I am not a courageous man. But I will try."

"Not courageous? You opened your mouth and questioned the priests, did you not? Some would not even have had the courage for that. And you are here, listening and understanding, are you not? You are more courageous than you know. Before I finish with you, Daniel will enter the lions' den only to find that the lions have been fed and are fast asleep at the feet of Didymus."

Lazarus turned red and laughed out loud. Merovee and Deborah exchanged glances. If only for the sense of self that Jesus was giving to the young man, they would both have loved him.

"Now, as to the three versions of Creation indicated in Genesis, there is actually a fourth version indicated throughout . . . and interesting truths about changing versions of 'God' and 'gods.' But those truths, regarding that fourth creation, are far beyond your abilities to comprehend at this time. Suffice it to say that there can be creations within Creation, itself. And our original 'Mama,' or 'Mother Goddess,' Ninkhursag . . . "

He was interrupted by a knock at the door. Surprised, and a bit annoyed, Merovee answered.

Salome stood without. The girl's eyes were larger than Merovee had ever seen them.

"I am sorry, Merovee. But I am not sorry. I want to hear him, too."

Merovee frowned.

"But Salome, we . . . " She was not good at lying—and she should not be. "We have spent some time talking of family business."

"Please, Merovee. Let me come in."

"Salome." It was Jesus, coming to Merovee's rescue. "We speak of nothing that you need to hear. Go back to the others, Child."

Salome set herself in a way that Merovee had come to know well.

"I am not a child and you *do* speak of things that I should hear. If it were not so, then why have I been unable to concentrate upon anything else since Merovee came to fetch Deborah and Lazarus? Why was I impelled to come here and make a fool of myself if there is not a reason?"

Jesus stayed firm.

"At this point, what I have to say is only for the ears of Merovee and her family."

But then Merovee had an arm about Salome's shoulders and was leading her into the room.

"You are not being a fool, Salome. Jesus has just been explaining that very thing. He finds Humanity foolish and amusing, for believing that Ideas can be kept a secret. He smiles at those in a position of leadership who assume that knowledge of What Is True can be kept from their subjects. Instead, he explained to us, Ideas are the common coinage of the species. Unconsciously, what *one* knows, *all* know. And there are families of consciousness, unrelated by blood, but who are the very closest of sisters and brothers, and who sense what is happening with one another most acutely."

She was grinning now, watching the face of Jesus.

"You just told Salome, Jesus, that what you have to say is only for the ears of my family and myself. I say to you that, since something inside this girl alerted her as to what we are doing here, and since she has been bold enough to search us out and demand knowledge of What Is True, that she *is* a member of my family. She is my sister. I dare you to tell me that I am wrong. I also remind you that you once cautioned me never to call any man 'fool,' since, at any moment, it might be yourself who deserves that appellation."

"Merovee," said Deborah tersely. "You ought not to speak in that manner to one such as Jesus."

"She put me much more firmly into my place at Machaerus," said Jesus softly. "How did you put it then, my love?"

"I told you that I do not care if you are God, himself. I will think for myself and speak my mind honestly and take responsibility for my own actions."

"On that day, she pulled me up short when I missed my mark and, hence, sinned against her. She has once more brought my poor marksmanship to my attention. Except that, this time, I sinned against Salome." He held out his hand to that girl. "I stand corrected. Come in, Little Sister."

Jesus did not go back over any of the points which he had already covered.

"You will have to understand as best you can," he told Salome. "I am as one who sows seeds. What will grow will grow. I will not cover the same field twice."

"What I do not understand, I will ask of Merovee at a later time."

"You do understand Greek?"

"Of course," she said with lifted chin."

Jesus nodded and went on, in Greek.

"What I am hoping to show you here is the futility of fixating upon Hebrew Scripture or upon any words, written or otherwise, as an infallible means of discovering *any* truth, much less Universal Truth. Words are Humanity's invention, not any god's. Words, spoken or written, have no intrinsic content of their own. Rather, to the one listening or reading, they are as vessels which fill themselves with the current understanding of that listener or reader. Whereas the originator of the words might have had a completely different understanding of them. That original writer or speaker could be likened to a potter who made a cup intended to be used for wine. But those who have inherited the cup now use it for water, vinegar, honey, milk, as a receptacle for coins, or as a vase for flowers—as they see fit.

"Understanding that, dispense your words as carefully as you would dispense your pearls. Give your words a shape which will cause as little misunderstanding as possible.

"Even I cannot hope to be understood in the manner of my own intent. That horrible dream I had in the boat coming here was a preview of the way in which my words will be changed, twisted, used, stretched, hidden, shredded, edited, and mistranslated by generations to come. Yet I try to give to the words a certain shape, a certain emotional tone, to design them so that, no matter how they are changed, or where they are hidden, they will open hearts, release feelings. For, in feelings—in E-motion, not words, you will find Universal Truth, and you will begin to know the true god.

"It is for this reason alone that we are enjoined from speaking the supposedly true name of the Temple's god. As is often the case, a religion intuited the truth, but ascribed to that truth the wrong reasons. The true god, itself, does not forbid its name to be mentioned. That mention would not offend the true god. If it took any notice of such attempts at all, it would more probably be amused. For the true god is *beyond* words. The names of the true god, no matter how many, how secret, how solemn or 'sacred' to that gang in the Temple, are Humanity's doing, pure and simple.

"The true god *has* no name! The true god is too vast to be named. So how could anyone utter that name?

"The true god is, quite simply, All That Is.

"And, as I told you at Obed's the other night, All That Is is composed of pure E-motion. That very word, Emotion, would be a much better name for the true god than any proper name ever devised.

"So try to rise above words. When you go out to teach, open your hearts to Feeling and to Emotion . . . to the Joy, the Exuberance, the Love—even the Angers—that will flow through you. Let those Feelings, those E-motions, shape your words. You will then have some hope of reaching Hearts.

"Now, I said to open yourself even to your Angers. Do not be afraid of Anger. Anger is dangerous only when it is denied expression. Anger, expressed, never turns to Hatred. Anger, expressed, never frustrates, eating at the body, manifesting itself finally in some sickness, or in the mental disturbances that our people mistakenly believe to be demons inside of a person, or yet in the hideous running sores of leprosy. That is one key that you will need to remember when you go out to cure. I will teach you all as we go. Salome, what is it? Why the wide eyes?"

"What do you mean, 'When you go out to teach'? And cure? Surely you do not expect that I . . . You are not including *me*, Jesus?"

"Did you not demand admittance to this room tonight?"

"I only wanted to listen!"

Jesus shook his head and grinned, as at a precious, baby animal.

"Then do so, my kitten. Yes. That is what I will call you. Nothing shall be forced upon you, Kitten. Only listen and learn. Your call will come from out of the depths of your own Self, just as it came tonight. When you understand it, you will not be afraid."

"Why do you insist upon giving people new names!" cried Salome in frustration.

"Is it not obvious? Are names not words? Have I not explained to you the plastic nature of words? There are cultures which insist that names be changed as the individual grows and develops. Those cultures recognize the fact that one name cannot describe a person for a whole lifetime. At the moment, our culture is not one such. Our culture is rigid. Our names are as graven in stone, and are not to be changed. The *person* is not supposed to change. What I attempt to do with my names, Salome, is, first, to apply a word that, to me at that moment, has the Feeling of the person whom I see. Now, the person that I see is not the person that anyone else sees. Every single person in this room, looking at you, Salome, has a different Feeling of you, and so sees something different. I attempt, with my names, to make you aware of other parts of your Self, of other views of your Self . . . to shake you out of a rigidity in regard to your own being, to open up new vistas. Today I call you Kitten. Next week, I may decide to call you Little Snake."

"Ugh!"

"Then just watch yourself." Jesus winked at Merovee, and held out his cup.

She refilled it thoughtfully.

"What you just said, Josh, is another reason why 'God' cannot have a name. If one name cannot describe just one human being in just one lifetime, how could any name possibly hope to describe something that is, not only, *everything that is*, but that is also constantly *changing*, in billions of ways each second?"

"There you have it," said Jesus. "So learn to rise above words. You must use words, yes. They are the recognized vehicle of communication currently in use in this experiment.

"But there is a higher and better communication. It is the language of the Universe, received and understood by each and every atom in that Universe. No lips speak it. No ears hear it. It consists of

162

feeling-tones between minds *and* objects. It is the communication that brought Kitten so unerringly to our door. Her conscious mind could make no sense of her actions. She felt a fool. Yet she would have swum raging rivers to get here. That deeper communication—the true language of the true god, of All That Is—suggested to her most urgently that she should join us.

"I will strive . . ." he smiled gently at Merovee, "in the little time that I will have amongst you, to teach you the vocabulary of that deep language of Feeling. I will help you to translate that Feeling into words, to shape your words with so much Feeling that listening Hearts will unconsciously know the greater reality of which you speak."

"Josh," said Merovee quietly. "Why were the others not invited tonight? How can you hope to teach in a uniform manner if all of your followers are not allowed to hear you?"

"What in this world is truly uniform, Merovee? Uniformity is a myth. Each and every person, *particle*, in this world is unique. Even twins considered identical are far from being identical. When snow falls on the Judean hills, can you compute the number of snowflakes? Yet each is unique. There never has been, and there never will be, two snowflakes absolutely alike.

"That is one of the glories of All That Is. Each unit of All That Is is a totally different expression of the potential of All That Is. Hence, Merovee, I can never hope to teach in a uniform manner. The others are each capable of that of which they *are* capable. I will train each of them differently, so that they will then go out and appeal to the ears of those listeners who have reached similar levels.

"But I am not sure as yet just what all their various levels are, how much flexibility or rigidity each of them has, how much of what I have to tell them they can absorb and understand.

"The men among them are an especial problem. By the mere fact of their *being* male—and, save Phillipus, Hebrews—they are burdened with very definite ideas of male superiority, and bound hand and heart by The Law. I must feel my way. You, too, all of you, will have to learn to gauge these things. You can teach to five-year-olds only what five-year-olds can understand, and in terms that they can understand. You teach those of thirteen in quite another fashion, and so on with each age group.

"But I do not wish to mislead you with this analogy of age. It is only an analogy. Because the sort of understanding capability to which I refer does not limit itself to one lifetime, or stratify itself so neatly. Understanding is gained by very hard work, through innumerable experiences, by unending trial and error, in existence after existence. And each Spirit reacts to experience in its own way, progresses at its own rate. So that each and every person of whatever 'age' is at a different level of development. Certain five-year-old children would be capable of understanding every single thing that I have said here this evening, while certain octogenarians would understand nothing. It is the work that has been put in, and the understanding that that particular Spirit has been able to achieve as a result of the work, that makes the difference.

"You here in this room tonight have turned your various experiences to good account. You are the lilies which float at the top of the pool, sopping up the sun, rather than the sediment which lays all gooey and stagnant at the bottom. You are ready to hear my innermost teachings. It was to find you that I came."

Deborah's brow had furrowed as she tried, diligently, to understand.

"You came of your own accord? I mean—you made up your mind to come?"

"I was called, Deborah, as I have been called so many times before. This is a two-thousand-year millennium. A major cyclical crest. On a mass, unconscious basis, at millenniums, and particularly at double-millenniums, the collective mind of Humanity calls for change, for upheaval which will lead to new understanding and further growth *on a planetary scale*.

"The collective mind of Humanity *dreamed me up*. Humanity created me. I am its dream made flesh."

There was a long silence.

Finally, Merovee spoke.

"What of such as Simon Yeshuah?"

Jesus shrugged as though attempting to drop an unwelcome cloak from off of his shoulders.

"As I told you in Machaerus, I am not the only teacher who responded to Humanity's call. There are many of us. Some are teaching right now in remote areas, in countries and lands of which you have no knowledge. Some are my brothers—and, where allowed, sisters—fragments from my own entity. Others, like Simon Yeshuah, are off of powerful, yet . . . " he shrugged again, "less advanced entities than my own. For even the great entities are at various levels of development and of understanding, while the teaching fragments which are sent out, even from the greatest, run the gamut of development from brilliant to asinine.

"Simon Yeshuah. Ahhh."

He shook his head, and looked suddenly old. When he spoke again, he lapsed back into Aramaic.

"I fear that that man will do much damage."

He laughed a bitter laugh.

"Then there is the other part of *me*. Saul. Between Simon Yeshuah and Saul . . . "

Merovee reached up and touched his hand.

"Let us return to words," she said gently. "You said that there is no Word of God. Yet human beings have invented words, and All That Is shares in the experience of human beings. So would words not be at least one aspect of All That Is?"

He squeezed her hand, grateful that she had drawn his thoughts away from such as Simon Yeshuah and Saul.

"Very definitely," he went on, in Greek once more. "Just as a hair of your head is an aspect of you. But if I fixated on that hair, thinking that, by devoting my life to its study, I would know Merovee, I would be sadly deluded. Oh my!" He laughed, coming fully back to himself, regarding her with eyes so filled with love that tears came to her own eyes. "How very sadly deluded. What I would miss if I did not stir myself to discover that greater Merovee.

"Now!" He clapped his hands efficiently. "These examples we have discussed as to the manner in which Scripture misleads are as a few grains of sand in a desert. But are you all beginning to understand the immensity of the misunderstanding under which the Sadducees and Pharisees and those of their ilk stagger when they fence their lives about with Scriptural words?"

"*I* certainly am," said Lazarus rancorously. "And their sin is very great. For they attempt to fence the lives of all their fellows as well."

The eyes of Jesus turned, gentle, to the young man.

"You think, of course, of the suffering which has been imposed upon you because of your slight, physical difference. But I say to you, Didymus, that these people sin only against themselves. And that you are as much of a sinner as they, against yourself. For you allowed them to impose their Ideas onto you. Anyone who sins, truly, in the Universal scheme, hurts only himself. And no one ever, in any circumstance, has to accept the dictates of others. There are always options. Always, there are doors for those with the courage to believe that those doors are there, and the courage to find them.

"What, now, of your understanding of the true history of this planet as opposed to what is currently believed by our people? Are you all beginning to have some mental image, some Feeling, some deep memory of the truth of what I am telling you?"

"It takes a complete rebuilding within the mind," said Deborah.

"Ah, but that should not be difficult," said Jesus, "You were born into a Noachite culture. A culture of Builders."

"That is something I cannot understand!" said Deborah. "I have never built anything in my life! Or wanted to. How can *I* be of this family of consciousness?"

"Think about it. What is the first error that you are making?"

Deborah sighed and was silent.

"Well," she said at last, "you say that we live again and again. My first mistake, then, might be that I am thinking only of the life I am living at this moment, rather than considering the whole picture. *Was* I a man who built things in other lives?"

"Oh dear. You just made another mistake."

"I was not a man who built things?"

"Oh you were. But what prejudice have you allowed to shape your thoughts?"

Deborah screwed up her brow, looking to the others for help.

"Oh!" cried Salome. "Why can *women* not build things as well?"

"I could kick myself," said Deborah mid the laughter. "All right. In other lives, have I been both men and women who built things?"

"Again and again. Both in the past and in the future. But I am pleased that you were able to see the prime error of limiting your understanding of yourself to one lifetime. I will help you with yet another error in your thinking, for it will not be as obvious. Again, it is a matter of semantics. You obviously, from your side of understanding, fill the word—the 'cup' of 'build'—with Ideas of *physical* objects."

"Oh. Of course. There are many other ways to build, are there not."

"Actually, the Old Hebrew of that second version of the Creation says that God 'built' the mate of Adamah from out of one of Adamah's ribs. And, by the way, in that bit of information is a clear statement of the fourth version of creation that I mentioned. Here again," he smiled, "we must be careful of just how that 'built' was meant. Old Hebrew, as we know it, is a comparatively recent development. There was an Ancient Hebrew before Old Hebrew. So that we now must translate from one language, Old Hebrew, into our current languages, New Hebrew, Aramaic, and Greek, while the language that we are translating from was only a translation from an older language to start with.

"The opportunities for error in this process are endless.

"Take the point that Didymus raised a few minutes ago, the name of 'Adamah' and 'his' 'wife.'"

He gestured for the papyrus and stylus again, and began to illustrate his words.

"In Old Hebrew, she is called Chawwah. In New Hebrew, it is Hawwah or Chava or Chavah, or Chavvah, or Havah, or Hava, depending on who is doing the writing and where. In Greek, it becomes Ava or Avas. In modern Aramaic, it is Ewwe. Our scholars and scribes of the Temple disagree as to what exactly the name, by whatever spelling, meant in the Ancient Hebrew before Old Hebrew. They have decided that it meant living, or life. They do not take into consideration the fact that Ancient Hebrew was not Hebrew at all, but a mixture which included Akkadian, Hurrian, Old Elaminian, and Aramaic . . . that there were a hundred dialects, combinations, and spellings . . . that meanings changed with the understanding and eras of speakers and scribes . . . that some placed a 'd' or a 'b' or 'l' in the place of the 'w' or 'ww' or 'v' or 'vv' . . . that some dropped the 'Ch' or 'H' and placed only a sign of aspiration, leaving 'Ava or 'Avah, and variations such as 'Adah, 'Abah, 'Avelah or 'Alah. They then argue over 'Adam,' and say that it springs from 'Adamah,' and means Man, or red, or clay. Lately our Pharisees have decided that it was the proper name of one man, himself. Because of the narrowness of the lives which they lead, exposing themselves to nothing but the organized prejudices of their own kind—because of their bias against women and their great need to see women as secondary beings good for nothing but the serving of food and breeding—they cannot see that, in Adam, or Adamah, or the many variations such as Chadamah, or Hadam, or Chavvam, or Hawwam, or Avelum . . . is also the name of the female.

"*All* are versions of exactly the same thing. They reach back to a time when the true god was known to be neither male nor female yet both. One could say that in the beginning was the word. Which became many words. All parts of All That Is, male and female in one.

"Witness the god name that we are forbidden to speak—but do attempt to speak anyway. Yahweh is the most frequent rendering. Look again at all the variations of Adamah and Chavvah. You will see that Yahweh is yet another variation.

"All these words indicate a duality that is multiplicity, and yet is still also only One. All of the words contain the true god which is All That Is, and its 'Children' or manifestations, and contain the unifying Spirit that is Oneness—a Trinity if you will.

"And, yes, these words mean living. Yes, they mean soil, and red, and clay, and Man. Yes, these words in their variations mean *all* those things. The unconscious aggregate wisdom in all the many versions is obvious when one looks for it.

"And only by ceasing to fixate on hairs, only by allowing oneself to feel, to experience, to intuit the whole, can one begin to know anything about particulars. These many words, *in the whole*, indicate the true nature of the true god in this world. God *is* earth, rock, soil, red clay, man, woman, animals, *all*, gloriously infused with Life and Spirit.

"The true god is all these things . . . and none of these things. The true god is simply All That Is. And so, automatically, also All That Is Not.

"Ah! Those Temple nigglers make me ill." Again the Aramaic. "I become furious when I contemplate their refusal to open themselves to the obvious. Pour me more wine, please, Merovee my dearest."

"Would you like not to go on?" she said.

"No, I would not like not to go on. It is impossible for me not to go on. And on. I must continue forever, whenever I am called, wherever I am called. Wherever even one mind calls upon my name, whatever my name might happen to be at that point—there I, or some fragment of me, must and will be. I chose it. Willingly. Consciously. Eons ago. So pay no heed to my angers, Merovee. After what I have told you of angers, you surely did not think that I would be without them."

"Of course not. I also remember a few rough words spoken at Machaerus."

That made him smile. He took a long sip of wine and cocked a brow at Deborah

"She nearly got her non-existent backside turned to leather."

"It is good that you did not waste your energy," said Deborah. "How do you think that her backside *got* so flat? I discovered early on that nothing can deter her when she has her mind made up. But you were telling me how I came to be one of these Builders."

"Oh. Yes. The word 'build' was what got me off onto Old Hebrew. Well, one could say that all creatures living in this system began as builders. Just as one of the versions of the 'Creation' tells us that God built a mate for the first man out of one of the man's ribs—which, by the way, is an egregious mistranslation—each living creature plans and builds its own body . . . . . . Oh yes! Do not all look at me that way. The body of each of you is your own creation. You used the stuff of your mother's body to build with, but the form and intent is your own. You maintain it throughout your entire lifetime with your own mental energy, which is *The Energy*, the stuff of which the Universe is made. At any moment, the state of your body accurately reflects the state of your Spirit. So, Deborah, you created and built, first, yourself. Then you lent the stuff of your body to two beautiful creatures named Merovee and Didymus."

Deborah hesitated, then smiled.

"You are only one-third right. I did lend my stuff to two beautiful creatures, but their names were Miriam and Lazarus."

Jesus spread his hands in the face of their laughter.

"The House of Nathan seems bent upon correcting me, and the point is well taken. Even I constantly fall into semantic traps.

"Miriam and Lazarus and Merovee and Didymus are *not* the same. 'Miriam and Lazarus' is what they were initially, to Deborah. They might always remain Miriam and Lazarus to Deborah, for mothers tend to be that way. It is difficult for them ever to see that their babies have grown and have become personalities with Ideas and goals of their own. Merovee and Didymus are, then, my own personal views of those grown and changed babies.

"Yet, in what I have just said, is the primary way in which you, Deborah, have been a Builder in this particular lifetime. Even though the bodies of these two people are not *your* creations, but their own, and even though you only provided the stuff with which their Spirits directed the building of their own unique bodies . . . yet you *have* helped to build them.

"For their Spirits *chose* you. From out of all the millions of wombs on the face of the Earth, they elected to build their Selves, and hence the lives that they would lead this time, out of the genetic stuff from which you sprang, *and* with the aid of the Ideas which they knew that you held in your mind.

"It is no accident that their father died when they were born. In most cases, a Spirit will choose a *pair* of parents, for the blend of influences which the two of them will provide. On very rare occasions, a Spirit will chose to be born into a family not on account of the parents, but in order to be close to a friend or relative of those parents, a kindred Spirit with whom they wish to travel. Sometimes that kindred Spirit is even one of the parents.

"The 'fact' of your husband, Deborah, and of his strict religious background, provided a necessary tension for these two children. He provided a necessary basis to their goals for this lifetime, an obstacle to overcome, that I will explain shortly.

"But these two people came here primarily for you. For your beautiful mind, your openness, your fairness, your willingness to learn and to allow them to learn and to search for themselves—supported by your love. Your price is far above rubies, Deborah. Your price is above all the treasure on this planet Earth."

He raised his glass.

"I salute you, my new mother."

For a moment, Deborah stared, her mouth working. Then she buried her face in her hands. Merovee turned and embraced her.

"Do not cry, Mother. It is true. I know it is. I certainly feel that way about you."

"I, too," said Lazarus. "I can understand it now."

"Thank you. It is just the nicest thing that has ever been said to me. All these years I worried so, that I was doing the wrong thing, even endangering your lives. Oh yes! If anyone had found the goddess, you might have been dragged out and stoned right along with me! Do you think that that did not weigh on me? Do you think I did not lie awake nights wondering at myself? And then, in the face of Martha's disapproval . . . "

"Oh poof to Martha," said Merovee. "She is our father's child. We belong to you."

"Yet always," said Deborah, "no matter how frightened I was, I just felt that the goddess was so important . . . that I just *had* to let you know about her, and about all the things I had learned as a girl in Greece. How could I doubt the wisdom? You know what your grandfather was like. Such a good man. Wise, compassionate, loving, curious, courageous, creative . . . all the things which I admired. All the things it seemed that a human being should be. And he revered the goddess, thought her important. How, then, could I deny her? I felt that, if I did, if I kept knowledge of her from you, I would be robbing you of so many vital things. First and foremost, I felt that I would be robbing you of free choice."

"And so, Deborah, you 'built' a *bridge*. That is what I was leading to. I said that most mothers will not allow their children to grow, to change. You are an exception. You not only allowed their growth and change, you carried them on your shoulders. In the face of your own quaking fear, you yet went ahead, toward a goal, a vision, that you saw imperfectly, but that you felt, deep down into the very core of your Self.

"You see, my dear, you came into this life with a mission. In a way, you were *called*, as was I. All these years, without understanding it consciously, you have been working for a new consciousness, the seed of which we are even now inserting into the womb of the world. One might call you a spy for the enemy, masquerading as a good little Noachite, but, all the while, working for the Aquarian Consciousness.

"Your Spirit chose a free-thinking father who built with Ideas . . . and a husband who, though beloved, was narrow, rigid, and the opposite of creative. With that very basis, you saw to it that the minds of your children were presented with many streams of thought. You saw to it that they learned of many cultures, mastered multiple languages. You surrounded them at the same time with love and approval, asking only that they use what you provided in order to discover their own best Selves. You made of these two young people a bridge, to be used by all brave explorers of the mind, and even by myself. The bridge leads from the old understanding, that is about to be displaced, to the new.

"We will not, any of us, see the end of this bridge in our lifetimes. No, not in a dozen more lifetimes. The world will not reach the end of this bridge until two more millennia have passed. But I promise you, that, when I get to the other end of this bridge, I will turn and say to the billions following after me, 'This is the bridge that Deborah founded. Let us never forget Deborah.'

"Do not give her any more wine, Merovee, she is becoming altogether too teary."

"Oh!" laughed Deborah. "And to think I objected to you simply because you are a Jew!"

"*Did* you now!"

"Oh yes!" said Merovee evilly. "She did her best to talk me out of you a few nights ago. Luckily, as you have all observed, I am hard to budge once my mind is made up."

Jesus shrugged.

"That, too, is partially her doing. Give her the wine."

"Jesus?" Salome tugged at his sleeve. "I, too, am a bridge, am I not? And my mother? Oh, I wish you could meet her, she is much like Deborah, I am here with her love and her blessings, though she puts herself at risk in keeping Antipas from realizing that I am gone. I, too, bridge many cultures. Idumean to start with, then Herod the Great married my Hebrew-Hasmonaean grandmother, but my parents were raised in Rome at the court of Caesar Augustus and were also exposed to the best of the Greek culture. All this was passed on to me, and now, into whichever marriage I am sent, to whatever place, I will carry all that Johannan taught, and all that I have heard here this night. I *am* then, a bridge, am I not? That Herodias founded?"

Jesus leaned back against his pillows, staring at the ceiling.

"I see an arch reaching up through the heavens. It is made of pink feathers. Every twenty feet there are caged birds, singing. They have to be caged, else they would be eaten, for the bridge is filled with gamboling kittens."

Salome burst into tears.

"Oh!"

Jesus sat up abruptly, got to his feet and pulled Salome into his arms.

"Forgive me, dear Kitten. Of course you are a bridge. You are brave and fine and wonderful to have recognized that fact, and yes, I would love Herodias if I met her. I love her without meeting her. How could I not, when she has produced such as you?"

"You mean that?"

"You would not be here if I did not mean it. I do not squander time on those who have no hope of understanding. But you must understand even more, Kitten, and tolerate my faults. I frequently relieve my tensions by teasing those whom I love best."

"Oh. Well. Now that I know about your faults, I forgive you."

"You will not dissolve into tears if I greet you in the morning with a query of, 'With how many little birds did you break your fast, my dear'?"

"I will answer that 'Birds were not to my taste this morning, I had ten pounds of pink feathers instead, and now I must rebuild an entire pilaster of my bridge.'"

Jesus held the girl away from him, regarding her with sober eyes.

"You have an excellent Spirit, Salome. You will do well. Now . . . "

He released her and wandered over to the window vents, there to breathe of the night air.

"It would be nice to take a walk, but then they would all follow us.

"Oh."

He leaned forward, peering through the vents.

"Hello there. Come out of the shadows . . . . . . so, it is you, Friend Nathaniel. And Susannah. Have you two been listening there for long?"

He shrugged.

"This room is getting busier than a money-changer's stall at the Temple. Well, come around and come on in, the both of you. It is better than skulking in shadows."

Chapter 7

The Stone Masons

Susannah and Nathaniel entered, eyes lowered, faces burning.

"What have you to say for yourselves?" said Jesus. "No! Do not tell me." He crossed his arms upon his chest. "You simply could not help yourselves, some little voice kept nagging, nagging . . . " His voice rose to a squeak. "Hurry! Go listen at his window! He is saying things that you ought to know!"

The others laughed. Nathaniel and Susannah exchanged glances.

"Sort of," said Susannah. "We . . . followed Salome."

"Then you have heard much. What do you think of what you have heard?"

"We wish to know more," said Susannah.

"You do not think that I am demented?"

"It all sounded sensible to me," said Nathaniel gruffly.

"Can the two of you be trusted never to reveal the presence of the honored guest in this house?"

Susannah followed the sweep of his hand to the idol on the bedside table

"I have offered to The Mother in my day," she said.

"Nathaniel?"

"I trust you, Jesus. If you tell me that that thing is right in the sight of God, then right it is."

Jesus nodded.

"Not only is it right in the sight of God, it *is* God. Just as everything in the Universe, each living thing, each object, each Idea, each concept, is God."

He relaxed back down onto the cushions of the bed.

"Let it be understood that, when I speak of God, I mean All That Is. It is unfortunate that I must keep using that word, 'God,' when speaking to Hebrews. It is confusing in the extreme. But it is by that word—that they use as a proper name in place of the name that they are forbidden to speak—that they have come to understand and think of that which they worship.

"The fact is that their 'God' does not exist, not as they assume 'him' to be. Neither does *any* supreme being exist. There is no supreme being because the very concept is too limited. Pathetically limited.

"For one thing, the word 'God' presupposes a supreme power that has a definite form—in our arrogance, human.

"It also indicates a definite sex. Male.

"All That Is has no form but endless forms. It has no sex but all sexes—even sexes not represented in this experiment. I am personally aware of thirty-six different sexual types in the Universe. All That Is is not one god or goddess, but all gods and goddesses, which are as numerous as are the stars throughout the Universe. All That Is. *All That Is.* If you think about those three words, you are forced into a much more expansive conception of a supreme power than that which comes to mind when you say 'God.' I would ask all of you to begin immediately to concentrate upon substituting those words, All That Is, for 'God,' both in your personal thoughts and when speaking to one another.

"*Words* again! Words, that so mislead and confuse us, and which so often stand between us and the truth of any matter.

"Well, sit down, Nathaniel. Susannah. I suppose I should have known that you two must be included into my inner circle. You are, after all, the originals of Machaerus, who ministered to my other part and to my wife."

"In that case," said Salome softly, "Mathiah and Judah should be here as well."

Jesus turned, staring at her. But his eyes were suddenly far away.

"Judah Sicarius. The world will remember that name. For the same reason that they will remember yours, Salome. You like the man, do you not?"

"He . . . I think of him as my brother."

"You are indeed a pair."

Abruptly, Jesus turned and shut the window vents tight.

"It might get close, but, for the moment, so are the rest of the minds out there."

He went back to the bed, propped himself up against the pillows and resumed as through there had been no interruption.

"Now. The point, Deborah, that I hope I have made abundantly clear, is that not all building is done with wood and bricks and stone. The contributions of both bodies and of Ideas are as much a part of building as setting one brick on another. Without the Idea of Brick, physical bricks would not exist. Without the Idea of Body, there would be no physical bodies to lift the bricks. *The Idea always precedes and literally creates the physical object.*

"Historically, Noachites contributed heavily in all areas of the building of physical objects and structures. Theirs was the genius that produced the Idea and so created the necessary material, and theirs were the bodies which fabricated the objects and structures. With this two-thousand-year millennium, however, the Noachites who are Hebrew prepare to move into a phase in which their contribution will be almost entirely in the realm of Ideas. We shall see what they do with this new manner of building."

Merovee raised her hand.

Jesus laughed.

"This is becoming as a schoolroom. You need not be quite so formal, Wife."

Merovee blushed. Though, by Hebrew custom, they were now so truly married that only divorce could dissolve the alliance, it was still disconcerting to hear him say "Wife" before all these others. He, for his part, seemed to enjoy her discomfiture.

"My question is out of the way," she said, "but I would like to understand it before you go on. It harks back to things you said earlier. You spoke several times about historical truth, what *really* happened historically. Yet you have also told me of the many probabilities which act themselves out side by side with one another. There could not then be any *one* historical truth, there must be histories without number. How then can you presume to tell us *the* historical truth?"

"The question is a good one. Nathaniel, Susannah, have you any Greek?"

"Enough to get by," said Nathaniel. There were few Galileans who had not been exposed to Greek.

"My wandering husband was Greek," said Susannah. "I have forgotten much, but it will come back."

"I will try to stay with Aramaic, but there are concepts which only the Greeks have bothered to put into words. What I am telling you, Merovee, is the historical truth that pertains, in the main, to the probability that you are living out right now.

"Go back again to my analogy of the grass with its occasional 'bulges.' You are living at this moment in one of those nodules. One thousand years ago, and for roughly a hundred years before and after that millennium—a period coinciding with the tail end, here in Palestine, of what were centuries of invasions and settling by various Hebrews and allied bands, and extending through the reigns of David and Solomon—both of whom were major organizational Spirits in regard to our culture as we now know it—there was another nodule. A vast number of probabilities came into being during that nodule, some of them in the mass dreaming mind. Gradually, they synthesized, merged, and, out of the synthesis, we selected those stories which we now accept as our official history. We then continued on with our slim, main stem.

"There are, however, phantom stems, which accepted other probabilities as their official history and which grew off at differing angles from the nodule. Out of the nodule in which we now exist, many more slim, clean stems will grow, each thinking that they are the only stem. Generally, most of us stay with our chosen stem of probability. It *is* possible, however, to switch over to one that is completely alien.

"One can often spot a place where major characters or whole groups have switched from one probability to another. There will usually be markedly divergent versions given for major historical events. Some people might even claim that the event or events never even happened. All involved will honestly believe that their memory is the correct memory, and all will find excellent evidence to prove their points. Scholars will come running and commence their nitpicking, attempting to discover which of the versions 'really' happened.

"What really did happen, of course, is that each side is legitimately remembering the same event, but, when the event occurred, each was in a different probability, and so experienced it differently. One group then switched into the probability of the other, bringing their alien memory along with them. There is no use at all to argue over which version is 'true,' for each is true, each did happen in the past of each group.

"And so what I give you when I tell you our true history—all that I *can* give you, is the main thrust of the probabilities which have culminated in the moment we are now experiencing. You look confused, Salome."

"Pay me no attention. I will catch up."

"Have I answered you, Merovee?"

"I guess so."

"Do you understand it completely?"

"I have a feeling that, were I to understand it completely, that understanding would only bring me to the brink of yet another mystery. I think that must be what it is all about. What—Life, what Existence, is all about—mastering one mystery only to be presented with another. Do *you* understand everything, Josh?"

"If I did, I would be perfect, and thus truly, eternally, and irrevocably *dead*. Because the very concept of perfection allows no movement of any sort one way or another, and certainly no growth."

"Even All That Is is not perfect, then?" said Merovee.

"There is no such thing as perfection, not in the way that Humankind perceives it. Perfection is one of the most ridiculous, ill-thought-out and *destructive* Ideas that the species has ever come up with. It is useful only in that individual concepts of perfection provide goals—targets for which to aim. As you said, however, the moment that one attains that individual goal of perfection, one realizes that there is a further perfection. The degrees of perfection are without end, ever growing, ever changing. One might even compare perfection to doorways in a never-ending house, each of which one must pass through to reach the next part of that house."

"Even All That Is does not know all, then?" said Lazarus.

"It would be very dull even to itself if it did. You did indeed hit upon the essence of the true god, Merovee. All That Is is constantly exploring, learning, re-learning, and re-membering itself, constantly growing, constantly changing.

"And it loves to surprise itself. Have you not had the experience of forgetting something that you know perfectly . . . " He grinned. "That word again. You see how our words trap and lie to us? . . . something that you know 'perfectly' well? Then some event recalls it to mind, and you find yourself saying, 'But of course! I knew that. How could I possibly have forgotten?' In the meantime, though, you have afforded yourself the fun of a surprise, of a different view, a different experience, a different attack on what you already knew but so conveniently forgot.

"All That Is is no different. Because All That Is *is* you, forgetting that thing and then re-experiencing it through *your unique vision*, in your unique moment. I spoke before of the snowflakes in winter—millions, billions, trillions of them—not a one of them alike. One would think that All That Is would grow tired of being a snowflake, of forming, falling, laying about, melting. But no. No snowflake has ever felt the same as any other as it formed or fell or laid about or melted.

"*Snowflakes* feel?" said Nathaniel.

"I have explained to the others that All That Is is Feeling and Emotion. You might define the entire Universe, and so each and every thing that exists, as a system of conscious, Feeling Energy.

"So yes. A snowflake feels. Not in the way that you do, but in a manner that is distinctly its own. And All That Is loves to experience the unique life of every one of those flakes, just as it loves to experience the unique life of each of us.

"Take any attribute, quirk, or quality that you have—'good' or 'bad'—and there you will see a bit of All That Is. Magnify that quality to the furthest degree, and you will still fall far short of the degree to which All That Is possesses that quality which you think of as yours.

"And glories in it!

"There is no end to the multiplication of All That Is, or to its experiments and expansion.

"And, in one of its aspects, All That Is is the supreme Noachite, the restless, insatiable, *Eternal Builder*.

"In a certain way then, Noachites can be forgiven for assuming themselves to be Chosen, or superior, people. Though All That Is does not, in reality, have any favorites, but loves all equally, it *is* true that the Noachite *consciousness* was chosen to lead this particular experiment."

"Then when you tell us the history of our world and of the Noachites," said Lazarus, "you are telling us but one small part of All That Is."

"Infinitely more small than is a hair there on the back of your hand in relationship to the Universe.

"But let me tell you more of the Noachites, for, as small as they are in the grand scheme of things, they are large to us. And, since All That Is in this experiment sees largely through the eyes of us creatures, and understands this part of itself largely through our minds and experiences, the Noachites are large to All That Is as well.

"This is the duality of what you have always thought of as 'God.' Beside the Universe, the sparrow is small. Yet, let one sparrow be snared, and its terror, its pain, is gigantic to All That Is. Because All That Is *is* that sparrow! The entire Universe, every part of All That Is, experiences, on some level, the terror and pain of that 'insignificant' sparrow, and feels unaccountable sadness as it physically dies. Conversely . . . "

He smiled at Merovee.

"Let one person laugh, and that laughter ripples out so that, soon, All That Is is laughing as well. Now. The Noachites . . . "

"But that is terrible!" cried Salome, leaping to her feet. "That is a horrendous imposition, a *crushing* burden!"

Jesus did not smile at her this time.

"Yes, Kitten. It is."

"You are saying that if I squash a bug, I kill God! That if I step on snow, I destroy God."

"All That Is, if you please."

"You are saying that my every action is in some way felt by the entire Universe. If I cry, God cries. If I laugh, God laughs. If I do wrong, I cause God to do wrong!"

"Aside from your choice of titles, you have seen the matter clear. That is what I said, it is what I meant, and it is the truth."

"But . . . " Salome ran distracted hands through her hair, her eyes wild. "That is not *fair*. It loads each of us down with such . . . responsibility!"

"It does indeed."

"We are, each one of us, representatives of . . . "

"All That Is, if you please."

"All right! All That Is!"

"Yes. You are."

"But . . . what should we do? How can we know which way to turn, how to act?"

"You begin by understanding that All That Is will accept whatever you chose to do. Whatever it is, it will be unique, done in a way that All That Is has never before experienced. So that, if you make a mistake—that is to say, if you do not make the 'best' choice in some circumstance—All That Is will not be angry with you. Disappointed perhaps—as many more learning experiences will have to be lived through until the mistake is *understood* to be a mistake—but not angry.

"Now though, knowing what you know, you can make your decisions more intelligently. You can recognize yourself as an emissary of All That Is and—knowing that All That Is reacts best to positive action—you can consciously choose positive action.

"You can, for instance, choose to be generous instead of stingy. You can give the world a smile instead of a frown. You can let that little bug go on about its business instead of squashing it. You can send greetings to the snow if you must step on it, sending your love and understanding along with it as it experiences being crushed and packed tightly, or as it experiences melting and changing to water.

"Would you believe me, Kitten, if I tell you that the snow will not forget? Somewhere, sometime, in this Universe or in others, you will again encounter the Consciousness that was in the snow. That

Consciousness will smile, and say, 'I remember you. I was being snow at the time, and you had to step on me. But you acknowledged me and sent me on my way with Love. Now what may I do for you?'"

Tears were streaming down Salome's cheeks.

"Oh, Jesus. I am not sure that I am glad that I came here tonight. The responsibility. My God!"

"My darling, your responsibility is only a little greater than it was when you arrived. If you think that Job had patience, it is as nothing compared to the patience of All That Is. The difference now is that you know the difference. Yes. 'Good,' 'positive' actions do affect the entire Universe. For the better. Negative actions affect it for the worse. And, yes, the poor choices *do* redound on you, in that, again and again, you will place yourself into positions where you must make similar decisions—and suffer the consequences—until you finally learn to choose the *positive* action.

"But the choice is always yours. All That Is advises, but never interferes. You have complete freedom of will, and All That Is will be patient through all of eternity if that is how long it takes your stubborn, little Self to figure it out."

"But All That Is is always *here. In* me. Spying! Right now, All That Is is listening inside me. Where is privacy? It is just not fair!"

"Your free will and the patience of All That Is are your privacies, Salome.

"Besides, there is a benefit to this situation that you are overlooking. You said before that the presence and participation of All That Is in you is an imposition. On the other hand, since All That Is is always *in* you, then no power on this Earth, or in any other world, can ever separate you *from* All That Is, or from its Love and *support.* You, the essence that is 'Salome,' can also never die. All That Is within you, that you think such an imposition, confers upon you immortality. You can never truly stray, never really get lost. All That Is will always be there, within your very footsteps, walking with you to the very ends of a world that had no beginning and will have no end. Is that not a fair trade, Salome?"

Great, dry sobs tugged at Salome's breast.

"It is a beautiful trade. It is just so overwhelming. Are you very, very sure, Jesus?"

"*I* am sure, yes. There is only one way for you to be sure, though, and that is to prove it to yourself. That will take a great deal of courage. It takes courage to make positive choices—negative choices always seem so much easier. It takes a towering *trust* in the basic goodness of the Universe, blind faith that a positive action will *automatically* produce a positive result. That sort of trust is hard to come by—almost impossible to develop when your intellect and all your senses, plus the 'physical' evidences around you, all say that the world is untrustworthy, that people are evil, and that positive action is foolhardy—even insane. To actually select the positive actions in the face of all this 'evidence,' to then observe the results and receive your own *private* proofs . . . ah.

"Overwhelming, you say? Terrifying is a better word. Terrifying to accept the fact that you are *totally responsible* for your own life, your own health, that you, yourself, create everything that happens to you.

"Most people will *not* accept the truth. They take to their heels, they find a nearby hole and crawl into it. They are simply not brave enough even to try to trust long enough to prove anything to themselves."

"But you will teach us how to trust?" said Salome quietly.

Jesus nodded. For a moment his eyes unfocused. Then he grinned.

"Yes. Sooner than any of you can imagine."

"And, when I die," said Salome, "'will I still stay Salome?'"

"Yes."

"I mean, will I *have* to stay Salome? You say I will be immortal. But I am suddenly thinking that being Salome for all eternity might get boring. I mean, I can think at this moment of a hundred different people I would like to try being."

Jesus laughed outright.

"You are, indeed, Merovee's Soul sister, you catch on fast, you imp. Yes, you will always be Salome and no, you will not always be Salome. 'Salome,' your essence, what you are now, is inviolate. It will never, ever, be forgotten, not by you, not by All That Is, neither, in simultaneous time, will it ever cease to exist. But The Energy that gave 'Salome' her existence will go on to other things, much as you have gone on from the seven-year-old that you once were. You can still remember that child. She is inviolate. But she is not you."

"I can see difficulties in all of this, Jesus."

"How so, Nathaniel?"

"As Salome said, the responsibility that this truth places on the shoulders of all who accept it is enormous. In my experience, Jesus, most people are not very keen on accepting responsibility, especially for themselves. I think a lot of people would turn on you if you told them what you have just told us."

"They will, Nathaniel."

A deadly quiet entered the voice of Jesus.

"But they have to be told. The seeds must be planted. Someone has to do it."

"When we listened at the vents, we heard you say that we are all to go out and teach to people. If we do, if we tell them those things . . . they might turn on us, too, might they not."

"If you go to them and tell them that they are immortal Spirits, particles of the true god, that they choose their own lives, their parents, their circumstances, build and maintain their own bodies with their own mental powers, create with those same mental powers each and every event which occurs in their lives, make themselves sick or keep themselves well, choose the hour and the manner of their own corporeal deaths, if you tell them that everything they have ever believed about the physical world is mistaken . . . yes. Many of them will turn on you. In their fury, in their terror at the responsibility that you place just where it belongs, squarely upon their individual shoulders, they will try to destroy you. They might even kill you."

Nathaniel nodded.

"I just wanted to get that straight."

"Does anyone wish to leave now?" said Jesus. "I will not take it amiss, I promise you."

"You might not, but what of us?" said Susannah. "You present us with a very definite choice, the most positive of actions according to you, or the most negative and cowardly. This is our chance to make good, to really prove things to ourselves, to make tremendous strides on an eternal scale."

Jesus looked at Merovee.

"Have you been coaching her?"

"I think that we have found another sister," said Merovee.

"My family grows more quickly than a racing frog covers ground," said Jesus.

He said it wryly. But he no longer looked old. His eyes sparkled, and there was a wonderful smile on his lips.

"I am very pleased with all of you. You gratify a teacher, you truly do."

He gestured, and Merovee handed him a bunch of grapes.

"Thank you, my dear. So," he continued, "I was going to tell you more about the Noachites. I insist upon finishing that general outline this evening, because they really are important to your further understanding. At first, in the millennium following the cataclysm, they included into themselves all who arrived by birth or by marriage. By the second millennium, however, their society had grown to enormous proportions. Leaders came and went, various attempts at organization and control were made. There were quarrels, splinter groups, even wars within this growing army of craftsmen. Generally, the eldest clan in direct line from the ancestor was considered paramount. This group guarded the 'secrets' of the science of building. They were the teachers, scribes, priests, and administrators to the 'God of the Fathers.' They made the rules, dispensed the justice, and assigned the junior 'provinces' of their wandering 'nation' to specializations and tasks.

"But, as is always the way, that which is secret becomes the target of those from whom the secret is withheld. By one means or another, over the centuries, the secrets of the dominant clans were gradually gotten away from them. The story of Noah's drunkenness, and of his 'nakedness' being seen by a traitorous son called Ham, is a case in point. It epitomizes the ways in which junior branches obtained information by stealth. It also signaled the end of the original significance of circumcision."

"What was that?" said Lazarus.

"Circumcision was, at first, a rite secretly performed only upon initiated males of the governing clan. A very ancient rite. To the Adamites, it was the 'mark of Cain,' that, when revealed, would keep people from killing him. That was so because, on seeing the 'mark,' other initiates could know that a stranger who came amongst them, claiming to be one of them, was telling the truth."

"Is that why Scripture says that one should not reveal one's nakedness to so much as an animal?" said Merovee.

"That was certainly the original intent. 'Ham' uncovered his 'father's' nakedness. 'He' obtained the secrets held by the ruling clan, including the sign of circumcision. Henceforth, he and his 'sons' would be circumcised as well, so that they could more easily spy out the secrets of the dominant elders.

"Gradually, then, circumcision came into such general use among the Builders that it no longer had any practical secret value. Gradually, the original reason for the mark was forgotten by all but a few, and the practice was carried forward as a 'demand' made by the 'God of the Fathers.'

"Ham, then, is symbolic of many who broke away from the original authority, who fanned out into the world and became the Builders of the cultures that you know, and who even traveled afar and built cultures of which you know nothing. Naturally, over the centuries, in the face of these defections, the old guard had to keep coming up with ways to protect its own interests. For that old guard had grown accustomed to power. And any group vested with power becomes jealous of that power."

"As the God of the Jews is jealous," said Deborah.

Jesus smiled ruefully.

"Exactly. In the main, Moses, the erroneous idea that Hebrews were essentially slaves in Egypt, the Exodus, the God of the Jews, and The Law were creations of the priesthood—one priest in particular, Ezra—and of the scribes, after the return from Babylon. Scraps of written or oral history were blended with bits and pieces of even more ancient information and writings, both of us Hebrews and acquired during the years in Babylon. The truth of much of this information was lost in the mists of time or understood by only a select few even when collected into what we now call the Five Books of Moses. Now, the writings are totally misunderstood, and daily distorted even further by the endless study and interpreting.

"And, as Deborah observed, in creating their 'God,' the priests made that god into the image of themselves. Jealous, restricting, Law-bound, ruthless, secretive, arbitrary, and consumed by a lust for power and glory."

He shook his head.

"Those poor 'sinners' of the Temple. How widely they miss the mark. Would that they would allow me to put my arms around them and guide their aim."

He held up a skeleton stem, stripped of grapes, and gazed at it as though it held some great truth.

"Those driven by ambition, and who lust for power, seldom stop to remember that they are mortal. Why do any of them do anything? Why did Alexander conquer half the known world? What good did it do him? He lived in a tent then died as easily as a poor desert dog. Why did Julius Caesar conquer half the known world, only to be cut down by his own friends like some pig at a Roman carnival? Why did he not forewarn himself with the fate of Alexander? What good did conquest do Caesar? Or Sargon, Darius, Cyrus . . . David.

"I will tell you what these men unconsciously strive for. Immortality. Which, translated, and in any language—is divinity. God-ship. They strive to lay such a lasting foundation that, for centuries afterward, Humankind will do their bidding, and, for millennia afterward, remember and honor them. To certain minds, that is god-ship, and immortality.

"The actual Moses was no different. Though, yes. He was. He was born into the royal house then current in Egypt—the story of the baby in a raft in rushes reflected a royal initiation ceremony practiced in many cultures of old. He was a royal heir who ran afoul of the politics of the time. And he was a genius. Greater than Alexander or Caesar could ever have been. At a certain point in time, the exploits of conquerors fade in importance and are finally of interest to none but historians. But what Moses did still affects every one of us on a daily basis. It will continue to affect us, and the whole world, for millennia to come.

"Moses was a great psychic, a master manipulator. The greater part of the 'Law of Moses' was, indeed, the work of the Jewish priests and scribes returning from Babylon. They were the ones who took the final step of placing absolute and irrevocable power into the hands of the priests. They were the ones who made the rules of the newly codified and regimented vehicle with which they meant to control and dominate a people, who made of that people, and that Law, a religion and a nation indistinguishable from one another. But the framework for theocracy was all there, latent, implied in what Moses had done.

"And he had made two moves of particular, consummate genius.

"The first move was the personification of and naming of 'God.' The second move was one cunningly guaranteed to perpetuate his memory. That was the creation of a hereditary priesthood, vested in the House of Aaron and backed up by a literal army, the Levite police . . . who were as dedicated as the priests to preserving that priesthood—and, automatically, memory of Moses.

"I know that this might be hard for you to believe, but Moses, with his Aaronites and Levites, and bands of both Hebrews and non-Hebrews which he managed to bring together, invaded a land that was already copiously peopled by various of their Hebrew 'brethren.' For, you see, the conquest of Canaan did not happen all at once. It was a gradual and sometimes peaceful thing, taking hundreds of years to fully accomplish."

"Oh, please!" said Susannah.

"Only believe me," smiled Jesus. "The Hebrews who found themselves invaded by the Moses peoples were already partially domesticated, having learned, from the Canaanites, agriculture, and the joys of permanent houses and towns. They knew nothing of this new, personified god who had been invented by Moses. They worshiped Baal and Astarte, as did their Canaanite neighbors. Some of them much preferred the settled life. Others were still Builders, who traveled to other lands when the call went out for Builders for this new project or that.

"Into the midst of these semi-settled tribes and clans came their largely Egyptian 'brethren,' led by the Aaronites and Levites, who wielded their new religion like a great club. Cheered on by their 'God'— in truth, the ruling hierarchy of the invaders—they invaded both their own kind and the indigenous Canaanites with equal ferocity, and proceeded to force their rule, religious and temporal, onto the vanquished. This they were able to do largely because, besides the religious structure bequeathed to them by Moses, they also had . . . The Secret. They carried this secret in an ark. Do you have a question, Salome?"

"No," she said, feigning disinterest.

Jesus laughed.

"With these 'weapons,'" he continued, "the Aaronites and Levites were not only gradually able to achieve dominance over the people of Canaan, they were even able to convince their silly new subjects that they, the Aaronites and Levites, should live at no cost to themselves, and in great luxury, supported by a portion of the people's wealth. Which, of course, made Aaronites and Levites, in perpetuity, the richest and most powerful classes in the nation.

"Returning to Moses, then, his genius had created a hereditary group whose very existence was bound up in the perpetuation of his edicts and of his memory . . . two classes which would lie, cheat, steal, kill, commit any deed necessary, to keep themselves in power.

"Implicit in their needs was a stationary nation. Farmers, not nomads—no more would they wander about in the wilderness—and carpenters, not Builders.

"But they did not have an easy time of it. The Noachite spirit is strong. It yearns to think, to create, to build and do. The body of a Noachite itches to move, to travel. Judges and Kings and Chronicles is full of hints as to the war that raged back and forth for close to a millennium after the invasion, between the priests of Aaron—who finally, under David and the tribe of Judah, situated themselves firmly in Jerusalem—between those priests of Jerusalem and dissident Hebrews who denied their authority, who still wished to travel and to build, who had grown attached to Astarte and Baal, and wished to continue to honor them alongside this Yahweh, the god of the 'Jews.'

" . . . which of course the priests of Jerusalem would not and could not tolerate. It had to be Yahweh and only Yahweh. Their entire claim to power and glory and financial support depended upon the oneness of Yahweh, and the destruction of rival gods and priesthoods.

"The exile of your Benjaminites, Deborah, is one example of this clash. The Benjaminites were among those who had arrived with the Moses invasion, but who grew to be devotees also of Baal and Astarte/Artemis, and also Asherah, another aspect of the Great Mother, who was worshiped by some as the consort of Yahweh. Benjaminites would not abandon their idolatrous, female-worshiping ways, and the persecution visited upon them drove them, first, out of their Judean lands, then out of Palestine, itself."

He smiled.

"Which was fortuitous for the rest of the world. For the Benjaminites scattered to Phoenicia and Greece primarily, but also to Italy, to Egypt, to Babylonia . . . and it is Benjaminite architects who have been largely responsible for the magnificent cities that one now sees in these places.

"Over the centuries, many from other tribes followed the lead of Benjamin and left as well—sometimes in large numbers, sometimes in small groups. Our priesthood would have us believe that all of us Hebrews have been united as a people since the days of Ibraham. Nothing could be further from the truth. There was no real cohesion, no real sense of being a nation, so that those who would not put up with the priests of Jerusalem often just left. Those who did stay were often rebellious, and inclined to gods other than Yahweh.

"Then came the Babylonian 'captivity.' There were actually two 'captivities,' first for some of the people of the northern state of Israel, then, about two hundred years later, for some of the people of the southern state of Judeah.

"Now remember, please, that almost everything that we know of either of these 'captivities,' or 'enslavements,' was written many years after the fact by priests who had a vested interest in obscuring the facts. Yes, there were invasions. Yes, many from Israel did go to Assyria, and later many from Judeah went to Babylon. But though some went under duress, many others went voluntarily, to take part in the vast building projects of the Assyrian kings, and later of King Nebuchadnezzar, who was rebuilding Babylon.

"The rebuilding of Babylon was a massive undertaking, one of the largest projects which had ever been attempted. Nebuchadnezzar needed, not only, the best Builders in the world, but, a great many of them.

"His chief architect was a man of the clan of 'Daniel,' a descendant of Benjaminites who had been forced out of Palestine over five hundred years before. This architect was quite a fellow, of the ilk of Moses, though the architect was a nicer man than Moses had been . . . "

"You do not seem to like Moses" said Deborah.

"I am sorry if I give that impression. I dislike no one. Perhaps I go too far in attempting to give you a realistic picture in comparison to the godlike picture that our Scripture paints for us.

"Moses was brilliant, ambitious, great, and unique. He was also a powerful psychic. He created a mental framework on which the world still builds and will continue to build. Personally, he was cold and withdrawn and unable to love, or even to like, his fellows. He had a vision and he made that vision happen, often with a ruthlessness that left me breathless. The Spirit that was 'Moses' had, of course, lived many times before and has lived many times since . . . always grappling with its personal lacks, and never quite conquering them."

He caught Merovee's eye.

"Moses and Elijah were manifestations of the same entity," he said softly.

At her intake of breath, he went on.

"So, as to the architect of Daniel, that man sent out a call to all his fellow Builders—to Greece, Egypt, Phoenicia, Anatolia, Cyrenia, Palestine, Italy—inviting them all to come and participate in the Builder's Banquet shortly to be served in Babylon. He was especially anxious to have the Palestinian contingent. Because they still had The Secret."

"I can not bear it!" cried Salome. "What in the world *is* this secret!"

"I thought you would never ask. Still, I am not going to tell you. Just yet."

"You really *do* have a mean streak!" cried Salome.

"It is no fun being nice *all* the time."

"You said before that the secret was housed in an ark," said Nathaniel. "Are you saying that this secret was housed in the Ark of the Covenant?"

"Exactly. Which ark supposedly now resides in the Holy of Holies in the Temple, and which supposedly contains *stone* tablets, graven with the 'Word of God.'

"Keep that in mind. Think about it. Stone. And with words written onto it by 'God.' How did 'God' so easily incise words into stone?

"Anyway, of course no one could examine what was in the ark except the High Priest, since it had been conveniently put abroad that anyone who touched the ark would be struck dead—convenient if a power structure wishes to keep curious hands off of a secret.

"And also a wonderful example of the sheep that people are, of the ease with which we allow the clever and ruthless among us to lie to us. For close to fifteen centuries, we have complacently taken the word of the High Priest as to what is in the ark . . . when, for that same period of time, it has been seldom that any except our High Priests could even officially lay eyes on the ark. Fifteen centuries of mindless sheep, baaing to be shorn.

"However, the Daniel architect knew what was in the ark. He knew because he was clan leader of the Daniel Benjaminites, and this was part of the secret knowledge that had automatically been passed to him.

"That is, he had been passed *general* knowledge of what was in the ark. Not the specifics. Those particulars were guarded by the Aaronites and their partners, the Kings of Judah. The architect wanted those particulars.

"For many years, Nebuchadnezzar had been harassing the Kings of Judah. A great many Palestinian Builders had responded to the call to work, heading, most of them voluntarily, some under duress, for Babylon. Just as, two hundred years earlier, many had, voluntarily or under duress, responded to the call of Sargon and other Assyrian kings. In each case, perhaps a quarter of the people went, mostly those who still had itchy hands and feet. But the Daniel architect was seriously intent on getting the formula from the ark."

"Formula?" said Lazarus.

"Yes, formula. And so, finally, the architect got Nebuchadnezzar to dispatch yet another army, this time specifically to get the ark and its contents. That army attacked Jerusalem and took the Temple. But the High Priest had hidden the ark, and he proved to be a stubborn and courageous man. No amount of persuasion could make him tell where it was hidden.

"King Jehoiakim, one of David's successors, but a puppet of Nebuchadnezzar's, was an easier target. As king, he knew the secret entrance into the hidden chamber beneath the Holy of Holies. Solomon, himself, had had the entrance built. It led from the king's own bedchamber. Jehoiakim accepted the wonderful gifts which Nebuchadnezzar begged to present to him, and led the Babylonians to the hiding place of the ark. The Babylonians then destroyed Solomon's Temple in order to discourage further use of that site and to encourage more of the Palestinian Builders to remove to Babylon. Jehoiakim also removed to Babylon, or Shinar as it was then called. He had not exactly planned to make the trip, the Babylonians insisted. He made the journey with 'part of the vessels of the house of God, which he carried to Shinar to the house of his god, and he brought vessels into the treasure house of his god.' I have never been able to understand why scribes feel compelled to repeat each bit of information at least twice, have you, Lazarus?

"Anyway, the ark got taken to Babylon. But the Aaronites who accompanied it still retained control. Because, even though the Babylonians now had the ark, and the stone that was in it, only Daniel and a few other chiefs were given the code that was needed to read this 'Word of God.'"

"Oh!" Merovee rose up onto her knees. "Does this have something to do with why Daniel and those others were put into the fire and thrown into the lions' den?"

"You see how it all makes sense once a few missing pieces are supplied," said Jesus.

"The Babylonians were trying to torture the secret of the stone out of them," said Merovee.

Jesus smiled.

"The attack of the 'wicked' Babylonians on the 'believers' in the 'God of Israel' takes on a different color, eh?

"Actually it was not that initial architect of Daniel, or any of his contemporaries, who were tortured for the secret. They were long dead. The tortures occurred during the reign of Cyrus, the first Persian king, so deified in Isaiah. Cyrus was determined to wrest the formula from the Jews once and for all. And the priests of Aaron did finally strike a bargain with this 'Messiah,' as Cyrus is called in Scripture. They would give him the formula if he would allow them to collect all the Hebrews that they could find, and return to Palestine. Cyrus even agreed to send troops to escort them home. For, by this time, not many of the people wanted to go. They had to be rounded up and escorted rather forcibly.

"Not only that, but the priests, with their bothersome rules and regulations, had been away from Judeah for seventy years. The people who had stayed behind had gone their own ways, to their own governments, their own gods. They were less than thrilled to see the priests return, and they offered not a little resistance. The troops of Cyrus helped the priests bring this ungrateful and ungodly rabble under control. Cyrus then, as part of the arrangement, even paid for the rebuilding of the Temple."

"But if they left the secret behind with Cyrus," said Lazarus, "what then is in the Holy of Holies?"

"The Ark of the Covenant. For appearances sake, the priests carried it back from Babylon. It is, however, empty."

"Empty?" Lazarus stared, dazed. "The ark in the Holy of Holies is *empty*? Then it is all a sham. The ceremonies of the priests are but one vast lie."

"They are. And have been for over four hundred years. *Any* priesthood is one vast lie, Lazarus. It cannot help but be. Priesthoods, like governments, bring out the worst in men, who make those institutions their careers and reasons for being and means of support and even riches. Interests become too vested. We will only be free of dishonest governments and corrupt priesthoods when, and as, each human being begins to accept total responsibility for his or her own self, and to demand that same honesty from those who presume to lead them.

"And now perhaps you can see why, when Aristobolus invaded Jerusalem a hundred years ago, and entered the Holy of Holies, he announced to the world that the God of the Jews was a golden ass. He opened the ark, found it empty, realized the trick that was being played upon the people, and was trying, in his own way, to tell them that they were being made asses of.

"But what difference does it really make, Lazarus, whether the ark is full or empty, when only the High Priest can enter the Holy of Holies, and then only once a year?"

"But . . . but . . ."

"Yes. But. It is as I said before. The people tend to focus upon the *outward physical circumstances and ceremonies* of any god, and not upon that god's *message*. The priests who carried an empty ark back from Babylon were well aware of that principle. They knew that, if the people ever learned that they were being asked to worship an empty ark, they, the priests, would be finished, and, with them, 'God.'

"Which is one of the reasons why they decided to miraculously find five books—that Moses had supposedly written a thousand years before—which books had been mysteriously hidden away during all that time in some still undisclosed vault under a temple that had not been there until about five hundred years after Moses lived—and that had then been totally destroyed.

"And people wonder at *my* miracles.

"It was genius. Sheer genius. It was, in fact, a new religion. They gave to the people who had been dragged back from Babylon—and to the belligerent population that had never left—a proud and dramatic new history, a new focus and reason for unity. Until then, the focus of all worship had been the Ark of the Covenant, supposedly containing the 'Commandments of God.' That ark was still there, in a new Holy of Holies.

"But now the people were given a focus that channeled their every thought and movement into worship of a different sort. The Five Books of Moses. Torah. The Law, accessible to all Hebrew males."

"I do not quite understand," said Merovee. "Do you mean that, before that time, there had been no Scripture?"

"Not as we know it, no. There had been writings and verbal traditions aplenty. But these things had been the property of the chief priests and scribes, to be read and discussed only by them. Never before had the *people* been given access to these 'sacred' things.

"Now, suddenly, they were given that access. They were invited to *read*, and *discuss*, the very 'words of Moses' for *themselves*.

"And so, what if the common man was still forbidden to so much as see the ark? What if he could never hope to so much as set a sandal inside the Holy of Holies? He suddenly had something better! The words of Moses, presented in such a way as to be his own personal property, there to be read, studied, discussed, interpreted, embroidered upon. Not only that, but he was now led to understand that he must focus his entire life on the study, and adherence to, The Law contained in those five books. Indeed, those who refused these sudden new religious 'duties' were cast out. As 'sinners,' some were even stoned to death.

"With this stunning stroke, the Temple seized absolute and total control over an entire people. They turned a polyglot of expansive, outward-searching creators into a nation of rigid, myopic slaves to the perpetuation of the 'God of the Jews,' and, incidentally, to 'his' Temple and the rulers thereof.

"Talk to any Sadducee, or to a Pharisee if you can get him to stop praying long enough. Ask him about Torah. He will talk the ears right off of your head. Ask him about the ark and the Holy of Holies. He will shrug.

"Because the ark in its Holy of Holies really does not matter anymore.

"He would not admit that. Not to you, least of all to himself. But every Hebrew male now has his Torah, and, after that, our Chameleon-like Oral Law. If he does not have the wealth and social position that would allow him to be a Sadducee, he can be a Pharisee.

"Before the people had Torah, anyone who was not a priest, scribe, Levite, of royalty or extremely rich, was *nothing*. Now *any* man, by applying himself to unending study of Torah, to mind-bending interpretations of Oral Law, and to the devising of ever more scrupulous ways in which to obey the 'Law of God,' can be *great*. People listen to him with respect. They bow to him on the street, look how holy he is. He gets the best and highest seat in synagogue. *He* dictates the new rules, and his fellows had better obey them or else.

"He does not have to do work of any kind, he leaves all that to his chief slave, his wife. Ask my mother about that, she will be happy to give you a short five-hour lecture on the subject. If he is not yet married, he still does not have to do any work. All he has to do is to be a student studying Torah and the populace must support him.

"*Any* man can finally be equal with a priest—holy, privileged, a man of leisure, and with *power*.

"At least so he thinks, not noticing that the rulers of the Temple giggle behind their hands.

"With all his 'power,' the Pharisee or Sadducee does not notice that he has given his life, his Self, up to playing the Temple's game."

"I am so glad," said Deborah, "that my new son is not a revolutionary."

Jesus smiled.

"You are accustomed to dangerous living, New Mother."

"I had hoped to retire from the ranks of the brave in my old age."

"As a man with a fine eye, I can tell you, Deborah, that your old age is not yet upon you. Besides, being brave is a habit that cannot be broken once acquired. Lazarus, are you all right?"

Lazarus shrugged, his eyes dull.

"You have pulled my whole world out from beneath me, that is all. Everything. Everything that our priests have told us, everything that I have been caused to believe during my whole life. Lies. All lies."

"When dealing with governments or priesthoods," said Jesus gently, "it is best to believe yourself in luck if one item in each hundred presented to you has even a faint whiff of truth. As to history . . . that is always written by those in power who have a need to present things in a certain way in order to maintain their power.

"Actually, Lazarus, knowing this can be a great deal of fun. Suddenly, one can watch the priests and the leaders going about their machinations . . . and one can laugh at their antics, and marvel at their endless creativity. It is truth that sets you free, Lazarus, not blind adherence to the lies of others."

Lazarus nodded. But he turned his head away.

Merovee put an arm around his shoulders.

"Talk about something else, Josh. Tell us more about the Noachites. What did they build? Where? And what was this secret that they kept in the ark?"

"Well, the Noachites from whom we genetically descend are combinations of the Adamite tribes of Seth and Cain, and then of Imenhotep."

"Imenhotep!" cried Merovee.

Even Lazarus perked up.

"Is he not an Egyptian god?"

"He was an architect whom the Egyptians revere as a god, yes. We will get to him later. But to give you a clue, is there not something suggestive in his name?"

"I-men-ho-tep," said Deborah.

"Play with just the 'Imen.'"

There was silence.

"It sounds a bit like Ibram," said Lazarus finally.

"It does indeed," smiled Jesus. "Ibram, you will all remember, was the name of Ibraham before 'God' changed it. Now, the Adamite tribe of Seth was first situated north of Assyria around the Caspian Sea. It migrated south to the area that is now the Chaldees, while the tribe of Cain migrated westward from Elam. Both tribes were Aryan and of the noble class, and they joined forces. You will note the reference in Genesis to the effect that, in the days of Seth's son, men began to 'call upon the Lord.' The name of that son was Enoch. He who, Genesis tells us, was taken up to Heaven without dying."

"Were you?" said Merovee.

"Yes and no, depending on your definition of the words Heaven and dying. Now, the life and ministry of the historical Enoch . . . "

"Ministry?" said Nathaniel.

"Exactly. But that life and ministry is of no particular value to this discussion except to say that most of what Enoch taught his people was misunderstood, distorted, and perverted by them after his departure from this planet Earth. His name was applied, however, to the amalgamation of Seth and Cain. 'Enoch' was the first confederation of what would, after the 'flood,' become the Builders.

"The 'Lord' that this confederation began to call upon was not the lord that Enoch had tried to tell them about. The 'Lord' that they called upon was the rule of their own order, the trade and guild hierarchy with the eldest chieftains in control. Their god concept—a god that could be neither seen nor physically expressed, was the ancient Aryan concept. Enoch attempted to tell them of All That Is, but they retained very few of his teachings, and they also clung to the unfortunate Aryan habit of sacrificing small animals and occasional people for the invisible enjoyment of their invisible god. We have now, in this day and age, finally dispensed with the sacrifice of humans—officially, that is. Little animals continue to suffer at our hands.

"Now. Before the 'flood,' most buildings were of sun-dried brick and a great deal of wood . . . for this was many thousands of years ago remember, and the land from Iran to Egypt and Palestine was still verdant, with magnificent forests. During this period, the Adamite 'Enochians' achieved an excellence in joining and carving of wood, and also began to dabble in the decorative uses of metal, tile, and stone. Very little could be found today of these early buildings, for wood and mud bricks deteriorate with time.

"Even less could be found of the period just after the 'flood,' for the climate changed, many of the forests dried, the desert began to take over, and building was done almost exclusively of mud brick. In the Chaldees, almost no stone suitable for building occurred naturally. Assyria had only a bit more, marble and limestone mostly, good only for use in facing and flooring, and for statuary and bas-reliefs, but not for basic structure. A certain amount of wood could be brought down the Euphrates from Anatolia, where forests still flourished, but the transport of stone over that long a distance was out of the question.

"This was also true in Egypt, by the way. From the Nile to the Chaldees, palaces and cities of enormous size and great beauty were constructed, but always in perishable, mud-dried brick. These structures had to be rebuilt periodically or else abandoned completely, left to crumble into heaps good for nothing but goats to climb on. In Egypt, the yearly flooding exacerbated the problem.

"Then, one day, shortly after the 'flood,' someone invented the kiln-baked brick."

"Yes!" said Merovee. "Genesis comes right out and tells us that that is why they decided to build the Tower of Babel. They could build much higher with fired bricks."

Jesus smiled.

"All right. And was there really a Tower of Babel?"

Merovee thought, then smiled back.

"Oh we know that there were towers aplenty in ancient Mesopotamia, and some were very high. But probably the tower mentioned in the first book of Torah is symbolic of a major event in the history of these Builders."

Jesus nodded his satisfaction.

"As far as that history is concerned, it is the true dividing line between Adamite and Noachite, and the real beginning of our present experiment. In whose lifetime does that first Book of Moses say that the 'Earth was divided'?"

"In the lifetime of Peleg," said Lazarus.

"Then Peleg is our man. Or rather our sub-dynasty. He is listed as a mere descendant of Noah, but his group, along with that of his 'brother' 'Joktan,' was of primary importance. Theirs was the amalgamation that invented the kiln-baked brick. They came shortly before a millennium . . . hmm? Always look for that millennium. It was also at the turn of a double millennium which began a new, six-thousand-year cycle. Four thousand years ago.

"With their revolutionary invention, Noachites could now construct buildings to a height that had never before been possible, using much thinner walls, and incorporating delicacy of design. The refinements and possibilities were endless, and the results were relatively lasting.

"The Mesopotamian world went literally mad in a collective frenzy to build, build, build. Cities, palaces, temples, public works—the frenzy spread, as rulers vied to outdo their predecessors and contemporaries. The demand for master Builders grew, the competition for their services became intense, and the rewards and prestige accorded to those Builders grew apace with the demand. Builders scurried here and there, hither and yon, in relays and segments. Those who laid foundations would move on to the next job the moment that their part of the work was complete, then those who raised the walls would move in, and then on to the next job when they were finished. And so on. So that the finest craftsmen in the fashioning or painting or carving of wood or stones and metals, those who finished off the interiors with the grandeur demanded by kings, were always the last to arrive and the last to leave. Never a moment was lost. No guild was ever idle.

"Especially rewarded were the chiefs, the *architects* of Noah, those who held the secrets of each guild, who controlled and directed the others. And, over all, as I told you, there was a supreme director—

186

the eldest group in descent from the ancestor. It was at this time that the 'avelum,' those privileged 'Sons of Man' that I told you about—whose rights equaled those of kings—made their appearance in Mesopotamian law. I am sure you can guess who the 'avelum' were. And you might, by the way, be beginning to understand why family genealogies have always been paramount to us as a people.

"With the passing of centuries, of course, Noah became less and less of a homogeneous organization. *Creativity cannot be contained*, no matter how assiduously rulers seek to contain it. Gradually, Noah split and splintered until there were hundreds of rival bands traveling the world, building in ever more far-flung lands after having been initially forced out of Mesopotamia by the more powerful tribes—or departed of their own accord. Most of these bands were large enough to be called nations, and these fringe nations fought tooth and nail for available work contracts, stealing techniques and master craftsmen from competitors whenever the chance arose. Competition for the available work was a matter of life and death, you see. The reputation of the head man—usually the architect—was often what decided the employment or the life-long poverty of thousands . . . for the contract to build an entire city could occupy a whole generation.

"And perhaps you can also understand now why the first book of Moses says that the world was divided, and why, with the building of the 'Tower of Babel'—the first use of kiln-dried brick—'God' directed the confusion of tongues."

"What had been essentially one nation to that point split into many," said Nathaniel, "and each began to speak a different tongue, for each invented its own codes and symbols to protect its secrets."

"Exactly," said Jesus. "Before that time, Noah had indeed spoken with one language, with one head and with a uniform set of secrets and symbols. The tribes of Peleg and Joktan, after demonstrating the height to which buildings could rise with kiln-fired bricks, broke away from Noah, hoping to keep the secret of fire-kilning to themselves. The 'God,' then, who ordered the beginning of the confusion between these people, was the supreme council of the Noah amalgamation. For that is exactly what the word that has come down to us as 'God' meant in those days. 'God' was the supreme leadership of the Builders. Nothing more."

"Which is why," said Merovee, "when the people of Heth called Ibraham a Prince of God, they meant something much different than we suppose today."

"They meant specifically that he was a supreme chieftain of the foremost nation of Builders. Only gradually, as those chieftains used the people's Idea of deity for their own ends—to frighten people and to control them—did *deity* become interchangeable with that leadership, and with the word for that leadership."

He smiled.

"So you see then, when the Romans invest their Caesar with divinity, they are only extending this confusion to its logical conclusion.

"Now . . . at a certain point, Noah's genealogy ends and we find ourselves figuring descent from Ibraham. This is for very good reason. At the end of a millennium nodule, some twenty-eight hundred years ago—much longer ago than Scripture leads us to believe—the dynasty of Ibram, later to be known as Ibraham, began to take the lead in building away from the Mesopotamian Noachites. As Peleg and Joktan had changed the face of Mesopotamia with their baked bricks, the clan of 'Terah,' whose men were the experts in stone—in carving, cutting, flooring, facing, and inlay—were, after a chance discovery, preparing to again change the face of the world. The chiefs of Terah understood the potential of their discovery very well, and they were not about to give their secret to the supreme tribal leaders. They preferred to take themselves to a more remote place, where there was plenty of stone, where they could get some work, but where they could also experiment in relative privacy.

"The entire clan of Terah, then, many thousand strong, defected. Extra stone masons were needed up at the head of the Euphrates near the present Carchemish. The first Elamite kings were building themselves several cities. A nation of Builders called 'Harran' had the contract, but not enough manpower. Terah sub-contracted itself to Harran and went to work. Several generations had passed before the elders of Harran began to realize that Terah was doing ever more astounding things with stone. Terah must, they then realized, be in possession of a very important secret. Harran determined to get it for themselves. By force if necessary."

"Which is when Ibram was suddenly advised to leave the land of his 'fathers,'" said Lazarus.

"Exactly. Ibram was the most senior branch of Terah. Its leader at that time was an architect of great vision. In order to preserve the secret, he and his people smashed all the work then in progress in their studios. The leader was hauled up for trial, but managed to escape and to leave the area. By prearrangement, in stages, most of Terah slipped away as well and joined him—and they set off with their secret.

"They were destined to become the rulers of the most powerful confederation of Builders that the world has ever known. So great that its name changed from Ibram, clan leader, to Ibraham, leader of a multitude of nations."

"I am beginning to understand," said Merovee, "why the King of Elam later captured 'Lot.' And why Ibraham went to such extremes to get 'him' back."

"And you say they were stone masons," said Salome. "Is that why stones play such a large part in their story? They were always setting up pillars of stone, and altars of stone, and then there was Jacob's pillow of stone."

"Yes! What a strange pillow," smiled Jesus. "Have none of you ever wondered why Jacob—who, after sleeping on that strange pillow, becomes Israel—chose such a hard substance upon which to lay his head?"

"I know that some people prefer those dreadful wooden head-rests," said Salome, "but I much prefer something softer."

She tilted her head. Her eyes narrowed.

"Softness. The softening of stone. Soft enough to be a pillow . . . I have it! The Secret. The Secret is the *Samir*!"

"Quiet," laughed Jesus, "you are getting ahead of things."

"It is, it is! Just tell me that it is and I will be silent."

"It is. So hush."

"What is the Samir?" said Merovee.

Jesus ignored her.

"Terah's initial discovery and the refinements made by the clan during several generations of experimentation in 'Harran,' changed the face of building. A guild that had been minor, good only for putting on finishing touches and ornamentation, could now take the fore and crack the whip over all the others.

"And it was at this point that the incest that we mentioned earlier became the law of the inner circle, so desperate was the need to keep The Secret to themselves.

"After escaping 'Harran' and reassembling, Ibram headed south. Now, you must realize that, in the story of Ibraham, Scripture compresses events that actually took hundreds upon hundreds of years to transpire, and the adventures of many men, into the supposed lifetime of one supposed man. There was an actual Ibraham. In fact, among his descendents, there were many Ibrahams. It will do us no good to try to discern just which was which Ibraham, or whether chronologies are correct. It is the first Ibram/ Ibraham who is the most interesting.

"We are told that, after escaping Harran, the clan built temple complexes for the Canaanites of Sechem and of Beth El—each probably only a year's work with the new technique, but temples such as the world had not yet seen. An Egyptian Pharaoh named Djoser heard of their activities and invited Ibram to come to Egypt. Djoser was, himself, of Noachite consciousness, and he wanted to build himself a very special city. He recognized, in the reports of these Canaanite temples, exactly what he was looking for.

"Once in Egypt, the architect of Ibram was taken straight into the royal house. In a move to insure brotherhood, Djoser took the architect's sister/wife as his own wife, and gave the man one of his own sisters."

"Was the name of Djoser's sister Hagar by any chance?" said Deborah.

"Hagar is a corruption of the sister's name. Djoser virtually opened his treasury to the architect, and, together, they embarked on the most astounding building project that that era had witnessed."

'The pyramids!" cried Merovee. "Are you saying that *we* built the pyramids?"

"Through the genius of the man that the Egyptians call Imenhotep, yes. Of course that man was dead by the time of the actual construction of the largest pyramids, but his were the calculations—and his was The Secret—that made them possible."

"Then Imenhotep and Ibraham are one and the same man?" said Merovee.

"Ibraham, by whose seed 'God' promised to *build mighty nations*, by whose seed all the nations of the world would be blessed. Ibraham, whose clan had, among other amazing things, discovered how to use stone in a monumental way, how to move stones weighing many tons each, and yet to fit those stones together with such precision that the seams could hardly be found. The same man who, says Scripture, went to Egypt, whose wife-sister became the wife of Pharaoh, the man who Pharaoh so richly rewarded. The man who, in Egyptian records, was Egyptian, the great architect who built the pyramid and the great stone city for the Pharaoh Djoser at Sakkarah. Yes. These two records speak of one and the same man.

"Neither view of him is correct, but the point is that this leader of Ibram was a genius who, with the aid of a great benefactor, catapulted the world into the age of monumental building with stone. And, for the next millennium or so, everyone was kept busy trying to get that ultimate Secret away from Ibraham. For, after the kings of the world learned what the Ibram-Djoser builders had done at Sakkarah, they would have no builders but Ibraham, so that Ibraham had really an unfair monopoly on *all* building."

"Now I have some more word games for you. I told you before, in regard to the name Imenhotep, to think only of Imen, and you recognized Ibram. What if I now tell you to think only of hotep—or otep."

There was a moment of silence.

"Joseph!" cried Salome.

"And what of the name Djoser?"

"Joseph, again," said Deborah.

"Pronounce Ibram-Djoser or Ibram-Joseph quickly."

"Both are somewhat like Imen-hotep."

"Now think of the story of Joseph."

"His brothers were jealous," said Salome thoughtfully, "because he was . . . oh, their *father's* favorite. They threw him into a well, but he got pulled out and taken to Egypt, and he became a great man, one of Pharaoh's favorites. And he was such a good man that, when he met his brothers again years later, he forgave them and made them his brothers again and gave them many gifts."

"This is a lovely example of how traditions become confused over the centuries, of how bits of this and pieces of that get jumbled together or separated completely. *Part* of the story of Joseph, and *part* of the story of Ibraham, tell of the same man and same events. In Genesis, Ibraham was advised to get out of his own country. To find out why, one has to skip over to Joseph, to the jealousy of the 'brothers'—who were really the rival clans of Harran."

"Harran!" cried Merovee suddenly. "*Aaron!*"

The jaw of Jesus dropped.

"You know, I think you are right."

"You mean that I figured something out ahead of you?"

"Do not make a habit of it, I have a reputation to maintain."

He rose, and began exuberantly to pace.

"Yes! Wonderful find, Merovee! It makes perfect sense all of a sudden. *That* is why Aaron was called the brother of Moses. I never could figure out where 'Aaron' had come from, how the group had become so powerful as to be the leading Josephite clan at the time of the departure from Egypt . . . why that clan was given the supreme prize, the priesthood. But the story of the brothers of Joseph coming down to Egypt, being welcomed by Joseph and deciding to remain, must be the symbolic statement of another amalgamation of Builders. When Harran found out where Ibram had gone to, they came to Egypt and subjected themselves to that group. They became second in command and formed a building nation that was essentially Egyptian-based as opposed to those operating out of Mesopotamia."

"Yes. Of course. The 'Ibram-Djoser Imen-hotep' Builders had power. But they also needed numbers, and craftsmen skilled in work other than stone."

He halted.

"You know," he said thoughtfully, "they might even have *sent* to Harran and invited their 'brothers' to come and join them."

"Yes!" said Merovee. "That would be one symbolic significance behind the story of the embassy of Ibram's servant to Harran to get a 'bride' for Ibram's 'son' Isaac from out of his 'brother's' family."

Jesus nodded.

"Exactly. I see it now. A 'marriage' occurred between the Ibramites of Egypt and the clans of Harran, or Aaron. Aaron got hereditary second place in the new federation."

Nathaniel had risen as well.

"Do you think, then, that the story of Jacob's sojourn with his father's relatives back in Mesopotamia, the years that he had to spend there, and the two 'daughters' that he was obliged to take to wife, indicates a rebellious branch striking off on its own and joining forces with allied clans in Mesopotamia?"

"And when," offered Lazarus, "that new nation of 'Jacob' finally returned to Egypt, it was greeted with open arms by 'Esau,' the current leader or heir of the Egyptian Ibrahamites! 'Jacob' then, by some dishonesty or trickery, wrested the leadership away from 'Esau.'"

"Perfect," said Jesus. "And now we can see why the name Jacob was changed to Israel . . . 'he supplanted,' or 'deceiver' was changed to 'may God prevail,' or 'Prince of God,' depending on what translation you accept. Yes. This indicated a rebellion against 'God.' Against the ruling hierarchy. We are told right out that Jacob wrestled with God. Jacob prevailed and, *'himself,'* became God—that is, the supreme leader of Ibraham."

He hugged Nathaniel and flopped back down onto the bed.

"Ah, it is fascinating. I never tire of mental sleuthing. Each new puzzle piece found is a treasure to me . . . a deepening of my understanding of Humankind's enormous mental creativity . . . and so a deepening understanding of my own Self."

He seemed at that moment as a young boy, excited over the gift of a new ball.

"And the thing I have discovered is that large periods of time, groups of millenia, make as much, or as little, sense as any one lifetime if one can free oneself from myopia and regard these vast stretches of time as a sort of mega-lifetime—of a people, not just of one person. Which, actually, those who wrote the Five Books of Moses did.

"Even more fascinating is that the major symbols unconsciously chosen by the people as a whole, and left as a record for later generations, will tell a beautifully cohesive tale. People living one thousand years separated from one another in 'time' will unfailingly use symbology, use words, have ideas, record events, which validate the story and add to it."

"But," said Deborah, "these symbolic levels that you speak of . . . are they not consciously known to the scribes and priests and leaders who keep the tales? Do they not know that they speak symbolically?"

"Only the greatest of them would have any grasp of overall significances. For the most part, they speak in such apt symbols despite themselves. It is the deep knowledge of the species forcing itself to the surface. They do not even know that they possess such knowledge, or that their deeper selves possess an underlying greatness of purpose. Certainly, if they are falsifying or twisting information for some immediate political gain, they do not imagine themselves to be performing any noble, cosmic deed.

"Yet they are. You see, each of our separate eras is as a breath that takes, on average, three score and ten, while, right along beside us, is what seems a silence, but is actually the greater breath in which we exist, that takes many millennia to 'happen,' instead of our puny span. Yet, in each one of our little breaths, one can sense that mega-breath if only one trusts that it is there."

He sat forward, eyes shining.

"In India, artisans do a wonderful thing. They take a big chunk of ivory and carve it so that it is beautiful to see, shaped like a ball, but all cut out into a wonderful tracery. Within that ball they then carve yet another ball, seeming to be just the same as the first, completely detached from the first. Within that second they carve yet another. Then another. In Benares, I saw a ball into which one could look and count one hundred more, smaller and smaller and smaller, until the eye could hardly see the last. Yet that, too, had been carved as lovingly as the first.

"We who reside in this system of reality called Earth are not as that smallest ball. There are worlds far tinier—in Spirit and in Intent—than our own, to whom one of *our* breaths would seem to take six thousand years.

"But neither are we the largest. There are systems of reality so vast in Spirit and Intent that they could not be understood or even glimpsed by us.

"Yet we should at least begin to accept that they are there. We should make ourselves as alert as possible to hints of these unending worlds which surround us—cradle us—within themselves, while also letting us ride free, like each one of those balls, so that we often think that we are the only ones in the Universe."

"And now," said Lazarus thoughtfully, "I see that, metaphorically, one of the balls which encircles us Hebrews so invisibly is Egypt. Again and again, Scripture connects us with that place, but never did I realize that our roots are as much Egyptian as they are Mesopotamian."

"Moses and the patriarchs had to be made to appear thoroughly Hebrew. Those who wrote the history of Moses, and codified 'his' Law into the form that we know today, had to cleanse him of any Egyptian taint.

"The religion that the priests invented—created out of bits and pieces of the past—had to appear to be ancient. It had to seem that we Hebrews had, since the day of the first Creation, worshiped essentially one god—this despite constant references to the God of Ibrahim, the God of Jacob, and so on. 'God' had to seem to have been one and the same throughout, and we had to seem an unbroken continuity of Chosen People, born, each one of us, to do nothing on this Earth but worship that god.

"Could the priests tell us that originally we were not Hebrews at all, but Aryans of Noachite consciousness, come down from the north and out of the east, who then mixed with the peoples that we found in Iran, and Mesopotamia, and Syria, and Canaan, and Midian, and the Sinai, and Egypt?

"Could the priests tell us that our sacred language is a soup made from the hundred languages with which we have come into contact?

"Could they tell us that the Law of Moses is a similar soup, filled with ingredients picked up over millennia from dozens of cultures, not the least of which is Egyptian?

"Could they tell us that they borrowed the stories of the Creation and of Noah's flood from the Babylonians, who had borrowed them from the Assyrians, who had borrowed them from the Elamites and Sumerians?

"And here, by the way, was wonderfully manifested that unconscious knowledge, that finds its way into symbology and makes one cohesive 'piece' out of vast periods of time. Because the Elamites, from whose records some of these legends were borrowed, were part of our own original Aryan stock."

"Then," said Nathaniel, "the stories that the priests used for the Creation were our own ancient legends?"

"I would say 'quite by accident,' except that, as I will tell you repeatedly, there is no such thing as an accident, neither is there coincidence. Anything that seems to be accident or coincidence is actually *deep unconscious understanding of the true nature of an event manifesting itself.* It is, if you will, that 'larger breath,' quietly working out its own course alongside our own.

"Rather a good joke on the scribe, who thought he was lying and cheating, no? And a lovely example of the way in which All That Is, that can see beyond the horizon, turns our most shameful actions to good account. That secret knowledge in each of us, that true god, that innate goodness of which, I promise you, Man *is* composed, is always seen to be triumphant if one will only leave the valley and climb up onto the mountain for a wider view.

"Could those priests and scribes of five hundred years ago, desperately seeking to unite a people, *needing* power, needing support from the nation that they were forging—for their own personal and family glory, yes, but forging no less—could they have told their people that their greatness had once made them kings of the world? In lands that they hardly knew of, north of the Caspian and of the Caucasus, and in Susa of Elam, in Shinar and Ninevah and Ur, in Harran, in Canaan, in Midian, in all the lands bordering the Mediterranean, in Egypt? Even if they, the priests themselves, had really understood it? Could they have told the people?

"No. They could not and would not have told the people. They needed a populace grateful to 'God' for saving them from supposed bondage, not a people resentful of that god for having sheared them of greatness as Delilah supposedly sheared Samson . . . a god who now refused to them even the simplest of creative outlets."

"The commandment against graven images," said Deborah. "That was the crux of the whole thing, was it not. I see their plan now, those priests. They needed to stop the Spirit of the Builders dead in its tracks. By refusing us the right to make representations of anything, either in Heaven or here on the planet Earth or in its waters, they effectively put our creativity into a jug and bunged it tight. The only creativity that has been allowed us for five hundred years has been the building of the last two Temples, the construction of synagogues, and the interpretation of Scripture."

"Is that, then," said Lazarus, "why Solomon was so free with representational art in his temple? And why the Ark of the Covenant is decorated with wonderful angels? Was there, quite literally, no commandment against the making of images until five hundred years ago?"

"Not as we know it, no. Until that time, Hebrews were forbidden only to make images of their god, in whatever guise they understood him. The men who negotiated the return from Babylon and 'discovered' the 'Books of Moses' in the Temple—a priest named Ezra in particular—were among the greatest geniuses of all time . . . the true patriarchs to the 'children of Israel.' They created a unique system, a male culture, a *nation of priests*, convinced that their purpose was not as that of any others on Earth, convinced that their only function was to worship."

"Note that I say worship, not 'pray.' There is a vast difference."

"Well," said Nathaniel, "we were also supposed to marry and have children."

Jesus nodded.

"To ensure a constant supply of worshipers. Which is why we are enjoined, in both the Creation and Noah stories, to 'multiply and be fruitful.' Organized religions, and governments, need populations to control and govern. The controlled and governed must therefore have many children . . . even if the parents cannot feed those children. Religions and governments also make sure that the controlled and governed teach their children what those religions and governments declare to be 'The Truth.' That is self preservation. For, without worshipers to worship and pay tithes and make offerings, and people to be governed and pay taxes . . . well, priests and governors and Caesars would have to find other ways to bilk the people of the fruits of their labor, and to live their lives of ease."

Nathaniel grunted.

"We also produce food," he muttered defensively.

Lazarus laughed.

"Enough to keep us from falling into dead faints as we worship."

"And of course," said Susannah archly, "it is the women who have to cook the food. Indeed, it is the women who do most of the work in this country if truth be told, while their men-folk amuse themselves in the synagogues."

Jesus studied them for a few moments and then continued as through they had not spoken.

"The people could not be told that their history was intricately entwined with that of Egyptian aristocracy, including the Hyksos who ruled Egypt for centuries. They could not be told that wandering bands of workmen sometimes called Hapiru were also a part of their history. They could not be told that much of the world now looks at the great works wrought by their ancestors and says that they were built by an Assyrian queen named Semiramis, who was the daughter of a fish goddess, and who ascended into heaven in the form of a dove. They could not be told any of these wonderful things. They had to be made to believe that they were one people, descended from one man, a simple shepherd, just one simple family that had remained intact and could trace its lineage from the first day of the world, that they had always had one god, one Law—that they had transgressed and offended repeatedly, of course, but still one Law, one god. They had to be made to believe that they had always been unique, always set apart, chosen by this god from the very beginning.

"And, again, we encounter that greater breath, that greater subconscious knowledge, surfaced in the twisted teaching of an ambitious priesthood. Because many of these things were true! They did descend from a people, the ancient Aryans, who believed in one god that could not be described or fully represented with any idol or statue or work of art. That original concept had been the one originally used by the ruling clan, and the very secrecy and exclusiveness of the ruling clan had preserved the concept with a purity unknown by any others of Aryan descent.

"They *could* trace lineage with great accuracy. The clans had always had to prove their lineage, and so their right to a place in the hierarchy.

"They *had* always had their own Law, peculiar to their own purposes and often different from the laws of the countries to which they traveled to work. Among those peculiar Laws were those to do with food and cleanliness, for, in traveling from country to country, one comes across oddities of diet and standards of cleanliness that are sometimes appalling, so that it is best, if only for the sake of digestion, to keep to a simple and predictable regimen.

"Last, but not least, they *were* unique, and they *had* been chosen. Noachites, whether Hebrew or otherwise, were and are, in truth, the current spearhead of the species, almost a new species of Humankind, the motivating consciousness of a brand new experiment, chosen subconsciously by the species, elected to formulate and embody the new rules and activities, to lead the way, blaze the paths."

"You keep speaking of a new experiment," said Susannah. "What is the experiment? Why is it so different from anything that went before?"

"The experiment is, quite simply, total fixation with, blind emphasis on, the manipulation of physical reality.

"Some of you look blank. You cannot imagine a world without physical reality. Without objects. Without physical impediments, without physical processes which must be observed before anything can be 'accomplished.' You believe that, to get to the central court of this house, you must first rise, walk across the room, open a door, cross a threshold, and walk into that court. It does not seem possible that you could walk straight through the wall, or yet that you could remain sitting here and send just your mind through either the door or the wall into the courtyard. It seems to you that, if you wish to communicate, you must open your mouths and speak, or at least make signs or motions with your bodies.

"It does not occur to you that you could have a conversation here in this room by thinking thoughts to each other. Even less does it seem to you that you could think a thought to a relative in Bethlehem, have it heard, and receive an immediate reply.

"It does not occur to you that you could fly, or walk across water, or be seen by that relative in Bethlehem while you yet sit in this room.

"Oh, you might entertain the idea that oracles, or seers, or prophets could do some of these things, or perhaps magicians, or sorcerers, those given power by some Prince of Darkness. But you would not consider yourself capable of these things.

"Yet I say to you, that, not only is the ability to do these things inherent within you, but, that it is your natural state. These things are more representative of the way that the Universe 'really' is than are the physical manipulations, and shackles, to which you are currently accustomed. Your dreams are even more real than are you right now at this moment.

"But that is the difference of this experiment. Before the cataclysm, that you think of as the flood, consciousness was organized in a much different way. It achieved its results by what are now thought of as 'female' methods, by the mental sending and receiving of thoughts, by full use of the psyche, and with intuition.

"The relationship between Humankind and other living creatures was also much closer. There was communication and cooperation among all living things, both animal and plant. There was also free communication between living things and what you think of as non-living things. But physical objects were not the focus. The innate consciousness of all matter, and the true nature of what you call matter, were understood and experienced by all.

"By all, that is, except the incorrigible Adamites, the outcasts, whose fascination with physical matter and with the creation of objects from that matter knew no bounds.

"Till, at a double millennium, about four thousand years ago as I said, the Adamite consciousness, which became known as Noachite, was given the ascendancy. In the dream state, on a mass basis, the species *chose* them to lead the next experiment. The species agreed to 'forget' about its real capabilities for a while, and to concentrate on, and become subservient to, the Adamites' fixation—physical reality.

"So that is the experiment that we are embarked upon. The experiment will continue until the objects which we create begin to possess us and then to destroy us . . . threaten even to destroy the world in which we live. Until we are as over-balanced in the physical direction as the last experiment was in a non-physical direction.

"Only then will we begin to remember our old abilities, begin to remember that it is mind that creates the physical and not the reverse. Only then will we understand how to achieve the necessary balance between mental and physical—between male and female—and go forward into the next experiment, that will combine the best of what we have learned in both areas.

"Until that time, in societies ruled by Noachites, 'God,' in whatever way 'he' is worshiped, will grow increasingly 'male.' Increasingly, reason and intellect—which are not at all the same as mind—will be worshiped. All that is female, including deities that are female, will be subjugated or destroyed. The God of Ibraham/Israel led, and will continue to lead, the assault upon, the annihilation of, every vestige of female power and worth in this world. Our 'God' is like a wheeled vehicle that I have seen in India, called a juggernaut. It is larger than ten elephants, and crushes everything in its path. The God of Ibraham/Israel is just such an efficient machine, meant to crush the 'female'—the memory of the mind's non-physical capabilities—into the dust, and to raise the 'male'—adoration of reason and logic and of physical objects—to the sky."

"If this is so," said Merovee tersely, "then what good does it do you to tell us all this? What use would it be for any of us to try to change things?"

"Apply the principles I have taught you. Probabilities, Merovee."

"But if this juggernaut cannot be turned, and if we will destroy ourselves and our world . . . "

"I said that our course will *threaten* to destroy us and our world. It is up to such as us to stop that juggernaut, and go forward with a people who have learned from their mistakes. I, for one, do not care to complacently accompany rigid, immovable, and yet unstoppable imbeciles into a spiritual chaos that will take another hundred lifetimes to right. If you care to do so, then go right ahead."

Merovee flushed, for there was an edge of anger in his voice.

"You expect too much of me," she murmured, "The fact that I understand some things does not mean that I understand all things."

"My sincere apologies." His shrug was rueful.

Then he grinned.

"But you really are slipping. You missed a chance to land a good one on me. You should have said, 'Now Josh, you have explained to me that one's anger at others is really only anger at oneself. Therefore, since you just got angry at me for what I said, I must have voiced something that you often say to yourself . . . "What is the use?" Remove the mote from your own eye, Josh, before you take a knife to mine.'"

Merovee smiled.

"Consider it said."

"Wherever religions based on the God of Ibraham/Israel spread to, or whatever offshoots they spawn, even far into the future, there the female will be trodden underfoot and down-graded. Cultures rich with the wisdom of the ages, which persist in remembering the 'old' ways, will be ruthlessly destroyed, their records wiped from the face of the Earth, all in the name of the 'God of the Jews,' who most certainly is a jealous god.

"The juggernaut has had four millennia during which to gather momentum. To bring any moving thing to a halt, you must begin to apply your braking pressure far in advance of the spot where you wish that thing to stop. The reversal of this process must begin now. It is to begin the reversal of that momentum that I come, to this place, to these people, at this time. It is because I need you to help me that I speak to you tonight.

"Merovee and I began our conversation with the 'stone that the Builders rejected.' She asked me who the Builders were. I have explained.

"You might also now understand that the composition of the rejected stone is the female and all that she represents. Our race will not be able to go forward again until it fully recognizes, remembers, that the female qualities—Feeling and Emotion, with, first of all, Love—comprise the cornerstone on which the very edifice of the Universe rests. Another glass of wine, please, my dear."

"You have had quite a bit," said Merovee.

"Ouch!"

Jesus turned to Nathaniel.

"Barely two hours married, and already she nags. Think you I should beat her?"

"Ah, no, Jesus. Remember, she is with child."

"True. Dreadful nuisance," said Jesus with a scowl. "How then shall I handle this insubordination?"

Nathaniel gave the question mock serious thought.

Susannah thought quicker.

"Why not simply pour your *own* wine . . . *Man?*"

"Brilliant!" said Jesus. "What a mind."

He rose and poured himself a full measure of wine. He drank it down with a sort of steady deliberation, staring at the ceiling as he drank.

Then he thumped the cup down onto the table.

"I have decided to take a walk."

"But you have not told them about the *Samir!*" cried Salome.

"I might even go for a swim. Any of you who care to come along, come."

He strode out of the room.

There was a moment's stunned silence. Then, as one, they rose and rushed after him.

Chapter 8

The Moon Dancers

The prolonged absence of the hosts, and then three of the guests, had penetrated the collective awareness of the others. Heads appeared at the parapet of the roof the moment that the door to Deborah's suite opened.

"Jesus!" hailed Chandreah. "What have you been up to?"

Jesus grinned, eyeing Phillipus who stood beside Chandreah.

"If you wished to know, why did you not simply dig a hole through the roof?"

Phillipus joined in the laughter.

"Come on up," he said to Jesus. "It is cool and we have been enjoying the full moon while your men gave me and Johannah some of your teachings. But, if you like, I will play the teacher and reveal my method of digging though wine-house roofs."

"Which could have more uses than one," said Jesus. "But some other time. My legs yearn to stretch after such long inaction. Come on along."

They hastened down the stairs and followed in his wake—Chandreah, the Sons of Thunder, Phillipus, Johannah, and Levi. Petros, they found hunkered down at the front gate.

"Ho! My faithful guard," said Jesus.

Petros gave him a long, accusing glare.

"Nothing else to do. Not when you seem to like certain of your friends better than others. Your new friends."

The smile melted from the face of Jesus.

"So. Jealousy. What do you think we were doing behind my closed door, Petros?"

Petros did not rise. He hugged his legs more tightly and looked away.

"What do you always do? You were teaching them. What was so secret that we others were not invited?"

The eyes of Jesus unfocused in momentary thought.

"I, myself, learned a lesson this night. These people taught it to me. Or, rather, they reminded me. No secrets can be withheld from those who actively seek the answers. If one seeks, one will find. If one asks, the answers will be given. If you believed that I was teaching these people, and you wanted to hear, why did you not come and listen at the windows, or pound upon the door?"

"I was not invited," said Petros. "I will not go where I am not invited."

"That is pride speaking," said Jesus. "And pride in what? If you think you were robbed, and are lessened by not having heard the things that I said in that room tonight, if you are now eating at your own peace of mind with jealousy, then you believe that you are not as good as you might be. You believe there is room for improvement. Why, then, are you so defensively prideful of what you do have?

"Pride is nothing *but* defense, Petros, a screen that you throw up to hide, from your own self, your own knowledge of your need for greater understanding and betterment.

"And do not confuse pride with self-respect. Pride hides a lack of self-respect. Pride is a negative and destructive attribute.

"Those who, from pride, limit their associations only to those who have invited or been invited, are throwing up the same screen, giving themselves just as short a weight. Both—the one who does not invite, and the one not invited—suffer from a need to protect themselves from examining their own inadequacies. They hurt only themselves.

"This, these 'new friends' re-taught me tonight after I, myself, had forgotten. Never, out of pride, turn away those who come knocking unbidden on the door of your life. And do not let pride stop you from knocking upon the doors of any whom your inner Self whispers have knowledge that will increase your own spiritual worth. Each of you will teach the other if you will both be courageous instead of prideful."

Abruptly, Jesus walked on. Salome ran to catch up, slipping her hand into his. Lazarus, too, hastened up beside him. Jesus put his free arm around the young man's shoulders and, thus, the three of them led the way out of the House of Nathan and down the packed-dirt road toward the town of Magdala.

"Are you coming?" said Chandreah, lagging behind.

Petros had not moved from his original position.

"He did not invite me."

"Stop being a numb-brain. Of course you are invited."

"He did not say so."

Chandreah opened his mouth. Then he shut it and shrugged.

"You are right. He did not. Well, I will shortly understand just how courageous my big brother really is. If you decide not to come, I will try to remember all that happens and tell you later. Farewell."

He trotted off after the others. Some yards down the road, his listening ears picked up the following footsteps. He grinned and caught up to Merovee.

"So. Did Jesus make the marriage contract with your brother?"

Merovee shot him a glance.

"I am sealed and delivered, like one of my grandfather's magdalia."

"Stop making female noises. It is obvious that the arrangement is to your liking."

"I can still resent the fact that you men consider my brother, and not I, the one qualified to make such a contract. Even before my mother!"

Chandreah shrugged.

"I do not know how to console you or to right what you believe to be so wrong. Where is he taking us?"

"For a walk is all I know. He said he might go swimming."

"Not a bad idea, it has been so hot, but with this mixed company? Does he intend to go in fully dressed?"

"I think," said Deborah, "that my new son is quite drunk. If he does go in, you had all better be prepared to rescue him."

Ahead of them, Jesus had been singing. Now he began to dance, progressing down the road with a swaying one-two-three-touch in which Salome and Lazarus were forced to join, Salome giggling, Lazarus laughing. The others could not help but smile.

Despite the lateness of the hour, the night was warm and sultry, smelling of jasmine. The moon was at perfect full, hanging directly before them there on the other side of the lake. The repetitive sing-song of the chanting of Jesus was not loud, but deep and compelling, while the rhythm of his steps seemed to pulse in the very air.

Deborah picked up the beat.

Then Merovee, Johannah, and Susannah.

Then Chandreah.

Soon even the two gangly Boanerges were moving to the pulse.

"To the Universe
belongs the dancer," went the melodic sing-song.
"He
who does not dance
does not know
what happens.
You
who follow my dance,
see
yourself in me, who speaks.
In the years
that will come,
when you grow frightened,
or weary, unto death,
and know not
how to proceed,
remember, this night,
and me, who is yourself.
Rise you up. Do . . .
One, Two, Three, Touch,
One Two, Three, Skip-Cross.
Feel the dust
smile at the rhythm.
Feel the sky
grin at the sight.
Feel All That Is
starting to laugh,
and the Universe
beginning to sing.
One Two, Three, Touch,
One, Two, Three, Dip, Cross.
Petros!
Stop your plodding!
Dance,
my moveable stone!"

"I cannot!"

Petros had caught up. He had been surveying the others in consternation, glancing up at the roofs of the quiet village houses that they passed. On such a hot night many might be sleeping up on their roofs. What if someone should look over his parapet and see this strange display?

"There is no such thing
as cannot," chanted Jesus.
One, Two, Three, Touch.
Snap the fingers
as you make the Touch.
One, Two, Three, Snap.
Lengthen your strides.
Glide as a bird.
Come, my rock.
Be the first
dancing stone."

"I have no rhythm!" cried Petros. "I feel a fool."

"If you feel a fool,
then a fool you shall be."

"But this is heathen dancing!" said Petros. "I have seen the Greeks of Bethsaida dance like this."

"Not like this,
Never like this.
They have not me
to follow.
Come my rock,
while yet you have me,
while I am amongst you.
To the Universe, belongs the dancer.
To the dancer, belongs the Universe.
Would you deny
joy to All That Is?
Feel All That Is
within your feet, my stone!
All That Is
yearns to dance!"

"Ohh!"

They had reached the closed and deserted market section—not so much chance of being seen and laughed at. Resigned and grumbling, Petros studied the feet of the others, trying to see how they did it.

"Forget the feet," Phillipus sing-songed, as, without missing a beat, he seized the shoulders of Petros.

"Do it with the shoulders. See? Four counts right shoulder down road, four counts left shoulder down road, four counts right shoulder, four counts left shoulder. The feet naturally follow. Yes! Petros is dancing, Jesus!"

"I am *not*! You call this dancing? Oh! Now you have me all mixed up again."

"Talk in rhythm," chanted Chandreah, "or you will have all of us mixed up."

"Right shoulder down the road," muttered Peter, "left shoulder down the road."

The swaying, laughing cavalcade progressed beyond the last of the village and started down the little road that led nowhere but past the factory of the House of Nathan and to the stone tower and harbor upon the shore. With the town left behind, and only the tower and the moon before them, it seemed suddenly that they had gone to another place, into a world that was theirs alone. There were not even any boats to be seen, or stars, with the moon so full and bright. And the road, heading straight down toward the water, seemed to continue right out into that water, becoming a highway of light across the lake and up to the moon.

Silhouetted against this highway, Jesus commenced to embellish his steps with spins and turns, and leaping, gliding swoops. He seemed suddenly to be composed, not of flesh, but, of a flowing liquid. Indeed, at moments Merovee was sure that she could see the moon right through him.

"Whhoooopah!" he cried, leaping high, swooping low.

Weeping for joy, a girl again, dancing beneath a Peloponnesian moon, Deborah, too, began to leap and to glide.

A madness swept through them. Each became lost in personal variations.

Like Jesus, Phillipus rose in expert leaps, bowed in swoops that all but swept the dirt, echoing, "Whhoooopah!"

Levi ran from side to side, forward and back, doubling the beat.

Nathaniel marched in wide, stately spirals, snapping his fingers.

Susannah dropped occasionally to her knees, where she beat the dirt in rhythm before rising again.

Johannah bounced, arms raised, fingers snapping.

Chandreah lifted his arms and coasted this way then that, like some great bird.

Lazarus studied Jesus, doing his best to copy every motion, beginning to move and leap with surprising grace in view of his limp.

Salome progressed forward with endless pirouettes.

"I cannot get my fingers to snap," she complained dreamily. "Oh, how I wish that Judah were here."

Merovee could not have said just what she was doing.

Petros had his eyes half-closed as he shoulder-danced along, sticking, like the Boanerges, to the basic step, but abandoning himself to the pleasure of rhythm for the first time in his life.

Suddenly his chunky body, that had all the lyricism of the stone that Jesus declared him to be, lurched into the air, attempting one of those swoops. The Boanerges burst into laughter. Petros took no umbrage.

"Let me see you do better, you two great clods."

202

Jacob executed a leap and landed akimbo.

"One of your father's camels would be more graceful," sniffed Petros, dancing complacently on.

There were no words to the song of Jesus now, only a driving, rhythmical sort of wail. His leaps went higher, his spins were more dizzying, his body was more fluid, seemingly more translucent. The road reached the water's edge and turned toward the tower.

Jesus did not turn. He danced straight onward, out onto the highway of moonlight.

Salome was the first to see. For a moment, she stood staring, her mouth working convulsively. Then that mouth opened wide, and a scream of sheer horror split the night.

The others froze, suspended as by the wand of some sorcerer, in their various positions of dance. Salome had dropped to her knees, her hands gripping her head.

"Oh, Jesus! Do not. *Please* do not be this way!"

"Follow me!" he called back to her, spinning along the surface of the lake, arms raised, fingers snapping.

"It cannot be," breathed Johannah.

"Are we bewitched to think that we see such a thing?" said Levi.

As though sleepwalking, Merovee moved to the water's edge. She had seen the multiplication of the fishes. Yet, somehow, that had been explicable. Making more and more stuff out of stuff was, however, not the same as dancing out onto water. She was dreaming. She had to be.

He had stopped now. He stood with his back to the moon, directly in the center of the beam, nothing but a silhouette in that brightness.

He raised his hands to them, beckoning. The moonlight glanced off his fingers and radiated toward them like needles, seeming to pierce each one of them, impale them there at the water's edge.

"Who will be brave enough?" he called.

Rhythm still pulsed in his voice, a rhythm filled with Love, and hope for each one of them.

Merovee realized that she, like Salome, was sobbing.

They were not alone. Even the men were crying, Petros with great huge gasps which seemed to struggle for air.

"Come to me," Jesus called again.

"How do we do it, Josh?"

"Simply come to me."

"Just walk out there? Should we think anything special?"

"Only that I stand upon the water and say that you may walk out to join me. Trust me. Believe in my words. The water is solid. Come."

Salome turned away.

"No," she said. "*No!* It is not fair. He asks too much of us!"

Merovee felt a hand slip into hers. Lazarus. His eyes were shining.

"Let us try it together," he said.

"Mother?" Merovee reached with her other hand. "Come with us?"

Deborah's face was whiter than the moonlight. Her eyes remained riveted upon Jesus. She shook her head. Her voice was barely a whisper.

"I am filled with fear such as I did not think possible. I would only drag you down, my children. This is where the generations separate. Go to him. Do it for all of us."

"Anyone? Chandreah? Johannah? Susannah? Nathaniel?"

"Come!" called Jesus. "While The Energy is still upon you! Come!"

Hand in hand, Lazarus and Merovee advanced till their toes were touching the water. So fierce was the trembling within Merovee that she wondered if she could continue to stand. She turned to Lazarus, imploring.

He shook his head, laughing almost maniacally.

"Girls first."

She felt, rather than saw, the others close in behind her, felt the tension, the fixed stares.

She stretched out her right foot, placed it on top of the water.

Oh. It was no dream. That water was cool, real, gently lapping.

'Believe,' she told herself. 'You know it is possible, for he is out there, making good his words, demonstrating with his own body. Do not disappoint him. Find courage in his courage. Believe. *Do* it.'

Her heart seemed to stop and the world grow silent as she transferred her weight out over the extended foot.

The bottom dropped at a good rate on this shore. Below that extended foot was already six inches of water.

And it was not going to work. The water was, as always, unresisting, her foot was sinking into it.

She realized that she was glad. Salome was right. He asked too much.

Then she gasped, and heard that gasp ripple through the watchers.

Her foot was not sinking after all, it had been only the gentle waves, lapping at her foot, that had made it seem so. Her weight was now fully centered over that foot. She stood on nothing that she could feel. Yet she was not sinking.

Emboldened, Lazarus stepped out. He sank immediately, into the six inches of water and to the bottom.

Quickly he released her hand.

"Go on without me."

Merovee stood frozen, staring down at the whiteness of that foot in the moonlight, screaming inwardly, begging it to sink. Sink!

From across the water, she heard his voice.

"There are various plateaus which lead up to the beginning of any journey. First, one conceives a desire to move from the spot that one is in. Some never find the courage to advance beyond that plateau of desire.

"If they do, they find themselves on the plateau where one decides where one wants to go, and when and how. What time-consuming decisions these can be. Some never do manage to make them, and so never reach the next plateau . . .

" . . . that is where one prepares for the journey. Even those who make the preparations sometimes never get around to the journey itself, for they can not bring themselves to make the *essential* move of the journey.

"The first step.

"You, Wife, have come a very long way to have made that first step. At what then is it that you now nearly faint in terror? Contemplation of the length of the trip ahead of you? Specters of the dangers and hardships you will encounter along the way?"

The night was no longer silent. A roar filled Merovee's brain.

Almost blinded by that sound, and by tears which flowed like a river, she transferred the last of her weight out onto her right foot and brought the left foot up beside it . . . so that she stood, firmly, very definitely, on top of the water, six inches above the bottom of Lake Gennesareth.

She heard Salome's moan, heard the renewed gasps and murmurs and sobs. Out of the corners of her eyes, she saw Nathaniel and Susannah drop to their knees, gazing at her.

Slowly, she lifted her eyes, and looked out across the path of light to that fluid, beckoning silhouette. His voice filled her.

"Come to me, Merovee. Come all the way."

She looked back down at her feet. She seemed suddenly to herself to be a gigantic, alien presence, gazing down through miles, millennia, worlds, onto some strange, white creatures.

But the waves around the creatures seemed to be growing, too, rising higher and higher, trying to swallow the white creatures and all of her own self as well!

Abruptly, she turned, stepped back onto the shore and kept walking. She went to a little hillock, sat down and wrapped her arms around her legs. She hardly knew what she had done. She knew only that she was suddenly cold . . . and that she wanted to go to sleep forever and never again have to think. She lifted blank eyes, not really seeing what was before her.

Jesus still stood there upon the waves.

"Is there no one else who will try?" he said quietly.

For a moment there was silence. Then Petros stepped forward.

"I will."

"I hoped that you would."

"Do you believe that I can do it?"

"It is for you to believe or not to believe."

"If I believe, then I can?"

"If you believe, then you can."

Petros gathered himself. He kept his eyes on Jesus and quickly stepped fully out onto the water. He looked down.

"Chandreah!"

He took another step.

"I am doing it!"

"Keep coming!" urged Jesus.

Those on the shore snapped out of their various trances and moved in behind Petros, calling encouragement.

Alone on her hillock, Merovee tensed.

"Go!" she whispered. "Do it, Petros. Do not fail him as I did."

Step after step after step, Petros moved out onto the lake.

He began to laugh.

"Look at me!"

He raised his arms, snapped his fingers, and did a One, Two, Three, Touch.

His audience cheered.

Moved to audacity by the approval, Petros gave a leap, intending to do a swoop. He landed hard and began to sink.

"Up! Think *up*!" called Jesus.

Petros took two quick steps forward, seeming to climb two shallow steps back to the surface of the water.

"Keep coming. Do not think of anything else now but coming straight ahead to me."

Petros did as Jesus bade.

But, after a few more steps, he chanced to glance back at the shore.

"Oh." He stopped. "We are very far out. How deep is it here?"

"Why do you ask?"

"I cannot swim."

"A fisherman who cannot swim?"

"Swimming is for fish, men use boats. How deep is it?"

"I do not know. But perhaps you had better not sink."

"You will save me if I do sink, though."

"I will try, but it has been years since I did any swimming."

"Ohh!"

Petros turned and began to run, back toward the shallows. With each stride, he sank deeper, until, finally, he disappeared beneath the water. He came up thrashing, calling to be saved.

Laughing, Jesus walked to his side, reached down, took his hand, and towed him to where he could touch bottom.

"My poor rock," he said fondly. "You gave way to doubt. And worse. Fear. You see what doubt and fear do to you? All of you. Look. Here is doubt and fear in action."

Jesus took hold of his nose, closed his eyes, and, with comical majesty, sank straight down, disappearing beneath the water. He came back up grinning.

"Doubt and fear will sink you every time."

The watchers burst into laughter. The men splashed in and raised Petros up onto their shoulders. Midst noisy acclaim, the hero was carried up onto the shore.

"But I failed!" cried Petros.

"The man walks on water," said Nathaniel, "and then says he failed."

"It is the way of Man," said Jesus ruefully, getting out of the water without assistance or cheers. "If things do not go exactly, down to the last detail, as Man has planned—if the ending is not exactly to his liking—his mind fills with bitter thoughts and angers, against himself and all his fellows. He can think only of the things that went wrong, while appreciation of the many things that went right is lost to him."

You are pleased with me then?" said Petros.

"It is not important that I be pleased with you, Petros. You must be pleased with yourself. Are you not? Just a bit?"

Petros grinned.

"I guess maybe I am."

"Then so am I. My rock. My gatekeeper . . . who has done his first miracle. More reason never again to look upon me as any particular master, for we are all masters if only we will believe it."

"Jesus, why did I fail so completely?" asked Lazarus. His manner contained no rancor, only candid inquiry.

"You quite obviously do not yet believe that you can do such a thing," said Jesus kindly. "You saw me out there, yes, but you obviously attribute to me powers innately greater than your own."

He gave the young man a hug.

"Rest content, Didymus. You tried, that was a mighty step. You wanted to believe, and you tested that belief. Next time, you will make a better showing."

"And I?" said Salome bitterly.

"Oh, my dear Kitten. What dreadful, squalling, cat noises you did make. But, even for you, I have good news. We, each of us, find our own areas of bravery. Then again, we each find our own areas of cowardice. You have been immensely brave in the last weeks, Salome, often in areas which would have set the others to squalling like cats. So do not be hard upon yourself.

"Think long and deeply upon this night. All of you. Remember each little thing that happened, remember your own thoughts, reactions, Feelings. Confront it all squarely. In a few days, after you have had a chance to do this, I will speak with each of you privately, and help you move forward."

His eyes flicked toward the hillock, to where Merovee sat, her face buried against her knees.

"That one is ready to talk about it right now. And it occurs to me that, though I have lately arisen from a two-day sleep, it is very late at night for the rest of you. And so good night. Return home at your own pace. Dance all the way if you wish. Merovee and I will follow after a time." He glanced at Deborah and at Lazarus for this permission, and found it granted.

He stood where he was until, laughing and chattering, they disappeared from sight. Then he walked over and sat down beside her.

"We seem always to be sitting on hillocks facing some sea," he said.

She did not lift her face.

"Please leave me, Josh. I am so ashamed."

"The only thing that should shame you is your own shame."

"I failed you."

"Me?"

"I ran from it."

"There I must agree."

"You and Jo. I have failed you both. I was not worthy of him and I am not worthy of you."

"Oh my! You have been watching too many Greek dramas. Should I call the others back? They could wail a mournful chorus in the background."

"Do not make light of it!"

"Why not make light? Is not the only way out of darkness toward the light? Come out of your dark hole, Merovee, or you *will* make me angry. You were magnificent! You and Lazarus both. You were the first! You joined hands and you tried it. And your own personal understanding is so far progressed that you did it. Your understanding is also so far progressed that you did not want to do it! You even tried to sink. I could hear your thoughts."

She lifted her head in shock.

"You could?"

"At times such as that, when I put my Self into what I term my 'excellent' state, I am aware of the workings of every scrap of consciousness in my vicinity."

"So! A scrap of consciousness is what I am? One of your many experiments! Well, who wants to be married to something like that? Some . . . freak! Or is it I who am the freak!"

He sighed, reached over and pulled her toward him.

"Let go of me."

"Sorry, but I think the time has come."

"What time? What are you going to do?"

"I am going to kiss you if you will stop squirming."

"Oh."

She did stop squirming. But she went stiff as a board, shoulders hunched, chin thrust down into her chest.

For a moment, he fought the position, trying to bestow a loving kiss upon her lips.

Then, with an expletive, he released her.

"For the life of me, I do not know how my cousin got you pregnant."

Merovee's head flew up.

"What a beastly thing to say!"

His next movements were so fast as to be a blur. As gracefully as the leap and swoop of his dance, he slid her out of her sitting position flat onto the ground, pinning her with his own body, holding her face with his hands.

"I would like to kiss you," he said, with gentleness that was quite shocking after the fluid violence of those movements. "Really kiss you. Please, Merovee. May I?"

In answer, Merovee's body went slack. That river of tears came flooding out again. She put her arms around his neck and offered her lips, opening, from top to bottom, rushing out to meet this man. He seemed to open in turn, allowing her to rush into him and mingle with his own self. All was liquid. And a strange fire struck, and began to burn wherever those liquids met.

Then, with a cry, she pulled her lips away.

"Oh, I did not want this! I did not. Because now that I hold you, how can I ever bear to let you go?"

He gave no answer. He wrapped her more tightly, covered her more completely and took her lips back, enveloping her into a warmth that shut out the world. She tasted his own tears and savored the salt, understanding that its quality would leave her thirsty forevermore.

"Do you still think that you are only a scrap of consciousness to me?" he whispered.

"No. I never did. I just wanted to make you go away and never come back."

"Really?"

"No. Damn it, no! I wish I knew what it is that I want. I just know that I understood Salome perfectly tonight. You *do* ask too much."

"Really?"

"No. Oh, just hold me. Hold me and never let me go."

"I never will. You have a unique husband, Woman. Even if you try, you can never again be free of me, or so far away as a sigh."

She did sigh. And she nestled closer.

"Your robe is dry. So is your hair."

"A convenient trick, no? I learned it in the mountains called Hima-alaya. In our final test before our teacher, we had to drench ourselves three times in one night, then go outside and generate enough heat to dry ourselves thoroughly while sitting in a snowstorm."

"So!" This time the anger was feigned. "The warmth I felt while kissing you was not the heat of your passion. You were drying your clothes!"

"Ah, but it is a proven fact that passion cuts the drying time in half."

She laughed, and the laughter turned back into tears. She buried her face against him, wishing she had a hundred arms with which to hold him.

"I am very happy to be your wife."

"If this is how you express happiness, I dread your sorrow."

"In that case, see that you have removed yourself from the scene before I must be sad."

"It is always possible that I will have done that."

She held him tighter.

"It always comes back around to that, does it not."

"It has to. Which is one reason why you refused to walk out to me tonight. You were confronted squarely with the predicament that you have gotten yourself into . . . with the 'freak' who you have married, and the extremely difficult future that you have chosen for yourself. And that is why I do not blame you for your actions. Or little Salome for hers.

"Do you know, you caused me to recognize her tonight. I had a suspicion the other night in Kapher Nahum, when she gifted me with the nard. But when you called her 'sister' tonight, I understood completely. She was my first wife. In India."

Merovee pushed him upward, staring.

"You have been married before?"

"You imagine yourself the only one so privileged? Despite my mother's belief, yes. I have had a wife. I had only fifteen years when I arrived in India, with all those hot young juices cooking my brain. I found Meore wandering alone, her family killed by a flood. She was barely thirteen, and endearing beyond words. I made her my wife." He laughed. "Even then, she made me act more the father than the husband. She has not changed in that wise. But I am gratified to see that the ideas which I was able to give to her then—callous boy though I was—took firm root. They are budding in the Salome that we see."

"Why did the nard make you suspect that she was Meore?"

"Meore obtained a bit of it and rubbed me with it as a wedding gift. She was so proud. I do not know how she ever obtained such expensive balm . . . I have always suspected that she stole it. As she lay dying, I took virtually the last of the money that my parents had sent along with me, and bought a whole pot of the stuff. While yet she had life in her, I soothed her with part of it. When she was dead, I prepared her body with the rest. She was the sweetest corpse that any ghat along the Ganges had ever seen. The man who burned her body was mightily impressed."

"When did she die?"

"She was with me but two years. She had given herself a consumptive cough. I am surprised to see her back so soon. But not unpleased. She was evidently determined to return so that she could learn, from the man, those things about which the boy was only able to supply hints."

He laughed.

"I can tell you that rebirth is not an easy matter. A certain period of reflection and synthesis is expected, and hasty comings back are frowned upon. How that little conniver must have twisted her teachers around her fingers to have gotten back here so soon. And into such a perfect position!"

Merovee thought back.

"Suddenly all that she has done is explicable . . . the way she took to Johannan. She recognized that other part of you. Of her own accord, then, she sought me out in the market. Then she followed after us as we went to bury him. And nothing could keep her from coming down to Galilee to meet 'Jesus.' Does she remember being your wife, Josh?"

"No. She knows only what she feels. Which is open-handed Love. You will not be jealous of her will you?"

"Salome is so very . . . Salome. I cannot imagine being jealous of the one who is now Salome. Did you love Meore very much?"

"I have never met a person who I did not love very much, Merovee. But there are thousands upon thousands of ways to love. I am no longer that young boy with the spiritual fire in his brain and the physical fire in his groin. I am a man well in sight of forty, who holds his life's desire right here in his arms. She answers the needs of both fires. And it is a large answer that is looked for, an answer that no other living woman could give. For those fires are no longer separate. They coalesced and formed a new sort of flame years ago. That flame is unified. It burns even and true under all conditions. It consumes me waking and sleeping, taking all that I am to feed itself. Yet, strangely, in the very act of consuming me, it gives back to me The Energy that makes me more 'I' with each day, and so ever more able to feed this consuming fire that does not consume. So, each day, I must give up more of myself to the fire, knowing that it will give back more than I gave. Once one is engulfed by this unified fire, Merovee, one burns forever, growing each day, that growth consumed by nightfall. There is no turning back. There is no way out, not once you have accepted it. Those who have never experienced it, who run and hide each time it draws near . . . I suppose those people would call the fire 'Hell.' They do not understand that the fire in which ones burns forever, is Heaven—that this is the true god, itself. Salome is walking toward her own fire, drawn as haplessly, so she thinks, as a moth. You are teetering on the brink of yours. That is what both of you understood tonight. That is why you both reacted as you did. My heart went out to you both. I well remember the moment in this lifetime when I remembered my past lives and began to understand what was in store for me—then the moment when something that I did produced 'miraculous' results, when I did something that was just 'impossible'—when I was forced to accept my own power, and when I understood what my mission had to be. Like you two tonight, I cried out, 'No! You ask too much!' Like you, I turned, ran away. I went out into the desert, crawled under a rock, and lay there for a month, begging to die. I would have faced lions, a pit full of vipers, an unforgiving All That Is, rather than live through what I suddenly realized I must live through. For all of eternity. You had this same thing thrust rudely upon you tonight. Perhaps it was cruel of me. But my teacher pulled much the same trick on me and my fellow students. Shock like that brings it home very quickly, and sends the chaff off to the four winds, if chaff there be. You and Salome . . . and, yes, your mother . . .

"Her face was so white."

"She will recover. Deborah has the strength of the entire Earth bound up within her. You three women have the greatest depth of understanding. But, of the three, it was you who received the greatest shock. The other two understood, yet only watched. You stepped out onto the water. You looked down and saw what you were doing. You looked out and saw what I was doing. And you had married yourself to this. The enormity of what you understood was simply too much. And you had to go and sit down."

"Petros did not flinch. Petros went nearly all the way."

"You silly girl!" he cried, and he kissed her once more. "Merovee, The Energy is neutral. That is one of the most difficult things for people to get through their heads. You do not have to be smart to use The Energy that you and I and Petros used tonight. You do not have to be young or old or pretty or ugly or foolish or wise or good or bad. The Energy is simply there—given—everyone's property, just as is the air that we breathe. Each of us uses that Energy every single day, as naturally as that air. But, as some people breathe more efficiently than others, so some people use The Energy more efficiently than others. If they are observant, they begin to catch on to the results of their efficiency, and to study on how to be even more efficient. It takes a very long time, however, before even the best of us begin to suspect the true nature, the staggering extent of this Energy. Until then, each of us supposes that personal goodness, or prayers, or amulets have produced the wondrous results. Or just the reverse, that evil manipulations, curses, or spells have done it. Which is why some doltish and seemingly unworthy people are often very successful and why also some very nasty and ill-intentioned bastards seem to have all the luck."

"And never get punished."

"Ah. But there is just the key. They do get punished. Though I do not like the word 'punishment.' It is better to say that, sooner or later, each of us gets taught every error of every way. All That Is, which is each of us, always provides situations which demonstrate and teach those errors to those who are ready to learn them."

"All That Is works through us? We punish our own selves for our own misdeeds?"

"We do."

"But how can we be trusted to do that? And how can we be trusted to punish ourselves enough?" Jesus smiled.

"Did I not just say that the true god is us? Do you not trust All That Is to see to these matters? And what is 'enough'? Who could measure the precise amount of enough? In practice, my dear, people punish themselves too much. People know only how to punish. Denying the voice of All That Is within, they refuse to forgive. Themselves, especially. But there is another aspect to 'punishment' that confuses most people and makes them suppose that an offender is not being punished. Because the punishment does not always come about immediately after an offense. Indeed, it seldom comes about immediately after an offense. It might occur years later—manifesting itself as a dreadful disease perhaps. Or the punishment might not manifest itself until another lifetime. Someone who has been cruel to a crippled child, for instance, might cause himself to be reborn as a cripple so that he can suffer similar cruelty and learn the injustice of his former actions. The automatic and inescapable 'retaliation' for any deed is almost never obvious to those without overall perspective. Hence, it seems that All That Is does not care, and allows all manner of injustice to proceed unchecked. One must gain trust, in this as in all things."

"But would it not be dangerous to teach a doctrine such as this to the general populace? Would it not encourage wrong-doers? If The Energy is neutral, what is the point of being good? If punishment is left to one's self, well, many people would rub their hands in glee and go on a rampage of evil and cruel deeds."

"Some would certainly do that. Poor souls. For how they would eventually suffer."

"But how could good people just sit by and not punish the wrong-doer?"

"What constitutes a 'good' person? Are you telling me that there are people who have never 'sinned,' who have never committed acts for which the All That Is within will not eventually teach them a hard lesson? No, my love. Even I have offenses that I will have to pay my own Self for. Until I am perfect, until I can go through a lifetime and never miss the mark—which will be never—I have no right to judge another human being, for anything, no matter how heinous. That is the great mistake, Merovee, for society to believe that it is responsible for inflicting punishment, and that it has the right to do so. 'Judgment is mine says the Lord.' Yet Humankind will not trust 'the Lord' to keep 'his' promise, and inflict all needed lessons. I tell you that anyone who takes the punishment of another person into his own hands, even by condoning his government's infliction of that punishment, not only perpetuates the very evils he thinks to punish. but renews his own personal cycle of 'items which must be atoned for.' The 'Lord' whose prerogative is judgment, is the Soul of each and every person. Drag an adulteress out to the pit of Jerusalem and lift a stone against her, and an 'eye for an eye' becomes your lot. You will have sealed a bit of your destiny. Someday, it will be you on the receiving end of someone else's missile. There will be no way to escape it—not until you learn not to judge others. For, once you draw back into that place between lives to rest and to consider how well or how badly you have done, you will tabulate for yourself all the 'good' things and all the 'bad' things. Each good thing will signal an area where you have progressed, learned. Each bad thing will signal an area that still needs work. In the new life that you then plan for yourself, you will include areas which will provide you an opportunity to experience the fruits of your own previous actions, of all that you have previously inflicted upon others. You will not do this to yourself out of cruelty, but out of Love, as a teacher makes a student write one hundred times an answer that he got wrong—so that, finally, the child understands his mistake and understands how never to make it again. This strange, seemingly unfair, world of ours is one vast schoolroom, Merovee, filled with students who range from rank beginners to consummate masters such as myself."

"But that is not fair! You say we provide reverse areas, and punish ourselves for what we have done to others. Do we never receive reward for the good things we do?"

He smiled, his teeth white in the shadow of his face.

"Why think only of punishment? Listen to what you have just said. Repeat my words and work it out."

"You said that, in each life, we will provide ourselves opportunities to experience the results of our own . . . things that we have inflicted . . . Oh!" Her cry was of happiness. She grabbed his face. "So, if we 'inflict' good, then those are the effects which we 'suffer.' If we inflict kindness, we get kindness back! Oh, Josh. Say it is so. Tell me it is so."

"It is so," he laughed.

"Promise."

"I promise. 'Surely goodness and mercy shall follow me all the days of my life, and I will dwell in the house of the Lord forever.' The promise is an old one, my darling. But I make it anew, to you. Just as, again and again, we must suffer the results of our cruelties before we understand that they flow from our own past cruelties, and learn, thus, not to be cruel, so we must find kindness done to us over and over and over again before we can understand—and trust—that the kindness flows from a goodness basic in our own Selves, from even our own 'past' actions—and so learn to be kind with a glad—no, a joyous, heart. I am sure you have seen people who simply can not accept the kindnesses shown them. They are still learning, even as the man who suffers injustice is learning."

"But what is the school for, Josh? Do we never graduate?"

"There are, quite simply, higher levels to which one cannot proceed until one understands the mechanisms of this reality. As to graduation . . . " He shrugged. "A personality can leave at any time. There are other realities of a like advancement available. You will get tired of hearing me say that Free Will is the rule of the Universe—but it is. And so, if a personality does not like this reality, nothing will make it return. The catch is that, if that personality thinks that, by switching, it can avoid having to learn a particular lesson, it will be sadly disappointed. The moment it enters that other reality, it will find itself on the horns of a like moral dilemma. There is only one way to enter a higher level, and that is to learn the lessons of the lower levels."

"Is Earth the lowest?"

"No. There are countless simpler realities. Earth is, though, the most important school for the teaching of the manipulation of what we call physical reality. By that token, it is a low level—while, in the reverse, it is an extremely important level that really should be mastered if a personality wishes to be well-rounded."

"But why then are you still here? Why have you not gone on?"

"I have. I thought I explained this down in Machaerus." He kissed her lightly and moved his fingers up along her temples and into her hair. "You have your arms around me. Your fingers are twined into my hair, and I have just twined mine into yours. What is it that we each hold between our two hands? What we each hold is a fragment, a representative part off of a much greater entity. In our case, there are not two entities involved, but only one."

"Is Salome off of our entity?"

"Strangely enough, no, though her entity is a great friend of our own. Deborah, however, is of our entity."

"Lazarus?"

"No."

"That is a surprise."

"Not really. His task is far removed from ours. And his parent entity is eons younger than our own. Now. You hold between your two hands a fragment that currently calls itself 'Jesus.' Jesus is one of the oldest fragments thrown off by a very old entity. Jesus, in one form or another, has been around for a very long time. The personality known as Jesus has become very old in knowledge, and has learned to be aware of much that is going on 'back home' with the parent entity, and also with many of its other parts. So that the parent and those other parts seem, to Jesus, to be just another part of himself. Why have I not graduated, you ask? Parts which I understand to be 'I' are operating, at this very moment, in higher realities, involved in activities that I could not even begin to describe to you. I share their

213

experiences even while I, seemingly, am only here. And I am here out of Love for this place. Between my appearances here, I can 'live' in many wondrous levels. But my greatest Love is to return to Earth. You have heard me complain, yes. But I Love Earth. And so, what I hold in my hands is 'Merovee.' It, too, is a fragment of my entity, though much younger than my own personality. Merovee is one of the adolescents of our group, still struggling to understand, and not yet aware of all its other parts living 'lives' on those higher levels. Perhaps one of the reasons that I was so eager to come at this time was because I would be introduced to Johannan's promising young Merovee. Will you promise, Merovee, that, as many times as I return to this Earth, you will try to manage your own schedule so as to be here as well?"

"As long as the Earth lasts."

"Oh, I have just trapped you. For, with time being simultaneous, the Earth will always exist in one form or another, and I will never cease to return. Knowing that, do you want to back out?"

She stared up into his dear face. What woman would not give the world to hear the words of truly undying love which had just been spoken. Yet she was not as other women, and he was certainly not as other men.

"Perhaps I should back out. For that was really what I ran away from tonight, was it not. My first glimpse of that eternity, and the responsibility that will be mine from hereon in. For the first time, Life stepped up, looked me squarely in the eye and said, 'For you, Merovee, the time of bargaining has passed.' Yet I turned and ran. How can I promise that I will not run again? And again, and again. Petros might be the rock that you truly need."

"Ah." He pulled her head to him and kissed her hair. "On a world level, rocks are not half as pleasant to hold or to kiss as are Merovees. But you still do not understand about Petros, do you. He used The Energy tonight, yes. But he used it unknowingly, do you not see? Petros has not the slightest idea of how or why he was able to do what he did. If I talked to him for one hundred years, I can promise you that he still would not understand. Petros walked across the water on pure faith in the truth of my words. Now. This places Petros far above many others. But Petros still has far to go before he catches you, my girl. You shared his faith and his belief, and you could have come to me. But you also had understood the immensity of what you were doing, of what that walk would imply in time and space and responsibility to your own Self in this Universe. That understanding caused you to turn around, to come over to this hillock, to sit down and cry and think things over. Petros gained in pride with every step, thinking of nothing but how big he was growing in the eyes of his fellows. I had to cut him short finally, play on his mortal fear of drowning—ludicrous in the face of what he was doing—and sink his ship of state. If I had allowed him to come all the way, I have no doubts but what he would have been out tomorrow, thinking himself a possible Messiah, preaching to some multitude on some hillside. His walk was ended by a mundane fear of drowning, based on worldly knowledge. Your walk was ended by fears based on knowledge of cosmic import—and, thus, of healthy humility. I will see you turn and run any day, Merovee, rather than allow Petros to walk all the way out to me."

"What if I had kept coming, Josh? Would you have allowed me to come all the way?"

"Yes. I would have."

"Is there a probability in which I did?"

"There is."

"What happened when I got there?"

"You became equal to myself. That world goes off at a different angle, and progresses much more rapidly than ours."

"I . . . that was another thing. As I stood there, fully on the water, I saw Nathaniel and Susannah kneel to me. I do not want to be anything other than human, Josh."

"None of us are."

"They look at me with enough reverence as it is."

"I understand. You see the fight that I have, to keep them from calling me master or lord. It is difficult for them. They want gods. They insist on deification. That way, they are never without their scapegoats. Your fight will always be to keep your human status while performing deeds which they think no human should be able to perform. Only in this way can you bring them forever around in a circle, right back to themselves, both in their search for gods and for scapegoats. This will not make you the most popular person in the village."

She burst into tearful laughter. He held her closer.

"My darling girl. Do you understand how much I love you? Just 'as a man.' Will you allow me that? Give me that? Let me be that lowly human when I am with you?"

It took her breath away. She could only cling to him. How could she say to him that that was another reason she had refused to walk on the sea this night. How should a woman love a man capable of miracles, a man who could lead her in a dance then turn her into a goddess to whom people would kneel and pray? How did a woman find the starting place of a love like that? Where did one begin?

Yet it seemed that she already had begun.

* * *

On the Sabbath, as Jesus had slept, Simon Yeshuah entered the synagogue of Kapher Nahum and spoke to those assembled. He was known to the people of the town. The eldest son of Jethro, the Nazorite carpenter and stone mason. Jethro had been a fine craftsman. The best-built homes in Kapher Nahum, in all the towns along the lake, in all the plains of Gennesareth, and in all of Galilee for that matter, had known the hand of Jethro, or of his father Simon, or of Simon's father Yeshuah, and so on back to the very founding of those towns. Simon Yeshuah was said by some to be nowhere near the craftsman that his father had been, but, still, the family commanded a good deal of respect. It was spoken that the eldest of each generation had been a life-long Nazorite since the days of Noah. It was spoken that the ways of Nazorites reflected the ancient and true nature of the Hebrews, themselves, a nature lost and forgotten in the settlement of the land of Canaan. Being Nazorite, the family traveled, from building job to building job, living in tents or caves or in shelters provided by employers. Honor, rather than disdain, was accorded their homelessness. And Jethro the Nazorite had descended through his mother from David, himself, while the mother of Simon Yeshuah, Meraiah, was the daughter of a poor but pious and respected farmer from the hills west of Gennesareth. This Meraiah was also sister to Micah, a lately deceased elder of the synagogue of Kapher Nahum.

So it was that, when Simon Yeshuah and his followers had entered Kapher Nahum the morning before the Sabbath, he had been greeted with respect, and given shelter at the home of Micah's widow. Yet there was an uneasiness. For Simon Yeshuah was also known to be a Zealot. Neither was there a one of his brothers or followers who were not known to be Zealots. It was whispered that Simon Yeshuah's chief lieutenant, bar Tolmei, had killed fifty Romans to date, while the youngest brother, Judah, had even been surnamed for his treacherous sicarius. Crispus Marcus, commander of the Roman garrison of Kapher Nahum, had been prepared for the arrival. He had had Simon Yeshuah under surveillance since his reappearance in Galilee some months before, and a rider had warned him that the band was headed for Kapher Nahum. Crispus issued orders that, while Simon Yeshuah was in town, legionaries were to travel in pairs, and stay out of tight, unlighted places after darkness. He doubled the torches around headquarters and barracks, and sent several of his informers from the town to loiter near the home of Micah's widow and report back upon all that they observed. Crispus Marcus had grown to enjoy the peace and ease of his post at Kapher Nahum. He was not about to let a bunch of wild-eyed fanatics ruin that tranquility.

Most of the townspeople felt the same way. They were business people, grown fat upon the stability provided by the presence of a Roman garrison in the town. Terms of barter were set, disputes were few, and quickly settled when they did arise. Caravan drivers knew that Kapher Nahum was a dependable place in which to halt, a reliable place in which to conduct business. Then there were the lucrative contracts which the Zebedee had with even Rome itself, which contracts provided much employment for the area. So what if some tax had to be paid, was prosperity not worth a little tribute to Caesar? The Roman Empire was a good and excellent invention, of which business people were happy to have the use.

So, though Simon Yeshuah was greeted politely as he entered the village, the informers of Crispus were not the only ones keeping an eye on things. Galilee was accustomed to wandering religionists, preachers, malcontents, and self-proclaimed prophets, expounders of this new idea or that. Galilee thrived on new ideas, and welcomed these men. Any who went too far could always be dealt with quietly by the religious community, without bothering the Romans. The man called Jesus had raised a few religious hackles, but he seemed to pose no immediate threat to the status quo. Simon Yeshuah was a different matter. He belonged to a political party dedicated to the ousting of the Romans from Palestine, and he traveled with men who boasted of killing Romans. More frighteningly, he did nothing to squelch the talk of his followers that he was the expected Messiah, the rightful King of the Jews, destined to throw off the Roman yoke and establish the Kingdom of God on Earth. Simon Yeshuah was both a religious and a political fanatic. A man such as that was perfectly capable of organizing a revolt against Rome in order to seize the Palestinian throne for himself. Such a move would be a disaster. Rome, the currently benign and useful machine of the merchants, would take the wraps off its greater machinery, of death, destruction, subjugation, conquest. Only a madman could believe that Rome, once aroused, could be beaten. Only a madman could believe that such a revolt would not be the end of the Hebrew nation.

Or so the elders of Kapher Nahum whispered amongst themselves. And they watched anxiously the comings and goings to the home of Micah's widow, alert for an increase in the number of followers, or the arrival of any more of the known Zealots of the district.

The fears of the elders came to naught, as did the expectations of the sick and crippled who heard of Simon Yeshuah's arrival, and who gathered in the street outside the house, waiting for him to come out and heal them. Simon Yeshuah, instead, spent the late morning and early afternoon with Judah and Mathiah, picking their brains and memories for every morsel regarding the man Jesus. He seemed especially fascinated by the story of the multiplication of fishes and loaves. Mathiah was made to repeat it so many times that Judah grew sick of hearing it, and grew bold enough to say so. Simon Yeshuah smiled and returned to more general questions. What was the temper in Jerusalem? Of the priests, the scribes, the Levites, the Pharisees, the Sadducees, the Romans, the people in general? Where were the Zealots the most active? Who led them? What was the temper of the Essenes? What were the rumors of his own ministry, which the south had so thoroughly confused with the activities of Jesus? He made them tell the story of their journey to and from Machaerus again and again. He asked for details of the burial, and descriptions of each conversation, each action of each and every one of the followers of Johannan and of Jesus, especially the man Simon called Petros. They were made repeatedly to recount details of the healings which they had witnessed, to remember any word that Jesus had spoken, every gesture which he had made.

Only one story did Judah withhold. He made no mention of Salome. For, just as everyone else in Galilee, Simon Yeshuah had heard the cover story of Herod Antipas and took it for the truth. Indeed, when Judah made the suggestion that it was not the truth, his brother became wroth and lectured them upon the wickedness of women. Trading covert glances with Mathiah, and seeing assent, Judah decided not to turn that stone.

Was it to protect Jesus, he wondered in the back of his mind as they talked? Perhaps. Simon Yeshuah might not be above sending word to Tiberias and having Jesus and his entire group arrested, on what might even be capital charges. How, then, would it go with Salome, herself?

He found himself wondering what all of them were doing that day, where they had all gone that morning. Back to Magdala? Very possibly. Was Jesus teaching to them at this very moment? In that soft, rich voice of his, laughing so often, understanding so much, seeming to forgive the worst that a person had to offer.

What foolishness was this? These thoughts were demented.

But would he ever see any of them again? Jesus? Merovee?

And Salome. Funny, little Salome. Pretty, sweet, little Salome.

"Brother."

Judah jerked back to the place where he really was, reclining on a couch on Aunt Sarai's roof.

"My words have moved you to tears," continued Simon Yeshuah. "I will use them in the synagogue tomorrow if they have that good an effect."

"Yes. Do," said Judah. He rose and walked to the parapet.

There were indeed tears in his eyes. How strange. What magic had this Jesus and his people done upon him to make him want to return to them?

Some distance away, on the roof of Obed's inn, he could see men working. The brothers of Phillipus, repairing the damage done the night before. They might know where Jesus had gone. If he could just get away on some pretext . . .

It was late afternoon before his aunt decided that she might not have baked enough bread to last her sudden army of guests through the Sabbath. Quickly, Judah volunteered to go to the baker. He sealed the offer by suggesting to Simon Yeshuah that he tarry, mix with the people, and find out what was being said of him. Simon Yeshuah never could resist knowing what was being said of him.

So Judah was off, at a trot. He went first to the baker, as they usually ran out of loaves in the hours just before the Sabbath. His sharp eyes did not fail to note that a man from the crowd outside the house followed after him. Judah laughed to himself. The man had no skill at all. Emerging from the baker's,

Judah darted into an alley, flattened himself into a doorway, then doubled back after the man had pounded past. He then hastened to the inn of Obed and took the stairs to the roof two at a time.

At the top, he stopped, stunned. It was not only the brothers of Phillipus who had labored at the repair of the roof, but Demetrius, himself. As a matter of fact, the sons now sat with their backs to the parapet, resting, laughing, and calling suggestions to the old man, who was down on his knees, bare-chested and sweating, applying the finishing coat of stucco.

The old man looked up, recognized Judah and grinned.

"What are you doing here? Did you not go down to Migdal with your master?"

"That is where they have gone?"

"So says Phillipus. He and Simon Petros sailed in a while ago to make sure that we were doing our job."

Judah relaxed, having got what he had come for.

"I had family business to attend to. I will join them after the Sabbath."

"Well then, you take a careful look at how we have fixed this roof, and you give us a good report. Tell Jesus it is fixed better than ever it was to start with."

"I could say that he has done the same for you," said Judah, studying the energetic movements of a man who, only the night before, had not been able to stand without assistance.

"Is it not the truth? I can hardly remember back to when I was young, but I could swear that I never felt any better then than I do now. And this cure will last, not like the overnight miracles of that other fellow. He is the false prophet, not our Jesus, I can tell you that."

Judah's thoughts went quiet within his skull.

"The other fellow? Are you speaking of the one called Simon Yeshuah?"

"Yes, that one. Oh, he cures them. He cured Elias of his scaling sickness over in our village . . . "

"And the wife of Isaac, the maker of nets," offered one of his sons. "She had a growth."

"And he cast the demon out of Samuel's wife," said another.

"But it is just as Jesus told me last night," said Demetrius sagely. "The cure did not last with any of them. A week later, Elias had his scales back, Isaac's wife had another growth, and Samuel's wife was out drooling in the street and trying to mount a goat. That is not going to happen with me. Not on your life. I can feel it, all the way through me, just as Jesus said. The Power is in me to keep myself whole. I am enjoying the wholeness and I will stay whole."

Judah hunkered down, regarding the old man intently. Yet he was not really seeing the old Greek. He was remembering the young Greek playmate whom Simon Yeshuah had murdered, then raised for just a few hours from the dead.

"Demetrius, this is important to me. I am the brother of Simon called Yeshuah."

"What?" Demetrius laid down his trowel, sank down cross-legged, and stared at Judah. "How then do you come to be following after Jesus?"

"It is a long story. But tell me Demetrius, do you know of any other cures done by my brother? Cures which have lasted?"

"The three we spoke of are all that we know of personally," said Demetrius.

"But we know of several others done by Jesus which have lasted," offered one of the boys. "Which is why we finally stopped trying to bring our father to the attention of your brother and carried him to Jesus."

"What are these cures done by Jesus?" said Judah.

"Well," said Demetrius, "there is the son of Samson of Bethsaida. The boy's leg was twisted when he was born, and he has always had to walk sort of sideways. Now he walks straight, and it has been near a month since Jesus cured him. You can look at that leg and wonder how you ever thought it was twisted. Then there is Lemuel. He had the bloody coughing sickness. Lemuel was one of the first to go to Jesus, oh, well over a month ago. The cough left him as though it had never been."

"And then Sarah," said one of the boys. "That poor girl was so filled with demons and evil things that her parents had to keep her tied like a beast. They say that Jesus went in and sat beside her in the place where she was kept and talked to her near half the day. You should see her now. Talk to her. She is beautiful."

One of his brothers punched his shoulder.

"Sweet on her are you?"

"Well why not?"

"But why should this be?" said Judah. "What does Jesus do that my brother does not do?"

Demetrius shrugged.

"You would have to ask Jesus I guess. For myself, I can only say that the things he told me made sense. It had never occurred to me before that the power to heal myself was in my own self, that I might be clinging to my pain for my own reasons. I thought I was afflicted by God, that I could do nothing to help my own self. Somehow, when Jesus told me that I could, I felt the truth of it inside myself. And then he said those two words. Release. Allow. And I actually felt myself releasing my infirmity and allowing the good health to flow in in its place." He shrugged again. "That is really all I can tell you. Except . . . " The eyes of Demetrius flicked over Judah's gird, searching for his weapon. "If you are Yeshuah's brother, you are a Zealot. I would keep my actions clean here in Kapher Nahum if I were you. The Romans are watching your every move."

Judah smiled.

"Thank you, Demetrius, but we are used to the ways of Romans."

He returned ever so slowly to the home of his aunt, allowing his shadow to find him again, noting the paired Roman guards and caring not. He thought only of the fact that he was returning to his brother's presence. That suddenly depressed him beyond words. With the Sabbath nearly arrived, he would be trapped for the next twenty-four hours with no way to escape Yeshuah's burning eyes, his righteous tongue.

And then for every day after that. Trapped forever.

Trapped.

He wanted to return to Jesus. He knew that now, with an internal certainty that he could not even begin to describe to himself. He wanted to know, understand, more of that strange man whose smile, whose laughter, whose generous attitude toward all of Creation was such balm to aching minds.

But he never could return. The vow that Simon Yeshuah had demanded of him that morning had sealed his doom.

Or had it?

Judah stopped. His eyes darted, looking at nothing, only following the rapidity of his thoughts. A slow, crafty smile lifted his lips. It might work. It just might.

His demeanor, upon returning to his brother on the roof, was studiously disturbed. He took a certain grim satisfaction in the fact that his mother was also there, conversing with Yeshuah and her other sons.

"What is this?" said Yeshuah, alert to his expression. "Have you heard ill tidings?"

"No, no," said Judah, altogether too quickly.

"Come, Judah, out with it. Is it the Romans?"

"Oh, the Romans. No. They are as always."

"What then? I insist that you tell me."

"They say that you are a false prophet."

Yeshuah sprang to his feet.

"Fools! Generation of vipers! The Son of Man stands among them and they know him not!"

"Never is a prophet recognized in his own country," soothed Meraiah.

"They say," continued Judah with seeming reluctance, "that you do not really heal. Worse yet, they say that you do not truly cast out the demons."

"What manner of imbeciles have you been speaking with?" cried Simon Yeshuah.

"Pay no heed to such gossip," said Meraiah, throwing Judah a look of fury.

"Not heal?" continued Simon Yeshuah. "Not cast out demons? Have they not the evidence of their own eyes?"

"That is just it. They have. They say that, within a week, afflictions and demons return to those whom you have cured."

"Judah, desist! You are disturbing your brother!"

"Silence, Woman. Judah. Explain yourself. What do you mean, those whom I have cured?"

Judah shrugged.

"It is foolish, of course. But they say that those whom Jesus has cured remain cured, and that, thus, only his power is demonstrated as to be from God. So that he must be the true Messiah."

The angry red in Yeshuah's face deepened to a purple.

"Have some of this nice pomegranate juice," said Meraiah.

Simon Yeshuah shoved her away.

"My power not from God?" he said ominously.

His eyes darted about the roof, and fastened upon his aunt's prized miniature fruit trees, each in its own pot in the corner.

He smiled.

"I will show you power," he said softly.

He strode over to the trees.

"You!" He pointed an accusing finger at a fig tree. "You offend me. I wished for a fig and you have not a single one to offer."

"Yeshuah," said Meraiah. "That is Sarai's best tree. She has picked all its figs for our Sabbath supper."

"Quiet! I say this tree offends me. And so you shall die, Tree. You shall wither before this Sabbath is ended, neither shall any of your seed grow nor prosper. Your life is ended. Thus is the fate of all those who offend God and the Son of Man. Their lives shall be taken from them. They shall be cast into eternal fire. This is the power of God!"

He spun back around, dark and threatening as the most towering of thunder clouds.

"Now leave me. All of you. Leave me alone with my father. I must calm my mind and prepare myself for his Sabbath."

He turned and dropped to his knees, facing Jerusalem, and so the Temple. The rest of the company hurried quickly down the stairs to the center court.

"Fool!" cried Meraiah as she reached the bottom. She raised up her insignificant height and swung with open-handed might, landing a blow upon Judah's jaw that snapped his head back. "Why did you tell him such lies?"

Judah put a hand to his jaw, trying to rub away the sting.

"They are not lies, Mother."

"Do not talk back to me! How have I offended God to have been given a dolt such as yourself? You are not to speak any ill to Yeshuah, do you hear me? He needs all his energy for the fight ahead of us. Now look what you have done to him. And how am I to explain the fig tree to Sarai? You know how she has worked on the cultivation of those miniatures . . . how she especially dotes on that fig tree."

"I grieve for Aunt Sarai. I also grieve for the tree. It had done Yeshuah no wrong. What right had he to curse it? If that is the way of God, I want none of it."

"What insanity is this? What blasphemy? To hear you talk one would think that a tree has sense, or feelings, or rights." In her indignation, Meraiah began to bounce up and down. "Nothing has rights, do you understand? Only God has rights, and his son, your brother."

"Mother." Judah's next eldest brother, Jacob, took hold of her arm, while Mathiah took hold of Judah's, trying to pull him away from Meraiah.

Judah shook himself free. All his pulses were pounding. He saw his mother as through a red haze.

"How does Yeshuah become the son of God, Mother? Is Yeshuah not your husband's son?"

Meraiah was struck dumb. She stared at her youngest, her mouth opening and closing.

"Do not tell me," said Judah evilly. He leaned down toward her, putting his forehead against hers. "Let us see. How could it be possible that Yeshuah is God's son and not my father's. Oh! I know. You could tell much the same tale that the mother of Samuel told. You could say that an angel of the Lord appeared to you. But you could go the mother of Samuel one better. This angel appeared to you before ever you married father, no? While yet you were a virgin. He told you that God had sent his own Spirit down from heaven and planted Yeshuah in your belly, is that it? It must be! How else does Yeshuah become the son of God and not of Jethro the carpenter?"

A look of marvelous craft passed over the face of Meraiah. She stepped back away from her youngest.

"Exactly," she said with bared teeth. "You are a clever boy after all, Judah, to have divined that secret that I have never revealed to a living soul."

Judah's jaw dropped.

"You would not." He slapped his forehead and wheeled away.

Then he stopped, thought, and turned slowly back, grinning from ear to ear.

"In which case, Mother, Yeshuah cannot possibly be the Messiah."

"Why?"

"The Messiah must be of the blood of David. My brothers and I descend from David through my father, Mother, not through you. And you claim now that Yeshuah is not of my father's blood."

Meraiah blinked.

"What an abomination you are."

"I have always thought so myself, so, in that one matter, we are agreed. Though how could I ever have thought anything else? From the first moment I can remember, I have never done anything right in your eyes."

"I suggest that you go off quietly and compose yourself," said Meraiah. "I suggest that you do some serious praying and find your way back. In the meantime, I will not tell your brother the dreadful things that you have said."

"Oh, by no means. Yeshuah should not be disturbed. Yeshuah must be allowed to believe what Yeshuah believes, and we should all follow him into Hell if need be."

"That is certainly where you are headed, my fine young friend."

"I do not think so, Mother." Judah realized, to his amazement, that he was crying. "For the first time in my life, I really do not think so."

He turned and walked blindly away, into the kitchen to where Sarai and her serving girl were preparing the Sabbath meal.

"Aunt Sarai?"

Sarai turned.

"Judah. My baby. What has happened?"

She came to him, a big, ample woman. She drew him into her arms just as she always had, since the days when he had been a skinny, stammering child, lost in the darkness of the shadow of his oldest brother, scorned and neglected by his mother.

"What has happened, Judalah? Tell Aunt Sarai."

"I can not. Only hold me, Aunt Sarai. Hold me for just a little while."

* * *

Yeshuah led the household in long devotions the following morning. Then he dressed himself in a clean robe and even combed his hair and beard. After the morning meal, he took up his tefillin and prayer shawl and led his followers forth to the little prominence higher than any other part of the town, where stood the synagogue.

The way was packed. Unlike the man Jesus, who had never been known to enter a Galilean synagogue in order to speak. Yeshuah was famous for doing so. Or infamous, since his violent expulsion from the synagogue in the place of his mother's birth. The crowd—much of it composed of strangers to Kapher Nahum, come specifically to see and hear the man rumored to be the Messiah—made way expectantly.

Yeshuah walked slowly, smiling graciously, making broad, loving gestures. The ill and the crippled called out to him as he passed.

"Rabbi, heal me."

"Rabbi. Please help, we have traveled so far."

"It is the Sabbath of the Lord," Yeshuah told them. "Desist. I will come to you on the morrow."

In front of the synagogue, Meraiah and Sarai separated from the men, entering through a side door allotted to women, to watch the services in respectful silence from behind an openwork screen. Inside the prayer hall, way was again made for Yeshuah, the crowd managing to part even though the men stood packed more closely than fish in a net. On the stone benches around the wall, where worshipers usually sat, men stood, getting a view over the heads of the others. On a raised dais before the Tabernacle sat those with the best view of all, the priests, Levites, scribes, Pharisees, Sadducees, and elders of Kapher Nahum. Among the elders were Jairus, ruler of the synagogue, and Alphaeus. Among the Sadducees was the Zebedee. None of their three faces betrayed a single emotion as Simon Yeshuah made his way through the crowd and took his place in the front ranks of those gathered about the central speaking platform.

There was no question as to who would be asked to do the reading. It was what they had all come for. The crowd fell silent as that part of the ceremony was reached, and the Master of the Worship called out the name of Simon bar Jethro called Yeshuah.

He mounted the platform solemnly, and went to the migdal, the tower-shaped wooden lectern on which lay the day's selected reading. From Isaiah. For a moment, he studied the place in the scroll where the master had indicated the passage that he meant to be read. Then, very deliberately, he searched further, found what he sought, and began to read.

"The spirit of the Lord God is upon me, because the Lord has anointed me to preach good tidings unto the meek, he has sent me to bind up the brokenhearted, to proclaim liberty to the captives, and the opening of the prison to those that are bound."

There was a stirring among the elders. Liberty, captives, the setting free from prison of those who were bound. It was as they had feared. The man was issuing a call to hotheads such as himself.

"To proclaim the acceptable year of the Lord, and the day of vengeance of our God, to comfort all that mourn, to appoint unto them that mourn of Zion, to give unto them beauty for ashes, the oil of joy for mourning, the garment of praise for the spirit of heaviness—that they might be called trees of righteousness, the planting of the Lord, that he might be glorified. And they shall build the old wastes, they shall raise up the former desolations of many generations, and they shall repair the waste cities, the desolation of many generations. And strangers shall stand and feed your flocks, and the sons of the alien shall be your plowmen and your vinedressers. But you shall be named the Priests of the Lord, men shall call you the Ministers of God—you shall eat the riches of the Gentiles and in their glory shall you boast yourselves."

He moved then to another section of scroll and read . . .

"For unto us a child is born, unto us a son is given, and the government shall be upon his shoulders, and his name shall be called Wonderful, Counselor, the mighty God, the everlasting Father, the Prince of Peace. Of the increase of his government and peace there shall be no end, upon the throne of David, and upon his kingdom, to order it, and to establish it with judgment and with justice from henceforth even for ever. The zeal of the Lord of hosts will perform this."

He then rolled the scroll, handed it down to the Master, and waited for the murmuring to cease.

"The day of this Scripture is fulfilled," he said evenly when at last there was silence. "The expected Son of Man stands before you."

There was a moment of stunned silence. Then the crowd broke into shouts, some angry, others jubilant.

Jairus rose and went down from the select dais, through the crowd and up onto the speaking platform. He waved his arms. Order returned. He turned then to Yeshuah.

"Are you telling us in no uncertain terms that you believe yourself to be the Messiah?" he said coldly.

A visible change came over Yeshuah. His stern, glowering features seemed to melt downward, into a mask of suffering. His shoulders bowed. Tears filled his eyes.

"I know myself to be the Messiah," he whispered.

Not another voice was heard.

The eyes of Yeshuah swept the crowd, gentle now, filled with such love that Judah's breath caught in his throat.

"I come to redeem the sins of the children of Israel. I come to make myself an acceptable sacrifice unto the Lord, to take onto my own shoulders the transgressions of his Chosen. In me is your salvation. In me, if you will reach out and grasp it, is eternal life."

"Rabbi," came a respectful voice, "what should we do to be worthy of you and of our God?"

Yeshuah smiled. He was a man different than the Yeshuah that Judah had always known.

"It is only this. Believe in me whom God has sent to you. If you will do that, you will be saved. If you will not, you will be cast into outer darkness, there to rot in agony for all of eternity."

There was silence once more.

Then another voice was heard.

"Rabbi, will you not show us a sign, that we may believe you?"

"Have I not showed you signs enough? Have I not healed the sick and cast out demons? It is the Sabbath. It is not mete that I should do aught but honor the Lord on this day. But, if you seek more signs, follow me on the morrow. You will see wonders such as no man has ever seen."

"Rabbi," said Jairus. "What of the man Jesus?"

To Judah's amazement, Yeshuah only smiled.

"What of him?"

"He, too, works miracles and gives signs."

"As do all sorcerers and magicians and traffickers with the Prince of Darkness."

There was an affronted murmur.

Yeshuah stepped out from behind the lectern and began a slow circuit of the dais.

"Is it not written that there shall be many false prophets in the last days? I say to you that the man Jesus is one of these false prophets. And I say to you that God has sent me to deliver you. Reject me and you damn yourselves. Oh you sinners, I am greater than the manna with which God sustained the children of Israel in the wilderness. It is written, 'He gave them bread from Heaven to eat.' But I say to you that Moses did not give the children bread from Heaven. For I am the Bread from Heaven, the Son, who has come down from Heaven to give life to the world. I am the Bread of Life! Here in this body of mine *is* that Bread."

He seemed to grow as he stood there before them. His eyes took on a power that dared a man to look away.

"He who comes to me will never thirst again. He who believes on my sacred body will never be hungry again. You stand there staring . . . the sheep I have come to lead back to the fold. You see me, yet you do not believe. Come to me. Come! The Father has given all power into my hands. He who follows me, I will never cast out, for I came down from Heaven not to do my own will, but that of my father. And this is his will . . . that all those who are given to me *shall* never be lost, but shall be raised up by me on the last day, that awful day when the world shall be judged. Every one of you who sees me, the Son, and believes on me, shall be given everlasting life. You and only you shall I raise up on that last day."

"How will you raise us, Carpenter? With a pulley?"

Chaos broke out, half the men laughing, half shouting in anger at the impudence.

"Silence!" cried Jairus. "Silence, or I will have the Levites clear the synagogue, and every single one of you shall be excluded from worship for a month."

Silence returned.

Yeshuah stood smiling.

"The man who asked that question is one whom a lever the length of Palestine will not be able to pry out of the darkness on the Day of Judgement."

"But how can you say you came from Heaven?" said another voice. "Are you not the son of Jethro the Nazorite and of Meraiah? How can you ask us to believe this, Simon Yeshuah? The man Jesus makes no such claims. He does as well as you or better, but he does not threaten us with damnation, or call himself the son of God, or even the Messiah."

"At least, then," said Yeshuah, "he has some shame left. Were he to proclaim such a thing, I have no doubt but what my father would cause the Earth to open beneath him and he would be taken down to Gehennah in a moment."

"If we are to believe that the Messiah has finally come and is in our midst," said Jairus quietly, "why should we not believe Jesus to be that Messiah? His house is the eldest of the eldest in descent from David and Solomon. After his father, Jesus is the ranking Prince of Judeah. Were the Jews allowed to freely name their own king, it would be Joseph of Ramah and, after him, Joshuah called Jesus. Explain to us, Yeshuah, why Jesus is not the Messiah, even though he does not go around insisting that he is. You share the likeness of blood with him. There is even a certain physical likeness. But his blood is of the highest, while yours is somewhere in between, and traced through a woman, your paternal grandmother."

Jairus turned to the crowd and gathered himself.

"I have something to say to this congregation. Jesus asked that it be kept secret, yet I think the time has come to tell you all. Many of you know my little daughter Rebeckah. She is the only such gift that God has seen fit to give to my wife and myself. We love her more dearly than words can tell. Some of you might know that she was sick unto death about a month ago. What you do not know, is that she did die."

There was an uproar.

"Jairus!" someone called. "I saw Rebeckah in the market just yesterday!"

"Thanks to Jesus, you did. And thanks to my wife. In the middle of that awful night, as our darling lay dead upon her couch, turning cold and stiff, my wife begged that we should send for the man Jesus. I finally consented. A slave was dispatched to the inn of Obed and Jesus was roused from his sleep. He came with all haste. He embraced us both and told us not to worry. He then went in to my daughter and touched that cold corpse and spoke to it. And my daughter sat up and began to cry. She called for her mother and said she was hungry. Now you can see her, playing in the market, happy and healthy with the other children."

"Have you witnesses to this?" called someone.

"My brother, myself, my wife, the physician Aristas of Bethsaida, and all my servants."

The congregation was silent, so shocking was the tale.

Jairus turned to Yeshuah.

"What say you to that, Simon called Yeshuah?"

"Even the Prince of Darkness can give his minions power to raise from the dead. You are accursed and doomed to outer darkness, Jairus. Jesus, has raised your daughter only to plant demons within her."

"How dare you!"

Jairus raised his fists to strike Simon Yeshuah. Two men leaped forward and restrained him, for to strike a blow within the synagogue was a grave offense. Jairus shook them off, regaining his composure.

"Go out and raise me something from the dead, Simon Yeshuah. Return it to bountiful health. When you do, send me your witnesses. Men might then perhaps begin to believe some of the claims to which your unspeakable vanity drives you. Until then, I will chance that outer darkness into which you promise I shall be thrown. For, if you are right, Jesus will be there, too, and I cannot imagine finer company in which to spend eternity."

Jairus turned and descended the stairs of the platform, elbowed his way through the crowd, and left the synagogue. Many departed with him.

Yeshuah watched after them sadly.

"No man will come to me except that my father, who sent me, finds him worthy and draws him to me. The prophets have told you. You have all been taught by God, himself. But only a few have truly learned what they have been taught. Those are they who will come to me, and those are the ones who will be saved. Johannan, who died at the behest of the Hasmonaean whore, proclaimed my coming."

"They say his followers went to Jesus," came a voice.

"Not so. Jezabel returned, a whore with seven demons, went to Jesus. My brother, Judah, and Mathiah are here with me. And Salmon and Eli and Ezekiel. As my fame spreads, all who ever followed Johannan will recognize the one of whom that master foretold, and they will seek me out. For no man has seen the Father except I, who comes from the Father. Such as I will surely be recognized by those who have honestly learned of God. Truly I say to you . . . he who believes on me shall have everlasting life. I am the Bread of Life. Your fathers ate manna in the wilderness. They are dead. I am the Bread from Heaven, that of which you may eat and not die. I am living bread. The bread that I will give you is my flesh. Eat of it, and live forever."

There was a murmuring. The man beside Judah tugged nervously at his beard.

"Does he mean to suggest that we literally eat his flesh?" he said to no one in particular.

The presence of Yeshuah upon the platform seemed more expansive by the moment. He threw back his bead and lifted his arms.

"Father. Make them understand."

With a riveting gesture, he flung down his hands, and then lifted his right hand, pivoting in an accusing circle, one finger outstretched as when he had cursed the fig tree.

"I say to you truly. Unless you eat of the flesh of the Son of Man and drink of his blood, you shall have no life everlasting."

A shudder rippled through the congregation. Even those who had lately cheered Yeshuah shrank backward.

"I shock you. Well, the truth is shocking. God has sent me to you. He has sent me to give my life for you. I am the sacrificial lamb. I am the perfect son of God, the only acceptable sacrifice, the only way by which you may be saved! I will take all of your sins onto my own self. I will leave you guiltless, clean. And your dirt, your sins, your foul treacheries, your idiocies, I will carry on my back to my father, who will forgive them because it is I who brings them. I am the way, the truth, the light. He who believes on me shall never perish. My flesh is your meat, and my blood is your drink. But it is not the meat or drink of this world, which spoils and perishes. It is the meat and drink of Heaven, which endures through life everlasting. You must eat my flesh, drink my blood. And yet you will see the Son of Man rise up whole into Heaven from whence he came, for it is his Spirit that is the true meat and drink—the physical flesh is as nothing. These words are the Spirit, these words are the Life."

The hall was filled with a silence made passive. No man knew what to say to speech so repulsive and incomprehensible.

Yeshuah's eyes swept the faces of the watchers, fastening for a moment on Judah before passing on.

"Yet still there are many of you who will not believe me. Among you here today are those who are of the Evil One, who will betray me." He shook his head sadly. "But what can I expect? No prophet is ever accepted in his own country. Even Elijah was forced to do his good works in Sidon and in Syria. The widows and lepers of our own country remained poor and uncleansed for their lack of belief in him."

He extended his arms.

"Come to me. Follow me. I will establish the Kingdom of God on Earth and show you the way to God's kingdom above."

"What is the place of women in this kingdom of yours?" came a solid female voice from behind the screen.

The Zebedee was seen to start.

Yeshuah's jaw dropped. It was unheard of for a woman to speak in synagogue. Quickly, he recovered himself.

"Whose was that voice from out of nowhere? One of God's angels do you think?"

As one man, the congregation gave way to laughter—a laughter near to hysteria in the need for release. All the townspeople knew that voice. And who was there who would dare to call the wife of the Zebedee to task? Certainly not even the Zebedee.

Yeshuah smiled, secretly grateful to the woman for breaking the tension.

"In answer to your question, oh Divine One . . . "

More laughter.

"There is always a place in God's kingdom for the helpmeet of Man. The Kingdom is closed to no one. But believe on me, and you shall find your place."

With an abruptness that shocked the watchers, Yeshuah then descended the steps of the dais and made his way through the crowd to the door. Hastily, his group followed.

He was in an excellent mood as they returned to Sarai's. He threw his arm about Judah and hugged him as they walked along.

"I think it went well, eh, my son?"

"They will have much to think and talk of this night. And for nights to come. But, Yeshuah . . . " He found himself hugging his brother back, leaning toward him, filled with a great love for the man. "What were you speaking of? What is this business of giving your life? Of being eaten!"

"Never you mind, Judah." Yeshuah laughed, and ruffled Judah's hair. Judah had never seen such a beautiful smile on his brother's lips, such radiance in his eyes. He told himself to remember that moment—to etch the picture into his mind, so that it could never be forgotten. Yeshuah—smiling, shining, splendid there against God's blue sky.

* * *

Judah could not sleep that night. He yearned to roll this way and that, to thrash against his quilt and sigh and mutter. But the quarters were cramped. He slept in a room with Salmon, Eli, and Ezekiel, who snored and licked their lips so peacefully that he had not the heart to disturb them. Finally he rose and padded quietly out in only his under-linen. It might have grown overly cool up on the roof, but he did not care—the ferment within his brain was creating enough heat to warm the whole world. He mounted the stairs and went to the parapet, looking out onto the lake. The air was pleasant, the moon at perfect full. He thought he could see . . . yes. The moon was so bright that he could see, not only, the beacon light, but, the tower itself, six miles down the coast at Magdala.

What were they doing down there tonight?

He lowered his face into his hands and rubbed his eyes.

He thought then that he saw Salome. She was dancing. Turning in dizzy circles.

"Oh, I wish Judah were here," he heard her say.

"My son."

Judah spun about.

"Yeshuah. Forgive me. I would never have come up if I had known I would interrupt you."

Yeshuah was kneeling upon the hard stucco, facing Jerusalem.

"It is all right." He rose stiffly and smiled. "Even the Messiah's knees grow sore. Come." He beckoned Judah over to the couches. They still held heat from the day. Yeshuah sank down and lay back, gazing at the moon hanging there on the other side of the lake, sending a path of light over the water to Kapher Nahum. "The world is so beautiful at times. I pray for them, Judah. They do not understand that I am their last chance."

"Why, Yeshuah? Why the last chance?"

Yeshuah turned his face to Judah, his expression tranquil.

"The end of days is coming soon, my son. That is why I was sent. To rescue as many as I can before it happens. It will be awful. There will be no stone left laying on top of another in the Temple."

"Impossible."

"I tell you it is the truth. There will be such a weeping, a wailing, and gnashing of teeth as has not been heard since the world began. Jerusalem shall be encompassed by the legions of Rome. Those shall be the days of vengeance. All things that have been written must be fulfilled. There shall be earthquakes, and famine, and pestilence, and great signs shall appear in the heavens. And woe betide those women who are with child, or who give suck, for the wrath of God shall overtake them, and they shall fall by the sword or be led away into slavery. And Jerusalem shall be filled with Gentiles, and they shall reign there until their time is done."

"But when will this happen?"

"All shall be fulfilled before this generation has passed away."

"But then what of the Kingdom of God on Earth that you spoke of today?"

"My kingdom will not be of this Earth, my son."

Judah sat up.

"But that is not what you lead everyone to believe."

"Ah, Judah. Listen more closely to my words. I am the Messiah. I come to redeem the children of Israel. I come to save them from the pit and to give them everlasting life. I will do this by offering my own sacred self to my father as the only acceptable sacrifice. Those who believe on me, who accept my sacrifice, and understand what I am doing, shall be saved. All others shall perish."

Judah sat straighter.

"You mean . . . a handful of people on the face of the Earth, who have heard your message—and all of that handful Hebrews—that handful shall be saved? All the rest shall perish?"

"Yes."

"But why did God create all those others only to leave them unsaved or unchosen and then destroy them? And you just said that Jerusalem would fall and be occupied by unchosen people, by Gentiles, until their time is finished. Yet you also say that all shall perish. How long is their time?"

"I do not know. I come to save the children of Israel, I have no knowledge of the Gentiles."

"But you said that the fall of Jerusalem would be the end of days. Yet, again, you say that Jerusalem shall be overcome and our people shall be led off into slavery. For whom, then, shall it be the end of days?"

"Judah, you ask too many questions."

"But . . . "

"That has become your favorite word."

"Yeshuah! You are stating some very awful things! And I am sorry, but I cannot seem to make sense of it all! Have I not the right to ask questions? Does not everyone have the right to ask questions?"

"No. You do not. Your lot is to obey. That is all."

"Obey whom?"

"God, of course."

"But how am I to know what God really wants of me?"

"I am telling you what he wants, my foolish boy! You have only to listen to me. I am the Messiah. I will show you the way."

"'But why does God choose to be so unreasonable, so arbitrary?"

"Unreasonable? Arbitrary? God laid down rules. The world has transgressed against those rules. The world must suffer for its transgressions."

"But you tell me now that redemption hinges on you, on your words, your actions. Yet you refuse to even speak to any Gentiles. If people do not have a chance to hear your words, and know of your sacrifice, and know that they are transgressing, how, then, can God justify their punishment?"

"Justify! It is not for such as you to question the actions of God, Judah. God does not have to justify a single thing."

Judah thought he heard a splash, and laughter.

The laughter of Jesus.

"What is going to happen to the world, Yeshuah?"

"To the world?"

"Yes. The fish and the animals and the plants and trees and sky. When God visits this wrath and destroys us all for being so sinful . . . what is going to happen to all the rest of it?"

"It will be burned in his fire, I suppose."

Judah looked over at the fig tree. It was drooping most pathetically. For a moment, Judah thought that he heard it sobbing.

"Why would God want to hurt these innocent and lovely things?"

"They belong to God, my son. They are his to do with as he pleases."

"What difference does that make? Have they no rights?"

Yeshuah smiled.

"What a ridiculous notion."

A strange thought came to Judah.

'If I were God,' he thought, 'I would love all these beautiful things. And even people. Most of them are not so bad down deep. If I were God, I could never bring myself to destroy them. And I would allow them some rights. After all, why did I create them in the first place? They must have some purpose. I must have had something in mind. And, if I am perfect, but my creations are imperfect, then the error is mine, so how is it fair to punish them? Why not help them, teach them, rather than destroying them?'

An even stranger thought came to him.

'Even Romans. They, too, must have some purpose, some worth to God. Have I, then, the right to go around killing them?'

"Ah, Judah." Yeshuah stretched, enjoying his rare moment of relaxation. "If only I could make them understand how much I love them. My people. This Palestine." He reached out a hand. "I will need you, Judah. Of all my brothers, you understand the most. I have it all planned. But I will need your help. Together—you and I—we will redeem the lost sheep."

"When were you first absolutely certain that you are the Messiah, Yeshuah?"

Yeshuah shook his head.

"How to point to one certain moment. I could not say. You remember the idolater that I killed and then raised up."

" . . . I was thinking of him only today."

"That incident made me know that I was different."

Judah smiled, but did not interrupt.

"And there were so many incidents after that, of which you know nothing. Still, I rejected the idea that I might be the Expected One. It is a hard thing to accept, Judah. The responsibility is immense. And the pain that I will have to bear . . . I faint within myself when I allow myself to think of what I must undergo."

Yeshuah's tone made Judah look over. For the first time ever, he saw fear in his brother's face.

"When we went to Johannan," Yeshuah continued softly, "you have no idea how I hoped, how I prayed that it was Johannan, and not I, who was born to bear this burden. But that was not to be. I am The One. I must face it with courage and bear it without a whimper. Pray God for me, Brother, that I will be brave enough to see it through and save these people whom I love so dearly."

For a moment, Judah had no breath. His brother's words had been so simple, so obviously sincere. He reached over and touched Yeshuah's hand.

"Yeshuah . . . are you very sure that Jesus is not The One?"

The question aroused no anger in Yeshuah. He simply shook his head.

"He is a false prophet."

Judah rose and turned away.

"You said that, together, you and I will redeem the sheep. Will I have to see men tear your flesh apart and eat it as you said today in the synagogue?"

There was more than a moment's hesitation. When Yeshuah spoke, the fear was in his voice again.

"Not quite. But almost. It is the only way. Can I count on you?"

Judah closed his eyes.

"You have already exacted one oath from me. Do not make me repeat it."

"Then I will give you your first assignment. I want you to return to the man Jesus."

Judah whipped around, staring.

"Why?"

"He is a constant danger to my plans. Your intelligence on his activities has been invaluable. You are in a position to go to him and pretend that you wish to follow him and not me, but then, secretly, to report everything back to me. Will you do it?"

Yeshuah was implementing his, Judah's, own plan. He was suggesting what Judah had, himself, been about to suggest.

He turned away again, hiding his elation.

"I am yours to direct. So of course I will do it." He kept his voice flat. "Do you wish me to slip away tonight, as though I have defected?"

"Yes. Be gone before the dawn, I do not wish to lose a moment. I will make an excuse for you. I will say that you are gone on my own business. As you know, our mother can be very hard." Yeshuah laughed. "Even the Messiah quakes before that woman, so I would not set her against you, else, when most I need your intelligence, she might bar you from our camp and from my presence."

He rose and took Judah by the shoulders.

"God go with you, my son. I will look for your reports weekly, by whatever means you can devise."

"I love you, Yeshuah."

"I love you too, Little Brother."

Judah pulled away.

"Yeshuah. The fig tree . . . "

"What about it?"

"Remove the curse. Bring it back to life. Please. Aunt Sarai loves it so."

Yeshuah shrugged.

"Brother, the tree is gone. Look at it. There is no way to put life back into those leaves. And why so concerned about a silly tree?"

Judah hesitated.

"It was only for Aunt Sarai," he said at last.

"She will survive, I promise you."

Yeshuah kissed him.

"Goodnight and goodbye, Judah. Remember how anxiously I will await your messages."

He walked slowly across the roof and disappeared down the stairs.

Judah, for his part, crossed to the fig tree and stood for some time staring at it. Finally he turned and, with quick and purposeful step, went to collect his belongings.

Chapter 9

Seven Demons and a Fig Tree

When old Jesse opened the gate to the House of Nathan the next morning, he found Judah asleep against it. Tethered to a nearby tree was an ass, bearing Judah's baggage.

"Now what would you be wanting?"

"Remember me? I am a friend to Jesus. I come to join him."

Jesse eyed the ass, and the baggage.

"I am sure he will be thrilled to have you," he said laconically. "Enter."

"Is anyone awake yet?"

"There was so much goings on last night I am not even sure any of them went to sleep." Jesse shook his head. "Out until all hours and the ceremony not yet performed . . . dancing and laughing . . . must have been the moon."

"Judah!"

Salome had only just entered the main court. She flew across the tiles and flung herself into his arms.

"Oh Judah! Brother! I have been wishing so hard that you would return. I am so happy to see you. I have so much to tell you!"

Judah's attempts to hide his pleasure were unsuccessful. He could not squelch his grin.

"Why of course I knew that, Salome, and it was just for you that I did come back. Only last night I dreamed that I saw you dancing and spinning and saying, 'Oh, I wish Judah were here!'"

Salome dropped her arms and backed away.

"What is wrong?" said Judah. "What did I say?"

"Why does everything have to be so *crazy* all of a sudden?" cried Salome. She turned on her heel and stalked away.

"What did I say?" said Judah to Jesse.

"Even if I knew, I would not tell you. I have decided to keep my mouth shut. If you want Jesus, you will find him in the kitchen with my mistresses. I will take your beast to the stable. What of your baggage?"

"Bring it to the kitchen I guess."

"The kitchen."

"I guess."

Jesse shook his head and continued on his grumbling way.

Judah's heart was pounding as he passed through the door to the kitchen. He could hear them, Jesus, Merovee, Deborah and the serving girls, talking and laughing.

The conversation halted as he appeared. For a moment they all stared. Then Jesus, who had been seated cross-legged before the hearth shaping bread cakes for the morning meal, rose and crossed swiftly to him. Before Judah knew what had happened, Jesus had gathered him into his arms and was hugging him.

"Welcome, Judah. I knew you would make it."

"You did?"

"Does your brother know that you have returned?"

"He sent me."

Judah pulled away and looked Jesus straight in the eye.

"I am assigned to spy upon you and report to him your every word, deed, and movement."

Jesus smiled, studying Judah's face.

"Had I known that he was so interested, I would have sent him daily pigeon reports. Thank you for your honesty, Judah."

"Do you want me to leave?"

"Do you want to leave?"

"No."

"Good. Not only are you frugal, but honest. Yes, you shall definitely be my treasurer. And perhaps you can do me the favor of telling me what your *brother* is up to from time to time, eh?"

Judah grinned.

"It is the least that I can do."

"Jesse heard that Yeshuah spoke in the synagogue of Kapher Nahum yesterday," began Merovee. Then she halted, puzzled, for Jesse, himself, came huffing in with Judah's baggage.

"Where do you want me to put it?"

"Oh . . . anywhere," said Judah.

Jesse set it down in the middle of the floor, shot Deborah a look, and left.

"I have brought you this," said Judah to Jesus.

"How very nice of you."

Jesus made a turn around the thing.

"It looks like a fig tree."

"It is," said Judah.

"In a pot."

"Yes."

"Did the journey not agree with it or was it dead before you began?"

"My brother cursed it. He ordered it to die. To show the power of God, he said."

"I can think of kinder ways," said Jesus mildly.

"The thing is . . . " Judah paced over to the hearth and turned. "He was angry because I told him that people were saying that your cures last while his do not. I said people thought that, therefore, your power comes truly from God while his does not. So he did this terrible thing to my aunt's favorite tree. Jesus, I thought I heard the tree sob. Is that possible?"

Jesus looked at him sharply.

"Your senses are finely tuned. Yes, it surely sobbed."

He bent and examined the plant. Its leaves and branches were not only drooped, but turned brown, and the trunk and branches were dry and brittle. It seemed that all moisture had been sucked from the victim.

"When did he curse it?"

"Friday afternoon just before the Sabbath."

"I am impressed. He certainly does know how to use The Energy. It is, however, a shame that he chose a destructive act with which to demonstrate."

"But he always does! I mean . . . that is why I brought it. Jesus. It has occurred to me that, rather than coming from God, my brothe's power comes from the Prince of Darkness."

"A common error in our thinking, Judah. The fact is that all Power, all Energy, comes from All That Is. *Is* All That Is. That true god gives it to each and every one of us, and it allows each of us to use it as we see fit in our own lives, constructively . . . or destructively, as we see here. For that is why we are here, do you not see? To learn of our own power, and to learn how best to use that power."

"Jesus," said Judah, turning squarely to him. "Jairus of Kapher Nahum told the congregation yesterday of how you returned his daughter to life."

Jesus frowned. Then shrugged.

"I suppose I could not really have expected him to keep silent forever."

"He revealed it only in order to protect your name and works from the slanders of my brother."

Judah came to Jesus, touched his arm.

"Jesus, please return this fig tree to life. It is very important to me."

"Believe it or not, Judah, whether or not the tree returns to life will be up to the tree. But we shall see."

He went to the corner where stood a vat of household water, filled an earthenware pitcher and returned to the side of the plant. Then he simply stood, cradling the jug of water between his two palms.

"I do not think water will help it," said Deborah.

"It is well and truly dead," agreed Merovee.

"In this moment, it is dead. But each and every moment is a separate fulcrum for The Power, independent of any other."

His hands kept moving, cupping and caressing the jug.

"Besides," he said finally, "if water will not help the tree, neither will it injure it."

With those words, he bent and poured the water over the base of the plant.

Judah dropped to his knees and commenced to stare at it.

"As Jerusalem was not built all in a moment," laughed Jesus, "so our corpse might require a few hours to think things over. Are you intending to serve the morning meal in the center court, Deborah?

"The girls have put out mats and cushions there in the sun."

"Then we will allow the tree to join us and share in our happiness, and perhaps rediscover a desire to live."

He bent to lift it.

"My word! How did Jesse carry this? Or you, Judah. Give me a hand here, Man. Merovee, get the door if you please."

They selected a spot just to the side of where they would eat, in deep shade, beneath overhanging branches.

"For I do not think it wants any sunlight just now," said Jesus, caressing the slim trunk, allowing his fingers to brush each branch and leaf. "Surely you did not carry this all the way from Kapher Nahum in your arms."

"I went to the home of the Zebedee. I knew his sons were with you, so I woke him to ask for the loan of an ass. I had not realized that he was stabling your own animal."

"So! You have brought me my Pharisee." Jesus grinned. "You must have had a very uneven trip."

"He does tend to balk a lot."

"Some creatures never learn to appreciate the goodness of the world around them, and so never cease their balking. Judah, you must stop staring at our patient, you will make the poor thing nervous."

Judah smiled. But his words were solemn.

"I asked my brother to bring it back to life. He laughed at me, and brushed me aside with smooth words. That is when I determined to bring it to you. If you can bring it back . . ."

He turned away.

"My brother killed a boy once. Remember, Merovee? I told you of the matter."

"I recall."

"When he realized that he might suffer for the killing, he brought the boy back to life. But only long enough to return him to the village, so that, next morning, when the boy was dead in his bed, it was assumed to be a natural death, with no onus attaching to Simon Yeshuah."

He turned.

"Everything my brother does is temporary. His cures last just long enough to astound people and send word abroad that he is the Messiah. He can raise from the dead, yes, but he does not return life to what he raises . . . they are as walking dead, who walk only long enough for Yeshuah's purposes. Perhaps it is not fair to ask this of you, Jesus, but I need to see that your power is greater. I need to know that there is a man in this world who can return my aunt's little fig tree to its prime and allow it to live out its normal span. After I see it . . . I want to understand it. I think you can teach me, Jesus. And I want to learn."

Jesus put a hand onto Judah's shoulder.

"Then learn you shall. Before I have finished with you, you shall know from first-hand experience that my words are true, that all of us have The Power within us. Then shall come your real test. For you shall have to decide for yourself how to use that power."

* * *

It was a busy day for the House of Nathan. As the entire company sat long over the morning meal, questioning Jesus and being taught, Jesse came to say that four men stood without the gate, seeking to know where Jesus could be found, wanting to become his followers.

The men proved to be Mathiah, Salmon, Ezekiel, and Eli. They were gratified to find Jesus at the spot where Mathiah had hoped he might be found, and stunned to find Judah there, sharing the meal with the rest.

"Yeshuah said he had sent you to Jerusalem!" said Mathiah.

"Not so," smiled Judah. "He sent me here to spy upon Jesus. Is that why he sent you?"

"He did not send us," said Mathiah uneasily. "We have left him. We spoke together of his strange utterances in the synagogue yesterday, and we decided. We think the man is mad."

His eyes dared Judah to blame him for breaking the oath he had sworn to Yeshuah.

"Jesus, we wish to follow after you and learn all that you will teach us."

"You are welcome. Have you eaten? No? Then sit. Here. Try the bread. I made it myself—under the tutelage of my wife and new mother, of course."

He leaned forward, watching for their reactions.

"Do you like it?"

"It is very good," said Salmon cautiously. He was accustomed neither to sitting down with strange women, nor to a man who would proudly announce that he had done a woman's task.

Jesus sat back, beaming.

"I thought it was rather good. For a first try."

His eyes took on a twinkle.

"And I assure you gentlemen that it is the only bread that has anything to do with my person—or body—that any of you will ever be required to eat."

Mathiah shuddered.

"Judah told you, then. What think you, Jesus? What in the world is Yeshuah planning?"

Jesus shook his head.

"I cannot be sure. It is amusing, in a way. We all know that Yeshuah is a man steeped in the letter of The Law, a man who would be the first to stone any idolater. Yet, ironically, he demands what many pagan religions demand. In Egypt, for instance, the 'flesh' of Osiris must be ritually cut into little pieces each year so that he can be reborn in his true glory. In Greece, there are several groups who suppose themselves to be eating the flesh and drinking the blood of their god, in order to achieve union with him, and assure both their own immortality and his own rebirth. There were ancients who killed their king every seven years and ate his flesh and drank his blood on the supposition that the rite would ensure another seven years of fertility, for the land and the people. Simon Yeshuah would be the first to condemn these forms of worship. Yet he seeks to form the same mythology and practice around himself."

"I can assure you," said Judah, "that my brother has never heard of any of these things."

"And so this symbology, this Universal Idea, has come to him naturally, from out of his own great, unconscious knowledge." He glanced at Merovee. "He draws on the many interesting concepts harbored by his parent entity. Were Yeshuah adhering strictly to Torah, he could not suggest such a thing. The aborted sacrifice of Ibraham's 'son,' Isaac, supposedly put an end to human sacrifice among Hebrews. Yet Yeshuah seems intent upon, at least symbolically, reinstating human sacrifice."

"But he is *not* speaking symbolically," said Judah. "I asked him myself if I would be required to eat his flesh. He said, 'Not quite. But almost. It is the only way.' He is planning to somehow make of himself a physical sacrifice, to save the children of Israel he says, for he says that the end of days is near, that one stone will not be left laying on another in the Temple."

"Josh!" said Merovee, "You told us the same thing in almost the same words."

"It is a strong probability, yes."

"Then the end of the world *is* at hand?" cried Judah.

"The world had no beginning and it will have no end, Judah. What we do encounter is change. I have already explained to the others that the most major of the changes occur each thousand years, with an especial emphasis at the turn of double millennia, which—in relationship to the six-thousand-year span of major experiments—this happens to be. We are, then, in the process of a transition that will be shattering to old ideas, old traditions, old ways of life. The changes which emerge from this period will set the direction for the last third of our current experiment.

"Now. Men like your brother, Judah, who are definitely talented in foreseeing major probabilities, but who are rigid in their thinking, allowing only one truth, one way—and that being *their* truth, *their* way—men such as that cannot imagine a world different from the one that they believe to be the only right or possible world. When they then look into the future and glimpse the vast upheavals which will accompany these changes, they assume that they are foreseeing the absolute end of the world, rather than simply the end of the world as they know it or would have it."

Jesus broke off a bit of his prized bread and chewed it thoughtfully.

"In a strange, symbolic way, your brother Yeshuah *is* his god. He is the old 'God of the Jews,' a narrow, restricting, punishing god of vengeance who must soon die . . . in order to be reborn in a greater form. A god 'come down to Earth' in order to 'die for his people.'"

"He called himself the Lamb of God," said Judah. "The only acceptable sacrifice. He says he will take all of our sins onto himself and carry them to the Father . . . so that, if we believe on him, we will then be saved from the wrath to come."

Jesus was still staring thoughtfully at nothing in particular.

"It is wonderful," he murmured. "Pay attention to the symbolism. And remember what I told you. Symbols are real things, powerful things, imbued with the energy of the living Ideas which create them. It is with symbols that each particular reality is created, that events are created, that any particular reality is perpetuated.

"The 'wrath to come.' Yes. The dying throes of gods *are* horrible to see.

"And that is what Yeshuah is up to. His greater entity knows of the vast change, the 'death' of Yeshuah's god that is about to occur. Yeshuah has borrowed much from the ideology of the Essenes, then translated it all into an impression of his own self as his god made flesh. He intends to physically act out the death of his god here on Earth, to, himself, bear his god's pain, and, in so doing, he believes, win pardon for us sheep.

"At the same time, by being his god come down to Earth from his lofty perch, made to live and love and hate and feel as the rest of us, then to suffer and die just as any mortal, Yeshuah plans to bring 'him' closer to Humankind, make 'him' more sympathetic to us and us to 'him,' so that a true mutual love and respect can develop."

Jesus shook his head appreciatively.

"Your brother *is* a great man, Judah. Deluded . . . far from any real understanding. But great no less. Men do not have to be wise, or 'right,' or even 'good' to be great. They have only to conceive within themselves a cohesive system of thought aimed at the goals that they believe to be good and of benefit to their fellows, and then act upon those beliefs with unremitting courage. Those with that sort of courage will always be called 'great' even if not 'good.'"

"Josh."

Merovee leaned over against him. He put an arm about her.

"I have seen a vision," she said. "Of Jerusalem."

"I heard you speaking of it to Deborah as I slept yesterday. You see men coming for me, you said. And then there is vast confusion. And you know only that you must lose me."

"What is it that I am seeing? What will happen to us in Jerusalem?"

He shook his head.

"Vast probabilities will be played out. I fear that, by that time—more and more I think because of this drama that Simon Yeshuah is intent upon—it will be beyond even me to fully control my own destiny, to chose the probability that I, myself, want to live out. I feel massive, emotional forces building.

"Understand, all of you, that I was not directly sent here by any 'God.' Instead, I was called. By the species. By you, yourselves. Since you, yourselves, each are units of All That Is, only in that wise could one say that I was sent by any god.

"So. I was born from out of a summons from the mass dreaming mind. That dreaming mind understood the approach of a double millennium, a unit in the Universal Cycle too vast, as a rule, for Humanity to consciously perceive. But, in the dream state, that mass mind understood the change that was approaching, and the new direction that Humanity craved to explore. That dreaming mind literally, out of its need, created such as Johannan and I . . . caused us to appear in our mothers' wombs.

"In other parts of the world, teachers such as ourselves—some of them actual parts of me or Johannan—have come to other populations, to teach, to guide them through the transition.

"But so great is the need, so hysterical is the energy being generated, that less developed Spirits, such as Yeshuah, also responded to the call. They act in complete sincerity. And that is the most difficult thing. As harsh as Yeshuah might be, as contorted and perverted as his teachings might be, he truly believes himself to be the Messiah. He believes that he, and he alone, was truly called, truly sent from 'God,' and that, thus, it is he alone who can redeem and save the children of Israel.

"There is nothing more difficult to combat than a man so convinced. Especially one who has mastered use of The Energy to the extent that Yeshuah has mastered it, and who is from an entity as powerful as his.

"And so what will happen to me in the maelstrom which the man is brewing? I might, in this probability, fall by the wayside, to be trodden under the convictions of Yeshuah's followers, to be remembered, if I am remembered at all, as a false prophet, or, worse yet, as a messenger from the 'Prince of Darkness.'"

"But Jesus!" said Petros. "How could that be? You are the Messiah, I know that you are. Is the outcome not thus foreordained?"

Jesus smiled patiently.

"Petros, you are not applying the principles which I have taught you. Repeatedly. Think back to what I have told you about probabilities."

"I cannot understand such complicated talk! I am a simple man, Jesus. You must talk to me simply."

"Simply, then, you do not have to understand. Merely believe that what I tell you is so, just as you believed me last night, and did a miracle as a result. Nothing is foreordained. Every single man, woman, and child, at any juncture, at every single moment of life, has freedom of choice. So how could anything be foreordained? *Probabilities* can be predicted, yes. But when the object of the prediction gets to that juncture, he may not choose the most probable course, he may choose to do something quite different.

"Which is why those who presume to predict the future often end up looking like great fools, and it is why there is so much furor and confused gibble-gabble over our Scriptural prophecies.

239

"Each man who prophesied was adept at seeing what was, from his standpoint—from his current understanding of the world—the most probable outcome of events. Each erred in believing that what he saw was the *only* possible outcome. Each one stated what he saw as an absolute that could not be changed.

"But there are no absolutes. Each of those seers had either glimpsed different probabilities from one another, or else each had colored the same probability with his own, individual prejudice.

"Hence, each story differed from the others just a bit.

"Our scrupulous scribes and Pharisees then, also believing there to be only one possible future, and believing all these prophecies to tell of one and the same situation, rubbed their brains, sat up night after night, and twisted words about until they found a way to make all the prophecies agree."

"But how, then," said Merovee, "can you tell us so confidently, as you did yesterday, that you will be present again in two thousand years."

"Tch, tch, tch. Apply the principles, Merovee. What happens each two thousand years?"

"Oh. The major upheaval, the turn of double millennia. And you just mentioned that that will be the end of this current experiment, so that . . . oh my. That will be *very* chaotic, will it not. So the mass dreaming mind will most certainly call you. You will appear in one form or another in every probability."

"I will actually appear in a large number of forms in all probabilities in that nodule. Do not forget also what I told you of time. Always take the true nature of time into account."

"It is simultaneous. Therefore . . . you, in all your manifestations, are already there, two thousand years hence, living . . . oh, so many lives, and in so many probabilities."

Jesus smiled at Petros.

"Have we made it simple enough for you, my friend?"

Petros sat scowling.

"No. What the two of you say makes no sense. If you are already there, living two thousand years hence, with all those people who must surely be more advanced than we, then why are we even bothering? Why are we even here? Why are *you* here if you can be there?"

Jesus considered for a moment.

"Did you go to synagogue school, Petros?"

"Of course."

"When first you went to school, did you know as much as you know now?"

"Of course not."

"Yet your teacher patiently taught you. A boring job, one would think, to have to, over and over, year after year, teach ignorant little creatures the very same things. According to you, your teacher should not have bothered. Why, he had friends his own age, who knew as much or more than did he. He could even have spent his hours in the synagogue listening to the sages. Why, then, did he waste his time teaching children?"

Petros nodded, understanding the parallel.

"We are newly born into this world," he said. "We have to learn. We are the continuation and the hope of our kind—and so of great value. We are greatly loved by those who know more than do we."

Jesus smiled.

"Splendid, Petros. And do you know—any teacher will tell you this—that teachers are constantly being taught by those whom they presume to teach. Teaching is far from being a boring job. The insights, the nuances that the teacher then takes to those of his own age and recounts to them, and tells to the sages in synagogues—those insights enrich those elders—who then cogitate upon that enrichment and speak words of wisdom which the teacher then cogitates upon and takes back to his children, the better to teach them. It is a system of constant mutual benefit, and constant learning, for all concerned.

"And so it is between time spans. Your advancement here enriches those living two thousand years into your future, while what they think comes back to you with us teachers and enriches you."

Petros nodded, but hunched down into himself.

"Ah Jesus. Just leave me to keep the crowds back from you. It is all I am good for. This talk of simultaneous time . . . how can a man be expected to understand it? Or even believe it?"

"How can it be more difficult to believe than walking on water? And you should understand simultaneous time as naturally as you breathe! You read Scripture, do you not?"

"Of course."

"Written in Old Hebrew. Have you never noticed that Old Hebrew speaks only in the present tense and does not seem to recognize either past or future?"

"Well of course I have noticed. It makes it almost impossible sometimes to understand what is being said, or when what they are talking about happened."

"Here again, we have a nice example of our unconscious knowledge of the true nature of reality. Old Hebrew somehow understood the 'Simultaneous Moment,' Petros, the simultaneous reality that is the body of the true god, All That Is, which is everywhere and all, and all that ever can possibly be, all *at the same time,* with no beginning and no end . . . only the Eternal Simultaneous Moment."

He smiled at Salmon, and at Eli and Ezekiel.

"What of you three? Do you boggle and wish for escape from my simple words?"

"Not I," said Salmon. He was only a boy, no older than the Boanerges. His eyes were shining. "I do not understand, but I desire to."

"I also," said Eli. He was older, with gray in his beard, and a roughness to his features. "I find what you say much easier than Yeshuah's insistence that we eat his flesh and drink his blood in order to be saved. You might say that I find it easier to . . . swallow."

They burst out laughing. Jesus nodded approvingly.

"You and I will get on splendidly, Eli. Ezekiel, what of you?"

Ezekiel was a dark and quiet young man, tall and handsome of face, smooth and polished as a sea-washed stone.

"Like Petros, I am a simple man, Jesus. I am not able to understand your words at this time. Until I do, I shall but listen and refrain from comment."

"A sensible course," said Jesus.

"Jesus," said Nathaniel, "those lives that you know yourself already to be living two thousand years into the future . . . can you see yourself there clearly? Are you aware of the details?"

"In my dreams I am. As I wake, most of it fades till I can remember only broad, general outlines. And that is as it should be. If, while here, I had to think about all the problems I am surely facing there, how could I concentrate on what I wish to do here?

"And by the way, Merovee, when you described your Jerusalem vision to your mother yesterday morning, you spoke of a place where all becomes confused. What you are sensing, that confusion, is your experience of the moment of intersection of major probabilities. Because of all the conflicting threads, you end up remembering nothing."

"Except that I must lose you," she murmured.

He shrugged, but pulled her close.

"Jacob! Lebbaeus!" said Deborah suddenly.

She rose and moved forward to greet two, short, stocky, pleasant-visaged newcomers. Merovee and Lazarus rose as well, going forward gladly to embrace the men.

"Jesus," said Deborah, leading the eldest of the men by the hand to where Jesus sat. "This is Jacob, son of my Uncle Alphaeus, he who sat with us in Obed's the other evening, remember? Jacob runs the pottery and dye works for me since Uncle retired. And this is his son Lebbaeus, without whom neither Jacob nor I would be able to get on."

"Welcome Jacob bar Alphaeus—and Lebbaeus bar Jacob. Do you, too, come to follow after me?"

"On the day before the Sabbath, I went up to see my father," said Jacob. "I found that he could also see *me*, for the first time in many years. When he told me why . . . my curiosity was baited."

"Curiosity is prerequisite to learning," grinned Jesus. "Sit you down. Have some bread. I made it myself."

* * *

They adjourned into the coolness of the sitting salon when the sun grew hot and the bread ran out. Jesus stretched out upon a divan and taught them with smiles and laughter, putting them all at their ease, answering questions with such understanding that no one feared to speak up, even if it was to disagree with him.

"I approve of your disagreement," he told Mathiah at one point. "It means that you are thinking about what I say and questioning within yourself. You will get tired of hearing me say that the answer to any question is always contained in the question. But you will never even find an answer, to anything, without first asking a question.

"There are worlds, universes, possibilities, which you cannot know of as yet. And you cannot as yet know of them because it has never occurred to you to ask whether they might be there.

"The moment that you ask, they *will* be there. This is one of the most delightful qualities of All That Is. Ask, and the answer will be given.

"And the amazing thing is that the answer might not even have *existed* until that moment when you asked the question! You see, with the question itself, you add a new dimension to the Universe, and to All That Is. Because the true god All That Is will immediately, from out of its endless possibilities, create an answer to your own creativity. And find great joy in doing so.

"This is what it is all about, do you see? You are a *partner* with All That Is, helping it to expand, push, test its own self to add to its Self.

"Seek without stinting, and you will always find. Without fail. All That Is loves to play the game with dedicated seekers.

"Seek not—and there will be nothing to find anyway. You leave All That Is twirling its thumbs."

"My brother said last night that we are not allowed to ask," said Judah. "He says that our lot is to blindly obey."

Jesus shook his head and spread his hands.

"What can I say, Judah? Your brother and I could not be more in disagreement."

"But which of you is right?" said Levi.

"Both of us and neither of us."

"You talk in riddles again!" said Petros in exasperation.

"There is no such thing as right, and there is no such thing as wrong," said Jesus. "There is only what is *considered* to be right or wrong by any individual at any moment.

"Judah told me that, yesterday in the synagogue, Yeshuah paraphrased the watchwords of the Essenes, saying to the congregation, 'I am the way, the truth, and the light.' And he added, 'He who believes on me shall never perish.'

"Well, what he said was absolutely true . . . as far as it goes. For himself, and for those who believe him, he *is* the way—their current way. He is the truth—their current truth. And he is the light—their current light.

"And those who believe on him shall *not* perish. Though that is because *no one* perishes, ever. It is not because Yeshuah has any special influence with any god.

"But Yeshuah does not know this. Deep within himself, he does know that eternal life is possible. Since he has never asked himself whether eternal life might not just be a natural gift from All That Is, the inalienable heritage of everything, living or non-living, in this world, he feels that he must make a special promise, offer a guaranteed way to achieve what he is sure is possible for those who have also never bothered to ask.

"Everyone then goes home happy. The people are assured that they will have everlasting life, while Yeshuah thinks he has fulfilled his mission and saved the world.

"I told you before, Judah. Those who do not care to stir themselves to ask questions—the Tortoises as I call them—who prefer to spend their lives alternately hiding in their shells or creeping fearfully along in the dust, will flock to Yeshuah. They will hear his words and be pleased with them, for those words will require not one jot of thinking or spiritual courage on their parts.

"'Do not ask questions,' Yeshuah tells them. 'Questioning is not allowed. Just believe what I tell you and you will be fine.'

"And so they *will* be fine! Because all are equally cherished by All That Is. And these Tortoises will return again and again to this life, and hide in their shells, and creep in the dust, and be buffeted by life with all its 'cruelties,' and by sickness, and pestilence, and tragedy, and they will cry out against a cruel fate and an 'uncaring' 'God,' not knowing that there is another way. They will just keep listening to the Yeshuahs of the world, who miss the mark as widely as it can possibly be missed, by seeking to enslave the minds, direct and control the thoughts, and curtail the Ideas, of their fellows.

"But no mind will remain enslaved forever. One by one, the Tortoises will grow bored with, or angry about, their lot, and venture to ask the questions which the Yeshuahs have forbidden.

"Then, and only then, will the Tortoises come to such as I, and hear my words, and find a happier way.

"Six of you came to me today. I did not tell you to come. I did not shout and fill you with guilt and fear and threaten you with eternal damnation if you did not come, neither do I threaten you with damnation if you do not believe a word that I say. You came because you wanted to come, because you have shed your Tortoise shells and have questions that must be answered.

"I will be your way, your truth, your light, then. But only for a little while. Only until you understand that, truly, it is your own self which is the way, the truth, and the light to your own Self.

"Like Yeshuah, I will also promise you eternal life. But without any strings. Even if you leave me, fail me, betray me . . . if you commit the foulest of acts, still, I promise you eternal life. I can do nothing else, for eternal life is the nature of reality."

He smiled.

"I would add, however, that I can show you ways to vastly improve the quality of your realities in that eternal life."

Petros shook his head.

"I can not agree with your words. You would have no right or wrong, no reward or punishment. You make it sound as though people can never really do wrong, are never really bad. But they can and they are! Look around us, you see evil every day."

"Yes, Petros, I do. The difference is that I see all that 'evil' from the mountaintop, while you have never ventured out of the valley. You have scarcely even lifted your eyes from the path on which you walk. So that, when you observe this 'bad' action, you see it at very close range. It fills your entire vision, it is massive in extent. You are as a man who has a bad cold, and who descends into despair and rage, wailing that 'God' and Life and Fate, each one, is cruel and unjust. You forget all the good days before the cold, and the good days that will follow the cold.

"Looking down from my mountain, I have better perspective. And All That Is sees from an even higher peak. It can see far into the distances. Its view is a multi-dimensional panorama . . . and it can see the whole life of that man with a cold. It can also see the lives that he lived before, and the lives that he has yet to live. It smiles gently at the man's petty rage, understanding his cold—which the man considers to be such a 'bad' thing—to be but a minor, though quite necessary, adjustment in the overall objectives of the eternal journey of the man's Soul and his parent entity."

"But a bad cold—or illness, any calamity—is not insignificant to the person it is happening to," protested Salome.

"Luckily not."

"Luckily?" said Salome. "How can you say that? Was it lucky for the Prophet that he was murdered? Or for my mother and me that my step-father placed the blame upon us two, while we yet had the heartbreak of preparing Johannan's dear head for burial?"

There was a stirring among the newly arrived men—save Mathiah—as the identity of the girl with the pale red hair dawned upon them.

Jesus was aware of that stir, but he continued smoothly on.

"Yes, Kitten. Lucky for you and for many other people in this world. If it had not been for Johannan and his tragic death, we would not all be here now. None of you would be embarked on your current path of learning and understanding. Generations, yet unborn, will profit from what you do here with me.

"And so this 'bad,' 'evil' thing done to Johannan turns out, when you climb up onto the mountain and see it in perspective, to be the focal point of a great good that will send its ripples into the farthest eternity. And it was for that purpose that Johannan came. So that, from the mountaintop, one can see his triumph.

"If you study each 'bad' event closely—no matter how small the event might be—if you simply stub your toe—you can, if you apply yourself, perceive the good that flows from that event. Allow yourself to be angry if you must, to cry at first, or to grieve. Allow your emotions to flow, for emotions, honestly expressed, never turn against you.

"But then allow yourself to ponder what possible good could have come out of the event. If you really try, you will find a good. Perhaps you learned something from the event, or others learned something. Perhaps you met someone new as a result. Perhaps the fact that it happened has made you or others swear never to make the same mistake or to be guilty of the same wrong. Perhaps it caused whole groups to change their attitudes toward that sort of event. Perhaps it has caused someone to put his arms around you and hug you and give you extra attention. Like old Demetrius, you might even have learned to appreciate such kindnesses, and have conceived a desire to return them.

"Begin, then, to dwell on whatever little good you can find. Start climbing the mountain as you do so, trying to see more and more of the view, to gain greater and greater perspective. Think, in your minds, of ways in which that good could ripple out, affecting others. See those ripples go forward even into the future, touching generations unborn, until you have imagined a hundred goodnesses that might flow from the 'bad' event.

"If you will do this often enough, you will begin to understand why the concept of a punishing, unforgiving god is sheer nonsense. The higher you climb, the more you understand, the more you forgive, the more you love. And the true god All That Is stands on the highest peak of all."

"But if good ripples out from a bad event," said Petros angrily, "does not bad ripple out as well?"

"It certainly does. Yet I will tell you a wonderful, joyful secret. Good is much more powerful than evil.

"I know. You think I am crazy. You look about and you see much evil. Forgetting the vast, loving base which *allows an experiment that has turned out 'badly' the right to exist*, you concentrate on the 'evil.' Its contemplation fills your entire life, till it seems that there is nothing other than evil, and that, hence, evil must be stronger than good.

"But the Universe is predisposed to goodness, Petros. All its workings are positive. How else could you even *be* here, in a world where the sun rises and sets, and grains grow, and your body lives. You ignore this vast, loving basis of your everyday life.

"And you fail to see that the ripples from a good action—which are totally good, and the good ripples hiding in a 'bad' action, will never cease traveling through time and space. They cannot be stopped once set in motion.

"The bad ripples of a totally 'bad'—what we would call 'evil'—action, *can* be stopped. You can stop them with good. With Love. You can stop them by understanding their basis and applying a new understanding.

"This takes great courage. The courage of a 'Daniel.' But, as the Daniels of this world increase, wave after wave of ancient evil, which have been traveling the Universe since time immemorial, shall be halted, made as though they never existed, replaced with understanding, and with Love. And then the lion shall lie down with the lamb, and Humankind shall enter the age that some have foreseen and called the Realm of the Blessed."

"I can not see that that will happen very soon," muttered Petros.

"You just sent out a ripple, my friend. A 'bad' one. That little bit of distrust, of negative expectation for your fellows and yourself, is off into eternity. And you are the one who is going to have to chase it. You will encounter it again and again, in life after life. The 'sins of the fathers' will be visited upon the 'sons' of your own Soul. Until, some day, one of those 'sons' develops into a 'Daniel,' and dares to nullify this evil that you, yourself, have put into motion—with Love, understanding, and trust. No one else can do it for you. Only the one who launched that boat can bring it to harbor.

"That is the other truth to the eradication of 'evil.' No one else can learn your lessons for you. No one else can take your 'sins' onto his own shoulders . . . for then *you* would have learned nothing."

"Is it that way with every word that we speak?" said Johannan, the youngest of the Zebedees. "Does it *all* ripple out into the Universe?"

"Every word, every thought, every action. And so, if only for selfish reasons, it stands to reason that you are best off trying to send out good."

"But how can we do that?" said Jacob, the eldest. "We would never get anything done if we had to halt before every word or thought and decide upon its merits."

"And how frightening," said Johannah, "to think that we could spend eternity atoning for the least little slip of the tongue."

"Any more frightening than the sort of thing that Yeshuah or the priests in the Temple would tell you? They give you no chance at all, consign you to punishment for all of eternity for any of a thousand arbitrary reasons, with no hope of pardon, not even a second chance." He smiled. "I think my offer is an excellent one, Johannah. With me, you get an endless number of chances to make good. While, to atone or not to atone—and when—is strictly up to you."

"I think it is that 'strictly up to you' that is the most frightening part," said Johannah ruefully.

"Clever woman. That is, however, the way things really are, so you might as well make your start now as later.

"But wipe the word 'atone' from your mind. It implies eternal, slavish bowing before some master. You do not have to spend eternity 'atoning' for a slip of the tongue. You have only to understand the truth of your error and learn how not to do it again. You may do that in the same lifetime or wait a million years, the choice is always your own.

"Now, in answer to your question, Jacob, you are right. It is silly to move as haltingly through life as a Pharisee, terrified lest you make an error. Remember that All That Is shares in your errors and learns more of itself from those errors, so that, even while erring, you never cease to be loved. The trick is simply to become increasingly ware of the things that I have told you, and to understand the greater extensions of your every word and deed.

"You will be amazed at how quickly you begin to think differently, speak differently, act differently. Being ware to consequences, understanding your own responsibility for what you are setting in motion, will become a part of you, so that you no longer have to *think* about acting with 'goodness,' you simply *will* act with goodness.

"Not with the false and sterile piety of the Pharisees and Sadducees and elders of Zion, mind you, who give their alms on street-corners to the clanging of bells, and proclaim their holiness with clothing designed to draw attention, and with behavior designed to do the same, and who demand the best, and highest, seats in synagogue, so that all may know of their piety and watch them pray.

"All That Is finds these people, not holy, but boring.

"You will do well to give your alms in secret, and find your goodness proclaimed only in the vast, loving reaches of your own Souls. You will do well to take the lowest seat in the synagogue with no demur. Not from meekness, but because of the fact that you have nothing to prove to anyone but yourself.

"Indeed, you will find that you do not even need a synagogue. You will come to recognize your own self as the house of the true god All That Is.

"You will find this secret goodness so easy after a while. You will find yourself rushing gladly to any point where you see that something may be done to right a wrong, knowing that the little evil to be righted is one of your own waves coming in, that was set in motion by an erring you on a distant shore."

"But if all this is to be done in secret," said Phillipus, "does that not preclude teaching to others?"

"Yes and no. Once you *Know* the truth, I enjoin each of you to speak it. But only to those who come seeking. There will be plenty of those, I assure you. Please, do not ever force yourselves onto any who do not want to hear you. For one thing, it is a tremendous waste of your precious energy. The Energy. And never threaten people with horrendous consequences should they not believe your words.

"I do not care what anyone tells you. *The Souls of others are none of your business.* Only *your* Soul is your business. You will have all that you can do to remove the mote from your own eye without messing about with the faulty vision of others.

"And so, Phillipus, the secrecy of which I speak is mainly this. Do not speak loudly or publicly of how much you love others. *Show* your love, quietly, in each movement and action that you take toward all living things, and even to the seemingly inanimate objects in the world around you.

"Be gracious, even as All That Is is gracious.

"Be patient, even as All That Is is patient.

"Be thankful, even as All That Is is thankful.

"Be humble, even as All That Is is humble.

"Forgive all, even as All That Is forgives all of you."

Old Jesse appeared in the doorway.

"Jesus, there are those at the gate who claim to be your parents and brothers and sisters."

"My parents and brothers and sisters? Who *are* my parents, my brothers, my sisters?" he said, smiling at each of them in turn. "They are yourselves. You are my sisters, my brothers. There are those among you who have even acted my parents in other lives."

"Shall I send them away?" said Jesse.

"I would hate to see you try it. My mother digs in deeper than any she-ass."

Merovee sat up in surprise.

"You think that it *is* them? How could that be? There has not been time."

"Did I not tell you yesterday," he said with a twinkle, "that it is possible to send a mental message to Bethlehem and to know that it has been received?"

"But then come!" cried Merovee, jumping to her feet. 'We must not leave them standing there. Mother, Lazarus, hurry!"

She and her family rushed out ahead of the others. Laughing, Jesus followed.

He was half way across the courtyard when he heard Judah cry out.

He turned.

The young man knelt beside the fig tree, sobbing.

Jesus walked to his side and placed a hand on his head.

"There. You see? A little water, quiet shade, and good company . . . that is all that was needed."

"Thank you, Jesus. Thank you."

"Do not thank me. It is our little green friend who deigned to lend itself to a demonstration of the real Power of the real god. The truth is, Judah, that there is no such thing as a dead fig tree."

Jesus turned and hastened to greet his family.

* * *

The House of Nathan resembled a beehive, in sound and activity, for the rest of the day. Servants were dispatched to the market of Magdala, while Petros set sail for Kapher Nahum, and the Boanerges for Tarichaea, to purchase the more exotic supplies which Deborah deemed necessary for the proper entertainment of such honored guests. Some of the men busied themselves setting up a dormitory in the stable, for the house would not take twelve more people with any kind of comfort, and one never knew when yet more would arrive. It was decided that Jesus and his male followers would sleep in the stable, leaving the house to his family, and to the women.

As for Deborah and Rosula, Jesus hardly gave them time to say hello. He sat them down and bade them compile their guest list before the afternoon was out, so that messengers could be dispatched on the morrow, and the wedding held in just over a week from that time.

Actually, those still to be invited were of Galilee, with not far to travel, for, besides Martha in Bethany. and two of her husband's cousins, there was no one in the south that Deborah cared to invite. The only other members of her husband's family still living were of such distant relationship that she had not seen them in years.

While Rosula had already sent word to Joseph's brother Cleopah and his wife Miriam in Mount Ephraim, to his sister Annah in Hebron, and to her own son, Jacob, in the Essene community at Qumran.

Rosula was vastly proud of herself for having responded to her dream.

"Oh, I learned to know when it was really he years ago. I always knew where he was in his travels, for he would come to me in dreams and tell me. There is a feeling to that sort of dream that is different to any other. You wake up and just know. So I would tell Joseph, 'Joshuah is in India. He is well.' 'He just reached Athens. His feet are sore.' 'He is at Mount Ararat, and the natives pointed out a dot up on the snows near the peak that they say is the ark of Noah.' And, when he would come home to visit us, sure enough, he would verify all.

"So! When I woke from sleep on Friday morning, I told Joseph, 'Joshuah is going to marry the granddaughter of Nathan. We are to go to the place of Nathan's factory immediately.'

"I sent servants off to Jacob and Cleopah and Annah, and also to some of Joseph's friends of the Sanhedrin, who I hope will come. Luckily, Jude was at home for a few days, as I would never have known where to send word to him.

"We set off as quickly as we could pack and journeyed straight through the heat of the day on Friday, so that we were well beyond Jericho when we stopped for the Sabbath."

She clapped her hands like a girl.

"We camped out! I have never done that before, it is really very nice, I think I shall not use inns anymore. You feel the earth, you know? And the sunrises and the sunsets! It takes the breath away out there in the middle of nowhere.

"And so there we were, camped near to the road on the Sabbath, when along came jogging Merovee's messenger. I realized that he was no Jew to be traveling on the Sabbath. I do not know what made me realize the rest, but I ran out and hailed him and asked if he was on business for the House of Nathan. He then verified the wonderful news and rode on to Bethany to collect your daughter and cousins.

"Joseph had to eat a handful of grass. He had made me a wager that I was wrong about the marriage, you see, and promised to eat grass if I was right.

"Is your stomach better now, Dear?"

The father of Jesus, the ranking prince of the House of David, was the human equivalent of a cipher. It was difficult to describe him. His features seemed non-features. His height was neither here nor there, and his hair and beard were no particular color. He hardly ever looked straight at anyone, so that the color of his eyes was hard to determine.

No wonder that the Romans had never considered him any sort of threat, but, instead, socialized with him, grew to genuinely like him, and gave him their confidences. He was not respected by Zealots on account of his Roman associations, especially with Praefectus Pontius Pilatus, but that same lack of commitment or threat kept him as safe from the sicarii of the Zealots as it did from the Romans. Rebels considered him to be stupid, ineffectual, committed to nothing in particular, and not worth bothering with. Romans thought they could depend upon him for guileless confidences as to the hidden Jewish climate.

Joseph was, thus, the Sanhedrin's most valuable man. Through Joseph's unthreatening socializing, the Sanhedrin kept always in a favorable light with the praefectus, while learning, through Joseph, much in the way of information that was privy and ought not to have been uttered to any Jew.

Joseph of the Triple High Ramah was, in fact, far from stupid. And he *was* committed . . . to the welfare and safety of, first, his family, second, his people. He was a kind man who wanted only to be left in peace, and who had never really been accorded that privilege.

His childhood had been steeped in fear. It was then that he had learned to blend into the scenery, and act the enemy of no man. For that childhood had been spent in the midst of dynastic wars between the remnants of the old Maccabean dynasty—the Hasmonaeans—and the appointees of Rome, the Herodians. In the matter of who should be King of Judeah, there were many who had felt then, and still felt, that neither the Hasmonaeans nor the Herodians had a legitimate claim, that the only legitimate claim was that of the ranking prince of the House of David.

But Joseph's father Jacob had been a peaceful man as well, eager only to be left alone. So that, finally, he had taken his wife and children down to Egypt, removing himself and his male heirs from the jealous arm of Herod the Great, and discouraging compatriots who talked incessantly of making the House of David the focus of a new battle cry.

Years later, the family ventured back into Palestine. But the low profile had been studiously maintained. The political climate of Judeah had still been treacherous, with Herod gone quite mad, so jealous of his power that he had taken to murdering his own family one at a time. So the family did not return to Bethlehem. Jacob took them, instead, into Samaria, to the family lands near Mount Ephraim, and, eventually, for greater safety, into Galilee.

It was in Galilee that Joseph had been betrothed and married to Miriam, daughter of a merchant of Tarichaea made wealthy in the tin trade with the Isle of the Britons. The marriage, though affluent, had purposely been far from dynastic, and, indeed, due to Miriam's Celt mother, problematical as to Hebrew blood lines. But, the less the House of David presented a threat to either Herodians or Romans, the better.

The death of Jacob shortly after that of the dreaded Herod saw the division of Jacob's holdings among his three children, and the departure of those three from Galilee. Joseph's younger brother Cleopah was allotted the family vineyards of Mount Ephraim. Their sister Annah was given the sheep-grazing lands of Hebron. While it was now safe for Joseph, the first heir, to take his pregnant wife home to Bethlehem, and repossess the rich ancestral wheat lands outside of that village—the same wheat lands which had belonged to his ancestor Boaz, where Naomi and Ruth had come to glean.

In that place, Joseph's children had been born. Through the years, he had continued his endeavors to simply blend into the scenery.

So it was that Joseph of the Triple High, the Ramahs of God—of Mount Ephraim, Hebron, and Bethlehem, the most exalted genealogy amongst the children of Israel—sat in the salon of the House of Nathan that day a very disturbed man, whose lifetime of careful colorlessness might have come to naught.

All of Jerusalem was buzzing about the mysterious Messiah preaching and healing along the shores of Gennesareth. Joseph, for one, had had no doubts as to the identity of the man, and there were many in high places who were beginning to put two together with two, so that Joseph had had to rise to elegant new heights of avoidance . . . of Romans, members of the Sanhedrin, of priests, Pharisees, his own Sadducees, and of the Zealots.

Yes, all of Joseph's sons were rebels of one sort or another. But Jacob, of the skinny, burning eyes and Essenic ideas, had never really disturbed the status quo, while young Jude, who mixed with Zealots, brought little more than shrugs from Joseph's Roman and Jewish colleagues.

The rumors which had drifted south from Galilee in the last month or so were another thing altogether. Joseph could hardly believe that his eldest would be foolish enough to declare himself the Messiah and rightful King of the Jews, issuing a direct challenge to both the Jewish hierarchy and to Pontius Pilatus—who, though titled praefectus by Rome, was the de facto King of Judea, Samaria, and Idumea.

Joseph's best hope was in this marriage. Despite the unorthodox manner in which it was being conducted, the girl was of good family, there seemed to be no dynastic complications, and a wife was a fine thing. A wife settled a man, even the wildest of them.

And Joshuah was no wild man. He was a good, responsible boy. His ideas were not to be countenanced, it was true, and his behavior, almost since birth, had been abominable. But he was good and responsible no less. Joseph loved his eldest a great deal.

What made things worse was the fact that it had occurred to Joseph that Joshuah would make a great king.

It was as the women got deeply into the guest list that Joseph was able to suggest to his eldest that they take a walk.

Jude rose as well. He, too, had guessed the identity of the "Messiah" of Galilee, and was aching for private converse with Jesus. Fiery Zealot that he fancied himself to be, he was all for instituting a blood bath in an attempt to put his brother onto the throne.

Joseph motioned him back down.

"I would speak to your brother privately."

"Do not let him talk you out of anything, Josh!"

Joseph answered for Joshuah.

"When have I ever been able to do that?"

The two men walked, not toward the town, but, westward, following a little-used path up into the hills, until they had a fine view of the entire Lake of Gennesareth. They sat for a while as they had walked, silent, enjoying the panorama. Josh's attention seemed especially drawn to a place on the heights behind Heptapegon.

"Do you not think it would have been considerate to confer with me before making your contract?" said Joseph at last. "After all, it is the prerogative of a father . . . "

"Would you have said no to the match?"

"No, it is a fine match, but . . . "

"I knew you would think that, so I saved time and got on with it."

"But there are monetary matters to be discussed!"

"Merovee . . . "

"Why do you persist in calling her by a Canaanite man's name, is she not Miriam?"

"She was. Now she is Merovee. She is freely given, her family requires nothing of us, and I require nothing of them. Finances are the very last worry in this match, Father, so all of that foolishness was passed by."

"Foolishness! We have customs, Young Man! Our people have customs, and they exist for good reason!"

"Name one."

"Finances are a reason unto themselves," Joseph spluttered.

"They have certainly become that to many people. If Merovee's mother and brother had asked a bride price, what would that have signified? That I was buying her while they were selling. If, on the other hand, I had demanded a dowry, what would that have signified? That they had to pay to be rid of her. Both instances imply that a woman is a piece of merchandise to be bought and sold. Well, I want no such merchandise. I want a friend, a lover, a free and equal partner to my endeavors."

Joseph shook his head.

"I do not understand what is happening in the world. You young people are going crazy, just crazy. I think the prophecies are correct. The end of the world must surely be at hand. What are my colleagues going to think of this hasty marriage? I hope to Heaven that none of them do come down for the wedding, I *told* Rosula not to invite them."

He shrugged.

"Me, you can handle. But I have the feeling that I have only just begun to see the improprieties that will accompany this marriage, and I want them witnessed by as few people as possible."

Joshuah laughed.

"Too late for that, I am afraid. From what I heard back at the house, my mother intends to invite all of Tarichaea and half of Galilee."

"Never have I seen a woman with so many relatives. And they never lose track of one another! She knows where to find even the great-great-great-grandchildren of the great-aunts and uncles of her great-great-grandparents."

He grinned ruefully at Joshuah's laughter.

"I should know. I have entertained them all at one time or another, each with their dozen or so children. Your new mother-in-law does not know what she is in for when she insists on paying half the cost of the wedding. Just that half might break even the House of Nathan."

He became serious once more.

"Joshuah, take care not to thumb your nose at too many customs in this matter. And, for the sake of us all, do not so much as dent Mosaic Law as clearly written. There will be Sadducees watching, waiting for you to do so."

They had not discussed Joseph's suspicions as to the identity of the supposed Messiah, but Joseph proceeded as though there were no need.

"The Pharisees and their interpretations of Oral Law can be gotten around. It is, after all, only interpretation. And, for every school that would rule one way, we can find another school to rule in the opposite direction. Just do not be found in direct violation of what is written in Torah."

"You think, then, that the Sadducees with their literalism are the ones to watch?"

Joseph shook his head.

"I wish I knew. I do know that they are the people who could have you executed the same day with no questions asked. I fear that they could somehow use the very haste of this marriage to make trouble."

"No period of waiting is outlined in Scripture, Father, so it is not a fundamental violation. Additionally, this is not a situation to which most of The Law and interpretation applies itself. Merovee is not a maiden, but a widow. And carrying a child."

"No wonder she was freely given!" cried Joseph.

"She would have been in any case, and I would have wanted her in any case. Her husband was the Prophet, Father. She carries the child of the Prophet."

Joseph put his hands to each side of his head.

"Joshuah! For the love of Heaven, what are you getting yourself into? You place yourself as enemy to every authority in the land. Do you not realize that I have pieced together all the rumors flowing south these last weeks and realized that you are the Messiah of whom they speak? It is only a matter of time before the High Priest and the Romans figure it out as well. And that girl whom you introduced in the salon . . . Salome. I know that I have seen her before. *Please* do not tell me . . . "

"I am afraid so, Father."

"Oh my God. My God."

"Do not take 'his' name in vain," Joshuah teased.

"I am not taking his name in vain!" cried Joseph. "I am *calling* on him."

He took Joshuah's arm.

"Promise me you will tell your mother none of this until after the wedding. Let her have her happiness and peace of mind for at least that long."

"I am afraid she will have to know of Merovee's widowhood," said Joshuah. "I have need of her amazing grasp of the intricacies of her family tree. I never did really understand the relationship between her and Johannan's mother. Johannan thought I was his most senior, unmarried, male relative. Only mother will know for sure."

"Joshuah, you really do not have to do this. Leverite marriage is disregarded more often than not nowadays, especially for unmarried distant relatives rather than brothers. No one would look askance if you turned away from this matter."

"The son of Joseph of Ramah—who might now be claiming to be the Messiah—ignoring Law and custom? And you think no priest, or Sadducee, or Pharisee would notice?"

"You are right. Well, maybe Rosula can come up with a more senior candidate after all."

"If she does," said Jesus, "we will get him here so that Merovee can spit in his sandal before she and I drink the wine."

"What if he will not renounce his right?"

"If he puts on that act, I will have to offer him such a handsome sum that he will drool at the mouth and appear, to all watching, to be spitting in the sandal himself."

"Ahhhh!" Joseph put his hands alongside his head once more. "Sometimes I wonder if you are really my son."

Joshuah patted Joseph's knee.

"Yes and no, Father."

"Yes and no, yes and no. What ever happened to a good firm yes? An unequivocal no? A person used to know that the ground he trod was solid. Now it is full of quicksand. Joshuah, you have got to stop calling yourself the Messiah and saying that you are the rightful King of Judeah."

"How could I make that claim when you are the rightful king?"

"Stop that! Be serious!"

"I am serious. I have never claimed to be the rightful King of the Jews. Neither have I said to anyone that I am the Messiah."

"But the talk in the Temple courts is that . . . "

Joshuah raised his arm, pointing north along the shoreline.

"Look up there about four miles, to that hill with an outline like a camel's hump."

"Yes?"

"Look carefully. Can you catch the movement? There are a great many people on that hillside. About two thousand I should say."

"Yes. What is going on?"

"I can only think that it is the man who calls himself the Messiah and rightful King of the Jews, preaching to his flock."

Joseph of the Triple High of God rose, staring intently at that distant hillside.

"Are you telling me that the rumors are of that man and not of you?"

Joshuah smiled.

"Yes and no."

"Do not play games!"

"I play only the games which that wonderfully capricious and delightfully droll thing called Life puts squarely into my hands—or mouth, as the case may be. I have never called myself Messiah or rightful king. That man has. He insists on it. But both of us are teachers, we are both capable of miracles, though he is more intent on 'driving out demons,' while I think in terms of healing. He likes to speak to huge groups such as you see there. I prefer selected intimates or small groups. He is fond of entering synagogues to proclaim his divinity. I have not been inside a synagogue since I entered Galilee."

"Shame on you."

"Show me in Torah where a man must attend synagogue.

"Both of us have followers. Both of our doctrines are at variance with the current understanding. We share a certain superficial resemblance, in stature and in coloration. And his name is Yeshuah."

"Yeshuah!"

The light dawned.

"His given name is Simon," said Joshuah. "But, when he was little, so his brother tells me, he began to be pet-named after a great-grandfather who was called Yeshuah.

"When I first met him, he was calling himself Simon Yeshuah. Since my arrival in Galilee, he has begun more and more to refer to himself only as Yeshuah.

"I think it is purposeful. He knows my superior genealogy and hopes to trade upon it. I think he wants this confusion. With such similar facts about the both of us circulating, who can know what is true of him, or of me—or even that there are two of us? They certainly do not know that in the Temple courts."

"How should they?" said Joseph ruefully. "Travelers come up to Jerusalem and rave on and on of the miracle man teaching in Galilee who must surely be the Messiah. The details they give are alike enough to speak of only one man.

"As to the name, I, myself, had heard Joshuah instead of Jesus, and Yeshuah instead of either of those. And yes, once I heard Jesus. I never thought but that all variations referred to you. So."

Joseph walked two steps forward, as though by doing so he could better see the man on the distant hill.

"He hopes for your genealogy to be confused with his own, does he? Well, I will see to it that the right people in Jerusalem are told what is what. He is a Zealot?"

"He makes our young Jude look like a Sadducee."

Joseph nodded.

"Yes, I quite agree with you. He means to use the initial confusion to add to his own prestige, to gather followers and convince those followers that his claim to the throne is so powerful that the people will rally behind him. What will it matter if his claim is found to be inferior once an insurrection is set in motion? There would be no going back at that point, and, after all, Scripture does only say that the Messiah will be 'of the loins of David.'"

Joseph stood for a moment, nodding in agreement with himself.

"Yes. I see his strategy clear. 'Borrowing' our genealogy could definitely win him the early support that he needs. There are always plenty of wild-eyed royalists to be had in this poor land."

Joshuah watched his father with respect. It was seldom that one saw the man in this light, was caused to remember the harried childhood, to understand the quick mind that had brought him safely through youth and middle age to the brink of old age . . . that had kept his family free from political intrigues and threats, despite the machinations of the Jerusalem hierarchy . . . and whose conduct, throughout a lifetime, had even allowed his sons to safely pursue religious and political ideals that were each, in their own ways, at variance with the establishment.

"What *is* his lineage?" said Joseph.

"Through David's son Nathan, not through Solomon."

"That is not so bad."

"The blood flows to him through his father's mother."

"Oh, a female line. Most unhelpful to a man with his ambitions."

Joshuah stared at the distant hill for a moment.

"I can see why you think that he has ambitions for the throne, Father. Yet I think that that is not quite it."

"What else could it be?"

"He told his brother that his kingdom would not be of this world."

"What sort of talk is that?"

"The talk of a man with a vision," said Joshuah quietly. "A man of potential greatness and potential goodness, but who completely misunderstands the nature of reality and the true source of his own powers, who thus must build for himself a mad dream in which to live and operate. I do not think he plans a revolt. He has stated publicly that he is going to offer himself as a living sacrifice by which the children of Israel will be redeemed."

Joseph stared.

"Redeemed from what?"

"Sin."

"Ah!" Joseph threw up his hands in disgust. "Another one of those, is he? What idiots they are, running around bemoaning the sins of Israel's children. While all the rest of Israel's children are running around being so holy that God must be gagging in the smoke. What more would they have us do? How much more holy can a people be and still be human? Not to mention getting any work done. From whom does he intend to obtain this redemption?"

"God."

"In person?"

"What else? Yesterday, he told the congregation of Kapher Nahum that he is God's only begotten son."

Joseph's mouth dropped.

"He says God cohabited with his mother?"

"That seems the implication."

"But that is pagan, is it not? It is as some of those Greek beliefs you told me about. The man *is* mad. So mad that his claims directly contradict one another. If he wants it to be believed that his father is not his father, then he loses his claim to descent from David."

"Unfortunately, when dedicated fanatics work their spells on gullible minds, all such seemingly obvious contradictions become locked away in dim recesses of those minds."

"All the more reason for him to trade on confusion with *your* lineage."

Joseph turned and took Joshuah earnestly by the shoulders.

"Joshuah, you have got to disassociate yourself from all of this immediately. At the moment, we have nothing but stories in Jerusalem, and both the Temple and the Romans are treating all 'Messiahs' as a joke.

"For there are more than just this Yeshuah and yourself, you know. There is a fellow teaching down in Hebron, and a madman in Samaria, and, only last week, we heard of a new one over near Gilead.

"But the tolerance cannot last. Suggestions have already been made in the Sanhedrin that spies be sent to listen to these 'Messiahs,' to determine whether any of them should be silenced.

"And the most concern is over the Galilean Messiah, for he is the one, not only, drawing the most attention, but claiming to be the King of the Jews. Believe me, more than a few of my colleagues have looked at me strangely, wondering, I know, whether this 'rightful king of the House of David' might be yourself.

"Take your bride away after the wedding. Next week, Joshuah. Rome would be nice, you have not been there yet. With a letter of introduction from Pontius Pilatus, you can see it in style, be treated like . . . a king. Heaven knows I do not wish to be without your company any longer. I think that you and I have had not more than an aggregate of a few months together during all the years of your manhood. Yet I would rather see you go traveling once more than to have you endangered."

Tears came into the eyes of Joshuah, now Jesus. He studied the Chameleon face lovingly.

"I am sorry, Father, but my time of bargaining has long since passed."

"I do not know what you mean," said Joseph gruffly.

"Yes you do. I have been telling you the same thing for years. In the existence of each consciousness there comes a point when, finally, it Knows, understands, who and what it is, where it comes from, where it is going, and why. At that moment of Knowing, the time of bargaining has passed it by forever.

"Strangely enough, most of us couch the realization in just those words.

"From that moment onward, no haggling, deals, or half measures. The full price and nothing but the full price. From that moment onward, that consciousness must act on what it knows, with unremitting courage.

"Those who posture in the Temple prate of sin, Father. I tell you that their little minds, worrying over how many stripes they must wear at the edges of their garments in order to please 'God,' or whether it is permissible to lift a pot on the Sabbath, cannot begin to understand the heights and depths that 'sin' can reach.

"Only those who *Know*, and who *fail to act* on what they know, can reach those heights and those depths. The miss of a master archer is a thousand times more egregious than that of the student. The greater the archer becomes, the more is expected of him, the more he expects of himself, the more stunning his mistakes.

"The mistake of a master can mean the defeat and loss of whole nations. And, should a person like that turn and run when faced with a battle, well . . . "

Jesus spread his hands.

"I am a master of masters. I may miss the mark. I often do. But not for lack of trying for the sure center. And not because I have turned and fled the field.

"I am here to teach, Father, and teach I will. I will attract to myself those minds which are ready to hear and to understand, and then, to the best of my ability, I will tell them the truth, so that they may tell others, so that, always, in the centuries to come, there will be a solid core, a sure nucleus of minds which do *Know*, and that will continue to speak the truth and pass it on. That nucleus will grow. Slowly. But surely."

"And for that you would risk your life?"

"Life does not end, Father. The only risk would be in not doing what I was summoned here to do. Because that slow-growing core of truth is the be-all of this earthly plane."

Joseph turned away again. He rubbed his hands over his face and sighed.

"So, like that fool up on yonder hill, you, too, would make of yourself a sacrifice."

Jesus laughed, most inappropriately, Joseph thought.

"To be a sacrifice is the last thing that I would plan, Father. Do you not see that a sacrifice implies that the sacrificed item somehow relieves the person for whom the sacrifice is made of the responsibility for his own past actions? Or in-actions.

"I have spent the morning explaining to my people that this is an impossibility. I would never be a party to any action that would further delude Humanity, give people further cause to believe that the responsibility for what happens to them belongs anywhere but squarely within themselves, or that anyone or anything other than their own selves can lift from off of them the burdens of what they must learn for themselves.

"To do so would be the most horrendous 'sin' of which I can conceive.

"No. I am a creature of *joy*, Joseph. What I do, I do with gladness, with Love, with pleasure! My whole message seeks to convey this joy and gladness to others.

"It is not 'saintly' to suffer. It is 'wrong' to deprive oneself of the loving pleasures of the Earth. And, to purposely visit suffering upon oneself just in *order* to suffer is 'sinful' in the extreme."

"Aha!" said Joseph. "I have you then. For, if you tempt the authorities, you might be purposefully bringing suffering, and even death, upon yourself."

"The authorities cannot make me suffer. Or even kill me, though they might believe that they have done so."

"What a cock-sure pup you are!"

Jesus shrugged, grinning.

"When one is sure, one is sure. That it offends you, is your problem, and not mine."

"You have got to take things more seriously, Joshuah."

"Heaven save me from *that* particular mistake of the human race," said Jesus, rising.

He gave Joseph a hug.

"Well, have you cautioned me as much as you had planned, and persuaded me as much as you are able?"

"I spoke truly to Jude. I have never been able to persuade you of anything. I do not know why I even try."

"That has been your role in many lifetimes, Little Father. You have followed me often, urging caution. By doing so, you constantly remind me that I must refrain from that very thing.

"Shall we return? I find myself moping now when I am separated from Merovee. I begrudge every minute."

Joseph did not move.

"What is it, Father?"

257

"*Are* you the Messiah, Joshuah?"

Jesus threw back his head and laughed.

"*A* messiah, Father. A messiah."

* * *

When Petros returned from Kapher Nahum that evening his brow was furrowed, his face was stern. He went straight to the salon to find Jesus.

"I have startling news."

"What *was* our friend up to there above Heptapegon today?"

Petros started. His frown deepened.

"You do not leave a man his own private thoughts."

"What is private about what Simon Yeshuah did today? Surely it is public knowledge."

Petros grunted.

"Well, he fed five thousand people. With seven loaves and seven fishes."

"What?" Judah jumped to his feet, exchanging shocked glances with Merovee and Mathiah.

"It is very bad, Jesus." Petros shook his head. "All of Kapher Nahum is buzzing. People are much impressed. I fear you have lost ground."

"I am not in competition with Simon Yeshuah," said Jesus easily.

"But he is with you," said Judah bitterly.

"And it is my fault," said Mathiah. "He insisted on knowing all that had gone on in Johannan's camp after he and Judah left. I told him what you and Johannan did with the bread and the fishes. Now he wishes people to think that he has the same kind of power. What trick could he have used to make it seem that he was feeding five thousand people with seven loves and seven fishes?"

"Why do you assume that it was a trick?" said Jesus.

"Well it must be! There could not be yet a third person alive with that power!"

"All have The Power, Mathiah. There are only varying degrees of mastery in using it. And Simon Yeshuah is a master. If it makes you feel better, though, the number fed was closer to two thousand than to five thousand."

"But . . . " The face of Petros was a study in confusion. "Yeshuah cannot have the same power that you have. You are the Messiah. Your power comes from God."

Jesus sighed.

"Petros, will you ever begin to hear the things which I tell you? All power comes from All That Is. The Power is *neutral*. Anyone can use it. Everyone does use it. Daily, whether they know it or not. The average person creates objects as easily as Johannan and I, and now, seemingly, Simon Yeshuah. The only difference is that such as we three create consciously, while the average person has not the slightest idea that he is creating everything around him."

"But you have said that this Yeshuah does not understand the true nature of God." Petros persisted. "If he does not understand God, how can he use God's power?"

"All drink from the stream, Petros. It is simply there. One does not have to know what the terrain is like a mile upstream, or where the source is, or where the mouth is, or if there are rapids or waterfalls. One does not have to know whether there are fish in the stream, or whether there are tributaries. One does not have to know what the water is composed of, or how it came to be there in the first place, neither does one have to know that all others drink from that stream.

258

"One only has to drink.

"Each, as he chooses, can search out this other knowledge—or not search it out.

"Each can drink as much water as he likes, in any posture he wants, at any time he wants.

"He can capture it in any vessel he wants.

"He can live by the stream all his life or range up and down or even far beyond it.

"He can live on the mountain or down in a cave and haul his water long distances.

"He can dam the flow and keep large volumes to himself.

"He can fish in it, swim in it, watch it, wash in it, drown people in it, raise ducks in it, throw rocks at it, sail boats upon it.

"He can drink it straight or add it to his wine. He can have it cold or heat it.

"He can even fold his arms over his chest, refuse to drink, and perish of thirst.

"All That Is simply provides the stream, Petros. All That Is never tells anyone how he must use what is provided.

"I would compare Simon Yeshuah to a man who has learned almost all there is to know about the stream *except* the true location of its source and the true location of its destination. Rather than seeking out the source and the mouth for himself, he has relied on the suppositions of ancestors who also never bothered to go exploring for themselves, and who based their own suppositions on the suppositions of their own ancestors who were just as lazy.

"So Simon Yeshuah has a large command of the use of the stream. Yet I beg you not to listen to him when he seeks to tell you from whence it comes and to where it goes, for he does not know."

"But he performs miracles," said Petros tenaciously.

"Petros," said Merovee. "You did a miracle last night. I did a miracle. Why are we each not out claiming to be the Messiah?"

Petros turned and stared at her.

"You could not claim such a thing. You are a woman."

Merovee glanced at Jesus and subdued her smile with effort.

"You miss my point."

She lifted her chin.

"Yet, now that you bring it up . . . Mother, did you not once tell me that I have descent from King David on my father's side?"

"Through your father's mother, yes."

"Ah. Well then you see . . . "

She was enjoying the surprise, not only of Petros, but, of Jesus.

While Joseph of Ramah turned ashen.

"Scripture," she went on impishly, "says only that the Messiah will be from the loins of David. I am from the loins of David, my genealogy is at least as good as that of Simon Yeshuah, and I can do miracles. So why should I not put myself forth as the Messiah? Why do you assume that the Messiah will be an anointed king? Perhaps the Messiah will be an anointed queen."

"This is blasphemy!" cried Petros, shaking his great head. "Simon Yeshuah is right. You *do* have seven demons within you."

With a movement so fast as to be hardly seen, Jesus stepped forward. He seized the shoulders of Petros and spun him around. Upon his face was a fury such as none of them had ever witnessed.

"What is this?" he said through clenched teeth. "Where did you hear such a thing?"

Petros opened his mouth, then closed it and lowered his eyes.

"It is said in the streets of Kapher Nahum. Everybody knows it. Yeshuah spoke of it in the synagogue, and again as he taught today. That you have taken up with an evil woman, Jezabel returned, who has within her seven demons."

For a moment, there was dead silence in the room.

"He called her Jezabel returned?" Jesus finally whispered.

"Yes, Jesus, he has said that," said Judah. "He also refuses to recognize the marriage to Johannan. He called her 'whore,' and said that he had had a dream in which it was revealed to him that Merovee has seven demons within her."

Jesus stood, still gripping the shoulders of Petros, staring at that man with something akin to hatred.

Then he dropped his hands.

"So be it. Merovee, come here."

It was Rosula who rose, placing herself between Merovee and her son.

"Joshuah, this is foolishness, the ravings of a madman, we all know that."

"Do we?" said Jesus. "Petros evidently does not. If he has doubts, what might creep into other hearts? I need you *all* for my rocks in the days to come. And Merovee and her child will need you. I can leave no doubts."

He held out a hand.

"Come to me, Merovee."

It seemed to Merovee that life and breath turned still within her.

"Come to me. I will drive out any demonic thing that might be lurking inside of you. I will do so in front of this whole company, so that they can never again wonder about you."

"Oh Jesus, do not hurt her!" cried Salome.

The ghost of a smile touched his lips.

"How could you think that I would ever hurt her? Come, Beloved Disciple."

As in a dream, Merovee rose, touched a hand of comfort to Rosula and to her mother, and crossed the room to stand before him.

"Be careful of the baby," she murmured, gazing trustingly into his eyes.

"Kneel down," he said, "for your legs will give way."

Obediently, she knelt and lowered her head. Her heart beat fast now, but her body was cold. So cold. And she had no breath.

She felt warmth then, as his hands en-capped her head.

He was silent a moment. Then he spoke.

"Yes. The vision of Simon Yeshuah was correct. This woman has demons within her. Though he, Poor Soul, cannot begin to understand what demons they are."

Merovee thought she was beginning to sway. She trusted to his hands to hold her upright.

"They are not the demons of the common herd. This woman is not a student, she is a master. Her demons are more powerful, more fearsome than most of you here can imagine. I will now remove them."

There was a moment of silence. Then suddenly his hands lifted and quickly descended, his fingers gripping like a vise.

"Fear to Know Self . . . Release."

She thought the floor was opening up. She tried to send herself upwards into her head so that his hands would hold her and she would not fall through.

His hands lifted again. She cried out. Her mind clung to those hands as they re-descended.

"Fear to Love Self . . . Release."

She was not cold anymore. Perspiration burst from her pores and flowed like a river. She had the insane thought that she would drown.

His hands lifted again.

"Do not leave me!" she screamed.

The hands came back and she burst into grateful tears.

"Fear to Know others . . . Release."

Merovee shrank down, sobbing. She seemed suddenly to be made of nothing but water. "Oh," she moaned as his hands lifted again, and as she waited only for their return.

"Fear to Love others . . . Release."

She thought then that she was laughing. She suddenly saw herself, and she was a laughing puddle of water. It made her laugh all the more.

"Fear to Know and speak Truth . . . Release."

Why did he keep leaving her? Come back!

"Fear to Know the true god All That Is . . . Release."

She was jerking. All her bits were leaping about, trying to go in all directions at once. Even inward. Inward! What if she could not find her way out again? But there he was.

"Fear to Trust your Universe completely . . . Release!"

He had tricked her! It was terrible! Some power! Some awful energy! It raced in through the fingers of her left hand. It surged up her arm and commenced to whirl round and round in her trunk. And it *did* hurt! It was ripping her heart and insides to pieces! There was no way to move, no place to escape to, she could not even think. She opened her mouth. She had to get that terrible energy out some way. Out!

She heard a shriek. It rose. It was going to split her head wide open. And then it did. She burst outward and inward, in all directions, into a void filled with nothing but silky blackness.

And a voice. Like a campfire in the darkness.

"Allow," it said.

She floated toward it.

Jesus caught her as she slumped downward. Deborah was quick to her side, feeling her pulse. Lazarus was behind his mother, eyes wide and frightened.

"She is fine. Trust me," Jesus told them.

But then he looked up at Petros, and the fury returned to his voice.

"Are you satisfied now, Simon bar Jonah? Have you seen the demons driven out of this woman?"

Petros was white-faced in a circle of equally white faces.

"Yes, Lord."

"Call me not lord!" cried Jesus.

He dropped his face into the abundance of Merovee's hair and breathed deeply for a moment, composing himself.

At last he raised his head.

"Petros . . . I would take it kindly if you would sail back to Kapher Nahum this night and begin to tell what you have seen here. Tell the people that the seven demons have been driven out of this woman and that she is forthwith sanctified. Will you do that, Simon Petros?"

"Yes, Jesus . . . . . . May I return after I have done that?"

"Only if you will try your best, ever afterwards, to give to my wife the love and respect which she deserves."

"I swear that I will do that from this moment on."

"I did not ask you to swear, Petros. Never swear an oath. Not by anything that is in Heaven above or in the Earth or waters below. Say only that you will try your best. And mean it."

"I will try my best. I do mean it."

"Good."

Jesus gathered Merovee more closely, hefted her into his arms, and got to his feet.

"She should be warm and quiet now, Deborah. Your room, I think. Has your friend departed?"

The goddess was safely locked in her box.

"Yes. Come."

They led a silent procession to Deborah's suite, where Jesus put Merovee onto the sleeping couch.

"Get more pillows," he said. "Elevate her feet. And coverings, she must be very warm, get those sheepskins from off the floor. Yes. Perfect. I will stay with her. She will sleep for many long hours. I have sent her to a far place, but she will return periodically to check on the well-being of the body. She will see me here and be reassured. She did the same favor for me over the Sabbath."

The subdued congregation began to drift out. Rosula and Joseph were among the last, Rosula's eyes frightened, Joseph's thoughtful.

Finally, Deborah and Lazarus, Nathaniel and Susannah, Judah and Salome were left.

"Will she be different when she wakes?" said Salome.

Jesus ruffled the girl's hair.

"Not so very much to you, Kitten. The real change will be understood only within herself."

"Only!" said Salome. Tears came to her eyes. "Your 'onlys' are like flying to the moon, Jesus."

He drew her into his arms.

"Have courage, Salome. You are doing very well."

Deborah was on her knees, holding Merovee's hand.

"Those 'demons' that you drove out for the sake of Petros . . . "

Tears come to her eyes as well.

"We all have them. How *can* one be rid of them for good and for all?"

"One cannot, Deborah, you are right. Not completely. Not ever. Ever!"

He, too, knelt. He smoothed Merovee's brow.

"I spoke truly when I said that she is a master. And I did truly banish the 'demons' which I proclaimed. But, as you understand so well, they were demons commensurate with her own current level of understanding.

"And I am not sure that I did her a favor. She has been accelerated—pushed before her natural time—toward a greater level of understanding. She is there now, being taught by those far greater than I.

"I could not have said this in front of Petros and many of the others. But she will return with even greater demons than when she left. For, the greater the understanding, the greater the demons. My own are taller than to the moon and beyond.

"I would never have done this to her but that I know she is strong enough. And she was nearly ready. Nearly."

He bowed his head for a moment, then raised it.

"Nathaniel. I want you to go with Petros to Kapher Nahum. Take Thunder's sons. Take Chandreah and Phillipus as well. Not Levi, he is not liked in the town. And do not take Judah or any of the men just come from Yeshuah. Will the son of Alphaeus go, Deborah?"

"I am sure that he will."

"Take all who are willing. I leave it to you, Nathaniel. Make sure that all of Kapher Nahum knows before sundown of tomorrow that the man called Jesus has driven seven demons out of this woman and that she is sanctified. It is essential that Simon Yeshuah's claim that she is Jezabel returned be countered. Yeshuah does not understand from whence he comes. He does not realize the danger to Merovee and her baby of this charge. And though I said that I am not in competition with Simon Yeshuah, or my entity with his . . . "

He shook his head in bitterness.

"It seems I have allowed myself to be forced into just that position.

"And now please leave. I do have your permission to stay with her, Deborah?"

"Of course. Should I bring some food or beverage?"

"Nothing. I have decided to try to follow her and help her with her lessons in the place to where she has gone."

Deborah rose and shooed them all out.

Only Judah lingered.

"What is it?" said Jesus, trying to conceal his impatience.

Judah drew, from the sheath at his waist, his wicked, gleaming sicarius.

"I only wanted to give you this."

He offered it hilt-first.

"It is a gift from the fig tree and from me. It comes with my oath that I will never again be responsible for the death of any person."

Jesus became alert, giving his full attention to the earnest young man.

"Judah."

He took the sicarius and hugged Judah to himself.

"I appreciate your intent. And I applaud it. But I will not accept your oath. Did you not hear what I told Petros? Do not swear any oaths. Never. Not by anything that is in Heaven or in the Earth or its waters."

Judah's face crumpled. He began to cry like a child.

"But what if one has already done so, Jesus? There is no going back from an oath once sworn and accepted."

263

"Yes there is."

Jesus held him tenderly, comforting him.

"Judah, oaths are invalid concepts. They are impotent at birth. To swear an oath is to impede the true god, to go against its will. For the crux, the vital essence of All That Is, of reality, is change. Oaths seek a state of *un*change. Oaths seek to guarantee that a thing will be one way, and one way only, forever. And I tell you that this is impossible. It is impossible for the simple reason that All That Is will not, cannot, allow an oath to stand. For *All That Is is change*. All That Is will not, cannot, stand still. So no oath can ever be truly, completely kept. If one is really acting for, doing the 'will' of All That Is, one is constantly changing, growing. Even those who do not think that they change, do change. It is a basic law of the Universe. Do you not see?"

"I am trying, Jesus."

"I know that. And I cherish you, Judah, lately of the sicarius."

Jesus could not stop his own tears. He kissed Judah upon the lips and hugged him once again.

"In place of your oath, I accept your pure intention and your realization, Judah. As I said to Simon Petros, simply do your best, at every moment. That is all that any god will ever require of you."

"Thank you, Jesus." Judah clung to him.

"Now I set you to guard this chamber. I must put myself into a deep sleep and follow Merovee, help her. She has been severely shocked. She needs a guide."

"I will not let anyone come near. And I will stomp on anything that dares to make a sound."

Jesus laughed, appreciating the hint of humor in Judah's reply. He gave the boy a slap on the back and sent him from the room.

Then, with a sigh, he turned back to the still, white form of Merovee there beneath the quilts and sheepskins.

He took off his outer robe and, in his under-linen, slid in beside her. He drew her into his arms, arranging the both of them into comfortable positions.

Then he began to breath deeply, from the abdomen.

Soon he was as far gone into sleep as was she.

An observer, simply perusing the two bodies, could never have guessed to where the two of them had gone.

Chapter 10
A Wedding in Kana

The marriage of Joshuah ben Joseph and Miriam bat Jeremiah took place a week later, at the farm of the bride's mother in Kapher Kana.

It was not a traditional wedding, any more than the farm was a traditional farm. For Nathan of the Magdalia had always built with flair, with a taste for beauty, and for the luxurious trappings of the Greeks and Romans. The house, itself, was several times larger than the house in Magdala, and there were extensive livable out-buildings. Nathan had made of it a sort of school, bringing promising young artisans from all over Galilee, Samaria, Judeah, and Peraea, to be taught more of their crafts. The most brilliant had been invited to stay on indefinitely, to create and to experiment at their leisure.

Nathan had died with his dream—a Hebrew art form of major and recognized proportions—unrealized. But Deborah had carried on the tradition, and a dozen young artisans, several with their wives and children, were still in permanent residence. Their total living was supplied, as well as any materials which they fancied for their creations. As a rule, they enjoyed complete privacy to work on whatever they pleased. Deborah then marketed their efforts for them, even to Rome, itself. The only thing asked of them in return was that they oversee the general running of the buildings and of the vineyards.

The buildings, themselves, were contained in the center of a great square windbreak of cypress trees, for, winter and summer, the winds which swept the Galilean hills were punishing. The square of cypresses was, in turn, in the center of many hundreds of acres of vineyards, and greater expanses of windbreaks.

The wine produced was the finest of Galilee, the soil in the immediate vicinity being admirably suited to a hearty, red grape that produced a dry, robustly flavored wine. Most of the villagers found full or seasonal employment in Deborah's vineyards, and the name of Nathan was spoken with love and respect.

So it was that the streets and houses of the village were gaily decorated in honor of the approaching marriage of Nathan's young granddaughter. An unofficial local holiday was understood, for, of course, all the villagers were invited to the festivities. They pitched in with glad hands, to erect the tent city needed to shelter the banqueting area and house the overflow of guests. The wedding would be a welcome rest. The harvest of the lower fields was done, and now they must wait for the grapes of the high fields to come prime. The festivities would last a week . . . longer if everyone was having a good time, which would be just about right.

In order to give lip service to the custom that required the groom and his attendants to go to the house of the bride, and conduct her in gay procession to his own home for the ceremony, Deborah had solemnly declared the farm to be the property of Jesus for the period of one moon.

Accordingly, he reluctantly parted from Merovee and went up to Kana for the week to oversee the wedding preparations and to greet arriving guests. With him went Lazarus, his parents and brothers and sisters, and all of his men save Petros, Chandreah, Nathaniel, Jacob bar Alphaeus, and Lebbaeus. These last were asked to stay behind to guard the women and to do errands on the Magdala end. Nathaniel's mother, a widow and a thoroughly competent woman, had already been alerted. With the help of Nathaniel's brothers and sisters and some of her fellow villagers, she had things organized and matters well in hand before ever Jesus arrived.

Deborah's eldest child, Martha, was one of the first guests to appear. She was small and plump, with lips seemingly carved from rock and a downward pitch to the carving. The expression in her eyes stated that nothing that they had ever seen had yet come up to Martha's standards, She studied Jesus from head to toe, sniffed at her young brother, and departed for the kitchen to take charge of the household.

Jesus wondered what would happen when Martha met Nathaniel's mother.

Arriving with Martha were her father's two cousins, Micah and Daniel. They brought with them a total of five married daughters and their families, two married sons and their families, plus diverse young, and as yet unmarried, siblings. Micah and Daniel were, of course, priests, as were their sons who were of age. The two men were grave, and conscious of their positions, but with a friendliness of eye that made Jesus decide, after only moments of conversation, that one could clap them on the shoulders and lay in a jest in confident expectation of answering chuckles.

Martha's intended, Boaz, was a different matter. Of a prominent Levitical family, he, too, seemed to be searching for some object perfect enough to suit him. Jesus offered no suggestions and gave the young man wide berth.

Then there came Jacob, the eldest of Joseph's sons next to Jesus, hastened to the wedding from his Essenic community at Qumran, despite the fact that such prolonged contact with the outside world would seriously defile his Essenic purity.

But 'Jac' had always doted on his big brother Joshuah. The two had been especially close as boys, the first of Rosula's two 'families'—for there was a fifteen-year gap between Jac and the next of the children, Jude. In order to share in this joyous occasion, Jac was more than ready to undergo the weeks of purification that would be necessary once returned to Qumran.

For this was the first marriage of any of Joseph and Rosula's children. What a disappointment the two oldest had been on that score, how remiss even in their duties as good Jews—Josh, going off to India, and Jac to an ascetic life at Qumran.

Oh, not that Jac would never be married. Many of his Essenic brothers married, fulfilling God's injunction to be fruitful and multiply. Maybe, someday, he, himself, would get around to marriage. Maybe. But, truly, he was looking to his younger siblings, now all of age, to make up for his lack.

Unfortunately, Jude had turned out as badly as his two older brothers, as passionately taken up by political matters as Josh and Jac were consumed by matters spiritual. Joses was, of course, only thirteen and newly a man. But even Annah and Rachel, both of them now old enough to be wed, were dragging their heels, rejecting all of their parents' suggestions for mates.

To console herself, Rosula had taken to saying that, someday, the dam would burst, and there would be six weddings in just one year . . . and six grandchildren a year later. Rosula was probably, thought Jac, thinking that very thing right now, that the dam had burst, and that, in the next year, she would see the other five married as well.

Actually that was not at all what Rosula was thinking.

"Did I not tell you?" she said to Jesus. "Does Jacob not look like a vulture waiting to die?"

"I have seen emaciation," said Jesus to Jac. "In India, there is almost no other way to be. But, Jac, you would win a contest even there. Why do you do this to yourself?"

"I starve the Evil One."

Jesus sighed, studying the Essene.

"Brother, I will tell you that you are misguided. You believe flesh to be wicked, corrupt, imperfect. You believe that Mind and Spirit is all. I tell you that the answer is in balance. The purpose of Earthly existence is to discover that balance. There is as much 'God'-consciousness in your flesh as in your mind. Your flesh mirrors the condition of your Soul. Your flesh is the conscious Temple of that Soul. And that consciousness has rights. You miss the mark when you mistreat your flesh, Jac."

Jac smiled. He had ever been a pleasant boy—and also stubborn in the extreme. One talked to him, counseled him, received his fond smiles . . . then discovered that he still went on with his own course as though no words had ever been spoken.

"*You* are looking well," he said, ingenuously and with heartfelt admiration. Jesus knew that there was no use in further conversation. And, after all, he thought ruefully, was not he, himself, just as determined to go his own way as was Jac?

Their father's brother Cleopah arrived from Mount Ephraim. Jesus had not seen him, or his wife Miriam, in several years, or yet his cousins and their children, so that there was a great to-do and happy re-introduction. Jesus picked the two-year-old daughter of Cleopah's youngest son, Benjamin, for his special pet, set her on his hip and would not be parted from her until she fell asleep, well past her nap-time, and was insistently reclaimed by her mother.

No one had heard from Aunt Annah down in Hebron, whether she and her family could come or not.

There were Rosula's uncles from Tarichaea. Micah continued the family business, trading in tin with Rosula's mother's family in the Isle of the Britons. Samuel dealt in animals for the caravans. Solomon imported spices. Saul built and leased boats, particularly to the Zebedee. There was Job, who had never seemed to get on well with anything. His mother had begged that he not be given that name. Then there was great-Aunt Tibah, sister to Rosula's grandfather, and a great-Uncle Samson, who had been hit on the head when only a child, and who had remained curiously childlike, even in appearance.

With all these patriarchs came their children, grandchildren, great-grandchildren and servants.

From Samaria came great-Aunt Judith and her children, grandchildren, great-grandchildren and servants, and a good many distant cousins from Samaria whom Judith had summoned and who brought their children, grandchildren, great-grandchildren and servants.

Judith had also made sure that stray cousins throughout Galilee, and as far north as Tyre, were informed. Being close-knit and cognizant of family duty, all came, with, of course, their children, grandchildren, great-grandchildren and servants.

To Joseph of Ramah's further horror, many members of the Sanhedrin to whom Rosula had issued an invitation showed up, with full retinue.

Even several who had not been invited showed up. Notably, Mattias, the grandson and right-hand man of the High Priest, Annas.

Strangely, Annas had not been High Priest for over twenty years. The titular High Priest at the moment was the son-in-law of Annas, Caiaphas. Yet, in truth, Caiaphas but conducted certain religious ceremonies in the Temple. That was the depth to which the office had fallen. Ask any citizen of the land for the name of the real High Priest, the power and ruler of the land. That citizen would say, "Annas." It was Annas who gave the final nod to each stoning, Annas who formulated each policy, Annas who manipulated Caiaphas, and all the other members of his family who constituted the Temple hierarchy, as a traveling showman manipulated his dancing bears. It was Annas who had grown so wealthy that he habitually lent large sums to highly placed Romans, thus keeping those Romans securely within his closed fist.

It was the right-hand man of such a powerful figure who had been sent to spy upon this wedding and then report back.

A second uninvited guest was only a little less unsettling. His name was Zakiah, the eyes and ears of the dreaded, pharisaic House of Shammai—that so frequent partner of the High Priest and Sanhedrin.

Both Mattias and Zakiah had been in the Temple delegation at Machaerus. But there was nothing to do but pretend, returning the smiles of the gate-crashers, that they had received the same invitations as had the others.

Yet there was one more surprise guest. A surprise, that is, to everyone but Joseph.

"Why is he here? How does he dare!" hissed Rosula when first she saw the approaching retinue of that guest.

"Was I not allowed to send invitations of my own?" said Joseph.

"*You* invited him? You *invited* him?"

"Whichever way you care to phrase it, yes."

"Have you gone mad?"

"No. Sane. Intuition told me his leavening would be needed at this affair, and I was right . . . though I did not expect him to come in person. I thought that he would send a delegate. With him here, no one will dare to make trouble. Not priests, not Sadducees, not Pharisees, or Zealots. Hopefully neither will our 'Jesus.'"

And, smiling in heartfelt welcome, cognizant of the honor being shown him, Joseph of the Triple High took his wife's arm and propelled her forward to welcome Praefectus Pontius Pilatus, de facto King of Judeah, Samaria, and Idumea.

"Do get a pigeon off to Yeshuah right away," grinned Jesus to Judah when he, himself, was informed of the arrival, Then he, too, strode off to welcome the might of Rome.

* * *

Hours before sunrise of the following day, Jesus donned festive garments, set off with his men on be-ribboned Arabian horses and camels supplied by Uncle Samuel from Tarichaea, and traveled the fourteen miles back to Magdala to fetch his bride, her mother, and her 'women.'"

Two of these women came veiled—friends of Susannah's it would be said, and left at that. The veil was not required of Hebrew women, and was uncommon. Yet there were those who preferred to go veiled, either from shyness or because of disfigurement from the pox. It was a matter of preference, which did not excite much comment one way or the other. Indeed, of late, some of the Sadducean women of Jerusalem had taken to wearing, as a matter of fashion, sheer, coaxing veils, scented and sewn with little bells.

But the veils of these two women were not sheer. Additionally, they were fashioned in such a way as only to reveal the eyes. Definite pox victims. No questions would be asked. People would be elaborately polite and gently sympathetic.

Yet, even Salome's courage faltered when she heard that Pilatus was among the guests.

"How many times has he seen you?" asked Jesus.

"Only twice. At the marriage of my mother to Antipas and at a banquet in honor of my late husband, Uncle Phillipus. But on those occasions he looked at me very closely, Jesus."

"I do not blame him. You are a marvelous thing to look at."

"Look?" said Salome indignantly. "He all but undressed me with that look! And he with such a beautiful wife, a cousin to Tiberius, himself. I do not know how he gets away with it."

Jesus smiled.

"And you, Johannah, has he met you?"

"No. I hide only from the eyes of my fellow Galileans. I have sent to my family. They will raise no alarm over my absence, but one never knows who might be at the wedding."

"Well, I should not worry then," said Jesus. "Only keep those flashing lights from out of your eyes when Pilatus is near, Kitten, for your eyes, more than anything else about you, shout, 'Salome'!"

Merovee, too, came veiled, but sheerly, out of deference to the bridal convention. She and her women rode in a festooned, cushioned, camel-drawn wagon.

Alphaeus rode in a festooned wagon of his own. His passengers were his son Jacob, Jacob's wife and their son Lebbaeus, Jairus and his wife and little Rebeckah, Chandreah, a young lady of Kapher Nahum to whom Chandreah was betrothed, and a certain woman of Kapher Nahum called Navea, a friend of Levi's.

Thunder was there, and her husband the Zebedee. They brought, in their wagon, Obed the innkeeper and his wife and young sons, Petros and his mother and wife.

Demetrius and his family were given Ruthie and Pharisee—the latter of whom could be depended upon not to balk as long as Ruthie was ahead of him—and such steeds as were necessary from the stables of either the Zebedee or the House of Nathan.

Nathaniel and Jesse brought up the rear, Nathaniel on Solomon, Jesse on Gilead.

Laughing, singing, ringing bells, calling out, and jesting with those they passed, the cavalcade made its way over the hills turned golden by the summer sun, to the farm at Kapher Kana. They rested, then, through the heat of the day.

Until, in the cool of the evening, when a distant, unmarried cousin—who Rosula and Aunt Judith had declared to be more senior than Jesus—obligingly handed to Merovee an old sandal that he had brought along for the occasion. Merovee spat into the sandal to register her displeasure at having been rejected by him as a wife, and the ceremony began.

Lazarus, flanked by his uncles Micah and Daniel, had the honor of administering the wine to the pair, while Jesus had shrewdly asked of Mattias, the grandson of Annas, that he pronounce the closing benediction. All in all, the ceremony took just minutes. The feasting and dancing continued till dawn.

A dancing such as none of the assembled, except the Grecian-born Deborah, had ever seen. As it began, Joseph of Ramah turned a color that was almost green.

For Jesus led it off by drawing his bride into the center of the court and dancing with her, right there in front of everyone.

The move was greeted by stunned silence. Only the crickets could be heard, and the orchestra— harp, zither, Greek reeds, and finger cymbals. The cadence they played was Greek—in itself no surprise here in Galilee.

But the guests, lying upon the many long couches, and sitting on the cushions and chairs which ringed the court, all sat up attentively, telling themselves that this could not be happening. Hebrew men danced alone. Hebrew woman danced alone. Never the two sexes met on a dance floor.

The effect was made more stunning by the beauty of the couple. Even in this last dusk, Jesus shone. His clean, combed hair had an inner glow, like a nimbus about his head. His mustache and beard and earlocks had grown to almost presentable proportions—they were full and carefully trimmed. His robe was of golden damask, his cap of crimson silk. Upon his face was a smile to make the angels sing. Tall, straight, healthy, sturdy, he moved in graceful rhythm opposite and facing his bride, not touching her—at least not physically.

She was hardly less tall than he. One felt that, somehow, her body, clad in rippling amethyst silk, was a physical manifestation of the music from the harp. She swayed like a plant responding to the flow of a tide, his tide, as sturdy and strong as he, but following his lines of force. Her smile reflected his. Yet her face was entirely her own. Calm and cool where his was bright, her eyes were as deep, endless pools which drew one inward—while his, shining with love, dazzled. They moved in hypnotic unison, holding their audience as collectively spellbound as a small animal is held before a swaying cobra.

And then the two-year-old daughter of Cleopah's son, Ben, toddled out onto the floor, gurgling with delight.

The audience gasped.

Laughing, other children ran onto the floor. Desperately, parents tried to call them back.

"Do not stop them!" called Jesus. "Let them come to us. They know. They still remember where to find the Kingdom of Heaven."

Laughing, he hoisted Ben's two-year-old onto his hip.

"Come!" he called to the adults. "Be as little children. Join us in the dance. Let the Universe sing as you move."

By unspoken agreement, he and his bride split apart, still smiling, still dancing, encouraging the children. With his little friend still on his hip, Jesus moved to Deborah and drew her onto the floor. Merovee moved to Lazarus.

"No, Miri! My foot!" he protested.

"Jesus finds you beautiful. Forget your foot. Come be a child again."

Groaning, Lazarus rose and moved with doubtful grace out onto the floor. One of the bride's women, one with a veil, rose and began to tug at the sleeve of the man named Judah. Susannah rose and beckoned to Nathaniel.

"By Jove!" said Pilatus, clapping Joseph on the back, "They do know how to enjoy themselves here in Galilee. After constipated Samaria and your lifeless Judeah, I had doubted the reports.

"This is capital, my friend, thank you for inviting me, had I known it would be like this I would have brought my wife. How Procula used to love to dance. Now she can only watch, but still she adores it."

He studied the dancers.

"I have seen Greeks do these movements of course, but I have never tried them myself . . . "

With which he leaped to his feet and extended his hand.

"Come, Rosula. Do me the honor to accompany me."

Rosula paled.

"Me?" she said.

"Do not be shy," grinned Pilatus.

He was a tall man, in his early thirties, slender and darkly handsome. He was of equestrian rank . . . which meant that he was a man of wealth and of good family, the sort from which senators and consuls of Rome were selected. Pilatus had a bright future before him. He was a proud man, often haughty, and, especially according to Zealots and to priests, and according to their own political needs, cruel.

Yet there was also a streak of commonality in the man, as though something deep within remembered other times, other places.

"Come along," he persisted. "Did I not say that this is my own first time at this dance? If you look a fool, I shall look an even greater one."

Whey-faced, looking numbly at her husband, Rosula allowed Pontius Pilatus to lead her out into the madness.

After all, it had been Joseph who invited him.

And what was wrong with it really? Dancing—even traditionally, men in groups with men, women in groups with women—had come into such ill repute of late. Both Sadducees and Pharisees considered it frivolous, hence, un-Godly, beneath the dignity of God's Chosen, who were so busy preparing for the end of the world.

A small sob of joy rose in Rosula's breast. So she was frivolous. This felt good. She loved music. She loved to dance. So what if a man did stand opposite her? Could anything that filled one with such joy be evil?

She caught sight of Jesus with Deborah, leading the children in the dance. Pontius Pilatus blurred in her vision.

"Why do you cry, dear Little Rose?"

"I am grateful that you asked me. It *is* fun, is it not?"

"I need your oath that you will not tell Procula of this. She would never forgive me for leaving her behind."

"My petals are forever sealed," said Rosula. They burst into laughter.

And the wisdom of Rosula's husband became manifest. Upon their respective couches, Mattias and Zakiah were thinking, quickly and ferociously. Both mentally re-skimmed Torah for any conceivable injunction against dancing, itself.

There was none.

Against dancing with women?

Still no definite injunction.

One was not *supposed* to dance with a member of the opposite sex, that was for certain. Clearly, however, that was custom, interpretation—Oral Law—not The Law.

The entire banquet was being done in a most disconcerting manner. Women had been freely assigned to places beside men on the couches, rather than curtained off by themselves as was proper.

Of course, it was largely a family affair, and Galilee was notorious for its laxity in regard to proper behavior. But dancing with women?

For Mattias, however, the fact that Pilatus was participating in the dance was a political problem. He could not afford to offend Pilatus. Did it get back to Annas that he had done so, and so jeopardized the latitude given to Jewish self-government—and to the private business enterprises of Annas—it would go very badly for him . . . perhaps even worse than if he did transgress against custom or Law.

Mattias rose and motioned to Abner, his scribe. The two of them went to the floor and proceeded to make token movements.

The problem was left squarely in the lap of Zakiah, the Shammite.

No, this was not forbidden by Torah. Surely, though, learned rabbis had spoken against it, since it was universally known among Jews that, if one *had* to dance, it should never, ever, be with a member of the opposite sex.

Why?

Zakiah tried to remember.

It might lead to sexual union, that was why. For, when male and female met, and unless that female was a sister or mother or other relative cooking or cleaning or somehow serving men, there could be only one possible outcome, one reason for the meeting, and that was sexual union.

Why?

Because sexual union and giving birth were, besides cooking, cleaning, and serving men, the only reasons for the existence of women.

Zakiah had often looked at some women and felt no lust, but, rather, a simple desire to talk with them. Memories of such urges shamed him. It was unnatural to want to talk with women. He worried secretly that there was a problem with his masculinity.

Now his problem was twofold. He could not offend Pilatus, but, most of all, he could not offend Mattias. If the House of Shammai was put out of countenance with the High Priest, all that the master had worked for, to gain political ascendancy over the House of Hillel, would be lost. And he, Zakiah, would be out on the street.

Zakiah rose.

"Joseph!"

Joseph of Ramah crossed to him.

"I find this dancing frivolous and unconventional in the extreme," said Zakiah.

"For once we are in agreement."

"However, I do not wish to dampen your son's festivities."

"And I see no violation," said Joseph casually.

"Not of Law, no. In Judeah, though, this would never be allowed."

"It is these Galileans," agreed Joseph.

"Exactly. I have always felt that they should be included among the Gentiles."

"Let me refill your cup . . . what! is your pitcher empty? Boy! More wine here!"

"It is most excellent wine. That I will give these Galileans. But why did you allow your son to marry one of them?"

"She is only half Galilean," said Joseph. "And do you not know that my own wife is Galilean?"

"She . . . Oh. Of course. Well, what I really wanted, Joseph, is the honor of your accompaniment in this dance."

And so that unlikely pair, a Sadducee, the true Prince of Judah, and a Pharisee, the spy of the House of Shammai, moved onto the floor and began, themselves, to make token movements.

After all, if everyone did it, who would tell on anyone else?

* * *

Most of the company slumbered until the next noon, having drunk and danced until the dawn.

There were entertainments then. The black man and his monkey had been gotten, and there were acrobats from Crete, and a puppeteer, and a troupe of traveling players from Ephesus. Deborah's protégés displayed their arts and crafts. Susannah set up a wheel and taught any child who cared to learn how to mold clay objects. There were storytellers and magicians, and Uncle Samuel's Arabian horses for the men to admire and to ride. The food tables were never empty, neither were the wine jugs. The company was lazy and happy, renewing old acquaintance, making new. There was almost an enchanted quality to the day.

Only young Jude was seen to sulk, and to sit in a corner worrying ants with a stick. Jude was sorely disappointed in his big brother, and completely disgusted with Judah, lately of the sicarius, who had gone so soft that he talked of nothing but fig trees. He, Jude, seemed to be the only true Zealot present! And he steadfastly refused to speak to Pilatus, or even to look in his direction.

Pilatus, for his part, was thoroughly enjoying himself. Certainly he would never have told Joseph, but the invitation to the wedding feast of Joseph's eldest had come at an opportune moment, just as Pilatus was contemplating a tour of Galilee.

Pilatus had never before been to Galilee, for the simple reason that it was not his territory. While entry was not forbidden, entry was . . . awkward. Yes, he was praefectus of Judeah, Samaria, and Idumea. Yes, he was the immediate, regional overseer of the Roman troops posted to Galilee. But Galilee was the territory of Herod Antipas. And Antipas was a bristly little fellow when it came to *his* jurisdiction.

Not that Pilatus could blame him. In the original will of Herod the Great, Antipas had been sole heir. He was to have been king, after his father Herod the Great. King of Judeah, Samaria, Galilee, Peraea, Idumea, and perhaps even the Decapolis.

And then something had happened, some peregrination in the crazed mind of the dying Herod, and Antipas had found himself only a tetrarch—the administrator of but a quarter of the inheritance— while the great prize, Judeah, with Jerusalem and the lucrative corruption of the Temple, had, of all things, been willed to Rome.

Small wonder, then, that Antipas defended his borders tenaciously, and shot complaints off to Tiberius Caesar at any moment when he sensed a trespass on the part of the praefectus.

With Antipas now down in Machaerus organizing a war, however, it had seemed to Pilatus an ideal time to go into Galilee and see to some business without Antipas being around to breathe on his neck. He could always say that news of a possible insurrection had reached him, and that, in the absence of his friend Antipas, he had rushed into the territory to safeguard it for Antipas.

Antipas would, of course, know the lie. He and Pilatus had never been friends. Antipas kept the Herodian Palace in Jerusalem, and came to it often. As a nominal Jew, he could not be denied a residence in Jerusalem. But the chief residence of Pilatus was in Caesarea. Seldom was he in Jerusalem, usually only for a month or so at the time of the Passing Over.

So that he and Antipas seldom met. When it was necessary to meet, at ritual and governmental functions, their exchanges were polite and nothing more. Not that Pilatus had anything against Antipas. It was Antipas who could not forgive Pilatus for being ruler of the territories that should have been his.

So Antipas would know the lie of any "friendly" movement to save Galilee for him. Still, the fact of his own absence from out of Galilee would preclude any complaint to Tiberius, for Tiberius would take the position that Pilatus had acted with prudence. In truth, and if Rome cared to force the issue, all of Palestine belonged to Rome anyway. And a Roman praefectus would be justified in moving to quell a possible rebellion in the absence of a mere nominal owner, a tetrarch.

Yet Pilatus had still hesitated, trying to think of a better excuse. He had thought of using this "Messiah," of whom they had been hearing so much. After all, if the man was plotting any sort of rebellion, Pilatus should know of it and take steps to apprehend him.

Of course spies could ferret out the truth of that. No one would believe that the praefectus, himself, had needed to journey into the territory of Antipas to hear the man.

So that Joseph's messenger, arriving in Caesarea with the wedding invitation, had been exactly what Pilatus had been looking for. No one, not even Antipas, could fault him for journeying to the wedding of the son of a friend, especially a friend of the importance of—as the High Priest referred to him—Joseph bar Ramathea.

He had set out immediately, accompanied by just twenty cavalry, and by Gallus Lucius, his executive tribune. It was always a sadness to leave Procula, especially now. Yet, with each mile up over the Plain of Esdraelon, he had felt more like a boy playing truant from his tutor, off on some wonderful adventure.

Was that how dull his life had become? That a trip into Galilee should be an adventure?

He had been in Palestine for nearly nine years. Certainly, Caesarea, his headquarters, was a jewel, and certainly it was cosmopolitan and relatively free of the Hebrews themselves, which was always a blessing.

But even Rome would grow tedious if Rome was all that was to be had.

Oh, there were the periodic jaunts up to Jerusalem, through those Jove-forsaken hills which surrounded it. And there was the society while there of the more sophisticated Sadducean sort, such as Joseph and Rosula.

But he had also at those times to deal at close range, sometimes face to face, with the corrupt Annas, and those pompous peacocks who roosted in the Temple. And with the general populace of Jerusalem, so holy that they made Pilatus sick in the stomach.

Officers of the legion had assured Pilatus that Jerusalem, with its pious bores, was not representative of the country, or of its people as a whole. Not that Pilatus really cared. Barring men like Joseph, and the amusing Rosula, Pilatus did not like Jews, and did not care to know more about them.

He was, however, ambitious, and intelligent enough to know that, to run a country successfully, the ruler should gain understanding of its people. He had lasted this long as praefectus by dint of his excellent spy system. And, whether he had wished to or no, he had learned a bit about the people . . . nothing, to date, to change his initial impression of them as fanatical bores . . . or as, in the case of the rulers of the Temple, hypocrites and criminals.

But this trip into Galilee would afford him first-hand experience of a wider range of Hebrew society. And many birds would be slain with one stone. Joseph bar Ramathea would imagine that the Roman praefectus had made the trip especially to honor him. Such a gesture of goodwill would carry much weight with the Jews, while his own men would understand his shrewdness, and the inevitable spies among them would send good reports back to Rome.

In the meantime, Pilatus was, indeed, getting to know the people, on a shoulder-to-shoulder basis seldom experienced by a Roman of his rank. As his officers had promised, Jews did know how to unbend after all, and were not half as bad as he had expected—at least not the Galilean sort. When the festivities were completed, he might even be able to search out this "Messiah" after all, and hear him speak. For reasons he could not even name, he found himself actually wanting to hear the man.

After that, he could proceed nicely and naturally into Kapher Nahum, and get down to the real point of the journey.

In a position such as Pilatus occupied, many interesting "business" opportunities were made available. On an almost daily basis, some word was whispered, some bribe offered, or a partnership, a share of profit, in return for official Roman blindness as to whatever was going on.

At first, being young and idealistic, Pilatus had refused the bribes. Then, little by little, he had begun to accept them. Not primarily because he wanted to amass a fortune, but because he wanted to be a good praefectus, to leave Palestine with such a fine record that his appointment to the Senate, or to some important governorship, would be assured.

It had finally become apparent to him that, to be a good praefectus, he *must* accept bribes.

An honest praefectus made his subjects nervous. Nervous subjects were apt to complain of him frequently to Rome, accusing him of this or that in order to be rid of him. So he had allowed himself to become one of them, a partner in their crimes, trusted and valued by them.

In the last years, he had amassed a fortune far in excess of anything left him by his parents. It was kept in coffers in hidden places in both Caesarea and Jerusalem. But he was running out of space. More importantly, he was running out of time.

If he was nothing else, Pilatus was a realist. His tenure of nine years as praefectus was unusual. These eastern provinces were notorious for the manner in which they "ate" administrators sent out to them by Rome. Their peoples were too different, too volatile, too quarrelsome, so that even the best of men ran quickly into trouble, crossed this one and that one, and finally one too many, got too many bad reports, and got relieved of their positions. Pilatus liked to believe that his own long stay was due to his fine spy system, and to the relative wisdom with which he had governed.

Yet he could not deny that part of his good luck was due to his wife—a cousin, and especial favorite, of Emperor Tiberius. Procula's husband would, of course, be given the benefit of every doubt.

Yet things were bound to change. Sooner than later. Each pouch from Rome brought ever more disconcerting news as to the mental state of the emperor—a once great man—as to his cruelties and growing perversions, as to his latest victims. One could no longer depend that his love for Procula would endure.

. . . as one could no longer depend that Procula, herself, would endure.

So now was the time to get his fortune smuggled out of Palestine and safely invested with reliable bankers. In Massilia of Gaul, perhaps. Its bankers had good report.

The smuggling must be done by those other than Romans. He could be sure that the emperor was not the only one with paid eyes and ears in Caesarea. The Senate would have spies among his men, as would members of Procula's Claudian family, and anyone else jealous of the position of Pilatus.

One simply did not know whom to trust. Only his tribune, Lucius, was completely in his confidence. But, since he was in his confidence, Lucius was certainly as closely watched as was he, himself.

Galilee was the place to find his smugglers. Galilee, that exchange depot to every point in the world, was the logical place in which to make new "friends."

Pilatus wished first to meet and size up Crispus Marcus of the Kapher Nahum garrison. He knew the man only through the weekly dispatches received by the garrison commander at Caesarea. Crispus seemed an able sort. And, having been assigned to remote Kapher Nahum, he was almost certainly no one's spy. He might prove to be an eager—if highly paid—overseer in the smuggling.

The second intent of Pilatus had been to search out the potential smuggler himself, a man called the Zebedee.

Now, conveniently, here was the Zebedee, a guest at the wedding.

This one stone was, indeed, killing many birds!

The fact that Mattias was also in attendance was the only embarrassment. Much of the fortune which now burned holes in the coffers of Pilatus had been "gifts" from Annas, messengered to Pilatus via Mattias, himself, most of the gifts in gratitude for the silence of Pilatus in the matter of "Lions' Fat."

If only the Jews understood the corrupt depths of the Annians, who possessed their high priesthood seemingly in perpetuity. Caesar, at least, made no attempt to hide his own corruption, and he did not hide behind sanctimonious smoke.

On nights when Pilatus had trouble sleeping, he had often lulled himself by attempting to calculate the amount of gold, jewels, silver, ivory, and wealth of every sort hidden in the vaults beneath that Temple. It was said that the hill called Mount Moriah was honeycombed with rooms and corridors dating from the days of Solomon, the entrance to which only the family of the High Priest now knew.

Each day, in addition to the outright payments and bribes to the High Priest in regard to his business interests, more treasure poured into the Temple in the form of dues, offerings, tithes, fees for concessions, and gifts. The treasure came, not only, from the Jews of Palestine, but, from Jewish settlements all over the civilized world. The treasure daily amassing in the Temple was called the Corban. It was sacred, not to be touched. It "belonged to God."

What a joke.

Did these Jews never stop to wonder where all that treasure was kept, and how much it amounted to? Did it never occur to them that someone other than their god might be making use of those riches? Oh yes, supposedly the Corban could be used to do good works for the people. Yet, somehow, that never seemed to happen. How well Pilatus knew. What trouble he had gotten himself into when he tried to use some of the Corban to complete Herod's aqueduct, and bring desperately needed water to Jerusalem.

What fools they were, these Jews.

It was the same with their Ark of the Covenant. Since, supposedly, no one but the High Priest was ever allowed to see either the ark or the Corban . . . who was to say that they were even there?

Pilatus smiled.

What he really should do was stroll over to Mattias and ask him which Galilean merchant the High Priest used to smuggle out his gold, and where the High Priest invested it. On Anatolian hillsides, Pilatus guessed, growing more poppies to produce more Lions' Fat.

How droll if the High Priest's smuggler should turn out to be the Zebedee.

At sundown, to cheers and applause, the newlyweds emerged from day-long seclusion. Chandreah, who had been appointed Governor of the Feast, raised his red and yellow baton and the music, dancing, feasting, and drinking began in earnest for the second night. Resolved to endure that loud-mouthed woman that he had heard called "Thunder," Pilatus made sure that he dined beside the Zebedee.

That second evening was the time of gift-giving. One by one, during the course of the feast, guests approached the divan of the bridal pair.

. . . who did not much seem to care for dancing on that evening. They seemed content to loll about, nibbling at the food placed upon the table before them, sipping wine, smiling often at one another, bursting frequently into laughter, the causes of which laughter neither was able to explain. Openly, the groom was seen to reach out, touch and tease, even kiss his bride. She lay to his right—"on his breast," as custom said of the person who laid beside, just in front of, the most honored guest at any banquet.

The gifts were varied. Rare foods, precious spices, ointments, gold and silver trinkets, inlaid vessels, silks, linens, bolts of brocade and other fine cloths.

The cousins of the bride's father gave a scroll of the Five Books of Moses, beautifully copied and adorned with golden decorations.

The bride's sister gave a box of cooking pots.

From Mattias, there was a purse of silver coins, and on and on.

Finally, at the last, one of the veiled friends of Susannah came forward carrying a box covered in gold tissue and poked full of holes.

The groom opened it and withdrew a tiny, yellow, tiger kitten . . . wearing a collar of pink feathers. The gift caused much merriment between the bride and the groom, seeming almost to eclipse the other fine gifts. Cradling and kissing the kitten, the groom finally tore himself away from his bride. He rose, drew the veiled donor out onto the floor, and led her in a dance. Soon the floor was full of dancers.

There was some magic, observed Pilatus, that happened whenever this Joshuah took the floor. There was something so compelling about the manner in which he moved—the way in which he laughed.

Thunder was watching Pilatus hopefully. Pretending that he did not see, Pilatus rose and moved quickly to the bride before another could claim her.

"Would you accompany me to the floor, Mistress?"

She was a beauty. Really a beauty Pilatus decided as she walked beside him, as she turned, smiling, and began to move to the music. There was nothing to her figure really. Yet, with some women, that did not seem to matter.

"Is it true that you are the widow of that prophet that everyone was so excited about?"

"Yes."

He shut from his mind the many tittle-tales he had heard regarding the Temple's involvement in the death of the man. It was not his place to interfere in the religious politics of these people.

"I hope you will forgive my ignorance, but, under these circumstances, I do not know just what words to say as to your bereavement . . . "

He made a gesture that eloquently took in a gala wedding feast after such short widowhood.

"I think I have much to learn about the customs of your people."

The bride's wide, full lips parted in a smile. Then throaty laughter bubbled out.

"I can understand your confusion, Praefectus. But I will hand you a clew. You will not learn of me or of either of my husbands by studying our people. The Jews, for instance, do not dance much of late. Neither do the sexes sit together at meals, as you see many of them doing here. And never do men and women dance beside each other upon the same floor."

"I had heard something to that effect. I thought perhaps in Galilee . . . "

"Galilee is more free in custom and usage, it is true. But what you see here flows from the presence of my two husbands, not from traditional Jewish thought. It is amazing even to us that everyone has accepted their lead so gracefully, and that such freedom of action is manifesting itself."

The rhythm being played by the musicians lent itself to a dignified promenade. Pilatus promenaded, adding embellishments as he was moved to do so. The lovely creature opposite him responded as though by magic, mirroring his every gesture. From the corners of his eyes, he studied her.

The tense she had used in referring to her husbands was confusing, sounding almost as though both were alive. His Aramaic was not the best, so he assigned the confusion to his own ignorance.

The thing that impressed him most deeply was the girl's calm, her manner of speaking. She was so sure, so certain, and so gracious in that knowing. He found himself wishing that he could draw her aside, sit down cross-legged at her feet, and ask a hundred questions, the nature of which he did not even know. Yet he knew that he wanted to hear her answers.

"Mistress . . . what is your name?"

"Miriam. But I am called Merovee."

"I did not bring you a gift, Merovee."

"The honor you bestow upon us with your presence is more than sufficient, Praefectus."

"Ah, but I wish to give you something. This is my first attendance at a social affair such as this among your people. I thought that I would watch, see what others gave, and then I would know what is proper.

"But you are so lovely, my dear, and your husband seems to be an outstanding man, fully as true and good as his father, of whom I have grown fond. Tell me what you wish of me. If it is within my power, I will give it to you."

Pilatus felt suddenly as though a cloud had sailed across the sun. It was already night, but, suddenly, it was darker. For a moment, everything about the girl seemed to draw inward. He felt a thrill of fear, and fancied that it was her own.

Then he had no doubts. When she spoke, the fear was in her voice.

"Do you really mean that?"

What had he let himself in for? But still . . .

"Yes."

She stopped dancing, turned and faced him. What worlds were in her eyes! What a fortunate man was this Joshuah.

"Would you grant," she said, "that we may wait to name our gift? Would you grant us the gift of an unspecified favor, which my husband or myself, or our messenger, may claim from you at any point, anywhere in the future?"

Pilatus swallowed.

"Merovee. You sound as though you already know what this favor must be."

She shook her head. Her voice came in a whisper.

"I only know that I will need the favor in Jerusalem."

There were tears in her eyes. He wanted to reach out, and did not dare.

"Please do not cry, my dear. It grieves me."

"Forgive me. Your Excellency, I do not know what the favor will be. Hopefully, I will never even have to claim it. If I do, it will not be light. When and if I ask, it will mean the world to me. But it might be politically dangerous to yourself."

Pilatus hesitated. What was there about this woman? And about the man Joshuah?

Jews! Inferiors to a Roman such as himself.

Yet he was having the oddest reaction to them. Of warmth. Of recognition. It tugged at his mind like a near-to-being-remembered song.

Where had he known these people before? Since arriving at this place, he had been filled with the same sense of comfort as he would have had in his parents' home, surrounded by his own family.

He wanted to help Merovee and her Joshuah. He wanted to know more of them.

If only to insure subsequent contact with them, he was prepared, at that moment, to promise anything she asked.

"As I said, if it is within my power at the moment of your asking, whatever you desire will be granted."

He drew a golden bracelet from off of his wrist.

"Present this with your request. It belonged to my mother. She was from the north of the Isle of the Britons. It had been handed down in her family. She gave it to me just before she died. No matter how busy or harassed I might become, the sight of this bracelet will remind me of this night, of the most beautiful bride that Galilee has ever known, and of my promise to her."

"From the north of the Isle of the Britons," murmured Merovee. "How strange." Reverentially, she slipped the circlet over her hand and slid it up her arm until it found a place to fit just below the shoulder.

"But if you do not have occasion to ask your dreadful favor," continued Pilatus, smiling, "you must promise to return this bracelet to me anyway. Someday. Somewhere. You must promise to visit me and return it personally."

"You are a very kind man," she said simply.

He flushed.

"There are many who would not agree with you, Mistress. I am not kind. I am not even honest."

Why was he telling her this?

"I am a Roman. Praefectus of Palestine. I shall rise to even higher station before I am through. A man does not rise to great station in life by being honest, and, especially, not by being kind."

"Yet you are. I like you, Pontius Pilatus."

He remembered having felt the same as a child, when an aunt he adored had complimented him on his lessons, smiling in just the same way that Merovee smiled at him now. He had wanted to turn himself inside out, to scream and shout, to hug her, to stand on his head and do childish stunts to further impress her.

Why should it matter that this woman saw good in him, why?

"I hope you get a chance to discuss these things with my Josh before you go," she went on. "He will explain to you how being kind and honest can raise a man to the most exalted position imaginable.

"But there. Do not frown, Praefectus. I talk in riddles you think. Do not disturb yourself. It will all come to you when the time is right. Do you not think that Mattias is most graceful?"

Pilatus threw back his head and howled with grateful laughter. For, the moment he had taken the floor with Merovee, Mattias and his scribe had followed dutiful suit.

"Zakiah is equally nimble," continued Merovee.

Zakiah had, once more, prevailed upon Joseph.

"Mistress, you astound me. Is there anything that you miss?"

"There is much. But I am working on the problem."

"Ah!" He smiled. "As am I."

Why did he want to prolong being with her? It was not sexual. If it had been, he would have been able to understand it.

The music ended. The musicians left the court for a few minutes of rest.

Yet still he stood there, a foolish boy, not wanting to let her go, wanting to ask all those questions, the contents of which he did not know, and hear her answers, the gist of which he could not begin to imagine.

"You say that your husband could tell me how to be great by being kind?" he blurted.

"Yes."

"I should like to hear his words."

Then the man Joshuah appeared beside them, smiling, stroking his pink-collared kitten.

"Listen to her purr," he said. "A cat's purr is blessed. It is unadulterated joy. It fills the Universe. Just this tiny, yellow mite fills all of Creation, is that not amazing?"

"Your wife tells me that you know how to be great while being kind, is that so?" said Pilatus bluntly.

"Why yes. Are you interested in learning the technique?"

"I am ambitious. I should be grateful for any knowledge that would hasten my advancement."

Jesus stood, still smiling, his eyes cast downward upon the kitten.

"You must understand," he said finally, "that the 'advancement' you would receive as a result of my words would not necessarily be the advancement that is recognized by the world. As a matter of fact, once you hear the words, you might never again be able to function in relation to the world as you did before the words. Think twice, and then yet again, before you decide to hear them, Pilatus."

Pilatus felt a madness, as though he were throwing himself off of a cliff in drunken abandon.

"I want to hear."

Jesus looked up, still smiling.

"The best place to invest your funds *is* Gaul, Pilatus. Massilia is, indeed, an excellent choice."

The face of Pilatus went blank.

"What funds?"

"You wonder how best to invest the fortune which you have acquired."

Pilatus shot a look toward the Zebedee, thinking back rapidly over the evening. No. He knew for certain that Joshuah had not been near the Zebedee since he and the Zebedee had spoken. So how could Joshuah know of the matter?

"You gave the same advice to my mother," said Merovee in puzzlement. "To sell all that she has in Palestine and invest the money in Gaul. Why Gaul?"

Jesus shrugged.

"Only a hunch. You may act on it or walk away from it."

His eyes met those of Pilatus.

"Think carefully for a night before you ask again to hear my words, Pontius Pilatus."

Pilatus felt held so that he could not move, and yet ever so gently, by the gaze of Merovee's Josh.

"If you say so," he heard himself say.

Yes. Best to go have some more wine and try to understand.

Understand what?

He turned and walked back to his divan, trying to remember.

* * *

The next day there were contests . . . foot races, spelling, language, and Scripture competitions for the children in the morning, camel and horse racing, slingshot and archery contests for the men in the afternoon.

The groom took part in everything. Moved by the spirits of both camaraderie and devilment, so did Pilatus.

Which forced Mattias and so Zakiah to test their own skills. Zakiah became seasick during the first camel race and retired from that particular competition, but Mattias proved to be a natural horseman, and won two out of five heats run on the Arabians throughout the day.

Pilatus won the other three. Yet he developed a slight respect for Mattias. Due to the rocky and hilly terrain of Palestine, these Jews did not often use horses, preferring tough, sure-footed asses, and the commodious camel. This showing of Mattias, on an unaccustomed beast against a Roman with the skills of Pilatus, was amazing.

And the man Joshuah—or Jesus—Pilatus could not quite understand why he was called by both these names—came in third in all five races, even over Tribune Gallus Lucius.

Pilatus made a mental note to pass on to Rome. Never underestimate these Jews, he would tell Tiberius. Simply because they did not do a certain thing did not mean that they could not. Immediately and well.

Naturally, Pilatus and Lucius were no match for any of the Jews in the camel races. The beasts were cranky beyond belief, seeming to obey no will but their own, and they were well named, these "Ships of the Desert." Their rolling gait took a strong stomach. And, when those "ships" went into full gallop, a storm at sea could not be more nauseating.

To wild cheers, led by that overbearing wife of his, the Zebedee came in first in all five heats, with Rosula's Uncle Samuel and, surprisingly, that big fisherman called Simon Petros shifting back and forth between second and third.

Jesus came in, each time, laughing along with Pilatus and Lucius, somewhere back in the pack.

It was in archery that the man Jesus showed himself to be a complete master. His every shot was square and center. He even, at the end of the day, astounded them all by having a linen cloth held four feet in front of the target, so that none of that target could be seen. His shot pierced the cloth neatly and the arrow was found to be, once more, squarely in the center of the target.

"How do you do that?" said Pilatus in amazement.

"Well, I certainly do not do it with the eyes of my body," said Jesus. "So I must do it with the eyes of my mind. Always trust the eyes of your mind over the eyes of your body, Pilatus. The eyes of your body are inferior tools, crafty deceivers, which will lead one astray if one puts his entire trust in them."

Smiling then, Jesus gave his bow and an arrow to his wife, and showed her how to notch it, hold it, draw it, how to aim. The other men drew round, listening, hoping to learn a thing or two. The veiled female who had given Jesus the kitten then demanded of the man Judah that he should allow her to use his bow, so that he had to put his arms about her, helping to adjust her aim. Laughing, others of the women joined in.

So that, in that hour before sunset, in a warm, red-orange glow, a hilarious and thoroughly enjoyable time was had. Pilatus was not the only one who was impressed—and touched—who said to his or herself, deep down inside . . .

"I shall never forget this moment."

The festivities of the evening were thus even more enjoyable, companionable, laughter-filled, as the events of the day were discussed and re-discussed.

Mattias did not even wait for Pilatus to rise for the dance, but made so bold as to escort the mother of the bride to the floor. Flushed with triumph over his showing in the races, he had drunk more than his share of wine. Recently made a widower, he could not help but admire the gracious Deborah. A man could do worse. Much worse. Of the tribe of Benjamin this woman might be, rather than of Aaron as was expected for the family of the High Priest. And some years older than himself. Yet he had already sired a goodly number of boys for the Annian dynasty from out of an Aaronite woman. Might not dispensation be made for a second wife?

An impossible dream. Yet tonight seemed a good night for dreaming. Certainly her fortune would count in her favor.

Jesus and his group watched with amusement the consternation of Zakiah the Pharisee as he saw Mattias asking the company of a woman on the floor. What to do?

His compromise was masterful. With a show of fatherly affection, he invited Ben's two-year-old daughter to join him.

It was late when Pilatus approached the bridal couch once more, and was invited to join them in the figs in cream then being served.

"I come to tell you," he said, "that I must depart the day after tomorrow. As long as I am up here in Galilee, it would be beneficial for me to review our garrison in . . . how do you say it? Capernaum or Kapher Nahum?"

"Capernaum is the Greek corruption," said Jesus. "Most Hebrews still call it Kapher Nahum. Kapher means 'place of,' and the tomb of the prophet Nahum is there."

"Ah. Well, I would like to go there and confer with Centurion Crispus. And, frankly, I did not understand just how long you Jews go on with wedding festivities."

"As you see," smiled Jesus, "many of the guests travel long and hard distances to attend, so that they prefer to stay a while, making it a real visit before starting back."

"I would that I could stay as well. I mean that truly. I cannot recall when I have had as good and as carefree a time. Not since I was a child at least."

"I am pleased to hear that." Jesus laughed as the kitten found his bowl and began to lap at the cream. "Because you are on the right road. To enter the Kingdom of Heaven, Pontius Pilatus, one must be brave enough to become as joyous, and as spontaneous and trusting, as a child once again."

"The Kingdom of Heaven. I do not understand what you Jews mean by 'Heaven,' Jesus. Is it what we Romans and the Greeks call the Elysium Fields?"

"I will tell you a secret. Even the Jews do not understand what they mean by 'Heaven.' Every one of them will give you a different story, and many of them deny its existence altogether. But, yes, in the most popular understanding, it is much the same as the Elysium Fields . . . a place of reward to which the great and good go after death.

"When I use the term, however, I mean something much different than does that popular understanding. One does not have to die to enter 'Heaven.'"

Pilatus hesitated.

"You told me to think for a night before asking again to hear your words. I have thought. I would still like to hear them."

"Why?" said Jesus simply and quite pleasantly.

"I do not know why," said Pilatus just as simply. "I thought perhaps you could tell me."

Jesus smiled noncommittally.

"My wife has told me of your gift to us. You have my thanks in advance. It gives her much peace of mind to know that she can rely on you."

Quick, foolish tears came into the eyes of Pilatus. Before any other couple in the world, he would have felt angry, shamed. Yet, before these two people, he remained comfortable.

"I cannot imagine what it is that your wife fears, Jesus. But I would not have her frightened for the world. If my promise gives her comfort, it is a great happiness to me."

"For that alone, Pontius Pilatus, whatever may happen in the days to come, you have my friendship and my Love forever. Remember those last words. You will need them as a ship needs harbor in a storm, again and again before your days are finished upon this Earth."

Pilatus frowned. This man Jesus was so unlike others. Pilatus felt suspended, floating in a dream world, confronting a man who was a phantom of his own sleep, who said and did things that would make no sense to a waking mind, but which made perfect sense to a dreaming mind.

"May I hear your words, Jesus?"

"By all means. It is time that even I got back to business."

He looked fondly at his wife.

"I can not hide behind merry-making forever, can I.

"But perhaps just for this last night.

"You shall hear my words tomorrow, Pontius Pilatus."

The morrow dawned warm and cloudless. No activities had been planned, a purposeful interlude, so that those who wished to could slip gracefully away, or at least prepare to leave the following day. Even those who had come down from Jerusalem had time to get home before the Sabbath if they left early enough in the morning.

But no one came to announce a departure as had Pilatus. Which meant that all, save Pilatus and his retinue, would be staying at least through the Sabbath.

"We are showing them too good a time," said Rosula to Deborah at the informal, but private, breaking of fast in Deborah's salon.

Deborah shrugged.

"As long as the wine holds out, so can I."

"The wine will not hold out if certain people do not stop drinking so much," said Martha with a meaningful glance at her new brother-in-law.

"There is much of importance in wine," said Jesus. "And in the vine. Perhaps someday you will understand that, Martha."

Deborah frowned, as mystified as Martha by the response.

"What of you?" she asked Joseph. "Is your side of the expense mounting too rapidly?"

"I will stand any expense," smiled Joseph, "so grateful am I to see this prodigal of mine married."

"It is mostly that I wrack my brains for new ways in which to entertain them," said Deborah. "And the sun has been so good that our grapes up on the high slopes have come prime a full week before we had expected."

"The mother of Nathaniel says that both of the top-most fields should have been picked yesterday," said Martha crisply. "If they are not gotten in, they will be good for little but vinegar. Why do you not set some of these rabble-rousers to picking grapes for their wine and board?"

"Do not be ridiculous," said Deborah,

"But why not?" said Jesus.

He gave Martha a solid nod, raising his cup to her.

"Sister, you have a good, practical head on your shoulders."

"Thank you," said Martha with something akin to shock. She was not accustomed to approbation.

Jesus rose.

"That is it exactly. I will organize them . . . trust me to infuse them with an eagerness to dirty their hands . . . Martha, can you organize a spectacular noontide feast to be brought up to us in the fields?"

"Of course!" said Martha, beaming, and she hastened off to begin at once.

"We will also need plenty of wine, Deborah, to nourish their enthusiasm. Even tomorrow's entertainment is then settled. Tomorrow we will have a grape-crushing festival."

"Jesus," laughed Deborah, "you are impossible."

"I stand before you, therefore I am quite possible. For their troubles, I might, however, be forced to offer each family a case of the vintage from the grapes which they pick."

"Offer as you see fit, Jesus. I know that I will never have short shrift by following in your wake."

* * *

The procession that Jesus led up the hillside that morning was large and merry. The day was so clean, mild without being hot, the company so congenial. For many, the gathering of grapes—indeed any manual labor—was enough of a novelty to be a lark. And what fun to look forward to serving the best vintage of the House of Nathan and then revealing to guests that one had helped to gather and crush it oneself!

For Pilatus, there was quite another thrill. This took him back to his boyhood, to the hills of Abruzzi, the beautiful old villa, and his father's vineyards. The father of Pilatus had believed that even the wealthy should know something of manual toil, so that, at each harvest, the whole family had labored with the slaves among the vines.

That villa and its vineyards had been sold years before, after the death of his father, then of his beautiful, fair-haired mother, a Pict from the north of the Isle of the Britons. Now the fingers of Pilatus itched for the vines. He fancied that, as he picked, he might glimpse his father again, if only in a clear mind's eye, and hear his mother's soft laughter. To be as a child once again . . . was that not what Jesus had advised? Yes. Pilatus wanted to be a child again. At least for this last day.

Lucius, trudging beside him, probably thought that he had gone quite mad. Lucius did not know. He did not understand. Jesus understood. How? Why?

Perhaps it did not matter. That he understood was enough.

The upper field was the first to be attacked. It was near the top of the highest hill of the area, a hill almost high enough to be called a mountain. Soon that mountain-top resounded with songs and jests. Only Joseph "bar Ramathea" was seen to be distracted, and slow to participate.

The villagers moved quickly amongst the amateur pickers, supplying baskets, carting off those that were filled, loading wagons and pack asses, driving them down the hillside for unloading, then back up again. The pickers were not exactly efficient, especially the children, who ate more grapes than they picked, but their number was so great that the first field was stripped clean and they had moved on to the next by the time that Martha's wagons arrived with the noonday feast.

The Zebedee was partially responsible for the success of that meal, for his wagon brought a daily supply of fresh fish from the lake. Martha had caused bite-sized cakes to be made from a variety of these fish, and there was a tangy radish sauce to dip them into. There were vegetables and fruits, cheeses, newly baked breads, and sweetmeats.

"Wonderful, Martha! It could not be better."

The pleasure that Jesus took in his meal was certainly not feigned. Martha commenced quietly to glow.

"Do you like the sauce?"

"Perfect. It does not burn the tongue from out of the mouth yet it has a good bite."

"It is my grandmother's recipe. My father's mother."

"This bread as well?"

"Yes. I understand that she was a wonderful cook. I hardly knew her. She died shortly after my father—just after the twins were born."

"Well thanks be that her recipes were passed down to one such as yourself."

Martha looked almost as though she might cry.

"I think they need wine over there," she said. She rose, seized an empty pitcher, and rushed off.

"Are you making up to my sister?" said Merovee with raised brows.

"I merely compliment those talents which she most certainly has."

He took another fishcake and used it to scoop up a plenty of sauce.

"All of us have talents. All of us have purpose. The talents and purposes of others might not be readily apparent, neither do they often agree with our own. Yet, if we take the time to search out those talents and voice our appreciation of them, magic is the result. One of the easiest ways to be 'kind' is to recognize and praise the talents and efforts of others, no matter how mundane or lowly they might seem. And that sort of kindness is a step toward wisdom, for, in the eyes of All That Is, anything well done, or honestly tried, is superlative."

The intimates of Jesus edged nearer. Pilatus found himself edging with them.

"Joshuah," murmured Joseph. "Please do not get started. Please. Not to these people."

"I have promised Pilatus that I will explain how to be great while still being kind, Father."

"*Anything* well done is superlative?" asked Pilatus. "Even something that the world would call 'evil'?"

"Even that," smiled Jesus. "No man intends to be evil. Each justifies his actions, and, in his own mind, believes those actions to be good—or at least the best or most advisable under the circumstances. And 'God'—working on a greater scale than your own little mind can encompass—turns to good account even the worst that is done. So that one should not concern oneself overly with 'bad' or 'evil' or 'unfair' things done by others. Truly, they do not concern one."

"But what if someone lifts his hand to strike me? Even to kill me," said Petros indignantly. "Does that not concern me?"

"No. Only in that you must deal with your pain after the slap, or with your 'death' if the blow should be fatal. But since 'death' does not really kill you, the fellow has not killed you, he only thinks that he has. And, in thinking that he has killed you, thinking that he *can* kill you—in that belief, is his 'sin.' He will be a long time 'atoning' for that belief . . . atonement that will be self-imposed, by his own greater consciousness.

"I say to you that, if a fellow comes at you to strike or to kill you, *in your own best interest,* upon an eternal and cosmic scale that takes in much more than this one little lifetime, you should in no wise hit that person back, or attempt to kill him to save yourself. In hitting back, you but set up for yourself a cycle of self-imposed atonement that will not end until you, too, understand the true nature of such an act.

"My advice to you is, if a man smites you on one cheek, turn the other cheek, and let him hit you there as well. Not from meekness, but from strength. Out of wisdom."

"But this is insanity!"

It was Tribune Gallus Lucius who spoke.

"Where would the Roman Empire be if it followed such advice?"

"In the Kingdom of Heaven," said Jesus with a smile. He took a slab of cheese and refilled his wine cup. "Or at least further along the road to that kingdom.

"I understand your disbelief, Tribune. My words are seemingly against all common sense. Yet the world has, for thousands of years, done things in the way that you think is proper . . . striking, fighting back, offending, defending. You Romans fight battle after battle, you occupy and subjugate, you strive amongst yourselves for the high offices, your Caesars rise to heights only to be struck down by those who oppose them. You accumulate wealth. You sacrifice to your gods. You do all that common sense and society says that you should.

"And what is your lot? Just more of what Humanity has always endured under this system. Disease, treachery, injustice, war, dissatisfaction, fear, insecurity, distrust, suffering, death."

"And what of it?" said Lucius. "It is the way of the world, the way of men. What more should we expect?"

"Oh, much more. Does it not occur to you that this system of behavior in which the species has engaged for so many thousands of years *does not work*? It does not get us where we say we want to go. It does not bring us happiness, security, health, well being, and joy. Indeed, it brings us the opposites. I repeat, our current system does not work, given what we say we wish to achieve.

"Now. There is an experiment that Humankind has never attempted, for which it has as yet gathered neither the understanding nor the courage. When it does find that understanding, and then the courage, a greater age will dawn.

"Do you not sometimes, Tribune, all secretly down in the depths of yourself, yearn for quiet, joy, beauty, for a chance to fulfill all of your finest secret aspirations in freedom and peace?"

Lucius shrugged.

"Sometimes I suppose. But it is mere foolishness."

"I beg to differ. What you consider 'mere foolishness' is the voice of . . . "

He hesitated. Semantics were such a problem. Romans did not understand the concept of one god, while others who had drawn near to listen would not understand "All That Is."

Yet there was no other way.

" . . . the voice of the Creator of this Universe—which I call All That Is, and of Truth, trying to get your attention, trying to tell you something. Those finer yearnings are your own, greater Self, whispering to you, telling you that there is a better way, if only you will have the courage to try it."

"But that way never works!" said Pilatus. "Certainly much less well than our current way of operating. I agree with Lucius. Just try being nice to someone. They will turn around and cheat you or betray you. All of Mankind is ruthless, scrambling, clawing."

"As long as that is what you believe, Praefectus, that is what you will create for yourself, and so encounter in your experience. Yet you do not wholly believe your own words. For you are here, with me. Have you seen me scrambling and clawing?"

Pilatus frowned.

"A man who is 'nice' will only get left in the dust," he said stubbornly.

"More often than not. But let me ask you this. That man left sitting in the dust behind the thundering herd . . . is he really the loser? Or is he the winner? Those who reach the top—the Caesars, the senators—even a tribune or praefectus—what do they get of lasting personal value for their efforts?"

"Wealth, for one thing," volunteered Petros.

"No man has yet been able to take his treasure with him beyond the grave—even if he has been able to keep the moths and rust and dust and rot from corrupting it through a whole lifetime, and if he has escaped the thieves who break in and steal, even kill him and his loved ones to get the treasure for themselves."

"He gets power," said the Zebedee.

"Alexander had power. Think you he cares for it now? Think you it sets him in good stead in the place where he is? I asked you what those who scramble to the top of the heap—wealthy and powerful as they may become—what do they get that is of *lasting value to them personally*?"

"Maybe . . . " Pilatus was still frowning.

"Yes?"

"They might at least learn."

"Learn what?"

"That . . . there *is* nothing of lasting value to be gained from wealth and political power. At least not to them personally."

"Ah." Jesus nodded, eyeing Pilatus with respect. "Now we are beginning to get somewhere. But, to finally get there, we must go back to our poor fellow sitting in the dust.

"He has been hit, spat upon, robbed, shouldered, and trampled, without returning a single blow. What has he gotten of lasting value from the situation?"

"Nothing so far as I can see," said Thunder, delighted once again to find herself in a position where women were free to contribute to the thinking. "Except that he is still alive."

Jesus did not fail to further her pleasure.

"Excellent, Zilpah! Yes, that is a start. For, where there is life there is hope.

"So our friend sits there, and the dust begins to settle. The herd has passed him by, there will be no one else to hit him or kick him, at least until the next ambitious herd comes thundering along. He has no need to compete with anyone, to defend himself, or—since he has been robbed—to jealously guard the gold in his gird. There is suddenly nothing there but himself, being supported by the Earth, surrounded by her bounty.

"Now. This fellow could do one of many things. He could decide that he had been a fool, jump up and go rushing off after the mob, shaking his fist, intent upon busting a few skulls and getting his gold back so that he can resume his place in the scramble.

"He could, instead, not rush after them, but sit there and fume at the others, call them terrible names, curse them, think how awful they are, and what a poor, good, innocent, mistreated fellow he is.

"He could curse his own self for being a coward.

"If he had let himself be trampled because he had listened to my words, he might even curse me, and call me a fool.

"He could even just curl up and go to sleep.

"If he is wise, however, he will take advantage of this moment of peace and quiet, free from any need to do anything but sit in the warm dust. He will put from his mind all that has passed. He will begin to look around and see the birds, the grasses, the flowers. He will ponder on their innocence, upon their trust.

"As, for instance, that songbird there on yonder vine. It does not sow, neither does it reap, nor gather into shelters against the fallow months as do we. It does not ponder the state of the world, or lay furious plans for survival.

"Yet all that it needs is provided for it—seeds, fruits, water, bushes in which to nest, a mate to love, air upon which to wield its wings. The bird greets each day with glad song, then goes on about its business, selecting, from the great available bounty, that which is sufficient to the day.

"Do you ever see birds sitting on the vines all screwed up in worry over whether the same bounty will be available on the next day? If birds began to do that, they would starve, or else have to work twice as hard the next day to make up for the time lost worrying."

"But we cannot be as birds!" protested Uncle Samuel. "If I ceased earning my living and laying up money and supplies, I would starve, and my family with me!"

"As long as you believe that that is the truth, so it shall be," said Jesus. "You shall be ever engaged in a mad scramble to insure against future deprivation, and have time for nothing else but that worry.

"Yet I think you might agree with me that much which you consider 'essential' to your life and station—and which you expect to give you 'happiness'—could be gotten along without if it became necessary."

"But you cannot compare us to birds!" insisted Uncle Samuel.

"Of course not. Birds and humans are totally different species of Spirit. And, humans, for one thing, are possessed of a greater ability to ponder.

"But the level of Humanity's pondering marks its level of progress. If the 'God' in which you profess to believe knows exactly what that bird needs, and provides for it so admirably, why do you not trust that 'he' would do proportionately more for you?"

"But . . . " Uncle Samuel sputtered. "It just does not work that way."

"And it never will, Uncle Samuel. Until you raise your level of pondering. Until you find the courage to give my words a try. Until then, you will consistently block 'God's' natural benevolence, and the great creative Energy that has been given to you in particular and to Humanity as a whole."

"Camel dung! Give it a try, my foot! I do not have to give it a try. I know. One has only to look at the world to know. If you do not work and earn money and put it away, you will starve. That is, unless you want us to get down on the ground and scramble around for seeds as does that bird."

"I have done so, Uncle Samuel. I have existed for as long as a year in wilderness, drinking from the streams so kindly provided by All That Is, eating its wild fruits, nuts, seeds . . . being very happy and healthy all the while."

"Well, of course one could live that way if one was forced to. But it would not be much of a life."

"Not much of a life? Ah, Uncle Samuel. You do not understand what true riches are. The gold in your coffers could never match the gold of a ripe melon, or of the hills at sunset. Or even pay for the joy that all of you have felt here on this mountaintop today."

"Hmmph. This is mere philosophy."

"What you dismiss as mere philosophy is the road to lasting value, Uncle Samuel."

"And what?" said Thunder. "Should then we all go naked as animals? Or did you also find fine robes hung about in the wilderness for you to choose from?"

"Do you see those lilies growing there beyond the vines? Those lilies do not toil. Neither do they spin. Yet even Solomon in all his glory was not arrayed so beautifully as they.

"Are you not greater than a lily, Zilpah? You profess to believe in 'God.' Why, then, do you not know that 'God' would clothe you at least as finely as a lily if you showed 'him' your trust?

"Even the grass, so unimportant that we tread upon it and cut it to fodder our animals and feed our fires, wears a fine green coat, and, each spring, is given a new one.

"All this our fellow, sitting in the dust, will begin to notice if he has come far enough along the road of wisdom. He will begin to think deeply, and widely, upon the 'philosophical' ramifications of the condition of that lily, and begin to understand what the bounty enjoyed by that lily indicates for every living thing on the face of planet Earth.

"With the dust settled, and the thunder of the mob silenced by distance, he will at last understand himself to be fortunate. He will understand, finally, the message that shouts, screams at us daily from the example of these simple plants and animals.

"If he is very, very wise, he will vow to begin at least to try to trust, to try to find the courage to begin a new experiment in living."

"Surely," said Deborah with troubled brow, "you do not mean that we should forsake our art, our architecture, our attempts to build fine and beautiful things, and return to the animal way of life?"

"Not at all, Sweet Mother. What I am saying is that the basis should be firm before one begins to build. Only when that basis is firm can anything of lasting value be erected.

"The man . . . " He smiled. " . . . or woman, who wishes to build, should build upon rock . . . rock composed of deep understanding and trust in the great benevolence of the vast sea on whose surface we sail.

"Any truly great piece of architecture—any immortal piece of art—will arise, can only arise, from out of this deep knowledge. The creation will be great for the very reason that something in its lines, in its composition, will convey to the mind of the beholder that which the artist understood, even if imperfectly. Without knowing why, generation after generation will be drawn to it. Those who gaze upon it will go away fortified, inspired, strangely elated, still without knowing why.

"No, Mother, I do not wish to rob Humanity of its creative endeavors. Those endeavors are the flowers, the fruits of our experience and progress. I seek only to better them, with a real understanding of the fountain, the source from which they flow."

"But you do seem to say," said the Zebedee anxiously, "that to possess money is wrong, and that to be successful is wrong."

"When did I say that? Not at all. Create all the money you want. By all means, be successful. But do it from your solid base of stone. Do not be a silly fellow who builds his house on the sand, so that the first tide brings it crumbling down in ruins about his head.

"There is full wealth and there is empty wealth. There is full endeavor and empty endeavor.

"Empty riches result when riches are the sole objective of those who scramble for them. Full riches are a mere by-product to those who understand the true nature of reality, and who trust that reality."

The Zebedee glanced at Pontius Pilatus.

"Should I, then, not try to gain more riches?"

"You may do exactly as you wish, Zebedee. I but tell you that to gain riches for the mere sake of gathering riches will not help you discover the Kingdom of Heaven—which kingdom is, very simply, interior wisdom and peace based on understanding and trust. When you devote all your time to making money—or to worrying about making it—you have no time to learn the things that will lead you to that kingdom. It would be easier to get a camel through one of those little, needle-eye gates in the walls of Jerusalem than for one obsessed with the procurement of money to find the Kingdom of Heaven.

"You would do much better to sit down in the middle of a dusty road on a warm day in the country and watch the lilies and the birds."

"But many good things can be done with money," said Judah. "One can help the poor . . . "

"The poor again, eh Judah? Tell me, just who are the poor?"

"Well, those who have not . . . . . . hmmm. Who have not much money."

Jesus smiled.

"There is more to being poor than having or lacking money. The poor come in all shapes and sizes and from all strata of society. There are rich poor people and poor rich people, and rich rich people and poor poor people, and all shades in between. A man can have no money at all and be happier than that songbird, and glow more finely than the lily. I say to you, do not notice the mote in your neighbor's eye, or his lack of funds. Do not pity others, thinking that you are above them, and, from that supposed position of superiority, attempt to correct them, or fund them, or help them . . . *not until you have helped yourself.*

"Spiritually.

"Remove the beam of wood from your own eye. Only then can you see clearly enough to help in removing a speck of dust from the eye of a neighbor. Find out whether you are truly rich or truly poor before presuming to help one 'less fortunate.'"

"Are you saying we should not give alms?"

The voice was strident, angry. Zakiah the Pharisee, spy from the House of Shammai, sent northward especially to lick at juice such as this, was the speaker.

"Joshuah. Please," muttered Joseph.

Jesus merely reached out and patted his hand.

"Why do all of you insist upon twisting my words? Why do you not simply listen to what I say?

"I did not say that one should not give alms. What I suggest is a new basis from which to give them.

"But since it is you who ask, Pharisee, I shall address myself to your kind.

"You make a great public show of your holiness, praying in the street, flaunting your tefillin, demanding the highest seats in the synagogue, giving your alms to the clanging of bells so that all may witness your generosity."

There came an apprehensive murmur from the assembled.

"How dare you?" said Zakiah.

"I offer no judgment. I merely make observations. Have I said anything that is untrue?"

"We but obey the Law of God."

"Show me where your tefillin are demanded by Torah."

"There is no demand, but it is implied . . . "

"Show me where it is written."

"It is not."

"Then it is an invention, designed specifically to make you seem even holier than the High Priest.

"Where is it written in Torah that the streets should be clogged with your praying, that you should have a seat higher than any other, that you should ring bells to attract attention when you give alms?"

"We but seek to give a good example for others to emulate."

"You but seek the approbation of Man and your own personal glory, that is what you seek. And I tell you, Pharisee, that, each time you ring a bell to attract attention when you do alms, you take yourself further from the Kingdom of Heaven.

"Just as the Zebedee removes himself further when he agrees to a contract that is not quite savory, simply in order to gather wealth.

"When Pilatus takes a bribe.

"When Uncle Samuel sells a twelve-year-old camel saying it is only six years old.

"When Mattias tells a lie for his uncle Annas.

"When Petros slips a few fish off of the weight reported to the Zebedee.

"When my brother Jac starves himself.

"When I do less than I could in any circumstance."

The silence of the listeners was charged, and many were the inquiring glances.

"All of these 'sins' are of the same ilk and magnitude. They are the result of imperfect understanding of the true nature of 'God,' and of a lapse of trust in the benevolence of the Universe.

"My advice would be, Pharisee, do not ring bells any longer. Do your alms in secret. Be so secretive that your right hand is unaware of what your left hand is doing. Trust that your god, that sees in secret, will reward you openly and lavishly.

"For only when alms *are* done secretly, is it true generosity. Only an act that seeks no public reward is worthy.

"And, when you pray, do not do so standing on street corners and upon platforms in a synagogue so that all can see and bow down in respect. Go into your closet, where none may know of your 'holiness' except the true god that sees all, that, indeed, dwells right inside of you, *as* yourself, as your every thought and heartbeat.

"If you will do so, if you will trust that the true god hears your secret prayer, you will receive open reward.

"Until you have the courage to do these things, and to trust, to believe that my words are the truth, you will receive only empty, ephemeral rewards, and you will come no closer to that which you seek. The Kingdom of God."

"But why?" said Jacob bar Alphaeus. "Why does God wish us to do these things secretly?"

'He' does not. Frankly, 'God' could not care less."

Jesus raised his hand to silence the shocked and affronted sounds.

"What is paramount, is that you begin to trust the infallible laws of this Universe. Only by going into yourself, only by doing your deeds so that only you know of them, can you see the results of these infallible laws and prove to yourself that what I tell you is the truth.

"For the Power of 'God,' the Kingdom of 'God,' is within. Within each one of you. You must purify your self, satisfy your self, teach and try your self, prove your self to your Self. What you do for your Self—not self*ish*ly, which is quite another thing, based on a *lack* of self worth and self confidence— what you do for the advancement of the Self, and not for appearances or standing in the world, you do for the true god All That Is. The course I recommend to you is, indeed, the *only* way to do anything for the true god, the only way to approach the true kingdom.

"I told you before that you would be better off turning your cheek than hitting back at one who hits you. That seems to you to be the most foolish advice imaginable. Yet, when you begin truly to understand the laws of the Universe, you understand that, by hitting you, that person hurts only himself. He will have to pay, again and again and again, until he learns, not only, not to hit people, but why he should not hit people . . . until he learns that he does hurt only his Self, and so 'God.'

"So, if the man sitting in the dust has already gained enough understanding not to hit back, and so understands that he was on the receiving end of the blow because he was once the one giving the blows, how far ahead of his attackers he is! He should know himself to be rich, and those other souls to be poverty-stricken."

"But to hold one's temper is often difficult," said Chandreah.

"That it is. And pure emotion should never be denied.

"But few angers are pure. Most are muddy, confused and petty, arising, not from the insult, attack, or unfairness received, but, from out of the private guilts and unadmitted feelings of inadequacy of the receiver.

"Be truthful with your self the next time that you are moved to anger. At what are you really angry? Perhaps you have let some matter slide, so that, finally, it turns out badly for you. The anger that you direct at others is really an attempt to hide your fury at your self from your self."

"Are we then not allowed to be angry?" said Susannah.

"To be angry is human. My last wish is to deny you any of your humanity. It is the reason for your being here. I would simply show you a more superior way to be human.

"There is tremendous Energy in anger, and the potential for great Creativity—which can show itself in 'good' or 'bad' creations. Make honest efforts, then, when moved by anger, to understand what it really is inside of yourself that you are angry at, and then to turn that tremendous Energy into some positively creative channel.

"If our friend sitting in the dust was of a mind, for instance, he could recognize his own anger at himself for having placed himself in the position that he did, and he could jump up and begin, with his own hands, to construct a new road to an entirely unexplored place."

"If everyone began to act as you suggest, society as we know it would disintegrate."

Jesus looked up and gazed for a long moment into the face of the speaker.

"Yes, Mattias," he said at last. "It would. And a better form of society would emerge."

A slow smile lifted his lips.

"But you and your family have naught to fear, at least as yet. Many will hear my words, few will understand them. Even fewer will have the courage to implement them in their own lives.

"The gate that leads from the countryside of Spiritual Emptiness into the City of Destruction is wide. Eager throngs run hourly through that portal.

"The gate *out* of that unhappy place is small and narrow, smaller even than a needle-eye gate. Very few even know of its existence. Fewer still would deign to use it.

"Why should they, they reason, when that wide, comfortable gate is there if ever they should care to leave the City of Destruction behind and return to mere Spiritual Emptiness.

"What they do not understand is, that the wide gate is a magic gate. There is only one way to it. Once you pass from Spiritual Emptiness into Destruction, you cannot leave . . . except by that narrow, difficult gate."

"To where does that narrow gate lead?" said Merovee.

"Back to your forgotten, native country. To Everlasting Life in the Kingdom of All That Is."

"The narrow gate is death then?" said Pilatus.

"Not at all. I know it is not a part of your beliefs, Praefectus, and it is not even officially a part of the beliefs of my own people. But you have lived and died many hundreds of times on this Earth, and you will have to keep living and dying until you finally understand.

"Death is no permanent escape. Neither does it confer automatic, all-seeing wisdom, or the sort of Everlasting Life of which I speak.

"One who is stupid and 'dead'—sleep-walking so to speak—while 'alive,' will be nearly as stupid, 'dead,' and somnambulistic in what we call death, and will have to come back again and again to get progressively less stupid and so more truly alive."

"But you have told us," said Merovee, "that Everlasting Life is automatic to each of us, is this not so? The City of Destruction, is that damnation? Hell? *Is* it possible that All That Is would cast us into this everlasting torment forever?"

"Apply the principles, Merovee. All That Is would do nothing of the sort. What is done to us, we do to ourselves. And the way out of the torments that we give to ourselves is always there—that narrow gate, which looks so difficult, and through which only the courageous, or those who are just plain fed-up with wallowing about in Destruction, dare to go.

"And when I tell you that the gate leads to Life Everlasting, I speak qualitatively. There is life and there is Life and there is *Life* and there is LIFE and yet again *LIFE!*" he said, his voice rising with each emphasis

"The Life Everlasting beyond that gate is a place of greater consciousness, of more acute awareness, of deepening understanding, and of a sure, certain Knowing that life *is* everlasting.

"All of which understanding makes each moment, each experience, rewarding in a way that is difficult for me to describe. One who has passed through the gate lives more dimensions of any given moment, it is as simple as that."

"But such people would not be fit for society," said Mattias.

"It is more a case of society not being fit for them, Priest. They are more than fit. They are the truly great amongst you. They are the ones who seem to glow, who radiate confidence and wisdom, to whom you are attracted as moths to a flame. They do not force themselves upon others, but neither do they hide their light beneath bushels. They simply allow their lights to shine before men, and those who behold them unconsciously understand that these are the ones whose mere being glorifies 'God.'

"These bright ones are the ones who have vision, courage, daring, trust. They are the ones who do not have to scramble to the top of any heap, but who rise as though on invisible wings in whatever their circumstance—hovel or palace—their ideals relatively intact, their integrity only chipped, growing better, rather than worse, as they live their lives.

"There is not a one of you who has not met such people . . . and secretly admired them, wished to become as they.

"Well, I have just told you the way to do it. That strait, narrow gate."

"But what of criminals?" The speaker was Reuben, a wealthy Sadducee, friend of Joseph and member of the Sanhedrin. "You enjoin us not only not to kill—and of course we are commanded not to do so anyway—but not even to defend ourselves, which . . . well, I have often wondered about that myself. If we are enjoined not to kill, it should mean 'Do Not Kill,' under any circumstance."

"Would that not mean animals as well?" said his wife.

"Hold, Woman. I am speaking. All right, Jesus, the commandment does not say, 'You shall not kill except in cases where you must defend yourself or others.' Therefore I might go along with you and say that one should not even raise a hand to keep from being killed. Ideally. But surely we are allowed to seize and punish criminals. Torah actually commands us to do so."

"Have you ever attended a stoning, Reuben?"

"Of course. It is my duty."

"Is it? Who did you kill most recently?"

" . . . an adulteress."

"Of course at the time you, yourself, were without sin."

"Well . . . certainly my sins were not as hers."

"'Sins' do not come in sizes, Reuben. If I miss my mark when I shoot my arrow, I might just as well miss by a mile as by an inch. A faulty aim is a faulty aim and must be corrected, and that is all there is to it, for that is where survival eventually resides, in the perfected aim. As a fair marksman myself, I can tell you that, often, that habitual slight miss, that mere inch, is harder to correct than is the miss of the amateur that flies out into the field and decapitates a daisy.

"I ask you to look more closely at a body of Law that tells you unequivocally not to kill, and then, you believe, enjoins faulty archers, who have missed the mark by an inch or a foot, to go out and stone to death one who missed by two feet.

"At the next stoning, Reuben, pick up your stone if you must, but then say to your fellows, 'Let he among you who is without sin cast the first stone.'"

Sweat broke out on Joseph's brow. Jesus had just stepped over the line. He was openly condemning The Law.

"This is all very interesting, Rabbi," said Mattias, giving the 'Rabbi' an ominous emphasis.

Jesus smiled brightly.

"Why I suppose that I *may* now be called Rabbi, may I not, now that I have done my Mosaic duty and become a married man. Thank you for being the first to so honor me, Mattias."

Mattias scowled.

"You tell us that the Law of Moses should not be obeyed. There should be no stonings."

"There you go again," said Jesus mildly, "twisting my words. Did I say that? No. I said only that he who is without sin should be the first one to cast the stone.

"Moses, you see, assumed that all who went out to do the stoning would be without sin. Had he not laid down his Laws? Would not all good Hebrews follow those Laws and, thus, be sinless? Of course they would, Moses thought.

"Therefore, he did not even consider it necessary to say, 'Oh, and by the way, if you, yourself, are not without sin, you have no right to participate in this punishment.'"

It was difficult to tell whether the smile on the lips of Jesus was merely a smile or incipient laughter.

"You are very clever," said Mattias, not without admiration.

"I do not come to destroy the Law, Mattias."

The smile was gone from the lips of Jesus. In its place was infinite tenderness.

"Neither would I mock any of our prophets. I come to build upon that solid base of stone which those great men prepared for me. In one way or another, all that they foresaw will be fulfilled, down to the last jot or tittle. The information they passed to us was good and right if one will consider the limitations of the viewpoints which their circumstances forced onto them.

"He who teaches in the *Spirit* of their Laws shall be great in understanding. He who tries to turn others aside from that Spirit shall be small.

"Yet I tell you that even words graven onto stone can be made flexible and plastic with the proper techniques."

He cast a mischievous eye at Merovee, who had been badgering him for the secret of the "Samir" that Salome had spoken of the night he told them of the Builders. His mischief turned next towards Mattias.

"*You* should understand the plastic nature of stone, Mattias, you and your family above all others."

The mouth of Mattias quite literally dropped. Quickly he looked about, and saw that the others had no clew as to the import of the words.

"Where do you get your information, *ben Joseph of Ramah?*"

The reference to the lineage of Joseph was both a guess as to the answer to the question, and a veiled threat. Aside from the family of the High Priest, only the scions of the House of David and of Solomon might somehow know the truth. And where the politically potent nature of Joseph's line had not been alluded to during the festivities, it was now quite definitely recalled to the minds of all.

"I get my information from that place beyond the strait, narrow gate, Mattias.

"But be of good cheer. Your secret is to me no more than a bauble of academic interest. The point is that words are symbols, and, as such, must and will naturally change with the times.

"I offer a change that is growth. I offer a deeper understanding of our Law and of the words of our great prophets.

"And I tell you to judge not others. By an inescapable law of the Universe, as you judge others, so you eventually shall be judged.

"What you measure out to others, shall be measured back to you.

"What you sow, you shall reap.

"Be it good or be it bad, what you give out, you shall receive back.

"Tenfold.

"I do not thus advise you to be 'good' for any religious reason, but out of sheer practicality. The path to real success is the ever-growing understanding of the workings of The Energy that composes and structures our Universe. Its rules are definite and may not be sidestepped forever.

"Our Law was a good beginning step in preparing us for an understanding of Universal Law.

"Some of you are now ready to take the next step, and that is why I am here.

"You *can* lay up treasure while here on this Earth that you *can* take with you into the place beyond the grave.

"As Pilatus so astutely observed, you do lay up that treasure even while you think you are gaining nothing. He observed that one who had scrambled to the top of the heap could learn, lastingly, that he had gained nothing from the possession of objects and riches and power of any sort.

"A person who has learned that takes incalculable treasure along into the time between lives, and then into the next life. For no experience, no learning, is ever lost. It is used as the foundation upon which to build the next edifice.

"If that basis is solid, the edifice will be better than the last.

"If the basis is weak, the edifice will crash as ignominiously as did the prior.

"The person who has learned the emptiness of earthly power and possession in one life will begin to look elsewhere for meaning in the next life, and will edge nearer to knowledge of the nature of true Power, and to a knowledge of the 'possessions' that are worth possessing."

"Tell me, 'Rabbi,'" said Mattias with narrowed eyes. "Do you approve of the animal sacrifices at the Temple?"

Jesus hesitated, collecting his thoughts. Joseph tensed. The sacrifice of animals was ordained under Mosaic Law—perhaps not in the mad profusion of recent years, but ordained no less.

"I tell my followers to 'apply the principles,'" said Jesus at last. "I . . . " he glanced at Zakiah the Pharisee, "along with the Pharisees, am far from entranced by the practice of slaughtering and burning helpless little animals on our altars. I know within myself that 'God' does not require the death and subsequent burning of little animals to know of 'his' own greatness. I know within myself that, far from condoning this practice, 'God' finds it abhorrent.

"What was the original purpose, the idea behind, this ancient practice? Sacrifice is, quite simply, a tangible means of expressing one's trust in the bounty and benevolence which I mentioned earlier.

"What does one do when one takes one's best calf, or kid, and slits its throat and burns it on an altar? It might be the only calf, the only kid that one has. Or, as we are told of Ibraham and the sacrifice of Isaac, an only son, dearly loved.

"What, then, does one demonstrate by sacrificing these precious things? One demonstrates trust in the bounty, in the ultimate benevolence, of the deity. When performed in that spirit, in full knowledge that one is giving up something precious expressly *to* demonstrate trust and belief in a generous 'God' who will straightway provide a substitute, rather than as a *bribe* to 'God' to get 'him' to do something for you, the act could be called pious—if also totally unnecessary.

"Yet one must follow the principles. I do not teach one rule for one instance and another rule for the next instance, each one contradicting the other. What applies to the judging of another and to the casting of a stone applies to sacrifices.

"You cannot win any favor by sacrificing an animal just to gain expiation for a 'sin'—neither will such a sacrifice purify you.

"Indeed, it will dirty you further.

"Neither can you win favor by hoping to flatter 'God' and tease his nostrils with the burning flesh. As a matter of fact, I can tell you that the true god would be nauseated and disgusted by a person who killed a dear little creature for such a ruthless purpose.

"I would advise you, then, to make no sacrifices unless those sacrifices are made in exactly the right spirit.

"You must not simply buy some poor little dove or kid at the Temple and take that stranger up to the altar to be killed. No. You must take your best cow or ass, or your pet dog, that creature that is dearest to you, and sacrifice that creature, your best and most beloved friend. That creature you must kill and burn, offering it to 'God' in perfect trust."

He steadfastly ignored the horrified gaze of his new wife.

"You, Mattias. Do you have a pet?"

Mattias went pale. His mouth worked pathetically.

"I have a little bird," he managed at last.

"Marvelous! You love this little bird?"

" . . . yes."

"Well then the bird must be your sacrifice."

"But there are doves for sale at the Temple . . . "

"Think you that any of those doves is less dear to the true god, who loves all, than your little bird is to you?"

"I . . . never thought of it that way."

"So why should you take one of 'God's' pets and kill it and save your own? What sort of sacrifice is that?"

"I . . . do see what you mean. It is no sacrifice at all, is it."

"None. So. When you return to Jerusalem, you will take your beloved little bird to the Levites and let them slit its throat and then burn it on the altar."

"It . . . I raised it almost from the egg. Its mother was killed and I found it. All its brothers and sisters were dead, but I fed it. And it lived for me. It trusts me. It . . . "

"Yes, yes, I know. But you are prepared, when you return to Jerusalem, to show 'God' how very much you will give up for 'him.' You are prepared to take your little bird to the Temple for sacrifice."

Mattias turned away, muttering some reply.

"Splendid, Mattias! That is the spirit! But now, if you apply the principals, there is just one more little problem. You may not make this sacrifice until you, yourself, are free of all sin."

One could have smiled at the expression upon the face of Mattias as he lifted his head.

"Oh?"

"Absolutely. What applies for the judgment and stoning of others applies for animal sacrifice. And if, for instance, you arrived at the altar and then remembered some transgression, even so much as an unjustified anger against a fellow human being, you would have to take your offering away, go out and correct the transgression, or make your peace with the person against whom you held the anger. Only when you had done that would you have the right to return—would you be worthy to return—and kill your little bird in sacrifice."

Mattias stared long at Jesus.

"Have you ever made an offering?" he said at last.

Jesus spread his hands.

"Alas, I always have some transgressions unsettled. I go out to settle them, but, before I get back to the Temple, I have incurred more yet, and must be off to settle those. I have just never found myself worthy enough to take the purposeful slaughter of one of my god's creatures onto my conscience."

Mattias stared for another moment.

"What monstrous evasion!" he blurted at last. "All this is but a way to flout The Law, to avoid your duty to God!"

"On the contrary, Mattias. I strive with every waking and sleeping moment to do my duty to the true god. My duty as I see it.

"One of the most important things left to us in our Scripture is the injunction to listen to the voice of our god in our hearts, always above the voices of men.

"My god's voice in my heart tells me that, just as Moses assumed that those who cast stones would be free of sin, so he assumed that those who made offerings would be pure.

"And I tell you that, by attempting constantly to correct my transgressions and make peace with my fellows, and thus improve myself before presuming to make any such offering, I do better duty to my god than if I were to go, in an impure or mindless state, and burn every animal on the face of the Earth upon your altar.

"And I say to all of you here today that, unless your own right-mindedness exceeds that of our priests and Pharisees, you will, none of you, approach nearer to the Kingdom of Heaven in this lifetime."

There was a moment of stunned silence. He had not allowed himself to be trapped in any infraction, but words such as these could make bitter enemies.

"I object," said Zakiah softly, "to your definition of the Kingdom of Heaven. You have told us that it can be defined as interior wisdom and peace based on understanding and trust. Do I take it, then, that you say that there is no physical Kingdom of Heaven to which those who are holy, and who keep God's commandments, may attain? To which we will go and be rewarded for our righteousness, and from where we will be able to watch those foolish souls who did not obey the commandments burn in eternal torment?"

Jesus cocked his head.

"Do you look forward to that, Zakiah? To watching fools burn in an eternal fire?"

"Frankly, yes."

What a shame. Well, if that is what you want, that is what you will get."

" . . . I do not understand."

"You create your own reality, Zakiah, before and after death. If you want to go to a Kingdom of Heaven and sit and watch people burn, then you will create, with your own mind, such a place. Teaching entities will join in, helping to maintain the reality of this little piece of theater for you, and you will stay there until you get good and sick of it.

"At which point one of your teachers will cease pretending to suffer in the flames, walk over, and politely explain the truth of the matter. You will then be ready to get back to business.

"But please do not call other people fools, Zakiah, no matter how wrong their actions seem to you. To call another fool shows such a lack of understanding as to the true god's true intentions, that you, yourself, might be in danger of that hellfire to which you would so smugly consign others."

"Jesus . . . " It was the veiled lady of the kitten who spoke. "I am still confused about the giving of alms. May we not give them?"

"Yes, of course. At any point when you are truly moved by love or honest concern for any of the creatures of All That Is, do all that you can to help. Give everything that you possess if it suits you. Only do it as secretly as the circumstances permit, and never in expectation of reward or glory for yourself.

"And, if you are *compelled* to help, I advise you to give thrice what is required.

"As for instance, any Roman can, by law, compel you to walk a mile with him, carrying his burdens. If you are so compelled, walk not one mile with him, but three.

"If a man sues you and takes away your tunic, I hope that you will give him your coat and gird as well.

"Give to any who ask of you, and do not refuse those who would borrow. Cast your only chunk of bread onto the waters to feed the fish and the ducks. Do it with a glad heart, understanding these acts to be in expiation of your own past errors, trusting the benevolence of the Great Consciousness in which you nest, never demanding a thing in return.

"And understanding, especially, that All Is One, that what you do for the least of creatures, you do for yourself and for the true god All That Is.

"I guarantee that, if you will give in this Spirit, all which you have given will return to you ten-fold. For that is the immutable law of the Universe."

He smiled at his brother, Jude.

"You have also heard it said that you should love your neighbors and hate your enemies. I advise you to hate no one, and try, as best you can, to begin to understand your enemies and so begin to at least like them.

"Does not the sun rise on the house of your enemy as well as on the house of your neighbor? Does the rain not fall upon your enemy's crops? Does your god not show to your enemy the same love as 'he' shows you? Would you make yourself more haughty than your god, and hate a person whom your god obviously loves?"

"What of the Gentiles?" It was the Greek, Phillipus.

"I have not noticed the sun shining any less brightly in Bethsaida than in Kapher Nahum," smiled Jesus.

"You ask us to love the *Gentiles*?" said Mattias.

"Why not?" said Jesus. "Show me where, in Scripture, it says that we should not love them."

"Some passages enjoin us to *kill* them," said Zakiah.

Jesus shrugged.

"You can kill something and still love it. So do yourself a favor and begin to love Gentiles."

He lifted the wine jug, found it empty, rose and went to the wine vat to refill his cup.

"Deborah!" he said, staring down into the vat. "Surely there is more wine."

"Oh dear! It has gone more quickly than I expected. I am so sorry. I will send for another vat. There is water there in the meantime."

"Water?"

Jesus turned with pained expression to the water vat.

"After the prime vintage of the House of Nathan?"

He hesitated. After a moment, he turned and looked long at Mattias, and at Zakiah. And at Pilatus.

Then he turned back and placed his hands on the water vat. He bowed his head and was silent for nearly a minute.

Then he raised his head, dipped his cup into the vat, sampled the beverage and smiled.

"Chandreah! Come try this!"

The Governor of the Feast rose, went to the vat and dipped his cup into the liquid. He drank slowly, a strange expression upon his face. Then he smiled, broadly, mischief dancing in his eyes.

"I congratulate you. At most weddings, when the good wine runs out, they substitute one that is less good. But you do not stint your guests. Even now, you provide the best vintage of the House of Nathan."

"Yes, I agree! Well! Come, Friends, let us return to work. Here is wine for all, and, when we have finished, my new sister will have an even more sumptuous feast awaiting us."

He grabbed Merovee's hand, startling her out of her open-mouthed stupor.

"Race you to the end of the row!"

And they were off, down the sun-lit slope, Jesus laughing, trying to tease Merovee out of her silence.

The others converged on the water-vat, pushing and shoving to see.

"It is a ruse of course," said Mattias. "There was wine in the vat all the while."

"I took a cup of water from that vat a while ago myself. I know the difference between water and wine."

The speaker was Lucius, the tribune of Pontius Pilatus.

The parents and siblings of Jesus had drawn apart.

"In front of Mattias," murmured Joseph.

"What does it matter, in front of Mattias?" murmured Jac. "He did a miracle. They say, and I believe it now . . . the daughter of Jairus. They say he raised her from the dead."

"Then why does he not declare himself!" said Jude. "He is the Messiah! Why does he not gather an army and march on Jerusalem?"

"Shut your . . . "

Rosula started to say 'foolish mouth,' remembered her son's words, and amended herself.

"Give more thought to your speech, Jude."

Her eyes turned to Joseph.

"I am sure that Joshuah knows what he is doing, Joseph. He must have his reasons."

Joseph shook his head.

"No doubt. But I wonder if even he knows what I learned this morning—in such casual conversation with Deborah. Sweet soul that she is. It had never occurred to her that it could be a problem. As it had never occurred to Merovee that descent from David could be a problem. You recall, my dear, that King Saul was of the tribe of Benjamin."

Rosula braced herself for what she suddenly understood was coming.

"Yes?"

"According to family genealogies, Deborah's father Nathan was the most direct male descendant of Saul, through Jonathan's son, Nephiboseth."

"God help us," said Rosula simply.

"What does it mean?" said Rachel plaintively.

"It means," said Joseph, putting an arm about his youngest daughter's shoulders, "that your big brother has unwittingly made a disastrous political move in wedding our dear Merovee. He is heir to the House of David. He has married one of the two available female heirs to the House of Saul."

"But Father," said Annah, "I do not understand what difference it makes. Saul was defeated. A thousand years ago. By David."

"Yes," said young Joses. "So who cares who the heirs of Saul might be? No one cares who *we* are."

Joseph smiled, and exchanged glances with Rosula. For all of her complaining, Rosula, before anyone on the face of the Earth, understood how Joseph had twisted and turned, sweating blood much of the way, to create a climate in which a son could, in all innocence, say, in effect, 'No one cares that we are the royal heirs to David.'

"You are almost right," he said to Annah and Joses. "Almost no one cares. The exceptions are those people who might wish, for whatever their own personal reasons, to make trouble.

"You see, my dears, politics and great affairs of state do not always make as much sense as you two just made, and a thousand years are as nothing to people who need to stir up trouble.

"Jerusalem belonged to the tribe of Benjamin before it was taken away from them by the tribe of Judah. There are those who would see, in the first heir to Judah, and a first heir to Benjamin, the perfect dynastic alliance. There are those who would say that Joshuah and Merovee, together, have more right to rule Judeah than any other two people on the face of the Earth. And their children . . . oh Lord," he sighed. "Their children."

"Surely Merovee's genealogy is registered in the Temple," said Jac quietly.

"No doubt," said Joseph.

301

"The scions of Judah and Benjamin wed," mused Jac. "The heirs to Jerusalem. No word of this must go beyond any of us standing here. For if Mattias and his family were ever to figure it out, the lives of our bride and groom, and of their children, would not be worth a thrice-clipped coin."

"And here Joshuah has gone out of his way to make an enemy of Mattias," said Joseph flatly.

Jac—the vulture waiting to die, the pure Essene who would not, as would his brother Josh, touch wine, whose ways were so strict, whose habits were, to his mother and father, so strange—turned and placed his hands firmly on the shoulders of his brother, Jude. From Jude's grimace, it was obvious that the grip did not lack strength.

"Zealot. Know this. If ever I find that you have repeated this information to a living soul, or in any way used it to foment any sort of rebellion with the object of placing our brother—who has no political ambitions of any sort—on any throne, I will forfeit my immortal Soul by killing you myself . . . with the most slow, the most agonizing method I can find."

The fight seemed drained from Jude.

"Keep your Soul, Jac, and help me find my own. Do you not know that I love him, too? After the way he spoke to us just now—who could but love him? Place your trust in me and worry no more."

Down in the field, Pilatus and Lucius were beginning to pick together, each rapt in his own thoughts.

At last Lucius said . . .

"Praefectus. You wanted to find this mad 'Messiah,' the miracle-worker of whom we have heard so much, and listen to his discourse while here in Galilee . . . "

Pilatus was holding a bunch of grapes—fat, rich, and red—just staring at it.

"Yes?" he said absently.

"Has it occurred to you that we have already heard that discourse?"

Chapter 11
Blood With Their Sacrifices

Pontius Pilatus and his escort left immediately after breaking their fast the next morning. Pilatus did not seem happy to leave. He hung back even as Lucius and the guard moved off at an easy lope.

Jesus and Merovee walked beside the steed of Pilatus, smiling up at him.

"Where do you go after Kapher Nahum?" said Jesus.

"Over to Akko to review their garrison, then back down to Caesarea."

"Must you spend so much of your time in Caesarea?'" said Merovee.

"But of course," said Pilatus. "It is my headquarters. Why?"

She shrugged.

"It is not always easy for us 'Jews' to come into Samaria. I only wondered when we would see you again."

Pilatus flushed, honestly touched.

"Anytime you wish to come, send word. I will dispatch a guard for your safe conduct. But, as a matter of course, I shall be in Jerusalem at the time of your festival of the Passing Over. You will be there at that time, will you not?"

"I can promise that we will," said Jesus, "for I will want my wife to be with her mother and sister in Bethany, and near to my own mother, when the time of her lying-in arrives."

Pilatus blinked, thinking that, once more, his own faulty Aramaic was to blame, and that Jesus had not said what Pilatus thought he had said.

"Of course. Well, will you come to me, then? Will you tell me more of your words?"

"You wish to hear them?"

"I do. I want Procula to hear them as well. I know that you will love her. She is such a wonderful person."

"We will look forward to meeting her," said Jesus, smiling as beneficently as though he were the Roman on the horse and Pilatus the Jewish subject walking alongside. "I send her my blessings. Have a safe journey."

Still Pilatus hung back.

"Jesus . . ."

"Yes?"

"The beliefs of your people have always been strange to me. I am accustomed to a freedom and tolerance in my worship that I thought no Jew could enjoy. Yet, in what you have said, I sense a freedom and tolerance beyond anything I have ever imagined. I only want to say that . . . I do not think that I can ever find the courage even to search for that strait, narrow gate that you spoke of yesterday. But I want you to know that I am greatly comforted to know that you believe that that gate is there. It almost gives a reason to live . . . for there is always the hope, is there not, that, one day, one *shall* find the courage to search."

With that, he touched heel to his mount and set off at a smart lope. Merovee laid her head against her husband's chest as they watched him mount the hill.

303

"I do not want to have my baby in Jerusalem," she murmured.

"Bethany is not Jerusalem. And I intend to take advantage of your estimable sister. Stern she is, yes, but the stuff of her is sure and good. You and the baby will have need of her solid arms."

"Bethany is all *but* Jerusalem," Merovee persisted.

"We have more time than only to the next Passing Over, Merovee. Quite a bit more, I feel sure."

At the crest of the hill, Pontius Pilatus paused and looked back down into the valley. The farm of Nathan was no longer visible, hidden as it was behind the cypress windbreak. But the two small figures were there at the break where the drive came through the trees. He saw their arms lift. He returned the salute, then turned and loped on.

Lucius was hanging back, waiting for him to catch up. They exchanged no words, though Pilatus could feel the frequent, inquiring glances.

They kept up the lope. The road was good, for they had joined the Roman Highway from the coast near Caesarea up to Kapher Nahum. Somehow, the businesslike motion of the horses, the dust and heat and clatter, broke the spell.

Had it ever even happened, Pilatus was wondering in only a few miles?

Yes. It had happened.

And how did one account for his own ridiculous behavior? He must have been mad these last three days.

Or had he been bewitched?

He pictured Merovee, how she danced, that calm, knowing look that she had, and her laughter, like a mountain brook.

And Jesus. Definitely a charlatan. How his teeth flashed when he laughed. Pilatus laughed himself, just thinking of it.

"Yes, Praefectus?" said Lucius eagerly.

The face of Pilatus straightened.

"Nothing."

He had been bewitched, no doubt about it.

On the other hand, perhaps it had only been that wine. Perhaps it was more potent than the normal.

Had he made as large a fool of himself as he felt?

He wished Lucius would stop throwing him looks. He did not dare to return them.

He was painfully aware of a lightness upon his wrist, an emptiness in the place where his mother's bracelet had always been. Why had he been so impulsive? He wanted his bracelet back.

No. He did not. For, when it returned to him, it would return with a request for a favor that he had pledged himself to grant. He did not want to know what it was, that dreadful event that the witch foresaw, that frightened her so.

'Stay away,' he silently commanded the bracelet. 'I never wish to see you again.'

Or them. Jesus and Merovee. He must have been soft in the head to have invited them.

'Stay away,' he silently called to them both. 'Live out your lives in happiness. Have a dozen Jewish brats and die in peaceful old age surrounded by your grandchildren. But leave me be. I have a good life, a bright future. Leave me be.'

"Should I send a man ahead to inquire as to the whereabouts of the 'Messiah'?" said Lucius suddenly. "Do you still wish to seek him out? That is if . . . "

"No!" Pilatus kicked his horse and galloped angrily ahead.

All this messiah business. After that wine trick, Lucius had obviously already decided that Jesus was the one about whom they had been hearing.

What in the world *was* a messiah? All whom one talked with had something different to say on the subject. They gibbled and gabbled of prophecies, none of which made any sense whatsoever.

All that the word messiah really meant was anointed king, or anointed leader of any major sort—even the High Priest was termed Priest Messiah.

But there seemed a huge difference in the people's thinking between *a* Messiah and *the* Messiah whom they were all waiting for. *The* Messiah, who was also expected to be a king.

King, indeed. The whole matter was ridiculous. Judeah no longer had a king, much less an anointed king. It had a praefectus, pure and simple. Why, for any man to have himself anointed and proclaim himself to be this particular, long-awaited Messiah would be . . .

Treason against Rome, that is what it would be.

The palms of Pilatus turned clammy.

Reports of various "Messiahs," preaching here and there throughout the land, had never bothered him before. Palestine sprouted a new crop of such lunatics every year, right along with its wheat. They strutted and preached for a season, then were gone. The matter was not even worth Rome's notice.

Oh yes, he had considered using the "Messiah" drawing such attention in Galilee as an excuse to enter the territory, but the matter would have gone no farther. Treason it might technically be to call oneself *the* Messiah, but it was beneath him to recognize such folly by punishing anyone involved. It would belittle Tiberius, making the emperor look as foolish as would a king of elephants who trampled a mouse that declared itself to be the elephant king's better.

Why, these Jews expected *the* Messiah to sweep aside all the other kings of the Earth, the Emperor of Rome included. They expected *the* Messiah to establish an empire more mighty than anything that Rome had ever even dreamt of, run, apparently, by the Messiah in partnership with the Jewish god.

The kingdom of this god right here on Earth! How could a rational man think of it as anything but a joke?

Until such a rational man met Jesus, and came under his spell.

Pilatus slowed his pace until Lucius was once more beside him.

"The prophecy regarding the Messiah . . . " said Pilatus.

"From what I can ascertain," said Lucius, "there really is no cohesive prophecy. The only thing on which these Jews agree—most of them at least—is that he will be of the House of David."

Pilatus seemed to draw into himself. It was a manner he had, that shut the mouth of Lucius whenever Pilatus wished for it to be shut.

Everyone knew the first heir of the House of David. Joseph "bar Ramathea" as he was referred to by the rulers of the Temple. Ramah had something to do with a high place. Pilatus was not sure whether that meant a high place like a mountaintop, or a socially high place. Or both. But Pilatus did know that, were there to be an election for King of Judeah this very day, Joseph would be elected. With Jesus his heir.

'Oh, Jesus,' came his silent cry. 'Do not force me to be your enemy. Please do not do that to me.'

"Praefectus?"

"What?" snapped Pilatus.

"You can count on me."

"I do not know what you are talking about."

"I will help you and support you, whatever you decide."

"Stop talking nonsense."

"He changed that water to wine."

"I have seen magicians do the same."

"They have special equipment. They have stages, curtains, assistants, special pots of their own. No magician on Earth can do what that man did, all spontaneously, out in the middle of an open field. I repeat. You can count on me. I will be your support."

Pilatus rode on in silence for a moment, then he said.

"I have changed my mind. I do want to learn the identity of the 'Messiah' that everyone is talking about. I at least want to know . . . "

"I understand."

"You are wrong, Lucius. Quite wrong. That man we just left does not consider himself a king. He makes no claims at all."

"There are those who do not need to claim kingship, Praefectus. They just naturally are kings. They are the most wonderful—and dangerous—of all."

"Yes," said Pilatus softly. "Because the people proclaim their kingship for them."

He realized then that he had tears in his eyes. The realization made him angry. He could not remember ever being angrier about anything in his entire life.

He would not be made mush of! He would not fall into the man's snare. Or hers, either, that temptress. He suddenly distrusted even Joseph, who had invited him to this debacle.

It was over! Soon he and his men would be in Kapher Nahum. Once there, he would demonstrate, in no uncertain terms, that he was still Pontius Pilatus, Praefectus of Samaria, Judeah, and Idumea, *King* of Samaria, Judeah, and Idumea, Lord of these foolish Jews.

* * *

Crispus Marcus had barely half an hour, after a lathered horse arrived at the barracks bearing one of his spies, to alert his men, get them into proper—and hastily shined—gear, straighten up his office, and get into his own full-dress uniform.

When Pilatus rode into Kapher Nahum, a guard was waiting in parade array in front of the provincial office, that was located in the centurion's quarters. Centurion Crispus stood at attention before them, his mouth dry and his palms wet inside his impeccable facade.

What in the name of Jove was Pilatus doing here in Galilee? *How* had he gotten here? Why had his spy network not alerted him well before of the approach of the praefectus?

Had Pilatus received intelligence regarding the Zealot activists staying in town, or elsewhere in the province, that had not reached his own ears?

Or had someone reported him for a lack of military discipline, so that Pilatus had purposely sneaked into the province, hoping to catch him unaware?

Galilee was popularly supposed to be a hotbed of Zealot activity, inimical to the Roman presence. Hence, it seemed that Romans stationed in Galilee should be doubly on guard. In practice, as a result

306

of the overriding business interests of the province, Marcus had found the Zealots to be even less of a problem than were the fleas of the area.

Yet his comeuppance might just have ridden into Kapher Nahum.

Pilatus did nothing at first to put the centurion at ease. Soberly, he inspected the troop, noting a still-wet smear of polish on one fellow's breastplate, and perspiration on all the brows.

He had, indeed, had intelligence of the relaxed manner in which Crispus policed the province. He had taken that as a good sign. Though young, in his first command, Crispus was of an ancient and honorable family, with a long tradition of responsible service to the empire. The centurion's career, not to mention the honor of the House of Crispus, and the good of the empire, rode on his judgment of the danger or non-danger. Pilatus had no doubt that, should anything alarming reach the ears of Crispus, the garrison would snap to attention on a moment's notice, ready to show these Galileans the cold steel of Rome.

Actually, it had been a comfort to Pilatus to know that Galilee was this quiet, this unthreatening. Pilatus wanted no trouble. The smoother things went here in Palestine, the better he would look, the sooner would come his own advancement.

The quarters of Crispus were luxurious. He lived, and had his office, in the house that had once been the house of the Zebedee, which accommodating gentleman had offered it to Crispus, moving himself and his family to one of his other properties. A good trade. Crispus had closed his eyes to many of the Zebedee's activities in return for the favor. For a rich, spacious, and splendid house it was, with cool fountains and tiles, and beautifully frescoed walls.

Servants were still at work, preparing the best sleeping chamber for the praefectus. Crispus led Pilatus and Lucius into the salon, and bade them partake of a noonday repast that had been hastily, but well, laid out. Hopefully, Pilatus would not inquire after the opulence of a mere centurion's quarters.

Of course "How come you by this fine house?" was the first thing that Pilatus asked.

"'Oh . . . " Crispus waved a negligent hand. "One of the local merchants insisted that I use it. The merchants are eager to maintain our presence here, as you know."

"Yes," said Pilatus.

He helped himself to some of the lovely, fresh fish. Strangely, he did not get much fish in Caesarea, for his cook was Roman, and the offerings were mostly of meat, fowl, fruits, and vegetables. Pilatus liked these fish patties of the Galileans. They virtually glided down the throat.

He cast Crispus a shrewd glance.

"I have just spent several days with your landlord."

Crispus changed color.

"Indeed."

There was another long silence as Pilatus ate another fish patty. He could hardly keep from laughing. Cruel it was, but it amused him to toy with the man. He could almost hear the fellow's mind working. 'Where, why, how?' he was asking himself. And just what had the Zebedee told Pilatus?

Pilatus nodded inwardly. Crispus was his man all right.

"I came over to Galilee to attend the wedding of the son of a friend," he said. "The Zebedee was also in attendance. I decided that, as long as I was in the area, I would continue on up here to Kapher Nahum and get acquainted with you."

Crispus partially relaxed.

"I am so glad that you did."

Yet wariness, and mystification, still hung between them.

"The only wedding of any consequence that I am aware of, that the Zebedee might attend, is the one in Kapher Kana."

Pilatus nodded. Relaxed Crispus might be, but he obviously had eyes and ears throughout the province. A good man indeed.

"That is the one. Whenever I go up to Jerusalem, I make it a point to suffer the society of the greater Sadducean families. The couple I have found most tolerable is Joseph of the Tripe Ramah and his wife."

"So. Yes. I am told that his eldest son has married an heiress of the House of Nathan."

Pilatus had been at that wedding for days? And his spies had not been aware of it? Crispus tightened his jaw. There were going to be some changes among those spies.

"The son in question is a man called Jesus."

Crispus had been pouring more wine as Pilatus spoke. The wine sloshed. Crispus raised stunned eyes.

"Jesus?"

"So," said Pilatus. "There are several things that you had not heard about that wedding. Perhaps it is time for us to stop sparring, trying to find out what each the other knows, and exchange our information honestly. You obviously know of this Jesus."

"I do. He was in the vicinity for about two months, teaching, and healing. Then, two weeks ago, he disappeared. Though we heard that he had thrown seven demons out of some woman, none of my men could get a line on just where he was operating."

"He was in Magdala, then in Kapher Kana, preparing for his wedding."

"And you say that this Jesus is the son of Joseph of the Triple Ramah?"

"You obviously understand the implications. Is Jesus the one we have heard about in Caesarea? Is he the one who calls himself *the* Messiah and claims to be King of the Jews?"

"That is the crazy part of this whole thing, now that you tell me whose son he is. No."

Pilatus and Lucius exchanged inadvertent glances, both breathing secret sighs of relief.

"Your 'Messiah' is a Galilean—Simon, also called Yeshuah. He is a Nazorite, who claims descent from David, and he is a Zealot . . . at least most of his followers are Zealots. But even he has never been heard by any of my men to come right out and call himself the Messiah or King of the Jews. It is his followers who say that he must be both of those things. If it is he who is putting those words into their mouths, then he plays a clever game by letting them speak for him. What he *has* called himself publicly, in the synagogue here a week ago, is the son of the Jewish god."

"What? Literally the born son of this god's body? The man is mad."

"That is my opinion."

"So there are two of them. He and Jesus have been preaching simultaneously."

"And curing," said Crispus. "Both work miracles. And certainly there are those who say that Jesus must be the Messiah, but not with the insistence with which they say it about Yeshuah. I have heard that, far from encouraging such talk, Jesus discourages it.

"You must have seen the crowds encamped along the route as you came into the town. They are as nothing compared to the crowds that were here a fortnight ago, before Jesus disappeared. Even more drifted away after Simon Yeshuah declared himself to be the son of his god. Many agree with us, that the man is mad."

"These miracles and healings you spoke of . . . are they legitimate? Or magicians' tricks?"

Crispus paused for long moment, staring into his wine glass.

"Those of Jesus are legitimate," he said at last. "I . . . have seen some of the people whom Jesus has cured. There is even a little girl in the town whom they say he raised from the dead."

"Rebeckah. She was at the wedding."

"Oh."

Crispus kept staring into his wine glass.

Suddenly he lifted his face.

"Jesus also cured my slave, Philogenes. It was a sudden fever, with dreadful shaking and chills, alternating with terrible sweats. It went on for days. He got weaker and weaker. We—he has been with me since I was a child. I did not want to lose him, and he did not want to die. So I took a guard and went to the inn where Jesus stays, and demanded entrance. Jesus would have come to Philogenes. But I told him no. 'But say the word,' I told him, 'and I know that my servant will be cured.'"

"How could you be sure of such a thing?" said Pilatus.

"I do not know. It was something in the face of Jesus. The way he smiled, the way he talked. And I know how these Jews are with their rules of cleanliness. I did not want to make him come here where he might feel contaminated . . . "

"He would not have felt that way," said Lucius softly.

"I think not, myself. Still, I just knew that he had only to say, 'Philogenes, be cured' . . . and it would be so."

"And it was?"

"When I arrived back at this house, Philogenes was up and polishing my armor, exactly as though he had never even been sick."

The thoughts of Pilatus seemed to leave the room.

"He does not even have to go to a person," he murmured. "He can send his healing over a distance. I wonder how far he can send it."

He sat deep in thought for a moment. Then he shook himself back to the business at hand.

"What of this Simon Yeshuah? Is he legitimate?"

"He does not seem to be the healer that Jesus is, but, with my own eyes, I saw him take a few loaves of bread and some fishes and keep breaking them into pieces until they filled seven bushels and fed close to two thousand people. You might think that I, myself, have gone mad to claim such a thing, but . . . "

"I do not think you are mad," said Pilatus shortly. "But why have I received no official reports from you on these matters?"

Crispus stood his ground.

"I have mentioned both men several times in staff reports, but I saw no reason to go into great detail upon what I considered to be a local situation, and escalate it out of proportion by calling it to your attention personally, Praefectus. There is always some 'prophet' or other running around Galilee, and, from what I understand, many of them have been able to do these miracles. It seems to be a Jewish talent. They claim that the power comes from their Yahweh, or whatever they call him. They are not allowed to pronounce his real name. They consider him superior to all other deities.

"And who knows? To be on the safe side, I offer him a dove once a month.

"But, so far, these 'prophets' have been nothing to be alarmed about. Half a dozen have come and gone in the three years that I have been here. The Jews are obsessed with this religion of theirs, concerned for very little except the observance of their Law and what will happen to them in some Last Judgment.

"As long as they continue to occupy themselves with such polemics, they will, in my opinion, constitute no danger to us. Neither of these current preachers has disobeyed our own laws. Neither has offered threats of violence to Rome. Neither has so far hurt anyone or anything. The worst charge we could lay against either of them is disturbing the peace by reason of the crowds they attract.

"And so, until such time as either of them made some overt move, I preferred to watch and to wait."

Crispus looked Pilatus square in the eye.

"I was also sure that you would hear gossip of these men—which you did—and I assumed that, if you, yourself, deemed it a pressing problem, you would send to me for further information."

"Bravo," said Pilatus, clapping politely. "A wonderful speech. How nicely you protect yourself. But also, I suspect, you seek to protect Jesus, lumping him in with all those other, silly prophets."

"I seek to protect no one!"

"It is quite all right, Crispus. After having just spent many days with the man, I understand your problem completely. Yet, as a military man . . . is it truly your opinion that Jesus—and the other one, Yeshuah—are they truly harmless?"

"I did not say that they are harmless. I said that, if they do have teeth, neither has yet shown them. We get along very well here in Galilee, Praefectus. I do not wish to agitate the waters. Why should we make trouble unless they do? These men seem no more politically motivated than any of the others have been, I truly believe that.

"Both Jesus and Yeshuah are of a totally different ilk than was Judah of Galilee thirty years ago, or that Maccabee who raised such a following and kicked out the Syrians a couple of hundred years ago. Even the one called Yeshuah is not politically motivated. He surrounds himself with Zealots, yes, and he uses them. But when one hears these two men speak, one realizes that their intents are . . . " Crispus shrugged. "Well . . . spiritual."

"You have heard them both, I take it."

"I made it my business."

"Then you are one ahead of me. I have had opportunity to hear Jesus. I wish for you to make arrangements for me to hear the one called Yeshuah."

"That will not be difficult. He is preaching today on a hillside north of the town. We will have to go dressed as Jews, however. The one time we tried to join his listeners in uniform, he ceased his talking and left. He will have nothing to do with Gentiles."

"But how can we appear as Jews?" asked Pilatus, indicating their cropped hair and clean-shaven faces.

Crispus grinned.

An hour later, three Jews in travel-stained tunics and sheltering burnooses slipped out the back of the centurion's house and headed north out of the town. Their wigs and beards were convincing even on close examination. They had to be convincing for the spies of Crispus to move about amongst the people as freely as they did.

What an odd feeling, thought Pilatus, to be so unknown, unnoticed out among the people. It filled him with a sort of elation, an unreasoning sense of freedom. It was almost the way he had felt while picking the grapes.

"We must not speak once into the crowd," said Crispus. "Our accents would betray us. I do not fear the sicarii among them. Zealots are jackals, they slay only from ambush, or at night in dark alleys. They would never risk daylight murder in a large group. Strangely enough, by their own Law, witnesses would have to punish them . . . or at least force them to make restitution to our families.

"But, if we are found out, either Yeshuah will leave or we will be ousted. I also do not care to have it known that we can come amongst them so well disguised."

So the three of them crept unobtrusively in among the listeners. There was no need to get close to Yeshuah. His voice had a quality that carried even his whispers to the farthest ear. Also, the crowd was smaller than Pilatus had expected.

And there was a tenseness in the air.

Yeshuah sat upon a rock at the top of the hillside. His garment was no different—and appeared no cleaner—than that of any of his travel-stained listeners. His hair and beard were uncombed. But— perhaps it was his elevation above his listeners, perhaps it was his eyes—there was a majesty to the man.

What was that tenseness in the air? One could almost taste it.

Having listened to Jesus, Pilatus was familiar with some of the concepts to which Yeshuah directed his preaching. He was speaking of sin and of salvation from sin. Of the Kingdom of God. Of Heaven. Of Hell.

Disturbingly, he spoke much of a Last Judgment, a day, not long in coming, when the world would end! When his god would come to judge the *whole world*. Upon that day, only those who listened to him now, and did exactly as he said from this moment onward, would be saved.

Pilatus frowned. Yeshuah also made it obvious that the only ones who could possibly be saved were Jews.

That did not seem fair.

How dared this Yahweh, or whatever his name was, march in and destroy everyone but his own favorites? Did he think Jupiter and Mars and Quirinus would let him get away with that? Or Juno, or Janus, or even Vesta? What was there about this god whose name could not be pronounced, and who the Jews often, most disconcertingly, called simply 'God,' as though there were no other—what was there about this god that made him so special?

He could not be terribly nice, for he did not even have a family. Not even a wife. How could a man get along without a wife?

Ah. Yes, Crispus had told them. This Yahweh was obviously in the habit of coming down and copulating with Earth women, that is how this disheveled man up on the rock supposed himself to have been conceived.

So that Jehovah did have a family. At least, according to this man, a son.

That wizened little female sitting at his feet, could she be . . . yes. The maternal expression was unmistakable. That was what Yahweh had chosen for a wife? Pilatus shook his head. Surely a god could have found something better.

"You are right," said the man beside him, speaking in Aramaic. With a shock, Pilatus realized that the man was responding to his shaking head. "He insists that the only salvation is through his 'word,' by his 'name.' And we are to drink his blood!" The man shuddered. "No sense. No sense at all."

Pilatus grunted, nodded, and turned away as politely as possible.

He understood now the tenseness in the air. The people assembled at the feet of this "son of God" were not all friendly to his ideas. They had come to listen, as had Pilatus and his officers, but there were very few adherents among them.

Pilatus wished that he understood the whole matter better. His own religious observances were simple and free. He had been raised to pay homage to both the ancient and the new Samnite gods of his paternal ancestors' native Abruzzi region, and the nature spirits of his mother's Pictish people. Especial favorites of the family had been the goddess Earth, the fertility goddess Bona, Ercole, or Hercules, Diana, Dionysus, and Jupiter, who his father had always referred to as Jove. Now, of course, Pilatus also paid honor to all the gods and goddesses of the Roman pantheon.

And things were very simple. One offered proper homage to the proper gods or goddesses for the appropriate functions and reasons. If one did that, then mankind and the gods stayed good friends and each the other prospered.

When a person died, he or she went to the company of the Good People, and, according to how great or prosperous he or she had been in life, was held in reverence by those who lived after.

It was all so easy. Why did these Jews have to complicate matters?

Sin? It was a concept that Pilatus could not get his mind around. One reverenced the gods. One did the very best that one could do with what one was given. One also honored one's parents and family, and Caesar and the Roman Empire. One did nothing to disgrace any of them.

Gehennah, Hades, Hell—by whatever name—was a concept in which Pilatus had never believed. It implied that a man could be blamed, then punished, for circumstances and events that the gods, themselves, had forced onto him.

It was not a rational concept. Neither was it fair. Pilatus prided himself on being both reasonable and fair, and he expected no less of his gods. Certainly a person received enough punishment in a lifetime without dreaming up more to come in some 'Hades.'

Heaven? The Elysium fields? Now that he could understand. He was all for such concepts. Even Plebeians deserved to go to a nice place where they could eat good food, look at pretty things, rest on silk pillows, and enjoy honorable thoughts sent up to them by their posterity. Pilatus supposed that Patricians such as he would have much better accommodations than Plebeians, but he did not begrudge anyone—even Jews—the company of the Good People.

Strange, he had never given that place beyond the grave much thought before. What would one do there? Just eat and sleep and float and watch what was going on down on Earth? The idea that Jesus put forth, of successive lives, was complicating and a bit confusing to the old concepts. It was also intriguing in the extreme.

But this notion that an alien god, of whom most people had never even heard, could just appear from out of nowhere and end a man's life, destroy the world around him, and throw anyone whom he did not like into some pit of eternal fire . . .

No. Jove and Ercole, in especial, would definitely not allow such impudence. For all the simplicity of the beliefs which Pilatus held, they were, along with the beliefs of most Romans, sincere. Pilatus felt a deep and abiding affection for the gods who had been the patrons of his family. He had always felt that the affection was returned. Indeed, those gods had seemed to him as extended family. Certainly his belief in their reality was as deep-rooted as was that of any of the Jews around him in their Yahweh.

Oh, it was true that Roman citizens were not now as pious in classical terms as they had been in the days of the Republic. In the days of the Republic, the strictness, the austerity, the deep sincerity of the Romans in the honoring of their gods had been remarked upon by all with whom they came in contact.

Now there were so many strange religions filtering into Rome . . . from Greece, Egypt, Persia, yes even from Palestine, for there was a large Jewish community in Rome, and many Romans were known to have converted to this strange doctrine, the men submitting themselves to the excruciating rite of circumcision.

The Senate had, at first, tried to make rules, to keep alien gods and ideas away from the people. But the very nature of Roman society was inquiring, thrusting. In the end, due to the many cultures that it set itself to assimilate, of necessity, it had had to be tolerant of differences, both in living and in thought. In the days of the Republic, only native-born Italians had been citizens. Now Anyone and his brother could earn citizenship. And the beliefs of Anyone and his brother had to be accommodated by the empire and honored in its capitol.

This, the Senate had finally realized. So that the religious beliefs of Rome and her far-flung citizens no longer had cohesion, and represented almost every spiritual concept known to man.

It suddenly occurred to Pilatus that the religious austerity of his forefathers had matched that of these Jews. And, in part, he supposed, it was that religious cohesion and purpose which had permitted those forefathers of his to conquer half of the world.

He frowned again. If one extended the parallel . . . then these Jews, as equally dedicated, following, believing that they had found, their Messiah, could also conquer half of the world—just as their prophets foretold.

The thought was shocking. One assumed that the Roman Empire was eternal. How could it but prosper? What could ever destroy it?

He knew the answer suddenly. He had just said it to himself in so many words.

Tolerance would destroy it. The chaos attendant on the presence of so many conflicting ideas. It was happening at this very moment. They talked of it at every party in Rome. The moral decay. The rebellious attitudes of the young. The strange cults. People spoke openly of the decadence and corruption of the empire, of its emperors, of the Senate.

Was the Roman Empire entering old age and approaching death? Was that the key to the rise and fall of civilizations? Austerity, such as had characterized the Republic, purity, morality, discipline, and clarity of purpose. Was that what made possible the birth and youth of . . . anything, a civilization or a human being? And was "age" a gradual emergence from that narrowness, a gradual broadening, a willingness to learn and to embrace other views?

In that case, he, along with Rome, must be growing very old. For, look at him, here on this hillside listening to a madman, comparing the words of that madman with those of another . . .

. . . No. Not another madman. Jesus was the most sane, the most rational and fair human being that Pilatus had ever met.

Was there something in this notion of Jesus? *Did* people live again and again? Were civilizations like people? Did they live repeatedly, growing somehow better or wiser with each life?

Surely, the citizens of any failing civilization thought that it would be the end of the world if their civilization was lost. Yet it never was the end. Another civilization always rose in place of the last, always better in some ways.

Perhaps . . . it would not be so awful if Rome died. Perhaps the Fates had something even better in store for Humankind. Perhaps this process was necessary and good, the way that the world—and gods—had of growing better, a process too subtle for Humankind to comprehend.

Treason. Absolute treason to be thinking this way.

But look how easy. The Roman Empire *could* crumble if such as he could entertain these thoughts.

Yes. These Jews, following a man whom they believed to be *the* Messiah—these Jews, pure, narrow, clear, and dedicated in purpose, could establish a kingdom greater than Rome's, reducing Rome and all her glory to a memory.

And he, Pilatus, was the trusted representative of Rome.

His eyes narrowed. He had to stop wool gathering and return to work.

Was this Yeshuah a danger to Rome? Should he be seized and given a free boat ride to, say, the Isle of the Britons?

If Pilatus understood him correctly, what he was saying was that everyone was born evil, that their bodies were evil—some sort of mistake on the part of his god—and that god blamed his imperfect creations for his own mistakes—blamed then almost for living—and that the only way that they could keep from being thrown into a fire when they died was to repudiate their own evil selves, beg forgiveness almost for having had the temerity to live, to have been human.

Now they must also believe that this Yeshuah was the only begotten son of that god, sent to excuse them from the terrible sin of having been born, and that they must also drink Yeshuah's blood and eat his body in some obscene ceremony, the particulars of which Yeshuah did not go into.

But first Yeshuah was going to make some sort of a sacrifice for them, and, because he was his god's son, it would be the perfect sacrifice, that would take away all their sins. Those who believed on his "name" and "word," regardless of how good or bad, nice or rotten, they had been, would then rise out of their graves on a Day of Judgment and go . . . somewhere. Pilatus was not quite sure if it was to Heaven, but somewhere fairly decent. While everyone else who had ever lived, especially everyone who was not Jewish, and again regardless of how good or bad they bad been, would be cast into the fire, which fire would not kill them, but would, instead, just keep cooking them for all of eternity.

Who but lunatics, sadists, and masochists would be attracted to such nonsense? Who but the most disgusting monster would subject anyone to everlasting torture? Who would want to live in a kingdom based on those principles?

Certainly no civilized peoples.

Yeshuah harangued the crowd to "believe on" his "word," but his words had no attraction, even to his own kind.

He called his god "perfect." Pilatus found him flagrantly flawed.

Were Yeshuah and his god any sort of threat to Rome? An unkempt man, albeit with fascinating eyes and a magnificent bearing, prating of an arbitrary god with as much appeal as a spoilt five-year-old throwing a tantrum?

How different a god than the reasonable and exciting concept of deity as taught by Jesus. Clearly, the two men were talking of two completely different gods.

For all of Yeshuah's prating of the love of his god for his people, and his willingness to forgive, the terms under which his god would forgive were so narrow, and the punishment for those who did not meet the terms so severe, so irreversible.

No. Yeshuah's god could not destroy Rome. Yeshuah could never gather enough followers. His god offered no more than any of the gods of the Roman pantheon, or of the Greek, and no more than any other gods which Pilatus had ever heard of. Indeed, in view of his severe terms for the "purchase" of the same reward, and the dreadful punishment promised to those who did not obey just exactly—a punishment offered by no other god—one could say that what Yeshuah's god offered was a woefully inferior product.

To Pilatus as to any other Roman—indeed, to anyone whom Pilatus had ever heard of, saving the Jews—the freedom to choose one's own favorite deity from among a vast assortment was basic.

Who could understand a deity who jealously insisted that he was the only one, denying other gods who quite obviously *were*?

Pilatus shook his head. The minds of the people that he had been sent to oversee had mystified him from the beginning. And this man, Yeshuah, was taking their strange ideas to such a ridiculous extreme that . . .

. . . that he was *murdering* his own god.

The greater part of the Jews would turn away from what Yeshuah described, and the doctrine would find no favor among any other people of the Earth.

What was any god without followers? Nothing, that was what. Without followers, a god might just as well not exist. The god of this Yeshuah would not, could not, have the power to do the awe-full things that Yeshuah said he would do. People would simply turn their backs and walk away from this god and his Yeshuah, as they would from two petulant children who threatened to knock down the house and kill the neighbors if people would not do things just their way.

Not so Jesus and *his* god, All That Is.

Nothing that Jesus had said, neither directly nor when talking to all the people on that hillside, had struck Pilatus as ridiculous, nor had his ideas outraged the religious beliefs of Pilatus, nor denied the gods of Pilatus their own due, for they were graciously included as aspects of All That Is. The words of Jesus had been eminently reasonable, dangerously inviting. Pilatus had felt himself stirred as never before, tempted to believe, or else to at least put those words to the test.

It came to Pilatus that Jesus, and the deity that seemed to be part and parcel with the man, were the most gracious creatures he had ever met.

He had the sudden image of Jesus as a round, smooth, beautifully fitted and greased wheel that one would be proud to have on his chariot, happy to ride upon and trust oneself to.

While Yeshuah could be likened to a square block of wood thrust onto an axle . . . a poor, unworkable joke.

Sitting there watching Yeshuah, Pilatus felt suddenly sorry for the man. How his eyes blazed. How deeply he believed the things he was saying.

At his feet, beside Yeshuah's mother, sat a boy of about thirteen, who gazed up into the Yeshuah's face, rapt in his every word. A son?

In a semi-circle between Yeshuah and the crowd were his adult followers. The face of one of them was known even to Pilatus. Bar Tolmei. He was suspected of being responsible for the killing or wounding of dozens of Romans and Sadducees in the past years . . . yet no proof had ever been gotten against him, so that, though he had often been brought in for questioning, they had never been able to convict him. The rest of the faces in the semi-circle were as grizzled and awe-inspiring as that of bar Tolmei.

What was going on here? Did these killers, dedicated to the ousting of the Romans from Palestine . . . did they believe Yeshuah's prattle as truly as did Yeshuah and that boy at his feet?

What did any of these people truly plan? Who was using whom?

And how could it be that this misguided fanatic was able to work miracles and cure people?

Pilatus found himself yearning—almost aching—to have Jesus sitting at his side, whispering in his ear, explaining it all, as surely he could. His words would render the most perplexing enigmas, the most insoluble mysteries, clear, simple, logical, reasonable. Jesus had the ability to give meaning to anything, especially to lives which had lost their zest, abandoned the search for—even the belief in—meaning. Jesus gave hope . . . eternally gracious encouragement and hope.

The god of Jesus was a god who *could* gain followers. A great many followers.

Pontius Pilatus, Praefectus of Samaria, Judeah, and Idumea, sitting at the feet of Simon Yeshuah, understood clearly that, if either of these men was a 'Messiah'—The Messiah—destined to lead the Jews to greatness and world domination, it was Jesus. If either of these men constituted a threat to Rome—could destroy Rome, that man was . . .

'Leave me alone, Jesus,' he silently prayed. 'Do not make me your enemy. Do not make me hurt you.'

Once again, he realized that there were tears in his eyes.

* * *

It was that evening, as Yeshuah sat at supper with his followers, that the driver of one of the Zebedee's wagons delivered what Jesus smilingly called the pigeon report—a message from Judah to his big brother. There had been no communication for nearly a week. Yeshuah smashed the clay cylinder with one blow and eagerly extracted the papyrus.

He read the letter with grunts, snorts of anger, and then an exclamation. When he was finished, he read it yet again. And again. Then he sat long in thought.

Those who sat with him, cross-legged upon the floor around a simple cloth that constituted the table in Sarai's kitchen, were silent, not daring to interrupt his reverie or to ask questions.

"Pontius Pilatus is in Kapher Nahum," he said at last.

Bar Tolmei leaped to his feet. In that instant, he was changed to a creature who hardly seemed human, his face distorted by his hatred. He did not even ask. His burning eyes did that for him.

"Staying with Crispus," Yeshuah answered. "He arrived this morning."

"There are enough of us. Let us go and kill the swine," said bar Tolmei.

"If you do, do not bother to return to my house," said Sarai.

She knelt by the fire, cooking yet more bread. She had lost weight in the last weeks. Her hair was stringy, for she did not have time to attend to her appearance anymore. She was kept hopping, cleaning up after this army, buying and preparing the food which filled its belly.

She, too, had just about had her belly full.

"I want no trouble as long as you are under my roof."

"Do not fear, Aunt."

"I do not fear, Yeshuah. I am simply telling you."

Yeshuah smiled.

"To kill the praefectus would be most ill-advised. Besides . . . we can put his presence to a better use."

"Who has sent you this message?" said Meraiah. She sat at a respectful distance from the men, on the floor by the hearth.

Yeshuah shrugged.

"The follower I told you of, who attends the wedding of this Jesus to the whore. Jesus has done another miracle it seems. He has changed a vat of water into wine in front of a throng of people."

He spoke lightly, as though it did not matter. Yet he did not truly take it lightly. Neither did his followers.

What could this Jesus *not* do? Feed a multitude, raise the dead, walk on water, now change water to wine.

"Truly, he is the son of the Tempter," said Meraiah darkly. "We must strive more strongly to combat him."

Everyone in the room was aware of the defections that had taken place after Yeshuah's speech in the synagogue . . . Mathiah, Salmon, Eli, Ezekiel.

They were equally cognizant of the manner in which the number of people who came out to the hillsides to hear Yeshuah speak, and to ask for his cures, decreased with each passing day. Yeshuah's own miracle, the feeding of the multitude, had caused a brief stir and, for a while, brought out many listeners.

But it was the listening that was the problem. What the people had been hearing ever since Yeshuah's proclamation in the synagogue was driving the people away. They all knew it, Yeshuah most profoundly of all.

"Few there are who will understand in time and be ready for the Judgment," said Meraiah, shaking her head sadly, voicing what was in all their minds. For not a one of those who remained would entertain the thought that there was a basic lack in Yeshuah's message. It must all be laid to the evil powers of the man Jesus, to his master, the Prince of Darkness, and to the basic imperfections of Mankind, itself.

"Eleazar, my son."

Eleazar rose eagerly.

"Go to the house of the Roman centurion. Do your best imitation of a street child. Ingratiate yourself with the cavalrymen who came in the train of the praefectus. Learn what you can. I need especially to know when he plans to leave Kapher Nahum. And by what road."

"If I get a chance, should I kill a Roman, Father?"

"With what?"

"Will you not let me take a knife?"

"No, my dear. Keep your patience. Bar Tolmei tells me that your lessons are progressing nicely. On the day of your manhood ceremony, you will get your sicarius. In the meantime, obey me. In so doing, you obey and serve God."

An hour later, Eleazar returned.

"The praefectus leaves on the morrow. He will take the road to the west, through the hills, for he wishes to review the garrison of Akko."

"So."

Yeshuah still sat at table with the rest of his company. The atmosphere was tense, for Yeshuah had hardly spoken since the boy had left—while bar Tolmei could ill conceal his eagerness to be up and at this most exalted of Romans in Palestine.

Now the fruits of Yeshuah's silence became known.

"Never think," he said quietly, "that I come to bring peace. I bring a sword. For, no matter my own mission, you who are my trusted followers will need to win the kingdom that I bequeath to you with that sword. God has given us this opportunity and delivered the praefectus into our snare. Our fellow Galileans have become as sheep, bleating mindlessly beneath the Roman staff. We will now begin to rouse in those sheep the memory of their ancestors who were lions, and who drove the Gentile oppressors from without our land. They will drive them out again. And the process shall begin tomorrow."

* * *

When Pontius Pilatus rode out of Kapher Nahum late the next morning, he rode in a state of shock. At himself. He had sat late the prior evening in conversation on various matters with Crispus. He had had opportunity after opportunity to broach the business that had brought him to Galilee, and to Crispus, in the first place.

Certainly there had been no doubt in the mind of Pilatus that Crispus would be amenable. It was patently obvious, from the bribe he had taken of the Zebedee's house, that he closed his eyes to the Zebedee's more clandestine activities. A man like that would never fail to do a few favors for his own superior, to accept a few gifts, and to close his eyes still further.

All had been arranged with the Zebedee. The plan needed only the cooperation of Crispus to go into effect, and to operate with the smoothness of a well-watered pulley.

It was a matter of Lions' Fat, the powder of the Anatolian poppies. The Zebedee had convinced him that it was in that commodity that Pilatus should invest his fortune, rather than merely transferring it to Massilia, to molder in some banker's vault. The Zebedee had all the connections necessary for the purchase of fields, the harvesting of the crop, its transport and sale. Why should Pilatus, he had asked, not be putting his money to as good use as was, say, the family of Annas?

Yet Pilatus had found himself unable to speak to Crispus, to make that last, crucial move. Why?

It was simple enough. He kept seeing the face of Jesus and of his Merovee. He kept hearing the words of Jesus, thinking of that strait, narrow gate, and of the better place to which it led.

Pilatus wanted to find that gate. He knew it now. Though he would not have been able to say in words how or why the concluding of his scheme with Crispus would have taken him farther from that discovery, he knew that it would.

Had not Jesus challenged him openly on it, telling Pilatus that he knew all about his plans?

'Invest your money in Gaul,' he had said, smiling so amiably, with such understanding.

Pilatus realized that, if he had made his deal with Crispus, Jesus would not have minded. He would not have been angry, or threatened Pilatus with eternal fire as did the man Yeshuah. He would only have been disappointed, and made sad for the sake of Pilatus. Because he, too, would have known that Pilatus had removed himself one step further from the discovery of the gate.

As Pilatus rode out of Kapher Nahum that morning, he fancied himself a tortoise. At least he would pretend to be a tortoise for a while. He would hide in his shell where it was safe and dark, and no harm could come to him. He would think and think and think and think, and perhaps finally he would understand what it was that this Jesus and his Merovee had done to him, and what to do about it.

The road to Akko—not a main highway, but little more than a trail for wagons—wound torturously through the Galilean hills, taking great detours around some of the stonier heights, searching always for the path of least resistance, narrowing at some points to the width of little more than one wagon. The trail was well-tended and easy on the horses' hooves, however, being the only caravan route from Akko.

It was more heavily traveled than normal this day, for it was drawing nigh onto the month of Tishri, during which the Jews had one religious observance after another.

It had taken years for Pilatus to get it all straight. First was their New Year, on which they set up a great wailing for their dead, and scurried about the countryside paying homage at the tombs of ancestors and prophets. They then beat their chests and fasted and bemoaned their sins for another ten days, after which ensued a week during which they went out to the fields and built themselves little huts. Then there was another week during which they lived in those huts, feasting gaily and telling one another stories. Only this last seemed worthwhile to Pilatus.

The many pilgrims on the road now might be on their way to anywhere, perhaps all the way up to Jerusalem to worship in the Temple during these holy weeks, perhaps over to some ancestral tombs in Peraea, or the Decapolis, perhaps only to Kapher Nahum, to do honor at the tomb of Nahum.

Others were surely traveling in search of the Messiah of whom they had heard.

Most were family groups, with women and children, sheep and goats, the latter intended as sacrifices when destinations were reached. They drew aside at the approach of the praefectus, his guard of twenty cavalry and supply wagon. They stood silent and gaping, friendly enough, the children shyly waving, awed by the horses more than by the men.

They were ten miles west of Kapher Nahum when it happened.

The road had just skirted a high, rocky hill. It then entered a narrow place between two other hills, with low cliffs on either side of the track—a natural trap, Pilatus afterward realized. Had they been on a wartime footing, the column would never have moved into such a position without scouting ahead. But they were not on a wartime footing.

An oncoming party of pilgrims, larger than the usual, Pilatus also later realized, had entered the narrow place between the cliffs before the Romans started through.

The pilgrims drew to the side to let the Romans pass.

The cavalry was forced into single file.

A pretty little girl with dark hair and sparkling brown eyes smiled at Pilatus as he rode past. He smiled back.

Then there was a cry. With no comprehension, Pilatus saw that an arrow was sticking out of the neck of the man on the horse ahead of him. He saw the man topple from the saddle.

At the same moment, a stone fired from a sling hit Pilatus on the forehead just above the eye. He reached up and touched the spot, looked at his hand and was astonished to see blood.

He heard Lucius yelling then, heard the smart ring of steel as Roman swords were whipped from Roman scabbards.

People began to scream, running in all directions, trampling one another.

Another arrow hit a horse. It fell, pinning its rider and one of the pilgrims, adding all of their screams to the terror.

Another horse fell, shrieking in pain, hamstrung by some invisible knife-slash.

The trapped cavalrymen laid into the pilgrims without mercy, seeking the source of the arrows and blades.

The bridle of the horse of Pilatus was seized. Jumping the wounded horses and men, trampling anything in their path, Lucius galloped the praefectus out of the bottleneck to the cover of a hillock beyond the draw, calling at the same time for those who could to follow.

Behind the hillock, the cavalrymen who had followed formed a wedge, the civilian praefectus safely in its center, awaiting the next move of the undefined enemy.

All that now issued from that place of horror between the cliffs were the continued screams of the horses and the groans of the wounded.

Over it all, rose a sharp, female keening, a sound of unbearable anguish.

Then Lucius pointed a finger. Disappearing away over one of the hills, traveling with practiced ease, Pilatus counted perhaps a dozen men. There was no use trying to pursue them. Aside from their head start, they were in their own territory, and knew the secret ways.

Pilatus and the others dismounted and returned to assess the damage.

Lucius dispatched the horse that had been hamstrung. The horse that had been hit by the arrow was already dead, his rider still under him, his leg broken. An old Jew was pinned with him. He appeared to be dead, probably from failure of the heart.

The man who had taken the arrow in the neck was dead. Two more cavalrymen had been unseated by stones from slingshots. One had had his neck broken in the fall. The other was stunned and bruised, but not seriously hurt.

Among the pilgrims, it was a different story. In their panic, the cavalrymen had taken anything that moved for an enemy.

One man sat dazed as an old woman desperately attempted to staunch the flow of blood from his left arm. It had been cut off above the elbow.

A cavalrymen crouched down and gently pushed the woman away, applying his own tourniquet with a rawhide thong from his kit.

The wounds and gashes were many, and many were the broken bones, most received in the crush of the pilgrims' own panic, or during the headlong gallop of the Romans from out of the draw.

That terrible keening came from a woman who bent over the motionless form of a little girl.

Pilatus walked slowly toward them and stood looking down. A sword thrust had taken the child through the chest.

He made himself look at the small, silent face, still so prettily framed by the dark hair. The brown eyes were still open. They would never sparkle again.

The mother turned and looked up at him. She was crazed with grief, but she recognized the enemy.

"Pig!" she cried. "Roman Pig!"

She rose, gathering her spittle, and spat it into his face.

A cavalryman seized her.

"Release her," said Pilatus.

He did not wipe the spittle from his face. He turned back to Lucius.

"We must help these people into Kapher Nahum."

"You have helped us enough, Roman."

It was the man who had lost his arm.

"Go on about your business," he continued with surprising mildness. "We cared for our own before you Gentiles came, and we can do it now."

Pilatus glanced up the road. A caravan and more pilgrim parties were approaching, slowly, not knowing what to make of the scene. Yes, surely those people would help, to bind and support the wounded, to make slings and litters, to bury the dead. The man was right. They had already done enough.

What was it that he had promised himself after leaving Jesus? That he would demonstrate, in no uncertain ways, that he was Pontius Pilatus, Praefectus of Samaria, Judeah, and Idumea, King of these foolish Jews.

Somehow it did not mean the same thing as it had used to. In his mind, he heard Jesus explaining that one creates one's own reality.

He turned back to the man.

"Is there a headman of this group?"

"You are speaking with him."

"Do you understand that brigands mingled among your number and set upon us? Do you understand that we did not attack you in cold blood?"

"Cold or hot, Roman, the result is clear."

"Did you get a look at any of their faces? Could any of your people recognize them again so that they could be brought to justice?"

The voice remained calm.

"Whose justice, Roman?"

The voice of Pilatus rose in anger.

"Your arm is lost! That beautiful child is dead! What does it matter whose justice?"

"To us, it matters greatly," said the man.

He was weak from loss of blood, near to fainting it seemed to Pilatus. Yet he maintained a dignity to which Pilatus could only aspire.

Pilatus lifted his hands in a gesture of defeat.

"So be it then. But, since you are headman, know that I will send to the centurion of the garrison in Kapher Nahum, and instruct him that all of your party who come to him to claim damages shall have fair measure in accordance with those damages."

A thin smile touched the headman's lips. He moved the stump of his arm.

"How shall I value this?"

Pilatus kept his face hard.

"Only you can judge that, Man. Tell the centurion and you shall be paid. Do I not offer recompense as honestly as possible and in accordance even with your own Law?"

The headman's irony softened.

"That you do. I suppose we should be grateful for at least that. Do you know that you are bleeding, yourself?"

Pilatus ignored the last and leaned toward the man

"The little girl's mother. I especially want to see that she is helped. Is she a widow?"

"No."

"Then she has a husband who can provide for her."

"He used to be able to. The woman is my wife. The dead girl is . . . was my daughter."

Pilatus drew back as though he had been slapped. It took him a moment to get his breath. In that moment, he wondered wildly whether, had Jesus been there, he could have magically re-attached the man's arm, touched the little girl and brought her back to life.

"You have been sorely punished this day," he said at last. "May I know your name?"

"I am Micah bar Amos, the baker of Cabul. And you?"

"I am Praefectus Pontius Pilatus."

Micah bar Amos only nodded. Clearly he was in shock. Nothing astounded or hurt just now. That would come later.

Pilatus turned away. The Roman with the broken leg, and the old dead Jew—please Jove the latter was not the unfortunate Micah's father—had been gotten out from under the horse.

"Can we splint our man and continue on with him in the supply wagon or should we return to Kapher Nahum?" said Pilatus to Lucius.

"The break is clean, he can go in the cart."

The soldiers were now rolling, pushing, dragging the two dead horses out of the road.

"I will continue on, then," said Pilatus. "Take two men and ride back to Crispus. Watch your back on the way. Tell Crispus to look alive for a change. I think the attack was specifically in my honor. On the other hand, there might be something major brewing."

"Praefectus . . . "

For the first time, Pilatus realized the anguish of his tribune. He stayed the man's next words.

"Neither you nor I had any reason to expect an attack, Lucius, so spare me your guilt. Perhaps it was the Zealots who surround Simon Yeshuah. Perhaps both of us should have thought more deeply about them. But we did not, and nothing could ever be proved, and maybe they are innocent. We can only go forward. Tell Crispus that I will send a rider to Caesarea and have reinforcements sent up to him. As a courtesy, he should send men and litters out to help these people into town if they will accept the favor, for it occurs to me that their Sabbath begins at sundown, so that they should get to shelter and medical aid before that time.

"Tell Crispus also that I have instructed their headman to come to him to obtain recompense for the injuries and loses of his people."

He took a purse from the folds of his tunic and gave it to Lucius.

"If this is not sufficient, I guarantee to reimburse him for whatever he expends. Cause him to know—without doubt, Lucius—that I grieve most truly for these people, and that he is to be generous rather than stingy with them."

A lamb standing nearby, one of the small, sacrificial herd, bleated.

Pilatus gave it a look.

"Would that the sacrificial blood had been yours as planned."

He started back to his own horse. Then he stopped, thought, and returned the Micah bar Amos.

"Since you but smiled at the recompense of gold that I offered, I will offer you recompense of a greater sort. Seek out a man called Jesus. He shall soothe your hurts better than any medicine or payment on Earth."

Without waiting for answer, Pilatus walked back to his horse.

The oncoming pilgrims and caravans had piled up into a crowd by the time that the two wounded cavalrymen, and the two who had been killed, were loaded, and the column proceeded on. That crowd was ominously silent. The hatred, the blame in the eyes of the pilgrims, was a force that was felt, like knives thrust into the heart. The silence lifted at the last, on the fringes of the crowd.

"Dogs."

"Swine."

"Murderers!"

A child, caught up in the anger of his elders, picked up a handful of dirt and pebbles and flung it at Pilatus as he rode by.

Pilatus paid him no mind. He kicked his horse and galloped away, eager to put distance, oh so much distance, between himself and that place.

* * *

Yeshuah was waiting, at prayer on his aunt's rooftop, when bar Tolmei and his men returned from their excursion. One look at bar Tolmei's smiling face told Yeshuah that it had been a success.

"You did not hurt the praefectus?"

"No more than a scratch for good luck. I doubt he kept dry under-linen though."

"I knocked a Roman right off his horse with my slingshot," said Eleazar proudly.

Yeshuah ruffled his hair.

"Good boy. What of the pilgrims, bar Tolmei?"

"A lot of flesh wounds and broken bones. Two are dead I think, a young girl and an old man, and one fellow lost an arm."

"They are blessed martyrs to the Kingdom of God. The old man shall be with the angels this night, and the girl shall have high honor among her kind. Angels shall note those who were wounded and save their places for them."

He got to his feet.

"Come, bar Tolmei, we must go out to meet the victims. We will minister to them and I will heal those who are worthy.

"Mother! Eleazar! Move out into the streets. Begin to spread the word of the dreadful and unprovoked Roman attack on these innocent pilgrims. Tell them of how Pontius Pilatus mingled their own blood with that of their sacrifices. See that the town is in full cry before they arrive, so that they are received as the martyrs and heroes that they are."

"Galilee is about to rise again, my friends, and she will carry the whole world along on the sweep of her gown."

* * *

It was, of course, not till after the Sabbath that word of the "massacre" could be taken to Kana. The Zebedee's driver left Kapher Nahum at the first possible moment after sundown of Saturday, and whipped his camels smartly along.

The number of guests had dwindled. Mattias, Zakiah, the guests from the Sanhedrin, Deborah's cousins, and Martha's intended, Boaz, had, after all, departed on the morning that Pilatus left, to be back in Jerusalem for the Sabbath. They were all well mounted, on asses, and, traveling in a band, they could safely take the short way home, through Samaria.

The others gathered around, aghast at the news . . . how Pilatus and his men had, for no reason at all, attacked a band of unarmed Galilean pilgrims on the Akko road, slaughtering even children and elders.

Oh, the carnage had been dreadful. Pilatus had been heard to make a dreadful jest, about mingling the blood of Jews with that of their sacrifices.

Then he and his men had ridden on, laughing.

Merovee sat beside Jesus, watching his face. It could not be possible. Surely, there was something that was not being told.

Judah had not a doubt.

"I do not have to be told that my brother, Yeshuah, is still in Kapher Nahum," he muttered.

"Indeed he is," said the Zebedee's driver. "They say that he rushed out the moment he had the news, met those who were carrying in the wounded and healed many of the wounds."

"How good of him," said Judah with a dreadful little smile.

"Were there any Romans hurt or injured?" said Jesus.

"Not a one, why should there be? But the tribune of the praefectus was seen to ride back into the village and go to Crispus. The garrison now wears its armor and goes fully armed. It is whispered that there is a Roman army riding on us from the south. The people are in great fear. Even on the Sabbath, the talk flew as though on wings. There are those who say that we should elect a leader and rise against the Romans now, overpower them before their army arrives, then sweep south into Judeah and . . . "

Judah rounded on the man.

"Simpleton! Tell me that it is not the people of my brother, Yeshuah, who rush forward with these suggestions. And have they as yet suggested that Yeshuah be made the leader? Bar Tolmei, it will probably be, and my mother, putting ideas into the heads of others until they think the ideas are their own."

The Zebedee and Rosula's uncles were conferring. The Zebedee came forward.

He was a short, broad tub of a man, his physique in almost comical contrast to that of his tall, big-boned wife.

"Jesus, under the circumstances we feel that we should return to our homes with all dispatch and try to oil the water. This news will sweep through the province like a wild fire. It would be a disaster for Galilee if any sort of uprising were to take place."

"I am in agreement," said Jesus. "As a matter of fact, I, too, will return to Kapher Nahum. Most of the guests will, I think, in any case, be ready to start for their homes for the advent of Tishri. Those who do not so plan may come to Kapher Nahum with us and continue their merrymaking until we must all grow solemn.

"I think it is Tishri that will be your oil for the waters, Zebedee."

For, the first two weeks of that season were the most solemn of the Jewish calendar, with many observances and daily obligations to be seen to, obligations which could not lightly be set aside . . . not an opportune time for a devout people to launch an uprising.

Many of the guests did leave that very night. Among them was Jac. He had attended on all the proceedings with good nature, but at the cost of all his beliefs and the proper observance of everything including the Essenic Sabbath. He left eager to get back to Qumran, to cleanse himself of his many transgressions, and to pass the high holy days with his Essenic brothers. At the behest of Jesus, he took Jude with him. A Galilee spoiling for revolt was no place for Jude right now. Maybe the desert sun would bake some sense into his brain.

After an early breaking of fast then, Jesus, his family and followers, left as well, the celebration officially ended. Many there were, though, who elected to go on to Kapher Nahum, having planned to spend the Season of Atonement in Galilee anyway, worshiping in Kapher Nahum's fine synagogue. Deborah invited Joseph and Rosula and various aunts and uncles to enjoy the comforts of the house at Magdala. Martha went along to see to the cooking. In Kapher Nahum, Alphaeus eagerly opened his house to as many as would fit. Jairus and his wife followed suit, and Jesus once more leased Obed's inn for himself and Merovee, his close followers, and left-over guests.

How word got around as fast as it did was something that none of them could ever understand. Less than an hour after Jesus had returned, the street in front of the inn was thronged with the sick, the maimed, and the crippled, all patiently waiting.

Lazarus stepped out to explain to them that the bridegroom still had the welfare and entertainment of his guests to see to, but that he would open the doors that evening and help whomsoever he could.

A one-armed man fought his way forward and called to Lazarus in low, urgent tones. Lazarus heard only a few words. Then he conducted the man inside to Jesus.

So it was that Jesus and his people heard the truth of what had happened on the Akko road, from the man who had suffered the greatest hurts, Micah bar Amos, the baker of Cabul.

"When I heard the lies they are telling in the street, I knew I must come to you as the praefectus bade me. He bade it for my welfare, but I come to you for his. I have no love for these Romans, but I do love the truth. Someone must speak it."

"Then let it continue to be you, Micah bar Amos, for you are the man they will believe best. Do you have the courage to stand up in synagogue tomorrow and tell the congregation what you have told me?"

"If I do, I will make myself the target of a Zealot sicarius, for you can bet your last shekel that that is who those brigands were. They will not forgive me for nipping their insurrection in its bud.

"Yet so be it. My life is not worth much now anyway. Dough cannot be kneaded with one hand. It would be better for my wife to be widowed and get herself a whole husband."

"What makes a man whole, Micah? You seem more whole to me than most other men on the face of this Earth."

As he spoke, Jesus came to Micah and lifted the dressing that bound the stump.

"Did the man called Yeshuah heal this for you?"

"He did. The blood flow ceased, and, over the Sabbath, I had no pain. I still have none. But it is beginning to stink and turn green, is it not. Perhaps the Zealots will not get the opportunity to dispatch me. God will beat them to it. I must be among the greatest of sinners for him to have visited such wrath upon me."

Jesus smiled.

"How you flatter yourself. Do you really think your sins so much greater than any other man's, that your god would take his valuable time and wreak such havoc just to punish *you*? What of your daughter? Was she a great sinner, too?"

Micah put his remaining hand to his face and began to sob.

"She was more innocent than the angels."

"Then search for the meaning of all this in something other than your god's wrath, Micah, and do not heed any who would look down upon you for your sins. Unless they, too, begin to re-think their beliefs about this life and the correct way in which to conduct it—and so change their behavior—they, too, will one day suffer some dreadful fate, which they will have brought upon themselves in order to teach themselves . . . just as you caused yourself to lose your own arm."

"What?"

"You visited this trial upon yourself, and you did it for you own good reasons. Perhaps you needed to find out just what does constitute a whole man."

"What of my little daughter?" cried Micah. "What did *she* need to prove to herself?"

"Each Soul enters this life at a particular moment, then leaves it at a particular moment, for its own reasons and purposes. I sense that, in this case . . . was your little girl exceptionally happy all her days?"

"A happier child you never met. She brought sunshine and laughter wherever she went. Even the stones had to smile when she came near."

Jesus laid his hands upon the man's head.

"She was an angel then. They seldom stay long, those creatures of light. They come only to brighten a place that is dark, then they move on—for there are so many dark corners which need them. Behind them, they leave a part of their light, in the memories that we keep of them. And so do not grieve for the child, Micah. Her vast Spirit has had to go on about its work, and you must not waste the great gift that she came to you specifically to bestow.

"Remember her light. Use the memory of her goodness to banish every shadow from your own life.

"Now. Do you wish to die? Or would you prefer to live, with a whole new understanding of life?"

Micah looked up into the bright, kind face. His cheeks were wet with tears.

"The Roman did, indeed, offer me recompense beyond gold, and for that I will always bless him. Yes, Jesus. Make me live. Teach me to be whole."

"Live you shall. Trouble yourself with the condition of your wound no longer. Do you write a good hand?"

"Yes."

"Can you do sums?"

"Passably."

"Jacob bar Alphaeus. Did you not say that you have need of a good clerk at the factory?"

"That I have, Jesus."

"So there is a job for you should you want it, Micah, in which your one remaining hand will be all that is needed.

"Or perhaps you should follow after me as my recorder, taking down my words so that, after I am gone, there can be no quarrels as to what I actually said.

"See? There is yet a second offer of work, you may take your pick."

"If you really want me, I will follow you, Jesus."

"Ah. Bar Alphaeus, I can understand your difficulty in keeping clerks. Each time you get a good one, someone comes along and steals him from you.

"And what of your wife, Micah?"

"I think, if you would speak with her, Lord . . . "

"I am not your lord and not your master. Call me Jesus, call me friend, whatever you wish, but not lord and not master."

"If you would speak with her, Jesus, I think you could give her the peace that I now feel. She can then decide for herself whether she wishes to come with me or to return to Cabul."

"I will see her privily before we open the doors this evening. And you will speak in the synagogue tomorrow?"

"I will."

"I must ask you two more questions. You buried your daughter on the Akko road, you say."

"With the Sabbath approaching, and the Laws of carrion—we could do nothing else."

"Would you that I should raise her, Micah?"

The color drained from Micah's face. His jaw grew slack. For a moment he could not speak.

"You could do it?" he said at last.

"I asked you if you would that I should."

Micah continued to stare up into the face of Jesus, his eyes dilating, the tears flowing unchecked At last he shook his head.

"If I understand you correctly . . . I should respect her own decision, her own . . . purpose. No, Jesus. Leave her."

"Would you that I should return the arm to your body, as though it had never been severed?"

Micah's face was crumbling.

"You are hard, Jesus."

"Am I?"

"You make me do it myself."

"We all do it ourselves, my friend. I only make you face that fact."

Micah drew himself together, as visibly as a man scooping up pieces of a broken jar.

"My arm lies in the grave, cradling my daughter. Leave it there, Jesus. I send it with her and dedicate it to her. May it continue to cradle her, support her, and comfort her as she goes about her task of lighting those dark places which need her.

"As for me, I can see now that the loss of my arm has been the most fortunate event of my life."

Chapter 12
The Last Disciple

Micah bar Amos, accompanied by Jesus and his people, entered the synagogue of Kapher Nahum during services the next morning. When the moment came for speech, Micah ascended onto the central platform and spoke his truth. He enjoined all present to go out and repeat the things he had said, and so put an end to the foolishness that could lead to a major clash between Romans and Galileans, and leave many more of their people dead or maimed.

Micah's eyes strayed often and thoughtfully to bar Tolmei as he spoke, for Yeshuah and his men were in the congregation. Yeshuah sat quietly throughout the speech, making no move to question or to contradict. Neither did he rise, as was his wont, and preach to those assembled. He conducted himself as a humble worshiper during the services, then, along with his followers, left without saying a word.

Many were the looks that were passed, though, to Judah by bar Tolmei and the others. Judah could even feel the eyes of his mother boring into him from behind the women's screen. The identity of Yeshuah's "secret follower" in the camp of Jesus was now obvious to all.

With that in mind, Judah borrowed a wagon from the Zebedee and went to Magdala, returning with his aunt's fig tree.

He found the mood, when he entered Sarai's house, staggering under the weight of the tree, to be dark and tense. Yeshuah was not in evidence, but Meraiah and the disciples sat silently, waiting for whatever they were waiting for.

Sarai was astounded and delighted.

"Meraiah! It is Judah! And look what he has brought. It seemed to disappear into thin air! Nobody would answer me as to where it had gone . . . and the mention of it made Yeshuah so angry that I grew frightened to speak. Why did you take it, Judalah?"

Judah exchanged glances with his mother.

"It would do no good to explain, Aunt. I will carry it back up to the roof for you."

"Oh no you shall not," said Meraiah. "Yeshuah is up there in prayer. We are not to disturb him."

At those words, Sarai's belly grew finally and completely full. The bile spilled out.

"Whose house is this?" she cried. "I do not care what Yeshuah said. Let him go out to the hills if he wants to be alone. I have hardly been able to tend my trees since you people moved in here, been hardly able even to gather fruit, so constantly does Yeshuah pig the roof and order us off. Well, I will not stand for it a moment longer. Come, Judalah. We will return my tree to its place."

With difficulty and several stops to rest, Judah got the tree to the top of the steps. If anything, it had grown heavier since its ordeal. New branches were starting throughout, while a fresh crop of figs was sprouting from the old branches.

"Yeshuah!" said Sarai sternly. "Get yourself over here. Help Judah carry my tree back to its place."

The expression upon Yeshuah's face as he turned and saw his brother and the tree could, in other circumstances, have been termed comical. He rose, came to the tree, and stood staring down at it.

"This is a trick," he said at last. "Your tree was dead, Aunt. Judah has brought you a substitute."

"Do you think I do not know my own tree? I raised it from a cutting. Look. Here is where a branch withered and I cut it off and put a plaster to the spot. And the bend in its trunk is from an injury that it received when it fell from off of the parapet.

"Now help him carry it, Yeshuah. And I must insist that none of you take it away again. Though you certainly have taken fine care of it, Judah. What sort of dung have you used?"

"None, Aunt. The happiness of your tree is due to a man named Jesus."

On the other side of the branches as he helped Judah carry the tree, Yeshuah's head snapped toward him.

"As Yeshuah said," continued Judah, "your tree looked very poorly. It withered very suddenly, on a very hot day. So I took it to the man Jesus, who I know to be the best of all gardeners, and I bade him make your tree live and thrive."

Sarai was neither deaf nor blind, and certainly not stupid, so she knew who Jesus was. She hesitated, looking from one nephew to the other.

"How did Jesus restore it?" she said slowly.

"As I recall, he watered it, ran his hands over the branches, then set it in a shady spot alongside himself as he spoke to me and to his followers of Love and of Beauty. My own heart revived from a state of withered death that day, and grew its own crop of new fruit."

They reached the tree's usual spot and set it down. Judah brushed the soil from his hands and smiled from brother to aunt.

"Well, I must be getting back to Obed's. Soon after our supper, Jesus will open the door to admit those who seek aid, and we are all needed to help with the crowds.

"If your tree should begin to do poorly again, Aunt, send for me, and I will take it to Jesus yet again."

He met Yeshuah's eyes squarely.

"No matter what forces are brought to bear upon it, what injuries it receives or how often, Jesus will always be able to make it whole again. For he dwells most truly in God, and God in him, and to God all things are possible.

"In God, there is no such thing as a dead fig tree."

Judah kissed his aunt and departed without further conversation, leaving Yeshuah staring at the traitorous giver of figs.

"You may continue with your praying now, Yeshuah," said Aunt Sarai. She headed for the stairs, throwing back over her shoulder, "And that tree had better stay healthy. I took a switch to you more than once when you were a boy, and I would not be afraid to do so again."

* * *

The supper at Obed's was large and merry. It was held in the upper room, a frequent feature of such establishments, intended, with its large size, for feasts and banquets, for merchants' gatherings, or simply for the privacy and comfort of Obed's wealthier clientele. The walls were frescoed, and the couches were covered in silk. It was built as a second story over the sleeping chambers, and opened out onto the roof over the common room, so that, on hot nights, those who rented it could take the air in privacy.

For all its size, however, it was crowded that evening. Besides Jesus, his siblings, followers, and die-hard wedding guests, more of the Greek kinsmen of Phillipus had come over from Bethsaida, and there were friends of Levi's—publicans such as himself.

Levi's woman friend Navea was also there. She was a harlot of the Romans, a Roman herself. The unfortunate woman had followed her legionary sweetheart to his assignment in Palestine and lost him to dysentery in less than a month. She had had to stay and earn her living in one of the few ways that a lone woman could. There was talk of marriage between Navea and Levi. For what did he care what people would say, he was already outcast by his people on account of his occupation.

As at the wedding in Kana, following the example of Jesus, the sexes were not segregated at table, people sitting as they willed, many upon the floors, for there were too many for the couches by half.

Into this scene, near the end of the meal, walked Simon Yeshuah.

Speech and laughter died raggedly, as, one by one, the diners saw him.

Jesus and Merovee were among the last to look up. They had been deep in conversation with Navea and Levi, who lay beside them.

"Simon Yeshuah." Jesus showed no surprise. Simon Yeshuah might almost have been expected. "Welcome. Will you eat with us?"

Simon Yeshuah held himself like a man who must needs walk through a pit of vipers to reach his destination. His eyes traveled around the 'U' of couches, seeing the women who dined freely beside the men—one of those men being Judah—seeing Greeks, who must certainly be idolaters, mixing with children of Israel, seeing publicans and a harlot given places of honor.

"I do not sit at table with publicans and sinners and idolaters," he said.

"Do you not? What a shame. For should physicians spend their time binding up those who are whole, refusing to go to those who are sick? Those who are whole have no need of physicians, and saints have no need of such as us. These people do."

Yeshuah hesitated. The word "us" had paid him subtle homage.

His eyes flicked over Judah.

"I also do not defile myself by sitting at table with women."

"So I recall, but that is your misfortune, not mine."

"It is not a matter for jesting."

"I was perfectly serious. If you will not join us, what may I do for you?"

"I only needed to see with my own eyes whether the abominations which are spoken of you are so. In truth, you are the agent of the Prince of Evil. You lead the lost sheep of Israel ever further from the fold, into the outer darkness, from whence there is no return, and no salvation. The solemn days are only one week away. Yet you do not fast, or purify yourself in preparation."

"Have you ever known wedding guests to fast while the bridegroom is still amongst them?"

"Fear not, Yeshuah. The wedding will soon be finished. The bridegroom will be taken from them, and then they will fast.

"And tell me, by what pronouncement of Scripture does the Day of the Sounding of the Horn begin a week before that day? Or even one day before that day? If it does, why not then a month before the day, or two months, or three? Where do you draw your lines, and by what authority?"

"Sufficient to each day are the tasks thereof, and to the season what belongs to that season. So suffer me and my bride and our guests our season of rejoicing, for it is brief enough, and will never return.

"As to the outer darkness into which I lead these people . . . what is outer darkness? It is those places which our people have feared to explore. What is dark remains dark only so long as we do not light it with knowledge of itself.

"For knowledge is light, and light is knowledge. Once your 'outer darkness' is lighted, it might just be that people would not want to return from it, would not care to be saved back into your mindless sheep fold.

"Now, is there something else I can do for you? I will invite the afflicted to enter soon. Perhaps you would care to stay and to help."

Again, Jesus accorded Yeshuah subtle recognition, as to an equal practitioner.

Yeshuah hesitated long.

Then, to the surprise of all, he said . . .

"I shall stay and watch."

And so he did. Taking himself to a corner of the room, away from accidental touch and possible defilement, he stood, arms folded, face expressionless.

All drew back when the last of the supper was cleared away, forming a gallery, and the men begin to admit the supplicants.

The press was great, for people had waited over two weeks for the return of Jesus, and word was spreading. Some had returned to their homes and there awaited news. Others had trudged about the countryside hoping to find him. Some had heard rumors and gone to Magdala, only to find that he had left. Some had gotten wind of the wedding and set out for Kana, only to hear that he was now back in Kapher Nahum.

Jesus was magnificent that night. He was happy, rested, smiling, relaxed. His vitality filled the room. What he called The Energy was at its peak, and he worked more quickly than any of them had ever seen him work.

Yet the flow of people did not cease. Hour after hour they came—the halt, the lame, the blind, the deaf, the dumb. A lunatic boy was brought in, and two who frothed with "demons." There were people with growths, with the coughing sickness, with palsy, and stiffness and pain of the joints. There were people with withered limbs, crooked spines, and swollen parts. Every known ailment seemed set to parade before Jesus that night, and, strangely, his vitality seemed to feed upon them, growing greater with each moment, flowing, even, into those who watched, filling them with an excitement that was almost past bearing.

Till, finally, at the approach of a blind girl, Jesus looked beyond her and motioned for the next two people to be brought forward as well.

"We can help more people if more of us work. Merovee. Do the blind girl. Judah. Take the lamed man."

Merovee, sitting with the gallery, and Judah, helping to conduct the supplicants, froze like two Greek statues.

"Come," said Jesus, voice clipped, inviting no nonsense "While The Energy is this great, I can carry you all along. Each of you can cut your teeth tonight. Petros, Nathaniel, Susannah, Lazarus, all of you. Watch, for your turns will be next."

He pulled Merovee up and forward, not in the intimate way of a husband, but in the detached way of a teacher. There was something quite alien about him suddenly. Even his face seemed that of a stranger.

"Simply do it. Do not think, just believe and do. Come, Judah, you have seen me work and you know the secret of the fig tree. Do each of you believe?"

"Yes," they answered in unison, strangely mesmerized.

"Do either of you have any doubts?"

"No."

"Then lay hands on these people and heal them."

Merovee reached out and did as she was bade.

"Do you believe that I have the power to heal you?"

"Do you truly desire to be healed?"

"Do you believe that you deserve to be healed?"

"Do you agree to release your infirmity?"

"Will you allow yourself to be whole once more?"

As if the chamber were filled with echoes, she heard Judah asking the same questions of the lamed man, and Jesus asking them of a man with a growth upon his lip, heard the replies of the girl, and of the two men.

She placed her hands upon the girl's eyes. As she did, The Energy surged into her—the same terrible energy that had filled her the night that Jesus expelled her demons. It whirled round and round in her chest and innards.

But this time she did not faint.

She thought she was growing, swelling. She seemed suddenly to be gigantic, looking down upon the blind girl from a great height. The Energy poured out her fingertips in fat, warm streams.

"Release," she said, and her voice seemed to fill the Universe.

"Allow." And her voice broke the walls of that Universe, rolling onward like a wave, into the outer darkness. She felt the streams of energy connect and mingle with a vibrancy in the girl's skull. Before Merovee's eyes, the milky films which had covered the girl's eyes dissolved, washing away in a river of tears.

The girl blinked furiously and lifted her hands to hide from the brightness she had never before seen. Beside her, her mother cried out for joy.

"Take her out into the dark," Merovee heard herself say. "Shield her eyes from light until they grow accustomed to sight.

"And know that, as she afflicted herself, it is she who has healed herself, for the Power of the true god is within each one of us. Laugh and be joyous, and use that power graciously for all the rest of your days."

Judah's lamed man was standing straight, happily testing his new strength.

Jesus touched both the girl and the man, as though to find out whether the infirmities were really gone. He nodded, smiled, and hugged first Merovee then Judah. Then he shooed them aside.

"Who is next? Petros. Where did he go? All right. You, then, Nathaniel, and . . . what? All right, my kitten. Step lively, men, get the people in here. Find a woman or child for our veiled lady to heal.

"Keep them coming! The Energy can ebb as easily as it flows."

So it went, until an hour past the midnight, and ended only because they ran out of patients. For the first time, all who had gathered hoping for aid had been seen in one evening, and helped to whatever degree they, themselves, would allow.

Every follower had been made to perform. Most had taken several turns.

Only Johannah failed completely, fainting as The Energy surged through her, then refusing to try again. She took scant comfort in Merovee's reminder that she, too, had fainted, and had had to be put to bed the first time that she felt that energy.

Several could obtain only partial results on the first try, so that Jesus had had to re-do those healings.

And Levi was not able to do a thorough job despite four tries.

"I can not get around the knowledge that I am despised," he sighed. "I guess I do not feel worthy to touch these people, much less to heal them."

"It is yourself who despises yourself, Levi. Be patient. You will learn to love, both your self and your Self."

It was difficult for any of them, followers or wedding guests, to calm down. Joseph and Rosula were with Deborah and Martha in Magdala, but young Joses, Annah, and Rachel were present, staying at the inn with Jesus. They were large-eyed and dumbstruck, for they, too, had been asked to come forward. Rachel and Joses had obtained partial results, while Annah had totally healed the scales from off of a hideously covered woman, producing pink, new skin instead. It seemed that the guests would remain all night, endlessly reliving all that had occurred.

Finally, however, prodded by Alphaeus, the wedding guests left in a chattering herd, returning to his house and to the house of Jairus, there, most likely, to continue in conversation until the dawn.

It was only then, as Obed moved about closing the shutters and doors after them, that Jesus remembered Simon Yeshuah.

"Did you see him leave, Judah?"

"Yes."

Judah's face was drawn. He had done four healings, all successful.

Yet he could find no joy in the accomplishment just now.

"He left just after I cast the demon out of the man."

"Ah. And what was his expression?"

"He looked . . . "

Judah turned away.

"Stunned. Betrayed. Confused. I felt . . . . . . it was all I could do to keep from running after him to beg his forgiveness."

"Forgiveness for what?"

"For doing what he thinks only he should be able to do. I am sure be is telling himself that what happened here tonight was the work of the Tempter."

"Do you think that it was?"

Judah hesitated. Not because he had doubts. He but searched for the best way to say it.

"No. How could it be? Can a wagon cut in half continue to function? If the Tempter aided us in driving out his own demons, he would be weakening himself and would eventually fall.

"No, Jesus. My urge to run after my brother and beg forgiveness stems, not from any question about the rightness and beauty of what I did tonight, but, from my own problem, which I wonder if I will ever overcome—from the awe and guilt and sense of inadequacy which Simon Yeshuah has always inspired in my breast."

"I am glad that you understand that. Pour oil on your thoughts, Judah. Be peaceful, and calm, for truly you are great among my followers. You can rise to a high understanding within this lifetime.

"And do not fret for Yeshuah. He, too, can rise to great heights this time, if only he will overcome his vanity. Trust in me. Be at peace until you must needs be otherwise."

His eyes swept the room. In the aftermath of the evening's excitement, those who had done miracles were manifesting a variety of emotions.

Salome clung to Merovee, chattering ecstatically, being her usual, eternally bright Spirit.

Sitting beside them, Lazarus kept recovering from, then bursting yet again into, nervous tears.

Susannah seemed sunk into deep depression.

Nathaniel was beautifully serene.

The Boanerges preened like young roosters, laughing and making silly jokes.

Phillipus sat grinning stupidly into space.

Mathiah was on his knees, praying in the direction of the Temple.

Salmon, Eli, and Ezekiel were immersed in a conversation that none of them heard, since all of them were talking at once.

Jacob bar Alphaeus sat staring at his fingertips as though trying to find traces of what had so lately poured through them.

Chandreah was having chills, while Petros, Levi, and Lebbaeus were getting quietly drunk.

Jesus smiled.

"I do not feel at all like sleeping," he announced. "Those of you who would like to sit up a while longer, let us speak of what has happened this night, and keep speaking until we all understand."

There was not a one of them who did not wish—crave, yearn—to talk, or at least to listen. There was not a one of them who did not have questions. And then more questions. There was not a one of them who was not shaken to the core.

So more wine was brought. And the sun had risen before they retired.

Merovee went almost fearfully to the chamber that she shared with Jesus. For he had remained that alien throughout the night—that kindly, but distant, teacher, who showed no more care for her than for any of the others.

Yet the man who crawled in beside her was once again Jesus. He took her into his arms and kissed her.

"Thank you for going first and so well. You never fail me. You showed them the way, and made it so much easier on me. I never dreamed that I would be able to initiate them in a group as I did, so quickly and so successfully. But, when I felt The Energy rising to such a peak that it wished to overflow my own Self, I recognized the opportunity. And you were there to help me."

He pulled her closer, squirming until her body fitted perfectly against his own in just the way that he liked. His lips turned again, seeking hers.

Before they found her, he was fast asleep.

Only then did Merovee begin to understand the magnitude of The Energy that he had put forth that night, for nigh onto twelve hours.

With nothing but the overflow—without ever diminishing himself—he had raised more than a dozen other people to superhuman heights, allowed them to wield power that was, to them, incredible, to him, an everyday tool.

Then he had sat with them for hours, answering their questions, hearing their excited recollections, calming fears, offering encouragement, nipping a few egos which threatened to grow overbearing, laying his hands upon each of them, sending The Energy into each of them once more, so that all could feel it again in a relaxed atmosphere, think about it, accommodate it to their own selves, accustom themselves to how it felt, and learn how to direct it.

With the stuff of his own Self, he had shown his inner circle what was possible, available to anyone who cared to try to understand, to anyone with the courage to try to believe.

Could any of them repeat the performance, raise The Energy without him there, without his energy to prime their own?

Maybe not. But they all now knew what was possible. It was now up to each of them to find his or her own way, to a sure and certain belief, to the trust that would make The Energy as familiar a tool to them as it was to Jesus.

Perhaps, to do a thing like that, one had to put favoritism aside, and be an alien for just a while.

For a moment, in the pale light of the new morning, Merovee studied his face.

Then she closed her eyes and breathed as he had shown her. If she hurried, perhaps she could catch up with him and accompany him on this 'night's' travels. He always tried to wait for her.

She did not always understand the things that she saw in the places where they went . . . but at least she was learning how to get there.

* * *

It was to a high hill bordering Lake Gennesareth that Yeshuah had gone that night, walking through the hours during which Jesus and his followers completed their healings, and during the hours in which they talked.

As the sun rose, and Merovee followed Jesus into sleep, Yeshuah arrived at the summit.

There he dropped to his knees, and then flat to the ground, his face to the dirt. He wished he could have found a higher place, for he needed to get as close to God as possible, to hear very clearly the things which God said.

Because, suddenly, the possibility loomed huge in Yeshuah's mind that he had not been hearing clearly up until now.

He could not have brought that fig tree back to life.

How, then, had Jesus been able?

He did not want to admit the answer that kept knocking at the back door of his mind.

Never in his life had he cured the variety or the quantity of people such as Jesus had cured during this last night. It had never even occurred to him that it was possible.

Actually, he shied away from curing, preferring to cast out demons.

Why did he shrink from curing?

Was it, as he had always told himself, that those with such afflictions were sinners who deserved their fates, which fates should not be tampered with?

Or was it that he knew, deep within, that he was not able.

It had never occurred to him that the power which he thought set him apart, marked him as the Messiah, and even—blasphemy—the son of God, could be shared around with others as easily as food or drink.

Yet, with his own eyes, he had seen this Jesus do it. The whore whom he called wife, fishermen, clerks, publicans, children, all manner of rabble, had done miracles before his very eyes.

And, yes, they had cast out demons as well.

That last hurt badly.

Judah hurt worst of all.

Such power could only come from the Prince of Darkness.

It must.

It had to.

Because if it came from God . . . then Yeshuah's whole life had been predicated on error.

"Father. Speak to me. I am so very confused."

He wrapped his face with his arms and sobbed.

* * *

Micah bar Amos and his wife Leah were waiting in the common room when Jesus awoke, officially reporting for work. Micah had got himself sheets of papyrus, ink and sand, pens of quill and reed, a light wooden board for a portable desk, and pins with which to fasten the sheets so that they would not slip and slide as he worked. To carry these materials, his wife was fashioning a great cloth pouch, with a strap so that it could be hung over the shoulder or looped over the head for travel.

This Leah could not have been recognized as the creature who had been brave enough to spit upon the praefectus and call him "pig." She was a tiny woman, of little speech. She was also less convinced than her husband in regard to the words of Jesus.

Still, the man had healed Micah's wound, taken away the green flesh, so that she would not lose her husband as well as her daughter.

And she would not leave Micah. She would follow where he led, supplying another hand when he needed it, though she kept herself well apart from her husband that day, and from Jesus and his followers. Having touched her dead daughter, and her husband's severed arm, her ritual impurity would last yet another three days after this one.

The man Jesus smiled at her scruples.

"Nothing outside of yourself can defile or sicken you, Leah. The things of this world are only illusions, created by the mass consciousness. It is not any of those things, touching or entering into you, which cause you to be impure. Defilement comes only from within. It is the things within the heart, which come forth from *out* of you *into* the world, in word and deed, that have the power to defile, corrupt, or sicken you."

His eyes swept his companions.

"Those with ears to hear, hear."

Then he smiled again, hearing the scratch of the stylus.

"Are those the first words which you record, Micah? That is well. Truly, you could stop right there, for they are the most important words you will ever hear me utter. Those who come truly to understand

336

those words, in all their ramifications, will have learned all that they need to learn on this plane. All other words are as mere embroidery."

It was upon that morning that the "army" which had been rumored to be heading north to despoil Galilee arrived. It was a century of men. Though, under the Republic, a century had consisted of one hundred men, under the empire it had been corrupted to eighty men, one-sixth of a cohort, each century commanded by a centurion of the lowest grade.

Eighty men. Just enough to flex muscle and display resolve without overly provoking, Pilatus had reasoned.

The gesture was understood by the people of Gennesareth in just that way, and reinforcements were redundant now in any wise. Micah's speech in the synagogue had been known throughout the province within hours of its utterance. Only malcontents and Zealots would continue to deny the truth and shrill for revenge.

And it was upon that morning that boats putting in from further down the lake brought word that Herodias and her women had arrived in Tiberias, there to await the return of Antipas from his campaign.

The news was not unexpected. Both public gossip, and idle comments from Pilatus at the wedding, had informed them that Antipas would be leaving for Petra momentarily—a safe distance behind his army—to oversee the war against his former father-in-law. Salome had confidently predicted that her mother would now be on the way north to Tiberias, impelled both by curiosity and by a need to legitimize Salome's presence in Galilee.

"You see, Merovee?" she cried when she heard. "I promised that there was no danger to you in bringing me north."

There was nothing for it but that Jesus and Merovee go with her immediately to meet her mother.

They set off that afternoon, sailing with Petros. Included in the party was, of course, Johannah, and Lazarus. Chandreah came along to help Petros. Micah and Leah—agog when they understood their destination—were also brought. For, if Micah was to take down the words of Jesus, he must become a constant shadow. At Salome's insistence, Judah came as well.

"For my mother must meet my new brother."

The city of Tiberias could be seen from almost any point once one was out onto the lake, both on account of its brightness and of its size. It was not yet complete, but already it contained the royal palace, situated on a hill, markets, theaters, administrative buildings, mansions of its many rich inhabitants, a library, gymnasiums, lavish public baths, and a hippodrome. Very few Jews had contributed to the construction of Tiberius, for the first excavation had turned up ancient graves. Fearful of defilement, most Jews refused to work in the building. Even fewer could be persuaded to live or conduct business in the town . . . only outcasts and publicans, and those Jews who placed the riches and favors which Antipas offered above The Law.

Tiberias was, therefore, an outright creation, as unnatural and out of place in the midst of Galilee as would be an eagle squatting among chickens, pretending to be one of them. Living and working alongside the few dissident Jews were Greeks, Syrians, Armenians, Romans, Egyptians, Phoenicians, Persians, Celts, Franks, Indians, even representatives from the Silk Lands beyond India—cosmopolitans and merchants for the most part, often outcast from their own lands. In lieu of local help, the town had been finished by Roman and Greek builders under the direction of one of the best Athenian architects, imported at great expense to make Tiberias the jewel of the Middle East, a fitting tribute to the emperor for whom it was named.

An oasis of marble, of graceful columns and peristyles, of gardens and fountains, tile and fresco, it was a beautiful city, and the passion of Antipas. He might, in the press of duty surrounding the administration of his tetrarchy, have few occasions to travel to his beloved Rome, to greet face-to-face once more the Imperial Family among whom he had been educated, with whom he had lived as a brother, until his father, Herod the Great, had died, forcing his return to Palestine and to duty. But he could make, of Tiberias, a mini-Rome. And he could pretend.

The crowning beauty of the small harbor was a vast, marble porch, which extended on massive fill—from the base of the hill on which sat the palace—out into the waters of the lake. A peristyle edged the entire expanse. Within its confines was a covered pavilion, gardens, places for entertainment, an animal menagerie and aviary, and a small, elegant house for the seaside pleasure of Herodias and her women.

It was at the end of this porch that boats arriving at the palace docked, and it was there that the party from Kapher Nahum alighted.

The guards who came forward relaxed at the sight of Johannah.

"Send to Herodias," she said easily. "Tell her," she gestured toward the veiled figure that was Salome, "that I bring a woman with whom she will wish to converse."

Within minutes, the entire party—save Petros and Chandreah, who sailed on to do an errand at the House of Nathan in Magdala—was ushered into the little house at the end of the porch, and into the quarters of Herodias. Salome pulled off her veil when at last the door was closed, and ran to her mother's arms.

"Thanks be that you have come!" she cried. "Oh, Mother, I have so much to tell!"

"You always have so much to tell," laughed Herodias. She held her daughter out to arms' length, then shoved her along to be inspected by her women. When it had been agreed by all that Salome was in one piece, though a few pounds lighter, Herodias turned her attention to the others.

"So. Jesus." Her eyes twinkled as he was introduced. "Your fame grows. You were much spoken of even in Machaerus in the last weeks. Indeed, my husband grew quite pale at the mention of you, for I told him that I had heard that you are Johannan, risen from the dead."

They sat down to wine, and to fruit and bread and cheese that Herodias ordered to be brought. With Micah doing his best to write it all down, Salome talked non-stop through much of the afternoon, omitting nothing, not so much as the courtship of Pharisee and Ruth.

Herodias was alternately gay and solemn throughout the telling. Her shrewd eyes studied each of Salome's new friends. Being schooled in keeping her judgments to herself, however, she betrayed none of her thoughts.

Herodias was not a beauty in the classic sense. She was too closely bred, a definite product of the incestuous Hasmonaean-Herodian dynasties.

Granddaughter of Herod the Great, she had been married, first, to her own uncle, Herod Phillipus, and had then been invited away from that match by his half-brother, Herod Antipas, yet another uncle.

So that Salome, born of the union with Herod Phillipus, was in the odd position of having a father who was also her uncle, a step-father who was her uncle, and of being a granddaughter of Herod the Great through her father, and a great-granddaughter through her mother.

She was also her mother's first cousin.

Phillipus the Tetrarch, to whom Salome had been wed, had been yet another half-brother of her father Herod Phillipus, and half-brother also to her uncle and step-father Herod Antipas, so that Salome had been married to a man who was both her uncle and her great-uncle.

The relationships in the family were so very confused that even the family had trouble keeping track. Herod the Great had gotten fourteen children out of his ten wives, and hardly a one of them had married outside of the family, while, inside those confines, there was much changing of partners.

Small wonder that Herodias had taken no serious umbrage at the report that Johannan had preached against her marriage to Antipas. It did not make sense that Johannan would have singled her and Antipas out from the whole mess, finding special fault with the illegality of the marriage of Antipas to the wife of a living brother. Not when more serious prohibitions concerning incest were violated by Herodians as a matter of constant policy—as they had been by the Hasmonaeans before them, which sinners had yet been made High Priests of the Temple with little demur.

It also made no sense when the annals of the House of Herod were black with every sin of which Jews could conceive, murder and idolatry not least among them.

Even if the Prophet had made a public remark, how would it have differed from what many others said, both publicly and privately?

And what would it have mattered anyway? While paying lip service to the Jewish god, and to The Law, Herodians had, in practice, ever done what was expedient for them at the moment. If that expediency entailed violating The Law, The Law was violated, and the old men in the Temple had better just turn their heads.

Witness the golden eagle that Herod the Great had caused to be affixed over the entry to his new Temple in gross violation of The Law, but in order to flatter his great friend, Caesar Augustus. The old men of the Temple had turned their heads, and the idol had remained—until some young hotheads took matters into their own hands, cut it down, chopped it up, and were executed by Herod for their pains.

Witness Herod's violation of the tombs, of the very bodies of David and Solomon, in his search for money and valuables.

Should then a granddaughter of Herod the Great by his royal Hasmonaean wife—and thus a descendant of the Maccabean saviors of Palestine—should that woman fear the censure of religionists where her own personal affairs were concerned?

The only displeasure that any Herodian had ever feared was that of Rome.

And the family of Augustus would have been the last on Earth qualified to censure incest, wife-trading, wife-stealing, or divorce.

No. Herodias was far from being a beauty. She was too thin, too nervous, too fine . . . and the fineness did not manifest itself in fragility, as in Salome. Herodias was as a lute string, drawn too tightly, seeming ready to snap at any moment. Her movements, of hand, head, eye, and body, were quick, seeming almost to have pointed edges. She was prone to fits of depression, and to sudden rages.

Herod the Great had murdered her great-great-grandfather, then her great-grandmother, then his wife who was her grandmother—the tragic and fabled Princess Mariamme—then Mariamme's young brother.

He had then murdered his two sons by Mariamme, one of them being the father of Herodias.

Perhaps out of guilt, Herod had then shown especial care in the raising of his fatherless granddaughter and of her three brothers. He had sent them to Rome, where they had been reared and educated among the offspring of the Imperial Family. The aging Caesar Augustus had bounced Herodias upon his knee. The Empress Livia had cosseted her with sweetmeats. After that splendor, the enforced return to Palestine at the age of fourteen to be married to Herod Phillipus, to whom Herod, himself, had betrothed her when she was only a child, had been like expulsion from Paradise.

It was supposed to help that Herod Phillipus had been King Herod's darling, the obvious heir, the only child of King Herod's next great love after the Princess Mariamme, ironically yet another Mariamme, daughter of the High Priest. But Herod Phillipus had been weak and pockmarked, and Herodias had hated him simply for living.

Then, after King Herod's death, it was found that that crazed old man had inexplicably and totally cut Herod Phillipus from out of his will. Herod's kingdom had, instead, been divided between his three youngest sons, leaving Herod Phillipus with no dynastic standing and without a shekel to his name—no better than any private citizen.

Herod Phillipus had been too spineless to fight for his rights, rights obviously superior to those of his younger half-brothers, offspring of later and junior wives. And the bitterness of Herodias had known no bounds. The pearl that was herself had been cast before swine, to be trampled and slimed in the mud.

It was in that bitter mental state that Antipas had found her when stopping at the home of his half-brother on the eve of a voyage to Rome. He had not seen Herodias in years. Now she was twenty-four, and, to him, beautiful beyond words. Her tension, her pent-up vitality, her diamond-hard brilliance, uncovered his own dissatisfactions, set him to dreaming of what might be possible. He had, at first sight, fallen into a love with her the intensity of which recalled the insane passion of his father, Herod, for the Princess Mariamme . . . a passion so intense that, finally, in mistaken jealousy, Herod had put his beloved to death so that no other man might have her.

How could Herodias have been expected to resist when Antipas begged her to leave Herod Phillipus and marry him? Antipas, ruler of Galilee and Peraea. Antipas, with an income of two hundred talents a year. Antipas, with a future before him.

Would that she had been born male. She would have fought for her rights had she been Herod Phillipus. *She* would have gotten herself provinces to rule. Fighting would at least have been something to do.

But she had not been born male, and Antipas might almost make up for that. She could see his weaknesses so well. She would only have to handle him properly, and she, Herodias, would finally rule provinces in all but name.

So she had agreed. But on condition that she would not be merely another wife. She made Antipas divorce his wife of many years, Phasaelis, the daughter of King Aretas. She made him promise, further, never to take either more wives or concubines. She would share him with no one. She would have all the power, the influence, all the possibilities to herself.

She had bargained ruthlessly, way ahead of the smitten Antipas, knowing herself to be on firm ground. For there was more than just herself to be loved in this situation, and she made sure to tell Antipas what else there was to love.

Despite his long marriage to Phasaelis, that lady had remained barren. A man needed heirs. What better wife to get them by than by Herodias, the senior granddaughter of Herod's Hasmonaean wife, thus of truly royal blood, a blood held almost sacred by the Jews . . . blood that even Antipas did not carry in his veins, for the parents of Herod the Great had been but wealthy Idumeans, while the mother of Antipas had been but the daughter of wealthy Samaritans.

Along with her own valuable body in marriage, Herodias was careful to remind him that there was yet another available body. Salome. Salome, too, was a chalice of precious Hasmonaean blood, a matrimonial chip that could be sold to the highest bidder while their own children were being gotten and raised.

Did he know, for instance, that his brother, the other Phillipus, tetrarch of the Decapolis, had already written to Herod Phillipus broaching the possibility of marrying Salome when she reached the age of thirteen? Tetrarch Phillipus obviously saw the importance of getting himself a Hasmonaean wife. Would it not be to the advantage of Antipas to get control of the girl and dictate the marriage terms himself? By means of Herodias, Salome, and future children, Antipas might even be able to consolidate his tetrarchy with that of Phillipus, then convince Rome to turn Judeah back to him. By means of these two marriages, the Palestinian empire over which Herod the Great had ruled could be revived.

Had Antipas never wished to be a king? Did he not wish to make her a queen?

So it had been settled. On the return of Antipas from Rome, Herodias took her daughter, left her husband's house, and sent him a bill of divorcement. Had not the maternal grandmother of Herodias, the Salome who had been the daughter of Herod the Great and the Princess Mariamme, done the same, in clear defiance of the Law of the Jews, which Law gave the right of divorcing to men alone? Had that grandmother not gotten away with it? Why, then, should her granddaughter not do the same?

So Herodias and Antipas were wed.

How clever she had thought herself. She had not bargained on the undying hatred that the divorcing of his daughter by Antipas would raise in the breast of King Aretas. She had not bargained on the harassment, the border skirmishes, the raids and incursions into the territory of Antipas. She had not bargained on having to go to war, on having to spend every penny that either of them possessed in order to fight that miserable old man.

She had not bargained on Johannan the Prophet, and on the eerie ways in which his life insisted upon mixing with hers, or on the pressures that had been brought to bear on her marriage as a result of his mere existence.

Herodias had also not counted upon falling in love, deeply, irrevocably, in love with the man she had thought only to use. She had not counted on trapping herself more deeply than she had been trapped by her first marriage.

It was frightening to care as she did. Were Tiberius, himself, to come to her, and ask her to be Empress of Rome, she would refuse. Only death would take her from this husband.

Herodias had also not counted upon growing to love her daughter so very much that she had been overjoyed when Phillipus the Tetrarch died as Salome was being taken to him, so that Salome was returned home to her. She had not counted on wishing to put off any future marriage, no matter how wonderfully dynastic, so that she could keep that Bright Spirit, who lightened her days and eased her depressions, with her as long as possible.

Now, on top of all else, there was Salome's embroilment in this strange new teaching. Was this Jesus as much of a spellbinder as Johannan had been? He must be. Look how Salome loved him. Even Johannan's widow had become his wife. While Herodias found her own eyes straying constantly to his face, finding indescribable comfort in what she saw.

Herodias realized that day that she went in deep dread of the future. Nothing was working out as she had planned. The world was constantly shifting around her, as it did in dreams.

Even her own actions seemed dreamlike more often than not.

She had listened to the man Johannan and been moved as never before.

She had forgotten her royal blood, her dignity. She had cried like a child when they brought his head, then sent her daughter off with strangers to bury it. She had lied and dissembled to hide the girl's absence, understanding that she must be traveling down to Galilee to find yet another spellbinder.

A royal Hasmonaean princess! The chip on which many of her dynastic schemes depended, sent cheerfully off to tour the countryside with who knew what low sorts, examples of whom she now welcomed to her apartments as if family.

And it was not even as though she understood, or even believed, the things that Johannan had told her and Salome.

Yet she had acted in this bewildering manner.

Perhaps Johannan had bewitched her. Or perhaps it was, indeed, all a dream.

She smiled gently as her vivacious daughter talked on.

Herodias was too honest to deny her own faults. She was equally as frank in assessing her finer qualities. And it often seemed to her that, by a fortunate whim of nature, all that was fine in her had been emptied into Salome, while all that was bad had been strained out, including the nerves and bad temper which came with the inbreeding. And when she was with Salome it seemed that even she, Herodias, could manifest only those finer things, that there was nothing to do in the world except to laugh, and love, and eagerly search for new knowledge.

Salome had nearly finished her narrative. Her voice dropped, her eyes shown. She took her mother's hands and told her of the previous night . . . how the disciples of Jesus, herself included, had lain hands upon the afflicted, and helped them to cure themselves.

Herodias heard her words with sinking heart.

When Salome was finished, Herodias rose, walked to the broad window overlooking the lake, and stared out at the blue-green depths through its ornamental frets.

What was she to do with the girl now?

For she saw only too clearly what was coming. Salome was ruined.

That fortunate girl had found purpose. She had a found a clear, bright reason to live, a definite direction in which to travel. She would never again be content to sit in some palace and embroider cushions, or to direct a husband from over his shoulder. When it came time for Jesus to leave, Salome would insist upon leaving with him. And, for sheer stubbornness, Salome was a match for Herodias any day.

Herodias knew that Jesus was watching her. She could feel his smile, sense the gentle twinkle in the eyes. She almost thought that he was reading her mind. She turned. Their eyes met. And she knew he was reading her mind.

"What *am* I to do,' she asked him softly.

"Who should decide that but yourself, Herodias?"

"It is not in my hands."

"Is it not?"

"I can control affairs only so far. I am a woman."

"Does that not make you one of the most potent beings on the face of the Earth?"

"Antipas is even now considering a new marriage for her."

"Do you see a problem in that?"

"She can not go running about the countryside any longer. What has possessed me thus far I cannot imagine."

"Can you not?"

"Stop asking me to answer my own questions!"

"As I said before, who else should?"

"What a maddening creature you are!"

He held out a hand.

"Come join me in my madness."

To her own amazement, Herodias burst into laughter.

Salome ran to her and hugged her.

"Did I not tell you that she is wonderful, Merovee? Does she not remind you of Deborah? Oh Mother, you must meet Deborah. And Joseph and Rosula."

"Would it surprise you to learn that I already have?"

"But how?"

"Do you remember our years with your father as having been lived under a rock? One can hardly move about in Judeah's social circles without meeting the most illustrious members of those circles. The heiress of the House of Nathan, but, especially . . . " she looked at Jesus once more, "Joseph bar Ramathea—Prince of the House of David.

"In the days when our grandfather Herod was made king, my dear, there were many uprisings which aimed at putting Joseph's father onto the throne instead. There were many then, just as now, who said that those born bar Ramathea are God's chosen kings. There are many who would say," her voice hardened a bit, "that you and I are no more royal than worms, while that man sitting there eating his third apple was anointed by Heaven before he was born."

"Oh well. I am sure that he was, but we are much better then worms, Mother, never you fear.

"Baramathea," she mused. "It sounds almost Greek."

"*Bar* Ramathea, two words," corrected Herodias. "Would you care to explain that name to my daughter, Jesus?"

"I was hoping that you would explain it," he smiled. "Frankly, though I have theories, I do not know for sure what it means. As you say, it is a name by which we are called, a name of which some few, privileged people know. It somehow became attached to the oldest living male representative of the eldest line of each generation. When my father dies, I will become bar Ramathea. Should I die without a son, my brother Jac would inherit the title, and so on.

"Likewise, should I die before my father and leave no son, the title would go to Jac after my father's death. But should I have a son it would go to my son, however young, evolving to Jac's line only if that son died with no son.

"Should all my father's sons fail in male issue, it would revert to the family of my Uncle Cleopah. Should his line fail in males, it would at last revert to the male issue of my Aunt Annah.

"Should my Aunt Annah's line offer no males, it would jump back to my line and search out the senior male issue of my eldest daughter, and so on down the line once more until it found bar Ramathea."

"And if it searched the entire line once more and found no males at all, would it then settle on the senior female?" said Merovee.

"I cannot say. It has never had to search that far. There is always a male to be had somewhere or other. When you study the genealogies, you can see it jumping about, searching. The end result is that it finds and marks the single living male who is the most direct heir."

"To what?" said Herodias. She wore a slow, sly smile. Jesus returned that smile in kind.

"One would expect my answer to be 'to the House of David.' Yet, as you obviously know, the genealogies show the title, or some semantic version of that title, extending back beyond David's father Jesse, beyond Jesse's parents Boaz and Ruth, back into records which we are not now able to read, some even on clay tablets.

"I am taken aback, though, Herodias. I can understand how you know of the title, itself, coming from the family that you do come from. But you also seem to be privy to the ancient mystery surrounding the name. That mystery is not widely understood or discussed outside of the upper echelon of the Temple."

"Do you forget," smiled Herodias, "that the mother of Salome's father was daughter to the High Priest? There is much information to be gleaned in a family such as that."

"Bar Ramathea," said Merovee. "The 'bar' seems to be Aramaic . . . it could be either 'son of' or 'from.' But 'Ramathea'—there is no person or place by that name that I know of."

"And so the title does not refer to any particular person or place," said Jesus. "Believe me, my father and I have puzzled over this often, and searched the Temple genealogies for clews. There are none. As the word 'Ramathea' stands, it is a strange mixture. It is possible that the Egyptian 'Ra,' and 'Maat,' have something to do with it. But I think rather that it is the Hebrew 'Ramah'—that can be taken for 'high place' or simply 'highest' or even 'all-high.' It is often found attached to places where altars have stood—while 'thea' seems to derive from Greek, to do with deity, with gods. All the manifestations of the title in the genealogies, in whatever script or language or dialect, render those same two elements. So that you could read 'from the high place—or altar—of god.' 'from the all-high god,' 'from the highest god,' or else 'son of the high place of god,' 'son of the all-high god,' or 'son of the highest god.'"

"Son of God?" said Judah. He stared at Jesus, stunned.

"No, not son of God," said Merovee. "I thought you knew your Greek, Husband."

"I do, Wife. I have been teasing, waiting for you to correct me."

"If this has to do with Greek, the male rendering would have to be theo. Thea would be female. It could mean simply 'goddess,' or it could refer to Thea, herself. She was a companion to Artemis."

344

"Merovee, how wonderful!" said Salome. "How do you know so much about these things?"

"I read a lot," said Merovee shortly. "Josh, does your father's title never take the masculine at any place in the genealogies?"

"It does not," smiled Jesus. "And that—mid genealogies so fixated upon males—is what is so perplexing. And tantalizing."

"From, or son of, the All-high Goddess," said Merovee softly. "And it is rendered with those elements back into time immemorial? Back to records so old that they cannot be deciphered?"

"Obviously," said Jesus, "extremely ancient information is being preserved. And extremely *important* information, for those records to have survived, been guarded, for thousands of years."

"But this is blasphemy," said Judah. "You are speaking of idols, of false gods. There is no such thing as a 'High Goddess.' There is no such thing as a goddess at all. There is only one god, and he is he, and he is male."

" Judah, you are reverting to old thought patterns," said Jesus gently.

"Oh. Yes. Sorry," said Judah. "But . . . "

"No buts if you please, not if you have been listening to my teachings. In addition, in this case it is not I who insists upon words which indicate a goddess. It is the records of the Temple which preserve those words. And *is* your god exclusively male, Judah? Did your god not say, 'Let *us* make Man in *our* image,' and was Man not then created both male and female?"

"Jesus," said Johannah, "who is it who preserves this strange title for your family?"

"It has to be some knowledgeable line among the priests or scribes, acting upon secret injunctions, handed down and known only to themselves. My father says he is sure that his father never made the necessary changes when his own father died. Yet they were made. And, when my father's father died, my father did not make any changes, neither did he ask that they should be made. Yet, when he went to look at the records, the title of bar Ramathea had been put beside his own name.

"Among ourselves and publicly, we have always referred to ourselves as being of the Triple Ramah, which refers to the high holy sites of David that have been handed down in the senior branch of the family as an inheritance . . . certain lands in Mount Ephraim, Bethlehem, and Hebron."

Judah's face was working.

"What is it, Judah?"

"It is what you are saying! Followed to its logical conclusion, you are saying that God is not one, but two. Male and female. This cannot be so, Man is obviously the heir! Woman is but . . . "

"Judah bar Jethro!" cried Salome. "What colossal ego! What am I? Do I exist? Have I a reason to be that is just as good as yours? Did I not heal right alongside you last night? If I have no reason to be here, then why am I here? How could I be here? Why would God make me if I were not part of his own image? I suddenly see that he would not.

"And why am I saying 'he' and 'his'? Those words are *male*."

"Which is why you find me privately referring to the true god as 'it,'" said Jesus. "The true god is One, Judah. But, in that oneness, is all. The true god All That Is is neither male nor female and yet both.

"And, by a process that even I do not understand, a secret remembrance of the female qualities of the true god has been preserved by the very priests who seek to promote a totally male god.

"I have always suspected that the story told of Ruth and of Boaz is a memory, a symbolic statement of what once was, what should be, and which hopefully will be again. Ruth would be a symbol of the Great Mother—forgotten, cast aside, looked upon as a stranger. She must creep into the field of the Great Father to labor as a servant and glean as a beggar—until she is once again noticed by the Great Father, and restored to her place at his side.

"Why my family was chosen to represent this remembrance, I cannot say. Somewhere in the Temple I think that the answer could be found. But, until it is, I simply accept the title, and the honor. To my way of thinking, the tradition seeks out the male, yet reminds him that he is the son of the Great Mother who is One with the Great Father.

"And, when I come again in my various parts, to demonstrate to Humankind the true nature of its source, I will often be as All That Is . . . neither male nor female but both."

There was silence in the room, each person staring at Jesus, trying to digest his words.

"Have I answered your challenge, Herodias?"

Herodias was open-mouthed.

"You have indeed."

"Do you have any intelligence to add to the name of bar Ramathea?"

She shook her head.

"I knew only that the male marked bar Ramathea was considered the true, secret king. And I knew that there was ongoing consternation over the obvious reference to a female deity. I knew—and know—that, politically, you are my enemy. I know that, should you choose, you could rally every Jew to your banner and displace, not only my husband, but, Pontius Pilatus, himself.

"Did you know that, Salome? That we are consorting with our natural enemy?"

"If I must be enemies with Jesus over inheritances, Mother, then I will gladly relinquish my claim. He has filled me with such riches that I will never want again."

"I should like to see you make that speech to Antipas," said Herodias wryly.

"I will," said Salome. "Gladly."

Herodias shook her head.

"Remind me to be on the way to Rome when you do, so that I can be clear of the furniture which he hurls. My dear, you do understand that you are going to have to make another marriage at some point? Antipas might even settle on the man within the next few months."

"I am looking forward to marriage, Mother. But, until it comes, I must follow Jesus. I must learn all that I can while yet I have the opportunity. Scota must keep on in my place."

"You promise you will not balk when it is time to be married?"

"I told you that I am looking forward to my next husband."

"Who is Scota?" said Jesus.

Mother and daughter burst out laughing.

"Can your friends be trusted with our secret?" said Herodias.

"Yes. Besides, if Jesus is to let me continue to follow after him, we must put his mind at rest as to the safety of that course."

Herodias nodded to one of her women, who went to an adjoining door and called.

Moments passed.

Then a girl of Salome's age, slight, fragile, with pale read hair and freckles, entered the chamber. She was richly dressed and bore herself regally. The resemblance to Salome was astounding.

The girl saw Salome and, with a cry, ran to her arms. As they stood together, embracing and laughing, the resemblance was even more striking.

"Is it not amazing?" said Salome. "She used to fool even my own father. Mother saw her in the market years ago and bought her, thinking that she would make me a playmate, and that the resemblance could sometimes be convenient. She is a Celt. Is she not wonderful?"

Merovee exchanged head-shakes with those others who had come north from Machaerus. It was now clear why Salome had been so confident when she had promised that she would not be missed.

"I am sorry I could not explain to you about her before, Merovee. But I could not have done so without my mother's agreement. We have kept Scota a great secret. Only our women and Johannah, here, know about her. Scota and I dress alike while I am at home so that anyone seeing her assumes they are seeing me."

"Salome has a great reputation amongst the staffs of the various palaces," smiled Scota. She even sounded like Salome. "They say that she is faster than lightening . . . so fast that she often seems to be in two places at the same time."

"No matter how loving the husband or exalted the situation," said Herodias with a shrug that was close to apology, "women are at a disadvantage. Witness my grandmother, so dynastically important, so beloved. Yet Herod had her taken out and stoned to death because of calumnies and unfounded suspicions.

"I can not tell you what it did to me as a child, when I began to understand about my grandmother."

She returned from the window and sank down onto a divan, speaking earnestly.

"I understood at a very young age that a female had to grab any opportunity, use any device which presented itself—even if it be underhanded or not quite honest—merely to stay head-to-head with men."

She held out an arm, and Scota went to her, sinking down beside her, hugging her as gladly as would Salome.

"We could amuse you for hours with tales of the uses to which this darling girl has been put, and the little freedoms which her presence has given to Salome and to me over the years. She is most dear to us."

Herodias kissed the girl's cheek.

"She has been offered her freedom, but she will not take it."

"Why should I, Mother?" said Scota, in such natural address that it was obviously of many years standing. "Where could I be happier than here with you and my sister?"

"Yet one day soon, Scota, I will find you a husband. One who is comely and kind and also rich, whom you can love and who will love you."

"I will always do as you insist, but I would rather stay with you and Salome all my days than with any husband."

Herodias hugged her again. Her face was troubled, her eyes, for a moment, faraway.

Jesus and his party remained at the palace that night and for much of the following morning. Herodias was boundless in her questioning, rapt in her listening. She did not openly agree with any of the words which Jesus spoke, neither did she openly disagree. She but listened, and thought.

Thought deeply. Merovee remembered Nathaniel's words back at Machaerus.

'The Prophet says their interest is genuine, their questions intelligent, and that they are both decent women,' he had said.

Herodias was, indeed, a decent woman. It was almost a shock to know that one of her breed could be humane.

Yet, knowing the daughter, she should have credited the mother.

Only one thing did Herodias ask repeatedly, as though having forgotten that she had already asked it, or else disbelieving the previous answer.

"Jesus, do you promise that you have no political aspirations? For I could not in good conscience be your friend, or allow my daughter to continue your friend, if you plan to declare yourself king and wrest this land from my husband and from Rome."

"I have no such aspirations," he answered repeatedly. "Neither have any in my family had them since the last of the kings.

"You spoke of the attempts to put my grandfather onto the throne in your grandfather's day. Yet you must know that my grandfather took himself and his children out of Palestine and went to Egypt expressly to discourage those attempts. When he returned to Palestine, he did not return to Judeah, but hid away in Samaria, and then in Galilee, living simply until he died.

"Were others to oust Rome and banish your husband, and then come to me offering to make me King of the Jews, I would refuse.

"I am not concerned with such trivialities, begging your pardon, Herodias. My reason for returning at this time has only to do with what is thought of as the Kingdom of God. I come as a guide, to show others the path that leads to that kingdom, which is within themselves. I ask nothing more than to be heard, and even then I ask only for the brief time that it will take me to train other guides."

That next afternoon, when Petros returned for them and they embarked, Salome was still in their company. But with a new chaperone.

She was Zana, who had been nurse to Herodias and her brothers, and then to Salome. Merovee recognized her as the woman who had overseen Salome's purchase of balm from the trader lad in the market at Machaerus that day.

Johannah, to her own disappointment, was left behind. Her month's holiday was ended, and Herodias would on no account extend it, for then Johannah's husband Chuzah might begin to ask questions.

"I think I will just ask him to divorce me," fumed Johannah. "We have never liked each other anyway."

"That will be your business," said Herodias. "But, while you are his wife, it is my business. Were Chuzah to begin sticking his nose into my business, or that of Jesus, there could be dire consequences."

She made a gesture at once petulant and apologetic.

"Present company excepted, men simply cannot be trusted. They are much more treacherous than women, even more so because they pretend not to be. They pretend so well that they even convince themselves.

"That is why I allow no eunuchs in my court, they are the most treacherous of all, poor things, with the worst traits of both the sexes."

Yet it was agreed that Herodias would develop a craving for certain fish, the freshness of which only Petros could be trusted to supply, so that Petros could come and go with reports of Salome's welfare and the doings of Jesus, while Johannah, herself, would often have to ride with him up to Kapher Nahum, to select just the right fish for her mistress.

Zana was chosen as the new chaperone for yet another reason.

Merovee's pregnancy was beginning to show—only slightly, so that it took a practiced eye.

But Zana's eye was practiced, and, when she inquired, and Herodias understood that Merovee carried the Prophet's child, there was nothing for it but that Zana must be sent along with her.

"For she knows all there is to know about the carrying and birthing of babies," Herodias assured Merovee, "and she is an expert with herbs as well, more accomplished than any physician. Trust Zana. Do as she says. Eat and drink the things she gives you. You will rest easily as you carry, then deliver a healthy baby with ease."

It pleased Herodias mightily, one could see, to be able to contribute thus to the continuation of the Prophet within Merovee's belly.

She did not go out to watch them leave. The arrival, the welcome, and the overnight stay of this mysterious and motley group was suspect enough without the wife of the tetrarch going out to wave them away as well.

She did her waving privately, from her window overlooking the lake. She stayed at the window, with Johannah and Scota and her women, till the boat became a dot and was lost in the chop of the lake.

Herodias then took Johannah's hand, and led her to a couch.

"Tell me more about Jesus, Johannah. If it takes a week. Tell me everything that you remember. Do not neglect a crumb."

* * *

A storm was brewing by the time they reached Kapher Nahum. A Thunder storm.

Thunder's sons were waiting at the shore and drew Jesus aside, shamefaced. They remained in quiet conversation for some time. Then Jesus patted them and continued to the common room of Obed's inn.

Thunder was waiting, her toe tapping, her eyes flashing. She was studying Micah and Leah with ill-concealed distaste. She wasted no time as Jesus entered, but proceeded to the attack.

"What an ungrateful wretch you are, Jesus."

"Ah. The dove-like Zilpah. How am I ungrateful, Sweet Lady?"

"You have been to the palace to visit Herodias and you did not take my sons to be presented. Instead you take these people, this baker and his mouse of a wife. Why? How do they come to be so special to have that honor? You only met them this week! Are not my boys your first followers after Chandreah and Petros? Have they not served you faithfully? Do they not deserve the foremost positions at your side at all times and in all matters? . . . Well? Do they not?"

Jesus poured himself some wine, took a deep draught, then turned to Zilpah.

"Let me tell you how things are in the Kingdom of Heaven, Zilpah, for the Kingdom of Heaven is what I hope to teach you. Perhaps for such as yourself a parable would be the best.

"There was a householder, who, needing workers for his vineyard, went out in the morning and hired men from off the street, agreeing with them that they should each get half a drachma for the day. Happy at that respectable wage, the men rushed off to the vineyard to work.

"But the work was heavy, and more workers were needed to get in the harvest, so, at the third hour, the householder went out once more, and, seeing men idle in the marketplace, he said to them, 'Go to my vineyard and work for the rest of the day, and whatever is fair, I will pay you.' And those men went off gladly, for the work was welcome to them.

"But still the harvest was great, and even more workers could be used, so, at the sixth hour, the householder went to the market once more and sent workers to the vineyard with the same promise, to pay them what was fair.

"He did the same at the ninth hour.

"At the eleventh hour, he went again, and found men standing idle. And he said, 'Why do you stand here idly all the day?'

"And they answered, 'Because we came to find hire and have waited patiently, but found none to hire us.'

"So the householder hired them, again for 'what is fair,' and they went gladly to the vineyard and toiled with the rest for the remaining hour of daylight.

"And when the men came to be paid, they received in order from the last to the first. And those that were last got half a drachma, and also those who came at the ninth and sixth and third hours.

"And those who had come at the first hour supposed that they would get more. But they, too, received half a drachma.

"And they grew angry, and murmured amongst themselves, and they said to the householder, 'These last have worked but one hour, while we have toiled in the sun and the heat all the day, yet you have made them equal to us.

"And the householder answered to them, 'How do I do you wrong? Did you not agree to labor the whole day for half a drachma? And is that not what I have paid you? Take that which is your own and go in peace, envying not your fellows. Is it not lawful for me to do as I will with my own money? These others went to the market, hoping for work, and would have toiled alongside you all the day had I found them earlier. They, too, stood in the sun, and, where you were bent with work, they spent much of the day bent with despair, thinking they would earn nothing to buy bread for their families. And they were content to rush to my field and work with zest for whatever their hours, trusting my word that I would reward them fairly. So why should your eyes grow evil with jealousy because I chose to be good to these men?'"

Jesus took more wine.

"It is not 'time' or 'duration' that is of weight in the Kingdom, Zilpah. It is intent. So that, often, those who you think should be last will be first, and those who you deem first will be last. And though I call to many, few will hear, and rush to my field with proper intent, and so be chosen into the Kingdom. Among those who do, all will be great, and all will be equal."

"Why do you talk in such riddles? Why do you not say things out straightly?"

"If I did, Zilpah, you would hear me no better. Now please. You try my patience. And you are most uncomplimentary to your own self."

He walked toward the corner, where was the corridor that led to the chambers. But Zilpah followed.

"Jesus! I would speak with you privately."

Jesus turned.

"If you wish to be private, I suggest you begin by lowering your voice."

Zilpah did so. She edged closer, casting a furtive glance back over her shoulder.

"I want your promise. My sons are ready to give up everything for you, to follow wherever you lead. But they are young and foolish. They do not understand that certain negotiations should be made, bargains struck, before making such a sacrifice. Today is an example of how they may be shunted aside if these matters are not worked out.

"I want you to guarantee the location of my sons' seats in the Kingdom. I want you to promise that they will be placed immediately at your left hand once there, and that they will never be demoted from your immediate left hand by anyone or for any reason."

Jesus stood staring at the woman. He realized that his jaw had dropped.

"Surely you jest," he said at last.

"I am perfectly serious."

"Have you heard nothing that I have said? The Kingdom has no banquet hall. There are no couches or seats. The Kingdom is not a place. It is a state of consciousness. Where is the left hand of your consciousness, Zilpah? Show it to me, and I will run to find a couch to put there."

"Then what are my sons toiling for? What will be their reward?"

"If they continue to follow me, Zilpah, I can promise you only one thing. Their reward will be as mine. From whatever cup I drink, so shall they. Is that good enough?"

"You are sure that there are no assigned places?"

"Positive."

"Then will you guarantee that they will drink immediately after you, before any others?"

Jesus looked up at the ceiling, sighed, and returned his gaze to Zilpah.

"Unfortunately, all drink at once, for the cup is very large, and it is round."

Zilpah pursed her lips.

"Like an animal trough," Jesus offered helpfully.

"In that case, you must drink at one particular position, and my sons should be to the left of that."

Jesus shook his head.

"Woman, you are incorrigible. Consider this. If the trough is round, then there is no head place. All in the circle are equal.

"Now, if all in the circle are equal with myself, why, then, should your sons seek to drink at the spot to my left, when, in so doing, they insist that I am greater than they, and, hence, they are less than I, and so automatically less than all the others in the circle who are equal to me?"

Zilpah's face went blank.

Jesus patted her.

"Work on it," he said, and escaped down the corridor to his chamber.

* * *

The first of Tishri, the Day of the Sounding of the Horn, came and went. Jesus attended synagogue, but refused to be mournful and solemn, as the Pharisees had begun to demand that good Jews should be upon that day.

"To beat one's breast is the very last way to go about pleasing All That Is," he told his followers.

His attitude continued the same throughout the ten days of solemnity leading to the Day of Atonement, during which period he taught daily and privately to his own friends at the inn of Obed, not going out to teach to multitudes, but opening the doors each night, save for the Sabbath, for healings—the latter done regularly now by his followers as well as himself.

"These solemn observances were never ordained by any god, but by Man. It is well to be reflective, to think on one's errors, and plan how to do better in the future, but one should not dwell upon those errors. One should study them with a glad, not a sad, heart. One should recall errors with joy, contemplating the wonder of the fact that he or she is now able to recognize them as errors, offering thanks and song to All That Is, that forever forgives, and that will wait eternally for improvement.

"The best way to 'atone' is to go forward gladly, trying one's best to do better."

In the week between the Day of Atonement and the beginning of the Feast of the Booths, Jesus did go out among the people, speaking to large crowds—on the western side of the lake one day, in Bethsaida another, down to Tarichaea, even all the way up to Caesar Phillipi.

He gave aid to all who came seeking to be healed and initiated many of his followers by sending them out two-by-two into the countryside, to teach and to heal all by themselves.

Chandreah and the youngest of the Boanerges returned from their first tour, into the hills to the west of the lake, with long faces. Many had come out to them, and the teaching had gone well enough. Yet, when they had laid their hands onto those who sought cures, nothing had happened.

"Why?" said Chandreah.

"Lack of belief in yourself," said Jesus. "Be patient. The days will be on you all too quickly, when you will go out into the world without me, and when your belief will be strong enough, and when you will handle great multitudes all by yourself without even a partner, and cry because you need rest, rather than because you have failed to heal."

Indeed, the next day both men reported good success in healing.

It was that way with all of the followers. As their confidence went, so went their cures.

The women, of course, were not tested in such a manner. No crowds would have come to hear them teaching by themselves. No Hebrew man would have allowed them to lay their hands upon him. Indeed, they might have been stoned for trying.

So that the women simply followed where Jesus went, listening and assisting as they could, helping with the workload by healing female supplicants as Jesus and his male companions healed the males.

Throughout it all, Judah became increasingly morose.

No one had heard from Yeshuah since he had disappeared from Obed's the night of the first healings. Refusing to hear any reassurances, Judah blamed himself endlessly for whatever had befallen his brother.

Then came the Festival of the Booths. All from Obed's, and those still staying with Alphaeus and Jairus and in Magdala, went out into the fields together. They built themselves little huts as directed by Torah, and lived in them for a week, feasting and telling stories and listening to what Jesus had to say.

This would be the end of the holidays. Even the most stubborn of the wedding guests could not justify staying longer. Joseph and Rosula would be heading home, escorting Martha and in company with Aunt Annah and her family, who had finally arrived from Hebron. Cleopah and his family and all the aunts and cousins from Samaria and Sidon and Tyre would likewise be leaving.

It was on the last night of that feast, as they sat together around a fire, singing and conversing, that a living skeleton emerged from out of the darkness.

Simon Yeshuah.

He was filthy and tattered. His eyes caught the fire and glowed as those of a wolf.

He came straight to Jesus and stopped before him.

"I have come to ask if you will accept me as your follower," he said.

There was a great silence.

"Please," said Simon Yeshuah.

"I am happy to accept you.

"Judah. Get your brother some of that broth.

"Sit you down, Simon Yeshuah. When did you eat last, Man?"

Chapter 13

Nigh to Jerusalem

At the end of the month of Tevet, Jesus and his followers went up to Judeah, to Bethany near Jerusalem, to the house 'bar Jeremiah,' where Deborah had lived with her late husband, and where her children had been born.

Merovee was in her seventh month when they arrived, yet she was not what would have been called big with child. Perhaps it was her height, perhaps her boyish, muscular build, perhaps Zana's concoctions and Zana's strictly prescribed diet, but she was one of the fortunate few who showed late and little, and who still moved with such ease that, in her loose, flowing garments, strangers seldom understood her to be pregnant. She was able to keep up with Jesus wherever he went, accepting all conditions, being no burden, her only concession being to ride Ruthie as they traveled, rather than to walk. She used the kitten to save face. Someone had to transport and care for Freckles.

For, in the nearly three months since the dwelling in booths, Jesus had traveled widely. He made a complete circuit of Galilee, then moved north through Tyre and Sidon, and east to Gaulanitus and Caesarea Phillipi. He then traveled south through the Decapolis and into Peraea, teaching daily to groups large or small, healing any who came, then teaching his own people by night. He rarely stayed in one place more than one day, seeming driven to give of himself to as many as possible in a very short time.

Thus they slept wherever they could. The hospitality of houses was sometimes extended, but, due to the size of their band, this was the exception rather than the rule. There were sometimes inns, or, on roads used by caravans and Romans, caravansaries, huge hostels of the simplest sort, where travelers could find bread and wine and a relatively clean sleeping palette sheltered from the elements.

But there were nights that Merovee liked the most, and which she filed away among the most precious things in her memory. Those were the nights when there were no civilized lodgings available, and Phillipus or Judah—who had assumed the responsibility of locating nightly shelter and obtaining provisions, and who traded the task back and forth, depending on whether they were in predominantly Hebrew or Gentile territory—found them some large cave in which to sleep.

Then a fire would be built just inside the entrance, so that it would draw off into the night and yet protect from the cold of that night. The female hands to make Merovee's pan bread that Jesus liked so well, and to cook stew, were many. When the meal was finished, all would draw in around Jesus.

There were beyond seventy-five of them now. Petros, the sons of Thunder and Thunder herself, Alphaeus, Jacob bar Alphaeus and his wife and his son Lebbaeus. Chandreah had hoped to be married to his intended and to bring her along, but the girl had refused such a mad endeavor and both parties had asked out of the betrothal. Levi had quietly married his Navea, and she was in the party. She was strong and resourceful, well-liked by everyone but Thunder. There was Phillipus and his wife, along with his three young sons, his father Demetrius, his mother Cleopatra, four of his brothers--Theo, Archimedes, Plato and Ulysses--and their wives and children. There were Micah and Leah, Mathiah, Salmon, Eli, Ezekiel, Nathaniel, Susannah, Salome, Zana, Judah, Lazarus, and Merovee. Jairus and his wife Esther and daughter Rebeckah had joined them, and the younger siblings of Jesus, Joses, Rachel, and Annah, traveled along. Three sons of Uncle Cleopah, Jacob, Simeon, and Reuben, had stayed, sending their families home with Cleopah, Aunt Miriam, Ben and his family. Two young cousins from Tyre had joined the band, Barnabus and Thaddeus. And five of the artisans from Kapher Kana had become followers—Moses, Jude, Jeptah, Elihu, and Samuel.

Finally there was Yeshuah. And his family—his mother Meraiah, his son Eleazar, his brothers Jacob, Joseph, Baruch and Isaac, and their wives and children

Of Yeshuah's Zealot followers, only bar Tolmei had remained loyal. The other three, Samuel, Ephraim, and David, had deserted, disgusted with Yeshuah's surrender to this Jesus.

Deborah did not accompany them.

"Jesus has taken my manager and my assistant manager and half of the staff from Kapher Kana," she had smiled. "Someone has to stay behind to mind things. Besides, there is some business to which I must attend."

They were a strange and mismatched throng that was, at the same time, oddly homogeneous. Merovee knew that she was not the only one who treasured those nights in the caves as they gathered around Jesus—some of the children pressing near, Rebeckah especially, falling asleep finally, snuggled up against him. And he would talk to all of them much as he had talked to his inner circle that night in the House of Nathan, telling them so many things, things which many in the group still refused to credit or even to try to understand. His smile was always so gentle, and the words, "Those of you with ears to hear, hear. Those of you with eyes to see, see," came so often. Indeed, his smile was the gentlest when he spoke those words.

Jesus had told Merovee that she would live to a great old age. She had known it without being told. She knew that her time—or times—with him would be short, and that there were great, long, lonely, and often confusing, years ahead. So she stored those nights carefully, missing none of their details, memorizing their textures, watching the formless, primeval, and strangely comforting vaults of the roofs, where the dancing firelight made warm, glowing patterns on the golden rock.

Somehow, away from man-made objects, and man-invented conventions, the words of Jesus took on even more validity, becoming part of the flickering gold shadows and seemingly molten stone. It was, at those times, as though the outside world did not exist.

She thought the child floating in her womb must feel the same way, warm and sheltered, nurtured and loved. It stirred often as Jesus spoke. She had the impression that it, too, was listening, and understanding perhaps even better than did she. Thinking that, she would take one of Johannan's sheepskins and crawl in among the children, laying her head onto the lap of Jesus alongside the purring Freckles, curling, belly toward him, welcoming his caressing hands to her hair, hoping that, in this way, his voice would be even more audible to the child.

Sometimes, despite herself, not having realized how tired she was, she would fall asleep that way along with the children. That was all right. Her mind would hear even though she slept, and, if she missed anything, the child in her womb would tell it to her, sometime in the years ahead.

Oh, her Jesus. What a wondrous creature he was. He told her it was possible to love much, much more than she already did. He said there were heights and depths and widths of Love which even he had not yet learned.

How could such a thing be? For her part, it seemed impossible that more love could be borne toward any one person.

For his part . . . how could one love more than he? For he loved everyone. She adored to watch his face, his movements, on those golden, warm nights in the caves, as his words blended with dancing shadows, and seemed a sort of truth being spoken by the Earth itself, while the love flowing from his eyes immersed them all.

Watching him, she did begin to see what Love really was, and to know why it was such a difficult thing to consistently achieve in relation to all one's fellows.

His love flowed from a boundless understanding of each one of his listeners, from his appreciation of all their foibles, his forgiveness of all their faults, an interest in, rather than censure of, their differences. His love often seemed to be one vast, warm chuckle, a humor-filled appreciation and acceptance of all that he saw. She realized that, in watching others, he learned to know his own Self better, to like his own self better, to be more amused at, and forgiving of, his own self, and that he thus thanked his fellows hourly for being there, for coming into his life to teach him about his own self and his own Self.

Love such as he manifested was rooted in just that . . . in self understanding leading to Self appreciation.

Was this how All That Is truly was? Only much, much more so? Boundlessly more so?

Jesus said that it was.

Even Simon Yeshuah seemed to believe it in those first months. The change in the man was almost frightening. Merovee did not trust it. Neither did Judah. Yet the man was sincere.

"And Simon Yeshuah is a vast resource of Humankind," Jesus told the two of them gravely. "I have told you this, Judah. Your brother is great. He but lacks the last, vital understanding. He has shown his greatness by admitting that lack."

"But I fear for you!" cried Judah. "Jesus, you do not know him."

"Actually, I know him better than you think. I must learn to know him better."

"You do not understand! It as though you took a viper for a pet. He will turn on you, Jesus. He believes too firmly in his own destiny. When he has finished using you, he will sacrifice you to his own glory."

"What do you imagine he could do to me, Judah?"

"He could—well, certainly he could get you into such trouble with the authorities that they might decide to kill you."

"Can the authorities kill me, Judah?"

"Well, as you say, no, not your Soul, but they can kill your body."

"It is usual, at some point, for bodies to die. But the 'I' cannot be killed, Judah. And I, like all other I's, am a unique packet of consciousness that is a beloved part of the true god. As such, I am eternal and indestructible.

"So tell me, what have I to fear from your brother? The only thing that I have to fear is my own self, Judah.

"This great man, your brother, has come to me. You and our friend the fig tree made him recognize a lack in himself. You showed him clearly that my powers are more advanced than his, and that they are more advanced because they flow from Love rather than from negative beliefs such as his own. He has been great enough to see that, to hunger for my teaching, and, far more, he had the courage to come and humble himself before me. And before all of the followers.

"Good Lord! Do you not understand the guts that took?

"Should I, then, out of fear for the well-being of my own body, should I fail this man? Should I refuse to show him some glimmering of what Love is really about?

"If I did that, Judah, I would greatly miss my mark. For Simon Yeshuah will return to this world, again and again, in body after body. Each time he appears, he will be large in the world.

"I have a chance to add Love to that largeness, so that, whenever he appears again, he, and those with whom he dwells, will come closer to understanding . . . closer and closer with each appearance.

"So be cheerful, Judah. You too, Wife. The true god is always in its 'Heaven.' The world is never anything but right, no matter how wrong it might seem to you."

As for Yeshuah, he stayed nearly as close to Jesus as did Merovee. His eyes still burned, but the burning now was a sort of fear, as though he worried that, should he leave the group for even a few minutes simply to attend to the calls of nature, he would miss *the* word, *the* phrase that would make it all clear. He had gained back his weight, for the women fed him solicitously. Yet he still seemed gaunt.

Because, Merovee realized, his gauntness was of the Spirit. The eyes in the mind of a beholder saw, and understood, that parsimony before the eyes of the body saw his outer form. Simon Yeshuah was as a fisherman's net, empty, trailing in the water, hoping to be filled.

Yet, there was a mellowing as well. There was no way to be with Jesus on a continuous basis, hear his words, feel his total acceptance of whatever one was, without responding to that Love.

Sitting at the feet of Jesus night after night, the hotness in Yeshuah's eyes was from tears more often than not. Yeshuah was a man still in shock, who looked to Jesus as to a savior. He seldom spoke, and he did not voice opinions or argue with that savior.

And never did he voice objections that would have been his of old, to the wine, to the free movement of the women in the group—even the obvious disregard of 'women's times,' when they should have drawn apart, and did not.

Neither did he remark upon the fact that Jesus and his followers made no attempt to seek out synagogues, nor to ritually purify themselves, nor to make sacrificial offering required by Law.

He ate beside the women without demur and complained of nothing. Not having renewed his Nazorite vows since cutting his hair in honor of his uncle, he washed and combed that hair along with the other men, and grew careful that his nails should be pared, his clothing clean.

There was now, at times, something almost gentle about him. To her shock one day, Merovee realized that she had grown to like the man.

His brothers and their families were equally as amiable. His son Eleazar had just had his thirteenth birthday, become a man, and now felt entitled to strut, to correct his elders, and to quote Torah with every other breath. But that was understandable. He would grow out of it.

Bar Tolmei and Mother Meraiah were different stories.

With each passing day. Merovee grew more hopeful that bar Tolmei would make good his threat and leave for Jerusalem or Caesarea to "get on with our work! There are Romans out there needing killing, Yeshuah! What has happened to you? I think this Jesus is a sorcerer, you are bewitched, your spine has turned to chicken fat!"

But still bar Tolmei stayed, following at Yeshuah's heels like some vicious, yet totally obedient, guard dog. And his teeth and brawn were all that he had left with which to guard, for he, along with all Yeshuah's people, had been obliged to dispose of their weapons.

"Those who live by the sword shall die by the sword," Jesus had told Yeshuah that first night. "To have sararii in my camp would be to draw to us those psychic energies which are also looking for a fight, men with swords of their own. Weapons will not win the kingdom that you seek, my friend, not by the longest and luckiest shot in the world. You must find the courage to lay siege to that kingdom with naught but the weapon of Love."

Mother Meraiah was even surlier than bar Tolmei—a very hard person to like. Merovee sometimes felt that Meraiah sat up late after all the others had gone to sleep, thinking up ways to be even more contrary on the morrow.

Yet, to see her son sitting at the feet of another—all her fine pride seemingly in the dust beside him—must be painful in the extreme. Somehow, between the amusement afforded by visions of Meraiah hunched nightly over the fire scheming at how to be disliked, and by frequently reminding herself of the woman's pain, Merovee found that she could like even Meraiah.

Of course, she could not tell Meraiah that, else Meraiah would have gotten even nastier. But Merovee found herself frequently smiling down onto that old, grey head. And often, toward the close of the day, she was even successful in convincing Meraiah to ride Ruthie for a bit.

Meraiah had steadfastly refused to have a mount assigned to her, so that Gilead and Solomon were ridden by Cleopatra and Esther. Alphaeus put up with Pharisee. Jacob bar Alphaeus had brought an ass from his own stable for his wife Michal. Herodias had seen to it that Salome had a fine Syrian riding mare. And the rest of the company were content to walk.

So that, to entice Meraiah onto Ruthie's back, Merovee had always to claim, often truthfully, that, even with the softness of one of Johannan's sheepskins, she was saddle-cramped, sore in the nether regions, and in desperate need of release. Fiercely proud was Meraiah, not wanting to admit when her old body was so tired that she wanted only to lie down and die—her feet so sore that each step was torture. No one must ever think, no, not for an instant, that Meraiah could not keep up with the strongest of them.

In return for Merovee's kindnesses, Meraiah returned none of her own. Not so much as a thank you for the rides. While Merovee's smiles seemed even more torturous to her than her aching feet. Still Merovee smiled. Still Meraiah accepted the rides.

Till, at the approach of Tevet, Jesus finally asserted his authority as husband. And it became obvious that he had planned the grand circle to be close to Bethany just at that juncture.

"It draws too near to your time, Merovee, and, as smooth a gait as Ruthie has, I insist that you spend your last months in the Bethany house, not upon Ruthie's back."

"It is too soon. Josh. You know how I feel about returning to Jerusalem. Please let us stay away until the very last minute. I can keep up. There is no need to pamper me.'"

"What of Ruthie? She is pregnant, herself. Might she not wish for a quiet stall and soft straw and no weight upon her back during this time?"

"She is early in her time, it will be months before she must be pampered."

"I can see why you lean toward Meraiah. You are both more stubborn than Ruthie could ever be. Merovee, do you not want Johannan's baby?"

"Of course I want him!"

"Then why would you endanger it?"

"I do not endanger him. Nothing can happen to him, he is meant to be. He will be strong and handsome and fine even if I bear him in a manger in some caravansary stable. Oh Josh, do not make me be parted from you. Do not shunt me off like a . . . woman."

They stood alone, enjoying a rare moment of solitude at the noonday hour. They were near Gilead. From their hilltop, they could look out across sparse, rocky, Peraean slopes to the emerald band edging the Jordan.

"What makes you think I plan to leave you?" smiled Jesus.

"But . . . you mean you will sit around the house doing nothing for these last two months as well?"

"I certainly hope not. No. I will use the time for concentrated work with my people. There is so much to teach them, and so little time."

She drew in her breath.

"Then please, Josh, let us go any place but towards Jerusalem."

"Come now." He hugged her. "I told you there is no danger as yet. And I must show up at the Temple for the Passover. It is important this year that I do all the things that a good Jew is supposed to do, and give the authorities no excuse to complain."

She had not thought of it that way.

"I suppose you have a point."

"Bethany is perfect. There you can be safe and well-tended while I can go about my business—at the Temple or even out to Bethabarah to teach. Yet, still, I can return to you each night. When the child is born, you can receive purification at the Temple, then the child as well. Which will give the priests even less of an opportunity to fault us."

He turned her to him.

"But there is something you must promise me. When we are nigh to Jerusalem, you must obey Law and custom as regards Jewish women, and appear in every way as the docile wife. We can get away with our behavior out here in the middle of nowhere, but not nigh to Jerusalem."

She lowered her head, sighed and nodded.

"I will be good."

He took her into his arms.

"What else could you ever be?"

And so, for the first time in over a year-and-a-half, Merovee returned to the house in Bethany . . . domain of the iron-minded Martha.

But Deborah, too, awaited her, having been escorted south by Old Jesse.

"So. You and my husband planned this in advance," Merovee accused.

"He is perfectly correct to make you sit for a while, Miriam. Never fear, it takes more than two months of sitting to grow roots, so you can be on your way again soon after the Passing Over."

Bethany was less than two miles southeast of the walls of Jerusalem, a suburb, actually, much of it wealthy. With no commercial enterprises or markets to speak of, the town was a place of peace and of quiet.

Many of the homes were grand, upon two or three acres, each enclosed by a high wall, which feature afforded the residents an unusual degree of privacy. Within the walls were manicured gardens, of flowers, but also of vegetables and fruit trees, and there were shade trees for respite during the notorious heat of Jerusalem summers. There was shade also behind massive boulders, which might have been scattered about the landscape by capricious gods, and in cool grottos as well, in the rocky cliffs and outcrops around which all must be built in this part of Judeah.

Most of the wealthy homes also included that feature which only the very rich could afford, a private family tomb, dug deep into one of those rocky outcrops.

Such tombs were composed of two rooms. In the first room, the newly dead were lain—wrapped in their linen, steeped in their spices—upon stone shelves, there to stay until they moldered away to nothing but bones. At that point, their bodies were reverently removed from their wrappings, the bones packed into an urn, and moved into the back room, to rest among the urns of generations of forebears.

The doors of such tombs were commonly sealed by a tall, flat, round stone, set vertically, and rolled over the entrance. The stone over the entrance of the garden tomb of the house bar Jeremiah was one such, beautifully carved with a geometric design. It was nearly five hundred years old. It had been there since the return from Babylon. That was how long the family of Deborah's husband had occupied this site, and how many centuries of urns were packed into that second room.

Who knew? Among the urns might be the bones of one of the geniuses who had "discovered" the Five Books of Moses in the Temple.

The house bar Jeremiah was also typical of the riches of old priestly families—those who had clawed their way to the top, who had played politics, and used their many advantages to lay up great fortunes. Begun humbly after the return, each generation had added to the structure. Its current size and opulence was in surprising contrast to the house in Magdala, the farm at Kapher Kana, or to the home of Joseph and Rosula in Bethlehem. Yet the riches of the House of Nathan, or of Joseph bar Ramathea, could each have bought and sold the riches of Jeremiah's family ten times over.

So telling, thought Jesus, as he entered through the gates and saw that mansion for the first time, the differing ways in which people chose to display their riches. He could understand now why Merovee had left it, and why Deborah escaped to Migdal any time that she could.

Yet he did not find this near-palace in Bethany unpleasant. As a matter of fact, it would do very well.

On the first night of their return, which was at the full moon, Ruthie and Pharisee were roused yet again from their stalls, and Jesus and Merovee rode out to Bethabarah. Merovee had suddenly just taken it into her head, and would have it no other way. It seemed only right, after all, now that she must be shut away in order to bring Johannan's child to full bloom, that she first take herself and her full belly as close to him as possible, and show herself to him so that he could know, and be happy.

Of course he already did know. He did not have to "see" her, she knew that. Still, she needed to go to him, as for a benediction, and she wanted to show Josh where they had put him, and hear him exclaim at the perfection of the site, the solid way in which they had piled the stones, and the secure manner in which the Prophet slept.

Perhaps she was getting crotchety in her pregnancy for all of this to suddenly mean so much.

After Jesus had made the required inspection and voiced the proper appreciation, he took the quilts, and Johannan's sheepskins that had been brought along, and made them a bed beside the tomb. They laid down and watched the moon and talked. Merovee cried often. Finally they slept.

When they woke, daylight was approaching. They packed up and returned to Bethany, Merovee silent and more docile than Jesus had ever seen her. Upon arrival, she dispatched Jesus and Lazarus to the bazaar of Jerusalem with a list of requirements. They returned laden with fine Egyptian linens and cottons, with homespun and good wools, with threads and needles. Sitting herself down, Merovee commenced to sew upon tiny garments for Johannan's son.

* * *

There could be no doubt about it. At first sight, approaching from the east, the Temple of Jerusalem seemed the most awe-inspiring edifice ever constructed by man. Jesus marveled at it yet again, as he always did upon approaching that monolithic sprawl atop the great rock called Mount Moriah. Second-best—after first-best, which was murdering disrespectful relatives—Herod the Great had loved to build. He had excelled in both lines of endeavor.

And how perfectly Herod, with so little Hebrew blood, had yet captured the spiritual essence of his subjects in his architecture. Even though not yet totally finished, Herod's Temple was a declarative statement.

It had been purposely placed on the edge of a chasm, so that the steep grade that fell away outside its eastern wall, hundreds of feet into the Vale of Kedron, seemed a part of the walls themselves. The effect was of a structure more immense than anything that even the Egyptians had managed.

Yet that was all it was. Effect. Subterfuge . . . like the machinations of the priests, and the lies as to what the Temple, itself, contained.

The majesty was in the hillside, not the buildings at the top. The walls which surrounded those buildings were thick, square, angular. Scarcely a curved line graced any part of that geometric sprawl, or of the buildings within, save in the rounds of supporting columns and their capitals, which rounds, amid such unremitting austerity, seemed not to be round at all, but only more sternly, more perfectly, squared.

The shrine, itself, the building that housed the Holy of Holies and the Ark of the Covenant, was an ungainly cube, slightly taller than square, and top-heavy with gold decoration. Its walls were white where not clad with gold. There was nothing to commend it save overstated monolithicism. It had once supported a breath-taking spire—or almost supported it—a spire as tall as the spire of Solomon's temple was supposed to have been. But it had collapsed while being built. Despite good intentions, it had never been rebuilt.

The Temple of Jerusalem was, thus, a perfect bastion, an accurate statement, in mortar and stone, of what the priests and scribes had made of the Five Books of Moses and the Law therein. Deceitful in its majesty, stern and unimaginative, unforgiving, ungiving, unloving, unliving.

Nowhere was there a soaring line, leading up, out and away, no hint that this symbol was capable of growth.

No. Herod's Temple was capable of nothing but a sordid squatting within, a contemplation of, its own squared self. Like anything that inflexible, it would eventually destroy its own self.

Sinking easily down two conscious levels, and even as he strode along with some of his followers, Jesus mentally entered another dimension, and looked at that same cliff from a viewpoint that was forty years into the future.

The Temple was gone.

How difficult it was for people to believe him when he said that not one stone of that Temple would be left sitting upon another. It was inconceivable to most minds that something that huge, that solid, that important, that "sacred," that "eternal," could simply cease to be.

How little they understood the nature of the true god. Why could they not see that All That Is was change, that it would, must, destroy anything that sought to imprison it, restrain it, keep it from the growth and change—from the death and rebirth—that was essential to its continued life?

In the place where Jesus had gone, he suddenly sensed another presence. He slipped back up to his ordinary level of consciousness and glanced at Yeshuah, walking beside him. There were tears in Yeshuah's eyes.

"You see it, too," said Jesus simply.

"Yes."

"Do not grieve, Man. Rejoice. This place has become a place of stagnation, of spiritual death for our people. To this place the priests bid our people endlessly come, to slay their small animals and commit their slow, spiritual suicide. There can be greatness ahead for our people, Yeshuah. But they will never find it until they have turned their backs on the Temple. The Temple must be destroyed, so that our people can go free.

"This is the seat of God on Earth!"

"It is one seat of the true god. One hill, one rock, one exceedingly dull group of buildings. Do you not see what you are saying, Yeshuah? Why do you insist upon imprisoning, upon limiting, your god? Why do you insist that 'he' can be seated nowhere but here? You are free to wander every hill on this Earth. If you so desired, you could visit a different hill every day of your life. Or a different valley, or town, or country, or people. Why—out of what arrogance—do you make your freedoms greater than those of your god?

"Yeshuah, do you believe in your god's commandments?"

"Of course."

"All right then, I will couch it in those terms. Did not your god command our people to have no false gods? Did 'he' not forbid them to make for themselves graven images?"

"Of course he did. Get to the point."

"The point is that that 'commandment,' that pure and real inspiration received by some Hebrew of old, has been wrongly and most grievously interpreted. The pure message said simply that the true god is All That Is. All That Is is everywhere and everything. 'I Am That I Am.' I am that, and that, and that, and that. I am. The 'commandment' did not seek to keep us from artistically picturing anything and everything, but, to save us from just such a mistake as we see here before us. It sought to guard us from imprisoning our god, and our thinking, in one place, or in one object, or sort of object."

"How can that be so when God commanded us to build an ark to house him?"

"God did not command that, Yeshuah. The narrow thinking of men, unable to deal with the magnitude of the truth that had been given, unable to deal with the multiplicity of All That Is, commanded that a simple, understandable, manageable box should be built and that the people should be told that it contained god.

"Then jealous, ambitious men, seeking to keep that god as their own special property, and as a guarantee for victorious conquest, commanded that the god should be kept in that box and never allowed to escape. To guard against any accidental escape, they put it about that 'God' would strike dead any man who dared to touch his box.

"Then greedy men, seeing the advantage of controlling access to that box, further encouraged the people's worship of it, and built a great Temple in which to house it . . . and also, by the by, to hide it.

"So that they gained absolute control of 'God,' a monopoly on his services, and they are now able to charge us an 'admission fee' to come and worship 'God' in a box we are not even allowed to see, while they claim for themselves the right to speak for 'God'—denying the voice of the true god All That Is within our own hearts—and they claim the right to withdraw or bestow 'his' favors at whim.

"Be ware, Yeshuah. Always be ware of those who, for whatever reason, put their gods in boxes of whatever nature, and demand payment from their fellows for allowing them the privilege of worshiping those boxes.

"I mean think about it, Man. Really think. If you do think, you have got to realize that this is the most ridiculous notion in the world! Keep the true god in a box?

"Can you really imagine it? All That Is. I Am That I Am. Asking to live in a box? Being content in there forever?

"I wonder what 'he' does with 'himself' all day besides twirl 'his' thumbs and count 'his' toes? Well, since 'he' does not have a woman, I suppose 'he' probably . . . "

"Stop! What blasphemy!"

The laughter of Jesus rippled out into the bright spring sunlight.

"Do you really hold your god to be such a boring, second-rate humanoid creature, Yeshuah? For, if you do, as far as I am concerned, you are the blasphemer, not I.

"A true blasphemy against the true god is to believe that it is such a pitiful and limited creature that it desires a box in which to contain itself, or could be so contained.

"A true blasphemy is to allow priests to imprison our god, and so our own Spirits.

"And I tell you, Yeshuah, that the Temple, itself, is a false god. The Temple is a graven image . . . that our people are enjoined to worship! Have you never seen that?

"Our misinterpretation of the 'commandment' deprived us of the right to vent our creativity in artistic representations of either our god or nature. But that need is inborn in every living Spirit! Man *must* make creative representations of All That Is—and of the world which *is* All That Is—or die. Literally die.

"And so we have made the Temple our representation of our god on Earth, and we have put all our passions into yonder heap of stones, all our thought, all our creativity, convincing ourselves that our god is contained there and nowhere else. If that is not 'building a graven image,' I am at a loss to know how else you could explain it.

"And this graven image must be smashed, Yeshuah. Our people *must* be separated from the worship of this god in a box. They must be expelled from Jerusalem, some to wander even among the Gentiles. Else they will never learn that the true god is with them wherever they go, in each man or woman equally, in each plant, each animal, each speck of earth. Only when the flower of 'Israel' understands itself capable of thriving on any hillside, or in any little pot by any doorstep, will it finally bloom. If our people stay here, attached to this Temple, 'Israel' will die. It will become extinct upon the Earth and have no place in the memory of generations to come."

"I can not—I will not believe this."

Yeshuah's jaw worked painfully.

"Leave Jerusalem? Our people leave Jerusalem? Go out among Gentiles? *That* would be our spiritual death, Jesus."

There was a touch of Yeshuah's old arrogance in that last, a reminder to Jesus that he was simply being used. Poor Yeshuah.

Jesus laughed outright.

Yeshuah did not understand that he, Yeshuah, was the one being used.

"What is so funny?"

"Life," said Jesus. "Life is so funny. And quite wonderful."

"Life is a vale of tears."

"I am sorry that you find it so, are we both living in the same place? It must be your diet. Too many onions perhaps?"

The impossible happened. Yeshuah grinned.

Then he reddened, angry to have been lured into levity in a situation so serious.

"The prophesies must be fulfilled, Jesus. The Kingdom of God must come at the end of days, and that kingdom will be in Jerusalem. A kingdom founded and ruled by Jews, a Nation of Priests, who will then guide the Gentiles to a knowledge and love of the one true God."

Jesus shrugged.

"Have it your way. As I just told you, it will be the end of days, at least for Jews, if they stay here in Jerusalem worshiping their Temple. But if you really want to show your god that you love him, Yeshuah, I promise, your best first move would be to let him out of his box."

The stream of Sabbath worshipers approaching by way of the Bethany road swelled as it joined the local traffic in the Vale of Kedron. Slowly, the multitudes snaked up the steep paths which ascended to the Temple from out of that valley—up onto the Orphel, entering the city through the Horse Gate into the Street of the Cheesemakers, and thus to the Court of the Gentiles, or up the even steeper path that led to the Golden Gate directly in front of the main sanctuary.

The private amusement of Jesus increased. These same people would think it sinful to pick a nut from off of a tree and crack it open to feed themselves today. Yet they toiled, sweating, up this hill to the Temple, and never considered that 'work.'

The songs of the Levites could already be heard. Did it never occur to Jews that their god might become annoyed at having to listen to the same songs endlessly sung? And did they never stop to think of how boring it might become to be constantly worshiped?

The cries of beggars without the gates, the babble of learned conversations, the preaching of would-be prophets blended with the Levite song..

Then there were the cries of the animal sellers in the Court of the Gentiles. The jaw of Jesus grew tight.

Ah, it would serve no purpose to grow angry.

But that wretched smoke. Could the priests never get enough of burning flesh?

How he despised this place.

And what a hypocrite he was to come here.

Why was he here?

For the sake of appearances, that was why.

For 'safety's sake.'

Buying time. Oiling the waters. He must not jeopardize his mission.

Or was it really his time with Merovee that he wished to prolong, to keep safe, to guard?

In that case, why not simply leave Palestine, go to Athens, Rome. There were any number of places in which he could teach that would be infinitely more safe than . . .

And that would be turning his back on all he had come for, betraying the united, dreaming cry of the species that had summoned him, and caused him to quicken within the womb of a particular mother in a particular time and place.

It was the collective Jewish mind that he needed to metamorphosize. The mind of the Supreme Noachite . . . of the Builders of old, whose parts had so completely, and so ignominiously, forgotten their greatness under the chains of priestly dogma . . . the Noachites, the leaders, the very creators of the current experiment . . . and they knew it not.

Theirs were the minds with the qualities needed to carry his teachings forward.

While theirs were the minds which most needed his teachings, which needed to have their downward spiral into paralyzed, soulless, lifeless "perfection" halted.

Each day, the culture became more ruthlessly male. And, with their far-flung enclaves, the priests were busily, purposefully proselytizing, remaking the world in their god's male image.

Increasingly, the people were fixating on the physical world, and the manipulation of its goods, bound up in so many Laws concerning any object or event which they encountered that they could hardly take a free step along the street, much less have a thought of their own, while creative thought was equated with sin and disobedience to "God."

The creators had stamped out creativity itself! They had grown as rigid as the rocks whose symbols filled their Scripture, and whose bulk comprised their Temple. . . while, each day, the ability to love and to know that they were loved by the true god, which ability they supposed they had mastered so perfectly, drifted further out of their reach.

The march of the Temple's victorious, male god had to be halted. The God of the Jews was going to have to be killed . . . so that that god could be born again, in a gentler version of itself, one that remembered the female in its own nature.

Jesus smiled. Symbolically, once more, the supposedly mythical Samir would be called upon . . . to soften rock, make it light, malleable, amenable to the creative hand. But, this time, that bird would be used to physically and emotionally pull the Temple down, not to raise it up.

The Samir was about to rise again, to soften the unyielding rock that Israel, itself, had become.

And bar Ramathea, the son of the All-High Goddess, would be the one to resurrect that Gentling Bird of All That Is.

They approached the first great portal into the Court of the Gentiles and the throng of beggars crying for alms. The eyes of Jesus swept their ranks.

He stopped beside one man, touched his withered hand, spoke softly to him for a minute, and passed on.

Just at the last, he put a drachma into another outstretched hand.

"Why only those two?" said Judah.

"The first man is an honest fellow who has not been able to work at his trade since his hand atrophied. The second is dull-witted, so that no one will hire him."

"And the others?"

"Each has a pot of silver hidden away. Shed no tears."

They climbed the terraced staircase and entered the Court of the Gentiles. It was the largest of the Temple courts, the only portion of the Temple into which non-Jews were allowed. It was also the entrance most frequently used by Jewish women, for it led directly into the segregated Court of the Women, the only portion of the Temple where they were allowed to worship. Indeed, the Court of the Gentiles was the entry used by most everyone coming to the Temple, since it was here that the money-changers and the sellers of sacrificial animals were to be found.

The scene in that court was thus far from sanctimonious. Moneychangers shouted to newcomers entering the gate, each claiming that his were the best rates. Dove-sellers swung cages, each calling that his were the whitest, most perfect doves. A seller of goats shoved a tiny, bleating, white kid under the nose of Jesus.

"Come for a sin offering, Friend? Be sure to give God the best. He will surely forgive you if you give him this one. Newborn yesterday, feel the coat, like silk, no?"

The young goat-seller's eyes met those of Jesus. His patter froze on his lips.

He turned abruptly and went in search of a new client.

"It gets worse all the time," said Lazarus softly.

"We are each our own sort of hypocrite," muttered Jesus.

For such commerce, such "work," such activity on the Sabbath, was strictly against Mosaic Law. Yet, within the confines of the Temple, it was allowed.

Not everyone could bring his own dove or kid along, argued the priests. People had to get their sacrifices from somewhere. Likewise, foreign visitors had to be able to exchange their money—which bore graven images—for unadorned Jewish coins, so that the sacrifices could be purchased with un-idolatrous funds.

Of course no Jew could damn himself with this Sabbath commerce, so the priests sold concessions to Gentile merchants—at prices rumored to be equal to the ransom of kings. But this was also all right, said the priests, because the money was for God. That money disappeared, into the Temple, into, the people supposed, one of the bottomless vaults where God's sacred money, the Corban, was kept.

Into those vaults, along with the merchants' money, went the required dues and tithes from the Jewish communities of every town and city throughout the known world. These arrived daily, by the bags full, brought by delegations who made the duty trip once each year.

Then there were the tithes from the residents of Palestine, itself, and special gifts and offerings from worshipers.

Conveniently for the priests, since God's money could not of course be spent by anyone but God, there was no need for mere men ever to count it, for surely God took care of that himself. Should a few shekels fall through the cracks now and then, well, was that not God's own will? And what man would there be who would ever know?

Besides which, old Annas had joked to his son-in-law Caiaphas one day within the hearing of Joseph of Ramah . . .

'What does God need with money anyway?'

"Will you offer a sacrifice?" It was Petros at the elbow of Jesus.

"No."

A hypocrite he might be to have come to this place, but he would not add a useless murder to his errors.

"I wish to make a sacrifice," said Yeshuah. "Will that be offensive to you, Jesus?"

Behind him, Jesus heard bar Tolmei snort at such subservience.

"It is not for me to be offended by any of your actions, Yeshuah, it is you who must learn to be offended. It is you who will have to pay and pay, ad infinitum, for each little death that you purposely cause to occur, until you learn that you must not kill for selfish and frivolous reasons. So exercise the free will which All That Is accords to you. The rest of you as well."

Yeshuah hesitated. Then, not meeting the eyes of Jesus, he went off to select a dove. Bar Tolmei and his brothers, excepting Judah, followed.

"I, too, would not feel right unless I did," muttered Petros, and he followed the others.

Jesus lifted an inquiring brow.

"Anyone else? Jairus?"

The Ruler of the Synagogue of Kapher Nahum shook his head.

"A man who has seen his daughter raised from the dead would be a fool not to trust the man who did the raising. I will kill no more animals in an attempt to smooth my own path to God. I will manage it all within myself, or bear my own consequences."

Jesus smiled.

"Anyone else care to make a sacrifice?"

There was no one. So Jesus led them to an empty position along the great gallery called the Porch of Solomon, which ran along the eastern wall. Micah prepared his writing materials. Jesus began quietly to teach.

As he taught, men strolled by, listened for a moment, and either stayed or moved on. It was Jerusalem's great Sabbath sport. to come to the Porch of Solomon and hear the diversity of speakers.

To the right of Jesus, a young man was arguing that the manna which God had supplied to the Hebrews in the wilderness had, in fact, been mushrooms, of an especially nutritious sort no longer extant upon the face of the Earth.

On the left, a grey-beard was thoughtfully proposing that the seven days during which God had created the Earth and then rested should be understood symbolically. The old man had done careful computations, and he reckoned that seven thousand days was the more likely figure.

Another man was speaking out against the wearing of tefillin. "God between the eyes" was meant to be a tattoo, he claimed, and that had been the true mark of Cain.

Beyond him, a man with wild hair and wilder eyes was drawing a sizable crowd. He had just come from The Wilderness of Judeah, where he had fasted and prayed for forty days and forty nights. He had seen visions of the end of the world. The destruction of Jerusalem would take place in just forty weeks. There was no time to spare, they must send word throughout the land and over the seas, inviting all children of Israel to hurry to this place, to await the arrival of God and his angels.

All this speculation, this questioning, was permitted, encouraged. Indeed, it was demanded of all pious Hebrew males that they constantly study, consider and interpret Scripture. It kept them busy—and also dizzy Jesus had often thought—so that they failed to notice that they but walked round and round in exactly the same circles. Circles prescribed by the priests.

The thing that no man ever did in this Temple court was to question the basic "God-given" validity of any part of Torah and its Laws, or of Scripture. For that would be sin and disobedience to "God," punishable by immediate death by stoning.

Jesus spoke that day of Love, of the need to love every person upon the face of the Earth equally with one's own self. And he explained the trap in that statement.

"For if you do not love your self, but, instead, hate and despise and punish yourself as do most people, and then love all others in that same way, I think they would rather you would go back to hating them.

"The key then is, first—learn to know your self. Learn to understand your self. For Love does not, *can*not happen, without Knowing, without Understanding.

"Because Love cannot happen until you forgive, and you cannot forgive until you know and understand.

"So that should be your first step upon the road to the Kingdom of God, my friends. Indeed, it is the only first step that can ever get you to that place.

"Love, and so the true god, cannot be found—not ever—until you become brave enough to take that step. Inward. Into your self . . . to remain for a million years if that be the length of time it takes you to know, understand, forgive, and so love your self, and so your Self, and so find the capacity to love the true god and Humankind as well."

It was edging close to the line, he knew, to speak of forgiving one's own self—to speak of learning to love one's own self before one loved "God." But lines had to be approached and walked, else he could never teach what he must. The crowd around him increased as those who stopped to sample his speech scented the subtle controversy.

There were no women among them, for women were encouraged to stop and listen to the philosophical disputations of the men no more than they were allowed to study Scripture. Such endeavors could not be allowed the daughters of Chavvah, the temptress of Eden. It was mete only that a woman should pass quickly and humbly through the Court of the Gentiles into her own segregated court, make sacrifice to purify her unclean and sinful state, then humbly leave. In synagogues, women were allowed to peek through the screens and see and hear the men in disputation, but not so in the Temple . . . which effectively dampened the enthusiasm of all but members of the pious Ladies' League of Jerusalem to go to the Temple on the Sabbath. Women came mostly upon festival days, or on weekdays, to be cleansed and then to make the required purification offerings demanded by The Law after each menses, after the birth of each child, after having been made unclean by carrion, or in any of the hundred other ways that a Jew could be sullied. Hence, none of the women among the followers of Jesus had cared to make the trip today. Even Mother Meraiah had been content to observe the Sabbath from her bed, having developed a cold as excuse.

What a shame, thought Jesus as he spoke. At Johannan's campfire, he had told Simon Yeshuah that if Heaven were without women he would not care to go there. He had been serious. The semi-circle of faces regarding him was, indeed, only half a circle without the softness of a female here and there.

. . . and without that one face in particular.

The day was so warm, the first day of real spring that they had had. What a waste to be without her, what a sadness to be deprived of sharing.

Would he ever again think time anything but wasted if Merovee were not with him?

He saw the faces leaning closer, straining to hear, and realized how his voice had softened. What would they think, these paragons of maleness, if they could read his mind as he could so often read theirs?

That Pharisee with the absurdly wide borders upon his garments, for instance, had been at the gate and seen him touch the man with the withered hand. He was beginning to put two and two together. Soon he would ask.

What would these "supreme images" of "God" think if they knew that he considered them to be only half complete on account of their rejection of the female?

"Pardon me," said the Pharisee with the wide borders. "But are you the rabbi who has been teaching in Galilee?"

"I am *a* rabbi who has been teaching in Galilee."

Jesus inclined his head toward Yeshuah, who had returned to his side after taking his dove to the Levites, silently asking if Yeshuah cared to be announced.

Yeshuah simply lowered his head and crossed him arms.

The listeners were murmuring. Some slipped out of the circle and ran to find friends and drag them over.

"Then you claim to be a healer," said the Pharisee.

"I do not claim to be a healer. I but facilitate healing."

"Why did you touch that beggar's hand as you passed through the gate?"

Jesus knew that additional saliva sprang forth into the Pharisee's mouth as he spoke.

"Did you heal the beggar?" said the Pharisee.

It was all that Jesus could do to keep the disgust from off of his face.

Did you heal on the Sabbath? was actually what this "saint" of "God" meant to ask. *Did you violate God's holy ordinance by helping a fellow human being on God's holy day?*

"No. I did not heal him."

"Then why did you touch him? And what did you say to him?"

"I said the words he most needed to hear in this world, for he believes that he is afflicted because of his sins. I told him that his sins are forgiven."

"You did what?" The Pharisee was honestly aghast. "It is one thing to speak of forgiving one's own self. Surely you make a point in that matter, for, if we will not try occasionally to forgive ourselves, then we can never sense when God has already done so."

"Exactly!" said Jesus. "You have answered your own question most masterfully."

The Pharisee frowned, liking the compliment, but still scenting blood.

"But by what authority do you presume to forgive the sins of others? Only God can do that."

"And where does your god dwell?"

"Here, in this sacred place."

"Do you then deny Scripture which states that your god dwells in the hearts of Humankind and so speaks to us from out of our hearts?"

"I do not deny that God sometimes chooses that method of speaking to Man."

"Good! Then we are in complete accord! For, as I was climbing the hill from out of the Vale of Kedron, I suddenly, in my heart, began to hear the voice of my god.

"'Jesus,' I heard, 'when you reach the gate of the Temple, you will see a beggar with a shriveled arm. The man is in great pain because he blames himself for an injury he did to his brother's hand when only a boy. So relentlessly did he blame himself over the years, that his own thoughts finally caused his own hand to shrivel in retribution, so that he could no longer earn a living, and his wife and children have returned to her parents to live on their charity, and he is cast down into the dust as he believes that he should be.

"'And the thing is, Jesus, that that brother's injury was the best thing that ever happened to the brother. That boy reached great heights of spiritual understanding in struggling to overcome his handicap and to rebuild his damaged muscles. With his Understanding, came Forgiveness, and Love, so that he truly loved his brother and completely forgave him, as did I.

"'Unfortunately for this beggar man, though, the brother, having understood so much in so short a time, and having accomplished exactly what he had come into this life to learn, died young. Before he died, he did tell our beggar man that he loved him and forgave him, but the beggar man—Malachi is his name—would not believe it.

"'Jesus, I tell you, I have been trying to get through to this man for years. I have grown hoarse, shouting at him from out of his heart, *You are forgiven, Malachi!* I simply cannot make myself heard above the din of his own constant shouting at himself, *You are guilty, Malachi, Guilt-guilt-guilty!*

"'And so, Jesus, I would take it kindly if you would just stop as you walk by him, and tell him what I have told you, and ask him please to stop shouting at himself for just a minute and listen for my voice, so that I can finally make him know that his sins are forgiven.'"

Throughout this pleasant and guileless speech, the Pharisee's mouth had hung slightly agape.

"God told you all that as you climbed the slope?"

"Yes, my god did." Jesus smiled brightly. "And it made the climb a lot less like *work,* I can certainly tell you. But tell me, Pharisee, do you think I did wrong in obeying my god's direct command, and whispering to Malachi to give his god a chance?"

The Pharisee reddened. It struck Jesus that the red went nicely with the spotless white of his robe, and the rich blue of its borders.

But the Pharisee's befuddlement, hence the spectacular red, lasted only a moment.

"Yes!" he said. "You did do wrong. You did evil. For you were deceived. It could not have been God who spoke to you, it had to have been the Prince of Darkness."

"How so?"

"Because this is God's day of rest. He would never conduct his business on the Sabbath, or tempt you to do so."

There was a beautiful cliff down the peninsula from Athens, at Sounion. The Greeks had erected a temple to Poseidon upon its crest. The grass was lush. Tiny, red field poppies grew by the tens of thousands. While the Aegean, at the foot of that cliff, was the most magnificent blue that Jesus had ever seen. How lovely it would be to go there with Merovee and the child. To sit on that bejeweled slope, day after day, and teach to one who understood.

"You agree then," said the Pharisee.

"What?"

"You have no answer for me. So you agree that, as God rests on the Sabbath, it had to have been the Prince of Darkness, and not God, who you heard."

370

"Well, it certainly is a creative theory. Let me see if I understand you correctly. Your god does not conduct business on the Sabbath."

"Absolutely none."

"Then why are we all here at the Temple today if our god cannot be reached?"

"Oh, God listens, he simply does not speak."

"Is that because listening is less like work than speaking?"

"Well of course. Listening is passive, talking is active."

"How strange," said Jesus pleasantly. "I know some people who listen actively and others who talk passively, running off at the mouth with all the thought of streams tumbling downhill.

"Well, in any case, all voices that we hear on the Sabbath, then, are the voices of the Prince of Darkness."

"No, not all. Not ordinary human speech."

"But if speaking is such work that our god will not do it on the Sabbath, why then do we not remain silent and uncommunicative as well, since our god forbids us to work on the Sabbath?"

"Because God wants us to speak. He wants to hear our prayers and praise."

"Where is that written?"

"Well . . . I do not think that it is, not in so many words."

"Then, if it is not written, you are merely deciding this for yourself, are you not, Pharisee.

"And see into what a broil you have put yourself. For, you have told me that your god closes shop and refuses to communicate on the Sabbath. What that means, is that your god abdicates on the Sabbath. And who is the only one to whom your god could possibly abdicate? Satan. And so, according to you, Pharisee, the Sabbath belongs to Satan. According to you, the Sabbath is the day of Satan, and not of your god."

"That is not what I said!"

"It most certainly is. You have told me, and all these gathered, that your god will not, cannot ever, under any circumstances, be heard on the Sabbath. So you are telling us that a seventh part of each week belongs to Satan. Therefore, every thought we have, every idea, every whisper that comes to us on that seventh day, comes from Satan. Of necessity, then, since we are such imperfect, sinful creatures, and your god never interferes with Satan's actions on that day, every word that any of us speak on the Sabbath is *inspired* by Satan. Even the services of the priests here today . . . "

"Stop! I forbid you to go further with this!"

"You forbid or your master, Satan, forbids? Ho! I have caught you out, Satan. I see you shining in this Pharisee's eyes. You do not want it known that Sabbath services are your doing, do you? You seek to silence me."

"I will silence you! I will call the guard and have you taken to the High Priest!"

"When we get there, will you tell him your remarkable theory or will I have the fun of telling him what you said?"

"This is insane."

"Now you are talking sensibly. How *dare* you so demean the true god, Pharisee."

The Pharisee took a step backward, shocked by the sudden, cold anger in the words.

Jesus closed the distance, towering over him.

"How dare you think for one moment that it is wrong, a sin, a Satan-inspired act, to do good on the Sabbath! What man is there here who, if one of his sheep fell into a pit on the Sabbath, would not stretch forth his hand and pull the poor, frightened, thrashing creature out? And how much greater is a man than a sheep? I tell you that the Sabbath was made for Humankind, not Humankind for the Sabbath.

"Petros. Go to the gate. Bring the beggar, Malachi, here to me."

"Master, please," muttered Petros, nervous at the growing crowd, more Pharisees, priests, and scribes among them.

"Judah, Petros is exhausted from the work of his climb. Fetch me Malachi if you please."

Jesus had said all of this without taking his gaze from the Pharisee's face.

"Woe betide you, Pharisee," he said as Judah slipped away. "Hypocrite! Tell us why the borders of your garments are so wide."

"To show my devotion to God, of course."

"Of course? What is of course about it? Think you the true god is so childish as to be flattered by the width of your pretty blue borders, when you believe that goodness done on 'his' day is evil?

"What is the true god if not Goodness and Love? And so what should we do upon 'his' day if not good and loving things?

"Would you prefer evil, Pharisee? You obviously do. For I tell you that, to see a kindness or an act of love that can be done, and block the impulse to do it, no matter what the day, is evil.

"And doubly evil on the Sabbath since that is the day dedicated to our lord of Love and of Goodness.

"Woe betide you, all of you, Pharisees, scribes, priests, hypocrites. You sit yourselves down in the seat of Moses, and presume to dispense The Law.

"Yet I say to honest men, take care to observe those things which these hypocrites direct you to observe, so that they cannot take you out and stone you. But do not do after their works.

"For they say—and do not. They invent heavy, moral burdens, and lay them on your shoulders, while they content themselves with ever wider borders, and think the true god to be as moronically content as they. Their phylacteries grow so broad that they stretch almost from ear to ear. Which is well, for this hides the emptiness in their eyes. They demand the uppermost rooms at feasts, and the highest seats of the synagogue, so that all should know of their holiness, and bow down to them. And, from the heights which they so hypocritically claim as their own, they presume to look down and judge their fellows.

"Woe unto you, hypocrites! You shut your god up in a box and keep your fellow beings from entering 'his' kingdom, entering not into it yourselves, and destroying those who would honestly try.

"You devour the houses of poor widows, purchasing them for not one-hundredth of their worths, while hiding your evil with long, pious prayers for those poor women.

"Woe to you, Pharisees, priests, scribes, you hypocrites. You have littered the known world with your settlements, which proselytize any who they can, the better to fill the coffers of the Temple.

"And what you teach the convert fills him with a greater lack of understanding than ever he had before.

"You blind guides! You even now presume to tamper with the injunction to make no oaths. I hear that some chicken-brain over at the House of Shammai has decreed that it is not sinful to swear an oath by the Temple, but, should one swear an oath by the Corban, that man becomes a debtor, and must forfeit all his gold to further swell 'God's Money.'

"Idiocy!

"What should be greater, a pile of gold or the Temple that supposedly sanctifies that gold?

"That same great thinker has declared that it is not sinful to swear by the altar of the Temple. But, if one swears by the gift that is laid onto that altar, one must forfeit yet more gold to the Corban.

"Our thinker seems fixated upon swelling the Corban at the expense of all else!

"Which is greater, I ask you, the gift or the altar that supposedly sanctifies the gift? If one swears by the altar, does it not stand to reason that one swears by it and all that is upon it? If one swears by the Temple, does it not stand to reason that one also swears by all that is in the Temple including the Corban?"

His eyes met those of a scribe, who he knew to be the Baruch, the secretary of Annas.

He should stop himself. Now. He might already have gone too far.

And he had meant to be so unobtrusive, so good, so obedient today. He had meant to make hardly a ripple as he oiled the Temple waters. What was it he had told Merovee as he convinced her to come nigh to Jerusalem? He had said that he must appear to do all the things that a good Jew should do, and give the authorities of the Temple no cause for complaint.

But he was sailing. Really sailing. And it felt so good!

So he smiled broadly at Baruch.

"If the Corban *is* still in the Temple, that is."

He returned his gaze to the people in general.

"Likewise, I hear that it is all right now to swear by Heaven, though it is still not right to swear by your god. I tell you that he who swears by Heaven swears by the throne that he supposes to be there, and the god that he supposes to be sitting upon it."

Some people had ingeniously hired the stools of money-lenders and sellers of animals, and were standing upon them, the better to see. Levite guards had shouldered into the crowd and were waiting, should Baruch give the signal to break things up.

Jesus heard his voice rising. So that even the god on that imaginary throne directly over the Holy of Holies might hear him.

"*Woe* unto you, Pharisees, priests, scribes, *hypocrites*! You blind guides who strain at gnats and swallow camels, teaching your followers to do the same . . . who pick at nits and, paying no heed, walk off the cliff, into the abyss, calling to your followers to hurry after you, lest you all be late for your appointment in Heaven.

"How carefully you Pharisees measure out your tithes of mint, anise, and cumin, while ignoring the real point of The Law. Justice, mercy, faith! Do those duties first. Be just, be merciful, have faith—faith that your god will return these things to you ten-fold. Then, and only then, should you worry about measuring out just the correct amount of herbs to please the priests.

"You make clean the outsides of the cup and bowl while leaving what is within full of extortion and excess. You deck yourselves as though whited sepulchers, all beautiful on the outside, while inside is moldering and rot, and a horrid, foul smell. You build tombs to honor prophets, and decorate the sepulchers of the righteous, while murmuring to yourselves that, had you lived in the days of those great men, you would not have helped to spill their blood.

"And yet, only months ago, you caused to be put to death the greatest teacher who has yet come amongst you."

The crowd burst into tumult.

"We of the Temple had nothing to do with Johannan's death!" shouted Baruch.

"Then what were you, yourself, doing in Machaerus just hours before he died?" Jesus shot back. "Why were you there, along with scores of priests, and scribes, and Levites? And with Zakiah from the House of Shammai?"

"It was the wickedness of Salome and Herodias that had him killed."

"Baruch, how long does it take to travel from Machaerus to the Temple."

"The better part of a day."

"Then how was the fact of the Prophet's death, and its manner, known in the priests' robing room of the Temple less than five hours after it occurred?"

A hush stole over the crowd. As one, the spectators turned and stared at Baruch.

Baruch's eyes fastened malevolently upon Lazarus, there beside Jesus.

"Whoever told you such a thing was mistaken," he said.

"Add not public lying to your shame, Scribe," said Jesus gently.

The crowd was parting, admitting Judah with the beggar man, Malachi.

Seeing Jesus, Malachi hastened forward.

"You wonderful man. Thank you! Thank you for your words. I listened, just as you said. And I did hear God. He *has* forgiven me, is it not wonderful!"

"It is indeed. And would you now like to be healed of your affliction?"

The murmuring again.

"Oh. Well, it would be nice," said Malachi, "but of course there is no way."

"Do you believe that the true god has forgiven you?"

"How could I not, when he has just told me so himself?"

"And do you forgive yourself?"

"If God has taken all this trouble to let me know of his forgiveness, who am I to hang onto the guilt for a single moment longer?"

Jesus raised a finger, and pointed it directly at the Pharisee.

"I see a kindness that may be done here. So I ask you one thing. Is it Lawful on the Sabbath to do good? Or should one eschew good, and so, by default, do evil? Name it, Pharisee. Tell me, if you dare, that it is not Lawful to do good on the Sabbath."

"Surely you do not really intend to try to heal him," said the Pharisee, honestly perturbed. "Well, I do not know! I just do not know. Healing could be considered work, you see, or the trying to heal, even if you are not successful. Really, you must not proceed! You must consult a master, for I am not sure just how to judge this matter."

With all his heart at that moment, Jesus wished to punch the Pharisee squarely upon his uplifted nose.

In his mind's eye, he felt his fist connect, saw the blood spurt, and he smiled.

"If you can not decide how to judge, why not try loving instead, Pharisee? My question is so simple, I cannot see why you hesitate. Or you, Baruch. Is it unLawful to do good on the Sabbath?"

Both men stood speechless. There was no way that they could answer "yes" to the question, yet neither wished to answer "no," and so go on record as having sanctioned a healing in Temple court on the Sabbath.

Jesus waited hopefully.

Then he shook his head and sighed.

"There is yet something else you should know, my friends. The kingdom of the true god is only for the courageous. No coward has ever yet gained admittance."

He reached out.

"Give me your hand, Malachi."

As one man, the watchers leaned forward, eyes fastened on that withered claw. The atrophy had traveled up through the wrist and halfway to the elbow. Bones, covered with hard, brown, seemingly mummified flesh, were all that was left.

Jesus smiled at Malachi, asked him what his god's voice had sounded like. Had it been loud or had it been soft? What had been the exact words spoken? What had Malachi answered?

As they talked, Jesus massaged the hand and arm almost absentmindedly, as though the touch were of no importance.

Only gradually did watchers realize that the hand was changing before their eyes . . . filling out, turning pink.

In the front rank, an old man began to cry, sinking slowly to his knees. Around the Court of Solomon, the other speakers were stilled, come with their own audiences, drawn by invisible strings. Had the Temple been a ship, it would have capsized, as its passengers crowded toward that eastern wall. Those in the front passed hushed whispers of what was happening back through the ranks, till all those present knew, even though they could not see, that the rabbi from Galilee was healing Malachi the beggar. Successfully.

As he worked, Jesus spoke softly to his disciples, and to Yeshuah in particular, which man leaned close, watching carefully.

"This sort of healing must always to be done slowly. The body has rights, and a consciousness of its own. It should not be shocked. This flesh has been shriveled a long time. And, though its natural bent is toward health, it has faithfully followed the dictates of Malachi's mind.

"Now we give it a moment to accustom itself to this change in Malachi's thinking, and so to the new directive. The body is singing with happiness at Malachi's decision, but still we must let it respond and begin to draw the life back into itself at its own pace.

"No big spurts of The Energy. Hold it off. Keep it steady. Watch the color, and see that the withered portions expand uniformly.

"And Love as you do all this. Love your Self as you heal. Love the world. Love the man. Love his flesh. Love the true god All That Is.

"This will be a lasting cure. For Malachi has heard the voice of All That Is with his own inner senses. He knows that he is forgiven by All That Is, and he has forgiven his own self as well.

"Since he has forgiven his own self, he can now truly begin to Love. He is going to return today's gift to the world by loving that world, and everything in it, for the rest of his days. Is that not so, Malachi?"

Malachi was watching his hand with fascinated detachment, exclaiming and commenting like any other spectator, as the tissues and veins expanded and filled with blood once more.

"My wife will be so happy. And her parents . . . they have been very good to her and the children. I will care for them now, so that they can end their days in ease. And I will go into the street every day, and tell people of this. I will tell them not to be arrogant, as I was. Yes, arrogant . . . to have been so unforgiving of my own self, to have talked so loudly to myself of my own guilt, so that God could not make himself heard. I can feel it in my heart as well, Jesus. I have felt it since you first you spoke to me, and touched me out at the gate."

"What do you feel?" It was Yeshuah asking.

Malachi looked at him quizzically.

"Why Love of course, just as Jesus says. That is what is filling my hand, can you not feel it as well? I never really felt it before. Funny, then, that I was able to recognize it immediately."'

Yeshuah looked almost as quizzical.

"What does it feel like?"

"Like . . . laughter. Like all of me wants to laugh. Yet I am crying. Is that not silly?"

Jesus taught no more that day. When Malachi's hand was whole, he gave the man five drachmas to see him to his in-laws' home in Hebron, and departed, the crowd making way respectfully.

"Which one is he?" some whispered.

"The tall one."

"The one with hair bleached fair."

"Which tall one?"

"Which fair one?"

"I am not sure."'

For Yeshuah walked on his right side, and Judah walked on his left, and many there were that day who mistook one for the other . . . and who would make the same mistake in the days to come.

Near the gate, the young goat-seller stood, the same white kid under his arm.

It was not really without blemish, not really pure white. And female at that. A second-rate offering, the last of the day, the continual reject. But someone would come along with not enough money to buy a first-rate kid, and pay him a copper or two. If not, he would toss it onto a dung-heap on the way home. It would not live out the day, he had bought it off a caravan driver the night before, minutes after its birth. It had had no sustenance, and was growing weaker by the moment.

He found himself edging forward as the healer approached. He knew which of the three men he was. For never would he forget those eyes when he had tried to sell him the kid as he had entered the court.

Just as Jesus passed, the kid lifted its head and gave a feeble bleat.

Jesus stopped, turned, looked down at the kid.

Hardly realizing what he did, the young man thrust it forward.

"Take it, Rabbi. It is really not fit for the altar, I would be cheating to sell it. Do with it as you will."

"I will be happy to pay you."

"You have already paid. I . . . know Malachi. We have talked often. I count him a friend, and I am happy for him this day. Take the kid. She would die soon, but you can make her live if you care to, and perhaps you could use an extra goat."

Jesus smiled and accepted the tiny creature. He held her, first, up to his face, seeming to breathe upon her. Then he settled her down into the crook of his arm, where she curled into a tiny ball and fell asleep.

"How do you know I can make her live?" he asked easily.

The young man was astonished to find his eyes filling with tears.

"There are things that one just knows."

Jesus stood stroking the tiny, white goat, his eyes bent upon the goat-seller. The man wore the garb of a Cyrenean Greek. The cloth was good, neat and clean as well.

"Since you are finished for the day, Alexander, why not make it your final day in this loathsome place? Why not make our little friend here your final sacrificial goat. Why not follow me?"

He turned, and went out through the gate.

The Pharisee was just leaving as well, a bloodstained cloth held to his nose.

"What is the trouble?" said Jesus.

"Just a bad nosebleed," was the terse reply.

"Oh! I am so sorry!"

"Why should you be sorry, it is not your fault," said the Pharisee, and he rushed off through the crowd.

"Wait!" called Jesus.

The Pharisee did not turn back.

"What is so funny?" said Lazarus.

Jesus shook his head.

"Red *is* nice with white and blue, is it not."

He headed for home then with eager strides. The tiny mite in his arms needed milk. And there would be Merovee. She will love the kid. Maybe Freckles would take to it as well.

Should he be ashamed of himself, or proud?

The day had certainly turned out differently than he had planned. By now, Baruch was in the salon of Annas, telling him all. And the Pharisee was on his way to the House of Shammai, nose-bleed and all.

Oh, he had made enemies this day. Bitter enemies. When his father heard of it, Hell might be a more pleasant place in which to hide than that man's presence.

So why was he laughing? Why did he feel so good?

The road to Bethany ascended between two hills, the crests of which were called, too grandly in relationship to their heights, the Mount of Olives and the Mount of Offense.

At the point where Jerusalem could last be seen before the road dipped downward into Bethany, Jesus turned, looking back at the Temple, and at the city.

For a moment, his joy turned to sadness.

"Oh Jerusalem. Jerusalem," he murmured. "You who killed your great teachers as soon as you were able once we were sent to you. How well I remember some of the stones, the knife thrusts. How often have I, and others like me, tried to gather you, as a hen gathers a chick in under a wing. And you would not have us.

"I think you still will not have us. However many more would come to you, those you would stone as well, or crucify, or scourge.

"So that the time of patience is nearing its end, Jerusalem.

"But go ahead. Bring yourself to desolation. Have it your own way. You always have."

For a moment, he felt defeated. The day had accomplished nothing.

Yet here came young Alexander, following after, not sure why, only sure that he must

Malachi was on the road south to Hebron, off to tell the world about Love.

There was Yeshuah, pondering on this latest demonstration of Love.

There was the kid, sleeping in his own arms, having, with its faint bleat, chosen life, rather than flames, or an inglorious end on a dung-heap.

And who knew how many others had been touched and changed that day?

"Jerusalem. There could yet be so much good in you.

"Perish you will. But may the best that ever was in you be saved. Like the spawn of shellfish, dormant in desert sands, may that good sleep. A thousand years. Two thousand. Then may the sweet rains come. May your good burst forth into new life that is Love. And may the whole Earth be fed on the Love that could flow from Jerusalem. Love, Jerusalem. Only Love can save you. Only Love can excuse you."

He realized that he had sunk to his knees. His friends gathered round, shocked. They had never before seen him on his knees. To anything.

"I will not forget you, Jerusalem. I will help you if you will let me."

He lowered his face into the fur of the sleeping kid and was silent for several long moments. Then he rose, smiling again. He turned, and his smile broadened.

For Merovee was hastening up the road toward them, the veiled figure of Salome at her side.

"I have brought milk!" called Merovee.

"Milk for what?" said Petros.

"The kid of course," grinned Lazarus, and he loped quickly off after Jesus.

* * *

"So *I* was to behave myself! I was to be the perfect wife and not get us into trouble," said Merovee when she found out what had happened.

The bearer of the news was Joseph, himself, arrived from Bethlehem as they broke their fast the next morning, so rapidly had word spread amongst the hierarchy. As expected, Joseph was furious.

"A wonder it is you were not arrested on the spot, you flap-mouthed, young fool!"

Jesus sat with head lowered, chastened before his father's wrath.

Yet he answered firmly.

"I was not arrested because I gave them no grounds for such action. At no point did I call The Law into question or disobey it."

"You cured a man on the Sabbath!"

"Tell me it is a sin to do good on the Sabbath."

"Do not split your hairs around me, Young Man. I care nothing for your fine arguments."

"But *they* do." It was Lazarus who dared to answer. "Joseph, he was magnificent. You should have seen their faces. They could not answer! Neither yea nor nay. And every common man in the crowd was for your son, I can tell you that."

"It is not the common man I care about, Lazarus. It is Annas and his crowd, and the Shammites."

"You *should* care about the common man," said Jesus softly.

"It is not they who will kill you!" cried Joseph.

"Please," said Jesus, putting an arm around Merovee. "You are upsetting her."

"*I* am upsetting her? I am not the one who has put her into prison. That is what you have done, can you not see it? You made fools of the rulers. You called their honesty into question. You even accused them of murder!

"And do not think that you have not plunged Didymus, here, into trouble as deep as your own. Baruch was quick to understand who had told you that the news of Johannan's death was known too early in the robing room. And Didymus they can get at even faster than you. I doubt not that he has already violated so many priestly Laws, trotting around the country after you, that they can take him at their leisure.

"You have signed the warrant on everyone whom you profess to love. The Temple will not rest now. Not until they do have grounds to arrest you. All of you. They will follow you everywhere that you go. In every crowd that gathers around you, there their spies will be, watching, waiting, baiting you. Until they trap you.

"Oh, Joshuah. Why did you do it?"

Jesus lifted his face.

"My poor father. What is Man that you fear him so? Tell me about the god that you profess to believe in. What does that god believe in? Anything? Did he put you here to do nothing but survive? Is there no reason to anything? No purpose? If there is not, why come into this life? Why struggle so hard to stay?

"I know that many of your Sadducean friends of the Sanhedrin believe that there is no purpose. They believe that what we are ceases to exist at death, as surely as does the flame of a candle engulfed by the sea.

"In so believing, they deny the testimony of their own hearts and impulses.

"The very persistence of life proclaims a purpose! Flowers know it, birds know it, ants know it. But we 'thinking' creatures, we with the greatest gift—that of reasoning minds—we cross our arms and demand to be convinced, to see proof . . . when that very proof, that we refuse to examine, is all about us every moment of every day.

"What is your purpose, Father? To sire children? You have already done that.

"To give them shelter and sustenance and raise them to adulthood? You have done that as well.

"To be a responsible member of the community? You have done that.

"So what? What is your purpose? Why should you go on? Why do you want to?

"Surely you must wonder. Surely something deep down inside tells you that there is purpose. Surely you long to learn what that purpose is. Surely some little voice must whisper that you have got to learn it. Or else truly perish.

"And that is the exact state of affairs, Father. Each time that you refrain from speaking the truth of what is in your heart and mind . . . each time that, just in order to stay 'alive,' you meekly surrender to others the right to own your body, your mind, your Soul—the right to direct your every action—you, in fact, die.

"Each time that you turn away from courageously searching for your purpose, you get 'deader,' and make the journey back to life that much harder.

"Each time that you cower in submission to the preferences of others, just to save your skin, or to be thought an 'obedient citizen,' you take a backward step away from the truth of why you are here, away from All That Is.

"The meek shall inherit the Earth, Father. And that is all that they shall inherit. Dirt and dust and temporal bodies or possessions, which wear out, grow ill, rot, or die. Repeated lives, repeated sufferings, repeated stupidities. Damnation. That shall be their lot.

"Until they find the spiritual courage to seek for their purpose, and be deterred by no man, no circumstance.

"Then, and only then, shall they leave the ranks of the damned, and enter into their true inheritance, which is the Kingdom of the Spirit . . . where one knows, not only, that life is everlasting, but why it is everlasting."

Jesus rose.

"You question my love for my family and my friends. Father. I tell you that, not to speak, not to show them the way to purpose, would be to withhold my love. I care for the continuance of their bodies, yes. But I know that true Life resides in a healthy *Spirit*, which is as independent of the body as you are independent of a chariot in which you ride for a distance.

"Should I, then, strive to preserve that chariot at the expense of the life of its occupant?

"You ask, why did I incur the enmity of the priests and Pharisees? I did it because it is part of my job. My reason. My purpose . . . to lead my fellows toward spiritual health.

"I did it because the time to do it had arrived.

"What thought you, that I would go on hiding in the provinces forever? No. I had to invite them to follow after me, and question me, and try to trap me.

"I have to invite a national focus.

"For I must bring our people face to face with an Idea.

"Which Idea is that there is something above The Law.

"Which something is Love."

"Then you went there yesterday planning to whip up a tempest?" said Joseph incredulously.

"Actually," grinned Jesus, "I went there to be a hypocrite. I went there prepared to put on a huge, false show and take my own step backward away from the Kingdom. I went prepared to play their game, by their rules, just in order to do what you so prize, and protect my wife and my friends and myself from bodily harm.

"But I could not do it. To be false is now so far from my nature as to be nearly impossible. What happened simply flowed. I was as surprised as anyone.

"But I do not deny the flow, Father. I learned eons ago to follow my own internal river of Impulse and Feeling. Done freely, joyously, and with love and understanding, one soon realizes that these Impulses and Feelings are All That Is, itself, speaking personally to or through each one of us, seeking to lead each of us toward our own greatest good—hence, automatically, toward the greatest good for the species.

"Did each of us follow our impulses as trustingly, each structuring our personal worlds based upon the voice of the true god that whispers to us unceasingly—rather than on rules and regulations and dogmas and social mores which seek to force all of us into the same mold—the Kingdom of Heaven would arrive on Earth tomorrow."

"What you speak of would be chaos," protested Joseph. "Every man running around, a law unto himself!"

"That is just the key. Every man *is* a law unto himself. That is what must finally be recognized. Father, do you believe in 'God'?"

"Of course I do!"

"Then why not give the god in which you believe a chance? Why not actively believe that that god cares for each of us, and would help us if we would allow it? Why not trust that god? Its voice. Its vision. Its personal suggestions, different for each and every man, woman, and child?

"Why not try to listen to the voice of your god above the voices of men?"

"It would be the breakdown of society."

"As we know it, yes. And would that be such a loss? What have we achieved with this fair society of ours? Not just us Jews, but every people, every nation on the face of the Earth?

"Order. Law. Men move about in carefully prescribed patterns, doing the things which an elect few—which other men—have decided that they should do.

"If they try to do something greater, or different, if they start listening to a higher authority, to the voice of the true god within, they are quickly ostracized or punished, sometimes imprisoned, even killed.

"Our way of thinking achieves nothing but riches and power for a select few, and slavery and continued misery for the masses. I do not care which country, which people, which government, which god. That is the end result.

"With these systems go unceasing war, unceasing hatred of one group or another, all manner of sicknesses—which always result when the natural Impulses sent by All That Is are denied and repressed—all manner of injustice, poverty . . . damnation.

"So what would Humankind have to lose by trying the experiment that I suggest, Father? Truly. Could the result be worse?"

"Yes! Much worse! People would run around killing and robbing. They would become animals. No decent person would be safe!"

"Is the current state of affairs any different?"

Jesus shook his head, his eyes sad.

"You have such little faith. And your assumption is that the core of each person is bad and animalistic.

"What an insult, by the way, to our lovely, natural, animal friends.

"Father, I tell you that people are intrinsically good. Left to their natural impulses, people are creatures of light and endless creativity.

"It is only when these natural impulses are blocked, when people are made to act unnaturally—counter to their pure, natural, individual flows—that they become 'bad.' It is the moral, social, and legal systems which we impose upon ourselves that are bad, not ourselves.

"'Father, I have already dwelt in the future. Many of them. Parts of me dwell in those futures now. Some futures are as bad as our own. Some worse.

"But there are other futures . . . ah, Father. If I could tell you the heights of greatness to which our species can, and will eventually, rise—no matter from what 'pasts' . . .

"But you have not the capacity to understand as yet."

Joseph stiffened, hurt to the quick that Jesus should think him in any way incapacitated.

"What nonsense you speak. Live in the future? If the future is already laid out, why worry about anything? When we get to that greatness, we will get there, and nothing can change that."

"That is where you are mistaken. You have heard me speak of simultaneous time, of past, present, and future existing at once."

"Pure idiocy."

Jesus smiled.

"In this probability, it will be one of our own, a Jew, who eventually 'discovers' principles which convince the world to seriously consider the notion of simultaneous time.

"Father, what we do right here now is effecting, and changing, all our pasts and all our futures.

"Consider this. If what I say is so, and time is simultaneous, then the Joseph that you think you are does in fact not exist. 'Joseph' is, instead, composed of millions, billions, endless trillions of moments of consciousness experienced by a master core or entity. Each moment, through that master core, is then intimately, instantly, in contact with each other moment in the 'bundle' that is the whole. What one moment does, learns, experiences, is instantly and automatically at the disposal of all the other moments, for them to use or not use as they please. Yet the interconnection goes further, for each entity is in contact with, and shares experience with, every other entity. All of Creation shares in each and every moment of every part of itself.

"So that each moment is precious beyond price . . . beyond rubies, or any of the riches which can be imagined.

"Had I acted the hypocrite in the Temple yesterday, I would have hurt, not only, my Self of the moment, but the Self in trillions of other moments that are 'I,' everything for which the core from which I spring, and that the 'I' that I am, has worked to achieve in all its pasts and all of its futures. All of Creation would also have been robbed.

"Each act, no matter how seemingly insignificant, has infinite repercussions, Father. Infinite. Worlds that you cannot even imagine are stirred by your every breath. New worlds are created by your every thought!

"Which is why you are well advised to make each moment, and each thought, the very best that you know possible.

"And I am come to tell people of even more 'better possibles.' What I do here, in this place, and in this 'time,' effects the whole of Creation, all of eternity.

"And the same goes for you. Joseph. You may believe me or not. I do not force myself. I only tell you. The rest is up to you. At every moment of every day, you have it in your power to improve all your yesterdays, all your tomorrows, hence, your present. By your actions right now, you can so improve your pasts that your present becomes better and your futures superlative, which will begin the process yet again, the even better pasts and more superlative futures reaching backward and forward, reaching out to all their other moments, and improving them as well.

"On the converse, you have it in your power to harm, not only, the Self of your moment, but the Selves of all your other eternal moments, by feeding them cowardice, rigidity, wastefulness, sloth, fear, hatred, callousness, thoughtlessness, and all things negative.

"All of which bounces right back upon you and your own present circumstances, making them worse, carrying you, and all that you are, throughout all your eternal moments, deeper into the pit.

"Those who speak of Hades, or Gehennah, or some punishing fire, have glimpsed this truth if only incompletely, and tried to convey the dangers of 'sin,' of missing the mark, to Humankind.

"Father, just . . . here . . . "

Jesus looked slightly down and to his right,

"Right where I am looking, there is a probability just like ours, in the same 'time' as are we. But, long ago, the people of that probability learned to be brave, and to listen to their internal voices. There is no way to describe them to you. You would not believe them. They have contrivances with which to fly, and they can send their voices, and their images, to any place in the world in seconds. But, more, they are working on the conscious creation of physical reality.

"Knowingly, each day, they create their own physical needs—food, shelter, whatever—with their minds. They have no need of governments, or 'authorities' to structure their lives, and so confine their thinking. They do not run around robbing and killing, because there is no need for such things. Anything a man wants, he can simply materialize, so that objects, and riches, are as nothing, and people reach out to the corners of their minds for new modes of expression. Their creativity knows no bounds. Many can already dematerialize their bodies and rematerialize them at other spots on Earth, or send their consciousnesses to the moon and beyond . . . "

Jesus looked closely at Joseph.

"We could have been those people, Father. We still can be. As each moment grows in understanding, that moment gets closer to its potentials.

"But we have a long way to go. And I am come to help us along the path.

"You can ask me to shirk my duty and turn aside from my purpose as much as you like, Joseph my Father. But I will not. I can not. All who join me know this. All who will eventually remain with me will do so because they accept my purpose and agree to carry that purpose forward. They will be as committed to the greater good as am I.

"I hope you will be one of those who are committed, Father, but I do not require it. I will understand if you turn away.

"You even have the right, under our Law, to declare me to the priests as a disrespectful and disobedient son and have me stoned to death. I will understand that, too."

Joseph seemed hard-pressed to find breath with which to speak.

"Think you I am as King Herod?" he managed. Then he remembered. "Excuse me, Salome."

"I take no offense."

"Joshuah. How could you think that I would turn away from you?"

"I do not think, or expect, one way or another, Father. The choice is yours and the choice is mine."

Joseph bowed his head. When he raised it, he was shaking with silent mirth.

"Did you really ask Baruch if the Corban is still in the Temple?"

Jesus smiled.

"In so many words."

"I do not suppose that he answered."

"No."

Joseph shook his head.

"Be patient with me, Joshuah. And just . . . be careful. Keep that fine chariot of yours as long as you can, eh? Good chariots are hard to find."

During the next weeks, to the relief of all—possibly even the rulers of the Temple—Jesus remained within the walls of the house at Bethany, quietly teaching his followers . . . which now included Herodias, who had returned from Tiberius to the Herodian Palace in Jerusalem on the pretext of waiting there for the return of Antipas from his war. After arriving there, however, and leaving Scota and her women to cover for her, she quietly removed to bar Jeremiah.

With her came a now-divorced Johannah.

"When I asked Chuzah to divorce me, he made out the writ so quickly that I knew not whether to be glad or insulted!" she laughed.

Five weeks before the Passover, it was told in the streets that Pontius Pilatus had arrived from Caesarea, to remain in Jerusalem till the end of the festival.

Within twenty-four hours of that news, Tribune Gallus arrived at the house bar Jeremiah, bearing a letter from Pilatus . . . asking that Merovee and Jesus be his guests for dinner that evening.

At the end of the message was one word, set apart and underscored.

Please.

Chapter 14

The Gentling Bird

The Hasmonaean Palace was antiquated by Roman standards. Even King Herod had forsaken it, building himself a fine new structure by the Corner Gate at the west of the city, which palace was now the Jerusalem town house of Antipas.

The old palace was, however, more comfortable for Procula than was the Antonia Fortress on the northwest wall of the Temple, palacial though the living accommodations in the Antonia were. Procula needed peace and quiet, something lacking at the Antonia, with the constant bustle and clang of six centuries of legionaries. The old palace was connected to the west side of the Temple by a raised private causeway, and then to the Antonia via a private tunnel. Pilatus and his personal guard could, thus, move back and forth between the palace and the fortress without going out into the streets of the city, or yet disturbing the Jews in their Temple courts. While, several days before the actual Passover, Pilatus and Procula would move to an apartment in the safety of the fortress, and stay there throughout Passover week. Should violence threaten in the meantime, Procula could be gotten over to the fortress in a matter of minutes.

For the Passover visits of Pilatus were not pleasure jaunts. His annual presence in the city, with six additional centuries of legionaries, was a police action, pure and simple. Because, during the Passover, much of the citizenry of Palestine, and Jews from enclaves throughout the civilized world, gravitated to Jerusalem like water seeking its level.

Would, Pilatus often thought when in a temper, that all the Jews would then disappear down a drain, into the caverns in Mount Moriah, which, fable said, reached to the very bowels of the Earth.

Not that he was expecting trouble this year. Except for the ambush on the Akko road, the Zealots had been surprisingly inactive of late.

But one never knew with those fanatics. If trouble arose, it would most likely erupt in Jerusalem, near the Temple, during the Passover, in the press of the mob, where tens, even hundreds, of thousands of pilgrims would be encamped in a ring about the city, and more tens of thousands would be packed into the inns, and the homes of relatives and friends. Already, a month before the Passover, the pilgrims were beginning to arrive—those who wanted rooms at the inns, the best quarters in the houses, the best campsites, close to the Temple, or closest to water.

There were traditional areas where regional groups banded together . . . Peraeans, Idumeans, Jews from the Decapolis, Phoenicia, Gaulanitia, Egypt, Greece, Italy, Cyrenea, Anatolia, Gaul, Iberia, Syria, the Caspian, Babylonia.

And there were outcast sections —not officially, but in the minds of the people—where those Jews of Samaria, who respected Mount Moriah rather than Mount Gerizim as the seat of God on Earth, camped. Then there was the campground of the oft derided Galileans.

What an intolerant people they were, these Jews.

But just who were the Jews? Pilatus had often tried to get it straight in his own mind.

And just who were the Gentiles?

The definitions would seem to be plain. Yet they were not, when, within the general group of the people who were regarded as 'Jews'—those who circumcised their male children, and worshiped the god of Moses—various groups scorned and reviled one another even when they had all gathered together to worship the same god, and when many of them would take heated exception to being called by the name of "Jew."

The appellation of "Hebrew" was no more helpful, as some Hebrews were not Jews, and some that Rome would label as Jew were not Hebrew.

"Israelite" was even harder to understand. Israel had ceased to exist as a nation some seven centuries before. Part of what had been Israel was now called Samaria. Yet, so often, he heard those who called themselves Jews also calling themselves Israelites, even while they hated the Samaritans.

It was enough to make a praefectus gnash his teeth.

Lucius said that the name Israelite probably had more to do with some ancestor of theirs, called Israel. But that man had also been called Jacob.

These people and their names! And not a family name amongst them.

Many of the males seemed to have no names at all, but were addressed merely as bar Jesse, or ben Levi, meaning simply "son of" some man called Jesse or Levi.

To further confuse matters, bar and ben could also mean that they were from a certain place.

And why some used bar and some used ben—and why both sometimes showed up in the title of one man—was a semantic mystery that Pilatus had not quite solved.

And why some men seemed to have no names of their own, but went through whole lifetimes known only as the sons of their fathers, while others were given names of their own from the very beginning, was another mystery.

The last mystery was why half the males in Palestine who did have names were either Jacob, Joseph, Judah, Johannan, Yeshuah, Joshuah, Isaac, or Simon. So that, at any gathering, there were several of each, and one had constantly to define which one was being spoken of or to. Jacob bar Joshuah. Jacob the Pharisee ben Joseph. Jacob the Pharisee ben Isaac . . .

Pilatus came from a people each of whom stated themselves clearly.

The wife of Pilatus was, for instance, Claudia Procula. One therefore knew that her name was Procula, and that she was a female of the Claudian family. Pontius Pilatus. Gallus Lucius, Crispus Marcus, Claudius Tiberius. A person was a person, clearly, simply, with a name of his or her own. Often there were third and fourth names as well, one perhaps stating the area of the bearer's birth, another usually being a nickname. Each Roman was himself or herself and no other. Romans did not prevaricate about their own presences or rights in the world.

Pilatus had often found himself distrusting a people who refused to be—who were perhaps afraid to be—solid, known individuals, each in his or her own right, rather than mere echoes of fathers or grandfathers.

He was also a representative of a people who had, especially since the reign of Julius Caesar, grown increasingly more tolerant of the differences of others, rather than less so.

Who was a Roman?

Nowadays, he or she was a person on whom citizenship had been conferred. That person might be Greek, Egyptian, or Persian, or a Briton, or born in any one of a hundred other places. But that person was a Roman, and that dignity equalized all. All citizens enjoyed the same respect, they were governed and shielded by the same laws, taxed in the same manner, rewarded or punished in the same way, accorded the same opportunities for advancement.

They were all also allowed to worship as they pleased.

Not like these Jews.

Pilatus had always hated the necessity of spending time in Jerusalem. But he had been sent to Palestine to govern, and govern he must. So he would put up with the narrowness of Jerusalem, the corruption, the putrid truths of their priesthood. He would not allow himself to think on those things. He would not dwell in anger.

And now there was Jesus. And his consort, the graceful Merovee. They were, to Pilatus, an oasis in a desert.

And much more besides. He had actually looked forward to the trip up to Jerusalem this time, counting the days before he might see them again. To assure himself that they would actually be there for the Passover, he had stooped to requesting reports from his various garrisons, and from his spy network, as to their whereabouts. Had it been possible, he would have rushed to Jerusalem the moment that he knew they had arrived in Bethany. And poor Procula. He had talked of them so much that she had finally laughed and covered her ears, and said she would not hear another word, that she would judge for herself.

His dear Procula. His beloved companion. He had not always been faithful to her. That knowledge pained him now. But never had he ceased to love and adore her.

Oh yes. Jesus represented much more to him than a mere oasis.

Oh do come, Jesus. We need you. So very much.

Those had been the unspoken emotions in the underscored, <u>Please</u>.

So that the arriving guests were paid an uncustomary honor. When the wagon, covered for privacy and sent by the praefectus, pulled into the courtyard of the old palace, the praefectus, himself, was waiting on the steps, to grasp the hand of Jesus, and to help Merovee to alight.

"My very dear friends! There are no words to tell you how happy I am to see you. What is this? My dear lady, a child on the way already? Congratulations!"

He did not look, at first, full into the face of a third person climbing out of the chariot. When he did, the smile froze on his face.

It was not that he knew for sure who the man was. Yet he did. Somewhere in the back of his mind, he knew very well. He knew him from a place of horror, of frustration and wild grief . . .

Then he realized that the man was missing one arm. That awful day on the Akko road came flooding back.

How could Jesus do this to him? He had thought they were friends! What awful accusations did they mean to . . .

He felt the hand of Jesus on his shoulder, and was immediately comforted.

"Praefectus, I hope we do not offend by bringing Micah. He has become my recorder, hired to follow as closely as a shadow and to put down the pith of what I say and what is said to me. I thought also to reunite you two, so that you might reconfirm to each other that most men are of very good will. Micah came to me immediately in Kapher Nahum, Praefectus, and told me the truth of what happened on the Akko road—how you and your men were ambushed, how the death of the pilgrims was not your intention . . . how you tried to help. Micah then stood up in the synagogue on the Sabbath and told the congregation the same thing, and it was his words which quelled the wild rumor that was circulating, and possibly even stopped some foolish uprising in Galilee. Truly, I felt it worthwhile for you two to come face to face once more."

Pilatus hesitated, the breath gone from him for a moment.

Then he reached out and took Micah's hand.

"Indeed. I have thought often of you and your family, Micah. And wondered. I thank you for your service, and I . . . am very glad to see that you . . . . . . How is your wife?"

"She is well, Praefectus. She is with the others at bar Jeremiah in Bethany. We miss our little girl most sorely. But, thanks to your suggestion, we have a great gift in return. The privilege of following after Jesus and Merovee."

"She was a lovely child," said Pilatus softly. "I saw her just before it happened, Micah. She smiled at me, and I at her. You did not know that day, Micah, that I was grieving with you, most personally. Such laughing eyes. Procula and I had a little girl once. Her eyes laughed, too."

He summoned a smile, for Micah stood smiling and serene.

"Yes. You are most welcome, Micah. Come in now, my friends. Procula is waiting."

The dinner was to be only the four of them, five now—though Micah had developed the knack of blending into the surroundings and being scarcely noticeable, except for the scratch of his quill and an occasional rustling as he began a new sheet—so that Pilatus conducted them, not to any state chamber, but, to his own private rooms, to the small dining chamber he shared with his wife, a place to which only close associates or the most intimate of friends would be brought.

It seemed to Merovee as she walked ahead of Jesus and Micah, on the arm of Pilatus, that the praefectus became as a man afraid to open a final door. His steps seemed to lag, wanting never to get there, never to have to face the truth of what he might be forced to face once the door of that private chamber was opened.

"So it is as I saw in my dream," she said gently as they reached that door. He looked down, not understanding, in torment, poor man. "It will be up to her," Merovee said simply. "If she wants to live, Jesus will make it so. If she is determined to die, nothing and no one can stop her."

He stared at her for a moment. Then he gathered himself and opened the door.

Upon one of the couches there reclined a shimmering creature—like a mirage that Merovee had seen as a child, in the desert outside of Alexandria. The eyes told you the woman was there, while something deeper said it was only a vision, as insubstantial as a mist, just a reflection of something belonging to another place, another time . . . or to something the Spirit of which had already passed on out of this world, leaving the semblance of a body simply to be polite.

She had been a beauty, light and bright, with, at one time, Merovee imagined, a healthy pinkness suffusing that brightness. Now there was no color at all. The woman was translucent.

"My darling," said Pilatus. "Here are Merovee and Jesus at last."

"Welcome." Her smile was sweet and genuine, but her voice had little energy or volume. "I warn you that you will be hard put to live up to all that my husband has led me to expect of you. Ah. You are with child, Merovee. What are you hoping for?"

"A boy, of course."

"Yes. Of course." Procula turned her sweet smile expectantly to Micah.

Micah spoke up hurriedly. Why disturb this fragile creature with long, sad stories?

"I am merely the recorder of my employer's words, my lady. Pay me no mind, I will set myself up in a corner."

Procula nodded. She was a woman used to slaves and servants. But slaves and servants did not speak boldly, as had Micah. Merovee noted that flicker of awareness on Procula's face, and smiled to herself.

"Jesus," said Pilatus. "Here. Sit beside Procula."

Merovee had also to smile at the attempts of the praefectus to seem offhand while shoving Jesus down onto the couch beside his wife. The couch bounced, and Procula laughed. Jesus laughed back, and reached for her hand. She gave it quite naturally.

"Now!" Pilatus gestured to a servant while conducting Merovee to the opposite couch. "Wine for our friends. The very best." He sank down beside Merovee. "And you know which that is. My pay for a day's labor in your vineyard."

A case, not of the new wine, but of the best, aged vintage or the House of Nathan had been sent.

"I am glad you received it." said Merovee, "but you do not need to waste your treasure on us."

"Waste?"

The most queer expression played over the face of Pilatus. One thousand emotions vied for first place.

"Waste," he repeated. He shook his head. "Oh, it is no waste, Merovee."

His eyes flitted anxiously to his wife's slim, white hand, held in the strong, golden hand of Jesus.

"Why is it you wish for a boy?" He was making conversation, yet he truly wished to know. "Do you have something against women?"

"Not at all. But you men do have all the advantages, do you not?"

Pilatus frowned. That was something else about these Jews and their aggressively male god that he could not accustom himself to.

"Among your people that is very true. But much less so in some other cultures that I know. Why, even among us Romans, women are . . . " He shrugged helplessly. "Romans. People. We worship female gods, women are often our priests. Women inherit, and wield power, in much the same manner as men—witness the Empress Livia. My mother was from the Isle of the Britons. She told stories of great women among the people of that isle. Mighty queens. Priestesses. Wise women. And, among her own people, women fought alongside the men." He grinned. "Perhaps you should move there, Merovee."

Merovee's eyes flickered, thinking again of the new life of the little Miriam who had drowned in that storm off Delos, already reborn a thousand years into the future, queen of a land in the far north of that isle.

"I might very well go among the Britons someday. For now, I hope for a boy because I want no bars on my child's life."

"Each of us makes our own prison," said Jesus quietly. "You can have the world's finest boy, and, if he decides to put bars around himself, he will do so. There will be nothing that you can do about it.

"Just as you can have a girl who refuses to believe in the existence of bars. And that girl will fly with eagles. As do you, Merovee. It amazes me that you do not see that for yourself.

"Oh! Do not set your chin so stubbornly." He grimaced comically to Procula. "She has the most dreadful mind of her own."

"A great failing amongst women," said Procula. Her fingers still curled happily about his, though she seemed not at all aware of it. "She has many more months of considering before her time, though. When will it be, my dear, late summer?"

"No. Within the month," said Merovee.

Both Procula and Pilatus hesitated. It was obvious that the girl was pregnant, yes, but not that pregnant. On top of which . . . they both counted rapidly from the date of the wedding.

"It is not my child," said Jesus smoothly. "Merovee was newly widowed when we married."

"Oh. Yes, of course," said Pilatus. "And so it is the child of . . . "

"The Prophet Johannan," said Merovee proudly.

Pilatus frowned and finished his glass of wine, wondering whether to tell them of the pressures from the priesthood which had surely been brought to bear on Antipas. Why, old Annas had even sent to Pilatus, asking that Pilatus invent a reason to arrest the Prophet and execute him. Pilatus had refused, vehemently, in a strongly worded reply.

"Do not fret yourself," said Merovee kindly, exactly as though she had heard his thoughts. "We understand. So did Johannan. He could have escaped in time. He chose not to. His task here was finished, you see, and he needed to go on."

Pilatus stared at her, feeling suddenly that he was part of a dream. Why was he sitting here with these Jews, concerning himself with their problems, their lives, considering them as friends, looking to them as to saviors?

But he was.

He chose not to. His task here was finished.

What would Procula decide, Pilatus suddenly wondered? Did she feel that her task here was finished? That she needed to go on?

If she wants to live, Jesus will make it so. But, if she is determined to die, nothing and no one can stop it.

What was Procula's task in life? He had never thought about it. He wondered if she had. To be a good wife to him, she would probably say. And that she had certainly been.

Been. Past tense. She had done it. Did she feel there was more, and that she must move on to find it? Did she even ache for more? If that was it, if that was why she was leaving him by way of death's door, then that was the answer.

He must find her some new purpose. Here. With him. Something to make her want to stay.

To do that, he would have to change even himself, make of himself a new challenge, become part of that new purpose.

He watched her with a yearning that was almost past bearing. He became angry at her so much of late, all secretly in his mind, ranting and railing at her, accusing her of perfidy, of not loving him, to be so treacherously ill, to be so obviously preparing to leave.

Love for him should be enough of a purpose, enough of a task!

Traitor! You traitor, Procula, to consider me not worth the staying! To consider my need of you not enough of a reason!

He felt Merovee's cool hand upon his. He turned and looked into her eyes.

She was reading his thoughts. How?

He felt light. The dream was becoming more pervasive. He remembered having felt this way at the wedding in Kana. He surrendered himself to it, giving himself to its flow even while his mind remained sharp, observing as from a place above the scene.

What must the servants think as they moved about, filling the goblets and setting out the first of the evening's delicacies, to see Procula lying on one couch, holding hands with Jesus, smiling into his eyes and laughing at nothing in particular, and he, himself, lying on another couch holding hands with Merovee?

And since when did he worry about what slaves thought?

"How *does* one give purpose to another?" he heard himself ask of her.

Merovee glanced at Jesus. He seemed to be paying no attention.

"One gives purpose to others by being the very best that one can possibly be," she began. "One works only with oneself, never presuming to force one's beliefs onto others, but, instead, endeavoring to be a worthy example of all that one believes. If you work unstintingly for what is right, true, good, beautiful, and if you work to make yourself a model of all this, understanding yourself and your fellows better each day . . . if your love of beauty in all matters shines like a sun, warming others . . . if it is obvious at all times that you are searching for the best, the most fair, the most loving conduct . . . if what you do is of consistent benefit and encouragement to others . . . if you make them smile and laugh and feel good about themselves, utterly forgiven and understood by yourself . . . if your example makes people glad that they got up that morning, and certain that there is no end to the wonderful things to be learned, the amazing skills to be mastered, the worlds to be explored . . . if the things that you do with your own life make them feel that there has just got to be a definite reason for all of being . . . . . . then you are helping them toward their own purposes, opening doors in their minds to those rooms where their purposes are locked away.

"Yet there is a hook catch to it all, Praefectus. Because, to accomplish it finally and thoroughly, you have got to believe implicitly in others . . . in their own needs and desires to be all the things that you, yourself, are trying to learn to be, in their abilities to recognize your example and, ultimately, in their own good times, put it to work in their own ways, in their own lives, with no force or coercion of any sort from you or from anyone else.

"I think that that trust . . . that confidence in others, to eventually be as wise as yourself all by themselves . . . is one of the very hardest of things."

She smiled over at Jesus.

"How did I do?"

"Very well."

"Very well indeed," said Pilatus thoughtfully. "I can see it now. That is what it is about you two. You both shine. One feels such trust. Such hope. You exude a certainty, a solidity . . . a serenity that can only come from a knowing far beyond my own.

"Yet you do not make me feel lessened for being just an ordinary, confused man, neither do you make me feel threatened or coerced. Instead, you make me feel that, secretly, down deep, I am more than my own self . . . or that I can be . . . will be, if only I study you two.

"It is really rather . . . exciting."

"That is the first thing that Josh made me understand," said Merovee. "He forbade me to call him master. He said he was no greater than I, but that . . . well, that he had managed to fit together more pieces of the puzzle than I had, and that, eventually, I would also have his wisdom, and his abilities.

"More than that, he helped me to realize that that greater, wiser 'I' is already in existence somewhere, due to the simultaneous nature of time."

Procula leaned forward.

"I had a Greek tutor when I was a girl. He taught me of his people's ancient philosophers. He also mentioned some philosophies of lands to the east. There are people there who believe as you seem to, that all things happen at once. The idea always intrigued me, yet I have never been able to feature it.

"Oh do go on. About time. Explain your beliefs, please."

"I think," said Merovee, "that Josh can do a better job."

Jesus shook his head and helped himself to some creamed fish.

"You begin. The exercise will be good for you."

Pilatus quite lost track of time. Neither could he remember afterwards whether he had eaten anything himself. Their conception of reality, of how the world worked and why, of its history, of its future, of its gods, was unlike anything that had ever occurred to him, even in his wildest dreams.

Yet how could he disbelieve it as explained by Merovee and Jesus? Had he, himself, not seen this man turn water to wine? So how could he say nay when they explained that the world and its goods—all of which seemed solid and unchangeable, so simply *there*—were far from solid . . . and only "there" by virtue of an agreement between the objects and those who perceived them?

How could he doubt that, should that mutual agreement change, then appearances and even results would change?

How could he doubt that the "world"—all matter—was composed of trillions upon trillions of tiny moving bits of energy, each of which was a parcel of consciousness itself?

How could he doubt that these conscious bits could appear to "form themselves into" whatever consciousness directed them to form, that the latent potential for all was in each part?

How else explain the ability of Jesus to direct water to re-form and appear to be wine?

How else explain his ability to do some of the healings of which Pilatus had heard?

It made perfect sense if one viewed a body, not as something solid and beyond one's control to change, but, as one's *idea* of oneself, formed by one's consciousness—as its own fluid representation of itself in the world—which representation would change its appearance as consciousness changed its idea of what it was.

As long as one's idea of oneself was "sick," one would appear to be sick. If consciousness changed its idea of itself to "health," the body would then represent health.

No wonder then that, as Jesus was careful to point out, he, himself, could work no lasting cures unless the patient had, himself, decided to be healthy. For, soon after Jesus was gone, the person's consciousness would change his idea back to "sick."

Pilatus was vitally aware of Procula as they spoke, how she leaned forward, listening intently, asking questions which made Jesus smile and say, "Good!"

More than anything, Pilatus was aware of the faint flush of pink that had crept into her cheeks, and of how well she ate as she listened, munching absentmindedly upon all the good things that he was forever, without success, begging her to eat to strengthen herself.

And a great excitement filled him. For his initial idea had been correct. She *could* stay. If she *decided* to stay. If she found a *reason* to stay. She was not at the mercy of her body. No. Or of any "Fates," or of the invisible disease that had turned her to a wraith. The disease was at *her* mercy. The mercy of her mind.

Procula, too, must be thinking upon this, for she asked a great many questions about the people whom Jesus had cured.

"Jesus," she asked finally, "if you and your recorder here, Micah, decided between the both of you to restore his lost arm . . . could you do it?"

Jesus smiled.

"He and I discussed that very thing the day that I healed the gathering green on his stump. The answer, at this point, is no. I could not now bring the arm back. At the moment of injury, or even within days, had the arm been available, and had Micah wanted it, I could have caused it to rejoin successfully.

"Even without the arm, had Micah answered yes when I asked him if he wanted his arm again, and had he truly meant it, I could have instructed him in the mental techniques needed to gradually materialize, or 'grow,' a new one for his own self."

"What?" said Procula in astonishment.

"That is what I said. It is an exercise demanding great trust and mental exertion, but it can be done if commenced immediately after such a loss.

"At this point, however, the restoration would be prohibitively complicated. You see, Micah made the decision not to want the arm back. Thus, 'time' has passed, and the Universe, in answer to Micah's decision and desires, has flowed firmly away from that arm, which was 'long ago' buried and rotted away—that is, transformed into other matter forms—while Micah has found an entirely new life as a result of its absence . . . a life that, I think, pleases him greatly."

Micah smiled and kept on writing.

"The thing is, Procula . . . one should be very careful about what one believes. For, as you believe, so your life shall be.

"You should be equally as careful about what you think you want, and about what you wish for, what you desire and ask for. You are very liable to get it.

"In order to restore Micah's arm back to his body right here in this room tonight, Micah's own desire would have to change drastically. He would have to desire most wholeheartedly to have the arm back, to know exactly why he wants it back, totally believe that it is possible for it to return, make the firm decision to cause it to do so . . . and then we would have to carry out a very involved and advanced exercise during which we would mentally change every single moment that has passed since the accident. We would insert a different version into each of those moments, in which things happened otherwise than we now 'remember' them to have happened. We would literally change the past, and so our memory and experience of it. And, if the new version had Micah getting his arm back just after the accident, then, in this moment, automatically . . . his arm would be here, well-attached and healthy.

"But then Micah would not be here! He would probably find himself back in his bakery, kneading tomorrow's bread.

"Or perhaps he might still have become a follower of mine, but in a different capacity, so that he would not have accompanied us here tonight.

"The thing is, you see, that this process would put him, and us as a result, into a totally different probability. The individual worlds of each of us in this room would be much different than they seem to us now.

"But, of course, we would not remember the world as it is now, so we would not be aware that the new one was different. All our memories, and all the physical evidence surrounding us, would support the new version.

"Actually, all of us do this quite naturally. And often. But to do it on demand, as a 'cure' or demonstration, is quite another thing."

"But . . ." The face of Pilatus was puckered in concentration. "You say the thing is possible, yet you started by saying you cannot do it. Why can you not?"

"One can know it is possible to speak Greek without being able to do so. As great as you think I am, Pilatus, believe me, there are entities in the Universe who are far greater, to whom I am the student. They could do what I just described as easily and quickly as I changed the water to wine. I, however, have eons of study ahead of me before I could attempt such an advanced manipulation with any reasonable hope of success."

"But the implications of what you say are staggering," breathed Procula. "Just how great do these entities become?"

"As one of your lessons for this night, Sweet Lady, begin to ban limiting ideas from your mind.

"There was no beginning . . . there is no end. To anything.

"There is no highest. Neither is there a lowest. There is always a less, and always a more.

"The only limitation is the amount of information that an entity allows itself—or is able—to focus upon at any one time. Hence, one should work constantly to extend the breadth of one's focus. It is difficult for you to conceive of this, but there are entities which live and function in dozens of realities all at once, with full awareness of every detail of each one of those realities known and held simultaneously in the 'mind,' and with each manifestation fully cognizant of all the other manifestations."

"Then . . ." Merovee hesitated a long moment. "I think I finally understand All That Is, Josh."

"Tell us what you understand."

"It came to me the morning that we rode back from Johannan's tomb at Bethabarah. At least part of it. Ruthie and Pharisee were frisky and happy, heading for home and their grain. I was suddenly so very aware of their animal joy and pleasure, just as though it were my own.

"At the same time, I was aware of the feelings of my own body, as apart from what I thought of as myself, as though my fingers and toes had thoughts of their own.

"Then I knew how my baby's body felt. It, too, was sharing in the joy.

"Then I realized the complicated baby growing in Ruthie as well, and I seemed to be it for a moment.

"I seemed also to be the dust beneath Ruthie's feet, experiencing her weight, being rearranged by her passing.

"Then I was the grasses and bushes that we passed, ready to flourish again after the winter, and I seemed to know all that they would have to do to grow and to survive.

"And then there were all the insects, and the tiny animals scurrying around amongst the grasses, and the birds flying above them. And I realized—felt—how vast and complicated is the world of just one little beetle. Or one small sparrow.

"And I was thinking so hard about Johannan, his life, his death, what he taught me, what the eternal implication of that teaching is. I was wondering where 'he' was at that moment, trying to think of the ways in which he might take form. And I wondered about my own relationship to him now, to where and what he is.

"But then I was also thinking about you, Josh, and being so afraid of the dangers to you, and of what the future will bring . . . "

She turned to Pilatus with an expression he had seen before.

"For we all know, do we not, Pilatus, that the Temple will try to destroy Jesus, just as they destroyed Johannan. We all know that, at some point, they will approach you and try to get you to do their shameful work for them."

Pilatus found himself answering with candor to match her own.

"They already have. At least they are preparing the ground. It seems you made enemies in the Temple court several Sabbaths ago, Jesus. Our dancing fool, Mattias, called on me yesterday, within hours of my arrival. He had a long list of notes from Annas and Caiaphas. One of the most important items was yourself.

"It seems," he said with great irony, "that Annas and Caiaphas go in huge worry for the safety of the might of Rome, and for the possessions of their friend, Emperor Tiberius. It seems they consider you to be a great danger to Rome. Not to them, of course. Their only concern is for Rome."

He looked hard at Jesus for a moment.

"I knew of your lineage, but I had not realized, until Mattias explained, quite how strong a claim you do have, at least in the emotions of the people, to the throne of Judeah."

Jesus smiled gently.

"I have a greater claim to a greater throne, Pilatus, in a kingdom that is not at all of this world. Go on, Merovee, Darling. What else did you understand as we returned from Bethabarah that day?"

"I realized . . . how incredibly complicated it all is. I even thought of you, Pilatus, and the things you have to think about and do each day, the problems you have that are so different from mine. I thought of the world you come from, and the customs you know. I thought of all the people, all over the Earth, each with his or her own customs, his or her own private, daily life. I thought of all the birds, and grass, and insects, and babies growing in all sorts of wombs, and of all the skies, and all the differing lands, and the seas, and all that goes on in them.

"I thought of all these things in relationship to how Jesus says they really are, and I realized that this is not even the only world, that the number of worlds is infinite, that other places and times were right there with me at that very moment, even though my focus was not broad or deep enough to see them, or sense them.

"And, as I tried to put it all together, I felt overwhelmed. How could I ever understand it all? What was the use of even trying?

"But then the strangest thought came to me. If I, Merovee, was so overwhelmed by just my own little problems and thoughts and philosophies, and by the relatively few things going on around me, in just my little space . . . if I felt so helpless before all the complications of my one, short, little life . . . if I felt there was no way I could ever understand it, ever experience it all, ever even know about it all . . .

" . . . then how must All That Is feel?"

Jesus smiled, lifting his goblet to her.

"And then," she went on, "it came to me that the basic structure of reality as we know it is particulate. It has got to be, there is no other way for it to work. All That Is has got to, must, work through each of these little particles—which are the particles of its own mind, its own consciousness. It has got to work through us, through the individual private moments of each of us.

"And that is the beauty of it! Because, as All That Is does that, as it experiences each individual moment along with each one of us—whether 'us' is a Merovee, or an apple tree, or a fish, or a rock, or a cloud—it not only explores more of its potential, it has the fun and excitement of re-experiencing, re-learning, re-discovering, re-membering, over and over, but in totally new ways each time, everything that it has 'forgotten.'

"So yes. As Josh just told us, as you grow greater as an entity you learn to handle more and more all at once, you do not have to think of just one thing at once, or live in just one world at once, you can think of thousands of things at once, and live in a thousand places.

"But, as Josh also says, there is always a more. So just think what All That Is has to juggle!"

She sat up, easing her belly.

"By a massive effort, I am sure that All That Is could 'think' simultaneously, bring into clear, conscious knowing, every single particle of itself in every single world and every single probability, past, present and future . . . that it could, for one, glorious, simultaneous moment experience the total content of itself.

"That moment would be one of wild, Universe-shattering insight.

"Has it ever happened to you, Procula? Have you ever had one of those supreme moments, when suddenly everything makes sense, and you feel all one with the world, and so filled with joy that it seems you will burst? You think you know it all, you have it all figured out, and you think you will never forget it . . . "

"Then, next morning," smiled Procula, "you cannot remember what it was that you would never forget."

"And neither can you get that feeling back," said Pilatus, "no matter how you try."

"So you do know what I mean. Well, that is a pale idea of how it would be if All That Is suddenly and simultaneously 'knew' all of itself. Yet the experience of All That Is would still be much as it is with us, that brief flash, that momentary knowing that would not last.

"And it should not. For then the point, the purpose, would be lost. All That Is *wants* to forget! That is what it is all about!

"You see what is happening to me now? I knew all of this the morning that Jesus and I rode home from Johannan's grave. And I forgot that I knew. So now I am rediscovering it, in a totally new way, on a new level, more deeply, more profoundly.

"And I suddenly realize that Josh has said much the same thing to me in one way or another again and again. And, each time, I have thought that I understood, and I have been able to expound at great length on the whole matter. On just the same thing.

"But it is not the same thing. It can never be the same. Each time it is experienced, it is different.

"That is why All That Is loves us. And why I suddenly really love All That Is. Because All That Is, itself, lives in and on the moments, in and on each little moment of each little one of us. All That Is, itself, has a hard time remembering. All That Is, itself, re-discovers and so grows greater in understanding with each moment. All That Is, itself, is us and we are it.

"That is what you meant that day up in the vineyard, is it not, Josh? When you told us to be as the lilies of the field. A lily understands how to ride the moment, in total trust that everything that is really necessary for its well-being will be supplied. The lily knows how to ride on the moments and in the moments . . .

"Oh!"

She put her hands to her face, her eyes shining.

"Now I do see. This is why you are always telling us to bless each moment, live each moment, trust each moment, regard each new moment as a rebirth, as a golden opportunity, why you are always pounding it into our heads that our power is in each moment . . . that The Power of the Universe is always with us because the moment is always with us."

She stared at her husband.

"The moment . . . is God. God is the moment. That is it. Is it not?"

"You have it, my dear."

Tears came to her eyes.

"So that is why God is always with us . . . why we can never be separated from the love of what is really God."

There were tears even in the eyes of Jesus.

"And now that you know it, Merovee my love, as you so aptly said . . . you will forget it. Again and again, you will forget it. Only to, again and again, remember it. Strive to make the remembering the more frequent occurrence. Strive to become ever more conscious. In that striving is 'godliness.' The way to the true god.

"You might say that that true god is composed of endless eyes. Those eyes are the moments, but not the moments as measured off by a sundial or hourglass.

"Though the example of an hourglass might provide a mental picture of what I am saying. Each grain of sand that passes through the narrow part of the glass, each of which we will equate with our perception of a passing moment, continues to exist, each one separate from the others, waiting to be cycled once more, in a different order and way, through that narrow part when the glass is turned.

"In reality, however, contained in each one of those separate moments will be endless trillions of moments, the relative views of each bit of matter *and* non-matter participating in that particular point of 'time.'

"So that a moment is not simply a term by which we express the passing of 'time.' Moments do not just 'happen,' one after another, like Caesar's legions marching neatly along the Appian Way. Moments only seem to march one after another. We make them seem that way by choosing to 'remember' them in a particular sequence.

"Each moment is an *entity*, as separate from all others as are the stars in the heavens . . . and tell me the order and sequence of the stars.

"Moments have personalities, histories, civilizations, heights, depths . . . *feelings, consciousness, life*. Some are greater, larger, brighter than others, for they have been developed more fully. But one could go into any moment and stay there for billions of 'years,' exploring all its potentials, always 'doing' a different thing, while still not reaching the limits of that moment's potential.

"Indeed, we do go into moments in that way. A portion of us remains in each of our selected moments for eternity.

"Which is one of the reasons why we can 'reach back' from 'future' moments, or 'ahead' from 'past' moments, and suggest new courses of action to those bits of our own selves busily exploring the possibilities of those moments."

He shook his head fondly.

"Very good, Merovee. My Beloved Disciple. We will make a lily of you yet."

"And so," said Procula thoughtfully as she helped herself to more fruit, "the thing one must do is learn to trust each moment and live it as fully as possible 'at that moment,' to let it have its own vitality." She cocked her head. "We can never really be 'wrong' about anything then, can we. It is only a matter of doing less well than is possible. But then . . . even those lesser areas of each moment must eventually be explored if a part of oneself is in it for all eternity, no?"

"One can, however," said Jesus, "be selective about the moments one chooses to explore in the first place. They are your creations, never forget that. There is no Fate telling you what you must do. You choose for yourself. Before your birth, you choose your own life circumstances, and then, at the moment of your birth, you became a completely unique, separate person-ality, a new eye, of All That Is, a new idea of Self, set loose to create your own drama, your own version of how things are or should be.

"Understanding that, and accepting responsibility for your own choices, is the first great step. You have it in your own power, then, within the structure of your chosen circumstances, to select the very worst or the very best of moments, or something in between. To my mind, it behooves you to try for the best." He grinned. "For, remember, once you choose, a part of you is 'trapped' there forever. I said before that we each make our own prisons. At least make good ones."

"And this is the basis of the endless forgiveness of All That Is, is it not," mused Merovee, "As Procula says, at some point, with all of eternity in which to work, one must at some point explore the least good aspects of any one moment. Actually, one has to. Have you ever had a bad pain? You never appreciate how good it feels to be free of pain unless you have had pain in the first place. And you would not know how awful pain is if you had never felt good! It is all a matter of learning what best, or better, is, and working to achieve that best more consistently.

"But, since there is always a best, there is always a better best. And since there is always a less, there is always a lesser. So *of course* All That Is is endlessly forgiving! It understands what we are up to even when we do not. God knows that we have to explore the valleys to even know that there are places more high."

She passed a hand over her eyes, wiping away more tears.

"We are all the partners of All That Is, that is it, is it not, Josh. That is the basis of all understanding. All forgiveness. All love."

The pink in Procula's cheeks had grown more pronounced.

"And what a challenge," she said, "to try to stay aware. To watch one's moments and try to understand each new one, its personality as you say, its histories, and feelings, and futures, and pasts. To allow it to touch you and guide you, even while trying to make *it* better. To let each moment be a process of coming to understand its own Self more fully. Of learning how to use its own particular power.

"By Jove!"

Her blue eyes widened.

"Jesus. We . . . are not really here, are we. We are not . . . continuous as we seem to be to ourselves. The Procula that is . . . . . . well, actually, that Procula already *was*, for that moment in which I commenced to speak is gone . . . that me is not at all the same as the one here now. But now even that now is then. We are not really people, none of us. We are endless billions of these packets of energy called moments."

"I am afraid so," smiled Jesus.

"Oh my stars," said Procula, still wide-eyed. "I think I will have more wine."

She did not join in their laughter.

"Jesus, I am frightened suddenly. Who is Procula, then? What is Procula? What if I should lose her? Where would . . . *I* be?"

It was Pilatus who answered.

"In your moments," he soothed. "How can Procula ever be lost when, as I understand it, there are billions of Proculas, each living in her moments, putting them together in endless new patterns with all the other Procula moments."

"Oh. Of course. Well, that does make sense, does it not." She nodded. "But I will still have more wine."

Pilatus rose, chuckling, came to her side and filled her goblet himself. He caught the eye of Jesus, and flushed at the respect he saw there. He felt a wild surge of joy, of hope. How quickly, invisibly, his life and that of Procula had changed. All because he had accepted an invitation to a Jewish wedding in Galilee. Procula had not been as alive in years. Not since the death of their own little girl with the laughing eyes.

"Now!" said Procula, bubbling like a girl. "There is something I am so curious about. I have wondered for years, and surely, if anyone does know the answer, it will be you, Jesus. After all the things you have just told us, it surely cannot be God . . . . . . so what *is* in the ark in your Holy of Holies?"

"Aha!" cried Merovee. She, too, was having more than her usual quota of wine. "Now I have you, Husband! You will finally have to tell. I think it is a bird, Procula."

"A bird?" laughed Pilatus. "I would sooner believe that Greek who entered the Holy of Holies and came out saying that the Jews worshiped a golden ass."

"This all has to do with the Noachites," said Merovee sagely, "and the Builders, and 'Father Ibrabam's' great secret. I think that the secret is something called a Samir. And a friend of mine told me that the Samir is a bird. By some means, it can make stone so soft and light that it can be transported over great distances with ease, carved as easily as clay, and fitted stone to stone so perfectly that mortar is hardly needed and seams scarcely show. Right, Husband?"

"Very vaguely, Wife."

"But yes!" said Procula. "I have indeed read legends of this Samir creature. Legends say that your King Solomon used it to help build his great temple. I thought, though, that it was a worm of some sort."

"A worm in the Holy of Holies?" grinned Pilatus. "That is the best theory yet."

"The legends also say," said Procula, "that Solomon had pet demons, who were able to toss the great stones up to the top of his Temple as though they weighed nothing at all."

"Demons in the Holy of Holies," said Pilatus. "The theories grow juicier."

"Pilatus," said Jesus, "I often get the impression that you do not hold our Seat of God on Earth in quite the esteem that our priests would have you."

"And I am evidently in sympathetic company, from what I heard of your performance in the Temple court. At least we know that the Corban is not in the Holy of Holies, eh, Jesus? How I applaud your nerve. It is about time someone began to question those filthy priests . . . "

"Oh, do not let him get off onto that topic," laughed Procula. "Corban, Corban, it is all that I ever hear."

"But it is a crime not to use those funds for the people themselves!" cried Pilatus. "They are supposed to use them for the people, but they do not. We all know that Jerusalem is in dire need of having the aqueduct that Herod the Great began finished. The city is desperate for water. Have you ever spent time here in the summer, Jesus? The heat is not to be believed. And there are only a couple of dilapidated excuses for aqueducts serving the Temple, and four, perhaps five, wells in the whole city that I would call adequate. People sometimes line up and stand for hours to get one jug of water, and they must make do with that for all their household and drinking needs, plus the endless washing they do in regard to their endless regulations as to ritual cleanliness. And, of course, the Temple requires an *enormous* amount of water for the ritual bath houses, and to wash away the rivers of blood from those disgusting sacrifices . . . more water is needed with each passing year. The stink of everyone and everything in the summer exceeds all imagination! And it is so unnecessary! Again and again, I begged Annas and Caiaphas to release some of the Corban funds to complete Herod's aqueduct. Our engineers could have had it finished and supplying all the water that is needed in little more than three seasons. But no! They grew apoplectic whenever I mentioned the Corban. So . . . well, you must have heard about what I did, Jesus. And how I suffered for it. What a howl and complaint against me was sent to Rome. Because I confiscated some of the tribute and tithes coming in from the provinces. Much of it arrives through the port of Caesarea, you see. And I grabbed some! And we set to work extending the aqueduct."

"Darling, calm yourself," said Procula. "He gets so upset about this," she said to Jesus and Merovee.

"And well I should! Had they let me continue there would now be an aqueduct supplying all the water that Jerusalem needs. But no. The priests loathe the loss of even so much as a drachma. They convinced Tiberius that there was really no need for more water in Jerusalem, that they have all that they need."

"Darling, it is in the past. Jesus, please go on. Talk right over him if you must. Do not forget that your wife is in a delicate condition and should be humored. She wants to know about the Samir and so do I. Is it in the Holy of Holies?"

"My apologies," said Pilatus, recovering his good nature. "Procula is right. And I would love to know just exactly what is in the Holy of Holies."

"Actually, I am not at all sure what is in the Holy of Holies at the moment. I can tell you what was once there. If it is still there, it is of no good to anyone. My dear ancestor, Solomon, took the key to its understanding with him when he died.

"There are many versions of what happened with the Samir. Some say it was a stone, some that it was a worm, some an insect. It is almost always associated with a mysterious Prince of the Sea, who has charge of it, and a moor hen—or sometimes a vulture or raven—who borrows it from the prince in order to cut through a glass that has been placed over her nest, separating her from her young ones." Jesus smiled at Merovee. "That is where your friend's 'bird' comes in."

"How did a glass get over her nest?" said Pilatus.

"In some versions, Solomon, himself, places it there. In other versions, it is the demons who work for Solomon. It is a ruse to make the bird fly out to the Mediterranean Sea, to the Prince of the Sea, and borrow the Samir, for she knows that the Samir will cut through the glass and she can then get to her young ones and feed them.

"But, when she comes back with the Samir, Solomon or his demons pounce upon her and steal the Samir, which is taken to the quarries, where the stones of the Temple are being cut."

"And," said Pilatus, "this Samir then magically cuts the stones, so perfectly that seams cannot be seen? And it makes them so light that stones of many tons can be easily transported?"

"That is what they tell us."

Pilatus shook his head.

"As children, we are told such fanciful things by our nurses. Later, we are told even more ridiculous things by our priests. I never did take such stories for anything but flights of imagination."

"And so you should have," said Jesus. "On a certain level. On the level of the 'reality' that you live each day, things simply do not happen that way. But, on deeper levels—the levels where hide the realities that build the realities which you think of as real, such fabulous stories are to be taken in all seriousness. And those realities forever bubble to the surface in what you think of as imagination. The reality that we know, that we see all about us, that we are 'living' at any given moment, began as a dream—a collective dream shared by many parcels of consciousness. At a certain point, the dream became so pervasive that it was accepted as the new experiment that that 'group' would try. And so, as a group, the consciousness that had acquiesced took the next step, and created a physical world modeled on the dream, and they then began to live out that selected 'reality.'

"These stories which you have difficulty believing, Pilatus, represent, in part, the collective memory of the original dreams, of the original patterns of successive experiments . . . and of their creators so to speak. In every myth, fable, or legend—of the Samir, the Bird, the Prince of the Sea, or whatever—eons of 'real' history are encapsulated.

"Not only that . . . this is difficult for you to understand . . . but these symbols are *alive*. We continue to draw upon them, to feed upon them in our dreams, as children at a mother's breast—which, by the way, is one meaning of the many-breasted Ephesian Astarte—and, in so feeding, we find the nourishment to keep our 'waking' 'reality' going.

"As opposed to children, though, we never stop nursing upon this 'mother.' As we grow and change, so our myths and symbols grow and change, always providing the proper nutrition, containing any and every element which we need in order to build each new 'day.'"

Pilatus was scowling in concentration.

"The Samir actually existed in our history then?"

"Actually, 'actually' is a pale word," grinned Jesus. "Legends contain depths and levels of 'actuality' without end. One level of the actuality of the Samir is a fabled Assyrian queen-goddess. Some call her Sammu-rumat. Most call her Semiramis."

"Oh, I have heard of her, too!" cried Procula. She was now, Pilatus noted with shock, sitting up cross-legged on the couch, exactly like the tom-boy he had first known. "They say that she, not Nebuchadnezzar, built Babylon and the Hanging Gardens."

"They say she built every city in Mesopotamia," said Merovee. "And in Syria, and Iran, and Armenia, and even some in Egypt. And all the roads and irrigation systems and monuments, too."

"I wonder if I could hire her for an aqueduct, " muttered Pilatus.

"She must have had help," said Procula, ignoring him. "I mean architects and masons and people like that."

"Oh, oh," said Merovee. She laughed, and grinned at Jesus. "We are back to the Noachite Builders again."

"What are Noachite Builders?" said Procula.

"That is a whole evening's lecture," said Jesus. "Go on, Merovee. Think about Semiramis and the Builders."

"All right. You have told us that the Noachite Builders are largely responsible for all the great cities and monuments in our world. But now we are considering the fact that a queen-goddess called Semiramis is also said to be the builder of these things. This is very queer, 'actually.' For the Builders, the Noachites—us, us 'Jews'—are so militantly male. Our legends allow no 'queen,' no woman, to have done anything besides be the adoring or conniving, thoroughly evil, bed mate of some man."

"Tch tch tch. Temper, temper," teased Jesus.

"You are the one who asked. Neither do any of our stories allow that one woman built half of the world as we know it."

"Exactly," said Jesus. "Semiramis is not a part of Hebrew legend. It is non-'Jews' who preserve her memory."

"Oh." Merovee hesitated, then she nodded. "I think I see, then. We Noachites, 'Jews' primarily, are pursuing a male experiment, so we give all credit for everything worthwhile to the male, banishing what is female to a corner to hang its head in shame. While other peoples—those who are not Noachite, seek to preserve memory of female power." She cocked her head. "And perhaps to preserve memory of the power structure of the world before the flood—by crediting a female for all the great works."

"Right you are. And, if you watch carefully, you can always detect the 'historical' male takeover by the Noachites in those legends. Remember that, in the story of Noah, the dove, symbol of the Mother Goddess, flew away, never to return, after delivering the olive branch of submission to Noah. In Greek stories, one repeatedly finds some goddess being conquered by a god. In the Assyrian stories of Semiramis, when Semiramis finds out that her son, Ninyas, is conspiring to wrest her domains from her, she decides not to punish him, but to abdicate in his favor. Like the loving and most superior being—and properly submissive female—that she is, she turns herself into a dove and flies away into the heavens."

Merovee grimaced.

"I would not have been that easy on such a horrid son."

"Wait till you have one of your own," laughed Jesus.

"Was there actually a Semiramis?" said Pilatus.

"There was a talented Assyrian queen, whose exploits and accomplishments were combined in the minds of the people with more ancient tales. This is the way you must study the legends you see, for that is the way that they are formed, one generation adding it own overlay of 'actual' data to the old, while also adding its own *emotion* in regard to those events, and often even adding an intuitive knowledge of other probable versions of the events, so that the actions and characters begin to seem fantastical and completely improbable.

"A legend is like a living book, written in code, requiring much study to decipher. If one learned to decipher the codes of all legends, one would know the entire history of Humanity, in all its probable forms. We would even have a hint of what Humanity was before it became Humanity.

"One would also be able to know all probable futures of Humanity, including what Humanity will be when it ceases to be Humanity. Because past and future are one, and all probabilities could be known from the given data."

"And so," said Procula, "one would be better off studying legends than reading our great historians."

"Indeed one would. Historians give limited and often questionably true versions of a few selected events. Legends tell you how and why those events were 'created to happen' in the first place. They help you understand the thrust and emotion of the mass mind that creates and supports the entire sweep of any epoch, not just the few paltry highlights upon which historians fixate."

"The real Semiramis must have been very great," said Procula thoughtfully, "to have become part of such a legend. Some stories say that, besides being beautiful, she was a military genius, a brilliant general. That she led the charges of her armies herself. She was always the first one up the walls. She even captured one city single-handedly."

"The magic is," said Jesus, "that she is anything you want her to be. Go to her for nourishment, and you will receive it to your fill."

"*Was* the real Semiramis a military genius?" Procula persisted.

"In one word, yes. Procula my dear, you seem to have had a very learned tutor."

"Oh, he was. A wonderful man. Andropos was his name. From the Peloponnesus, but educated in Athens. When he was still a young man, he went to Alexandria for further study and got pressed into naval service by Cleopatra. He was with Antonius Marcus at Actium—part of the booty awarded to my grandfather after that battle. Grandfather said ever afterward that it was almost worth having lost his leg in the battle to have gained Andropos." She smiled at Micah, realizing the similarity of experience. "Andropos was my father's tutor, then tutor to me and my brothers and sisters. He was the only slave to whom Father ever gave freedom. And dear Andropos stayed with us even then. He was more like a grandfather than a slave."

Tears stood out in Procula's eyes.

"I remember so well the morning we heard that Father had given Andropos his freedman document. I ran to him, and my sisters and brothers with me. We threw ourselves upon him, children that we were, and held him and sobbed and begged that he not leave us.

"Poor man. Perhaps he would rather have gone. Perhaps he would have liked a life of his own. But he wrapped us all in his arms and told us that we were not to worry. As long as there was a child of our father who needed teaching, Andropos, would be there."

"He kept his vow remarkably," offered Pilatus. "He seemed to be on his deathbed when Procula's mother announced that she was having another child."

"Very late," said Procula. "The rest of us were all grown, off and married. Mother was nearly fifty."

"Old Andropos sighed and got up out of his bed and said that Death would have to wait a while. He asked Procula's father for a leave of absence and went off to Alexandria for four years to study at the academies and learn all the newest ideas. Then he came back and commenced teaching Procula's little brother."

"And," said Merovee.

"He is still there, teaching," smiled Procula. "My brother is fifteen now. Andropos laughs and says that in just a few more years Death may have the prize that was snatched from it all those years ago. Though then he laughs still harder, and says that my brothers and sisters have children who need a good tutor, so that perhaps Death will still have to wait a bit."

"How old is he?" said Merovee.

"He says," said Procula, "that he was born at about the time that Julius Caesar invaded the Isle of the Britons for the second time. Which makes him around ninety. You would never know it to see him these last years. He seemed to be born again along with my little brother. It is amazing how young and healthy one can stay when . . . "

She glanced at Pilatus, flushed and grew silent.

"Yes," said Jesus softly. "Every once in a while people of large Spirit come along and afford us glimpses of what is always possible in the way of human achievement. Did Andropos tell you of the nativity of Semiramis, Procula?"

"She was the daughter of some goddess, was she not? Yes. The one with the fish tail. A woman up top, and a fish on the bottom. But the goddess just 'had' her, then left her all alone in the desert. The baby was found by doves, and they took her and put her in their nest and fed her till a man came along and . . . "

Procula stopped, frowning.

"Well now there are the birds. And a nest, and a human being concerning himself with what is in the nest just as in the legend of the Samir. And you spoke of a Prince of the Sea. The mother of Semiramis was half fish. Was her father or grandfather then a Prince of the Sea?"

Jesus cocked an eyebrow.

"My cup still runs over. All right, Procula, think more carefully about the mother of Semiramis."

"She was a Syrian goddess, I think. Agarta . . . Ataritis. Something like that."

"Atargatis," prompted Jesus, glancing slyly at Merovee.

"Yes, that was the name," said Procula. "She had centers of worship around Carchemish."

"A few miles from Harran, where Father Ibraham received his inspiration," said Jesus, still watching Merovee.

"And she was worshiped at Ephesus, too," said Procula. She frowned. "You mentioned Ephesus just a minute ago. The Ephesian Astarte or Artemis, with the many breasts. Are they one and the same? The Ephesian Artemis and Artargatis?"

"They are," said Jesus. "And, from that goddess who was worshiped in Carchemish and Harran—that goddess who eventually became Artemis —was 'born' Semiramis, who 'built' most of the cities and monuments that we know today."

"Incredible," murmured Merovee. "Just incredible."

"I do not understand," said Pilatus.

"I do," said Procula. "It is all one. Somehow. If only we can figure it out. All these things are facets of one main thing. Some very ancient truth. The very basis of our existence. Atargatis, Astarte, Artemis, Diana as we Romans call her, and Semiramis . . . they are all aspects of the same core . . . all differing *emotional* versions of that core.

"Look at the two legends. The same elements surface in regard to Semiramis and to the Samir. Each is a version of the other."

"And both are female versions of the Builders," murmured Merovee.

Procula studied Jesus with narrowed, thoughtful eyes.

"Each culture uses the same information, but presents it in a different way. And what a mockery that makes of differences between peoples, does it not . . . of hatreds and prejudice. No one should hate his fellows. No one should seek to destroy the cultures of others. We should glory in the differences of others, study them and support them with great joy. As though they are master art works. For they are. And no one has the right way, no one the wrong way. No one has the right god, no one the wrong god. What everyone has is their own wonderfully creative version of one central core."

For a moment there was silence. Procula's translucence seemed to have become a glow, as though a lamp had been lighted within her.

Pilatus broke the silence, turning away as though in anger, speaking gruffly.

"I still do not understand what was in the Holy of Holies."

"A stone, have you not heard?" smiled Jesus. "Inscribed with the 'Word of God.' We Jews worship a stone. Just look at Scripture. It is filled with stones. Jacob even made a pillow of one—and had a wonderful dream."

"Then that is really it?" said Merovee in confusion. "After all this teasing of the last months you are telling us that the priests are telling the truth and that the Ark of the Covenant really held stone tablets given to Moses by 'God'?"

"Did I say that? I do not recall saying that. I said 'a stone' inscribed with the 'Word of God.' The question is, then—what sort of stone, and just what really is the writing referred to as the 'Word of God'?"

"If you do not stop torturing me and tell us, I will throw such a fit that I will have the baby here and now!"

"Heaven forefend. Zana would hound me to the ends of the Earth if she missed the birth."

He rose then, and commenced moving about the room, head lowered thoughtfully, fingering the lovely jeweled inlays in the marble of the walls, touching the statuary.

At last he turned.

"The truth of the Samir, and what is or was in the Ark of the Covenant, is as complicated as the legends of which we have just been speaking. And that complication, by the way, is but one root of the Great Vine of this world. The roots of that vine reach back to ages and to places that would astound you. As to the Samir, it is many things. And what was contained in the ark is many things.

"Part of the difficulty of explaining all of this to you is the fact that none of you, at this point, are able to travel into the future in your mind as, to a certain extent, am I. I have been able to take Merovee with me on some of my journeys, in the dream state . . . but she is still unable to comprehend much of what we see. Even I do not always comprehend it all. But, to tell you how complicated the truths of the Samir and of the ark are, let me give you an example.

"As you might know, Pilatus, we have, among our 'learned' men, a growing tradition of interpretation of Scripture. Five books of our Scripture, supposedly written by Moses, we call Torah. Accompanying Torah is our Oral Tradition. Again supposedly conveyed to us by Moses. This tradition was not to be written down. Instead, it was to be committed to memory and passed from one generation of the upper echelon to the next." He smiled. "Wonderfully convenient for those who wished to change and amend things as they went along, eh? The Sadducees, and some others among us Hebrews, reject Oral Tradition. But not our Pharisees. For Oral Tradition, even more than Scripture, lends itself to interpretation. And Pharisees just love to interpret—to invent new Law to suit themselves. As they busily embroider upon Oral Tradition, the Pharisees are also freely inserting into that tradition stories of their own." His smile broadened. "Though they would bridle at the suggestion, they are, in fact, building legends.

"One very curious story has arisen amongst them, and is being woven into their new legends. The story speaks of thirty miraculous pieces of silver—sometimes called coins, sometimes talents."

"There is a large difference between a coin of whatever domination and a talent," said Pilatus.

"There is indeed. But we are dealing with symbols, not reality. I would say that 'thirty' and 'silver' are the things to watch for.

"It seems that, originally, this silver was turned into coins, ingots, whatever, by Terah, father of Ibraham, in Harran, near to Carchemish—even though, by the way, coins had not yet been invented in Terah's day."

"We are not dealing with reality, remember?" grinned Pilatus.

"You are catching on," laughed Jesus. "Well, many years later, learned men tell us, Ibraham used those thirty pieces of silver to buy a field as a burial place for himself and his family near Hebron.

"These very same coins later came back into the hands of the sons of Jacob."

"He who is also most confusingly called Israel," said Pilatus.

"They received the coins from the slave merchants when they sold their brother, Joseph, into bondage in Egypt. Many years later, they again used the same coins to buy corn from Joseph in Egypt."

"How did they know they were the same coins each time?"

"Hush, Procula," said Jesus. "You are not supposed to ask reasonable questions. We are in the presence of legend, of stratified super-truth.

"The coins were again used to buy spices for the body of Jacob—Israel—when it was laid in its tomb."

Pilatus winked at Merovee.

"If those spices were bought with talents, they must have been made of gold."

"You concern yourself too much with value," smiled Jesus. "These thirty silver what-evers then passed into the hands of the Queen of Sabaea . . . "

"Oh please!" cried Merovee. "From Jacob to the Queen of the South? That is a gap of at least a thousand years."

"Closer to two thousand if the truth be known," said Jesus. "Be that as it may, the queen then journeyed in search of the remarkable King Solomon and gave him those thirty pieces of silver as a gift. From thence, they somehow again made their way back down into Arabia and waited most patiently for yet another thousand years, until recent times."

His eyes grew serious and fastened on Merovee.

"You know of course, my dear, that the legend builders are already busy with Johannan."

She nodded.

"He mentioned it himself . . . that last night. Some were already saying that his mother was impregnated, not by Johannan's father, but, by 'God,' himself. Can you feature it? That 'God' descended from heaven in the form of a . . . . . . "

She looked up at Jesus in shock.

"Of a dove. You said it was doves which found and raised the infant Semiramis after Atargatis-Artemis abandoned her."

"Another facet of the same core." said Procula eagerly. "Now that I think about it, since doves are sacred to Artemis, maybe Semiramis was not abandoned after all. Her mother was there in the doves, taking care of her baby as a mother should . . . you did say that those of more advanced consciousness can be many things at the same time, did you not, Jesus?"

He smiled.

"You take my breath away, Procula, you progress so rapidly. But allow me to remain with my thirty pieces of silver . . . "

"Ah!" said Merovee. "Silver is the metal of the moon, and the moon is the symbol of Artemis."

"So this all somehow has to do with the mother goddess," said Procula.

"Of course," Merovee agreed, "because if it had to do with a male, the coins or talents would have been gold, for gold is the symbol of all the great male gods."

"Ladies, please have lunch next week and talk about it then. I am trying to tell you the newest facet of the legend concerning Johannan. Had Johannan heard about the Magi who came to worship him when he was born, Merovee?"

"I think he was spared that one."

"Well, the learned rabbis are now suggesting that the Magi, knowing Johannan to be Elijah reborn, journeyed from afar, bringing precious gifts, among them those thirty pieces of silver, which they presented to his miraculous mother."

"Hmm. Well, if so, Johannan certainly never had the use of any of them," said Merovee. "Where do our learned rabbis say that his mother buried that silver? I will go and dig it up. It would make a fine inheritance for my son."

"Your son will have to find other means of support," said Jesus, smiling gently. "As you know, these thirty pieces of silver are thirty pieces of magic, with no 'real' substance at all . . . yet, they carry the substance of millennia. Their odyssey is really the odyssey of the Samir, and of Semiramis. And that odyssey has not ended, I promise you."

He turned solemn eyes to Pilatus.

"This is the difficulty of explaining such things, you see. Things like the Samir, and the Ark of the Covenant. Such living symbols. Because an unspoken part of each one of those living symbols is the future, which I know partly, and you know not at all.

"But, someday, you will be able to see for yourselves the vitality, the true reality, of these symbols. You will see at first hand how we create what we think of as reality from them.

"I somehow know—and do not ask me how, because I do not know—that you, Pilatus, will hold these thirty magic pieces of silver in your own hands before all is said and done. You, too, Merovee. As will I . . . after, once more, a man is sold for that symbolic price. And, once more, one would be able to say that a burial field has been purchased.

"When that comes to pass, understand the glittering jewel passing through your lives, like a star streaking across the night sky. Recognize the simultaneous millennia of human emotion swirling in those 'solid' pieces of silver."

The faces looking up at him had all grown quite pale.

"I am sorry," he said. "I did not mean to cast a pall over the evening. You are still waiting to know of the Samir.

"Procula, my little scholar, did Andropos tell you of the fabled Atlantis?"

"Oh yes!"

Jesus refilled his goblet.

"Atlantis flourished in a time 'long before' the flood, long before even the 'Eden' experiment. Its culture was extremely advanced. Its sciences developed machines for travel, including flight, and conveniences of living that you would find hard to believe.

"Among their developments was an extraordinary harnessing of light. By means of specially-made sheets of glass . . . "

"There is the glass over the moor hen's nest!" said Procula, recovering her spirits.

"Exactly. The Atlanteans' glass was polished in a way that enabled it to channel, to focus, light rays. This concentrated light was used to heal, to cut stone, metals, all manner of difficult materials, and to do many other amazing things.

"From a culture even older than their own, the Atlanteans had also received an advanced knowledge of sound frequencies, and they used those frequencies as a power for lifting and for locomotion."

"Sound?" said Pilatus skeptically.

"In a way," said Jesus, "the Universe is composed of sound and the frequencies of sound. Each of us gives off our own particular 'music,' which we could hear if our ears were tuned to the frequencies upon which those 'songs' play. Some of the frequencies of the Universe have tremendous power. There are frequencies one note of which could make the whole Earth burst apart and float off into the skies as a cloud of dust."

"But what is a frequency?" said Procula.

Jesus frowned thoughtfully.

"I could explain it my means of a vibrating string on a lyre, but it might be best at the moment if you think of it simply as an invisible channel in the air, through which an equally invisible substance flows."

"I think I see now," said Merovee. "Father Ibraham—the clan of Terah—they discovered some of the lost secrets of Atlantis?"

"They did not physically discover them. That is, they did not unearth long-buried formulas. They came upon them mentally.

"The individuals comprising the clan of Terah had, of course, each lived many times before. As is often the case, those particular Spirits preferred to travel together, so that almost all of their incarnations had been taken as a family or social unit. Their Atlantean existence had been one such close social venture . . . they had been foremost among the Atlantean people of science.

"Reborn as 'Terah and family,' they applied themselves to yet a different expertise. Building. Specializing in stone. But, as is always the case with people of genius, places in their minds remained receptive to the information and accomplishments of their other existences.

"All discoveries are really only rediscoveries you see, new versions of old information—and no knowledge, no experience, is ever lost. Ideas are the common property of the species, always there, ready and waiting for those who either consciously or unconsciously open themselves to them. So that, spontaneously, from out of nowhere it seemed, even to the Terah clan, they 'invented' a glass that focused light and cut stone as finely as a newly sharpened razor cuts a hair.

"Then the one we know as Ibraham, a genius who has seldom been surpassed, 'invented,' or found a means of producing, sound that could lift a monolith of many tons as if it were a feather.

"Think for a moment, of the stories of the 'demons' who worked for Solomon . . . of the 'magical' ways in which his Temple was built. There was one demon, they say, whose specialty was tossing stones, each of which weighed tons, up to the masons as they worked, even as high as the roof.

"Where do you suppose such stories came from? They were not made up, not the imaginings of ancestors suffering from the heat. Stones did actually float up to the roof of the temple. Lifted by sound frequencies. Between the 'magical' appearance of the thing, and the quite unearthly sound that accompanied the feat, what were those who had not been admitted into the secret supposed to think? That Solomon had demons working for him, of course."

"And that is why Ibraham was so sought after," said Merovee, "and why he and his group went to such lengths to keep their secrets to themselves."

"So the real basis of the Samir legend was . . . what?" said Pilatus. "The special glass that cut with light, and . . . what was it that made the sound that lifted things?"

"A stone. A small black stone which fits into the palm of the hand."

All three stared.

"But . . . " said Merovee, "stones do not do anything except . . . clunk when you drop them."

"As you believe, so it shall be," said Jesus lightly.

"Oh, come! If I believe that a stone will make a sound that will lift things, it will?"

"You, who stood on water and who heals the sick and makes the blind to see, can ask me that?"

"Stop teasing me. This had to have been a very special stone."

"It can be found on any riverbank or seashore. A most unremarkable stone. Before Ibraham, it had been a stone that builders would easily have rejected."

Merovee looked up sharply.

"And now it became the head, or cap, stone," she said.

Jesus smiled.

"Yet another facet of King David's mysterious comment."

"The legend says that the Samir was gotten from the Prince of the Sea," Procula murmured. "And this stone can be found on seashores. What is so special about it?"

"What is special," said Jesus, "is the mental relationship between the stone and the person holding it."

"The thoughts of the person cause the stone to make its sound?" said Merovee.

"Exactly."

"What sort of thoughts?"

"We are back to frequencies. Your consciousness works through the brain in your skull. In some ways, this brain is much like the lyre I mentioned earlier. It is a delicate instrument upon which consciousness, the mind, 'plays.' And, as the brain is 'played,' it emits a sort of music, tones of varying 'frequencies' of vibration, which frequencies of vibration change as the thoughts change. It just so happens that one particular frequency reacts with this particular sort of rock, and causes the rock to emit yet a second sound. With that second sound, my dear, you can move mountains."

"And Ibraham stumbled onto this by accident," said Pilatus.

"All great discoveries are 'accidents.' A more astonished man than Ibraham you never saw. And, if he had been as most men, the moment, the opportunity, would have been lost. For, as his thoughts changed, the right sound was interrupted and things stopped moving about. Most men would have fallen down gabbling and frothing in fear, or just walked away, assuming that their imagination had been working overtime. Ibraham, however, had the presence of mind to persist in his wonderment, until he duplicated the circumstances and caused the phenomenon to repeat.

"Now, it just so happened that he had been importuning a particular god when the right frequency was produced, so he got the idea that the phenomenon was a sign from that god, and, at first, assumed that it was the combination of words that had caused the god to be so pleased and to show his 'sign.'

" . . . which is, by the way, a common misunderstanding amongst those who try to work magic by the use of pre-set spells . . . or, for that matter, amongst those who do a great deal of praying. They suppose that they have only to procure certain items and then mumble certain words over them to obtain miraculous results. It is neither the words nor the objects which produce the results. As Ibraham at last realized, it is the mental frequencies, produced by particular attitudes, or thoughts, in combination with the things, which produce results.

"Those results are not magic, and they have nothing to do with religious devotion or 'righteousness.' They have only to do with The Energy on which the Universe is founded."

"But in that must be . . . " Merovee hesitated. "Since the true god is the Universe, and the Universe is the true god, in learning to use that force—that Power or Energy—is one not venturing toward the highest—or deepest—'religion'? Is not one venturing closer and closer to true awe of the true god, and thus to true veneration?"

Jesus leaned down, picked up a cluster of grapes and stared at it before breaking off the first morsel.

"Ever closer to the true face of the true god . . . or closer to true 'damnation.' In those few words, my dear, you have encapsulated the striving of the ages, the confusion of the ages, and the key to both sainthood and to evil of the most appalling sort.

"Let us suppose, just for amusement, that Pilatus and I left you two ladies to chat for a while, and slipped over the causeway to the Temple, then into a tunnel that leads to a particular hidden door to an ancient secret tunnel that leads to an even more ancient passageway, built by Solomon, into the vault beneath the Holy of Holies . . . "

"If you think that you are leaving me behind while you take such an adventure," said Merovee, "you are crazy."

"Is there such a passage?" said Pilatus eagerly. "I have heard tales, and I have had Lucius poke around, but he never found any door. Do you know where it is?"

Jesus grinned and popped another grape into his mouth.

"We are being hypothetical here, Pilatus. So you and I and Merovee . . . "

"And Procula," said Procula.

"And Procula. The four of us . . . "

"Five," said Micah.

"The five of us get into the vault under the Holy of Holies, and we climb the stairs and lift the trap door, and there we are, in the Forbidden Place, that room into which only the High Priest may venture, and then only once a year. There is the Ark of the Covenant, covered with gold on its every inch, so dazzling that it nearly blinds us even in torchlight. We stand for a moment, in open-mouthed awe. Then we walk over and we lift its lid."

"Who lifts the lid?" grinned Merovee. "I am not going to lift the lid."

"How about you, Pilatus?" said Jesus.

"Uh . . . is one not supposed to get struck dead or something?"

"Procula?"

Procula hesitated. Then she smiled up at Jesus.

"If you will stand beside me and hold my hand, Jesus, I will lift the lid."

Jesus walked to the couch, reached down and did take her hand.

"I will be standing beside you and holding your hand forevermore, my darling, Open any lid you wish. You need never fear again."

He gave the hand an extra squeeze, released it and strolled back to regard a bust of a young Caesar Augustus.

"Pilatus, how did you smuggle all of these graven images in here?"

For, shortly after becoming praefectus, Pilatus and his men had aroused the ire of the rulers of the Temple by carrying shields with images on them. To avoid a riot, those blasphemous shields had had to be gotten quickly back to Caesarea.

"In the dead of night in barrels of flour," said Pilatus. "And only those I can trust are ever allowed into this apartment."

The two men exchanged fond glances.

"So!" Jesus continued. "Procula lifts the lid and, at my bidding, she reaches in and takes out the stone. Again at my bidding, she gives it to . . . "

He turned, smiling.

"To you, Pilatus. We rummage about a bit more in the ark, and come up with a great many tablets, incised in various ancient scripts. But I am able to translate those dead languages, and tell you the words which should be spoken over the stone. I am also able to translate the instructions—the description of the mental attitude that you must have while saying the words. Everything is right there for you.

"With all of that, Pilatus, do you think you would be able to point that stone at so much as a pebble and cause the pebble to lift?"

Pilatus opened his mouth. Then shut it. He turned his head and thought for a moment. Then he nodded.

"I see what you mean. That 'essential attitude' is probably very hard to achieve."

"What if," said Jesus slowly, "I give the rock and the instructions to Procula. Think you she could make miracles happen?"

A slow smile spread over the face of Pilatus.

"Yes. I think Procula could do it. I can see already . . . " His voice was almost wistful. "She believes. Therefore, according to you—she can."

The eyes of Jesus upon Pilatus darkened in hue. The blue flecks seemed almost to glint.

"Never undervalue your own self or Self, Pilatus. You are quite right. Procula could probably do it. In a very short time, Procula could do a great many astounding things. Procula is quite naturally at a 'place' in her development where she is ready to take giant strides.

"But so are you ready to take strides forward from your own place. You start from a different place than does Procula. Not lower, not inferior. Different. If you were not, yourself, ready, you would not recognize Procula's readiness."

Jesus stroked the marble pate of Augustus.

"The truth is, Pilatus, that anyone could do it. If he or she managed to achieve the right mind frequency. It is difficult, yes. Very difficult. One must have a great deal of mental discipline, or else natural talent. Again, it does not matter whether one is good or bad, a saint or a sinner. The Power is neutral. The Power simply is."

"But . . . " Pilatus frowned. "If it works equally for those who are good or those who are evil, why bother to be good?"

Jesus glanced at Merovee and laughed.

"That is always the first question asked. Yet one could as well say, 'Why bother to be evil?' You speak as though there is something qualitatively superior, happier, about being evil. Have you ever known any really evil people, Pilatus?"

"More than my share."

"Have you ever known any good people?"

"A precious few."

"Precious. Interesting that you should call them precious.

"Which of the two classes would you rather spend your time with?"

"Those who try to be decent."

"Why?"

"They are . . . . . . more pleasant to be with. A person can relax, you do not have to be frightened, and on your guard."

"They are more pleasant. Is that because they are happier than those who are evil?"

"Generally. Yes. Definitely. Those who are evil are so eaten by their ambitions and jealousies, their egos, their greeds, and lusts."

"So evil people are not happy?"

"Well . . . "

"Have you ever met an evil person who was happy?"

" . . . No. What passes for happiness with them is momentary elation, triumph, satiation . . . but the thing is, that they are never really satisfied."

"Would it be fair, then, to say that evil people never know a moment of true happiness or contentment? Of peace?"

"I think that would be fair."

"Why would you ever then, given a power that works equally for saint or for sinner, say, 'Why bother to be good'?"

Pilatus shrugged, honestly bemused.

"Just habit, I suppose. We have been taught to fight and claw for what we want in this world. We have been taught that certain achievements bring happiness, and that being good will not get us those things which we desire . . . at least not speedily.

"Yet none of that is necessarily true. You are right."

"Indeed. And let us understand that those who are good and those who are evil can be found among all strata and levels of society. Riches do not make evil. Poor does not make good. There is only The Power, All That Is, that is available equally to all, to use as each sees fit.

"Most use that force unconsciously, never even suspecting its existence. Here and there, an individual comes to know consciously of its availability and uses it actively. Those individuals do not have to have possession of any particular amulet or charm or rock or animal or words. Yet they can do much more than simply lift stones.

"In lesser manifestations of its conscious use, The Force can make Caesars, conquerors, winners of contests, great lovers, kings, queens, generals, successful farmers, rich merchants, great cooks, prosperous fishermen, praefecti of Roman provinces, successful courtesans, builders of cities, high priests and priestesses, great tyrants, and notorious brigands.

"At more concentrated levels, it can make sorcerers, sages, great teachers, scientists, immortal artists and writers and musicians, scientists, and other bringers of love, light, laughter, and healing. Merovee spoke rightly when she said that All That Is is the Universe and the Universe is All That Is, and that, in learning to use The Power of the Universe, we approach the deepest religion, that we venture closer to the 'face' of All That Is. The Power of All That Is, The Force that is All That Is, is there for us to use as we will. All attempts to learn its true nature and use are, in the overall development of a Soul, 'good'—for only by doing, can one learn.

"But there is a best way to use The Force. And that is what all those who reach the point of consciously using it eventually learn. Some know the truth of that best use immediately. Others might use up a hundred lifetimes, applying The Force negatively—for 'evil,' for personal gain, for riches, for dominion over their fellows—before they finally understand.

"The legend of Sisyphus is a marvelous statement of the principal.

"Sisyphus was among the cleverest of men. But he used his cleverness to lie, cheat, steal, rape, and to get his way in all things. So that he became very rich and very powerful, and all the world knew of him.

"Until, in his inflated presumption of his own power, and of his personal immunity from reprisal, he undertook to cheat and steal from the gods, themselves.

"Well, that was just a bit too much. The gods took Sisyphus by the ear and led him over to a boulder at the base of a hill, where they condemned him to an eternity of pushing that boulder up that hill.

"They arranged it so that, each night, when Sisyphus reaches the top, the stone goes tumbling back down to the bottom, so that, the next morning, he must start all over again, pushing that miserable stone up that miserable hill.

"That is how it is with those who use The Power—who use the gifts provided them by 'the gods'—in any negative way. All their work is for naught. Each night—at each death—all they have worked to achieve, of earthly power and possessions—just goes pouf! And they must start all over again at the next birth."

"Will the stone ever stay up there?" said Procula. "Can Sisyphus ever gain release?"

"Oh, in a moment!" said Jesus.

"But how?" said Merovee. "The gods have condemned him for eternity."

"That is what they told him. And that is what he believes. As long as he keeps believing that, he will remain in that damnation, in that underworld of his own making."

"He has only to believe that he is free and he will be?" said Merovee.

"Almost. He must first understand that he is there for eternity only if he believes that he is. Then he must do something to demonstrate to the gods that he has learned something from the experience, that he is ready to try it another way."

"But what could he possibly do?" said Pilatus.

"Think you," smiled Jesus, "that Sisyphus is the only poor fool toiling on that mountain? If he would stop thinking of himself for a moment, and look around, he would see that the slope is littered with people, many toiling at rocks much heavier than his own. What Sisyphus would have to do, you see, is to find the courage to defy the gods yet again, have the courage to trick them, go against them yet again . . . but for a completely different reason, a reason that would be the opposite of his usual, grasping, selfish mode of operation.

"He might one day, for instance, take notice a man who has an even larger stone to roll, who is so exhausted and dispirited that he can hardly sleep, who sits up all night and cries. Sisyphus could decide to give that poor man a day off, and use his own great strength to roll two stones up the hill, his stone and the other man's stone, so that the other man could have a rest, take a nap, enjoy the sun, perhaps even laugh, or sing a song. Knowing that he might be bringing even graver punishment down onto himself, Sisyphus could make the first completely unselfish and genuinely loving move of his entire existence, and strain his innards rolling both stones up that hill."

"And the gods would be so impressed that they would be waiting for him at the top and release him from his bondage?" said Pilatus.

Jesus ate a few more grapes.

"I wish I could tell you yes. But no. It would seem that the gods had not even noticed. Both stones would roll right back down to the bottom again."

There was a united groan from the listeners.

"But, that night, the man who had been given a rest would sleep soundly, and next day he would offer to roll the stone of Sisyphus for him, so that Sisyphus could have a rest. And, the next night, both men would feel better, if only for their mutual rests, and their newfound friendship, and they would have the energy to build a fire to warm themselves, and cook a stew, and they would tell stories and sing. And others would draw near, and share their own food and drink. And Sisyphus and his friend would tell them the cause of their happiness, that, by helping one another, by caring and loving, their lots had become measurably better.

"The next day, all over the mountain, you would see people rolling two stones while others rested, and the next day you would see those roles reversed. And the nights would be brightened with the dancing lights of many fires, with laughter and with singing.

"And then one day Sisyphus would have another idea.

"'It has not escaped my attention that the gods have not interfered with us even though we have defied them,' he would say. 'And I wonder if we have struck upon a way in which the gods love to be

414

defied. Let us test this theory still further. Let us, each one of us, roll his own stone to the mountaintop today. But let us do it with gladness and with singing. Let us call out to the gods to witness our happiness. Let us shout of the love we have learned to express, and of our gratitude to them for making us roll our stones in the first place, so that we could learn the path to true success and happiness. And when we get to the top, quickly, before the stones begin to roll back down, let us build something with them. Let us build an altar to the gods.'

"And there would be cries of approval, but also voices of dissent.

"'Why not simply take our stones and build a great warm hall down here at the base of the mountain,' some would say. 'It can house us all, so that none will be cold, and so that travelers can find shelter. That would be the most fitting tribute to the gods.'

"'Would it not be better to build a warm place to tend those who grow sick?' others would ask.

"And so the toilers would split into groups, some toiling yet again up the mountain to build an altar, others remaining at the bottom to build a communal lodge, others to build a shelter for the sick and infirm, and some a school . . . but both the hills and the valleys would ring with joy and with thanksgiving.

"And still it would seem that the gods had not noticed. But the altar and lodge and place for the sick and the school would get built and would not be destroyed by the gods, and no one would have any longer to roll a stone up the mountain each day. There would be prosperity and plenty, and warmth and caring, and laughter and song, and the zest of discovery with each new day.

"And all of the original builders would know why. Their hymns of praise and gratitude would be based on real experience, real learning, so that each would strive, for all his life, to be just and fair, loving and helpful, to all of creation.

"And when each died and was reborn, each of those founders—who had once thought that evil was the way to happiness, and who had then thought himself condemned to roll stones for all of eternity— each would find himself living as easily and as beautifully as a lily on the hillside, so that others would wonder at his luck, and say that he must be a favorite of the gods.

"But, of course, there would be new generations on the mountain, the children, and the children of the children of the founders, who would not know, would not understand, how or why their village had been built.

"Ah yes. There would be wise ones among them who did know, and who would try to tell the others. But they would be as voices crying in The Wilderness. The others would grow greedy, they would strive for earthly power and earthly glory, forgetting what their elders had taught them of the superior benefits to be had from loving and sharing. They would war amongst themselves for control of the buildings, and riches. Their evils would know no bounds, transgressing, finally, even upon the gods, for they would use even the altar as a means to gain earthly riches and power and glory, assuming that the ends justified the means.

"And one day they would wake to find their world shattered, their buildings reduced to huge stones laying about, and the gods would be standing amongst them . . . leering.

"'You! You! You! Yes, you, too. All of you. Each of you. Get yourself a stone. Start pushing. And this shall be your lot, your damnation for all of eternity. Push!'

"And a great wail would go up.

"'How capricious, how cruel are the gods!' the toilers would cry."

Jesus stopped speaking and applied himself to the remainder of the grapes. The listeners sat silent for a some moments. Finally, Pilatus spoke.

"You would take from us all our excuses."

He shook his head ruefully.

"Jesus, I would not be in your shoes for all the riches of the Silk Lands. Not only do you rile the priests, you will rile the people by stealing their scapegoats. How many will be able to accept the fact that they, and they alone, are accountable for their own misfortunes?"

Jesus smiled.

"Many fewer than will crow of their own accountability when things go right. But I do not seek popularity, Pilatus. I seek a few fertile minds, here in this time and place, in which I will plant my seeds. You have worked in the fields. You know that even the best seeds, cast upon rock, or sand, or poor soil—even though cast one-hundred-fold—will produce but a few sickly plants which are gone after a season. While even one prime seed, delivered to prime soil, will produce one strong plant, then, the next season, several, while, by the third season, there will be a patch of lusty fruit fit most truly for the gods.

"You and Procula, each in your own way, will provide such lusty fruit, Pilatus. And I want you to remember always, come what may . . . the Universe inclines toward the positive. Whatever the appearances, whatever the situation, have the courage to make a positive choice from the many alternatives. If you do, your results will not only be quick, but lasting. Your eternal incarceration in your moments will be pleasant indeed.

"And so." He patted Augustus. "What a handsome man he was. Have I answered you as to the Samir? And the ark?"

"Perhaps just enough to help us to form more questions," laughed Procula. "The Samir, and what was in the ark, they were many things. But, on the level of our reality, it was a formula . . . "

"Many formulas," interjected Jesus. "Secret techniques for the achieving of seemingly magical effects."

"But why, then, are we told that the ark contains the Ten Commandments of God?" said Merovee."

"Because it did. Those ten rules were contained in the other instructions. The names that have come down to us, of the great patriarchs and leaders, have not stood the test of time by accident. Those men were truly great, each in his own way. Each, to a certain extent, understood what I have just told you. That The Power should never be used for evil, or for selfish purposes, and that the most efficient results are obtained by those of good intention. And so they included those rules in an attempt to guide those who came after them to that goodness.

"Unfortunately, as is so often the case, things went awry.

"First, as Merovee pointed out a while ago, a great obstacle to overcome as one grows in understanding is the notion that others are not as well-intentioned as oneself. One must get over the idea that others must be shielded from the truth, or given false, childish stories, directed, by dint of rules and regulations, into paths of 'righteousness,' or just plain terrified into 'doing right.' None of our leaders overcame those hurdles in thinking, with the result that the very truths and 'goodnesses' that they sought to ensure were destroyed by their own falsehoods at the outset.

"Second, as I pointed out, having all the particulars and formulas of the ark at your disposal does not guarantee that you will be able to produce miracles. Throughout our history, there have been only a handful of men who did manage to consistently produce astounding results. Ibraham himself, Isaac, Esau. Jacob, Joseph, two men not generally known, Sheiim and Nabata, then Moses and Aaron, Solomon, Hiram Abiff, and Daniel. Those individuals never failed to 'make the magic happen.' Others got spotty results."

"Not David?" said Merovee.

"Not even David. But we do have David to thank for the glorious Solomon. Remember the story of David going into the Holy of Holies and laying hands on the ark in defiance of his god? What he was actually doing was defying the priesthood, the descendants of Aaron. He walked in and opened the ark and seized the formulas which the priests had been keeping to themselves. Though he was himself unable to make them work, his son, Solomon, was able. Which is why, out of the many children that David had got out of many wives and concubines, Solomon was designated heir.

"He was the greatest of all, was Solomon. He was another incarnation of Ibraham, actually, and so a genius of the first order who added to the 'miracles' already contained in the chest, though all the keys to those miracles died with him. You have heard of King Solomon's mines, for instance, where worked some of the genies and demons of the great king—genies who lighted the darkness of the mines with miraculous, oil-less lamps. There were no genies or demons, only ordinary men who had at their disposal one of the king's many inventions. The core of the invention was coils of thin metal which produced bright light even in underground chambers."

"And none of the workers tried to steal this idea?" said Pilatus.

"Like those who watched boulders float up to the roof of Solomon's temple, they assumed it to be the work of genies and demons, with which creatures they would never have dared to interfere. Besides, whenever a shift of men finished their time of working in the mines, Solomon had them slain. Just to be sure.

"Actually, the principle used in Solomon's coil can be duplicated in the body of a human being. If, that is, that person knows how to harness the spiral energy within his or her own body."

"Could you light a dark cave with just your body?" asked Procula.

"If ever I must needs try it, I will inform you of the results," smiled Jesus.

"And Solomon took the keys to all of this with him when he died?" said Pilatus, shaking his head. "What a crime. How some of these techniques would have helped his fellow Man."

"In some probabilities, he did give the secrets to Humankind. You would be hard-pressed to recognize the worlds of the people who live now in those probabilities. In our probability, Solomon began as a good man. He ended as a debauched, inflated, crazed creature who wished not only to destroy the keys to his own discoveries, but to all of the information that David had removed from the ark. He was determined that no one ever again would be able to equal his achievements, or build an edifice as magnificent as his temple. He had already had all the master builders who had labored on the temple slain—all those privy to, or in possession of any of the secrets of the Builders—including the current head genius of the Builders, who we incorrectly remember by the name of Hiram Abiff. You see, though the secrets contained in the ark were the central core of the knowledge of the Builders, certain of the groups still guarded secrets of their own. Since most of the great masters from all the groups of the Mediterranean and Eastern worlds had come to Solomon, eager to be part of such a momentous project, Solomon, in killing them, effectively destroyed the Builders as a unified force. With their head masters and geniuses killed, and the ark robbed of the most crucial of its contents, the bulk of the secrets, the most important understandings of the Builders, were gone. What was left of those groups scattered—some to very faraway lands—taking with them the tatters of their knowledge and skills. Here in Palestine, the Nazorites are a remnant of one group of Builders who did stay, though they have lost understanding of their own history. Most Builders who remained here in Palestine simply turned to the land."

"How large is the rock that Solomon is currently rolling up the mountain each day?" smiled Pilatus.

"Ten times the size of the Earth," said Jesus.

"The distant thunder in the hills at night," said Procula dreamily. "It is not the anger of the gods at all. It is all those stones, rolling back down into the valleys."

"I have heard of a Key of Solomon," said Merovee. "Some Pharisees claim to have a document written by Solomon, himself, that tells them how to command jinns and genies and demons."

Jesus nodded.

"One of Solomon's little jokes. He did indeed write it. But he garbled those instructions so that no one has ever been able to obtain results. The real keys, he took with him to his grave."

"So the Holy of Holies has been empty for a thousand years?" said Merovee.

"For only half of that time. Even Solomon had enough residual awe to refrain from destroying certain prime objects and writings. Those, he returned to the priests and to the ark. But all the important details which had been handed down with the instructions, the helpful hints which successful practitioners had added over thousands of years, the bits of wisdom and experience added by patriarch after patriarch . . . those essential adjuncts to the basic instructions, he destroyed."

"Which is why," said Merovee thoughtfully, "that our history after Solomon becomes lackluster for hundreds of years. Until the Captivity. And Daniel."

"Exactly. Daniel was a scholar, chief of his clan in Babylon, and an architectural genius who was privy to at least cursory information as to what was still left in the ark. He believed that, if he could get his hands on the ark, he would be able to resurrect the old magic.

"And he was right. Working only from the prime documents—those not destroyed by Solomon— he, and those who followed him, were able to work such wonders in the construction of Babylonian cities—and then Persian cities when the Babylonians were ousted by the Persians—that Persian authorities finally went to great lengths of torture and intimidation to try to pry their secrets from them.

"The compromise finally struck was that the Jews would give the Babylonians the secrets in return for their 'freedom' and safe conduct back to Judeah. This was negotiated by the priests, led by Ezra, who realized that they had much more to gain by enlisting Persian aid in the re-building of Jerusalem and of the Temple—and the setting up of a purely priestly state—than in the continued ownership of the contents of the ark. Those contents were as worthless as dust to anyone who did not have the luck or talent to understand.

"And what did it matter that the ark that was carried back to Jerusalem was empty? As long as the people believed that what the priests said was in the ark was indeed in the ark, all would be well."

Jesus stood facing the bust of Augustus Caesar as though in deep contemplation of that countenance.

"And that—the return of some of our people from Babylon—the enforced return of the few who could be rounded up, then whipped along the roads by Levites and by Persian soldiers—that marked the true end of the Golden Age of those peoples whom the world is coming to know collectively as 'Jews.' For it was the total end of an innocence, of a basically pure desire, even amongst priests, to do great things through the auspices of goodness and truth.

"What the priests set up once returned to Judeah was a sham, a parody of truth and goodness, a state designed solely to confer riches and power upon themselves . . . which sham I am called upon to expose. And to destroy."

He turned. His eyes seemed fastened on a place not of this world, and his voice held a dry, faraway quality that Merovee had heard only once before.

"I charge each of you three. Strive always to speak and do the truth as you see it. and to represent that truth to your fellows as clearly as possible. Do not make the mistake of Ibraham, and of all those who followed him. Do not assume that good results can be obtained by lies or dishonesties or by any acts which are not loving and fair to any and every creature. Do not hide truth under rules and regulations and prevarication. Think not that you can lead your fellows in paths of righteousness if you, yourself, are dishonest. Think not that you must hide truth from others in order to insure their goodness. Trust your fellow beings to be of good intent and able to respond to truth. Keep trusting until they are and do. For they are of basically good intent, and, somewhere in simultaneous time, there is a part of them that does understand, and that does respond. Humanity discovers its own good intent quicker by the light of truth than in the darkness of lies and cruelties, however well-intended. Think not that the ends justify the means. Dishonest means always result in dishonest and dishonorable ends."

The brittleness faded. He smiled.

"That is, if you would stay out of the stone-rolling business. Believe me. I know. I have rolled my own fair share."

During the ensuing laughter, he walked to Procula's side, reached down, took her hand, put his thumb to her pulse and was silent for a few moments.

"Merovee and I will take our leave," he said at last. "You need rest."

"Oh no, please! I have never felt better! I could not possibly sleep now."

"Trust me. Go to your bed. Not only will you sleep, but you will sleep more deeply and comfortably than you have in years. During that deep sleep, you will think upon these things that I have said to you, and confer with teachers far greater than I.."

The time? Pilatus had lost track. Checking with a slave, he was shocked to learn that it was well past the midnight hour. He, too, grew concerned for Procula. Automatically, he appealed to his dear new friend.

"Merovee. We have been thoughtless of your condition. You must be exhausted."

A smile tugged at those wide, warm lips.

"I suspect that, by the time your wagon returns us to Bethany, I will be grateful for my bed."

"Ah, Pilatus." Procula still clung to the hand of Jesus. "Would that we had come up to Jerusalem even sooner. Think of the time we have wasted. I must hear more of this. And more and more. Jesus— oh say yes, please. May I not come out to Bethany each day and listen as you teach your people?"

"Procula!" Pilatus rose. "It is quite impossible. My dear! You are simply not strong enough for such activity."

"I fear that I will not be strong enough without it. Not now that I have heard these things. I will surely expire if I do not hear more."

Hurriedly, she rose, and went to embrace Pilatus.

"Please. Pilatus, what harm could it do me? I certainly cannot get worse than I have already been in the last weeks. And, if it must be that I should die, think of the great gift you would be allowing me, to take with me into my next life."

Pilatus felt the sudden hot tears pressing. Briefly, the political ramifications darted through his mind.

This Jesus was an enemy of the priesthood. An enemy of Rome! To condone the man . . . to send his own wife to sit at the feet of the man, might cost him his career. This Jesus could be his ruination.

All he could see was his wife's shining face.

He allowed the tears to flow.

"You must promise to remember every word and repeat it to me when you come home each night."

He felt weak, and dreamlike again, as Procula gave an excited cry, like the girl he had first known, and threw her strong, young arms around his neck.

Strong, young arms?

He watched her seize the arm of Jesus to conduct him out to the wagon.

Slowly, on the arm of Merovee, he followed.

Who was that glittering creature chattering to Jesus?

He stumbled, suddenly blinded by a new spate of tears.

He felt the solid, uplifting pressure.

"You thought to save her life," he heard Merovee whisper. "You thought to find her a new purpose. And that you have done.

"But you assumed that a new purpose would fit into the old framework . . . that the life you were saving was the one you had known, that her purposes would be as of old.

"Such a thing cannot be, Pilatus. Procula is reborn. The old Procula died shortly after we walked into your dining chamber tonight.

"I mean that literally. That Procula expired, and this probable version was born, complete with an infusion of energy from the one who died. The person on my husband's arm is a totally new Procula.

"And the question for you now will be . . . will you be able to abide by what you, yourself, have wrought?"

Chapter 15

A Child Is Born

Petros sat as still as his nickname, his back against something equally as still, the tomb in the garden bar Jeremiah. The weather had turned unseasonably warm, and that secluded corner happened to be the coolest spot. Besides, he wanted to be alone. Bar Jeremiah seemed busier and even more crowded than the Temple courts of late, and he needed to sort his thoughts.

Not only was the place crowded, but the visitors grew ever more exalted. The Princess Salome had been intimidating enough, but he had grown accustomed to her. Just as he did get used to her, her mother, Herodias, had appeared.

Why could the woman not have stayed in her palace? Why did she have to come here?

And now the wife of the praefectus arrived all secretly each morning, having walked all alone from the Hasmonaean Palace, veiled and dressed as a common serving girl, so as not to draw attention to herself.

It was more than a simple man should have to deal with.

And Petros was a simple man. Only a fisherman.

Yet, did he not do that job so well that he had become a master at it? Had the Zebedee not made him the foreman over all the other workers?

Yes, that was what he was. Not just a simple man. Not just a fisherman. He was a fore man.

And that was not a light thing. A man had to work a long time to be fore of all others. To be fore was to have talent, a good head on the shoulders, a favored place in the eyes of God, so that fortune smiled upon the fleet. To be fore was to be honest, so that an employer could delegate the work in complete trust. To be fore was a proud thing. And fore man of the Zebedee, one of the greatest merchants in all of Palestine, was a doubly proud thing. So that, certainly, when his young brother Chandreah had come to him and told him of this Jesus, and asked Petros to join him in following after, Petros had had a perfect right to expect that he would be the first follower afterer.

And when Jesus had given him a name meaning piece of rock, it had seemed obvious to Petros that Jesus did intend that he be the fore man. Was a rock not a hard, steady, durable, dependable thing? Was a rock not something with which one could defend oneself? Or with which one could build?

It had not worked that way. Not at all. The degradation which Petros had suffered since joining up with Jesus had often made him feel more like a pebble than a rock, a pebble on the footpath, dustier with each day, fit only to be trammeled, or kicked aside. More than once, Petros had considered leaving, returning to his work, where he was accounted of import.

And that was why he was sitting in the shade today, gathering his thoughts. Once more, he was considering leaving.

The Big Fisherman, they called him on the lake. And they said it with respect.

This Jesus accorded him no respect. This Jesus admitted no man to be more than any other. The twin, 'Didymus,' and Judah—those two might be closest to his favorites. Among men.

While the real favorite of Jesus, the one whom Jesus loved, was clear for all to see.

A woman.

A whore as far as Petros was concerned. No one would ever convince him that the Prophet Johannan had made a contract of marriage with her, gird or no gird. The respect paid this woman by most of the others was sickening to see.

The Beloved Disciple, they called her, the one who received the secret teachings of Jesus, the one who accompanied him upon his nightly journeys, the only one, so they said, who truly understood the things that the Prophet, and now Jesus, taught.

Beloved Disciple she might be to the others. To Petros, she was simply "the Magdalen." That was what he called her behind her back or when speaking to others, filling the words with all the contempt that he could summon. Heiress of Migdal-Magdala, vendor of Magdalia, so rich that it was obscene. Yet she traipsed around the countryside like a man, refusing to admit her own womanhood or even to call herself by her woman's name of Miriam.

Well, she knew that she was a woman now. She had been brought to bed, attended by a bevy of solicitous women, and even by Jesus, to that man's everlasting shame so far as Petros was concerned. They said that he had not moved from her side for twenty-four hours, that he sat there sponging her head, rubbing her, talking, laughing, encouraging, waiting upon his cousin's bastard for all the world as though it were his own.

"Dear Lord of mercy and justice," Petros prayed to God in the sky over Jerusalem. "May the bastard never see the light of day. May it die in the womb and take the whore of Magdala into damnation with it."

What a joke that the strong young Magdalen should be having such a hard time of it. It was those slim hips, which had so successfully passed her off as a boy. She had offended God in using those hips to trespass against his rules concerning a woman's proper attire. Now God was getting back at her. And Petros was glad.

He lowered his face into his hands. A great, dry sob shook the massive shoulders. He should not feel this way. He should not hate her so. If Jesus were to find out, what would he think? What, after all, had the Magdalen ever done to him, Petros, except to be gracious and kind? Did she deserve to die merely because Jesus loved her above all others?

'Yes!' came the answer, echoing viciously from out of some fetid cavern in the mind of Petros, some demon calling to him. 'Let her die! She interferes with Jesus, she makes him soft. It is she who is responsible for the foolishness he spouts, those ideas of his which go against all righteousness. It is she who keeps him from his destiny. For he is the Messiah. But he turns from it. All because of her.

'And she steals that place in his affections that should be yours alone.'

He heard the crunch of gravel, slow footfalls along the manicured garden path. Cursing the disturbance, Petros let his head fall farther forward onto his arms and knees, pretending to sleep. The footsteps halted as the intruder spied him. But then, rather than retreating, the steps continued. Petros waited, trying to sort out a soft swishing, a confusion of sounds. Had the person sat down near to him?

After long minutes of silence, Petros peeked sideways.

It was Simon Yeshuah. He knelt some feet away, in profile. His head was bowed, his hands were clasped, his eyes were closed and his lips moved in silent prayer. Petros lifted his head and went back to his own ruminations. The man had obviously come to this secluded spot for the same reason as had he, and would bother less than the ants.

Yet Petros found his thoughts straying to that silent, upright figure. Finally, he turned and simply watched Yeshuah.

What a fine sight he presented as he knelt there. How like Jesus he was. Yet how unlike Jesus. There knelt the sort of man that Petros wished Jesus would be. Devout and God-fearing in the time-honored sense, and according to the highest tenets of The Law. Solemn, decorous, dignified, a man unswayed by feminine blandishments—except for those of his mother, of course, which was as it should be.

Why could Jesus not be that way?

Petros tilted his head sideways. His eyes, which were the milky sea-green of Lake Gennesareth after a rain, dilated.

The inside of the head of Petros often felt the same, even to Petros. Like Lake Gennesareth after a rain. Cool, calm, slightly opaque and yet teaming with activity, each bit of action separate, safe, and secret from all others because of the opaqueness. Much went on in the mind of Simon called Petros that even Simon called Petros did not know about. For, by the time that he realized that something was going on in some area, and sent his thoughts there to find out what, by the time they got there, whatever it was would have disappeared into that cool, slightly opaque sea-greenness.

But now a thought, clear and completely defined, swam out of the gloom and hovered, metaphorical gills and fins undulating lazily, so that Petros had the leisure to examine it from all sides.

This Simon Yeshuah had, himself, claimed to be the Long-Awaited One. Not a common messiah like the messiahs David or Solomon, or the Priest Messiah Caiaphas, but the supreme leader of the end of days, appointed, anointed, supported, and instructed by God, more than a general, much more than a politician, a holy man as well, the greatest of rabbans, able to usher in the Kingdom of God on Earth, able to conquer the Gentiles and bring them under the rule of The Law, with Jerusalem as the capitol of the entire world . . . after which, the world would end.

It was not unusual for men to proclaim themselves as the Messiah. Street talk had it that the fellow in Hebron had gathered quite a following. And, in just the last weeks, there had been news of a teacher and miracle worker among the Jews of Athens . . . while, in the last years in Galilee, half a dozen rabbis had been thought for a time to be the Messiah. They were as fish in the depths, these messiahs. A silvery flash . . . and they were gone. Simon Yeshuah seemed to have been just another flash.

Yet was he?

How arresting he was as he knelt in prayer. Not a man to be discounted. No, not at all. He had taken great pains to announce himself in Galilean synagogues as the Messiah, while Jesus had taken equal pains to announce to any and all that he was not the Messiah. Yet he, Petros, and all of the followers of Jesus, persisted in believing that Jesus was the Messiah.

Why?

As Petros examined that lazy, clear idea hovering in the coolness of his mind, he saw the answer.

One had only to study the habits of fish. A fish laid thousands of eggs. This was not because the fish expected there to be thousands of baby fish. On the contrary, the great number of eggs lain was because relatively few of those eggs would last long enough to hatch. They would be eaten by other fish, crushed by rocks and tides, or, in some other way, destroyed. From those thousands of eggs, perhaps only a few hundred baby fish would eventually hatch. From those few hundred, perhaps only a hundred would last into adulthood. From that hundred, perhaps only one, lonely fish would die of old age, having escaped the nets of the fishermen season after season.

Might it not be the same with the Messiah?

If God wished to save his Chosen People by sending to them a supreme Messiah, to govern and to lead them to their true greatness, would God cause only one possible Messiah to be born? Being the Messiah was trickier than being a fish, and certainly as dangerous. God would be taking a terrible chance to create only one. What if something happened to that one Messiah on the way to his destiny? What if he fell down and hit his head and forgot who he was? What if he got leprosy, or went blind? What if he tumbled into a well and drowned, or was put into prison? What if no one believed him? What if he was lazy, or a coward? What if even he refused to believe that he was the Messiah? Any number of things could occur to make it so that the planned Messiah would not happen at all. The way for God to be sure that at least one Messiah would happen would be to send many dozens qualified for the task.

Petros examined the kneeling Simon Yeshuah with sudden new interest. Was it this man, and not Jesus, who was destined to establish the Kingdom of God on Earth?

If so, then Petros was following the wrong man.

He frowned. That thought did not meet with his favor. He was a simple man, yes, but also a fore man. A fore man he would stay. Surely, the friends of the Messiah—the one who would finally establish the Kingdom—would be counted great among men. They would have honors and privileges while living, and positions of first importance when they got to Heaven. And the fore man of the Messiah would be second only to the Messiah, himself. If it were true that Jesus was not *the* Messiah, but only one possible Messiah, and that this man kneeling beside him had equally as much chance to attain the final glory, then it behooved Petros to figure out which man had the best chance, and to back that man to the hilt . . . indeed, to work night and day to insure that his man was the blade which found its mark and drove home. Surely, God would then thank him doubly for seeing to it that at least one of the Messiahs fulfilled his destiny.

The frown deepened. How then to proceed?

Well, for one thing, did it not make sense to back a man who *called* himself the Messiah, who *thought* of himself as the Messiah, who *wanted* to *be* the Messiah?

Did it not make sense to back a man who would be an inspiring leader in war, who was not adverse to killing Romans? For, to establish God's Kingdom on Earth, Romans aplenty would have to be killed. Rome was not going to simply surrender Jerusalem without a fight, that was for sure.

Did it not make sense to back a man who believed in, who practiced, the highest and best ideals of The Law?

Did it not make sense to back a man who placed his best confidences in men instead of in women?

Jesus, with all his jabbering about simultaneous time, and probabilities, and reincarnations, and love, would never be able to lead great multitudes, or hold the confidence of right-thinking men. Who could understand such prating? Only a handful. And handfuls did not win kingdoms.

He realized with a start that Simon Yeshuah had turned his head and was regarding him.

"I am sorry," said Petros. "Did I disturb you?"

"I had finished."

"For what do you pray on such a hot afternoon?" said Petros in an attempt at levity. "A cool evening?"

Yeshuah smiled, and settled back against the cool of the tomb.

"I was praying for Merovee. That she be released from her ordeal and delivered quickly of the fine young son that she has been hoping for."

Petros turned away, hiding a face gone red.

"You are a saint to wish good to one whom you hate."

"Hate? I do not hate Merovee."

"But Judah has told us of how you despised her when you followed the Prophet, and in Kapher Nahum you said that she had seven demons.

Yeshuah stared at Petros. Then his gaze unfocused.

"Yes," he said almost to himself. "I guess that I was very hard on her at one time. Strange. I can hardly remember that man that I was."

"There might be some who would wish that you were still that man," said Petros, more tartly than he had intended.

Yeshuah's eyes refocused. They would always be arresting, those eyes of his. But they were not now composed solely of fanaticism as of old. Something deeper, something eternal, had taken up residence, tempering that raw fanaticism to a knowing that was as soft as it was strong.

He smiled.

"Has bar Tolmei been chewing your ear? Have you become a Zealot, Petros? Do you wish me to lead an army and wrest Palestine from the Romans?"

"I have not been speaking with bar Tolmei, but why not wrest Palestine from the Romans? Is that not what the Messiah is supposed to do?"

So it was out.

The words hung in the sultry air. More red-faced, but resolved, Petros supported the words by meeting Yeshuah's gaze squarely.

"You would turn traitor to your master, Petros?"

"He does not allow us to call him master. And so I have none. Unless I decide to choose one."

"And so you would choose me," said Yeshuah softly. "You would name me the Messiah. But on your terms, just as does bar Tolmei. Like him, you believe that *the* Messiah must be essentially a general, a conqueror, a priest-king. Like bar Tolmei, you think that the Kingdom of God is meant to be only a place in this world."

Yeshuah heaved a sigh and settled further down against the rock.

"I can hardly blame you. I thought the same myself once. Poor bar Tolmei cannot understand my change from that fiery Zealot that he first knew. The man follows me like a confused sheep . . . no, not a sheep, for a sheep has little thought and even less love for its master. And bar Tolmei has much love, for me if for no other.

"Do you know how many Romans I have killed, Petros? How many silent, untraceable executions on darkened streets? One hundred and six. They call my little brother by the nickname of Sicarius. But I was the real master of that instrument. And proud of it. I counted up those hundred and six Romans so carefully." His brow wrinkled. His voice softened. "It is amazing, really, the trust that Pilatus places in Jesus. As well he should, of course. And how admirable, both, to be able to give and to deserve such trust. Procula must have told Pilatus of whom Jesus is harboring within these walls. And Pilatus is no fool. He must at least suspect the identity of his attackers on the Akko Road. Micah and Leah must as well. Yet still they trust. And, in trusting, forgive. Neither Micah nor Leah look askance at Judah, nor bar Tolmei, nor myself. While Pilatus continues to allow Procula to come here each day." His face grew wistful. "It is really . . . wonderful."

His face brightened, then, with a sort of boyish enthusiasm that shocked Petros.

"What an astounding person is Procula! Is she not marvelous, Petros?"

Petros grunted.

"I suppose. I am not overly fond of women."

"Ah, but she is not a woman. She is a person. That is the difference. It is a lesson I had to learn. I learned it from our Merovee. I no longer think of Merovee as a woman. I think of her only as a person. There are certain people, Petros, male or female, who are quite simply . . . above, outside of, the rules, who simply must not be judged by, or bound by, the mundane little standards which society invents in order to regulate itself.

"Procula is one such. Procula is a very special person. Were Procula free . . . "

He smiled.

"I would woo her."

"I thought you were above such things!" said Petros in indignation.

"Why should I be above such things? Do you not have a wife?"

"That is different."

"Why so?"

"I am only I. You are you."

"Thank you so much, but I decline the distinction."

"You are beginning to talk just like Jesus!"

"I do believe that that is the nicest thing that has ever been said to me."

"You are going soft. All right. You want Procula. Why not see to it that Procula's husband goes the way of the sicarius?"

"I have thought of it. Were I the old Yeshuah it would be already accomplished, and I would have Soul One Hundred and Seven upon my list of 'Items To Be Atoned For.'

"But no. I am not destined, as Jesus, to have a Merovee. I tread a different path."

"And fortunate you are. A woman does nothing but weaken a man."

"I am afraid I must say that we benefit from that weakening."

Petros threw up his hands.

"You are lost. What good is it? What good is anything if a man such as yourself can be so changed?"

"It is the other way around, Petros. All would be lost, and nothing would be of any use, if a man such as myself could not be changed. But fear not, my friend."

He reached out and gripped the hand of Petros.

"You are looking for the Messiah and you have come to the right place. In that, I have not changed. I am the Messiah. Not Jesus. Jesus is . . . "

His eyes unfocused once more.

"Jesus is beyond such trivialities."

"Trivialities?"

Petros sat up in shock.

"You call the Messiah a triviality?"

"In comparison to Jesus, yes. Petros, the concept of the Messiah is of Man. And a small group of men at that. The concept is of Earth, and, though I once thought the Earth was all, now, because of Jesus, I know that the Earth is only one, tiny corner of God.

"Jesus speaks with the wisdom of a million worlds. He comes to us from places that are beyond our comprehension, while you and I know only this one small place.

"I have pondered long over who and what Jesus might be. I have decided that he must be the supreme archangel, a direct envoy from God, sent into this life expressly to teach me, and to prepare me for my own mission."

Yeshuah turned to Petros, eyes forbidding.

"So speak no ill to me of Jesus. I will hear nothing against him. Or of those whom he deigns to love. He is an elder of Heaven, sent to Earth by my father to guide me. But the Messiah he is not. He was never meant to be. To be the Messiah is my lot.

"I cannot know why my father has chosen to exalt me on one hand, by making me his Sacrificial Lamb, and to bring me low on the other hand, by allowing me to know this Jesus, so to understand how parochial my own efforts will be. But I do not question. I merely accept. I accept my lot, my mission, my destiny. I accept it with humility and with joy. I will climb by whatever path my father ordains. I will do his bidding, and pray that he is well-satisfied with his son.

"And I shall be happy if you choose to follow me, Petros. You are already exalted for recognizing me for who I am. But, if you would follow me, your understanding of the Messiah must change. You must accept my teachings on the subject."

Petros sat open-mouthed and slightly glassy-eyed.

"What might those teachings be?"

"Do not look for me to raise and lead armies. I am not meant to be that sort of king. And my true kingdom is not of this world, but of the world to come. Up until now, that world to come, Heaven, has been a place to which perhaps one man in a million could go. For only those who were pure, who were perfectly blameless, were allowed in."

"What happened to all the others?"

"They were cast into a pit of eternal fire."

"Seems a terrible waste," said Petros.

"Yes it was. And it made my father very sad. And now the end of days is near. So that he has sent me into the world to suffer, and to die a horrible death, so that even the sinners can be redeemed and taken up to Heaven."

" . . . How can sinners be redeemed because you? What sort of suffering? What horrible death?"

"It is written that the Son of Man . . . "

"Wait. You just said that you are the son of God."

Yeshuah smiled patiently.

"'Son of Man' is a title, Petros. Have you not read the prophecies?"

"Many times. I know that the Essenes call the Messiah the Son of Man. But now you tell me that the Son of Man is really the son of God, and so why should he be called the Son of Man?"

"These things are of no import," said Yeshuah with a wave of the hand.

"A triviality?"

"A triviality."

"But men go to war over things much less trivial," frowned Petros. "Jesus would say, I suppose, that God is in Man and Man is in God and that that is why the Messiah is the son of both God and of Man. Is that how you see it?"

"No."

"But . . . you said that Jesus is greater than yourself. How then can you disagree with him?"

"Ah," said Yeshuah with a grin, "you have not been listening to Jesus if you can ask that. Jesus, himself, teaches us that we each have our own vision, that no two of us are alike, that no two visions can be alike.

"Well, I have my own vision, and I have it clear. And it is my own vision that I will—must—act upon.

"I have told you that I understand that the vision of Jesus is greater than my own. Infinitely more great. But I am not Jesus. I am only I. I can do only what I am capable of doing, and only to the limits of what I can understand. I told you that my messiahship is a parochial matter pertaining only to our little corner of the Universe. I do not, even myself, understand why I must do the things that I must do, especially as they are so at variance with what Jesus has taught me. But my own vision has been presented to me too clearly for it to be turned away from.

"I thought—even hoped—that coming to Jesus might change things, that I might find a different understanding, and so escape the horrible fate that my vision demands. I *have* found an expanded understanding. But, as to my vision, it has only grown more clear, while my resolve has become stronger than any iron or rock on the face of Earth."

"This horrible death that you speak of . . . "

"Crucifixion."

"God in Heaven!"

"I used to think he was only there," smiled Yeshuah. "Now I realize that he is everywhere . . . even supporting your ample buttocks, Petros."

"Do not make jests! You are mad, just as I first thought. Do you mean that you are actually planning, looking, to get yourself crucified?"

"Exactly."

"Yeshuah! Have you ever seen a crucifixion?"

Yeshuah turned away.

"As a matter of fact, since I realized who I am, and what I must do, I have made it my business to attend every crucifixion of which I hear. Bar Tolmei reports that there will be a trial at the Antonia in the morning, so the man will probably be hung by noon. Will you accompany me and watch?"

"No!"

"I wish that you would. There is much to be learned from watching." He turned back. "Oh. I am sorry. Have I made you ill?"

"Blood," breathed Petros. His face was flushed. Flashes of heat raced through his body, and he fought the bile, trying to keep his stomach in its place. "Ever since I was a child. At the sight of it, I faint. At the thought of it, I grow sick."

"Ah. Well, if you are to follow me, Simon bar Jonah, and become *my* rock, you will have to get used to talking about blood, seeing blood, shedding blood . . . even drinking blood."

Petros hove to his feet and managed to reach a mass of tall grass before emptying the remains of his last meal onto the earth. Behind him, Yeshuah laughed lightly.

Somehow Petros did not mind. There was the strangest quality to the laughter. Not derisive, but loving.

He turned.

"I am really sorry, Petros. On the other hand, I was serious. If you follow me, you must deny yourself everything. Eventually, you might have to take up your own cross. A man who vomits at the thought of blood is not a man on whom I can build."

"Did you mean it though? Would you build on me if I could surmount my problem? Would I be your rock? Your fore man?"

"Yes."

"But what of bar Tolmei?"

"Bar Tolmei is indeed a rock. I could not hope for a more trustworthy bulwark while in this life. But bar Tolmei has not the . . . wherewithal, neither in brains nor in spiritual understanding, nor yet in spiritual caring—not even in ambition—to carry on with my doctrine once I am 'dead.' No, Petros. I need a bar Tolmei who is more than a bar Tolmei. And you are the man on whom I have settled."

Petros stared.

"You did not come here accidentally at all. You purposely sought me out."

"I did. I want you, Petros. Follow me, Big Fisherman, and I will make you a fisher of men."

"But what of young Judah? Why is he not to be your fore man?"

Once more, Yeshuah turned away, and was silent for long moments. When he spoke, it was as though to himself.

"How to explain it? At first I counted him a traitor. I had always assumed . . . just assumed . . . after all, was he not my little brother? Was he not almost a son to me? A man just takes for granted that juniors will follow after him, do his bidding, agree with him in all things, uphold him, come what may. A father or senior brother comes to regard such unquestioning loyalty as his right. Indeed, our Law has codified such behavior. It is mandatory.

"But Judah has taught me that my assumption, and the assumption of The Law, is misplaced. The fact that I was born first of all my mother's children does not give me the right to dictate what Judah may think and believe."

Yeshuah passed a hand over his face, as though to clarify his thinking.

"Judah is like Procula, you see. He is special. There are so many special people, Petros, so many more than one would think . . . most of them hidden, buried, squelched by laws and rules and conventions. Especially squelched by their own lack of realization as to how very special they are. And it is a mistake—no, a sin—that they should be so squelched, so kept down. Because to imprison a mind is to imprison a Spirit."

"But you are saying that you think our Law is wrong. You!"

The shock of Petros was genuine. All his fine assumptions about Yeshuah were being demolished. First the man had shown himself sympathetic to the Magdalen, now he even talked against The Law!

Yeshuah sighed.

"Yes The Law is wrong, and no The Law is not wrong. Ah, forgive me for being so slow and bumbling with my words, Petros. This is the first time that I have tried to put my beliefs as regards Jesus and me into words.

"Petros, I, Simon Yeshuah, will personally try to uphold The Law for as long as I live. Because that is how I believe that I should live. But the thing is, Petros, that there are other ways to do things, other ways to think and live. And those ways are just as valid as my own. Perhaps this is the greatest understanding that being with Jesus has given me. I have not only learned that there are other ways, but I have learned to respect those other ways . . . to know that there are an endless number of legitimate exceptions to any rule.

"I know my words are confusing, for I am groping at them, trying to find ways to explain to you what has happened to me, when even I do not fully understand what that something is.

"On top of which, of late, I find myself believing two things about almost every matter, each belief diametrically opposed to the other while each is also completely true. It is as though a door has opened . . . " he gestured toward the shrubbery on the other side of the walk, "right there, in those bushes. An invisible door. And I think suddenly that much the same thing happened to Moses when he saw his burning bush. He was looking through such an invisible door, into a greater world. Now you and I know—our eyes tell us, and our common sense repeats—that there is nothing there on the other side of the path except common ordinary bushes, and, behind those bushes, a vegetable garden. We know that there is no magic door there among the leaves, opening to an anteroom that leads to totally different worlds, each with totally different 'truths,' all of which somehow exist in the same space as the vegetable garden. All 'right-thinking,' 'rational' men would agree that there is nothing there.

"Yet, perhaps such a door *is* there. Or there, among the rocks. Or in the sky above us. I am convinced now that such doors do exist for those with the eyes to see them. The mental eyes. For I am convinced that Jesus is right, and that many worlds exist all at once in the same time and space, and that we 'see' of those worlds only what our minds allow us to see.

"And so, Petros, I am as a man who has been shown the location of such a door. All about me are friends and family eager to enter in through that door, to explore those other worlds, and perhaps even abide by some of their rules, their truths.

"Not that they plan to leave this world. No. They are, rather, eager to expand their horizons, to make those other worlds extensions of their total experience and understanding. The thing is that, once they explore those other worlds and understand them somewhat, this world will never be quite the same to them. What they learn of those other worlds will automatically change their experience and perception of this world.

"Not only will this world not be the same to them, but they will never be the same again within themselves, not once they have gone through that door, taken a look around, and begun to understand those other places.

"Neither can they ever seem the same to the denizens of this world . . . to those who do not know that the door is there, or to those who, for whatever reason, and even though they have heard of the existence of such a door, refuse to seek it out or to enter through it.

"And all of this is by way of explaining to you, Petros, why Judah cannot be my fore man. Judah is one who has entered into those other worlds and is forever changed. While I am one who, for whatever reason, has refused to enter. Judah and I do not think alike anymore. We no longer perceive the world

430

in the same way. Actually, in a strange way, though we seem to inhabit the same world and to share the same circumstances, we are each living and perceiving totally different realities. To ask Judah to do more than an occasional favor or task for me, to ask him to consistently uphold me, agree with me, follow after me, to deny his own burgeoning greatness, to leave off exploring the world that Jesus has shown him, would be a dreadful imposition. Judah would do it. Yes he would, for he loves me that much. If I demanded, he would comply . . . at least I think that he would. But my love for him is as great as is his for me, and now I even have the understanding to go with it. Judah has his own way to go, his own reality to create."

"His own reality to create." Petros spat in disgust. "Next thing I know, you will be babbling about simultaneous time and reincarnation."

Yeshuah laughed. But not with gladness.

"Not I, Petros. Remember. I am one who refuses to enter in through the door that leads to the worlds where one begins to understand such matters. So, my friend, are you."

Petros huffed. Then he puffed. Then he grew silent and obviously thoughtful.

"I guess I refuse to enter because I am lazy," he finally said.

He thought for another moment.

"No. Laziness has nothing to do with it. There is not a lazy bone in my body. Is it because I am a coward?"

He thought that one over as well.

"It may be so. Yet I think not. Aside from the sight or thought of blood . . . and oh yes, water—I cannot swim . . . but aside from those things, I cannot remember ever being really afraid of anything in my life. I think it is just that . . . "

He turned those milky green eyes to Simon Yeshuah.

"I think it is simply that I do not give a damn about any of the wild imaginings of Jesus. I like my life just as it is. I like my God just as he was taught to me. I like those bushes and the vegetable garden that they screen. If there is a door there, I really do not want to know. Even less would I want to enter into that door and see what is on the other side."

"And yet," said Yeshuah quietly, "along with all of us, you have learned more and more of healing in these last months. You have caused the lame to walk, the blind to see, the deaf to hear. You have cast out demons. You have even healed a leper. And, though I did not see it, I believe the witness of others . . . one night you walked on water."

"I would rather forget about that."

"Why?"

"Besides, I think maybe it was only a dream."

"In which case a great many people were invited to your dream."

"Or maybe Jesus is a magician, and he somehow made us all think that we went down to the water that night."

"Can you honestly think that Jesus has any need to fool you in that cheap manner? Jesus has no need of tricks, Petros. The truth is that he walked on water that night, you walked on water . . . and so did Merovee."

"She did not! She but stood upon the shallows! I was the one who walked, all the way out until the water was over my head."

"Oh," said Yeshuah. "So you have not forgotten the incident after all, neither do you insist that it was a dream."

"Certainly not if people would end up giving her the credit."

"And still, after doing that miraculous thing, you want to forget about it. You do not 'give a damn' about entering in through the door, to worlds where such feats are made understandable, where, indeed, they are common-place. Why, Petros?"

"Why do you dun me? I am not alone in my preference. You admitted that you do not want to go in either."

"I am not backing away from my admission. I will give you my own reasons. But first, I want yours."

"Why should I go first?"

"Because I am the master and you are only the fore man."

"Oh. Well . . . I guess it is not a lack of courage. Truly it is not. I guess it is . . . vanity. I am a very clever man. Anyone who has worked with me will tell you that. I am very good at the things I know. And I have worked very hard to know the things that I do know. But there is another sort of cleverness."

He shook his head.

"It is astounding how some people just pick things up without working for them. You mention a concept and . . . pouf! They have it. You show them a thing and . . . pouf! Just as though they have been doing it all their lives, they can suddenly to it as well as you, plus which they can dream up a whole lot of ways to do it even better. Which hardly seems fair. Well . . . here with Jesus, I find myself surrounded by so many of these pouf people. Just a few words, and all of a sudden they understand lifetimes. While I have to plod along and think so very hard to understand so very little.

"I do not like being left behind in the dust, Yeshuah. So I do not want to go into a new world where I have to learn a lot of new things and look the fool when others learn those things faster and better. I prefer to stay right here, where I already know what I am doing, where everything makes a certain amount of sense, and where I am a big man.

" . . . . . . Maybe there is a bit of cowardice to it after all."

"At least," said Yeshuah, "you have the courage to bare your secret inadequacies, which is more courage than most would have."

He hesitated a moment, gathering his thoughts.

"My own reasons are like yours while being quite unlike them."

He plucked a leaf from off of a weed and commenced shredding it to minute ribbons.

"I cannot remember a time, Petros, when I did not feel . . . special. Big. Important. Great. I have always been able to do miraculous things. My childhood was made lonely because of that fact. I could not play with the other children. Strange things were always happening when I was around, and either they came to fear me, or they taunted me.

"Then came the day in synagogue school when I first heard of the Long-Awaited One, the Messiah. Quick as a wink, I spoke up and told the rabbi that people did not have to wait any longer, the Messiah had come, he was I.

"I got sent home in disgrace, accused of vanity, deceit, and blasphemy. My father was a harsh man. He beat me severely. Later, my mother came to me and comforted me, and whispered that she believed me, but that we must keep it a secret between the two of us until I grew too big to be beaten by my father.

"Which is why, despite her failings, I will always love and defend my mother, and keep her with me. She was my first friend, and she has been the most steadfast. Still, despite her assurances, that awful day filled me with doubts, and with fear to proclaim myself. Only after leaving Johannan did I finally re-discover the courage.

"Yet always, always within myself, through all those years of doubt and suffering, I have known the truth of the Messiah, understood the mistakes of others in interpreting the prophecies. Always, I have known what the Messiah must do, and why he must do it."

The leaf carefully shredded into strips, Yeshuah commenced rearranging the parts into a fan-like design upon a flat stone.

"And so, on being confronted with a man like Jesus, by such a superior Spirit, the like of which I can only aspire toward . . . on being exposed to his teachings, in which I earnestly believe, and which I think I almost fully understand . . . on being shown the invisible door to new worlds, and being invited to enter into it and to explore . . . why do I, along with you, refuse to enter?

"I refuse exactly because of people like you, Petros."

Yeshuah examined the rearranged leaf as intently as though it provided answers of cosmic importance.

"After meeting Jesus, and understanding him, I was faced with myself and with my role as Messiah more forcefully than ever before. Did I still believe in the Messiah? And in myself as that character? Were all the great plans, the great understandings which had filled me since childhood, now shown to be the blathering of a fool or a mad person? How could I still believe in the Messiah as I understood the Messiah when I knew what I now knew, when I understood the realms where Jesus is king, when I knew that the very things which I meant to proclaim and teach as Messiah are false false false when weighed on that greater scale that Jesus has shown us?"

He laid back against the stone, eyes still upon the leaf.

"It has been a time of great trial for me, Petros. And that is why I say that Jesus was sent to be my final teacher, to put the finishing touches onto my preparation. I have a new understanding of Satan. The Tempter."

Petros sat bolt upright, his allegiance to Jesus rushing to the fore.

"Do I understand you rightly? Are you saying that Jesus is Satan?"

"Sit back, Man. Do not glare so. Yes, I am calling Jesus 'Satan.' Do you know that the word originally meant 'Adversary'? And the original understanding was the true understanding.

"Must an adversary be evil?

"No. That is what has been so terribly misunderstood. How could we ever have thought that a loving God would invest evil entities with power over us? How could we not have understood that God but sends challengers against us, to test us, to see what we have learned, to determine whether or not we are steadfast and trusting of that learning, and so ready for even higher learning. An adversary is one against whom you pit your strength, your intelligence, your skill, your endurance, your knowledge, your courage.

"Did I not tell you that I have a new understanding of this 'Tempter'? This 'Adversary'? I am not saying that Jesus is evil. On the contrary, I have ready told you that I believe him to be the highest angel of God. He is sent by God on only the most important of missions, because only the greatest of men have any hope of withstanding his testing.

"And only the greatest men need his testing. Only those with a great calling can stay true to their own personal vision in the face of his greatness, his superior ability in all things."

Yeshuah rose onto his knees. Tears stood in his eyes.

"And I thank God my father—my dear, loving, blessed father—for having honored me by sending the most potent of his angels to carry out my personal testing."

"What of the demons then? Are they only for the tempting of lesser men?"

"They are. And Petros, I tell you that, for all the fury that they can arouse, their mission is good. It is only the failure of us students to combat them that makes them seem evil. Evil is purely and simply our own weakness. 'Evil' resides in us, not in the Tempters."

Yeshuah's attitude was not exactly one of prayer, yet he seemed prepared to pray at any moment should the need arise.

"You see before you a man who has 'wandered in The Wilderness,' and wrestled with the great Satan himself.

"Yet I have emerged unscathed. Victorious.

"Exactly because of my victory, I refuse to enter in through the door that Jesus has shown me. My vision is true. My vision is right and needed . . . for this place, this people, this time. It might not be the ultimate vision. Indeed, it is not the ultimate vision. But it is good enough for now. It is the best that anyone has come up with, the best that anyone has to offer at the moment.

"In another two thousand years, at another double millennium, perhaps people will have changed enough so that the majority of them will be ready for the worlds to which Jesus invites us. Perhaps they will be lining up five abreast, crushing through that door, in their eagerness to understand those further worlds. I hope that they will be.

"For now, the majority are like you, Petros. If they *could* understand Jesus, they would *not* understand him, for they would not *want* to understand him. They are too comfortable in their unknowing, or too lazy, or too smug, or too ornery, too vain, or too frightened.

"And someone has got to take care of them, Petros. Someone who understands them has got to stay behind, so to speak, and teach them something better than what they know now—show them a better way, a closer truth, a greater understanding of what the world is all about . . . and teach them how to love one another. Someone has got to help them make their mistaken version of reality a little less mistaken, and turn their cruelties to charities. Someone has got to save them, show them how to get closer to what God really is, tell them how to be better, so that they will climb higher and more quickly. Someone has got to gather those lost lambs. I am that someone.

"And I need you to help me, Petros. I need you to be my right-hand man. I need you to carry on when I am gone. I need you to understand, not only Jesus, but, me—to support me, and my purpose, and my teachings, with your very life. Will you do that, Petros? Can I count on you?"

" . . . You will make me your fore man, and allow no others to be more important than I?"

"The stone that is yourself shall be the cornerstone of the edifice that I will build, an edifice to shelter my congregation of redeemed Souls, an edifice that shall stand for two thousand years."

Petros frowned.

"Did you not just say that the end of days is near?"

"Yes I did, and it is. The end of days as we have known them. The end of our Law as we have known it. The end of our Temple as we have known it."

"The end of the Temple?"

"As we have known it. And you and I who will destroy it, Petros."

Petros drew back. The horror on his face was genuine.

"I suddenly think that it is you rather than Jesus who is Satan."

Yeshuah smiled.

"If you mean by that that I am your 'Adversary,' perhaps I am. For I test you, tempt you, and challenge you.

"What do you believe in, Simon Petros? What do you believe about yourself? What will be your destiny? Speak up, Man, I have little time to waste! If you will not be my fore man, I will find another. Or perhaps two others. The Sons of Thunder jostle for position, and Thunder herself—what a juggernaut of a person—she would sell her Soul, and those of her sons, for one stinking copper if, for that price, the buyer would promise them preferred seating in Heaven and immortal names here on Earth.

"What do you want, Petros? How cheaply or dearly do you hold yourself?

"Do you wish to be worshiped for centuries to come? Shall Humankind forever say, 'It is Petros who holds the keys to the Kingdom. Do not cross Petros, or you shall not get in.'

"Do you wish buildings, cities to be named for you? Shall you be remembered as long as Humanity endures?

"Do you wish to move into myth, and, finally, be thought of as a sort of angel?

"Or do you want all those honors to fall to Thunder's sons, while you return to your murky, little lake and spend the rest of your life reeking of fish?"

Yeshuah rose to his feet.

"Name it now, Petros. Quickly! With no further thought! Else you are not the man that I thought, and I will go forthwith and seek out those pimply-faced boys."

"I do not want riches," Petros muttered.

"You will get not one penny from what I offer. Hard work, heartache, and, finally, most likely, blood and torture will be your lot.

"But glory you shall have. And the highest 'seat' in the Kingdom.

"Speak, Man! Do you accept me as your Lord and as your Savior?"

Petros stared up at that towering, threatening figure. His mouth opened.

But then it closed. His eyes narrowed.

"I am not sure. And I refuse to be rushed. I am no son of Thunder, Yeshuah. I hold myself more dearly than half a copper, and I will not sell myself to wild promises. So, if you are in such a hurry, go to Thunder and her sons and good riddance to you. If you are so poor a judge of men as to make that trade simply because you are in a hurry, then you are no man that I could ever work for anyway."

For a long moment, Yeshuah stared. Then he threw back his head and roared with laughter.

Petros waited, trying to maintain a straight face. Then a chuckle escaped. And another. Soon he was laughing as helplessly as was Yeshuah.

Yeshuah sank back down beside him, wiping the tears from out of his eyes.

"Ah, Petros. Congratulations. Perhaps I *was* playing your personal Satan. And you have emerged the victor.

"All right. I can see that I have, indeed, picked the right man, a solid rock in fact, that can never be given a fool's rush. I can see that I must explain the entire plan to you in a businesslike manner. You question. I shall answer."

"Oh. Well . . . you have me confused. You began by speaking of a place of eternal fire, and of something like nine hundred ninety-nine out of every thousand Souls who are there to burn because they are were not pure and perfectly blameless. Not only does this not agree with anything that our rabbis have ever taught, and even less with anything that Jesus teaches, but it does not agree with my own common sense."

"Why?"

"Well, as I said before, what a waste. And how senseless. I mean . . . did God not create us? Why, then, did he do such a very bad job of it? Why should so much of his product be worthless and fit only for the fire? It seems to me that this should be God's fault and problem, not ours. It is as foolish as if I gathered dead fish from the shore and tried to sell them in the market as fresh-caught. I would soon lose my reputation and have not a customer left."

"You call God less than perfect?"

"I was not the one who called him less than perfect. You called him less than perfect by default. For a god who makes so much worthless product is far from perfect, and, for my money, is not much of a god. His creations necessarily mirror him and can be neither better nor worse than is he. And so why should the product be punished for its imperfection, rather than the maker? How could that maker help but hang his head in shame for punishing that product so mercilessly when the whole thing is his fault in the first place?

"No. I can not go along with you on that, Yeshuah. I can not believe in such a god. Why, even I would have more mercy, more common sense, than the god you describe. The most inept man in my fleet down on the lake is a better workman than that god seems to be. No. God cannot be that way.

"Neither can we be so very bad that almost all of us deserve such irreversible punishment. I cannot think of anyone who deserves to be sentenced to eternal torture.

"And where did you get this idea of fire anyway? Is that not a Greek idea?"

"Petros, I do believe that those are the greatest number of words I have ever heard you speak all in one bunch."

"If you were one of my men, and you fouled your net, or came in with a scant catch, you would hear me speak much more. Yeshuah, I think I must have misled you. I think that you think that my ambition is so great that I will clutch at any straw, follow anyone, in order to be first man.

"This is simply not so. I have to believe in what I am doing."

He turned away, pondering his next words.

"I suppose that, to a certain extent, I am like you. I love Jesus. I would not have followed him if I did not care about matters more spiritual than fishing. I also believe that what Jesus tells us is the greater truth. And I . . . sort of understand some of the things he says. I wish, with all my heart, that I could understand them better. I would like to join hands with my own younger brother, and go through that door. For I, too, know that it is there.

"But I am not able. Not yet. I flounder in the words of Jesus as though drowning. And I end up resenting him, and all these young smart-scribes with whom he surrounds himself.

436

"But, there the resemblance between the two of us ends. I have no personal vision to turn to. I am not a boss. I am a fore man. I am not a creator. I am . . . a perpetuator.

"I am, however, the best sort of fore man and perpetuator. So that, even though I am not . . . good enough to be first man to Jesus . . . even though I must personally settle for something . . . less . . . that less will have to be no less than the next lower notch . . . which next lower notch might rightfully be yourself.

"But you will have to convince me of that fact before I contract my most excellent services to you.

"So you speak, Yeshuah. You perform. I am the one who is interviewing. Show me that you are the Messiah. Convince me that you are worthy of my service. Present me with a plan that makes sense to my own mind. If you can show me, convince me, I will serve you with my life and perpetuate your 'Kingdom' as no other man could. But talk sense. Be straight. For I know no other way, I am not a devious man."

"Yet, you are a fisherman. Do you not deal in lures and baits and hidden nets and snares as a matter of livelihood? If you serve me, Petros, you will have to become even more devious."

"What?"

"To perpetuate my plan, you will have to get used to lying, each minute of each day for the rest of your life. You will have to get used to telling people things which you know to be less than the truth. You will have to do it with a straight face, and a sincere and loving heart."

"You speak in contradictions."

"Yes. There is no other way. Not for those who will not, or cannot, understand Jesus . . . all those sheep whom you and I are going to gather into a safe fold. We must develop a cohesive lie to tell to them. We must give them something halfway between what they believe now and what Jesus would show them. We must lure them, as you lure your fish.

"Except that we will not lure our human fish to destruction. Instead, we will lure them in the direction of salvation. For Jesus has convinced me. We do live again. And again and again. If we can help people to be better with each life, then they will arrive at the door of Jesus that much more quickly.

"But people are children, Petros. We can not tell them that they have more than one chance. Like children, they must be threatened, baited, even terrified, into doing things correctly. Now. They must be made to believe that they have one chance and one chance only, and that, if they are not good and perfect during that one chance, they shall be thrown into something like my pit of fire, there to roast for all of eternity."

"No. This is madness. Have you spoken to Jesus about this?"

"Why is it madness? What is the world as we believe it now to be, Petros, and what is the God that we Jews currently believe in? Both are made-up stories!"

"I should not be listening to this."

"I tell you that they are conglomerations of lies, put out by people like Noah and Ibraham and Jacob and Moses and Ezra. You told me to speak plain. Well I am speaking plain. Do you think that what we are doing now is anything different than what Moses and Aaron did? Were those patriarchs bad men? Of course not. They were the best of men, the best that their times had to offer, as are we. They were men of vision, men who saw beyond their own times, men who saw the way, in whole or in part, to something better. Each of them glimpsed a path that seemed to lead toward the great central light, and they created myths for their fellows to believe in, and made up laws to help those who were less gifted, and who could not see the way, to help them toward that light.

"And that is what we are going to do, Petros, you and I. We are going to create a myth, a whole new belief, with a congregation of believers more powerful than ever the Temple has had. We are going to create a Messiah. Me. We are going to create a new version of God, and of this Earth, and of the life to come. We are going to create something for people to believe in that will take them beyond what they are now.

"And this shall not be only for Jews, Petros. We will reach out to the Gentiles as well. We are going to give God to the whole world, and, with that God, the world shall also get a son of God . . . oh yes, I know that would have been your next objection. My reference to myself as the son of God. It smacks of paganism you think. There is only one God, you say, and that god is one. Well, there is only one Simon Yeshuah, yet I have a son. Does that destroy my oneness? Of course not. So why can God not have a son? Myself. A representation of God in the flesh, a gift sent to sinful Humanity by a merciful god in order to save its members, redeem them, in order that each man, woman, and child may have a personal invitation to the realm of the blessed.

"My death shall save them, Petros. I, the perfect, supreme sacrifice, will take their sins onto my own shoulders and suffer for them. Whosoever believes that this is true shall be saved. Only those who do not believe shall suffer in the flames."

"You are going to go out and get yourself crucified on that ridiculous pretext? It will be laughed at."

"Not at all. For it is totally new, totally different. Tell me when anything like this has ever been tried. Think of it, Petros. A god, in effect manifesting himself in flesh, living among the people, then dying, making of himself his own sacrificial lamb—what more perfect sacrifice? Never before has a god allowed a part of himself to be born as a common man, and then deigned to relieve his worshipers of their sins by sacrificing his own flesh to himself! It is revolutionary. It is what they want, what they need. Something different. They will flock to you, Petros . . . because, aside from the novelty, people are lazy, people are cowardly, they will never be able to resist what seems an easy way out.

"But, after they come to us—to you, rather—after you have them in your net, then they will learn of the hard part. Our way will not be easy at all. In fact, it will be more difficult than anything they have ever encountered. It will require bravery and spiritual fortitude that will test them and keep on testing them.

"By the time that they realize even a small part of this, it will be too late. They will be trapped . . . caught on the hook of their own belief. Then our true work—your true work, for I will be 'dead'—your true work shall begin.

"Oh, do not scowl so. Petros, I have worked this out to the last iota. I have been thinking and planning for close to forty years now."

"But it is all to be a sham."

"No! A creation! Petros, were you not listening? Our whole way of life, all our beliefs, our God, our Law . . . all those things were shams to start with. They were the creations of men like myself, great men. But, once the people begin to believe the shams, the shams are no longer shams. The shams become truth, reality!

"What, do you think I am not the Messiah simply because I speak to you in this manner? Quite the opposite. It is because I am the Messiah that I have had the vision to plan this thing. Is the Messiah not to be a general, a strategist, a conqueror, a politician? Would you be happier were I laying out battle strategy to kill Romans, instead of strategy designed to save Souls and elevate Humanity? Petros, before we are finished, I will take you through scriptural prophecy line by line. I will explain to you how others have gone wrong, and I will show you exactly where it says the things which I tell you. The Son of Man must be reviled and persecuted. He must be delivered up to the authorities by his own people, the priests and the scribes. He must be killed by crucifixion, and placed in a tomb. After three days, he shall be seen to have risen from the dead."

The mouth of Petros fell open. Unabashedly, he sat thus.

Yeshuah regarded him kindly.

"You still think that I am mad. I promise you that I am not."

He turned his head away.

"Do you think that it is easy for me to talk this way, Petros? Do you think that my own flesh does not shrink at the thought of nails . . . being . . . "

He shook his head and turned back.

"Oh. I am sorry, I forgot your aversion, have I made you sick again?"

Petros ignored his nausea.

"You really think that you will rise from the dead?"

"Read the prophecies. They promise that I will."

The eyes of Petros unfocused.

"Well . . . I suppose . . . Jesus brought back the daughter of Jairus . . . "

The eyes refocused.

"But Jesus was alive, and filled with Power, and the girl had just died, and they sent for him immediately, and he went to her, and was able to call her back. You will be all alone in the tomb, just lying there dead, with no one to help you. You think you will have the Power, while dead, to somehow call your own self back?"

"God will care for his Messiah, who, by his act of suffering, shall become God's son in fact. The mechanics by which I will return are not your problem. At least not at the moment. You need only believe that I can, and will, return . . . What is it? Why do you look so strange?"

"He must be placed in a tomb, you said. What tomb? Hung men are not accorded an honorable burial, that is The Law. They are outcast, disgraced, merely shoveled under when dead. What do you propose to do, rise up out from out of many feet of dirt after three days? You promised me you had this whole thing planned, but you seem to have forgotten a detail or two."

"I have forgotten nothing, Simon bar Jonah. I will be laid in a stone tomb, Law or no Law. I guarantee you that there is no detail that I have not foreseen, no contingency that has not been provided for. And that is one reason why I am certain of the identity of Jesus as archangel of God. It is he and his family who have supplied, and shall continue to supply, all that is required for the success of my plan. Stop shaking your head."

"It simply cannot work. It cannot be believed."

"The entire civilized world will eventually believe it. Because they will want to. They are ready to believe. They are not ready for Jesus. Jesus demands too much, too soon. But they are ready for me, and for the drama that I will create for them to focus upon.

"And, Petros, we must move quickly. We must get to them before some charlatan captures their attention. I know of what I speak. Look at the frenzy, the chaos around us right now. Look at all who claim to be the Messiah. Look at the competing ideologies. The Assideans, the Pharisees, the Sadducees, the Zealots, the Essenes, the priests and scribes, the Levites, the Samaritans, all of them shouting something different, everyone rushing in a different direction, everyone at each others' throats, thieves and brigands everywhere, no one knowing what to believe about anything.

" . . . while the mental and operational magnificence of Rome is in decay and already beginning to stink since the death of Augustus. Something called Rome will, no doubt, flounder on for a few centuries, but Rome as we know it, the usefulness of that Idea to the world, is ended.

"It is just as Jesus says. It is the end of a double millennium in the cycle of our Universe. The world awaits its new focus. Only let a master mind—let *me* move into the situation and supply that focus, and we will have them.

"Can you not see for yourself that things are ready to bust wide open? But as a bud from a seed, a bud that will be a magnificent new bloom. For it is at the double millennium that the seed of the new mental flower is planted. It is then that old gods die, and are reborn with new 'bodies' and personalities. So let the exotic new bloom of the next two thousand years be our doing, Petros—mine as creator, yours as . . . the gardener.

"And let the personality of God-reborn be of our design."

Surely, a bolt of lightning would descend from Heaven to strike this blasphemer dead. Petros regarded the sky so openly that Yeshuah smiled.

When the bolt did not come, Petros found himself thinking something that he had never before allowed into his consciousness.

There had been no bolt because there was no God to hurl one.

"So in another two thousand years," he said absently. "What will happen then?"

"I think then that our Jesus will come to Earth again. I think that the world will be ready for his teachings."

"Then you are not going against him. I mean . . . in what you propose, you are not trying to undermine him . . . his work."

"Far from it, Petros. So very far. Rather, as I have explained, the real reason for the presence of Jesus among us now is to help me. To supply what I need for my mission. Perhaps, when his time comes to truly take the fore, I can be there, too, helping to supply what he needs . . . will you be my man, Petros? May I count on you?"

There came a light, quick footstep along the path.

"Yeshuah!"

"Mama?"

Yeshuah rose.

"Thank the good God that I have found you. You, too, Petros. Come quickly."

"What is it?" said Yeshuah in sudden trepidation, for there were tears streaming down Meraiah's face. "Oh please do not tell me . . ."

440

"No, but she is totally spent. She cannot deliver the child. Jesus is coming to pieces. I would never have imagined it of him. He is calling for you. He says that he needs you. You also, Petros."

"He calls for me?" said Petros.

"Hurry, hurry!" Meraiah seized her son's hand and pulled him along the path. "It is not fair. She is such a good girl."

The old woman stumbled, blinded by increasing tears. The two men took hold of her, all but carrying her as they hurried along.

"Yeshuah. If you get a chance . . . I never told her. If you get a chance before she dies . . . whisper to her that I thank her. Tell her that I love her. Tell her I always knew she was only pretending that she was tired of riding Ruthie.

"Oh, why are we so proud! Why do we always wait until it is too late?"

"Do not cry, Mama. We will not lose her."

"You do not understand these women's things. She has given everything that she has to give. She is just too small in the hips."

"No! Yeshuah is right!"

It sounded to Petros as though he were shouting. How did one reverse a curse? Oh, why had he wished such a dreadful thing upon the poor girl? . . . and so upon his beloved Jesus, to whom she was the sun and the moon and all the flowers.

"We will keep her, Mother Meraiah. Has not Jesus prophesied that she will live to a great old age? He is calling for us because he knows that we can help."

"Men," moaned Meraiah. "You all think that these things are so simple."

* * *

The scene in the central garden of the house bar Jeremiah, just outside of where Merovee lay in labor, was a scene of emotional devastation. Some whispered together compulsively, needing to hear their own voices. Some stared, others prayed. Faces were tear-stained regardless of sex. This simply could not be happening. It was not possible that they could be losing Merovee and her child.

Not Merovee.

And not that long-awaited remnant of the Prophet.

All That Is would not allow it.

Would it?

The room in which Merovee lay was the main reception salon. It had been hastily converted for the delivery on account of the unseasonable heat, for it had a large number of vents near the ceiling, and that ceiling was fitted with fanning panels. The vents had been opened to allow the escape of heat, while servants worked the cords of the fanning panels frantically, trying to send cooling air in Merovee's direction.

About the room were those of the inner circle. Old Jesse. The parents of Jesus and his young brother and sisters. Susannah and Nathaniel. Alphaeus and his family. Judah. Chandreah and Mathiah. Micah and his wife.

. . . while Merovee's sister Martha sat alone, bolt upright on a stool, staring at nothing, for once in her life unable to command a situation.

Other hands besides Meraiah's seized Yeshuah and Petros as they entered, and hurried them along, straight to the screened-off end of the room where Merovee lay. Petros felt his stomach flip. Did they expect him to go in there with her? What if . . .

But there was no blood. Behind the screens was only another hushed group. Zana and a physician, Simon of Cyrene, father of Alexander, the goat-seller from the Temple. At the head of the couch were Salome, Herodias, Johannah, and Procula, gently fanning the silent wraith that lay beneath the sheet. Lazarus crouched at his sister's side, his face buried against her. Deborah was on the floor in the corner. Beside her curled the kid and the kitten. Like Martha, Deborah stared at nothing. Her hair was unkempt, and there seemed suddenly to be more gray in it.

Jesus sat on the side of the couch, holding Merovee's hand, leaning toward her, speaking earnestly. He turned to look at Yeshuah and Petros. Both halted, stunned.

He, too, had given everything that he had in the twenty-four hours since labor had begun. He was the same man, yet there was an ineffable difference . . . as though he had spent, not only his vitality, but, his Spirit. As though those things had departed forever.

"Yeshuah. Petros."

His voice was all but gone, too.

"Please help me."

"Anything," said Yeshuah, moving forward quickly. "Tell us what to do."

"It is no use."

The words came from Merovee, and could hardly be heard. Her body was as though already dead. It had given up any effort to expel the child. Beneath her head was one of Johannan's treasured sheepskins. Laying beside her was Johannan's marriage token, his great gird.

"Let the physician cut it out of me. I beg you, Josh. Do not let Johannan's baby die with me."

"You are not going to die!" said Jesus harshly.

He turned back to Yeshuah. His eyes were bloodshot.

"I cannot understand it," he whispered. "I cannot understand why I have failed to help her through. Without a massive infusion of The Energy, she is lost. And I am spent. I cannot raise it alone. I need transformers."

"You need what?" said Yeshuah.

"Petros, my friend."

Merovee managed a smile and beckoned faintly. Petros swallowed and went to her side.

"We walked on water, did we not, Petros? But you were more courageous. I guess women are the weaklings after all."

Her thin, white face, the enormous violet eyes—dilated now, seeming even larger—dissolved into a sparkling mosaic as the tears of Petros came stinging out. He took her hand.

"You were the one who went first, remember? I would never have found the courage had you not shown me the way."

"Jesus." It was Simon the physician. "If we are to save that baby, the decision must be made quickly."

"Cut!" cried Merovee with the last of her strength.

Petros moaned.

"No!" Jesus rose unsteadily. "Judah!"

Judah appeared from around the screen.

Jesus hesitated a moment, gathering all his strength.

"Call everyone into the room. Everyone."

"Jesus," said Judah, "I think you should know that the praefectus has arrived. He has come to see Merovee."

"I sent for him," murmured Procula. "He loves her so."

"He will see her soon enough," said Jesus. He glanced at Yeshuah. "Where is bar Tolmei?"

Yeshuah nodded.

"Judah, keep an eye on bar Tolmei. Tell our friend that, should he try any tricks, I will personally carve out his heart and feed it to swine. Make him know that I have never been more serious about anything."

"When you have all the people in, Judah, come and tell me."

The mere activity was bringing color, if not life, to the face of Jesus.

"Didymus, get up. Nathaniel. Come help us."

Nathaniel appeared so quickly that one would have sworn he had been waiting just outside the screen.

"Carefully now. Let us move her couch to the center of the room so that there is space for people to stand on all sides of it while still the couch is screened. Gently!"

Petros and Nathaniel took most of the weight between the two of them—there was remarkably little anyway . . . as though Merovee and her baby were already gone, or standing on tip-toe, poised for flight.

"Lazarus, Joses, bring the screens along. Girls."

It was to Johannah, the two Herodian princesses, and the wife of the Roman praefectus that Jesus spoke.

"Forget the fanning. Deborah, up! Where are there more screens? And linens. Go with your servants and get them, quickly. I will need a complete circle of privacy for Merovee. Physician. Do whatever you need to do to be in readiness for the birth."

"I have been in readiness since last night. Shall I wash my hands again?"

"Any positive gesture. Zana, is the oil to anoint the child warmed and ready?"

"I will warm it again, Jesus."

Judah returned.

"The people are all coming in."

"We will let them see her for a moment before we surround her with screens once more."

"No."

The small protest came from Merovee.

Jesus leaned over her.

"You want to live, do you not?"

"Yes. But the child, Josh . . . "

"Do you want to live to see the child?"

"Yes."

"Then trust me. Forgive me for failing you so badly up to now. How ironic that, when it means the most to me personally . . . "

"No. It was I. My weakness. I had no idea . . . I was so very cocksure."

"Do not waste energy worrying about it now. Only humor me. I have had a bad day."

Despite it all, Merovee laughed. Those just entering the room saw this. A murmur of hope rippled through their number. If Merovee was laughing, it might not be so bad after all.

Even Jesus was now managing a show of vigor, and he wasted no time, for there was none to waste.

"Martha, Rachel, you two keep out of all this, I will want you at Merovee's side. The rest of you, form a spiral around her. Man, woman, man, woman, I need the energies alternated as far as possible. Didymus, you take first position—at the outside wall, facing inward, leaving your left hand free. Come on, join up. Take my brother-in-law's right hand, Mother. Now a man. Keep coming."

He watched the lengthening arrangement.

"Wait, here we have too many in a row who have never healed. Susannah, trade places with Meraiah . . . Joses, trade with Father."

From behind him came soft laughter. Merovee.

"Is this a new dance?"

The lightness of her tone was a tonic to Jesus. His weariness dissolved into a grin.

"Behave yourself. I happen to be constructing a baby-birthing mechanism so sophisticated that every physician will want one. Remember our conversation about Solomon's coil? Alphaeus, switch places with Mathiah. Pilatus. Thank you for coming, your energy is completely fresh, it may be just the factor that will take us over the top. Stay where you are. Procula, come take his left hand and—yes, when Deborah returns I want her on his right, leave her a space . . . "

The line spiraled inward, ending several females short of a complete alternation, so that female servants were inserted here and there. When he was satisfied with the composition, and Deborah was back with the additional screens, he asked that they all join hands, and he called for silence.

"I have left the screens down for the moment so that you can see Merovee clearly. Study her. Memorize every detail of how she looks at this moment."

"I will get you for this," said Merovee.

There was a ripple of nervous laughter.

"Yes! Laugh!" cried Jesus. "Do not hesitate. Laughter is the true god's favorite sound. It calls up The Energy.

"Now. Not only are we alternated as to male and female energies, but I have interspersed among you those of my followers who have accomplished healings and so who are acquainted with The Power, with what it feels like. They have learned how to handle it, and each will be able to increase it as it reaches them, and pass it on in even greater strength. In other words, it will gain in intensity as it travels inward along the spiral."

He smiled at the last three people in the spiral before himself, his sister, Annah, Judah, and the innermost, Salome.

"Which is why I have arranged that these three people who I know will be able to withstand the full Force are here in the center with me. For those of you who have never felt The Power—Energy—Force—it will come in through your left hand . . . or, in Micah's case, through the left stump . . . "

The laughter now was full and unafraid.

"It will dash up that arm and into your trunk, where it will whirl in circles, using you, and your vitality, to transform itself to a higher cycle before leaving by way of your right arm and hand. You will think that lightning has entered you. But do not be afraid. You will not be harmed. Stand firm. Let it use your strength. At the worst, you will want to sleep for a day or two afterwards. If anyone faints, release that person and close ranks immediately, regardless of male and female, for the most important thing is to keep an unbroken flow traveling from left to right. I will have hold of Salome's right hand, and, when she passes that magnified energy which she has received on to me, it will enable me to re-energize certain areas within myself. Standing between me and Merovee will be Petros and Yeshuah. Because of the manner in which I will arrange them, and their own very great energies, they will amplify what I am able to pass to them many times over. Merovee will, then, receive The Energy in plenitude. And we will have our child. Are we ready?"

There was a murmured assent.

"Then look at Merovee again. As we work, hold that picture in your mind and mentally send The Energy toward yet another picture . . . toward the baby that will shortly be born. Give the child any features or sex that you wish . . . "

"I insist upon a boy."

"All right, a boy," said Jesus over the laughter. "A boy, happy and healthy in his mother's arms. So that, as The Energy comes in from the left, you will see Merovee as she is now. As it goes out the right, you will see your own imagined image of our dear lady and her child. Give it all the force of your Intent. Try to think of nothing else but what I have described. Be patient in waiting for The Energy to reach you, and stalwart in conveying it to the next person." He nodded to the servants. "Put the screens back around her."

Within the screens, at Merovee's side, he arranged Yeshuah and Petros.

"I will hold the left hands of both of you in my right. Both of you will hold Merovee's left hand with your right. This will double the amplifying bodies between her and me—each a most excellent sort of amplifying body—besides which, the two of you will form a circle between her and me, which is of great importance.

"Jesus." Petros was ashen. "Please do not place me so that I have to . . . I cannot stand the sight of blood."

"I would not think of subjecting you to anything like that," smiled Jesus. "Nor Merovee. Martha. Rachel, dear. Take that linen sheeting. Hold it between the two of you to screen Merovee from the sight of these men. Would you also like some sheeting to put over your head, Petros?"

"No. Not if . . . can I close my eyes?"

"Close or open what you will, simply do not faint until we have our baby safely delivered."

He went to Merovee, leaned down and kissed her.

"You have felt The Power."

"Yes."

"What you have felt up to now is pale in comparison to what you will shortly receive. What is going to come to you after I, then Petros and Yeshuah finish with it, would literally move a mountain. Be prepared. Hold on tight. Do not faint when it hits. It will be overwhelming for only a moment. Then it will become comfortable. Relax into it. Let it re-energize you. It will take a few more moments to reactivate the womb. When you feel the contractions again, picture . . . well, picture whatever you will."

Merovee pulled Johannan's gird up onto her chest.

"You will not mind if I picture Johannan."

"His Energy has already been attracted to this room and is waiting to help. Picture him so vividly that you could touch him. Then deliver his child into his waiting arms."

"I will do my best."

"That is always more than sufficient."

He started to straighten. He could not look into those violet eyes any longer, not without breaking down, for his facade of businesslike strength was only that. He had failed so utterly in the last hours. He was not at all sure . . .

She caught at his arm, holding him with surprising strength.

"I love you."

He averted his face, the tears so close.

"Not now."

"We shall have to decide on a priest for the circumcision."

His laughter burst out, mixing freely with tears.

"Exactly right," she said. "Laughter generates the best sort of Energy. Now you go do your bit, Jesus, and I will do mine."

"Well someone do something!" said Simon of Cyrene.

Jesus straightened.

"Lazarus!"

"Yes!" came a voice from the far end of the room.

"As on the day of your own birth, when you were Alpha and she was Omega, so it is still. You are the beginning, while she waits on the end. Give it a good start, Didymus, and keep it coming."

"Should we not pray first?" came the voice of Meraiah.

"You are about to engage in the highest prayer possible," said Jesus. "Deborah. You are in the middle for good reason. Are you ready?"

"Yes."

"All join hands. Make yourselves comfortable. Wait until I say ready . . . "

He reached to his left, through the opening in the screening, and took the small, but determined, hand of Salome. He smiled at her, wondering if she remembered, even in dreams, the girl who had been his first love. She smiled back.

"I can feel Johannan around," she said. "Do not be afraid, Jesus. We will do it."

He laughed again, and reached to his right, entwining grips with Petros and Yeshuah.

"Do both of you have Merovee's hand?"

"I have her," said Yeshuah.

"I will not let go of her," said Petros.

"All right then."

He took a deep breath.

"Ready!"

A hush came over the room.

Up and down the line, they waited, in various stances of apprehension, of private thought, of belief or disbelief.

At the beginning of the spiral, Lazarus waited with bowed head. The fingers of his left hand flexed, searching the air for the promised Energy. He had been a failure for so much of his life. Now Miri was there, waiting for what he was supposed to send, her life depending on it . . . his beloved twin.

. . . who had always been better than he, infinitely more favored. Did he really love her?

A thrill of horror swept him.

What if, instead of loving her, he hated her? What if some dark, evil thing within him chose this moment to get back at her?

In the center of the spiral, Deborah fought her tears. On her one side was Pilatus, clasping her hand warmly, even helping her with a gentle upward pressure. On her other side was Mathiah. Deborah was thinking what she had been thinking for hours. Artemis should have been brought out and allowed to stand beside Miriam in her labor. She had slipped the Astarte amulet, given to Miriam by Nathan just before he died, under Miriam's bed mat. The amulet had saved Miriam that day. But would it be enough on this day? Why should she lose her beloved child because of The Law of the Jews? It was not too late. She could run to her chamber now and bring Artemis. So the truth would be out, and she, Deborah, might be stoned to death before sundown. So be it. At least Miriam and her child would have been saved.

Perhaps the praefectus could somehow keep the Jews from stoning her.

No, that would embroil him in an incident for which even Rome would call him to account. Better that she just let herself be stoned and have done with it.

Meraiah held fast to Alphaeus on one side and to the youngest of the Boanerges on the other. It did not seem to Meraiah that she could have many years left. More than anything of late, she had been yearning to square accounts. Had Yeshuah remembered to tell Merovee the things she had said? If he had not, and Merovee lived . . . would she have the courage to tell Merovee herself?

Herodias worked to keep her mind a total blank, except for the picture of Merovee as she had lain upon her couch. She also tried to make that mind move out of her head and down her left arm to the fingers twined with those of Joseph bar Ramathea. Herodias doubted most strenuously that anything would come of this, but Jesus and his Merovee deserved her best effort. As did Johannan. And, if this thing was to work at all, a person had to obey instructions.

Yet a vision kept intruding. Antipas, riding at the head of a column of soldiers. Was he on his way home from his war in the south? If so, her strange adventure here in Bethany would end. She would have to keep to the Herodian Palace, and act as though she were happy to see Antipas when he arrived.

Of course she would be happy to see Antipas. She loved Antipas.

But it was amazing how little thought she had given him in the last months.

This simply was not going to work at all. What was it supposed to feel like, this "Energy," this "Force," this "Power"?

In the mind of bar Tolmei was nothing but hate and confusion. There stood the Roman praefectus, not half a room away, and he was not allowed to kill him. What had happened to the dream? The Romans driven from Palestine. Yeshuah reigning as King of the Jews. Life was hardly worth living anymore. Maybe he should go down to Hebron and see about the supposed Messiah teaching there.

Judah was wrestling his shame. Because, somehow, the only thing he could think of was that Salome's hand was entwined with his own. He had to stop thinking, dreaming about that girl. There was just no future, no chance. She was royal for Heaven's sake, and probably already promised to some king.

But if that king were another uncle or close cousin, and if he, Judah, went to the Temple authorities and pointed out that the betrothal was incestuous, they might forbid it.

So what if they did? He would still be nowhere. Unless he abducted her . . .

'Stop! Concentrate on Merovee.

'Merovee. Do not die. I need you to tell me what to do.'

In Jesse's mind, the world was black. About him raged the sea. He was fighting to keep his head above water, flailing against the inexorable waves. It was no use, why even try? Drowning was not such a bad death he had always heard.

Then some screaming thing was thrown against him. He realized what it was. Suddenly it was impossible to drown. He seized hold of her hair, and started to swim. There had to be a piece of wreckage that he could get her up onto, or a rock . . .

He sniffed unabashedly, waiting for the promised Energy. He would send it to his little girl if it took his last breath.

Joseph bar Ramathea strove to keep his mind blank. Joseph did not want to think. Arriving in the wee hours of the morning, summoned from Bethlehem with word of the impending birth, he had discovered, not one, but, two Hasmonaean princesses, hovering beside his daughter-in-law's bed like common midwifes. On noticing that a third midwife was the wife of the Roman praefectus, Joseph had gone into a catatonia that the recent arrival of the praefectus, himself, had done nothing to relieve.

Vaguely, he wondered if Pilatus had noticed that this house was teeming with Zealots.

Then he began to wonder where one could go to find a simple life. Into the mountains of the north, perhaps. Some seed. A few simple implements. He could put together a lean-to . . .

Ah, but for all of Rosula's enchantment with camping out, she would never agree to it.

Rosula, next in line to Lazarus, only stood, watching Lazarus sideways from beneath lowered lids. What agonies he was enduring. The perspiration rolled from his forehead. While he sweated and hesitated, what was happening to poor Merovee behind those screens?

Rosula found herself smiling, remembering the "boy" who had walked in with Jesus and Chandreah that first night.

. . . the very night that this child had been conceived.

It simply must not end this way!

How lovely Merovee had been in her wedding robe. She was such a good girl.

'Damn you Lazarus, *do* something!'

Rosula's cat eyes flashed, no longer hiding behind lowered lids. Yet Jesus would not have put Lazarus into first position had he not expected . . .

She stiffened. There was a funny feeling in her left hand.

Lazarus had been looking to his left as well. Someone had taken hold of that hand.

But there was no one there.

He studied the air. There had to be someone there, the hand that held his seemed so real. He could even sense the size of the person, there was a "dead" space in the air, that gave away a presence as surely as it did when one was blindfolded, playing the game of Blind Man's Catch. The presence was a man, much taller than was Lazarus . . .

Then Lazarus forgot the presence. Something that was hot and cold all at once was pouring in through his fingers, charging up his arm. It rushed into his chest and started its circuit, down to his bowels, up the other side, across the top of the chest and down again. Why did it do that? Why did it rush in those mad, ever quickening, circles? And what did it matter? He had caught a good stream, just as Jesus had hoped he would. He had to stay on his feet—his uneven, malformed feet—let it pour into him, let it use him, so that it could rush on to the next person in greater force. He had to stay strong. Miri and her baby were waiting.

He heard Rosula gasp. Involuntarily, her hand tried to leap out of his. He held fast.

"Got it?"

"Yes!" cried Rosula. "Oh! My goodness!"

Lazarus did not realize that he was laughing.

"Miri! It is on its way! Wait for it! Wait for it!"

Rosula vaguely remembered that Jesus had said something about visualizing the infant. She tried, but all she could see was something round, pink, and plump, like a fat cloud on a summer's day.

The whole room was astir, the excitement gripping them all. Hairs stood on end. All along the line, they waited, gabbling and nearly jumping up and down in anticipation.

"Do not let go! Hold on to your neighbor's hand no matter what!" came the voice of Jesus from behind the screen.

And his cry was none too soon. Whatever it was picked up momentum, racing along the line like a wind-driven fire that had found a field of dried grass. Before Salome realized it could be possible, it was upon her. She heard Jesus again.

"Hold on, Kitten!"

Salome held on. Though she was not inside of her body anymore. She was suddenly floating up near the ceiling, looking down upon the scene. How tiny she was beside all the others. How strange that Jesus had put her at the end, next to himself, a big strong man would have been better. Yet look at her little self. How straightly she stood, eyes closed, a smile upon her face . . . she looked like an angel. Where was her mother? Oh, there she was.

Salome examined Herodias critically. Not really a beauty. Yet she was a beauty. Had she always been so pretty? Salome looked back at herself. A definite resemblance. She would be satisfied to look like Herodias when she, too, got old.

Then she laughed, for Freckles and Phoenix the kid were rolling and tumbling together, caught up in the excitement in their own little ways. What a shock it would be for poor Freckles when the kid grew up and was ten times her size. And how strongly Judah stood.

Her Judah. He looked a lot like Jesus. Of course so did Yeshuah. Strange to see them all in a row like that, only herself in between and Merovee at the end . . . Merovee.

Oh. The baby. She was supposed to visualize the baby. But she could not see to visualize. What was that light coming from within the screens? So bright. Blinding. What was making such a brilliant light?

With a thud that nearly made her let go of the hands she was supposed to keep hold of, she was back in her own self. She was filled with a roar that was not a sound. She heard screams, shouts, laughter. Meticulously, her mind sorted out directions, and fought its way through the whirlwind that filled her, toward the hand that was supposed to belong to Jesus.

Why did someone not take care of that baby that was crying? Did it not have a nurse? Where was Zana?

Chapter 16

Naming Day in Bethany

All who saw him agreed. And there was no need to prevaricate.

"Magnificent!"

Only Zana was scandalized, and slightly at odds with him during his first hours.

"In all my born days I have not seen . . . babies simply do not come this big! No wonder our poor lady nearly died trying to get him out."

On the other hand, he won immediate favor with his step-grandmother and distant cousin, Rosula.

"He is what I saw, Joseph, just exactly. Remember that Jesus told us to picture the baby? Well, when I did, this is what I saw. A big, fat cloud, round and plump as on a summer's day. And now I see why Miriam stayed so slim. She gave it all to her boy."

They ohhed and ahhed almost without exception, none crowding, or wanting to seem over-eager when finally the screens were taken down, but all of them staying near, watching the oiling, smiling—even applauding—as he was delivered to his mother's waiting arms. Each then stole close whenever the opportunity arose, to congratulate Merovee, and to delightedly examine the child's tiny, plump hands, his exuberantly pumping feet, to exclaim at the profusion of fine, fair hair, and, especially, to remark upon the way in which his blue eyes seemed to focus, and to regard each of them as intently as they regarded him. Not a one of them was uninterested . . . for there was not a one of them who was not partly responsible for his glowing new existence . . . not a one who did not feel almost a parent to this strapping, new son of the Prophet Johannan. All had felt The Energy as it had flowed along the spiral. No one who had stood in that line would ever again wonder at how miracles were done. No one who had stood in that line would ever again wonder, in the secret reaches of the heart, 'Is there really a God?'

One of the most obviously effected was bar Tolmei. Refusing to speak to anyone, even Yeshuah, he approached the couch on which Merovee lay cuddling her infant and simply gazed. Nathaniel would never have been able to say why, but he was drawn to the man at that moment. He went to his side, put a hand upon his shoulder, and just stood, enjoying the sight of the infant along with him.

Close beside that "dangerous" Zealot, was Pilatus . . . not standing. Lucius had brought him a stool. It was Procula who stood, gently fanning her husband's ashen face.

"I know how you feel, my darling. I, too, was stunned the first time I felt The Power. But you will grow accustomed to it."

Pilatus looked up in horror.

"Accustomed to it? Why? When will I ever have to feel it again?"

"When you learn to heal."

"Oh. No. I mean . . . no thank you." He managed a smile. "I will leave the healing to you, Procula." His smile turned wry. "You are obviously much stronger than this poor wretch who is your husband."

Joseph bar Ramathea had only one wish, and that was for Rosula to stop prattling so that he could think. He tried to think what he would think if he could think. He could not think.

Martha had managed to avoid getting drawn into the teaching sessions, which had gone on hour after hour, day after day, since the arrival of Jesus and his people. She had never felt this Force, this Power, The Energy about which everyone raved. She counted herself fortunate to have escaped yet again, lucky to have been called upon by Jesus to help hold the sheeting.

Holding a length of linen had given her something to do. Screening her sister from the eyes of the men had been a positive, assertive action that had restored her own self-esteem. Now, with the baby arrived, that terrible, out-of-control feeling, that had reduced her to vacant staring during the last hour of her sister's labor, was gone.

And what a good thing it was that she had held herself aloof from this Energy foolishness, else there would have been no one to see to the really important things that needed doing, and decisions that must be made, like, should everyone be cleared out of this main salon and Miriam left here to take her rest and subsequent convalescence, or should she order that the men lift Miriam right now, couch and all, and carry her back to her own familiar bed chamber? The salon offered space, for Miriam and Zana and the baby, plus the physician and the visitors who would come and go—while the fanning panels kept the air fresh . . . . . . And what of tonight's supper? With the heat and worry, Martha had planned the lightest of repasts. Now, with the excitement and celebration, the guests would probably turn voracious and want to feast until midnight! It was one thing for Deborah to invite this swarm of locusts to stay at bar Jeremiah—indefinitely so it seemed—and Martha was not at all impressed that some of the locusts were now royal, or exalted Roman, locusts. They still had to be fed, two of them housed, and they ate as much as the more common sort of locust while also dirtying bedding just as quickly. Of course, it was not Martha's place to voice disapproval, for certainly the money which fed and housed the horde was Deborah's own, and she could do with it as she liked, but what would Deborah ever have done without her? Perhaps one day Deborah would come to understand that it was best for daughters to keep their feet on the ground, instead of running off into the clouds. Who else but a daughter with sense could have seen to the feeding, and bedding, and management of this multitude?

Angrily she suppressed tears. Look at that child. Look at that rosy, wonderful boy. And Miri had done it first. Miri, running around in boy's clothes, had gotten herself two husbands and a beautiful boy in less than a year.

Miri, who had nearly died.

Martha's mind went stubbornly blank at memory of what her thoughts had been when it had seemed certain that her sister was about to die.

Miri, the favorite. Always Deborah's favorite, no matter how Deborah tried to hide it.

Martha laughed despite herself as the infant made a sound that was almost a chortle of delight, and went into a new spasm of kicking. A wonder that Miri had a belly left if he had kicked like that in the womb.

More than anything in the world, Martha wanted a boy like that of her own. Boaz, her intended, was anxious to give her her heart's desire.

Why did she hesitate? Why did she continue to delay the marriage? Boaz would lose interest and look elsewhere for a wife if she put him off much longer.

But look at them! Deborah, Lazarus, and Miri. What would they do when she was no longer here to run bar Jeremiah, seeing to all the mundane household details that they were too feather-brained to think about? They would be lost when she married and went to a home of her own.

Except that it would not be her own home. It would be the home of the parents of Boaz. The ruler of that household was the mother of Boaz. Martha would have to fetch and to carry, and to obey that woman's whims. How many years, she wondered, before the mother of Boaz would have the courtesy to die, leaving her, once again, in control of a great household?

She felt an arm around her shoulder and looked up with a quick smile, bestowing upon the man an adoration that only he could inspire.

"Martha, my prize. Thank goodness for you as always. What we would have done without you in these last hours I do not know."

Martha commenced to glow, not bothering to wonder what Jesus thought she had done to have been indispensable. It only mattered that, as always, he could be counted upon to recognize her worth.

"Is it not a fine boy that we helped into the world, Jesus? I am envious, I must admit." She cast him a sidelong glance. "Are you not envious, too? Just a bit?"

"What, that my wife's first child is not my own?"

He seemed honestly to examine the possibility.

"No." He shrugged. "Children are nice, I enjoy them. But I am afraid that I am not a terribly good Jew in that wise. I do not agree that, to be a true man, I must beget children. There are more than enough people eager to do that. We are in no danger of running out of babies. To tell the truth, if Merovee and I do have children of our own, I would prefer girls. Boys are so noisy."

Deborah came to them, slipping in under the other arm of Jesus.

"Well?" said Jesus. "What do you think of your grandson?"

"He will do. Very nicely. But I have come to you to confess and ask your pardon. I was guilty of despair at the last. I lost trust in you and I lost trust in All That Is. I should have known that neither of you would let her die." She smiled. "Not in this probability anyway."

Jesus hugged her.

"Promise not to tell, Deborah, but I, too, was in despair. I, too, nearly lost trust in the very things that I know so well, and teach with such confidence."

"But you did not let it defeat you," said Deborah. "You rose above it."

"Ah yes. That is the trick. But do not beat yourself. You, too, will have learned the same trick after only a few more lifetimes."

Martha pulled free.

"If you two are going to talk nonsense, I am going to go to the kitchen to arrange a more fulsome supper for these people. And far be it from me to make suggestions, but I do think that Miriam should be resting instead of holding court like the Queen of Sabaea. I have decided that she shall stay here in the large salon for her convalescence. But really, you should shoo the people out and let her get some sleep."

Jesus bent fond eyes onto Merovee. She was propped up now by all of Johannan's sheepskins, intent on the study of her son, lapping up the compliments of those who came to adore that jewel as eagerly as a cat laps cream.

"Leave her be for a while yet," he said. "She would not be able to sleep on any account, for she is still riding the crest of The Energy. She received an extraordinarily large dose of it you know." He patted Martha's shoulder. "Do not worry. The crest will end soon. When it does, she will plunge into the trough as though the floor has dropped out from beneath her, and no power in the world will be able to keep her awake. In the meantime, my excellent sister, I find your talk of supper most appealing."

"I should think so!" said Martha. "You have not eaten a thing all day."

And she bustled off, clear in her purpose, secure in her worth.

"Everything is so simple for Martha," sighed Deborah.

"Is it really?"

"You do not think so?"

"Martha is of a different species of consciousness than ourselves, Deborah. I mean that literally, for there are species of consciousness just as there are species of living things. We of our species cannot truly appreciate her difficulties and occasions of Soul-searching any more clearly than she can appreciate ours. Let us simply be content that she is here, and that she finds her own greatest joy in serving us." His eyes twinkled. "For I am very hungry tonight."

As Jesus had predicted, the floor dropped out from under Merovee long before Martha's fine supper was served. One moment she was fondling the child, laughing with Procula and Pilatus. The next moment she had laid her head down and was fast asleep, the smile still upon her lips. Zana snatched up the child, her nurse's fingers having been itching to hold him, and the guests tiptoed out into the courtyard.

Jesus lingered, bending to kiss his sleeping wife. He smiled up at the physician.

"You must be exhausted, Simon. Come out and have some wine and food. Zana will call us if there is any problem."

"I could do with some wine," admitted Simon.

Jesus went to Zana, leaned down and kissed the child's fair head.

"Welcome to the world yet again, my little friend."

"Jesus."

Zana's voice had the bristling quality of one bracing for a fight.

"No, Zana. Absolutely no."

"The child must be swaddled. It is not natural to leave him free. Please give me your permission."

"His mother will not hear of it, so that is all there is to it. I must admit that I find the practice as objectionable as does she. And distinctly unnatural."

"All right. Just you wait. A boy, and so big and energetic? Without the swaddling to teach him quietude and docility, he will become a monster. Before you know it, he will be crawling, and then, before you have had a chance to wink twice, he will be on his feet and walking, getting into everything, breaking pots, refusing to mind his betters, thinking himself the little Master of the Universe. You will not be able to control him, Jesus. And then you will pull your hair and wonder why you did not listen to old Zana, why you did not allow her to make of him a quiet and obedient child."

"I dare say that you are correct, and that, to achieve a quiet and docile child, one should wrap the child in swaddling. And I dare say that there will be all too many times when I will devoutly wish that this particular child was quiet and docile. But I would not have that wish granted at the price of his being wrapped like a mummy for the first year of his life in order to break his Spirit. In addition to which, to wrap this particular child now, after the infusion of Energy that he received along with his mother, would be cruel beyond words. So, may I always understand and forgive when he breaks my best pot. May I always, no matter how busy I might be, take a moment to pat or hug him, compliment or discipline or teach him, if he decides to crawl or walk in my direction.

"In short, Zana, Merovee's order stands. No swaddling clothes. And no more discussion of the matter."

He started to leave, then he turned back and planted a kiss on the brow of the nurse.

"But thank you, Zana. For all you have done. Not just for today, but for all these months."

"Jesus!" She grabbed his arm, and suddenly started to cry. "I was to blame."

"To blame for what?"

"For nearly losing her. My potions should have given her an easy birth. I failed."

"Oh dear dear dear." He took the old woman into his arms. "The fault was far from yours, Zana. And look at the healthy child that your potions produced." He put her out to arms' length, gently, playfully. "You have been so stern, Zana, so demanding. But all of us have known that you know what you are doing, and that your demands were for the good of mother and child. It has been a wonderful comfort to have had you with us, Zana, to have been able to relax, knowing that an expert had her eye on things."

The nurse laughed outright, batting at her tears.

"Jesus, you certainly do have a way with you."

"To recognize what is good and worthwhile and say it aloud is the only way I have, Zana. I will have wine sent to you, and food. I will not waste words asking you to join us, for I know that wild elephants could not drag you away from our boy, here."

"Neither from her, Jesus. My lady and her child are as one to me."

"They are much more one than you know, Zana. Much more."

He kissed the old lady again, put an arm about Simon's shoulders, and, together, the two men went out into the court.

The dusk was cooler than the day had been.

Lazarus was waiting, his face troubled.

"What is the problem, Didymus?"

Lazarus glanced at Simon of Cyrene.

"Surely you can speak in front of our new friend," said Jesus.

Alexander the goat-seller had brought his father to bar Jeremiah the week before, along with his brother Rufus, suggesting that Simon would be of use in the pending birth. In the city of Cyrene—originally an Athenian outpost, now, like the rest of the world, Rome's vassal—Simon was a physician of note, while, in all of the Mediterranean world, Cyrenean physicians were held to be the best, surpassing even those of Athens. The two, young sons of Simon were not accounted Jews. If they had been, Alexander could never have won a goat-selling concession in the Court of the Gentiles—for Simon, born a Jew in a tiny village just north of Jerusalem, had defied Jewish convention as a student in Cyrene and married a Cyrenean girl of Greek parentage. Since Jews traced Jewishness, or Gentile-ness, through the mother rather than through the father, Simon's sons were, thus, considered Gentile.

"It is an embarrassment to speak to any but you, Jesus," Lazarus persisted.

"Then I shall go on ahead and get some wine," smiled Simon.

"Well?" said Jesus when he had left.

"I have a great sin to confess."

"You, too? Dear me. Deborah came running to confess her fault as well."

"Mother? What could she possibly have done?"

"She started to lose faith and trust"

"Oh, well that is nothing."

"Actually, Didymus, it is everything. But what is your great sin?"

Lazarus turned away.

"For a moment . . . . Jesus, I am not sure that I really love Miri. As I was waiting for The Energy, for the first time in my life I realized how jealous I have been of her. I always told myself that I was not jealous. I told myself that I did not mind that she was perfect, while I was blighted. I believed that I was happy for her when she got to travel the world with Grandfather, while I had to stay home. But, suddenly, I realized that I have always resented those things, maybe even hated her because of them. When you called out to me to send The Energy . . . I actually thought of not sending it . . . so that she would die."

"And what did you in fact do?"

"Do? Oh, well, then I felt the presence standing beside me—it must have been Johannan, Jesus—and I felt The Energy he gave me and knew it was good. I just braced myself and sent it."

Jesus put an arm around the shoulders of Lazarus and hugged him in the affectionate way he had with male or female, young or old.

"And you wonder if you truly love your sister? Didymus, here is a rule of thumb by which you can never go wrong. Do not look at what they say, or think . . . look at what they do. What you did was to start The Energy moving along the spiral in exactly the way I was expecting, with all the strength that I was depending upon. As a result, Merovee is alive and well and so is her son. If that makes you her enemy, then I am sure she is happy to have such a one."

"But Jesus, I actually thought of trying to kill her!"

"Good. It is about time."

"What?"

"Your attitude has been unnatural, Didymus. It is natural, and totally permissible, to be envious in some matters. It is natural to have angers. It is even natural to want to kill some people some times. Such feelings are only human. You have not allowed yourself to be fully human until now. You have been trying to be a saint. I am glad that you can finally recognize your emotions and bring them out into the light of day. You have hidden them in darkness for too long. Sunlight is the great purifier, Didymus. So bring more of these fearful things out into the sun, and take a good look at them. Do not be afraid of them. When feelings are allowed an outlet at inception, when they are not blocked, then they do not build up till the pressure is so great that they finally burst out in a destructive way. The only 'bad' emotions are those which are held in, which are not recognized and acknowledged. I want you to go to Merovee when she feels better and tell her about this."

"I can not! Oh, please, do not make me do that, Jesus."

"I insist. I will wager that she will admit to having had secret jealousies against you."

"Miri? Jealous of *me*? Never."

"You were born a boy, were you not?"

Lazarus frowned.

"But that never bothered her."

456

Jesus laughed outright.

"Talk to her. You will be surprised. Now come. I need a cup of wine as never before."

The main courtyard of bar Jeremiah was Martha's pride and joy. In the days of her father, the priest Jeremiah, and of his father and his fathers before him, it had been used for many a princely and priestly gathering, so that it was beautifully tiled, and equipped with delightful fountains. In her own lifetime, and since the death of her father, there had been few large gatherings, for Deborah had observed only those occasions that were ritually and socially necessary, to keep her in-laws satisfied, and the wag-tongues stilled.

During the life of Grandfather Nathan, the courtyard had, of course, seen endless gatherings, but small ones—of merchants from far countries, dickering with Nathan over a contract for Magdalia, of the men from Tyre and Sidon, whose ships Nathan purchased, and whose crews usually sailed them, and of so many strange people—Greeks mostly, for most strange people were to be found among Greeks—philosophers, sculptors, architects, mathematicians, scientists, orators, historians, poets.

And then there had been the more dangerous sorts of guest, at least to Martha's way of thinking.

Priests and priestesses of one pagan god after another! Seeresses and oracles!

And actors, whole troupes of them. Oh yes, King Herod had built a magnificent theater in Jerusalem. But, after his death, both the Pharisees and Sadducees had begun to talk against theatricals as blasphemies, so that, gradually, the theater had been abandoned. Yet, here in this courtyard, situated less than two miles from the Temple, itself, every major work of the Greek repertoire had been performed before Nathan, Deborah and her children, and carefully selected guests. After Nathan's death, the entertainments had continued, though with diminishing frequency as the years had progressed.

In the last two years, the courtyard had welcomed not even one gathering, which hurt Martha down in her secret heart. For, while disapproving entirely of the sorts of guests who had once graced the place, Martha had yet proceeded, over the years, to turn the courtyard into a place of beauty. Showing her aptitude for household management when only a small girl, she had been given full rein by Deborah, and had worked with the flowers and shrubs until she succeeded in guaranteeing some bloom, some color, no matter what the season, even in the winter . . . while that color was so planned as to be aesthetically pleasing in its arrangement at all times.

She had had a huge covering, and arrangements for drainage, made. The covering fastened cleverly to fittings sunk into the stone of the building itself, and was able to roof the whole courtyard. This "roof" she caused to be put into place each winter, so that, in all but the worst cold or rain, the courtyard was habitable, and available for entertaining. She had further outfitted the courtyard with lovely furniture, arranged in groups—cushioned couches, tables, benches, stools, and chairs of Egyptian style.

Like an eager bride, decked in finery, the courtyard had waited during the last few years to show herself to a truant groom. Certainly Martha did not approve of this rabble that accompanied Jesus and her sister, anymore than she had approved of the pagan priests and the actors. Yet, how good it was to see her courtyard filled each night, how wonderful to hear the talk and soft laughter, see people enjoying the food and drink set before them. This courtyard had been born for such gatherings. Even the flowers seemed to glow more deeply in their own chosen ways, to smile and nod, listening contentedly. Martha stood in the door leading from the kitchen, arms across her chest, alternately enjoying the sight of her beautiful courtyard filled with happy people, and checking the salvers as the servants brought them out, assuring herself that everything was just as she had planned.

Jesus passed among the diners, his wine cup always full, sampling from this dish then that. He spoke and laughed with each of them, ascertaining their reactions to the day's events and to The Energy, assessing the mental states of everyone there, trading remembrances. Yet he moved on non-existent legs, powered by energy that he did not feel. He would gladly have been stretched out, asleep on a quilt, on the floor beside Merovee's couch. Part of him already was.

He was a humbler man than when he had started the day. For he had failed. Utterly. None of these people thought that he had. They thought him a great success. How could they know or understand his measurement of success or failure?

His Power—'God' as he knew it—had seemingly deserted him when most he had needed it. Were it not for these people, and the fresh Force that they had been able to generate, to replenish his own spent self, Merovee would be dead, and perhaps the child with her.

Yet he knew that it had not been The Power, or All That Is, which had deserted. He had deserted himself. His love for Merovee had made him fearful, over-anxious. He had expended too much before she was ready, so that, when she was ready, he had had not enough to give.

Yet he should have had. The Energy was always there, always available. It never ran out. It was trust that ran out, blocking the ability to use The Energy.

He looked across the court to where Deborah sat, with his parents, with Herodias, Pilatus, Procula, Lucius, Salome, and, ironically, Judah the Sicarius. Dear, gracious Deborah, coming to him to confess, and to ask forgiveness for having lost trust.

He turned his face away from the people with whom he was sitting, for sudden tears pushed at the backs of his eyes. If only Deborah knew.

Ah. How long was the path? How far did one have to go?

He had been upon the path for such a long time. He had come far. Still, trust had deserted him today.

For that had been the trouble. Oh yes, he could not avoid it.

"What is it, Jesus?"

"Perhaps you should rest."

"No. I am fine. What are these? Ummm. Rice in grape leaves. I shall have a few more if you please."

He had been so eager of the prize, so needful of Merovee, so suddenly terrified of losing her, that he had panicked. Like a neophyte in the marathon, he had burned himself out in the first mile, forgotten everything he knew, given in to despair, collapsed into the dust . . . and nearly lost that which he most loved as a result.

Oh, he had much more work to do with himself. Much more. Perhaps he should go out into The Wilderness for a month or so, and bake some sense into his brains.

But that would be precious time away from Merovee.

He wondered again, as he had so many times since meeting her, whether people such as Petros were right . . . whether Merovee, this new probability in his eternal life, would be the ruination of his mission, of all that he had come here for this time, worked so hard to achieve, in this life and in all the thousands of other lifetimes of which he knew.

He had been a gone man at first sight of her, as she stood knee-deep in the Jordan, one of the lean, sun-baked young "men" in the cordon about Johannan. He had not even questioned, as his eyes fell upon her, whether he was looking at a male or a female. He had only known that he loved that person. A closer look, at the eyes, had told him that his beloved was female. A jolt of surprise, an inward sigh of contentment. And he had begun to envision their marriage.

He had thought that he never would marry again. What was the use? He could not devote himself to a mate as could other men, while, to do the things that he must, it was better to be unencumbered.

Merovee's eyes had changed all that.

Had he made a dreadful mistake?

He could not believe that. Rummaging through memories of his many lives, he found loves aplenty. But never a love such as he shared with Merovee. Never such union with another Soul. He was better, more complete, for knowing and loving Merovee. Any difficulties that the marriage presented were more than recompensed by the opportunities for greater Self-understanding that those very difficulties gave to him.

Look what had been revealed today, for instance. Jesus, the great one. Jesus, the one who presumed to teach his fellows. That Jesus was prone, along with the most poor in Spirit, to lose faith and trust during crisis and plunge into the abyss of despair, there to rail at the Fates, curse the cruelty of life, and wonder at the reality of All That Is.

He moved on to where Yeshuah sat with Mother Meraiah and other intimates. It had not escaped his notice, even in the confusion of the delivery, that Petros and Yeshuah had arrived together. It did not escape his attention now that Petros sat beside Yeshuah.

Well, so be it. It had been bound to come. Petros had been like a fish out of water these many months. He was simply not ready to understand. Yeshuah's simplistics were much more in line with the capabilities of Petros, much more the thing that Petros wanted to believe.

They made room, and he sank down cross-legged onto a cushion beside Mother Meraiah.

"Have some of this nice chicken," she said, selecting a plump thigh and handing it to him. "Always take the dark meat, Jesus, that is where the chicken keeps its vitality."

"Thank you, Meraiah, I will remember that."

"And I will remember today," said Meraiah. "Till the day I die, I will remember the day when the Power of God flowed through me. Through *me*."

She sat straight and smiling, slightly puffed, like a bird preening itself. The novelty of being allowed to sit at table with the men had not yet worn off her mind. She had been scandalized by the practice when first they had joined Jesus. Now she enjoyed it. And never, in all his teachings. had her Yeshuah suggested to her that she, a lowly women, could partake of, feel, administer, the Power of God.

Meraiah's mind swam now in song. Joyous notes and melodies flowed to and fro, colliding, laughing as they collided, trilling to one another, then gushing onward. She could hardly find a serious thought mid all that merriment and splashing.

"May I come and listen with the others, and learn how to heal, Jesus?"

Jesus glanced at Yeshuah. Yeshuah did not hide his surprise. Neither did he seem displeased.

"Of course, Meraiah. You have always been welcome. And what of you, Eleazar, will you, too, learn to heal?"

Yeshuah's son had been to the Temple and made his first sacrifice as an adult. As the body follows the mindset, the body of Eleazar was muscling up, lengthening to manly stature. There was even the beginning of a straggly beard upon his face.

Eleazar frowned at Jesus. He did not glance at his father, or his grandmother. His statement was his own.

"I do not think I am cut out for such matters."

"Eleazar," said Meraiah good-naturedly. "Surely you felt The Power. You stood in the spiral with us."

"Of course I felt it, Grandmother. Who could have missed it? But I am not moved in the same way as are you. I do not feel the desire to learn how to use it as an everyday tool. I have no desire to rush out and cure people, or cast out demons, or do miraculous deeds. I do not see my duty to God in that light. I see my duty in no other fashion than that which is outlined in The Law."

The young man's jaw set in a way that Jesus had seen often, from Judeah to India and from Greece to Egypt, particularly among men whose zeal for their god made them eager to slaughter any who did not believe as they.

"Shall we get you a Pharisee's tefillin and broad borders?" said Yeshuah gently. "Or perhaps you crave the white robes of an Essene."

"Or a Zealot's sacarius," said bar Tolmei. The man's voice was oddly flat. His eyes regarded a place faraway. He seemed not even to know that he had spoken.

"I wish only to serve my God in the pureness of his Law," said Eleazar sullenly. "And I do not see much of that around this place."

"Eleazar!" snapped Meraiah. "Do not speak disrespectfully. If your father says that what we do here is right, then what we do here is right."

"You!" cried Eleazar, turning on her. "You should not even be sitting with us! And what of the uncleanliness of the childbed? That woman in there is unclean now for seven days. Not a one of you should have gone near her. Yet all of you hung around her bed, some even touching her, and the child. Then you come here to eat! Half of you did not even wash your hands first! Were I to go to the Temple and describe to the priests your actions here today, you would all be arrested, and perhaps even stoned to death."

There was a long silence around the circle. Some might have become aware of the decadent picture that those around the courtyard presented, lounging on their pillows and cushions Roman-style, plucking morsels from the tables, everyone well-supplied with wine, and Jesus just refilling his own cup. Eleazar's words brought harshly to mind the Laws of Moses which had been ignored in the excitement and elation of the birth. Yes, according to those Laws, they were all unclean, sunk in sin. All should go to the Temple to make offerings before they might become clean once more.

Yeshuah's face was devoid of color.

"You have become a man with a vengeance, Eleazar."

"A Jewish man, Father. Which is the sort of man you seen to have forgotten how to be."

Eleazar's angry voice, warbling between that of a boy and that of a man, had reached other tables. Conversations dwindled. Heads turned.

Meraiah was in tears. She started to rise.

"I will leave the table," she murmured.

Yeshuah thrust out a hand and forced her back down.

"It is not you who will leave, Mama."

"Ah!" said Eleazar. "Am I outcast now, Father, for reminding you of your duty?"

460

"Only if you want to be, my son. It is my suggestion that you stay here, keep your mouth shut, and attempt to absorb some of the wisdom which Jesus is at pains to impart to us."

"I see no wisdom in this man who goes against The Law at every turn."

"Oh, to be young again," murmured Jacob, the brother of Yeshuah, "and so very sure of oneself."

"You mock me," said Eleazar. "But I am the only one who sees things clear. What can you teach me, Jesus, that is better than The Law?"

Jesus polished off his wine and filled his cup yet again. He was so tired. Almost past caring. To be challenged right now by a thirteen-year-old pup was almost beyond bearing.

"Obviously, Eleazar, I cannot teach you a thing. For no teacher can reach a mind that is not ready to receive the teaching. I can tell you something though." He waggled a finger. "And you pay attention, for it is the most important thing that you will ever have heard. If you had bothered to listen to my teachings, you would have heard it a hundred times before this. It cannot be repeated too often. You worry, Eleazar, of contamination from the great miracle you saw, and felt, here today . . . the birth of a child. You believe that touching the mother or the babe has defiled these people. You think that, if they eat with unwashed hands, or sit beside a woman as they eat, they become contaminated, and will contaminate you. And, oh my, the thousand other ways that both written and oral Law warns that you and your fellows can be defiled, and insists that the way to purity and sanctity is through not touching certain things, and in the washing of hands."

Jesus shook his head. How had his cup gotten empty again so fast?

"The truth is, Eleazar, that it is not what proceeds *into* a person by way of the mouth, or by any other means, that defiles or sickens the person physically. Or spiritually. It is what comes from *out* of a person, out of the heart, that defiles and sickens. Because it is in that heart, in the mind of the heart, that we create all realities and send them forth. Including those that then appear to originate outside of us, and which then enter back into us. If what we create in our hearts is good and pure, then that is what we will give out, and that is what we will get back. There is no reason, ever, for a truly good and loving heart to fear its outward surroundings. Despite any appearances, outward manifestations are as good and pure as the heart from which they proceeded. No more, no less.

"So pay less attention, Eleazar, to the washing of hands, or to those items of the outside world with which you come into contact. Work always in your heart. Keep your heart scrubbed, honest, loving, forgiving, sympathetic, striving, unprejudiced, giving. Fill your heart with light and song and laughter. Trust unswervingly in this great, benevolent Universe that is the true god All That Is. And I promise that you can swallow any filth or poison offered you, be it the offal which fills the Ganges or a cup of hemlock, and be totally unharmed."

"But what of The Law?"

The courtyard was beginning to spin.

"What *of* The Law?"

"The Law says we must not do certain things!"

"Then do not do them!"

Jesus rose, swaying.

"Obey The Law, Eleazar, see if I care. Wash your hands scrupulously. Hold your sacred body aloof from contamination. Call dirty the supreme miracle of birth, while your heart steeps in hatred, and vitriol drips from your tongue. I will see you again when you have lived a thousand more lives. By then, you might be ready to understand."

His stomach did not feel so good.

"Now if you will excuse me, I am very tired. I must lie down or else fall down. Yeshuah, Petros . . . I wanted to tell you . . . Thank you."

He swayed again, and pawed at his eyes.

"I have just lectured this young man about keeping his heart pure, and believing in the benevolent Universe. But I was guilty of mistrust today myself. My own heart was not pure—and I nearly lost Merovee because of it. Your strengths made up for my lapse, and brought her through. I will never forget that. My remembering and my thanks are for eternity. Good night, now."

He started to turn, then he stopped. Bar Tolmei was swimming in the frame of his vision.

"Do not be afraid of what you are feeling, Zealot. We will talk of it tomorrow when I am rested. It is nothing to fear, I promise. Rather, it is the beginning of the light for you."

Bar Tolmei lowered his face into his hands and began to sob. Jesus patted him clumsily on the back and lurched toward the salon where Merovee lay. He felt sustaining arms, heard teasing comments.

"I think he is quite drunk."

"No, he would just rather be with Merovee than with us."

"But she is asleep."

"Some would say that Merovee asleep is better company than all the rest of us awake."

"Well, there are such things as sympathy pains, you know, and he has been through a lot today. I heard of a man who gave birth to a stone-weight sigh, just as his wife gave birth to a boy."

"All right, all right," smiled Jesus. He walked in a haze, hardly seeing anything—perhaps the wine had gone to his tired head—but he could tell that one set of the guiding hands belonged to Salome.

"Kitten, if I were to fall, I would squash you like a bug. Did you know that you and I were married in India?"

"No. I presume, then, that I am dead."

"Yes. Pity. But you are almost nicer now."

"Married in India?"

"Hello, Mother Dear."

"You were married and you never told your father and me?"

"There are a lot of things I never told Father and you. There are still a lot of things I will never tell Father and you."

"I will take him in."

"Do not give me sedatives, Cyrenean, I will sleep without them."

"I only want to see that you get laid down without crashing into your wife and knocking her out of her bed. Do you always drink like this?"

"Only on very special occasions. Like when confronted by a twit like Eleazar, or at the birth of a son. For the child is my son, too, Simon. You would not understand, but Johannan and I . . . and there is a third one of us. His name is Saul. I do not like him. He does not bend. I will not let him be father to this boy. What shall we name him? Merovee, what shall we name him?"

"Shh. Do not wake her. Lie down here . . . Zana made you a nice, soft pallet on the floor beside her."

"Look at her," said Jesus, obligingly sinking to his knees on the palette. "Is my Merovee not the most beautiful woman you have ever seen?"

"In deference to the memory of my own wife, I must place her second."

Jesus chuckled, stroking Freckles and Phoenix, cuddled beside Merovee.

"Poor Phoenix. You will soon be so big that you will be ousted from the paradise of her couch. That Eleazar is going to be trouble, Simon."

"Do not think of it now. Lay your head down. That is a good man. Now sleep."

"He is worse than ever his father was."

"Sleep. Are you comfortable? There are more quilts here if you need them."

"Simon?"

"Yes?"

"Is Merovee all right?"

"Yes."

"Are you sure?"

"She is resting splendidly, did you not see? You do the same."

"I think . . . yes. Oh yes. That would be the perfect name for him."

Those were the last drowsy words before Jesus slept.

Simon of Cyrene straightened, smiling. He checked Merovee, felt her brow, took her pulse, then tiptoed over to where Zana slept beside the infant's cradle. That was a healthy boy all right, no problems there. And he heartily agreed with the decision to keep him unswaddled. Barbaric practice, swaddling.

He turned and went gratefully to where his own palette had been prepared. Let the others carouse till dawn. He had not had that much wine, but he knew how Jesus had felt. Exhausted unto death.

He drew a long, shuddering breath as his head touched the pillow, and, himself, went fast asleep.

* * *

The house bar Jeremiah was silent the next morning, as though enchanted. Even the infant slept soundly on, breathing deeply, his rosebud mouth slightly opened, eyelids occasionally fluttering. He, too, had been exhausted by the ordeal, and needed time to recover.

Merovee was probably the first to wake. Memory of the child came before her eyes had opened.

Secondarily, as she tried to move, she realized areas of stabbing pain.

Oh, so much pain, in so many places. While every other morsel of her body just plain ached.

Carefully, eyes still closed, she began to move, finding places where she must be very gentle with herself, easing muscles out of frozen positions. She could tell that it was still morning, sense that she was surrounded by sleeping people.

Would she ever be able to walk again? Even to sit up?

She opened her eyes and got her bearings. Phoenix and Freckles were cuddled on her left. Beyond them was a light, fluttering snore. She smiled. Josh, there on the floor. She would know that snore anywhere.

Fighting through the stiffness, she turned her head to the right, till she could see the cradle.

She had to see her baby once more, she simply could not wait.

She got up onto one elbow, eased her legs over the side of the couch, and pushed up into sitting position. She sat for a minute, allowing a dozen pains to subside, then she began to move her legs and wiggle her feet and toes.

How strange to have the bulk gone from her abdomen.

She pushed herself up into standing position and paused yet again, letting pains and dizziness pass. She began a step and paused yet again. Her knees were not working right.

She tried again, and managed to move forward, but a wave of faintness rushed through her, and sweat burst out upon her brow.

She stiffened herself and took another step. A woman who had walked on water could certainly walk a dozen feet to the crib of her son. Mind over body.

'Obey me, Body!'

With slow, careful steps, she skirted the sleeping Zana and went around to the far side of the crib.

He took her breath away.

Could any child ever have been more beautiful? She bit her lip, silencing a giggle at the way his little arms were flung up on each side of his head. How relaxed the little hands, how graceful the tiny fingers. She ached to pick him up, but what if she fell?

'Oh, Jo. Can you see him from where you are? Did we both not do a good piece of work that night at Bethabarah?'

He must have a name. She had thought and thought, but had reached no conclusion. One thing she knew for sure. He would not be Johannan. She had always despised the practice of naming children after parents or grandparents, making of them just a little Levi, or little Naomi. Johannan had been great enough. He did not have to have another human being named after him in order to be made a big man, to have been of worth, to be remembered. By the same token, the child was his own self, not just a shadow of his father

The child stirred and wrinkled his face. He smacked his lips and uttered a petulant sound. He must be hungry. And wet. She took a linen from a pile beside the cradle and made him comfortable. Then, oh so carefully, she gathered him into her arms and sank down onto the floor.

Would her milk have started yet?

She drew her gown aside and showed him a breast. He hardly hesitated before seizing the nipple with rosebud lips.

A lusty sucker, as Zana would put it, sign of a child who would go far.

She watched him in wonder. How different the world suddenly was. Yesterday, she had been just Merovee, with Merovee's business to attend to. Now . . .

A whole new human being had suddenly appeared, attached to her by invisible cords, depending upon her for every need of his sweet existence. It would be years before she would again be able to make a move without considering his welfare before her own.

Or even before the welfare of Josh.

She felt a stab in her heart. Things would never again be the same between her and Josh, as they had been only yesterday. With the arrival of this child, a tiny wedge was driven. She was a different woman than she had been yesterday, with a new set of duties, and priorities.

So it was beginning already. The separation from Josh.

Tears stung her eyes. He had said it must come. But he had promised her that they still had time. Neither of them had taken the inevitable wedge of the child into account.

'Dear, fat baby. What is your future? And what is mine?'

How much longer before her idyll of happiness shattered like a goblet of glass, that could never be put back together again, each shard of which was sharper than any sicarius, dangerous, liable to cut, and slash, and draw blood from the incautious.

Without thinking, she hugged the child closer. He spluttered in protest at the squashing. Which sound woke Zana on her pallet on the other side of the crib. Merovee smiled in sympathy as she heard the slow, stiff movements, heard the small sounds of discomfort as Zana roused her old bones.

"I am here, Zana," she whispered.

There was an exclamation as Zana evidently looked toward Merovee's couch and found it empty. She came around the crib on hands and knees.

"You should not be up! Ah, the young master is dining. Is he getting anything?"

"He obviously thinks that he is," smiled Merovee.

"Probably not much thicker than water at the moment, but he is fat enough to live for months on water if need be. Have you had him on the other side? Switch him for a while." She stuck out a finger and chucked his chin. "Hello, little Johannan."

"No, Zana, that is not to be his name."

"But it has to be. A boy child ought always to be called by the name of a dead father."

"My brother Lazarus was not named after my dead father."

"That is because your mother has strange, Greek ideas."

"So do I."

"Do you not wish to do proper honor to the Prophet?"

"Johannan's honor does not depend upon this child."

"No swaddling, no respect for a dead father . . . poor little fellow," said Zana to the child. "What is to become of you with a mother and step-father like yours?"

Merovee laughed aloud, not at all offended by the heartfelt lack of tact.

"What is going on here?"

The face of Jesus appeared over the crib. He came around and sank down beside them, patting the baby's head.

"Good morning, little friend."

"Nothing for me?" said Merovee.

He kissed her on the cheek.

"You are feeling well, I see."

"I thought at first that I might need sutures and crutches, but things are gradually working out."

"I thought of the perfect name for our boy. It gives him his own name while still remembering Johannan. The Hebrew for 'substitute' or 'compensation.' Seth."

"Seth." Merovee rolled it around in her mind. "I have always liked that name." She frowned. "But no. It still takes away from both Johannan and the child. First of all, it implies that there could be a substitute or compensation for such as Johannan."

"Oh?" said Jesus with raised eyebrows.

465

"Yes, 'Oh,'" smiled Merovee. "Even if that compensation is a man called Jesus. Neither could there ever be a substitute or compensation for you. No. As much as I love the name, it robs them both. There can be no substitute for Johannan, while the child is not just some substitute or compensation, and that name would forever suggest to him that we consider him to be only that."

Jesus shrugged.

"Seth will still have my vote."

"I was not aware that it would be subjected to ballot," said Merovee.

Jesus looked up.

"Good morning Simon. Did you sleep soundly?"

"As the dead," said the Cyrenean. "You seem remarkably well, seeing as how I nearly poured you into your bed last night."

"Last night was then, now is now. Once you understand that, nothing can hang over from one moment to another."

"Doctor," said Zana, "tell our lady she should not be out of bed."

"I will not do that, as I happen to believe that women should be up and about immediately after a birth."

"She is not up and about," said Zana sullenly, "she is on the floor. But, since it seems that no one around here will listen to a thing that I say, excuse me. I shall go to a necessary and conduct my morning business before the lines begin to form. I will take your animals and put them into the back garden for a run as well."

"You are a dear."

The sounds from the grand salon gradually awakened those slumbering in the courtyard. Sounds from the courtyard traveled to the sleeping chambers. Lugubriously, the house bar Jeremiah woke to another day. Merovee had not, in fact, been the first one awake. The servants had been up for hours, preparing the morning meal according to Martha's previous instructions. Soon the courtyard was, once again, filled with munching locusts.

Deborah went straight to the salon before breaking her fast. She had a proposition to put to Merovee. Others had gotten there before her. Martha and Lazarus, Rosula and Joseph. A dispute was in progress.

"Mother!" Martha came to meet her and seized her hand. "Uphold me for once. I say that the child should be called Jeremiah after our dead father. It is only right that his first grandson should bear his name."

Rosula shook her head.

"He must be called after the paternal grandfather. The name of Johannan's father was Zacariah."

"No. Merovee is right," said Lazarus. "He should have his own name, not the name of someone else. He is blessed, is he not? Then give him such a name. Baruch is nice. Baruch means blessed . . ."

"The Greeks have a word for blessed that is even nicer," mused Merovee. "Cherub."

"You can not give him a Greek name," said Joseph in horror. "How about Elidad—'beloved of God'? What could be better?"

"Cherub," Merovee murmured again, gazing at the infant to see if the name fit.

"Mother!" cried Martha. "Tell her to name him Jeremiah."

"I can hardly do that, Martha, Darling, when I came here to ask her to name him after my father Nathan."

Merovee looked up quickly.

"Oh. That would be nice."

"You simply can not do that," said Martha. "The paternal must take precedence."

"Exactly," said Rosula. "Which is why you have got to name him Zacariah."

"I despise that name," grumbled Joseph.

"Why, in the name of all that is sensible?" said Rosula.

"Because it reminds me of Zachariah, himself," said Joseph. "A more disgusting man I never met. All his teeth were rotting, Merovee, and . . . "

"You hold it against a man because he had bad teeth?" said Rosula.

"There was just something about his bad teeth that was worse than other people's bad teeth," said Joseph "What do you say, Joshuah?"

"I do not remember Cousin Zacariah's teeth."

"No, I mean what name do you think is best?"

"I stand by Seth."

"Seth?" said Rosula. "What on Earth for? Seth was nothing but the third son of Chavvah and Adamah."

"The more ancient traditions name him as the first son, Mother. And 'Adamah' means Mankind. The first Son of Man. While Chavvah has come to mean 'Living.' First Son of the Living. I think the name is most apt, and I will call him Seth no matter what the rest of you decide."

"Oh you will, will you," smiled Merovee.

"Yes. I will."

She grew pensive.

"What a shame really, that we must choose a name for him—only one name that is. I mean—look at me. I was named Miriam, which mother still calls me, while my brother and sister still most often call me Miri. I remember looking over my shoulder once as a child, when I heard them calling 'Miriam,' wondering what little girl was being summoned. Miriam just never sounded like me to me. So, the moment I had an excuse, I chose a new name, one that did feel like me to me, as did 'Jesus' here."

She smiled at him.

"Yet, for all our private choices, people will still call us as they see us. I still most often persist in calling you Josh. I have to stop and think in order to call you Jesus. When I do, I feel as though I am addressing a stranger. For, to me, Josh fits you and Jesus does not.

"As for my current 'Merovee,' I sense that that will not even be my own final name. I sense that, before I am finished, I will grow through several more. Petros has taken to calling me by a name of his own devising, I have overheard him speaking to some of the others. It is a name that reminds me of the little girl who went traveling with her grandfather, and of my mother at her happiest in the house in Magdala, and of my own happy times there. 'The Magdalen' is what Petros calls me. He means it unkindly. But I love the appellation."

"Never let Petros know that," smiled Jesus. "It would spoil his fun."

"One name simply should not be expected to fit a person for a whole lifetime!" said Merovee, looking earnestly at her family. "Not when 'fit,' by its very nature, implies something that confines, restricts, something carefully measured and sewn to enclose its subject, to strain and fight against its growth. Which is why Josh calls so many of the followers by other names, to free them from the restrictions that a name imposes upon a psyche . . . and of the need to be something that other people, long ago, decided they should be.

"You, Lazarus. You have been burdened with your Jewish name, and with the strictures of priesthood associated with it. Now you answer also to Didymus. Just twin, but in another language. It is as a blank tablet, a return to the womb, to a time before you were named. Your idea of yourself and of your potential is changed, your idea of 'you' enlarged. You can now think of yourself in more ways than one, be many things all at once, make your own choices, find your own ways, define, 'name,' your own self.

"So it should be with all of us. Each of us is constantly changing, constantly different, to ourselves as well as to others. Is it not ludicrous that one group of sounds should be expected to describe any of us for a whole lifetime? Especially when what we are is beyond language. It is as Josh said. The name of 'God' is unpronounceable, not because it is a sin to pronounce it, but, because the true god is beyond words. There are no words, no names that can describe the true god. Even if there were, the true god is changing so rapidly from one moment to the next that the names would have to change just as rapidly. So, to a lesser degree, it is with us."

She sighed and gazed down at the bright, pink cloud of a child sleeping in her arms.

"How shall we call you, Little Friend? How can we find a word for all that you are now and might become? For what you make us feel?"

She shook her head.

"I have got to think on this matter. No need to rush. We have time."

* * *

The company naturally gravitated back into the salon after the breaking of fast, so that soon all were engaged in the quest for a name. Few were without ideas.

Salome's suggestion gained many adherents.

"He was born through the combined efforts of us all. Why not chose a name that bespeaks that very thing? Something that means 'union,' 'together,' 'joined hands,' or even 'spiral,' or 'energy'?"

People wandered off to murmur in groups, all searching their Hebrew, Aramaic, Greek, and even Latin for a proper word, one that would also sound well as a name for a boy child.

Judah made an audacious suggestion.

"How about 'Jordan'?"

Susannah topped him.

"How about 'Bethabarah'?"

It was unheard of to name a child after a place. Yet even Merovee gave the suggestions long, smiling consideration.

Jesus wandered among his muttering, oh-so-serious followers, and came finally to where Yeshuah and Petros sat alone. He squatted before them.

"Do you not have a name to propose, Yeshuah?"

"There are already too many," smiled Yeshuah.

"What of you, Petros?"

468

"Well—I am fond of Jonah, but that is because it was my father's name, which has no bearing on this child. Besides, she would not listen to my suggestion."

"Go try her. She is open, Petros. It will all boil down to what strikes her fancy."

Petros shook his head.

"It does not matter."

Jesus hesitated, then addressed Yeshuah once more.

"I have not seen Eleazar this morning."

"He seems to have departed during the night," said Yeshuah quietly.

"I am sorry," said Jesus. "I hope that I did not . . . "

Yeshuah held up a hand.

"Do not make polite noises. Not you. You know that what will be will be. This was bound to come. I have watched his anger growing ever since I joined you. He has made his own decision, and now he will make his own way."

"Bar Tolmei did not go with him," said Jesus reflectively.

"No." Yeshuah smiled a thin smile. "You seem to have given the Romans in Palestine a further lease on life. That Zealot is tamed."

"I hope so. For the sake of the Zealot, himself, for his own new lease on life. Do you mind if I speak with him?"

"I feel certain that he is waiting for someone to render assistance."

Jesus clasped Yeshuah's hand, rose and walked to the corner where bar Tolmei sat scrunched, staring at the floor. Some distance away, Nathaniel was leaning against the wall, paring his fingernails, a hovering guardian angel for all of his studied nonchalance.

"May I join you, bar Tolmei?"

The man looked up blankly. Then his eyes focused. He straightened himself and nodded.

Jesus sank down beside him, his back to the cool wall.

"I told you last night that we would talk."

"Yes."

"What are you feeling, bar Tolmei?"

"I do not know exactly. I seem to be floating mostly."

"No feelings?"

"No."

"Good."

"Good not to have feelings?"

"For you it is good. For a while. You have run too long on feelings, my friend. Un-useful and self-destructive feelings. Martial, negative. Feelings of anger, frustration, hatred. You have concentrated only on enemies, and not at all on your self or your Self. All the lack you felt in your self, you have projected outward, onto Romans. Each time you killed a Roman, you were secretly killing a bit of your own, unworthy, self."

Bar Tolmei turned his great, shaggy head.

"Me? Unworthy? Who thinks that I am unworthy?"

"You."

"Me?" Bar Tolmei stared more closely. "Not at all. Just look at how I have fought for freedom."

"From whom?"

"Why the Romans, of course."

"What have the Romans ever done to you, bar Tolmei?"

"They have curtailed my freedom."

"To do what?"

"Why . . . to live my own life."

"Have you not been doing that?"

"No. I have had to give up whatever I might have naturally done, to try to remove the Roman yoke."

"What do the Romans do to stop you from doing that which you could naturally do if they were not here?"

" . . . But we have to pay taxes to them!"

"What about the taxes that the priests of the Temple demand of you and all our people each year?"

"Oh, those aren't taxes. That is money for God."

"Have you ever seen God out in the bazaar buying melons? Never mind. Have you ever, in fact, paid any taxes to the Romans, bar Tolmei?"

"Well, not me. I keep on the move. But others have to, and I fight for them."

"Why do they not fight? Why do they pay and go quietly, even contentedly, about their lives?"

"Because they are cowards."

"And what are you?"

"I am a fighter. For our Jewish freedom."

"Who asked you?"

"Who asked me?" Bar Tolmei frowned. "Me. I asked me."

"And who are you?"

"I am bar Tolmei."

"That tells me who your father was. He was called Tolmei. Or Ptolemy. But who are you?"

"I am . . . I am I! The son of Tolmei."

"If you had left it at 'I am I,' I would have been satisfied, son of Tolmei. But, again, you identified yourself only as the son of another. Is that your only identity? If I waved my hand, and the Romans were miraculously gone from this land, what would you do with your precious liberty?"

"I . . . " The man's face grew blank. "I . . . "

He looked down at his square, rough hands. For a long moment he sat thus.

"I never thought about it," he said at last. "Up until now, I have only thought of killing the Romans, driving them from our land. That was who I was, I guess."

"Who are you now?"

Bar Tolmei shook his head.

"You know the answer to that, Jesus. I do not know who I am."

"Do you want me to tell you?"

"Yes."

"All right. You are a divine fragment of the true god All That Is. You are you, totally individual. There has never been another like you and never will be again. You have already lived thousands of lives and will live thousands more. 'You,' through all of eternity, have a particular stamp, a particular way of looking at things, of doing things, that gives All That Is a unique perspective that can be obtained from no other creature. As such, you are beloved of All That Is. As such, you are a part of All That Is. No one of its parts comes before you in its eyes, but neither does any part come after you. And you do have a name. Somewhere there is something, perhaps a musical tone, or a feeling, that expresses you. If you could hear that tone, or feel that feeling, you would recognize it immediately. You would know that that is you, out of all the Universe. After you learned your own true tone, you would never again be angry, or hate, or feel the need to kill."

Bar Tolmei bent his head.

"I think . . . I understood a little of that yesterday. Was it All That Is that we felt, Jesus? Is that the wonderful, frightening Power that poured into me and whirled round and round in my breast?"

"That was one manifestation of All That Is . . . a bit more immediate than some lowly posy growing quietly on a hillside, undemanding of your notice. Tell me how you felt as The Energy surged through you. Try to recall."

Bar Tolmei's eyes filled with tears.

"I do not need to try. How can I ever forget?"

He lowered his head, overcome by a sob.

"Jesus, it had all been so much talk up until that moment . . . God, that is. As a boy, I learned what I was supposed to learn. I obeyed The Law and made my sacrifices. I sort of believed that maybe it was all the truth. But, somehow, I grew angry. Somehow I saw my duty, my part in this as . . . a killer. I thought I had been born to kill the enemies of God's kingdom wherever I found them, even among our own if they sympathized with Rome.

"Until yesterday, when I felt—when I knew—that God is something much bigger, so much more wonderful than anything that my puny mind can imagine. And what is confusing me now . . . the thing I cannot understand is . . . ever since yesterday . . . I keep loving everybody!

"Do not smile at me Jesus. I cannot tell you how frightening this is! To love! I even loved the praefectus last night. Poor man." Bar Tolmei was crying and laughing at once. "His legs were giving out, and his tribune had to run for a stool, and his little wife had to fan him. I knew just how he felt. And I loved him for it! I could have seized him in my arms and kissed him! This is terrible, Jesus. I just do not know how to deal with all the love that keeps welling up in me!"

"Your cup runs over, bar Tolmei."

"I wish it would stop. Just for a minute. I did not even sleep last night. Eleazar came to me and asked me to go with him, to find Yeshuah's old Zealot comrades and form a new force to fight the Romans. I laughed at him. Giggled. Like an insane fool. But what I really wanted to do was to hug him. Not because he was going out to kill Romans, but because I loved him. And I wanted to explain it to him, but I did not know what to explain. And still I keep fighting this desire to embrace people, Jesus.

"And that baby. Oh, how I would love to take that child into my arms."

"Come then." Jesus leapt to his feet, seizing bar Tolmei's hand.

"No! Oh no, I could not. I might drop him, I have never held a baby."

Yet a man big and powerful enough to resist allowed Jesus to lead him to Merovee's couch.

"Merovee, my darling, our friend bar Tolmei is filled with love, and a vast need to hold our little Seth."

"His name is not Seth, but of course. Come around to the other side of the couch, bar Tolmei. Come. Do not be afraid, he has no teeth with which to bite you as yet. Sit down facing me. That is it. Now carefully. Support his head with your arm and get the other hand under his back."

"Oh, I can not! He is so small! How can anything this small be so large!"

"There. You have him now."

"He weighs nothing, just nothing. Oh. He opened his eyes. He is looking at me."

"So look back."

Bar Tolmei giggled.

"I think he really sees me, he . . . he just smiled at me. Look! He is smiling. He likes me!"

"Gas," said Zana flatly.

No one paid her the slightest heed. People crowded around, peering over bar Tolmei's shoulder, eager to see the baby smile.

"Can I keep him for a while?" said bar Tolmei shyly.

"My son will have need of staunch friends such as yourself, bar Tolmei. By all means, get acquainted. Walk him around the room. Jiggle him. Babies like that."

Bar Tolmei rose.

"Like this?"

"Exactly. You have a natural way, bar Tolmei. You will make a wonderful father when finally you marry."

Glowing, bar Tolmei moved off, jiggling the child, showing him off to all that he passed.

" . . . be spoiled like a rotten apple if this keeps up," grumbled Zana.

Jesus laughed, bent and kissed Merovee upon the mouth.

"Thank you, Darling. You have made a friend for your son for life."

"Do you realize that bar Tolmei has held him even before you have?"

Jesus sank down onto the couch and took her hand.

"Yes, I have realized that. So now you see what a coward I can be. I do not want to hold him, Merovee. Not just now." Tears welled into his eyes. "If I did, I would stand in danger of becoming the blubbering, wet clay that bar Tolmei is in that child's tiny hands at this moment. I might be tempted to lay aside my own purpose in order to just be his father, to stay with him, to see him into adulthood, to watch that glorious little body grow, to know a smile that is not just gas, but only for me—lovingly for me, to teach him, guide him . . . "

Merovee's own tears welled out.

"Then go get him. Do hold him. Do stay with us."

"I cannot. Rather, I will not."

Jesus lowered his head to hide his tears, though most eyes were now upon bar Tolmei and the child, everyone appreciating the change in the Zealot. A sort of euphoria was building in the room, as people began to understand bar Tolmei's emotion and to participate in it.

"I must do what I must do, Merovee. I could say this to no other woman with any hope of being understood . . . but you and our love together are peripheral to me. At one and the same time, you are the core of my existence, the most important thing that has happened to me. And I have got to trust you to understand why that very fact makes you peripheral in this lifetime. You, as you are here and now, are a delight and a treat—a partner—which I dreamed of but never expected, and in which I now gratefully indulge myself. You are what I would want for myself for all of the rest of eternity if I did not have other immediate purposes. And, Darling . . . someday those purposes will be realized. When they are, when we have both become what we are meant to become on our particular levels, then we will have leisure to be together. We will have leave from any Powers That Be to dally and romp in the 'Elysium Fields' for as long as the fancy moves us, till we are sated, until we are so sick of one another that we will cry for release, begging to go on to the next level. I am asking you for the utmost of belief Merovee. I am trusting you to believe that what I say is so."

"I do . . . Damn it. . . . Though I cannot imagine ever growing sick of you."

"Better to say that you will mature . . . find a need for more. Personally. Within yourself. And you will go questing after that something. Do not fear. No matter how many times we are together and then grow apart, we will always find each other again. You, Johannan and I. We will always find one another."

Merovee lowered her face to hide her own tears.

"Merovee!" It was bar Tolmei. "May Mother Meraiah hold him?"

She took a deep breath and called back with such good nature that one would never have known.

"Mother Meraiah has raised enough of them. I am sure that we can trust her not to drop him."

She watched as the eager old woman took the child into her arms and commenced to parade him, bar Tolmei shadowing lest she should stumble.

"I love you," said Jesus.

"I know," said Merovee. "Sometimes I wish I did not know."

During the next minutes, or hour—or however long it might have been in the framework known as 'time'—the child was passed from arms to arms. Everyone seemed to want his or her own turn. Even Yeshuah took the child for a minute, and felt the tiny hand wrap around his teasing finger.

And Petros. The wife of Petros had proven barren. By Law, he could have put her aside and chosen another. But she was a good girl. Quiet, amiable. She kept a clean house and denied him nothing. She had made not a peep when she learned that he was leaving. And he knew how she cried inside at her lack. Should he further punish her, shame her, by divorcing her? No. He had looked, instead, for Chandreah to marry so that he would have a baby to jiggle. How cruel that the first into his arms should be the child of the Magdalen.

But what an engaging little fellow! A man had to chuckle at those penetrating blue eyes. And what a grip! He would be strong, make a good fisherman.

As for the child, he seemed, if a newborn could seem to be anything, to enjoy his odyssey from person to person, face to face, from crooning voice to crooning voice.

"He needs feeding," growled Zana.

"I am sure he will let us know when he agrees with you," said Merovee.

Jesus sat on the floor beside her, his back to her couch, holding her hand and watching the spectacle.

At last he rose, and spoke in a voice peculiar to him, not loud, but carrying to all, and silencing all.

"I have a suggestion to make. You are all searching for a name to adequately represent this child. I invite each of you to search for new names for yourselves as well."

"What on Earth for?" said Joseph bar Ramathea.

"For absolutely nothing but the fun of it. The names do not have to be serious. They need not even be known outside of this group. But it would be a fine exercise for each one of you to try to find some image, or some group of sounds, that would, as Merovee said earlier, say you to you more clearly than your present name. It does not have to be a 'name' name. It can be gibberish, or something from nature, an object, an animal, an action, an emotion . . . "

There was silence for a moment.

"What if we already have such an unofficial name and are content with it?" said Miriam, the mother of Jesus.

"Then by all means, 'Rosula,' Darling, hang onto it."

"I would not mind thinking up a new name for your father. I never did like the name Joseph."

"What makes you think I am not capable of thinking up my own name, Wife?"

"Because you have no imagination. And no daring."

Joseph's mouth fell open.

"I will show you who has daring. I choose the name . . . "

Joseph cast through his thoughts for the most daring name of which he could think.

"Careful, Father," said Jesus. "It has to be something that says you to you more strongly than does Joseph."

Joseph nodded, his honor, his dignity before his wife, at stake.

"It can be anything? Even in another language?"

"Anything," grinned Jesus.

"Then I choose the name Apollo," said Joseph quickly, getting it out before his courage failed.

Rosula let out one of the shrieks for which she was infamous.

"A Greek god? You can not call yourself by the name of a pagan god."

"Mother, you are not allowed to interfere," said Jesus.

"But what will people think?"

"'People' do not apply, Mother, only us."

"Why Apollo, Joseph? Why not something nice, like . . . "

"Because I like the name, that is why."

"You never said so."

"Why should I have?"

"What is so wonderful about Apollo?"

"It sounds like what it is meant to sound like. Sun. And that is what I feel like to myself. The Sun."

"Leave it to you to feel like the most important thing around," snorted Rosula.

"Try getting along without me and you will think that you have lost the most important thing around," snapped Joseph.

"So be it then," said Jesus. "My father is Apollo." He smiled at Deborah. "The twin of Artemis. Who is next?"

"I," said Susannah. "I shall be Clay. I shall be malleable, but capable of becoming everything from a water pot to a house. I shall be the stuff that holds cities together, and the blob with which children play. And I shall be the whole Earth."

"I am content with Kitten," said Salome. She grinned. "Though I might grow up to be a cat."

"I shall be Moon," said Deborah.

Chandreah chose First. Procula chose Lily. Lazarus decided on a version of twin in yet another language, the Aramaic Thomas. Petros grunted when prodded, and declared himself content with Petros. Thunder's sons became Lightning and Storm. Annah, the sister of Jesus, chose New. Nathaniel chose Support. Johannah chose Free. While Herodias re-named herself Pursuit.

"For, all my life, I have been pursuing something. I know not what. But I think I might finally be gaining on it. When I do catch it, whatever it is, I will let you know, and tell you my real name."

Zana snorted and said she had been named Zana by her parents and that what was good enough for her parents was good enough for her. Simon of Cyrene felt the same.

Alphaeus chose Sight, in honor of his newly returned vision.

Phillipus, Lover of Horses in Greek, decided on the Roman name Marcus.

"Why?" said Jesus.

Phillipus shrugged.

"I just always liked the name."

And so it went around the room, some people declaring new names immediately, others taking time to think. Some, like Zana and Simon, kept their own names. Others, like Herodias, declared interim names. Names like Lightning and Storm, applied by the mild-mannered sons of Thunder to their own selves, were self-applied spoofs. While Clay, Support, and First were deeply meaningful yet capable of infinite expansion within the minds of Susannah, Nathaniel, and Chandreah.

Surprisingly, even Martha took a new name.

"I am Bread. I feed foolish waste-abouts such as yourselves."

Mother Meraiah came hesitantly to Jesus.

"I know this sounds silly and awful, but, when I was a girl, I used to imagine that I would grow up to be a queen." She reddened. "As long as this is just for fun . . . could I please be Queen Meraiah?"

Jesus rose and bowed.

"So it shall be, Your Majestic Highness."

He turned then, to where Yeshuah still sat, smiling, enjoying the game.

"And you, Yeshuah. What new name would you have us call you?"

"I have already proclaimed it," said Yeshuah softly. "I call myself The Messiah."

The good-natured chatter stilled.

"The Messiah is the name you choose?" said Jesus.

"Yes."

"It is a hard one, Yeshuah."

"I am prepared for the consequences."

"Just do not get my son killed, Fool," cried Joseph.

"Peace, Father," said Jesus. "No one can kill me except I decide to withdraw from my present body. So The Messiah it is, Yeshuah. The Anointed. Which makes Queen Meraiah even more a queen if you have decided to be our king. You know, the Greek for anointed has a nice ring to it. Christos. Yeshuah Christos." Jesus nodded, pleased with himself. "A fine ring."

"Yes, I like it," said Yeshuah serenely. "I will accept Christos. And what of you, Jesus? Have you no new name to adopt?"

"As a matter of fact, I do." Jesus sank back down beside Merovee's couch. "You may call me Wine." The company chuckled. "I do not take the name lightly," he said. "The symbol of vine, grape, and vintage is one of deep and mystical importance to Humankind. The roots of that which gives Wine are the roots of Life, and of the Earth itself. Now. Bar Tolmei. What of you? What name have you decided upon?"

Bar Tolmei hesitated.

"I was never called by my own name. I detest it anyway. Job. I was wondering . . . there is one here who has been kind to me. He has sat with me and tried to quiet my fears and answer my questions. I admire him and want to learn to be like him. Since he chooses now to be called Support . . . "

Bar Tolmei turned to Nathaniel.

"I wonder if I could borrow Nathaniel for a while. It would help me feel like the thing I am learning to be."

"I will gladly loan it," smiled Support.

"I know, Jesus, that I am still making of myself a mere reflection of another, but, until I find my own true Self, will it suffice?"

"It is a fine start," said Jesus. "And it is certainly as valid as the image chosen by Pursuit here. Both of you characterize yourselves as searching for your true Selves, and I promise you that there is no holier pastime. Judah. What of you?"

Judah reddened, at first avoiding the gaze of Yeshuah. Then, as he answered Jesus, he lifted his eyes to his brother.

"There is only one name possible for me, Jesus, by which symbol I mark my entrance into true life. I am Fig Tree."

There was a murmur of approval. Even Yeshuah gave him a rueful nod.

The naming continued midst pleasantry and a good deal of laughter, as those who could not decide upon names received suggestions from their friends. Jesus sank down beside Merovee.

"And what of you, my lady?" he murmured. "Will you not choose a name beyond Merovee?"

"Indeed I will. You have chosen it for me. For, if you are Wine, then I am that which yearns to be filled by you. I am Chalice."

Jesus smiled and arched a brow.

"Beware, then, Lady, lest I intoxicate you and take advantage."

"Only fill me and keep filling me. My thirst for you is unquenchable."

"And what of our son? Have you found a name for him as yet?"

"It is so obvious I wonder that I did not see it immediately. Look at him pass from person to person. Yes, now he is young and must be helped along. But the impetus is his, never doubt it. They pass him because he has called to their minds to do so. He wished to meet his friends. And look at the change he makes in all whom he touches. Look how he is liking it, loving each one of them equally. I know his nature already, Josh. And it is not just my fond hopes speaking. He has shown me his name, told me what he is. I know I cannot wrong him, or saddle him with a name that is not himself, by calling him by a Greek verb. Agapo."

Jesus sat back and rolled the sounds around his tongue.

"Agapo. 'I love.'" He smiled. "It is a fine name, Merovee."

"And will you still call him Seth?"

"Yes," he teased.

"Oh! You are impossible!"

"If I were impossible, I would not be sitting here beside you. Stop calling me Josh, and I might consider Agapo. Merovee, have you noticed what happened here today . . . just among us and some of our own family? Think what we have said. My father is the sun, your mother is the moon. I am wine, your sister is bread. You are the chalice, and our little son is love. While my mother is a rose. Between just us few, we can light the world, provide food and drink, and satisfy Humanity's need for love and beauty eternally."

Merovee tilted her head, staring at him.

"You are serious."

"Yes."

"I mean . . . I think I am coming of age . . . Wine. You do not speak symbolically, or metaphorically. This is how it is done. This is how reality is constructed. By naming ourselves thus, we have become a living unit of Energy that will actually give that sustenance to the world."

"We have and we will."

"The responsibility is so great. If only Humanity could understand . . . the import of every thought, of every word, the living Energy in the symbols it selects . . . "

"Do not dwell on the responsibility, Chalice. It is all a game. A wonderful game. The more you look upon it as a game, the better a player you will become, the more effective a player you will be. If you never remember another thing that I say, remember this. Do not take yourself seriously. All that is good and creative arises out of a spirit of joy and play. Only when you begin to take life and self seriously, do things get sour. It is the one who 'plays' with love and joy and trust in the Universe who moves ever closer to what is 'seriously' the true god. While those who are intense and pompous stagger deeper into farce."

A light, but imperative, hand touched his shoulder.

"Jesus." It was Procula. "Do not alarm the others," she murmured. "Go quickly out to the court. Pilatus has sent Lucius with a message."

The smile left the face of Jesus. He rose. Exchanging pleasantries with this one or that one, he made his way to the door. Once outside, he walked swiftly to the corner of the colonnade where Lucius waited.

"What has happened?"

"The High Priest has applied to Pilatus for permission to stone a priest who has transgressed the Law of Moses."

"Lazarus."

"We think they intend to have it over and done with before sundown."

"Has Pilatus granted his permission?"

"Unfortunately, just before the request came in, Pilatus became ill and took to his bed, leaving word that he was not to be disturbed for several hours. Naturally, none of us dared to disturb him with such a routine request.

"But we cannot put them off much longer, Jesus, and the permission is only a formality anyway. It is not our policy to deny the priests and so interfere with your internal religious matters. They are well aware of that. They might even decide to move without the permission."

"They will, no doubt, send Alexander and his Levites to arrest him."

"For all I know, they are on their way here at this very minute."

"Ah, the filthy, errant Souls! I did not think they would make any move at this point . . . the Passover not a week off."

"That is just it. Thousands are already encamped in the Vale of Kedron and all about the city. The priests want the excitement of a mob. So many are eager to throw that first stone. Once it is thrown, there is never any stopping the stoning, you know that, yourself."

"Yet they cannot stone a man without a meeting of the Sanhedrin."

"They have already had it."

"What? My father was not informed."

"Of course he was not informed. They summoned only the legal minimum and all those their own adherents. That is how much of their business is done of late. You can not save Lazarus with the technicalities of your Law, Jesus. Annas and his people snap their fingers at those technicalities, even while pretending to uphold them. They have evidently decided that putting your brother-in-law to death will stop you. They hope that such a show of force will cause you to retreat in confusion, and be heard from no more."

"But what charges are they using?"

Lucius threw up his hands.

"You ask me to make sense of your Law concerning priestly conduct? All I can tell you is, get Lazarus out of here. Fast! And you get out, too. For who knows but what, at the last moment, they might decide to make a clean sweep and arrest you and your more political followers as well."

"You were not observed coming here?"

"Naturally I took precautions."

"We must somehow get Procula out as well. And Herodias and Salome. It would be a catastrophe if Alexander and his ruffians found them here."

"Of course. That was what I was going to say next. The enclosed wagon should have arrived by now."

"Wait here, I will send them out to you." Jesus started away.

"Your God be with you, Jesus."

Jesus turned back. For Lucius had choked on tears as he said it.

"Our God, Lucius. Which God is always with us. All. All ways."

He continued on into the salon. Procula was waiting.

"Come with me," said Jesus.

She followed after him as he moved to where Salome and Herodias sat in conversation with Judah.

"Kitten, Pursuit," he said lightly, "you must leave with Lily at once. No!" He silenced their beginning protestations. "Just leave with Procula now, as though you are going for a walk in the courtyard. Lucius has a conveyance waiting for you."

"Is Antipas back from Idumea so soon?" said Herodias in astonishment.

"I know naught of your husband's movements, this has nothing to do with him. Procula and Lucius will explain on the way back to the city. Just trust me and help me by going quietly. And do not be frightened by anything terrible that you hear of any of our friends after you leave this place. Any terrible news will not be so. Keep your faith and wait for me to send word to you."

"We will see you again?" whispered Salome.

"I promise, Kitten."

Salome rose, drawing her mother to her feet as well.

"I need some air, Pursuit, it is growing close in here. Come with us, Lily."

"I will come too," said Judah quickly.

Jesus stayed him as the women moved away.

"They have a Roman guard and the immunity of position, they will come to no harm. Stay with me. My need of you is great."

He strode then, smiling, to Merovee's couch. He bent and kissed her on the lips, ignoring the agonized questions in her eyes.

"The priests will be sending the Temple guard soon to arrest Lazarus. Stay calm and do as I tell you. Most of all, believe what I tell you. You have seen me do miracles."

"Yes."

"The best is about to be. I am going to round up most of the men and go out to Bethabarah for a few days to teach, vain and undutiful husband that I am. Naturally, the new mother will stay here, with the women and her family, including Lazarus."

"But . . ."

"The police will not be able to take Lazarus when they arrive. They will be confounded and leave in confusion. Just watch. Is Artemis hidden away so that she can not possibly be found?"

"Yes."

"Then do not fear. And do not believe the thing that will appear to happen. Do you understand me?"

"Yes."

"How I love you!"

He turned and strode over to Yeshuah.

"Up. We must leave immediately. Petros, Support, 'Nathaniel,' Levi, Boanerges, up. All the men who are not family, up. Alphaeus, you stay, you are family. And you, Jacob bar Alphaeus, you and Lebbaeus stay. Lazarus, you stay. And you, of course, Physician. No women are coming. Mother, Father, Joses, Annah, Rachel, you stay as well."

Amid the general cries of dismay, the mind of Jesus worked furiously. It must all look natural. To everyone. He could not tell them what was happening. He could not ask them to dissemble and practice deceit. And they were not professional actors. The life of Lazarus depended upon the conviction of the players in this drama.

"Judah, move them out. No one is to stop for so much as a quilt. Jesse, if you please, be so good as to load up a wagon with quilts and provisions. Bring it down to us at Bethabarah as soon as it is safe to do so."

"Is it the Temple police?" whispered Yeshuah.

"Yes. Pilatus sent warning. I do not wish to overly frighten the women. I told Merovee that I was suddenly possessed of a need to go to Bethabarah and teach. You and Judah get the men well away down the road. I will catch up with you."

"Do not linger too long."

Jesus turned and saw real concern on the face of Yeshuah. He embraced the man, kissing him upon the lips.

"I will not. Go, Christos."

Yeshuah did as he was bidden. Soon the salon was emptied, peopled now by confused and frightened women and family members, and, of course, old Zana and Simon of Cyrene.

"This is only a precaution," Jesus told them smoothly. "Our friend Pilatus was afraid that the Temple authorities might try to make trouble for me or for Yeshuah here today, so I thought it best that we rush down to Bethabarah for a few days. There is no danger to any of you, so please just relax and see that my wife and baby are well cared for."

"I should go with my son," cried Meraiah.

"Begging your pardon, Queen Meraiah, but we can travel faster and better without you. And your expertise here with my wife and her new babe will be welcome."

He wheeled, taking Lazarus by the hand.

"I leave Merovee in your explicit care, Thomas, my love."

As he spoke, Jesus pulled the man toward him till he had reached up and had his head between his two hands. He stood thus for many long seconds, staring into the eyes of Lazarus, his fingers bringing such pressure to bear on the young man's skull that Lazarus winced.

Then, suddenly, Jesus released him.

"Goodbye, then."

He glanced at Merovee, wide-eyed and pale upon her couch.

"Remember what I told you," he said, and he strode rapidly out of the salon, out the gate, and down the road toward Bethabarah.

In the salon, there was silence for a long while. It was all so inexplicable, and doubly shocking, in the way that violence cutting into gaiety and happiness is always worse of a shock.

Even Agapo reacted. He began to fuss, and then to cry out loud. Zana put up the screen so that he could be fed.

Those left outside gathered into knots once more, murmuring apprehensively.

Then there was a scream.

Uncaring of the startled and protesting child, Merovee shoved him into Zana's arms and vaulted from the couch. By the time she rounded the screen, Deborah and Martha were already crouched over Lazarus, moaning. He clutched his head and writhed in agony. Simon of Cyrene pushed through to his side.

"What is it?" cried Deborah.

"A seizure of the blood in the brain, I fear. Joseph, Alphaeus, help me lift him. Put him on Merovee's couch.

Merovee stood back, watching in horror as her brother was carried to her bed. For some minutes, he continued to writhe, making ghastly noises, his eyes bugging out, his sense gone.

Then, suddenly, his body went slack, his open, screaming mouth relaxed, his already sightless eyes rolled back in his head.

Simon worked feverishly. The only sounds now were Martha's sobs.

Behind her, Deborah and Merovee silently clung to one another.

So intent upon Lazarus and Simon were all in the salon, that they hardly heard the shouts at the gate, the tread of many feet. The Levite police who entered the room might have consisted of vapor for all the attention they were given.

For a moment, the guards stood gaping at the tableau. Then Alexander, their leader, announced their errand.

"We have come in duty to God, to arrest the priest Lazarus bar Jeremiah for sins against The Law."

All but Merovee turned wondering eyes.

Simon of Cyrene straightened. He stood for a moment, staring down at his patient in anger and disbelief. Then he turned to Alexander, a macabre little smile upon his lips.

"You are too late, Levite, unless you wish to return a corpse for trial. Lazarus bar Jeremiah is dead."

Chapter 17

He Is Risen

The wagon from bar Jeremiah arrived at Bethabarah at sundown. Jesus and the men had waited in Johannan's grove south of the ford. Most rushed forward, eager for food and drink, and for news.

Jesus followed more slowly.

The driver of the wagon was not Jesse, but Lebbaeus.

"Jesse was too distraught to come. For I bring tragic tidings, Jesus. He who you love, my cousin Lazarus, has died."

A shocked cry went up. Support laid a consoling hand on the shoulder of Jesus as Lebbaeus haltingly, with many tears, recited the events of the hour after their leaving.

"So your mother bids you return with all haste, Jesus," he said in conclusion. "For there is no danger to you, it was Lazarus who the police came to arrest. She says to say to you that your wife and her mother and sister are beside themselves."

"Yes, Jesus, surely we must return," said Jairus. "For, as you raised my daughter from the dead, so you will be able to raise Thomas."

Jesus shook his head.

"Your daughter had not long stopped breathing when I reached her side, Jairus. Lazarus is now several hours dead. By the time I got back to bar Jeremiah, he would be even more hours on the journey to decay. I have a mind to go into The Wilderness and meditate for a day or two. Then I shall return."

"But . . . . . . this is heartless!" cried Lebbaeus. "Even if you cannot raise him, your women need you! Your wife is still weak of the childbed, she should not have to bear this without you at her side. And poor Deborah. And Martha. They can do nothing but wail. All of Bethany rings with their mourning!"

"Good. Let those sounds reach over the hill and to the Temple, itself, so that Annas and Caiaphas may be sure that Lazarus is dead. Return to bar Jeremiah, Lebbaeus. Tell my wife that the weather continues hot, so that Lazarus should be quickly entombed in the morning. Tell her that I shall return to her after three days time."

Lebbaeus stood stupefied.

"I can not believe this of you," he finally managed.

"Then do not believe it of me, Lebbaeus. Trust your Intuition always above Appearances. Judah, I would that you return to bar Jeremiah with Lebbaeus."

He led Judah aside.

"Tell Merovee, though I am sure she knows . . . Thomas is not dead, he only sleeps."

"But how?"

"At the moment, that does not matter. Tell none of the others about this. Let them think the worst of me. Speak only to Merovee. It is imperative that appearances are kept up, that the grief is real, and that the priests believe Thomas to be dead, laid in the tomb, gone beyond any recall.

"It is also imperative that his mouth and nose be left free when he is wrapped in the linens, so that he can continue to breathe. There will be no breath apparent, but, believe me, he does still breathe. You and Merovee prepare him. As his twin, she may demand the right. The two of you will then have to be closeted away with uncleanness, and that will be fine, you will not have to feign grief and be false before the world. To any who ask, do not lie. Tell them that Lazarus only sleeps, and that you are sure of his resurrection. They will assume that you deceive yourself to assuage your sorrow.

"Oh. Be sure to use only enough of the spices to send out aroma and make others believe he is properly wrapped, else his flesh could dry and atrophy."

Judah was hardly listening. Instead his eyes were far away, but glowing with excitement.

"It is the Seventh Sleep, is it not."

For Jesus had begun, with his most receptive followers—Merovee, Lazarus, Deborah, Judah, Salome, Procula, Nathaniel, Susannah, Johannah, Annah, and Chandreah—to teach techniques that he had learned in India and then among the priests of Isis in Egypt, instructing them in slowing the pulses and stilling the breathing, with an eye to finally becoming proficient enough to leave the body for indefinite periods and roam time and space at will. None of them had as yet reached that level of excellence, and, hence, experienced, the Seventh Sleep. Merovee had come closest.

"You somehow catapulted him into it," said Judah. "Did he understand what you were doing?"

"He knew I was up to something, but I doubt he knew just what."

"Oh, Jesus. What an adventure he must be having right now. How I wish I could go and die with him, and see the things he is seeing."

"You will accomplish the sleep soon enough, Judah, do not seek to enter it as did Lazarus, through the agonizing seizure I was forced to induce in his brain."

"How long will his sleep be?"

"He must be awakened after three days."

"You will be able to bring him back?"

"He will be brought back."

"Then Jesus, I wish you to do it to me when we return. I will endure the seizure. Please let me die like Lazarus, so that I may visit other realms and be born again in wisdom."

Jesus laughed and gave him a shove.

"Only when I hear that the police are on their way to arrest you will I do such a thing." He laughed again, ignoring the confused, and accusing, glances of his other followers. "Give Merovee this message. Tell her that Wine sends the Chalice a Fig Tree as a sign that there is no death. Supervise the twin's wrapping. See also that the stone over the door of the tomb is rolled just short of its mark, so that fresh air seeps in to him. Send to Salome and Herodias and Procula, for those three may also know the truth. Tell them to stay away from bar Jeremiah until they hear from me. In two nights beyond this night, I will arrive at the home of Simon outside of Bethany. Tell him to expect us."

"Simon . . . the one you cured of his leprosy."

"Keep your ear tuned in these next days for any rumblings against me or against Yeshuah. Procula and Pilatus will have the best information. Trust them implicitly. Send to me at Simon's at the noon if you deem it safe for me to bring all the men back to the house. If it is not safe, I will have to find a way to slip in alone. Go now."

He hugged Judah and kissed him upon the lips, then stood silent as the young man sprinted to the wagon and climbed up beside Lebbaeus.

His men were equally silent. Sullenly so.

"Anyone who wishes to return to bar Jeremiah right now may do so," he said as the wagon rattled away. "The rest of you come with me."

Without waiting to see who followed, he headed south, along the Jordan, into the Judean Wilderness that edged the Dead Sea. Yeshuah soon caught him up.

"So it was Lazarus they were after and not us."

"Correct."

"Incredible coincidence that he should up and die just as they came for him."

"The Lord moves in strange ways."

Yeshuah burst into laughter.

"Jesus, you are a marvel. I thank God that I came to my senses and joined up with you. How did you do it?"

Jesus was not laughing.

"By disrupting the rhythm of his brain. And with much danger to him, Christos."

Yeshuah's face straightened as well.

"You mean you might not be able to get him back?"

"Oh, I will get him back. But what his mental condition will be, I do not know. The sleep I have put him into is the ultimate. Self-induced, after proper preparation, it is perfectly safe and more than beneficial. It is the sleep into which the High Priest of Isis puts himself each year."

"Yes, I know. A sleep so profound that one seems dead. They even put the priest into a tomb. Yet, after three days, he 'rises' from the 'dead' . . . just as did the god Osiris after three days."

Jesus glanced sideways. So Judah had been mistaken. Yeshuah had, indeed, made himself conversant with other religious practices.

"I have been working with Lazarus, among others, giving him some of the initial understandings and abilities necessary for such a 'journey.' But he was not ready to take one. I had to force such an advanced state onto Merovee once. Because of you, Christos. Petros returned from Kapher Nahum with news that you had called her Jezabel returned, a whore with seven demons."

Yeshuah reddened.

"I have gained much understanding since that time, Jesus."

"I know. But, on that day, I felt it necessary to publicly remove seven 'demons' from out of her. The technique and the trauma was somewhat the same as I was forced to give to Lazarus today, though nowhere as severe. Merovee emerged from the experience greater in Spirit and understanding. I pray that it will be so with Lazarus. What emerges from that tomb might be a great man. There is also the possibility that what emerges will be a man—damaged in mind."

Yeshuah walked silently for a moment.

"Since each of us creates his own reality, is the decision of what emerges not up to Lazarus?"

"Thank you for understanding that, Yeshuah Christos."

"What arrangements did you just make with Judah?"

Jesus told him.

Yeshuah fell thoughtful once more.

"Jesus, if what you did to Lazarus was so dangerous, why did you do it? Why did you not merely have Lazarus flee along with the rest of us?"

"In crisis, one must quickly choose from an array of possible actions, and pray that the choice is wise. As I saw it, if Lazarus had fled, it would have been an admission of guilt on his part . . . any guilt that the Temple decided to proclaim. Right now, if he had fled, Lazarus would be a fugitive, a hunted animal, with formal and public charges of a capital nature against him. While all who fled with him, any who harbored him, would be attainted as well. General guilt would have been established for all of us, perhaps even for Deborah and the women.

"And what of little Agapo? The son of the Prophet Johannan, a future rallying point for activists, and a constant reminder to the priests of their own crimes. The priests could well have seized the chance and arrested everyone left behind at the house. And I can guarantee you that little Agapo would have met some 'accidental' end, while the priests would have turned the countryside upside down looking for us men, until they had every last one of us—with full sanction of Law and cooperation from the people. For Lazarus to have fled would have played right into their hands . . . I think."

He looked toward Yeshuah almost beseechingly.

"Do you think I made a wise choice?"

"You did. And Lazarus loves you and Merovee so much. He would far rather risk only himself than his loved ones."

"If I could have thought of a way to take the punishment myself, I would have. For it is really I, and you, too, Christos, who they aimed at through Lazarus . . . myself primarily at the moment, as I was the one who ruffled the priestly feathers in the Temple court, and it is my genealogy that is the most provocative. But they have no real grounds against me yet, or against you. Their aim, then, was to take Lazarus and kill him as warning to me, and to you. They hoped to frighten us into silence. Now their plans are destroyed in the bud. No charges have been set forth against Lazarus in any court, and any that were intended have been dropped, while nothing can be settled on me or on you for simply coming out to The Wilderness to meditate. Whatever momentum Annas and Caiaphas had got going, is halted in its tracks."

"What will happen when they find out that Lazarus is still alive?"

"They will have to re-think their strategy. He will have been seemingly dead, as witnessed by a physician and even by Alexander and the Levites—dead for three days, in the tomb. When I wake him, I will tell everyone the truth. I will even have it proclaimed in the Temple court . . . that he was only in a sleep. Few will believe it. Most will prefer to believe that I called him back from death.

"I do not relish that. I do not like being in this position of . . . untruthfulness. Anything less than full honesty always harms the Souls involved.

"Yet Lazarus will be safe as though charmed, for a man suspected of having risen from the dead is not as easily arrested and stoned as a priest guilty of sinning against The Law. 'Why was he raised if not by the grace and will of God, himself?' That is what the people will whisper. So that Annas and Caiaphas can talk themselves hoarse and still not get anyone to agree to a second arrest. Confounded, they are. For a while. Only a while. Miracles in the wilds of Galilee are one thing. A 'miracle' such as this, so near to Jerusalem just before the Passing Over, is quite another."

He sighed and shook his head.

"There is no going back from what I have done this day. Soon the entire Judaic world will know of Lazarus. The one consolation will be that, just because of the fame, the priests will not be able to proceed against any of us except with great caution and firm charges under The Law."

"Yet they will find a way. You have only bought time."

Jesus nodded.

"But is that not what we need? Both of us?"

Yeshuah walked silently for a while.

"What is your mission as you see it, Jesus? Why are you here?"

"I am here, first, in response to a summons from the mass dreaming mind of Humankind. It is the double millennium, time for a change. I come to initiate that change. Ultimately though, Humanity will use me and my 'life' led in its midst as it sees fit. People will make the things I do, and the things I say, fit their own notions of what should have been done, what should have been said. And they will invent pretty stories about my origins, and about the nature of my being. I cannot control, or fully foresee, all that future generations will do with what I now give to them. All that I can do is to give them the very best of which I am capable, plant my finest seeds, so that the tree that grows upon my life will be better than any tree previously grown."

There was another long silence.

"And that is it?" said Yeshuah finally. "That is all there is to your mission?"

Jesus smiled a faint smile.

"All?"

"Do you not want to give people a framework? New beliefs? A new code to live by, so that they may be guaranteed the Kingdom?"

Jesus halted and dropped to one knee, adjusting the thongs of a sandal.

"No."

"But without organization . . . "

"Yeshuah, one day the Tempter was walking along a highway with a friend when, just ahead, they saw a young man stoop and pick up some shining object from out of the dust. For a moment, the young man studied the object. Then, with a glad cry, he ran off.

"'What did that young man just find?' asked the friend of the Tempter.

"'A piece of the Truth,' replied the Tempter.

"'Well,' said the friend, 'are you not going to try to stop him? It could be very dangerous to you if people learned any part of the Truth.'

"The Tempter only smiled.

"'Not at all,' he said. 'I will let him play with it for a while, and even show it to his friends. Then I will simply move in and help him organize it.'"

Jesus rose and studied Yeshuah's face in the starlight.

"Do you grasp the message, Yeshuah?"

"I am afraid not."

"Work on it," shrugged Jesus, and continued on over the rough, rocky ground.

Yeshuah hastened up beside him.

"Make me understand, Jesus. Teach me. I want to learn. I am here to learn."

"Yeshuah, if I talked for the next thousand years I could not make you understand what you are not ready to understand. Those with ears to hear will hear, those with eyes to see will see. Do you not understand that this is why so much of what I say when I speak to the multitudes is couched in parables? I can help people only so far. Beyond that point, they must help themselves."

"You act as though you do not care whether people understand you and grow towards God because of your words."

"You are right. I do not care. Do not look so shocked. In that not caring are dimensions of care which you will be many more lifetimes understanding, Yeshuah. All is relative, my friend. You cannot teach any person who has not come to a point, relative to you, where he can, and, very importantly, has made the choice to, understand. You cannot legislate or enforce 'God' or 'goodness' in hearts. You cannot guarantee some idealized 'Kingdom' to anyone, and, most certainly, not through any rituals or regulations or organized beliefs or priesthoods. These things can only come in their own time, into each heart, into each mind as each heart comes to understand through its own journeys, through its own joys and sorrows.

"No. I do not care a clipped copper whether people understand my words or not. I care only that I have said the words to them. Somewhere, in the backs of their Souls, they will remember. On the day when they have journeyed far enough, and experienced enough, at that point in which they are finally positioned in proper relativity to my words, then those words will spring forth from out of their minds, like new species of flowers. Someday, somewhere, the Earth will bloom because of them. Since time is simultaneous, it matters not whether these blooms appears now or in a thousand years or two thousand." He smiled. "Or whether they appear two thousand years into the past as we think of it."

Yeshuah strode along, frowning. Jesus glanced sideways, his heart going out to the man. He was trying so very hard to understand.

"I want you teach me the Seventh Sleep," said Yeshuah finally.

"If you wish."

"I have been waiting for you to do so. I know that you have already begun with my young brother, he whom I look upon as a son. You teach the son these great mysteries and neglect to invite the father. Why?"

"Because, Yeshuah, once you have learned the mysteries, I am sure that you will leave me. So great is your personal command of The Power, that you will probably only have to be shown or told once, and you will have it. I have wished to prolong your time with me, so that I could implant some of my finest seeds in you." He glanced sideways again. "Is it not so, Christos? Will you not leave me when you have learned the sleep?"

"I shall have to. I, too, have a mission. It does not agree with yours."

"More is the pity."

"Petros will be coming with me when I go."

"I know. And probably the Sons of Thunder. Take any who wish to follow after you, Yeshuah Christos, each must do as he sees fit in his own time. Yet, I still have hopes of convincing you that no physical Kingdom of God can be established on Earth, since any such kingdom is non-physical, interior, and individual to each person.

"Neither can the sacrifice of any one man take the sins of those who believe in his teachings from off of their shoulders, so that they automatically enter your proposed kingdom."

He smiled at Yeshuah's own sharp, sideward glance.

"Oh, do you not think that I know what you are planning, Yeshuah? Your speech in the synagogue of Kapher Nahum was well reported to me. Tell me, Yeshuah, do you still, after having been with me these many months, after hearing my teachings again and again, do you still seriously consider yourself to be 'the only begotten son of God'?"

"Yes."

Jesus shook his head in amazement.

"After all I have explained as to the true nature of 'God,' after I have made clear the equal divinity of each one of us, you can still think that. So who do you suppose that I am, Yeshuah?"

"You are God's highest and chief angel, sent to Earth to ease my own mission in this time and place."

Jesus could not help chuckling.

"In a way, I have to admire you. You certainly do stick to your thesis. But I am no angel, Yeshuah, if only for one very good reason. I would not work for a god such as you envision.

"What a hideous concept, Yeshuah, that a father would require his son to suffer agony in order to redeem the creations which he, that father, himself, made so 'badly.' What a sadistic, even cowardly, creature is your 'God.'

"No, believe me, I am sent by no such monster. It is good news that I bring, glad tidings, from the true god, that does not want its parts to suffer—for, when they suffer, it suffers—that true god that, instead, bids its parts be happy, healthy, prosperous, glowing, laughter-filled—that bids them allow their exuberant creativity to fill the world.

"I come expressly to explain that grief and suffering, and sickness and cruelty, and injustice and rigid laws and restraints, are not wanted, not needed, for all that they appear to be needed and inevitable.

"I come to explain that organization and dogma is the automatic death of any Idea, any true creativity, that it is the antithesis of 'godliness.'

"I come to explain the beauty and divinity of each individual 'eye of All That Is' in this world, the validity and purpose of each one of those eyes.

"I speak only of love and joy and laughter, of trust, and belief in the goodness of the Universe around us, of its consistently benevolent intent, and of the consistently positive results that you will achieve when you do finally learn to love and revere and trust your own Self and so the Universe.

"Suffering, sacrifice—those are not things that All That Is wants of us, Yeshuah. The doctrine that you have chosen, the path you intend to follow, will do nothing except lead you, and any who follow you, further into error and confusion."

Yeshuah had listened intently, as he always did. Now he smiled.

"There, you see? You have proved my case for me."

Jesus threw up his hands.

"How?"

"You have just repeated the divinity and validity of each 'eye' of God. I am such an eye. Therefore, in your own terms, my view, my creative version of my own life, is as valid as any other. You have also proven me the only begotten son of God in your own terms. For you have told us repeatedly of the unending multiplicity of God, each one of those versions valid in its time and place, and you never cease to impress us with the relative nature of all things. Each man's view of God is different from that of any other man's, you have always told us, while each view is yet valid. So, since I, like any other man, have a unique and valid god of my own, I have got to be the only begotten son of that god! And I have a perfect right to live my life in accordance with what he expects of me."

Jesus walked on, struck momentarily speechless.

"Well? Is it not so?"

Jesus gave a noncommittal grunt.

"And see here!" said Yeshuah, warming to his argument. "You say my god is cowardly, to expect his son to suffer in order to redeem his own imperfect creations. But you also say that the true god experiences through each one of us. So, if I suffer to save all of his sinning creations, then my god is suffering with me. He is not cowardly at all. He intends to do his own penance for his own incompetence. But, since the true god of whom you teach, with all his versions, is so huge, there is no way he could appear among us except through an individual man, or son. He has chosen me, caused me to be born. Through me, he will catapult all who believe on me and my sacrifice into a state of grace, into the Kingdom. For, if they believe as I, and believe in me, they will be believing in him. And if people come to believe as I, then they will see the same god that I see, and all the benefits of 'children' of that god will be theirs. I thank you, Jesus! I had never seen it quite so clearly before."

"My pleasure."

"And so you agree with me?"

Jesus walked on for a long moments, shaking his head, sighing, even laughing to himself.

"Well, Christos," he said at last, "it is this way. You have grasped most of my teaching very well. As is to be expected, you have fitted those teachings to your own mental form. As sculptors work with clay, you have taken my words into the hands of your mind and turned them into a new and unique creation that is all your own. And yet you believe on me, do you not?"

"With all my heart, Jesus. I know that your wisdom is greater than mine, but I also know that you are for the ages and for all peoples, while I am meant, in this one place and time, and for my people the Jews, to do one certain thing, to the best of my ability and in my own way."

"But you do believe on me, and in the true god All That Is that I have described to you."

"Yes, Jesus.

"Yet, even though you *believe*, you do not *see* the same god that I see. You have but taken my words and re-worked your own original version of that god."

" . . . I suppose you could put it that way."

"Then why do you expect any of these 'sinners' whom you intend to redeem, whom you expect to believe on you and in you—why do you expect them to do differently than do you? If you believe on me and in me, and yet do not see the same god that I see, how do you expect them to do anything other than slather your new ideas onto their own old ideas, and create their own new versions of that god? This is one of the elements of my teaching that you have not yet truly understood, Christos, even though you think that you have understood. And it is a most crucial element. If you do not really understand the 'relative view' then you understand almost nothing.

"Those who believe on you and in you and in the sacrifice you plan to make to 'save' them, will not see the same god that you see. They cannot. No two sets of 'eyes' can ever see exactly the same thing. No two perceptions can ever be the same. No two sets of 'eyes' can ever be in exactly the same point of time or space or circumstance. Hence, there is no final, legitimate perception. There is only what each consciousness sees from its own standpoint in its own 'moment.'

"You seem to envision your followers, your believers, as mindless, clay dolls, all lined up, all washed clean, all individuality, you assume, wiped away, so that all of them see and believe exactly what the 'Master' tells them to see and believe.

"Only imagine them in their row—that you would have be endless—all of them looking towards you. That very model will show you that each one of your clay people will see a different view of you, and so understand you a bit differently than does the next clay fellow in line. Some will be so far away that they will not be able to see you at all, but will have to rely on the murmured descriptions traveling down the line.

"Have you ever played the children's game of Whisper? All sit in a circle, and one child whispers a phrase of his own devising into the ear of the next. That child then turns and whispers what he thought he heard to the next child. And it does not matter whether there are only several children or a dozen. By the time the message has been whispered round the circle, it will be somehow changed from what was originally said.

"No, Yeshuah. Your view of your god is yours alone, and can never ever be shared by any other. Because individuality and the relative view is the structure—indeed, the whole point—of the Universe. Individuality can never be destroyed and must be reckoned with. All teachings, all religions, all governments, all disciplines which ignore, or aim at extinguishing, the individual view, the individual creativity, which attempt to reduce Humanity to rows of identical and obedient clay figures, are doomed to eventual extinction.

"And the more repressive and inflexible they are, the more quickly they topple. One hardly has to fight them, they collapse of their own ignorance. The individual human Spirit will not be denied, or remain long enslaved. Until this is learned, religions will rise, religions will fall, governments will rise, governments will fall.

"So, if you maneuver yourself onto your cross, Yeshuah . . . oh yes, I know that that is what you are planning . . . if you get yourself up there, know that you die alone, and you die for yourself alone. No one will ever be able to understand your suffering as you will understand it, No one will ever understand your god as you understand 'him,' and your sacrifice will not redeem one single sin. Of anyone. Including yourself. Neither will you save anyone.

"For this is another point of my teaching that you fail to understand. There are no 'sins' to redeem. No one needs to be 'saved.' Because no one is in any danger. There are only good intentions which have been badly executed, understandings to be perfected. All That Is does not blame its parts for their mistakes. All That Is expects only that we actually learn from our mistakes, find a better way of doing things.

"And there is yet another element of my teaching with which you quite obviously have not come to terms. Where do you think you are going after your 'death'? To some kingdom in the sky where you will sit and converse with angels and listen to music for the rest of eternity? No, my friend, sorry to disappoint you. You, like all others who leave the flesh, will be given all the time that you need to reflect on Simon called Yeshuah, on what he did well, and what he did less than well. Then you will come right back into the flesh, into the womb, out the birth canal, and you will have to start all over again, trying to do better than you have this time.

"So where is your Kingdom of Heaven in that scheme, Yeshuah? Where is the realm to which your blessed and sanctified clay people will go? Where is the 'salvation' you promise them? It is right here, Christos!"

Jesus jumped straight up in the air, landing with feet apart and well-planted.

"Here! This is the only Heaven, just as it is the only Hell. This is the only realm of the blessed, just as it is the only realm of the damned, and you lie if you promise people that they can leave this sort of training ground for 'higher' realms before they have learnt for themselves that they create their own realities, before they have learnt for themselves the results of their every thought, their every action, before they understood the true nature of this reality.

"Live out your creative vision if you must, Yeshuah, but do not delude yourself that you are providing anything but negative example, an example that will do not a fig of good to anyone."

He quickened his steps, drawing ahead. For he suddenly, unaccountably, found himself near tears.

But Yeshuah would not be left behind. He hurried up alongside once more.

"I am sorry to have distressed you, Jesus."

"No more sorry than I. Yeshuah. What words can I say? What words would it take to make you understand? You are great. And you are going to throw that greatness away."

Jesus stopped again. They had come to within a mile of the Essenic community of Qumran. Its first evening lights were lighted. Jac would no doubt be sitting beside one of them.

'Ah, fools!' he cried to himself, remembering, even as he thought the word fool, his own injunction to his followers never to call others by that name.

But they *were* fools! Jac, the Pharisees, this Yeshuah—fanatics, who persisted in denying the truths that their own daily lives and beautiful creaturehoods presented to them, who developed elaborate tales of heavens and angels and demons and sin, maniacal laws of cleanliness, and constipated rules for behavior, who assiduously, and often viciously, set out in the name of their god to deny and annihilate the very essence of All That Is—their own individuality and that of their fellows.

Yeshuah was still prattling.

"I think I understand more than you assume that I do, Jesus. One important thing that is bothering you is that you think that I will ask my followers to wallow in guilt and sorrow over my own suffering. No! Not at all. That is just it! I will set them free of guilt, free from sorrow. I will bid them be joyous. They can go forth singing gladly, shouting the tidings to all who will listen, that I have lifted all sin, all sorrow, all guilt from off of them. My followers will be a congregation of joyous saints!"

Jesus groaned.

"Yeshuah! The ends never justify the means. Never. And you cannot get an apple by planting an onion. If you plant suffering and blood and sorrow and martyrdom, that is what you will reap! When, oh when, will you people understand what the lowliest plant teaches? You reap what you sow, there is no other rule, there can be no other rule. You cannot reap joy from seeds of suffering, or forgiveness from seeds of guilt. You cannot bring peace by brandishing a sword. Never. No matter how high-minded and 'fine' your intentions. You cannot find love by dwelling on hate. You will never see good if you think only of what is bad."

He halted suddenly, and leveled a finger at Yeshuah.

"And I call you Coward, Yeshuah Christos. For you seek the easy way out."

"Easy! You call the death I contemplate easy?"

"Yes, easy. Two, three days of agony, then it will be all over for a while. You will not have to stay, to fight on, to keep trying to understand. You will not have to endure the unending disappointments in your own self when you miss your mark, you will not have to pick yourself up by the straps of your own sandals and keep going, you will not have to develop the courage to trust. Or to love. You will not have to suffer fools. Just out. Pouf! You have done it again and again, run like a rabbit, and thought yourself a saint for so doing. It takes no courage to run, Yeshuah. The courage is in staying. Why do you not try it, Yeshuah, just for once. Try staying instead of running."

He wheeled then, and shouted back to Nathaniel.

"Support. We camp here." To their right was a good-sized hill, part of the cliff structure of the palisades which ringed the Dead Sea at distances of a mile to two miles from its shore. "I am going up onto yonder hilltop for the night. Or longer. I wish to be alone and undisturbed."

Without even taking a bedroll, he started off.

Nathaniel braved his displeasure by overtaking him and shoving a quilt and a skin of wine into his hands.

Jesus stood for a moment, looking down at the offerings. Then his anger faded, and he laughed.

"You are indeed a Support. Thank you. In an hour, I would have been cold, and probably before that I would have been thirsty. But, after such a dramatic exit, my pride would not have allowed me either to come back down or to call for aid."

"Let me come up and sleep near to you."

"No. Thank you, but I really wish to be alone, Support. I might need to curse, or rant . . . or even to sob. It is best to be alone at such times, with nothing but Mother Earth to hear one. You will serve me best by guarding my privacy. Goodnight."

"Jesus!" said Nathaniel quickly, stopping him. "I have placed all the money that I possess on a wager with Petros and Mathiah. I say that Lazarus but sleeps. Do you think I have a chance of winning the wager?"

"You placed all the money you have?" mused Jesus. "What a shame."

Nathaniel studied the face of the man he had grown to love and to trust above all others.

"You mean I will lose the money?" he said slowly.

"No. I mean what a shame you did not have more to wager. Here." Jesus reached into his gird and drew out some coins. "We will be partners. Go back and cast our net. Catch us some more of those doubting fish."

He turned then, and strode on up the slope. For a moment, Nathaniel watched after him. Then, grinning, humming and counting the coins, he was off on his fishing expedition.

* * *

Yeshuah, too, drew apart from the others that night, up onto a hillock of his own. He needed the height, he thought, to gain an overview of his situation.

Of one thing he was certain. If Jesus returned to Bethany and was thought by the world to have raised Lazarus from the dead after three days in the tomb, his own plans to gain the public's eye and ear would be finally and utterly crushed. There were tens of thousands already encamped around Jerusalem. In another week, there would be ten times that number come for the Passover. Even the most idle gossip spread through Passover crowds like wildfire. Word such as this would cause a firestorm, a conflagration that would burn to the end of time, that could never be quenched.

'Joshuah ben Joseph bar Ramathea, who calls himself Jesus, has raised a man from the dead! A man already three days in the tomb! Surely this Jesus must be the Messiah. A first heir of David who can do such miracles? Who else could he be but the Promised One, here at last, praise be to God!'

Did Jesus seriously think he could throw water on the fire and put it out by telling people that Lazarus had only been sleeping? What nonsense. The glad tidings would be carried to all the Judaic world within a month, as pilgrims returned to their homes throughout Galilee, Judeah, Peraea, Moab, Phoenicia, Syria, Anatolia, Greece, Egypt, Cyrenia, Babylon, Italy, Gaul, Iberia, the Caspian. Thus it would be the words and teachings of Jesus upon which the Jews of the world would wait, to which all would hearken . . . while he, Yeshuah, would become less than a piece of chaff on the wind, just some false, foolish prophet, his voice drowned out by the adoration of Jesus.

And it would be Jesus who gained the honor of dying for his people, not Yeshuah. For the Temple authorities would close upon Jesus as soon as possible.

Jesus must be mad not to know this—not to foresee it.

But, of course, he did foresee it. Jesus was no fool. That was it. His assurances that he would proclaim the truth and not take credit for raising Lazarus were false. He meant to take credit all right. He meant to pull the path right out from under Yeshuah, put an end to Yeshuah's ambitions before ever Yeshuah knew what had struck him. Jesus meant to get all the glory for himself, get to Heaven before him and usurp Yeshuah's promised throne.

No. That could not be it. As chief of angels, Jesus already had a throne of his own. Why would he wish to steal Yeshuah's?

There was something else going on here. What was he missing?

Yeshuah sat munching on his fingernails, trying to understand exactly what Jesus was up to, for it never occurred to him that Jesus, unlike himself, ever made any move that was not calculated.

As he sat munching, Yeshuah thought he began to see the true plan.

Had he not already recognized Jesus as having been sent to help him along his own path? If that was the case, Jesus was not working against him, but for him.

This newest turn of events was meant to be his, Yeshuah's, big test then, and the protestations of Jesus against his plans were nothing but a ruse, a trick, a trial, to see if Yeshuah could be turned from his course—while, all the while, Jesus had prepared for him the means to be finally and universally proclaimed the Messiah.

It was all there, in Bethany, ready and waiting, if he but had the wits to seize the moment.

Jesus expected him to use his ingenuity and do just that.

Yeshuah's eyes traveled to the last lights in the Qumran community. Some of those lights would be the sheep fat lamps of the lay brothers on kitchen and scouring detail, cleaning, endlessly cleaning, making everything immaculate for the following day. Most full brothers would be already abed, or engaged in solitary prayer beside their mats. Some few of them would be in the meeting room, singing songs to the Lord until the sunrise, for the community never truly slept, prayers were offered up to Heaven twenty-four hours a day, the brothers taking turns at the all-night vigils. When the lay brothers had finished their cleaning, they would leave the central enclosure and go to the caves that were their homes, for that central enclosure could by no means accommodate all the lay people. It could not even accommodate all the full brothers. Hence, it housed only the most senior, unmarried, full brothers. Surplus full and unmarried brothers slept in tents just without the walls. Full brothers who had wives and children lived in a tent city in a valley atop the cliff behind the community—a valley where there was a spring, so that crops could be grown, and where the community grew its food. While lay brothers took shelter in some of the caves which honeycombed the cliffs.

At last, the lights of the kitchen staff were extinguished and only the singers were left awake in the night. For the day came early in Qumran. All rose for prayers and ritual bathing at four each morning. Devotions were accomplished and fasts broken by six, so that they were about their labors with the sun.

Yeshuah knew their routine well. He had lived among them as a lay brother for four years after his wife's death.

Was old Ephraim still alive, still their overseer? He had been so last summer when Judah and Mathiah had sojourned in the community, and past his hundredth year.

Better if that old saint were dead by now, better if Reuben, the second most respected of the community, were the new overseer . . . for Reuben had new ideas, a political mind, and a goal that was more emotionally Zealot than Essene.

Reuben could be counted upon to see reason. Whatever the leadership down there at the moment, it was to Reuben that he must speak.

He called his brother Isaac to him. They whispered together until long after the other men had wrapped themselves in their quilts and gone to sleep. Finally, Yeshuah lay down and slept as well, with Isaac keeping watch.

At the first faint sign of morning, Isaac roused Yeshuah, who rose and moved silently off, toward Qumran.

* * *

During the following day, the disciples of Jesus camped at the base of the hill on which Jesus sought solitude. None would disturb him. Indeed, most, themselves, took the opportunity to draw apart and to meditate. It was a time-honored tradition for a man serious about his relationship with God to come into this barren, rocky, sun-baked strip along the western shore of the Salt Sea, known as The Wilderness of Judeah, and cleanse himself spiritually. It was thought that the sun and the harshness of the land was beneficial to the Spirit, and that, here, a man was even apt to find God strolling, and so have opportunity actually to speak with God.

Nathaniel had always thought this rather silly . . . or else God rather silly. Why choose a place like this to stroll when there were so many more comfortable and attractive locations? He, himself, tried praying, but the sun beat on his head, and the rocks cut into his knees. He could not get comfortable, or concentrate on his prayers. So he went and sat in the shade of a boulder.

What was there to pray for anyway? Prayer had become silly in light of the teachings of Jesus. Prayer made it seem that God was something or somewhere 'out there' rather than 'in here.' Prayer made it seem that God was some irascible and detached superior from whom one had to beg, to whom one must continually plead for mercy or any sort of fairness . . . rather than one's own self.

Rather than pray, Nathaniel had decided, one should do and be the very best that one could do and be at every moment. One should live every moment as fully and as well as possible. Instead of praying conventionally, waiting for some voice, some sign, some response from without, one should sit quietly and go within, ever more deeply within, listening inside oneself for the whispering of the divine, for hints of how to do even better, live even more fully, and love. Love ever more deeply.

The other Nathaniel came and sat with him, and Support told him his thoughts.

They had quickly developed a comradeship, these two, big, burly men, both with the sort of bigness that made people automatically assume them to be doltish and stupid.

The new Nathaniel sat listening to his hero, nodding occasionally as Support spoke. Then Support fell silent, waiting patiently for Nathaniel to formulate his reply.

"Well," said Nathaniel at last, "I have not had much experience with the old sort of praying. I memorized what I was to say just as the priests instructed, but I never felt it. Oh, once in a while, when I was a boy, I would be seized with pride in our people, and with sheer happiness to be alive, and I would feel for a moment that maybe there was a God out there, and that he was very good.

"As I grew older, though, I could see no good in anything.

"It is very different, you are right. Reciting memorized prayers to something 'out there,' as opposed to . . . living the truth within your self."

He reached over and grasped Support's hand.

"Just being with you, the two of us together like this. This is the best sort of prayer. I feel things within myself that the priests' prayers were never able to give me. I have that boyish feeling again, that there is a God, and that that God is good.

"But now that God is no longer 'out there,' I know that you are God, and I am God, and the feeling that I feel in my breast at this moment is God. God is the love I feel for you and Jesus and Merovee and her Agapo.

"And so, yes, why go out into the sun and kneel upon stone hoping to talk with God, when I am hearing God speak right now in my heart?"

"How did you feel when you followed Yeshuah? Was there none of this goodness, Nathaniel?"

Bar Tolmei grinned to hear himself called by that name.

"We were about other business, Support. The business of hate, not of love."

He looked up toward an opposite hill, where Isaac said that Yeshuah had retired to pray during the night.

"I can hardly believe it now, when I think of the man that I was, that one who followed Yeshuah. Surely it was a different person."

Support hesitated long.

"And what business do you think Yeshuah is about now, Nathaniel?"

Bar Tolmei grunted.

"Exactly the same business as before. Certainly his outlook is different. He has softened and learned. You will not find him sticking blades into any more Roman ribs. No one can know our Jesus without being improved at least that much. But . . . Yeshuah is unlike other men. It is not that Yeshuah is ambitious. I truly believe he has no ambition for worldly goods or worldly acclaim except as a means to an end. Instead of ambition he has . . . a fire in his heart and mind. He burns for something higher than mere acclaim. And the goods for which he strives are not of this world. He burns for a heavenly throne. He will have it if he has to build it himself when he gets there."

"I have often thought that the man is quite mad."

"Oh, I have never doubted it, not for an instant."

The sun passed its nadir and sank, an orange ball, into the palisades just to the west. The men dined on bread and wine.

"If Jesus is not down from his hilltop by tomorrow evening, I will take him up more provisions," vowed Support.

Soon all save Support were rolled into their quilts and falling off to sleep. The night was turning exceeding cold, giving Support more cause to worry for his master.

Master. He would call Jesus that in his thoughts, never to his face.

He finally could not sleep at all from worrying. At about midnight, he rose and walked a short way up the hill. He almost kept going. Then he stopped.

Jesus was, after all, a grown man, and would certainly come down or call out if he were in need or distress. Jesus would tease him for being a mother hen if he went up there.

He turned back toward the camp.

It was then that he heard it, clear in the cold night air.

"Oh!"

He froze, listening for more sounds. None came.

Had it been his imagination? It had seemed so clear.

Mother hen or no, he was going to assure himself of his master's safety. He set off up the hill at a run.

Then he stopped again.

'I might need to curse, to rant, or even to sob . . . and it is best to be alone at such times.'

The big man put his arms about himself, not from cold, but by way of comforting his own self. Slowly, he turned and went back down the hill. Reluctantly, he rolled back into his quilt. After more fruitless listening, he fell asleep.

* * *

Yeshuah rejoined the group, coming down from off his own hill late the next morning.

"What, Jesus is not down yet?"

By sunset, Support was pacing like a caged bear. Yeshuah took it upon himself to go up to the hilltop to see how Jesus was faring. At Support's insistence, he took a loaf of bread, and skins of both water and wine.

He was gone less than an hour.

"There is no cause for worry," he said when be returned. "Jesus is in a transcendent state. What a wondrous thing to see. He glows with an inner light that illuminates the darkness. He is so bright I could scarcely look at him. Come. Look for yourselves."

The men rose, went away from the campfire and looked up at the summit of the hill. Indeed, reflected upon the rocks, there was a strange, flickering glow.

"He wishes to remain thus for as long as the Spirit is upon him," said Yeshuah, speaking into the hush. "So he bids us return to Bethany without him."

"No!" It was not only Support who protested.

"We can not just go and leave him here alone," said Chandreah.

"You do not understand," smiled Yeshuah. "He will be there ahead of us. He says he will soon be snatched up, as in a whirlwind. In the twinkling of an eye, that will yet seem as the journey of a thousand years, he will be shown all this world and many others. When he returns, it will be to Bethany.

He will meet us at the home of Simon the Leper. We are to go there this night. Jesus has made plans with Judah to send word there at noon on the morrow if it is truly safe for us to return to bar Jeremiah. So come. Pack up. We must not be guilty of disobeying the wishes of Jesus."

It was a confused and hesitant band of men that Yeshuah led out of The Wilderness that night. Many there were who stopped again and again, looking back at the eerily illuminated hilltop.

Support found himself crying in his own confusion. And hurt. Why had Jesus revealed his splendor only to Yeshuah? How came it that Yeshuah was now ordained their leader? Why had Jesus not, instead, seen fit to speak to his oldest and most trusted friends?

"I wish that Judah were here," muttered the new Nathaniel as they trudged along.

"Why?" said Support.

"He can read his brother better than can any other man on Earth. I do not like this. I do not know why, but I just do not. Jesus was a fool to trust Yeshuah like this."

"He must have good reason," said Support with a confidence he did not feel.

"He may think he has, but he is wrong to give Yeshuah this power over his men."

The confusion of the men deepened when, well after the midnight, they knocked at the back door of Simon the Leper's house in Bethany. Simon speedily answered, having, as arranged, been alerted to their scheduled arrival by Judah.

He was not a pretty sight to behold, this Simon. The cure of Jesus had arrested the disease and healed the sores, but not rebuilt or replaced those parts that the disease had already ravaged. Still, one almost forgot the unsightliness when confronted by the warmth of disposition that had characterized Simon since the cure.

"Come in, come in! You must be freezing. Go to the hearth, there is a kettle of honey ale simmering there for you all, and my wife Judith baked the date bread fresh just this evening."

He stood nodding and greeting all in turn as they entered. When the last man had passed in, he hesitated, then stuck his head out the door.

"But where is Jesus?"

"He is not here yet?" said Yeshuah.

"You mean he is coming separately?"

"That he is," smiled Yeshuah. He repeated to Simon the tale of the transfiguring light that had filled Jesus upon the hilltop.

There was nothing that Simon would not believe of Jesus. His eyes grew wide as Yeshuah spoke, and he looked about his kitchen reverently.

"Do you suppose he will simply appear, as from out of nowhere?"

"I think we might hear a rushing of wind before he appears," said Yeshuah sagely. "He might even seem to form as from out of a whirlwind."

For an hour they all watched and waited. Until, one by one, they fell asleep upon their quilts, lulled by the honey ale, the surfeit of warm bread, and the warmth of the fire. Finally, only Yeshuah and the leper kept vigil. Then Simon gave up and went to join his wife in sleep.

Alone beside the fire, Yeshuah sank onto his knees and commenced to pray.

When the company woke, Jesus was still not in evidence. And it was Martha, rather than Judah, who arrived at Simon's door at the prearranged noonday hour, to say that all was safe. She, too, was stunned by the absence of Jesus.

"But Judah said he would be here. Judah could not come himself, for he and Miri wrapped . . . the carrion, so that they are unclean and remain apart. But he promised that Jesus would be here!"

"Jesus . . . was transfigured and snatched up by a whirlwind," said Petros lamely. "He should arrive at any moment."

Martha's voice rose to a wail.

"Oh, why did he leave in the first place? If he had been here when Lazarus had his seizure, my brother would never have died! If he had returned immediately that he was sent for, he might still have brought Lazarus back. And now he will not even put in an appearance. I thought he was a great man. Now I call him a coward!"

"Martha, dear sister in heart," said Yeshuah.

He had been sitting on a stool by the fire. As he rose, all eyes went to that man. Bar Tolmei's hand reached out to grasp Nathaniel's arm.

For bar Tolmei knew very well what he was seeing. It was the old Simon Yeshuah. The spellbinder of Galilee, the leader of men, the worker of miracles, the caster-out of demons, who dared to rise in synagogues and declare himself to be, not only the Messiah, but, the only son of God, sent to redeem his father's people from their sins.

Nathaniel had never seen the fabled Simon Yeshuah in action. He knew only the broken man who had come to the fireside of Jesus on the last night of Tabernacles in Galilee, the penitent, quiet and respectful man who had followed after Jesus these many months, who had sat at his feet night after night, gratefully learning.

The man who now rose to his feet there upon the hearth of Simon the Leper seemed a giant, in every conceivable way. Yet how had he changed, Nathaniel wondered? He had not. Yet he had. Even he, Nathaniel, felt his mouth dropping open at the power, the certainty that radiated from the man.

"It is time to tell you all of the grand design that Jesus, that angel of God, has prepared. When you understand the design you will be happy, Martha, that he was not here when your brother died, and you will understand the heavenly purpose that made Jesus refuse to return and raise Lazarus from the dead. For, without this definite death of your brother, the power and glory of God, and of his son, the Son of Man, who is myself, could not have been made apparent to any of you. Cry no more, Martha. Your brother is going to serve a heavenly purpose, for I will go now and raise him from the dead."

Martha's mouth was agape.

"You intend to raise him? No, Yeshuah, you do not understand. It is three days ago that he died. He has been laid in the tomb for two days, his body . . . it must have begun to stink by now."

"Have you so little faith in the power of God, Martha?"

"I revere God! And I know that my brother will rise again in the resurrection. But . . . "

Yeshuah raised his arms. His flashing eyes bore into each of them.

"*I* am the resurrection. I am the life. He that believes in me, though he were dead, that man shall live. And he who lives and believes in me shall never die."

He seized Martha by the shoulders and forced her down till she knelt before him.

"Do you believe my words, Martha? Do you believe the words of your Messiah? Say it Martha! And Lazarus shall be raised."

"I believe," she whimpered.

"What? What do you believe?"

"I . . . "

"That I am the Messiah!"

"Yes."

"Say it!"

"You are the Messiah."

"What else am I?"

"The . . . "

"Son of God! Say it!"

Martha's face was devoid of color as she contemplated the blasphemy.

"Say it!"

"You are the son of God," she whispered.

"Good girl!" beamed Yeshuah. "Up with you then. Run and tell your sister and all the others. I come now to raise Lazarus."

Martha rose and backed slowly toward the door, never taking her eyes from Yeshuah. Then she turned and ran.

The disciples broke into a clamber.

Yeshuah laughed and pushed through to the door.

A furious Chandreah grabbed his arm.

"How dare you! You fraud! What are you up to? How dare you try to take the place of Jesus?"

"But follow and watch, Chandreah. Then call me fraud if you can. And why do you think Jesus opted out of this? He wants me to be the one to raise Lazarus. It is all part of the heavenly plan. Stop scowling, Man, and come along."

Martha ran as she had never run before, for once throwing decorum to the winds and losing her head-covering to the same. She arrived at the gates of bar Jeremiah in a terrible state, in tearful disarray and gasping for breath. Boaz, her intended, was waiting there. With a cry, he ran to her and caught her. She pushed him off and struggled on, to the grand salon where all the uncleanliness of bar Jeremiah, of birth and of death, had been consolidated and quarantined.

Judah caught her at the door. Martha did not fight off his unclean embrace, but dissolved into tears upon his breast.

"My God!" Merovee leapt up off her couch and ran to her sister. "Martha, what is it? What has happened?"

"I do not know! Jesus was not there! Yeshuah is leading the men instead! He made me say that he is the Messiah. He made me call him the son of God! God forgive me! He says that he is going to raise Lazarus. Oh Miri, I am so confused. You promised Mother and me that Jesus would raise our brother. I cannot see how, but I trust Jesus. Jesus, not this Yeshuah!"

Over the hysterical woman's head, Merovee and Judah were staring at one another.

"I told you that my brother could not be trusted," said Judah. "He is making his move."

"But what has he done with Jesus?" cried Merovee.

"Jesus was transfigured and snatched up by a whirlwind," moaned Martha.

"Lady," said Zana, "your boy has awakened and is crying for his milk."

"He will survive," snapped Merovee. Her eyes were wild. "I do not know what is going on, but Yeshuah does not know how to do this. He may think that he knows, but he does not. If he makes some terrible blunder—if Lazarus is not brought out of the sleep correctly . . . ."

She thought for only another few seconds.

"Come on, Judah, we have got to get to Lazarus ahead of Yeshuah."

She ran out of the salon and down the colonnade to the door that led into the back gardens and to the tomb.

"Bring some men to roll back the stone!" she called after herself.

The order was unnecessary. The court was filled, not only with companions of Jesus, but, with the priestly cousins of Jeremiah, with friends and acquaintances come to sit and mourn with Deborah and her girls. Already alert as a result of Martha's dramatic entrance of moments before, they now rose and streamed after Merovee and Judah, thinking that Merovee had gone mad in her mourning, to be running to the tomb this way.

Merovee wasted not a moment once they reached it.

"Come on!" She threw her own weight against the stone. "Roll it back, roll it back!"

"Miriam. Dear Cousin!" Jacob bar Alphaeus did not touch her, as she was unclean. He tried, instead, to put the force into his voice. "He is dead, Miri! You have got to accept it!"

"Shut up and help us push, Jacob! Lebbaeus! Mother! Help us! Push! Everybody push! Jesse, run to the front gate. Bar it, do not let them in."

"Who?"

"Just run! Bar it. Come on, damn you all, help us!"

"Oh Miri," cried Martha even as she pushed. "He must smell so."

"Push!" It was Judah who called out now.

Somehow the stone got rolled back, just far enough for Merovee to wiggle in through the opening, Judah behind her.

"Mother. Come in with us. Do not be afraid. Close it behind us, Martha."

Sobbing, Deborah scrambled in through the opening and the stone was rolled back into place, leaving them in darkness.

Merovee embraced Deborah quickly.

"It is only in the Seventh Sleep, Mother. I could not tell you before. It had to appear to the priests that he was really dead. But things have gone awry. Jesus has disappeared and Yeshuah is coming to try to wake Lazarus, and Yeshuah does not know how. If we are to be sure that Lazarus is properly wakened, we have got to try to do it ourselves."

Deborah shuddered, then took control of herself.

"When you promised that Jesus would raise him, I dared to hope that it was only the Seventh Sleep."

The three of them groped their way to the back of the chamber, where Lazarus lay upon a stone platform. Together they knelt beside him.

"You begin it, Mother. You remember how we called Jesus out when he put himself into the sleep for us. Gently and lovingly. We must remind him of the time and place in which he belongs."

Deborah took a deep breath and laid her hands upon the wrapped head of her son.

"Soul of the one known as Lazarus . . . . My voice is so shaky, Miriam."

"It is fine. Go on."

"Soul of Lazarus. You are summoned back. It is Deborah speaking, she who inhabits the body that gave you birth in this lifetime."

"And I, the one who inhabits the body that is now your sister, Miri. I summon you, too, Soul of Lazarus."

"And I, the one who inhabits the body of your friend, Judah. I summon you back to this time and this place, in Bethany, near to Jerusalem."

"We are in the year following the departure from this plane of the Soul that inhabited the body of the Prophet Johannan," said Deborah. "We summon you for the love of our fellow Soul now corporeal as Jesus. Your adventure must terminate now, Soul of Lazarus. For the love of the master Soul Jesus, you are needed here with us."

There was a growing clamber outside the tomb. Jesse had not gotten to the gate in time.

"There is a body waiting for you here, Soul of Lazarus. Follow the energy in the sound of my voice and you will find this body. Allow yourself to enter back into it." Deborah's voice had become smooth and even. "Do it easily. The body might at first seem as an unknown house. The limbs will at first refuse to respond, the body will feel as though made of stone. Do not be frightened, and do not be discouraged and depart away from us. Revitalize all the body parts slowly, lovingly. They have lain asleep so long, they have almost forgotten you, as you nearly forgot them. Come now, Soul of my son. Become ever more conscious. Try to move the hand that I hold. Signal me that you have returned, move that hand."

Outside the tomb, they heard Martha's strident cry.

"You may not roll back the stone! My brother has been dead three days and surely he stinks!"

"Soul of Lazarus," said Merovee, "I hate to rush you, but you are just going to have to get back into your body. Right now."

There was no response of any kind.

"I call you in the name of Jesus!" cried Merovee.

Still no response.

Then all the small hairs at the back of Merovee's neck stiffened.

Someone had placed a hand upon her shoulder. There was someone behind her in the darkness of the tomb.

She turned and lashed out, every ghost tale from childhood filling her mind.

"Who are you?"

There was nothing there.

Yet someone was there. Deborah and Judah felt it too, and they all pulled back with startled murmurs as the presence passed between them. They could not see, yet they knew that the figure bent and touched Lazarus.

"Come forth now, Thomas. I will soon have great need of you."

"Josh!" gasped Merovee. "What has Yeshuah done with you? Where are you?"

No answer. The presence was abruptly gone. But there were now muffled moans beneath the linen wrappings.

"Ahhh. Ohhhh! Oh, I ache. I cannot see. Oh. What has happened to me?"

"Help me sit him up, Judah."

"Oh! Slow down! My bones! Am I now an old man? Miri, is it you? Why can I not see?"

She was fumbling at the bindings covering his face.

"There is no light here. We are in the garden tomb."

"Tomb?"

But then there began to be light. The stone was again rolling back, and they could hear Yeshuah's voice, throbbing, nearly sobbing with emotion.

"I promised you, Martha! I told you that, if you believed on me, you would see the glory of God. Now you shall.

"Oh, my dear father in Heaven, I thank you for having heard my prayers, and for bringing me to this place, and to this demonstration. I have always known that I was heard, but I thank you now publicly, in front of all these assembled, so that they may understand that you have sent me here, and that what they are about to witness is your doing, that the Father has given his power—of bestowing life—to his son."

He came forward boldly then, toward the door of the tomb, even as all the others retreated backward into the garden, some in dismay, some in horror, and all in fear of ritual contamination.

As he reached the doorway, Yeshuah raised his arms and called in a loud voice.

"Lazarus! Come forth!"

Lazarus peered between his mother and his sister, blinking at Yeshuah's silhouette, unable to see against the light and still thoroughly disoriented.

"What does he want, Miri? Where is Jesus, he was here just a moment ago, did he return to the Essenes? Oh Miri, how I love that man. I never wish to leave his side again."

Yeshuah was leaning forward, peering into the dimness of the tomb.

"What are you two doing in there?" he exclaimed as he saw Merovee and Deborah.

Before another word could be spoken, Merovee rushed forward. In view of all those watching from their safe distances back in the garden, and as if in adoration, she knelt at Yeshuah's feet.

"I have been waking my brother from his sleep," she said through gritted teeth. "Tell me what you have done with Jesus."

"He is safe. That will have to suffice."

"It will not. I will know where he is. Now."

"Not until I have accomplished my purposes."

"Now. Else I will tell everyone watching the truth, and send my priestly cousins to the Temple Court to make a similar proclamation."

Yeshuah smiled condescendingly.

"You would not do that. You would place Jesus and Lazarus, yourselves, this whole group, in dire jeopardy."

"I will also rob you of your messiahship. I will squash you as a bug. 'Fraud,' they will call you. They will throw dung at you and hoot you off the face of the Earth."

"You do not frighten me. You would not do it."

Merovee lifted her face and looked squarely into his eyes. In her own eyes was an icy and malevolent glee.

"Try me."

Yeshuah hesitated.

His mind worked furiously.

"All right. My fight with Eleazar was a sham. He and his friends followed us in secret. Two nights ago, as Jesus was alone upon a hilltop above our camp, they crept up and overpowered him. They have taken him to a cave near to Masada. Isaac can lead you there. I will give orders for Jesus to be handed over."

"Do you swear that this is the truth?" said Merovee.

"As God leads me and advises me, it is true."

"Merovee," Judah whispered. "It is not true."

Yeshuah started, finally seeing Judah behind Deborah in the gloom.

"You, too, my darling brother?"

Merovee got to her feet.

"It is all right, Judah. My intuition tells me to trust Yeshuah's information."

"You are going to let him get away with this?" hissed Deborah.

Merovee turned away from those watching back in the garden.

"We need the return of Jesus, Mother. Things have already gone too far. However the matter is decided, the consequences will be dire for all of us."

She looked up into the eyes of Yeshuah. Despite it all, she had come so to like the man that she felt concern for him.

"Yeshuah . . . if you are believed to have raised my brother from the dead, you will have guaranteed your own early trip to the grave."

"The Son of Man must be delivered up to men and they shall kill him. But, on the third day, he shall rise from the dead." He gave a strange little smile. "Which your brother has already proven possible."

"You promise that your brother Isaac will lead some of my people to rescue Jesus this very night?"

"I promise."

She sighed.

"Then do your worst."

She and Deborah and Judah stood aside. Yeshuah went into the tomb and re-emerged in triumph, guiding the stumbling Lazarus.

Some who saw the dead man emerge cried out in joy. Some broke into sobs. Some fainted. Some stood as though frozen. Some dropped to their knees. Others retreated still further, certain that Yeshuah was leading an abomination from the nether regions.

Only as Yeshuah began to strip the linen bindings from his head and torso, and the young man was seen to be clean and whole—as they saw his bemused smile, heard his shy greetings—did they begin to press forward to see him more closely, to hear him speak, some even to touch him. Martha, for her part, stood back from the crowd, alone, and with tears of both joy and confusion streaming down her face.

Merovee, Judah, and Deborah drew aside.

"He did lie to you, Merovee," said Judah.

"I know."

"The fight with Eleazar was no sham, and there is no hideout cave near to Masada. We have never operated that far south."

"But we are now sure of a few things. Jesus has been abducted, and by Yeshuah. Most importantly, he is being held in a cave, and I know where that cave is. Do you remember when I cried out to . . . it *was* Josh, was it not."

"It was his voice," said Deborah.

"I would know it anywhere," said Judah.

"When I called out and asked him where we was, there was no answer. But I saw a quick image in my mind. I was in a cave. From where I sat in that cave, I could look out and see the Qumran community."

"That is what Lazarus meant when he asked if Jesus had returned to the Essenes," said Deborah. "I thought he was delirious."

"Josh obviously managed to impress both of our minds with the same information. When Lazarus said the word Essene, I was almost sure. Yeshuah's confession of an abduction and a cave made me certain."

"You really should go to Greece in your boy's disguise and become an actor, Daughter. Your performance in these last days has been remarkable."

"Oh Mother, I am so sorry that you had to go through such sorrow. But the grief had to be real, the priests had to be convinced that he was dead. And I did promise you that Jesus would raise him."

"You did, and you did not lie. So do not fret yourself. Now, if you will excuse me, I am going to go and give my son a hug. Then I must tend to the mental state of my other daughter."

"Merovee, we have got to act quickly," murmured Judah as Deborah moved off.

"I know. Have you ever mentioned to Yeshuah that Jac is at Qumran?"

"I am sure that I have not."

"Do you think that Yeshuah heard Lazarus say the word Essene?"

"No. He was too rapt in astonishment at finding you in the tomb."

"The look on his face . . . "

"The same as the day I returned the fig tree."

They allowed themselves the luxury of quiet laughter.

Then Judah's face straightened.

"I know who he has pressed into service at Qumran. Reuben ben Hezikiah. He is second man to old Ephraim, and he was a Zealot before he joined the community. He and Yeshuah are old friends. But Reuben is at least halfway honorable. Yeshuah must have had a very convincing argument to have gained Reuben's cooperation."

"We have the advantage as long as Yeshuah believes that you swallowed his story, Merovee. But, while we are sending to Masada ostensibly to rescue Jesus, Yeshuah might get him moved to an even more secret spot, just to be on the safe side."

"Judah, he would not . . . "

"He would not have Jesus killed. He has come to love Jesus. What a foolish thing to have to say. He absolutely adores Jesus, yet he does a thing like this."

"My brother is mad, Merovee. How else to explain his actions?"

"So, no, he would not kill Jesus. But he might keep him a prisoner for a very long time."

"And we have no leverage left," said Merovee. "I gave it up the moment I let him lead Lazarus out of the tomb. Before a day has passed, half of Judeah will have heard of this 'miracle.' I could stand before the Temple shouting the truth for the next hundred years, and no one would hear me. Yeshuah will be proclaimed the Messiah."

"The cave that you saw in your vision—the view of Qumran. Would you recognize it again if you saw it? The exact same angle?"

"Yes. We have got to go there tonight, have we not. We have got to make our move ahead of Yeshuah."

"Are you up to it?"

"But of course," she said lightly, ignoring the throbbing pains that still plagued her woman's parts. "Even my physician agrees that a woman should be up and about immediately after a birth."

So plans were made, quietly and swiftly. The first order of business was to dispatch Isaac south to Masada, leading Petros and the sons of Thunder, supposedly to retrieve Jesus from the place to where—they were told that Merovee had seen in a vision—the whirlwind had taken him. It was then necessary for Merovee and Judah, joined by Deborah and Lazarus, to retire back to the quarantine of the grand salon. For, after deliberation, the priestly cousins decided that, while Lazarus was not now dead, he had been dead, and so anyone who had touched him while he was still dead was ritually impure for another seven days . . . including Lazarus, who had, of course, touched his own self while he was still dead.

As to Yeshuah and any who had touched only the living Lazarus, they were deemed only to have touched a man who had touched a dead man—that is, Lazarus, who had touched the dead man that had been himself. This was a much less serious degree of impurity, lasting only till sundown.

All this was arrived at after a great deal of quoting of Torah and arguing of Oral Law.

The funereal bindings gave the priests the most trouble. For Yeshuah had touched those, too, so that impurity of almost first degree was possible.

But he had touched them only after Lazarus had become alive. Had he then touched the bindings of a dead man, and so technically touched carrion, or had he merely touched the 'apparel' of a living man?

It was decided that the latter was the case. For, surely, when God had performed his miracle and 'cleansed' Lazarus of the taint of death, the cleansing would have extended to his wrappings.

And, surely, the solemn priests also agreed, if their judgments were wrong, none could blame them, for who had ever before needed to make judgment in such an extraordinary case?

The decision to excuse Yeshuah from full uncleanness was a welcome one to those closeted in the grand salon. Plans would have been impossible to make and execute with him sitting in their midst.

Not that Merovee and the others were forbidden to leave the salon, or that people were forbidden to visit them. Indeed, people kept peeking in the door to look at Lazarus. It was simply that the unclean could not touch others, neither could they touch any articles with which others might come into contact. Pharisees even claimed that the unclean tainted the earth or floors on which they trod, so that any who accidentally touched the same spots became secondarily tainted.

All in all, it was best for the unclean to keep to themselves, and best for visitors to stay away. It was doubly best this close to the Temple, and with priestly cousins running about, to stick to the letter of The Law. This could not be like the trip down to Galilee after Johannan's death, when they had made up their own rules as they had gone along.

To decrease the danger of discovery by those who would inevitably brave uncleanness to gawk at Lazarus, Merovee got sick, and had the screens, which were usually put around her couch only at night, or when she was feeding the baby, put up permanently. Understandable. The events of the day had been too much for her. Everyone already understood, after her dash to the tomb and insistence upon crawling into it, that the girl was close to nervous collapse, possibly already unhinged.

There were already screened places at the far end of the room for the men. Living in such close quarters with the women, modesty demanded it. So that those who came to peer in at the door could not be sure who was where, and, in relative privacy behind Merovee's screens, with Martha coming and going as messenger, plans were laid.

Martha first ran out to hire a wet nurse for Agapo. Understandable with Merovee so ill. Besides, the child would soon have to be separated from his ritually unclean mother so that he would be free of taint when the day came for his circumcision and then presentation at the Temple.

Through Martha, Joses was then briefed. One of the lesser members of the company, his absence would never be noted by Yeshuah. He slipped out of bar Jeremiah and set off with all speed across the hills to Qumran. With his youthful vigor, he could be there in several hours, while, as they were to most children of the area, the hills were the playground of Joses. He knew every trail, every wadi by heart, knew each shepherd, almost every sheep, by name. Often, on his rambles, he had happened by Qumran, and called to his brother Jac, working in the fields. On those occasions, Jacob had always paused for a few minutes and squatted in the shade with his young brother, exchanging family news and gossip. So that the appearance of Joses at Qumran on this particular day would be nothing out of the ordinary.

"And you can count on Jac," he told Martha. "He is not so bad an Essene that he will not dirty his hands to save Josh, and look to his purity afterward. I hope, though, that Jude is not still at Qumran. That hot-head always messes things up."

The only other two people immediately informed of the situation besides, necessarily, Zana and Simon of Cyrene, were Nathaniel and bar Tolmei. Both would give their lives for Jesus—Nathaniel, a trained soldier, strong enough to overpower ten times his number in Essenic guards . . .

"And you would not believe the speed, the stealth and cunning, of bar Tolmei," said Judah. "He is the best mountain fighter we ever had. If anyone can help us find that cave and get Jesus out, it is bar Tolmei."

On one thing, Merovee insisted. It was part of the message sent to the two men. They were to carry no weapons. Jesus would be rescued at the price of no lives.

They both agreed. They would slip away separately, well after the evening meal, and be waiting at a designated place outside of the town.

There was nothing to do then but wait. Deborah, and especially the quiet and still bemused Lazarus remained much in sight, in order to satisfy the curious who kept poking their heads in the door. Word was spreading, for even the neighbors were beginning to come to look at him. Merovee remained totally behind the screens, while Judah was sometimes visible and sometimes not.

In a way, to Merovee, the wait was welcome. She spent it quietly with Agapo, holding him, feeding him, gazing at him, filling her being with his own.

And she talked to Johannan, entrusting their son to his care while she was absent.

At seven in the evening, Simon of Cyrene had the door of the salon barred and curtained, explaining to the company that those within had had a trying day and must get some rest.

Indeed, this was true of Lazarus. The man was pale, still quiet and relatively uncommunicative, as though part of his Soul still lingered in the far regions to which it had traveled.

The Cyrenean's announcement was hardly noticed by those in the courtyard anyway. For Yeshuah, still at a discreet distance from any other person despite the setting sun, was holding court and teaching. Almost all of the company were gathered about him, some disgusted, some curious, some wavering, a few wholly convinced now of Yeshuah's shared divinity with God, who was his father. Those in the salon were far from Yeshuah's mind now. They had played their roles in his grand design. It was those who listened to him that night who were essential. He must convince as many of them as possible, while the impact of his raising of Lazarus was still upon them, so that they would go out into the streets and onto the by-ways on the morrow, and proclaim to the world that he was the Messiah.

On that morrow, he, himself, would put in an appearance at the Temple.

So Merovee and Judah were free to slip out a service door at the back of the salon and into the garden. Once more, Merovee wore the clothes of a boy. Her breasts were bound . . . she had fed Agapo one last time, teasing him awake each time that he slept, making him drink far more than he wished to, in order to empty those breasts. All too soon, they would fill again, and ache to feed him . . . and there was long, fast walking to be done.

They went out a small gate in the back wall near to the tomb, and made their way through alleys to the place where Nathaniel and bar Tolmei waited. Then they set off across the hills on a line as close to direct as possible.

Merovee, like Joses, knew the hills well. From Temple Mount, the Salt Sea seemed to be just a good bowshot away. Beyond Bethany, in some places, one could look down across what appeared to be a gentle slope, and see patches of that opaque green expanse less than fourteen miles away. While, from Bethany to Qumran, itself, following the shepherd's trails over the hills, it was only about eleven miles.

But the slopes were not gentle at all. They were rocky and treacherous, filled with steepnesses and gorges, which grew increasingly more treacherous as one neared the palisade of cliffs that ringed the sea at a distance of anywhere from one to three miles from its shores. There was a moon near to full that night. There was also a dense cloud cover, so that one had to step carefully.

Merovee led the way. No one spoke much at first, conserving breath and energy. Though, often, Nathaniel sighed or moaned.

"Stop it, Support!" Merovee finally called. "It is not your fault!"

"It is. And I don't deserve to be called Support. I should have known. I should never have left him. The glow on the hilltop . . . I see now that it was nothing but a lamp that Yeshuah lighted when he went up. I should have gone up and looked for myself."

"Who could have imagined that my brother would abduct him?" said Judah. "Come on, Support. Jesus has more foresight than any of us, and even he was taken by surprise."

"I will never leave him again," said Nathaniel. "I do not care what he says, I will not leave him, not for one moment."

"Oh really? I might have a thing or two to say about that," laughed Merovee. "And if you and Susannah are to be married as you plan, things could become doubly awkward."

"You know what I mean," growled Nathaniel.

They returned to silence. But it had been good to laugh for a moment, good to act as though it were a foregone conclusion that Jesus would shortly be back with them.

And that was the way to do it, Merovee realized. Jesus always said that the spirit of play secured the fastest and best results.

"Laughter is God's favorite sound," she said aloud. "And when God smiles, everything grows, and the rain falls from blue skies filled with rainbows."

She began to sing of the very fat priest jogging toward Jerusalem. Dutifully, the others joined in.

And the miles did seem to fly. The cloud cover even lifted, so that they had the moon, and the going got easier.

They lapsed back into silence well before the palisade. As prearranged with Joses, they stayed north of the garden valley where was the tent city of the married brothers. Instead, they approached a particular formation of rocks on the crest of the cliff, known to countless generations of the children of the area as the Dromedary. Figures were waiting beneath the hump.

Merovee ran forward. But what had seemed to be two figures was only one.

"Jac. Where is the boy? Is he all right?"

The Essene seemed taller, more cadaverous than ever. Yet his voice and mien were vigorous. He had shed his customary Essenic robe of brilliant white and was camouflaged, instead, in brown homespun.

"Joses is fine, Little Mother. He tells me that you have a fine boy, may God bless him with wisdom and long life. Joses is hidden in a place where he can survey all the terrain between the community, the tents which surround it, and the cliffs. If anyone comes away from the community during the night, and heads for any of the caves, he will warn us with three adult wolf howls, then as many cub barks as there are men. He does wolves wonderfully well."

Bar Tolmei grunted approval.

"That leaves us free to move about and search without fear of surprise from behind."

"What of Jude?" said Merovee.

Jac shrugged.

"What of him? He stayed with me here for only one month, then set off again to find trouble with his Zealot friends. I am not my brother's keeper, and we are better off without him, as I am sure that Joses has told you."

"Do you have any idea which cave they might have Jesus in?" said bar Tolmei.

"There are hundreds. He could be in any one of them. You make a very handsome boy, Merovee."

"You are not offended?"

"'Before I could be offended by you, I must be offended by my Essenic brothers, that any of them should have stooped to this shameful thing."

"Yeshuah has a way of persuading people to shameful things," said Judah bitterly. "I suspect that your second in command, Reuben, is Yeshuah's cohort, for the two of them were Zealots together."

"Which does not excuse Reuben. Essenes are sworn to keep aloof from politics and to tend only to God and to the Spirit. I am sad to say that, of late, more and more of our brothers concern themselves overly with worldly matters." He offered his skin of water for them to drink.

"The priests declare Judah and me to be unclean," said Merovee, drawing back.

"Joses said Lazarus was not in fact ever dead, so Judah is not unclean. You, though . . . " He hesitated. "You have not completed your unclean days since the birth. Drink last after the men and then keep the skin, I will get myself another. Joses says that you had a vision. Describe to me what you saw, and we can narrow the area that must be searched."

Merovee described as best she could, drawing a map with a pointed stone in the dirt.

"Could you see a little building, a tool shed, outside the wall of the corner tower nearest you?"

Merovee closed her eyes and thought.

"Yes. From a greater angle, not square on."

"That shed is on the north side of the northwesterly corner." He thought a minute. "Could you see any of the roof of this tower?"

" . . . Yes. All of it."

"So the cave is high up," said bar Tolmei. "Can one get down to the caves in that section from up top here?"

"Not without ropes. We must go to the bottom and climb back up."

"Do you think they have guards on him?" said Nathaniel.

"I can remember no brother who has been absent from meals or devotions, either at bedtime or at waking. I took note this evening, and again found no one absent. There are many lay brothers and sojourners—they come and go, so that I do not know them all. Still, if any man were to be absent for a long while, it would be noted and reported to Ephraim. Hence, if there is a guard, it could be no more than one man, and that guard would have to change often. That would necessitate many participants in this affair. Many men, repeatedly disappearing, if only for an hour or so during the last days, would have caused comment. In short, I am sure that he is not guarded. He is probably securely bound, gagged, and tethered, and they check on him and take him food and drink when they can."

"Then it is likely that someone may slip out of the community during the night and go to the cave," said bar Tolmei.

"Which is why I posted my brother sentry," smiled Jacob, pleased with himself. "If someone comes out, we have but to hide and watch and we will see the way."

"In the meantime, we must search," said Judah. "We cannot afford to be wrong, or to waste this night."

"Of course," said Jac "Time is already wasting, so come. Single file and carefully. This particular track is seldom used and is treacherous even in daylight."

The trip down many hundreds of feet of the palisade face was a sobering preview of the trips they would have to make upward from the bottom. Merovee remembered nearly scampering down this path as a child. Was this what it was to grow older? Was growing older to grow fearful? Footholds were nearly imaginary. Of handholds, there were few. And it was impossible to move quietly, there was too much loose dirt and stone, too many ways to slip and slide and send debris showering down the cliff-side.

"It will not be heard in the community," Jac comforted. "All is farther away than it looks. Besides, there are natural rock-falls on these cliff-sides hourly, so that we who live here no longer take notice. Only keep your ears peeled for the wolf."

Once down, they moved along the base of the palisades till they reached the stretch that Jacob reckoned most nearly approximated the angle of Merovee's vision.

"And it stands to reason," he said. "None of the caves above us are used for housing by lay brothers. All are either currently used as storage by the scriptorium or meant for the scriptorium's eventual use. One who is privy to the doings of the scriptorium could hide someone here with confidence."

Dozens of chasms, the erosion of millennia, zigged and zagged. Jacob pointed out a multitude of nearly invisible trails leading upward.

"You will not be able to lose your way once you start, for there will be no choices on the climb. Either you will step in the right place or you will step into nothingness. Some of the paths pass small caves on the climb. Once near to the top, most paths divide and broaden, and connect with a number of caves, some large, some hardly big enough to contain one man. Be sure that you explore them all before descending and starting up a new trail. And remember, I am only supposing that there are no guards."

"Would guards be armed?" asked Merovee.

"No Essene should have a weapon."

"There is always the possibility that Yeshuah summoned some of our old Zealot friends here to guard Jesus," said Judah. "Merovee, I think that you had better wait here at the bottom."

"I am up to the climbing. I am probably more sure-footed than any of you. And no harm will come to me in a search for Jesus, Zealots or no. I have that trust."

They each chose one of the first five paths and the search began. It was torturous going, more from lack of light than from steepness of climb. One had to be sure, very sure of where one was stepping, and then search with the hands for the next certain niche, many of which seemed to have been cut out of the rock with hammer and chisel. There were five caves on Merovee's first path, two on the journey up and three at the top. Most were little more than crevices. The last was large, and she crawled through it on hands and knees, making broad sweeping gestures along the floors with her hands, making a circuit of the walls, to be sure, absolutely sure, that she was not missing her husband's inert form in the darkness. If he was 'on a journey,' as he had surely been when he managed to come to Lazarus, his body would be lying as though dead.

She had forgotten to mention that to the others. Did she dare call out?

"Judah?" she called softly once out of the cave. His response came from quite near, about thirty feet further on along the cliff face. "If he is in trance, he might be lying as though dead. Do not count on him to hear you and make a sign. Pass it on."

She could hear the message traveling from man to man along the cliff as she made her careful descent. Her next path was the sixth path. She removed the oddly shaped stone they had chosen as a sign, and placed it upon the seventh, to show that that should be the next choice.

Most of the caves of the sixth path contained tall, thin earthenware jars. Merovee opened the lid of one and found a scroll. Active scriptorium storage, hardly a place for smart abductors to hide their abductee. Yet she searched each cave carefully.

The stone was on the tenth path when she got back down to the bottom. She moved it to the eleven and started her climb. It was dark once more, with clouds hiding the moon. Would Joses be able to see in this blackness? Poor little fellow. She could imagine how hard he was straining to see, the weight of the world on his shoulders, lest he fail, and allow his friends to be surprised from behind.

The caves on that tenth path were all pregnant with possibility, large, and empty of jars. She searched each of them carefully. It was as she entered the last one that she was seized with recognition.

She turned, peering down through the darkness to the obligingly white buildings of the community. Her heart skipped a beat. The little tool shed was there, beside the northwestern corner, its entire roof visible. And at the right angle.

She wheeled.

"Josh! Josh, are you in here? Make a sound. Move."

She waited, holding her breath the better to hear. Nothing. She dropped to her knees and commenced the search, haphazardly, in excitement at first, then slowly, methodically.

Jesus was not there.

Except that she found an empty wine skin that yet contained a few last drops of wine, un-soured. And there was a crust of bread. About a day old.

Her vision had been right. But he had since been moved.

It was all she could do not to sit down and cry. What would they do now? What oh what?

Then she did sit down, cross-legged, as Jesus had shown her. She laid her hands comfortably onto her knees, palms up, calmed her breathing, slowed the pulses, and sank down one level of consciousness, to what Jesus called the Tunnel of Communication. He had managed to tell her of the first cave. He could do it again. Mentally she called to him through the tunnel.

'Josh, I am here at Qumran.'

She projected a careful mental image of Qumran into the darkness of her mind. Then she pictured herself, pictured Jesus, and visualized her mental image traveling from her mind, along a tunnel behind that darkness, to the mind of Jesus.

'I am in the cave they have just taken you away from. Send me an image of where you are now.'

She visualized a haze, an image, coming out of his mind and traveling back along the tunnel toward her. She waited, trusting that it would be received, keeping her mind black, in readiness for his image to register itself.

Nothing came. Except an annoying light behind her closed eyelids.

It ruined her concentration. She banished it, and got her darkness back again.

'Josh. Jesus. Send me a sign. Show me where they have taken you.'

She got nothing. Nothing except the persistent light.

Again and again she tried.

Finally, with a sigh, she rose. Taking the evidence of the cave's prior habitation with her, she climbed down to the bottom. Nathaniel was just starting up the thirteenth path. She called him back, told him the bad news. Together they waited until the other three came down.

"I do not know what to suggest," said Jacob, " . . . except to mount watch and follow everyone who leaves the community. That would work if they have simply transferred him to a nearby cave, but if they have removed him to some other area . . . " He shook his head.

In defeat, Merovee traced the upsilon-shaped curve of the chasm, those towering cliffs with their endless hundreds of caves. Tears stung her eyes, blurred her vision. And that annoying light was there again.

She froze.

She wiped her eyes.

The light was not part of her tears.

"Look!"

They followed the line of her frantically pointing figure, to the far side of the chasm, to a place halfway up the cliff. A dim, steady light shone from out the mouth of a cave there.

"I asked for an image and he sent the light, but I was too impatient to understand. How do we get there, Jac?"

"By a steep climb and then by ladder. That cave-mouth is flush with the face of the cliff. But I know where the ladder is hidden. Come."

They set off at all speed.

"I can see why they switched him to that cave," Jac huffed as they hurried along. "It is seldom used, and its secrets are known only to senior brothers. If one must leave a man unguarded, then a place from which he could not escape without a ladder, even if he did manage to escape his bonds, is perfect."

"If there is a light, then at least one of his jailers must be with him at the moment," panted Nathaniel.

"We will be equal to any who are there," promised bar Tolmei.

"If it becomes necessary, I will run to the community and rouse all the brothers to his rescue," said Jacob.

They reached the base and began the climb, slowly, so carefully, so as not to make a sound and alert the guards. Bar Tolmei would have preferred to have had a weapon in his hands. If there were Zealots up there, hand-to-hand fighting would go only so far. But the days of weapons and violence were gone from him forever. He pictured Jesus, and felt an immediate comfort. As Merovee had faith, so would he.

They were halfway up the path to the base of the cave when they heard the wolf. It howled three times. Then a cub barked.

They halted, looking back toward the community. It was too dark to see anything.

"Either it is the changing of the guard or a reinforcement," whispered Nathaniel. "Let us get up into the cave and overpower whoever is there, and be waiting for this next one."

They hurried on to where the ladder was hidden.

"If the new man is to be taken by surprise, I will have to stay down here and put the ladder back into its hiding spot after you are up there, so that nothing seems amiss," whispered Jacob. "I will hold it with all my strength as you climb, in case the guards hear you and try to topple it."

Soundlessly, then, they put the ladder up against the rock. Nathaniel insisted on going first. Bar Tolmei was right on his heels, then Judah, then Merovee.

She had hardly begun her climb when she heard Nathaniel cry out. There was silence after the cry. Ahead of her, bar Tolmei and Judah hurried on.

Merovee scrambled after them, all her senses alert, ready to punch, kick, bite, scratch, seize rocks and split skulls if need be. But she found bar Tolmei and Judah waiting at the top. They took her hands and helped her into the cave.

"Jacob, come up," called Judah. "We will pull the ladder up after us and to Gehennah with whoever is coming."

The floor of the cavern sloped downward from the entrance to a distance of twenty feet. Against the back wall sat Jesus, bound and gagged . . . Nathaniel was removing the gag. The big man was crying.

"I would that I could cut the bonds from off of you quickly, Lord, but your wife forbade us to bring knives."

Merovee but stood, staring at her husband, while Judah and bar Tolmei went forward and knelt before him, bowing their heads before his radiance.

For Jesus shone as if he contained the sun. His hair glowed in a halo about his head and his garments were a white more brilliant than any Essene had ever dreamed possible. There were no other lights in the cave. The glow that had led them to the place had been Jesus, himself.

Jacob climbed into the cave and stood beside Merovee, staring at his brother. When he spoke, his voice was flat and angry.

"We will not pull the ladder up. I want whoever is coming to see this. I want whoever it is to understand just how grave an error he has committed."

Merovee went forward slowly, feeling as though she had no feet, or as though her feet were not making contact with the stones. She had always known that Josh was beyond them all. And he had said only recently that it was possible for a human being to light himself by using the spiral energy of his own body. Yet this demonstration brought it home with awe-full force. She knelt with the others, and would have bowed her head as well, had Jesus not smiled and brought her back to her senses.

"My darling, rather than kneeling in adoration, please help Nathaniel undo the knots. These ropes cut rather painfully."

Obediently, she began to work at the knots, all the while studying his face, but unable to return his smiles.

It was as if he were made of molten gold . . . or else molten iron, glowing white hot before being plunged into water. Yet his body beneath her hands felt exactly the same. Just her Josh.

Indeed, as his hands were loosed, he reached out and pulled her to him, hurting her breasts with the strength of the embrace. She did not care. She wrapped her arms around him and let the tears flow.

From the mouth of the cave came Jacob's voice.

"Keep coming, Reuben ben Hezekiah. Yes, it is I, Jacob ben Joseph. Keep coming. Hurry. Your prisoner awaits your most kind ministrations. He has even lighted a lamp for you, to show you the way."

Jacob turned back to regard his brother, his own face lit by new internal light.

"A lamp to show all of us the way," he murmured.

Chapter 18

Departure

Reuben ben Hezekiah, like most of the leaders of the Essenes of Qumran, was a hereditary priest, a descendant of Aaron. Yet he had no dealings with the priests of the Temple of Jerusalem. Indeed, the Essenic order had originally been formed by Samaritan priests, in protest of the defilement that the Temple of Judeah had endured—not once, but repeatedly, as one invader after another, most recently Greeks, then Romans, had desecrated the sacred courts, even entered the Holy of Holies. While, since the advent of the Hasmonaeans nearly two hundred years before, even the sacred office of High Priest had become profane, usurped by the conquerors themselves, given to conquerors' lackeys as a political prize, or sold to the highest bidder. The upstart family of Annas was such a high bidder, in the saddle almost since the death of Herod.

They got on well with Rome, did Annas and his crew, and cared nothing for God's Law or sanctity as did the Essenes and Samaritans. For the Judean Temple continued to follow the Greek calendar, rather than insisting upon a return to the holy Jubilee calendar, the ancient Hebrew method of reckoning time, a system of twelve months of thirty days each, with one day added for each one of the seasons and with a short Jubilee "year" each forty-nine years to catch up to the sun.

The Jubilee calendar had been used and ordained by God at the creation of the world. With divine simplicity, it caused each appointed festival to fall on exactly the same day of the same week, year after year, and so upon the day ordained by God for its observance. By means of the Jubilee calendar, one could reckon with precision back to the creation of the world and know with certainty that God had created light on Wednesday, so that Wednesday, not Saturday, must be the proper Sabbath.

To the Essenes, Jerusalem, her Temple, her High Priest, the reckoning of the holy festivals, the observance of the Sabbath, all, all had been desecrated, had remained uncleansed, all had become profane, abominations before God, works of the Prince of Darkness. All who followed the dictates of the "Jews" of Jerusalem dwelt in mortal sin and error. Torah clearly spelled out the rules—for the maintenance of the purity of the Temple, for the perpetuation of an inherited, rather than appointed, high priesthood, for the timing of festivals, for the observance of the Sabbath—none of which rules were being followed by the rulers of the Temple, or by those who worshiped there. All who followed the Judean priests sinned weekly by observing the Sabbath upon Saturday, yearly by observing the holy festivals upon the wrong days, daily if they worshiped each day at an unclean Temple ruled by usurping priests.

And so the prayers of most of the children of Israel had become useless. God did not hear prayers said at the wrong times, and in unclean places. Each year that followers of the Judean Temple practiced according to the Greek calendar they fell deeper into the pit of the Evil One. Each year that they supported, and worshiped at, a profane Temple, they removed themselves further from salvation. Each year that they allowed political appointees to wear the sacred robes of the High Priest, they more thoroughly assured their damnation.

Heaven be praised that the children of Israel had their Essenes. Only through the Essenes and their sacrifice might all the children of Israel be saved.

Zadok, the founder of the Essenes, their Teacher of Righteousness, had recognized the mortal danger to the greater portion of the children of Israel and had set himself to save those wandering sheep. Gathering disciples among disaffected Samaritan priests such as himself, he had drawn apart into the desert places, to establish ritually clean temples to God, to ordain a proper High Priesthood, to observe the Sabbath on the proper day, to celebrate festivals according to the Jubilee of God, to live lives of sacrifice and strict dedication to The Law, to become perfect and acceptable offerings to the Lord in token of all the children of Israel, not just the Samaritans.

It was almost two hundred years since Zadok led that first handful of "saints" out into wilderness places. There were now many thousands of Essenes, living in numerous settlements which stretched from Caesar Phillipi and Galilee to Egypt, with the largest, and most important, settlement—their capitol so to speak—and their central temple and Grand High Priest—at Qumran. Many there were, even among the "Jews," who recognized the sacrifice of the Essenes, who gave thanks each day that those saints were there, quietly praying for their erring brothers, making of themselves that acceptable sacrifice to the Lord.

They lived quietly, the Essenes, according to an ironclad and unforgiving discipline. They did not seek converts. Those wishing to become Essenes came to them. Many years and many degrees of probationary servitude were required before one could be considered for full admittance to the community, before one was allowed to give all his worldly goods to the order and to live in saintly poverty. Even after years of probation, many were denied the final brotherhood and sent away.

Such a one had been Simon Yeshuah. The saints would have among their number only those who had proven themselves to be, not only, truly repentant and holy, but, truly humble, obedient, and unambitious of any aim but the sanctity of the order and the redemption of the entire body of the children of Israel upon the Day of Judgment. Essenes refused to adulterate their sanctuaries with any who were less than the best.

Essenes, Saints, Zadokites, The Many, or People of the Way as they were variously called, their sanctuaries were the only true and undefiled sanctuaries of God's Chosen. Their Grand High Priest, selected on the basis of prime Aaronite genealogy, was the only true High Priest of Israel. Essenes were the real custodians of The Law, the only hope of their people. The end of days was fast approaching. One had only to observe the chaos abounding in the world to know that soon God and his angels—all the forces of Light—would begin to gather, to fight it out with the angels of the Prince of Darkness in the skies over Jerusalem, and the Kingdom of God would be established on Earth. The Essenes would be ready for God, heads held high, pure, clean and blameless, in sacrificial token of their people. Was not it said that the messenger was to be considered as the one who sent him? The Essenes were the messenger, sent by erring Israel. Perhaps God would honor that old axiom and accept the sacrifice of the Essenes as the sacrifice of all of Israel. Perhaps he would be lenient toward those who had followed the dictates of the Temple of Jerusalem.

So that, almost in sight of Jerusalem, there dwelt a group of Israelites who quite literally lived in and according to another time, observing another set of rules than did adherents to the Temple of Jerusalem, denying the leadership of the Jews of Judeah. That they remained unmolested by that leadership—which could, according to the Temple's interpretation of Law, have had them all stoned to death—was largely due to the fact that they did keep to themselves, that they conscientiously refrained from any political advocacy, that they did not invite—indeed, that they almost discouraged—converts, that they were seldom, except on the most necessary business, found outside their communities . . . and then, on their returns, what bathing went on! What penances and apartnesses were endured for having exposed themselves to the impurities of the world.

As the Essenes now stood, Temple authorities agreed, they were harmless. While to molest them would be to arouse the indignation of the populace, which indignation could be a greater danger than the Essenes could ever be.

They *had* been a danger at the inception of the order, so much so that Zadok, their Teacher of Righteousness, had been seized by his rival, the Temple High Priest Alexander Jannaeus. Casting about for the most hideous, painful, and humiliating way in which to exterminate his rival, Jannaeus had borrowed a Gentile method of execution . . . crucifixion. It was held by the Hebrews that any sort of hanging, a form of which crucifixion was deemed to be, rendered the one so punished irretrievably defiled, inexorably damned.

No graver insult could have been offered Zadok. His crucifixion had been the first ever allowed in Palestine.

But the death of their teacher, and the dishonor of its means, had served only to give the Essenes new faith. Crucifixion became, to them, an honor. They had felt no need to take revenge. Indeed, they had ceased to involve themselves politically. For they had realized that they had only to wait.

It was suddenly obvious to them that Zadok would come again, that, indeed, his Second Coming was the whole point of his death upon the cross. At the end of days, reborn into a new body, he would once more be found amongst them, sent by God to lead them, to guide them as they took their well-deserved places as rulers of God's earthly kingdom, one of two Messiahs which God would send to Israel.

Zadok reborn would be the Priestly Messiah, the Spiritual Guide, Teacher of Righteousness, Giver of the Way.

The second Messiah would be subservient to Zadok, a secular Messiah, sprung from the loins of David, a soldier, a deliverer, an administrator, a king.

Together, these two men were destined to bring about the Kingdom of God on Earth.

Reuben ben Hezikiah was convinced that he, himself, was the reincarnation of Zadok. It could be no other way, with him so close to the rulership of Qumran, and with the end of days so near. There simply were no other candidates. After old Ephraim, none among the Essenes had a genealogy superior to his. His pedigree of descent from Eleazar, son of Aaron, was incontrovertible. Certainly, among the profane, there might be many with superior lineage, but the profane did not matter. Only an Essene could be the Priestly Messiah.

Reuben was equally convinced—had always been convinced--that his old comrade in Zealot arms, Simon Yeshuah, was the one who would one day be revealed as the Davidic Messiah.

What could be more perfect? It was no accident at all that the two of them had met, fought together for their people's liberty, and come to Qumran together. No accident that one had been "rejected," sent back out into the world, into the arena in which his messiahship would be enacted, while the other had been taken to the bosom of the order, where his own messianic destiny lay.

So convinced had Reuben been of all this that it had never even occurred to him to question Yeshuah, to doubt his word or sincerity, when, some days before, Yeshuah had appeared from out of the morning mists and proclaimed to Reuben that the time was fulfilled, that the end was near, and explained his situation—explained that the means by which he would be recognized as the Davidic Messiah was within his grasp, for the price of the detention of just one man.

Reuben had been delighted to help. If Yeshuah's time was near, so was his own. Praise be, that stubborn old Ephraim was finally going to die. For, surely, the events of Yeshuah's messiahship would be concurrent with his own. As Yeshuah was proclaimed Messiah by the masses, as he set about the physical ousting of the Gentiles from the land, Reuben would take control of Qumran and begin the spiritual preparation of the brotherhood for their high offices in the Kingdom.

Soon, so soon, he would be able to reveal to his brothers that he was Zadok returned. Perhaps within the year, in league with Yeshuah, with God and his angels, Reuben and the brotherhood would enter Jerusalem in glory and begin the cleansing of its holy places.

Ah, what hosannahs, what tears of joy there would be. What a jewel they would make of Jerusalem. How the Gentiles and unrepentant of Israel would cry from out of the depths of the pit into which they would be cast.

God's Kingdom on Earth. And himself God's Anointed, the Saint of the Saints, the Teacher of Righteousness.

Yes, Simon Yeshuah and Reuben had come before the Council on the same day after their probationary periods, and the Council, in its wisdom, had sent Yeshuah away while taking Reuben to its bosom. Yet the only real difference between the two men was that Yeshuah had not known how to hide his ambition behind a mask of humility as had Reuben.

So Jesus had been abducted by only three men, Reuben, Yeshuah, and Yeshuah's brother Isaac. Yeshuah and Isaac had merely approached Jesus and engaged him in conversation while Reuben had stolen up behind him and applied a choke hold that had put Jesus to sleep just long enough to be rapidly gagged, then bound. He had then been thrown over the back of a pack animal and trundled off to that first cave.

Not until that very afternoon had it become necessary for Reuben to bring anyone else into his confidence. At that point, however, he had had to act quickly. The Master of the Scriptorium announced that he planned, the very next day, to transfer a load of newly copied manuscripts to the cave in which Jesus was concealed. Quick Reuben's actions might have been, but cunning. He selected three probationers, each of whom had been at Qumran for four years—bright, dedicated men, who had worked their ways through the levels of probation with honors. Each was also ambitious—if anyone could spot ambition, it was Reuben. Each man was due shortly to appear before the Council, seeking full admittance to the brotherhood. In the Council, the most weighty vote—indeed, the deciding vote now that old Ephraim had begun to act childish, and refuse to bathe—was Reuben's.

Reuben had had only to call in each of the three men and speak kindly, but plainly. He had had only to make it clear to each of them that his vote would be positive *if.* Each had been more than happy to ask no questions, and had helped him move his captive to a safer location immediately after darkness of that very night. Those three could be trusted implicitly, and would be of great use to Reuben in the days to come. In the way of all ambitious men who commit forbidden acts in unison, they were now united into a brotherhood within a brotherhood—a brotherhood of guilty men who dare not accuse each other for fear of ruining themselves, and from which there is no escape except into further service of their master.

Reuben ben Hezikiah had felt himself perfectly safe, his messianic destiny assured.

Now, as he climbed the ladder towards that oddly lit cave, it occurred to him that he might have destroyed his entire life's work by helping Yeshuah. The man awaiting him at the top of the ladder was as fearsome to Reuben as God, himself.

Jacob ben Joseph was indeed a saint, the type of man that all Essenes should be, were supposed to be, a man devoid of personal ambition, a man who truly sought The Way.

A man like Jacob ben Joseph could never be bribed.

Yet, as he reached the top of the ladder and stepped into the cave, Reuben forgot Jacob ben Joseph.

What had he done?

Oh, what had he done?

He dropped to his knees, staring at the radiant man who had been his captive.

"Forgive me," he managed to say.

Jesus came forward, bent and took the wine skin from Reuben's trembling hands. He unbunged it and took a deep draught.

"Excellent," he said at last. "For wine such as this, you are forgiven."

Reuben could not take his eyes from that shining countenance. Every Essene knew that God and his angels came bathed in light, while Satan and his demons were Darkness, itself. Every Essene knew that, at the end of times, the Forces of Light would begin to gather for the final conflict. Surely, this man was no man at all, but a harbinger arrived from Heaven.

"Who are you?" he whispered.

Jesus laughed—and the laughter could be seen, a sparkling shower of light.

"Did Yeshuah not bother to tell you?"

"He told me that he had obtained the means to become known as the Davidic Messiah. He said you were a false prophet, who stood in his way. I meant you no harm. You would have been released as soon as Yeshuah's army was raised. I believed him to be the King Messiah. Is he not?"

Jesus shook his head in sorrow.

"Reuben, poor deluded man. How can you imagine that any good could come from bad? How do you think that you will learn to walk in the light if your business must be done in darkness? Humankind professes to seek righteousness. Forever it is asking, 'What is right?'

"What is right is so obvious. Were it a snake it would bite you. What is right has been given to you, told to you again and again by those of us who have come amongst you. Yet, as blind men sitting on a river bank, dying of thirst, but unable to find water, you ignore what we tell you and do what is wrong and bad, all the while making pretty excuses and explaining that the bad things must be done in order to obtain a good end."

"Who are you, Lord?"

"I am, first of all, no one's lord." Jesus cast a glance toward Nathaniel, who, in his excitement, had used the same title. "My name is Joshuah ben Joseph bar Ramathea."

Reuben's face drained of color. He, Reuben, might be a direct descendant of Aaron through the first grandson. But the shining creature who stood before him was *the* descendant of David.

Could there be any doubt that this man, and not Yeshuah, was the Davidic Messiah?

A surge of excitement swept him. When the time came for him to proclaim his own messiahship before the community, would he shine in the same manner?

"Does it make you feel hot? The light?"

Jesus laughed so heartily that the cave was lit as by sunlight.

Reuben charged on.

"Joshuah, I acknowledge you the Kingly Messiah and I beg your forgiveness."

"You have my forgiveness, but I am not your messiah. You must be your own messiah, Reuben."

"Oh but I *am*! I am the Priestly Messiah. Surely you recognize me, for we two are destined to work together for the Kingdom of God on Earth."

"You misunderstand me, Reuben. What I mean is, to each his own messiah. And that messiah will ultimately be found to be his own self. Only you can lead your own self out of the morass that you have gotten your self into, Reuben."

He shook his head.

"Our people yearn for a supreme 'Messiah.' This country is mad with Messiah Fever. It is the way of all Humankind, always looking for someone else to do it for them, to lead them out of misery and bondage, to explain themselves to their own selves, to tell them how to act, what to do, when to visit the private, and to take them to 'God.' Humankind will just keep floundering, keep suffering, until each of its parts, one at a time, finds the courage to lead its own self out, think for itself, and finally understand the true god."

He took another long swallow of wine, bunged it, slung the skin onto his shoulder and motioned to Merovee.

"Come. We must start back."

"I am coming with you," said Jacob.

"What is this?"

Jesus turned. The light became incredibly soft.

"You would leave your community, Brother?"

"What choice have I? If I went back, I would have to denounce Reuben. I could not live in the community, or with myself, if I did not. Yet what good would it do? If I denounced him, he would be banished, and those in the community who are truly saintly would be last among the candidates for his successor. That successor would surely be Jaddah, whom I deem to be a most evil man."

He shook his head as a man stunned by blows.

"How can this be? How can it be that I am left with a choice of seeing to the banishment of one evil man, or leaving him in power to keep an even more evil man from coming to power? There is something very wrong here. We Essenes are supposed to be a company of saints."

His eyes filled with tears.

"No. No, I can not stay in this community in any wise. I may have been a fool these many years, but I will not also be a hypocrite. Our community is fallen so far short of its boasts! I see now that it is as riddled with deceit and rot as is the Temple it so despises."

"You are harsh upon all because of a few," said Jesus gently.

"No! I am not too harsh at all. Perhaps it is not possible, this saintliness, the perfection I told myself I had found here. But I must keep striving for that perfection. If it is not to be found here, then I am bound, by my love of God, to go in search of it."

He turned and looked Reuben squarely in the eye.

"And so I leave you to Heaven, Reuben." A terrible laugh escaped his lips. "That is the best curse I can call down upon your head. And as for the community . . . Heaven help it. How far it has strayed if such as you can reach its heights. Go back and become their leader. Tell them you are the Messiah if that is your ambition. As for me, I will follow the Light I see here tonight. I go with my brother to seek God in a new way. I can certainly do no worse than I have done here. Indeed, I am now sure that, with my brother's help, I will do much better."

They descended the ladder, leaving Reuben to his own thoughts. Jacob gave three owl hoots. Soon Joses came running from out of the darkness. He threw himself into the arms of Jesus, in no awe of the man's glow.

"Thanks be to God. I was so worried. I did not know whether to come and help you fight or to stay at my post."

"Always stay at your post," smiled Jesus. "Always do what you have promised to do, and be where your allies depend on you to be until the job is finished. With that simple rule, you can never go wrong."

With all haste, then, they went up the cliffside, openly taking the pass, an easy path that led to the top of the cliffs and into the valley where was the tent city of the married brothers. It did not matter now that their passing might awaken some of those brothers.

Jesus lighted the path as they went, his glow fading gradually, until, with the first rays of morning, he was as ever before.

"Do you need to rest?" he asked Merovee when it was full morning and they had come several miles.

"I am not tired. Only my breasts ache."

He smiled.

"That you should have such trouble on a march. I remember accusing you of being flat as a boy."

"How things do change," she said.

"While staying ever the same."

She looked at him, puzzled for a moment, then she grasped his meaning.

"Ohhh . . . you!" She threw Jac's water skin at him.

Laughing, he dashed ahead.

Laughing, herself, she ran after him . . . after that creature of Light who still, so wonderfully, remained Josh.

* * *

Bar Jeremiah was nearly deserted when they arrived. The family of Jesus, and Deborah, Martha, and Lazarus waited anxiously in the salon with, of course, Zana and the Cyrenean.

Oblivious to all else, Merovee rushed to Zana and Agapo and withdrew behind her screens. He might have had a wet nurse, but she had milk aching to flow.

The few others assembled were Susannah, Johannah, Micah and Leah, Chandreah, and Meraiah. Of them all, only Meraiah had not, as yet, had the truth of the situation explained to her.

"Jesus!" she cried at sight of him. "Thank God you are back. I am so worried. Yeshuah and all the others left at first light for the Temple of Jerusalem."

"We are sure that he plans some mischief," fretted Joseph.

"That is the one thing about my brother of which you can always be certain," said Judah grimly.

"Of all days to go to the Temple," said Rosula. "I tried to stop him, but he would not listen to me, or to Meraiah here. The man must be mad. Does he not understand that all Jerusalem will know of his raising of Lazarus? He will surely attract a mob of people about him . . . some fool could even start a riot. And would not the rulers of the Temple just love such an excuse to seize him and as many of your people as possible?"

"Jesus," said Meraiah, "you must go to the Temple and find him and convince him to leave. He should start for Galilee, or Samaria, right away, tonight, and stay there until all this is forgotten. He loves you, Jesus. He will listen to you."

"Forgive me, Queen Meraiah," Merovee called from behind her screen, "but, Josh, if you go near that Temple today I will never forgive you."

"Miri is right," said Lazarus. "You must not even think of it, Jesus. It would be nearly as suicidal as for me to go there. But I do think that Queen Meraiah's suggestion of a rapid journey to some safe province should be acted upon. By all of us."

"I have already set the servants to packing for you all," said Martha quietly.

Jesus walked to the screen and stood looking in at Merovee and Agapo.

"Did Yeshuah notice the absence of any of my rescue party?" he said at last.

"Rescue?" said Mother Meraiah. "What rescue?"

"We will explain later," said Deborah. "He did not suspect anything, Jesus. We kept the doors to the salon closed."

"Then he has no idea but what I am still safe in my cave at Qumran. It will unsettle him when he realizes that I am not."

"Cave?" said Mother Meraiah.

Deborah drew the old woman aside, and commenced, in low tones, to explain all that had happened.

"'Unsettle' is a tame word to use for the way he will react," said Judah. "The moment he learns that you are here, he will return hot-foot. I will leave for the Temple this minute, to convey the glad news."

"No!" cried Merovee from behind the screen. "In the eyes of the priests, you are ritually impure, Judah. You could be seized for contaminating the sacred precincts."

"Better that than that my brother jeopardizes all the rest of you."

A commotion of arrival was heard in the court. Jesus hastened to the door.

"Father," he said in puzzlement, "it has been a great many years since I have seen him, but is this not your friend, Nicodemus?"

Joseph grunted and came to his side.

"Weeks ago I asked him to keep his ears open around the Temple, and warn me if ever he felt we were in immediate danger. Nicodemus! In here."

The gray-bearded man hastened toward them. Though Nicodemus ben Hiram was a man of wealth and position, and so a member of the Sanhedrin, he was also a Pharisee. It was highly unusual to find a wealthy man adhering to the Pharisaic discipline, but Nicodemus was a man with his own mind, who yet managed to bring balance, fairness, and reason to all that he did—so that all factions trusted and respected him.

"What a perfect spy you have got us," murmured Jesus.

"I came as quickly as my mount would travel, Joseph. Hello, Joshuah. My, how you have grown. And you, too, Jacob. My, how you have . . . " Nicodemus clucked his tongue and shook his head at Jac's emaciation. "Joshuah, it is nice to see you home from your travels, yet maybe it would have been better had you stayed away. Why have you let your followers get so out of hand, young man? Do you know what they have done in the Court of the Gentiles this morning?"

"No. Was it perfectly dreadful?"

Nicodemus maintained his stern visage for only another moment. Then, seeing the cocked eyebrow and the twinkle in the eyes of Jesus, he lowered his face, hiding a grin.

"Old Annas will certainly think that it was dreadful. You have struck at his most tender part, his money bags. As for myself . . . " He raised his face. "I wish that I had been courageous enough to do it."

"What, for Heaven's sake?" said Judah.

"The one who they say raised Lazarus . . . "

Merovee had come from behind the screen.

"He is called Yeshuah," said Jesus. "Nicodemus, this is my wife Merovee."

"Yes, Joseph told me of her. The Lord's blessings upon you both. Well, just after sunup, this Yeshuah led your people into the Court of the Gentiles. And another huge crowd as well, for word spread rapidly as to who he was, and everyone wanted to see and hear him. I must admit that I was one of the curious, especially since he did not even bother to go to the Porch of Solomon to teach, he began to speak just where he stood."

"In the Court of the Gentiles?" said Joseph in astonishment.

"He taught to Jew and Gentile, man and woman alike. The rulers heard of it within minutes. I saw several of their most clever scribes, and Zakiah and Uriah of the House of Shammai, who work side by side with the High Priest in all things. They slipped into the crowd and made their way to the fore. They began to ask your Yeshuah baited questions, trying to trap him into some utterance that the High Priest could use against him if the need arose.

"But this Yeshuah is clever. They could not trap him. Rather, he confounded them. They asked him, for instance, by what authority he taught the things he did, who had given him the authority? He answered with a question of his own, and said that, if they would answer it, then he would tell them by what authority he spoke.

"'The immersions given by Johannan,' he asked them, 'were they authorized by Heaven, or were they only the pretensions of a misguided man?'

"Well, they knew not how to reply. If they said that the immersions were authorized by Heaven, they knew that he would retort, 'Then why did you not believe in Johannan's words and practice them and follow him and protect him from all harm?'

"Whereas, if they replied that Johannan had no authorization from God, that he was a foolish man who only imagined that he did, they knew that the people would turn against them, for most now hold that Johannan was Elijah returned. So that they could only mutter that they could 'not tell.'

"To which Yeshuah answered, 'Than neither can I tell you by whose authority I do the things that I do.'

"The Pharisee Zakiah then asked him if he considered it Lawful for us Jews to give tribute to Caesar."

Bar Tolmei grunted sharply.

"A question already raising passions, what with tribute having to be paid this year. How did he answer?"

"He asked a Gentile to loan him a coin. He stared long and hard at it. Finally, as though he did not know, he asked Zakiah whose image and superscription was on the coin. When Zakiah said that it was Caesar's, Yeshuah simply said, 'Render unto Caesar the things that are Caesar's, and unto God the things that are God's.'"

Jesus let out a hoot.

"Perfect! No one could fault him for that . . . yet, while giving an answer that could not be challenged, he also managed to imply that Caesar is not a god as he claims to be. Ah. He is good. Yeshuah is good."

"He made so bold as to fault them on the matter of Johannan as well," said Nicodemus. "He told some parables which as much as said that tax-collectors and harlots who had harkened to Johannan would enter the Kingdom and Heaven before scribes and priests and Pharisees who had turned their backs on him."

"A dangerous game," muttered Joseph.

"But exciting!" cried Nicodemus. "Joseph, you should have been there. And I have not even come to the best part. They stopped baiting him finally, seeing that he could not be trapped, and that they were getting the worst of it. So he went back to teaching. He told us that the greatest commandments were, first, to love God with all our hearts and minds and strengths. Secondly, we should love our neighbors as ourselves. These were the two greatest commandments, he said. And, as he taught—here comes the good part—he took a great many leather strips from out of his gird, and commenced to plait them all together at one end while tying knots into each strip at the other end. When he had finished doing that, and with the court filled, and almost every eye upon him . . . "

Nicodemus began to giggle.

"Yes?" said Joseph.

"He got to his feet and strode over to the tables of the money changers."

Nicodemus strode to a table in the salon and raised an arm dramatically.

"Then he knocked those tables right over!"

"Lord help us," moaned Meraiah.

"Right and left, left and right, he struck!" cried Nicodemus, throwing himself into a re-enactment of the gestures with such gusto that Agapo woke and began to cry.

"He sent that money flying in all directions, and beggars rushed in to scoop it up. Then he laid into the moneychangers, themselves, with his whip! Ah, Joseph, you should have seen it. He sent them yowling out into the streets. But then, then!"

The Pharisee clasped his hands in delight.

"Then he went after the animal sellers! He moved down the row like a man possessed. He broke every dove cage and set them all free so that doves whitened the sky. Then he drove the calves and the goats and the sheep out through the gate and down the ramp into the Street of the Cheesemakers! What yelling, what screaming, what confusion, what laughter. The people began to cheer him on. Some helped to drive the animals. Others got angry, and fell to quarreling and fighting with their fists. You have never seen anything like it! The press was so frantic that the Temple Police could not get through, and many like myself, who saw them trying, moved into their way to stop them. And all the while Yeshuah was shouting.

"'My father's house should be a house of prayer!' he screamed. 'But you have made it a den of thieves! Out! Out!'"

Nicodemus remained for a moment, face shining, his Pharisee's heart warmed by the memory. For Pharisees abhorred the animal sacrifices of the Temple, and considered the money-changers as vermin.

Then the sternness returned to his face.

"It was a very bad thing that was done, Joseph."

"Yet still," said Joseph uncertainly, " . . . did Yeshuah violate a Law?"

"That is of secondary importance. What is of first importance is what everyone in that crowd was whispering. By now that whisper is all over Jerusalem and halfway to Hebron. They were already thinking it when they heard the news of Lazarus yesterday. Now, with this open warfare on the Temple, itself, they say aloud that he *must* be the Messiah—that, at the Passover, he will be revealed—that God and the angels will arrive for the final battle."

Martha headed for the door.

"I will hurry the servants with the packing."

"Leah, dear," said Jesus, "get all of Micah's writings packed up if you would, please."

"Yes, yes." said Nicodemus. "So you do plan to flee. That is what I came to tell you. Go. Quickly. Take this Yeshuah with you. If he stays in Jerusalem, the Zealots will rally to him. With all the pilgrims in the city . . . ah, the consequences might be dreadful. The Temple will have to move to stop him, they cannot risk open rebellion.

"And what if there *were* rebellion, and we managed to drive the Romans out of the city, even from our shores . . . they would come right back! Tiberius would send legion after legion until we were crushed.

"So go without delay. Hide. Do not make yourselves prominent. If the rulers of the Temple can find none on whom to vent their spleen, and if they see from your actions that none of you truly intend to initiate a rebellion . . . well, in a year, or two, it might be over and forgotten."

Jesus could not help his smile.

"Your advice is sound, Nicodemus. By the world's standards. But something has always puzzled me in the attitudes of the priests of the Temple and pious men like yourself. You all look for the Messiah, yearn for the Messiah, believe that the Messiah will come, that he is promised by God, and that God, himself, will aid this Messiah in overthrowing and subjugating the scriptural Edom, that you interpret as Rome. At least those are the things which you profess to believe.

"Yet, when a man appears and it seems that he might actually be the Messiah, you try to crush him, or ask him to run and hide for fear of the Romans. If Yeshuah *is* the Messiah, Nicodemus, then, by your own beliefs, the Romans cannot prevail against him, for you insist that God and all his angels will come in clouds of light and fight his battles for him.

"Can you explain this paradox to me? Why you cry to God for the Messiah, yet show yourself afraid to trust that he has actually been sent?"

"Joshuah," said Joseph. "You insult this good friend who has come to help us."

"No." Nicodemus raised a hand. "His question is just."

The man turned away and thought for a moment. Then he sighed and turned back.

"As for the priests and scribes of the Temple, the answer is that they are hypocrites. They are not holy men, they are politicians and businessmen. Even if they do believe in the Messiah, they do not *care* for him. They care only for riches and power."

He spread his hands.

"So that theirs is a lesser sin than mine, is it not. As a Pharisee, I profess to care nothing for my own fortune or position, but only for God's. Yet, as you say, when God might have answered my prayers, made my dream come true . . . I turn my back."

His arms had dropped lowly to his sides as he spoke.

"You make me face a terrible thing, Joshuah. Do I trust and believe in my God and in Scripture, or do I not?

"Joshuah . . . . . . *is* this Yeshuah the Messiah?"

The gentle smile had not left the face of Jesus.

"What do you think?"

The old man shook his head.

"I do not know what I think. The man speaks with a power seldom seen. He does not come right out and proclaim himself the Messiah, yet his utterances hint at it.

"And did he not make such a proclamation in the synagogue at Kapher Nahum? Did he not say that the time was fulfilled, and did he not call himself the Son of Man? One does not have to be an Essene as your brother, here, to know that Son of Man is an Essenic appellation for the Kingly Messiah. While today . . .

" . . . he did say one dangerous thing. In the heat of battle, as he was driving out the animals, a Pharisee of Shammai shouted at him that he was destroying the Temple. He shouted back that he could tear the Temple down and, in three days, build it up again. People whisper that he meant that he is the Messiah and that he knows that God and his angels will be arriving shortly, and would help him rebuild anything that had been torn down. Others mutter that his words were treason against The Law, sacrilege against God, himself, that he assigns to himself power equal to God's."

The gray head was still shaking.

"The man comports himself and speaks as we would expect the Messiah to speak, while he seems to be in fear of no earthly power—as though he knows something that we do not know. Yet there are those who say . . . "

Nicodemus looked beseechingly at Jesus.

"Some say that it is you who will finally be revealed as our deliverer. From what I had heard, from what your father has told me of you . . . I had hoped it would be so."

"Yet," said Jesus gently, "you would send me away as well. You would send away any possible Messiah, lest one of us be real, organize an uprising, cast Rome from our shores, and initiate the Kingdom on Earth. How do you explain this, Nicodemus?"

"I guess . . . I do believe it could happen, will happen someday. But I would rather it happened to others, and not in my lifetime. I guess I have not the courage to take part, to put my trust and belief to that test. I guess I prefer to dream, and to prate of my dream, but have not the courage to actually experience that dream."

Jesus put an arm around the old man's shoulders.

"In that, you are not a sinner, Nicodemus, and certainly no worse than the hypocrites of the Temple. You are just very human. It is part of the journey each of us must take, a lesson each of us must learn as we search for 'God.' Each, in his own time, must finally find the courage *to* make his dreams come true. After one has found that courage, one must then come to understand that only good and loving dreams are worth the effort. When a person has finally and thoroughly learnt that, he will look around and, to his shock, discover that he is already in the Kingdom of God right here on Earth . . . that the promised Messiah did come, and that it was himself.

"And I will tell you a secret, Nicodemus. In coming here today to warn us, to help us, in putting your own self at risk, you did begin to find the Messiah, who has been right under your nose all along. You have taken a step toward making your dreams come true."

Nicodemus gazed up into the face of Jesus as through hypnotized.

"I can continue to help you," he said. "You will still need eyes and ears at the Temple. And if ever you must slip into Jerusalem, I can hide you in my house on the Orphel. The authorities would never suspect such a thing."

"Good man. Micah, make out a list for Nicodemus of the names we have all chosen for ourselves. We will use them as codes in messages to and from one another. I was Wine, Merovee is Chalice, Martha is Bread . . . "

"I had already made a list," said Micah. "I am copying it right now."

"And what code name will you choose, Nicodemus?" said Jesus.

Nicodemus turned to Joseph.

"What name did you choose?"

Joseph colored.

"Apollo."

Nicodemus stared, then burst into slightly hysterical laughter.

"Dear oh dear, my good old friend, what have you led me into here? Well, let me see. All right. Why not just that? Friend. I should be proud of that name in relationship to you, Joshuah."

"Then Friend it is," said Jesus, embracing him. "But please call me Jesus. Joshuah is too much like Yeshuah. Now, more than ever, I prefer not be confused with Yeshuah.

"Jacob, my brother, what of you? You must choose a code name as well."

The Essene stirred from the deep and sad reverie in which he had been sunk. He gave his father a wry smile.

"Apollo, is it? While, only hours ago, I saw your son shining like the sun, so that he lit the darkness. Names of light are apt then, but I am a lesser light to you both. Is Moon taken?"

"I am Moon," smiled Deborah, "and I will never give it up."

"Then I shall be the Evening Star, that tiny point that braves the light of day, that dares even to approach the sun, then shines bravely through the night, as though trying to light the Earth when the sun has gone and the light has fled."

"You choose well," said Jesus softly.

Then he turned, his voice all business.

"Nicodemus, where did you last see our friend Yeshuah and my followers . . . if my followers they still be."

"Oh, they are on their way back, they got off the grounds of the Temple immediately he had driven out the last animal, for Alexander and his Police would have been justified in seizing them simply for making a disturbance within those precincts. But huge crowds followed after him. They surround him, and the sick and infirm plead for healing. It will take him some time to get here. And he is perfectly safe for the moment. The authorities would not dare to follow and arrest him while he has that army with him, for that could touch off the revolt that they wish to avoid."

Joseph could not help laughing.

"I can just see old Annas and Caiaphas and their crew, buzzing like angry bees, trying to decide what to do."

"I am not sure that he did violate any Law in turning out the merchants," said Nicodemus. "And, in the Sanhedrin, there are many who abhor the commercialism, who will applaud his actions. It will take a good deal of thinking for Annas to find a proper charge to lay against him."

"Something for which the Sanhedrin will be forced to issue a warrant," mused Joseph.

"Exactly. Yeshuah's retort about tearing down the Temple might supply what they need. Yet, even then, with the eyes of the nation trained on the man, they will wish to take him by stealth and in the black of the night. But Jesus, it does not matter that it will take them time to think things out. You must not tarry. You should leave this place no later than tonight, before they gather their wits and think to have you all watched."

"I suspect they will think of that long before tonight," said Jesus.

He walked back to the door and stood looking out at Martha's beloved courtyard.

"In line with that," he said finally, "get your own self gone, Nicodemus. It would be ill for the minions of Annas to see you here. Is the list finished, Micah?"

"Just," said Micah, sanding the last notations. Nicodemus took the document and scanned it.

"You will find a few surprising names," said Jesus.

"Pilatus's tribune? Surely you jest. And . . . " Nicodemus stared at the list. "The Lady Procula and Pilatus himself? How can this be?"

"It is too long a story. Only know that they are my friends and followers and may be perfectly trusted to do their best to protect us all. Procula, especially, is most dear."

The old man's eyes found the names of the two Herodian princesses.

"But . . . " His mouth worked soundlessly for a moment. "They killed Johannan."

He lifted stunned eyes to Merovee, who was gentling Agapo.

"How can you associate with those women? You, his widow, mother of his child."

"What you have heard against them are lies," said Merovee kindly. "Trust us, Nicodemus. And trust them."

"And so," said Jesus, "you have company in watching and listening, Nicodemus. Allies in high places. Micah, please copy off two more lists. We will find a way to get one to Procula and one to Salome, so that all can be sure of who is who, and be able to read and write coded messages. Tell them especially of Nicodemus, our new Friend, so that they will know to trust him. Get you gone now, Friend."

"I will escort him out," said Lazarus, rising. "We will get your mount from Jesse, Nicodemus, and I will show you the back gate."

"Lazarus," said Nicodemus abruptly, "did Yeshuah really raise you from the dead?"

Lazarus grew still.

"No," he said at last. "It was not he." He glanced at Jesus. "I am told by Jesus that I was not really dead, that I only slept. I would ask seriously then—what is death and what is life? I think the division between the two is thin. I do not know if I would ever have come back from where I was had I not been called by . . . . . . I heard my mother calling, then Miri and Judah. But I was so happy where I was. I might not have come. Then Jesus called. When he called, I had to come." He sighed. "I am not fully returned even yet. I feel such distance from all this . . . wrangling. It seems so foolish all of a sudden. Why do we fight and strive so amongst ourselves?" He shrugged. "Ah well. Come. We will get you gone."

There was silence for long minutes after the two men left. All eyes were fixed on Jesus, who commenced to pace, eyes lowered as though in deep contemplation of the floor tiles.

Finally, in front of Merovee and little Agapo, he halted. He seemed about to take the child into his arms. Then he just reached out and touched the little cheek.

"Support. Get you down the Jerusalem road. Find Yeshuah and my followers and whisper to each that they are to return to Bethany immediately. Tell them . . . tell them that the Master has need of them."

Nathaniel's mouth dropped.

"I am to use that title?"

Jesus grinned ruefully.

"It is sure to convince them that I mean business, and to bring them running, all agog. It is sure to bring our friend Yeshuah hotfoot as well."

"I will go and help," said bar Tolmei, rising.

"No. The crowd will contain spies from the Temple. This is no time for a Zealot of your notoriety to be seen whispering to Yeshuah or to any of my people. Besides, I have other work for you. Get moving, Support. 'Nathaniel,' I want you to take Merovee and Agapo down to the house of Simon the Leper."

Merovee let out a cry.

"I will not go. I will not leave you."

"Only as a precaution, my darling. I want you away from this place while it is still unwatched."

"No! We will stand or fall with you."

"Merovee, how would you feel if Agapo were taken and 'accidentally' killed, and you were left alive?"

" . . . What?"

"It has occurred to me that the rulers might eagerly avail themselves of the first opportunity, the most flimsy pretext, to lay hands on Johannan's son. And, right now, their pretexts might be more than flimsy. Even should all this fuss pass over, the rulers will know that the child could be a rallying focus for rebellion in years to come. They would be happy to be rid of him. And they are without scruple. Please. I can think more clearly, and do the things that must be done, if I am not simultaneously worrying about him. Go with our new Nathaniel. Wait at Simon's till I send for you."

Merovee had heard his words in horror, understanding for the first time that they were all too true. Her eyes lowered to Rosula's fat, pink cloud. It was as she had realized the morning after his birth.

Things would never again be the same. It was no longer just her and Josh. Her first duty now was to Agapo, no matter what she, herself, would wish.

"I will go," she whispered.

"Thank you."

"Josh?"

"Yes."

"You always promised that we still had time. Do we? Still?"

There was a long pause.

"You see me now naked in fallible humanity. I had not foreseen that Yeshuah would rush to destruction quite so soon. The answer to your question is that I do not know if there is still time. I will do my best."

"I am going, too, of course," said Zana.

"Of course," said Jesus. "Both of you veil yourselves. Get a burnoose from Jesse, Nathaniel. Take Ruthie with you."

Martha had prepared a bundle of clothing and linen for Agapo. Johannan's sheepskins and the gird had also been tied securely together.

"The kitten. The kid," said Merovee.

"There must be some sort of cage in the stable. Have Jesse sling it onto Ruthie. One of you women ride and carry the baby, the other one walk. Go out the back gate and meander the streets like Passover pilgrims until you are certain that you are not being followed, then go to Simon's. Nathaniel, you will remain there with my wife and child."

The Zealot grunted an affirmation. The reasoning of Jesus was two-pronged, to provide a bodyguard for Merovee and the child, and to remove his own Zealot self from out of the group during this dangerous period.

Jesus leaned forward and kissed Merovee upon the brow.

"Be off with you," he said.

At the door, Merovee looked back. He was watching after her with as much heartache in his eyes as she felt within herself.

She summoned a smile.

"We will see you later. Probably tonight?"

He nodded.

"Yes. Probably tonight."

* * *

The followers began straggling into bar Jeremiah within the hour. They found the numbers of those who awaited them much reduced.

Joseph and Rosula, Joses, Annah, and Rachel had, at the bidding of Jesus, left by way of the front gate, and ridden off toward their home in Bethlehem. The three women wore veils, the faces of Joseph and Joses were covered with burnooses, and Rosula carried a bundle that might have been a newborn infant.

At the same time, Susannah, veiled, riding Solomon, and carrying a bundle that might have been a newborn infant, had also ridden out the front gate. Riding with her, on Pharisee, his face covered with a burnoose, had been Lazarus. These two set off toward the Jericho road.

At the same time, from the back gate, Micah and Simon of Cyrene had gone, dispatched into the city with the lists—Simon to Salome and Herodias in the Herodian Palace, Micah to Procula in the Hasmonaean Palace. Deborah, accompanied by Chandreah, left along with them, off on a business matter that she had been negotiating and had now decided to conclude. A short way from the back gate, the three parties split, heading in different directions.

Should spies already have been watching at the front or the back, they would have been thoroughly confused, and torn as to whether to keep watching the gates or to split up and follow these parties.

So that bar Jeremiah was virtually empty. There were only Martha, Johannah, and Leah, working at the packing with the servants, and Jesus, Jac, Judah, and Meraiah, waiting in the salon.

The returnees were in a festive mood, riding high after the morning. They greeted Jesus with pleasure, still unaware of the abduction, believing him to have returned from some mystical journey. They fell over one another in their eagerness to tell him of the clever things that Yeshuah had said, and to describe the rout of the money changers and animal merchants. Even Jairus and Alphaeus were as excited as two boys returned from a raid on a detested neighbor's date palm grove.

Jesus sat silent and smiling, listening to each of them.

When Yeshuah appeared in the doorway, Jesus rose, went to the man, and embraced him.

"I am told that you were brilliant in the Temple, my friend. I am in especial awe of your answer as to Caesar's tribute."

Yeshuah stood stiff and wary, unable to return the embrace.

"How fine to see you back. So soon."

"Yes. Well, the whirlwind ran out of wind . . . or maybe it was whirl."

Yeshuah's eyes came to rest on Jac.

"I do not believe," said Jesus, "that you have met my brother Jacob, until early this morning a member of the community at Qumran."

Yeshuah paused, absorbing that information, beginning to understand how Jesus could have been rescued.

"He has left the community?"

"Regrettably, yes. It was either that or denounce a certain Reuben ben Hezikiah before the membership."

Jac rose from the cushions upon which he had been sitting and crossed the room to stand toe-to-toe with Yeshuah. In that position, tall as Yeshuah was, Jac, with his long, gaunt frame, seemed to look down upon him.

"My brother has the grace to embrace you," he said tersely. "Never look for the same grace from me."

He turned then, his eyes sweeping the chattering followers.

"I would have all of you know what I, and the soon-to-be ruler of the Qumran community, and several of your company witnessed this morning."

He spoke quietly, yet with such command that all fell silent.

Without betraying the truth of what Yeshuah had done, he described what he termed the 'transfiguration' of his brother . . . how, in the darkness, he and Merovee, Judah, Nathaniel, and bar Tolmei had been led to the place where Jesus was. Such a display of inner light was not a new concept to those assembled. Yeshuah had already described such a phenomenon, claiming that he had seen Jesus so illuminated just before he was snatched up into the whirlwind. Indeed, those at the bottom of the hill had seen, for themselves, a light in the darkness.

Now the testimony carried the weight of many more witnesses, including Essenes—saints every one of them—who could always be counted upon to speak the truth.

"When I saw this light emanating from my brother," Jacob continued quietly, "I realized that he *is* The Light. We Essenes call ourselves The Way. We call ourselves The Truth. And we call ourselves The Light. But, this morning, as I looked at this man Jesus, I realized that it is in what he has to teach me that I will finally, truly, find the way, the truth, and the light. And I made a difficult decision. I have been at Qumran, an Essene, for many years. It has been my whole life . . . all I ever looked forward to. Yet, this morning, I put it all aside, for I saw that everything I had prayed for, believed in . . . the Promised One, had come. He is here, in this man, my brother. And so I left the community to follow after him. I think all of you here will shortly need to make a similar decision—to decide who and what you will follow after. I only wanted you to know of my experience. and what I, myself, decided to do."

Abruptly, Jacob turned, went back, sank down onto his cushions, and returned to his reverie.

"What does he mean?" said Mathiah. "What choice will we have to make?"

All eyes turned to Jesus. His somber face reminded them that the summons had been . . .

'The Master has need of you.'

The elation of the morning faded.

"Where are all the others?" said Levi, realizing for the first time how many of the company were missing.

"They have kindly agreed to remove themselves to places of safety," said Jesus simply. "Others are off on errands. I, myself, will leave here before nightfall, heading northward. All who wish to join me are welcome."

"Leave before the Passover?" said Jacob bar Alphaeus. "That will not look very good."

"And what of our little Agapo?" said Lebbaeus belligerently. He had still not forgiven Jesus for not immediately returning to help his cousin, Lazarus, and he was in a state of confusion as to all that had happened since. "He must be circumcised in two days' time."

"And then he must be presented at the Temple," added Alphaeus.

"Both of these matters are of no account compared with the child's safety," said Jesus evenly.

"Circumcision of no account?" said Lebbeaus. His shock was genuine. The most basic tenet, the sign of a Hebrew's covenant with God, was the circumcising of male children.

"I have told you again and again, Lebbaeus, that I bring a new covenant. By that covenant, yes, circumcision is of no account. Your bond with All That Is does not reside in the presence or absence of a foreskin. Your bond is in your heart. After the events of these last days, by no means would I take our child anywhere near the Temple. In no wise would I deliver Johannan's son into the hands of the rulers. And if that means that, in the uncertain days that we face, the time shall pass during which he should have been circumcised, then he shall not be circumcised."

His eyes moved searchingly from one to another.

"Can none of you see what Yeshuah has done by his actions of yesterday and this morning? He has taken all of us beyond the point from which return was still possible. At this moment he—and I by association, perhaps even our families—are on the Temple's death list.

"Oh no," he said as a murmur of protest arose. "Mistake it not. Yeshuah plays a deadly game. By deed and inference yesterday and this morning, he has caused it to be openly and widely suggested that he is the Messiah, and within the Temple precincts, themselves. He has chosen to bring this suggestion into the open just as Jerusalem and its surrounding valleys are filling with tens, hundreds, of thousands of Passover pilgrims, in a tax year, when emotions and resentments run highest, with our praefectus present, and extra centuries of Romans garrisoned in the city, so that any insurrection would involve Rome in a major way."

"Insurrection?" said Mathiah. "Who is planning insurrection?"

"No one," said Jesus. "But the rulers do not know that. All they will be able to see is that a major candidate for Messiah, for King of the Jews, whose supposed aim will be to expel Rome from these shores, and lead our nation to world dominance, is declaring himself to the people. All they will be able to see is that every hot-head in the land will flock to this man, and that insurrection against Rome, and maybe even against themselves, will result. At the very least, a declaration of the messiahship is treason against Caesar . . . at least as the rulers understand the messiahship."

Jesus smiled.

"They could never be expected to understand the very different way in which Yeshuah understands the messiahship. And that, of course, is exactly what Yeshuah is counting on. Yeshuah enters the cage of the Lion of Judeah, not as did Daniel, trusting in his god to deliver him out of that cage, alive and unharmed . . . but, rather, trusting in his god to see to it that he is mauled and treated to agonizing death."

All eyes turned to Yeshuah . . . most deeply puzzled.

"Possibly all the rest of you are now on this death list, too," Jesus continued. His voice was gentle, and held no rancor. "Thus, I think it is only fair to educate you all as to what is going on, so that each of you can make your choices with opened eyes. Yeshuah, do you believe yourself to be the Messiah?"

"I know that I am the Messiah," was the quiet answer.

"But Jesus, I thought you were the Messiah. Have my boys been following the wrong man?" said Zilpah plaintively.

Jesus laughed outright.

"Still worrying for your sons seats in the Kingdom? Well, no one in the world can answer your question for you except yourself, Zilpah. You, and your boys, must follow where your own hearts lead you. There is no other way. Now. You all know where I stand, how I feel, what my teachings are . . . "

"*Are* you The Messiah?" Zilpah persisted.

"As you think of it, no."

He surveyed the stunned faces.

"Because, as you think of it, there is and will be no Messiah. You must each, in your own time, learn to understand the Promised One symbolically. But, if you care to understand me as one 'sent by God' to show you the way to that Long-Expected One who is your own self . . . to that limited messiahship I will gladly own."

He smiled again.

"How confused you all look. Yet you have heard my teachings, again and again. You have heard me tell you that the Universe is mind-stuff, that you literally create your own reality, both the good and the bad of it.

"You have heard me tell you that 'God' is not some white-bearded, old man in the sky, but is, rather, All That Is, and so, naturally, also All That Is Not—that vast mind, of which you are each an essential and beloved part.

"And so you have heard me say that the Kingdom of 'God' is within. Within you and within each leaf, stone, drop of water, star, creature, clump of dirt, or blue patch of sky.

"You have been told of The Power of All That Is that is within each of you. Most of you have done feats of healing, and so have seen—and felt—that Power at work.

"You have heard me say that there is no real sin, only human error, fear, and misunderstanding.

"You have heard me say that guilt is counterproductive, literally fruitless, and that no one is guilty in the eyes of All That Is.

"You have heard me say that All That Is wants only for you each, individually, to develop your own particular talents and potentials, which are yours and yours alone out of all the Universe.

"You have heard me tell you that the only real sin is to refuse to develop yourself to the utmost of your capabilities.

"You have heard me tell you that you live countless lives, and that all those lives are constantly and continually interconnected in simultaneous time.

"You have heard me tell you that you are the true god, itself, learning about itself.

"You have heard me tell you that you do not have to beg to be forgiven, and certainly do not have to go in fear of the true god.

"You have heard me say that All That Is automatically understands, and so forgives, those things which are, at base, its own mistakes as it tests and learns about its own Self through your Selves.

"You have heard me caution you that, in your development, as you select ways in which to grow, it is best to remember that you always reap what you sow.

"You have heard me tell you that the Universe is predisposed to the positive, and will respond faster to good than to ill.

"You have heard me tell you that nothing which comes into you from 'outside' of yourself can harm you, but only those things which come out of you, from out of your hearts, into the world, can harm you.

"You have heard me ask you to be as trusting as the lilies of the field.

"You have heard me say that Love is all.

"Perhaps, most importantly, you have heard me tell you that laughter, that sounds of joy, are the true god's favorite sounds."

He paused, staring at the floor tiles, wishing that Merovee were with him.

"I said before that I would own up to a limited messiahship, as one sent by All That Is, to show you the way to All That Is. But, since All That Is is within your own selves, then it is you, yourselves, who both summoned me and sent me to yourselves.

"The question now is . . . will you hearken to what you, yourselves, called to yourselves and sent to yourselves?"

He turned and regarded Yeshuah.

"With us is a man who also feels that he was sent. Not summoned. Only sent. For he allows Humankind no divinity, no mechanism with which to summon. He thinks that I am an archangel, and he understands messiahship in a much different fashion than do I. To him it can only be *the*

Messiahship. My brother spoke truly when he said that you each will shortly have to make a decision. You will each have to decide which of us you believe in."

Abruptly he went to the door.

"Martha? Martha, there you are my darling. I do not wish to trouble you when you are so busy, but do you have something around that I could eat? A hunk of bread will do. I am utterly famished."

"Oh my God! Of course! I did not think!"

"Anything will do."

"Right away!"

He turned back and smiled, straight at Yeshuah.

"So much for archangels. And now, my friends, I think you would be well advised to ask our friend the Messiah some pointed questions. Ask him what his aims are. Find out from him his true goals. I can in no wise disassociate myself from him. When I accepted him as a follower and undertook to teach and train him, I became as much a part of him as he became a part of me. My own work, it seems, my own success in this world—in this probability --is inextricably mixed with Yeshuah's. I will not disown him. With his permission, I will not abandon him. But I tell you here and now that my own aims and understandings are diametrically opposed to his. My message to the world is one of light and love, joy and life. One does not impart light and love, joy and life, by suffering or dying. One does that by living, beautifully and fully, by being the shining, successful example of what one teaches, an example to inspire the emulation of others. Ah. Thank you, Martha. What an artist you are, how attractively you have arranged each morsel."

"What is this about suffering and dying?" said Levi.

"I can tell you about that," said Judah. "Yeshuah intends to get himself crucified."

A clamor erupted among the followers. Meraiah lowered her face into her hands.

"Yeshuah, what insanity is this?" demanded Yeshuah's brother, Jacob.

"No insanity at all," said Yeshuah quietly. "Have you not studied Scripture? I fear you have not, at least no better than could those who are blind and deaf. It is clearly written that the Son of Man must suffer greatly. He is the Suffering Just One, the only perfect sacrifice to the Lord, by which the children of Israel may be saved, their transgressions forgiven. The Messiah must be delivered up to the High Priest and to the scribes and to the elders and be killed."

"Where is that clearly written?" said Mathiah. "I know Scripture as well as you. Nowhere does it say such a thing."

"You are as one blind. The Messiah is a second, hidden meaning behind almost all that has been written. The Psalms of David speak not only of David. Each line must be read doubly, and there you will find the prophecies of what must befall The Anointed of David's loins. Isaiah and Zachariah and Hosea must also be so read. 'The kings of the Earth set themselves, and the rulers take counsel together, against the Lord, against his anointed.' 'He is despised and rejected of men, a man of sorrows, and acquainted with grief.' 'All that hate me whisper together against me—against me do they devise my hurt.' 'And one shall say to him, What are these wounds in your hands? Then shall he answer, Those with which I was wounded in the house of my friends.' 'I gave my back to the smitters, and my cheeks to them that plucked off the hair. I hid not my face from shame and spitting.' 'He was oppressed, and he was afflicted, yet he opened not his mouth—he is brought as a lamb to the slaughter —cut off out of the land of the living for the transgression of my people was he stricken.' 'All they that see me laugh me to scorn. They shoot out the lip, they shake the head, saying, He trusted in the Lord that he would deliver him. Let him deliver him, seeing he delighted in him . . . I am poured out like water, my bones are out of joint . . . you have brought me into the dust of death . . . like a lion they are at my hands and feet . . . They part my garments among them, cast lot upon my vesture.' 'I looked for some to take pity, but there were none . . . They gave me gall for my meat and in my thirst they gave me vinegar to drink.' 'They shall look upon me whom they have pierced.' But, 'Though I walk in the midst of trouble, you will revive me . . . your right hand shall save me. The Lord will perfect that which concerns me.' 'The bands of the grave compassed me about . . . the snares of death prevented me. In my distress I called upon the Lord . . . he heard my voice . . . Then the earth shook and trembled, the foundations of the hills moved and were shaken.' 'After two days will he revive us . . . and on the third day he will raise us up, and we shall live in his sight.' 'You will not leave my soul in the grave, neither will you suffer your holy one to see corruption.' 'God will redeem my soul from the grasp of the grave, for he shall receive me.' 'You set a crown of pure gold on his head. He asked life of you, and you gave it to him, even length of days for ever and ever. His glory is great in your salvation—honor and majesty have you laid upon him.'"

Yeshuah's eyes traveled from bewildered face to bewildered face.

"You *are* sheep," he said. "But God has finally sent your shepherd. Jesus and his brother are right. You must soon decide which of us two you will follow. Those of you who follow after me will each have to deny yourselves completely. You must turn your backs on your former lives, upon your families, and strive only to spread the news of my death and resurrection, and of the consequent redemption of the sins of all who believe in my name. Most of you will eventually have to take up your own crosses, and suffer and die as I will have suffered and died. But those of you who lose your lives for my sake and for my good news, those are the ones who will save their lives. Those who deny me will be cast into the deepest of pits for ever and ever. So what will it benefit any of you to deny me and save your lives if, in so doing, you lose your souls?"

"And he calls this good news," said Judah dryly.

Levi's head was shaking.

"This is ridiculous. He has taken all sorts of verses completely out of context and strung them together to make a story they were never meant to tell!"

"It is the way of the Essenes," said Mathiah. "But they go even further. They take half of a line from Isaiah, for instance, then tack something from Zachariah onto the end of it and claim that this mis-marriage is divinely inspired prophecy that proves whatever point they wish to prove."

" . . . and we hid as it were our faces from him—he was despised and we esteemed him not,'" murmured Yeshuah.

"Yeshuah," said Alexander the goat-seller. "Surely Judah is mistaken. You cannot really want to die on the cross."

"Of course I do not want to die on the cross! Or anywhere else! But I am the Messiah. So I must. I will teach to all of you who wish to hear me, show you all the reasons. When I have finished, you will understand. The verses that I just quoted are but a very few of those which reveal most clearly what the Messiah must do, to gain his full glory, and to institute the Kingdom of God on Earth. Do you not see that it has taken the Messiah, himself, to finally understand their hidden meanings?"

"How can you have followed Jesus all this while," marveled Alphaeus, "heard his words, and still believe as you do?"

"I do not deny the teachings of Jesus," said Yeshuah. "I deem him to be far greater than I. But the teachings of Jesus are beyond the understanding of men at this moment. After the Kingdom is established, then we will be able to understand, and then all the Gentiles will be enlightened as well. But I am sent for this time, this moment, this people. The Kingdom cannot be established until the children of Israel are redeemed. I am, thus, sent by the God of Israel *to* Israel. Exclusively. I am the *Messenger,* can you not see that? I am the Messenger sent by God. The Messenger is to be regarded as the one who sent him. So I *am God* in the flesh. I, God, in my love for my Chosen People, have provided the truly perfect sacrifice . . . that of myself. I will suffer and die upon the cross, and, at the moment that I do, the sins of my people will be forgiven. They shall have only to believe in me, and on my word, to be saved, and to be granted everlasting life."

The assembled sat silent, looking from one to the other. Yeshuah's words in no way matched anything they had ever heard, believed, or expected of the Messiah.

"What of the Priestly Messiah of the Essenes?"

Yeshuah shook his head.

"The Essenes are sorely misguided. In their ignorance, they even suppose themselves to be the perfect sacrifice on behalf of Israel to the Lord, and they suppose that their High Priest will be the one to teach truth and righteousness in the Kingdom. I tell you now that there is only one Messiah, and he is myself. After my resurrection, I will be both King and High Priest. I will deliver our nation from the yoke of Rome, and I will teach righteousness to all nations."

He cast a look of irritation at Jesus, who was crunching his bread rather noisily.

"Pay me no mind," smiled Jesus. "The heel has always been my favorite part."

"You mock me."

"Never, Yeshuah. Because, when all is said and done, you are still rare and beautiful, for you are a man with the courage to try to turn your dreams into reality. Well now friends, you have heard from Yeshuah and you have some idea of what he plans. You know the outcome he expects to achieve from his actions of these last days. His every move has been premeditated, calculated, to bait the authorities and force them to move against him. I, however, do not intend to die just yet, and so, as I said, I am going north. Who is coming with me?"

"I," said Jac.

"I," said Alphaeus.

"I," said Levi.

"I," said Alexander.

The I's repeated until only Meraiah, Yeshuah's brothers, and Thunder had said nothing.

Meraiah's eyes were red with tears.

"Yeshuah, why did you never tell us that you intended to set yourself killed?"

"Mama, I *have* told you. But you are not to worry. After three days I will rise from the dead. You saw me raise Lazarus. How can you doubt but that God will raise me as well?"

Jesus tilted his head. Was Yeshuah beginning to delude himself? Surely he could not be basing expectations for his own survival on what he knew to be a fraud.

Besides, Lazarus had been laid in a tomb, above ground, ventilated. Whereas, by Law, felons who perished on the cross were barred from such honorable burial, and were merely shoveled into common graves. Such felons were, after the three days that it took most of them to die, hideous wrecks, wrists and feet ripped and torn, bones smashed by the nails, arms pulled out of shoulder sockets, muscles, sinews, and tendons destroyed—while, if mercy had been shown and the death had been hastened, the felon's legs would have been broken, smashed with a mallet, so that the man could no longer support himself with his feet, so that the entire weight of his body would then press upon his lungs and rapidly asphyxiate him.

What sort of a body did Yeshuah expect to be resurrected in? Did he expect his God to give him a new one, totally healed, strong and shining, clean and uncorrupted by the earth? What, did he expect an earthquake to come along on the third day and heave him up out of that grave?

Jesus shook his head. The man must not be allowed to waste himself on this madness. Surely it was not too late to influence him.

"And what of you, Yeshuah? Will you come north with me, too?"

"I had not understood that I was invited."

"Of course you are invited."

"Then I will come."

For a moment, Jesus was speechless, thrown completely off his stride. So it was *not* at this Passover that Yeshuah planned to stage his grand drama. There *was* still time.

He rose with a glad smile.

"Come then. Let us start moving out."

* * *

They slipped out of bar Jeremiah during the afternoon hours, singly, in pairs, or in small groups, while those with children went in family groups. Again, some went by way of the front gate, others went out the back. All took different directions—toward Jerusalem, Jericho, Bethabarah, or Bethlehem. Others seemed merely to want a stroll around the village. If, by now, there were spies watching at the front or back, there could not be enough of them to follow everyone.

The meeting point was set for the farm of Joseph's brother Cleopah, about thirteen miles northwest of Jerusalem on the slopes of Mount Ephraim. Once all were sure they had not been followed, or had shaken any followers, they were to head across the hills, keeping off the roads until they were well north of Jerusalem.

The farm of Cleopah was some miles inside the border of Samaria. Yet, at the time of the Passover, it was perfectly safe for non-Samaritans to travel north upon Samaritan roads. Samaritan antipathy would be directed only toward those going south, toward Jerusalem, to observe the Passover at the hated Temple. Those who turned their backs on the Temple at this season would be accounted friends. Indeed, they would be taken for pilgrims journeying to Mount Gerizim to observe Passover according to the Samaritan tradition, and on the proper day of Wednesday, rather than on Thursday as in Jerusalem. No one going to Jerusalem would therefore be journeying through Samaria at this time, so that the chances of Jesus or Yeshuah or any of the followers being seen, recognized, and their whereabouts reported in Jerusalem, were non-existent.

Yeshuah had been one of the first to be sent off, by way of the back gate, in company with Zilpah and Meraiah, Yeshuah's face hidden with a burnoose, Meraiah riding Merovee's Gilead, and Zilpah walking at her side. Just a family group, a man and his wife with their old mother.

"Do I see a subtle punishment of Yeshuah," said Leah to Jesus," to make him travel with Zilpah?" That woman seldom spoke, but she missed nothing, and, when she did speak, she revealed a wry humor.

Jesus grinned and winked. The two of them were the last, beside the servants, left in bar Jeremiah . . . last also except for Judah, who had flatly refused to leave without Jesus. They were waiting for the return from the city of Micah, the Cyrenean, and of Deborah and Chandreah.

Deborah was subdued when she arrived, her tears near the surface.

"I did not imagine that parting with this place would affect me so."

For, the sale of bar Jeremiah had been what she was up to.

"It is a large part of your life that you leave behind," Jesus empathized.

"Soon it will be the farm at Kana, the house in Magdala—and the pottery works."

During the months in which she had stayed behind in Magdala, while Jesus and his followers made the circuit of Galilee, Phoenicia, the Decapolis, and Peraea, Deborah had been quietly acting upon the advice of Jesus, transferring her business records, and the bulk of her fortune, to her office in Caesarea and the protection of Pilatus—thence out of Palestine, to offices in Alexandria, Athens, Rome, and, in particular, Massilia of Gaul. Trusted officers of her company had also been contacted and transferred to those cities, so that the groundwork was done. It had only remained to sell her physical properties.

And, during the months at bar Jeremiah, she and Jesus had had many a private talk. He had revealed to her much of what he believed would come to pass in his own life and in the future of Palestine. So often had he reiterated his advice to sell everything before it was too late that she had reluctantly initiated arrangements to do just that. By way of the twice-weekly caravans of the Zebedee arriving and departing Jerusalem, the Galilean sales were now being negotiated. For a handsome fee, the Zebedee had made discreet inquiries among his Gentile customers and found exactly the right buyers.

"Oh Jesus, how can I ever do it? How can I part with Magdala and Kana? If I weep for bar Jeremiah, which I never before knew that I loved, how can I sell those places which are all the world to me?"

"If they are all the world to you, do not sell them."

"No. No of course they are not all the world to me. They are only places, things. The safety of my children and of my new grandchild, and our freedom, our new life and our new understanding of that life . . . those are the things which are all the world to me. But you know what I mean."

"I do indeed, Dear Mother." He took her into his arms, consciously transferring Energy to her. "To pull up the roots of a lifetime takes bravery that few possess. Most would stay and die at the hands of their enemies before they parted with their homes or their riches. Your husband's cousin gave you a fair price?"

"Daniel was most fair. He has always been kind to me. As my late husband's eldest, unmarried relative, he was obliged to offer me marriage after Jeremiah's death. I did not desire it, neither did my father. I know that Daniel was secretly grateful that I declined, for he was already much in love with the girl who is now his wife.

"I am sure that he suspected my desperation today, for why else would I come running, wanting to sell immediately and for cash? He could have driven a shrewd bargain, gotten the place for half of what we had discussed earlier . . . yet he made no attempt to reduce the price by so much as a copper, and immediately sent his son to the vault for the gold."

"Happy news indeed. He will be blessed for his graciousness and generous regard, while that positive energy will actually impart itself to the funds. They will be used with equal generosity for generations to come. You will never regret having them."

Deborah's tears came forth.

"I regret having them already. For Martha's sake. I feel such a traitor to her, my poor, dear first-born. This is so unfair to her! Her whole life is being torn asunder, all without her leave, without her even suspecting.

"Forgive me for saying it, but we have all thought of Miriam's concerns, and those of Lazarus, both of whom follow you and care nothing for this place. In all the excitement, no one has thought of Martha and her life, her wishes, her future. She loves bar Jeremiah as deeply as I love the places in Galilee. What will she say when she knows I have sold it out from under her?

"Yet now I wonder if she ever can marry Boaz. I wonder if his family will allow it with all that has happened and might happen. We have turned her into a homeless, unwanted fugitive, Jesus.

"Why do you laugh? How *can* you laugh?"

"Forgive me, Dear Mother. But really, the girl who was buzzing around here today packing and preparing for our departure, closing up the house with such dispatch, did not seem unhappy at all. And how long is it that she has been affianced to Boaz?"

"They have known each other since they were children, but, formally—almost two years now."

"Rather a long betrothal, do you not think? Trust me, Deborah. Martha is far from being an unwilling participant in the matter. She understands more than you think. When she left . . . I watched. She stopped and took a very long, hard look around. She was engraving it all onto her memory. She knew she was saying goodbye, Deborah. Yet her chin was up, her eyes were dry . . . she called to me not to forget the packet of food she had prepared for me, said she would see me at my uncle's, and hustled Mathiah out the gate with, I am sure, the intent of getting to Mount Ephraim before any of the rest of us, so that she can take over my aunt's kitchen and be sure that we will all be properly fed on the morrow.

"For someone like Martha, Deborah, there is no greater reward than being needed. And we do need her. We will never cease to need her. Therefore, whilst she is with us, Martha will never cease being happy.

"Now. What of the transfer? Who did Procula send to collect the money?"

"Lucius was waiting outside Daniel's home when Chandreah and I emerged."

For Micah had carried a double message to Procula, and previously discussed emergency means of moving sale proceeds safely and secretly out of Palestine had been implemented.

Pilatus, himself, had suggested the plan. He had not, in fact, ever gone through with arrangements for the investing of his fortune into Lions' Fat, but he had been using the services of the Zebedee to, as Jesus had suggested, transfer his funds to Massilia of Gaul—for which purposes he had become one of the fish merchant's most passionate customers. Deborah's money would travel along with the next "deposit" of Pilatus, returning down to Galilee with the Zebedee caravan that had delivered the pickled fish for which Pilatus had developed an insatiable craving. From there, the Zebedee would send the funds, along with proper instructions, in a shipment of pickled fish to Massilia of Gaul. There a certain businessman involved in the handling of funds, who had also developed a passion for pickled fish, with whom Pilatus had been enjoying fine relations since meeting the Zebedee, and who both Pilatus and the Zebedee had assured Deborah could be trusted, would, for a fee, transfer Deborah's funds to the safekeeping of the office of the House of Nathan in that city. As the Galilean properties sold, the Zebedee would convey their proceeds to Massilia in the same manner. So that, long before the rulers even began to suspect the complete sell-off of all of Deborah's Palestinian holdings, the funds would be out of the country, safe in the vault of her office in Massilia. And the means by which it had all left the country would never be known.

. . . unless the Zebedee, himself, revealed it. Which was unlikely. In business, and despite many questionable and conflicting arrangements with a variety of people, the Zebedee was close-mouthed, a man of "honor," who could be trusted not to reveal any of his arrangements or "clients," and to carry out his end of any bargain. Indeed, the deals—his own growing fortune and his safety and freedom to operate—depended upon his firm reputation as a man who kept the secrets of his clients . . . even from his large-mouthed wife.

Jesus gave Deborah another hug. She was a brave lady. She could not at this point understand the great, good purposes to which her homes, turned to cash—indeed, that her entire far-flung business fortune—might one day be put. He did know that he could depend upon Deborah, and upon her heirs, to continue to use that fortune in the way that it had always been used, graciously, and in the service of Humanity and its creativity.

There would be no similar monetary fortune forthcoming from his own father. Just as, at the instruction of Jesus, Deborah had warned members of her family, including Daniel, of the destruction of Jerusalem that Jesus foresaw in the near future, Jesus had warned his father, giving Joseph the opportunity to sell his own possessions and spirit the proceeds out of the country.

No one had taken Deborah seriously, and Joseph had not believed Jesus.

Oh, perhaps to placate Jesus, Joseph had indeed sold off some few trinkets and holdings not associated with his Bethlehem wheat lands—the garden and new tomb outside the walls of Jerusalem, for instance, where Joseph had fondly imagined that he and Rosula and their children and children's children would be lain, had been sold to Nicodemus. Other real estate in the city, along with shares in business establishments, had likewise been quietly disposed of. So that Joseph had a fat purse of gold hidden away in case of emergency.

But, for reasons that Jesus understood, Joseph refused to sell any of the Bethlehem property with its wheat lands. Those wheat lands were, after all, not only a family treasure, but a treasure and tradition of the entire tribe of Judah, handed down for over a thousand years in a direct line from David, himself. Those wheat lands, upon which Ruth and Boaz, grandparents of the great David, had been united in marriage, were royal lands in the deepest sense of their people. They must never, said Joseph, be sold away from the family of David's first lineage.

'Dear Father,' thought Jesus.

Joseph refused to comprehend the extent of what was soon to come. He could not conceive of a world in which the Temple would be no more, in which most of the Jews of Jerusalem and surroundings would be slaughtered, enslaved, or fled into exile. He could not picture a land of Judeah in which The Law did not reign supreme, a Jerusalem in which the royal genealogies were not safely filed in vaults beneath Mount Moriah. Joseph would never have been able to accept that, within a hundred years, there would be few, if any, Jews left alive who would know that the wheat lands of Bethlehem were the rightful royal lands of the Princes of Judah bar Ramathea.

Jesus had not found the courage even to hint of this last to his father. Come to pass it would. But let not Joseph have been the heir, the traitor, who had sold those lands into un-royal hands. Let him keep imagining that, in another thousand years, in two thousand years, even until the sun grew cold, his precious wheat lands would remain the legacy of his heirs.

With Micah and Simon the Cyrenean returned from the city as well, there were only two problems to be dealt with. The first was the matter of the servants.

Deborah called them into the salon and told them of the sale.

"Daniel bids me tell you that he will be happy to have any who wish stay on at bar Jeremiah. He has bought the house as a wedding gift for one of his sons, who has no staff of his own at yet. On the other hand . . ."

There were no slaves in Deborah's household. Nathan had not approved of slavery, and had insisted of Jeremiah, as one of the conditions of obtaining Deborah's hand, that all their servants be free.

Still, most of these people had been with Deborah for years, many since she had come to bar Jeremiah as a bride.

"I would be happy for any of you who wish to come with me and follow after Jesus."

There were few of them who had not been touched by his teachings. In their off-hours, many had sat with the disciples, hearing his words.

"It will not be easy. It might even be dangerous. But you are welcome to come with me, and you will be to me, in all ways, as my own family. The choice is yours."

There was then the problem of Petros and of the sons of Thunder, still off with Isaac on the wild duck chase to Masada. It was decided that Jesse should stay behind until they returned, to inform them of events and send them north.

It was further decided that Jesse should remain at bar Jeremiah indefinitely, until he was sent for. That would raise no eyebrows, for the house had to be looked after and guarded, and the animals in the stable seen to . . . one she-ass in particular had just foaled and needed attention. Jesse knew the premises backwards and forward, and could be of great aid to the new owners. They would take it as a graciousness that Deborah had lent them her beloved Jesse to help smooth their way . . . while his presence in Bethany, to receive and transfer messages, could be invaluable to Jesus.

Likewise, Simon of Cyrene agreed to help, to stay behind in Jerusalem, so that he could be in touch with Procula and Salome, with Jesse and Nicodemus and Joseph and Simon the Leper if need be, to keep his eyes and ears open . . . their man on the spot.

It seemed then that all had been attended to, everything thought of. Chandreah, Micah and Leah—packing Micah's precious writings—went first. Then the servants who had elected to throw in their lot with Jesus left, most singly, at five minute intervals, some out the front gate, others out the back.

Five minutes after the last of them left, Jesus and Deborah and Judah slipped out the back gate. They had no beast of burden and no luggage, except that, under one arm, Jesus carried something wrapped in homespun.

The sun was near to setting. The alley was quiet and deserted. Sedately, they walked to the end, turned right, walked to the end of that street, went left down another street . . . and finally agreed that they were not being followed.

They went then quickly to the outskirts and knocked at Simon the Leper's back door.

The door opened a crack and a suspicious eye appeared. With a glad grunt, bar Tolmei opened it wide.

"My lady. They are here."

Merovee leaped up and was across the room, throwing her arms about Jesus before he had even crossed the threshold.

"Careful, you will make me drop her," he laughed.

"Who?"

Then she saw the cloth-wrapped package.

"You brought her."

"Naturally."

Quickly, Jesus explained to Simon the state of affairs, told him of Jesse still at bar Jeremiah, of Simon the Cyrenean, of Nicodemus, of the web of communication available.

"I might not have to call upon you at all, my friend. But if I do . . . "

"I will be ready."

There was not a great deal left of Simon's features, yet his eyes sparkled with life—and now they held a hint of mischief.

"I have heard of the summons you sent to your followers out on the Jerusalem road today. Since you have finally proclaimed yourself, I will hold you to it. It will be our signal. You have but to instruct your messenger to say, 'The Master requires . . . ' and whatever it is that the Master requires shall be performed."

"I can see that I will be some time living that one down."

"May that 'some time' be at least fifty years," said Merovee quietly.

They left, then, in three stages. Merovee, Zana, and Deborah went first, with Agapo, just three women out for a sunset stroll, heading down the Jericho road. Bar Tolmei watched at the door till they were nearly out of sight, then he slipped out and followed after them. Judah followed bar Tolmei at the same distance. Jesus waited yet the same length of time, scrutinizing the road for signs that any of the others were being followed. Astride Ruthie, then, he set off after them.

A mile out of town, knowing themselves to be safe, they joined up. Beyond the intersection of the main route from Jerusalem northeast to Jericho, they struck out cross country, to intersect the road that ran northwest from Jerusalem to Mount Ephraim.

Zana rode Ruthie, carrying Agapo. Bar Tolmai guided the pregnant mare in the gathering darkness, picking easy footings for her. Deborah, Merovee, Judah, and Jesus walked behind, with the goddess.

"How can I help but love this man," said Merovee, "when he agrees to bring her along at a time like this?"

"He did not 'agree,'" said Deborah. "It was he who first mentioned her, and he who insisted that we bring her. I had planned to weight her securely and throw her into the well."

"Mother!"

"Well, I could not risk having her found once we were gone, and it seemed too risky a business to bring her."

"That would have been like drowning a member of the family to insure our own safety!" said Merovee. "Thank God that Jesus was there to rescue her."

"My feelings exactly," said Deborah, and they all laughed.

"Is she getting heavy?" said Judah.

"She is a weight I am happy to bear while yet I may," said Jesus.

All too soon, these people, and the goddess, would have to go forward without him.

Chapter 19

Mount Ephraim

As the plague of locusts had descended upon Pharaoh and his fields, so Jesus and his followers descended upon Cleopah.

"Fortunate all way round that I am a rich man," he spluttered into his supper wine on the following evening. "Though, if you and this army encamp much longer, I shall no longer be rich. We thought certainly we were being invaded when the first of your people arrived. And, my dear Merovee, that sister of yours . . . "

"I do not mind her," said Aunt Miriam. "This is the first rest I have had from supervision of the kitchen since Joshuah's wedding. And her stew is superlative."

"What a trying man your husband is," said Cleopah to Merovee as though his wife had not spoken. "What a blow, what an unhappiness it was to his poor parents when Joshuah abandoned them those many years ago."

"Now Uncle . . . " said Jesus.

"Well what would you call it? At thirteen, less than a week after his ceremony of manhood, Merovee, off he went. To India. India! For twelve years, none of us saw so much as a hair of his head."

"I wrote."

"You wrote. Every couple of years a trader would wander by and hand his mother some filthy piece of parchment so cracked and stained from the various hands through which it had passed that it could hardly be read. You call that writing? You call that keeping in touch? My youngest boy had had his own manhood ceremony before ever he laid eyes on you. He thought we had only made you up. Twelve years, Merovee. Then back he came. But only to say hello. And goodbye. Because off he went once again. To Greece for a few years. Or was it Ephesus? Or Alexandria, or Damascus, I have forgotten which went where.

"I must admit, though, that, during these last years, we have sometimes seen him. Just as one sometimes sees migrating ducks. Always and ever, Joshuah is 'just passing through.' Sometimes you do not even get to see him as he passes, you just hear the quacking up there above the clouds.

"Your wife thinks that is funny, Joshuah. Go on, laugh now, Merovee. Laugh while you may. You will find out."

"I already have, Uncle Cleopah."

Cleopah snorted and helped himself to more stew. He was worried for Joshuah. Very worried. He would never have admitted it, but he had a love for Joshuah that was greater in some ways than for his own sons.

There was something else he would never have admitted. He was glad that Joshuah had stayed away so much. Each time, through the years, that Cleopah had seen Joshuah, the same thought had come to him.

'He knows what he is doing. He has always known. He stays away for good reason. So go away again, Joshuah. Quickly. Before you come to harm.'

Joshuah was a consummate Prince of David. Cleopah had long considered it possible that he was *the* Prince of David. The ultimate, the Long-Awaited One. It positively shone forth from out of him, the dimmest of wits could spot it after five minutes in his presence. It had been that way with Joshuah since he had been a boy. So different from his brother, Jacob, for all of that man's Essenic saintliness, or Jude, or young Joses. They were merely . . . men. Joshuah was more. Had he stayed in Palestine, the Zealots would long ago have rallied behind him—with or without his consent. Inevitably, had he stayed, there would have been open rebellion and terrible bloodshed.

So why had he come back now? Why had he made himself so conspicuous, teaching to thousands, gathering this army of followers, consorting with Zealots, making scenes in the Temple courts? Why was he bringing calamity down upon all their heads? Why, after being so sensible for so many years.

Yet, if he was, indeed, the Long-Awaited One . . . he had to make himself known, did he not?

Cleopah sighed. He and Joseph had talked of it often. What would they do "if"? It had to happen someday if the prophecies were true. Someday, one of the generations of their house was going to have to deal with the Messiah in its midst. Cleopah, like his brother, had fondly continued to hope that it would not be their generation to be so afflicted.

Blasphemy to consider God's Messiah an affliction?

Perhaps. But it was one thing to view a whirlwind from afar, and another thing to be snatched up into its very heart.

His eyes met the eyes of Jesus. Jesus smiled. Cleopah melted.

"You know," he told Merovee, "it is not really true, what I said about not seeing a hair of his head for twelve years. His mother saw him often, and Joseph admits that even he saw him a few times. I and my eldest, my own Jacob, we saw Joshuah one day as we were riding home from Jerusalem. Of course we did not recognize him at first. Neither of us had seen him since he was thirteen. He seemed just suddenly to be there, in the road ahead of us . . . a tall, path-dusted stranger, who was yet so familiar. He hailed us, called us by name. Then he laughed. And I realized who it was. I called out to him, 'Joshuah!' As I did, he vanished."

"Were you aware of that meeting?" Merovee asked of Jesus.

"On that occasion I was on my way back from India, on an especially miserable stretch of road south of Babylon. I began thinking of Uncle, remembering my good times here at his farm as a boy. I wanted very much to communicate with him, to send him my love. Then I saw him and Jacob coming down the road toward me. I called out, and laughed in happiness. I heard Uncle shout 'Joshuah' just as they disappeared. I was well content. I knew the communication had been made."

"What of the times your mother saw you?" said Deborah.

"Sometimes I had a glimpse of her as well. Most times not. Most of my appearances to her were images formed by my waking mind as I thought of her with special emotion or longing. We all do that all the time . . . send out 'thought images' of ourselves to others. If the emotion that sends the image is strong enough, and the recipient is in just the right state of consciousness, those images can sometimes be seen. Whether or not the image, itself, can see, depends on many and varied conditions."

"And so, Merovee," said Cleopah kindly, "it is not quite as bad as I made out, being separated from him. If it comes to pass that this must happen, he will still find a way to show himself to you."

Merovee lowered her face, and Cleopah whispered even more gently . . .

"And I can just imagine the very strong emotions with which he will think of *you,* and so send himself to you."

"Uncle speaks truly," said Jesus. His eyes swept those of his group who were gathered for the meal. As in the home of Joseph and Rosula, formal dining restrictions were relaxed, and the women customarily ate beside the men, so that this group was varied and comfortable, the family reclining before low tables on Roman-style couches, the rest of the company sitting on the floor around mats.

Some of the followers had not arrived as yet. Some of those who had arrived had, indeed, been followed, and had traveled many miles in a wrong direction before losing their shadows. It might be another day before everyone arrived.

Then there were poor Petros and the Sons of Thunder. Who knew how long it would be before they put in an appearance?

So that Jesus had decided to relax in this place of happy memory, and to wait until even Petros and the two boys had caught up, before deciding upon the next move. They were safe here. No arm of the Temple would dare to touch them within the borders of Samaria, even if anyone found out where they were. They might even stay on indefinitely. Despite Cleopah's grumblings, they would be welcome.

However long the stay, though, he would use the time to teach to his people, free of distractions and interruptions. After all, teaching was what he was among them for. His only hope of success in this current mission was to teach then teach some more, watching the eyes of his students for those sparks which told him that he had hit home.

"I do have the ability to appear to you," he went on. " . . . both in dreams and in your waking hours. None of you will ever be without guidance. The time will come when we must part. Yet I will be with each one of you always, even to the end of worlds that never end."

He felt a thrill upon his spine, and tears sprang into his eyes.

"I make you a promise," he said softly. "And how wonderful that I know I can make it. If only each of you could understand the road that I, myself, have traveled, the thousands of lifetimes, the million mistakes from which I have learned, the evils which I have done, the pains and sorrows which I finally learned how to turn into joy . . . if only you could understand how firmly I know, how triumphantly I can say to you . . . . . . I *will* be with you always. I will be there for you and yours, and any that you teach, or that they teach, forever. Each of you, and those yet to be in the future, you are all my family. Each is my friend, by beloved. Each of you is my own self. And I am each of you. And each of us is a part of All That Is. You will have only to call to me, and believe that I will be there, that I will give answer to you, and I will. Wherever I am, whatever I may be doing, in whatever time or place, part of me will come flying to your side.

"Sometimes I will answer you as a still, small voice in your minds, or as a flash of understanding. Or I will appear in your dreams. Then again, I might come to you in the flesh . . . but in a flesh that will not look or seem to you as I look and seem now.

"Repeatedly, in the days and years ahead . . . " unconsciously, he reached out, took Merovee's hand and pulled her to him, so that her head rested upon his breast, "I will stand beside you in body. And you will not know me. In the centuries to come . . . I will appear to Humanity more often than the seasons. Very few of those to whom I appear will know me either. It has been ever thus. We come, those of us who are your teachers, your guides and helpers, in so many guises. Yet seldom are we recognized for what we are." He smiled gently. "So I advise you to give love and respect to all whom you encounter. As has been said, you might, unaware, be entertaining an angel. Or myself."

There was a long hush, each of them touched to the core by the pure Love with which Jesus had spoken.

His cousin, Benjamin, nearly whispered as he said . . .

"Joshuah, how is it that you can appear in so many forms?"

Jesus hesitated.

"Ben, on the face of the Earth at this very moment, I can name you a hundred people who, in a way, are a part of 'me,' fragments of the Living Energy that I manifest to you now in this time and place. And so it shall be, in every time and place. For the entity from which I flow is so large, so grand, that it keeps splashing over its sides with joy, casting abroad everything from seas, to pools, to puddles, to droplets of itself. Some of this exuberant moisture provides sustenance to people in places so far away that you do not even know that they exist.

"The entity of which I am a part is so vast, Ben, so Energy-filled, so old, so wise, so powerful, so brimming with creativity and with Love. It could never contain itself, or express its totality, in just one body, or one form, in any one time or place. The individual Soul that 'I' am has 'been,' in a multiplicity of forms, in every generation that this world has known. And 'I' will 'be,' in a multiplicity of forms, in every generation that it will know in the 'future.' In each of those forms, the Soul that is 'I' has attempted, and will attempt, to reach out to those of my fellows who are ready to hear my words, to help them, guide them, tell them of Love and truth and beauty, show them a better way.

"Most often my forms will be ignored, trampled underfoot . . . especially if they happen to be female. Once in a while, however, the circumstances will be exactly right, and my forms will make a major impact upon the entire species.

"As now. Conditions are prime at this double millennium. At this time and place there is a . . . window, you might say. The world, and all within it, can be likened to a building that has been closed and dark for centuries.

"Then a star falls from the sky, and knocks a hole in its side. Suddenly, the light streams in, and people can see things inside the building that they could not see before.

"And so, in this time and place, when and where the light can come in, 'I' have come in force . . . along with two other entity 'Soul Brothers,' if you will. Johannan was one of them. A man named Saul is the other."

"I do not know any Saul," said Judah.

"None of you have met him as yet. Before most of you are finished, you will.

"And I give warning to each of you. In dreams, I have felt this man's Energy. To be perfectly honest, it manifests itself much like that of Christos here." He smiled over at Yeshuah. "And I have made no secret of the vast chasm between the teachings of our Christos and of myself."

"How can that be?" said Judah. "If you and Johannan and Saul are all of the same entity . . . "

"Free will, Judah. All That Is allows every manifestation of itself to develop itself as it sees fit. Each of us, from his or her own relative position, does just that. So that even those who are part of great teaching entities have the freedom, while they are in the flesh, to develop their own ideas, follow their own paths."

Again he met the eyes of Yeshuah.

"In my opinion, some of those paths are a great waste of any Soul's time. They are dead ends. Those who follow them must eventually retrace their steps and start all over again.

"I think that this Saul will be one such, who, himself, will pursue a dead end path and take his followers with him. I can but warn you. When you meet him, remember my words. *My* words. I fear they will be as different from the words of Saul as my words are different from Yeshuah's.

"I urge you here and now, as I urge you in regard to Yeshuah. Follow Saul not."

He shifted Merovee upon his breast and took a sip of his wine.

"Anyway . . . added to the three primary manifestations off of my parent entity that I have just mentioned, there are numerous 'fragments,' junior, fledgling versions.

"My wife—our wife, Johannan's and mine—is one such. When you see her, you see me. You see us. When she speaks to you, you are hearing the truth and Love which we, ourselves, would give you."

"But where is God in all of this?" said Aunt Miriam.

"Right here. All That Is never left . . . *can* ever leave. All That Is is the very fabric of which we are composed. Of which all is composed. So that, when you see me, you see the 'Father.' When you see yourself, you also see the 'Father.' And the Mother. And all. All That Is."

"But . . . how can that be?" said Aunt Miriam.

"By your own belief, how can it not be?" smiled Jesus. "Your Scripture says that we were made in the image of 'God.' 'Man and Woman made he them.' Is that not what you profess to believe? Why, then, is what I have just said so strange? Or have you never bothered to think about what being made in the image of your god implies?"

"I guess I never have," said Aunt Miriam. "But, certainly, I do not consider my*self*. . . "

"By what right do you presume to limit your god?"

"What?"

"You put yourself outside of your god, outside of its Creation," Jesus said with a twinkle. "What cheek."

Aunt Miriam stared at him.

"But no. That is not what I mean."

"What do you mean then?"

"Well, it is blasphemy to think, when I look into my Egyptian glass and see myself, that I am looking at God."

"I beg to differ. The blasphemy is to assume that you are not. I repeat. By what authority do you presume to limit the true god All That Is? All That Is is not limited. Cannot be limited. All That Is is you, and I, every one in this room, and in this world. It is every house, jar, animal, blade of grass, drop of water, clump of earth, and inch of sky. All That Is never runs out of things to *be*, for, through each one of us, it is always discovering new things—and ways—to be.

"The next time you look in your glass, Aunt, for the first time in your life, face the truth of yourself squarely. Admit what you are—a part of All That Is—experiencing one facet of itself which is yourself.

"And then say to yourself, 'Now that I know who and what I am, am I doing the very best that I can? As a representative of All That Is—am I representing All That Is as well as I am able'?

"If you fall down, Aunt, All That Is falls down. If you get up and try again, so does All That Is.

"If you lie or cheat or steal or kill, so does All That Is.

"If you are lazy, so is All That Is.

"It might almost be better to say that, when All That Is makes images of itself, it gives all power to the images themselves. It then waits, and faithfully reflects the doings of each one of those images. In so doing, it experiences and learns more and more of itself."

"But you make God out to be passive! A slave to *us*," said Zebulon, one of the servants who had come from bar Jeremiah.

"Passive, you say." Jesus smiled. "Zebulon, what makes you breathe?"

"I . . . do not know. I just do."

"By what means do you think the thoughts that you think?"

" . . . I do not know."

"Rise from where you are sitting. Thank you. Now, please walk to the door. Ah, what a vigorous stride. Open the door, please. Now shut it. And come back and sit down.

"Now, Zebulon, tell me how you did all those things. How did your body know to rise, and how did it then do so? Did you shout to your legs to move? Even if you had shouted, would they, then, have obeyed you?

"Did you concentrate on each step? Heel toe, heel toe, heel toe?

"I hope you noticed, by the way, how cleverly the floor remained in place, and held you up as you walked.

"Think how smoothly your arm reached for the door, how intelligently the hand made the movements that opened it.

"How much concentration did you give those movements? Or did they just seem to happen?

"And why did the door indeed open?

"What of the bread in front of you? How did it get there? Uncle might have planted the seeds, and Martha saw to the cooking of it, but where did the seeds come from in the first place? What made them grow when they were placed in the earth?

"What of the rain? Where does it come from? Why? Why does the seed wait for the rain? Why does the rain come to the seed?

"What makes the sun rise up each morning? Why does it go to bed?

"What makes the love of a man and woman become a child in the woman's belly?

"Passive, you say? Think again, Zebulon. Think of the coordination, the vast, unseen *cooperation* going on all about you at every moment. Think of the Energy that, yes, keeps you breathing without your even knowing it.

"I can promise you, Zebulon, there are things going on in your body which, if you had to think about every one of them in order to so much as get to your feet, you would spend all day getting up.

"Yet I say to you 'Rise!' and you rise. 'Walk!' and you walk.

"Passive? Oh no, my good new friend. That unseen Energy is All That Is, our support, the 'always there,' that holds us up in the most loving of hands, and watches with the most open and allowing and loving and curious mind, to see what its wonderful creation might do next.

"We are each a partial image of the true god, Zebulon, each a reflection of the multitudinous aspects of All That Is. Each and every thing about us a reflection of some part of that great mind.

"But Aunt got me off of my original point. What I started to say was that . . . you all have my promise. You will never be without me so long as you call upon me and know that I will, in some way, answer you. And I empower you to pass that promise on to those whom you will teach in the years to come . . . who will never have seen me, yet I will support and come to them as readily as to yourselves.

"Indeed, they will be doubly blessed, those who have never seen me and heard the words spoken by my own lips, but who yet have the good sense to believe your teachings and call upon me for aid.

"This promise is good for all generations to come. In each of those generations, in every place, with every people, 'I' will be there in body as well, living amongst them . . . some part or parts of me, of what I am, will be there, teaching to those with the ears to hear . . . showing the way to those with the eyes to see."

"All of these 'you's,'" said Susannah, "those now living and those which will be . . . you say they do not look like you . . . do they also think differently from you, or do they think with your mind?"

"No one else, now or ever, can think with my mind, Susannah, just as no one else now or ever can think with yours. The current Jesus is Jesus. The current Susannah is Susannah. Each of our personalities remain eternally valid as they explore the probabilities of their eternal, simultaneous moments. There will never be another exactly like either of us. And the manifestations that my entity sends out, the fragments that I, myself, send out—and that you, all of you, send out without knowing it—also have complete individuality, their own manners of presentation.

"Then there are your reincarnational selves. While, in one way, they are all 'you,' and you are in conscious or subconscious communication with each one of them, each of those selves has its own eternally valid personality, and explores its own probabilities in the eternal, simultaneous moment—all of those moments also in communication with you. It is quite wonderful really."

"Wonderful? It is a nightmare!" said young Alexander. "How can we ever keep track of all this, or understand it?"

"You do not have to. Just as Zebulon does not have to think about all that must take place in order to get to his feet and walk across the room, and breathe while doing so. All That Is keeps track of it all. Only know that your sources of information, and aid, are literally infinite. And the more that you do make yourself aware of this greater network, the more you learn about it, the better. You are privy to the knowledge and experience of all the varied 'children' of your parent entity. While the underlying thrust and idea behind each of those children will, at base, be a working out of the 'personality' of your great, parent entity.

"Think of it in terms of sunsets. Have you ever seen one sunset exactly like another? Yet, what you see proceeds from the same sky, the same elements, and takes place over the same Earth. The basic ingredients are always the same. Yet each sunset is different.

"The great difference between me and all of you here is . . . duration. The entity from which I spring is ancient beyond words in the *emotional intensities* which comprise this particular reality. I am one of its earliest offspring. I, and other major manifestations who come to you from that entity, have had the benefit of its great knowledge and expertise for eons, and have been exploring and learning during all that 'time.' We are very advanced. I have demonstrated that to you. When we seniors manifest ourselves in the flesh, we always, sooner than later, know who we are and why we have had ourselves born into a particular 'time' and place. We are expert in communicating with all other parts of our entity and even with the greater Universe."

"Who here besides Merovee is of your entity?" said Judah eagerly.

Jesus laughed.

"Oh no. I will not play that game."

"What of me?" said Yeshuah quietly.

"I do not think you need to be told that we have differing parent entities, which do not see eye to eye," said Jesus kindly. "Beyond that, and beyond Merovee, I shall never tell. Besides, it is best for each of you to work it out for yourselves. If you are 'of me,' you most probably already know it deep down inside. And if you do not already know, you will know before you are through with this life."

His gaze returned to Yeshuah.

"I am of a mind to give instruction. What would you that I teach this night?"

Yeshuah sat up.

"You promised to instruct me in the Seventh Sleep."

Jesus hesitated. Then he nodded.

"That I did."

His gaze broadened to include the whole group once more.

"So that is what we shall do this night. There will be no more secret teachings, no more special instructions. I will teach all of you, any of you who desire to learn, anything that you want to learn. For we never know when our physical time together may come to an end. Use me while I am still amongst you. Question me without end, do not allow me to sleep for your questioning. And apply what I tell you with vigor."

He smiled.

"It is as the story I told to a multitude one day—the one about the wise and the foolish virgins. Be you as wise virgins. Trim and fuel your lamps on my teaching so that you will be ready for whatever comes."

* * *

Petros and the Boanerges arrived just before supper the following evening . . . in less than congenial spirits.

"Do you mean that you knew that Jesus was not to be found in any cave near to Masada?" raged Petros to Merovee.

He and the Boanerges had been brought into Cleopah's office for a private conference. Jesus still refused to embarrass Yeshuah by allowing the entire company to know the truth of what he had done.

"Yes, I knew. And yes, I misled you. I did have a vision of Jesus in a cave. Only not at Masada. But Petros, it was you who I had to send!" She both played on his vanity and told the truth. "You and the Boanerges. Yeshuah considers you three to be the foremost of the retainers of Jesus. In sending the most important followers, I allayed any suspicion that Yeshuah might have had that I knew where Jesus really was and was planning to rescue him."

Petros grunted, mollified.

"Still, you should have told me the truth," he said.

"Petros. Be reasonable. You are no actor. You do not know how to dissemble, bless your heart. If I had told you the truth, you would never have been able to carry off a deception. Indeed, you would probably have insisted upon going to rescue him."

"Well of course I would have! And I would have given Yeshuah a piece of my mind!"

"And so," said Jesus, "he would quickly have sent to have me hidden away more securely and there might have been no rescue possible. Petros, I would have reasoned just as did Merovee. I would have sent you to Masada. Would you then rant at me?"

Petros gave another grunt.

"Have you ever been down to that God-forsaken place? I fear I will not be able to eat for a week, my lungs and gut are so full of dust. And hot? I have never felt anything like it. Thanks be that we had asses to carry us, else I do not think I would still be alive. I could kill that Isaac! How soon do we leave this place, Jesus? Let us return to Galilee. I yearn for my cool, fresh lake."

His ill humor only increased the next day as he talked with the other disciples and learned of Yeshuah's speech in the Temple, and of the driving out of the moneychangers and animal sellers.

"I missed all the fun!" he moaned.

It was when he learned of the miraculous transfiguration of Jesus, witnessed by Merovee and Judah and Nathaniel—even by bar Tolmei—that his anger boiled over once more.

"We were shunted off on a chase after shadows," he told the Boanerges. "We, the first and the best of the disciples of Jesus, while lesser men, and that woman, were privileged to see such a wonder."

Zilpah sat with them, in a shady corner of the garden.

"As far as I am concerned, Jesus has treated the three of you shamefully."

"Were we not the first disciples?" Petros demanded angrily.

"No," said young Johannan. "it was Chandreah, then Merovee, Nathaniel, and Susannah . . . "

"Oh shut up," said Petros.

"Yes, shut up," said Zilpah. "As usual, Johannan, you do not know what you are talking about."

The young man's face changed color.

"I simply will not take this any longer, Mother. There are those who would say that you are the one who does not know what you are talking about."

"Sit down and be quiet," said Zilpah. "I will not repeat that again."

Johannan hesitated. Then he sat down.

Zilpah nodded.

"Tell us more of what Yeshuah offered to you as you talked together just before the birth, Petros."

"I am not sure I want to have anything to do with Yeshuah now. The trick he played on Jesus—on all of us, was unforgivable."

For Petros was not one to keep a confidence. He had freely told all who would listen about the abduction of Jesus.

"Do not be a stiff-necked fool," said Zilpah. "It becomes increasingly clear to me that Yeshuah is the man to follow. He is making all the moves. He it is who aims to be the Messiah."

"But I am not sure that he is the Messiah!"

"Think you that the Messiah came out of the womb with a tablet affixed to his bottom saying 'Messiah'? The Messiah will be the man with the nerve to make himself so. Can you not see that? Jesus is a nice man, yes, do not get me wrong, I like Jesus. But he is totally useless with his prattle of the Kingdom of God being nothing but a state of mind. How can you expect a man with such ideas to be the leader that we need? Think you God would choose a do-nothing pacifist to establish his Kingdom on Earth?"

"Jesus is very good with a bow," muttered Johannan.

"It will take more than a bow to oust the Romans," said Zilpah. "Petros. Be sensible. The time to make the proper decision is now. God will honor those who choose rightly, who support the man who has the talent to make himself the Messiah. I say that that man is Yeshuah Christos. I say that we ought all to approach him and pledge him our support. I say that we ought to persuade him to return to Jerusalem for the Passover.

"You did not see him in the Court of the Gentiles, Petros. He was magnificent. And he taught there so that even we women could hear. The entire populace is behind him now. They believe that he is the Messiah and they expect him to make his move.

"How many Roman troops are there in the city? Six, seven, eight hundred? What would it matter if there were a thousand? By the day of the Passover there will be several *hundred* thousand of us. We can overthrow the Romans before they know what has hit them."

"What would happen to Procula and her husband in that case?" mused young Johannan.

"Johannan! We are dealing here with the establishment of God's Kingdom! Procula and Pilatus are Gentiles. They are sinners and of no account."

Zilpah gritted her teeth.

"Oh, that I had been born a man! I would show you how to act. We must move! Now! While Yeshuah has an army, ready-made and expectant, awaiting him in his capitol. We can travel back secretly and hide ourselves in your father's Jerusalem house while we alert the populace. Then strike! We have only to take the city and prove ourselves to God—and he will arrive with his legions of angels and our nation will be invincible forevermore.

"And you three will be the leaders of the Kingdom after only Yeshuah. Think of it. The greatest of greatness can shortly be yours, if only you will reach out and grasp it. Perhaps God will be so impressed with your initiative that he will eventually give you kingdoms of your own to rule.

"Now, Petros, as to the details of our bargain . . . you say that Yeshuah has already offered you first place beside him in the Kingdom."

Petros hesitated. Zilpah had just voiced the thoughts that had been his own that day beside the tomb at bar Jeremiah. Once again, he was impressed by the very good sense of those thoughts.

"Yes. First place."

Zilpah made a snuffling sound.

"Well, I suppose that is as it should be, you were before my boys. On which side of his throne is your seat to be?"

"I did not think to ask. The right, I suppose."

"Then I must have a firm promise from Yeshuah that Jacob will be on his left, with Johannan just to Jacob's left."

"Can I not be just to the right of Petros?" said Johannan.

"Quiet! Those must be their seats in the earthly as well as the heavenly kingdoms, Petros. Those must be their places for all of eternity, they must never be supplanted."

"We can probably get that promise," said Petros.

"We must have it if my boys are to join him. Oh, and I must have a place close to the throne as well. I do not care where, but I must be close. After we have made our bargain with Yeshuah, we will approach some of the others for support. Certainly his own brothers will be with him . . . "

"Except Judah, of course," said Jacob. "Judah has became a man of Jesus through and through."

"I would not be that sure," said Zilpah. "Blood sticks together in times of testing."

"Zilpah," said Petros, "there is a problem that you do not seem to understand."

"What, that business about Yeshuah wanting to get crucified? Do not be a chicken brain, Petros, of course that is not what he intends. Even if it is, I can talk him out of it. I will speak with him as soon as he wakes."

For Yeshuah had been sleeping as though dead since last evening's teaching sessions.

Judah slept beside him, with Nathaniel and Susannah and Johannah. And Merovee, for Ben's wife was nursing a new baby and had plenty of milk for Agapo.

The Seventh Sleep, they called it. Many of the others had tried it, but only those six had finally been able to make their heartbeat and breathing seem to cease, to turn white as shrouds, and to resist any efforts to wake them.

How strange they all looked, lined up on the floor of a guest chamber like six corpses. Corpses. Yet they would wake.

Some of the disciples were now speculating that Lazarus had not been dead at all when he had been laid in the tomb—that he, too, had but slept this Seventh Sleep.

A good trick, thought Zilpah, though she could not see what use there was in it.

While, at the moment, it was a distinct nuisance! It made it impossible to confer with Yeshuah. And time was wasting . . . not much more than a week to the Passover.

Ah well, Jesus had said that he would wake the six of them this evening if they did not awaken themselves before then.

She flexed her shoulders and stretched.

Queen Meraiah would of course be titular first lady of the earthly kingdom. But Meraiah was an old woman and would soon be gone. She, Zilpah, was in her prime.

It was she who would be the real head woman of the kingdom. It would be to Zilpah that supplicants came, craving her indulgence, bringing gifts, begging that she intercede with her sons or Petros, or with even the Messiah.

She chuckled a deep, angry chuckle. Even her husband, the Zebedee, would come crawling to her . . . especially after she had ruined him, helped to drive out the Romans, from whom he derived most of his fortune.

Ah, the power she would wield. Sweet, succulent power.

* * *

Jesus in fact awakened all six of the "corpses" before suppertime. Truth to tell, he had resented Merovee's absence. He had hesitated even to let her try the sleep, and to waste their precious waking moments together. Yet he had wanted her to master the technique while still he had a chance to supervise.

Of all six, Johannah was the most difficult to call back.

"I was so happy there," she told him. "I wanted to stay. I could have stayed, could I not. I was 'Free' to do that."

"The choice to return or not was, indeed, yours, Free."

"Yes," she said thoughtfully. "But *you* called. To *me*. You *needed* me to return, did you not, my Jesus. So I let you raise me. I accepted life anew. Freely, I accepted the responsibility of that new life. Now, in all the days left to me, I will do what you need me to do. I will devote myself to giving to others the gift of what you have taught to us."

Jesus embraced her.

"Sister. You lift my spirits. You remind me that, even if I leave only a handful such as yourself, I should count my effort as having been a success. For I can be certain that the truth of what I have taught will survive, find nurture, and grow in more and more hearts such as yours . . . until the next great call from the species, when my entity shall be happy for me to make a major appearance once again. And, again, I will call, to all of my beloved sisters and brothers—with me now or yet to be born and taught my truths—to come into that time period with me. Together, then, we will teach, and assist Humankind to its next level of evolution."

After dinner he proceeded placidly with his teaching. Yet he was aware then, and even more so the next day, of the currents beginning to swirl about him, of a growing number of whispering groups and thoughtful faces.

The disciples were choosing sides, weighing his teachings, his goals, his performances against those of Yeshuah.

The ring-leaders were obvious. Petros steadfastly refused to meet his eyes. The Boanerges blushed crimson whenever he glanced their way. While Zilpah looked like a cat that had just had a fish.

It mattered not, as long he could keep Yeshuah at his side . . . as long as he could keep teaching that wonderfully talented soul. Who knew which word, which phrase, might tip the balance, show Yeshuah his error, and bring him toward his full greatness? He, Jesus, must just keep on planting his seeds, in Yeshuah and all the others.

Yet, after waking from his sleep, Yeshuah began to slip away from Jesus, to absent himself from the teachings, to stroll in the gardens with this one and that, speaking earnestly, in low tones.

Jesus watched sadly. Had that been the only reason why Yeshuah had so readily agreed to accompany Jesus north? Only to learn the Seventh Sleep?

It had indeed been one of the reasons, and perhaps the most important one. The ability to put himself into the Seventh Sleep was crucial to Yeshuah's burgeoning plans. Now all was accomplished. Along with the obnoxious Zilpah, he agreed that it was time for the man who would be the Messiah to make his move.

Ah, how he abhorred that woman. Yet he needed her. And her mewling sons.

There was no reason to delay, while there was every reason to go ahead. Every new pilgrim reaching Jerusalem was hearing the stories, about the raising of Lazarus, about the manner in which he, Yeshuah, had confounded the scribes and Pharisees in the Temple court, about his rout of the moneychangers and animal sellers. All of Jerusalem, from pilgrim to High Priest, was watching and waiting, asking, "Will he come? Will he dare to show himself in Jerusalem at the Passover?"

To fail them—pilgrim or High Priest—would be to declare himself no Messiah at all. In their disappointment, the pilgrims would turn away. They would forget him, perhaps even revile him. Never again would he have their enthusiasm and full support. While the High Priest, in his relief, would also lose interest. He would consider Yeshuah a toothless lion, not even worth capturing and killing.

There must be a triumphal entrance into the city, exactly as Scripture foretold. The entrance of a conqueror—the Messiah, King of the Jews. The entrance must cause such an expectant tumult among the people that revolt would seem a certainty before the end of the festival. The rulers of the Temple must be driven to seize him at the first possible moment, to try him, turn him over to the Romans as a traitor to Caesar, and have him crucified.

Crucified.

His skin grew clammy now each time he thought of it. Up until now, it had all been abstract, almost a game, to lay his plans, consider each possibility, discover the way to turn the rulers of the Temple, and Pontius Pilatus, himself, into unwitting accomplices.

How many crucifixions had he attended? How many scourged and bloodied felons had he followed as they dragged their crosses through the streets of Jerusalem, or Caesarea, Joppa, Akko, Jericho, anywhere where there were Romans and their tribunals.

How many times, and with what cold, analytical eyes, had he watched the nails being driven into the wrists of how many struggling, screaming men? Then into the feet.

How patiently he had watched, to see how long it took them to die, how severe was the pain, and at what points in the long ordeal was it the worst?

Did the pain finally turn to numbness?

How much blood was actually lost?

Did the victims faint? Did they thirst?

He knew it all.

And he had carefully planned just how to make it happen to himself.

Yet it had somehow never really been real. Now it was. In only a little over a week it would be his flesh into which they drove those spikes, he who would be hung on some prominence outside the walls of Jerusalem.

Except that he would not die of the ordeal.

That is . . . if everything went as planned.

The timing of the entire operation must be perfect. It ordinarily took a healthy man about three days to die on his cross. But, when a Sabbath or festival day intervened, the suffering was cut short. Jewish Law forbade that a felon be left hanging upon sacred days. It demanded that the felon be taken down and buried before the sunset that began that festival.

In deference to this, the Romans had devised a way of killing a hanging man quickly. Throughout his ordeal, and painful as it might be, he was always able to support part of his body weight on his feet. To hasten death, the Romans simply broke both his legs. Unable then to support himself, his entire weight pressed down onto his lungs and he rapidly asphyxiated. The body was then removed from the cross, thrown into a rude grave, and it was over.

For a dozen years, Yeshuah had known that he must suffer on the cross. The prophecies were explicit when one knew what one was looking for.

'And one shall say to him, What are these wounds in your hands?'

'Like a lion they are at my hands and feet.'

Certainly these passages referred to the nails driven into the wrists and feet.

'I gave my back to the smitters.'

Surely this referred to the thirty-nine lashes administered before the felon was taken out to die.

'I hid not my face from shame and spitting.'

'Or from them that plucked off the hair.'

'They cast lots upon my vesture.'

The felon was given to the soldiers of the crucifixion squad before a hanging. They had him all to themselves in the guardroom, and were allowed to make sport of him, pluck out his beard, spit upon him, bash him, and play the game of "King," in which they cast lots for the privilege of "crowning" the "King" with a crown of thorns. The winner of the lot would also present the prisoner with his staff, and with his cloak for a royal robe. The soldiers would bow before him, giving mocking obeisance—then take him out to be killed.

'I am poured out like water, and my bones are out of joint, my heart is like wax, it is melted in the midst of my bowels.'

The terrible downward hanging, the arms pulled from their sockets. What could be more clear?

'For my thirst they gave me vinegar to drink.'

Vinegar was the drink offered to a man hanging upon the cross, in a soaked sponge that was held up to the man, and on which he was meant to suck.

'They shall look upon me whom they have pierced and they shall mourn.'

Oh yes. The whole world would mourn this particular hanged man.

He had been some time in figuring out how to undergo the ordeal and still survive. For survive he must.

Because the Messiah was meant only to suffer, not die, on the cross.

'After two days will he revive us, and on the third day he will raise us up and we shall live in his sight.'

'Though I walk in the midst of trouble, you will revive me, you will stretch forth your hand against the wrath of my enemies, and your right hand will save me. The Lord will perfect that which concerns me.'

'For you will not leave my soul in the grave, neither will you suffer your holy one to see corruption. You will show me the path of life.'

'God shall redeem my soul from the grasp of the grave.'

The Lord would perfect all that concerned him. He had long ago begun to trust that, and to watch and patiently wait for the Lord to show him all the means by which he could suffer but not die, be revived on the third day, then take command of the Jewish people and institute the Kingdom of God.

Which was one of the ways he had known that Jesus was an angel sent by God. Jesus had provided all those means.

Yeshuah needed now only to enlist his most important accomplice.

"You swore a solemn oath to me once, my son."

Judah walked beside him, along a garden path. The young man's head was bent, his heart had seemed to stop. He had hoped that Yeshuah had forgotten—or would never call in—the debt that was owed him.

He should have known better. He must now pay the price.

"I have forgiven you your deviation from my service in these last months, Judah, for I understand your love of Jesus and I respect your right to your own beliefs. But I now call upon you to lend me your services and make good your vow. You swore to me in Chorazin that you would uphold me in all that I do or say and obey my will without question."

Judah nodded.

"I did so swear."

"My time is accomplished. Soon I go to Jerusalem to suffer upon the cross, to rise from my grave on the third day, to demonstrate that all prophecies are complete in me, and to institute God's Kingdom on Earth. I need you to carry out certain duties which will make this all possible."

"You are insane."

"Not at all. Will you honor your pledge to me?"

Judah hesitated. To the people of The Law, an oath was more binding than chains. A man who did not keep his oath was outcast . . . he might just as well be dead.

Yet, instead of demanding, Yeshuah asked. Perhaps he, too, had been touched by the teaching of Jesus, that proclaimed it a wrong either to require or to make an oath. Perhaps Yeshuah could still be bargained with.

"I will do nothing that would endanger Jesus and Merovee or any of those who have become our comrades. Including Pilatus and Procula and the princesses. Anything we do must include plans to protect these last."

"Of course, my son, I have thought of them. They shall be protected. While, by helping me, you shall be saving Jesus and our comrades. Once all is completed with success, any danger to any of them shall be a thing of the past. Once I declare myself the Messiah, Jesus shall pale to insignificance in the minds of both the people and of the authorities. He shall be left to teach as he wishes, and to live to a great old age, content with his beloved Merovee.

"Indeed . . . " Yeshuah's voice was soft. There was almost a hint of moisture at the eyes. "He and she shall be among the most honored of my kingdom.

"Please believe me, Judah. I care as fervently as do you for the safety of Jesus and his people. That is one of the reasons why I so readily agreed to accompany him to this place. I wanted to get them, and him, out of Bethany, away from Jerusalem, away from harm. I wished to lull Jesus into a sense of security about me, then slip away and have it all over and done with before ever he had a clew as to what I was, am, up to."

The man's sincerity was unmistakable. What he said was true.

"Once you were known as the Messiah," said Judah, "the authorities *would* no longer concern themselves with Jesus, would they."

Yeshuah did not answer the rhetorical statement.

Judah sighed.

"What do you want me to do?"

"You will stick by your oath no matter what I ask?"

"As long as you keep to your own promise of safety for our friends."

"Then listen carefully. For I will want you to slip away this very night."

Judah listened, for the rest of the day, to every detail of Yeshuah's astonishing plan.

It *was* insane.

It was so insane that it might just work.

Was it possible? Judah glanced often at his brother's face, his old awe—and love—returning.

What sort of man was this? To dream such a dream in the first place. To conceive of such a . . . magnificent enterprise. Who but one inspired from above could have come up with this plan?

Was Yeshuah the Messiah? *Was* God lighting his path?

A confusion crept into the mind of Judah as Yeshuah revived the old spell. Deep within, repressed Zealot sentiments stirred.

Of *course* the plan could work. Certainly the Passover throngs could overpower the few Roman troops in Jerusalem. After that victory, there would be nothing in the world which could stop those throngs. Under the banner of the Messiah, their risen Lord, in whom all prophecies were fulfilled, they would sweep through all of Palestine, adding to their number as they went. They would drive the Romans right into the sea.

Surely, then, the rest of the promise of God would come to pass. God, himself, would arrive and institute the Kingdom on Earth. There could be no Roman retaliation. Tiberius could hurl every legion of his empire at their shores, and those legions would break as glass on stone.

It might work. It might.

But if it did not . . .

And, according to Jesus, there would be no Kingdom of God on Earth, or in Heaven. The Kingdom was within, a state of mind, individually achieved by each in his or her own time. And God was not some person-like creature who would suddenly arrive from out of the sky.

"Yeshuah, something that bothers me . . . your whole plan is based on a lie. You plan to lie to people, to make them believe that you actually died, and were raised from the dead. Is that fair?"

"Was it fair that Jacob stole Esau's birthright by lying to his blind old father? Yet God applauded Jacob's deed and rewarded him above all men. It is not for us to question God's methods, my son. I know that I am the Messiah and I know that I am commanded by God to do these things. That is good enough for me. It ought to be good enough for you."

"Jesus would say that what you intend to do is wrong. He would say that the end never justifies the means. Not ever. He would say that, by beginning with a lie, you set in motion a wrong that will only become more wrong the farther it travels."

"I know what Jesus would say. But you have sworn to obey me."

" . . . Yes. What of your wounds, Yeshuah? They will be grievous. Even if the plan does work, and you do survive, you might never be able to walk again."

Yeshuah laughed outright.

"My silly Judah. Myself a healer and surrounded by healers, but you seriously worry for my injuries?

"'Come, and let us return to the Lord, for he hath torn, and he will heal us, he has smitten, and he will bind us up.'

"Stop questioning, Judah. It is all there in the prophecies. For any question that you can ask, I will give you God's answer. Now do you have it all straight? You understand it all?"

"I fear that I do."

"Then as soon as you are able to be off, be off. I will make excuses for your absence and send our brothers off one at a time in the next days so that they may complete their own tasks."

Yeshuah put his hands onto the shoulders of Judah.

"Judah, Petros and the Boanerges have asked for special favors in the Kingdom. What will you ask for yourself?"

"I want nothing."

"Come. Ask me now. I will grant it."

Slowly, Judah raised his eyes.

"All right. I will ask. The moment that I have accomplished all that is required to secure your crucifixion and 'resurrection,' I wish to be excused from my vow and service to you. Forever. I wish to be left free to return to Jesus."

Yeshuah nodded. His eyes were sad, his voice gentle.

"I expected as much. So be it." He dropped his hands. "God be with you, my son."

With not another word or glance, he strode away.

Judah watched after him, wondering.

How could he be so cool? The man had just arranged for his own mutilation! How could such courage and dedication exist?

It was a courage which he, Judah, would certainly never have.

While, within his own self as he walked away, Yeshuah was saying . . .

'And so it is done. The juggernaut is in motion and cannot in honor be halted. Thank you, Father. Thank you for getting me through it. For I felt my heart growing faint, my flesh beginning to quake in fear.'

He wiped a sheen of perspiration from his brow. As he took his hand away, he seemed to see a great black spike driven through the wrist.

He shuddered and hastened on, to the room where Jesus sat teaching. It would calm his spirit to listen to Jesus for a while.

His dear angel Jesus, sent from God.

How fortunate was Judah to be only a man, not the Messiah.

How Yeshuah would have liked to become Judah so that, in the end, he, too, could return to Jesus.

* * *

Judah arrived at the home of Jesus in Bethlehem at sunrise of the following day. He asked to speak privately with Joseph bar Ramathea and was conducted by that man to a private chamber.

"Apollo," said Judah without preamble, "you want to see your son Jesus safe—and his family and yours?"

"It is my fondest desire."

"My brother Yeshuah can make that happen. He has sent me to secure your aid."

"What is his plan and what must I do?"

"I must have your promise that, even should you refuse to help us, you will not reveal our design to our enemies, neither will you try to stop us."

Joseph hesitated.

"I would not be here myself," prompted Judah, "did I not believe that Yeshuah's plan, succeed or fail, will leave Jesus free and safe, at least for a while."

"All right. Even if I refuse to help you, I will not reveal the plan to your enemies or try to stop you."

"Early on the morning two days before Passover," began Judah without further ado, "my brother Yeshuah will arrive in Bethphage. There, by means that I and my other brothers will have arranged, he will be provided with the colt of an ass. He will ride the colt into Jerusalem and to the Temple."

"Deliver himself into the hands of the rulers? It is suicidal! Surely they will devise a means and arrest him immediately."

"He will be surrounded by adoring crowds, the rulers will not touch him. Know you not the prophecy of Zacariah, that the Son of Man will come riding upon an ass, even the colt of an ass? The Bethphage road will be thronged with Galilean pilgrims heading for Jerusalem. They will grasp the significance of his gesture and know that it is his open declaration . . . that he is the Messiah."

Joseph jumped to his feet.

"I am beginning to wish I had never even heard that title!"

"You might as well wish that you had never been born for all the good it will do you. The Messiah is a fact of our lives in—as your son would put it—this time and place, and matters are coming to a head whether you or I like it or not. We might as well bring them to the head that we want, in such a way that we are all maintained in safety. Does that not make sense?"

Joseph sat back down.

"Go on."

"My brother will proceed into Jerusalem in triumph, well guarded by crowds hailing him as the Messiah. He will ride straight to the Temple and there he will spend the day in teaching and healing. In the evening, again guarded by crowds, he will withdraw out of the city to a place that need not concern you."

"Why?"

"The less that each person who helps in this plan knows about anything other than his own little part, the better."

"That makes sense."

"My brother will also return to the Temple the following day. His words will grow ever more inflammatory. The rulers will discover the courage not only to arrest him, but to put him to death during this Passover. We will enable them to do so."

Joseph sat quietly, a quizzical little smile upon his lips.

"I must have misunderstood you," he said at last.

"You understood perfectly."

Joseph shook his head.

"What is your brother up to, Judah? You, yourself, just pointed out to me that Yeshuah will be protected by the sympathies of the mob. The rulers might want to arrest him. They might long to put him to death. But they would not dare to seize him at this particular time. The only means at their disposal is stoning. They could never convince so many as a handful of men, even with pay, to drag him out of the Temple and stone him in front of the Passover crowds. Why, any who tried would, themselves, be stoned. People could even turn against the rulers and stone *them*.

"And do not think that Annas and his bunch do not know it. Believe me, Judah, I know. My servants have been circulating around the Temple courts continually for the last days, with their ears wide open. Fully half of the people are already calling Yeshuah the Messiah. The way he has captured their imagination is quite beyond belief."

"We are aware of all that, Joseph. Yet the rulers will have my brother killed. They will turn him over to the Romans and he will be crucified."

Again Joseph just sat.

"What madness is this?" he finally said.

"After his inflammatory speeches, still accompanied by crowds, my brother will again withdraw from the Temple to a place outside the city. But that will be the night of the Passover, so that the crowds will finally disperse and go their own ways to their tents or lodgings to celebrate the Passover. My brother and his followers will celebrate the Passover as well. Then he will remove himself to a lonely, appointed spot where, without interference, the minions of the High Priest can arrest him and take him to the High Priest."

"But how will they know where to find him?"

"Again, this is information that need not concern you. He will be taken to the High Priest, tried, found deserving of death on religious grounds . . . "

"Tried? In the middle of the night? After the Passover meal? They would need the Sanhedrin for a trial. The Sanhedrin is not allowed to meet at night, and certainly not on Passover night."

"What better time to do the deed, to have it all accomplished while everyone is indoors, observing the holiday? All those crowds who, in daylight, and if they knew, would protect him. Who would expect Annas to make his move on Passover night? No one. For that reason, it is the very time when they shall move."

"But they cannot do that! It is not legal, Judah,"

"Think you that Annas and Caiaphas will care for legalities? They will do the deed and deal with excuses later. Their continuance in power will be at stake. They will have had it explained to them most fully that my brother intends to lead an immediate revolt that will put them, as well as Rome, out of business. They will have a sufficient number of the Sanhedrin—those whom they can trust—ready and waiting to meet in secret session during the night.

"It will be done, Joseph. Believe me. And then, at the first hour when it is respectable to wake Pilatus, Yeshuah will be taken to the Antonia and there tried for treason. A man who calls himself King of the Jews—when Caesar is our only king. A man who fully intends to instigate a revolt against Caesar. He will be found guilty and he will then be taken out and crucified. The blame will fall on the Romans, not the High Priest. The deed will freshly enrage the populace against Rome."

"Has no one ever bothered to tell your brother that dead men find it difficult to lead revolts?"

"He will not die on the cross."

"Do not be ridiculous. No one survives the cross."

"Not without friends. Yeshuah has friends. Consider this closely, Joseph.

"The timing of the Passover is perfect. The feast will be held on Thursday evening. Yeshuah will be arrested and given the religious trial by the Sanhedrin during the night, gotten to Pilatus on charges of treason at about dawn on Friday. Even with all haste, they cannot get him onto the cross before late morning. Which means he will not be left hanging for days until he dies. So that they can have him buried before the Sabbath, he will be taken down about an hour before sunset."

"Of course. But before they do that they will have broken his legs and he will have suffocated."

"They will not break his legs. Now listen, Joseph. He will be up there six or seven hours at the most. Yeshuah is strong and healthy, he can endure that. But he will appear to die well before sunset. It will not be the first time that a man's heart has failed him and he has died more rapidly than others. They will suspect nothing. Thinking him dead, they will not bother to break his legs."

"How will he feign death so convincingly?"

"The same way that Lazarus appeared to be dead. There will be a pain-deadening drug in the vinegar from the sponge, administered to him at regular intervals so that his mind will be free of agony and he can apply the concentration necessary to achieve the Seventh Sleep. As a last resort, in case he is unable to do it, there will be a sleeping draught that can be given him on the sponge."

"Who is going to give him these drugs?"

"Simon the Cyrenean physician, I hope."

Joseph's head had not ceased its shaking from side to side for many long minutes. He shook it even harder now.

"Judah, it cannot work! So very much could go wrong. And even if Yeshuah does fool them—even if they do take him down without breaking his legs, they will then put him in a grave and shovel him over with dirt and he will suffocate anyway."

"According to Jesus, a man in the sleep can be buried alive and still survive. The ascetics and holy men of India often have themselves buried for days as part of their training. It would only be necessary to cover his face in such a way that dirt would not clog his mouth or nostrils. Respiration is so very slow in the sleep, you see, so little air is needed, that the air in the new loose soil above him would suffice till he was dug up by his friends after darkness."

"Dig him up? On the Sabbath? If you were caught you would, yourselves, be arrested and stoned to death the following day."

"Which is one reason why we can not allow him to be buried, we can not chance that discovery.

"And this is where you come in. We need him to be put into a tomb, above ground. We have heard of your garden tomb near the northwest wall, at the Place of the Skull. We will see to it that he is crucified in that place, and the tomb will thus be right at hand. Will you allow us to use your tomb, Joseph?"

"It is no longer mine to allow. I am sorry, Judah. I sold the garden tomb."

For the first time, the air left Judah's sails.

"Oh," he said blankly.

"Thinking that we might have to flee the land, I have been selling a few things here and there, and my friend Nicodemus . . . "

"Nicodemus? Friend? He is the new owner? Oh well. That can be arranged then." He grew thoughtful. "Actually, this is an excellent turn of events. Nicodemus. It is perfect. So," he said, resuming his pace. "Yeshuah will be crucified at the Place of the Skull . . . "

"How can you arrange that exact place of the execution? They have been hanging them in the Valley of the Tanners of late."

"Yes, as an example to the ruffians there. Zealots particularly," he said ruefully. "The Valley of the Tanners is a spot calculated to draw attention to an execution. But neither the priests nor the Romans are going to want attention drawn to this execution. They are going to want it over quickly and quietly, as far from public view as possible. The same timing that will work for us will work for the priests.

"It will take most of Friday for people to realize what has happened, the priests will reason. So that, by the time that the people do catch on, their Messiah will be dead and buried. Any threat of a mob demonstration will be nipped in the bud by the arrival of the Sabbath and the necessity to sit down and be quiet for twenty-four hours. By the time that the Sabbath is over, the priests will think, Immediate angers will have dissipated and the pilgrims will be wanting to start out on their return journeys to home. The crisis will have passed. On top of that, it will be the Romans being blamed for the killing. Before any information as to the Temple's role gains circulation, the crowds will have dispersed, time will have passed, crops will need harvesting . . . and people will forget. As they always do. So the priests will tell themselves."

"My God. Your brother has thought this out well."

"Very well. And lest the priests be too dense to figure it all out for themselves, the plan will be supplied *to* them. So, Joseph, a crucifixion in a private tomb garden—on the northwest, away from the Temple and most of the pilgrim encampments—will be arranged."

Joseph sat thinking.

"How do you intend to get around The Law requiring that felons be put into an earthen grave? Assuming that all goes as your brother has planned, how does he intend that the Romans shall be persuaded to allow the use of the tomb?"

"You are going to go to Pilatus and ask that the body be handed over to you."

"I am?" Joseph had given up protesting. Numbness was setting in.

"Pilatus is not going to be happy about this execution in the first place, as well you know, Joseph. He does not know Yeshuah that well—I doubt if they have exchanged two words on the occasions when Pilatus visited bar Jeremiah. But Procula knows him. In the way of that good woman, she loves him. She will be distraught over the matter, and her word means much to Pilatus. It will be the most natural thing in the world for you, as friend of both Yeshuah and Procula, as the father of Jesus, the absent friend of Pilatus, and as a member of the Sanhedrin and ranking Prince of Judah, to go to Procula the moment that Yeshuah is 'dead,' and humbly ask her to go with you to Pilatus and get him to grant this one concession—that you be allowed to take the body and inter it in your own tomb that just happens to be in the place where he was crucified."

Joseph sighed. It would work. Dear, sweet Procula would argue the case for him, while Pilatus would be relieved to be able to make some gesture of good will.

"Surely, though, the Temple authorities would become alarmed at my intervention and seek to stop me from taking the body."

Judah smiled.

"What Temple authorities? Joseph, the moment they have secured a conviction, every man responsible for the deed will scurry for cover. Not one of them will want to be seen anywhere near Pilatus or the place of execution, and certainly not around a dead body or burial! Goodness me, they would defile their holy selves for the Sabbath.

"Neither will they send their spies to watch. The faces of those spies are well-known. People would notice and comment.

"No. The culprits will have no cause to think other than that the execution will be carried out with the usual Roman efficiency. They will go on about their businesses leaving us to our businesses."

"And what is our business, Judah? What is the point of this hideous deception?"

"Know you not the prophecy concerning the Messiah? The 'Suffering Just One.' The kings of the Earth set themselves against him, and the rulers take counsel together against him. He is despised and rejected, and led like a lamb to the slaughter. He is scourged, his flesh cruelly tortured. He is dead and buried. But the grave will not contain him. On the third day he will rise from the dead and lead his people in the establishment of the Kingdom of God on Earth.

"Joseph, every well-known prophecy concerning the Messiah will be fulfilled. If all goes according to plan, and my brother emerges from that tomb on the third day alive and well, and presents himself to the people . . . no power on Earth, not even the Romans, will be able to stop him and our people from establishing the Kingdom."

Joseph lowered his face to his hands and was silent for a long time.

"Does Joshuah know about this?" he asked at last.

"Of course not. The point is to keep him ignorant and safe at Mount Ephraim until it is accomplished. And Joseph, as you see, your son shall be safe. If Yeshuah succeeds, the Annians will be deposed and just men, who are subservient to my brother—who would make Jesus one of the most honored men in the land—will rule in their place.

"While, if things go wrong—if Yeshuah should die, still, unless Jesus then proclaimed his own self as the Messiah, and proceeded to make himself prominent and threaten rebellion, the rulers would forget to pursue him."

Judah had presented the matter with confidence and aplomb, but now there was anxiety in his gaze.

"Can we count on you, Joseph?"

Joseph rose, walked slowly to the door of the room and stood gazing out at the peace of his courtyard.

"What will happen if I say no?"

"It will be more difficult, but we will still do it. Since you have given your promise to tell no one, and not to try to stop us, we would use the garden and the tomb in any wise. Now that Nicodemus has been drawn into this, and I must go to speak with him, I could work everything out with him. I guess I, myself, would have to go to Procula and Pilatus and beg the body . . . or perhaps Nicodemus would do it."

"You should not involve Nicodemus in this dangerous matter."

"Fate has already involved him, Joseph. And what is the danger? If the scheme succeeds, all your worries will be over. If it fails . . . well then, we will simply have a dead Messiah on our hands, all decently entombed. And who will be the wiser?"

Joseph turned back.

"You sound so cool about that last possibility."

"If my brother can become the expected Messiah, then he *is* the expected Messiah, and the whole world will be better for it. If he fails and dies, then he is not the expected Messiah. The world will still be better for it.

"In either case, as soon as I have discharged the debt of service that I owe to him, I will run back to sit at the feet of Jesus, and there I will happily stay."

Joseph felt the sting of tears. What an unhappy young man this was. To be sent to arrange this terrible thing, to have his love and loyalty so cruelly used.

"You will do this with or without me then."

"Those are my orders."

"What of Pilatus and Procula and the Herodians if the insurrection succeeds?"

"I had the same concerns. Yeshuah has great adoration for Procula and would never see her harmed, nor Pilatus for her sake. The moment we are sure that Yeshuah has survived and will be fit to lead the rebellion, we will devise a means to hide them and then to spirit them to safety outside of Palestine. We will do this by force if necessary. The same for Salome and Herodias. Yeshuah has given his word. You may rely upon it."

"Pray God that Yeshuah could so control matters. Well . . . all right. I will help. As you have said, in a few days, after the Sabbath, we will know the truth of the matter one way or the other. Perhaps it *is* best to bring the matter to a head. Insecurity and fear is a terrible thing to live with. I have carried it on my back too long already."

Within himself, Joseph bar Ramathea then silently prayed . . .

'God of my son Joshuah. No. Jesus. Grant that I have made the right choice.'

* * *

They went to Nicodemus together. Much the same story was told, many of the same questions were asked. But now the weight of bar Ramathea was behind Judah's persuasion.

Officially, Joseph and Nicodemus were as unalike in religious observance and belief as a sheep was from a goat. Joseph, the Sadducee, officially disbelieved in any afterlife other than a shadowy existence in the shades of Sheol. He did not officially believe in reward or punishment for worldly deeds, in a resurrection, a Messiah, or in a heavenly or earthly Kingdom. Man was to live for the moment, not for future promises.

Those were the official tenets of the ruling party that counted him a member. They were not necessarily Joseph's tenets.

But what were his tenets? He realized that day that he did not know. He realized that he had spent his life hiding from tenets, adroitly sidestepping commitment. Now here he was, up to his skullcap in a plot to create a resurrected Messiah, overthrow Rome, and institute the Kingdom of God on Earth.

On the other hand, Nicodemus the Pharisee had not a doubt as to what he, himself, believed. Nicodemus had spent his life accepting commitment. He believed in the resurrection of the dead on a Day of Judgment. He believed in Heaven and Hell and reward and punishment. He believed that the Messiah would be sent, and that God's Kingdom would be instituted both on Earth and in Heaven.

Now here came two men asking him to help make it all happen.

If Nicodemus had not been present the day that Yeshuah spoke in the Court of the Gentiles and cleansed that court of its moneychangers and animal sellers—if he had not later spoken with Jesus—he would have dismissed the two men out of hand.

But he had witnessed the magic of Yeshuah . . . Christos on his code list. He knew the power of the man.

And he had talked with Jesus about his cowardice in regard to the Messiah.

Why should Yeshuah not be the Messiah. Why not?

Before him stood the father of the man whom he had always believed would be that messiah . . . but which man had disclaimed such a role, saying, 'Each man must finally come to understand that the Messiah is his own self. Each man must finally lead his own self out of the mess into which he has gotten himself. No one else can do it for him.'

And Jesus had challenged him.

'You say you believe in the coming of the Messiah, yet, if any man declares himself to be that messiah, you ask him to go away. Explain that to me, Nicodemus.'

Nicodemus had thought long and hard on the words of Jesus, Since that meeting, his prayers had not ceased. He had prayed for guidance, so that he would know what to do in the crisis that, somehow, he knew must come—and soon—a crisis in which he would be deeply involved.

He had no hesitation now. He would not run from his destiny, or turn a coward's back. In a way, Nicodemus would become his own messiah in order to aid *the* Messiah.

Good heavens. The man was ready to sacrifice himself on the cross in order to be the Messiah! Who could turn away from such courage, such daring? The man had spent his entire life studying upon how to unite the erring, turbulent, and confused children of Israel into a veritable band of angels.

What other man had bothered?

The children of Israel a band of angels. Perhaps, Nicodemus suddenly thought, that was the true meaning of the prophecy anyway. Perhaps God would not come out of the heavens with angels at his back to fight the Romans and establish the Kingdom. Perhaps the angels would be there ahead of God, waiting right here on earth, listening for God in their hearts, ready to obey his instructions and institute the Kingdom.

All because of a man like Yeshuah.

If Yeshuah would give his hands and feet to the nails, chance a felon's death and an unsanctified burial, Nicodemus would undertake to support him in whatever way he could. If his choice was wrong, Nicodemus was very sure that God would understand.

* * *

Judah moved through the next two-and-a-half days like a sleepwalker. It was all happening so easily, as in a dream . . . of which Nicodemus was now a part. Judah even began to wonder whether Yeshuah was right—that God *was* directing the operation. How else to explain the smoothness with which everything went?

The next most important man after Joseph and Nicodemus had been Simon of Cyrene, whom Judah found in his lodging in the Upper City late in the afternoon, after hours of planning with Nicodemus and Joseph.

With Simon, Judah had expected to be on shakier footing. The Cyrenean had no cause to risk his neck. He had only passing loyalty to Jesus and none to Yeshuah. He was not a Palestinian, he had come merely to pass some time with his sons and to see some old great-uncles, probably for the last time. His stay had been prolonged at first in giving medical aid to those failing uncles, then by his involvement in the birth of Agapo, now by the request of Jesus that he tarry in Jerusalem to give aid if it were needed.

Why should he be expected to agree to help Yeshuah in this mad scheme?

The saving grace was that Simon of Cyrene was more than a physician. He was a scientist, never able to keep up with his own curiosity, always eager for a willing body on which to experiment.

"Something strong enough to dull the agony of crucifixion, but which will still leave him clear-minded enough to put himself into this sleep," he mused, pacing to and fro, eyes bright with interest. "Something that will not make him lethargic, or stupid, so that the soldiers will not suspect a drug."

"A certain amount of stupidity might be expected," offered Judah. "The felons are given thirty-nine lashes while still at the Antonia. Those lashes alone could kill some men. Then they must endure the game of 'King' that the soldiers play. I understand that, depending on the mood of the mockers that day, it can be brutal. Then the felon drags his own crossbar to the site of the execution. In the case of Yeshuah, however, he will be dragging an entire cross . . . for the Place of the Skull in no longer used, and there are no uprights in place there. That cross will weigh more than most men. Then will come the nailing, and the hanging, with great loss of blood. I do not think that stupidity or lethargy would be found remarkable."

"True," said Simon thoughtfully. "And your brother is no doubt overestimating his own physical stamina. He has also not admitted to himself the toll that all of this will take upon his mental processes, plus you say that he has only done the sleep once."

"Yet Jesus remarked upon his precocity. Yeshuah did it on the very first try. It takes most students several tries, I, myself, included. My brother has astounding control of his mental powers, Simon. I could tell you stories which you would not believe, but which are quite true."

"Still he is no expert at the sleep. Neither is he an expert at being crucified. He will be up against an agony that he can imagine but never understand until it happens to him, and he could be in for a rude surprise, his powers quite gone.

"What I am thinking, Judah, is—it is very possible that a stimulant would be of more benefit to him than a drug."

"He says the vinegar works as a stimulant."

"To a certain extent, yes. But to achieve the concentration you tell me is needed for this sleep, one must be completely alert. The whole scheme fails if he cannot convincingly feign death, for, even with a sleeping draught, Judah, breathing continues—a rise and fall could be seen in the chest . . . on top of which, he might moan in his sleep, or cry out, especially when taken down, and when the nails are pulled out of his flesh."

"No. We need exactly the right drug to allow him to attain his sleep, for that sleep is the only thing that will make it look right."

"Lions' Fat?"

"No, not opium. Nor any of its derivatives neither. The alertness assumed by the user is an illusion. In reality, the processes and abilities are slowed and distorted."

Simon stopped his pacing.

"Judah. I do know of something that I think would work. I have always suspected its potency and yearned to test it upon an extreme case. Laserpitium radix."

"I have never heard of it."

"It is from the Silphium plant, which grows almost exclusively in my country. The plant and its juice were once Cyrenia's major export. Unfortunately, it was over-harvested. It is difficult to find nowadays and expensive when one does find it. I am sure, though, that, if I canvas all of the spice traders in the bazaar, I can gather a sufficient volume of the juice. I will need about a water jug full. That will cost dearly."

"Nicodemus will give you the funds. What is the juice used for?"

"Flavoring. It is highly popular among the wealthy of Rome and Athens. *Was* highly popular I should say, which is why it was harvested near to extinction. Only the extremely wealthy can afford it now. It is said that laserpitium, added to the food, makes a man wiser than he already is while also curing whatever ails him."

Simon's face took on the enthusiasm of a boy.

"I think there is good reason for these claims. The plant has properties which we have yet to understand. I have learned to boil the juice down to a concentrated gum. The strange thing is, that, while there is nothing observably different about the juice itself, this concentrate glows in the dark! I allow it to harden, then I cut it into little cakes. One can suck on one of these cakes for hours before it is gone."

"You have used them on patients?"

"And upon myself. I am prone to excruciating back pain at times. I usually carry them with me, but I have overstayed here in Palestine and have run out of them. I have not taken the time—or had the money—to make more. Would that I had had one to give Merovee for the birth."

"What do these cakes do for you?"

"They take away any pain or fatigue. At the same time, they make me able to think very well, and to accomplish excellent work in half the normal time. And the effect is not illusory as it is with Lions' Fat and its cousins. The work really gets done, better and quicker than without the laserpitium.

"Also, it has worked miracles in some of my patients, especially the old ones, whose minds have begun to wander and become childish. Those with the money to keep a supply of these little cakes to hand often return to their trades, seeming years younger.

"As I say, however, I have never tested the cakes upon anything as drastic as that which your brother contemplates."

"What is your opinion, though, Simon? Knowing how important this is . . . that there must be no miscalculation. Will this laserpitium concentrate do the job?"

"I would stake my life on it," said Simon. Then he smiled. "But that is no guarantee, so I hope that my life will not be forfeit should I be wrong."

Judah returned the smile and shook his head. Idly, he took a fig from a bowl on Simon's table and started to eat it.

Then he held it out, staring at it.

"Did you know that there is no such thing as a dead fig tree?"

"I shall file the information in that place in my mind where I keep other such impenetrable gems."

Judah looked up questioningly. Then he laughed.

"It is a long story." He ate the fig. "Well . . . my brother has empowered me to make his decisions for him. There will be precious little chance to confer with him, and that almost upon the eve of the deed."

"If I am to find a quantity of the juice and boil it down, I must set about the task immediately."

"What will be your plan then—for its use?"

"I must station myself outside the place in the Antonia Fortress where he will emerge, carrying his cross to the crucifixion.

"Oh, very importantly, Judah. Members of the Ladies' Society of Jerusalem—bless their hearts—when they learn of a crucifixion, some of them wait at that gate and offer drugs to the felons to deaden their pain. If any of these kind women are there, Yeshuah must refuse their offer to drug him.

"So. The Place of the Skull you say? Weakened by lashes, lugging the cross, it will take him about thirty minutes to get there . . . thirty minutes before the agony of the nails.

"It takes about twenty minutes for the cakes to take full effect. So he should stumble a great deal. Finally, about a third of the way, he should collapse entirely. I will rush forward to help him up, offering to carry his cross. As I do, I will contrive to slip one of the cakes into his mouth. When the nails are pounded in some twenty minutes later, we will know whether the cakes, alone, will carry him through. I will have other drugs with me—though, if I have to use them, as I told you, I think the plan will fail.

"It is, of course, necessary that I be the man who tends to the vinegar and sponge, and who offers it up to him. How do you intend to arrange that? Will Pilatus and Lucius be privy to this matter?"

Judah hesitated.

"To a limited extent," he said. "Pilatus can of course not be told that my brother intends to live and to lead a revolt against him. The plan is . . . . . . the plan is . . . "

He put his hands up to his face in sudden anguish.

"Oh Simon. The terrible thing my brother is making me to do. It is I who am to betray him. I am to go to the rulers, pretending to hate my brother and to want him dead, pretending to be worse than a viper, asking a bribe in order to betray him. It is I, then, who am to tell them of the best hour, and of the place where he will be alone and undefended. It is I who will lead them to that place so that they can arrest him. It is I who am to make sure that they think and act exactly as we want them to think and act."

He raised his face.

"After he is taken, I am to rush to the Antonia and beg an audience with Pilatus. I am to tell him that my brother has been seized, and will be brought to him for trial at sunrise. I will ask the boon that, if he is found guilty, I be allowed to find you and have you at the foot of the cross. I will admit quite honestly that I want you there to give my brother a drug for pain should it become unbearable."

"You have had more contact with Pilatus than I. Think you that he will agree?"

"Yes. He will be grateful for the warning of what the rulers are up to, and of how they plan to use him. But I will also offer him a bribe, using the silver with which the priests will have bribed me."

"How much will it be?"

"Thirty pieces of silver is what Yeshuah instructed me to demand."

Simon's brows lifted.

"I suppose even a praefectus would not sniff at that."

"Yes," mused Judah. "Yeshuah chose the figure because, in his teachings, Jesus has spoken of a symbolic thirty pieces of silver which tradition says were the price of Ibraham's burial field, the sale price of Joseph into slavery, and many other things. The figure intrigued Yeshuah. The 'three,' that is. After hearing the teachings of Jesus, Yeshuah has decided that God is a Trinity. The Father, the Son—himself—and a Holy Spirit that is in all. They are three and separate, yet they are one, so he has decided.

"Though how he could confine All That Is to just three of anything after listening to Jesus is beyond me. It is amazing how those who attempt to confine the beliefs of others also insist on confining their god. And amazing that I was once one such."

He shrugged.

"Anyway, I think that Pilatus will grant my request while refusing the money. If so, when this is finished . . . I will take those thirty pieces to the Salt Sea, weight them with rocks, and throw them in, hoping that they never again pass through mortal hands."

"But you feel confident, Judah, that I will be left free with the vinegar and the sponge. The soldiers will have orders to allow this."

"I do not see Pilatus refusing such a simple request, especially one so seemingly harmless to anyone including himself. He is not the beast that his enemies make him out to be. He is a Roman, yes, but he has been touched most truly by Jesus. Anyone so touched will show compassion if given half a chance.

"Oh, Simon. One of my greatest guilts in the whole matter is the deceitful way that we must use Procula and Pilatus. They will be the ones truly betrayed."

He shook his head.

"Jesus would tell me that this revolt is doomed from the start, if, to accomplish it, I must betray those who have trusted me."

"Yet you will go ahead with it. You will obtain the permission of Pilatus for me to wield the sponge."

"I must. I am sworn."

"In that case, the moment that I get possession of the sponge, I will cut a crevice into it, just big enough to hide a cake. Each time that he finishes a cake, he should call out that he thirsts, and I will offer him up another. While appearing to suck the vinegar from out of the sponge, he will draw the cake into his mouth. Should other drugs be needed, I can hand them up in the same way.

"All right now. Let us say that we succeed. Yeshuah attains the sleep and is thought to be dead. What happens then?"

"As he feels himself ready for final entrance into the sleep, he will signal by saying, 'It is finished.' Immediately that we see he is, indeed, in the sleep, we will get word to Joseph, who will be waiting nearby. He will then rush to Procula, and hence to Pilatus, with news of Yeshuah's early death. He will obtain permission to take the body then rush back. Nicodemus will be waiting along the route with water and linens and spices. There will most likely be a messenger sent along with Joseph to inform the soldiers of the orders of Pilatus. The soldiers will take Yeshuah down from the cross, and they, or we, will carry him over to the tomb."

"You intend to be at the foot of the cross as well?"

"For every moment."

"All right. Yeshuah is placed in the tomb. The soldiers leave you to your burial preparations. The Sabbath sundown approaches. It is time for all good little Jews to scurry home to their dens. Will you just roll the stone into place and shut this grievously injured man up in the tomb, hoping against hope that he makes it, and is, indeed, alive when you are able to return? The first opportunity will be after sundown of Saturday. But activity at the tomb at night could draw unwelcome attention."

"And suspicion. Unfortunately, we will have to leave him. Not to leave would be in clear violation of the Sabbath, and could well raise questions as to whether or not he was truly dead. I fear that the first we can return without arousing suspicion will be dawn of Sunday."

"But, Simon, we had hoped that someone not as obviously involved as I, or Joseph and Nicodemus, would agree to be shut up with Yeshuah and tend to his wounds."

Simon laughed.

"Well, a good physician should stay at his patient's side, should he not.

"All right, Judah. So. I must get into the tomb before anyone realizes that it is to be used. I will be considered, after all, an uninterested party, merely a compassionate physician visiting the city, who took the time to help this man. Once I have declared him to be dead, my departure will excite no comment.

I will take a look at the site tomorrow, and decide upon a way to get into the tomb without being seen. It should not be difficult. After all, this scheme is so unthinkable that no one will be suspicious or apprehensive.

"So. I get into the tomb, and I wait in the back chamber, coming out into the antechamber only after the soldiers have left you there with the body. You must make sure that the stone is rolled back a bit so that I can get in."

"The tomb is new and unused. Joseph says the stone already stands open."

"Fine. Now let me see . . . "

Simon took up quill and papyrus.

"I will have my bag and tools and remedies right along with me, but I am making a list of the more unusual pharmacopoeia and dressings that might be needed. These should be waiting in the back chamber. We will need several oil lamps as well, so that I can see to work once the stone is over the entrance, and flint and steel and tinder, and plenty of extra oil . . . oh, and leave the stone just a bit short of its mark when you roll it back, so that fresh air will come in. Some food and some wine, for me if not for the patient. I will need more fresh water than Joseph would customarily bring for the washing. Several jugs full. And several slop jars. And though a shelf of stone is fine for a corpse, Yeshuah will need something softer to lie on. So will I Four fairly thick straw pallets, two to put under him, two for me. Four quilts of the warmest sort. Despite his sleep, his system will be in shock and he should be kept warm. With his heartbeat slowed to the rate that you claim, his additional loss of blood will be minimal, which is one thing in his favor.

"Oh. Make sure that he eats very little at the Passover meal the evening before, maybe just a little bread and wine, and that he has no food or drink thereafter. I have found that, for pain relief and mental acuity, laserpitium works best on an empty stomach."

"I have a feeling," said Judah, "that neither he nor I will feel much like eating."

Simon studied his list thoughtfully.

"Well here," he said at last. "Procure these items and have them hidden in the back of the tomb. If I think of anything else, I will let you know, or pick it up myself. I assume that we will be in close contact."

"No. Thanks to whatever is guiding this thing, Nicodemus has agreed to help us. It is worked out that we will exchange messages through him. The poor man has just developed another one of his sick headaches. Hearing of the presence in the city of a distinguished Cyrenean physician such as yourself, and in hopes that you might have some new remedy for this chronic trouble of his, he has asked that you call upon him in his house. This will also give you an excuse to go buying expensive items in the bazaars . . . remedies for Nicodemus. And you can come or go to his house at any hour. All my messages to him or to you will arrive at that house by various messengers, so that none of us are seen so often together that suspicion is aroused."

There was little more to say then. Simon went bustling off to get money from Nicodemus and get to the bazaar before closing.

Did he even care about the Messiah, Judah wondered? Did it even occur to him that he might be helping to foment a revolution?

Or was his only concern the testing of his precious laserpitium radix? Was this nothing more to him than a scientific experiment?

Whatever the case . . . it was good to have a clear-minded professional like Simon of Cyrene involved in the scheme.

* * *

Judah spent the night outside the city in a walled garden of olive trees that, with supreme irony, also belonged to Nicodemus. It was named for the ancient olive press on the site. Gethsemene. Just as Yeshuah had supposed, it was the perfect place in which to get arrested.

It was at the base of the Mount of Olives, just beyond the bridge that crossed the Kedron at the northeast corner of the Temple—hardly a quarter of a mile from that structure and from the walls of Jerusalem. Yet, in only that short distance, one was away from the city, surrounded by the stern simplicity of primeval rock, and trees which were centuries old.

The question had been whether the gathering press of pilgrims, encamped along the Kedron, would spill into the garden, making it less than private.

But no. The pilgrims respected the walls and the fact that it was private property. It was also known to belong to Nicodemus, and to contain the tomb of his ancestors. There were few who did not have respect for that Pharisee almost above all others. True, throughout the evening as he lay watching, wrapped in his quilt in a shallow cave in the midst of the garden, Judah heard a few passing voices. But only people strolling, looking for a bit of tranquility before bedtime, away from the babble of pilgrims and the dancing campfires. By midnight, there were no more strollers, the campfires were damped to a glow, and the pilgrims were snoring in their quilts.

Yes. Yeshuah had selected the perfect place.

In his mind's eye, Judah saw himself coming through the gate, leading the hirelings of the High Priest. Yeshuah would be here, in this very cave, kneeling in prayer. Waiting. Alone. His disciples would be out snoring beneath the trees, drugged by the last wine served to them at the supper.

Oh. He had forgotten to tell the Cyrenean to obtain that sleeping draught to put into their wine. Well, he would send a message tomorrow.

Yeshuah wanted no problems, no well-meant attempts to fight off his captors and save him from that which he desired above all things. The disciples were meant only to know that he had been taken. They were meant to mill about in sorrow, confusion, and guilt as Yeshuah played out his grand drama, then bear witness to his "resurrection" and go forward as his chief lieutenants, convinced of his divinity.

'Where,' Judah wondered, 'will I be in all this?'

The traitor. Known forever as the one who had betrayed the Messiah.

For the first time, it occurred to Judah that his brother had, not only, asked of him the utmost of what should be asked of a brother . . . but that he had also found a subtle and most terrible way to repay Judah for leaving him and turning to Jesus.

"There is no such thing as a dead fig tree," Judah mumbled aloud as he fell into sleep.

Which had nothing to do with anything. Yet the words were so comforting.

Chapter 20

The Last Suppers

Jesus wondered afterwards how he could have been so dense, so easily gulled. It was late on Sunday, the day after Judah's departure, before he realized that he had not seen Judah at the teachings since the night before, and asked where he had got to. No one, including Yeshuah, seemed to know.

"But he has been quiet and thoughtful since waking from the sleep," said Yeshuah. "I have assumed that he went up onto the mountain to meditate."

Which made sense. Mount Ephraim was a holy mountain, upon which it was a tradition to meditate. It was also proper to leave those who meditated to their solitude. Though thinking that it was strange that Judah had not informed him, Jesus questioned no more. People were often vague after waking from the sleep. Nathaniel and Susannah were both still quiet, each sitting alone, gently contemplating their newly found Selves, unaware, for the most part, of their surroundings, seeking no conversation with others.

On the following morning, Judah was still missing. Jesus begin to worry.

At which point, Mathiah remembered that, indeed, Judah had said that he was going up the mountain for a few days.

"I hope," Jesus half joked to Yeshuah, "that he has not tried to fly off the mountain as he was able to fly during the sleep."

"I will go up and see if I can find him," volunteered his brother, Jacob.

On Tuesday morning, Judah still had not returned. Neither had Jacob. Their brother, Isaac, went looking for them. By the hour of retiring that night, all three brothers were still missing.

"Are people ever set upon by brigands upon the mountain, Uncle?" asked Jesus.

"Never to my knowledge," said Cleopah. "Those who go up go stripped of possessions and usually without even food, so that they may fast as they meditate. They would not be worth a brigand's time or effort."

"What of wild animals?" For, of old, wolves, lions, and bears had been abundant throughout Palestine.

"It has been years since I have heard of animals bothering," said Cleopah.

"Still," mused Jesus, "if none of them return by the morning, we must all spread out over the mountain and find them.

Just before sunrise of Wednesday morning, Jesus and Merovee were awakened by Meraiah.

"Yeshuah is gone."

"After his brothers?"

"I do not know. I did not sleep all the night long. I sensed something wrong. Just now I went to wake Yeshuah, to tell him of my fears. He is gone. And his quilt and pack."

"He took his quilt and pack?"

The realization descended upon Jesus like a pall.

"He has returned to Jerusalem after all."

Meraiah began to cry.

"Allow me to dress, Queen Meraiah. I will be with you directly."

The entire house was roused. A check of the sleeping chambers and pallets revealed that Yeshuah was not the only one who had gone. The families of all of Yeshuah's brothers were gone. Thunder and her sons were missing. Petros. Merovee's cousin Lebbaeus, Rufus, the brother of Alexander, Mathiah, Salmon, Eli, and Ezekiel—these last the same men who had come to Jesus, abandoning Yeshuah, on that sunny morning at the House of Nathan in Magdala. So they had thrown their lots back in with Yeshuah's had they?

"Do you know aught of this, 'Nathaniel'?"

Bar Tolmei shook his great head.

"It was kept from me most carefully, I can see that, Jesus. Yeshuah knew that I would have stopped him had I known."

"What of the rest of you? I saw many whispered conferences and thoughtful faces in the last days."

"He came to me, for one," said Phillipus. "He recited all his scriptural quotations as to the Messiah. He said that the Kingdom was nigh, that he would soon be proclaimed the Messiah. He urged me to follow after him rather than after you. He promised me honor and glory in the Kingdom if I would do so."

"The same with me," said Levi.

"He talked to many of us," said Alphaeus, "but we did not pay much attention. He was not saying anything different than what we have all been hearing out of him of late."

"He certainly said nothing about returning to Jerusalem," said Jacob bar Alphaeus. "Are you very certain that that is where he has gone?"

"As certainly as I live," said Jesus. "Ah!" He turned and slapped angrily at the wall. "What an idiot I have been. How badly I am creating my reality at the moment."

"But Josh," said Merovee. "It does not make sense that Judah would have joined him again."

"Yes. It does. The day that Judah came to me in Magdala, lugging his beloved fig tree—do you not recall the mental agony he was in? Or perhaps he spoke of it only to me. I gathered that Yeshuah had extracted from him a vow—that Judah felt he had broken by coming to me. I tried to assure him. I explained that, since the essence of a vow is rigid unchangability, it is invalid by its very nature. He has seemed content enough these many months, seeming to put the guilt away. Now, obviously, Yeshuah has reminded him of that vow and demanded that he live up to it. Judah has felt bound to obey."

"But Judah loves *you*!" said Lazarus.

"He also loves his brother. He has been called upon to fulfill an obligation to that brother and so expunge his guilt. Yeshuah sent him ahead, up to Jerusalem to prepare the way."

He gave a bitter little laugh.

"As Johannan prepared my way and made it straight, so Judah makes the way straight for Yeshuah. Let us hope that Judah does not come to the same grief for his efforts."

"I hope you are not thinking of going to Jerusalem yourself," said Aunt Miriam.

Jesus gave no answer.

"Josh!" said Merovee. "You must not. If Yeshuah is determined to get himself hung . . . well let him!"

Jesus turned with gentle gaze.

"Do not speak like a wife, Merovee. Remain my comrade."

"Why should she not speak like a wife?" snapped Deborah. "That is what she is. Do not raise an eyebrow at me, Son-in-law! Why do you not try acting like a husband for a while? Like a husband who cares for his wife, and a tiny little baby who . . ."

She turned away. Lazarus took her into his arms.

"I do not know what the fuss is about," said Martha. "Tonight is the Passover. Jesus is not going anywhere. He would not dream of leaving, and so insult me and the meal that I will prepare."

"Indeed," said Cleopah. "He would insult me as well. As your host and uncle, I must insist that you remain to celebrate with us, Joshuah."

For the family of Cleopah, living inside the borders of Samaria, celebrated the Passover according to the Jubilee calendar as did Samaritans and Essenes. Their Passover would be celebrated on Wednesday eve instead of Thursday eve as in Jerusalem.

To everyone's surprise, Jesus smiled almost cheerfully.

"Of course we will celebrate together, Uncle. Please allow me, though, to at least find out what Yeshuah is planning. 'Nathaniel'?"

"Yes, Jesus, I will go," said bar Tolmei. "For if Yeshuah is putting himself into grave danger, forgive me, but I must be with him."

"I thought as much."

"I will go, too, and report back to you," said Support.

"Take my older Arabian mares," said Cleopah. "They are well-schooled and dependable enough for novice riders. Even my grandchildren ride them in safety. The road to Jerusalem is a good one, with sure footing. Gallop along until you are out of Samaria. On galloping horses, no one will be able to set upon you, even if they recognize you for Jews."

The two men set out with the rising sun. As though nothing had happened, Jesus began once more to teach.

One by one throughout the morning, the women dropped out of the sessions, heading for the kitchen as per custom, to search out leaven and help with the meal. Most needed those mundane tasks just then anyway . . . painstaking repetition which required little thought. Time enough to think later.

Only Merovee stayed at the feet of Jesus, shirking her female duty despite complaints from Martha.

"For me, this is the better part," she told her sister, looking wistfully up at Jesus. "Like the wise virgins, I trim and oil my lamp. But not in preparation for the coming of the master. I prepare, instead, for the time when he will be gone."

Nathaniel returned in late afternoon, leading the second horse. All rushed out to meet him.

Nathaniel's face was grave as he dismounted.

"You found him?" said Meraiah anxiously.

"There was no way to miss him," said Nathaniel. He rubbed his backside gingerly and accepted the wine brought by Susannah. "Fast these beasts are, Cleopah, and I suppose one gets hardened in the rear if one sticks with it, but I shall walk from hereon in, thank you."

"On with it, Man!" urged Jesus.

"We stabled the horses by the Old Gate and walked to the Temple . . . such fine beasts would have drawn attention." As he spoke, he walked into the house and to the room of teaching, the others crowding along to hear. "All was as usual in the courts, no sign of any disturbance, no sign of Yeshuah or any of the others. We ambled around listening to this speaker and that. Still nothing. We were just talking of going to Nicodemus to see if he knew anything when we heard it."

"What?"

Nathaniel settled onto a pile of cushions with a grateful sigh.

"A roar. People. Thousands of them, coming over the Mount of Olives. It is a wonder that the Temple did not upend and tumble right down into the Kedron, for about everyone in the courts who would be allowed rushed into the Porch of Solomon and up to the Golden Gate to look out across the valley and see what was happening."

"I know what was happening," sighed Jesus. He sank down onto a couch, put his elbows onto his knees, and lowered his face into his hands.

"For all the sound and uproar it might have been a Roman legion coming along that road, but it was only Yeshuah, riding the colt of an ass and surrounded by pilgrims gone mad. They were capering and laughing, waving their arms and shouting hosannahs. 'Hail to the King!' 'Save us, oh Son of Man!' 'He has come! The Messiah has come! Glory be to God!' And Jesus, we also heard the name 'Christos' being called. The crowds ruined every palm tree they passed, shinnying up and chopping off all the fronds to throw in front of Yeshuah's colt as a carpet for him to walk on. That was the old salute to the kings, was it not Jesus? A carpet of palms all the way into the city?"

"It was."

"The numbers swelled with every encampment he passed, and he stretched out the procession. He did not come straight up the hill to the Golden Gate. Instead, he rode all the way down along the Kedron to the Water Gate, then up the Street of the Cheesemakers to the gate of the Court of Gentiles. Jesus, there must have been ten thousand people by the time he got there, jamming the street behind him, circling the blocks, drawn from all directions, pouring in at all the Temple gates "

"What did the Romans do?" said Lazarus.

"Not a thing. Very sensible, seeing as how there are only about six hundred and fifty of them. The sentries just kept lounging around at their posts up on the roof of the tower that overlooks the Temple. They did not even double the guard, they just let the people laugh and sing and shout . . . though I saw Pilatus and Lucius up there at one point. They watched for a few minutes. Then Pilatus shrugged, and they went back in."

Jesus nodded.

"Good man. He has the sense not to stampede. It would only play into the hands of the demonstrators."

"Neither was there a Levite in sight," grinned Nathaniel. "The rulers were obviously lying low as well. The mob swarmed into the court . . . Yeshuah made no offering . . . and you should have seen the moneychangers and the animal sellers cringing. Some closed their stalls and ran. But Yeshuah never even gave them a glance. He began preaching immediately, again there in the Court of the Gentiles, so that all could hear. He was still there, preaching, when I left."

"Did you talk with any of our men?" said Jesus.

"It took a while to get to them. They surrounded him as a bodyguard. What lovely shades of crimson when they saw us. All except Thunder. I do not think she knows how to blush."

"Who did you speak with?"

"Judah came aside with us. He would tell us nothing of Yeshuah's plans . . . except that they take the Passover in the upper room of an inn on the Mount of Sion tomorrow eve."

"The Mount of Sion!" said Jesus in surprise. "Almost next door to the house of the High Priest. Why would he choose such a dangerous location?"

"Judah says that it was upon Sion that David built his palace and his city—and it is upon Sion that David has his tomb. This inn is near to the tomb. Judah says that it means a great deal to Yeshuah to take this particular Passover upon Sion and near to the tomb of his ancestor."

"'Rejoice greatly, O daughter of Sion,' said Jesus quietly. 'Shout, O daughter of Jerusalem. Behold your king comes to you, a lowly man, and riding upon an ass, upon a colt the foal of an ass.'" He sighed. "Did Judah say more?"

"He said you are not to worry about our Roman or Herodian friends. Yeshuah promises to protect them. He asked me to beg you to stay away. He said to tell you that he has grown to love you—love all of us—more dearly than words can tell. He said that Yeshuah has promised that, when he has fulfilled his vow, he will be free to return to you. He said that he knows you understand."

Jesus shook his head.

"And the others? The Boanerges? Petros? Did you speak with them?"

"Petros. It was like being granted an audience with the Grand High Whatever. He is so jumped up you would not believe it, strutting like a cock for all the world as though Yeshuah is his hen. He is now First Man after the Messiah he told me in no uncertain terms. He is to have a throne just to Yeshuah's right in the Kingdom."

"Has he cleared that with Thunder?" asked Jesus.

"Oh, the Boanerges are to have thrones on the left."

Jesus could not help laughing.

"Thank 'God' that there are two sides to Yeshuah."

"And two faces," said Levi.

"But what in the name of their god do they think is going to happen?" said Lazarus. "How is this 'Kingdom' going to come into being? How is Yeshuah going to get this power, has Yeshuah told them that?"

"I think that Judah is the only one privy to his plans," said Nathaniel. "The rest of them are in a kind of dream, just plain drunk with exhilaration and the prospect of power. Young Johannan kept looking up at the sky as though he really expected 'God' to arrive at any moment. Jesus, if I may give you my advice . . . stay away. Yeshuah is consigning himself to Heaven. Leave him to Heaven."

"Easy enough for you to say," said Jacob bar Alphaeus. "You do not have a son in that 'drunken' company. I have got to go down there and try to talk some sense into Leb before he gets himself killed."

"Be at peace," said Jesus with unexpected calm. "We have promised my uncle to take the feast of unleavened bread with him, and so we shall. It is fortunate timing that Samaria celebrates the Passover a day before Jerusalem."

"Who cares about timing?" said Jacob bar Alphaeus. "And how can you be so sure that there is time in which to dissuade my son?"

"Because Yeshuah cares about timing. And I trust Yeshuah. I trust him to be a master strategist. If he has made plans for a Passover meal at an inn on Sion tomorrow night, you can be very sure that he and all those with him will be safe until at least that time."

* * *

Except for the laughter and chatter of the children of the household—whom Jesus not only tolerated, but forever welcomed near to him—the supper was subdued.

For the purposes of the gathering, Jesus was declared head of the household—indeed, as the heir bar Ramathea, he outranked his uncle. He declared all those present to be his brothers and sisters, and so of one family, else, by Law, they would have had to split up into interminable family groups, some with only one representative, all forbidden to mingle during the supper.

Reclining on the couches and gathered around mats, they drank the first of four compulsory cups of wine and recited a verse of sanctification. Raw greens were brought in and placed before Jesus, who dipped the greens into salted water and distributed portions to all present. Then the unleavened bread was brought, along with haroseth—a paste of apples, nuts and dates—and the bitter herbs, along with the paschal lamb, roasted whole.

That very morning, Ben had taken the lamb, a fine, unblemished male, to the Samaritan Temple on Mount Gerizim, to be slaughtered according to the Samaritan rite. Its blood had been smeared on the door lintel of the house to inform the Angel of Death that children of Israel dwelt within, and that he should pass over without smiting any of their first-born.

With those symbolic foods in place upon a central table, the second wine cup was filled, and Ben's youngest son came to sit at the feet of Jesus to ask the traditional questions. He was five, and it was his first time at the questions. He had rehearsed most diligently.

"Cousin Joshuah, why is this night different from others? Why do we eat only unleavened bread upon this night?"

Jesus grinned, and glanced at Ben.

"Only the traditional answer if you please, Josh. Do not confuse the boy with any of your historical, symbolic, economic, spiritual, and cultural analyses."

"So be it," laughed Jesus. "Well, David, we eat only of unleavened bread on this night firstly because The Law commands it, unleavened bread being regarded as the bread of affliction.

"Secondly, we eat only of unleavened bread this night because this night is said to be the anniversary of our ancestors' flight from bondage in Egypt. The story says that they had to sneak out of the country in the middle of the night, you see, so that Pharaoh would not catch them and keep them in slavery. They had, therefore, to pack their belongings and prepare their provisions in great haste, so they had no time to allow the bread to rise.

"That is also why we eat the meal quickly, and it is why we have all come to the meal wearing our sandals, with our loins girded and with our staffs handy. Our ancestors are supposed to have had to eat quickly and then rise from the table and depart upon a long and momentous journey. We eat the unleavened bread and do all these things here tonight in symbolic remembrance of that supposed night. And because . . . "

His eyes traveled kindly from one loved one to the next.

"We, too, some of us, must get up after this meal and go upon a momentous journey."

The boy waited a moment, then he smiled.

"Are you finished?"

"Yes."

"Well then . . . ummm . . . oh! Why do we eat bitter herbs upon this night?"

"We eat bitter herbs upon this night firstly because The Law commands it, secondly because we wish to remind ourselves that servitude is bitter indeed."

"But I sort of like horseradish."

"That is beside the point. Next question."

"Why do we eat only roasted meat upon this night?"

"Moses has supposedly told us, 'And they shall eat the flesh in that night, roast with fire, with unleavened bread and with bitter herbs they shall eat it. Eat not of it raw, nor sodden at all with water, but roast with fire, his head and his legs and with the purtenance thereof.' Next?"

"Ummm . . . Why are there two dippings?"

"We eat the raw greens dipped into salted water to remind us of many things. Of the salt of our tears whenever we are in bondage . . . of the salt of the sea, that will part and allow us to pass whenever we truly follow 'God.' It reminds us of the salt of our sweat as we toiled as Builders in the cities of the pharaohs." He smiled at Merovee. "Likewise, we dip the bitter herbs of servitude with the haroseth because the haroseth represents the mortar that we used as we built those cities and monuments.

"And there, David, are all your pretty and official, but largely inaccurate, answers."

"Thank you very much, Cousin Joshuah."

"You are quite welcome. And now we have to sing some songs. Will you try to sing along with us?

"Hallelujah!" Jesus began, launching, with a full, clear baritone, into the Psalms which comprised the Hallel. "Praise ye the Lord! Praise, O ye servants of the Lord, praise the name of the Lord."

No one felt like singing. But the Rabban Gamaliel had said that the Hallel must be sung joyously. So they sang joyously.

The One Hundred and Thirteenth Psalm, the One Hundred and Fourteenth, the One Hundred and Fifteenth.

Poor Martha's roasted lamb was getting cold, thought Merovee idly as they worked their way through the interminable verses.

The One Hundred and Sixteenth, the last of the group to be sung before the supper.

"I love the Lord because he has heard my voice and my supplications. Because he has inclined his ear to me, therefore will I call upon him as long as I live. The sorrow of death compassed me, and the pains of hell got hold of me. I found trouble and sorrow. Then called I upon the name of the Lord. O Lord, I beseech you, deliver my soul. Gracious is the Lord, and righteous. Yes, our Lord is merciful. The Lord preserves the simple. I was brought low and he helped me. Return to your rest, O my soul, for the Lord has dealt bountifully with you. The Lord has delivered my soul from death, my eyes from tears, and my feet from falling. I will walk before the Lord in the land of the living."

Merovee heard her husband's baritone softening. She glanced over her shoulder to where he reclined behind her on the couch. He was thinking of Yeshuah, she could read the look in his eyes.

"I believed, therefore have I spoken. I was greatly afflicted. I said in my haste, all men are liars. What shall I render to the Lord for all his benefits to me? I will take the cup of salvation and call upon the name of the Lord. I will pay my vows to the Lord now in the presence of his people. Precious in the sight of the Lord is the death of his saints . . . "

The voice of Jesus trailed off. He but listened as the others went on.

"0 Lord, truly I am your servant, and the son of your handmaid. You have loosed my bonds. I will offer to you the sacrifice of thanksgiving and will call upon the name of the Lord. I will pay my vows to the Lord in the presence of his people. In the courts of the Lord's house, in the midst of thee, O Jerusalem. Praise ye the Lord."

"Amen."

All were silent, watching Jesus. Finally Merovee spoke.

"Josh?"

"Hmm?"

"Will you give us a special benediction before we partake of the meal?"

Jesus pushed himself up onto one arm and was quiet for a moment. Then . . .

"Dear Power that is All That Is . . . give us the wisdom to see beyond formulas and set verses. Let us someday stop answering the questions of children with gibberish, and, instead, speak the truth about you.

"Our father and mother that are All That Is and are within us and all . . . holy is the name that can never name you. May the Kingdom come to fruit in each of us. Let us know that all that is, and that is done, is you, whether on Earth or in the heavens above. Help us to trust in our daily sustenance even as the lilies of the fields trust and so receive. Help us to know that to find forgiveness we need only find the grace truly to forgive all others. Help us to choose what is positive when faced with temptation, so that our existences become ever more joyous, with no room for those sadnesses which the world knows as evil. Help us to know that you in us and us in you is the Kingdom, is the Power, and the Glory, with no beginning and no end."

The meal was eaten in haste, as The Law demanded. To Martha's disappointment, neither Jesus nor Merovee could bring themselves to eat of the lamb, its little body so reminiscent of Phoenix. Jesus made up for the insult by eating heartily of the bread, herbs, and haroseth, fulsomely complimenting the cook.

The third and fourth mandatory cups of wine accompanied the closing of the Hallel, the singing of the One Hundred Seventeenth and One Hundred Eighteenth Psalms.

"The stone which the builders refused is become the head stone of the corner," said the One Hundred and Eighteenth.

How long ago, it seemed to Merovee, was that day in Magdala, when Josh woke from his sleep, and they stayed in Deborah's room, with Deborah and Lazarus. Then Salome came, and Susannah and Nathaniel were caught lurking without the vents. And Jesus taught them all that afternoon and on into the night . . . of the Noachites, and the Builders, of Ibraham and Joseph and of the vast, forgotten heritage of their people, the pitiful remnants of which history were reflected in the ceremony that was now taking place, and in the codified little story that accompanied it.

Then they had danced through the streets of Magdala, down a path of moonlight, straight out along its beam, out and over the waters of Lake Gennesareth.

As the hymn ended, as the company relaxed from ritual, and a fifth cup of non-compulsory wine was poured, Merovee laid her head back so that it rested against his breast.

"You are going to Jerusalem."

"I have to, my love."

"Why?"

"How many reasons do you want? You can give them all yourself."

"To save from harm the men who have accompanied Yeshuah . . . dear bar Tolmei and poor Judah very especially.

"And oh, if Salome discovered that Judah were in danger, she might do something really foolish.

"And what of Pilatus and Procula? There could not really be an uprising because of all this, could there? There could. There are countless thousands in Jerusalem by now, all in a frenzy, thinking the Messiah has come. As formidable as the legionaries are, sheer numbers could overwhelm them. If a mob were to overrun the Antonia, Pilatus, Procula and Lucius might be slain.

"And might that mob not also vent its anger on the Herodians? On Antipas and his family, especially believing Salome and Herodias to be responsible for Johannan's death? Oh, they would do horrible things to those two women.

"Yeshuah just does not realize how things can get out of hand. He might intend to shield our friends from harm, but, in the fury of a mob, would he be able? He has got to be stopped, and any such uprising and bloodshed averted.

"He has also got to be stopped from whatever it is that he plans, because it is all based on a lie, is it not, or multiple lies, deceits, misunderstandings, graspings for power and—if Yeshuah gets himself killed—upon the shedding of blood. Something like that is doomed from the start, it can never be right. It will only set off a wave of more lying and cheating and deceit and graspings for power and bloodshed that will take millenna to undo."

She closed her eyes.

"Besides which, as you have taught me—Jesus—one always has to *try*. Whatever the odds, whatever the personal inconvenience, whatever the danger, one must always try to right a matter that directly presents itself to one as wrong.

"How am I doing?"

"You never fail me."

"I wish that I could. I wish that I did not understand. I would rather just hate you for being . . ."

"Oh Josh, with all your powers, why could you not have just stopped this thing?"

"You know the answer to that, my love. When I took physical form I accepted to abide by the limitations of the system, the rules by which this game is played. Besides which, it is not right or even possible for me to interfere using force. Nothing can ever be forced on anyone or anything at any place at any time. And nothing is ever certain. Free will is the Law of the Universe. People just will not get that through their heads! Free will is King! All That Is advises. Through teachers such as myself, All That Is often even begs and pleads. But, when it is time for the doing, Humankind is allowed to do exactly as it chooses. Both All That Is and Man must then abide by the consequences."

"Josh . . . is it getting near to the end for us?"

"Oh Merovee. What can I say? Maybe so, maybe not. We can only live each moment as it is chosen."

"In your considered opinion."

"Probably."

"Why can you never be sure about anything!" she cried with such vehemence that heads turned. She felt his chest shake with laughter.

"Because," she answered herself bitterly, "there is nothing that is sure. There are only probabilities. Lord! I wish I had never heard that word."

"If you do not like the system, send a Magdalia to the Powers That Be. If anyone could charm them into changing it, it would be you."

"Oh Josh." She flipped over so that she faced him. "How can I even think of a life without you?"

"Less than a year ago you did not know that I existed."

"I have always known that you existed."

"And I always will exist. We will never be parted. Merovee. I have taught you the ways to reach me, to be with me. You do not even have to see me, to see this body, to be able to touch it, to have me with you. You, even more than all the others—the others to whom I have given promises of constant support . . . you, Magdalen! You have from me a love that is beyond love. So be of good cheer. Come. Lift your chin. Do not make my own heart break as well."

"I am coming with you to Jerusalem."

"All right."

"You are not going to fight me?"

"I am as selfish as yourself. I want every moment, even if those moments be difficult or even tragic. I do insist, however, that Agapo be left here at Mount Ephraim. Ben's wife will feed him."

Merovee glanced back over her shoulder, at the angel sleeping on the tiny cot beside her.

"I agree. And please All That Is that this will be the last time that I must be parted from his dear little Self."

"Have another glass of wine," said Jesus.

Her laughter floated through the room.

"I think that, at a previous time, you must have been Bacchus."

"You have found me out. Oh, laugh again, Merovee. I want that sound. Wherever I go, whatever and whenever I am, I want always to have your laughter as a background melody to all that I do. Promise me that you will never stop laughing. Promise me that, when in doubt, you will laugh—without restraint. Each time that you do, you can know that I will be listening, and made so very happy by the sound."

"Jesus?"

"Yes."

"I love you."

He kissed her upon the lips.

"Maybe you ought not to, my Chalice. For the Wine with which I fill you will often be poisonous to your own self."

"Strange. I thought of something like that—the day after you stilled the storm on the lake, as I sat beside you in my mother's chamber, watching you sleep. I had a sudden vision—of having to drink real poison. And I thought then that, if I held the thought of you firmly enough in mind, I could drink it and remain unharmed."

"Then remember my face now. Remember this moment. In all future dangers, conjure me up as I face you now, and hear my voice as it speaks to you. If you will do that, I promise that you shall drink any poison, face any peril, and remain unharmed."

"Jesus," said Jacob bar Alphaeus. "When do we start for Jerusalem?"

Jesus sighed.

"In the late hours, Jacob, when all are abed with none to protest our passage."

* * *

They had not many miles to go to the border of Judeah. Whilst in Samaria, they were technically sinning with their travel, which was "work," and forbidden within the twenty-four hours from sundown to sundown of the first day of Passover. But both their number and the hour gave safety from attack. Once into Judeah, there was over half-a-day before the Passover began.

Many of the company did not make the trip. Alphaeus stayed behind. His bones had had enough of traveling for a while, he said. Martha stayed with Zana and the baby, with Ben's wife and children and the wives and children of Ben's older brothers. All the children stayed behind, in fact, and many of the wives stayed to care for them. Jac stayed. According to his Essenic beliefs, he had already celebrated Passover properly. He had no mind to defile himself in the mob at Jerusalem.

And Lazarus stayed, for all agreed that he must not show his face in Jerusalem at this Passover.

The women who went wore head coverings with which to veil themselves if necessary. All had coats, and each carried a quilt, for who knew what they would have to deal with? There was scant hope of finding lodgings in or near Jerusalem at this time. The day before the Passover every house in Jerusalem was supposed to be already filled to the ceilings with pilgrims, for it was expected of each householder that he open his doors to as many pilgrims as he could shelter. In practical usage, most householders saved their space for friends and family who would be coming in from the country . . . or else they rented their space at exorbitant prices. Whatever the case, even a month before the Passover, most housing in Jerusalem had already been occupied or promised.

Those who could not find or afford space in the city gradually filled the valleys around Jerusalem— Hinnom on the west, Tyropoeon on the south, Kedron on the east. The camps sprawled back over the Mount of Olives to Bethphage, along the Bethany road, the Joppa road, the Bethlehem Road . . . some few camped along the northern wall of the city and along the Ephraim road, though, due to natural topography and to the way in which the Temple and the Antonia were situated, the north was not a popular campsite.

On one Passover, in an attempt to estimate an unusually large number of pilgrims, the priests had counted kidneys as they slaughtered the lambs. Five hundred thousand pairs had been counted. Estimating a family group of at least six to consume each lamb, the priests had come up with the figure of three million pilgrims that year.

The numbers were seldom that overwhelming. Yet it was also seldom that there were less than five hundred thousand pilgrims—men, women and children—thronging Jerusalem and environs at Passover. The number fluctuated so drastically because, while, technically, it was The Law that all Israelites must come to the Temple at the Passover to have their lambs killed and consecrated—and usually bought from the concessionaires of the priests—in practice it was recognized that not everyone could make the journey to Jerusalem every single year. A trip every other year, or even every third year was acceptable. Those who did not make the trip took their lambs to their local synagogues to be slain.

The number of pilgrims would certainly be large this year, however, since it was a year in which taxes must be paid to Rome. Malcontents would want to gather with their own kind and discuss the injustice of the whole thing, speak wildly of rebellion, and perhaps even stage a demonstration or two.

Additionally this year there was the excitement of the Messiah.

It was always both amazing and amusing to Jesus that the people so bitterly resented the Roman presence and Roman taxes, yet made not a peep against the tyranny of the Temple, the priests and The Law, or ever wondered where all the money that they poured into the coffers of the Temple went.

And it was astonishing that Rome held Palestine with a force of only a few thousand legionaries, spread throughout the entire country—that the praefectus came to Jerusalem and policed it during the Passover with what was, comparatively, but a handful of those legionaries. Whether this spoke of Roman overconfidence or of hot air exhaled by Zealots and malcontents . . . . . . well, perhaps it was a bit of both.

With it all, who knew where they might have to sleep that night? Deborah had suggested going straight to bar Jeremiah. Certainly her cousin Daniel's son and his new wife would take them in. They could sleep in the stable, or even on the grounds if he had already filled the place with pilgrims. Or perhaps Nicodemus would have room for them.

"Let us wait and see," said Jesus, "what the situation is when we get there, and what place will be safe for us."

The number of pilgrims was indeed great in this year. That was obvious once in sight of the city, even approaching by way of the unpopular north side, and just at dawn. It would take them several hours to work their way to the Temple. Every road and street leading to that place was filled with heads of households carrying white, male lambs. The stench of droppings and the heart-rending bleats of the little victims was overpowering.

The Law said that the lamb should have been taken from the householder's own flock. Yet, in this day and age, many Israelites did not own flocks. For the Passover, therefore, the animal sellers who usually sold in the Court of the Gentiles set up huge pens in the valleys and on the hills around the city, and sold the tens upon tens of thousands of lambs that would be needed from there.

The householders then lined up, in lines that eventually snaked all the way out of the city and to the pens of the animal sellers, but which eventually led to the two Temple gates on the west, the three gates on the south, and the Golden Gate on the east. The north was occupied by the Antonia Fortress and the Court of Herod, the latter used only by priests and Levites, so that, on that side was only the Sheep Gate, adjacent to the sheep pens, used primarily, on days other than Passover, for bringing sheep to be sold for sacrifice into the Temple courts

The waiting heads of households were admitted to the Temple courts in three relays. Once a relay had filled the courts, the gates were closed, the shofar was blown, and the slaying of the lambs of that relay began. Tens of thousands of priests and a thousand Levites—men who had passed all tests of ritual cleanliness, purity, and perfection in preparation for the event—labored with practiced precision, blessing and slaying the terrified little creatures, draining the blood, and burning it upon the altar. A great column of smoke rose continuously to the sky, up to the eagerly twitching nostrils of the god of the Jews, while a chorus of yet another one thousand Levites sang the entire Hallel.

If the slaying of the first relay was not completed by the time the Hallel was ended, the chorus repeated it, and was prepared to repeat it a third time. Yet so efficient was the slaughter, that never in anyone's memory had the Hallel had to be sung more than twice per relay.

As the householders took up the limp, drained, little bodies and headed for their lodgings, to roast the carcasses whole, the gates were opened and more tens of thousands of pilgrims surged in, filling every available foot of standing space. And the whole process began again.

Between the scent of burning blood and eliminations from hundreds of thousands of terrified lambs, Jerusalem on the day before the Passover was, Jesus had always thought, the most disgusting place on Earth.

'How long,' he cried out internally, 'will you demand the bloody sacrifice of your lambs, Jerusalem? How long will your god relish the smeared blood of innocents? How long will your god love to smell them burn? Will you ever truly cleanse yourself, Jerusalem? You, whose name means City of Peace. Will you ever learn that peace cannot be gotten by the shedding of blood? Will you learn before it is too late that those who live by the decree of blood of whatever kind will, themselves, roast in a fire? Oh, my people. How I cry for you. Will you ever be brave enough to stop trying to please your god by killing?'

Now yet another lamb went to be slaughtered. Went of its own accord, demanding to die—confused by this heritage, this lust to sacrifice blood—thinking to please its god by offering up its own sticky, sweet core.

"I will shed my own blood," he could almost hear Yeshuah say. "I will smear the redness of myself upon the lintels of the houses of Israel, and this will be pleasant in God's sight, and when he comes to establish the Kingdom he will pass over those houses, and smite only the Gentiles and those who are not enraptured by my oozing."

It made Jesus sick to the stomach. The man sought to found a new religion, a true "Kingdom of God," based upon all the most obvious mistakes of the past, upon lies and trickery and avarice and blood, upon suffering, smashed bones, torn flesh, gore, and guilt.

"Ah, Jerusalem," he muttered aloud, "you have much to answer for, that your children should so misunderstand the true nature of that which is god."

The closer they came to the city walls, the more oppressive the mob.

And one could smell Messiah Fever in the air.

Ah yes. This extraordinary number of people was not due just to the tax year. Word had traveled far and fast, of Yeshuah's royal entry, of his open declaration of messiahship. These people were here to see their king! To, perhaps, oh wonder of wonders, be in Jerusalem for the arrival of God, himself! They laughed too loudly, talked too much, were boisterous when such conduct was forbidden during sacred preparations.

And they gathered in too many whispering groups.

"Jesus, I do not like this at all," muttered Chandreah.

"You feel it, too."

"The hair at the back of my neck is standing on end. We must not take the women into the city."

Even on a normal Passover, passage through the streets was difficult. While, on any Passover, it was completely unthinkable for women to enter the Temple courts. The Temple, on preparation day, was a place for "heads of households," for men only.

Only once in Passover history had anyone been actually killed by the mob filling the Temple courts, and that had been an old man, trampled and suffocated. Perhaps the mob had not actually killed him. Perhaps, being old, he had died naturally, and sunk down with no one to notice.

Still, Chandreah was right. The physical strength of a woman should not be tested, even in the street throngs . . . especially with violence liable to erupt at any moment. It was even impractical to try to take the women from this northwesterly side of the city to the house of Nicodemus on the Orphel at the southeast.

"I know a place that will be relatively quiet and where the whole group can wait," said Jesus.

And so, as they reached the Ephraim Gate in the wall of Hezikiah, instead of entering the Lower City, he led them westward, along the broad path that followed the base of that wall.

They had gone not a hundred strides when he stopped dead, staring into the jostling throng that approached them.

"Merovee!" he said sharply. "That Pharisee."

Merovee followed his rudely pointing finger. Coming toward them was a student, his vestments marking him as a follower of Rabban Gamaliel of the House of Hillel.

"Memorize his face!" said Jesus with a stridency that Merovee had never heard.

She marked his face. His whole body. He was of ungainly build, with a large trunk set upon what she imagined must be short, bowed, and skinny legs. His face was dominated first by his nose, then by his eyes, then by his forehead. The nose had a spectacular, out-flaring arch to it. The eyes glowed with a fanaticism that Merovee had seen only once before, in the eyes of the Simon Yeshuah of yore. The forehead was high, balding despite the man's youth, and bulbous.

The Pharisee drew close, moving along with the flow of the crowd, but rapt in his own world of unceasing prayer.

"Saul!" said Jesus as he passed them.

The Pharisee stopped, turned. His bulbous brow furrowed.

"What do you want, Fellow? Should I know you?"

"Yes, Saul. Look closely."

The furrows deepened.

"I have an excellent memory for faces, and I have no memory of yours. If you want to apply for study with the Rabban, apply for yourself. Do not attempt to gain my patronage by pretending to be an old acquaintance."

Jesus laughed.

"Saul, you have no idea just how old that acquaintance is."

The Pharisee stiffened. His angry glance took in the group of people who had stopped behind Jesus. Then it fastened on Merovee.

"Why do you stare at me, Woman?"

"I am memorizing you," said Merovee with a mischievous grin.

"Is this how you govern your women, Fellow? You allow them to stare at their betters and to answer back?"

Jesus hesitated.

"'Better' is relative," he said kindly. "Go on with you, then. We will meet again. When we do, you will not be able to put me away."

The Pharisee sniffed and turned to go on. Abruptly he turned back.

"Where will we meet again?"

"Each night in your dreams, Saul, and then, I think . . . " Jesus closed his eyes. "Yes. I will meet you on a street called Straight."

"You are mad," said Saul. He turned and walked on.

"Who was that?" asked Phillipus.

"That was . . . Oh dear God."

Jesus shook his head and walked quickly on. Merovee caught up with him.

"He is worse than I thought," said Jesus.

"How can that ugly little man be the third part of you and Johannan?"

"I have been asking myself the same question. But an entity manifests every side of itself. Not all those sides are pretty. Or even congenial."

"He does not think much of women, does he."

"At this point he does not even think much of himself, for all his arrogance. My love . . . you will have endless trouble with that one."

"What are you talking about?"

"I fear that you will often have to handle him."

"I? Handle that pompous little toad? Not on your life! I might get warts."

"You have time to grow into the idea. It will not happen immediately. And not in this land."

"Josh!"

"We will talk of it later."

Despite her queries, he would speak no more on the subject.

But the meeting seemed to have saddened him deeply.

In about a third of a mile, they came to a walled garden set off to the north of the Joppa Road. Jesus opened the gate to usher his people in.

"Hey there! Keep out!" A gardener rushed at them, brandishing a hoe. "Can you not see that this is private property?"

"Good morning, Nehemiah."

The gardener halted.

"Reb Joshuah. Well . . . " It was almost a growl. "I suppose it is all right then. All these people are with you? Watch out where you are stepping! I will not have a single cabbage left if this keeps up, what with trespassers treading on them or just stealing them outright."

"Nehemiah, these are our friends. And my wife, Miriam of Magdala."

"Aha!" Nehemiah's irritation dissolved. "*Welcome*, my lady. This boy's parents are made joyous by you." He shot Jesus a look. "It took him long enough."

"And I am sure," grinned Jesus, "that you remember my father's brother and his wife."

Nehemiah's manner grew respectful. He bowed.

"Of course. Reb Cleopah. Lady Miriam. And all you boys!. What a surprise. Welcome to my garden."

Jesus smiled at the company.

"Nehemiah has been my father's chief gardener since I was a boy."

"And precious little we have seen of you *since* you was a boy," said Nehemiah.

"He considers any garden belonging to my father as his own private property."

"Without me, the whole passel of you would have starved. And it is the same each Passover. I have to get myself in here to the city and stay for weeks protecting the plantings, else every one of them gets trampled or stolen. I do not care what anyone says, there should be a lock on that gate, especially at Passover time."

There never would be a lock. Nehemiah knew that. Locks on tomb gardens were forbidden by usage and good sense. For, with the increasing popularity of the doctrine of resurrection as preached by the Pharisees and Essenes, it had become the vogue for the families of Jerusalem and environs to purchase plots of ground outside the walls and as close to the Temple as possible, there to make for themselves stone tombs and sepulchers. This was so that, on the day of resurrection, when God came down to Earth—to the Temple, naturally—and when he called to the dead to rise and come to him, when his call rolled back the stones from the doors of the tombs and lifted the lids of the sepulchers, and the dead did arise, they would not have far to walk.

But if there were locks on their gates, they might not be able to get out to walk anywhere! For there was nothing in Scripture about God opening locks.

It made no difference that the tomb in this particular garden was new and empty. The symbolism must be maintained, the unlocked gate a constant invitation to the call of God.

Some families could afford no more than a few square meters of ground. Others joined with friends and bought larger areas in common, constructing as many tombs or sepulchers as there were families in the consortium. A man of great wealth like Joseph bar Ramathea could afford a large area all to himself, and a choice and picturesque site as well, such as the Place of the Skull.

Whether large or small, however, these tomb plots were put to dual use. The people made their projected resting spots into kitchen gardens, utilizing every inch of soil for vegetables and fruit trees, tending them assiduously. Most consumed the produce in their own home. Some, like Joseph, who had a kitchen garden in Bethlehem, sold his produce in the market place.

"Stay on the paths and steps now. Mind that young lettuce. There are benches over before the tomb, and a bit of grass on which you can make yourselves comfortable."

He led them through terraced levels and to the far side of a high dome of rock in the midst of the garden—the "skull" from which the place had had its name for as long as anyone could remember.

The tomb was cut back into the rock of that skull. Its door looked eastward, toward the Temple, the outlines of which could be clearly seen over the roofs of the Lower City.

"Nehemiah," said Jesus as they got to the entrance. "Why is the stone levered partly back?"

Nehemiah motioned to him. They walked away, back to the other side of the skull.

"Reb Joshuah, do you know that your father has sold this place?"

"Yes. Despite Father's sentimental noises to the contrary, I have always suspected that he bought it on speculation anyway." He grinned. "You know his opinion of the final resurrection of the dead."

"And I concur. The idea turns my stomach. All those rotting corpses and skeletons getting up and walking to the Temple. Would God resurrect a cabbage that had rotted? No. And if not a cabbage, then why a man? Since, in my opinion, the poorest cabbage is of more worth than most men."

"I can not agree with your judgment of most men," said Jesus dryly, "though you are correct to revere the Spirit of a Cabbage and to reject the resurrection of long-dead bodies, human or cabbage."

"But you worry that Nicodemus will object to our using this place now he has bought it?"

"The thing is, Reb Joshuah, that your father asked me to look after the garden till Reb Nicodemus could get his own gardener onto it."

"I am sure that Reb Nicodemus purchased the site for the same speculative purposes as did my father. The tomb of his ancestors is over in the garden of his olive press. Surely Nicodemus plans to be entombed there. I assure you that he will not feel violated by our use of this place for just one day."

"No, of course not. That is not what I was going to say. Young Master, there is something strange going on. You saw the stone of the tomb partly rolled back. That is because Reb Nicodemus has been here several times yesterday and this morning and has hidden things in the tomb! He has instructed me specifically to leave the stone rolled back just that much—just enough for a man to crawl in. And the lever is hidden there in the bushes."

"What sort of things did Nicodemus hide?"

"Well certainly I have not looked, after all it is not my business . . . "

"*What*, you old sticky-nose?"

"Medicines. Herbs. Water. Bandages. Lamps and oil. Mats. Quilts. Slop jars. Food and wine."

Jesus turned away abruptly, his mind reeling at the implications.

Slowly his eyes scanned the garden . . . the neat beds of cabbage, the young lettuce, the sprouting leeks, onions, garlic, the orchard of fruit trees. Such an innocent place.

Yet, many years before, the Place of the Skull had been a popular site for crucifixion. In the days of Judah the Galilean, hundreds of his supporters were crucified on this spot. There must still be . . .

Yes . . . there in that clump of grass . . . and there in the midst of the cabbages. Mortared shafts, well sunk into the earth . . . each shaft meant to accept and stabilize the upright beam of a cross.

Had he stumbled onto both the place and the plan?

Such a plan was not possible. Even Yeshuah would not have conceived of such a thing.

But why not? A man who could achieve the Seventh Sleep could conceivably carry it off . . . just as could he, himself.

Abruptly, he turned and strode back to the group.

"All of you remain here, except . . . Nathaniel, you are big and handy at clearing the way in crowds. Come with me."

"What has happened?" said Jacob bar Alphaeus anxiously. "Have you heard something that effects my son? Let me come, too."

"Trust me, bar Alphaeus. I think I know the fastest way to discover Yeshuah's plans. I can move more quickly if I move alone. None of you stir from this place until I return. If you get hungry . . . " he threw Nehemiah a glance. "There is plenty of cabbage."

* * *

On an off-chance, they went to the headquarters of the Zebedee just inside the Fish Gate, so called for being the terminus of caravans from Lake Gennesareth, and the place where the people of Jerusalem came for their Galilean fish.

The Zebedee's headquarters was basically a shop and a stable. But, on the second floor, there were sleeping and living accommodations for the caravan drivers, and for the Zebedee when he was in town. The place was shuttered and barred, however. No one answered their knocks.

"What do you reckon is our fastest way to the Orphel?" said Jesus.

The Fish Gate was close to the Antonia Fortress and to the western wall of the Temple precincts. There was a choice of following directly south along that wall into the Lower City and the Tyropoeon Valley, hence up onto the Orphel, or else going completely around the fortress and the Temple, along the foot path at the base of the Temple's eastern wall, hence down onto the Orphel.

"On a day like this, neither is better," said Nathaniel. "It is shorter to cut through the Lower City. Going at angles to the lines waiting to get into the Temple, I think we can get through well enough. What are you thinking, that Yeshuah is crazy enough to be preaching in the Court of the Gentiles *today?*"

The head of the Orphel gave entrance to the Court of the Gentiles, where Yeshuah had taken to preaching. On the day of Passover preparation, however, there was hardly enough room for a teacher to stand within the Porch of Solomon, much less within any of the courts. So that, in practice that had become custom, no one expected to teach or to be taught within Temple precincts on this day.

On top of which . . .

"The people have been raised to too great a pitch by Yeshuah's declaration of messiahship. If he were to appear in the court today it could well be the spark to the tinder. Yeshuah is not ready for his rebellion to erupt just yet. It is to the house of Nicodemus that we head now, Support."

They plunged into the press of bodies. Most of the crowd, as Nathaniel had predicted, faced to the east, each man waiting his turn to get into the Temple. Traveling south, they were thus able to thread their way through with reasonable speed.

The Orphel, to the south of the Temple, the original Mount Sion, was a peninsula of rock high above the valleys to the east and south of the city. It had been the Ursalim, known to Egyptians for a thousand years before even David had been born. At the time that David had set his mind to the conquering of the city in order to make it his capitol, it had been the impregnable stronghold of the Jebusites.

David conquered it by sending his men up a well shaft, from a spring in the Kedron Valley beneath its walls. Thus it became the City of David. There David built his 'modest palace.' Somewhere at the northern end of the Orphel, in a tomb dug back into the bowels of Mount Moriah, into the rock that he had purchased as the site for the Temple he never lived to build, lay David, himself.

The exact location of the tomb, and its entrance, had been known only to the kings and to the priesthood. It was said amongst the people that King Herod had plundered the tomb of King David during his reign, and those of Solomon and Rebohoam, who slept at David's side.

It was also said that something terrible had happened to Herod as he did that deed—something so awful that Herod had never had an easy night's sleep from then until the end of his life, and so that a man great in many ways had descended ever more deeply into madness.

Certainly, so the people said, the tragedy which still stalked the House of Herod was the result of that desecration—the sins of the father being visited upon the sons. The curse of David lay upon every Herodian seed. So the people said.

The house of Nicodemus was at the southernmost tip of the peninsula near the Fountain Gate over the Pool of Siloam. The Orphel was no longer a fashionable section of Jerusalem. Most men of wealth and power, including Annas and Caiaphas, lived in the Upper City, a wider peninsula of land directly west of the Orphel, on the other side of the Tyropoeon Valley. The Upper City enjoyed greater elevation and so, it was imagined, more frequent summer breezes. Yet the Orphel was an honorable place to live, especially among the Pharisees.

A servant threw back the panel of a peephole in the door as they knocked.

"We are full, and this is the house of a Pharisee who must stay pure for the Passover. Go away."

"Go to your master and tell him that his wine has arrived."

"He has ordered no wine."

"Go and tell him."

It was Nicodemus, himself, who opened the door but a minute later.

"Come in. Hurry." He slammed the door behind them. "Were you seen?"

"No one can see anybody in that mob. Where will I find Yeshuah today, Nicodemus?"

"Yeshuah? Who is Yeshuah?"

"The man for whom you have secreted the supplies in the new tomb. Oh my. What wide eyes. Nicodemus, Friend, what have you gone and gotten yourself into?"

"I do not need to ask your permission for my activities."

"No you do not. Yet I hope you will not mind telling me what those activities are."

"Joshuah, surely you must understand that I am fasting and deeply engaged in purifying myself for the Passover. Those are my only activities."

"Is that why you are giving lodgings to no pilgrims?" For, despite the servant's statement that they were full, the house of that widower was quiet and empty of strangers. "You are keeping yourself private this year, Nicodemus. You do not want witnesses as to who comes and who goes."

"Joshuah, what are you doing here anyway? We thought you were safely away from this place?"

"Who is we?"

Nicodemus turned away, his shoulders stubbornly set.

"Was Yeshuah going to the Temple courts today?"

"Do not be silly."

"Where is he?"

"I have no idea."

"Nicodemus! Please!"

"I am telling the truth!" The Pharisee turned back to face him. "Surely he is out preaching somewhere, wandering as it pleases him—he would want to keep moving, not stay in one place for too long, while showing himself to as many people as possible . . . down along the Kedron, up on the Mount of Olives . . . I do not know."

"I have had information that he will take the Passover at an inn near to David's tomb. Which inn will it be?"

"I do not know. Do not look at me like that, I do *not* know. That part of the plan does not concern me. We have each been told only what each must know."

"Who else, Nicodemus? Who else has been drawn into this perilous . . . "

Jesus stopped. His mouth dropped open.

"My father?"

He stared at Nicodemus. The Pharisee was unable to meet his gaze.

"They wanted to use the tomb," said Jesus. "They went to Father and discovered that he had sold it to you. That is how you became involved."

He found his head swinging stupidly from side to side.

"My father involved in something like this? Joseph bar Ramathea has dedicated his life to *non*-involvement. In *any*thing. Now he joins forces with Yeshuah? How was it accomplished? What persuasions did they use on him?"

"I do not know. We did not discuss it. But you can blame your own self for my involvement. It was you who challenged me, who as much as called me a coward for turning away from a man who would declare himself to be the Messiah. I decided to be a coward no longer. Yeshuah might be the Messiah, and I am going to help him prove it, one way or the other."

"Do you mind if I sit down someplace?"

"Forgive my rudeness. In here. Timothy, bring us some wine."

"For you, too, Master?"

" . . . Yes, for me, too."

The old slave went off, shaking his head. The comings and goings in these last days! Now, on the day of preparation, the master was breaking his fast with wine and endangering his purity with dust-covered strangers.

"I have got to think," Jesus was saying. "I have seldom been so confused as to what to do. Is my father in the city, Nicodemus?"

"He is at home in Bethlehem."

"You are certain?"

"He is not to come here until late tomorrow morning."

"For what reason is he to come?"

Nicodemus hesitated. Yet Judah had not actually sworn him to secrecy. He had merely said, 'You must promise that, should you refuse to help us, you will not divulge the scheme to our enemies, neither will you try to stop us.' Jesus was not an enemy, and Nicodemus was not trying to stop them.

So he told the plan to Jesus and to Nathaniel.

There was a long silence when he was finished.

"Unthinkable," said Jesus at last.

"Which is why it could work," said Nathaniel.

"The audacity is beyond comprehension. I knew he meant to get himself crucified, but *this*."

Jesus suddenly put his hands up to his face.

"Oh my god."

"What? What?" said Nicodemus.

Jesus lifted his face.

"Nicodemus . . . I have lived many lives. I have seen many a good man given worldly power. Worldly power corrupts faster and more completely than any army of worms set loose on a corpse. Nicodemus, any who are helping Yeshuah to this, any who are involved, or who even suspect the truth . . . if Yeshuah succeeds, all of your death warrants are signed."

"How so?"

"A Messiah resurrected by human hands shall have pressing need to silence the mouths attached to those hands. Even Yeshuah does not now understand this, I promise you. He is pure enough now to still be thinking his divine thoughts. But this plot is conceived in lies and deceit, and it shall end covered with blood. What is sown shall be reaped. Judah, you, even Timothy, my father, the Cyrenean, and any of the followers who come to understand what has really happened—Yeshuah shall find means to be rid of you all."

"But no, Jesus! If he succeeds, the Kingdom will be established! *God* will be here, right in Jerusalem. All will be fair and just and happy."

"If Yeshuah succeeds there will be revolution and bloodshed such as our people have never known! Yeshuah will be a totally inexperienced general facing the wrath of the most efficient war machine that this experiment has known to date. For troops, he will have hundreds of thousands of untrained, but pompously opinionated, civilians, whose only common bond is a pressing need not to dirty their hands, and the belief that, at any moment, their god will arrive to fight their battles for them. To keep such a ridiculous army in line, Yeshuah would have to keep them believing in him. He would never be able to risk the truth of his 'resurrection' being told. Such information might tend to dampen the ardor of his troops."

"Our people will be as one," insisted Nicodemus.

"When have our people ever been as one? Our entire history is one of brother killing and cheating brother, of endless fighting and rivalry between our tribes, and now we are so divided by political and religious factions that a person does not know what to believe from one day to the next."

"But *God* will be the general," said Nicodemus.

"Oh? What sort of uniform will 'he' wear? Will 'his' armor be of gold? What is 'God' going to look like, Nicodemus? How tall is he? Does he have a long white beard? Where is he going to sit when he comes down? Can he handle a chariot? Will he lead us into battle, lusting for blood and vengeance? Or will he hide himself in the Holy of Holies and reveal himself only to Yeshuah?"

"Yes!" said Nicodemus. "Surely only the Messiah will be allowed to look upon God and speak with him."

"Then *you* will never be sure that 'God' is really there, just as you are not sure now. You will never know whether pronouncements are coming from your god or from Yeshuah, will you? As a matter of fact, nothing will change except that Yeshuah will replace Annas as the ruler of the Jews.

"It will be the same old story, told a little differently to make it seem new. But it will produce the same sort of corrupt and bloated priesthood, more tyrannical rulers, and more oppression of the Individual Spirit.

"And that Individual Spirit is the only thing that *is* holy, Nicodemus. For there is your true god. The Individual Spirit of each human, each plant, each rock, each star. Each is a particle of the great body that is All That Is.

"And may a particle not talk with itself? See itself? How can you imagine that only the Messiah should be allowed to see and talk with your god when the true god lives in each one of us?

"All That Is denies no one the right to see and speak with itself, Nicodemus, neither does it play favorites. Each of us is an important enough son or daughter of All That Is to enjoy the most intimate converse.

"Believe me, Nicodemus, All That Is is not going to descend into Jerusalem and take up abode in the Holy of Holies for the sheer joy of chatting each day with Yeshuah."

Nicodemus was covering his ears.

"I do not care to listen to any more of this. I have agreed to help Yeshuah and help him I will."

"Please listen to reason."

"I have agreed. It is a matter of honor."

"What if I talk my father out of it?"

Nicodemus hesitated.

"It would be difficult without Joseph. I am not as well known to Pilatus."

"What of the physician? Do you know where he can be found today?"

"No. There was no reason for any of us to be in contact today. There is nothing left but for each of us to do our assigned tasks on the morrow. I doubt that you will find him at his lodgings at this hour. I do know that he will take the Passover at the home of his uncles this night. Their house is next door to his inn."

"Judah was not scheduled to contact you today?"

"No."

"And you have no idea at which inn Yeshuah will take the Passover?"

"You seem to have acquired more information than was given even to me."

Jesus rose.

"Come on, Nathaniel. Nicodemus, I may have need to shelter some of my people with you this night."

"They will be welcome."

"I pray you will have a change of heart as to this endeavor, Nicodemus. You have sought so long, given your life to a search for holiness and right-doing in the eyes of your god. But you cannot do good by doing what is wrong. The end never justifies the means. No endeavor born of deceit and trickery will ever be righteous. Goodbye for now, my Friend."

"What are we going to do?" said Nathaniel once out onto the street.

"I was hoping that you would tell me," said Jesus ruefully. "Yeshuah has been too clever. Each man knows just enough to do his part and no more, it would do us no good to talk with the Cyrenean or with my father. Neither of them could tell us where to find Yeshuah. And it is Yeshuah that we *must* talk with.

"I could probably dissuade the Cyrenean . . . I could probably dissuade my father. Yet, if Yeshuah does not know they are being dissuaded, he will allow himself to be taken and the crucifixion would go ahead without the support he is counting on. Which would be a really vicious trick to pull on him. I will not be a party to that."

"I could run out to Bethany. Simon the Leper might have heard something of his plans."

"Yeshuah will not misstep that easily. Simon will have no more idea than did Nicodemus. No. We have got to keep searching, moving, watching. Yeshuah will attract big crowds wherever he goes."

"How do you see a crowd in a mob?"

Jesus smiled.

"It is a different color. Come up to the top of the street, let us take a look at the inns. Judah said nothing more than that it was an inn near to where Yeshuah believed the tomb of David to be?"

"That was it. I fault myself that I had not the wits to ask for the name of the inn."

"Fault not yourself for lack of wits, Support. I am doing enough castigating of self in regard to that for all of us."

They fought their way through the crowds to the upper end of the Orphel, their every step contested by those who thought they might be crowding ahead. The Orphel ended at the south wall of the Temple, below the Court of the Gentiles. Through the two gates that led up into that court, not only Jews, but, tens of thousands of visitors from all over the world passed during the course of a year, the Temple of Jerusalem being high on the list of places that should be seen by the well-rounded traveler. Hence, it was just in this area that there were to be found a hundred inns to accommodate those travelers.

The Street of the Horse Gate led along the base of that southern wall.

"This is about as close to the tomb as one could get," mused Jesus. "Solomon's Palace was over there on the western rim.

"Now why did Solomon choose that particular place for his palace? Does it not stand to reason that he built it over, and incorporating, the entrance to the great David's tomb? A tomb that he would one day share?

"And would it not again stand to reason that a tomb that we know to have been excavated back into Mount Moriah, and known only to the kings and the priests, would be caused to join through passages to both the palace and to the Temple? Both of which were on the west of the hill.

"Hence, if I were to guess, I would say that the tomb is some distance back in under the Temple wall by the western rim.

"Let us hope that is exactly how Yeshuah reasoned and that he did manage to engage an inn as close to that spot as possible.

"Start with the inn at the western end of the street and work your way back to this point, then do the side streets to this point, then the street behind this to this point. Which ought to keep you busy for a few minutes."

"What shall I ask the innkeepers? Surely the right one will have been paid to keep his tongue to himself."

"Act with authority. As you enter each inn, say that you are a friend of Judah, the brother of the Rabbi, and that you have been sent to reaffirm the arrangements for the upper room—which is truthful enough.

"Watch the proprietor carefully as he answers. Note any who get shift-eyed. Only one will not be able to tell you honestly that you have the wrong inn. On the other hand, you might catch the right one off guard.

"Be in this same spot in an hour. I will be back by then with some of the others. We will then spread out through the city and the valleys until we spot him."

He stopped at a vendor on the way back, and bought several breads and cheeses and two jugs of wine. He did not truly mean for his people to eat Nehemiah's cabbages.

The going was difficult only when he traveled in the same direction as the lines, when the men in the lines assumed that he was trying to get ahead of them. Cutting through, going at angles or in opposite directions, travel was relatively easy.

"I have this day re-discovered a great truth, a scientific principle," he grinned to Merovee when he got back to the garden. "To travel quickly and well in this life, never go in the direction of the herd. The place that the herd goes to will never be the place where one ought to go anyway. The herd only thinks that it is the place to go because its shepherd has told it that that is the place to go. If one goes in that direction, one will waste time and energy and end up nowhere except in the pen of the shepherd to be shorn or slain. Be your own shepherd, your own herd rolled into one. Decide your own course, designate your own pen. Shear and slay yourself for the benefit of yourself."

"Has the heat gotten to you?" said Jacob bar Alphaeus. "What news of my son?"

"We must go out and search, Jacob. No one can help us but ourselves. And here is my plan."

In this plan even the women would participate. They gratefully ate their bread and cheese, passed the wine and listened.

To establish a central means of communication, there were to be sixteen sentry points ringing the Temple, permanently stationed. Twelve runners would continuously circle the Temple precincts, six moving in each direction, from sentry to sentry, picking up any bit of information from sentries or opposing runners, passing it on to all others.

Each man could make a full circuit in about an hour, depending upon the crowds. By the use of the opposing runners, each segment of the network would be fairly current at all times.

The rest of the company was to fan out into the city and into the valleys, watching for Yeshuah or any of his people. Anyone with anything to report would report it to one of the sentries or to one of the runners. Those field people would also check in each hour to learn what success others might have had and to receive new instructions.

Merovee, Johannah, Esther the wife of Jairus, and Navea the wife of Levi, were assigned the north end of the precincts. Merovee was stationed by the main gate, at the base of the sheer hill of stone that was part of the northern fortifications of the Antonia. The other three women were stationed at equal distances eastward down the wall outside the priestly Court of Herod. Merovee knew why Josh had assigned her to her particular station. It was selfish of him in a way, for, should trouble develop—something that would threaten her safety—she would have but to run through the gate into the Antonia and find protection with Pilatus. Selfish, yes. But he had enough to think about. And was he not allowed a selfishness once in a while?

Aunt Miriam, Susannah, Leah, and Thera, the wife of Phillipus, took the narrow path on the cliff ledge along the eastern, Kedron wall.

Mother Meraiah and Deborah, Cleopatra, the wife of Demetrius, and two of her daughters-in-law took the western wall, Deborah and Meraiah being stationed together.

The southern wall—along the Street of the Horse Gate—was given to men—Uncle Cleopah, Ben, and two of the servants from bar Jeremiah. This was the point of the greatest crowds, leading into the Court of the Gentiles. It was also the point at which disturbances in regard to the Messiah were most apt to occur.

Besides which, while Cleopah and Ben and the two servants could all recognize any of Yeshuah's followers who came into the Street of the Horse Gate to see to the Passover preparations, they, themselves, were not nearly as well known as some of the other followers, and were less likely to be spotted.

"If any one of us sentries sees one or more of these men, should we leave our posts and follow?" asked Aunt Miriam eagerly. Her eyes were shining. She had not had this much excitement, this much responsibility, in her entire life.

Jesus hesitated.

"No. Instead, mark as much as you can about the man's destination, then walk with all speed toward the runner you know will reach you next. Send that runner after the man and return to you post."

"You think we women are not capable of following a man in a crowd?" Susannah bristled.

"My love, you and any of these ladies are capable of anything. You might even be able to follow better than a man. But I must be a good general. I abhor warfare, but some of its rules were formulated for sound reasons. Sentries must stay dependably in place else the entire system breaks down.

"Likewise, if one of you runners spots the quarry, report to the nearest sentry before following. No matter what the temptation. Do you all understand?"

They did.

"Lastly, there is the matter of our second Nathaniel. Bar Tolmei. He is one of us. He can be counted upon. If any of you see him, attempt to tell him of our system, or else the location of the nearest sentry, or of this garden, so that he can get information to us.

"If you see Judah, approach him as well. Give him the same information and tell him that I beg to know the name of the inn where Yeshuah takes the Passover so that I can speak with the man and try to talk him out of his plans.

"Are you ready to go? Nehemiah, you will remain dependably here in the garden?"

"Yes, Reb Joshuah."

"If all else fails, Nehemiah is our center. Get your information to him or simply return to this place."

They set off. Alexander, Micah, two servants from bar Jeremiah, and two of Cleopah's sons, Simeon and Jacob, were to begin running west to east, north to south, east to west, and south to north. Along with Phillipus, his two youngest brothers, Jacob bar Alphaeus, and Chandreah, who were to move immediately over onto the Mount of Olives and into the north of the Kedron Valley, they escorted Merovee and the women for the north and east walls to their places.

Jesus and the others escorted the ladies for the western wall to their places. While Levi set off to canvas the city to the west—where they really did not expect Yeshuah to be found—Jesus and the other men continued on to the Street of the Horse Gate and the appointed meeting with Nathaniel.

That man was waiting as instructed.

"In the hour allotted I was only able to canvas the inns facing upon this street. The proprietor of the Inn of Sion just over here either has a most unfortunate twitch or he is lying. Otherwise, I deem the responses to have been honest."

"The Inn of Sion," mused Jesus, looking at the inn. "It has a symbolic ring, does it not? Uncle Cleopah, keep especial watch on the door of that inn."

Jesus, himself, and Jairus, then left to search the south of the Kedron Valley and the area of the road to Bethany. Demetrius and two Kapher Kana artisans took over the canvas of the inns upon the side and back streets below the Temple. Nathaniel moved off to search to the direct south, in the Valley of Hinnom. The counter runners, the last two of the bothers of Phillipus, Barnabus, Thaddeus, Cleopah's son, Reuben, and one of the Kapher Kana artisans, began their circuit of the Temple precincts.

It was the third hour after sunrise when this system went into operation. For comfort's sake, the women adopted the appearance of beggars, veils and shawls drawn about their faces, squatting or sitting back in whatever angles created by jogs in the wall that they could find, away from the trampling of the crowds.

"What shall we do if people offer us alms?" Merovee had asked of Jesus.

"You labor to save them from blood and destruction, and the worker is worthy of her pay. Be sure to thank them nicely," he had smiled.

It was the fourth hour when word came around the circuit, sent in by Phillipus via one of his brothers from out on the Mount of Olives. Yeshuah and his followers had been out on the Bethphage road at dawn. He had healed a blind man and preached to a large congregation. No one knew where he was now, but people in the encampments upon that mount talked of nothing but Yeshuah Christos.

At the fifth hour, word came from Phillipus that he had just missed Yeshuah down by the Kedron. Opposite the Golden Gate! People said that he had been heading south. Surely Jesus or Jairus or Nathaniel would spot him. Merovee sent word around for the sentries themselves to watch more carefully, especially those with a view of the Mount of Olives and the Kedron Valley.

For the next hour, the only news to make the circuit was its own idle chatter. Aunt Miriam's back was killing her. The wisdom of posting Deborah and old Meraiah together became apparent, for Meraiah had gotten chilled, even with both her quilt and Deborah's. Deborah had gone to a shop and bought her a sheepskin to sit upon. Johannah, outside the Court of Herod, and the nearest to the Levite chorus, was so sick of listening to the Hallel that she hoped never to hear it again. Susannah, near the Golden Gate, had collected enough coins to buy another jug of wine. Alexander darted aside, bought it, and carried it around for all to share.

At the sixth hour, an alarm of hope was raised. Ben, down near the west of the Orphel on the Street of the Horse Gate, had spotted Petros! Demetrius had been alerted and had ran off after him, down into the market section of the Tyropoeon Valley.

On the next circuit, news came that Demetrius was back, chagrined. He had lost Petros in the crowds at the market place. But Petros had obviously been buying provisions—for the Passover meal, no doubt. It seemed that the guess of Jesus, as to the area of the inn, had been correct.

At the eighth hour, came word that both of the brothers of Phillipus had been drawn to a huge crowd up near the summit of the Mount of Olives. It was Yeshuah, no doubt about it, but they could not get near him for the mob. One brother had stayed to keep track of Yeshuah, while the other had run back to report.

`In the meantime, Aunt Miriam, looking out across the Kedron from her spot on the east wall, had also noticed the throng and sent word around to get the next scout who checked in out to that spot. The very next runner said that Jesus had checked in just at that time and was, himself, heading for the Mount of Olives.

A sigh of relief ran around the circuit. The vigil was nearly over. Johannah could escape the Hallel, Meraiah could be gotten to some warm place, Aunt Miriam could rest her back, Susannah, who, they were jibing, seemed to be the most convincing beggar of them all, could buy them all several more jugs of wine.

Outside the Antonia, even Merovee had grown cold and stiff, sitting so long in the shade created by the fortress wall. Her breasts were beginning to hurt, filling with milk for her Agapo. Oh, why was she here, and not with his radiant little Self?

The skies were clouding over. There was a threat of rain in the air.

Alexander was the next runner by, coming from the direction of Deborah and Meraiah on the western wall of the fortress. He had nothing new to report.

But then Barnabus came running from the eastern wall, running hard.

"There is trouble," he panted. "sudden shouting and fighting in that crowd around Yeshuah. Real fighting. We think perhaps Zealots have mixed in and are making trouble." He rushed on with his news.

Merovee rose to her feet, fighting the urge to run to the brow of the hill overlooking the Kedron to see for herself. Everyone in the street outside Herod's Court was running to take a look. The disturbance must be spreading rapidly to gain such attention.

Indeed, coming from the direction of the mountain she could now hear a roar. The full-throated cry of thousands. Many thousands.

Overhead, on the ramparts, Roman sentries began to shout. There came the sounds of many feet, the clanking of armor and weapons.

Surely Pilatus was not going to send men out into that! After complacently watching Yeshuah's palm-strewn entrance into the Temple? Why?

She knew the answer. The thousands accompanying Yeshuah to the Temple had been happy and peaceful. Fighting, angry thousands were quite another matter, a matter that must be nipped in the bud.

But a handful of men, no matter how well-armed, against thousands?

With a blast of trumpets, a century, eighty men, issued forth from the gate just to Merovee's right. Then a second century. Magnificently confident, their movements in precise harmony, they set off at the double-time in the direction of the Mount of Olives. And there was suddenly no doubt in Merovee's mind that just that "handful," just one hundred and sixty men, could destroy any undisciplined multitude in their path.

A slow, dull horror filled her. It was her first, direct experience of the Roman military in action. She realized that it would probably not be her last.

Prancing with frustration, still she held her place, watching for Reuben, her next runner from that direction. It seemed forever before he appeared.

"The crowd is dispersing, they can see the Romans coming. Most are running back over the Mount of Olives. I doubt there will be a confrontation."

Another brother of Phillipus, coming from the opposite direction, said that Levi was back from the western city and, hearing that Yeshuah was definitely over on the Mount of Olives, had gone down to the Orphel to add his eyes to the search for Petros.

The next word was that the two centuries were returning to the fortress, the disturbance having evaporated. Breathing a sigh of relief, Merovee turned back to her niche in the wall.

As she turned, however, she spotted a familiar face.

It took a moment for realization to sink in, and more moments for the implications to become apparent.

She turned slowly, her horror renewing itself. The numbers and composition of the crowd between the Antonia Fortress and the brow of the Kedron had subtly changed. There were suddenly a great many men who carried no lambs, who did not seem to be going anywhere—who were just loitering, waiting.

The face that had caught her attention was that of Yeshuah's son Eleazar.

Had she but known them, she would also have recognized many of the seasoned warriors from the Zealot days of Yeshuah.

The disturbance over on the Mount of Olives . . . could it have been a Zealot ruse? To draw the legionaries out? All these men had appeared so suddenly between the centuries and the safety of the Antonia . . . there were hundreds of them, faces grim, eyes watching. Did they mean to . . .

It was too late. There was no chance to cry out, to give a warning even if it had been clear whom she should warn. The first ranks of the centuries appeared back over the hill, trotting smartly.

It was Eleazar who was the Zealots' leader. She saw him make the first move, bare his sword, issue the battle cry. From all sides, the Zealots poured in upon the Romans, whipping their swords from beneath their cloaks.

Even taken by surprise, and surrounded by superior numbers of armed fighting men, the Romans, with cool precision, simply reformed into a number of hollow wedges and continued toward the fort, clearing their way with ease, leaving a trail of maimed Zealots. At the same time, more Romans issued forth from the Antonia, commencing a pincher movement as they went to the aid of their fellows.

It was over almost as quickly as it had begun. Those Zealots still standing broke and ran, escaping in all directions.

A pitiful display. One of utter futility. What had they meant to accomplish? Had they thought that they could wipe out the entire Roman garrison? Take the Antonia? And Jerusalem with it?

With what? Wild-eyed courage?

Ah, this brief display was all it took for a person to see, both, how Rome had conquered the world, and how it was keeping it. She suddenly understood the devastation that would ensue if Yeshuah succeeded with his plan, and, as the resurrected Messiah, inspired hundreds of thousands of his people to revolt.

Where she had worried before for the Romans and their small numbers, now she ached for those hundreds of thousands. Those numbers would count for nothing, just as the superior number of Zealots had counted for nothing against the professionalism of the centuries. Yeshuah's enthusiastic rabble would go down even more easily than had those Zealots, who at least pretended to be trained in the use of weapons.

An entire generation of her people would be decimated if Yeshuah had his way.

She huddled there in her angle beside the gate, watching as the soldiers cleaned up the street, piling the dead into a wagon, carrying the injured into the fortress. Eleazar was led past her, still very much alive, shouting invective.

He would be tried immediately, along with any others who were not too far gone, though most looked to be in poor shape. Roman justice was swift. They would all be found guilty of course.

It must be almost the tenth hour by now. No crucifixion would be commenced this late in the day, especially on the eve of Passover. Eleazar, and any of the others who were fit, would be crucified on the morrow.

Merovee sat looking at absolutely nothing, her eyes batting with the rapidity of her thoughts.

This was going to effect Yeshuah's plans drastically. He had certainly not expected his own son to go to the cross with him. Depending upon how many of those men were still whole enough to be tried, there could be a *mass* execution tomorrow, with Yeshuah only thrown in for good measure, separated from any chance at special or preferred treatment.

More then ever, it was necessary to get to him, to tell him and warn him.

She sent the message on with the next runner.

"But be gentle with Meraiah when you tell her of Eleazar."

Poor Queen Meraiah. If Yeshuah was the apple of one eye, Eleazar had been the apple of the other. A woman could go blind, having both eyes gouged out.

The next word around the circuit was that all was lost. Jesus had returned, with Phillipus and his brothers. They had lost Yeshuah and his men in the panic that greeted the approach of the Romans. Yeshuah and his people had escaped up over the Mount of Olives. There had been no way, in the frantic tides of people, to follow after them, or even to mark the direction in which they had fled.

And now the day was too far gone. The Temple's third relay was finished, people were heading for their lodgings in anticipation of the sundown and the official beginning of the Passover. There would be no more willing crowds for Yeshuah this day. He would show himself publicly no more. He would, instead, as soon as it was dark and safe, head for the inn that he had engaged for the feast.

The runners brought the sentries in on that last sweep, around to the Street of the Horse Gate on the Orphel where Jesus waited. He had already sent Nathaniel down to Nicodemus to ask that he shelter the women.

But the women would not go. Not even Meraiah.

"So my bones are cold! You think I have not had cold bones before this day? You think I am old and of no use? I will certainly be of no use if I cannot help you try to save my son. If I die in the effort, I will at least have died trying. Is that not what you always say, Jesus? One has at least to try."

"Yes, I have always said that, Mother. Come then, all of you. We must get food to fill our bellies and fortify ourselves before the sun sets, for we will not be feasting this night. Instead, we will be gliding like Angels of Death, watching the doors of the inns."

Vendors, preparing to close, were happy to turn unsold remnants into coins. The food would have been burnt anyway, since, during the seven days of Passover, none but ritually pure food was supposed to be consumed. Susannah, as promised, bought the wine, and the company went to sit in a jog in the wall of the Temple, out of immediate sight, but where they could see the street. Particularly the Inn of Sion.

They were all back on their feet before the sun had fully set, employing a new system.

The entire premise was based on the assumption that the inn to be used was within a certain area. The point was to keep as much of that area as possible under surveillance at all times.

Each person thus began at a street corner. Slowly then, they all began to walk, all in the same direction, by an agreed upon, snakelike route, round and round, in and out of the streets at the northwest of the Orphel. No one was to round a corner or angle till he or she was sure that the person following had come into view. At each little side alley, a person was to wait until, at the other end, a companion came into view. They would not have to keep this up for long. If they had the right area, Yeshuah and his men would arrive soon after darkness. Yeshuah's self-proclaimed time plan ruled out a late dinner.

But they had not reckoned on the darkness of the streets. It was a night of full moon—the Passover being tied to the full moon—but the skies were overcast, still threatening rain, so that the moon could not help them. Here and there, torches outside of inns threw brave crescents of light at the darkness, and parties of people came by with torches to light their own ways to Passover celebrations. Other than that, the watchers had to feel their ways along, and it was impossible, in practice, to see much of anything.

Still, it would be difficult for a large group of men to come into the area without being seen by at least one of the watchers.

Yet it seemed that they had. Or else the wrong area was being watched. Hours passed, with no sign of Yeshuah. Jesus found himself stumbling as he walked along. Not from fatigue, or because of darkness. He was blinded by tears.

He had failed. Utterly failed. If he could not find Yeshuah and talk with him this night, he would have to let tomorrow's events go forward just as Yeshuah had planned, without interfering. He simply could not, would not, pull the floor out from under Yeshuah without warning him.

Was this the way it was supposed to be? Was Yeshuah's view of God and salvation the one that would be carried forth in this probability? Was the confrontation with the Romans to come this soon?

No. It could not be. He refused to give up. As Meraiah had reminded him, 'You have to at least try.'

It was Meraiah, herself, who had been walking in line ahead of Jesus, who came stumbling back to him.

"Judah just came out of this inn up ahead!"

Jesus took her arm. Together they rushed forward, to the torchlight outside that inn.

"Did he see you, Meraiah?"

"No. I called, but I was too far back and he did not seem to hear. His head was down. I think he was sobbing, Jesus. He rushed off down the street."

Jesus looked ahead. At the end of this particular street were steps down into the Tyropoeon Valley.

He felt his own tears flooding out.

"Oh Judah!"

The house of the High Priest was somewhere in the Upper City on the other side of the Tyropoeon Valley.

"Wait here for the others, Meraiah, I have got to try to catch him."

He took off, running full out despite the darkness, stumbling, falling headlong, scrambling to his feet and rushing on. He got to the steps, grasped the rude rails, and rushed down the steps, using those rails for support and guidance, ignoring the slivers that drove into his flesh, and the occasional nail heads that ripped and tore.

"Judah!" he shouted as he went. "Judah! It is Jesus! Stop!"

He could not see anything ahead—the market was closed for the night, there was not even an occasional torch to light the way.

"Judah! Wait for me! Judah, *please*! Where are you?"

So that two sobbing men stumbled into the Tyropoeon Valley that night. But one was too far ahead of the other. He could not hear the voice begging him to stop.

And would he have stopped if he had?

Unfamiliar with the market section, and unsure of the route to the house of the High Priest in the Upper City, Jesus had to turn back. To press on would only waste time—when Yeshuah had finally been trapped there in that inn.

By the time he got back, the others had caught up to Meraiah.

"Did you stop him?" said Merovee.

"Your hands are bleeding!" said Susannah.

603

"I fear I shed but drops in comparison to what is to come," said Jesus. "Phillipus, Levi, Chandreah, bar Alphaeus. Come upstairs with me. Nathaniel, lead the others down to the house of Nicodemus, then return and wait here by the door."

"Josh, let me come with you," said Merovee.

He embraced her.

"We are in Jerusalem now, my love. Custom would frown on a woman invading their seder."

"Be careful then."

"Of course!"

He smiled.

"What harm could come to *me?*"

* * *

The seder had been subdued. Yeshuah had been morose and withdrawn throughout, answering young Johannan—who asked the traditional questions—automatically, hardly seeming to hear the Hallel as it was sung. He had refused the innkeeper's excellently roasted lamb, and barely touched his matzoth bread, building little pyramids of the crumbs, and swirling his wine, staring into its depths.

Petros had lain to the right of Yeshuah, signifying, as Yeshuah had told them, that Petros was to have first place after himself in the Kingdom. To Yeshuah's left, as arranged by Thunder, had been the Boanerges. Mathiah, Salmon, Eli, Ezekiel, Rufus, Lebbaeus, Isaac, Jacob, Baruch and Joseph had ranged about the serving tables in no particular order. Bar Tolmei sat apart. He had signaled his disapproval of a messianic uprising—they knew that he was there out of loyalty and not commitment.

At the far end of the room, even more pointedly apart, had been Judah, his eyes downcast, his face pale, showing as little interest in food as his brother.

But then, all the followers agreed, Judah had been acting strangely ever since they had arrived in Jerusalem.

At last, with the Hallel finished, Yeshuah seemed to come back to the room.

"I have looked forward for so long . . . yearned to celebrate this Passover with you here in Jerusalem, near to the tomb of my blessed forefather."

The men leaned forward, waiting to hear Yeshuah's plan for initiating the Kingdom. Surely, he was about to announce it. And, surely, with many hundreds of thousands of Passover pilgrims, plus the citizens of Jerusalem, ready to rise up and sweep him to the throne of Judeah, all that silly talk of crucifixion would no longer be a part of the plan. If, indeed, it ever had been any serious part. Flushed with triumph after the last two days, made happy by the wine, such a thing was unthinkable to the followers.

Yet there was another long pause as Yeshuah took up a portion of matzoth and lay staring at it. Finally, with a sigh, he rose and went around the table, breaking off a piece for each man.

He kept Judah for last, and put the matzoth, not into Judah's hand, but, onto his tongue.

"This is my body. Eat it. Chew it well. Henceforth, remember me always when you eat of unleavened bread. For, as Moses took our ancestors out of physical bondage in Egypt after the eating of the matzoth, so I will shortly take the children of Israel out of spiritual bondage."

The men murmured in appreciation and did as bidden. This must be part of some new ritual that Yeshuah had gotten from God.

Yeshuah, for his part, waited, looking down at his youngest brother as Judah dutifully chewed the matzoth. When Judah had finished, he said . . .

"Now get you gone, Judah. Go and do that which you must do."

Slowly, Judah raised his eyes. It seemed that he had had too much to drink, for he was crying.

"The night is cold. Let me stay, Yeshuah."

"Finish off your wine. It is my blood. It will be proof against cold."

Dutifully, Judah drained his cup.

"Goodbye, then," said Yeshuah. "Go. Quickly!"

Judah rose. Without a backward glance, he went to the stairwell and disappeared down into the hubbub and Hallels of the common room. Yeshuah followed after him and stood at the stop of the stairs for quite some time.

The men began to exchange glances.

"On what errand do you send Judah?" said Isaac finally. "All the shops are closed now, Yeshuah."

For a moment, Yeshuah did not answer. He did not turn to them when finally he did answer.

"Judah goes to get us the Kingdom."

"Get us the Kingdom?" said Salmon. "How?"

Yeshuah still did not turn.

"With holy money from God," he said. "Thirty sanctified pieces of silver which shall deliver the Kingdom of God on Earth to us."

"God gave you this silver?" said Eli in awe.

"God will cause it to be delivered to my messenger."

"But . . . "

Yeshuah held up a hand.

"Zilpah!" he called loudly.

"Yes, Master!" She rose from where she had been sitting, at the foot of the stairs, waiting for the summons.

"Bring up the special wine."

Yeshuah turned then, and walked in silence around the room. The men watched him just as silently.

At last Zilpah could be heard, carefully making her way up the staircase. She entered the room just as carefully, balancing a large tray upon which there were cups already filled with wine.

The woman was flushed and beaming, honored beyond words to be the woman chosen to serve this special wine, to do the secret biddings of the Messiah. She was splendidly dressed for the occasion, having purchased a magnificent robe in the bazaar. It was of a heavenly blue, and was richly laced with real gold threads, while copious gold dangled from her ears, hung from her neck, and jangled on her wrists. A single, enormous ruby adorned the front of her golden headdress. For, after all, she had reasoned as she had bought it on the Zebedee's credit, the price of a virtuous women was beyond rubies. And it was necessary to impress Yeshuah with her value as an ornament to the head table of the Kingdom.

The followers stared. Even Yeshuah raised a brow at the picture she presented.

For she had also applied lavish kohl to her eyes, and a redness to her lips and cheeks.

She looked . . . beautiful, actually, as she might have looked on her wedding day.

Slowly, ceremoniously, she circled the men, halting beside each one, decorously leaning down, inviting each to take a cup. Only for Yeshuah was there no cup. Having finished her impressive performance, she stopped before that man.

"Do you have further need of me, Master?"

"Not at the moment, Zilpah. Thank you."

"Then I will take my leave."

Gracefully, she disappeared down the stairwell.

Nervous snickers broke the silence. Yeshuah's expression stilled them.

Again he circled them. Their eyes followed intently. Now. Now he was going to tell them the plan. But he just kept circling.

"Do you not drink with us?" said Petros finally.

"From this moment, I will not again taste of the vine until God's Kingdom has come. Take this sacred wine into yourselves."

Obediently, each began to drink.

"Savor it. Feel its warmth as it goes down. More. Take more."

They obeyed.

"Understand what you imbibe. As the unleavened bread was my body . . . so this wine is my blood, which will, on the morrow, be shed for you and for the remission of your sins."

Young Johannan choked. Petros looked up in alarm.

"What are you saying, Yeshuah?"

"Drink!"

"Who is going to shed your blood?"

"How many times have I told you, Petros? The Son of Man must be delivered up to the rulers."

"No! Let us leave Jerusalem quickly!"

"Petros, my poor fool . . . "

"But the rulers dare not touch you now!" said the eldest of the Boanerges. "The people would rise against them."

"They will do it cleverly, in league with one of my followers, who has already betrayed me," said Yeshuah quietly.

The uproar was immediate.

"Who has betrayed you?" cried Petros. "It is certainly not I!"

"No. But you must deny me, Petros. All of you, any of you. At a certain point, you must pretend that you do not know me."

"I will never deny you!" The square, bluff face of Petros was red with wine and with anger. "I have made my choice. I am your man to the end."

"My man? You, any of you, will no doubt take up your own crosses before you are finished if you are my men, and die the sort of death that I will die. Yet I say to you that that death is the only way to life. Those who die in the way that I will die shall save their lives, while those who save their lives shall lose them, and find no place in my Kingdom. I prepare to save my life, and, in so doing, save the lives of all my people. My death shall be your model. It shall teach you how to die in order to bring your own eventual flocks into our Kingdom. Do not be frightened, any of you. Simply trust me and wait.

Even though the rulers of the Temple shall seize me this night. Even though I will be crucified on the morrow."

"No!" they cried, on their feet now.

"Tonight?"

"How could such a thing be?"

"It is impossible!"

"*Listen* to me! I want all of you to keep yourselves safely. None of you are to let yourselves be taken, neither are you to come near me, nor try to save me after I am taken. Do you not see that God shall not allow the grave to keep his Anointed? His Christos? On the third day, I will rise from the dead and come to you, and then you shall have your Kingdom. You have my promise."

"Stop! You may not go up there!"

It was Zilpah, and a sudden commotion on the staircase.

"Master, Master!" she cried.

Then Jesus was in the room. Behind him were Phillipus, Levi, Jacob bar Alphaeus, and Chandreah, fending off blows from the outraged Zilpah.

"Yeshuah!" said Jesus. "You started without us. We are offended."

Bar Tolmei ran forward to join them.

"Jesus. Thank God. Thank God you are here."

"Yes!" cried Petros, joining bar Tolmei. "Jesus, he means to get himself taken this very night. He is going through with that insane plan to get himself crucified. Stop him!"

"Master," said Zilpah, "what should I do?"

Yeshuah had turned deathly pale at the sight of Jesus.

"Go back down, Zilpah. I will call you if you are needed."

"But Master!"

"Go."

She went.

Jesus and Yeshuah stood looking hard at one another for a moment.

"Yeshuah," said Jesus finally. "You and I need to talk. Privily."

"I see no need."

"I promise you that there is."

Yeshuah hesitated. Then he nodded and walked with Jesus to a corner of the room.

"I have been to Nicodemus," said Jesus. He saw Yeshuah start. "I know the entire plan."

"Ah! There is, indeed, a traitor in my camp!" His eyes flew to bar Tolmei.

"Bar Tolmei is innocent."

"Judah, then," said Yeshuah bitterly.

"My discovery of the plan was accidental."

"Then how did you find me this night?"

"With a great deal of difficulty, and through the labors of a great many people who love you. Including Meraiah. She froze herself to the bone helping to search for you this day, and this night she has walked the streets with us endlessly. It was she who spotted Judah running from this inn."

Yeshuah's head snapped upward.

"Never fear," said Jesus. "He got away from me."

Yeshuah relaxed.

"Is my mother all right?"

"Your mother is a valiant and special Soul. It is hard to sink her. She has been taken to the house of Nicodemus for the night. Merovee has grown to love Meraiah as her own, Yeshuah. She will see to her comfort.

"Yeshuah, you need to give it up now. I will get to the Cyrenean, and then, on the morrow, I will intercept my father. I will stop them from supporting you. You cannot succeed without them. Judah and Nicodemus will not suffice."

For a moment, Yeshuah stared at Jesus as though, indeed, trapped and defeated. Then he shook his head.

"You are wrong, Jesus. Because I have an ally who you cannot dissuade. God. He shall open all doors for Judah and Nicodemus."

"I said a moment ago that I discovered your plan accidentally. Yet, do you not see that it was no accident at all? I was meant to learn of it. And to stop you."

Yeshuah frowned. Then he shook his head irritably.

"God shall guide Judah's steps, give him all the right words. God shall see to it that Pilatus grants everything that is necessary. Besides . . . "

A slow, soft smile came across the face of Yeshuah.

"I have learned you too well, Jesus. You will not stop the Cyrenean. When you see that I am determined, you will not have it in your heart to take my support from me."

"There are places and reasons in my heart the depths of which you cannot begin to know, Yeshuah. What you say would only have been true had I not been able to reach you and warn you. Now you are warned. And you have my solemn promise that I *will* stop my father and the Cyrenean."

Yeshuah paled. He stared closely at the face of Jesus and found the truth. He turned away.

"So be it then. Yet I will not be deterred. You only make it more difficult for me—more painful and dangerous.

"But on the other hand . . . "

He turned back, a new light in his eyes.

"Of course! As an angel sent by God to guide me while seeming to oppose me, you, in truth, come to show me the better way. Without the support on which I had planned, I will suffer so much more. In trying to lessen my suffering, I was being a coward, was I not. But the Son of Man must suffer. Suffer dreadfully. He must overcome seemingly insurmountable odds. Then his triumph will be complete, his glory the greatest."

"Yeshuah!"

"No. No, I want it this way now. I have to have perfect trust in myself and in my father. Whatever you are able to do to take away my support, be of good cheer while doing it, Jesus. And thank you for helping me see the light. I am I, and I will prevail. I will be able to do the sleep even if I do not have the Cyrenean's magic cakes. And Judah *shall* find a way to manage the tomb.

"Even if he is not able, even if they shovel me under, I will still rise on the third day and lead the children of Israel into the Kingdom of God on Earth. Thank you, my angel, thank you."

"Yeshuah, Eleazar attacked the Roman centuries this afternoon and was taken prisoner. He will be crucified on the morrow."

Yeshuah stepped backward as though he had been struck.

"... Eleazar? How? Where?"

"We think that the disturbance that brought up the Romans and caused you to flee back over the Mount of Olives was part of the plan. Eleazar and hundreds of Zealots were waiting as the centuries returned to the Antonia. They attacked and were routed."

"The fool. The young fool. I *told* him ..."

"You had spoken with him?"

"The day of my triumphal entry. He came to me all aglow, ready to support me now that I had declared myself. I told him to wait. I told him to trust me!"

He spun away and laid his head against the cool stone of the wall.

"The young, young fool," he said.

He remained thus for many long moments. Then he straightened.

"Ah well. He, too, shall see resurrection. I thank you for warning me of these things, Jesus. Go ahead and do as you must. And I will do as I must. Do not worry for me. God showed me this plan. He shall see that it is accomplished." He smiled a wan smile. "It will take a miracle. But that is just it. In God all things are possible. The Age of Miracles is only beginning. You shall see many of them in the next days."

"Yeshuah, you might end up in a mass execution with Eleazar and his cohorts."

But Yeshuah was walking to the head of the stairway.

"Zilpah. Bring more of our good wine for Jesus. And for Phillipus and Levi and Chandreah and Jacob. Give our friends a double draught, they have to catch up with us."

He turned.

"This is an excellent vintage. You must all drink to me on this special night."

A sullen Zilpah appeared, carrying a jug.

"I have no more cups."

"Ah well, we have some empty. Our friends will not mind drinking after others."

He filled five empty cups from the tables, handed them around, then emptied what was left in the jug among his men.

"Drink to me, please, all of you, share the cups amongst yourselves. Drink to the coming of the Messiah."

"He tells us that the wine is his blood," said bar Tolmei quietly.

"I will not drink it then," said Jesus.

"Please," said Yeshuah.

"No, my friend. I will not be a party to such a gross misunderstanding of 'God'—which understanding you seek to eventually impress onto the whole of Humankind. The true god asks for love and light, beauty, mercy, health and happiness. That god does not ask for suffering and it does not find delight in having your blood either shed or drunk. You are the one who asks for that, Yeshuah, you are the one who delights in the idea. It is time that you all stopped calling your own perverted desires the commands of any god!

"Have you given one moment's thought to what you intend to do to others, Yeshuah? To the rulers, to Pilatus, to the soldiers who drive the spikes—to your own dear brother? You seek to force them to kill you. In so doing, you would force blood-guilt onto them for all time.

"But not only onto them. You would force it onto Humanity. Yeshuah, each human action, no matter how small, travels outward in waves through all time, touching all who ever lived or will live. These actions which you intend to commit *stink*!"

He turned to the followers of Yeshuah, eyes blazing.

"Listen well, all of you. And think! You have ambitions for greatness? I promise you that, in helping this man, you become the smallest of the small in 'God's Kingdom.'

"Yeshuah, if you succeed in your mad design, what you send out into time is not love, light, mercy, or forgiveness, but blood, guilt, blame, complete misunderstanding, and rampant intolerance. What you contemplate is a *terrible* sin against your fellows. You, who says that he comes to initiate God's Kingdom on Earth. Well, Yeshuah, if you do as you plan, you will take Humanity further away from the Kingdom than ever it has been. You will magnify every error ever committed by Humanity a thousand-fold. The Kingdom of God? What you seek to institute is the Kingdom of Satan. And that is my answer to your cup of blood."

The followers were shuffling and murmuring among themselves.

While Yeshuah, after standing stock still for a long moment, seemed suddenly to sag. His spirit appeared to drain from him. He bowed his head, turned and walked to the far corner, motioning Jesus to follow.

Yet he stood without speaking for another long while.

Finally he looked up.

"I realize that you are convinced that you speak the truth, Jesus. You were also telling the truth when you promised to dissuade the Cyrenean and your father on the morrow."

"I disapprove of vows, but that is one that I did make and that I will keep."

"You are convinced that it is wrong of me to go ahead with the plan."

"Completely. Wrong for many reasons. Please, Yeshuah. Give me a chance to tell those reasons to you. What is the place where Judah is to get you arrested?"

" . . . Here. He has gone to Caiaphas now. But they will not come for me for hours. Not until the dining rooms of the inns have emptied and the populace is abed. Then, as we emerge from this inn, Judah will have the men of Caiaphas waiting in the next alley. In the darkness, they will overpower my men and take me."

"Then leave this place with me now, Yeshuah. Let us get out of Jerusalem—to a place where we can be safe, and where we can talk."

Yeshuah stared at him, A slow smile spread over his face.

Then he turned away, turned back, turned away once more and put a hand to his face.

"I wish this thing with Eleazar . . . . I must admit that the news has quite put me off my stride. I did not realize how it would affect me.

"You should have seen his mother, Jesus. Such a beautiful woman. Eleazar looks much like her."

He turned back. There were tears in his eyes. Jesus had never seen a face so earnest, heard a voice so terse.

"Jesus. Answer me honestly. Think you there is any chance—*any chance at all*—that we could save Eleazar? Perhaps if we went to Pilatus together . . . or if Merovee went to him. Pilatus loves Merovee. Or we could go to Procula . . . "

"Merovee witnessed the attack," said Jesus gently. "Eleazar led it—led an attack on Rome, and thus upon Emperor Tiberius. It is out-and-out treason. Pilatus has no choice but to convict him. Not to convict him would be treason on the part of Pilatus."

Yeshuah nodded.

"I thought as much," he said flatly. "I just had to be sure."

He was silent for long moments.

Then he shook his head, seeming to fight off some imaginary gnat.

"So be it. The air grows close in here anyway. Come. Empty your cup against the cold night. We will do as you say, go out to a place where the air is clear, and where one can think. The Garden of the Olive Press, that is where we shall go, it is not far. Then, if you do not convince me, I will still have time to return here."

He reached out and grasped Jesus by the shoulders.

"I am so very confused at this moment, my friend. The Kingdom of Satan, you say. Such a thing had never occurred to me. If you are right . . . if I could be convinced, then maybe . . .

"But go on! Drink your wine."

He wheeled.

"All of you, we are going for some fresh air. Drink up! I no longer insist that it is my blood."

Heaving a large inward sigh of relief, Jesus drained his cup—as did all the others.

"What of Zilpah?" said Jesus. "Nathaniel will be waiting outside. He can take her to the house of Nicodemus where the others are waiting."

"That will be fine. Perhaps we shall all join them there later."

With a faint smile, Yeshuah led them out of the upper room, down the stairs and through the common room, where family groups of pilgrims with enough silver to buy luxury were celebrating the Passover. Out on the street, Zilpah was entrusted to Nathaniel.

"Should I come to Gethsemane when I have delivered her?" Nathaniel whispered to Jesus.

"No. I think all is well. Stay with the others."

They left the city by way of the Horse Gate. Technically, travel was not supposed to occur from sundown to sundown of the Passover day. But the needs of Jerusalem's population and of the pilgrim throngs simply to live and to function during that time had long ago caused that rule to be set aside.

Where the streets within the walls had been dark, the Kedron Valley and surrounding hills were bright. Tens of thousands of families sat about their campfires, digesting their Passover lambs and enjoying extra wine. And still the Hallel was to be heard, for those families who had not gotten their lambs slaughtered until the third relay were late with the roasting, and thus with the dinner. Indeed, some purists preferred the third relay and a late seder, for had not the flight from Egypt occurred in the middle of the night?

The men walked at a leisurely—and progressively more stumbling—pace along the Kedron toward Gethsemane. Remembering it later, Jesus berated himself for having been so gullible, so easily tricked. Yet, in the doing, it had seemed so innocent. The men had had too much wine. The Mount of Olives was a natural place to go for fresh air. The Garden of the Olive Press was a perfect place for a safe and private talk.

It was also a perfect place for the men to sleep it off.

Jesus remembered depositing them beneath a tree.

"Keep watch, Petros," said Yeshuah.

"Yes. Yes. Keep watch," Petros repeated.

He was snoring almost before he finished the words.

Jesus laughed, and thought oddly that his laughter sounded far away.

"These fellows are thoroughly drunk! You must have had the required four cups and then four cups again."

"Actually they had a cup for each of the Twelve Tribes of Israel," smiled Yeshuah. "Come. There is a cave up here where we can talk."

Jesus remembered only that it was a very hard climb, though the cave was not that far up the hill. His strength seemed to drain away as they climbed. He remembered entering the cave. He remembered Yeshuah talking, but he was suddenly so sleepy . . .

* * *

Yeshuah sat as though alone in the garden. The followers slept in a huddle beneath their tree, all of them, save those who had come with Jesus, drugged with a double dose of the "special" wine. Yet the single dose seemed quite as effective, since Jesus, too, was slumbering in the cave. The Cyrenean evidently knew what he was doing. His drugs produced exactly the response required, exactly at the time desired. A great shame that Jesus would deprive him of those most excellent services on the morrow.

Ringing the garden were still campfires, and sounds of the Passover. But they were lessening now. Soon most would be asleep. In about an hour, Judah would arrive, leading those who would take him. It would not be the Levite Police who came. Levites might attract attention. Damaging stories might be told afterward. Judah had, instead, suggested to Caiaphas that he send some of his Arab servants to do the job, along with some hired Gentile rabble. People like that would not be as remarked upon traveling through the late night streets.

All that Judah had suggested to the rulers had been accepted by them. It had been so easy, so pathetically simple to bend them to his will.

And how easy it had been to dupe Jesus.

Of that, Yeshuah was not proud. Jesus was a pure creature, who operated on trust. He did not expect people to lie to him. Even though Yeshuah had lied to him so often, Jesus wiped the tablet clean each time and trusted anew.

At one time, Yeshuah would have thought Jesus a fool. Now he knew that he was not. Jesus operated in a certain way, for certain reasons, that were above and beyond Yeshuah's. He, Yeshuah, must act in his own way for his own reasons. Jesus said that the ends never justified the means. Yet Yeshuah could see no other way than to use unjustified means. If lying was necessary—then one had to lie. Even to angels.

Across the ravine, he could see the long, darkened mass of the Temple wall. And the towers of the Antonia.

Eleazar slept in that fortress this night, to die horribly on the morrow.

If Jesus only knew how close he had come to obtaining his objective. Calling everything off to try to save Eleazar would have been the perfect—honorable—excuse. Everyone would have understood. No one would have called him coward. If only, when asked whether he thought there was any chance to save Eleazar, if only Jesus had said, "There might be a chance. Let us at least try."

But Jesus had told the truth. Even if he had known that a lie would win the day for him, Jesus would still have told the truth. That was the way of it with Jesus.

That realization unsettled Yeshuah. If Jesus would never lie, then it stood to reason that everything that Jesus had been telling him was the truth.

What if Jesus was not an angel come to test him? What if Jesus was the one who was right, the one who had been right all along. What if what he, Yeshuah, was about to do was wrong, wrong, wrong.

He must shut out such thoughts. What had he been thinking about?

The Antonia. And, back beyond the Antonia, out of sight . . .

No, he did not want to think of that either, not the Place of the Skull, and its waiting tomb.

Yet, suddenly, he could think of nothing else.

His shivers were not from the cold. They arose from the terror that was rapidly engulfing him.

Just another hour. Only another hour. He must keep himself together until then. Once they had seized him, there would be no going back. The hardest part, the fear, the desire to run, to call the whole thing off, would be over.

He must keep thoughts of that other garden out of his mind.

But without the physician's magic cakes . . . how would he bear the pain when they drove in the spikes?

Absently, as so often in the past, he fingered his left wrist, finding the spot just at the beginning of the hand where they did it. Driven in there, the spike could not rip out through the flesh when the weight of the body was hung upon it. It could rip out if nailed into the hand itself, oh yes, for there were no bones in the hand at an angle to support a nail. The Romans knew all these things, knew just how to do it, where to find that place in the wrist that seemed to have been designed just for crucifying a man, a perfect loop of bone to encircle the spike and hold the weight of the body. The soldiers knew just the size spike to use, and the weight of the mallet necessary to drive it through the wrist.

They were not as particular about the feet, any place would do to support the weight from above. Usually they placed one foot over the other and drove one large spike through both feet between the metatarsal bones. They saved on spikes that way.

Yeshuah rose and walked a few steps, as though the distance would remove him from the idea. A rancid bile kept rising up into his throat, and waves of nausea swept him, leaving him sweating and trembling.

He had never been able to stand pain. More than anything in the world, more than death, he feared pain.

He dropped to his knees and lowered his face into his clasped hands.

"Dear Father. Give me strength. Still my trembling. Why is my flesh so weak, Father? Why did you make me so strong of mind and so weak in the flesh?"

Some victims fainted when the spike was driven into the first wrist. They did not even feel the spike going into the second wrist, or into the feet. They just woke up hanging, horribly, inescapably suspended on their own bones.

He could not keep the bile down. It rose and spewed out of his mouth.

It would be best if he was one of those who fainted.

But some men just kept fainting. He must not be one of those. What the physician had told Judah was so. To achieve the sleep, he must first be fully awake, alert.

Ah, how grandly, confidently he had told Jesus that it did not matter if the Cyrenean were deterred from aiding him. Jesus did not know how his stomach had turned over on itself in sudden horror. None of them knew, not Petros, not Judah, not his mother—how utterly terrified he was. Had always been.

"Stop thinking about it!" he told himself angrily.

He bowed his head once more, and told God how happy he was to be the Chosen One. He told God that he trusted him to see to all things. He thanked God for sending him his angel to make sure that he really and truly suffered upon the cross.

He was already suffering just thinking about it. Was the thinking worse than the actual experience, or would it be . . . ?

He threw up again. With not much in his stomach to throw up, it became a terrible retching.

He was beginning to feel cold. And he could not stop his trembling.

The matrons of the Ladies' League of Jerusalem would be waiting with their drugged wine when he was brought out the Antonia gate. He had sworn to the men in the upper room that he would not taste of wine again until the Kingdom had come. That vow had been nothing more than an excuse not to drink the drugged wine, Yet he had made it.

He licked his dry lips. Perhaps he would have to take the matrons' wine after all. One could say that, the moment he was taken by the minions of the rulers, the Kingdom had begun. One could say that.

And so he could drink the wine.

The drug would dull his mind, make it infinitely harder to achieve the sleep.

Yet what would terror, sickness, and agony do?

The drug might be the lesser of the two evils. If, sitting here in Gethsemane, with many hours still to go before the beginning of pain, he was reduced to this state of quivering terror—what would it be like with only minutes to go?

Strangely, he had never thought much about the flogging. Suddenly he began to. Romans used a particularly vicious instrument, a short, stout whip with many leather thongs. At the end of each thong was tied a chunk of heavy, spiked metal. Thirty-nine strokes were the number required. They were supposed to be administered to the back. Yet some of the soldiers took delight in inflicting the strokes so that the thongs wrapped around the body, breaking and tearing the chest and stomach as well.

There was a sound behind him. He leaped to his feet, instinctively poised for flight.

Nothing. A scurrying rodent must have dislodged a pebble.

He began to wish that he had not drugged the others. It would be good to have someone to talk to. Talking to others, he could keep his mind off the tortures he had chosen for himself . . . no, not that he had chosen for himself . . . that God had chosen for him. Talking to others, he could hear his own fine ideas, and take comfort and inspiration from them. Talking to others, he could fool even himself.

He had somehow to tell Judah when he came. There would not be much time. They had arranged that he would be waiting in the cave, and come out when he saw Judah, and Judah would come to him and kiss him. The men accompanying him would have been told that this was done in order to identify the man they were to seize. In fact, Yeshuah had suggested a kiss for just this eventuality, in case either of them needed to whisper some last minute instruction or information. After the kiss, there would be scant seconds before they actually took him.

He must think of the exact words to say. Was it necessary to waste time telling Judah of Eleazar?

Yeshuah sank down against the rock at the mouth of the cave and commenced to chew upon his knuckles for companionship.

The young fool. He had thrown such a variable into the plans, and here it was the eleventh hour. Surely they would go ahead and crucify him, Yeshuah, at the Place of the Skull as planned. Eleazar's pathetic little revolt would not change that. Caiaphas and Annas had been delighted to be contacted by such a clever traitor, one who had thought it all out for them. Yes. They would specify the Place of the Skull when they took him to Pilatus in the morning, whispering to Pilatus the very good reasons for using that secluded place. Pilatus would have no reason to refuse—every reason to comply. As a matter of fact, were he Pilatus, he would use Eleazar and his fellows to divert attention even more firmly from the "real" crucifixion. Were he Pilatus, he would hang Eleazar and his fellows with great fanfare down in the usual place, in the Valley of the Tanners. With the attention of the people fixed on that place, he would quietly hang Yeshuah in the Place of the Skull.

Yes. Eleazar would be crucified separately. Yeshuah was made strangely happy by the thought. He would not have to see Eleazar's suffering. Eleazar would not have to witness his. And, if his courage failed, if he became a coward in his pain, Eleazar would not see that either.

"Thank you, Father, for your continuing love and tender mercy."

Yes. Eleazar would be no impediment to his own plans. God would see to it that he was not. Hence, mentioning Eleazar to Judah would only confuse the issue.

Oh! it was wonderful to have things to think out right now! Yeshuah seized upon the thoughts more eagerly, for they would keep his mind away from the other thoughts, the ones he must not think, about nails, about pain.

What he would say to Judah as they kissed was simply, "Jesus is going to stop the Cyrenean and his father from helping me. You must do it all. Do not fail me. You have sworn."

Judah would take it from there. He would understand that, when he went to Pilatus later this night, he must ask that he, himself, be allowed to handle the sponge and administer a drug to his brother on the cross. He would know that, if at all possible, he had to get to the Cyrenean before Jesus did, and get those cakes from him. He would know that, once Yeshuah was "dead," he, himself, would have to go to Procula and beg the "body" and get it into the tomb.

What then? Could Judah manage to stay in the tomb to nurse him without it being known?

Yeshuah licked his lips, wondering what would happen if he was left in the tomb alone, deep in that awful sleep, his body pierced and ripped and broken, so much of his blood drained from him.

No! He must not fear! He should not worry about such things, God would take care of the whole matter. God would sustain his Messiah, heal him, raise him.

"Oh, I *do* trust, Father. I do. It is the pain that I cannot bear! Why did you pick me, God? Why not a man who is a man, not a child, when it comes to pain?"

Because the suffering, the sacrifice, would then be real.

"I am the Messenger. I am to be considered as the one who sent me. I *become* the one who sent me. So I become you, God."

He was going to throw up again.

"God, do you fear pain, too? Is that what I am feeling and why?"

Could it be possible?

"Jesus told me that you are love and light and laughter and happiness. He said that you abhor pain and suffering and bloodshed, that pain and suffering and bloodshed is *our* choice, not yours. Is that why this is happening to me now? Are you trying to give me a message, God? Are you telling me that I am wrong, that you do not want to suffer?"

That was the Tempter talking. Jesus, the Tempter, the Adversary, sent by God to try his Messiah.

Resolutely he turned to his pack. It was time to prepare.

He had bought a robe of the finest linen, of the most pure white, as spotless as any that ever an Essene had worn.

Shivering in the chill, he stripped off his clothing. He would wear nothing but this white robe. No profane or sullied garment was good enough for the entrance of the Messiah into the Kingdom. He would go with just his body, the perfect offering to God, draped with a robe of purity.

They would take the robe from him soon enough, give him a loincloth for his man's parts, while the rest of him was left naked for the torture. But, in those first moments, he would be the perfect, unblemished lamb, the ultimate sacrifice to the Lord.

And then he heard a sound down at the gate.

Oh. Yes. They were here. So soon. He had not had time to pray! Why had Judah brought them so soon?

He could pick out Judah, starting up the hill toward the cave, the other figures furtive, darting from bush to bush, tree to tree, some distance behind.

They had swords and clubs! He could see them in the soft light. They might hit him, get blood onto his perfect, white robe. They must not do that.

Yeshuah backed away.

'Why do you come so fast, Judah? Do you *want* to see your brother done for? Why did you listen to me? Why are you doing this?'

He was going to throw up again. He must not, he might dirty his robe. God was love and light and laughter, God did not want his son to suffer. Jesus had said so, and Jesus must know. This was all a terrible mistake. But it was too late.

No!

Why should he endure this horror when he had only to say the word to have every pilgrim in Jerusalem behind him? If he let these men take him, they would drive nails into him! Nails! Into his screaming flesh!

Yeshuah turned and ran, up the hill, into the trees. They would not be able to find him. They had brought no torches. They could chase him all night in this vast grove, and never catch him.

Judah, climbing the hill, saw the flash of white and wondered who or what it might be. Had an Essene bedded down for the night here in the garden? Yes, that was it. An Essene, fleeing at the approach of others, to avoid defilement.

He reached the mouth of the cave and called softly for Yeshuah. There was his pack against a rock. He called again, loudly.

A mumbled answer. Within the cave, a figure stirred.

"Yeshuah, it is Judah. Come out, Yeshuah."

"Judah . . . Judah? . . . Judah! Thank God you have come."

The man lurched to his feet and stumbled out of the cave.

"Thank you, Judah, thank you. I must talk with you."

Before Judah realized, before he could think, Jesus had taken him into a drugged embrace and kissed him upon the mouth.

"No-o-o-o!"

It was an animal howl. Judah snatched the arms from off of himself and backed away, pawing desperately at his mouth, trying to get the kiss off, trying to undo it.

"No!" He wheeled, raising his arms. "This is not Yeshuah!"

But the men were upon Jesus, pinning him, binding him with ropes.

"You have the wrong one! This is not my brother!"

"What? The wrong one?" Malchus, the Arab under-steward of Caiaphas, was in charge of the band. He seized Jesus by the shoulders and studied him closely in the dim light.

"Pay no attention to the traitor. He has grown weak-livered at the last. This is Yeshuah all right, I have seen him preaching in the Temple precincts with my own eyes."

"He is Joshuah, not Yeshuah! He is not my brother!"

"Then why do the two of you look alike? Get out of our way, Scum, you have your silver. Now let us earn ours."

"Jesus! I did not mean it! I will get you out of it! Annas and Caiaphas will know the mistake the moment that they see you!"

Jesus was trying to understand what was happening, remember even where he was.

"Drugged," he muttered. "Yeshuah."

"Sure, we know you are Yeshuah," laughed Malchus. "Come on, walk on your own two feet if you do not want to feel this club."

Desperately, Judah ran alongside as the men roughhoused Jesus down the hill.

"The Chalice, Jesus. Where is the Chalice?"

Merovee. Oh, Merovee!

"The house of the Friend."

A hulk rose up before them, roaring in anger.

"What are you doing? Where are you taking Jesus?"

"Keep back, Petros." Jesus was beginning to understand.

But Petros reached out. With one swipe of a mighty arm, he flattened one of the captors, took the fallen man's sword and swung at Malchus, grazing his ear.

In the confusion, Jesus shook free of restraining hands and jumped in front of Malchus.

"Put it down, Petros. Put it away, I say! I will have no weapons of death used in defense of me. Swords do not solve problems, swords make problems. And *you!*"

He wheeled on Malchus.

"What a brave lot you are to come after one unarmed man with all these weapons. You say you have seen me teaching in the Temple. If you have, then you know what I teach, and you know that I am no criminal to be taken with this force and disrespect. Now keep your hands off of me. All of you. I have my wits back and will walk quietly with you to the High Priest. Get back, Petros. Do not cry, Judah. You say I am not your brother. Yet I am. And more. Do not cry. I love you."

"I will not let you die!"

"I cannot die, Judah. There *is* no such thing as a dead fig tree, remember?"

As they took Jesus out through the gate from Gethsemane, yet another man sought to redeem himself. A figure clad in pure white linen ran out of the shadows and clutched at Jesus.

"Forgive me, Lord!"

"Get away from the prisoner," said Malchus.

"It is not he who you want. *I* am Yeshuah."

"How many Yeshuahs are there?" laughed Malchus. "Well, if you want to come with us, come along."

He reached out, but Yeshuah backed off, leaving Malchus with nothing but a handful of linen. Malchus laughed again.

"Make up your mind, 'Yeshuah.'" He tugged mischievously upon the garment.

Another man grabbed at it, and another.

Taunting, they tried to pull their quarry to them.

With a dreadful sound—a cry such as no human being had ever before heard or uttered, Yeshuah tore himself free. He then threw the garment up over his shoulders and dashed it at his tormentors.

For one long moment, he stood naked before them.

Then, uttering sounds so terrible that Malchus knew he would remember them until his dying day, he ran back into the darkness of the garden.

It was Jesus who broke the spell, for Malchus and his men seemed frozen to the spot.

"You were about to take me to the High Priest, Good Men. Pray . . . let us proceed."

Chapter 21

Behold Your King

The company at the house of Nicodemus sat quietly waiting. Despite—or maybe because of—the tension, Aunt Miriam and Mother Meraiah had fallen asleep upon couches. The rest of them conversed in low tones, sipped wine, and nibbled on matzoth. Nicodemus had told them as much as he knew of Yeshuah's plans.

Pure insanity.

Surely Jesus had been able to talk him out of it. Surely.

Merovee, though, was drawn apart. Her face was pale, her eyes dull. She could not put words to what it was that she felt. But, for over an hour, a dreadful chill had held her heart in its grip. She tried to fight back, from the chill, to warmth. It was like trying to rise from the grave.

She kept seeing Josh's face. Only his face, in a sea of swirling black. He was calm, almost smiling, strangely amused. Yet, in that swirling blackness, was something terrible. She kept trying to see through the blackness, to know what the terrible thing was.

Then came a stealthy, but rapid, knocking upon the front gate. In those knocks was an urgency that brought them to their feet.

Nicodemus gestured to Timothy, who hastened to inquire through the peephole who it might be at this hour. He hastened back.

"It is Judah, Master."

"Judah!"

They said it at once, and the fear that had gripped Merovee entered them all.

"Something has gone wrong if he is here," said Nicodemus. "Quickly, Timothy, bring him in."

The man whom Timothy ushered into the room could scarcely be recognized as Judah. He had aged by twenty years. His demeanor was such that Merovee thought for a moment that be had gone mad.

Yet his voice was calm as he came directly to her.

"My dearest lady. Beloved Sister. Forgive me."

"They arrested Jesus, too," she said flatly.

"Not too. Instead."

Nicodemus let out a cry.

"How can such a thing be?"

"Because my brother ran."

In a voice so even that it seemed he was discussing the weather, Judah told them. Only if one watched his eyes could one hear the screams so carefully kept out of his throat.

"When they took him away, Petros and I followed after," he finished. "And young Johannan. He was the only one we were able to rouse. I guess the rest of them are still asleep out in Gethsemane. Johannan is known in the kitchens of Caiaphas, for he has often delivered the Zebedee's fish. Johannan and Petros are still there, loitering about, trying to hear what they can hear. It is a busy place tonight with all the comings and goings, and with part of the Sanhedrin meeting.

"For my part, I went directly to Caiaphas. Old Annas was with him, of course. I told them of my brother's cowardice, and of the mistake. I was sure, so sure that they would release Jesus!"

The stridency finally escaped his eyes and entered his voice.

"But they would not," said Merovee flatly. "Of course not. Why should they?"

"They *laughed* at me!" cried Judah. "I tried to return their silver. I promised that I would find Yeshuah and, myself, deliver him to them. I threatened the people's wrath should the heir bar Ramathea be crucified. I got down on my knees before them, and begged that they release Jesus."

"What reason did they give for not releasing him?" said Nicodemus.

There was anger, and authority, in his voice. For the first time, many of them remembered that Nicodemus was a member of the Sanhedrin. An influential one.

"Old Annas said, 'When one lays his net for a particularly big fish and fails to catch it, but catches an even bigger fish, does one throw that second, great big fish back? One would be a foolish fisherman indeed.'"

"They were after Jesus, too," said Nathaniel darkly. "Even before they were after Yeshuah. It is only Yeshuah's actions of the last week, starting with the raising of Lazarus, that made him their first objective at this time. They meant to have both of them eventually."

"Caiaphas congratulated me," said Judah bleakly. "He said my plan was a superior one, and would work just as well for Jesus as for Yeshuah."

"But what charges have they against Jesus?" cried Deborah.

"None," said Nicodemus. "Not a one that could get him crucified or even stoned. Jesus has made none of the claims that Yeshuah has. They cannot possibly convict him of anything."

Judah shook his head helplessly.

"Nicodemus, the validity of the charges will not matter in this trial. Illegal it might be to convene a Sanhedrin at night, especially on this night. Technically illegal. Yet, as well we both know, they will have summoned a legal minimum number from among the members of the Great Sanhedrin, and every man summoned is of a like mind to the Annians. Every single one of them wants both Yeshuah and Jesus silenced. They already have witnesses waiting down in the guard room . . . people to swear to all sorts of things . . . that the prisoner called himself the Messiah and the King of the Jews, that he called himself the Son of God, that he said he could destroy the Temple and rebuild it in three days."

"But it was Yeshuah, not Joshuah, who said those things!" said Nicodemus.

"Look at me, Nicodemus. Of whom do I remind you?"

"In appearance?"

"Yes."

"Well, you greatly resemble your brother Yeshuah, of course. He is filled out a bit more, but he is so much older . . . "

"Who do both Yeshuah and I resemble? In height, weight, girth, coloring?"

Nicodemus hesitated. He did not voice the answer, but went on to argue it.

"Superficialities! Anyone who knows the three of you can tell you apart, you each carry yourself differently, you speak differently, smile differently, think differently, walk differently . . . "

"Yes, anyone who knows us knows those differences, and would never mistake us, or even particularly think that we resemble one another. But most of those men of the Sanhedrin, convening even now at the house of Caiaphas, are not that familiar with any of us.

"If they have seen Yeshuah or Jesus at all, it was fleetingly and probably from a distance in crowds. Think you those men, who want them both dead, will go beyond appearances and question the true identity of the prisoner?

"And the witnesses . . . men who have been dug out from who knows what dung heap, who have been paid to sit up this night and appear at a trial to testify exactly as they have been paid to testify. If, in fact, they ever did see Yeshuah or Jesus, if they ever actually were in some crowd and heard the things to which they will testify, do you think they would know that they are testifying against the wrong man?"

"You are saying that Caiaphas means to try Joshuah as though he is Yeshuah?" said Nicodemus. "What of Joshuah? Will he not open his mouth and tell them who he is?"

"Of course. What will it matter?" said Judah. "The confusion of appearances is great to start with. But even the names—Joshuah and Yeshuah—can be turned to confusion. being but regional versions of one another. Can a witness who saw a man he thought was called Yeshuah be sure that this man called Joshuah, who looks like the man he saw, is not one and the same? The confusion will be insurmountable in a prejudiced court. It will be the easiest thing in the world to make it seem that it was Joshuah, not Yeshuah, who said every damning thing.

"And any protest by Jesus or his supporters that they have the wrong man will be looked upon as merely his way to confuse the court and escape from the situation.

"Indeed, this works out even better for the Annians, do you not see? They have two birds with one stone. You said yourself, Nicodemus, that Jesus has not made public statements which could be construed as treasonable against God or Rome. He has given the rulers no real grounds to try him, or would he ever! Yet, as the heir bar Ramathea, and as the rabban and healer and leader that he obviously is, he is still a prime candidate for Messiah. A constant threat to them. And will be as long as he lives.

"If, then, they can dispose of him quickly and efficiently, and later say, 'Oh forgive us, we are so sorry, Joseph, we thought he was somebody else'—if they can achieve this based on charges that they had prepared against Yeshuah—the truth of which could never afterward be untangled—it is greatly to their benefit. They know that the momentum which my oh-so-brave brother—our admirable 'Messiah'—has built up, for a takeover at this Passover, is now thrown into confusion.

"In all practicality, my brother is thwarted. Either he will go to ground, never to be heard from again—which is likely, for how could he ever show his face again?—or he will re-surface and supply the rulers with even firmer charges, at a time when they will be even better able to deal with him.

"In any case, they cannot lose. They will use the plan with which I supplied them, and the," his voice broke, "kiss that my beloved Jesus bestowed upon these traitorous lips. And they will kill him."

"Yes! A traitor you certainly are!" cried Zilpah.

Merovee whirled upon the woman.

"Keep your miserable mouth closed, Zilpah. Close it and do not open it again in this company. Jesus knew of the pledge that Judah was fulfilling for his brother and he understood. If you are unable to understand that, then take your pack, get over to your house at the Fish Gate in your paint and finery, wait for a caravan back to Galilee, and never again disgust us with the sight of your face. Who was the one who drugged that wine at Yeshuah's bidding, Zilpah? The same wine that drugged Jesus and made him so stupid that he did not know where he was or what he was doing when he came forth from that cave. Do not talk to me of traitors, Zilpah."

She went to Judah and took him into her arms. He put his face down onto her shoulder, wrapped her into a desperate embrace, and began to sob like a child.

"There now. All is not lost. Judah. Brother! It is not lost. No. I have perfect trust in Jesus, Judah. You saw him shining in that cave. Jesus has a command of this reality that we cannot begin to understand. If he wants to, Judah, he can get himself out of this.

"Besides which, the final key is Pilatus. It is Pilatus who must pass any death sentence upon Jesus and carry out the execution. We must go to him, you and I, right away, tell him the whole thing. and plan between us what to do."

"While I must get myself over to the house of Caiaphas," said Nicodemus. "There has got to be someone there to speak for Jesus, and to refute the charges.

"Timothy, come here. There are honest men in the Sanhedrin, I promise," he told the assembled. "But, since they are honest, they have obviously not been called to this particular meeting. Timothy, help me think. Who can I lay my hand to immediately?"

"I would send servants hotfoot to the homes of Rebs Amos, Elias, Abner, Manasseh, and Jonah, " said Timothy.

"Exactly. Good man. Tell the servants not to fear to wake them. Have them tell those men that the Annians have convened an illegal Sanhedrin at the home of Caiaphas to try the heir bar Ramathea on capitol charges for execution on the morrow. They must join me there with all haste."

He turned to Merovee.

"I will do what I can, my lady. And Judah . . . "

He put a hand to the bowed shoulders.

"You are not the only traitor to Jesus. You must move over and make room for me . . . for I was a major party to this scheme that has ensnared him.

"And how do you think Joseph will feel? Or the father of Alexander, here? The only thing we traitors and fools can do to help ourselves is to pull ourselves together and do the best that we can in these new circumstances."

"Thank you," Judah managed.

He felt yet a new pair of arms trying to encircle hem, seeking to comfort. The arms belonged to Meraiah.

"There are many of us who have been at fault, Judah. Forgive me for my own faults, especially for my misunderstanding of you. Cry if you must, Judalah. It is all right, my dear, fine, baby son. We are all in this together now."

He turned his sobs to Meraiah and hugged her small body up to himself.

Yet it did not really help. Nothing could help what he had done.

Except perhaps one thing.

It was Merovee who took control.

"Alexander. Go to the lodgings of your father. Tell him what was happened and bring him here. We must keep this house as our center of information.

"Nicodemus, do you have mounts for Cleopah and Ben?"

"I have no stable. I rent mounts when I must ride, and, at this hour . . . "

"You want someone to go to Uncle Joseph?" said Ben. "I am a fast and sturdy runner. His farm is at less than six miles. I can reach it in little more than an hour."

"Then be off and bring Joseph here. If anyone accosts you for traveling during Passover night, tell them you travel in regard to the business of the High Priest. That will silence them without being a lie.

"Nicodemus, report back here when you have aught to report. Take Jeptah as your messenger. Judah and I are off to the Antonia to see Pilatus. We, too, will report back. Nathaniel, come with us as messenger. Jairus, get out to Gethsemane. Rouse the others and bring them here."

"What should the rest of us do?" said Susannah.

"Think positive thoughts," said Merovee. "No matter how difficult that might seem, think positively. Envision a world where Jesus does not die upon the cross."

* * *

The profession of praefectus did not always afford easy sleep. So it was that Pilatus was neither surprised nor alarmed when a lamp shown down upon him in the middle of the night.

"What has happened?"

"Praefectus, a woman is at the gate demanding to see you immediately. She will say only that she brings the chalice that you ordered for your favorite wine, and a support for your fig tree."

Beside him, Procula sat up. Pilatus forestalled her utterance.

"Bring her into the salon."

"Uh . . ."

"Yes?"

"There are others with her."

"Of course. Show them all in. Then wake Lucius and send him to us."

"Oh no!" cried Procula as the three of them were ushered into the salon. Their expressions left no doubt that tragedy had struck. "What has happened?"

"Jesus has been seized by Caiaphas," said Merovee without preamble. "An illegal and hand-picked Sanhedrin is trying him at this very moment, using paid witnesses. They will find him deserving of death on religious grounds, but bring him to you at dawn to be sentenced to crucifixion for treason against Caesar."

Procula gasped. Pilatus sank down into a chair.

Merovee drew from off of her upper arm the golden circlet that Pilatus had given her in token, and that she had worn since her wedding night. She went to him, hand extended.

"I have come to collect my wedding gift, Pilatus. Remember?"

He hesitated. Then, with a sigh, he reached up and took the bracelet.

"How could I forget. The most beautiful bride who ever graced Galilee. I promised to, at some time in the future, here in Jerusalem, grant you the favor that you would ask . . . a favor that would mean the world to you . . ."

"But that might be politically dangerous to you," she finished for him.

"What is the favor?"

"Before I frame it, is there any way that you can release him? If they give you testimony that he has named himself the Messiah—by inference King of the Jews, which would be treason against Tiberius—is there any way that you can refuse to execute him?"

Pilatus rose, shaking his head. In troubled thought, he walked to a table and poured himself a goblet of wine.

"Technically, no. Certainly it is a ridiculous claim, and, were it not specifically forced upon us, we would pay it no attention. Tiberius knows of the religious situation here in Palestine. It has been his own decision to simply ignore these messiahs, to let them burn themselves out. Good Jove! At any one time there are half a dozen of them running around this country, each thinking himself to be *the* Messiah. For Rome to search out each one of them, and execute them on charges of treason, would be as ridiculous as for a bull to search out field mice and stomp them to death for daring to nibble at his grass.

"No. These messiahs do not worry Tiberius. He even looks upon your Zealots as mere bothersome gnats. He knows that your people are too divided, too busy with religious wrangling amongst themselves, to mount any serious rebellion against him.

"If I were, myself, to seize one of these messiahs and crucify him, Tiberius would want to know why. If I had no good reason, I would be seriously rebuked for taking such provocative action, for creating trouble where there had been none.

"But for a man to be brought to me by the Temple authorities themselves . . . "

He shook his head again.

"That is very different. They must want him out of the way very badly. Cowardly scum. They dare not stone him themselves, they want Rome to do their dirty work."

He turned back to Merovee.

"I am sorry, do you want a cup of wine?"

She shook her head wryly.

"My chalice already overflows with wine."

"I can use some," said Judah.

"Nathaniel?"

"No thank you, Your Excellency."

Lucius had entered.

"Lucius?"

"Yes, please."

Pilatus poured out the wine.

"The answer to your question is, Merovee . . . it will depend upon how insistent the rulers become. I fear they will be most insistent.

"A trial in the middle of the night! And on Passover night. They are in dead earnest. If they present me with clear evidence, and absolutely demand his death . . . "

"Whose death?" said Lucius.

"The rulers have seized Jesus. They mean to deliver him to us on charges of treason and get him crucified."

Lucius blanched and turned away.

"If," continued Pilatus, "they threaten to inform Tiberius of my failure to execute this 'dangerous' revolutionary, who threatens both their peace and his . . . then I really should execute him or risk my entire career. Not to execute him would, among other things, be unnecessary provocation, do you not see? Tiberius has kept peace in his empire these many years by pursuing a policy of moderation and fairness in the provinces. He listens very closely to the complaints of provincial officials. Did those officials understand quite *how* closely, they would complain to him more often."

"Then you will have to sentence Jesus," said Merovee.

"I said that I should. But my dear lady! How *can* I? Sentence Jesus? I would almost rather . . ."
He turned troubled eyes to Procula.

"Of course," she said. "You can not do it. You must not do it."

"It might mean my recall, Procula. Or worse."

"No. I would go to Tiberius, talk with him, explain."

"Procula, you know the stories we have been hearing."

"He will always listen to me. He would never turn against me."

"He has turned against many who believed the same thing."

"I was as a daughter to him!"

"You have not seen your cousin in ten years. In all that time, he has been living like a recluse on his beloved Capri, playing with his astrologers, becoming more and more secretive. While, since the rebellion of my old friend, Sejanus, my dear . . . the treachery of such a trusted official did terrible things to Tiberius. He is no longer the man that you knew. And do not forget that the fact that Sejanus was a friend to me might count against me."

"He would listen to me, Pilatus. I know him like no other. He is a philosopher, himself. He is a recluse because, like us, he is searching. He has always been searching—for meaning, for right. And he has been misunderstood for doing so.

"Oh Merovee, he is such a gentle man at heart, you would love him, too. If Jesus were to go and talk with him, I swear that Tiberius would become his follower."

"Pilatus," interjected Merovee, "what was the 'or worse' that you indicated could happen to you?"
Pilatus shrugged.

"Banishment perhaps. To Gaul most likely, that is the favorite dumping ground of late. I suppose it would not be so bad. Half of Rome is languishing along the Vienne or the Rhone. We could renew many old acquaintances.

"Funny," he mused. "Jesus advised me to invest my money in Gaul, do you remember, Merovee? And I have done so."

"Anything worse than banishment?" said Merovee. "If you refused to execute a traitor . . . might that refusal also be construed as treason? Is not treason to Caesar automatic death?"

Pilatus hesitated. Again he glanced at Procula. Then he nodded.

"It is a possibility that cannot be discounted. The stories I referred to . . . they say that Tiberius has gone quite mad, that, for instance, he hurls his astrologers over the cliff and into the sea if their predictions do not suit him. While, since the betrayal of Sejanus, they say that his distrust and suspicion knows no bounds, that no one is safe from his mad fears.

"And the record speaks for itself. In only the last two years, fourteen senators have been dragged down the stairs and drowned in the Tiber. On the flimsiest of accusation and proof. All of Rome sits holding its breath so they say, waiting for the 'Monster of Capri' to breathe his last."

He shook his head.

"And yet I wonder. There was a time when Tiberius was great. He has been as able an administrator as ever Augustus was. To this day, in my own dealings with him—in the dispatches and replies and commands—I can see no slackening of skill—none of the cruelty and viciousness or madness that everyone insists is there.

625

"One almost wonders whether these stories are being hatched by his enemies as an excuse to be rid of him. For he keeps the same even, fair hand upon the reins. While always, at the end of each communication, he inquires after his sweet, young cousin's health, and sends fond personal regards to us both.

"So I do not know, Merovee. How can I say? If I refuse to pass sentence and the rulers complain directly to Tiberius, it *will* go badly for me. Just how bad the bad would be . . . "

He shrugged.

"Then," said Merovee, "you must pass sentence."

"Merovee, no!"

Merovee silenced Procula with a grim smile.

"The end never justifies the means, Procula. If it were only a matter of censure or even banishment, I would have asked Pilatus to risk it. But Jesus would not countenance putting the life of Pilatus in jeopardy to save his own. I can tell you that most certainly. And I can not tell you to jeopardize your husband to save mine. This must all be done clearly, with as much 'right' as is possible under the circumstances."

"On the other hand, my dear," said Pilatus, "how can I have his blood upon my hands? If I refuse to sentence him, I might die. If I do sentence him, he will surely die."

"Not necessarily," said Merovee.

"Do not be foolish," said Lucius. He was still visibly shaken. "No one survives the cross."

"There is always a first time for everything," said Merovee, somehow summoning a smile. "And now I can frame the favor I need from you, Pilatus. I need your complete cooperation in what transpires tomorrow, and your forgiveness for anything that has already transpired. The things I will ask you to do will be unorthodox, yet within your province. And I can think of no ways in which they will endanger you . . . while, if you do do as I ask, Jesus will emerge from the experience alive. Will you trust me? Promise to do all that I say?"

"Yes, my dear, I will trust you and do all that you say."

"And forgive anything that has already transpired."

"Whatever it is is forgiven."

She reached over and took the hand of Judah. She had hoped that it would not be necessary to reveal everything to Pilatus. He would not take kindly to the story of that original plot that had been meant to overthrow him and Rome.

"Tell him all, Judah."

Pilatus heard the telling with a mixture of astonishment, incredulity, and cold fury.

"If Yeshuah *had* survived," Judah told him limply, "if it seemed that he could actually spark the rebellion that he planned, we were going to warn you . . . to get you and Procula and the princesses away, or at least hide you until it was safe."

"Do you expect me to thank you?" said Pilatus. "Lucius, get out to Gethsemane with a few of our best men. Wear civilian clothes. If the Messiah of Rabbits is still hopping about in the shrubbery, bring him in."

"No, please," said Merovee. "Have Lucius remain. He needs to hear all that we have to say."

"Dispatch a detail then, and get yourself right back here," said Pilatus.

He turned dangerous eyes onto Judah as Lucius hastened out.

"Your brother is a great fool, Judah, but you are a greater one. Were it not for my promise to Merovee . . . "

"Praefectus, I am in complete agreement," said Judah evenly. "Yet I, too, had made a vow—a sacred promise—to one whom I loved."

Vows were sacred within all civilized cultures. Pilatus was sensible to the dilemma in which the young man had found himself—while, at the moment, the face of Judah seemed to be all but disintegrating under the pressure of his emotion.

Angrily, Pilatus snatched the empty goblet from him, refilled it, and handed it back.

"Drink!"

He turned to Merovee.

"You are very brave to come to me with this story. The night of your wedding you told me that I am kind. You must have great trust in that judgment of yours."

"I do."

"I should arrest all of you! Clear out the entire nest! What you have told me is indeed treason to Tiberius. I would not gain censure for my action, but advancement."

"I remember our conversation very well, Pilatus. You told me that you were not kind at all, but cruel and ambitious, that you desired greatness, advancement, which could not be gotten with kindness. I said that you were wrong, and promised that Jesus could teach you how to be great by being kind. While Jesus warned you that the advancement he would teach you to achieve would not necessarily be the sort that was recognized by the world, that, once you had heard his words, you might never again be able to function in relation to the world as you had in the past.

"He told you to think carefully before hearing his words . . . before understanding how to be great by being kind. And you said to him, 'I want to hear your words, Jesus.'

"Judah, here, was foolish, yes. Yet he but did what he had to do, what his heart and honor insisted that he do.

"And so did you, Pilatus. You said to Jesus, 'I want to hear.'

"In that moment, you committed yourself as surely as did our poor, suffering brother in heart, Judah.

"So here we all stand. Committed. In so many ways. Chiefly, as brothers and sisters in the words of Jesus.

"And the problem now is to keep Jesus with us, to bring him through alive, yet without harm to ourselves or to others."

"Merovee, swear to me that I do not make myself party to a rebellion against Rome. For, as Judah swore to Yeshuah, so I am sworn to Tiberius. Jesus would not mount a rebellion if 'resurrected' would he?"

"I swear it, Pilatus. You know his thinking."

"Yet he might not be able to avoid it. When the people saw him alive, after being dead . . . "

"Could I have that wine now?"

Procula hastened to pour it.

"Sit down here, my darling."

"I have not wanted to face this, Pilatus. You are right. It will be impossible for him to go among the people except in secret afterwards. He will obviously have to . . . leave. For somewhere."

Pilatus came to her, squatted before her as she sat in the chair.

"That night when he advised me to invest my money in Gaul. He had advised Deborah to do the same thing. As we know, she has taken his advice."

His smile was wheedling, an attempt to comfort.

"They say that Gaul in the summer is the most beautiful spot in the world. Perhaps Gaul is the future, Merovee. Perhaps Jesus has always known it.

"And think what it would be like . . . you and Jesus and your Agapo, your friends and family, far from the clutches and suffocating restrictions of the Temple. You could live and love and spread your good news unhampered. Tiberius is more than tolerant of divergent beliefs in the provinces. I can arrange transport for you on one of our own merchant vessels."

"It would be lovely, you are right. If only it could be that simple."

"Why should it not be?"

She patted his hand.

"Perhaps it will be, Pilatus. My beloved friend."

She sent Nathaniel back to the house of Nicodemus then, to assure those waiting that all was well.

"Alexander should have returned with his father by now," she told him. "Tell the Cyrenean that he is to proceed exactly as he and Judah had planned. Tell Joseph when he arrives that he, too, is to proceed exactly as planned."

"Return to us if there is aught of importance to report," said Pilatus, "just as we will send any important information to the house of Nicodemus."

They talked then for two more hours, going over it all, considering every possibility, rehearsing every move.

"And perhaps I can stave them off after all," said Pilatus. "I will be most unwilling, drag my feet endlessly. I will question him and find no fault. I will ridicule the title 'King of the Jews,' call him a demented fool, and let the rulers know that Tiberius, who has, himself, always refused the title of king, would find it just as ridiculous, see no reason to fear this madman. I will refuse to condemn him. I will flog him and tell them that that should be punishment enough. Perhaps they will give up."

"But would they then take him away and stone him themselves?" said Procula.

Pilatus shook his head.

"If they had the guts to, themselves, take responsibility for his death before this Passover throng, they would not be bringing him to me. They would simply apply for permission to stone a person for blasphemy against their God. And they would receive it. Never have we refused them. But, if I were successful in convincing them to be satisfied with just the flogging on this occasion, they would certainly regroup, and find another way and time to seize, charge, and kill him. We, though, would have time to spirit Jesus away, out of their reach." He shook his head. "Yet I cannot believe that they will let me get away with mere flogging. They have tasted blood. They will want their whole meal."

"Praefectus, could we not use those men that we took in today in the fracas in front of the fortress?" said Lucius. His men had returned empty-handed from Gethsemane. Yeshuah had disappeared. "Perhaps . . . it is their Passover day, a major festival. You could show great beneficence, Praefectus, parade out all the prisoners, including Jesus. Tell them that, as a gesture of good will for the festival, you will release to them one prisoner." His enthusiasm grew. "Yes. We could pack the courtyard with the people of Jesus, have them yell for his release!"

"Too many of us would be recognized," said Merovee. "The rulers would know it was a ruse."

"Then we could haul people in from off the street! We could send runners out into the valleys, let the people know what is happening, get them here by the hundreds, even thousands . . . "

The words of Lucius trailed off. He glanced at Pilatus and grinned sheepishly.

"Your enthusiasm is charming, Tribune, but our job is to avoid the gathering of excitable mobs, not to create them.

"And if we must go forward with this crucifixion . . . " He sighed. "As friend Yeshuah's plan takes pains to point out, it is best to keep it as quiet as possible."

"Pilatus," said Judah. "You should know the identity of one of your prisoners. He is Eleazar, my nephew. Yeshuah's son."

"Eleazar?"

Perplexed, Pilatus went to his writing table and shuffled through various sheets of papyrus.

"Here it is. Those scheduled for execution on the morrow are Noah, Jacob, Isaac, their leader Barrabban . . . "

Judah laughed outright.

"Barrabban."

A common Gentile mistake, to assume that two words of description were one proper name.

"Try *bar Rabban*, " said Judah. "Son of the Great Teacher. So Eleazar has rediscovered that much pride in his father, has he? He wishes to go to his death with only that appellation. I hope you will allow me, Praefectus, to visit my nephew in his cell and tell him, as you say, that the rabban turned into a Rabbit."

"Would that not be unnecessarily cruel?" said Pilatus mildly.

Judah turned his face away.

"He should know. He should share in the knowledge and the shame with the rest of Yeshuah's family. He should know what fools we have all been."

"He is to endure crucifixion," said Pilatus gently. "Surely that is enough. Leave him his ideals. So that he, at least, can endure the pain bravely, and return some honor to your family."

At two hours before the dawn, Nathaniel returned. Jesus had indeed been found guilty and deserving of death.

"They had a hard time of it," said Nathaniel. "Nicodemus and his friends questioned the paid witnesses at each turning, until they had them in such confusion that each testimony contradicted every other.

"And Jesus would not speak. To whatever they asked, he remained silent, except to say that he had often taught openly in the Temple courts, that many of them had, themselves, heard him, and did they not remember what they, themselves, had heard?

"Caiaphas was nearing his wits' end. Finally, he cried out at Jesus, 'Tell me straightly! Have you ever called yourself the son of God?'"

Merovee groaned and lowered her face into her hands.

"'No,' Jesus answered. 'but I have called, and do here name myself, a son of the true god. But then so are you, Caiaphas. We are all sons and daughters of the true god.'

"At which Caiaphas leaped to his feet and rent his garments and cried out, 'He has blasphemed against God! Do we need to hear more?'

"And of course they did not."

"He convicted himself?" said Pilatus in puzzlement. "Why?"

"Nicodemus asked him the same question as they were taking him out.

"'They were bound to have me one way or another, Friend,' he said, 'and I was tired of standing.'"

Merovee started to giggle. It built to a laugh. Her head fell back helplessly, and she let the mirth roll out.

"How long since you have had any sleep?" said Pilatus.

"Come," said Procula. "Come in and lie on our bed, my dear."

"I will not be able to sleep."

"Yes you will. And there is no point in staying awake. We all know what we must do and we will do it. But they will not bring him here till the dawn. Nothing can be done until then."

"Go," urged Nathaniel. "It will be a very long day, Merovee. You can serve him best if you are rested. Those at the house are napping as best they can. I, too, will go back and get some sleep."

"Keep them all there, Nathaniel. Do not let them come here to the Antonia for the trial by Pilatus. They must not put themselves in jeopardy. It would make it all the harder for Josh."

"I will tell them."

"The Cyrenean and Joseph and Nicodemus are to proceed just as planned. Pilatus and Lucius will see that all goes smoothly for them." Her voice broke. "Josh will take care of the rest."

"I know, I know, we have been over it repeatedly. Now stop thinking and go with Procula."

Merovee allowed herself to be led from the room, into the adjoining bedchamber.

"As Merovee says," said Nathaniel to Pilatus, "we will all stay at the house until at least midday. Only the Cyrenean will have to be here, waiting at the gate."

"He, too, need not arrive until at least the third hour after the dawn," said Pilatus. "I am going to keep Jesus away from that cross for every moment possible."

At last, Pilatus was left with only Lucius, and with Judah.

He fastened a baleful glare onto Judah.

"And what do you intend to do with *your*self during these hours, my poor young traitor?"

Judah was silent for long moments.

Then he drew from his gird that which the rulers had paid him for his betrayal. Thirty pieces of silver. He crossed to the writing table of Pilatus and meticulously stacked them on its surface. A slow, weary smile lifted his lips.

"I am going to spend part of it in bribing you, Praefectus. Just as originally planned."

* * *

At sunrise, the titular High Priest Caiaphas and his chief priests and scribes arrived at the gate of the praetoreum courtyard with Jesus and a paid mob and demanded to see the praefectus.

They were told that that worthy was sleeping. Caiaphas demanded that he be awakened.

Tribune Gallus appeared and argued for quite some time against such a premature awakening, since Pilatus had not been feeling at all well of late.

Finally, the tribune was persuaded to go and see what the body servant of Pilatus had to say on the matter.

After half an hour, Lucius returned and told Caiaphas that Pilatus was really very ill, and could definitely not be disturbed.

Caiaphas, magnificent in his regalia, drew himself up and said that he had brought a traitor to Caesar to be tried and crucified, and that Pilatus had better get up or Tiberius would hear about it.

Still Pilatus tarried, letting the mob cool its heels outside the gate as he watched down upon it through a window slit in the salon.

Merovee was still asleep in the adjoining bedchamber. They had promised to wake her the moment that Jesus was brought. It was a promise that would not be kept. The longer she was kept out of this, the better.

"They have already beaten Jesus badly about the face," he muttered to Judah. "Lucius can see to that."

"I will be only too pleased," said Lucius.

"Well, I suppose I have got to be dressed by now," sighed Pilatus. "I shall go down to find out what all the fuss is about. You two get on about your business."

Procula embraced her husband. Then Lucius. Then Judah.

"I pray," she said, "that we are doing the right thing."

"We are," said Pilatus.

The morning was nippy. He feigned drowsiness as he descended the stairs from his apartment and crossed the court to the main gate. As always, in approaching these priests, he felt a wave of disgust, of pure dislike. Caiaphas came forward so that he could speak without being heard by the rabble, but still he refused to cross the threshold. For fear of contamination. Gentile contamination. They must be so pure during their Passover. It irked Pilatus no end to be looked upon as a source of contamination, especially when the priests were the ones with the long, greased, smelly hair, and the great, grizzled beards which hid who knew what vermin. And whose hearts were black with lies and injustice beneath their sanctimonious facades.

"What do you mean, waking me at this hour, Caiaphas? Is this not a festival day during which work is banned? I had thought to take my ease along with your people."

"We have a matter that will not wait, Praefectus. We have apprehended a revolutionary."

"What, that bound fellow there?" To the relief of Pilatus, Jesus kept his head bowed, not meeting his eyes. "He does not look dangerous to me. Bring the prisoner forward. What has happened to his face? How now. Do I know this man?"

"I am told that you attended his wedding, Praefectus."

"His wedding? Oh. The wedding in Galilee. Why it *is* the same man. The son of Joseph of the Triple Ramah. But he is no revolutionary."

"I beg to differ. Besides which he has blasphemed against our God by calling himself the son of that God. He considers himself divine, Praefectus."

"He looks rather ordinary to me."

Blast Jesus. He actually *laughed*.

"He certainly bleeds in an ordinary way," said Pilatus angrily.

"And that is why he deserves to die."

"For bleeding in an ordinary way?"

"No, for considering himself divine."

"Why kill a man for being mad? And why bring him to me?"

Oh, stop smiling, Jesus! This is your life that we argue!

"He deserves to die, but we have no Law that allows us to kill him."

"No law? Do not be absurd, you have ten times more laws than Rome. We processed two orders for stonings just last week. Give Lucius the proper documents and take the fellow out and do the deed yourselves."

"He is a traitor against Caesar, Pilatus."

"If that is so, then all the better that you should stone him."

"Caesar's right to kill him is superior to ours, Pilatus."

"What do you want me to do, ship him to Capri?"

Oh! It was just too much! Pilatus wheeled upon Jesus.

"Why are you laughing, Fellow? These men want your life. And you think it is funny?"

"Your pardon," said Jesus. "I have grown giddy from lack of sleep."

"Or perhaps you are tired of *standing*," said Pilatus caustically. "Get him out of here, Caiaphas."

"You must try him."

"On what charge, for Jove's sake?"

"He has called himself the Messiah."

"Every madman in this country thinks he is a messiah."

"He claims to be King of the Jews, which is direct treason to Tiberius, for we have no king but Caesar."

"Caiaphas . . . "

"And this man has prime messianic genealogy. He is the direct heir of David. Some call him the Prince of Judah. On top of which, he has made a dynastic alliance with one of the two heiresses of the House of Saul."

Pilatus stopped in his tracks. His eyes flicked to those of Jesus and saw the same surprise.

"What are you talking about?"

"My scribe Zakiah . . . " Caiaphas smiled. He had very thick lips. "You remember him, Praefectus, he attended this man's wedding along with you. Zakiah has found the evidence in our Temple records. The woman he married, Miriam of Magdala, and her mother and sister and brother, are the primary descendants of King Saul."

Pilatus spread his hands.

"So? A petty king, dead a thousand years. Who cares who his descendants are?"

"We do, Praefectus. Time is meaningless to us Jews. A thousand years ago is as yesterday. We are vitally a part of Saul and he of us. For these thousand years there has been enmity between Benjamin, the tribe of Saul, and Judah, the tribe of David . . . for David took this land from the Benjaminites. The wedding of these two heirs heals that breach. The two of them together constitute the ultimate claim to the ancient throne of Judeah. Their children would be princes of sacred and even holy blood in the eyes of our people. So that, were the people to learn of the combined genealogies of this man and his wife . . . . Suffice it to say that this man is a clear and present threat to Rome, Praefectus. He has only to say the word, and the entire populace will rally to him. He was ready to say that word when we apprehended him. He was ready to overthrow you, to push you and your troops into the sea, to institute his own kingdom among our people."

"You are telling me, then, that this man *is* the legitimate King of the Jews?"

"No, but he claims to be."

"You just said that he *is*, that he has the genealogy."

"He cannot be our king. We have no king but Caesar."

"So why does he upset you? I can assure you that he does not upset Tiberius, who worries himself not at all about your tribal quarreling over petty kings a thousand years dead. Tiberius knows very well that you have no king but himself. Go home, Caiaphas, you try my patience."

"He has plotted against Caesar. He is guilty of treason. You are bound to execute him."

"Where are your witnesses?"

"Right here." Caiaphas gestured at the crowd behind him. "The Sanhedrin and my priests and scribes listened for most of the night to their testimony. It is completely damning. They have come here with us, but, of course, you have no time to hear them."

"Do I not? You." Pilatus gestured at one fellow, from his dress one of the High Priest's Arab servants. "What have you to say against the prisoner?"

"I have heard him call himself both the Son of Man and the Messiah."

"That is it? What of you, Fellow?"

"I heard the same thing. And I have seen him plotting with Zealots."

"Where did you see him?"

"Um . . . in the Court of the Gentiles."

"Upon which day?"

"It was . . . I think that it was the day before yesterday."

"You only think?"

"No, I am sure now."

"Jesus, were you in Jerusalem the day before yesterday?"

"No."

"Have you witnesses to your whereabouts?"

"About seventy."

"I think you must have mistaken Jesus for someone else then, Fellow. Do you suppose that is possible?"

"I suppose it is possible."

"Stand aside. You there. What do you have to say for yourself?"

"I saw him ride into Jerusalem on the colt of an ass."

" . . . Yes?"

"He allowed the people to strew palm branches in his path."

"Are you distressed about the trees? Why should this be a capital crime?"

"It is our prophecies," said Caiaphas. "The Messiah, the one who, our people believe, shall oust the Romans, is to do just that, ride into Jerusalem on the colt of an ass. While, in ancient days, the people strewed palm branches in the way of our kings as they entered the city."

"Your dusty old kings again. Can you not let their bones lie in peace?"

Caiaphas smiled his thick-lipped smile and proceeded, unperturbed.

"The entry of this Yeshuah into Jerusalem was, then, a clear announcement to the people that he is their Messiah and their rightful king. He made this declaration before tens of thousands, Pilatus. It was an overt attempt to organize the Passover throng into an army. Against you."

"Why do you call him Yeshuah? Does he not call himself Jesus?"

"Jesus is the Greek for Yeshuah."

"But is he not called Joshuah by his father?"

"Joshuah and Yeshuah are one and the same name, Praefectus, one originally an Aramaic version, the other the Hebrew rendering."

"I shall never be able to keep up with you people. Everybody has a dozen names, in as many languages."

"It is not our fault that we are situated at the crossroads of the world, Praefectus, and that one conqueror after another has overwhelmed us and forced its ways onto us."

"E-gods! Do you mean that soon you will all have Latin names as well? I hope that I will have gone on to better things by then."

"We hope so, too, Praefectus."

Pilatus grunted and returned his attention to the witness.

"Fellow, on what day did you see whatever-you-think-his-name-is make his 'royal' entry into the city?"

"Three days ago."

"Jesus, were you in Jerusalem three days ago?"

"No."

"Do you have witnesses as to your whereabouts on that day?"

"About seventy."

"Fellow, do you think it is possible that you are mistaking the prisoner for someone else?"

" . . . Maybe."

"Caiaphas, have you no better testimony than this?"

Another man spoke up.

"One day in the Court of the Gentiles I heard him instruct the people to refuse to pay tribute to Caesar"

"When was this?"

"The day after he raised that Lazarus bar Jeremiah from the dead."

"Jesus, were you in the Court of the Gentiles on that day?"

"No."

"Do you have witnesses to the fact that you were not?"

"About seventy."

"Pilatus, this is ridiculous!" said Caiaphas.

"I agree. I see no fault in this man. The testimony of your witnesses is not worth the hot air of their breaths. Why do only those who accuse come here as witnesses? Why have you not called some of his seventy?"

"They are all thieves, Zealots, and brigands, Praefectus, hiding for their own crimes. We could not find any of them,. The testimony of such people would not be credible in any case."

Pilatus cocked his head and said very softly . . .

"I am sure that the Zebedee will be thrilled to know your opinion of his wife and sons, Caiaphas. I wonder, would he be quite so willing to carry your 'goods' for you did he know that opinion?"

Caiaphas shifted his weight. His voice went deadly quiet.

"Pilatus, I must have this man crucified. I, uh . . . will see that it is made worth your while."

Pilatus stepped back, unconsciously sweeping his robe away from the priest as though to keep it from filth.

"Caiaphas, despite all opinion to the contrary, Roman justice attempts to be just. You should be ashamed, coming to me with this passel of fools for witnesses. And I have an idea. Why do I not make it worth *your* while to be an honest man and let this fellow go in peace? How much would it take, Caiaphas, to buy your honesty?"

A dangerous glitter crept into the eyes of Caiaphas.

"I will have this man crucified, Pilatus."

"Ah, then your honesty has no price."

"Do not force me to take measures against you, Pilatus."

"You threaten me?" For a moment, Pilatus looked angry enough to strike the man.

Then it seemed that a happy thought occurred to him.

"I have the solution! Antipas has just returned from his war. He is over in Herod's Palace."

"What does that have to do with anything?"

"Well, as the Tetrarch of Galilee, he has jurisdiction over this man, not I."

"But this man is not Galilean."

"Is he not? I attended his wedding in Galilee."

"But . . . "

"And I am not as without information as you seem to think, Caiaphas. My spies have told me about this 'Yeshuah,' and they have all said that he is Galilean."

"That is a different man."

"But my spies say that that different man is the one who has said the things you are now attributing to the prisoner. Is this man the one who said those things or is he not?"

"Yes he is."

"Then he is Galilean. Lucius!"

"Listen to his speech!" cried Caiaphas. "Is that a Galilean accent?"

"You cannot have it both ways, Caiaphas. Lucius!"

Lucius came running from the door of the corridor to the guardroom.

"Take this fellow over to Antipas to be tried. He is a Galilean and not of my jurisdiction."

So Jesus was marched through the deserted morning streets to the Palace of Herod by the Joppa Gate.

"Where is Merovee?" he muttered to Lucius as that man led him along at the head of the mob.

"Asleep in the bedchamber of Pilatus. The rest are with Nicodemus."

"Merovee is all right?"

"Only exhausted."

'Keep her there in the Antonia. For her own safety. And if I die . . . "

"You will not die. Everything is settled. You already know the plan."

"The best-laid plans are the ones which most often stray. If I die, beg of Pilatus secret passage out of the country for Merovee and the child, and for both of our families. This business of King Saul . . . if it is so, not only Merovee, but both our two families are in mortal danger. Even my father and Deborah. The rulers will seek to destroy them lest there be more marriage amongst them, lest our two families people the world with 'sacred princelings.' And Judah, Lucius. Tell him that I love him. Tell him that I forgive him."

"It shall be as you say."

"Tell Pilatus the same. What a magnificent effort he made! Why is he sending me to Antipas?"

"To waste time. We want your hours on the cross to be as few as possible."

"Of course. Thank him for me. I will not need the Cyrenean's drugs."

"You are very sure?"

"I have slept on beds of nails," smiled Jesus. "I am a master of conscious suspension and will not feel the pain."

"We will have the Cyrenean there no less. Just in case."

"As you please."

"Jesus?"

"Yes?"

"Do you love me as well?"

"Do you want me to kiss you?"

"No, but . . . "

"You are my friend and brother for eternity, Lucius. From this day forward." He reached up and grasped the man's forearm as though to steady himself. "Do not cry. It would not look right if you tripped and I had to stop *you* from falling."

Lucius could not stop the laughter.

"Oh Jesus. Jesus my friend. We will not let you die."

Antipas, taken truly by surprise, had no need to feign drowsiness, or irritation. He appeared in a rumpled purple robe with his hastily set diadem askew. He was an unremarkable man, of middle height, even features, sandy hair, and elusive personality.

Yet his irritation dissolved and his eyes sparked when he learned the name of the prisoner.

"So. At last."

Jesus had been brought into the audience chamber. Again, Caiaphas and his people had remained outside for fear of contamination.

Antipas made a circuit of Jesus, looking him up and down.

"I think they have lied to me. You cannot be Johannan returned. You are too old. Would not Johannan returned be yet a babe?"

Jesus smiled easily through his contusions.

"Your Highness makes an astute observation."

He continued to smile. Antipas found himself rather liking the man.

"I have heard much concerning you, Jesus. Your teachings have quite captivated my wife and her daughter. They often donned disguises whilst you were in Galilee and came to listen to you. I will wager that you did not know that!"

"Disguises? Both of them? I had not heard that."

"My wife is incorrigible, always off on some new adventure."

Antipas beamed, and, in his unremarkable eyes, was a remarkable love for the woman of whom he spoke.

"She also tells me that you stole the wife away from my overseer in Tiberias!"

"Johannah left him to follow after me, it is so. But I think, Your Highness, that the parting was agreeable to them both."

"True, true. They never did get on. Ah, Manaen!"

A tall, quietly handsome man had entered the chamber.

"Jesus, this is my foster-brother Manaen. Manaen, this is Jesus, the man we have been hearing about."

Jesus looked closely at Manaen. Then he reached out and took the man's hand.

"Manaen. We were just talking about Johannah, late the wife of Chuzah."

"Oh? Yes. Johannah"

Jesus smiled at the quick, tell-tale flush on the face of Manaen, and released the man's hand.

Antipas was gesturing to a slave.

"Pour some wine for our guests. No! Better yet, bring us a pitcher of fresh water. We will see if what we have heard is true. Now, Lucius, tell me what this is all about. Why has Pilatus sent me this man?"

"Caiaphas wants him crucified."

"Oh dear."

"Pilatus thinks that he is Galilean, hence, of your jurisdiction."

"He does not sound Galilean. Are you Galilean, Jesus?"

"No."

"Well, that settles that. You must take him back to Pilatus, Lucius. Which is a great relief to me. The blood of Johannan is enough upon my poor head, will the High Priest never be satisfied? Tell Pilatus that, from all I hear, this is a good man, Lucius. What are the charges against you, Jesus?"

"Treason against Caesar."

"How so?"

"They say that I have declared myself the Messiah and so King of the Jews, which is treason."

"Have you?"

"No."

"Be sure to tell that to Pilatus, Lucius. My wife thinks that Jesus is a most special teacher, an honest and gentle man. She is a wonderful judge of character. I have never known her to be wrong—except perhaps when she fell in love with me."

"Now Antipas," said Manaen.

"Well, it is true. I could not even win one little war. The only war I ever fought, and I could not win it.

"Ah, here is the water. Please, Jesus, while you are here, do one of your tricks for us. The wine trick that they say you did at your wedding."

Jesus stood silent.

"Is it the wrong sort of water? Do you need it to be in a different container?"

"The water is fine, and the container makes no difference. But why do you reside in the miracle of yourself, in your own body, your own vitality, and still ask for signs?"

Antipas drew himself up in startled and wounded majesty.

"I only wished you to show me what you have shown to so many others."

"Perhaps I think that you are better than many others, Herod Antipas. Perhaps that is why I will not perform tricks for you."

Antipas looked up at Manaen in confusion, then back at Jesus. His eyes narrowed.

"You mock me."

"Not at all."

The eyes remained narrowed.

"You really hate me. You blame me for Johannan's death."

"Even Johannan did not hate you, or blame you, Antipas."

Quite suddenly he reached out and put his hands to either side of the head of Antipas, his fingers pressing the temples.

"And now I will do a trick for you that is better than all the wine you will ever have. I forgive you and absolve you of my cousin Johannan's death—a death that has been filling your dreams with nightmares, and your innards with pain. I assure you that I speak with his own voice, his own words, his own thoughts. And, with these words, I am removing from you, taking out of you, the pain that has been troubling your belly. You will ache no more. I also give back to you your happy vigor with your wife. You can lie with her once again, while your dreams, from this day forth, will be sweet. When you dream, you will see my face, hear my words of love. You will find peace. And you will become a true prince at last."

Abruptly he released Antipas. The man sat speechless, staring up at him.

"How did you know those things?" he said when he found his voice.

Jesus only smiled.

"Give my great love to your beautiful wife and to her daughter, Antipas. Tell them that I rejoice that they came to hear me teach. Tell them not to mourn for me. Tell them . . . tell them that there is no such thing as a dead fig tree. Will you do that?"

"No such thing as a dead fig tree," said Antipas obediently. "Yes. I will tell them when they wake. Help me remember it, Manaen."

"I will help you," said Manaen, his own gaze upon Jesus both puzzled and thoughtful.

"Trust Manaen to help you in many things, Herod Antipas. Goodbye, then."

"Oh. Are you going?"

"I must return to Pilatus."

"Thank him for sending you to me. Tell him I will call upon him this afternoon and thank him myself."

Manaen whispered something to him.

"Oh, of course. He will be busy today, while we, ourselves, must prepare for the Sabbath. Tell him that I will call on him the day after the Sabbath."

"I will do that."

"Good fortune to you, Jesus. I hope they do not kill you."

"I appreciate the sentiment."

"What a shame you are not Galilean. I could have pardoned you."

By the time they arrived back at the Antonia, there was another mob waiting. Caiaphas had called up reinforcements. They spat upon Jesus as he was led through their midst, screaming for his crucifixion. After many minutes, Pilatus reappeared.

"What is this? Why has this man been brought back to me?"

"As I told you," said Caiaphas, "he is not Galilean."

"Is this so, Joshuah?"

"I am Judean."

"Well why did you not say so in the first place? What a waste of time!"

"I think not, Praefectus," said Jesus. "The Tetrarch was pleased by your deference regarding his possible jurisdiction in this matter. He will call upon you the day after the Sabbath to thank you in person for your courtesy."

Pilatus frowned.

"I can think of better ways to spend my time. But to business. Caiaphas, I have been thinking about this."

He had reworked the earlier idea of Lucius.

"I have decided that what this man needs is a good lashing. I will give him the thirty-nine stripes then release him. For I have decided to begin a new custom as a gesture of my goodwill to your people. On each Passover, I will release, absolved from all blame, one of your people. One criminal. I think this is an excellent compromise in this situation. Everyone should be satisfied.

"Take him to be flogged, Lucius. Tell the head centurion to use his strongest, cruelest man to inflict the punishment. The High Priest's need to punish must be well served. Then let the soldiers have their sport with him. Their game of 'King' will be most apt in this case. Call me when they are finished."

He turned on his heel and left the courtyard, while, with a show of roughness, and ignoring the protestations of Caiaphas, Lucius seized the arm of Jesus and jerked him away over the flagstones toward the corridor to the guardroom. Once through the door, he pushed Jesus into a dark, side room.

"What . . . ?" began Jesus.

The blow came from behind and fell upon his head.

He did not remember falling. Neither did he know that his clothes were stripped from him.

"We are ordered to give him an especially severe beating," said Lucius.

"That will be my pleasure," said the one who had knocked Jesus unconscious. "Pray, let us begin."

* * *

Simon the Cyrenean left the house of Nicodemus near to the third hour after sunrise and proceeded to the Antonia. In front of the courtyard was a mob of some hundred men, milling and muttering. At its head, at the threshold of the court, stood Caiaphas and his priests and scribes and elders of the Sanhedrin. They were all obviously waiting. Simon eased into the crowd, making himself a part.

"What is happening?" he asked the fellow next to him.

"Who are you?"

"I am a physician. From Cyrenea. Just passing through. Is this some part of the Passover festival?"

The man laughed rudely.

"Nothing to do with Passover. We are here to see that a traitor to Caesar named Yeshuah gets crucified this day."

"A traitor to Caesar? I am a most faithful subject of Rome. What should I do to help?"

"Well the praefectus does not like our evidence and is loathe to crucify this Yeshuah, so he has sent him to be flogged and made 'King.' Then he means to release him. He has started a new custom, he says, to release one prisoner free of blame on each Passover. But the High Priest has figured how to get around it. Yesterday, the Romans took some other prisoners. They are to be crucified this day as well. One is known to call himself bar Rabban. So, when this Yeshuah is brought out to be released, we are all to yell at the top of our voices demanding that it be bar Rabban who is released, not Yeshuah. The praefectus will be caught on his own promise and will have to release bar Rabban and execute Yeshuah."

"How clever of the High Priest."

"He is a fine and generous man."

"How generous?"

"All who yell are to receive an extra gold piece. Will you yell as well?"

"I am sworn to uphold life, my friend, sorry, I will not yell to end it."

It was another hour before Jesus was brought back out to the gate.

At the sight of him, Simon's stomach turned and tears rushed to his eyes.

He was naked except for a loincloth. Over his shoulder was a length of purple cloth. In his hand, as scepter, he clutched a soldier's staff. On his head was the soldiers' traditional "King's Crown," a plaited circlet of brambles, the thorns of which had been pushed down into his skull with especial cruelty.

He was a mass of blood. It ran in rivers down his lacerated face, in hundreds of rivers down his shoulders, chest, back, stomach, and legs. The man who had wielded the whip had missed nothing, and the upright man that Jesus had been was no more. His shoulders were stooped, his head hung foreward, his disarrayed hair was matted in the blood upon his head, face, and beard.

"Behold your King!" cried Pilatus. "He has been sufficiently punished. And so now, by the power vested in me by Tiberius Caesar, I hereby . . . "

"No!" came the first cry. "Bar Rabban. We want bar Rabban released!"

"Bar Rabban!" came the echo from another hundred voices.

Pilatus stood as though frozen.

"But what do you want me to do with this man?"

"Crucify him! Crucify, crucify!" cried the mob.

"You would have me crucify your rightful king?"

"Crucify him! Give us bar Rabban! You said you would release one man! We want bar Rabban!"

"Listen to me!" cried Pilatus. "My wife has come to me, telling me of a dream she had last night. She begs me not to crucify this man. She tells me that, in the dream, I and all of you will be damned before your god if we kill him! Would you have us all be damned?"

"Crucify him!" It was Caiaphas who renewed the cry.

Fighting for control of his breath, Pilatus went to the High Priest.

"You know that this man is innocent."

"Crucify him."

"I will not."

"Then I name you traitor to Caesar. He who is a friend to this man is no friend to Caesar. Indeed, I wonder if you now consort with Zealots and seek the overthrow of your own emperor, seeking to place yourself in a high place in a new government. That is what my people shall tell Tiberius, for, if you refuse to crucify this man this day, they shall be on the road by Sabbath's end, in Capri within the time of one moon, and returned in another. Which will give you just enough time, Pontius Pilatus, to settle your affairs in Palestine before being relieved of your duties. And time enough to make your will."

Pilatus turned away. He gestured to a servant.

"Bring me a basin of water and a linen."

It was brought. Slowly, elaborately, Pilatus washed his hands.

"You see what I do here?" he said loudly. "You, who are so concerned with cleanliness and purity. I wash my hands of this man's blood. I wash the blame and damnation promised by my wife's dream from off of myself. Let the everlasting guilt be on your heads. You, Caiaphas, and every man among you who has plotted, schemed, and now cried for the crucifixion of an innocent man. Let it be on your heads for all of eternity."

"We will take the blame and handle it nicely, thank you," said Caiaphas. "Now. Can we trust you to carry on with the execution?"

"You can trust me."

Once more, Caiaphas motioned Pilatus aside.

"We have decided that it should be carried out at the Place of the Skull, a walled tomb to the northwest, do you know it?"

Pilatus summoned Lucius.

"Lucius, do you know of a tomb garden called the Place of the Skull?"

"Yes, Praefectus. It was used of old for crucifixions. But it is private property now."

"It belongs to one of our Sanhedrin," said Caiaphas smoothly. "He will not mind its use."

Caiaphas smiled, thinking of the diligence with which Nicodemus had questioned the witnesses, nearly to the point of ruining the whole thing and getting Jesus excused from the charges. There was a certain satisfaction and justice then, that his should be the garden used for the crucifixion.

It was only at that point that Caiaphas realized two other odd coincidences. The Place of the Skull had once belonged to the prisoner's father, Joseph bar Ramathea, and only recently had been sold to Nicodemus . . . while Jesus had been taken at the Garden of the Olive Press, also belonging to Nicodemus.

Caiaphas shook his head and chuckled inwardly. God certainly did work in mysterious ways.

"Is there a post hole there for the upright of the cross?" Pilatus was asking Lucius.

"There are many post holes," said Caiaphas. "And that spot is out of the way, do you not see, Pilatus. It is of benefit to both of us not to draw attention to this execution. This way it will be, shall we say—a private execution? Execute the others down in the Hinnom as you have been wont. That will draw the greatest attention."

"As always, Caiaphas, you seem to have thought of everything. It shall be as you say."

And, since it was now really to be done, one might as well pay attention to practicalities.

"But do you think we should hang him up there completely alone, Caiaphas? Would that not, in itself, be questioned? After the release of bar Rabban, there are ten more left to be executed. Would it not be wise to hang a couple of those men with Jesus? Then, if passersby ask, they can honestly be told that it is only some of those Zealots who attacked the Romans."

"How assiduously you guard your honesty, Pilatus. But the suggestion is sound. Manage this thing as you see fit. Well, I have duties to see to at the Temple, and must be getting back. Have a fine day, Pilatus."

"I wonder if I will ever have a fine day again, Caiaphas."

He let the man get halfway down the steps from the courtyard before he called out.

"Oh, by the way, Caiaphas . . . do you know the identity of bar Rabban, the *truly* dangerous revolutionary even now being released from the guardroom?"

Caiaphas shrugged.

"A Zealot. The son of some rabbi."

"He is the son of Yeshuah."

Pilatus turned on his heel and strode away, savoring the last expression upon the face of the High Priest.

It was a small triumph. And no comfort at all.

* * *

The Cyrenean was waiting at the gate out of which prisoners were brought on the way to execution. As expected, none of the High Priest's rabble had come around—they had disappeared back into their holes the moment their job was done. Those gathered were not many. Matrons from the Ladies' League waited, with their myrrh-drugged wine, along with members of the victims' families, and some sympathetic, or merely curious, passersby.

Eleazar's Zealot companions were the first out the portal. Eight of them emerged, each naked but for his loincloth, each marked by his flogging, each wearing the crown of thorns from the soldiers' game, each dragging the crossbar for his own cross. These eight had the easiest crosses to bear. Only those crossbars. For the execution site in the Valley of Hinnom was used so frequently that uprights were kept always in place, waiting.

The uprights had long ago been removed from the Place of the Skull, so that those scheduled for hanging there would have to drag both the uprights and the crossbars.

At sight of the first prisoners, the matrons rushed forward and the execution squad stood back, allowing them to give each man a full cup of drugged wine, allowing friends and family to bestow embraces, gabble words of encouragement and love.

Then, taking up their crossbars again, those eight began the trip toward the Valley of Hinnom.

Only after the bulk of the crowd had gone off in their wake did the gate open again. Two more Zealots emerged, dragging full crosses. Jesus came last, dragging his cross.

The matrons offered the wine. The two Zealots accepted the dulling drink. Jesus shook his head no.

The Cyrenean fell in beside the execution squad as they set off, west along the outside of the city wall toward the tomb garden. Lucius was there as well, unobtrusively allowing the Cyrenean to get closer and closer to Jesus.

As planned, the steps of Jesus faltered often. With growing frequency, he stumbled. Yet Simon wondered if this was mere play-acting. The man had been whipped with a viciousness that had not been shown to any of the others. Had that really been necessary?

The loss of blood was already tremendous—there was hardly an inch of his skin not covered. One could hardly see his face for the gore, for his hair was matted into the congealing goo.

The leader of the execution squad kept his whip singing, urging the stumbling steps onward. The Cyrenean watched the every movement of Jesus. The first little cake was waiting in his sweating fingers.

Then Jesus stumbled badly. He collapsed onto the rocky path, taking the fall on his knees first, and then on his hands as he released the cross, allowing it to tumble sideways.

The Cyrenean darted in.

"I will help him! I will carry his cross!"

Seeming to reach out in a gesture of sympathy to the fallen man, he forced the little cake into the waiting mouth.

"Move away, Stranger!" cried the leader of the squad. He cracked his whip. "On your feet, Prisoner!"

"Oh forget it, Longinus," said Lucius. "He is too weak. He is falling behind the others. At this rate he will be dead before we have the fun of hanging him. You want to carry his cross for him, Stranger? Well go ahead. What, are you a physician? Give me your bag. I will carry it."

So the Cyrenean stepped across the fallen body of Jesus and took a grip on the cross.

Good God it was heavy!

He got it up onto a shoulder and glanced sideways. Lucius had just gotten Jesus to his feet. Jesus was looking straight at Simon, his face—his eyes—for the first time, and at close range, fully visible.

It was all the Cyrenean could do not to cry out. He lowered his head, humped his back, and threw his weight into dragging the cross. From that angle, all he could see of the man beside him were his feet, stumbling along.

They were not the feet of Jesus at all. The man who walked beside the Cyrenean, traveling to the Place of the Skull to be crucified, was Judah.

Chapter 22

The Messenger

The shouts of "Crucify him!" were the sounds that had awakened Merovee. Yet she had not been able to go to Jesus, or even to look down upon him from the window of the salon. For, when she rose and went to the door of the sleeping chamber, she found it locked. No one answered her calls.

Wine was on a table, and food. She could stomach neither, but set to pacing, watching the door until her eyes ached.

No less than her breasts ached for Agapo.

What had happened? Had Pilatus turned traitor to the plan? To Jesus?

She could not believe it.

Then why was she a prisoner?

It seemed an eternity before she heard voices in the other room. Pilatus and Procula. The bolt was thrown back and the door to her chamber opened.

She burst forth, rushing to the window slit to look down into the court.

"I heard them crying against him! Why did you lock me in? Oh, he is gone. Gone! And you would not let me see him!"

"Calm yourself," said Pilatus. "Jesus is not gone. He is safe, Merovee. He, too, is locked in for the moment . . . in a storeroom of the soldiers' quarters. We will retrieve him when Lucius returns."

"Then there will be no crucifixion?"

"The crucifixion is proceeding as scheduled. The victim is on his way to the Place of the Skull at this moment."

Merovee started to speak once again. Then her eyes widened. She sank down into a couch and just stared at Pilatus, waiting for him to continue.

"Merovee." It was Procula. "Forgive us. We think we did the best thing."

"After you went to sleep," said Pilatus, "Judah put forth his own plan."

He went to his writing table and scooped the silver into his hands, came back and emptied it into the hands of Merovee.

"He bribed me to agree to that plan. For his sake, I took the bribe."

"Thirty pieces of silver," whispered Merovee.

"Jesus told us that they would pass through our hands. We will have to think on how to turn them to a good cause.

"Though perhaps the actions of Judah have already done that."

"What Judah said to Pilatus made so much sense, Merovee."

Merovee felt the tears coming. She covered her face with her hands, the silver showering onto the couch.

"In short," said Pilatus, "he told us that it was both his duty and his right to go to the cross. He, Judah, was responsible for the capture of Jesus in the first place, he said. He, Judah, was the one who had involved all of us in this mess. It was his brother who had conceived the scheme, and who had made of him, Judah, 'the Messenger' when he fled.

"To uphold and redeem Yeshuah's honor and his own, he said that he had to do it.

"To save his beloved Jesus from a torture and possible death that he had not planned, he had to do it.

"For all reasons and for all people, he had to do it.

"And, he said, Procula and I had to let him do it."

"He explained to us about the Messenger," said Procula. "Your people have a special conviction, it seems, held more strongly even than in some other cultures. Any messenger, no matter how lowly, becomes as the one who has sent him, even if that someone is a great lord. Legally, in spirit, by an almost mystic trans-substantiation, that messenger becomes the one who sent him, and must be treated exactly as the sender would have been treated.

"This is what Judah told us. At first Pilatus and I thought he was mad. Then we saw the . . . exultation that filled him. He said that, when he went to the cross, he went as the Messenger for two masters, Yeshuah and Jesus. He said that, in that case, he would *become* both Yeshuah and Jesus. He could thus be Yeshuah on the cross and erase that man's shame. While he would also be Jesus on the cross, and conduct himself with that man's love and forgiveness and majesty. It was his delegated responsibility to represent those two men. He accepted that responsibility joyfully, Merovee. He assured us that he could do the sleep."

"We had to let him do it," said Pilatus. "He would have been destroyed anyway had we not. He would have been so ruined in Spirit that he would never have recovered."

Merovee nodded, staring at nothing.

"Yes. You did right, Pilatus. I, too, would have allowed it. You need not have locked me in."

"When first I heard Judah's story last night," said Pilatus, "I hated him. But now I think . . . he is the finest Messenger that ever two masters had. I sent a superscription to be nailed above his head. It says 'King of the Jews.' And I meant it. The Jews could do much worse. Everyone could do much worse. I hope that, if my time ever comes, I will have the honor and love and courage—and vision—of Judah."

Merovee sat dull-eyed for another minute.

"How was the change accomplished?" she asked at last.

"Lucius bashed Judah's face up a bit first, for Jesus arrived from the house of Caiaphas in a battered condition. They had to match. Then, as Lucius was taking Jesus to the guardroom to be whipped, he diverted him into the storeroom. Judah was waiting and knocked Jesus unconscious. They took his clothes for Judah to wear, bound and gagged him, put a pillow under his head, a blanket over him, locked the door, and continued on to the guardroom just as though Judah were Jesus.

"I am afraid that the most brutal of floggings was then administered. Lucius rather egged the soldiers on in their 'King' game with the crown of thorns. When all was finished—the bashing coupled with the blood—even you would have been hard pressed to distinguish Judah's features, and know that it was not Jesus."

"So now," said Merovee, "Judah is out there being nailed to the cross."

"Soon. They will arrive at the Place of the Skull within the quarter hour."

"I must go to him, Pilatus. I must be there to give him what support I can. That would be natural, would it not? For the wife of Jesus to follow after him and stand by him?"

"It would be natural. I will give you a plain-clothes bodyguard to the garden, however. Throughout this whole day you must not stray out of the sight of that bodyguard, or of my soldiers, is that clear?

Caiaphas mentioned something this morning that has Jesus worried for your safety, and that of both families. Do you know aught of your descent from King Saul?"

Merovee frowned.

"Grandfather Nathan often said that we are descended from King Saul by the son of the grandson who was taken into the court of King David. Why?"

"Lucius only had time to warn me that Jesus fears that it puts you in mortal danger. I can only let you out if you promise to be prudent."

"I will be prudent. I do not suppose that I could see Jesus now."

"It would call attention if any of us were to go to that storeroom. Besides which, Lucius has the key. We must wait until he returns from the Place of the Skull."

"Please send one of your men to the house of Nicodemus, Pilatus. Have Nathaniel come to me in the garden."

"It shall be done. Merovee, for my sake, and that of Lucius—of even perhaps Procula—it must not become generally known that the man on the cross is not Jesus."

"I realize that. I do not know how we will handle it. I will confer with Nathaniel when he arrives at the garden. Some of our people will have to know, but only those who can be trusted. Your secret will be kept."

She threw her arms about Pilatus, then about Procula.

"Bless you, Friends. Do not fear for anything, neither of you. What you have done this day . . . "

She smiled.

"You have learned how to become great by being kind. Though empires rise and empires fall, through all the lives that you have yet to live, you will retain that ability . . . nothing, no one, will ever be able to take it from you. That is riches beyond all the gold in all worlds."

The streets were still relatively quiet as Merovee walked to the garden with her bodyguard, a cousin to Lucius, a young centurion named Philadelphus. This being a day that was only a little less restrictive than the Sabbath, during which work was forbidden, most would remain in their houses or in their camps during the early hours. By midday, many of the men would be heading for the Temple for worship and to hear the speakers, while others would throng the hundreds of synagogues in the city. But no shops would be open. There would be almost no through travel on the roads into or out of the city. Most people would move within narrow confines and to prescribed places.

A perfect day for a private crucifixion.

The men had been hung by the time she reached the garden. She was grateful not to have witnessed the nailing. One of the execution squad stood at the gate, ready to discourage gawkers from entering.

"Let her pass," said Philadelphus. "She is wife to one of these men."

Across Nehemiah's cabbages—many of them already trampled—she saw the three crosses. The soldiers of the squad lounged about, casting dice or snoozing in the late morning sun. Lucius and the Cyrenean sat apart, pretending not to know one another, and to be personally unconcerned as to the men on the crosses or as to who came and went.

She started through the cabbages, seeming to have neither feet nor legs as she approached that cross bearing the superscription, 'King of the Jews,' seeming to rise up out of her body and hover above herself, divorced from sensations, as in a dream.

The man on the cross saw her coming. A smile of such gladness lit his features that everything about him seemed suddenly to glow. She drew in her breath.

She had seen that glow before.

"Merovee. Oh no, my love. My wonderful lady. Do not shed tears for me. I am so happy. Be happy with me."

"My tears are of happiness—Jesus." She must be so careful not to say Judah.

He sighed, relaxing in the knowledge of her acceptance.

"Have you met my friends?" As though introducing guests at his party, he inclined his head to indicate the other two hung men.

"They are of your old band?"

"Yes. Amos and Noah. I have explained to them the joy that awaits them. I have told them not to fear. I am going to do this well, Merovee. As well as would Jesus. For him. As him. I really feel . . . marvelous. Filled with power. And light. It seems that everyone should be able to see the light that I feel within myself."

"I can see it."

She realized then what was happening. Awake by now, back on the floor of that storeroom, Jesus had figured things out.

"Remember his light in the cave? He is sending that light to you. You are not alone up there."

"I thought I saw him. As they set my cross upright. I thought I saw him standing up on that dome of rock, watching. I thought he smiled at me."

Merovee turned and looked up at the top of the "Skull." He might be there even now, out of body, watching.

She felt giddy suddenly, as though she could give a hop and sail right up into the sky as in dreams. She felt like laughing. And laughing and laughing.

If only these soldiers knew what was going on before their unseeing eyes. If only they could grasp what was possible.

And poor, foolish Caiaphas, who thought that he could really kill people.

She was filled with a sudden love for them all, with the compassion of a mother, who knows that, someday, her foolish children will learn, and who is content to wait for that day.

If she had never before fully understood, she did understand at that moment why Jesus always told her, "We can never really be separated, Merovee. Not when we know so many ways to be together."

It was all open-ended. Nothing was closed. Nothing was ever finished. No life, no person, no universe, no time, no place. It all flowed together, in an endless "becoming," in ever-changing patterns, with eternal vitality.

Suddenly she could feel The Energy radiating from that cross and from the man who hung upon it, from even the rocks and cabbages, and lolling soldiers—feel that Energy rushing out into the world in all directions, like the rays of the sun.

But not only into this world. Into all worlds, all times, places, peoples, hearts.

"Perhaps this is what the Messiah really is," she whispered aloud to herself. "The Messenger."

From the gate came a light, female voice, imperious, slightly hysterical, arguing with the guard.

"Oh! Salome has come!" said Judah, sounding as though yet another, particularly welcome, guest had just arrived at his party.

Merovee turned and skimmed back through poor Nehemiah's cabbages.

"It is all right, Soldier. The lady is the sister of Jesus."

She led the veiled figure to one side.

"I came as soon as I could learn where they had brought him!" moaned Salome. "Oh Merovee!" She darted a glance at the crosses, then threw her arms around her friend and burst into tears. "Is he in terrible pain?"

"No. The Cyrenean has given him a drug. He is happier than he has ever been."

"How did it happen? How came they to seize him? We thought that you were at Mount Ephraim. You were all safe. How could Pilatus do it? He and Jesus were such friends!"

Merovee let her cry and gabble, only patting her and making reassuring sounds until the storm had subsided. Then she told her.

"Salome, you have got to get yourself together and be very brave. Braver than you have ever been. Jesus is safe, Salome. Pilatus has him locked in the Antonia."

"But . . . "

Salome turned and looked long at the man on the cross.

"That is not Yeshuah, is it."

"No, Darling. You can see now who it is. You must not cry out. No one must know that it is not Jesus."

Salome remained transfixed, staring at Judah. Merovee took her hand.

"Come. Say hello to him. He was so happy when he heard your voice. Come and be glad with us. Mind the cabbages, do not trip."

She led the girl to the base of the cross.

Above the veil, Salome's eyes swam.

"Hello . . . "

"Jesus," prompted Merovee.

"Hello, Jesus."

"Hello, Salome."

Still the glow, the transcendent quality that none could ignore.

"I love you, Salome."

"I love you, too . . . Jesus."

"Will you stay with me now until I am dead?"

"I will stay with you until then. But my heart will stay with you forever."

Judah smiled . . . even summoned a touch of mischief.

"You had better tell her what she has just sworn to, Merovee."

Nathaniel arrived some minutes later. Salome stayed by Judah while Merovee walked apart with the dumbstruck man.

"We must keep knowledge of what has transpired here as much of a secret as possible, Nathaniel. The life of Pilatus could be forfeit if the rulers learn that a substitution was made."

"Ah, Merovee." There were tears in the big man's eyes as he gazed toward the cross. "How the men are already talking against Judah. How they revile him."

"They must continue to do so for the time being. Later they can be told. You must keep them all at the house, Nathaniel. Use their safety as an excuse. Say that Jesus commands them to stay hidden. It makes sense, however, that his father should come here."

"Rosula and the two girls and Joses came along with him from Bethlehem."

Merovee smiled.

"I could have guaranteed that Rosula would not be left behind. Let them come here to the garden as well. And Uncle Cleopah and Aunt Miriam and their boys. And Meraiah. Bring Meraiah. We should not keep this from her, for, in her own way, she will be proud."

"Susannah will want to come. She is a rock, and you might need one. And what of Deborah?"

"No, not Mother. There is some danger to my immediate family that I do not understand as yet. Tell her the truth of the matter, but tell her also that she should remain at the house. Bring Johannah, though. She is known at the Herodian Palace and can run messages.

"So only those people, Nathaniel. If you must, say that Jesus has asked for them only. There will be hurt feelings, but that cannot be helped. Tell bar Tolmei and Chandreah. And of course Nicodemus. They can be trusted both to keep their lips sealed and to keep the others in order while you are gone.

"Once you are away from the house, give the truth to those whom you are bringing, so that they will be ready to play their parts."

"May I speak with Judah before I go?"

"But of course."

Nathaniel went to the foot of the cross. Wordlessly, he put an arm about Salome's shoulders and stood looking up. At the moment, Judah's eyes were closed. From the expression upon his face, one might have imagined that he was viewing fields of spring flowers, bright in the sun. Nathaniel's eyes lifted to the superscription over the head of Judah. Without having been told, he understood the tribute from Pilatus.

"I love you, Nathaniel."

Nathaniel started. For the eyes were still closed.

"I love you too . . . Jesus."

"Are you going to bring my mother to me?"

"I go to fetch her now."

Judah sighed and lapsed back into reverie. Nathaniel left the garden with fresh tears in his eyes.

* * *

By the seventh hour after the sunrise, the sun had turned cruel, and the atmosphere was strangely and oppressively humid after the chill of the day before. Rivers of sweat ran with the blood from Judah's wounds. Increasingly, he seemed to be suffering. The Cyrenean had been ministering to all three of those hanged, waving flies away with a branch of hyssop, putting up the sponge for them to suck upon—a sponge circumspectly doctored, soaked with dulling drugs in the case of the other two men. So that, when Judah murmured, "I thirst," and the Cyrenean offered Judah the sponge with a second concealed cake, the soldiers did not so much as look up from their gaming.

Lucius had returned to the Antonia some hours earlier, to release Jesus from his bondage in the storeroom. Fondly, Merovee imagined that he had been taken up to the apartment of Pilatus and Procula, given food and drink, perhaps provided with a bath. He must be resting comfortably now. Maybe he was sleeping on the bed where she, herself, had slept his trial away.

Certainly, however, he would not be allowed to show his face in this place.

To the astonishment of all, another dared to show his face.

Meraiah saw him first. She had been sitting at the foot of the cross, her head leaned against it, shaded by Judah's own body. Her eyes, as she looked toward the gate, gained such sudden venom and fire that all sitting near her noticed and looked in that direction.

Yeshuah walked slowly toward them through the cabbages. Poor old Nehemiah sat to one side, watching with dull acceptance as yet another cabbage was bruised beyond recall. His lettuce was still untouched, and the onions and leeks and garlic, thank God.

Oblivious to anything but the man on the cross, Yeshuah came to its foot and stood looking up. With that uncanny sight that he seemed suddenly to have gained, and again without opening his eyes, Judah said his name.

Yeshuah started, and stared more closely at the man above him.

Judah's eyes slowly opened. His smile was such a dear thing to see. Salome turned her head away, lapsing into silent tears. Rosula blew her nose.

"Brother," said Judah gently.

"Oh my God," breathed Yeshuah.

"I am free of you now, Brother. I have done all that I swore to do. And more. Never again, in this world or any other, can you enslave my Spirit.

"Thank you for making me your Messenger, Yeshuah. Thank you for allowing me to become yourself. Here you hang, the perfect sacrifice to the Lord. Here you hang, for the redemption of what you think are the sins of your people.

"And, as such, those sins are certainly forgiven. For I am so filled with Love that the whole world must feel it. It is as though some unseen hand pours it in through the top of my head, and I fill and fill, till I think that I will burst, that, surely, I can contain no more. Yet still the hand keeps pouring. And still I fill. And I begin to see that, when one finally accepts *the* Love, the container expands infinitely.

"Ah, smile, Brother. Rejoice. For the Messiah has come. A sprig of the House of David. Here you hang. Rejoice. For the Kingdom of God has come. It is here within me, and I am you, and we are all, and they are us."

Yeshuah's voice came as from a great distance.

"I wish I could believe you, Brother. But this splendor does not belong to me. It is yours alone."

"If you believe that, then you never believed your own words, Brother. You never believed that your cross would accomplish Love and redemption for all. What I do here, I do for all whom I love. And right now I love all. What I feel, I am feeling for all.

"It is as nothing that I can describe, Yeshuah. Open your heart. The feeling is yours as well. Allow what is now in me to enter into you. You have no one to blame but yourself if you do not take it. You create your own prison, and only you can dissolve its bars."

Yeshuah shook his head.

"I will find no joy from this day forward. No love, no peace . . . no forgiveness."

"Have it your own way," said Judah softly. "You still have my everlasting love and thanks. This day you have set me free of the cramped prison of you—and turned me loose into the Universe of my Self."

"Yeshuah." Merovee came to his side, using low tones. "No one must know that it is not Jesus up there on the cross."

"He is safe?"

"Thanks to Judah, yes."

Yeshuah could not keep back the tears. He lowered his face into his hands, hardly able to speak.

"For that tender mercy I give thanks. To the true god. Though whether All That Is will ever listen to me, I do not know."

"All That Is never ceases to listen, Yeshuah. You are welcome to remain here with us, but I advise against it. Pilatus has sworn to have you for the true treason you intended. If Lucius should return and recognize you, you would be arrested."

"Why do we not alert the guards and have him seized anyway?" said Meraiah venomously.

"Ah, Mother, no," said Judah. "Behold your son. He whom I love. Yeshuah, behold your mother. I would that the two of you be reconciled."

"Never in this life," said Meraiah. She rose and moved away.

"Is it then all a sham?" mused Judah. "Is what I am feeling only within myself? Am I unable to impart any of it to anyone else? How very sad if it were so."

He sighed and closed his eyes. There, in the sunlit fields of himself, he found his smile again.

"No. I will not believe it," he murmured. "I can hear a thousand million hearts trying to open. A great groaning of rusted hinges. I will go and pour my oil upon them."

He lapsed into silence, breathing evenly and deeply. Yeshuah stood for only another minute. Then he turned and, wordlessly, left the place.

No one bothered to note the road he took.

At the ninth hour after the sunrise, Merovee went to the base of the cross.

"Jesus?" she said softly.

"Is it time to begin?"

"Yes. Should the Cyrenean give you another cake?"

"Yes. I am having difficulty keeping my mind on any one thing. I keep floating away."

Merovee turned away, giving the Cyrenean a slight sign. After a minute, Judah called out . . .

"I thirst!"

Simon rose and offered up the sponge. Judah sucked out the cake, nodded, and lapsed back into silence.

Of those attending at the base of the cross, only Merovee, Susannah, Johannah, and Nathaniel had ever completely accomplished the sleep. Yet they all knew what Judah was trying to do. Every eye was on his features. Every breath, every movement, was noted.

Joseph motioned Merovee aside.

"How long will it be?" he said.

"If he is successful, he will arrive at the last gate in about half of an hour. If he can get through it, we can call him dead, and you may leave for the Antonia."

"That will get me back here well before the eleventh hour. Which will be perfect. By the time that the soldiers get him down, and we get him into the tomb, it will be time for them to break the legs of the other two men and get them down and buried. The soldiers will be much diverted, and lose track of our goings and comings."

Salome came to Merovee and laid her head against Merovee's breast.

"What if he is unable to do the sleep?" she said.

"If he cannot, he will call for the vinegar again. He knows that the Cyrenean has a sleeping drug ready to give to him just in case. We would then have to hope that the soldiers would be fooled and consider him dead."

"But if it did not fool the soldiers . . . "

"He will do the sleep, Salome. I feel sure."

"As soon as we know that he has done it, in the excitement as the Cyrenean tells the soldiers that he is dead, I am going to go behind the rock."

"Yes?" said Merovee in mystification. The grove of fruit trees on the other side of the dome had been a convenient place of relief for the entire party during the day.

"I will go quietly and I will not return. I am going into the tomb."

"Salome . . . "

"Do not argue with me. I must be with him. Did I not swear to stay with him until his death? I can help the Cyrenean, I can give Judah comfort. I love him, Merovee. Do you not see that we love one another?"

"We have all seen it since before either of you knew it, Kitten. How will your failure to return to the palace be explained?"

"Johannah will carry word to my mother." Johannah had already been to the palace twice with reports for Herodias. "Scota is there should Antipas call for me."

Merovee shook her head. Yet she could not refuse the girl. It was true that she had sworn to stay with Judah. Had it been Jesus up on that cross, she, too, would have insisted upon hiding away in the tomb.

The vigil continued. Judah was so still. One could not tell how well he was doing.

Except that less and less fresh blood appeared in any of his wounds. And the rivulets of perspiration were lessening. He was successfully slowing the pulses.

But oh, the heat and humidity seemed worse by the moment.

Strange. By this hour, the heat should have lessened.

Fanning herself with a hand, Merovee looked up at the sky.

It had been cloudless and bright an hour before. Now a haze had formed around the sun—a haze that both darkened and intensified its rays. A strange, green-yellow light was descending onto the garden.

Peals of thunder were heard, far away. Merovee looked toward the distant hills. The thunder continued. Strange that there was no lightning. Only the thunder.

The livid quality of the air in the garden intensified. Merovee exchanged glances with the others. All were beginning to notice. Even the soldiers stopped their gaming. They began to mutter, some to pace, looking up at the sky, and becoming aware of the distant thunder that contained no lightning.

"They say that your husband called himself the son of your god." Philadelphus edged close to Merovee, casting nervous glances at the sky. "Do you suppose that he really is? Perhaps your god is getting angry that we dare to kill his son."

"Have no fear, Philadelphus. My husband said only that we are *all* the sons and daughters of the true god, by virtue of the fact that each of us is a part of that god. Each of us is a little universe, Philadelphus. Each of us is a representative of the true god."

Her eyes went yet again to the silent figure on the cross.

"Each that god's Messenger. Each a Messiah."

"Then what of this sky? And thunder where there is no lightening?"

"It is happening because . . . this is all only a dream. A dream in which the entire world is sharing. In its dreaming, all the world knows what is happening here today."

"How could all the world know?"

"By the deep channels of mind upon which our usual thought rides, Philadelphus. The under-thoughts of all of Creation are with us now, focused upon this place. Not just the under-thoughts of our time, but of all time. It is all those thoughts which you are seeing in the sky, those emotions that shake us as thunder."

"How can you be so calm? Your husband is dying. Soon we will break his legs and shovel him under! Yet you stand there serene, and prate of the under-thoughts of the world.

"And you smile at me! How can you smile? He is crazy, too, up on that cross. Speaking of love, and of forgiveness. I have heard him. He seems to shine, and he floats as on a raft upon a cool lake, taking his ease, not even feeling the spikes. I do not understand you people!"

"But you would like to, would you not?"

The young centurion hesitated.

"Yes," he finally said.

She patted his hand.

"Then you shall. Someday."

Judah should be nearing the last gate. She left Philadelphus and went to the foot of the cross. Unobtrusively, the others also drew near.

He was absolutely still. The blood of his wounds had totally caked. His perspiration had dried.

Then it seemed that the peals of thunder began to march toward them, treading upon the land, itself.

And Judah's lips moved. One could never have heard. One who knew and was waiting could but read the lip movements.

"It is finished," he said.

His body went completely slack.

Behind them, a soldier cried out.

"Look!"

The man was pointing to the sky above the cross. They all looked up. For a moment it seemed that the air there shone with a brighter, even more sulfurous, light than any which suffused the garden.

Then whatever it was gone.

The Cyrenean called for a ladder. It was brought and propped against one of the arms of the cross. He climbed it, carefully tested a number of pulses on the body of the hanging man, lifted the eyelids, and touched the eyeballs. Then he climbed down.

"You will not have to break the legs of this one," he told Longinus, the leader of the squad. "He has died."

"So fast?" said Longinus in surprise.

"With all the blood he lost just on account of his whipping? I told Tribune Lucius that I doubted he would even get here alive to be hanged. A body can take just so much. Then the heart gives out. He was quite delirious during the last hours. I am sure that you noticed."

"I suppose so," said Longinus.

The family group had drawn together, embracing and weeping. It was necessary for the sham, yet how easily the tears flowed. Joseph came to Longinus, his face own streaked with tears.

"Soldier . . . do you have to do anything with him just yet?"

"It will be another hour or so before we must bury him."

"Then I ask of you. I am a patrician of this land and a friend of Pilatus. Let me go to him and beg a proper burial for my son."

"We are supposed to shovel him under."

"Nevertheless, there is an unused tomb in this garden belonging to a friend of mine. Let me go to Pilatus and seek his permission for us to lay my son's body there. Please, Soldier."

A clap of thunder rumbled straight through the garden, shaking the very ground upon which they stood.

"Yes, go!" cried Longinus, looking up fearfully at the slack, white body upon the cross. "Hurry, for the sake of Jove!"

Joseph did as he was told, moving off as quickly as his legs would carry him.

"They say," said the Cyrenean mischievously to Longinus, "that, on the Day of Judgment, when the Jewish god comes down to Jerusalem, the very sepulchers will rupture and spew forth their dead, and that all those corpses will rise up and walk to the Temple."

He appeared to scan the surrounding hills with their many tombs and slabs.

"I wonder if that is what is about to happen."

Then he laughed, and slapped Longinus on the back.

"Hey, Fellow, I but jest. It is merely a superstition of these Jews. We Roman citizens know better, do we not."

He went off then to offer vinegar—and more drugs—to the other two hanged men. When he had finished, he took his bag and bade them all farewell.

"In my wish to be of aid to these suffering fellows, I have already tarried too long. Goodbye, my poor people. May life be better to you than it has been this day."

And he left. In minutes, he would be climbing up a ladder hidden at the back wall, letting himself down into the orchard, and crawling into the tomb.

Where he would not be alone. Salome had slipped away as the Cyrenean had checked Judah's "corpse."

Within the hour, Lucius came hurrying into the garden, followed by Joseph, Nicodemus, and Timothy, laden with spices and herbals, linen, and water jugs.

"Longinus. Philadelphus," said Lucius "Reb Joseph tells the praefectus that his son has already died! The praefectus could not believe it."

Lucius went to the base of the cross and peered up at Judah.

"I guess we whipped him too harshly."

"That physician—that Cyrenean," said Longinus. "He got up on a ladder and felt him all over. He said he is dead."

"Well, if any physician would know, it is a Cyrenean. Take him down and give him to these people. The praefectus has given permission for the body to be put into the tomb here in this garden."

"But that is illegal," said Longinus.

Lucius pulled him aside and spoke in confidential tones.

"The man is dead, and, as it turns out, his father is a big man here in Jerusalem and a personal friend to the praefectus. The Praefectus is severely embarrassed by this whole thing. And what does it matter to us where the body is put? Do *you* want to go back and tell Pilatus his business?"

"No sir," said Longinus.

And then, so unexpectedly that no one even had time to cry out, much less to act, Longinus turned, reached up with his spear, and thrust it deep into Judah's right side.

"That will just make sure. It would be horrible if he were wrapped up and put in that tomb alive. I have nightmares about being locked in my own tomb alive. All right, men, step lively. Let us get this body down."

Merovee and the others could only watch dumbly, as blood and water poured from the wound in Judah's side.

"In deference to Reb Joseph," said Lucius weakly, "take the spike out carefully, Longinus. Do not rip the corpse any more than it is already ripped."

"Shall we carry him for you, Reb Joseph?" said Longinus when the spikes were out.

A moment of hesitation. Judah's loved ones might handle him more carefully. Yet there would be less suspicion if the soldiers saw the body laid in the tomb.

"Yes, carry him," said Joseph. "But please. Have respect. You have had your justice of my son. You can afford to bear him gently."

Perhaps it was the still sulfurous sky, the occasional rumbles of thunder, or the threat that the body might later get up out of its tomb, walk to the Temple, and perhaps pay them a call of retribution if they were not careful . . . but the soldiers carried the body to the tomb as tenderly as though it were a Grecian marble of incalculable worth.

"Oh!" said Longinus as they approached, "you had best make sure there are no little animals in there to gnaw at him. See? The stone was not properly rolled into its place, anything could have gotten in." And, when the stone had been rolled back, "Should we take a look around in there for you?"

"I am sure that they can see to matters themselves," said Lucius crisply. "Put him down and let us return to our work."

Yet Longinus could not stop worrying. He glanced around as his soldiers lowered the body onto the central platform.

"With this gloom you can hardly see to work in here. Maybe we should get you a lamp from somewhere."

"It will not take us long," said Joseph. "Please!" He lowered his face into his hands with a show of grief. "Leave us now."

"Oh, of course." Longinus backed hastily away.

Yet Merovee reached out and stopped him momentarily.

"Thank you for your many courtesies today, Longinus. And for your kind thoughts in regard to this body and to our welfare."

"It was my pleasure, Lady. I am sorry about him. He looked a decent sort."

Trying not to seem to be actually herding them, Lucius got the soldiers away from the tomb and to the other side of dome. As the last of the Romans disappeared, those in the tomb swung into action.

"Joses," said Merovee, "Keep watch to the left of the rock. Ben, take the right. Simon! Quickly! Longinus pierced him. Oh God, he meant so well. But I am afraid he has really killed him."

Simon appeared from out of the back chamber.

"Joseph, bring two mats from the back, we must get him up off this stone. And get the quilts out here. And the water. Elevate his feet, someone, and someone get those lamps lit. I need my bag. Damn. This is bad. The pleural cavity has been pierced. Maybe even the heart, I cannot tell."

Simon worked feverishly, the lamplight mixing strangely with the greenish glow of the waning day. Salome knelt at Judah's head, cradling him, whispering in his ear. Meraiah sank wearily down onto another shelf.

At last Simon rose.

"It is no use. I am sorry. Sorry."

Salome held his head closer. Meraiah did not move.

"Simon," said Merovee. "Can you be positive? The sleep is as death anyway."

"Merovee, I have not been able to find a pulse of any kind in all the time I have been working."

"Yet it might be too faint for you to sense."

"It could be. But if it is that faint, Merovee, he will not be able to get back. With this wound there will be no viable body for him to get back *to*."

Lucius appeared in the doorway.

"They are taking the other men down. How goes it?"

He saw their faces.

"*Damn* Longinus!"

"He meant well," said Merovee.

"Jesus," moaned Salome. "Bring Jesus!"

She lifted her face, a mass of flaming, wet freckles in the lamplight.

"Lucius! Merovee! Bring Jesus!"

"I was just going to tell you . . . " said Lucius.

But there was a sudden, collective sigh of dismay. Those in the tomb shrank back.

For there appeared in the door beside Lucius a centurion. He wore insignia of the highest rank. His uniform was immaculate. The silver of his helmet and upon his breastplate was so highly polished as to glow almost gold in the strange light. How had he come past Joses and Ben without an alarm being raised?

"Do none of you remember what I look like without long hair and whiskers?"

For one moment, Merovee stared at the clean-shaven face. Then she flung herself into his arms, bruising her breasts gladly on his breastplate. Salome was right behind her.

"Save him, Jesus. Heal him. A soldier ran him through with a spear."

Jesus first embraced Rosula and his father and sisters.

"They said you had been battered," said Rosula, stroking his face. "I see not a mark."

Jesus only smiled and hugged her again. Then he knelt beside Judah. Before anything else, he bent and kissed the cold lips.

"Any broken bones, Simon?"

"None in the wrists. The metatarsals seem fine, though they are probably chipped."

"'Not a bone of his body shall be broken,'" Jesus quoted. "Only possibly chipped. The prophecy also forgot to mention spear thrusts, eh?"

"Does Pilatus know that you are here?" asked Merovee foolishly.

"Who do you think had me shaved and gave me instant citizenship?" said Jesus. He smiled up at Lucius. "Our friend Lucius dug odds and ends of 'centurional' paraphernalia from out of a storeroom and pieced it all together into something resembling a uniform. I understand that some of my insignia accords high rank. Primus Pilus at the least. I am probably a special envoy from Tiberius, himself. Lucius and Pilatus got things all polished up as Procula relieved me of my long hair and whiskers. And here I am, sent to oversee this interment on behalf of Pilatus."

His hands had been running from one end of Judah's body to the other as he spoke.

"Is he still alive?" said Simon.

"The body consciousness is still functioning."

His fingers now concentrated on the forehead between the eyes of Judah.

"His Spirit is still connected to the body. He might come back and he might not. It will be up to him."

He rose.

"If the rest of you are to be back at the home of Nicodemus before the sunset, you should leave immediately."

Merovee grabbed his arm.

"You must let me stay with you, Josh."

"If I want an arm left, I guess I had better. Change veils with Susannah so that the soldiers will think they see 'the widow' leaving."

"I am staying, too," said Salome.

"I would not dare to say no. The rest of you, roll the stone back. Leave it just short of the mark for air. Then be off with Nicodemus. Except you, Johannah."

"Yes, Jesus. I will go to Herodias to tell her what is happening and spend the Sabbath with her."

"Thank you." Jesus bent and kissed Meraiah. "I will do my best for our beloved Judah, Queen Meraiah. You, Rosula, Aunt Miriam, Susannah—Johannah, you can meet them here as well—return at sunrise on Sunday morning after the Sabbath, as you would normally come to mourn. We will call out to you then what should be done."

"Get your stories straight before you get to the house," said Merovee. "Do not lie. Simon and I have stayed with the body just in case there should still be life. Do not even say that it is Jesus. Say just 'the body.' The situation does not look good. He seems dead. If they inquire as to where Judah has gone to, you do not know. Which is the truth. Heaven only knows where his Soul is at this moment."

"What a strange feeling," said Salome as, moments later, the huge stone disc was being rolled back over the opening. "I wonder where I shall be entombed."

"You are already strewn into the Ganges, Kitten, your ashes long ago washed to sea to feed the fish which feed the men." As he spoke, he fumbled with the fastenings of his centurion's attire. "Before that, you died in battle. You lay in a field near Babylon, and the vultures ate you. This time? You shall leave your body in a distant land. Again, there will be no tomb. You do not like to enclose your corporeal creations in stone. Always, you give your body to the chain of life, to look out through the eyes of other creatures, and so experience life more fully."

"And I?" said Merovee.

"For you, my love, various stone tombs or rumors of same. In widely distant places. And none shall contain you. Simon, I am confounded by my attire. No wonder that Roman officers need body servants."

Together, the two of them managed to get the helmet off, and work out the buckles, straps, belts, and clasps, till, finally, Jesus was released down to the under tunic.

"Now let us get Judah into his burial linen," he said.

"No!" cried Salome. "Why the burial linen? You said he still lives."

"Of course he still lives, is there such a thing as a dead fig tree? You must learn not to quake at the trappings of death, Salome, they are only symbols of change. Judah set himself to carry out Yeshuah's design. If he returns, he will be truly reborn, a new and golden child. His 'resurrection' should have some of the attendant symbols."

He glanced at a length of linen that had been provided.

"That will do nicely. Simon, you will help me lift him. When we do, Girls, stretch that linen out flat beneath him. I will want it to go up over his head, then lay down flat over the top of him. Ready Simon?"

"Shouldn't we treat his wounds first?" said Simon.

"And wash him?" said Merovee.

"Time enough for that later," said Jesus.

So they got the length of linen stretched beneath him, ready to come down over the front of him, and turned their attention to arranging the body.

"His leg muscles are so spasmed. I cannot get his knees to unflex," said Simon.

"His poor nose," said Salome. "They must have hit it, see how it has swelled? Can I at least comb his hair?"

"No time, Kitten. Tie a band of linen around his head and under his chin, though. Fold a quilt and slip it under his head and shoulders as a pillow. Being lifted up will be more comfortable for him with his knees flexed. Simon, let us get this loin-cloth off of him, it is too binding, I want the body to be as comfortable and unconstrained as possible . . . Cross his hands on his pelvis . . . What flowers and herbals have we? Do we have balsam? Excellent. Let us surround him with balsam, it encourages respiration and discourages infections. It will even aid our own breathing in this close air.

"Now lay the linen down over him."

"Are you going to heal him now?" said Salome when all was finished, and they stood looking down onto the linen-covered body.

"Apply the principles," said Jesus. "A healing only works if there is a mind for the healer to contact. Judah is far away. Not in distance, but in intensity. What is here in the body is the simple body consciousness, that takes its orders from the mind. That body consciousness is set at a level of minimum maintenance and will remain in that state until it receives an order from the mind. Time enough, if the mind deigns to return to the carcass, to do my healing. So we will let the carcass rest. You might want to warm it with a quilt or two."

He went to the back chamber, got a quilt for himself and laid down on one of the shelves.

"You are going after him?" said Merovee.

"Sorry to leave you yet again, my love, but yes. Give me a kiss."

"Careful," she laughed. "I am aching for the ministrations of Agapo."

He took her gently into his arms, and they lingered for many moments.

"You do not want me to come with you?" she asked.

"I will have all I can do to find him without keeping track of you as well. Besides, someone who understands the sleep should be awake here just in case."

So, there in the tomb, they took a true Sabbath. And more. Pharisees would have applauded such scrupulous observance. They took turns sleeping, Simon, Merovee, and Salome, at least one of them always awake to keep watch upon both men.

There was no way to tell the time. While air came in at the edge of the great stone, no light could be detected.

It seemed that the whole of the Sabbath and most of the night thereafter must have passed when Simon finally lifted Judah's shroud, thinking to, in his own poor way, check upon his condition.

As he touched the flesh, he pulled back, catching his breath.

"What is it?"

Salome leapt up from where she had been sitting and ran to lay a hand on Judah. She, too, pulled back. But slowly. In resignation.

"Dead. He is dead, Merovee."

Merovee came to his side and, herself, touched the body. Cold and stiff.

"Yes."

"I wonder if Jesus found him before he let go," said Salome softly. "It would be nice to think that Jesus had been there—to help—to say goodbye for all of us. I hope he knows, Merovee. I hope Judah knows how much we loved him. How much . . . ."

She turned away, went back to sit upon her shelf. There were no tears in her eyes.

"Strange. Death is not what it used to be. The old 'reality' is gone out of it. And the finality. He was so radiant, Merovee. So very happy. How can I be anything but joyful for him? I would like to be a mouse where he is now. I would like to see and experience it all with him. But I must wait. My own time will come. Until then, I must live as beautifully as he died."

She was silent for another moment. Then . . .

"Antipas has decided upon another husband for me. A cousin, of course, a nephew to my mother. I met him once. The one with pimples. He probably still has them."

"When does the marriage take place?"

"In the month of Augustus. But it will not be I who marries him, Merovee. Scota will go to the wedding cup as Salome. From that day forth, she will be Salome. Of what she does with her life from that day onward, history will say, 'Salome, granddaughter of Herod the Great, did thus and so. These were her children. These kings and princes are descended from her.'

"Scota was sad at first. To leave me. And mother. To know that she will probably never see us again. But she is getting used to the idea. From slave to princess. An exciting journey."

"Your mother agrees with this?"

"With all her heart."

"The enterprise entails a basic lie at the onset, Salome. Have you thought of that?"

"Yes. And I pondered it for days. I considered . . . would the lie do harm to the cousin whom I am to marry?

"The answer is, no. In Scota, he gets a wife eager to belong to him, eager to fulfill her role as princess and wife.

"Will his children be robbed? His blood is fully as Hasmonaean as my own. While, though Scota is now a slave, her father was a king among the Gaels. I will, thus, return to Scota the royalty that was hers by birth, while her children will inherit blood as royal as though I had been their mother. And there will be added benefit to them—a mother who *wants* princelings to child.

"If that had not been enough, Judah showed me yesterday that, as Messengers of one another, Scota and I will become each other. I think that everyone involved—indeed, the entire world—will only benefit from this lie.

"And is it a lie? What *is* identity, Merovee? Scota has been Salome for so long that she is now more Salome than am I. While I . . . I am . . . I."

Merovee studied Salome in the lamplight. How she had changed from the girl who had come to her stall that first day in Machaerus. In such a short time, she had become a woman. A wise and noble woman.

"And what do you plan to do, Salome?"

"I—had thought that I would marry Judah. That we two would follow after you and Jesus—and go out to teach for ourselves when we were ready. Now . . . I will still follow after you and Jesus."

"Your blood and heritage and position mean nothing to you?"

"Oh, you are mistaken. Those things mean a great deal to me. So much that I swell with pride to know that one of my blood and heritage and position should have been among the followers of both Johannan and of Jesus.

"I can do nothing prouder for my blood than renounce its earthly royalty at this time, Merovee. I have been an earthly princess. I have done that. Now I must use my blood and heritage to seek another kind of royalty, based upon my accomplishments in a kingdom to be found within myself.

"The world might never know of that new royalty. But I will."

Merovee smiled.

"Kitten, I think your greatest talent has always been doing exactly as you wish, while making that wish seem just right to everyone around you. Do not lose the touch. It will be of use to us all."

Her smile faded.

"We are going to have to leave Palestine, Salome."

"Yes. But then . . . " A twinkle lit Salome's eyes. "We have done Palestine, have we not. It is time to move on."

Merovee shook her head, the smile returning.

"I am so glad that you are coming with us."

"And will you not need a physician?" said Simon. "Even with Jesus around, a physician might have some few uses."

"We shall certainly need a physician, Simon. I wonder . . . would you consider to be that physician?"

"I shall consider the matter."

They all laughed.

"Let us celebrate," said Salome.

"I will get the wine," said Simon.

They passed the jug around, each taking a deep swallow, toasting Judah, and Jesus, the future, and their fellowship

Merovee would tease Jesus afterward that it had been the scent of wine that had awakened him. Yet there were equally pressing reasons to return.

He came out slowly. It was many minutes from the first twitch of a finger to full wakefulness.

"Judah's body is dead," Merovee told him when she saw that his attention was fully returned.

He nodded, yawned, stretched, and got himself slowly up onto an elbow.

"Give me some of that wine."

He drank slowly, small sips at a time.

"Do you want bread?" said Merovee. "Cheese?"

He shook his head no.

"Did you find him, Jesus?" said Salome.

"Yes." He addressed himself to Merovee. "He had created a garden of flowers and calm blue water for himself just outside of that Lloyd Wright structure that we visit so often over in the Sixth Dimension. My own teacher was searching for him as well. You remember Felliemme?"

"The one who so often appears as a rectangular cube?"

"Yes. We met up and found Judah's garden. He had been waiting . . . pleased with his garden, but very confused by that spear wound. He was not sure he could get back to the body, or that he was meant to. He was just waiting, knowing that someone would come along to advise him sooner or later."

Jesus smiled.

"How he shouted when he saw us. How he hugged us." He glanced at Salome. "How he asked after the Kitten he had left behind."

"Yet you advised him not to return," said Simon.

"No. He is coming back."

Salome gave a cry of delight.

"But . . . " Simon shook his head. "Jesus, the body is gone. It is in rigor mortis. There is no way."

"Simon, begin right now to put away your former beliefs as to what is death and what is life and what is possible and what is impossible."

He rose, easing his joints after their hours on the stone, and went to Judah's body. He removed the quilts, but not the linen shroud, and passed his hands over the body at a height of a few inches.

"Yes, you see? Here, pass your hands over him, Simon? Do you feel or sense anything?"

"I can not say that I do."

"Well, you will learn. The body consciousness is still alert, waiting. It can be reactivated."

"How long could it remain in that state of waiting?"

"Weeks. Months. Years even. In India, often, when a great teacher 'dies,' the body remains pure and sweet indefinitely, laid out for all that teacher's followers to see.

"Among our own people, were we not so hysterical about disposing of 'carrion,' we would see the same phenomenon. Strong Spirits have strongly allied components. The sympathy and love between Spirits and the atoms which are their vehicles is quite wonderful. Most often, they have been allied with each other time and time again.

"In such cases, then, at the 'departure' of the Spirit, the atoms of the body will wait indefinitely for a possible return. The atoms have a vested interest in the progress of the entity. . . while the Spirit feels the same kinship with the body atoms. So that it refuses to entirely sever the cord that unites them. Hence, the body atoms wait, ready to serve again if needed. Only when the Spirit definitely abandons that prior life, and so the body—cuts the cord to take another incarnation, or move on to other systems of reality—do those atoms cease their vigil and seek to join other forms."

"But does this mean," said Simon, "that the Pharisees are right? That, on a Day of Judgment, all the dead in these sepulchers around Jerusalem can be magically reactivated and returned to life?"

"Not at all. 'Resurrection' is impossible in those terms. Only 'restoration' is possible, and that is limited to sympathetic bodies such as I have just described, which are still 'physically' attached to exceptionally strong Spirits who have not 'decided' as yet.

"And this attachment—the Power even to maintain such an attachment, is rare. The Spirits of those who lie in the graves around Jerusalem have long ago severed the cords and moved on to other endeavors, while the atoms which housed those Spirits have long ago joined with other forms. They will not be magically reassembled, Spirit and atoms ripped out of their new forms to recreate old forms. There will be no great march to the Temple, Simon.

"For one thing, the 'dead' would have learned better than to approach that corrupt place."

He leaned closer to Judah, and put his hands onto the linen shroud over Judah's head.

"We will bring him back now. Felliemme is waiting with him in the garden, to help on that end."

"How far away is this garden—this Sixth Dimension?" whispered Salome.

"A breath away in 'distance' as you understand it. Yet so very far in true distance, which is emotional intensity.

"All of you now. Shield your eyes with your hands. Close the lids tight and do not peek."

They did as they were told . . . stood with their hands over their closed eyes.

Yet the flash that filled the tomb moments later was so intense, so blindingly white, that, through their closed eyelids, and the flesh of their hands, they could see the silhouettes of their own finger bones. At the same time, there was a great rumbling.

Then the blinding light was gone. And the sound.

"You may take your hands away now," said Jesus.

Slowly, each of them obeyed, still blinking against the flashing lights behind their eyelids, trying to restore normal vision.

The rumbling had issued from the great stone blocking the door.

That stone had rolled back.

From beneath the linen came a faint moan. Jesus lifted the shroud.

"Merovee, get all the quilts, he needs to be thoroughly warmed now. Simon, get that chin strap off and try to get him to sip some wine."

"He is bleeding!" cried Salome in horror. "His wounds have reopened!"

"Rejoice, my little ninny," said Jesus, ruffling her hair. "His blood is pumping again."

"What of the spear wound?" said Simon.

"We will see to that now. Judah. Judah, open your eyes."

Slowly the eyes opened.

"Can you hear me?"

An almost imperceptible nod.

"Do you know who I am? Say my name."

The lips moved.

"Jesus."

"I am going to heal the spear thrust. You understand?"

Another slight nod.

Jesus simply placed his hands upon the wound and stood for a minute, eyes closed.

"Now we will do the other wounds. Cover him, Merovee, I will work under the quilts."

Slowly and quietly, taking close to an hour, rolling Judah to and fro, sponging away blood and grime as he went, Jesus explored the body.

When he was finished, Judah was whole again.

"I would not have believed it if I had not seen it," said a voice in the darkness outside the doorway.

Jesus whipped around.

"It was worth getting my cabbages ruined."

Jesus relaxed, grinning.

"You are abroad early, Nehemiah."

"Who can sleep with lights and thunder dancing around the place?"

He entered the tomb, came to Judah's side and stared down at him.

"Young man, you are *dead*."

Judah smiled a wan smile.

"So are you. As dead as you will ever be."

"Humph!" said Nehemiah. He then glared at Salome. "Why are you giving him all that wine? I am the one who needs it," and he took the jug.

"Actually I am glad that you have come," said Jesus. "You saved me the trouble of waking you. I need the use of your sleeping shack up in the orchard. How soon to sunrise do you think?"

"If you was to get up on the Skull, you could see the first hint now."

"Come on, then. Simon, Nehemiah, help me carry him up to the shack. Girls, bring the mattresses and quilts, we will make him a nice bed."

They ensconced Judah in the small, low-ceilinged building, soft and warm in his nest. In that place they also hid the provisions that had been in the tomb.

"He will sleep now," said Jesus when all was packed away. "For perhaps a day. He needs many hours of comfortable, normal sleep."

"Let me stay beside him," said Salome. "He might need food—wine—water."

"It would not be proper for you to stay," said Jesus with a twinkle. "You are not man and wife."

"But we will be!" cried Salome. She shook Judah. "Wake up! You will marry me when you are better, will you not?"

His lips lifted in a drowsy smile.

"If I do not, I will never hear the end of it."

"In that case," said Jesus, "give Judah a sip of that wine, Salome. Now you take some yourself. Good. You are now husband and wife. Go back to sleep, Judah."

"He already has," laughed Merovee.

It was well and truly dawn when they left Salome cuddled down into the quilts beside her new husband, and returned to the tomb. While Simon and Nehemiah puzzled out how to buckle him back into his centurion's apparel, Jesus thought aloud.

"The women will be here soon," he said. "It is possible that some of the other followers will be with them, so I must get myself out of here. You wait for them, Merovee, and return them to the house of Nicodemus. Tell the men whatever you wish. We are obliged to keep the truth of the substitution a secret only until the Passover crowds have dispersed, and until we are sure that Pilatus is not endangered. I leave it to your good judgment, Merovee, what you tell our people. Now that we are into this thing—the damage is done. Our only course is to turn it to the best advantage that we can. Simon, get back to your inn. Get some sleep yourself. Could you have other people in your room do you think?"

"I am sure that the innkeeper would accommodate me."

"Then have pallets gotten for Judah and Salome." He gave Simon a gold piece.

"That is not necessary, Jesus."

"No, please, there is more. Buy some clothing for Judah today . . . and different apparel for Salome. And whatever items you think of that they might need for their immediate comforts. Toward evening, return and check on the two of them. I think he will sleep straight through to tomorrow morning, but perhaps not. When he can walk without stumbling and drawing attention, get them to your inn. If he proves too weak to walk all the distance, an enclosed public chair can be used as long as those carrying the chair neither pick him up at this very place nor deliver him right to your door. Nehemiah, if anything goes wrong with Judah in the meantime, get over to Simon at the inn of . . . "

"Reuben."

"Yes. You know it, Nehemiah? In the Upper City?"

"I can find it."

"I do not expect any complications, but just in case."

"In the meantime," said Nehemiah, 'where am I going to sleep this coming night?"

"Have you any foolish notions that Judah is unclean on account of being dead?"

"I dig in dirt each day."

"Then we left you your bed. Those two will not know when you crawl in to join them."

"They are newly wedded!"

"Which they will not be able to do anything about for quite some time. As I was about to say, if asked, you know nothing about anything, Nehemiah."

"That is no lie. I think I will never know anything about anything ever again."

"Answer no question, shoo people out of your garden, mourn your cabbages, be your usual sweet and friendly self.

"As for my own self, I must return to Pilatus, who released me only on great sufferance. He wants me kept safely out of sight until the greater part of the pilgrims have departed Jerusalem. It is prudent that all of us should follow that example. I will contact you all in a day or so.

"In the meantime though, Merovee . . . yes, send Micah to me. I can spend this time in dictation. Now I must be off. Goodbye again, my wife." He gave Merovee a peck and started for the gate.

"Have Procula send word to Herodias about Salome right away," she called after him.

"I will remember. Oh . . . gather up that linen shroud and take it with you. I will show you something curious about it later."

Still calling of this or that to one another, they parted yet again, off in separate directions. Would it always be so? And could separate directions eventually lead them to the same place?

Nehemiah set to work salvaging his cabbages. Waiting for the women to arrive, Merovee went back into the tomb to see that no telltale items were left behind. Only the burial linens. She folded the chin band, and then the shroud.

She was standing there holding the shroud, wondering how it had gotten scorched and darkened in so many places, when she heard people arguing with Nehemiah.

The voices were male!

She tossed the linen down onto a shelf and ran out, hiding at the far side of the rock till she was sure that it was only her own people . . . Susannah and Rosula, Meraiah, Johannah and Aunt Miriam.

Except that, with them, were Petros and the Boanerges.

They were gathered in consternation before the open and empty tomb as Merovee emerged from hiding. Petros had gone in and was just emerging, carrying the folded linens. He spotted Merovee.

"What has happened? Where have they taken his body?"

Merovee stood dumbly. What to say? She had not had time to think.

"Speak, Woman!" said Petros.

Merovee tilted her head, staring at the man, considering his tone of voice and the expression upon his face.

'So, Petros,' she thought. 'You think my husband is dead. And suddenly I am "Woman," to be shouted at and bullied by your superior male self.'

"Have you gone silly, Woman? Answer me this instant."

A slow, sly smile lifted Merovee's lips. She raised her chin. He would get no speech from her. Not till she had decided what to say and until he could ask with a civil tongue in his head.

Rosula read her thoughts. With the authority of her relationship to Jesus and of her age, she all but knocked the big man over backward with a sharp shove to his chest.

"How dare you speak to my daughter in that tone. I will thank you to remember who she is. The most beloved disciple of Jesus. We told you men that you should stay at home.

"Come, Ladies, let us take my daughter aside and soothe her. Perhaps she will speak to us. She is evidently in great shock and distress."

So saying, the women walked apart with Merovee, up into the orchard.

"Judah lives," she whispered, bestowing a caress upon Meraiah's cheek. "He is sleeping in Nehemiah's shack over there. Salome is with him. The Cyrenean will see to their needs. Judah did actually die—early this morning. But Jesus brought him back and also healed his wounds.

"Oh! You have a daughter, Queen Meraiah. Jesus married them, so that Salome could stay with Judah in propriety."

"Congratulations!" cried Rosula, hugging the old lady. "May you live to bounce their children upon your knee."

"A princess to daughter," beamed the old woman. "I am truly made a queen."

"How did the stone get rolled away?" asked Johannah more practically.

"There was a blinding flash of light when Jesus brought Judah back to life. The stone rolled back of its own accord. I do not know how else to say it."

For a moment, the women stood in silent wonder.

"I wish I had been there," said Susannah.

"My son was truly dead?" said Meraiah.

"Cold and stiff, Meraiah."

There was another moment of silent awe.

"Where is Jesus?" said Rosula.

"Returned to Pilatus. He wants all of us to stay out of sight for another day or so, until the worst of the Passover crowds have departed. He will send to us then.

"In the meantime, let us return to the house very slowly. I need time to think. I must find my tongue soon, and the words which I speak must be good.

"Only, please, keep Petros away from me, so that I do not punch the nose he is suddenly holding so high."

"He has been insufferable," said Susannah, "strutting and ordering us about and telling us that he is our new leader."

"With Zilpah cheering him on," said Aunt Miriam. "What a disgusting person, seeking to turn the entire world to her own desires—all on behalf of those boys of hers, or so she would have you believe . . . while the boys have less stuff to them than does her shadow."

"Do not worry," said Rosula. "They will all have their comeuppance when Jesus walks in."

It did not happen that way. Should she have spoken immediately? Merovee was to wonder so often in the years that followed. Should she have blurted out the full truth before things got out of hand? If she had done so . . . would things have turned out differently?

Or was Petros so set upon his course of self-aggrandizement that no words would have changed his intentions?

She thought so hard on the way back to the house, allowing the women to guide her halting steps as they would have guided a sleepwalker . . . the poor wife, shocked into speechlessness.

The stone had been rolled back, that much was obvious to the men. The burial linen had been folded neatly, the body of "Jesus" was gone. The wife was found standing by the tomb in shock. The Cyrenean had disappeared.

What she told them must not contain lies. But how to refrain from lies in this matter? At least from lies of omission.

Why had Josh placed this terrible responsibility squarely onto her shoulders? Why had he not told her what to say?

'Oh Josh. When I get my hands on you.'

It was young Johannan who swung around abruptly as they walked, who came back to Merovee with shining eyes.

"Merovee. I see it now. It was as Yeshuah said. What he expected for himself. But it was Jesus who was the true Messiah. That is why God made it so that Jesus went to the cross instead. Poor Yeshuah was only God's vehicle to deliver Jesus, so that all of the prophecies which Yeshuah had expected to be fulfilled in himself would be fulfilled in Jesus.

"Jesus is alive, is he not. God raised Jesus from the dead. This morning, on the third day . . . Jesus was raised before your very eyes, that is why you cannot speak. Was it an angel who rolled back the stone? Jesus lives. He does. Oh please speak, Merovee. Tell me that Jesus lives!"

She had to say something.

"It is true that Jesus is alive . . . "

"And an angel rolled back the stone," Johannan persisted.

"There was a flash of light and the stone rolled back. I saw no angel."

"Petros! He is risen! Jesus is risen! An angel came from out of Heaven!"

"I saw no angel!"

"But where has Jesus gone?" demanded Petros as he and Jacob came running back to the women. "Why did he not wait for us? Has he been taken up to Heaven?"

"He . . . left with a Roman officer."

That set them back onto their heels.

"A Roman officer?" said Petros.

"A senior centurion."

Petros stared for a moment, then he laughed outright.

"Did this centurion have a sword?"

"Most centurions do."

"Was his armor bright and shiny?"

"Yes."

Petros leaned toward Johannan.

"It was the archangel Michael, with his sword and shining armor. The Magdalen is so unhinged that she mistook him for a Roman."

Merovee's mouth dropped.

"No. Petros! The truth is that Jesus, himself, was wearing the shining armor."

"Yes, of course, we all know how Jesus can shine. Where did this 'centurion' take Jesus?" Petros grinned.

His eyes were so small and piggy.

"To Pilatus."

Petros snickered and elbowed Johannan in the ribs.

"Of course. Angels get on so well with the praefectus."

"Why not?" she snapped. "Does not Jesus also get on with him? You want to know where Jesus is? He is in the Antonia under the protection of Pilatus until the Passover crowds disperse. The armor was worn by Jesus as a disguise."

For this was getting out of hand. The entire truth might have to be revealed.

"And Jesus will come to us then?" said Jacob. "After the Passover crowds have gone?"

"Yes. And then he will explain everything. We are all to wait patiently at the house of Nicodemus. And we are supposed to stay out of sight, so I suggest that we move on before people get up and about."

By the time they arrived back at the house of Nicodemus, however, the thing was already out of control. And being embroidered upon with every utterance. The rest of the disciples crowded around, eager for news. Everyone talked at once, Petros and the Boanerges loudest of all.

"God raised Jesus from the dead, exactly as the prophecies foretold."

"Angels came and rolled away the stone. They have taken Jesus away."

"You should have seen the whiteness of their robes," said Petros.

"You actually *saw* them?"

"There was one sitting in the tomb when I entered. He spoke to me. He said, 'Why do you seek the living among the dead?' Here. Here is his burial linen, just as the angel folded it."

"Let me touch it."

"Let me kiss it."

"It was the archangel Michael who bore Jesus away, he had a flaming sword, and armor that shone as the sun. Jesus will return to us. We are to wait."

"All this is not so!" cried Merovee. "There were no angels! Jesus *walked* away. He is staying with Pilatus in the Antonia."

"The Magdalen has been made mad by the experience. Pay her no heed," said Petros.

Those who knew, or suspected the truth—the family of Jesus, Deborah and her servants from bar Jeremiah and her artisans from Kapher Kana, Meraiah, Susannah, Nathaniel, bar Tolmei, Chandreah, Nicodemus, Alexander, Micah and Leah, Jairus and his family, and Johannah—drew close to Merovee and watched the gabbling mass that surged around Petros and the Boanerges.

"It was not Jesus who went to the cross!" Merovee kept telling them all. "He was not raised from the dead because he did not die. The truth is even more wonderful! Listen to me, please! You must wait for Jesus to come. There are reasons why I may not tell you the full truth just now, but Jesus will tell you. Wait for him!"

They did not hear. Or they would not. And they did not wait for any truth from Jesus to set about the creation of their own truth.

"How can they take Petros and the Boanerges as authorities and ignore the only one among us who was actually there?" wondered Joseph.

"Because Petros is telling them what they want to hear," said Susannah.

"And because that one who was there was a woman," snapped Rosula.

"A suddenly mad woman," said Merovee sadly.

By evening, an entirely mythical version of the crucifixion had been conceived, explained, vouched for, and had passed into the belief system of Petros, the Boanerges and Zilpah, Levi and Navea, Jacob bar Alphaeus and his wife, Lebbaeus, Barnabus, Thaddeus, Phillipus and Demetrius and all their family, Rufus the brother of Alexander, Mathiah, Salmon, Eli, Ezekiel, and even the brothers of Yeshuah and their families.

Merovee sent Micah off to join Jesus at the Antonia, then went to sleep, exhausted beyond telling. So it would happen.

Whatever "it" was.

But that would be then. For now, she just had to sleep.

* * *

Jesus and Micah appeared at the door at dawn on Tuesday morning. Timothy, then Nicodemus, greeted him with relief.

His reception by those sitting about the salon and courtyard was not as cordial. The wife of Demetrius screamed as the centurion primus pilus appeared beside her.

Petros rose up menacingly.

"What do you do here, Roman? Who let you in?"

"Petros. Have you forgotten me so soon?"

"I do not know you.'

"No, and you obviously never did." Jesus removed his helmet. "Does this help?"

Petros leaned forward, looking hard.

"Jesus?"

Merovee came to him and they embraced. Gently, protecting her aching breasts.

"I have made a mess of things," she said. "Right the situation if you can."

Those of Peter's faction were encircling Jesus, staring at his apparel as though they assumed it to be constructed of moonbeams, examining his body as if it should be transparent.

"Phillipus." Jesus offered his hand. The Greek jumped back, staring at the hand.

"Are you afraid to touch me?" said Jesus.

Gingerly, Phillipus reached out.

"You feel real," he said in wonderment.

Jesus went through the entire group, shaking hands, embracing them.

"Now you all know that I am solid."

"Of course," said Petros, gathering his wits and instructing his people. "A resurrected body would be as the former body."

"Petros, this is no resurrected body that you see before you."

"No. Certainly. God has given him a new one, for, look, all of you. All his wounds have gone."

Jesus held up his inner wrists.

"Wounds are not difficult."

There was a gasp. For a moment, upon the wrists, lesions opened and blood appeared.

Then, abruptly, the wounds were gone.

"I can give you all the wounds you want. But wounds are not the point."

"Jesus, how soon before God and the angels arrive?" said young Johannan.

"Should we arm ourselves for the battle?" said Petros.

"Numbskulls! Have you never listened to what I taught? Have you learned nothing in all your time with me?"

"Teach us, Lord," said Jacob bar Alphaeus. "We want to hear your words. How soon will we join you in Heaven?"

Jesus stared at the man, his mouth working soundlessly.

Abruptly, he turned to Petros.

"It has come to my attention that you have ridiculed my wife and called her mad. For one thing, she spoke of a centurion in shining armor—who now stands before you—and you assured her that she had seen an angel. I would have to question which is the more mad of the two of you. I am also informed that none of you will listen to what she tells you as to events in the tomb."

"Who has said these slanderous things?"

"Micah."

The face of Petros reddened, not in embarrassment, but in anger.

"How came Micah to see you before those of us who are first among your disciples?"

"*My* disciples." Jesus seemed to be examining the idea. "Last time I looked, Petros, you and the Boanerges and others in this company were drinking wine with Yeshuah Christos in an upper room, having pledged unswerving fidelity to *him*. What can possibly have changed your mind?"

"We have seen the error of our thinking."

"Said without even blushing, " said Jesus with a shake of the head. "Well, Petros, you have already heard the parable of the workers summoned to the vineyard. Often the last shall be first and the first shall be last. It is as a thorn in your sandal that those other than yourself always seem to be in the right places at the right times, is it not Petros. Micah saw me before you saw me because I had bidden my wife to send him to me in the Antonia and she did so."

"Lord, we must get our order of precedence settled," said Zilpah. "Now, while you are amongst us, else we will be in confusion when you leave."

Jesus flinched and set his jaw.

"If I tell you people the truth of what happened in the tomb . . . will you hear my words?"

"Yes, Lord," said Zilpah's Jacob. "We believe upon your words and will die for them, for you are the way, the truth, and the light."

"I ask no one to die!" Jesus cried. "Those are Yeshuah's words, Yeshuah's ideas that you prate at me! Get things sorted out in your minds, will you please? Listen to me all of you. Are you listening?"

"We will always listen to your voice, Lord," said Petros.

"And stop calling me 'Lord.'"

"Yes, Master."

Jesus looked apoplectic. He went on through gritted teeth.

"I was not crucified. Do you hear me? I did not die on the cross."

"He is not dead. Hallelujah!" said Phillipus.

"In collusion with Pontius Pilatus and Lucius, Judah bravely took my place. I was kept bound and gagged in the Antonia while Judah was nailed onto the cross and hung in my place. Are you listening?"

"You were bound by Pontius Pilatus," said Levi.

"Pilatus allowed me to come to the tomb just before sundown, disguised as you see me now. I was shut in over the Sabbath with the Cyrenean and Salome and Merovee."

"You were shut in the tomb," repeated Petros.

"Judah did actually die. But I brought him back into life."

"He was raised from the dead," said Jacob bar Alphaeus.

"He is lodging with the Cyrenean in the Upper City at this moment."

"Who?" said Mathiah.

"Judah."

"Oh no," said Zilpah. "In the market only this morning I heard that the man who had betrayed you has hanged himself at a place outside the city."

"Well, in a way that is true information, Zilpah. Judah did hang himself at a place outside the city. It was at the Place of the Skull, upon a cross."

"Others say that he threw himself off a cliff in an old quarry and dashed himself upon the rocks," said Navea.

"The Place of the Skull is an old quarry. But I assure you that Judah is alive. If those rumors are true, sadly, they must pertain to Yeshuah."

Still they all stared at him, their faces as blank as though he had not spoken.

"Do none of you hear me?"

"Jesus," said young Johannan. "How much longer will you be with us?"

"I would be with you for years, Johannan. For a lifetime. But I wonder if you really want me."

"Of course we want you, Lord, but we know that sometime soon you must go to your heavenly father."

"Where did you pick up that bit of information?"

"Petros has told us."

"Petros seems suddenly to have grown very wise."

"Did you not name me your rock, Jesus? It is upon me that the Congregation of Souls is to be built."

"What Congregation of Souls?"

"The Congregation of the Kingdom."

"You are confusing my words with Yeshuah's once again. Can you not remember which of us said what? Our messages could hardly be more opposed.

"I do not want or need souls to be congregated, Petros. The basis of reality, of the true god All That Is, is individual. Congregations by their very nature deny individuality, and so they deny the very god for which they search.

"And congregations breed that evil against which I have fought all my life. Priesthoods.

"Petros, look at me. All of you. Come back to your eyes. You have left them vacant. Where have all of you gone? Can it have happened this quickly?

"I am not dead!"

"Hallelujah!" said Mathiah.

"I never did die. I was not crucified. Judah was crucified."

"He seeks to be kind to his betrayer," said Levi to the group. "He tells us that we, too, must forgive Judah and pity his soul."

"Surely," said Petros. "For do you not see? He tells us that, just as Yeshuah was the vehicle sent by God to lead his son to the cross, so was the betrayer the instrument of God. He tells us to pity Judah and pray for him."

"Stop talking about me as though I had left the room!"

"Oh, you must stay with us, Lord, you must not go so soon."

Jesus turned to Merovee. She shrugged.

"At least it was not only I."

No, it had not been. Jesus motioned to her and to those of his remaining inner circle. Together, they adjourned to the study of Nicodemus.

"The Builders are reborn," he said, shaking his head. "New Builders, for a new double millennium."

"What are you talking about?" said Joseph.

"Right before our eyes, and in contradiction to any fact presented to them, those people out there are building a psychological edifice, which is the strongest kind of edifice in the Universe. They mean their edifice to reach to the sky, where they expect to bask in glory. All they can see now are their plans for that edifice, and they will listen to no sounds except the clashes and clangs of their own building."

"They seemed to hear you as through a veil," said Nathaniel. "As though your words were magically changed somewhere between your mouth and their ears."

"Yes," said Susannah. "They were not being devious. They were all so sincere."

"What you have witnessed," said Jesus, "is, first, a demonstration of the true nature of perception. We see and hear that which our beliefs tell us to see and hear, and nothing more, even if a something more should be standing right in front of us, waving its arms and making very loud noises to attract our attention.

"What we do not believe in remains invisible and unheard.

"You also witnessed a probability of major proportions sliding into its groove. At such times . . . reality wobbles and wavers, and perception is even chancier. Witnesses to any one event will tell widely varying stories, each story most sincerely believed to be the truth.

"You people will go forward with one reality, in which my words are remembered rather clearly—though, even amongst yourselves, there will be variations.

"The others, I fear, will go forward with a reality in which my words are remembered only as they fit their preconceived belief in my death and resurrection."

"How is it that you dared to tell them the full truth of Judah?" said Merovee.

"Pilatus has given his permission. Aside from that . . . " Jesus shrugged. "I could see that they probably would not hear me. I have seen this sort of thing many times before, in so many lives. Yet, each time that I encounter it, I hope that things will turn out differently. If any of them did hear me without major distortion . . . if any of them did realize that Judah took my place . . . you can be sure that, soon, that understanding will have drifted off to closed places in their minds. You can be sure that the secret is safe with them for all time.

"Because their edifice is too far progressed into the clouds of glory for them to worry about a little thing like the truth, do you not see? They are too dazzled by their resurrected Messiah and the power and honor that will be theirs as his disciples.

"They do not even care whether the Kingdom, so central to Yeshuah's teaching, comes or not. Did you notice that? A rebellion, and a 'Kingdom on Earth,' ruled by a *living* Messiah, has been put from their minds—a fact that Pilatus will be delighted to learn. My only role now, according to Petros, is to disappear into clouds of glory to join some 'Heavenly Father.'

"They will now achieve their ambitions by gathering about them their own followers, this Congregation of Souls. They will tell their students that, one day, 'the Kingdom' will finally, magically, arrive. They will satisfy their lusts for power by dictating to their new followers the terms of those followers eventual entrance into that kingdom. While always, from this day on, they, and those who come after them—the priesthoods which they will spawn—will justify a delay in the coming of 'the Kingdom' in trade for that power and sway over the lives, and purses, of their fellows."

"In that case," said Merovee, looking closely at Jesus, "all of us here in this room have become . . . superfluous to them."

Jesus smiled and shrugged.

"Even I, their 'Risen Lord,' the object of their adoration . . . have become a nuisance and an embarrassment to have around. They can proceed much more efficiently in the formulation of their rules and regulations and required beliefs if I am not present to stick my shekel in.

"That is another thing you witnessed here today. You have seen god-making in action. Our Builders have shown you just exactly how 'divinely inspired' that process is, and how much of the 'god' is actually left when the god-makers get finished."

"Why did Pilatus give his permission to reveal the truth of Judah?" said Merovee.

"The greater part of the pilgrims have departed. The danger of a massive revolt or demonstration has passed. Caiaphas and his bunch have asked no questions, they seem perfectly content that the execution was carried out according to plan, and that I am shoveled into an unmarked grave with those other two men. They seem, thus, to have received no wind of the diversion of the body to the tomb, so that they do not question the emptiness of that tomb.

"Most importantly, within hours, almost every principal and witness to any of the events will have left Jerusalem. Even if Caiaphas were to get some inkling of what had occurred, he would have little to investigate, almost no one to question, precious little evidence to go on."

Jesus leaned back against the wall, arms crossed, surveying them all soberly.

"This evening, at sunset, Pilatus and Procula leave for Caesarea in company with all but the two centuries of soldiers usually garrisoned here. You can be sure that no soldier who was in any way involved in the crucifixion will be left behind. Merovee, you and Deborah, my father and mother and brothers and sisters . . . all of you, and any of the rest of you who so desire, are to accompany us to Caesarea. There is a merchant vessel in that port at this very moment. The sea lanes are safe now with the season of winter storms passed. That ship is waiting for its cargo to arrive from the Decapolis. When it does, the ship sails for Massilia of Gaul."

"Agapo!" cried Merovee.

"Soldiers are at Mount Ephraim by now with a letter from myself to Lazarus and Martha. Lucius leads them. He will bring to Caesarea the baby, and those from Mount Ephraim who wish to go to Gaul."

He laughed at Merovee's stricken eyes.

"Yes, and Ruthie and Pharisee and Gilead and Solomon and Freckles and Phoenix. How could you think that I would leave behind friends who have been through so much with us?"

"Joshuah," said Cleopah, "you are not expecting me and my family to leave are you?"

"No, Uncle. You were brought lately and willy-nilly into this matter, and are not overly associated with me in the minds of the rulers—or even our friends the Builders. There is no reason for you to uproot yourselves. While, in staying, you can be of great use and comfort to us, our secret anchor in this land."

"What of Jesse?" said Merovee.

"Send for him, of course. Send also to Simon the Leper. He and his wife may join us if they wish. I doubt that he will, but, in view of what I foresee for Jerusalem and its immediate surroundings, he would be well-advised to come." He smiled. "Tell him that the Master has need of him. That might do the trick. All right now, we have got to move quickly on all of this. Father, I will have Pilatus send a messenger to Bethlehem. Prepare freedom documents for the servants right away, so that the messenger can take them to them. I will also send along a letter warning them of the destruction that I have told you and Uncle Cleopah that I foresee, and inviting them to accompany us. Mother, are there any whom you would particularly wish to accompany us?"

"My Naomi. And little Coel. They are as my children. I would hope that they would want to come with me."

"I will see that they know of your hope."

Joseph was in shock.

"You warned me that this was coming. I had prepared. Yet, now that it is here . . . Cleopah, I will also make you a document. It will all be yours now. And our sister Annah's. But I should really go out to Bethlehem, myself, Joshuah. I had sold quite a few things, gathered a fair amount of gold, and it is hidden there in the house. We will have need of it in this . . . Gaul."

"No. You and Mother and my siblings must not expose yourselves more than is necessary at this point," said Jesus.

"Tell me where to find the gold," said Cleopah. "I will transfer it to Massilia when you send word of a trustworthy agent to handle the matter."

"I can give you the name of the man with whom I deal. Use the Zebedee as go between," said Deborah.

"Good," said Cleopah. "And Joseph, by no means will I take your land for myself or my heirs. Annah will feel the same. We will manage it for you and reimburse our just expenditures and salaries—Annah's youngest son and his family will doubtless be pleased to live there and handle things. But you and your heirs will continue to receive the revenues. In honor, it can be no other way."

"Also Joseph, do not worry about funds," said Deborah. Her eyes swept all those assembled. "None of you are to worry about funds. Thanks to Jesus, there are ample funds already waiting for us in Massilia . . . enough to maintain all of us indefinitely—as a community—in whatever our pursuits may be." She looked at Jesus. "You knew all along that this move to Gaul would be necessary."

"I could see it as a prime possibility. Only that."

"Oh, this is all so fast!" Rosula suddenly cried. "Just to leave everything. Our home, the families of Cleopah and Annah, all my people in Galilee, and Jude, my poor, crazy Zealot son. I cannot even let him know that we are leaving. I might never see him again. I *will* never see him again. And what if Jacob will not come with us? He, too, will be lost to me.

"Where *is* Gaul, Joshuah? Are the people civilized? I do not know, I just do not know. Why must any of us leave?"

"For one thing, the priests have found out that Deborah and her family are the first heirs of Saul."

"I *told* you, Rosula!" cried Joseph. "Before they were married, did I not tell you?"

Jesus was somber.

"Without realizing it, Merovee and I made what the priests consider to be a dangerous, dynastic alliance. With the importance of our two families called to their attention, they could well move to annihilate both of our families, to prevent more marriage between us. As for little Agapo, his jeopardy is doubled, having the blood of Johannan and now of Saul. No. Tripled. For did you not once say, Merovee, that you also have descent from David?"

"I am afraid so."

Jesus shook his head.

"At the very least, Deborah, Merovee, Agapo, Martha and Lazarus, Annah, Rachel, and Joses must be gotten out of the country. Jac and Jude . . . " He shrugged. "They are both headstrong enough to take no one's advice. But even Father could be in danger."

"Well, they are certainly not going to go and leave me behind!" huffed Rosula.

"What of danger to me and my children?" said Cleopah.

"With the rest of us just disappeared, I feel certain that you will be safe, Uncle. They will not know whether the first heirs are dead or alive or where we have got to, and their efforts would be spent in trying to learn the answers to those questions. As for Aunt Annah and her children, they should have no problems at all.

"I would, however, if I were you, have whomsoever you install in Bethlehem come to you in Samaria with his reports. I would stay inside the borders of Samaria as much as possible and away from the grasp of the High Priest."

He straightened and walked thoughtfully over to the writing table.

"There are yet other reasons for removing as many of you as possible from this land. Every one of you knows the truth of what happened at the Place of the Skull. That not only leaves you open to interrogation—or worse—by Temple authorities if ever they did launch an investigation . . . but it makes you the enemies of all our Builders out there in the other room. You know things that they will not want their own new followers to know.

"Oh yes, do not look surprised. Do you not see that they mean to become the teachers? The masters. The *priests*. Priests of a new way of thought.

"None of them fully realize at this moment what it is that they intend. But I do. I have seen this process occurring all too many times, in too many lives, as small people take the largeness that has been offered to them and squeeze it down to their own size, and keep on squeezing, till all truth and love, joy and beauty and life, is gone from the original offering, and only a self-perpetuating priesthood is left.

"Those people out there, and those who become their followers, will soon be so very serious about their work, so convinced of their mandate from Heaven, that they will feel justified in committing crimes to silence those who might tell opposing stories . . . which will not be regarded as opposing stories, but as heresies, and crimes against their new version of 'God.'"

"You are saying . . . they might seek to kill us?" said Nathaniel in disbelief. "But they are our friends!"

"No longer, Nathaniel. They are busy hatching themselves into wild-eyed fanatics with a cause. There is nothing more treacherous and potentially lethal in this world.

"Merovee, especially, is in mortal danger of them. The jealousy of Petros is already large. It will continue to grow daily, as he seeks to make himself first in the eyes of all. It will rankle constantly, gnawing at his insides—the secret knowledge that Merovee—a woman—was always first.

"And forever will be. I enjoin each of you to listen to Merovee always as you would to me, for we two speak from the same heart."

His eyes regarded each of them gravely.

"The truth is that none of you are now safe from yonder 'Congregation of Souls.'

"In your case, Uncle Cleopah, Petros and his followers could be an even greater threat than the rulers. So that, if I were you—Uncle, Aunt Miriam, you boys, any who elect to stay behind . . . as a matter of self-preservation, forget the truth of the crucifixion. If you speak of it with Petros and his people, agree that it must have happened the way they say. If you speak with the rulers, as far as you know, three men were hanged, and the soldiers took them down just before the Sabbath and did something with the bodies, you know not what."

"How can we ever forget the truth, Joshuah?" said Aunt Miriam. "That shining boy, hanging on those spikes, and knowing only love."

She turned away, her eyes brimming.

"I do not mean that you can really forget it, Aunt. I mean for you to keep the truth in a secret garden within your own selves. I merely give you permission to prevaricate to the world. I absolve you of any blame in advance for any prevarication. Keep the truth sweet and pure within yourselves, while keeping your own selves safe in the maelstrom that this land will witness in the next generation.

"The fault . . . the grievous fault in this whole matter, is mine entirely."

"Oh, Josh . . . "

"No. It was too soon, Merovee. I thought they were ready to hear the truth spoken plainly. They were not. Only a handful of you were ready. The others still want parables, and children's tales of angels, demons, Heaven, and Hell. On such simplistic notions they will go forward with their damned edifice . . . their Congregation of Souls. They will mislead and enslave another whole era of Humankind.

"But I do have you people. I have my nucleus. You are my real rocks, you few, who know the truth, who will carry it on, teach it to an ever-broadening circle, and ensure that always, somewhere, some people know the truth, and dare to speak it.

"You will go forward for me. But, to truly go forward, I need that most of you are out of this land, to a place where you are free to speak.

"Yet I do not demand that any of you either go or stay. I will honor your various decisions."

There was long silence.

"Jesus," said Nicodemus, "I am getting on in years. My stature among my colleagues is such that I fear nothing from the High Priest. And I do not fear Petros and his friends. Like Cleopah, I assume that I am exempt from all of this."

"Only for a while," smiled Jesus. "As you say, Nicodemus, you are getting on. Your time is relatively short. But would you like to know where you will be reborn, and into what circle?"

"No!" cried Nicodemus, covering his face against their laughter.

"Nicodemus." Jesus went to the man and embraced him. "We can ever thank you enough for what you have done for us in the last days. I know how upsetting it must have been . . . your Passover disrupted, your own concerns as to cleanliness and purity . . . "

"Ho!" laughed Nicodemus. "Worry not on that score, Jesus. Frankly, I have never had as much exhilaration as you and your people have afforded me in these last days. And my ideas of cleanliness and purity . . . well, the place will be worse than any tomb when all of you leave, with just myself, and Timothy and the servants, rattling around in it, being, oh, so very clean."

"At what time did you say that Pilatus marches?' said Nathaniel.

"He hopes to be off at sundown."

Susannah looked around.

"Are there any of us who would not relish a stroll to Caesarea?"

"I have always wanted to see Caesarea," said Rosula wanly. "Some say that it is a wonder of the world."

"What of Judah?" said Mother Meraiah.

"He and Salome will be taken in Procula's covered conveyance."

"Then I am with you," said Meraiah. "My other sons and their families are in there with Petros, participating in his madness. I no longer know them. I have only one son now, and that is Judah. Where he leads, I will follow."

"Will you all come then? Johannah? Bar Tolmei? Chandreah? All of you from bar Jeremiah and Kana? Jairus? Alexander, I believe that your father will be coming. You, too? Excellent.

"Throughout the day, then, slip out singly or in pairs. Ladies, wear your veils. Father, Joses, you two, especially, should wear burnooses Come directly and with all speed to the main gate of the Antonia. The centurion Philadelphus will admit you. The password is Gaul. Uncle, I will have Pilatus arrange for a guard to escort you and your family safely home to Mount Ephraim."

"I have a better plan, Joshuah. Rather then sending a messenger from Pilatus out to Bethlehem, have a guard escort me and my family there immediately. We can pack up things for your parents, arrange things with the servants, send those who want to come with you hotfoot to the Antonia, and make temporary arrangements for administration. We will need a few days for all of that. An escort home to Samaria, with a wagon to transport things, would then be most welcome."

"Much better, Uncle. It shall be as you say."

"Should we bring our quilt rolls?" said Johannah.

"Yes, though all else for the journey will be provided." He smiled. "And we have Judah's thirty silver pieces for gird change, you know."

"To just leave after all these years with naught but the clothes on our backs," said Joseph. "It will be again as it was when Cleopah and I were boys, and our father dragged us from Bethlehem to Egypt, then to Samaria, and up to Galilee. I thought I had left those furtive days behind forever. Cleopah, brother, I envy you the staying."

"And I thought I would pass grandmother's golden oil lamp on to Annah, and the silver bowl to Rachel," moaned Rosula. "Oh, all my beautiful things! How can I leave them?"

"You will not," soothed Miriam. "We will pack all that you tell us to pack and have everything sent to you when you are settled."

"Settled?" said Rosula. "Ha!" Her green eyes flashed. "We will never again be settled, I will warrant you."

There was but one more piece of business to be seen to. Jesus went to Petros on his way out.

"You have taken my shroud."

"Yes, Lord, here it is."

"Thank you," said Jesus. He tucked it under his arm and headed for the door.

"But Jesus," said young Johannan. "When will we see you again? What are we to do now?"

"Go back to Galilee, Johannan. Go back to your fish."

Chapter 23

The Chalice

She had forgotten the blue of the Mediterranean. A blue of such crystal clarity, and of such dancing, lighted depths, that one would wish to be left in peace, to stare at it all day, each day for a lifetime.

Far to the north in that water, a child who had been herself had been drowned. Did the bones of that little body lie on a probable ocean bottom, patiently gathering a blanket of silt for an eternity of rest, even as, simultaneously, The Energy that had activated those bones filled a woman who was living right 'now,' a thousand years into the future?

Even farther to the north, in a probable Athens, was there by now residing a Merovee who had decided not to marry Jesus . . . the one who had given in to her mother's fears, who was intending to study women's ills with a physician, and become a practitioner for women, or else considering life as a priestess? Was that girl even now seeing flashes of Mediterranean blue as she went about her day? Did she ever wonder what it would have been like had she married the insufferable Jesus? Would she hear that he had been crucified . . . and believe it?

Or would her own current knowledge bleed through to that probable Merovee, so that a voice somewhere in that Merovee's mind assured her . . . It is not true.

The column could move no faster than the marching soldiers. But it was pleasant to soak up the sunlight, along the edge of a sea that many in the party had never before seen. Simon the Leper and his wife Judith had, indeed, responded to the summons from Jesus, and were as wide-eyed children at a street festival. Even the soldiers seemed to be drinking in the beauty, and there was a feel to the column that was, indeed, festive, as all involved breathed unheard sighs of relief to be away from the stark, Judean hills, free of Jerusalem and its oppression.

Longinus and his men served as personal escort to both of the families, full of nothing but sympathy for those who had been close to the shining young Jew whom they had helped to kill, who, it was beginning to be whispered, had been the son of the Jewish god.

Merovee rode horseback for the first time in her life, both she and Jesus mounted on docile geldings. Her breasts were tightly bound. Toward the end of this day, Longinus had promised her, they would intersect the road from Sechem. There, Agapo would be waiting.

Riding beside her, Jesus was accepted by the soldiers in his guise as a senior centurion . . . though none were quite sure just what rank of centurion he was. Primus Pilus, perhaps, as some of his varied insignia indicated. But, whatever, he was a friend to Pilatus and attached to no legion. Rather, all had decided, he was on some mysterious errand for Tiberius. Mere soldiers did not question the uniforms or actions of the secret emissaries of emperors.

They just whispered among themselves.

Could the mission have something to do with the crucified son of the Jews' god? Had not this centurion come to the Place of the Skull to supervise the entombment?

Tiberius was known to be strange, a philosopher, a student of the stars, a patron of soothsayers. Perhaps his stars had told him something about this Yeshuah Christos—or Jesus as he was known to family and friends. Maybe that was why such elaborate courtesy was being shown to his family . . . and why such an exalted centurion was spending all his time talking with the widow.

It was said that the party meant to sail to Massilia.

Privately, the soldiers wondered if, instead, their destination was Capri . . . if the family of the son of the Jews' god was being taken to Tiberius to tell him the sayings of Jesus.

Years later, that was what many of them would tell their grandchildren.

"The Emperor Tiberius was one of the first converts to Jesus. I know, for I had the honor of escorting his family to the vessel that took them all secretly to Capri. Tiberius had foreseen the crucifixion in the stars, and he sent to try to halt it . . . but his emissary arrived too late. All that could then be done was to give Jesus an honorable burial in a tomb. Dead? Oh, Jesus was most certainly dead when we laid him in the tomb. Longinus had run him through with his spear just to be sure."

Another story would inform listeners that Jesus had been the son of a Roman centurion—that story the result of some lascivious remarks in regard to the centurion's attentions to a widow with a newborn babe, and, thus, a compilation of bits and scraps of innuendo with no regard to logical chronology or events.

There would be other odd stories circulating in the years that followed, having to do with the gardener who had tended the cabbages in the Place of the Skull. It had been the gardener who had spirited the body of Jesus away from the tomb, some would say, in order to keep gawkers out of this garden and save his cabbages.

Some would claim that the gardener had buried Jesus right under those selfsame cabbages.

Certainly, the soldiers accompanying the procession agreed, the gardener was more than a gardener, else why was he being brought along on this mysterious voyage to "Massilia"?

Additionally, those soldiers who had been at the Place of the Skull took note of the fact that the Cyrenean physician who had helped Jesus to carry his cross, then later declared him dead, was also traveling to "Massilia" with the family of Jesus.

And what was being so closely guarded in the Lady Procula's closed wagon? Certainly not the Lady Procula, who rode horseback beside her husband, enjoying the blue sea. Could it be, some storytellers would ask, that the gardener had also been a secret agent of Tiberius, and that he had spirited the body of Jesus away from the tomb during the Sabbath, not in order to protect his cabbages, but in order to take the body to Tiberius, himself?

Was that what had ridden to Caesarea in that enclosed wagon? The body of the man who had died upon the cross?

Or . . . had he not, in fact, been dead?

In the making that day, throughout all of Palestine, among homeward-bound pilgrims, the citizens of Jerusalem, the priesthood, the disciples, and among Roman soldiers, were hundreds of such tales, compiled from bits and pieces of this and that, of truth, eyewitness, gossip and hearsay, mixed and matched with wishful thinking and imagination gone wild. Each version would, of course, claim to be truth, and each storyteller would claim in some way to be an expert upon the matter.

Legend would inevitably grow even in the family, until descendants were not quite sure just what had really happened.

Most of the stories would fall by the wayside, to be heard only as echoes and whispers in the centuries to come. Others would be shouted from mountain tops as The Truth—till they conquered the world with their mandate from "Heaven."

Nehemiah, for his part, rode along steeped in gloom, ignorant of the whispers that he and his cabbages would engender in the corridors of time. Yes, surely Reb Joshuah had been right. It had not been safe for him to remain in Palestine. But, happy though he was to continue in Joseph bar Ramathea's employ, he was not at all happy to be leaving his gardens behind.

His plantings needed him! Another gardener would not know their idiosyncrasies as did he.

And Gaul? Who had even heard of the place? With a name like that, surely, despite all Reb Joshuah's assurances, nothing grew there.

"Poor Nehemiah," smiled Merovee to Jesus.

"The innocent bystander snatched up by the whirlwind?" he smiled back. "Do not worry for him. There are no innocents, and no accidents. We each create our own realities, and Nehemiah would not have put himself into the place where we found him, and witnessed the events that he did witness, had his Soul not fully intended for him to accompany us.

"Ah. This sea. It is food for the Spirit. There is a place down the coast from Athens, Merovee, at a place called Sounion. There, on a cliff, there is a temple to Poseidon. Millions of field poppies cover the slope, and the sea is just this color. Often—so very often—I have wanted to run away to that place, with you and Agapo . . . to forget who I am and why."

"We will go there together someday," said Merovee softly.

"If not . . . then remember the beauty of this day, and this sea, and realize what I would have wished to give you for all of your life."

"Pilatus says that Gaul is reputed to be the garden of the world. We will have plenty of beauty other than the sea. Oh Josh, I am beginning to be anxious for that place! A land in which we can be free."

It was at Apollonia, at the end of that second day—where the road from Sechem joined the Joppa-Caesarea road—that they looked ahead and saw the small troop of Romans encamped. Philadelphus rode up beside Merovee.

"That will be Tribune Gallus Lucius with your baby, my lady. The praefectus bids you ride on ahead of the column if you wish."

She needed no urging. Ruthie saw her coming and began to bray in welcome. Pharisee, thinking, no doubt, that Ruthie was praying, joined in. Gilead and Solomon took up the song and, in their shared cage, Freckles meowed and Phoenix bleated.

Agapo was equally vociferous, but not at all welcoming.

"Do not cry, Sweetheart! Do you not remember Mommy?"

"He might if you would give him a breast," snapped Zana. "He has had nothing but goat's milk since leaving Mount Ephraim. All this trotting around. It is not good for a child."

Merovee needed no further prodding. She and Zana commandeered a soldier's tent.

"We will be lucky if your milk has not dried too far or gone bad," said Zana. "We will have to find another wet nurse if so."

"No, I think it is all right. Oh, I am so sore. Oww! But he is getting something. Oh, he has grown. In only one week. I must never leave him again."

Lazarus had come, and Martha. They greeted Jesus politely, concealing their joy, remembering that he was a "Roman" and a stranger.

Alphaeus was there.

"Uncle," said Deborah when the situation had been explained, "Jacob and Lebbaeus . . . they are with Petros. If you sail with us . . . "

"I will probably never see them again. But Deborah, for so many years I could not see them anyway. Then Jesus gave me back my sight and allowed me to see them and you and all of Palestine as well. Now he is giving me the opportunity to see the world." He took her hand. "And to see you and your children *as* I see that world. What better bargain could a blind old man make?"

He shrugged.

"Besides, from what Jesus tells me, I would not get on with my son and grandson now anyway. The Cyrenean and I can console one another. He has left a son behind as well."

Jac had also come.

"But only to say goodbye," he told Rosula gravely. "I am too set, Mother. I can not leave our people. I am not capable of that bold a change."

"You left Qumran."

"But I am still among my own people, do you not see? I can still work to redeem them with the understandings which Josh has given to me, but still while living in this Promised Land, with the people of The Law. And do not fear for my safety in regard to this dynastic thing. First, I am not attracted to Martha. Second, she is thankfully being removed from these shores."

He laughed, then shook his head seriously.

"Mother, I thought that I could follow Joshuah and his light to wherever he led. But I have not the courage, I guess. I would perish among Gentiles. I wish that I were different. Believe me, I wish that I were as flexible as are you, for I suspect that you have the better part."

"I am the one who should be inflexible. I am the old one."

Jac smiled.

"You will never be old, Rosula."

It was the first and last time that he ever used her pet name.

Martha had been careful to bring Merovee's prized gird and sheepskins. She had also brought another treasure, carrying and guarding it personally.

"After all," she shrugged, ignoring Deborah's sudden tears, "Artemis has been a member of this family for even longer than I. I could hardly have left her behind. And if she was good enough for Jesus to carry to Mount Ephraim, well . . . . . . Ah! Here comes the kitchen wagon. I must talk to the cook to see what he is planning to feed you this night."

* * *

Caesarea was as lovely as they had been told, a marble jewel, set in a crescent around a small, man-made harbor.

The palace of the praefectus—built by Herod the Great—was out at the end of the harbor jetty, seeming to float upon the blue sea. Roses and lilies and flowering shrubs were everywhere. In the city, there was a stadium, an amphitheater, a hippodrome, endless temples, a roofed market arcade with permanent stalls for vendors from all lands, a library, a museum of Canaanite, Egyptian, Hebrew, and

Grecian antiquities, a gymnasium, a vast public bath, schools of history, philosophy, art, and science, banking agents, mercantile establishments—and peoples from all the Mediterranean world.

It came flooding joyfully back to Merovee what some of the cities of the Roman and Grecian world were like. Soon she would be seeing them again. What an adventure awaited them all!

The family and followers were ensconced in the palace with one whole wing to themselves.

"I feel like the princess that you used to be," laughed Merovee to Salome.

Salome responded as she had responded to almost everything on the journey. With a flood of tears. She had had but a few hours with Herodias in the Antonia before leaving.

"I never dreamed how much I would miss her. I mean—I will never see her again. Most of you have someone with you, but I go off to this new life all alone."

"What of me?" said Johannah. "You are my only solace. Can I not be yours?"

"And what of me?" said Judah gently.

"Oh yes, of course. But you know what I mean."

Yes, they knew. They did not begrudge the intrepid Salome her tears.

As for Judah, who had been treated as an invalid throughout the three-day trip, strictly confined to Procula's wagon, he was beginning to want to be up and about.

So Pilatus ordered that he, too, should have his hair cut and his beard shaved off in the Roman manner. When this was accomplished, he was provided with a toga belonging to Pilatus.

"Your own mother would not recognize you," said Meraiah when she saw him.

They were all free to wander the city. Word was that their ship's cargo from the Decapolis was not due for another week. So, with the air of children let out of school, truants partaking of the forbidden, they enjoyed Caesarea to the hilt.

Many of them wanted nothing but to lie on the beach, soaking up the sun. Simon the Leper and his wife and the servants from bar Jeremiah had never known such leisure, and, though it was spring, the coast was as warm as summer in the Judean highlands, but with a wonderful breeze. It was as the very best of Judean summer days every day, and bones dank from the Judean winter could not get enough of the warmth.

Meraiah's bones where the dankest. She could seldom be lured from the beach. Jairus and his wife sometimes joined her, but Alphaeus was always to be found with his quilt spread beside hers. Meraiah began to laugh a great deal, and to look years younger.

Rosula could not get enough of the temples. She dragged Joseph through each one again and again, astounded at their variety, at the friezes and decorations, at the statuary, at the rituals, and at the myths that willing priests and priestesses told them of each god or goddess.

Annah, Rachel, Joses, Rebeckah, Coel, and Naomi frolicked in the surf, guarded anxiously by Jac—his anxiety occasioned by that fact that he could swim no better than could they.

Jesse made himself at home in the stable of Pilatus, using the care of Ruthie—widening each day with her foal—as excuse, but eagerly helping to care for the horses, learning the ways of those beasts from the head groom.

The artisans of Kapher Kana haunted the museum and the school of art.

Nehemiah seemed to be taking inventory of each plant in the city.

Nathaniel and Susannah disappeared, hand-in-hand, every morning, leaving bar Tolmei twiddling his thumbs. Sitting about, he struck up a friendship with Longinus, and spent enthralled hours listening to that old campaigner's tales of duty in the land of the Britons and in Gaul, of action against the German tribes and in Syria, and of his soon-to-be retirement to a legionary village in Merida of Iberia. There he would be given a pension, a house and land, a wife so that he could have some children, entertainment and games—everything that a man would wish, for the rest of his life. Had his own life followed a different course, bar Tolmei decided, maybe he would have joined the legions.

Funny. And here all these years he had hated, fought, and tried to kill these people—good men like Longinus.

Judah and Salome spent most of their time in their room. When they wandered out, it was to the bazaar. The thirty pieces of silver had been broken down into small change, and distributed equally to each member of the party. So the two of them shopped, spying out little wedding gifts for one another . . . a carved kitten of pink, Iberian quartz for Salome, an ebony-handled razor for Judah, six els of pink silk for Salome, and a seamless coat of finely woven linen for Judah.

Deborah took those days for business, remaining closeted in the office of her company with agents and men skilled in international laws and regulations, restructuring the enterprises of the House of Nathan. There was also the awkwardness of arranging for settlement with Boaz over the disappearance of his betrothed. In this matter, the truth as to Martha's Gentile grandmother would, no doubt, convince that dedicated young Levite of his great, good fortune in losing Martha. He could also be trusted to keep that information to himself, as the shame of having it known that he had been affianced to a woman who was technically Gentile must be avoided.

Johannah, Chandreah, Lazarus, Martha, and Alexander went back to childhood and joined in a contest to see who could find the greatest number of absolutely perfect seashells before it was time to leave. None of them could say exactly what the winner would win, and they were all too busy collecting to wonder.

The Cyrenean, and Micah with Leah, spent most of their hours in Caesarea's fine library.

Only Zana found herself adrift during the daytimes. In desperation, she joined Jac in guarding the youngsters at surfside. At least, she huffed, *she* could swim.

Zana's need for an alternative activity was caused by the fact that Merovee and Jesus found a secluded little bay down the coast and went there early each morning, taking Agapo, and leading Gilead, whose back was packed with the kitten and kid in their cage, Johannan's sheepskins, and a basket of bread and wine, fruit and cheese. They swam and sunned naked, gloried in the beauty of Agapo, laughed at the romping of the animals set free along the surf, made love and talked. And talked and talked.

Evenings were spent at the theater. There were poetry readings, storytellers of ancient myths, and a troupe of actors from Athens, who did *Antigone*, *Medea*, and *Electra*.

Then one day a saddle-sore Nicodemus arrived into their midst. With him was Timothy.

"I decided," said Nicodemus, "that I cared not to clatter around my oh-so-clean house any longer. Timothy, too, has grown fond of defilement. So I am re-born into your midst more quickly than Jesus expected."

He immediately joined Deborah in her office.

"For I have left behind many matters in regard to my properties. Then there is the freeing and paying off of those of my servants still under slavery contract, and documents of recommendation for all of them. I will need Deborah's agents to help me settle it all."

Came the day when Pilatus told them that the caravan was in from the Decapolis. The ship was being loaded. It would sail on the pre-dawn tide.

A pall settled over the group. It had not seemed real until now. Only a holiday, after which they would go back to their old lives.

But they had no old lives. There was only the future, and what they would make of it.

Jesus showed them the shroud that night at dinner, a dinner shared with Pilatus, Procula, and Lucius. Jesus had arranged for a bar to be suspended from the ceiling of the dining salon, and he caused the length of linen to be hung over this bar so that they could see the figure on each side of the cloth.

"But . . . it is a weird, dark sort of image of Judah," said Salome softly, holding her new husband's hand. "Judah. It is you. As you must have looked just as Jesus brought you back to life."

"The burst of light," said the Cyrenean. "Is that what put his image onto the cloth? Look, here is the front of him—and, come around to this other side—come around everyone. There is the back of him. The image is just as we put the cloth under and over him. But how, Jesus? What is the process that made this image?"

"It is an energy that is beyond your ability to comprehend at this time, Simon. Though, strangely, your Laserpitium Radix aided in the definition of what you see here.

"Suffice it to say that the Energy of Life made the image. I only wanted all of you to understand the importance of this cloth—to be aware of the information recorded upon it."

"Oh Judah," said Salome. "you look so old and so hurt on the cloth. And now that I have a comparison, I much prefer you with your hair and whiskers off, so that we can see your beautiful face."

Jesus smiled.

"How you stare, Judah my friend."

The mildness of Judah since his time upon the cross had been remarked upon by all. He seemed to see things now as through a rosy gauze. Even in repose, his lips smiled, while his eyes viewed the world with wonder and love.

"It is a curious thing to sit here alive and well, married and so very happy, going off to a new world. And yet now to see the hurt, dead man that I so lately was. I think I felt it happen. I remember . . . such light as I returned. And a great sound that was not a sound, but . . . joy."

"You—all of you in this group," said Jesus. "Keep this cloth safe amongst your number and look at it often. It will remind you of many important things, the most important thing being, if ever you should forget, if ever you should be in doubt . . . that there is no such thing as a dead fig tree."

Tears filled the eyes of Judah.

"I wonder how Aunt Sarai is. And the tree."

"Write to her when you get to Gaul," said Jesus. "Perhaps she will come out to join you . . . and bring her tree . . . though I am sure that its exuberance will soon outgrow that pot!"

They all laughed. It was good to laugh. Good to have something to laugh about at this moment.

Perhaps the most difficult part, for Merovee, was taking leave of Pilatus and Procula.

"To think," she said, "that we might never meet again in this life."

"Cheer up," shrugged Pilatus. "I am sure to get myself banished. Now that I know how to be great by being kind, I fear that I shall not fit in very well, or see things quite as my superiors would wish me to see them."

He exchanged a long, loving look with Procula.

"Things will never be the same for us. With your sailing . . ."

His voice caught and he turned, busily pouring himself more wine.

"With your sailing," Procula continued for him, "Pilatus and Lucius and I lose everything in the world that has become dear to us. And essential. This place, this Palestine, will seem more of a forbidding desert than ever before. You have introduced us to a freedom of action and thought and loving that cannot be forgotten. Not to continue to use what we have learned, not to seek to grow further, would make us to be as three cripples, given back the use of their arms and legs, who yet refuse to use them."

She glanced at Pilatus.

"We have almost decided that—some way, as soon as we can—we will follow after you."

The face of Pilatus became animated.

"That day as we worked in your vineyard, Deborah, I remembered for the first time in years my love of the vine, and the supreme, golden joy that was mine as a lad in my father's vineyards. The soil of Gaul was made by the gods, so they say, especially for the growing of the grape. You can hardly go wrong, no matter where you plant. I want to get us some land along one of those beautiful river valleys, and terrace the hills and grow the finest grapes in Gaul."

"If you keep picturing that future vividly," said Jesus, "it shall be yours. If it is what you really want, what you really believe you deserve, you shall have it."

"Then, if I picture that my mother will be banished and join me, it will happen?" cried Salome.

Jesus laughed.

"Not unless Herodias wants it as well, my dear."

"Then I will write to her and tell her to start wanting it right away. I wonder if she would leave Antipas behind if I asked her. Probably not. Poor lady."

They sat up, then, late into the night, none of them wanting to sleep . . . talking of all that had happened and might happen, listening to Jesus.

Till, in the wee hours, Jesus drew Pilatus and Procula aside and spoke to them for some minutes in low tones. Then he excused himself and Merovee and led her to their chamber.

His face turned grave as they walked. A chill settled over Merovee's heart.

He drew her to a table once into the chamber, and poured out two glasses of wine.

"I drink to us," he said. "To the two of us forever."

She drank deeply, never taking her eyes from off of him.

"You are not sailing with us," she said when she had finished.

"No."

She turned and walked away, to the window that looked seaward, toward the deep, dark west of the world.

"I guess I knew it all the time. I thought that, if I pretended that I did not know, it might go away."

But then she had been as calm, as high-minded and understanding as she could be. She turned with a scream and flung her wine glass at him, missing him only because her eyes were blinded by tears.

"Noooo! You *will* come! What is there here for you now? You said, yourself, that it is a lost cause. Can you not teach in Gaul? In the Isle of the Britons? In Iberia, Greece, Egypt, Italy, in any one of a hundred places? Are there not minds in those places to be reached? Are those minds not even more willing than those in this place?"

"'That is why I send you to them. In those lands, you will be free to teach. A woman will not be stoned for presuming to teach.'"

"I will not go. I will not. I am your wife. Is there nothing for me? Do I not have some rights? Do you not have some duty to me? And what if I should be with child again now after these last days?"

"You are."

Merovee froze, staring at him.

"What makes you so sure?"

"I am in touch with the Spirit involved. It is quickening within you as we speak."

Her mouth worked soundlessly. Her hands pawed the air as though searching for something else to throw.

"*Damn* you! After my difficulty giving birth to Agapo you would send me off pregnant and alone?"

"You will never be alone, Merovee. My Energy will be with you. You will be in no danger."

"So. So! All right. So you believe that you owe me nothing. What, though, of the child? Will you not owe something to the child?"

"Yes. And I have given her that something. I have given her you."

"'She.' You even dictate the sex! You and Johannan both."

She backed away from him.

"You *are* one and the same. He is you and you are he and you have both *used* me! Used me to get your pups, as though I were some wandering bitch!"

"Do not say these hasty things, Merovee, you will have to remember them for the rest of your life."

"I do not want to *have* a rest of my life! I cannot do it without you, Josh! I cannot be you."

"You can."

"You expect too much."

"Yes, and I will never stop expecting it. Yes, you are my wife. Yes, you were Johannan's wife. And why *you*? Think about it. Why not Salome, or Martha? With Salome, we would always have been charmed. With Martha, we would always have been fed. Why did both of us choose a tall, skinny, flat-chested misfit with a mind so definitely her own that no one can own her?"

He took a step toward her.

"Do you remember the day we walked out of Machaerus, and looked down upon the sea? I told you that day that you are a part of myself. A fragment of my own entity."

He took another step.

"Merovee, Judah went to the cross as Messenger. He became Yeshuah. But he was already a part of myself. He is a fragment of our entity who opted to undergo that actual, physical ordeal."

"Judah is . . . a junior part as am I?"

"Our entity is vast, Merovee. Are you less courageous than Judah? Would you refuse to be a greater sort of messenger?"

She turned away.

"That is not fair. It is different between the two of us. And Judah had an agony of only seven or eight hours, with full restoration immediately following. Ask me to do that. Bring me the nails! I will pound them in myself!"

She whirled back to face him.

"What you are sentencing *me* to is perhaps a lifetime! A lifetime of acting for you, as you . . . but maybe without ever seeing you again."

"Exactly. Because you are stronger and greater even than Judah."

"No! How can I act like you? How can I speak like you, teach like you? How can I do the things that you can do? Where will I find the authority? Within myself? When the doubts assail me—how will I find the means to go on?

"I am only I, Josh. Just I. How can you think to leave me all alone, perhaps for all the years that you tell me I have left to live, and yet ask me to do all these things?"

"I can do it because I know you. And it is because you *are* you that you are our wife. Trust me, Merovee. Trust your Self. You have become greater than just a fragment. We have poured the best of our Selves into you. You *are* the Chalice, containing the sweetest wine of Johannan and of my own Self . . . in your mind and Soul . . . now in your body."

He smiled gently.

"I wish you would stop fighting. You will do it. You know that you will do it. You cannot help yourself. It is what you were born for. Even as you fight me, images come to your mind, of Gaul, of freedom, of a future filled with challenges which you can only begin to imagine."

She turned away again.

"You love it, Merovee," he continued. "You thrive upon change and challenge. I will not even tell you again that I need you, want you, to do it for me. Because what I want and need is beside the point. You will do it for yourself."

She stood for some time, her back to him, shoulders bowed. Then she straightened slightly and turned.

"Yes. I suppose that I shall. What else is there for me? A tall, skinny, flat-chested misfit who was taken to wife only because she was proper mental material for her masters.

"Stop laughing! Stop, damn you! That is what you have just told me. Stop!"

She hurled a vase.

He would not stop laughing.

She picked up a carved, marble ornament.

He rushed to the bed and armed himself with a pillow.

The energy drained from out of her.

"Tell me that you love me Josh. Tell me that you married me for me, not because I was some pre-ordained fragment foisted upon you just to get the job done."

"You really wonder?"

"Tell me. Please. I need it now."

He came to her and took her into her arms.

"Do you know that I heard you laugh?"

"When?"

"As I lay in a cell at the house of Caiaphas, waiting for the dawn, waiting to be taken to Pilatus. The space about me was suddenly ringing with your laughter. I thought the sun had come out in my cell. I had a brief glimpse of you . . . I knew you were with Pilatus, laying plans for my 'resurrection.'"

"That must have been when Nathaniel came and told us how you had convicted your own self before the court. He said that Nicodemus asked you why you had done so, and you said, 'They were bound to have me one way or another, Friend, and I was tired of standing.' It was so like you. Suddenly all I could do was laugh."

She pulled back, looking up into his face.

"Do you know, even as I laughed, the thought came to me, 'I wonder if he hears me. He said that he always would.'"

"And I always will. Your laughter will always make the sun to shine in my life. Merovee. Do you not see?"

His own eyes filled with tears.

"You asked me to tell you that I love you. And I, who would teach Humankind of Love, find my tongue all tied, unable to form words which would explain the love beyond all loves that I feel for you. We two are bound with cords so close that I often think that you are closer to me than is my own heart. Do you think that this parting is easy for me? My insides are crumbling at the thought of it. I will need all of your bravery to help me put you onto that ship. I will never stop hurting without you, my darling. Never."

He pulled her to himself once more and rocked her.

"Oh, it would be so easy just to be 'people,' would it not? Just to sail off together and make a home in some idyllic, new land.

"But it is that which is 'easy' that such as you and I will never have, Merovee, because of who we are, and *why* we are.

"Yet, in exchange for the difficulty of our paths—we two will know joys and rewards such as most can hardly imagine."

"I still do not understand, Josh. Why must you stay here? What can you do here that you could not do in Gaul?"

"Merovee, you know all the answers if you would only think."

He stroked her cheek gently.

"Think. Without feeling. Just for a moment. I came here for a reason. As did Johannan. We were summoned by the collective dreaming mind of Humankind. It was time for a change, time for new learning, new direction. Yet, as I told you, many entities responded and sent teachers. Such as Yeshuah. And it seems that Humankind was not quite ready for Johannan, or for me. While I dread to think of what our friend Saul will get up to. Whatever the case, it seems that Humankind is going to, largely, accept Yeshuah's twisted preachings. It seems that, in this probability, Yeshuah's view will go forward as the new understanding, even while it travels under *my name.*

"Yet I can not give up. I can not, Merovee. My darling, you are the delight, the reward, which I never expected to experience, to receive. Yet you happened. And yet you are peripheral. I have told you that. Merovee, this drama is occurring in this place called Palestine because Palestine sits upon the main entry point of The Energy of All That Is into our system of reality. In this area, every thought, every idea, every belief, every emotion, is magnified a thousand-fold. It is in this area that the new direction of the next double millennium will be forged, and it is here where I must stay, to do whatever I can do, to right the course, to make it better, to keep it at least from being a complete disaster."

"And I am to act for you—as you—outside of this place."

"To you I have entrusted my truth, Beloved Disciple. In you I have placed my trust that my truth will be preserved and handed forward. My own lot is to remain here in Palestine to, in whatever way possible, clean up the mess that I have made of things. While, in the Chalice that is the Magdalen, I send my gift to the greater portion of Humankind. Do you not love the manner in which I so freely bandy you about? You, my most precious 'possession.'"

She studied the strong, sun-darkened face. Nearly for the last time?

"Will I ever see you again?"

"I will visit so often in the Spirit and out-of-body, nag and suggest so incessantly, that you will grow tired of me, and cry, 'Be gone, Josh! This is for me to decide, you gave it to me to do.'"

"You know what I mean," she whispered.

"Will we be together again in the flesh?"

"I am a creature of flesh. I cannot help it."

"Neither can I. My flesh will ache for you every moment of every day. While my heart . . . Ah! I, myself, cannot bear the thought . . .

He smiled suddenly.

"Sounion. Let us promise each other at least Sounion."

"You would not . . . leave . . . without letting me know, would you?"

"I would visit you wherever you were, to say my farewell."

There came a sound from outside the window that looked onto the harbor. A clunk, of cargo being moved. Then the voices of seamen.

Merovee flinched as though she had been stabbed. Jesus drew her more closely into his arms.

"We still have a while."

* * *

They came silently onto the torch-lit wharf, like specters of the night, all those who were leaving, and those who had come to say goodbye.

Jesus called them together and told them that he would be staying.

Each had to make his or her decision anew.

And all agreed to continue on.

"Because I send you forth as my disciples. My messengers. As bringers and guardians of the truth of All That Is," Jesus told them. "I need you to go with Merovee. She is, her Self, sent forth as my Self. She is, indeed, a part of my Self. So that, in supporting and defending her, you support and defend me."

Micah and Leah were, of course, staying.

"You knew all along," said Merovee.

Micah did not meet her eyes.

"Jesus swore me to secrecy."

"You played your part well. I envy your staying, Micah."

Micah lifted his eyes.

"At least, leaving me with him, you can be sure that he will write to you."

She summoned a smile.

"I had not thought of that. Thank you, Micah. I will depend upon you. Leah, do not allow him to forget."

Pilatus and Procula had been told only hours before that he would be staying, promising to remain in Roman or Greek disguise for their safety as well as for his own. They had been made both glad and sad by the news.

"We will watch after him," said Procula, clasping Merovee to herself. "As best we can, we will shield him. Bless you, my darling. Oh, bless you."

Merovee cast a desperate look toward the ship. The shipmaster waited at the plank. His men were at their stations.

She took Agapo from the arms of Zana and held him up to Jesus.

"Will you hold him now? Finally. Just this once before we go?"

"With all my heart," said Jesus. He took the baby from her and enfolded the tiny, sleeping body. He stood for long moments, his face buried against the little head. Then he handed the child back to Zana.

"I must have your people on board," the shipmaster told him, "else I will lose my tide."

"The animals," said Merovee.

"They are on board, Lady."

"And the chest of writings?" said Jesus.

"Yes, Reb."

There was nothing to do but to say goodbye.

They came to Jesus, each in turn, to embrace and kiss, and exchange words of love.

The artisans of Kapher Kana, the servants of bar Jeremiah.

"Sometimes the last shall be first," he said as he embraced each in turn. "You people came lately to me. Yet you go forth with, and as, my dearest disciples."

"Farewell, my darling Martha. My Bread. I will daily remember your excellent care. Without qualm, I entrust to you the well-beings of my people."

"Lazarus, Thomas. Brother. Your beauty shall shine as the sun in the east."

"Deborah. My wise and beautiful Moon. Share the Great Mother with the world."

"Nathaniel. Support. I commissioned you once before. Guard my wife."

"Bar Tolmei, my other Nathaniel. Watch over Agapo." He winked. "And my daughter who is soon to be."

"What is this?" said the next in line, Zana.

"A good nurse's work is never done," said Jesus as he embraced her.

"Susannah. My Clay . . . "

Susannah grabbed Nathaniel's hand.

"We thought you were coming with us, but now . . . say words of marriage for us, Jesus."

He smiled.

"You are husband and wife."

"That is it?" said Nathaniel.

"That is it."

"Had I known it would be so easy, I would have done it before."

Joseph wrapped both of his sons, Joshuah and Jacob, in wordless embraces. Rosula only touched their hands, refusing to look at either of them. Then she allowed Joseph to guide her tear-blinded steps aboard.

"Annah. You have the gift, Sister. Use it."

"Rachel, my beloved imp. Keep on lightening hearts."

"Joses. Look after Mother and Father."

"Naomi, new sister. Coel, new little brother. You have chosen well."

"Chandreah. My First."

"Johannah. Watch for Manean."

"What?"

"You shall see."

"Simon of Cyrene. The world shall remember your services."

"Alexander. Teach the world of creature kindness."

"And you, Jesse. Name Ruth's colt Seth. Just do not say that I said so."

"Queen Meraiah, dear Mother. You are more royal than you know."

He touched the face of Simon the Leper and embraced Simon's wife.

"I would make his face smooth and perfect, Judith, except that, as he is, he can better demonstrate beauty to the world."

"Jairus, Esther, Rebeckah. Use your new lives with joy and pass that joy to all."

"Alphaeus. Let your sight light the blind of heart."

"Nicodemus. Never cease searching for new ways to defile yourself."

"Timothy. Make sure that Nicodemus takes a bath in mud at least once a week."

"Nehemiah . . . "

"You and Reb Cleopah stay to your promises now! I have not worked all these years upon your father's planting to find out that you have let them die. There are some as is like my children . . . "

"Your plantings shall outlast the Temple, Nehemiah, that I promise you. While my people shall have need of your talents in Gaul."

"Oh, I will not fail them, I will grow them things to feed themselves with even in that awful land. But, Reb Joshuah, to the right of the gate of the house in Bethlehem . . . that old olive tree. She must be more than a thousand years old. Be especially kind to her, will you? I call her Ruth, because I have always had the feeling that . . . "

"That Ruth, herself, planted the tree."

"She is going to miss me. Ruth. The tree, I mean."

"Wherever I go, Nehemiah, I will always find ways to ensure Ruth's care, and to visit her occasionally and give her your love. While, wherever you go, you have but to think of her strongly, and she shall feel your thoughts, and sense you as though you stood beside her."

He turned then to Judah and Salome. The three of them stood for some moments, looking at one another. Finally he just shook his head and embraced them both.

"Farewell, my darlings. Judah, ask Merovee of what entity you are a part."

Then only Merovee was left. He took her into his arms.

She could control her tears no longer.

"I can not do it, Josh."

"The shipmaster is waiting."

"Oh Josh!" She clung to him fiercely. "Come with us."

"I do come with you. I will always be with you. To the end of a world that has no end."

"No! Not that way! Josh, why do you do this to the two of us?"

"I do it *for* the two of us."

His voice broke as he said the words. He made a motion of desperation. The shipmaster stepped forward.

"You have got to get on board now, my lady. I will take her other arm, Reb."

Sobbing unashamedly, with Jesus at one arm and the shipmaster at the other, Merovee allowed herself to be led onto the plank.

Then, suddenly, Josh had let go, and the shipmaster was forcing her forward. She fought to turn, to go back to the wharf. Nathaniel came onto the plank, swung her up into his arms, and carried her onto the deck. Before he had even set her down, before she could turn, the seamen had withdrawn the plank, the lines had been cast off. She threw herself against the side, reaching out helplessly toward Jesus.

"I can not be brave!"

"Do not bother to be brave. Be Merovee. That will always be brave enough."

How quickly the ship slipped sideways and forward, moved by oars, the unfurling sail searching for a breeze. Jesus followed along the jetty, keeping pace, his eyes fastened upon her.

"Goodbye," he called, a panic entering his voice.

She could hardly get the words out through the tears.

"Do not say goodbye. Say Sounion!"

"Yes! Sounion!"

"Promise."

"I promise!"

Then the sail caught. The ship lurched forward. Jesus speeded his steps. But tears were blinding his own vision now, and he did not see the posts at the end of the jetty. He walked straight into one of them—stopped, shook his head, and peered at his assailant.

Merovee's laughter came bubbling out. His face lifted in grateful surprise. Grinning, he backed off and bowed to the post. Then, unable to keep following without walking on air, he slung a companionable arm around his adversary and leaned himself against it.

Hanging upon the rail of the ship, clinging to it, Merovee was glad that he, too, had something to cling to at that moment.

She did not move from her place at the rail until the sunrise. She stayed there, watching back towards the east, thinking that, somehow, the wood of that rail united them, that, back on the jetty, he still clung to his post with the same idea.

But then the slanting rays of the new sun became too bright, so that she could no longer look to the east.

She turned and looked toward the west. There was not a cloud in the sky. It was going to be a beautiful day.

There is no such thing as a dead fig tree.
It is never the end.

ABOUT THE AUTHOR

Bonnie Jones Reynolds was born in Utica, New York, and raised on the dairy farm that had been in her family since 1820. Immediately after graduation from Clinton Central High School, she headed for New York City, where she had a multi-faceted career as model, dancer, and actress, with one lead in a Broadway show to her credit. Relocating to Hollywood, she appeared in many a popular TV series, including M*A*S*H, which was produced by her then husband, Gene Reynolds. During the years of her marriage, Bonnie also wrote her first two, best-selling, novels, *The Truth About Unicorns* and *The Confetti Man*. After her divorce, Bonnie lived for some years in Australia, and wrote *Bikram's Beginning Yoga Class* at the request of her Yoga teacher, Bikram Choudhury. This book has been in continuous print since 1978. In 1982, Bonnie's father became an invalid, and Bonnie returned to the family farm to help her mother with the care-giving. One thing led to another. Bonnie adopted one, orphaned, abandoned, or unwanted animal after another, until, in 1991, in partnership with renowned Interspecies Communicator, Dawn E. Hayman, she incorporated the not-for-profit animal sanctuary, Spring Farm CARES. Their book, recounting the first years of Spring Farm CARES, *If Only They Could Talk, The Miracles of Spring Farm*, was published in 2005 by Simon & Schuster. Work at the farm is pretty much 24/7/365—check out springfarmcares.org—but Bonnie keeps up her Yoga, makes ample time for her writing, and for her hobby, the study of family genealogy, which genealogy includes multiple Mayflower descents . . . and multitudinous Merovingian descents. Additionally, there is fascinating descent from both Benedict Arnold, English immigrant and first governor of Rhode Island, and from Prince Henry Sinclair, Scots-Viking pre-Columbian explorer of the northeastern coast of America. Was it Governor Benedict or Prince Henry who built the mysterious "Old Stone Tower" in Newport? Pick your theory. Of further great interest to Bonnie are her various descents from Prince Henry's grandson, Earl William Sinclair. He's the guy who built Roslyn Chapel. Bonnie did not know of her Sinclair descent until late 2008. Coincidence? There is no such thing as coincidence. Those with the ears of corn to hear, will hear.

LaVergne, TN USA
17 March 2011
220598LV00003B/84/P